The Thirteen Trials
of
Dr. Marion Bailey

Felicity St. John

Tiny Boar Books

2020

Tiny Boar Books
Water Street
Port Townsend, WA 98368
www.tinyboarbooks.com

The Library of Congress has catalogued this edition as follows:
   St. John, Felicity
      The thirteen trials of dr. Marion Bailey / Felicity St. John –1st Tiny Boar Books paperback ed.
         1. Espionage—Fiction. 2. Historical, World War I—Fiction. 3. Occult and Supernatural—Fiction.
Library of Congress Control Number: 2020901337

ISBN-13: 978-1-7344833-0-7 (pbk)

The Thirteen Trials of Dr. Marion Bailey

Contents

Prologue: London, 1967

London, England
May, 1967

"TORTURE the woman." John Willcox ran a fingertip along the aging twine that held the loose folios together. "A questionable life philosophy. But I suppose it made sense at the time."

"To your father, perhaps."

"No." He glanced, humorous, across at his friend, enjoying the afterglow of the unseasonably warm sunset. They were perched on the narrow balcony of John's Georgian flat. Wrought iron chairs. Unstable wrought iron table between them. The manuscript on top of that. "That one was my mother's. Though she would have denied it. As she denied everything. Always."

"Will you open it?"

John examined the package, ignoring the nausea it provoked in him. "Are you certain it's for me? This seems more in Lydia's line."

"I haven't seen your sister for ages. Where is she?"

"Southeast Asia, I think. Starting a war."

"Hmm." John's friend straightened the package and pointed to the writing, modern Arabic, that obscured the top page. "Addressed to you alone. In your mother's hand. I'd never have taken it from the Museum if it weren't for your family's association with that collection." And then, with the innocent arrogance of a curator: "you can read it, can't you?"

"Yes." He laughed. Unhappy. "The languages won't go away. Despite the studious neglect. The physics degree. Mother started me too early." He tapped his index finger against the page. "It was with the Iraq material?"

"Yes. The Baquba Library. Your father plundered it and brought it back with him in the thirties when that sort of escapade was respectable." He paused. "Hidden, though. Under a crate of miscellaneous scrap."

"Oh. I see." The nausea coiled itself into a knot in his stomach. "She wanted it away from Maugham. It frightened her."

"Not Richard Maugham. The trustee? He would have been twenty years old at the time. Hardly a threat."

"Richard Maugham," John replied, "has been of spry, indeterminate age since I was a child. Father used to say he'd made an unspeakable bargain with something squalid stored in a box in the bowels of the Museum. At the time, it was a joke."

"That's silly."

"The Museum's a large building."

"Fine. But will you open it?"

"Maugham," John continued, "used to run them. Or, he ran father, and father tried to contain mother. He'd taught them at Cambridge just after the First World War. Though mother escaped all that in the early 1920s, fleeing some dodgy business with her mentor there. Never would talk about it."

"Yes, I've heard the rumors about Maugham's—other—unscholarly—networks." Uncomfortable. And ignoring entirely the commentary on the professorial privileges of Cambridge University's interwar faculty. "Never leant them much credence. And professionalism's put an end to that. The slippery shifting from occupation to occupation. Nowadays, scholars are scholars. Curators are curators. And spies—"

"Make for the very best television," John finished for him. "Though I wonder sometimes about the world that's disappeared in the wake of the specialization. You know, my father's title, from the day he left Cambridge to the day he died, was 'cataloguer.' For the Museum and Library. Yet nobody thought twice about the years he spent, still as a 'cataloguer,' overseeing intelligence in the Iraq Mandate. Or—or looting Yemen. There was an openness in those days to—to—"

"The brazen violation of international law?" Not to be outdone.

"You sound like my mother." But it wasn't a criticism. John was smiling again. "That's where they reunited, you know. In Baghdad. When my father was cutting his teeth on the mandate. She'd been protesting. Or resisting. Whatever they did then. He interrogated her."

"Of course he did."

"It was a different era." John stopped himself and considered. "Sort of. She'd been married before to an Egyptian. Helped to politicize her, from what I could get out of her growing up. He died, and my father stepped in. But she was quiet about that as well. Didn't trust the emotion. Or, really, any social interaction. I felt sorry for her when I was older."

John's friend nodded again at the package on the table. "Open it. Who knows? Perhaps there are answers there."

He tilted his head. "I think I recognize it. It came from Morocco. She crossed a courier in the park, and then she tried to hide it from us. I was eight or nine at the time. Pretended I was interested in the geese on the pond."

His face clouded. Troubled.

"Why are you hesitating?"

"Let me explain."

Turkey, 1927

Istanbul, Turkey
Asian Side
February, 1927

CONSTANTINOPLE *must be approached by water, at sunset. The sparkling waves of the Golden Horn will set off to perfection the striking Romanesque lines of Galata Tower, and a sensitive visitor might well imagine the breezes of the Marmara Sea darting playfully up and about the imposing minarets of Sultan Suleyman's mosque—*

Marion shut the guidebook and looked out the window of her Turkish Railways sleeping car. At the window of her Turkish Railways sleeping car. No view. And the sun had set. After a few seconds, her peaked, white reflection bothered her, and she averted her eyes. Scowled down at the book in her lap instead.

She'd purchased it in a moment of bored despair, hoping that laughing at a Baedeker would help her to pass what had become a nightmarish four-day wait in Alexandretta on her already meandering journey from Baghdad to Istanbul. Her movement had ground to a halt in the city when a fight had broken out there among the various—French, Turkish, Hatay, and, at one point, particularly resentful Italian—officials manning passport control. All claiming sole right to stamp her papers. Product of post-War order and rationality.

And so, she had waited. Worried. Because, in fact, her papers were false. The personal information was accurate. Name, age, date and place of birth. And any bureaucrat who interacted with her would assume her British citizenship without a passport. But she had married an Egyptian three years earlier, thereby forfeiting her British status in both International and British law. She hadn't taken Egyptian citizenship. And the statelessness that before the War had struck her as a bit of a joke now left her scarcely human. Immobile. She disliked it.

When she had resolved to return to Istanbul, therefore, she had appealed to an old contact who had conveyed her not to Turkey, but, invisibly, from the Iraq mandate into the protectorate of Transjordan. In Amman, she had walked into a branch office of the British High Commissioner for Palestine and had renewed the papers she'd carried with her from Great Britain in 1921. Then, enjoying her clean passport, she had tested her mobility across the new borders.

First, from Transjordan into Iraq. Then, from Iraq into French Syria. And then—and then, just has she had begun to feel secure in her anodyne identity, the mishap in Alexandretta had landed her in the bookshop that had refused to sell her anything but the Baedeker. As she'd passed hours in Alexandretta's humid, desperate customs offices, she had chastised herself for not drawing on the extra-, and occasionally not remotely-, legal resources that had moved her about the region five years earlier. If she had, she'd have been in Istanbul less than a week after she'd left Baghdad.

Looking back out—at—the window as her train slowed into Istanbul's Haydarpaşa Station, no longer trapped in Alexandretta, she was pleased that she'd been patient. Yes, she would have been in Istanbul sooner had she slipped illegally across what she still thought of as fanciful, only vaguely national borders. But she would have remained in diplomatic limbo, something between an insurgent and a refugee, at best undesirable and at worst subject to official attention from clerks who would make their counterparts in Alexandretta charming by comparison.

She removed her innocent passport from an interior pocket of her carpet bag and smiled at it. Then she placed it, along with the insufferable guidebook, at the bottom of the bag next to the carefully wrapped five-hundred-year-old manuscript that was her true reason for returning to the city.

THE guidebook told her that if she did have the misfortune of approaching Istanbul by land and on the Asian side of the Bosporus, she ought to take a ferry across to the European shore and find herself a room in the Pera Palace Hotel, "to experience the cosmopolitan delights of Constantinople at the site of their beating heart." An unpleasant image. She pushed it from her mind as she stepped down from the train into the refurbished station on the wrong side of the water. Clutching the key that she had kept pinned to the inside of her travelling coat throughout her journey.

It opened a *yalı*, an Ottoman villa, owned by Mehmet, a friend from before the War, and situated further up the Bosporus in the suburban village of Çengelköy. Still on the wrong side. Marion had telegraphed him from Transjordan in a moment of optimism, asking whether he'd be in the city a month or two later. She'd almost heard his laughter in the return message he had cabled back to her. No one who had a choice spent February in Istanbul. But Marion was welcome to the house if she wanted to stay while Mehmet was in France. There would be a boat waiting for her at the ferry dock once she'd notified his household of her train's expected arrival.

A stinging wind off the Marmara hit her in the face as she left the warmth of the station. Threw a few pellets of hail against her exposed neck. Despite her sensitivity, she was having difficulty imagining the weather as playful. She withdrew into her coat, shouldered her bag, and trudged further into the street, making for the ferry dock three piers down the shore.

But before she could walk more than a few steps, a polite voice stopped her. Asked in English whether she was Dr. Bailey.

She put her hand to her hat to keep it from blowing away. "Yes?"

"I'm Sinan—Mehmet Bey's student. He's asked me to take you to the house." Sinan turned and pointed to a forty-five-foot Hacker-Craft cabin cruiser that was docked with egregious illegality on the pier adjacent to the railway station. "The boat is there."

"How do you do, Sinan?" Marion had switched to Turkish. "Thank you."

Sinan relaxed, relieved not to be speaking English. Then he spoke again. "I've heard something from Mehmet Bey about your work. May I take your bag?"

She refused his offer, but let him help her onto the boat, and they escaped from the menacing weather into the cabin. She placed the bag on the seat beside her while Sinan started the boat's engine from the wheelhouse and reversed into the channel. Appreciated the ostentatious interior and the fact that Mehmet had refused to let war, imperial dissolution, or global destruction get in the way of his enjoyment of life. The room gleamed.

Once Sinan had the boat cutting through the choppy water, he opened a cabinet in the galley and retrieved a bottle of *rakı* and a glass. Held them up. "Drink?"

"Thank you. Join me?"

He smiled and poured the drinks. Marion was grateful to him for not trying to make conversation. The sound of the water against the hull was going a long way toward restoring her equanimity after the journey. A few minutes later, he slowed the engine and docked the boat outside Mehmet's villa.

Marion took her bag, climbed from the cabin, and jumped to the dock. Sinan offered to carry it into the house, but when she refused a second time, he didn't insist. Instead, he secured the boat, smiled at her again, and walked toward the bicycle he had ridden from the rooms he kept down the Bosporus in Üsküdar.

Before he'd gone far, he stopped and turned. "Dr. Bailey? Something else. Mehmet Bey told me that you were unsocial to the point of eccentricity, and he's sent his household away so that you'll have full run of the *yalı* while you're here. But if you find that you need anything, please contact me without hesitation. I've left my information on the table in the hall."

"I will, Sinan. And once again, thank you."

"I hope to see you soon, Dr. Bailey."

Marion watched as Sinan pedaled off into the wind and hail. And then, feeling oddly at home, she turned to the grandiose door of the eighteenth-century wooden structure and let herself into the entry hall.

MEHMET'S father had been as eccentric as Mehmet liked to think Marion was, obsessed with any and all technology, the more obscure the better. In a more prescient moment than those which had led him to purchase the flock of mechanical clockwork ducks and the anti-drowning hat with the United States patent, he had wired the house for electricity in the 1870s. Now that Istanbul's public utility had caught up to Mehmet's father's foresight, Marion could flip a switch to illuminate the ground floor of the building. Which, gratefully, she did.

She half set, half dropped her bag to the ground and removed her damp hat. Mehmet's great-great- great-grandfather, who had commissioned the villa in the first place, had found baroque European architecture appealing in much the same way that his late nineteenth-century descendent had appreciated the robotic ducks. Eschewing the conventional Ottoman-style Bosporus villa, he had built instead an improbably displaced Venetian Palazzo—decorated, however, by some perhaps Orient-obsessed Italian aristocrat who couldn't decide whether to privilege the marble busts of Claudio Monteverdi or the Hereke carpets and silver mirrors facing the walls. Looking at the grand entryway with the sweeping central staircase leading to an exposed upper gallery, Marion felt culturally dizzy.

Cosmopolitanism confused her. An imperial failing she wished she could repair, but knew, to her distress, she never would.

Focusing on hanging her dripping coat in a massive piece of furniture to the side of the hall so that she wouldn't be forced to think about the inoperative fountain that was its centerpiece, she considered her next move. She had intended to sleep for at least a day before embarking on her work. But Sinan's *rakı* had been as restorative as his welcome silence and the sound of the boat breaking through the waves. She was awake again. Eager to commence her project.

She registered, only half consciously, Sinan's note on an unnecessary, yet quite pretty, table flanking the door to the salon. Beside an elaborate Swedish telephone. Ignoring the note and telephone, and recognizing her decision to go to the salon, rather than to her bedroom, as the wrong one, she retrieved her bag. Then she walked through the door, lit a La Farge lamp resting on a Spanish Renaissance oak desk she remembered from previous visits, and sat in the tapestried chair behind it.

After waiting for a few seconds, thinking she might go to sleep after all, she bent over to open her bag. Removed the manuscript, careful to prevent its linen wraps from rubbing the edges of the vellum pages, and placed the book on the desk in front of her. Stared down at it. She had brought it from a library she'd unearthed in Iraq—literally unearthed, the library was cached under the river town of Baquba—knowing that she could decipher it properly only on site in Turkey. Having it with her now in Istanbul set her heart beating faster. The book was home.

As she unwrapped the manuscript, the wind squalled through the sea outside the house and hurled spray against windows that ordinarily framed a relatively placid Bosporus. But she ignored the sound. Instead, she ran her fingertip across the brittle cover of the volume. Her perfect original copy of Taceddin Ibrahim Ahmedi's fourteenth-century *İskendername*, the epic poem commissioned by the Ottoman imperial family in the early years of their military and political expansion.

Marion could think of at least five librarians who would commit acts of atrocity to read these pages. If those same librarians had access to the marginalia scattered throughout this, as far as she was aware, unique version, they would faint dead away. Marion nearly had. If nothing else, the markings had resolved one of the great problems facing scholarship surrounding the work.

On its surface, Ahmedi's *İskendername* was a book of kings describing regal history from Alexander the Great through the Ottomans. A rare Turkish-language source produced during the earliest years of Ottoman-Turkish history. But its value to scholars had always been equivocal because Ahmedi had been charged with writing the poem by the Ottoman Sultan, Bayezid I, whose career had ended in military defeat and capture by Timur, or Tamerlane, in 1402.

The historical loser, Bayezid had been portrayed by all sides in the struggle as at best a bad Muslim, and at worst a drunkard with questionable personal proclivities who had wrecked his family's claims to sovereignty. Ahmedi's treatment of Bayezid, his disgraced patron, was fraught. More than difficult to parse. Too confused for effective scholarship.

But the marginalia in Marion's copy of the *İskendername* pointed to a different explanation for Ahmedi's baroque descriptions of Bayezid's reversal of fortune. It read less as the history of a patron who had left his poet lacking a respectable subject, and more as a cryptic message to that patron's future line. Now that she was on-site, Marion meant to decode that message. She was looking forward to it.

She yawned and pressed the heels of her hands to her eyes. Not, however, at the moment. Intellectually stimulated, or over-stimulated, though she might be, her fatigue was catching up to her. She couldn't work. Forcing herself to stop, she pushed back her chair and stood. Wobbled. And then, prodding herself into a final act of responsibility, she checked the locks on the glass doors, re-wrapped the manuscript, and, leaving her bag behind in the salon, took the book with her up the stairs to her bedroom.

When she'd reached the room, she fumbled with the light switch, slipped the wrapped manuscript under her pillow, stripped off her damp travelling clothes, and crawled under the covers. Then she switched off the lamp on the bedside table and lost consciousness. The wind and the hail outside the house were whipping up again, but Marion was too deeply under to hear them. Unaware, she slept.

SHE woke to watery sunlight shining through one of the three walls of windows that framed her room. Product of Mehmet's eighteenth-century ancestors' unhealthy fascination with transparent and reflective glass. Or their ironic fascination with it. Mocking the equally light- and mirror-obsessed French.

Turning over in the carved bed, an off-putting mixture of the sleek Hacker-Craft and the pornography of Delacroix at his most harem-obsessed, Marion concluded that whatever their motivations had been, she approved of them. The house was so solid, so pleased with its impassive presence on the shores of the Bosporus, that it made cultural anxiety unthinkable. No need to worry about subtext or subtlety when the wood, glass, crystal, and marble were so very material.

Luxuriating, she curled up on her side, shut her eyes for a moment longer, and checked with her hand that the manuscript was still in place. It was. Then, becoming decisive, she pushed off the bedclothes and stood. And began shivering. She hadn't lit the wood-burning stove the night before, and the room was frigid. Annoyed with herself for the oversight, she dragged a blanket off the bed and threw it over her shoulders. Took a step toward the bath. And stopped.

Something wasn't right. She remained motionless for a few seconds, trying to determine what had tugged at the edges of her vision. Testing the air. But then, unwilling to let her rampant sensitivities assault her conscious mind so early in the morning, she shook her head once, sharply, and crossed the silk carpet to her bag, which was sitting on a low bench. Just to the side of the bath. Had she brought it upstairs?

She stopped again, confused. And then, with an effort, she pushed down her disquiet. Refusing to ruin the morning. Stubbornly grateful that it was waiting for her here rather than useless downstairs in the salon. After that, she dressed, pulled her manuscript from under the pillow, and stuffed it into a messenger bag that she had salvaged from the First World War. It was strong and canvas, and she could wear it across her shoulder, which helped her to work and also to ride a bicycle. She meant to purloin one of Mehmet's fleet to travel to Anadoluhisarı, the fortress built by Sultan Bayezid on the Asian side of the Bosporus. She finished by tugging on men's lace-up boots.

Feeling more prepared for her morning now, she wandered toward the grand staircase—sheepish as she trod across Mehmet's pristine floors in outdoor shoes—stopping periodically to admire the sculpture that adorned the empty spaces between the gallery and the hall. She lingered for some time over a graphic re-creation of the mutilation of Uranus by Saturn. Appropriate given that Anadoluhisarı stood on the site of an old temple of Uranus. Sacred ground. Then she stumbled again, perplexed, chasing a thought that remained half-formed in her mind. Nothing. Blinking, she continued down the stairs.

Where she found the kitchen, also ostentatiously well-stocked, and made herself a pot of tea. She always had the nagging impression that Mehmet, even when he wasn't present, was mocking her austerity with his profligate generosity. But his unspoken commentary was, like the bedroom, a variation on mockery that she appreciated.

As the water boiled, she grabbed a pastry and jam, smeared the latter on the former, and ate absentmindedly as she wrapped up bread, cheese, and olives to take with her on her journey. Then she poured herself a glass of the tea, dropped a couple of sugar cubes into it, and crossed the hall to the salon. Put the bag and glass of tea on the desk she had used the night before, sat in the chair, and bumped her knee against a half-open drawer. Annoyed, she pushed the drawer shut.

Once the caffeine from the tea had hit her bloodstream, she thought for a moment. She couldn't have left the drawer open last night. Frowning, she examined the room. Everything was in its place. She stood with her tea and walked to the windows that opened, during milder weather, onto the terrace overlooking the strait. The wind had blown debris across the tiled deck, but there was no evidence of human visitors during the night.

She rested her hand on the knob of the glass door and chastised herself. Her paranoia became worse every year. Drank the remainder of her tea and turned back to the desk. As she did so, the knob of the door gave way under her hand. It was unlocked. But still, she refused to react. To indulge her suspicions. Not here. She didn't want to know. And so, shouldering her bag, she returned to the kitchen, washed her glass and plate, and went out to inspect Mehmet's bicycles.

On her way, she locked and bolted the rear door and slipped the key into her pocket. Then she pushed open the gates to the outbuilding that had once held carriages and peered into the ranks of bicycles that extended into the dim interior of the building. Mehmet had too much time on his hands.

Choosing the bicycle closest to the door—a Dutch Omafiets—she wheeled it out to the road. Left it on its stand and returned to close the doors of the carriage house. They were shut and barred. She blinked again. This wasn't an accident, pilfering, or professional surveillance. Someone was baiting her. And she couldn't ignore it any longer.

Fuming, she retrieved the bicycle and pedaled off, away from Anadoluhisarı and her research, and toward Üsküdar at the other end of the strait. There, she stopped at a café heated inside with stoves and ordered a coffee. Tried to look as though she were enjoying a quiet afternoon, watching the February scenery. Looked, instead, impatient, petulant, and fidgety. Until eventually she gave up, left coins on the table to pay for the coffee, and rode back to the villa, taking out her anger on the Omafiets.

When she returned, the doors to the gate as well as the villa were unlocked and open. She pushed through both and walked loudly into the back hall. Called out. No answer. She hadn't expected any. Still moving loudly, and still guilt-ridden for wandering through Mehmet's house in her outdoor boots, she made as much noise as she could, touring every room of the *yalı*.

Every room had been visibly searched. There had been no attempt to hide the disorder. But there also had been no unnecessary destruction. A message. She instinctively put her hand over the bag holding the manuscript. The problem was that she couldn't fathom what that message might be.

She waited, uncertain, in the hall. Then, chewing her lip, she walked to the table on which she had left Sinan's information. It was still there, a bit askew, undoubtedly copied and replaced. Using the bewildering nineteenth-century telephone to its side, she rang through.

"Sinan?"

"Dr. Bailey. So pleased you've rung."

"Sinan, I think someone's been searching Mehmet's house."

Silence at the end of the line. Then: "are you certain? Could it have been a servant?"

Marion considered. She didn't want to sound as paranoid as she felt. "I don't think so. Do you know whether any of Mehmet's students have been in the area?"

"Yes." Relieved. "I'm confident that's what's happened. Mehmet Bey gives us unfettered access to the place, and there are certain to be a few doctoral students who haven't heard that he's in France. I hope you weren't startled. I feel terrible."

"No Sinan, not at all. Please—don't worry about it."

"But I know a way to make it up to you!" She could hear his smile. "Today is the 17th of February. Do you know what happened this morning?" He didn't wait for a reply. "America established diplomatic ties with the Turkish Republic. We're sovereign! There's going to be a party at the United States Consulate near Beyoğlu. You must come."

"Oh, Sinan. That's really not my—"

"Don't be silly. No one will recognize you. And Americans are entertaining to watch near alcohol—they aren't allowed to have it at home."

"Sinan—"

"I'll be there with a driver at 8:00. And if you need a frock, Mehmet Bey has a room full of them—"

"Yes," she said shortly. "I know. He has a room full of everything. I'll look forward to it."

She hefted the receiver onto the phone. Things were emphatically not going according to plan.

MARION looked blankly at the paper containing Sinan's information for a few seconds and set it back on the table next to the telephone. Then, finally obeying her conscience, she removed her boots, arranged them in the rack beside the door, and put on house slippers. She noticed that she was gripping the strap of the messenger bag so tightly that her knuckles were white. But this time she didn't chide herself. She did, though, pursue a thought. Lifted the receiver again.

"Dr. Bailey?"

"Yes, Sinan. I'm sorry to ring back so soon. Can I meet you on the European side of the city, in Ortaköy, this evening, rather than here? I'll take Mehmet's boat across the strait and dock it there."

"Absolutely. I'll be waiting for you in Ortaköy, same time."

"Wonderful, Sinan. And thank you."

She replaced the receiver a second time, feeling more confident. She would take the manuscript across the Bosporus and hide it away from both the *yalı* and herself. Whoever was harassing her would have no compunction about attacking her or breaking into the house while she slept. It was better out of her hands.

Failing to quell her frustration, she marched up the winding staircase and made her way to the third-floor room where Mehmet kept his dresses. She had never inquired about why there should be a room in the villa devoted to women's fashion, but she knew that it was a family fascination. Some of the material in the collection had been preserved, unworn, from the mid-eighteenth century. And, whatever its original purpose, the room suited her purposes. If she could find it, there was a dress in the collection that Mehmet had put aside for her—the clothing she wore, repeatedly, whenever there was a gathering in the *yalı*.

It was dark blue, thin velvet, high in the neck and plunging in the back, ankle length but clinging enough to turn black where it curved along her body. She wore it with buttoned satin ankle boots and her hair swept up into an unfashionable twist that she nonetheless preserved because she felt daring showing her nape and back. She rarely indulged in vanity of that sort, but Mehmet brought it out in her. Even now, she felt only mildly ashamed.

She found the dress hanging off to the side of the room, where she had left it last in 1924. After trying it on to be certain that it was intact and fit, she wrapped it in tissue, picked up the boots that went with it, and returned, in her working clothes, to the entry hall. She looked into one of the many mirrors to fix her hair into a respectable upsweep and then slipped the tissue-wrapped dress against the manuscript in her messenger bag. Another benefit of the thin velvet was that it travelled well.

The boots could handle the boat ride and a short walk through Ortaköy, and so she pulled them on to wear with her trousers. Glanced through the door at the grandfather clock Mehmet kept at the other end of his salon and saw that she had two hours to spend before meeting Sinan on the other side of the Bosporus. Realized that she was famished.

Keeping tight hold of the messenger bag, she walked back to the kitchen to fix herself a salad. She had no intention of eating the offerings at the party—she'd arrive with Sinan, sit against a wall for a half hour, and then leave as early as she politely could. But as much as she was dreading the Consulate, it did give her cover for crossing to the European side to deposit the manuscript. She'd do all she could to avoid appearing resentful.

When she had finished her food and washed her dishes, it was getting to be a reasonable time to make her way to the boat. Trying to look innocuous—and failing, just as she had in the café—she collected her wool coat, strode to the dock, threw her bag into the cockpit of the Hacker-Craft, and started its engine. Casting off, she put the boat into gear and turned it slowly toward the European shore of the strait.

The sun had gone down, and the air on the water was close to freezing, but she remained above deck as she maneuvered the boat. If her visitors had their own means of crossing the Bosporus, they would reveal themselves to her. They couldn't remain hidden on the water. And if they had no access to a boat, Marion gained forty minutes of her own time on the other side. Either way, she had an advantage.

She turned to look back at the *yalı* a few times as she sped across toward Ortaköy, but she saw no other suspicious vessels. A relief. And a few minutes later, still unaccompanied, she docked in a makeshift marina. After securing the boat and stepping off the deck, she took one last look at the water. Seeing nothing, she walked with what she hoped was touristic purpose into the side streets of Ortaköy.

The neighborhood had changed and grown over the past four years, but most of the businesses she remembered were still in operation. And she was more than familiar with her target. A narrow townhouse, halfway up one of the steeper cobblestone streets, with a green door and no storefront or sign. Unobtrusive, but recognizable.

The townhouse was an unofficial library for researchers, and she had spent days and nights working there when she had lived in the city after the War. It wasn't a secret or criminal institution. Anyone with an interest in Ottoman history found it. But it also wasn't advertised in the usual guides. Nor was it known to the government agencies that policed politics. It was what it appeared to be: a private collection of Ottoman and Turkish manuscripts that had become semi-public when its owner began inviting visiting academics to sample it.

Marion paused and looked up to her left. There was the green door. There was the gas lamp lit invitingly over it. And there was the wet, pockmarked sculpture of the lion to the right of the step. Mourning the evening she wouldn't be passing in the townhouse, she took the manuscript from her bag and lifted the head of the lion. It protested, creaking for a moment, before giving way. Then she deposited the manuscript in the recess, letting the lion's head fall into place.

The sculpture had been a drop during and just after the War, but it hadn't been used since the establishment of the Turkish Republic in 1923. Her volume would remain there undetected until she felt secure enough to retrieve it. And even on the off possibility that the drop was still in play, whoever was using it wouldn't compromise a pre-existing exchange. Her hiding place was as reliable as it could be, at least under these less than ideal circumstances.

Recalling her circumstances, she inspected her satin boots. They were damp, but they would pass. Then she glanced up the street one last time, saw no one, and walked—unhurried—down the hill to Mehmet's boat.

She stepped into the cockpit, unlocked the hatch, and descended into the cabin. There, she pulled the shades, turned up the lamps, and changed into her dress. Ducked to look into a mirror hanging against the door to the forepeak, combed her hair back into its upsweep, and put on an expression of enjoyment as she climbed out of the cabin. As she jumped to the dock, Sinan was walking toward her, wearing a genuine look of enjoyment to go with his white dinner jacket.

"Dr. Bailey, I admit it. I thought you wouldn't come. Mehmet Bey has done you an injustice." He pointed toward the road, where a menacing yellow Studebaker Commander was waiting.

She wrinkled her forehead. "This is yours?"

He grinned. "My fiancée is driving. İnci. Her family's in textiles." The grin turned into a blush when Marion, not quite comprehending, nodded. Polite.

As they approached the car, İnci rolled down her window and waved to them. The light reflected off the wet stones accentuated her red lips, shingled hair, and the diaphanous sequins floating about in the driver's seat. Beside her, in the passenger seat, was a pale, sullen boy wearing a tuxedo and a great deal of acne. İnci showed them both her bright, white teeth and pointed to the back seat. Sinan opened the door for her and sat down next to her once she'd slid across behind the boy.

When they were settled, İnci stepped on the accelerator while simultaneously turning back to Marion, thereby nearly colliding with a man selling chestnuts on the street. She laughed and waved at the man. "I'm so very pleased to meet you, Dr. Bailey!" She was speaking English. "I've been terribly jealous of the attention you've been getting from Sinan—" She swerved around a horse and a newly minted city cab, and then aimed the Studebaker up the hill toward Beyoğlu. "But now that I see you, I know we'll be such friends! Oh, and I forgot. This is my brother, Mustafa. He's already got a crush on you. Ignore him."

The boy scowled over at İnci. "Oh, shut up," he said in Turkish. "I'm only here because mother told me I had to—"

İnci glared back at him, in the process bumping the car over a ridge at the edge of the street. "*You* shut up. It isn't as if we *wanted* you to—"

She swerved again out of the way of the tram trundling up İstiklal Avenue. Sinan, unmoved by the chaotic ride, looked puzzled out the window at the tram. "İnci," he said, also speaking Turkish, "I'm not sure automobiles are allowed on this street. Perhaps you ought to—"

"Not you too!" She pouted back at him. Veered into a side street, slammed on the brakes of the Studebaker, and turned off the engine. "But never mind!" She threw open her door. "We're here!"

Marion opened her own door as well and got out of the car. It was parked diagonally, blocking any entrance to or exit from the alley, and smelling of burnt rubber tires. She felt old. Even so, this area at least looked familiar to her. Peering back toward İstiklal Avenue, she thought she could find the American Consulate again on her own should she need to. She let Sinan, İnci, and Mustafa lead her the three blocks along what had, under the Ottomans, been Embassy row, to the lighted, celebratory entrance to the Consulate.

As they walked toward the formal entrance hall, they stepped past a young man clutching a top hat, leaning over on his hands and knees, retching. İnci gazed at him with delight and grabbed Marion by the arm. "I *adore* Americans," she said in English. She squeezed Marion. "This will be loads of fun. Sovereignty is the best reason I can think of to have a party."

Marion glanced over at Sinan, who was visibly dazzled by his fiancée's love of life, Americans, and alcohol poisoning. Tried to smile.

When the four of them reached the entrance, security didn't vet them. They were waved through the door immediately and, interestingly, because of İnci and her brother rather than because of Sinan or herself. The guards came close to doffing their hats to İnci as she passed.

Sinan saw Marion's look and blushed again. "Her family," he explained. "Textiles."

Marion nodded sagely. "Textiles."

They left their coats with a porter, and İnci, still holding her arm, led her into the ballroom, where a few State Department types were already dancing to a mix of nineteenth-century waltzes and twentieth-century foxtrots. Sinan and Mustafa trailing behind. Most of the rest of the room was occupied by clusters of diplomats and industrialists sitting at tables or standing with drinks doing whatever it was that diplomats and industrialists did at these events. Mustafa spied a friend of his from Galatasaray high school and slipped away from İnci's already less than enthusiastic chaperonage.

When the band played "Ain't She Sweet," Marion could see that both İnci and Sinan were yearning to join the younger couples. She extracted her arm from İnci's grasp and pretended to recognize an acquaintance from before the War. Failing to hide their pleasure at being left to themselves, İnci and Sinan made for the dance floor while Marion sought out an unobtrusive corner of the ballroom.

She imagined she could leave, without offense, after forty-five minutes. Picked up a flute of champagne to nurse throughout her penance there and found a comfortable chair and table between a pillar and a potted yucca. Settled into the chair to watch the players watch each other. Pleased that she was no longer part of this world.

"Ain't She Sweet" was followed by "Heebie Jeebies," and Marion relaxed into her chair, set her champagne on the table to her side, and surprised herself by beginning to enjoy the evening. İnci and Sinan were entertaining to watch. Perhaps she would stay longer than a half hour, after all.

"I think you ought to."

Startled, she looked up. And gripped the edge of her chair to steady herself. "You—"

"Stay, that is." He was leaning against the pillar, smoking a cigarette, also observing the dance floor.

"How did you know?"

He stubbed out the cigarette in an ashtray on the table. "I've been watching you since you arrived. When you came through the door, you looked as though you were being led to your own execution." He glanced down at her to gauge her reaction. "But then you tucked yourself away in this dismal corner and noticeably calmed. The young love on the dance floor even had you questioning your determination to escape at the first opportunity." Something like a smile crossed his face and then vanished. "Ah yes, but there's the flight impulse front and center again." He signaled for a waiter to bring him champagne. "I've missed you, Marion."

She had regained her composure as he was talking. He was boasting, which suggested uncertainty. But she didn't trust herself to speak. When the waiter had brought the champagne, he took a sip, eyeing her. "Do you mind if I sit?"

She shook her head, the exhaustion from her journey through Iraq and Syria catching up to her. "Jeffrey, what do you want?"

He half shrugged and sat in the seat against the wall on the other side of the small table, both of them now facing the increasingly well-populated dance floor. The band had switched back to waltzes, and some of the older couples had ventured out. "It would have been impolite of me not to talk with you once I'd seen you. Besides, I was curious. What could have brought Dr. Bailey all the way back to Istanbul, after all this time?"

"It was you in Mehmet's *yalı.*"

"Not me personally."

"Your thugs."

"Associates."

"You can't do that here." She was becoming angry, which she knew was his purpose. Which made her angrier.

"What? Here in the American Consulate? No, of course not. No point among Americans. Open. Honest. Self-determination."

"This isn't Iraq." She felt herself ranting, tried to damp it down. "Turkey is a sovereign country."

"Yes, I did read the party invitation."

"You—"

"I've mentioned before how I've missed you, no?"

She stood to leave. If she left now, perhaps she wouldn't do herself or her project damage. He didn't make a move to stop her, but as she turned toward the door, she saw Sinan and İnci walking hand in hand back from the dance floor. They were beaming. She paused, wanting to thank them for the evening before fleeing the building. Jeffrey, still sitting, was pulling another cigarette out of its case.

When Sinan and İnci had reached Marion's corner, İnci didn't give her a chance to talk. Instead, she clapped her hands like a child and bent down to kiss Jeffrey's cheek. Then, still sparkling, she turned to Marion. "What a perfect turn of events! I was hoping to introduce you to Sir Jeffrey, Dr. Bailey, but here you are already deep in conversation. I knew you'd want to know one another—so very much in common."

Sinan was also smiling, a little shy. "I hope you don't think us forward, Dr. Bailey. We couldn't resist surprising you with one of your countrymen. Sir Jeffrey is something of a scholar too, as well as a statesman, from what I understand."

Marion could think of nothing to say to either of them. But Jeffrey, his cigarette safely lit, now stood and greeted Sinan as well. "But you see, we've surprised you instead. Dr. Bailey and I are colleagues. We worked together at Cambridge."

They all looked at her, and she swallowed. Nodded. Couldn't speak. Sinan and İnci, missing the tension, grinned at one another. And then, as the band switched to modern music—something by Gershwin—they turned toward the ballroom. On their way out, İnci cast a teasing look at Marion and Jeffrey. "Don't you dare sit there all night talking, You two are going to dance if I force you out here myself."

Marion lowered herself into the chair. A few seconds later, Jeffrey sat as well, pensive, smoking his cigarette. It was Marion who broke the silence. "*Sir* Jeffrey? They *knighted* you?"

He was blowing smoke up at the ceiling, looking delinquent. "'Services to Cataloguing.' And it was a baronetcy."

"What?"

"Not a knighthood. A baronetcy. Drove Langton batty."

She felt a headache coming on. Signaled for another glass of champagne. When it came, she drained it completely. Tapped her fingernail against the rim of the glass, wondering whether she could leave the building despite Sinan's and İnci's insistence that she stay longer.

"They'll be so terribly disappointed if you do, Marion." She threw him an exasperated glare, and he shrugged again. "The 'eluding capture and execution' expression. It's back. Suits you. Always has."

She closed her eyes. "You still haven't answered my question. What do you want? Why are you here? How do you know İnci and Sinan? If Iraq was such a monumental success for you, why aren't you still there, clawing your way to the top? Isn't an American Consulate party in a not-quite capital of a country unlikely to welcome British interference a bit beneath you now?"

"More than one question."

"You haven't answered any of them."

"No," he agreed. "I haven't. But then, I tend not to. Occupational hazard. I become nervous when I'm not the one doing the interrogating."

"Must we do this?"

He relented. "I was bored." He paused. "Oh. And her family. Textiles."

"Textiles."

"Yes. Everyone knows İnci. I'm surprised you weren't introduced to her before. I suppose industrialists were never your interest. Royals. Resistance fighters." He looked at his fingernails. "Radicals."

"You were explaining why you're here."

"I thought I was gossiping about İnci."

"Boredom," she prompted. "Something about being bored."

"Ah yes. Boredom. They offered me an array of tempting appointments, after Iraq. After you. But I told them I wanted back in the field. Five years is a long time to spend filing paperwork and tormenting peasants. My languages were rusty. So here I am." Gesturing toward the room at large. "Back in the field."

"I don't believe you."

"Wise. I wouldn't believe me either."

The band had started in on the first few strains of the Blue Danube waltz. Jeffrey stood, bowed, and offered her his hand. "This one is ours."

"You're off your head."

"Marion, if we don't dance to something soon, İnci will make good on her threat. I've seen her do it. Would you rather try your luck with the Charleston?" He sensed her hesitation, took her hand, and pulled her to her feet. "Besides, the Blue Danube is a good eleven minutes long, which will give us a chance to talk in private. I don't trust that yucca tree. Americans may be open, but they have a fascination for hiding in foliage. Tiresome national trait."

As he led her out to the other dancers, he put his hand against the bare skin of her lower back. "I haven't complimented you on your dress."

She turned to face him. "Stop it."

Without responding, he pulled her closer to him, his hand still on the small of her back, his other hand holding hers out in perfectly respectable, textbook waltz posture.

JEFFREY led them unostentatiously through the crowd of nostalgic pre-War power brokers occupying the dance floor, until they reached two tall, narrow doors that led to the Consulate's courtyard. Partially open to let air into the room. Then, still not talking, and his hand still firmly on her lower back, he walked her through to the outside.

She looked behind her to find Sinan or İnci, and although she did catch İnci's eye at the last moment, İnci entirely misconstrued Jeffrey's intent. She smiled, winked, and gave Marion a little wave as Jeffrey pushed her into the night air. Brought her to a wooden bench under a bare quince tree. No foliage.

"Are you cold? Would you like to wear my jacket?"

"No."

He removed his jacket and put it across her shoulders. She didn't protest. The air had the clean smell that precedes snow, and her dress was inadequate for more than a few minutes outside. She was trying to strategize, but the foggy anger that always dogged her interactions with Jeffrey had returned. She also had a tactile memory of his hand on her back, which was bothering her.

He sat next to her on the bench, six inches away, not touching. Leaned back and crossed his legs. "I was telling you about my boredom."

"Maybe I'm less interested than I thought I was. So here you are in Istanbul. I do hope you enjoy your time in the city. I suspect we won't see one another again." She stood to leave.

"I think it's in your interest to hear what I have to say."

"Talking to you is never in anyone's interest."

"Fair enough. But aren't you curious?"

"No." She began to walk away.

"I'll call off the surveillance."

She stopped. "In return for what?"

"Five minutes here. Finishing our conversation."

She threw the jacket across her shoulders and sat back down on the bench. Hating herself. "Five minutes."

"I'll have you spellbound in one." She didn't respond, and so he continued: "as I was saying, I considered returning to take up the Baghdad position again. Happy memories. Run of the place. And I did spend a few months there cleaning up what was left of your hapless organization." He glanced at her, but she kept her expression carefully blank. He looked up at the sky. "Interesting problem arose during our conversations with your friends there. It seems that Dr. Bailey had given up politics. Disappeared completely. No more banditry or bombings. We asked where you had gone, and no one knew." He considered. "And they had every reason to aid us in our investigations."

She made an involuntary movement, and he stopped talking. Looked at her to invite a comment. She didn't speak.

"So," he resumed, "we kept a few people on the trail, but for the most part we closed up the file. Consensus was that you'd returned home. And even if we could get to you there, the legal kerfuffle that would accompany any pressure on our part wouldn't be worth whatever outdated information you could provide to us."

"You've been talking for a good forty-five seconds now," she said, "and I'm still as uninterested as I was before."

"Ah, but here is where the story does become curious," he replied, a smile in his voice. "You see, consensus was that you'd gone home. But I didn't believe it. You're an addict. You'll never quit."

Angry again, she stood. "That's it. I have no reason at all—"

"Four more minutes, Marion. Sit." The smile had left his voice. "Unless you want to spend the rest of your life under one hundred percent surveillance."

"You can't possibly—"

"One telegram."

A second passed in silence. She sat.

He continued as though nothing had happened. "I didn't believe it. I knew you were still in Iraq. And I had a feeling I knew why."

She said nothing, trying to control her breathing.

He gazed out at the courtyard. "I put a few of my own people on you, and they found you easily. Not that you were hiding."

"I had no reason to."

"Of course not. Far be it from me to suggest that your activities have been anything but transparent and loyal. But they did report a pattern of inexplicable, even evocative, behavior. Your former colleagues, I was pleased to see, had been telling the truth. There was no evidence of radicalism. But there was evidence of—research?"

She leapt at the chance to lead him in a different direction. "That's hardly shocking. I've made it clear to anyone who troubles to ask that my interests now are scholarly. I'm back in the archive."

She sensed that she had made a mistake. He relaxed for the first time that evening, the uncertainty gone, and she felt an almost physical change in his manner. Her own anxiety skyrocketed.

But his reply to her claim was innocuous. "The archive? Do tell."

She shook her head. "No incentive. And by my count, you have one minute left to talk before I leave. Unsurveilled."

"Then I'd best come to the point. Your trail went cold—underground—repeatedly, in Baquba. You visited eighteen times. Every time you were there, you vanished. Sometimes for a few hours. Sometimes for over a day. They hadn't the faintest idea of what you were doing."

"You ought to hire better help."

"Perhaps. But then, I didn't push them."

She swallowed again, but she didn't speak.

"You see, Marion," he explained after a few seconds of silence, "I didn't want them to discover whatever it was you were doing. I felt it might be more strategic for us to speak in person. Before I sent a corps of soldiers blundering into—or under—Baquba."

She faced him on the bench. "You were wrong."

He kept looking out into the bare garden. "No, I think not. Because I'm rather certain I know what you were doing. And what was there."

"But you aren't completely certain. And you can't have found whatever it is you're looking for, or we wouldn't be freezing out here in this ghastly courtyard."

He turned and held her eyes. "I think it's the library. I think your husband left you a message before he died. And I think you deciphered it."

With an effort of will, she kept her own gaze level. "You delusional, self-aggrandizing pig. I will never, ever speak to you about Tariq. And you have truly lost your touch if you think that mentioning him will persuade me to say anything useful to you."

The hint of the smile was back on his face. "But why?"

"Because you killed him?"

He returned his attention to the garden and put his hands behind his head. "I didn't kill him, Marion. I employed him. If you persist in confusing the two, I really don't see how you'll ever integrate into civilian life."

She stood again. "You killed him just as certainly as if it had been you who'd slit his throat."

"But it wasn't I who slit his throat, was it? And if you want to go spinning out webs of contingent fault, consider your own. If you hadn't been wandering about in the desert annoying our intelligence services, he'd never have felt obligated to contact us to plead your case to begin with." He looked at his wristwatch. "But, oh dear, that's five minutes."

She nodded. "And you've accomplished nothing. I'm leaving. Goodbye."

"Nothing at all?"

"Goodbye," she repeated.

"I'd very much like to know where the library is."

"Your misfortune."

"So there is a library."

She put his jacket on the bench and turned to walk away. "I'm not doing this with you. You have no leverage."

He stood and slung the jacket over his shoulder. "I would never have initiated this conversation if I hadn't any leverage."

He was walking beside her. Opened the door to the ballroom for her, his fingertips on her back again. The band was playing New Orleans jazz.

She glanced back at him. "My papers, you mean?" She shrugged. "Yes, it would be an inconvenience if you flagged them. But I have other resources. And I'd disappear before I'd ever let you at my—" She caught herself.

He was putting on his jacket. "At your research."

"Yes," she said. "And I would go home. As you said yourself, you can't touch me there."

They were walking together toward the exit now. He had kept his hand on the small of her back, but she didn't want to give him the satisfaction of pushing it away. She signaled to İnci and Sinan that she was leaving, ignoring their gratified smiles at how well she was getting on with Jeffrey.

Before she reached the porter to ask for her coat, Jeffrey stopped her. "And that would be a shame," he said. "I mean, your disappearing underground again. At the very least, the office would no longer be able to amuse itself with your always creative itineraries. That paper trail you left for us from Amman was some of the most entertaining fiction I've read in years. Inventive."

She signaled to the porter without troubling to reply. The porter returned and gave her coat to Jeffrey, who helped her into it. "Apologies for Alexandretta," he murmured as he did so.

"I should have known."

He began buttoning his own jacket. "Well, what did you expect? You make a mockery of our diplomatic service, we will respond in kind." He looked up at her under his brows. "But it was wise of you not to lose your patience. If you had tried to cross the border using your—what was it?—'other resources,' you would have been talking to me under far less pleasant circumstances, far sooner."

She looked him in the face, cold. "As I said before, no leverage. I'm getting a cab now."

All his playfulness was gone. "And as I said, I would never have spoken to you if I hadn't any leverage." He took her arm and led her out the door, past security, toward the street. "No, Marion. We're not going to flag your papers. Though we could. Easily. And you shouldn't take your vulnerability there so lightly. There are a number of paperless refugees moving about just now, and they're not having a good time of it."

They had reached the line of new Republican cabs, waiting for customers. "But even so," he said as he cast a professional glance over the street, "I prefer less direct methods. Oblique pressure lends itself to a closer approximation of consent."

She disengaged her arm and walked toward the cabs. As she reached the first of them, he called after her: "do you know where Mehmet is? You haven't heard from him recently, have you?"

She stopped and turned. "What?"

"Mehmet. Haven't you wondered where he is?"

She took a step back toward him. "He's in France."

"Indeed. In France. But do you know *where* in France?"

She felt a twinge of fear. Shook her head.

"Not surprising." He made a show of looking about and then spoke in a stage whisper. "It's supposed to be a secret. But I'll give you a hint—if the President of the Republic found out, he'd be more than a little displeased."

"Jeffrey—"

"Ah. Then you do have a guess. And I suspect you're correct. *Gossip* has it that your friend Mehmet has become uncomfortably chummy with the self-styled 'Caliph' and romantically exiled head of the defunct Ottoman royal family. None other than your old friend, Abdülmecid."

"Mehmet isn't that—"

"Stupid? No. He wouldn't be. The Ottoman royal family is finished, and he knows it. But then," he added, "Mehmet, like you, is a fantasist. Surely you can empathize with his inclination? Aligning oneself with doomed causes for the thrill of it. Dead friends and husbands bobbing along in one's wake—"

"Jeffrey, this is *not* the place to talk about—"

He spread his hands. "Marion, I've been trying my damnedest to talk to you about it in every other conceivable place, but you keep jumping up to leave. I've become dizzy."

She collected herself. "Even if he were doing something like that, he'd never leave enough evidence to prove his involvement."

"Proof." He nodded thoughtfully. "Yes. How many supporters of the former Ottoman government were executed in Izmir last summer for the treason of 'trying to restore the Caliphate?' Fifteen? Twenty? Brilliantly efficient trials those were." He paused. "Although I admit I missed the 'careful compilation of evidence' part of the process. Granted I wasn't following too closely."

"He's not—"

"No," he agreed. "They wouldn't execute him. Such a shame, though, to lose that beautiful *yalı*, the house in Izmir, the automobiles, the boats, the servants, his position at the University, and really any reason at all to go on living." He took a few steps toward her and slipped her hand through his arm. "And all because he had the bad luck to invite you to be his house guest." He patted her hand. "Shades of Tariq, don't you think? You're like a natural disaster." He led her away from the cabs. "My driver is waiting round the corner. May I offer you a ride home?"

She didn't say anything as he walked her to his car. But she could feel his smile, perfectly relaxed now.

"I thought so."

*T*HE car was a government issue black Bentley 4 ½ Litre with a Weymann body and right-hand drive. As they neared it, a uniformed driver emerged and opened the door for them. Jeffrey helped Marion into the back and then slid into the seat next to her. The driver closed the door, returned to the front, and maneuvered the car into the nighttime traffic. Jeffrey was looking out the window.

"We're going to Ortaköy," he said. "I thought we might start with the boat."

She didn't say anything.

"My impression," he continued, "given the relative normality—at least for you—with which you accepted my offer, was that you were willing to continue our conversation." He paused. She still didn't speak. "That will be difficult if you don't talk." He looked at her. "I'm not kidnapping you, Marion. Say the word, and I'll stop the car and let you out."

She looked out at the Bosporus as they reached the bottom of the hill, turned left, and sped up the shore toward Ortaköy. "You could have started with Mehmet. Was the rest of that farce really necessary?"

"I have a process," he replied. "So far, it's served me well regardless of whether I'm applying electricity or mediocre American bands playing mediocre Austrian waltzes. Besides, I wanted to see how cooperative you'd be in the absence of pressure. And I got my answer: not at all."

She leaned back in the seat and closed her eyes. "Just so I'm clear, then. You're threatening to do some unspecified harm to my friend Mehmet, unless I—what? I still don't understand what you're wanting from me."

He looked back out the window. "I'd very much hoped you'd take me to your library."

She laughed. Her eyes still closed. "Unlikely."

"You're willing to sacrifice Mehmet?"

"No," she said as though talking to a particularly slow child. "I simply know Turkey. Despite your high handedness, you haven't got free rein here. Whatever you think you can do to Mehmet must be done fast, and it must be run from inside. If you drag me back to Iraq," she opened her eyes to look at him, "and believe me, I would not come quietly—you lose your hold on your people here." She closed her eyes again. "So, no. No imaginary library for you."

"Hmm." He nodded. "All right. I'll settle for whatever it is you brought back with you in that bag of yours."

She felt a stabbing pain between her eyes, the beginning of the unique headache she associated with him. She knew that telling him was inevitable, but she also wanted to put off the moment as long as she could. "Really, Jeffrey, why do you care?"

"I know what you're doing. But we'll get there eventually. So yes, I'll have this conversation with you. Again." He folded his hands primly on his knees. "As you know, I have a number of employers. But I remain loyal only to the one—the British Museum. We've been through this before, Marion. I want your archive for the British Library, and I want whatever objects the archive uncovers for the British Museum. It's perfectly evident at this point that our system is falling apart. In a few decades, all we'll have left are the artifacts, the culture, and an unpleasant imperial hangover. No more territory. No more military. No more economic influence." He unfolded his hands and wiped his palms on his trousers. "Unlike you, I know where my loyalties lie. History needs a center. And that center will be London."

She regretted opening this exchange with him. It only incensed her. And made her careless. "That made a reprehensible sort of sense in Baghdad, in the middle of the mandate. But—and I do realize I'm repeating myself—Turkey is independent. Sovereign. Autonomous. Why wreck its heritage as well?"

"Consider it the cultural equivalent of arming the Kurds. An homage to Mark Sykes."

"The whole post-War region is an homage to Mark Sykes."

"Not Turkey. Not Anatolia. That slipped away."

"I've told you, I'm not political anymore. I've nothing to say about Turkish policy in the southeast."

"Of course you haven't. As you yourself said, Turkey's complicated. Difficult to determine who the oppressed underdog is here, and until you do, you can't make a commitment, can you? It would be such an embarrassment, wouldn't it, to find yourself on the winning side?"

She surprised herself by not reacting. "'The cultural equivalent of arming the Kurds?'"

"Yes. Turkey may be independent. But it's by no means invulnerable. We'd like to keep it that way." He paused. "Stability is all very well, but we want to maintain at least a few explosive fault lines should regional politics go in an undesirable direction. Most of that is effected by our people on the ground. But a healthy reminder—in, say, the form of a well-placed exhibit at the British Museum—that global power emanates from Great Britain can also keep a population gratifyingly docile." He smiled to himself. "It's a niche operation, but it's mine. And so far, no one has complained."

"No one?"

"Not yet. But I must, at some point, demonstrate progress to my superiors." He considered. "Such as they are. Which brings us back to the matter at hand." He looked at her with something like fondness. "You've neither attacked me nor attempted to leap from the moving car. May I take that to mean that you're willing to work with me? Provisionally?"

"I have no choice."

"No."

"Provisionally, then."

"I'll watch my back."

"Good idea."

The car slowed to a stop in the small square at the edge of the dock in Ortaköy. The driver opened Marion's door, and the cold air off the Bosporus hit her face. A few snowflakes fell as she exited the car, and she slid on the wet cobblestones before finding her balance. Jeffrey followed her out and said something to the driver, who nodded and maneuvered the preposterous Bentley out of the square.

They were alone this late in the evening, and even the street sellers had packed away their stands. A few boats kept lamps burning, which would light their way down to the Hacker-Craft, but Marion was uncertain what Jeffrey's next move would be. And she was in no mood to help him. Content to let her mind wander, even for a few seconds, she inhaled the smell of the snow, the water, the city. It calmed her.

Jeffrey brought her back to the present. Holding her by the elbow again, he walked her to the boat and gestured into the cockpit. She noticed that he wasn't taking chances now. He kept behind her, watching her hands, prepared for unexpected activity on her part.

She could have laughed. She was so tired that she could scarcely walk, much less fight him. But she chose to be flattered that he rated her potential danger to his control of the situation so highly. She unlocked the hatch and climbed down into the cabin, followed by Jeffrey. He buttoned the cloth cover over the hatch and turned up a paraffin lamp and heater.

"I'll give him credit for committing fully to his vision," he said as he examined his surroundings. "I've seen a few of these custom Hackers, but nothing like this. Is that a Dollond barometer?"

She sat on the edge of a cushion that curved around the main cabin of the boat. "I think he borrowed it from his father's collection."

"Hmm." He leaned against the chart table and folded his arms. "So, let's see it, then."

"The manuscript isn't here."

"Well, it also isn't in the *yalı*. And your frock leaves little to the imagination, so I know it can't be on you." He turned to release the teak bench folded up behind the table, sat, and rested his chin in his hands. "Can you be a bit more forthcoming?"

"It's safe."

The heater had already warmed up the interior of the boat. Rather than responding, Jeffrey removed his jacket and tie and hung them on a hook next to the chart table. He busied himself with his cuff links, slipped them into a pocket of the jacket, and rolled up the sleeves of his shirt. He also unbuttoned its collar. Relaxed, he gazed at her, his elbow on the table, his chin on his fist.

"According to that horror of an Augsburg clock embedded in the bulkhead there," he said, "it's well past midnight. I don't need professional observational talent to tell me that you're on the verge of collapsing from sleep deprivation. I'm perfectly willing to extract this information from you slowly and painfully, fighting every inch of the way—especially since you've already *agreed* to work with me, and, I admit it, I do take a perverse sort of pleasure in these situations. But Marion, wouldn't it be easier, just this once, to share information like ordinary colleagues?"

"You aren't my colleague."

"I am now. Unless you'd care to start this tedious business from the beginning." He considered the room. "I wouldn't be surprised to find that Mehmet has a gramophone stashed somewhere, complete with a few choice works of Johann Strauss—"

"All right. Yes. You've made your point."

"And?"

"I've left the manuscript in safe keeping. In the city."

"Where?"

"The European side."

"More specific."

She sighed. "Here in Ortaköy. Up the hill."

"Getting warmer. *Where* up the hill in Ortaköy?"

She looked down at her hands. "I can't tell you."

"Oh, for God's sake." He stood and took a few steps over to the galley, opened a cupboard and found the bottle of *rakı*. Examined the label, retrieved two thin glasses, and poured them each four or five fingers. Then he walked to the edge of the galley, handed her a glass, and sat across from her in the main cabin. "What do you suggest, then?"

She took a sip and held the glass upright in her lap. "You stay here. I'll retrieve it and bring it back tomorrow."

"Alone? No."

"Jeffrey, I can't let you come. I used a drop."

He lifted his eyebrows. "And here I thought you weren't political anymore." His tone was nasty. "I wonder what else you've been up to?"

It was her turn to be exasperated. "Not a recent one. From before."

His expression turned to amazement. "You're concerned about compromising a decade-old dead drop? Unbelievable. I hate to be the one to tell you this, Marion, but your side—or whichever side you thought you were on—in fact lost that war. I think you can put your ghost scruples to rest."

"There was a time when people like you had a sense of professional propriety."

"This isn't professionalism. It's incapacitating nostalgia." He finished off his *rakı*.

She drank the last of hers as well. "I won't—"

"You will. Non-negotiable. If you don't, then tomorrow His Majesty's government will share, regretfully, with the proper authorities attached to the Turkish Republican Government, the sad news that Istanbul University Professor, Mehmet—"

"All right. I understand." The *rakı* had done nothing to alleviate her headache, which now threatened to move into her spine as well. She reached back to rub her neck, remembered her cocktail dress, and caught him looking at her. "Tomorrow," she agreed. "Is that all?"

He rose and collected their glasses. Set them in the galley's sink. "Do you have anything appropriate to wear?"

"Yes. I changed here before I met Sinan and İnci."

He smiled to himself. "God knows what they think we're up to."

"Right. Amusing."

He grinned at her. "You'll take the forepeak. More privacy, and I don't want to risk you regretting your decision to cooperate and absconding in the night."

She stood. "There is a hatch, you know."

"Bolted. The eyes tested it last night."

She was reclaiming her everyday clothes from the storage space under the cushions. Glanced up at him. "Jeffrey, your constant certainty is truly obscene.

He slipped off his shoes and stretched out on the other bunk. Looked back at her as she disappeared into the forepeak. "So I've been told."

She tried to slam the door behind her, but it merely swung silently into place. And so, disgruntled, she let her dress slide to the floor and crawled into the bed that Mehmet kept prepared for guests in the bow of the boat. She had thought that anxiety would keep her awake, but the minute she closed her eyes, she was asleep.

SHE woke to the sound of waves hitting the hull of the boat, loose halyards slamming against the masts of the sailboats moored nearby, and wet snow obscuring the wintry light filtering through the hatch above her. Bolted, she remembered. Then, as full consciousness of her situation reasserted itself, she heard Jeffrey moving about in the main cabin.

Feeling more affected by last night's champagne and *rakı* than she should have, she pulled herself out of the bunk, drew on her trousers, shirt, and jumper, slipped her feet into the now ruined satin boots, and used her fingers to pull her hair into a knot at the base of her neck. She folded the dress and left it on the bed before opening the thin, swinging door and stepping out into the main cabin. Refusing to acknowledge the pounding in her head. Or the wrecked state of her project.

Jeffrey, busying himself in the galley, was wearing a fitted blue pullover on top of his dress shirt from the day before, and his blond hair was covered by a black knit cap. He held out a cup of coffee for her. She took it without speaking. Drank a few sips, looking at the cabin. It hadn't all been a nightmare. She was disappointed. And, despite the sleep, she still felt too dull to develop a plan to respond to Jeffrey's reappearance in her life. Wondered what was wrong with her. Drank a bit more coffee.

He had finished his own cup and was wrapping a black muffler around his neck. When he raised his arms, she noticed a revolver secured to the waistband of his dress trousers, under the pullover. He watched her, without impatience, drink the last of her coffee. "Are you ready?"

She nodded, slipped her arms into the sleeves of her coat, buttoned it to her chin, and preceded him up the stairs to the cockpit. The snow was falling in earnest now, but still melting when it hit the ground. She watched it for a few seconds, vanishing into the grey water of the Bosporus.

Then she stepped off the boat and onto the dock. The wood was perilously slick, and she nearly lost her balance. She considered for a moment simply shoving him into the freezing water the moment he set foot on the dock. But before the idea could form itself into anything like a plan of action, she felt him behind her.

"The thought is beneath you, Marion," he said. "You're not an amateur."

"I have no—"

"You might as well have been musing aloud. It's beyond me how you found yourself privy to so much sensitive information." He adjusted his muffler. "But you have other assets, I suppose."

"You utter—"

"I was referring to your remarkable talent for decoding obscure dead languages. No need to be obstreperous." He walked with her across the square and toward the collection of narrow roads leading up the hill behind the water. Then he gestured toward the tangle of alleys. "After you."

She trudged up the hill, Jeffrey walking close, too close, behind her. When she reached the green door to the townhouse, the lamp was unlit. No one would be looking out the windows of the library as she exposed what had been one of Istanbul's most effective drops of the last twenty years. She stopped for a moment and considered her options. Could she make a move toward the lion sculpture and then turn, surprise, and incapacitate him? But she must do more than incapacitate him. Unless she killed him, he'd ruin Mehmet.

She glanced back at him and saw that he had drawn his revolver and had it trained efficiently in two hands at her head. The knit cap and top gave him a military look that she'd never noticed in him before. On his face was a half-smile that didn't go with his stance. "Really, Marion. This is becoming tiresome. Will you do it so that we can escape this wretched weather?"

"Wanker."

"Perhaps. Do it."

She pulled her coat more tightly over her shoulders and crossed the street to the lion. Lifted its head, reached into the cavity, and extracted the manuscript. He, meanwhile, had tucked the revolver back into the waistband of his trousers and followed her to the steps.

Rapped his knuckles on the head of the lion. "Convenient, that."

"As you said, it's old. I'm certain it hasn't been used in years."

"I'll be certain to put someone on it nonetheless. Who knows what ghostly flotsam from the War years will pop up now that we know where to look? Might yield all sorts of unexpected treasure."

He held out his hand for the manuscript. She gave it to him.

"Shall we take it home?"

When they reached the Hacker-Craft, Jeffrey slipped below to stow the manuscript in the chart table. The snow was still falling heavily, but there was little wind, and he had no difficulty once he'd climbed back on deck in starting the motor, untying the mooring lines, and pointing the boat toward Çengelköy and Mehmet's *yalı*. They both stayed in the cockpit, ignoring the weather, and they reached Mehmet's dock twenty minutes later, just as the snow was starting to stick.

A slushy veneer on the wooden planks of the moorage made walking nearly impossible, and the treacherous sheet of half melted ice on the flagstones that surrounded the entrance to the villa was close to fatal. Nonetheless, Jeffrey continued to walk behind her and to the side. Holding the manuscript under one arm. Maintaining his professionalism.

But his position, she suspected, was more to catch her should she slip and fall than to preserve an advantage should she attack him. Neither was in a position to attempt acrobatics. And so, reconciled to his presence, she walked obediently in front of him, the key to the house and the sadly worn cocktail dress in one hand, her other hand up and out to keep her balance in the sodden dress boots.

They both relaxed when they reached the entrance. And once Marion had turned the heavy key in the lock and pushed open the door, she sat on a bench just inside—gilt legs supporting a tapestried cushion depicting some classical Greek rape story—to rip off her boots. Jeffrey removed his equally ruined shoes, standing on one foot, while looking at the Venetian hall in fascinated incredulity. He pulled off his drenched knit hat and set it on top of the cupboard—monstrous carved wood, Albrecht Dürer on hallucinogenic drugs—that held the house slippers.

"Has his family ever been sane?" he asked looking down at a twisted soul in torment that served as a hook for drying wet socks. "Ever?"

She pulled on her own house slippers and stood, dusting off the front of her trousers. "It grows on you."

"I suppose," he replied, pushing damp hair off his forehead. "If one doesn't topple into the bottomless pit he keeps in the pantry." He spied a leather kit bag set to the side of the table that flanked the door to the salon. "Excellent. They've delivered it." Walked to the bag and opened it, examining its contents. Then he slipped the manuscript into it, re-secured it, and picked it up by the two handles. He also lifted a card resting on the table, glanced over it, and turned back to her. "From Sinan and İnci. Thanking you for a charming evening."

"That wasn't there before."

"They likely slept late. Eventful night."

"The bag."

He looked down at it. "Associates brought it early this morning."

"You said that you would call them off."

"I did call them off. The driver gave them their instructions last night. But I also need a change of clothing. Surely you don't expect me to rely on Mehmet's wardrobe. Given this house, I'd be reclined on a chaise longue in a silk dressing gown tippling absinthe within a day or two if I didn't import something normal to wear." He shouldered the bag and turned to walk up the curving staircase. "He makes your own cultural confusion look superficial. Which takes some doing."

She remained standing at the bottom of the stairs. Looking up at him. "Where are you going?"

"My bedroom." He continued walking, his back to her. "I plan to change into something dry, look at your manuscript, and decide whether or not you're still useful. If you are, I'll use you. If you're not, I'll have someone collect you and explain to you the seriousness of forging transit documents."

"You said you weren't going to flag my papers." She felt dizzy. Unable to keep up with his aggressive conversation. And her neck ached glaring up at him.

He had reached the top of the staircase, and he turned again, smiling down at her from the gallery. "I won't. But a week or two detained by passport control will keep you out of the way while I work. I'll be certain to find some particularly incorruptible officers to run the interview."

She rubbed the back of her neck, unimpressed. "Your Ottoman Turkish is scanty. You won't be able to read it."

"I don't need Ottoman," he retorted. "Anything worthwhile will be reproduced in Arabic or Persian. Always is."

"You're an idiot."

He disappeared into the room adjacent to hers without responding.

AFTER two or three seconds of quiet annoyance, Marion climbed the stairs after him. And then, once she'd pushed open the door to her own bedroom, she stretched herself out with a childish sort of rebellion on what was, indeed, a silk chaise longue. Positioned to take advantage of the windows overlooking the Bosporus.

Grateful for both the solitude and the silence, she adjusted a pillow beneath her neck and pulled a white fur blanket over her legs. The snow was piling up on the railing of the balcony and dusting the hills on the other side of the water. Jeffrey was touched, she told herself, for failing to appreciate the virtues of this piece of furniture. She could inhabit the chaise for hours without complaint. Weeks.

Despite the blanket, however, she began to feel cold, and so she rose, dragging the fur with her, and started a fire in the wood stove. Once it had warmed the room, she returned the fur to the chaise, retrieved her carpet bag, and dug through it to find her own change of clothing. She noticed that the bag had been rifled again, but at this point, she took it as a given that her possessions were under constant threat of contamination by unknown hands. Setting aside her irritation, she extracted wool socks, grey wool trousers, and a white knit jumper.

She left the clothes on the bed and went into the toilet to clean her teeth, turn on the water heater, and run a bath. Hot water was another novelty Mehmet's father had introduced into the *yalı*, although he hadn't built sufficient plumbing to heat the entire structure. She enjoyed moving from a steaming bath to a dry bedroom heated by wood stove. But she suspected that the next round of improvements would leave the stoves an anachronism as well. An aspect of Mehmet's hospitality she'd miss.

The tub was made of thick marble and stood on cabriole legs that mimicked not only the feet of some ungainly prehistoric bird, but the entire lower anatomy of what she took, without wanting to inspect it too closely, to be a goat. When it was full, she turned off the water and the gas, dumped half a crystal container of bath salts into the tub, stripped off her damp, wrinkled clothing, and eased herself into the water.

She had been looking forward to using this room since receiving Mehmet's telegram in Amman. And although her plans had gone awry, she wasn't about miss her opportunity. Entertaining herself with the thought of Jeffrey trying to decipher the *İskendernâme*'s marginalia next door, she slipped her head under the water to wash her hair.

After longer than she'd intended, she emerged dripping from the bath and dried herself with the *yalı*'s ostentatiously Venetian towels. Wrapping one of the towels over her hair, she walked into the now warm bedroom and pulled on her clothing. Then she combed her hair, left the towels to hang over the tub, and sat on the edge of the bed for a moment, uncertain. Coming to a decision, she stood. She'd eaten nothing this morning, and she was hungry. Light headed. Leaving the bedroom, she walked down the hall and stairs to the kitchen. Rummaged about in the pantry. Considered poisoning Jeffrey.

Then, turning up a burner on the stove, she cooked a skillet of eggs and sausage, annoyed with herself for shying away from the idea. Put her plate of eggs and sausage on a tray, along with bread and a large glass of tea, and crossed the hall to the salon. Still thinking. The salon was cool, and so she lit a fire in the green marble fireplace before settling into an armchair to eat. Chose a volume at random from the wall of books surrounding the fireplace to read while she ate. Waiting for Jeffrey's next move.

As she sipped her tea, she opened the leather cover. *Émaux et Camées* by Théophile Gautier. Which, she supposed, explained in part the classical Greek rape motif that ran throughout the villa's interior design. Perhaps Jeffrey was correct. Mehmet's family was more than a little bit demented. But the book was addictive, and she continued reading it even after she had finished her eggs and left the empty plate on the coffee table in front of her.

She was well into Gautier's meditation on blindness when Jeffrey walked into the room, hair also damp from a bath, wearing a white cotton shirt and dark wool trousers. He was carrying the manuscript under his arm. Radiating irritation.

She marked her place in the Gautier and looked up at him from the chair. "Are you handing me over to your passport officers, then? Or did you overestimate your mastery of my field?"

He sat in the chair opposite her, tossed the manuscript onto the coffee table, and lit a cigarette. Glanced at the empty plate she had left in front of her. "What, nothing for me?"

"Make your own."

He exhaled smoke. "I think I understand now why Tariq kept tempting death."

She looked back at him, cold.

He held her eyes, appraising. "It's a copy of the *İskendername*."

"That's what it says on the first page, yes."

He nudged the pages with his foot. "I remember it from some tutorial or other."

"But not all that well, I imagine." She dropped her eyes and smiled to herself. "Occupied as you were with that Abbasid *qasida* and its 'secret code' by the time we were reading the early Ottomans."

He took a slower drag of the cigarette, and set it, still burning, into an ashtray placed away from the pages. "Well, I wasn't half wrong about that, was I?"

"Weren't you?" Mocking. "I really can't say."

"Oh, do shut up, Marion." He stood and walked with repressed energy to the windows overlooking the Bosporus.

She raised her eyebrows. "Why not simply admit that you can't read it?"

He turned back. "I can *read* it perfectly well."

"All right then," she said brightly. "Shall I pack up my things and wait for your people to collect me?"

"Don't tempt me."

"You're the one who engineered this situation. If it isn't working for you, you can hardly blame me. And if you're too arrogant to admit, *again*, that you haven't the background to decipher the pages then it's your own problem."

He had regained his calm while she was speaking, and he walked back across the room, sat in the chair opposite her, and took up his cigarette. "When you went out on that bicycle yesterday morning, your initial objective wasn't coffee at a café on the coast. You were planning to go somewhere else. Where?"

"Anadoluhisarı."

"Why?"

"Architectural interest. It's a fascinating site."

"Try again."

She looked down at her hands. "I'm working on early Ottoman military strategy. I wanted to see the fortress in person. It's been a while."

He blew a contemplative smoke ring at the ceiling. "I remember enough from those soul-destroying tutorials to know that the copy of the *İskendername* you have there is no different from any other copy. At least as far as the central passages are concerned. Older. But no different. The marginal markings, however, are unique." He stubbed out the cigarette in the ashtray, not looking at her. "And, obviously, it hasn't escaped me that Ahmedi's patron is none other than the same Bayezid who built Anadoluhisarı."

He leaned back in his chair and crossed his legs. "I grant you, Marion, you are in a better position than I am to translate this volume. But don't underestimate me. There's something in the marginalia of that manuscript that has made it worth your while to come out of hiding, forge transit papers, and risk exposure to all sorts of attention from unsavory characters like me. It must be something big. What is it?"

She took a sip of her tea, which was now cold, and said nothing.

He watched her for a few seconds, sighed slightly, and continued. "Let me remind you, once more, of the two ways this can work. On the one hand, you can summarize for me the relevant points of interest in the marginalia so that we'll make progress, as colleagues, tomorrow." She still said nothing, and so he continued: "on the other hand, I can sit here with you for the rest of the afternoon and evening, going over each and every marginal marking in excruciating and humiliating detail, until I have an idea of why you've risked at the very least your freedom of movement to follow this lead. As I said yesterday evening on the boat, I personally would enjoy the second option because it would give me the chance to exercise my skill set. You, I suspect, would not."

She raised the glass of tea to take another sip, but he interrupted her. "The tea is cold, Marion. It's time for you to decide. Which is it?"

She put the glass on the table in front of her. Touched the vellum cover of the manuscript with the tip of her finger. Then she looked up at him. "In summary, then."

"Yes?"

"You know the basic story?"

"Broadly, yes. Ahmedi had a challenging task in front of him, writing that last set of verses, because his patron, Bayezid, was not only a drunk, an admirer of dancing girls, and prone to aligning himself with his Christian in-laws against his Muslim subjects, but eventually a catastrophically short-sighted military commander. It's surprising the Ottoman state survived at all after Timur captured him and paraded him in that cage all over Anatolia. Ahmedi's solution was to play up the piety and success of the *other* members of the Ottoman imperial family, both before and, implicitly, after Bayezid."

She nodded. "Right. But the marginalia in that text, which seem to date from 1401 and 1402, refute that story."

"And? He still lost. History isn't kind to losers."

"The marginal markings suggest that the poem isn't a history at all. It's not telling a story. It's not a book of kings. It's a message to posterity."

"I don't understand."

She resisted the urge to make a snide comment, and contented herself with saying: "you want a summary? Very well. By late 1401, Bayezid knew that he was going to lose to Timur. His support in the region had evaporated. The marriage to the Serbian princess hadn't done him any favors, and his ideological message was compromised. He had tried to prove his credentials by finishing Ulu Cami, the Grand Mosque, in Bursa in 1399, but no one was convinced. So his last move was to preserve the symbols of Ottoman power for his descendants—the swords and the cup. He hid them away where no one would think to find them, instructed Ahmedi to include a message to his offspring in the last part of the *İskendername*, and then wrote those famous, insulting letters to Timur to provoke him into an attack in 1402. By the time the dust had settled and Bayezid had killed himself, the Ottoman family had re-established itself as the ruling dynasty in the region." She looked back down at the manuscript. "But they had lost the swords and the cup."

Jeffrey had been nodding as she spoke. But then, pausing, he thought for moment and shook his head instead. "That can't be right."

"Why not?"

"The family never lost the sword," he said. "They used the Sword of Osman in the girding ceremony from the fifteenth century until 1922. I attended the last investiture of royal power myself. You did too. There's no lost sword. It's in Topkapı Palace now, if you want to look at it."

"I said 'swords.' Plural. Not 'sword.' And there's a cup as well."

"I don't understand," he repeated.

"Perhaps you ought to limit yourself to passport control."

"So enlighten me." Cold.

"Did you notice the shape of the sword during the girding ceremony?" Ignoring his tone.

He tapped his finger on the arm of the chair. Nervous energy again. "Relevance, Marion?"

"This is why your scholarship never amounted to anything."

"*Relevance*, Marion?"

"The Sword of Osman," she said, equally cold now, "is a *yatağan*."

"Yes?"

"It's a short, straight sword with a slight curve at the end. It's not a scimitar. It has no extended curve and it doesn't broaden before the tip."

"Your point?"

"In combat, soldiers use two *yatağan*s, one in each hand. Even into the eighteenth century. If a Janissary armed himself with a scimitar, he carried the one, but if he carried *yatağan*s, he carried two. And did you pay attention during the girding ceremony? There's a pause, a moment where you expect a second sword to be offered to the Sultan. But the second sword never materializes."

"So you're saying—"

23

"When Bayezid's son, Mehmed the First, re-established the Ottoman state, he found one of the two swords, the so-called 'Sword of Osman.' But not the other. And he never found—or perhaps never even thought to look for—the cup."

Jeffrey raised his eyebrows. "And this is what your reading of the marginalia in that manuscript suggests."

"I'm not sure. I need to take it to Anadoluhisarı to test my hypothesis."

"Ah." He leaned back, satisfied. "Hence your willingness to leave Iraq and risk falling into the power of one of your many waiting enemies."

She stood and picked up her empty plate and the dregs of her cold tea. "My advice to you is not to get in my way. You say you want these artifacts for the British Museum? I wish you the best of luck. But you won't get your filthy hands anywhere near them if you don't let me take the first step."

Then she walked with the plate and glass out the door and into the kitchen. Hoping she'd enraged him as much as he had her.

*H*E followed her into the kitchen and watched, insolent, as she washed and dried her plate. She was still hungry. The eggs hadn't been enough to counteract the chill of the boat ride and the dissolution of her plans. She looked out the window over the sink at a dull, greyish wash of thick snow, dejected. The storm hadn't abated. Jeffrey, meanwhile, was leaning, his arms crossed, against a solid iron oven on the other side of the tiled room. It took up more than half of the wall.

"We ought to wait until the snow has stopped before going out again," he said.

"Hmm."

He looked up at the ceiling. "That means we must entertain ourselves somehow until tomorrow morning."

She dried her hands on a kitchen towel. "Why don't you look for that bottomless pit?"

He looked around a corner and then peered, curious, into a section of the pantry installed at the back of the oven. "I am hungry. What does he keep here for guests, I wonder?"

"For uninvited guests? Nothing."

He turned his head to smile at her, and then he returned to the pantry. Muffled inside, she heard him exclaim, "perfect. I thought so."

He emerged, triumphantly holding a package of *yufka* dough and a bottle of olive oil. Found some white cheese, parsley, and butter in the cooler, lit the ancient iron oven, and spent ten minutes putting together a remarkably competent *su böreği* while the oven warmed. Then he slid the layered casserole inside, closed the door, and turned back to her, smug. She watched him, astonished.

"Fieldwork," he said.

When she still didn't speak, he busied himself with plates, silver, and napkins, made up a salad from ingredients he rescued from cold storage, and then looked about, stymied. "He must have a wine cellar here somewhere. Any thoughts?"

She walked silently to a wooden door set low in the stone foundation of the kitchen, turned the metal ring that served as a knob, and pushed it open. A few shallow steps led to a cellar of Ottoman-era bottles.

Jeffrey had followed her and gazed over her shoulder into the dim room. "Let's try something Bulgarian. For old time's sake."

He reached across her and pulled a bottle of Mavrud red from a steel rack.

She turned back, confused, but he had already pushed the door shut and uncorked the bottle to let it breathe.

"I don't think that goes with *börek*," she said.

"Let's be adventurous." He pulled the pan out of the oven and placed it on the counter to cool. "Besides, I haven't decided yet whether I'll share this with you. You were parsimonious with those eggs."

She watched him, still not believing what she was seeing. He poured two glasses of wine, slid two pieces of the *börek* onto heavy plates, added the salad, put everything onto another large tray, and nodded toward a second door at the end of the kitchen. "We haven't tried the dining room."

Then, smiling to himself, he lifted the tray, pushed open the door with his shoulder, and walked into the room. Set the food on an oak banqueting table that looked as though it belonged in Valhalla. Marion had been in this room only a few times before, during Mehmet's most crowded parties. Seeing it now, nearly empty, through Jeffrey's eyes, left her unexpectedly, disloyally, embarrassed. But she would never admit that to him. Instead, she watched as Jeffrey used his matches to ignite the eight candles, each two feet tall and the thickness of a child's arm, that were mounted, sentry-like, in the middle of the table.

Once the candles were throwing light across the room, Jeffrey frowned up at the ceiling, a mural depicting something out of Wagner. "Hmm. Is that Thor up there menacing us with a lightning bolt? Cozy." He moved the tray to one end of the table and arranged the plates and wine glasses across from one another. Gestured to Marion to sit. "I've decided to relent. And I hope you don't mind if we sit crowded together here. As Teutonic and fancifully medieval as it might be, I don't want to chat separated by an eighteen-foot slab of solid wood."

She sat and put the napkin in her lap. Ate a small bite of the *börek*. It annoyed her that it was as well put together as it was. Jeffrey, reading her reaction, took a satisfied sip of his wine and then began eating as well. Once he had finished most of his *börek* and picked at his salad for a while, he leaned back in his chair, holding the glass of wine. "We ought to make an early start of it tomorrow. Do you know what we'll be looking for? Anadoluhisarı isn't large, but I don't fancy going there in this cold without a plan."

She put down her fork as well. "I think it's something similar to the flute motif in the manuscript."

"Symptom of his decadence, wasn't that? The love of flutes and dancing girls. Are you certain he'd want to pass that to posterity?"

"That's the point," she said. "If it wasn't an accurate description of his character, his sons would have known. It would have struck a false note and encouraged them to think. To look. Besides, Ahmedi is ambiguous about Bayezid and music. At another point in the poem, he writes that Bayezid was an ascetic because he never listened to flutes at all."

"True. But what if the description *was* accurate? You have quite a bit of faith in Bayezid's good character. Despite five centuries of history to the contrary."

"I could be wrong," she admitted. "But I want to test it."

He finished off his wine without speaking and loaded the empty dishes onto the tray. After a few minutes, she heard him through the partially open door to the kitchen washing the plates. And then, putting both palms flat on the table, she rose and followed him.

He was drying his hands on a dish towel when she walked back through the door. And unbidden, an image of him at home, some home, somewhere else, domestic, flashed violently across her mind. She stumbled and shook her head to clear it of the thought. Held her hand to the wall to steady herself.

He watched her. "Are you all right? You look as though you've seen a ghost."

She pushed herself up off the wall, turned away from him, and moved in the direction of the salon. Blinking unhappily. "Worse."

Perplexed, he followed her out of the kitchen. When he reached the salon, she was already sitting in the armchair next to the marble fireplace, reading the Gautier. The snow outside the wall of windows was thinning, but the clouds were low, and daylight was fading. The wind was also picking up. He sat opposite her and retrieved the manuscript to start reading. She glanced at him from under her brows but didn't say anything. He was engrossed, his frustration evident. And so she turned back, smiling, to her Gautier.

A little over an hour later, they were both startled out of their reading by the sound of another of Mehmet's grandfather clocks, this one the size of a small pipe organ and embedded in an upstairs wall, alerting the house that it was nine o'clock. The reverberations from the chimes lasted for a good thirty seconds after the bells themselves had ceased ringing. Jeffrey had nearly dropped the pages of the manuscript.

"It doesn't do that every hour," he said. "I would have noticed."

Marion had also been surprised, though she had known about the clock from earlier visits. Put down her book. "No. Only at nine."

"At nine."

"Yes. Nine in the evening and nine in the morning."

"I know I'll regret asking this. But why?"

"Mehmet's father had an obsession with the number nine." She kept her finger in her book to mark her place. "He wanted to commemorate it."

He thought about this for a moment. Began to reply, but then asked a different question instead: "what about Mehmet himself? Same mania?"

"Mehmet told me once," she said, "that he had considered shutting down the bells altogether. But doing so would have defeated the purpose of owning the clock. He also didn't want to set it to chime every hour because, well, you heard. So," she finished, embarrassed, "he left it. Set for nine."

Jeffrey had stood and was fitting the manuscript back into its vellum cover. "And these are the people you consider your friends."

She stood as well, irritated. But she didn't respond. Instead, leaving the Gautier on the table, she walked up to her room, her headache reaching down into her spine. Unperturbed, he banked the fire, switched off the lamp, and followed a few steps behind.

SHE woke the next morning to painfully bright sunshine reflecting off the water into the windows of the bedroom. Having forgotten to draw the curtains the night before. Blinking and still half-asleep, she responded to the intrusive light by reaching instinctively under her pillow for the manuscript, finding nothing, remembering the past two days, and groaning.

Then, still squinting, she rolled over and dragged herself out of the bed, glancing up through the window at the grotesquely blue sky. There were small whitecaps on the Bosporus, and for the first time since she had arrived, one might call them playful. Or at least as close to playful as the wind and current on that body of water ever got. She disliked them. Mourned the low clouds and spitting rain.

The room was cold, but she didn't waste time starting a fire. Instead, shivering, she found the jumper she'd left on the chaise the night before and pulled it over her head. Then she walked barefoot into the bath, plaited her hair, and twisted it into a chignon before returning for an unused pair of trousers. She noted that the bag was as she had left it. And although it bothered her that she felt grateful to Jeffrey for keeping his word about the surveillance, she did. Slipped into brown tweed trousers, buttoned them, pulled on wool socks, and picked up her work boots to put over them before leaving the house.

When she glanced down from the gallery, Jeffrey was already prowling about in the hall, dressed in a black top, black wool trousers, his knit cap, and an oilskin coat, open. He was also wearing boots that evoked trenches to anyone old enough to remember the War. He looked military again, which she didn't like. At the bottom of the stairs, he handed her a glass of tea and then remained standing to watch her drink it.

"You slept well." Irritated.

She raised her eyebrows. "It isn't even nine yet. I would have heard."

She took a sip of the tea, still looking at him. He hadn't troubled to hide the revolver, which was properly holstered now in a belt. He noticed her looking at the gun and buttoned the coat. Then he pulled on leather gloves, his expression neutral. "We'll take the boat and dock it in the creek next to the fortress."

"No Omafiets?" She had finished the tea and set the empty glass on one of the tormented souls that decorated the shoe rack.

"Whimsy doesn't suit me."

She retrieved her travelling coat from the wooden stronghold on the other side of the hall. "Clearly not. You look as though you're planning to assassinate someone." She bent over to slip into her boots.

As he made for the door, the wrapped manuscript under his arm, he looked behind him. "I will be if you don't hurry."

She pulled on her hat, pocketed the key, and walked behind him, deliberately sedate. Then she turned to lock the door, still moving slowly, and smiled to herself when she heard him start the engine of the Hacker-Craft, the motor itself sounding impatient.

He had nearly cast off by the time she had climbed into the cockpit, and he was holding the boat in place by a single line off the stern. Once they were free of the dock, he slammed the throttle unnecessarily as he pointed the boat up the Bosporus toward Anadoluhisarı, jolting her when she lifted the fenders out of the water. She smiled more broadly.

The journey lasted only a few minutes. Soon, they were tying the Hacker-Craft to a makeshift dock in the creek that bounded one side of the fourteenth-century fortress. There was a brittle crust of ice over the snow that had fallen the day before, but it was thin, and the ground was no longer treacherous. Together, they approached an anonymous stone wall, a silent threat to the European side of the city since 1394. Marion rested a bare hand against the structure.

Jeffrey watched her, his expression still unreadable. "It's not open to the public."

She removed her hand, put it in her pocket, and shook her head. "No. But there also isn't any security. The Republican government has other concerns." She looked up at the towers. "There ought to be entry points."

He kept his hands in his pockets, the manuscript still under his arm, calculatingly casual. But his posture was deceptive. The reckless energy was very much present, and she knew that he was watching her closely. Without speaking, she turned and walked to the back of the structure. It was as she had suspected. One of the five watch towers marking the corners of the fortress was missing a door. A gaping, rounded passage through the cylindrical turret passed into the interior of the building.

She looked back at Jeffrey to be sure that he was following and then ducked through the passage. Smelled cats, and something worse, as she crossed the perimeter of the main tower. And then, under the open sky, with a dusting of snow beneath her feet, she paused to find her bearings. Jeffrey drew up next to her, looking about him with something like contempt.

Ignoring him, she walked toward a partially walled-off area of the central, pentagon-shaped floor. "I'm looking for a masjid."

"A mosque?" Skeptical. "Here?"

"A little one. He built it into the original structure of the fortress. Where the temple of Uranus had been. Sacred ground."

"Guilt."

She shot him a look. "Piety."

"As you like. My interest is the map."

She examined a set of regular indentations marring the crumbling interior wall. Ran her finger along them. "I don't think it will be a map." She wasn't looking at him. Instead, she was peering at the wall. "There would have been tiles here."

He walked over and crouched beside her. Removed his glove and touched the wall as well. "Hmm." He stood and pulled on his glove. "Any thoughts?"

"I'd like to see the manuscript."

He unwrapped the volume and passed the pages to her. Treating the vellum as gently as she could, she turned to the fourth folio. Ran her finger along the marginal images. Looked back at the wall. Nodded. "Yes. This is it. The tiles were calligraphic representations of flutes." She handed the manuscript to him without looking in his direction.

He took it from her and wrapped it in the linen. "I don't see it."

She knelt, the stone floor cold through her trousers, and scraped at the ancient mortar along the edge of the interior wall. "You're not supposed to see it. 'Calligraphy is music for the eyes.'" She looked up at him, then back at the base of the wall. "You know?"

He shrugged. "No. But you seem to have convinced yourself of something. I'll wait."

It hurt her fingers, but she kept rubbing at the joint between the wall and the floor until she broke through into a gap between them. Widened it with her hand and then pried up a rectangular stone. Underneath it was a cavity about the length of her arm, within which was cached a rotten piece of cloth, wrapped repeatedly around itself. She extracted the cloth and put it on the ground in front of her.

Jeffrey squatted down again. "Cup or sword?"

"Neither. But it's as close as you're going to get to a treasure map." She unwrapped the cloth, which partly disintegrated in her hands, producing a twinge of guilt. She was no archaeologist, and she hated disturbing sites like this. Pushed the shame away. No choice. And when she brushed back the cloth, she felt almost optimistic. What she'd exposed was a small, five-inch-long flute—a truncated *ney*, almost a whistle—ornately carved bone, set with lapis in a floral pattern. Three holes. She left it resting on the floor of the fortress.

Jeffrey stood again, brushing off his knees. "That looks like it could whistle up a nasty little spirit, given half the chance."

"What?"

"I'm from East Anglia," he said, as though that explained something.

Shaking her head, confused, she turned her attention back to the whistle. And shivered.

"Perfect," he continued. "And you're from Edinburgh. Perhaps we can hire someone to play it for us."

She placed the whistle on what remained of the cloth, wrapped it up again, stood, and began to slip it into her pocket. But Jeffrey stopped her. "Nonetheless, I'll overcome my superstitious horror of protective ghosts just this once." He held out his hand and, reluctantly, she gave him the wrapped flute. He examined the cloth and slid it into an inside pocket of his coat. "You can tell me what it does when we return to the *yalı*."

They rearranged the stone over the cavity in the floor and removed as much as they could evidence of their visit. Then, feeling but not seeing the cats watching them depart, they returned to the boat and Mehmet's villa.

I think it's supposed to evoke water."

They were sitting in the salon in front of the green marble fireplace. They had eaten the remainder of Jeffrey's *börek*, and Marion was drinking a cup of sweetened orchid root *salep* that they had brewed afterward in the kitchen. Jeffrey, who had removed his coat and put on another dark top, was turning the flute over in his hands. She set down her cup of *salep* and reached for the manuscript resting on the coffee table. Opened it and turned it so that he could see.

"Look at the upper left of that page."

He took the manuscript and wrinkled his forehead. "Yes. I see it. Next to this description of Bayezid's shock forces."

"The *akıncılar*," she confirmed. "Mounted archers who preceded the regular army into battle. They had a reputation for being, explicitly, off their heads. A force of nature. They're described by contemporaries as 'flowing like water.'"

"Then that also explains this bit of exegesis in the margin," he said. "Refers to them flowing out of the end of a 'flute,' or a 'whistle'…?" He looked up at her and she nodded. "And then into this—cup, I suppose? A nice metaphor. Bit arcane."

"My interpretation of it is that whoever holds the cup also holds the loyalty of the *akıncılar*. In his hand. They were instrumental in solidifying the early Ottoman conquests. Bayezid rallied them. And, according to this, he passed along the legitimacy to rally them to his sons. Via the cup."

"Hmm. So, whoever plays this flute somehow—what—summons the cup? And hence Ottoman legitimacy?" Intrigued.

She shivered again. Tried to identify the draft in the room but couldn't. "Yes," she said, pushing down her uneasiness. "But it must be played in the proper place. Not anywhere."

The wind, which had been intensifying outside the windows as darkness fell, heaved a splatter of drops against the glass. When the water hit, the window itself swung open, spraying the room with a salty mist and a few stray shards of ice. Jeffrey jumped up and slammed the window shut, turning the knob and locking it. He tried to peer out onto the dark flagstones surrounding the house, but gave up, annoyed.

"That wasn't open before," he said.

"They're old locks."

He looked at her levelly for a moment and then sat down again across from her. Held his hands out to the fire to warm them. "The proper place," he echoed. "And where would that be?"

"I think we ought to try the Köprülü family's *yalı* in Kanlıca."

"The Köprülü family?" He rubbed his hands together. "The Grand Viziers? They didn't come to prominence until a good two centuries after Bayezid. And isn't the *yalı* a ruin?"

"I've read commentaries on the *İskendername*," she said, "that hint they were entrusted with a secret by the descendants of Bayezid's Serbian wife and brother-in-law. My thought is that the wife, Olivera Despina, and the brother-in-law, Stefan, hid the cup and transported it back to Serbia until it was safe enough to present to Bayezid's line. Then history intervened, and—two centuries later, it became the duty of the Köprülüs to pass it along."

"Tenuous."

"It's a hypothesis," she said. "I find the timing of the *yalı*'s construction suggestive. Amcazade Köprülü Hüseyin Pasha was appointed Grand Vizier in 1697 solely because of his promise to retain the Balkans as Ottoman territory. But he didn't. The Ottoman military was routed in Europe throughout the 1690s. And yet, he wasn't dismissed. If anything, he was rewarded. And the first thing he did with his new power and influence? He built the *yalı*. In 1699. Same year that the Treaty of Karlowitz formalized the end of Ottoman influence in the region. And *then*, rather than maintaining a low profile, he filled up the *yalı* with all sorts of, I suppose you might call it 'Serbiana.' Objects salvaged from defeats on the battlefield. Or given to him by loyal subjects about to be loyal to someone else."

She rubbed the back of her neck with her hand. Still unsettled by the unlocked window. "He also installed a stone water wheel in the villa as a kind of early interpretation of the folly craze that became popular in Europe in the 1700s. People mocked him for it. It apparently made Marie Antoinette's little mill house a century later look agriculturally functional." She stood. "I want to see the water wheel. Or what's left of it. But now I'm going upstairs to sleep."

"It's not eight o'clock."

"I haven't slept properly since I arrived."

Without waiting for a response from him, she left the room and walked up the stairs. Meditating on their movements tomorrow. But when she reached her room and turned on the light, her contemplative mood splintered.

There was no damage and nothing to indicate a violent search. But someone had ransacked her things. The bed was wrinkled, her bag was open, and her clothing disordered. And the window to the balcony was ajar, letting in a thin, cold stream of air.

She crossed the room to look out at the balcony on the chance that someone was still there. Empty. She closed and locked the window. Then, blood rushing to her face, she stalked out to the gallery and nearly ran into Jeffrey, who had followed her up the stairs. He was coming out of his own room, the wrapped flute in his hand.

"Your *one* concession," she raged at him, "the *only* promise you made to me in this reprehensible arrangement, was that you'd call them off. And you can't even—"

He ran a hand through his hair. "They weren't mine."

"Piffle."

"'Piffle?'"

"Fuck you."

"Yes. More in character." He glanced briefly through the door to her room and then back at her. "I have no interest in keeping them on you. You spill more without them. I called them off. These weren't mine." His eyes moved hectically across the gallery. "And they searched my room too."

"Then who—"

She was interrupted by the sound of the clock, just a few feet down the hallway, starting to chime. Squeezed her eyes shut as it thundered through the house. When it had finished, and the reverberations had died off, she tentatively opened her eyes again.

Jeffrey had narrowed his own and was scrutinizing the hallway. "That was eight."

"Eight?"

"Eight. It's eight o'clock. Not nine." A smile was playing about the corners of his mouth. "One feels sympathy for Mehmet's father."

Marion's heart was beating hard in her throat. The wind was keening outside the house. She cast an involuntary look at the flute Jeffrey held in his hand. "I don't like this."

He was still peering into the hallway off the gallery, but his posture was now relaxed. "They've overplayed their hand." Then he turned back to Marion. "All you're missing is the flickering candelabra and the white lace nightdress."

"Whatever it is, it's—"

"It's clumsy."

"Jeffrey," she repeated, "I don't like this."

He turned and walked toward his room, throwing a glance back at her. "Poor Marion. Shall I stay with you tonight?"

She stood rooted in the hallway. "You're repellent."

He paused at the door to his bedroom. "I'm not certain what else I can offer you. You're the one falling to pieces over a novelty grandfather clock."

And then he disappeared into his room, closing the door behind him.

THE blinding, frigid sun and porcelain blue sky returned the next morning, but Marion was already awake by the time the light reflected through her window. She had spent a brief moment in bed, just before dawn, wondering whether she could convince Jeffrey to return the whistle. Then she had decided that she couldn't abandon her project for so little reason. Not to mention that he would laugh at her. Reconciled to their plan, but unhappy, she had sat up.

When she'd looked about the room, she'd felt, rather than observed, that her things had been disturbed again during the night. Her clothing not as she'd left it. Her pins and hairbrush rearranged— although she couldn't have said precisely how. She half wished that Jeffrey had admitted to retaining his own surveillance over the house because at least then she could be angry rather than afraid. She changed into her clothes from the day before and descended to the kitchen.

Jeffrey was awake, wearing his dark top and wool trousers, but he hadn't yet finished preparing the tea. He had the double kettle boiling on the stove, and he had begun arranging olives, white cheese, and slices of tomatoes and cucumbers on a platter.

The corner of his mouth went down when he saw her pallor. "A glass of tea will dispel the chill. I've been trying to prepare breakfast for us as well, but it's difficult given that your ghosts have appropriated our kitchen knives."

"What?"

"Indeed. What I thought. Odd behavior for angry spirits."

She considered the kitchen. It also wasn't right. "Jeffrey, I think we—"

"You're not going to ask me to return the flute to its place of rest, are you?"

She blushed. Didn't respond.

"Too late," he said. "My memory of these stories is a little vague, but isn't the first one to touch it always cursed regardless of the remorse that comes later? You're already neck deep in it. Might as well see it to its conclusion, don't you think?"

"I don't believe that it's cursed," she clarified, annoyed. "I simply think there's something wrong with—with how we're proceeding. We ought to reconsider our strategy."

He smiled to himself as he turned down the stove and poured two glasses of tea. "Of course there's something wrong with how we're proceeding, Marion." He glanced up at her and then back down to concentrate on the food. "I'm blackmailing you to loot Turkey's heritage for the greater glory of England. You're hysterically uncertain, as you always seem to be, about whether your goals are political, scholarly, personal, military, or some lurid combination of all four." He ran a critical eye over the platter. Shifted a slice of cucumber into place. Nodded. "You can't even remember whose side you're on, much less your deeper motives. So, yes. You're correct. Our activities are wrong. Dastardly. Unethical. Likely to attract the displeased attention of both divine and mundane observers."

He looked back up at her. "But that happens to be the way we work." He held out a glass to her. "Tea?"

"Return the flute," she said.

"No."

He put her glass of tea on the kitchen counter, picked up his own glass as well as the platter of food, and walked out the door to the salon.

She stared at the glass for a few seconds, took it, and followed him. Noticed when she entered the salon that the Gautier had returned to its place on the bookshelf. Shivered again. He was sitting in the armchair, sipping his tea.

She sat across from him. "You can't take the next step without me."

"I cannot," he agreed.

"I won't help you."

He put down his tea. "This again? Must we do it *every* morning? Even I'm becoming bored."

"I can't."

"Or perhaps this time you're doing for the benefit of the vengeful ghosts?" He turned and shouted out the door into the hall: "Dr. Bailey would like you all to know that she is cooperating with me under duress. Ordinarily, she would leave well enough alone." He paused for a moment and then shouted again. "Except that she wouldn't. She never does." He turned back to her. "Satisfied?"

"Twat."

He lifted his tea. "Yes, you've noted that before." Took a sip. Ate a few bites of cucumber and a piece of cheese.

She finished her tea and forced herself to swallow an olive. She wasn't hungry. "I want to ring Sinan before we leave."

"We are leaving, then?" He ate another piece of cheese. "I needn't dance with you or take you for a ride in the Bentley to remind you of where your interests lie?"

She stood and walked out the door to the telephone. Unwilling to let him goad her. "I'll ask him to look for me here if he doesn't hear from me later today."

Jeffrey followed her out of the room. Stood over her, leaning against the wall, as she rang through to Sinan. Lazy and mocking. "Will you ask him to look for me as well? Your illicit lodger? Vulnerable and exposed in a strange land?"

She ignored him and waited for the connection. Sinan wasn't in, but she left a message for him with his assistant, telling him that the *yali* was insecure and that she'd be grateful to Sinan for seeking her out if she didn't contact him that evening. She wasn't pleased by the plan, but at least there was the beginning of a safety net in place should whoever was reconnoitering the house take a new step.

She walked, still feeling a dull premonition of failure, over to the wardrobe to retrieve her coat and boots. Jeffrey, jovial as he always was when faced with an unpredictable adversary, trailed a few steps behind. As he was buttoning his own coat, he spoke to her. "We'll take the boat again?"

She nodded and walked out toward the dock. They cast off without speaking, and Marion sat in the cockpit, shivering with cold, at least, rather than with fear, and waiting for the ruins of the Köprülü villa to come into view. Staring at the choppy water.

Unlike Mehmet's family's *yali* the Köprülü house was an unassuming structure from the outside, unadorned wood held up on pilings and surmounted for at least a century by shattered windows in ill repair. They tied the Hacker-Craft to a rotting support and climbed up through a cracked hole in the floor of the main audience chamber. Marion thought for a moment that the building would collapse down over them, but she reminded herself that it had been there for over two centuries already and was unlikely to fall apart now. Jeffrey looked about him with his customary expression of arrogant contempt.

She crossed the creaking floor, examining the room. The walls were covered with decorative wood panels, etchings of vases and flowers in keeping with the very early eighteenth-century Ottoman fashion that the structure represented. They weren't what she wanted. A marble fountain in the middle of the room, now fractured and empty, was more promising.

She approached it and then stepped around it. It had an odd affinity, she thought, with Ulu Cami, the Grand Mosque that Bayezid had built in Bursa at the end of his reign. Same arrangement of twenty domes. Same two minarets. Although anyone looking at the two without first thinking of a connection would never see it. She circled the fountain a few more times, looking under it and then into its dry central pool. Jeffrey had walked up behind her, his hands in his pockets.

She pointed into the center of the square fountain. "This is where the water wheel was set. You can see it would have been a bizarre addition to the décor."

He looked at where she was pointing. "It's not there now."

"I think it may be hidden."

He shrugged and looked about the room. His breath showed in the cold air. "What do we do?"

"The same as before," she said. "I need the flute."

"You're volunteering to be the sacrificial victim? Summoning the angry spirits?"

"I need the flute," she repeated flatly.

He took it from his pocket and unwrapped the cloth. Held it out to her. "Very well." More amused than awed.

She took it and turned it over in her hands. Intuition told her to play the three notes from high to low. Although intuition also told her to put as much distance between herself and the object as she could. To drop it and leave. Annoyed by her uncertainty, she squeezed her eyes shut, clearing her head. And then she put the whistle to her lips. Blew gently and covered each hole in turn with her fingers.

The sound was both purer and more intense than she had expected. And Jeffrey shook his head, as though disturbed, when the first note sounded. Then, as she finished, an echo of the eerie wail reverberated through the room and across the rafters near the ceiling.

They waited for a few seconds. Nothing happened. She looked over at Jeffrey, who raised his eyebrows, unimpressed. Sensed a shudder coursing through the floor of the building. Then nothing. But a moment later, the room shook in earnest, and she put out a hand to steady herself. Convinced that she had weakened the underlying structure of the *yalı*. Jeffrey was frowning up at the trembling wood panels decorating the walls.

"Brilliant," he muttered. "Shall we get out before it crushes us?"

He turned to go, but she grabbed his arm. He turned back, looked down at her hand on his sleeve, and, self-conscious, she released it. Then she pointed at the fountain. "Look."

Rising up out of the center of it was a small water wheel made of Kütahya porcelain. It was pristine—no age markings, no cracks, the paint still bright. They watched as it reached the top of the fountain and then began spinning. The motion of the wheel was slow, but eventually a brightly colored, jeweled bucket—dry, unused, the fountain itself derelict—ascended to the top of the wheel and stopped.

Marion and Jeffrey looked at each other. Then Jeffrey stepped toward the bucket, peered inside, and retrieved a wrapped object. He held it in one hand and, with the other, removed the cloth, laughing when he saw what the water wheel had delivered to them.

It was small, no more than five inches high. A tinned copper goblet or wine jug, nearly spherical—a *mashrabe*—with etchings of lotus flowers and vines, and punctuated with sapphire and emerald petals. Immaculate.

Jeffrey grinned at Marion. "An ascetic? This is a wine jug, if I've ever seen one. No matter how many tiny soldiers he claims to have stored in it."

"It's symbolic."

"I think the term you would use is 'piffle.'" He wrapped the goblet back in its cloth and secured it inside his coat. "That cup has seen some celebratory use. I can feel it."

The spell was broken when Jeffrey hid the cup away, and she shook her head, looking down at the flute, which she still held in her hand. "Yes. And you can leave Mehmet in peace now."

"I want the sword too."

"Isn't this enough?" On the verge of tears. "You'll lose it all if you keep pushing."

"Still frightened of the ghosts?"

"No!" She looked about the decaying room as though it might help her to explain. "There's something—something—"

"Blasphemous? Heretical? Disrespectful? Impious?"

"Stop it," she nearly shouted. Her voice echoed through the *yalı*. She shivered again. Violently this time.

He touched the water wheel with the tip of his finger and set it spinning again, faster. Shook his head. "Northern upbringing." Then he nodded toward the flute. "I'll take that as well."

She gave it to him without speaking, unable to articulate her discomfort, and he glanced, contemptuous once more, at the fountain. Turned to go. "I'll look forward to learning how Bayezid's highball glass here leads to his missing *yatağan*. An engaging holiday we've arranged for ourselves, no?"

He crossed the floor and lowered himself through the gap and into the waiting boat. She followed, angry with herself for showing weakness. But then, deciding that what she was feeling, chaotic though it might be, wasn't a weakness at all, she looked back at the water wheel. It was still spinning, more slowly now. They hadn't disguised it again. She wondered what the next chance visitors to the *yalı* would make of it.

Dismissing the thought a few seconds later, she climbed through the gap in the floor, felt a splinter lodge in her hand, cursed, and hunched in the cockpit of the Hacker-Craft. Jeffrey had already started the motor, and they reversed out into the Bosporus. Pulling her coat tightly across her shoulders, she sat against a bulkhead, staring at the water passing beneath them. Jeffrey, she noted sourly, was whistling as he brought the boat into the center of the strait. Relaxed and confident. She rubbed the splinter in her hand with the tip of her finger, meditative.

MEHMET'S *yalı* was brightly illuminated and busy when they returned the boat to its moorage. And figures were moving inside, thrown into stark relief by the lights behind them. Active. Uninterested in their arrival.

Jeffrey scrutinized the extravagantly lit windows adorning the façade as he tightened the lines holding the boat to the dock. But he didn't speak. Marion, also puzzled by the change in what had been a neglected house, concentrated on arranging the fenders. Then, uncertain as to what else she could do, she stepped off the boat and started toward the flagstones. Sinan or İnci must have elected to visit earlier than she had expected them.

Before joining her, Jeffrey climbed into the cockpit and opened the hatch over the cabin. "I'll join you in a moment," he said. "I don't trust the house and I want to secure Bayezid's patrimony here in the chart table."

Clouds were gathering off the Marmara, and Marion hugged her coat over her shoulders as she nodded her assent. Then she felt the first few spatters of rain on her face and, impatient, watched the hatch. A few seconds later, Jeffrey emerged, locking the wood door and snapping the cloth flap into place over it.

He hopped off the boat. "Shall we see who's come to call?"

She felt the military aggression in his posture again and tensed. But this time, when he noticed her discomfort, he didn't take advantage of it. She looked up at his face, which was focused on the house, thoughtful. Then they walked together up the flagstones and toward the cheerful, well-lit door.

Before she had time to remove the key from her pocket, the door opened from the inside. She stepped into the house, followed by Jeffrey, and recognized Mehmet's valet. He bowed to her, and she smiled, still confused.

"Dr. Bailey. Sir Jeffrey," he said. "Welcome back. May I take your coats?"

She scoured her memory, trying to come up with his name.

Jeffrey handed him his coat. "Thank you, Hikmet." He was speaking Turkish.

Marion murmured her thanks as well, embarrassed by her forgetfulness and perplexed that Jeffrey knew him. She looked a question at him as he removed his shoes.

"İnci brought me to a few of Mehmet's crushes here," he said in response to her look. "Surprising, actually, that you and I didn't cross paths sooner."

She felt the beginning of a sick doubt lodge itself in her stomach. Chose to ignore it. Removed her own shoes as well.

"Mehmet Bey is waiting for you in the salon," Hikmet continued, indicating that they should walk through when they were ready.

When she didn't move, Jeffrey thanked him again, held Marion's elbow, and propelled her into the salon. Mehmet was sitting at the oak desk, writing in a leather ledger under the lamp. He was wearing a blue Lanvin suit, Parisian, and an ascot. When they entered the room, his face lit up, and he stood to meet them. He kissed Marion on both cheeks, shook Jeffrey's hand, and pointed them toward the fireplace and the armchairs.

"Marion. Forgive me for invading your privacy. I found that I had to be home, and I didn't have time to cable you." He spoke English with a slight American accent. "And Jeffrey. Wonderful surprise. How long has it been since you and İnci were here?"

Jeffrey made himself comfortable in the chair and crossed his legs. "Nearly a year, I think. You were in France?"

Mehmet sat as well. "Paris. Shopping. It was a nightmare dragging myself back here. February is worse every year." He gestured toward a silver platter holding three ostentatiously geometric glasses and a filigree decanter that, equally ostentatiously, clashed with them. "Drink?" And then: "Marion, sit. You look as though you've seen a ghost."

Marion smiled automatically. Sat.

Jeffrey leaned forward. "Thank you, Mehmet. Is that absinthe?"

"A weakness," Mehmet replied as he poured. "But there must be a verse somewhere in the Quran absolving a poor sinner of a taste for wormwood."

He handed a glass to Marion, who took a sip and put it on the table. Jeffrey left his glass untouched. Mehmet seemed not to notice and leaned back in his chair with his own glass.

"So, what have you been up to?" he asked both of them. "I heard about the party at the American Consulate. I wish I'd been able to attend."

"It was awful." Jeffrey smiled.

Marion nodded. "It was. You were fortunate you had an excuse not to be there."

Mehmet chuckled. "I thought as much. We won't tell Sinan and İnci." He turned back to Marion. "And the scholarship? You said something about a new project?"

"Mehmet, it's bigger than I imagined—"

"But then I turned up and distracted her." Jeffrey made a mock contrite face. "I haven't been in Istanbul for anything but business for ages. So when we chanced to meet at the party, I dragged her away from the books and forced her to show me the sights. I admit it. I'm well and truly a civil servant now. No appreciation for the life of the mind."

She shot him an annoyed look and opened her mouth to speak again, but Mehmet laughed and replied first. "The hazards of a career in government. Thankfully, I've avoided the temptation to put my academic skills, such as they are, to work on state building. Though opportunities here abound."

There was a hint of irony in his voice, but he didn't elaborate. Instead, he stood. "I hope you don't mind that I've reinstalled my household, Marion. Unlike you, I can't live in a freezing shell of a waterfront house in the middle of winter eating scrambled eggs. I've had my cook devise a real dinner." He paused thoughtfully. "And shall we try the dining room? I believe that it may be more than a year since I've eaten there."

Marion stood to follow him, but she abruptly felt dizzy and put out a hand to steady herself. A fleeting expression of concern flickered across Jeffrey's face as he stood as well. Then he held out an arm, his expression bland once again, and she grabbed it more tightly than she had intended to. She couldn't understand what was wrong with her head. Whatever it was, though, it was lifting. Her vision cleared, and the three of them walked through the tall doorway into the dining room.

Approached from the hall, the dining room was more impressive than absurd—especially now that the places were properly set and there were servers helping to arrange the food and chairs. But the three of them still sat together at one end of the table, which was spread with an embarrassing assortment of late-Ottoman *meze*s. Marion sensed, once more, the faintest hint of irony.

Mehmet offered them *rakı* topped with ice and cold water and told them to help themselves to the food. He also began to eat, informally, before turning back to Marion to ask her more about her work. She took a few sips of the *rakı* and prepared to explain to Mehmet the entire project, regardless of whatever it was Jeffrey was attempting. But before she could form the words, she felt the vertigo return, the edges of her vision turning black, and her speech becoming slurred. She was unable even to ask for help.

The nightmarish quality of the situation was heightened by the fact that neither Mehmet nor Jeffrey noticed her condition. Rather than recognizing that she was losing consciousness, they were switching in and out of English and Turkish, having what seemed to Marion's muddled mind to be a bizarrely heated argument. She tried to shake her head to clear it, but doing so nauseated her. Sweat beaded on her forehead.

Jeffrey, not touching his food, had glanced briefly in Marion's direction and then turned, angry, across the table toward Mehmet. "You're early."

"It's my house. I come and go when I please."

"Not at the moment, you don't. This is just about to come together, and your appearance here is, to say the least, awkward."

"You think I work for you?"

"Yes, as a matter of fact I do."

Marion saw Mehmet dip bread into a dish of yogurt. Take a bite. "I'm a billionaire, Willcox. I could buy you a hundred times over. And I'm sure as hell not one of your little Arab errand boys. I work for no one."

Marion's vision had almost completely clouded, but she was still trying to follow the conversation. What she heard couldn't be right. Her senses leaden, she shook her head again. She must have misunderstood the exchange. But rather than coming to herself, she felt her body collapsing. With an effort of will she remained upright in her chair. Forcing herself to continue listening. It wasn't possible that she had drunk enough absinthe or *rakı* to react in this way. She tried to catch Jeffrey's or Mehmet's eye, but they were looking hard at one another instead, ignoring her.

"Mehmet," Jeffrey was saying patiently, "unless you regain your senses, and now, I will cut you loose. Permanently All the money in the world won't protect you from Atatürk's people."

She heard Mehmet laughing. "And who do you think is giving me my orders, you smug, English bastard? They want you out of this. They've wanted you out of it from the beginning. But, unlike her, you simply won't go, will you? Fucking British. *She* would have dropped it—put the material straight back where it belonged. Buried. Dead like the empire. Not you, though. You couldn't resist pushing her, could you—"

She felt the room spinning about her, looked up at the mural on the ceiling, exchanged a glance with Thor, and then felt Hikmet catching her as she fell. After that, there was only darkness.

Istanbul, Turkey
European Side
February, 1927

MARION felt cold, damp stone beneath her cheek, and she rolled over onto her back. Whimpered in pain. Tried not to regain consciousness. It didn't work.

And so, forcing herself to accept whatever she would see above her, she cracked open an eye. A bulb suspended from the ceiling on a wire, throwing an unhealthy yellow light across the room. All she could discern from her vantage point on the floor.

Slowly, carefully, she sat up. Grateful that the only pain that hit her was a headache. Her wrists, she deduced after a few seconds, were shackled together in front of her, and a loose chain ran from the cuffs to a loop in the wall. Old metal. At least two centuries.

She peered across at the opposite wall of the room. Racks of wine. And, to her surprise, Jeffrey, who was sitting on the floor in a position similar to her own, shackled to an identical loop. His eyes closed and a threadlike trickle of blood along his temple.

When he heard her moving, he opened his eyes. "Miscalculation."

"What?"

"I miscalculated," he repeated. "I apologize."

She cast her gaze over the room. "What just happened?"

"It didn't just happen. You've been unconscious for six hours." He closed his eyes again.

"*What?*"

"As I said. A miscalculation."

"Jeffrey, what happened?" She looked at him more closely. "What's wrong with your head?"

He lifted his hands to touch the line of blood with a finger. Opened his eyes and looked at it, annoyed. "Unlike you, I am not a complete cretin, and I didn't touch the drinks Mehmet was throwing at me. Which meant that they were obliged to incapacitate me in a different way." He rolled back his shoulders and tried to stretch. "Hikmet, it seems, possesses some unexpected martial talent. And then, of course, there were no weapons for me to appropriate in the kitchen, and so—here I am."

"I don't understand. Why is Mehmet doing this?"

"One could grant him the benefit of the doubt and hypothesize that he has misunderstood his brief. But I don't think that's the case."

She felt the tug of dread at the corners of her mind again. "What?"

"Obvious, isn't it? Mehmet's one of mine." He considered. "Or, he was one of mine. I'm giving serious thought to terminating his relationship with His Majesty's government."

If she hadn't been chained to the wall, she would have attacked him. "You haven't done this. You *haven't*. You twisted *prat*. How—"

"Why not? It worked so well the last time." He paused. "Not so well this time, I confess. It was supposed to be you chained to the floor of the cellar. Not both of us."

She glowered at him. "How long?"

"Mehmet?" He thought for a moment. "Always, I suppose. Though I personally have been running him for only a few years. Seems he's had a change of heart about the virtues of Republican governance."

She leaned her head against the wall and looked blankly up at the ceiling. Couldn't begin to think of a response. But, after a few minutes of enraged cogitation, she calmed and let her eyes fall on Jeffrey again. "Did he tell you what he was planning to do?"

Jeffrey shook his head. "Too busy ordering his servants to attack me. But he did let slip that he'd hoped you'd react to their laughable campaign of terror by replacing the flute. I expect his orders are to dispose of artifacts that might encourage Ottoman pretenders." He closed his eyes again. "Along with witnesses to the existence of those artifacts. He'll be forced to kill us."

Marion tried to think. She had a small hope that Sinan might respond to her message and return to the *yalı*. But the likelihood of that happening before Mehmet made his next move was slim. In fact, she thought she heard the scrape of the handle at the top of the steps already.

Light from the kitchen shone into the cellar as Hikmet and two other servants opened the door and descended toward the wine racks. Hikmet carried what looked like medieval keys, on a ring, enormous and crumbling with rust. He glanced apologetically at Marion as he bent over to remove the chain from the loop in the wall. Then he handed the end of the chain to someone waiting at the top of the stairs, and the five of them, Marion and Jeffrey still shackled, walked up to the door.

Mehmet was waiting for them in the warm kitchen, wearing herringbone trousers, a white foul-weather coat and hat, and rubber soled boat shoes. He was smoking a cigarette, looking rested and relaxed. When they emerged from the cellar, he held out a package of Lucky Strikes. "Cigarette?"

Jeffrey, his wrists still manacled, took one. "Thank you."

He bent over for Mehmet to light it and then straightened and inhaled. Mehmet offered one to Marion, but she shook her head. He tossed the packet onto the kitchen counter. Looked at Jeffrey.

"You can finish it on the way," he said.

Jeffrey tilted back his head and exhaled. "Yes. Of course."

Mehmet said nothing as they walked out of the kitchen and through the main hall. Marion was still feeling as though she were in a bad dream, that somehow this wasn't happening, that she'd wake up alone in her bed in the *yalı*. Or even back in Baghdad.

Jeffrey, finishing his cigarette, looked toward the door. "Mehmet, is there anywhere I can put this?"

Mehmet stopped and nodded to Hikmet, who brought an ashtray from the gilt table. Jeffrey tossed the remainder of the cigarette into the ashtray and then addressed Mehmet again. "Would you consider a counter offer?"

Mehmet put his hands into the pockets of his foul weather jacket. Rolled up onto the balls of his feet and back again. "Let's talk about this on the boat."

They walked out the door to the dock. When the morning air hit her face, Marion noticed that for the first time since she had arrived the weather was neither glaringly bright nor whipped up into an incipient storm. The clouds were low and dull, the wind mild. It felt like typical February weather for Istanbul. She almost allowed herself a flicker of hope.

Hikmet separated the chains linking Marion to Jeffrey so that they could climb into the boat, and each of them, led by a servant, stepped down into the cabin. Hikmet followed them with the key ring, and while the two other servants held Jeffrey, he removed Marion's shackles. Told her to sit on the cushion in the main part of the cabin and fastened her wrists behind her back and then to a bracket ordinarily used for securing paraffin lamps.

When he had finished, he positioned Jeffrey in the same way, so that they were sitting across from one another, their wrists behind their backs, on facing sides of the cabin. Having finished their work, Hikmet and the two servants disappeared into the cockpit, snapping the cloth flap over the hatch. Marion and Jeffrey stared at the floor, not speaking.

A few seconds later, the boat's motor started, and Marion felt it pushing them out into the Bosporus. Rather than heading toward Anadoluhisarı, she had the impression that Mehmet was taking them in the direction of the Marmara Sea. And after he hit the throttle, the boat quickly picked up speed, the bow rising over the small waves. She suspected that the Coast Guard rarely stopped Mehmet for exceeding the established speed restrictions in the strait.

As they moved, she raised her eyes to Jeffrey's, preparing to speak. But he had now closed his own, and he appeared to be readying himself for something violent. Which made her uncomfortable. She dropped her gaze again.

After a half hour of travel at the Hacker-Craft's top speed, Mehmet slowed and cut the engine. She heard stronger waves hitting the hull of the boat, but she had little idea of where they were. Somewhere in the Marmara. And when she heard what she thought was Mehmet making his way back across the cockpit, her curiosity evaporated. More concerned with Mehmet's motivations than with the boat's position in the choppy sea.

A few seconds later, the cloth cover disappeared from the hatch, and Mehmet climbed into the cabin. Once down the ladder, he opened the chart table and removed the manuscript, the flute, and the cup. Then he unfolded the wooden bench and sat down. Observed them.

"This," he eventually said, lifting the cup, "is beautiful." He ran his finger along the engravings decorating it. "It belongs in a collection."

Jeffrey had opened his eyes while Mehmet was speaking. "I can help you with that."

"A collection in Turkey," Mehmet amended.

"Agreed," Jeffrey replied. "I'm not wedded to removing them."

"You were. You would have."

"Yes," he said. "And under changed circumstances, I would still."

"But not under these circumstances." Mehmet continued to examine the cup. "How do I know you'll keep your word?"

Jeffrey laughed. "Mehmet, I'm in no position to negotiate. You've won. And I respect you. I'm not lying to you."

Mehmet smiled in turn. "I respect you as well. And," he added, "despite losing my temper last night—for which I apologize—I also like you. But are you capable of not lying?" He turned to Marion. "You haven't said anything. What do you think?"

"I don't know what to think." She blinked, uncertain of how to speak to him. "I'm still grappling with the fact that one of my oldest friends has drugged me and imprisoned me in the hold of his boat. What happened?"

Mehmet set the cup on the chart table. "Politics?"

"Mehmet, we're *friends*." She felt tears welling up and, embarrassed, she pushed them back. Tried to mimic Jeffrey's professionalism.

Mehmet, watching her, looked irritated for a moment. And then tired. "You're right. This is a fatuous conversation. I felt it would be impolite not to entertain Jeffrey's offer." He stood and started back up the ladder.

"You haven't let me make my offer."

Mehmet stopped, turned, and sat again on the top step. He put his chin in his hand and looked down at Jeffrey. The swell was growing, and the boat had begun rolling. "All right, then. Let's hear it."

Jeffrey drew a breath. "I understand your situation, Mehmet. You've been trained since birth as an aristocrat and a scholar. But five years ago, aristocratic status became an encumbrance rather than an advantage, didn't it? Not fatal, obviously. This isn't Russia. But you're losing ground. Ground that you'll never regain. And then, more recently, scholarly status went the same way. Nothing cataclysmic. The universities are still functioning. But anyone can see that intellectuals who came of age at the end of the Empire will never move out from under the cloud of Republican suspicion."

Mehmet nodded. "Correct."

"And so, you're reinventing yourself. Because you're an intelligent person. And you're doing so with the help of the new guard."

Mehmet gestured at him to keep speaking.

"But Mehmet," Jeffrey said, leaning forward, "in addition to securing Atatürk's political blessing—which you've already done, if what you said last night is true—you must also protect your financial interests. Your *businesses*. Otherwise, no political connection, no matter how exalted, can maintain your standing in the world."

"I have been protecting my financial interests." Mehmet sounded almost sullen.

"No, you haven't." Jeffrey adjusted his manacled hands. "Because you can't. Not on your own. You know that the Republic's economic policies are an absurdity. But people like you, former aristocrats, have no choice but to support them, to allow their families' business concerns to be incorporated into the protectionist fantasy that Atatürk is erecting here. If you don't, you're traitors."

Mehmet nodded again. Curt.

"Which means that in ten years' time—at best—your capital will have evaporated. All for the greater good of the Turkish People, of course. But will that be a consolation to you? I admit that in your position it wouldn't be for me." Jeffrey paused and watched Mehmet for a reaction. "Your property," he emphasized, "will be gone. Permanently."

"Hmm." Mehmet gave nothing away.

"And this is where British support can help you," Jeffrey persisted. "We, and we alone, can provide you with a sound, international corporate foundation that will remain invulnerable to the tremors of this grand Republican economic experiment. With our help, you can prove your political loyalty without jeopardizing your family's property. Without our help, you can't. Without us, yes, you'll be alive. Loyal. Protected." He paused again. "And salaried."

"I see."

"What I'm offering you, Mehmet, is the best of both worlds." He flicked back his hair from his forehead. "You want to demonstrate your loyalty to the new government? My office gives you its blessing. You want to toss those artifacts into the sea? Go right ahead—"

"*What?*" Marion interjected.

Jeffrey ignored her. "Go right ahead and do so. Marion here, as she said, is your friend. And she is faithful to the point of mental illness. She'll never expose you. I may be incapable of telling the truth, but I do know where my interests lie. I'd far sooner keep a line of communication open to you than mourn the loss of some dissolute, five-hundred-year-old tribal leader's drinking vessel." He smiled, wry. "Neither Marion nor I is prone to resentment, Mehmet. You know that as well. You can remove these manacles, dispose of this Ottoman flotsam that so enrages Atatürk—while she and I discreetly admire the view of the Islands—and then the three of us can be back in front of your fire sipping absinthe before the sun sets. Although I prefer to take mine without the phenobarbital."

Mehmet shook his head. Rather than responding to Jeffrey, he turned to Marion. "Do you remember Abdullah?" he asked her. "He and my father used to buy race horses together."

Marion nodded. "I think so. He used to beat me at backgammon."

Mehmet smiled for a moment. Then the smile disappeared. "They executed him in Izmir. He was guilty as sin, so legally, of course, he deserved his punishment—" He interrupted himself. "Do you remember his wife?"

Now it was Marion's turn to smile. "Yes. Nilüfer. She was beautiful. And she used to help me cheat. At the backgammon. When he wasn't looking." She felt a dart of concern. "But they wouldn't have executed her. She wasn't involved in Abdullah's work."

"No," he said. "She's alive. Quite healthy from what I understand. She and her daughter run a brothel that specializes in *ci-devant* Russian countesses. The occasional princess."

"But—"

"Oh, of course," Mehmet answered her unspoken question. "We all tried to help her. That they confiscated Abdullah's property shouldn't have affected her. I would have given her everything I have. And I wasn't the only one. But she refused. Wouldn't take a *kuruş*. Lira. Whatever." Mehmet looked down at his hands. "And she is only one of very, very many victims of—" he looked back up at her, "—politics."

Jeffrey tried again. "Mehmet, these stories are horrific. You know it. So why give in to it? Why not fight it? You can. You have the resources. And," he emphasized, "let me repeat. You have the full support of the British government. For the asking."

Mehmet smiled wanly at Jeffrey. "Now that was a masterful move, Jeffrey. Lightning fast shift in the message. But no." He reached for the handles at the edges of the ladder. Pulled himself up. And then, thinking, stopped. "There is something else," he admitted. "I don't know how to say it without sounding offensive. Or at least inhospitable. But I'll say it nonetheless." He looked steadily at Jeffrey. "This is my country. It is not your country. You appreciate it only enough to plunder it. Which I can respect. I've inherited enough five-hundred-year-old tribal blood to feel the temptation there."

He turned to Marion. "But it's also not your country, Marion." His expression was apologetic. "And for what it's worth, there's something nearly as narcissistic in your guilty attempts to return these artifacts to us natives, instructing us as to their value, or whatever it is you imagine yourself to be doing, as there is in his," he nodded toward Jeffrey, "naked aggression." He thought for another moment. "Although it could be that I'm merely saying that to absolve myself of the shame of taking this step. Hospitality is a difficult habit to break. And, as I mentioned before, this situation sickens me."

They heard the sound of a smaller power boat drawing alongside the Hacker-Craft. Mehmet looked back. "I think that's for me."

And then he climbed up through the hatch into the cockpit.

THERE was a bump against the hull as the runabout rafted onto Mehmet's boat.

Marion swallowed. "What do you think he's going to do?"

"Kill us and leave, I'd imagine."

"Any plan?"

"No."

She stared at him. "So we simply sit here and let it happen?"

He laughed. "Surely your organization—or one of your various organizations—has taught you to recognize a futile effort when you see one? If not necessarily the symptoms of narcissistic guilt. It was the first lesson we learned in mine. Recognizing a futile effort, that is. The narcissism went without saying." He was enjoying the situation. "Just try not to embarrass yourself."

"I refuse—"

She was interrupted by raised voices in the cockpit. The cloth flap over the hatch went up again, and İnci, wearing a white fur coat, white gloves, and strapped high heels clamored down into the cabin. She looked back and forth between Jeffrey and Marion while she removed her gloves. The fur on their cuffs matched the fur of her coat.

She spoke to Marion first, in Turkish. "Sinan received your message. He passed it along to me and asked that I check on you. Said he was worried you might be in danger." She let her eyes run over the cabin. "He was right."

"Sinan doesn't know about this?" Marion was also speaking in Turkish.

"Sinan's a doctoral student," she replied, as though it were an answer. "A darling with his documents, but not all that observant otherwise. I don't think we'd get on as well as we do if he had any idea what was happening around him." She turned to Jeffrey with a happy smile on her face. Planted herself next to him on the cushion and put her bare hand on his thigh. "Do you know what this reminds me of?"

Jeffrey looked at her hand. "I can't imagine."

She peered up at him. Big, bright eyes. "That time in the suite at Pera Palace. Remember?"

"I think this is more fun when our roles are reversed."

"I think this is nice too." She patted his thigh, stood, and drew on one of her gloves. "Pity we won't be able to compare our impressions."

Marion was staring at them in disbelief. Jeffrey and İnci exchanged a glance.

Then İnci raised an amused eyebrow at her. "What? You think you're the only one he's—"

"I have *never*—" Marion started.

"Hmm. So he told me. I didn't believe him. Your loss." She pulled on her other glove. "And it's a moot point now." She straightened the seams on her glove and watched Marion under her eyebrows. "Because it's true, you know. I *had* heard so much about you. And I *was* terribly jealous. Not anymore." As she walked toward the hatch, she paused at the chart table. Picked up the bone whistle and blew a few experimental notes. "Pretty," she said, tossing it back on the table.

But before she could begin climbing out to the cockpit, a hand moved the cloth cover from over the hatch, and İnci's brother lowered his sullen face into the cabin. "İnci, will you hurry up?"

She glared up at him. "I told you, you little donkey, to stay in the runabout. Mother will be furious if she knows you saw this."

His voice was whiny. "Mother said I should stay with you no matter what—"

"I told her I was taking you to get almond pudding at Hacı Abdullah. I swear, Mustafa, if you tell her you were here, I'll make your life a complete misery."

"But—"

"Just get in the boat."

"Fine." His head disappeared from the hatch.

Jeffrey was laughing.

İnci glared back at him. "Oh, shut up."

Then she climbed up out of the cabin as well.

Marion looked hard at Jeffrey. He shrugged as well as he could with his hands shackled behind his back. "Tell me you don't find her attractive," he said.

"Do you know? Every time I see you, you disgust me a little bit more. I keep thinking you can't sink any lower—"

"Inopportune metaphor."

She stared up at the ceiling. "I am *not* going to spend my last moments having these inane exchanges with you."

"You're reconciled to them being our last moments, then?"

Before she could respond, Mehmet stepped back down into the cabin. He was carrying a revolver.

"Sorry for İnci," he said. "She insisted on seeing you, and since she'd agreed to collect me here, I didn't think I could argue." He examined the gun in his hand. "I'll be sinking the boat with you both on it. Make it look like an accident." He looked back up at them. Addressed Jeffrey. "And before you go complacent about the unnecessarily Oriental complexity of that plan, I want you to know that I'm aware that it leaves you with a healthy opportunity to escape. But, you see," and now he was including Marion as well, "there's something objectionable to me about shooting two unarmed prisoners point blank. I can't bring myself to do it. And although I could order Hikmet to do it instead, and he *would* do it, even if he wouldn't like it, I'm not certain even then that I could live with the cowardice that would imply. So, I've decided to wreck the boat, and let fate take its course." He laughed to himself. "I suppose that does sound Oriental, doesn't it? Kismet?"

"Aristocratic, perhaps," Jeffrey offered.

Mehmet considered. "Yes. Perhaps. İnci is furious with me. She thinks I should shoot you both, toss you overboard, and keep the boat. I imagine that's the difference between being in textiles and being the final, tragic scion of a decayed, four-hundred-year-old family." He spoke to Jeffrey again. "But you're a baronet now, aren't you? You understand?"

"Technically baronets are common."

"If you were in my position, you'd kill your prisoners?"

"Without hesitation."

Mehmet turned to Marion. "What about you?"

Jeffrey answered for her. "It's a flawed premise. Marion would never find herself in your position. She'd keep reading her bloody manuscripts as the boat and everything else sank about her."

Marion opened her mouth to retort, but Mehmet grinned at her. "Abdullah was always astonished that someone so intelligent could be such a disaster at backgammon."

"Mehmet." Marion's voice was weak. "You needn't do this. You truly needn't."

"Yes," he said. "I do." He sighed again. "And I may as well finish it."

He examined the gun again. "This is yours, Jeffrey. It's a Webley, I think? Six bullets?"

"Standard issue. I can't get used to American weapons. Though things in my profession seem to be moving in that direction."

"This would be your work for the British Museum and Library?" Mehmet had placed the gun on the chart table and was kneeling on the floor between Marion and Jeffrey, pulling up the teak boards that covered the bilge. As he worked, he continued to speak. "The problem with hiring a company like Hacker to design a cruiser rather than a runabout," he was telling them, "is that they always leave the hull flimsy. And they embed the pumps as an afterthought. Cosmetic. It's a design flaw, but I've always liked the speed, so it's never concerned me. And now, the thin hull and minimal pumps aren't flaws at all, are they?"

He set the floorboards against the bulkhead separating the main cabin from the forepeak. Then he hopped back across the exposed bilge to the chart table and picked up the revolver. "It's possible that you'll work some ghost magic to get yourselves out of here before the boat sinks. And maybe you'll even make it to the Islands. And maybe I even hope you'll succeed. But if you do, I don't think you'll be able to salvage Bayezid's relics in the process. And I know you won't come after me. I have nothing left for you to expose."

"Mehmet—" Marion repeated.

"I'm sorry." He took careful aim at the base of the bilge and squeezed the trigger of the gun. The boat shuddered.

"That's the pump," he informed them, unnecessarily. Then he methodically emptied the rest of the cartridge, certain to space the holes such that they'd do the most damage. When he had finished, enough of the bottom had been splintered that water began seeping in immediately. He watched as three or four inches flooded into the bilge, and then he put the empty gun on the chart table next to the manuscript, flute, and cup. Looking grim.

"Here's to Republicanism, Populism, Nationalism, Secularism, Statism, and Reformism," he said. "Six Republican principles for six Republican bullets. It should take about two hours to go under. Good luck."

Without looking back at them, he climbed up the ladder and departed through the hatch.

MARION and Jeffrey watched silently as the water rose over the level of the bilge and spread out along the floor of the cabin. They could tell from the motion of the boat that İnci's runabout was still rafted to it. Mehmet hadn't yet cast off. But they could also hear a continuing argument between İnci and Mustafa.

"I won't leave my book," Mustafa was insisting.

"We'll get you another one, Mustafa. Come back here *right now*."

Marion and Jeffrey looked at one another, bemused. And then Mustafa's head reappeared over the hatch. After casting his eye over the cabin and climbing down the ladder, he minced with disgust across the sodden floor toward Marion. Without speaking, he produced the rusted ring of antique keys, unlocked her cuffs, pocketed the keys, and turned to go.

"Mustafa," she said in Turkish, rubbing her wrists. "Thank you. *Thank you*. How can we ever thank you for this? You've saved our lives."

She stood and held out her hand for the key ring, but he shook his head, still sullen. "They'll be angry with me if they know I took the keys. I'm taking them back to the runabout."

Marion looked at Jeffrey. Back at Mustafa. "But we need them to unlock both sets of cuffs."

Mustafa also looked at Jeffrey. "He seduced my sister," he said dully. "She's such a bitch."

Then he turned and stumbled back up the ladder, taking the keys with him. They heard İnci yelling at him to get the hell back into the boat. A few seconds later, the Hacker-Craft shook as the runabout cast off. And the boat started tilting.

Marion turned to Jeffrey. "What are we going to do?"

"You," he said, "are going to get yourself into a life jacket and try to make it to the Islands. The water is cold, but you ought to survive."

She glanced at the objects on the chart table, and he smiled. "I'm afraid those must stay here with me. They'll keep me from feeling lonely as the water level rises."

"I'm not leaving you here."

"I'd never forgive you for rescuing me," he said. "You'll regret it if you don't leave now."

"Jeffrey," she replied patiently. "The boat is sinking. I'm not leaving you here. I could use ideas."

"May I take that as blanket authorization? Consent for everything that results from this decision?"

"Jeffrey," she repeated, tense, "*the boat is sinking.* And you're still playing at psychological manipulation? Are you out of your head?"

"Legal manipulation. Consent?"

"Fine. Anything. Ideas?"

A smile played across his lips. Then he nodded. "My dinner jacket is hanging on the hook over the chart table. There ought to be a set of picks in the inside pocket. I trust you know what to do with them."

She splashed through the sea that now reached four or five inches above the waterline of the boat, ripped his jacket from the hook, and searched through his pockets until she found the small leather case. She chose a pick and a tension wrench and glanced up at him.

"These locks are eighteenth-century at the latest," she said, nervous. "Early pin-tumbler. No more than three or four chambers."

His smile broadened. "I adore it when you turn your scholarly single-mindedness toward criminality. İnci's no rival to you."

She walked back over to him, bit her lip, and began to work on his wrists. "I can still leave."

He raised his wrists to help her. "And I've told you that it would be very much in your interests to do so."

She held her breath as she felt the third and fourth driver pins fall into place. Adjusted the wrench minutely, and the lock opened. Then she exhaled, and Jeffrey stood, examining his hands.

"But now it's too late," he said.

"You're an idiot," she replied calmly. "I think there are two life jackets stored under the bunk in the forepeak. We'll use those."

He stepped across the bilge and examined the ladder leading up to the cockpit. Then, pleased, he removed the ladder and the teak board beneath it to expose the boat's motor. "We don't need them."

She watched him, impatient. "Why not? What are you doing?"

He was ripping components out of the motor and piling them up on the chart table next to the manuscript.

"Induction coil," he was saying. "Battery. Interrupter." He stepped back across the bilge and smashed the decorative barometer on one side of the bulkhead. Extracted a piece of metal. "Key." Then he destroyed the clock and pulled out a length of wire. "Antenna."

The water was rising faster now. Marion stared at him as he began attaching bits of his collection together on the chart table.

"What are you doing?" she repeated.

"Isn't it obvious?"

"Not remotely."

"It's a spark gap transmitter."

"A what?"

He glanced up at her as though disappointed. Looked back down at his work. "Remind me not to recommend you as a Girl Guides Leader."

"What are you doing?" she asked a third time.

"Shh," he said. He was leaning down, concentrating on the plate, tapping out what she took to be Morse code. After he had repeated his message several times, he tossed his hair off his forehead and stood. "Now we wait. Wearing the life jackets."

She looked dubiously at the machine that he had cobbled together. "Someone can hear that?"

"We'll find out. If they received it, they ought to have a picket boat here for us in the next half hour or so. If not, we'll swim." He gathered up the manuscript and the artifacts. "But I'll be damned if I let these go down with the ship."

They put on life jackets and climbed out of the cabin into the cockpit and fresh air. She looked across the water. Mehmet had chosen his spot well. They were behind the outermost of the Princes' Islands, out of view of any chance pleasure boat or ferry, and far enough away from land to make swimming difficult.

She settled herself against the bulkhead, protected from the wind, and scrutinized the horizon without optimism. She had little faith in Jeffrey's technical skills, but she saw no reason not to be patient. Jeffrey himself sat behind the wheel of the boat, leaning back, relaxed against the side, his hands behind his head. The boat was listing in earnest now, but neither of them mentioned it.

I believe that's the cavalry approaching."

Jeffrey had sat up and was shading his eyes with his hand, looking into the distance at a speeding boat coming from the direction of Karaköy, on the European side of the city. The boat was travelling at a good twenty knots, throwing up an enormous wake, and manned by a skeleton crew of eight or nine sailors. It reached them in minutes.

The half-submerged Hacker-Craft, overwhelmed as the vessel reduced speed alongside it, lifted and then rolled back into the sea. Marion gripped a varnished teak rail, and then she stood, keeping her balance with difficulty, and walked toward the stern. A sailor was waiting there to help her up onto the deck of the picket boat. Jeffrey followed her, protecting the manuscript, cup, and flute from stray sprays of water. Then the sailor jumped back onto the higher deck.

The crew maneuvered the military boat a few hundred yards away from the sinking Hacker-Craft and repositioned its twelve-pound gun. Before Marion understood what they were doing, four sailors had fired the gun at Mehmet's boat, which disintegrated upon impact into unrecognizable pieces. She jumped at the recoil and put her hand up to her cheek.

There was something gratuitous about the display that seemed spiteful to her. She watched, with a feeling irrationally close to tears, as what remained of the devastated boat floated in the churning water. Jeffrey was standing beside her, his life jacket now in his hand, also watching, with a neutral expression on his face.

"Imperial decline," he murmured.

Surprised, she looked up at him, about to ask which Empire, but he turned away to greet an officer approaching him across the deck.

"Stephenson," he said. "You received my transmission."

"Half the world received your transmission, Willcox. Wrecked our bandwidth. You're lucky we haven't arrested you." Disgruntled.

Jeffrey dropped his eyes. "I haven't built one since I was fourteen. Though I suppose that excuse wouldn't hold up in court."

"Necessity. Can't fault you for using what was available. Quite the mess you've created here, though." He nodded in the direction of the eddying water. "Thought we ought to get rid of it altogether to discourage the curious. Speaking of which—" He threw a quizzical look in Marion's direction. She had also removed her life jacket.

"Yes," Jeffrey said. "Forgive me. Dr. Bailey. An Associate. Commander Stephenson."

She thought he gave her an odd look, quickly checked. His reply was studied and polite. "Dr. Bailey, how do you do? You must be chilled to the bone. Let me find you a blanket."

She held out her hand. "Commander Stephenson. Thank you."

He bowed, not taking her hand, and signaled to one of his crew. "Well. Let's get you to shore."

He walked aft as a midshipman appeared with a brown wool blanket that Marion hugged across her shoulders. She was glad to have it as the boat turned back toward Karaköy and picked up speed. For although the weather had cleared, and a watery sun was shining through the dissipating clouds, the wind was damp and biting. She started shivering.

Jeffrey, who had been standing beside her, looked sidelong at her, thoughtful, and then spoke. "I hope you don't mind my leaving you here. I'd like to store these," indicating the artifacts, "and speak to Stephenson for a moment."

She nodded, and he disappeared toward the stern of the boat. After that, she tugged the blanket more tightly over her shoulders and watched as the European shore of the city spread itself out in front of her. Her situation when they reached the dock would be unpleasant, given that her belongings were still in the *yalı*. But she had a half-formed plan to throw herself on the mercy of a friend who lived up the hill from Karaköy, in Cihangir, off İstiklal Avenue.

She would borrow clothing, and then once she had something suitable to wear, she would visit her banker to withdraw sufficient money to salvage her project. She had an idea of where to look for the sword. And although doing so would be difficult without the material that Jeffrey had confiscated, she refused to give up now. She didn't know how she would find herself a new passport, but if she didn't try to cross borders, she needn't worry about that yet. If all else failed, she would use her post-War knowledge of crossing points, at least some of which must still be viable.

The picket boat slowed and threw up a roiling green foam as it reversed into the slip reserved for British naval vessels. A few crew members jumped to the dock with mooring lines to pull the boat into place, and Marion shrugged off the blanket. She was folding it and looking for a clear space to leave it, when Jeffrey returned, followed by Stephenson.

He nodded farewell to Jeffrey, and then Jeffrey turned to Marion and walked with her down the lowered gangplank to the dock. She stopped abruptly once they were off the boat. Irritated to see his car idling near the shore road.

"This is where I leave you," she said.

"Marion," he replied, annoyed, "look at yourself. Your clothing is sodden. Your shoes are falling apart. You have no coat. No money. No papers. Let me at least drive you to the top of the hill."

"No."

"After everything that's happened, you think I'm going to arrest you? Detain you?"

"Yes." She turned to go.

He put his hand on her arm. "You're correct. But I'd hoped to avoid a scene."

She shook off his hand. "You have no authority. No leverage. Nothing. I'm going now."

"I have nine of His Majesty's sailors waiting about a hundred yards away. Would you like to try to fight them off?" He considered. "I might actually enjoy that. A modern variation on Gilbert and Sullivan."

She looked at the boat. The crew hadn't boarded it. Then she turned, with deliberation, toward him. "I will give you no information."

"You always say that. And yet here we are again."

*I*T was the same driver. Marion stared into the middle distance, just behind his head, as the Bentley retraced its original path, back toward what had been Embassy row. They passed the American Consulate.

"We're going to the British Consulate?" she asked.

"For now, yes," he said.

She tapped the window with her knuckle a few times. "This isn't like last time. You haven't Mehmet's vulnerability to hold over me."

"True," he admitted. "But the last time I wasn't kidnapping you. This time I am."

"To take me to the Consulate?"

"For now," he repeated. "It eliminates the legal difficulties that tend to surround these operations. If I took you elsewhere, there'd be a jurisdictional fight. The Consulate is, despite the garden parties, something of a legal black hole. We'll be discussing your papers. At some length. After that, we'll see."

She turned and glared at his profile. "I will give you *no information*."

"Hmm."

"If it weren't for me, you'd be dead."

He nodded, not looking at her. "Multiple times over." He glanced at her, then back out the window. "I resent that. And I told you that you'd regret your decision."

She dug her fingernails into the palm of her hand to keep from losing control completely. The car turned into the first set of security gates protecting the Consulate. Soldiers saluted, let them through, a second set of gates opened, more saluting, and then the car rolled to a stop.

A guard opened the door on Jeffrey's side, and he got out. He spoke to a soldier, who nodded and disappeared into the building. A few minutes later, two more guards emerged from the interior of the Consulate, opened the door on her side of the car, and helped her out.

Jeffrey walked back and stood facing her. "I've told them to treat you as a guest," he said. "An occasionally oblivious, but ultimately inoffensive, scholar who has found herself in some difficulty with her papers. But—and I want to make this clear to you—there are also holding cells in the cellar. We'll use them if we must. It all depends on you. As of now, you'll have a nice view over the rooftops of Galata, I've ordered you clothing, which they're delivering now, and if there's any food you'd enjoy, they'll do what they can to find that for you. Try not to do anything too typically unreasonable."

He turned toward the car, and she stopped him. "That's it? You're going?"

"You'd like to get right to it, then?" A flicker of amusement.

When she simply stared at him, he gestured at his clothing. "I must change first. And I might also pay a visit to İnci's father. Explain to him that His Majesty's government takes a dim view of her uncontrollable behavior. A discredit to her family."

Marion felt tired. Her eyes wandered vacantly across the façade of the Consulate building, and she realized that she had nothing to say to him. Jeffrey, also saying nothing more, settled himself into the car, which reversed and then drove back through the security gates. One of the guards held out his arm, solicitous, not classifying her as a prisoner. Without useful alternatives offering themselves to her, she let him guide her toward the entrance.

After crossing through the public sections of the building, they reached the second floor, which was residential. He opened a door to a clean, if not luxurious suite, asked her to ring if she needed anything, indicated, discreetly, a bedroom containing a change of clothing, and told her that staff would bring her tea in a half hour.

When she replied, to his question, that she had no additional requests, he withdrew and closed the door with a quiet click. Marion wondered whether he had existed in some previous civilian iteration as a valet. Then she felt ashamed of herself. She was in no position to pass judgement on unwise decision making.

She took a few steps into the room and considered. Jeffrey's promise held. A panoramic view from the window opened out toward the rooftops encircling Galata Tower, and beyond that, to a small, framed prospect of the Golden Horn with its playful wind. The room itself was carpeted and modern with recessed ceiling lights.

She tested a switch and saw that the lights were strong enough to illuminate the entire living area. There was a window seat at one end, two armchairs facing it, the ubiquitous potted palm, a round steel and white marble table with four matching, cushioned dining chairs, and a bookcase that she reminded herself to examine later. She peeked into the adjoining room and saw a low bed, the wardrobe that her porter had been too polite to mention, a lamp, a chair, and a bedtable. A third door led to a functional tiled chamber with sink, tub, toilet, mirror, and more than sufficient white towels.

She walked through the third door, planning to wash away the lingering effects of Mehmet's drugged absinthe, her encounter with the Marmara, and what was now some sort of extra-legal imprisonment in the Consulate. After filling the tub with water, she stepped into it, closed her eyes for ten minutes, and savored the dark. Then, opening her eyes and washing her hair, she put the past week out of her mind. She'd find an intelligent way to react to it when she was rested. Tomorrow. For now, satisfied by her decision, she pulled up the plug, stepped out of the tub, and wrapped herself and her hair in towels.

When she walked into the living room, the steel table sported a three-tiered tray of tea sandwiches, a silver teapot, a jug of milk, a container of sugar, and a cup and saucer. Without changing out of her towels, she made herself a cup of sweet, milky tea and examined the food. It was ostentatiously English. The assortment of sandwiches verging on the hysterical. But she certainly didn't think to complain. Instead, picking up a tiny cucumber butter sandwich, she returned to the bedroom, eating it and pondering who would have thought to mix dill and lovage in Istanbul in February.

She finished her sandwich and opened the door to the wardrobe. It held three identically cut women's day dresses in different colors. She missed her trousers. Irritated, she removed the black version of the dress and held it up to the light. The tag read Jean Patou. Thin, expensive wool. It was wasted on her, mourning as she was her favorite jumper with its unravelling hole in the sleeve.

She arranged the dress on the bed and rummaged about in a drawer, pulling out stockings, garters, underwear, and, finally, a pair of strapped black high heels. She stared at all of them, still annoyed, and then decided that she would store her sartorial worries along with her concern about her stalled project in some, for now, inaccessible part of her mind.

Dumping the clothing on a chair beside the bed, she walked out to the dining room, finished the sandwiches, including the dill and lovage, and returned to the bedroom. Then she let the towels she was wearing fall to the ground and climbed into the bed. Despite the tea, anxiety, and uncertainty about what would happen tomorrow that had insinuated themselves into her bloodstream, she was asleep in minutes.

She woke late in the morning, feeling energetic in a way that she hadn't for days. And after staring resentfully at the pile of clothing waiting for her on the chair, she rose, truculent, and dressed herself. Even without looking in the mirror, she could sense that the dress had foregone the drop waist she associated with women like İnci.

Instead, the black wool was tailored close to her body, almost nipped at the waist, and looked more like a man's suit than the floating layers she had become used to seeing fashionable women wearing. She rolled her eyes as she walked out of the bedroom to clean her teeth. The ensemble was entirely alien to her. She'd never even shingled her hair.

She emerged from the toilet with her hair combed back into the chignon that had served her since she had entered Cambridge during the War. Glancing out the window, she saw that the air was still damp, clouds and fog crowding in off the Marmara. She flipped the light switch in the living room and made for the bookcase, pausing for a moment next to the table to take a croissant.

She hesitated. Someone, after all, had come into the room while she'd slept. Surprised not to have noticed. But the service here was impeccable. In addition to clearing away the empty tea set and tray, they had arranged a laughably complete array of pastries, alongside a pot of coffee and a jug of orange juice. She poured herself a glass of juice. The last time she had drunk orange juice with breakfast had been before she went to school. She looked down at the croissant in her hand, considered it again, and replaced it with *pain au chocolat*. Smiling, she continued toward the bookcase.

The books had been chosen by the same committee that had governed the relentlessly neutral design of the room. Cool, shallow, and inoffensive. She deliberated among Edith Wharton's *Twilight Sleep*, *Arrowsmith* by Sinclair Lewis, and every novel ever written by Zane Grey, while wondering what sort of masochist would choose to read John Erskine's *The Private Life of Helen of Troy* while under indefinite, quasi-legal arrest in a downgraded diplomatic building.

She also looked thoughtfully at Anita Loos's *Gentlemen Prefer Blondes*, but she wasn't confident that a satirical feeling of intellectual superiority was the proper attitude to bring to whatever would happen during the day. The last thing she needed was for fate to teach her another lesson. And so, she settled on *Twilight Sleep*, licking the crumbs of the pastry from her fingertips as she brought the book back to the window seat. Letting her eyes wander for a moment across the rooftops, past Galata Tower, to the Golden Horn, where the wind, once again unequivocally not playful, had begun to howl through the minarets of Sultan Ahmet's mosque.

THERE was no clock in the room, but it felt like a few minutes before noon when she heard a knock on the door. She stood and was about to open it, when instead it opened from the corridor. Jeffrey entered, damp from the weather outside. He was wearing a dark grey suit, a white shirt with silver cuff links, a lighter grey silk tie, and a dark blue wool overcoat with the collar pulled up. His shoes looked hand made. Once he'd entered, he stood in front of her, appraising.

"Yes," he finally said. "Better than the moth-eaten bluestocking look. And thank heaven Paris is moving away from sequins and kohl. I've become sick to death of women mimicking my haircut."

She was still holding her book. "Good morning."

He collected himself. "Forgive me. I've just returned from a turbulent meeting with İnci's father. If I'd known that he'd try to fight back, I'd have worn the uniform. Remind him that, despite appearances, the sun continues not to set and all that." He pushed his hair off his forehead, distracted. "But it's been sorted. She's harmless. You'll likely be receiving an invitation to her wedding to Sinan in the near future."

"I have a future, then?" She hadn't moved. "That might involve attending a wedding held outside of consular limbo?"

"That depends on you." He opened the door for her. "And indeed, that is what we'll be discussing today."

She remained immobile. "Not here?"

"In the building. It's an official discussion that will happen in official surroundings. And you can leave the book here," he added. "Tortured domesticity hardly sets the tone for a productive conversation." He glanced sideways at the title as she left it on the marble table. "Surprised you didn't calm yourself with the Zane Grey, to be honest."

He gestured with his arm toward the corridor, and she walked out of the room. There weren't any soldiers, which was further evidence that no one, at least yet, considered her a criminal or a political threat. And the two of them walked alone down two flights of stairs to the main floor of the building through a series of secure doors, before stopping at an anonymous office at the end of a narrow hall. Jeffrey used his own key to unlock the door and stood to the side to let her enter.

The room was even more neutral, if that was possible, than the suite had been. Aggressively neutral. If it hadn't been for the flags of Great Britain and Turkey standing in a corner, it might have been a midlevel conference room at a bank. A window looked over Meşrutiyet Street, but it was protected by a metal grate, and she couldn't get more from it than impressions of foot and street traffic outside.

Jeffrey followed her into the room, let the door close behind him, hung his coat on a hook beside a functional, unostentatious desk, and invited her to sit in a cushioned wooden chair placed in front of it. He walked to the other side of the desk, tossed a thin file folder on top of it next to an unused ashtray, and sat in a second wooden chair, on casters.

He saw her looking at the folder, and half smiled. "I left the complete file in Baghdad. Too bulky for travel. This is all we need for now."

He leaned back in the chair and watched her for a few more seconds. She sat still and upright, focusing on the desk in front of her. She wasn't going to help him.

Eventually, he sat up, opened the near empty file, folded his hands on top of it, and spoke. "The Home Office has looked into the difficulties you've been experiencing with your passport, and unfortunately there's nothing they can do to help. Your marriage to a non-British alien was witnessed and legally valid. According to both British and International law, you forfeited your native citizenship upon your decision to become the wife of a citizen of a foreign country. The death of your husband has not altered your own status. That you chose not to pursue Egyptian citizenship at the time of your marriage also does not change your status. We cannot, under the circumstances, issue you British papers. You are currently stateless. We recommend that you contact the Egyptian Embassy to request an official passport."

She nodded slowly. "Is that all?"

"Yes." He closed the file.

She waited, suspicious. He didn't say anything more.

"I can leave?" she ventured.

"Unless there's anything more you need from us?" His voice was bored, bureaucratic.

She stood, doubtful. Started to open the door.

"You'll want to try the office three doors down on the right," he said.

She turned. "What?"

"Until five years ago, Egypt was a British Protectorate. We continue to administer Egyptian foreign policy. You'll make your request for papers three doors down," he repeated. "On the right. I'll meet you there, if you'd like." He was fighting a smile.

She took a breath, forced herself not to react. Kept her voice neutral. "What are you doing, Jeffrey?"

He looked up at her from the desk, all injured innocence. "I'm trying to help you. Red tape can be brutal. And I must warn you, the clerks over at the Egypt bureau are willfully officious. They don't take kindly to British women fraternizing with Arabs. Turks." He waved a hand. "And so forth. I admit that I haven't a great deal of confidence in the success of your application."

"I know what you're doing. You're trying to scare me. It won't work. I've moved about perfectly well without papers for years. I'll take my chances outside. Goodbye." She turned to the door.

"See you shortly."

She spun back. "What's that supposed to mean?"

He had his elbows on the desk. His chin in his hands. Looking mild. "They'll ask you for your passport on your way out. It's protocol. When you haven't one to show from *any* sovereign state, they'll return you here—with due concern for your welfare, of course—to me." He leaned back again, reached into an inner pocket of his suit for his cigarette case, and tapped out a cigarette. "I'll smoke a cigarette while I wait."

She lowered herself into the chair. "I don't know where the sword is."

He pushed the unlit cigarette back into the case. "I don't believe you. But that's not what we're discussing at the moment."

"What are we discussing?"

"I've told you. I want to help you resolve this paradox involving your papers. A nightmarish situation, isn't it? I suspect that the absence of any Kafka in that bookcase upstairs is a deliberate choice."

"All right," she said carefully. "Tell me, then. What is the solution? I admit that I am utterly defeated by this."

"Like backgammon."

"Fine."

"The people at the Home Office," he said, "suggested that you re-marry."

She laughed. "Thank you for that. I'll take it under consideration."

"But you must do it here."

"What?"

"Here in the Consulate," he said. "In order to leave."

An appalling thought began forming itself at the corners of her mind. "I don't understand."

He looked perplexed at her lack of comprehension. "It's perfectly obvious to me. In order to leave the grounds of the Consulate, you need a passport. In order to acquire a passport, you must marry—ideally a British citizen. Ergo, you must marry, here, before you leave."

"Jeffrey—"

"You might think of it as an international law variant on being tied to a railway track." He paused to consider. "Although not as messy. And without the screaming. And, of course, with no urgency whatsoever. You have all the time in the world to make your decision. Along with what looks to be a more than sufficient selection of reading matter to distract you while you ponder."

"Jeffrey—"

"Would you like me to go down on one knee?"

"Why are you doing this?" She nearly sobbed.

"I like you," he said. "You don't bore me. I must be married to advance my career." He thought for a moment and then corrected himself. "All of my careers. Men without domestic anchors become suspect at a certain age. *And* you know what I do. For the most part, at least. I have a growing dread of retiring thirty years from now only to have the trusting, devoted mother of my children learn from some slip that all those excursions she thought I was taking to promote the work of the Northern Lighthouse Board were in fact spent in dank cellars in Aleppo having arguments with my French counterparts about whether whips or water are more effective on people like you."

She was holding her forehead in her hands, looking down at her lap. "'Domestic anchor.'"

"In a manner of speaking."

She looked back up at him. And surprised herself. Because rather than feeling defeated, she felt a slight hope, the early glimmer of a counter strategy coalescing in her mind. "There's also my library," she said slowly. "Tariq's library."

"Yes. There is that too."

"But," she continued evenly, "if it were established, somehow, that the library *is* my property— which would be difficult in its own right—you'd have no claim on it. As my—my husband." Stumbling on the word. "The property that a wife brings to her marriage in Great Britain remains her own. That's been the case now for more than two years."

"Excellent," he congratulated her. "We're both up on our recent statutes, then. Yes, as a matter of fact, I am aware of The Law of Property Act. In effect as of 1925. Quite the blow for the women's movement, wasn't it?" He tapped the cigarette back out of the case. Lit it. Inhaled. Blew smoke up at the ceiling. "I even read the Dorothy Sayers novel that made such an entertainingly clumsy plot point of it. 'Unnatural death,' indeed."

He looked at the cigarette and continued. "But do you know what else I read?"

She shook her head.

"I read," he persisted, pedantically, "the actual text of the law. Enjoying, as I always do, a good comedy. My favorite section is Part Eight, on 'married women and lunatics.' And do you know, Marion? Given your customarily insane behavior and the logic of that section, it would take a mildly competent barrister approximately fifteen minutes to have me, as your husband, as you say, assigned as your guardian. And, of course, as guardian of any property that you might bring, freely and independently, principles of modern womanhood intact, to our union." He shifted his attention to his right cufflink and then gazed back across the table at her. "But we're getting ahead of ourselves. You haven't yet consented."

"If I don't consent?"

"You remain a guest of the Consul General."

"For how long?"

"For as long as it takes."

He ground out his cigarette in the ashtray and leaned back in the chair, watching her with interest.

She stared at a spot on the desk in front of her, working out the details of her strategy. Then, satisfied, she looked up and held his eyes. "Yes."

His eyebrows went up. "I wasn't expecting that. No fight?"

"No fight. I will marry you." She found it difficult to say the words, but once they were out, she was certain that she had made the right decision.

He kept his eyes locked on hers. "I'm afraid I'll insist on my conjugal rights."

"I understand." She spoke calmly.

"Such poise," he said, looking away from her, standing, and retrieving his overcoat. "It will calm the clerk. Consular officials don't ordinarily preside over marital ceremonies, and this welcome docility will prevent him from losing his wits completely." He held the coat over one shoulder with his finger and let his gaze run over her dress. "You chose the black. Appropriate, I think."

THEY walked along the main floor of the Consulate until they reached another bland office staffed by four bored clerks. The clerks stood when Jeffrey entered the room, but he waved them back into their seats and stepped between their desks to speak to their superior, the registrar. When Jeffrey had finished speaking, the registrar cast a confused glance at Marion and disappeared through a door at the back of the office. He reappeared a few moments later carrying two sets of documents. Remaining standing, he arranged the documents on the desk in front of him and beckoned two of the clerks to the table, where they hovered, also uncertain.

The registrar cleared his throat. "Miss Bailey?"

"Yes?"

"Would you and Sir Jeffrey approach the desk, please?"

She and Jeffrey stood side by side in front of the desk.

The registrar addressed Marion again. "We are here to witness the marriage of Miss Marion Bailey to Sir Jeffrey Willcox. Do you, Marion Bailey, know of any impediment to this marriage?"

"I do not," she said.

"Do you, Marion Bailey accept Sir Jeffrey Willcox as your husband?"

"I do." Her voice was cold.

The registrar repeated the questions to Jeffrey, who answered lightly, without emotion. He turned the first document on the desk toward Marion. Pointed to a line on the paper.

"Would you sign here please, Lady Willcox?" he asked.

"No."

They all looked at her.

The registrar colored. "But, Lady Willcox, you must sign the marriage certificate for the ceremony to become valid."

"I take Sir Jeffrey Willcox as my husband. I do not take his name."

The registrar gaped at her, bewildered. "But Lady—Miss—"

Jeffrey was laughing. "Try 'Dr.'"

"This is most unusual." He looked at Jeffrey. "We cannot issue a family passport under separate names. You had mentioned that the passport was a significant, er, incentive for this ceremony? You must travel as Sir Jeffrey and Lady Willcox."

"Precisely," Marion said. "I will marry Sir Jeffrey. But I will remain Dr. Bailey. And I will carry my own, *separate*, papers."

The registrar looked at Jeffrey, who nodded almost imperceptibly, still smiling.

"Very well, Dr. Bailey," he said, disgusted. "Please sign here." She signed. "And you, Sir Jeffrey." He signed. "Anderson, Davies, please make your marks as witnesses."

The two clerks looked at one another, shrugged, and signed. The registrar stamped the document with a satisfied flourish, folded it, and placed it at the corner of the desk.

"It gives me pleasure to tell you that you are now legally husband and wife." He waited for a moment, and when they made no move to embrace, he exhaled in irritation and motioned Marion and Jeffrey into two empty chairs at the other side of the room.

As they waited, he fussily worked through the second set of documents he had retrieved from the back room, filling in blanks and occasionally making use of the stamp he had slammed onto their marriage license.

Jeffrey watched him for a few minutes and then turned to Marion. "Was it all you'd hoped it would be?"

"Yes."

"I see what you're trying to do, my dear." Delighted to be annoying her. "You think that your separate papers will enable you to take advantage of your devoted husband's position, use him mercilessly for your own nefarious purposes, and then desert the poor fellow at the first opportunity."

She nodded toward the registrar. "I think he's about finished."

"But it won't work." He put his hand over her own. "Because you see, 'Dr. Bailey,' even your separate papers declare you to be—if no longer my property, what with your women's rights and your advanced politics and your charmingly competent unraveled jumpers—still nonetheless my wife and my responsibility. Abandonment is a serious marital crime. No one, least of all a civil court, would fault me for posting a watch on every border crossing between here and Calais once I'd discovered your betrayal. Nor would they fault me for having you declared, immediately upon your apprehension, incompetent." He removed his hand from hers and stood as the registrar made his way across the office. Looked down at her, still in her seat. "And then we would have the opportunity to revisit that intriguing question of what guardianship over 'married women and lunatics' entails."

He smiled at the registrar and shook his hand.

Marion stood as well, waiting impatiently for her papers.

The registrar held her passport in front of her between two fingers and spoke in a serious, patronizing tone. "These papers," he said, "are not to be taken lightly, Dr. Bailey. I understand that you've been having no end of difficulty with your status, largely as a result of your own heedless behavior. This passport is, as you've requested, in your own name. Its pages are blank. And I have used a photograph provided by Sir Jeffrey for the purpose. But please, Dr. Bailey, think of the honor of your native country when you use it. Not to mention the honor of *your husband*." Waspish.

"Thank you," she said, calm. "I am grateful to you for both your consideration and your patience in this matter."

She held out her hand for the papers.

"You are quite welcome, Dr. Bailey." He handed the passport to Jeffrey, who slipped it into an inside pocket of his suit. Before she could protest, Jeffrey led her by the elbow out the door. He put on his overcoat in the corridor.

"Don't fight with clerks, Marion. Even you ought to know better than that." He held out his arm, which she took automatically, and they walked toward the main entrance of the Consulate. "We must find you a coat," he said as they exited into the drizzle. "And a ring."

"I'll buy one for myself," she said. "I planned to visit my banker anyway."

"No time." He signaled for the car, which was waiting at the other end of the circular drive. "We'll be leaving for our honeymoon this evening. Any thoughts on a venue?"

"Bursa," she said without hesitation.

"If I didn't know better, I'd think that this compliant streak hid some dishonorable motive." The car had moved into place in front of the main entrance to the building, and Jeffrey opened the door for her. "But perhaps marriage simply suits you."

She balked at the open door. "I hate this. Can we walk instead? Or take a cab?"

He put his hand on her shoulder and pushed her into the back seat. "No." Then he closed the door. Walked to the other side and got in himself. "I myself have nothing but happy memories of our time spent here. An excellent place to begin this new chapter of our lives."

She watched, irritated, out the window as the car drove past the two gates and two sets of soldiers. At the second gate, Jeffrey reached into his pocket and pulled out Marion's passport. The guard gave it a superficial perusal, handed it back to Jeffrey, and waved the car out into the hectic Galata traffic. Marion sat, pensive, in the black, tailored Jean Patou dress, still looking out the window.

Jeffrey glanced over at her, an unreadable expression on his face. "Enjoying your freedom?"

She ignored him.

I thought you'd choose Bursa," he said.

They'd been on the road longer than Marion had expected. Having left the center of the city, the car had bypassed the Golden Horn and was now speeding along the Marmara coast.

"But there aren't any trains to Bursa," he continued. "And I don't think either of us could stomach a boat just now. Not to mention your unfortunate aversion to this beautiful automobile." He looked at her. Looked back out his window. "You know, you're doing it an injustice. It's hiding an 8 Litre engine. Not, despite appearances, a 4 ½. The first of its kind. A Bentley like this won't be available to the public for a good three years."

She continued to look resolutely at the passing shore.

"Unimpressed? Ah well," he said. "I have something better. Taking the chance that I was correct about both your compliance and your choice of honeymoon spots, I've arranged with a colleague from the Royal Air Force—"

"This would be one of your colleagues who currently govern the Iraq mandate by repeatedly dropping bombs on it?"

He nodded gravely. "The same." He waited for her to say more, and when she didn't, he continued. "He's in Istanbul on leave, and he's got access to a spanking new Armstrong Whitworth Argosy. Any excuse to try it out."

"Will he be bombing anyone?"

"Don't be silly. It's a cargo plane. The most he could do is fly low and strafe villagers with a Tommy Gun. *He* happens to like American weapons."

She closed her eyes. Didn't speak.

"When I told him about my hopeful prospects, he replied that he'd be honored to fly us from the airfield in Yeşilköy, just up the road, to the airfield in Yenişehir outside Bursa." He was smiling to himself. "I've also arranged to have a car, hopefully one without painful associations, meet us there to take us to the center of the city. And—you'll enjoy this—I've pulled some strings to have one of our secure villas in town emptied for a few weeks."

"Romantic."

"It's one street over from Ulu Cami, the Grand Mosque."

"Ah."

"I've asked my associates there to receive our trunks before they depart." He looked down at his fingernails.

Finally, she turned to him. Frustrated. "Jeffrey. What precisely do you think is going to happen when we get there?"

He frowned at her. "Surely some older female relative has explained it to you?"

She leaned back against the seat and closed her eyes again. "This is unbearable."

Smiling, he relented. "In addition to the obvious, I foresee an enlightening conversation with you about the location of Bayezid's sword. Bursa is the only reasonable resting place for it. I would have been disappointed if you hadn't suggested it. Indicative of a less than cooperative frame of mind."

"Don't be deceived, Jeffrey." Her eyes were still closed. "I'm very much in a less than cooperative frame of mind."

"And yet you're hitching a ride to the vicinity with me? Where you'll locate it without my noticing?" His smile grew. "I can only imagine the methods you'll employ to distract my attention so completely."

She squeezed her eyes more tightly shut. "Are you going to be like this all the time now?"

"Only when you obstruct me. You can't begrudge me my own defenses."

She opened her eyes and looked at him levelly. Cold. "It's true, Jeffrey. I can't stop you from following me. But know this now. I will tell you nothing. Not where we're going. Not what we're seeking. Nothing"

"The house is well-equipped for addressing that sort of obstinacy." He put his hand over hers. "And who knows? Perhaps our two purposes there will complement one another."

She leaned back in the seat again, pulled back her hand, and placed it over her eyes. "Tell me when we're at the airfield."

Ten minutes later, the car slowed and turned into a dirt car park. A few hundred yards away, a single plane was on an adjacent apron next to a deserted runway. Marion stepped out of the car before the driver could help her, closed her door, and began walking toward the plane, hugging her waist with her hands. She was cold without a coat.

Jeffrey, moving more slowly, emerged from his side of the car and walked up to the driver's window. There, he leaned over, said a few words, laughed, and then stepped back to watch as the car drove away. After that, catching up to Marion, he walked alongside her to the waiting plane.

As they approached, a man of Jeffrey's age in a worn leather trench coat open over civilian clothing materialized in the door of the plane. He climbed down a few rungs at the top of the ladder that led from the door to the ground, and then he jumped the rest of the way, landing athletically and trotting over to Marion and Jeffrey. He was tall and tan, with straight dark hair falling over his forehead, and he leached the obscene healthiness that had driven her originally into scholarship and then out of the country. She disliked him instinctively.

Jeffrey beamed at the pilot, and they shook hands with competitive robustness, slapped one another on the shoulder, and turned toward Marion.

"Marion," Jeffrey said, "this is Aldous. We grew up together. Aldous, my wife, Marion."

Marion tried to smile naturally.

Aldous gave her a slight, and slightly ironic, bow. "So, you're the one who managed to pin him down. I wish you the best of luck."

She couldn't think of anything to say in response. Glanced for help at Jeffrey. But he was looking instead, interested, at the plane.

Aldous raised his eyebrows. "Willcox," he prompted after an awkward moment. "Your bride here is wearing black and appears to be on the verge of tears. What have you done? Abducted her?"

Jeffrey turned back to Aldous. "Proper country for it, anyway. And what if I have?"

Aldous winked at Marion. "I'd aid and abet. No good throwing over a lifetime of friendship for one badly judged crime of passion. Say the word, and I'll take you to the isolated dungeon of your choice."

"Bursa's fine for now."

Aldous peered behind them. "No trunks?"

Jeffrey shook his head. "I've sent them on ahead."

"Very well, then. Let's get the crate up in the air."

Aldous and Jeffrey stood aside to let Marion precede them up the ladder. As she climbed, she heard Aldous ask quietly: "she's not the one who—?"

"In the flesh."

Aldous whistled to himself. "I suppose you know what you're doing. But I don't envy you."

50

She felt herself blushing as she stepped through the door. But what she saw in the interior of the plane distracted her from her embarrassment. The Armstrong Whitworth had been converted from a military cargo plane to a passenger plane, and it was far from comfortable. Behind the cockpit, there was nothing more than an empty area with three spare metal seats bolted to the floor. But there was also a package covered with cloth near the tail. She crossed to it, knelt, and drew aside the covering. It was her manuscript. She was digging beneath it for the flute and cup when the edge of Jeffrey's shoe appeared to her left. Startled, she looked up.

"Put it back, Marion."

Irritated, she re-secured the manuscript into place on the floor. Stood, dusting off her dress. Neither of them spoke further. But Aldous, who had climbed into the cockpit, leaned over and poked his head out into the main cabin of the plane. He was wearing goggles.

"Care to ride shotgun, Willcox?"

"Delighted!" Jeffrey shouted back. He was holding a wool military blanket, which he handed to Marion. "Fear not. Nothing more than an American expression." He turned to go. Looked back at her. "At least so long as Turkey retains its fragile sovereignty. Someday soon, darling, you and I must go flying over Iraq together. It will be educational."

He stepped into the cockpit and sat in the seat next to Aldous. Marion, chewing her lower lip, chose one of the three vacant metal seats in the cabin, attached her harness, and pulled the blanket across her shoulders.

Bursa, Turkey
February, 1927

ALDOUS brought the plane down in Yenişehir with the same skill he had shown taking off in Yeşilköy. And Marion amended her impression of him. Yes, he represented everything that she found repugnant about the Empire. But he did have expertise. If she focused on that, she'd perhaps manage to avoid hurting him in the few minutes she'd be forced to interact with him before leaving for the center of Bursa.

She sharply reminded herself of her decision as Aldous bounded from the cockpit, high on adrenaline. Followed by Jeffrey, who also looked uncharacteristically boyish. She concentrated on folding the wool blanket and rising to her feet while Aldous heaved open the door of the plane and Jeffrey moved the ladder into place. Still with the hint of gallant mockery, they gestured for her to exit.

She glanced back at the manuscript secured to the floor and then obediently climbed down the ladder. Aldous and, a moment later, Jeffrey followed, each jumping past the last few rungs. Jeffrey had taken off his tie and the jacket of his suit. He was wearing the long, blue coat over the grey tailored trousers and white dress shirt. He carried the package containing the manuscript, cup, and flute under his arm.

He shook hands with Aldous and then tossed his goggles back up through the door of the plane. "Thank you for dropping us here, Parker. Saved us a world of trouble."

"Any time," Aldous said. "And any excuse to trial a new aircraft. But I admit it, I still miss my Brisfit."

"Aren't they testing a new Bristol now?" Jeffrey asked. "Bulldog or some such, wasn't it?"

Aldous brightened. "Listen, Willcox. You get me signed up as a test pilot for the Bulldog prototype, and you can consider your debt here paid."

"Consider it done."

Aldous turned back to Marion. "You've landed yourself a brick of a husband, Lady Willcox. Treat him well, will you?"

She failed to come up with anything polite to say in response. She hated them both. Stared down at her feet.

After a few seconds, Aldous looked at Jeffrey. "She does talk, doesn't she?"

"When properly motivated."

"To each his own." Aldous shrugged. "Look me up when you find yourself in Baghdad, will you?"

And with that, he loped back to the plane, climbed the ladder, and closed the door.

Jeffrey and Marion, meanwhile, turned toward the road. There was a Daimler coupe, empty, bright blue, and right-hand drive, waiting for them at the edge of the apron. Jeffrey smiled when he saw it. "Our transport." He and Marion walked toward it. "Less imposing than the Bentley. It suits you?"

She nodded, not wanting to argue, and he walked to the left side to open the door for her. She folded herself into one of the uncomfortably low seats while he crossed to the driver's side, secured the package with the manuscript in a side pocket of the door, and positioned himself behind the wheel. She realized as she watched him start the car and put it into gear that she had never seen him drive before.

He brought the car onto the empty road, flipped on the lights, and picked up speed. Marion relaxed. He wasn't going to try anything impressive. But then, having difficulty remembering where she'd been when she'd woken that morning, she shook her head. Exhaustion abruptly overtaking her. Gave in to her fatigue, closed her eyes, and drifted into sleep to the sound of the car's motor.

It was dark when Jeffrey stopped the car, left the driver's seat to open a gate, returned and inched forward into a courtyard. Then he exited the car again to close the gate, this time taking the manuscript. Marion, still sleepy, opened her own door and got out. She looked about her, shivering. The air was dry and cold, and the sky above the house bright with stars. She could see her breath. Jeffrey, holding the manuscript under his arm, walked back to her and nodded toward two wooden doors set under an interior awning. All the windows of the house were tightly shuttered.

They approached the doors, and Jeffrey pulled a rope hanging from a bell. Almost before the bell had the chance to ring, both doors were pulled open by a soldier, short, pale, and in uniform. He began to salute, but Jeffrey stopped him.

"No need for that." He led Marion across the threshold of the house.

"Yes, sir." The man stepped back. "We're on our way out. Once we've completed our inspection of the property."

"Good," Jeffrey said. "Thank you. You've been more than accommodating on short notice."

"Not at all," the man replied, studiously avoiding looking in Marion's direction. "We're empty now. Things are quiet." He glanced behind him down the dark, wood-paneled corridor, where Marion could hear what she sincerely hoped was cooking. Then he turned back to them. "We've left the cleaner and the cook for you. Dining room is upstairs. Accommodations on the second floor." He forgot himself, glanced for a split second at Marion, and his pale face flushed. "Best not go down to the cellar. Although we've cleaned it up as best we could."

Jeffrey nodded. "As I said before, this is more than suitable. I will remember it. But it's late. Go rest."

"Yes, sir." The man kept his eyes on the ground to avoid seeing Marion a second time, turned, and hurried back down the corridor.

Marion heard him walking heavily down a flight of stairs to the cellar, and then a few seconds later the sound of a door closing with a substantial thud.

Jeffrey, meanwhile, removed his overcoat, draped it across a trunk set inside the doorway, and looked at the carved wood paneling, the flickering oil lamps, and the mosaic floor. Put his hands in his pockets. "Like something out of a fairy story."

"Right," she said. The hall was narrow enough for her to be uncomfortably aware of him standing next to her. "Bluebeard."

The corner of his mouth went down. "I've always felt that he was misunderstood." He walked with her into the corridor and put his hand on the small of her back to indicate that she should walk up an oddly placed wooden staircase situated halfway into it. "The dining room is upstairs. They ought to have something waiting for us."

When she reached the top of the stairs, which ended abruptly at the floor above, she found herself in the center of an open area, low-ceilinged, wood-beamed, and hung with carpets. There were narrow windows along one wall, but they were also shuttered, and she could see that even when open, they would be covered with latticework.

As Jeffrey reached the top of the stairs behind her, she took a hesitant step toward a wooden platform, something between a military mess table and a butcher's block. There were wooden benches along either side of it, thinly cushioned. It was also set, one place on either side, with plates, glasses, silver, napkins, and four bottles of mineral water.

Jeffrey put his fingertips on her waist to guide her toward the table. "This would be it."

They sat across from one another at the table just as a servant emerged from a door at the other end of the room, accessed by a second staircase that led down to the kitchen. The servant was carrying a platter, which he arranged with a flourish between the two of them. Jeffrey thanked him in Turkish, and the servant replied by wishing them a good appetite and withdrawing through the doorway.

It was the most generous portion of İskender Kebab that she had ever seen, and she stared at it, astonished, before Jeffrey began laughing. "I have a feeling that this was on the menu before the men agreed to vacate for us." He opened a bottle of mineral water and poured half of it into her glass before filling his own. "But eat. You must be hungry after what you've been through. And you'll be needing your energy."

She glanced up at him, colored, and focused on moving a few pieces of the lamb and bread onto her plate.

"Did you blush?"

"No." She was still looking at the plate, arranging a tomato and some yogurt over it.

He hadn't moved. His expression was half incredulous, half entertained. "I'm not vulgar, Marion. I was referring to those." He gestured toward the package on the table. "The manuscript? The sword? Not to mention your papers. Remember those?"

She flushed more conspicuously and then forced herself to look up at him. "I don't know how vulgar you're capable of being. Shall I venture into the cellar to find out?"

He helped himself to some kebab. "You're getting ahead of yourself. Wait until I give you the key and order you to stay away from it."

She cut into her meat. "I'm not certain that the Bluebeard analogy holds in this situation, Jeffrey. After all, I'm the one with the information, and you're the one trying to pry it out of me. Perhaps you ought to look after your own inquisitive head."

"I told you he was misunderstood."

She placed her fork and knife down carefully beside her plate. "I'm not hungry."

He half shrugged and ate a bite of kebab. Chewed. Swallowed. "Suit yourself. I think you'll regret it." He cut himself another piece of meat, taking his time. "Would you rather we begin?"

"Begin what?" She was having difficulty keeping the rage from her voice.

"Not what you're thinking about. Although it's darling that you're dwelling on it. Maidenly." He brightened, held up a finger. "In fact." He left his napkin next to his plate and reached into the pocket of his trousers. "I have something for you."

He put a small, antique box on the table in front of her. She looked at him, hostile, took it, and opened it. Inside was an ancient gold band set with light blue stones.

"It's a family piece," he said. "My mother wore it."

She shut the box and pushed it back toward him. "I don't want it."

He wasn't offended. "Bursa's a conservative town, Marion. You must wear something. Half the city will already know you've arrived with me. Our entrance wasn't inconspicuous."

"No."

"Wear the ring, Marion." Irritated now. "I give you my word of honor that I won't attach meaning to it. I've also ordered you the trousers and shapeless overcoats you fancy so much. They're waiting for you in a trunk upstairs. Not because I wanted to please you, mind. But because, as I said, Bursa is a conservative town, and it's better to dress the part." He exhaled in annoyance. "Any normal woman would accept the jewelry and be disappointed to put away the Patou."

"Perhaps you ought to have blackmailed a normal woman into marrying you," she spat at him.

He had regained his composure. Took another amused sip of his water. "Is this our first row?" He set the glass of water on the table. "Let me put this in a way that will perhaps be more familiar to you." He unwrapped the package and held up her passport, which he had secured on top of the manuscript. "I give you this ring as a symbol of my undying devotion to you. If you wear it, I'll let you have your passport." He placed the passport on the table and covered it with his hand. "I understand that writing individualized vows is all the rage these days."

Without speaking, she grabbed the box. Wrenched it open, took out the ring, and jammed it painfully onto her finger. He looked at her hand, sympathetic, and uncovered the passport. She reached across the table, snatched it, and realized that she had no pocket of her own in which to store it. Caught his laughing eyes and slammed the papers into her lap. She wanted to cry.

He detached a piece of bread from the kebab on his plate, dipped it in yogurt, and ate it while watching her. "But don't think that possession of those papers gives you the liberty to drop the ring down a drain or throw it out the window or feed it to a stray dog, dear. I still have the manuscript. Your access to it is contingent on your good faith. I'll consider your wearing the ring a symbol of that. Undying devotion, and all the rest."

"I'm not going to talk about the manuscript here," she muttered.

"Yes, you've made your position clear. I understand. We'll work through that tomorrow morning." He stood and stepped over the bench. Picked up what remained of the package. "Shall we continue this conversation upstairs, then?"

SHE stared at a spot on the table for a moment, nodded slightly, and stood. Avoided his eye as they walked to the staircase leading to the second floor, just as oddly situated at the edge of the room as the lower stairs had been. At the top was a narrow hallway, similar to its counterpart on the ground floor, running the length of the house, with five closed doors widely spaced along it. The hallway was carpeted with an old but attractive silk rug. Jeffrey, emerging from the stairs behind her, pointed down the dim extent of the corridor.

"It will be at the end," he said.

Nodding again, she walked the length of the corridor and turned the knob of a heavy wooden door painted a cheerful, at least for this house, green. The door opened smoothly, and she walked through it, followed by Jeffrey. He turned to close and lock the door behind them.

The room was modern compared to the rest of the villa. The windows, tightly shuttered, ran along two full walls and were wider than any she had seen thus far in the building. The oil lamps, which Jeffrey had turned up as soon as they had entered, were bright, and there was a wood stove already burning low and heating the room. The carpet, which covered the entire floor, was traditional, but no more than a few decades old, and it retained its thick pile. And the bed was English, with a double cotton mattress and a wood frame complete with headboard, footboard, and bedposts. It was made up with white cotton bedclothes. Across from the bed, against a wall, were two trunks, also new, and an equally English looking wardrobe. Next to the trunks was a carved wooden chair with a tapestried cushion.

Jeffrey crossed the room and set the package containing the manuscript on top of the wardrobe. Removed his cuff links and wristwatch, placed them beside the manuscript, and rolled up the sleeves of his white shirt. Then he slipped off his shoes and turned to face Marion.

She hadn't moved. But then, as though remembering something, she found the chair, sat, and peeled off the heels. After that, she hesitated. Jeffrey was watching her with a blank expression. Though as she watched him, a hint of something like remorse crossed his face and disappeared.

He lowered his eyes and toyed with one of the cuff links on the wardrobe. "You needn't do this, Marion. At the very least, we'll wait until—"

She shook her head. "I agreed."

He raised his eyes. The same remorse, tinged with amusement. "You weren't in a place where refusal was an option. It's an option now."

"And I should feel what? Gratitude? That you've chosen to present me with an option now? Appreciate your chivalrous concern for my delicate emotional state?" She stood. "Will that make you feel better about this situation?"

He was taken aback. And then, interested. "No. Rape is fine too."

She strode toward him, confident now, stopped in front of him, and began unbuttoning his shirt. He looked down at her hands, still smiling, but also doubtful. "What are you doing?"

She opened his shirt and pushed it down off his shoulders. It landed on the floor behind him. "What does it look like I'm doing?"

He glanced behind him at the shirt on the floor. Back at Marion. "But—"

She ran her hand down his chest. "I'm not some abject victim you can choose, on a whim, either to spare or to despoil." She locked her eyes on his. "I refuse to let you turn this into one of your domination fantasies. Overcoming my inadequate resistance. Or whatever else you dream up in those 'dank cellars' of yours."

She began unbuckling his belt with her fingers, but he grabbed her wrist. "Fair enough," he said, matching her belligerence. "But I do think we ought to take turns, don't you? In honor of the equality and mutual respect that characterizes our union?"

He spun her away from him and used the hand not holding her wrist to let her hair out of the chignon, which he watched fall down her back. Then he unbuttoned the top of her dress and pulled it off her, still keeping her back to him. After that, he moved her hair and brushed his lips against the nape of her neck. "I've wanted to do this since Cambridge. I fully *intended* to do it in Baghdad. No one would have faulted me. A perquisite of the position." He turned her back and, with a fingertip, pushed a strap of her chemise off her shoulder. Ran his finger along her collar bone. Looked at her face. "But I couldn't. I needed—" He paused, uncharacteristically, thinking.

"Consent?" she suggested.

He pushed the other strap down and watched the chemise fall as well. "An approximation of consent, perhaps."

She shoved him onto the bed, straddled him, and kissed him hard on the mouth. Then she reached down, finished unbuckling the belt, and began unbuttoning his trousers. "I've told you. No domination."

He was laughing. Just as she had finished with his trousers, he flipped her over and held both wrists above her head. She arched her back to try to free them, but he kept laughing and secured them in one hand. Then he brought his other hand along her neck and down to her waist. Rested his fingertips against her bare skin.

"Not even a little bit?" he asked. "Because, Marion, you see, I don't know any other way."

THE room was dim the next morning against the shuttered windows, but the stove had kept it warm. Marion woke curled up in the bed, with her head on Jeffrey's chest. He was already awake, his hands behind his head, gazing up at the ceiling. When he saw her open her eyes, he leaned over and kissed her temple. "I may very well learn to like your radicalism."

She sat up and pushed her hair off her face. "Prat."

He didn't change his position, but he smiled, still looking up at the ceiling. "I can't help it." He rolled over and put his arms around her waist. "Care to educate me further?"

"No." She pushed off his arms, stood, and walked over to the trunks, while he stayed in the bed, watching her. She opened the first, saw men's shirts, closed the lid, tried the second, and saw an approximation of her own wardrobe, abandoned in Mehmet's *yalı*.

She felt his eyes on her, straightened, and looked back at him. "Are you going to get dressed?"

He had leaned against the headboard again, his arms now crossed. "I'd rather not."

She turned back to the trunk, extracted tweed trousers, cotton shirt, wool cardigan, underwear, and socks. "Are there shoes?" she asked without turning.

"At the bottom, I think."

She found serviceable work shoes, removed them from the trunk, and stood. "So that's all it takes, then? One night, and the calculating, disciplined interrogator gives way to some soppy schoolboy willing to throw over his mission for another day in bed?"

He stretched, put his hands back behind his head, and kept watching her. "You have that effect. They all say you're a dangerous woman." He yawned. "You underrate yourself."

She pulled on her trousers. "Is that a compliment?"

"From one professional to another."

She buttoned the cotton shirt and put an arm through the cardigan. "I'm leaving now."

Pulling on the other arm of the cardigan, she took a step toward the package on the wardrobe. Jeffrey was out of bed in an instant, standing between her and the manuscript.

"My wristwatch," he said, teasing. "Don't touch it."

She looked him the eye, unimpressed. "Put on some clothes."

He took a step toward her, the provocative smile not wavering.

"I said," she repeated, "put on your clothes."

When he reached for her, she was already across the room, near the door. "Unlike you, I don't turn into a halfwit after one night and one compliment."

He gave up and opened the first trunk. "I suppose we'll keep working away at it, then." He was rifling through the clothing. Holding the manuscript, along with his wristwatch, in his other hand.

She turned and walked out the door without responding.

The corridor was nearly as dim in the morning as it had been the night before, but the lamps were still burning, and she had no difficulty making her way to the staircase and down into what she thought of as the mess hall. The table was already set with mineral water, tea, apricot juice, large bowls of yogurt, and honey. Enough for a corps of soldiers.

She didn't feel like sitting on the uncomfortable bench, so she poured herself a glass of tea, drank it quickly, and drizzled honey over a bowl of yogurt. Then she picked up the bowl and a spoon, and took them over to the windows, such as they were, to eat. She pried open one of the shutters and tried to peer out through the lattice to the outside. She could make out the anonymous, dusty courtyard, which was empty. Nothing else. The house felt simultaneously sinister and deserted. Rarely had she visited a building with such an unnerving atmosphere. She shivered.

"See anything interesting?" Jeffrey had walked up behind her. Silently. He was still grinning.

He was also too close to her, and she had to edge to the side to walk past him and back toward the table. She was annoyed with herself for letting him surprise her.

He was wearing khaki trousers and a brown pullover, ribbed and fitted. She thought she could make out the outline of his gun underneath it. He followed her to the table, carrying a bundle of clothing as well as the package with the manuscript.

He held out the clothes to her. "You left in a hurry. Forgot the overcoat and the headscarf for the mosque."

She set down the bowl and took them. "Thank you."

Pulled the coat on over her cardigan and trousers and left it unbuttoned. It fell to just above her ankles. The scarf, simple but silk, she stuffed into a pocket. Jeffrey had poured himself a glass of tea and was taking a careful sip.

"Care to tell me anything about our itinerary?" he asked.

"No."

"But we'll be starting at Ulu Cami?"

"Yes."

"I must admit that I'm surprised," he ventured. "You don't seem the sort to loot a mosque."

"No one will be looting any mosques."

He finished his tea and put the glass on the table. "I will. What they don't know can't hurt them."

"They'll know." She walked toward the stairs leading to the ground floor without looking at him. Didn't want to talk about it.

He walked behind her down the stairs, still too close, and then along the narrow corridor toward the main doors of the house. She was buttoning her overcoat as they walked, and he grabbed his own, still draped over the trunk, and put his arms through the sleeves as they left the house. She passed the blue Daimler, parked now to the side of the courtyard.

She looked behind her. "You said it's a few streets down?"

56

He nodded, caught up to her, and held out his arm. She paused for a second, sighed, and took it. They walked out to the public road and turned right toward the twenty domes of the mosque. They could see it rising up in front of them. And in five minutes, they reached the north portal.

Marion stopped, removed her shoes, took the scarf from her pocket, and covered her hair. Then she looked sidelong at Jeffrey, who had also removed his shoes and seemed impatient. "We're British tourists?"

"Yes."

"I'll want to speak to the imam."

"So we're well-educated British tourists. We'll tell him your governess was a Turk. Confuse him."

They entered the tranquil interior of the mosque, light seeping through the glass ceiling of the central dome, the calligraphy that decorated every wall gleaming. Marion took in the domes and pillars, getting a feel for the space. She needed the manuscript, flute, and cup. But she didn't know how to get them from Jeffrey without raising his suspicions. As she mentally worked through her options, she felt his hand close over her upper arm, firm, and pull her to the side of the room.

He bent over and whispered to her. "Marion, I've said it to you before, and I'll say it to you again. You are an excruciatingly easy read. Whatever you are planning, you can stop. I will not let you out of my sight while we're here. If necessary, I will hold you like this until the exercise is complete. You will *not* undermine my work." He let go of her arm. "Do you understand?"

She nodded, rubbing her shoulder. "Yes."

"Good. Now you said you wanted to speak with the imam. He's working over there." He nodded to an alcove at the other end of the vast room. "The next prayer isn't for an hour. Perhaps he has time to satisfy the curiosity of some keen British visitors."

They walked across the carpeted floor, casual, appreciating the calligraphy, until they reached the imam, who was standing, reading a volume open on a wood stand. He turned as they approached and greeted them in Turkish, asking whether they had questions.

Jeffrey responded in Turkish, saying that they were with the British diplomatic corps in Istanbul, and that they were in Bursa now for the first time on holiday. He said that his wife, who was an art historian, had stumbled upon some artifacts in the covered bazaar, in Istanbul. She'd be grateful for his expertise.

The imam complimented Jeffrey on his Turkish and turned, mildly curious, to Marion. She took the package from Jeffrey and began to unwrap it. As she did so, pretending to be having difficulty with the ties, she spoke rapidly in fourteenth-century Ottoman, which she trusted the imam to recognize, but Jeffrey to be unable to follow. She worked at the knots in the linen without looking up at either of them.

"He's lying," she said. "He's not a diplomat. He's a thief. I'm unwrapping an early copy of Ahmedi's *İskendername*. Its marginal markings have already led us to the Sultan Bayezid's flute and chalice. I believe his sword is here in Ulu Cami. My companion wants to steal it and smuggle it to London. Five minutes without him watching would be time for me to find the sword and deliver the objects in this packet into your care. Can you help?"

As she finished speaking, she lifted the cloth wrapping and revealed the edge of the cup and flute. She stole a glance up at the imam. His expression hadn't changed, but he nodded.

"Bayezid's sword has always been here," he said in perfect early Ottoman. "But we've been waiting many generations for the cup and flute. I can help you."

Then, switching to modern Turkish, he turned to Jeffrey. "Your wife's artifacts are intriguing. I would be pleased to escort you anywhere in the mosque to establish their provenance. As well as their proper place of rest."

Jeffrey nodded, suspicious, and tried to take the unwrapped package back from Marion. But the imam, still slow and gentle—and as though it were more the most natural move in the world—bowed and retrieved it from her instead. "As I was saying, your wife's artifacts may have significant value. I am grateful to you for bringing them to our attention. Let us reflect on how to proceed."

He motioned to Jeffrey and Marion to follow him to a small room, partially enclosed, in a corner of the mosque. Jeffrey, angry now, kept hold of her arm as they followed the imam. But when they reached the door to the interior chamber, the imam handed the package back to Marion, and Jeffrey was forced to release her.

He turned once again to Jeffrey, apologetic. "Unfortunately, women aren't allowed in this part of the mosque. Perhaps you would tell me the story of these marvelous objects while your wife waits outside?" The imam briefly held Marion's eyes. "Madam may enjoy the carved wooden *minber* at the far end of the building."

He gestured in the opposite direction, stood to the side, and waited, still patient, for Jeffrey to precede him into the chamber. Jeffrey opened his mouth to say something, looked between the imam's and Marion's impassive faces, threw Marion a threatening glance, and walked with ill grace through the doorway. The imam followed, paying no attention to Marion, who was standing just outside, gripping the manuscript, flute, and cup.

When she could see that Jeffrey was well ensnared in talk, she turned and walked quickly past the one hundred ninety two calligraphic wall inscriptions decorating the walls of the mosque, and toward the intricately worked *minber* at the other side of the twenty domes. The *minber* was a single piece of meshed wood, inscribed with interlocking flowers and geometric designs.

She smiled to herself when she saw it. Nothing would be simpler than fitting the cup into the monumental wood structure. The floral motif perfectly matched a repeated theme not only along the base of the cup, but also in the marginalia of the manuscript. She ran her finger along the edge of one of the larger pieces of wood, and then stopped, considering.

At a familiar looking lotus flower, she paused, held up the base of the cup, and fit it gently over the wood. The carvings on the base slipped easily into the wooden carvings on the *minber*, and once they were joined, a small clicking sound suggested the unlatching of a door further along the wall. She walked in the direction of the sound, still running her finger over the woodwork, until she felt the wood give. She pushed, gently, with the palm of her hand, and a door swung open on well-oiled hinges. She was surprised by its look of familiar use.

She passed through the opening and found herself on a clean, maintained, and yet ancient spiral staircase. And then, sensing her way as much as seeing in the sparse light from the open door above her, she descended until she reached a stone landing, in the middle of which stood a solid plinth about the height of her waist. She approached it, breathing shallowly now, and stared down at it. Positioned at its center, polished, cared for, and resting on a silk cushion, was an ancient *yatağan*. The imam already knew about the sword. It was part of the mosque's legacy—never lost to begin with.

She arranged the cup, flute, and manuscript around the sword, trying to make them look as natural as the sword itself did. So engrossed in her work that she didn't hear steps on the stone platform until they were behind her. At which point, startled, she twisted back.

Jeffrey and the imam were standing at the bottom of the stairs, the imam still calm, holding a wooden key that replicated the floral motif, and Jeffrey looking like he wanted to kill someone.

Jeffrey pointed to the plinth. "There they are. I've been telling you—"

The imam nodded. "Yes. There they are. The Sultan Bayezid's patrimony. They are, and always have been, the pride of Ulu Cami."

"What?" Jeffrey was livid. His Turkish deteriorating. "What are you talking about?"

The imam looked perplexed. "The mosque's treasures. Here. Where they always have been."

Comprehension slowly transfigured Jeffrey's face. He nearly smiled. "Why, you duplicitous thief," he said, half laughing. "You know we brought these here ourselves." He pointed at Marion. "She—" When he saw Marion's expression, he stopped. The smile left his face, and he took a step toward her. Controlled himself. "You witch."

She tried to match the imam's bland look. "Why are you angry? It was kind of him to take the time to show these artifacts to us. But perhaps we ought to leave now so that he can return to his duties."

Jeffrey turned toward the plinth. Neither Marion nor the imam moved to stop him, but Marion put a hand on his arm. "Jeffrey," she said in English, "I don't think even diplomatic immunity would protect you should you be seen, by two witnesses, ransacking a house of worship."

He drew a breath, forced his face into its customary expression of blank contempt, and put his hand around Marion's arm again. "Thank you," he said in once again fluent Turkish to the imam, "for this educational introduction to Ottoman culture. You are fortunate indeed to be the caretaker of these historically valuable treasures."

The imam bowed and addressed not Jeffrey but Marion. "You are always welcome to view them here. When I am no longer strong enough, one of my students will take my place. Waiting for the next claimant. Who may or may not come. Time will tell."

She started to reply, but before she could, Jeffrey walked her, nearly dragging her by the arm, back up the stone stairs and out from under the *minber*. He said nothing to her while they were in the mosque, when they replaced their shoes, or when they paused on the street so that she could remove the headscarf and return it to her pocket.

In the courtyard of the villa, though, he twisted her back before they reached the two wooden doors. "Cute."

She looked at him warily. "I couldn't let you take it."

"Apparently not."

When he didn't say anything further, she took a doubtful step toward the house.

"I'm not angry," he added.

He looked angry. She'd never seen him like this. "I'm pleased."

"Because," he continued as though she hadn't spoken, "there is, after all, more where that came from." He took her arm again and walked with her toward the doors. "In fact, I believe that the next stop on our honeymoon tour will be Baquba." He opened one of the doors and pushed her through it into the hall. "I'll enjoy having you back in Iraq."

"I won't let you near the library." She had stopped, after stumbling against the wall, and was taking off her long coat.

"Not your decision," he replied, ripping off his own coat and draping it over the trunk.

"Jeffrey, look. I'm not staying with you. It's finished. You lost. I'm sorry."

"You're my wife. Not your decision."

She laughed. "You can't be serious. What will you do? Keep me shackled to your luggage?" She paused. "Don't answer that."

"I needn't shackle you to anything. You know that. If you run away, if you fail to cooperate, if you *ever* hinder me again, you will never cross another border. Never." He almost smiled. "And believe me, immobility of that sort will destroy you."

She waited for him to say more, but he didn't elaborate. Instead, he walked down the hallway and climbed the staircase to the first floor, alone. A few moments later, she heard him climbing to the second floor and stalking into the bedroom. She expected a door to slam. But it was quiet.

Central Anatolia
March, 1927

THREE weeks had passed, and Marion was looking out the window of the sleeping car of a Turkish Railways train headed east toward Kayseri. Her destination was, eventually, Iran. Rather than following Jeffrey up the stairs, she had turned and left the house, visited a branch of her bank in Bursa, and bought a few changes of clothing as well as a new bag. After that, she had checked into an unobtrusive inn and waited for him to leave the villa. Two weeks later, he had, and she had ventured out to buy her train tickets. She had kept her passport.

As she sat on the train, she considered her options. She knew that her papers were flawed. Again. But, despite his certainty, Jeffrey couldn't have every border crossing alerted to her potential presence. And she had already hidden from him successfully in Bursa.

She imagined that he would now expect her either to travel south toward Iraq or, more likely, north through Europe and then home. Even should he suppose that she'd flee to the east, the borders along the eastern edge of Turkey were porous. She was confident that she could cross, and after that, she'd be able to use her papers with confidence.

Her plan was to spend a year or two in Iran or Central Asia. She hadn't visited Isfahan since the Pahlavis had taken power, and she was curious to see how the city felt. After that, when West Asia was less dangerous, she might test her mobility back through Iraq. And then, gradually, into Baquba. She would be patient. She knew that the library was well hidden, and that Jeffrey would give up eventually. He could recognize, as he had said, a futile effort when he saw one.

Settling back into her seat on the train, she closed her eyes. She felt relaxed for the first time since the party at the American Consulate. In fact, all that concerned her now was an intestinal virus that she must have picked up during her stay in Bursa. It wasn't debilitating, but she also couldn't shake it, and it had begun to irritate her.

She took a steadying breath. At least it only bothered her in the mornings. And eating a few pieces of dry toast did wonders to alleviate it. Her hand, still wearing the ring that she had forgotten to leave at the villa, rested lightly, unconsciously protective, over her stomach, as the train sped east. Into Kayseri. And then eventually to Isfahan.

Italy, 1933

Wiltshire, England
August, 1930

AN empty road wound through the wood, hugging the River Avon. There was no wind, and the turgid air was heavy with pollen, even this late in the summer. A woman in a pale green dress and a large brimmed hat waited, standing under the partial shade of an alder tree. Her hand rested on the seat of a bicycle, sadly abused, missing a wheel. She used her other hand to hold a handkerchief against the sweat that had accumulated on her cheeks. She had been waiting in the thick heat for an hour already, and chances were another two or three would pass before she could move. She was bored.

But luck was with her. She heard the car approaching before she saw it turn along a bend in the road. Leaving the shade of the tree, she stepped to the edge of the forest and held up her hand. Tried to project delicate, harmless appeal. The car slowed, its driver making up his mind whether to notice her. After a moment, it rolled to an irritated stop. The hood was down. And the driver, an old thin man wearing a moustache left over from the First World War and a shock of grey hair that he plainly took care of, looked up at her with rude brusqueness.

"What?"

She took another step forward and put her hand on the wing mirror. He glared at her hand, which left a mark on the polished metal, but she pretended not to notice. "I can't thank you enough for stopping. I wonder, would you help me—?" She waved vaguely toward the broken bicycle leaning against the tree.

He grunted. "Blasted women and their blasted bicycles. Kindly unhand my vehicle, madam, I have business elsewhere."

He made as though to start the car again.

She turned helpless eyes on him. "Please. I don't know what else I can do—"

He hesitated and leaned sideways to get a better look at the bicycle. Just as he was thinking that this one at least spoke proper English, she took his head in both her hands and, with a practiced movement, twisted it and broke his neck. The wood and the road remained silent.

Disengaging her hands, she stepped back and examined her work. He was seventy-two years old, his bones had been brittle, and it had hardly required strength. Now, dead, his face had taken on a vulnerable, infantile look that it almost certainly had never worn in life.

With mild revulsion, she pushed him back into an upright, seated position behind the wheel of the car. She didn't enjoy this sort of assignment, and at these moments she always had difficulty convincing herself to carry out the rest of her brief. She tried to prod herself into more dedicated action by thinking about the brutal colonial police force that he had helped to build in Egypt. About his servile, lifelong friendship with Herbert Kitchener. Or, for that matter, about the troops that he had commanded during the Fashoda incident in 1898, which had now come back to haunt him, more than thirty years later, as equally old, equally angry French statesmen—likely wearing the same moustaches— hired people like her to settle old scores. It didn't help. All she saw was a prematurely decayed corpse behind the wheel of a car that ought to have been driven by a twenty-five year old.

She shook her head to clear it of these less than useful thoughts. Then she reached over his body, released the handbrake, and forced the driving wheel toward the precipice beyond the edge of the road. Still sweating, she pushed the car to the drop, waited for gravity to take over, and watched as the vehicle careered down the hill and slammed into a tree.

When the dust had cleared, and when she had ascertained that the road and the wood were still empty, she scrambled down the hill after the car and its driver. His face was smashed up against the wheel and blood was oozing out of a gash in his forehead. She took a step back to observe the scene. Yes. A car accident.

Looking about the wood one last time to be certain that she was unobserved, she climbed up the hill, lifting her sun hat and wiping her forehead with the handkerchief. She pulled an undamaged second bicycle from its hiding place behind a fallen oak tree and pushed it into the wood on the other side of the road. Balanced it against the alder and walked further into the forest, where she had left her two-year-old son engrossed in a game involving last autumn's fallen oak leaves and a rivulet that trickled into the Avon.

The sun filtered through the trees above him and lit up his blond hair like a parody of a Boucher painting. She felt faintly embarrassed by his angelic look. When he heard her step toward him, he turned, jumped up, and ran to her, two oak leaves still clenched in his hand. "Mummy's finished?"

She scooped him up in her arms. "All done. Thank you for waiting quietly."

He pressed his cheek against hers and wrinkled his nose at her perspiring face. But he didn't say anything as he let her carry him toward the waiting bicycle. She strapped him into a makeshift child's seat she had attached to the frame, put her leg over her own seat, and began peddling down the road toward the Chippenham railway station. If she hurried, they'd be in London Paddington before the sun set.

She felt a breeze stir the leaves above her as she pedaled her way closer to the river. She could tell from the inert heaviness in the seat behind her that her boy had fallen asleep. And after puzzling for a moment as to how, at the age of thirty-eight, she had found herself living this life, she shook her head again, resolutely appreciating the yarrow blossoming along the edge of the road. Heard the train whistle in the distance and pedaled harder.

Durham University, England
June, 1933

MARION stared hard at the manuscript unrolled on the table in front of her and tried to ignore the insistent ticking of the clock mounted on the wall above her head. She refused to look up at the clock's face. She already knew that she was late for her tutorial. Pressing her fingertips against her temples, she willed the letters on the page to coalesce into something like sense. They refused. She closed her eyes and concentrated instead on not hating Alfred for keeping that vile clock in his office. There she met with more success.

Alfred Guillaume, who in 1921 had built Durham University's Arabic and Islamic Studies program, had saved her life. Limping home to Britain in 1929 after a decade of failures and false starts across the Middle East and North Africa, she had harbored low expectations of resurrecting her scholarly career. The impediments to her finding a teaching position were daunting: a reputation for militant activism, an unexplained infant son, and a Cambridge D.Phil. in Oriental Studies as tarnished as her political past. Working in her favor was a small income. And languages. As well as a sincere desire to devote herself to scholarship, and *only* to scholarship, in the future.

Alfred had always struck her as reasonable. And when, quietly, she had contacted him, he'd repaid her faith in him. Avoiding questions about her past, he'd been interested in her new project and had offered her a temporary lecturer position within his newly formed faculty. Her position came with use of Alfred's office in the seventeenth-century Palace Green Library, a cadre of postgraduate students pursuing work in the post-Abbasid Middle East, and three tutorials to be taught over the academic year. Now, at the end of Easter Term, she was completing a seminar devoted to translating and comparing the Persian and Arabic versions of Rashid al-Din Hamadani's fourteenth-century *Compendium of Chronicles*. It was a demanding course, but she was pleased by the progress her students had been making.

Without looking at the madly ticking clock, she knew that, despite her satisfaction with the course, she was currently five minutes late to it. She also knew that her persistent tardiness was her own fault for teaching in a separate room rather than in her own research space. This decision to shift her teaching out of Alfred's office had been unusual enough to raise eyebrows among the other faculty in his orbit, but at the time it had made sense. She didn't want curious students damaging irreplaceable documents. Better to seal off the room entirely.

Now, though, staring with hatred at these very documents—an eleventh-century Seljuk fragment to her left and a twelfth-century North African manuscript in front of her, both of which refused to offer up useful information—she was feeling less protective. She pushed back her chair, stood, and eyed the papers. Resentful.

Vulnerable and unique as they were, she didn't hide them when she left the room. Instead, arranging them at haphazard angles on the desk—angles she'd check upon her return—she reached for her bag. Shouldered it, brushed bits of dried paper off her sleeves, and tried to shift into her teaching mindset. When she'd been immersed in research, she found it difficult to pull herself back to the surface to communicate. Shaking her head to clear it of the medieval prose, she stepped into the corridor.

Where she collided with Nick, her research assistant. He was walking rapidly, trying to maintain a dignified stride down the exposed gallery that surrounded the library's reading room. He had large, startled brown eyes, a weakness for patterned cardigans over corduroy trousers, and—what kept him from descending into mousy mediocrity—an extraordinary aptitude for modern languages. This last skill, uncommon at Cambridge, and, as much as Marion hated to admit it, even more so at Durham, had led her to invite him to work with her when he had joined Alfred's collection of postgraduate students.

Marion hadn't regretted her decision. His facility with every conceivable variation on modern Arabic and Persian was unmatched. And when on occasion to amuse herself, she challenged him with idiomatic translations that only the most brilliant student could complete, he always made the task seem simple. But despite his talent, she did wish that he'd show an interest in medieval languages. There wasn't a great deal she could do with him if he refused to concern himself with anything written before the eighteenth century.

Now, as he caught sight of her locking the door at the end of the gallery, he appeared less brilliant than aggrieved. When he wasn't focused on his research, Nick's default state was an increasingly annoying combination of anxiety about, and criticism of, her lack of professionalism. Marion could feel the disapproval radiating off of him as he waited for her to close her office. She focused on his hideous cardigan to sidetrack her irritation at the unspoken reproach.

"I've instructed them to start on the assassination of Nizam al-Mulk," he said. Panting, trying to hide it. She passed him, and he turned to walk down the gallery at her heels. "It seemed best. You assigned it last week."

"Yes. That passage ought to hold their interest for a few minutes. You've explained to them that it's a copy of the Topkapı rather than the Edinburgh manuscript this time?"

He nodded, giving up and trotting to keep up with her. She hadn't slowed her pace for him. His tone bothered her.

When they reached the classroom—hidden behind a protruding wall, lined with books, and furnished with a scratched oak table and a collection of mismatched and uncomfortable oak chairs—her six M.Phil. students looked up at her, already bleary eyed. She placed her bag on the table, opened it, and pulled out her own copies of the text. Nick sat to the side and behind her.

"So, which is it?" she asked the table at large. "History or geography?"

"Geography." Christopher Welby. Radley College. He was always the first to speak in seminar, and as much as he tried to project the arrogance of the ruling class, his father's disappointment that he had attended Radley rather than Winchester and Durham rather than Oxford lurked beneath his conversation.

She nodded. "Unconventional. Why?"

He continued, relieved that she hadn't contradicted him. "It purports to be a world history," he started slowly. "And it's always been described as literature or history. But even a moment as dramatic as this—this assassination," he rested his fingertips on the pages in front of him, "is an excuse to describe the territory held by the Seljuk state rather than an attempt to add to the historical record. Rashid al-Din's world is defined more by, I suppose, space than it is by time."

"Well put," she said. "Any other thoughts?"

Margaret Allen, belligerently disheveled, pushed her spectacles up to the bridge of her nose. "I think it depends on which manuscript you read."

"Go on."

Margaret blinked. "It's difficult to compare the three versions of the text because the different manuscript fragments recount different moments. But it seems to me that the Arabic is more concerned with the passage of time. The Persian versions are more interested in space."

Gwendolen Clark, Margaret's flatmate, interjected. "The Persian version of the story is looking to defend the Ilkhanid state's place in the Islamic world."

Marion smiled to herself. Margaret and Gwendolen had prepared this argument before coming to class. Likely to pre-empt Christopher's monopoly of the conversation. She nodded again. Then she returned her attention to the copies of the text she had in front of her.

She was about to shift the tone of the discussion by directing all six of her students toward a closer reading of one of the thornier passages of the Persian Topkapı manuscript, when the door to the classroom opened. She glanced briefly, without curiosity, in its direction. Alfred, and on occasion interested auditors, sometimes visited her tutorials, and she paid them little attention beyond a welcoming smile.

This time, though, she faltered when she recognized the figure in the doorway. He walked into the room, leaving the door ajar.

"I'm teaching," she said. Her voice flat.

A ripple of apprehension passed through her students. This wasn't how she ordinarily interacted with visitors to her seminar.

He paused and considered the room. "Yes. Quaint."

He hadn't bothered to dress the academic part. Wearing a blue suit, a light blue and white striped shirt, and a pale pink tie, a concession to the June heat. There was a handkerchief in his breast pocket. He looked like someone pretending to be a bureaucrat and not caring all that much whether anyone believed the act or not.

She tried again. "We'll finish in two hours."

He wandered to the other side of the room and looked out the mullioned windows into the afternoon sunlight. Put his hands in his pockets, still facing away from the class. "No. I think you're finished now."

She felt her temper rising. "Jeffrey—"

"Really, Dr. Bailey." He didn't turn. "Look at your students. I realize little is more captivating than five-hundred-year-old bits of manuscript debris left over from those half-civilized

Turkic barbarians you like so much, but there's no way your students will be able to concentrate after this. You keep them here for another two hours, and they'll be even more hopeless than usual. Their little minds will be entirely occupied by possible explanations for this distraction." He turned back toward the room and leaned against the window, crossing his arms. "Surely you're not that cruel."

She ran her eyes over her students and saw that he was correct. All interest in the course material had dissipated. They were watching her exchange with Jeffrey in undisguised fascination. Christopher and Gwendolen had responded already to his easy authority and were leaning in his direction. If it came to a question of following his orders or following hers, she wasn't certain they'd favor hers.

Marion felt her throat tighten, but otherwise she didn't show her anger. Instead, she stood and collected her papers. When she trusted herself to speak calmly, she addressed her students. "I'm sorry about this," she said with unconvincing brightness. "I wasn't expecting the interruption. We'll start with this passage next week."

Jeffrey watched from the window as the six students stood, subdued, and filed from the room. "Don't count on it," he murmured at their retreating backs.

When the door had closed, she rammed her papers into her bag and turned to Nick, who had remained in the room, standing but uncertain. "Nick," she said. "I don't even know where to begin apologizing to you for this. But would you leave us while I resolve this misunderstanding? I'll contact you tomorrow morning, and you and I can devise a way to address this material before the end of term."

"No." Jeffrey had his hands back in his pockets. "Lieutenant Trelawney will stay."

"Lieutenant—Trelawney?" She stared at Jeffrey for a moment until understanding dawned. Then she stared at Nick. Nick shrugged, apologetic. The mousy expression had evaporated.

"Oh." She put a hand on the table to steady herself.

"Dr. Marion Bailey, meet Lieutenant Nicholas Trelawney. Eton. Oxford. Royal Corps of Signals." Jeffrey paused. "Sort of."

She felt the blood rush to her face. Pressed her hand harder against the table. "Damn it." Jeffrey and Nick exchanged a look.

"I hope we haven't led you to question your loyalty to your adopted institution. But admit it, Marion. You must have wondered how someone with his *darija* wound up at Durham." He looked at the seminar room as though it were contagious. When she said nothing, he continued. "Or perhaps you did wonder, but you chose not to question it too carefully?" He ran his fingertip along the edge of the window and looked with aversion at the dirt that accumulated. "The boredom here must be brutal."

She clenched her fist on the table, still not responding.

Jeffrey dusted off his hands and moved toward the door. "I think it's best to continue in Alfred's office. More privacy." He glanced at Nick. "And dispose of the cardigan, Trelawney. No sacrifice too great for the glory of His Majesty's government and all that, but there is such a thing as going beyond the call of duty."

Nick nodded once, curt but smiling. "Sir."

As they were speaking, Marion evaluated the windows and the exits in a half conscious memory of her political training.

Jeffrey followed her look. "What will you do, Dr. Bailey? Crash through this lovely seventeenth-century transom and abseil to the ground? Mad break for liberty?"

She reached for her bag, but he was there before her. Handed it to Nick. "Lieutenant Trelawney will carry that for you."

"'Lieutenant Trelawney,'" she said, finally finding her voice, "is a model of thoughtfulness, isn't he?"

She was pleased to see that Nick had the grace to blush.

*W*HEN they reached the door to her office, Jeffrey addressed Nick. "Wait here. We may be a while, but make it look as though you're following some eccentric request of Dr. Bailey's. No curious visitors. None."

"Yes, sir."

Jeffrey retrieved Marion's bag from Nick, pushed open the door, which was now unlocked, and gestured her into the room. When she saw her work table, she stopped. Her manuscripts were not only out of her meticulously placed alignment, but they were now lined up side by side in a precise row.

Jeffrey grinned at her. "Sorry. Couldn't resist."

She walked to the other side of the desk, sat, and looked up at him with a carefully neutral expression. "It's habit."

"It's not habit. It's slavish adherence to training. And training in a field that has little to do, I'm afraid, with the life of the mind." He sat in the chair opposite her, set her bag on the floor next to him, and unbuttoned his jacket. "You can't even leave your desk for a few minutes without making obvious your absurd unsuitability for this role. Alfred must have been out of his head letting you near his precious halfwit recruits."

He sat up straighter and looked at her impishly. "Incidentally, is this where they sit? Waiting anxiously on your judgement?" He leaned back again. "Terrifying thought."

She kept her eyes on him. "I would like very much to collect my bag, walk out of this room, return home, and not see you again for another six years. What must I do to make that happen?"

"And then you go and assign them the assassination of Nizam al-Mulk as a translation exercise?" It was as though he hadn't heard her. "Honestly, Marion, why not the bit about the fruit trees? Poor, hapless incompetents. You'll leave them all deranged."

"They are perfectly capable students," she shot back at him. "I *enjoy* teaching them. Why are you—" She stopped herself. She could see from his face that his goal had been to provoke her, and her response had been textbook. She took a breath. "What can I do to make you leave?"

He reached across the table and pulled the North African manuscript toward him. She made a move to stop him and then thought better of it. Watched, impatient, as he perused the first few pages. His hair had fallen over his forehead, and he read intently. The ticking of the clock was bothering her again.

Eventually she spoke, irritated. "It's a copy of Idrisi's geography. King Roger's Book. Any questions?"

He gazed up at her under his brows and flicked his hair off his forehead. "It isn't. It's not *Kitab Rujar*. You've doctored the first couple of pages to make it look that way to a casual reader. But this isn't the geography." He peered back down at the manuscript and turned a few more pages. "This is *The Gardens of Humanity*. The missing volume. The Idrisi work no one has seen." He let his gaze wander throughout the office. "I wouldn't be surprised if you had a copy of his lost study of medicine stashed in here as well."

He closed the book and set it on the table in front of him.

Marion refused to be drawn. "Is that why you're here?"

He half shrugged but didn't say anything.

She pushed the manuscript toward him. "Take it. If you want it." She shoved back her chair and stood. "Goodbye."

He looked up at her. "Sit down, Marion. I'm not going to steal your manuscript. At least not yet." When she didn't sit, he pointed to the chair. "Sit. Or you'll never get rid of me." She sat, and he ran his hand through his hair. "Why is it that every time I see you, your reaction is to jump up out of your chair and run away? It's hardly flattering. You haven't even asked me how I've fared the past six years."

"Why are you here?"

"What are you looking for in that manuscript? Why did you remove it from your library?"

"What library?"

He smiled fondly at her. "Right." He nodded toward the Seljuk document. "Why are you reading it with that?"

She looked at him in disbelief. "Are you insane? You show up after years of absence—and quite welcome absence, I might add. You interrupt my class with your high handed Britannia Rules the Waves arrogance. You corrupt my research assistant. And now you want to sit here and play at solving scholarly mysteries?"

"I'm more concerned with the territory adjacent to the waves than the waves themselves," he said. "And why not play at solving scholarly mysteries? It's what you do now. I like to take an interest." He thought for a moment. "Besides, your decision to read the two together had Lieutenant Trelawney completely baffled."

"Well, next time don't send a modernist to spy on me," she snapped back at him.

"Ah Marion," he said. "You have so little pity for a poor, understaffed bureaucracy. We did the best we could. And consensus was that you'd be better served by someone personable and pleasant to look at than by someone who knew his dead languages inside and out. We even toyed with the idea of sending you a girl. But we all knew that would be a non-starter. Despite your supposed principles."

"That is loathsome."

He was enjoying himself. "Hardly. You're the one who invited him into your parlor the moment you set eyes on him. We didn't even need to invent an excuse to get him near you." He looked down at his fingernails, demure. "But obviously your interest in him was purely pedagogical."

She stood and grabbed her bag from beside his chair. "That's it. I'm finished. You can harass me all you'd like, but neither of you will assault me in the middle of the University Library. I'm leaving now."

He stood as well, gathered up the Idrisi and the Seljuk document, and faced her. "For the best." He looked at his watch. "We haven't time to finish our conversation here anyway. We'll continue when we get home."

She nearly dropped her bag. "Home?"

"Yes—home. With one's family."

She took an involuntary step back. "I'm not letting you into my house."

"I've already been in your house. It is, I must say, also quaint. It doesn't suit you, Marion. I much preferred your flat in Baghdad."

"You—"

"But I'll suffer through it for now. I understand that motherhood affects women like this. Please tell me you haven't taken up fancy embroidery."

She tried to think of some way to redirect the conversation, and she failed utterly. Instead, she hugged the bag to her chest in an unconscious protective gesture. "Motherhood," she repeated stupidly.

He walked to the office door to open it for her again. Securing the manuscript under one arm, he rested his other hand on the knob and looked back at her. "Yes. I'm very much looking forward to meeting the boy."

She hadn't moved, but she felt panic rising. "Surely after all this time you're not going to—to make any claims," she said. "You can't—" She stopped when she saw his expression, deliberately and maliciously noncommittal.

"As I said, we'll discuss this at home." He turned back to the door and opened it. Then he stood to the side to let her through, in front of him.

She didn't move.

"For heaven's sake, Marion. Don't go and faint on me. I can see your pulse racing from here." He stepped back into the room to take her arm and guide her through the door. "If it's the sleeping arrangements that are concerning you, you needn't worry. I've been staying with the local gentry up at Lambton castle. My older brother was at school with the son and heir, and they still feel protective about me. They'll expect me back snug in their drafty guestroom long before I have the chance to assert any 'claims' in your purgatorial cottage."

She let him propel her out of the office. "You still haven't told me what you want."

He let go of her arm so that she could lock the office door and watched, impassive, as she fumbled with the keys. "I've told you exactly what I want," he said as she finally managed to turn the ancient lock. "I want to talk."

Yet again, she almost collided with Nick on the way out. But his appearance had changed completely. He had, as Jeffrey had suggested, removed the awful cardigan, and she noticed for the first time that he was too fit to pass as an ordinary, starving postgraduate student. More than that, though, his bearing was different to what it had been when he'd been playing her research assistant. He took up space in a way that he hadn't before. Marion found herself feeling afraid of him. She glanced over at Jeffrey, who was already speaking to him.

"I want more people at Dr. Bailey's residence tonight and for the next few weeks," he was saying. "Can you arrange that?"

"Easily, sir. Anything else?"

"No. Just make it happen fast."

"Yes, sir."

Marion watched as Nick loped—his prudish, skittering trot now forgotten—down the gallery and out of the library. She wondered how she could have been taken in by his neurotic postgraduate act.

"He's one of the best we have," Jeffrey said, also watching Nick's retreating back. "It wasn't you."

Marion shouldered her bag and began walking down the gallery as well. "You're a pig."

Jeffrey easily kept pace with her. "All right, then. It was you. You should have seen the reports he sent back to the office on his progress. Laughably easy target you were. We all enjoyed them."

She reached the stairs and took them two at a time, but Jeffrey still stayed at her side. He gazed out a passing window set into the thick wall of the stairwell. "It's a beautiful evening," he said. "Shall we walk? If we do, we'll arrive in time to wish the boy goodnight."

68

She pushed open a side door to the library and stared hard at the ground as she stalked in the direction of her house. She wasn't going to think about it. She'd worry about it all when she'd had time to process. She pretended not to notice when he pulled her hand through his arm and slowed them to a more sedate pace. They thread their way, leisurely, through the grounds of the school and toward the path that led home.

THE air was still warm as they reached the River Wear, crossed the bridge, and continued toward the moor. Marion had purchased a farmhouse with grounds that ran along the open countryside. Its brick walls were well-preserved for their age, the kitchen was sufficiently updated for her meagre cooking skills, the baths were new, and the three small bedrooms were clean and bright. Most important to her, though, was the land. Two acres of meadow and a well-established, if overgrown, garden that her son had adopted on sight.

Now, in mid-June, as she unlatched the gate that led to the drive, and as she stood silently to the side to let Jeffrey pass, the rhododendrons were still in flower, the late-blooming lilacs were at their peak, and an early climbing rose had begun to blossom. Jeffrey looked, bemused, at the shabby yet riotous growth along the front of the house.

"Marion," he said, "this house is obscenely healthy. I find it worrisome."

She let the gate swing shut and walked toward the wooden front door. It was painted yellow. "Good."

"Yellow," he muttered as he followed her. "Cheery." Put his hands into his pockets and continued gazing about him as she found her keys. "I suppose I can comfort myself with the fact that although the house itself looks as though you're expecting the Cottingley Fairies to drop by at any moment, you've at least chosen to live actually *on* a moor. And a moor, I understand, with not one, but two, tormented ghostly women wandering the night harassing passersby with their illegitimate infants and maudlin shattered families."

She was about to retort when she heard her son's voice shouting from the meadow at the back of the house. A few seconds later, he ran around the edge of the lawn and nearly barreled into her. He stopped short when he saw Jeffrey. After a long pause, during which he appraised Jeffrey, cold and suspicious, he turned to Marion.

"Hullo, Mummy."

She bent down to hug him. "Hullo, Ian. Aren't you meant to be getting ready for bed?"

He was wearing his pyjamas, also striped in yellow, but otherwise he was nowhere near sleep. He opened his mouth to try an excuse, but he caught himself when a short, plump, pretty woman with black hair and an apron jogged around the house from the same direction. She halted in front of the door as well, caught her breath, glanced at Jeffrey, dismissed him as unimportant, and turned a tense smile on Marion.

"Good evening, Dr. Bailey," she said. "Ian had just finished his supper and he was *just* about to wash his face before kissing his Mummy goodnight and going to bed—"

Ian grinned up at her. "But then I climbed out the window."

Marion tried to hit a jovial note. "It's all right, Cathy. No harm done."

Ian and Cathy blinked at her. And then, in the awkward silence that followed, Ian looked up at Cathy and whispered, loudly: "why is she talking like that?"

Cathy shook her head at Ian and risked another glance in Jeffrey's direction. Marion, feeling herself blushing, unlocked the door and pushed it open.

She left her bag on a wooden chair to the side of the entry and watched as Ian, closely followed by Cathy, ran into the living room and threw himself into an overstuffed chair about to collapse under its age, weight, and Ian's abuse. Jeffrey paused just inside the door. He eased it shut and leaned over to remove his shoes.

Marion shook her head. "No. Please don't bother. We don't. It—it's England."

He straightened, fighting back a smile. "Indeed, it is." He considered the scene again. "We ought to record all of this and send it along to inspire our soldiers when next they're called upon to fight a foreign war." He peered into the living room. "'Cathy?' Are you joking?"

Marion took a quick breath to steady herself. "Wait here. I'll get him into bed."

She walked to the living room and spoke quietly with Ian. He looked sullen for a moment, and then he nodded. She spoke with Cathy, who also nodded, and the three of them returned to the entryway and made for the stairs leading to the bedrooms. Ian paused at the foot of the stairway and stared hard, once again, at Jeffrey.

This time, Jeffrey held the boy's look. After an excruciating, drawn out silence, Jeffrey turned away and spoke to Marion. "I'll wait in the living room."

She nodded and let Ian and Cathy precede her up the stairs. After she had coaxed Ian into his bed and kissed his forehead, she thanked Cathy and descended to the ground floor.

Cathy lived with her family in a cottage much like Marion's, less than a mile down one of the old grazing paths. She rarely spent the night at Marion's house, but she stayed with Ian most afternoons. Marion was dumbfounded by Cathy's skill with her son. Other nannies had lasted at most two to three months before leaving with unflattering and sometimes violent haste. But Cathy was going on almost a year. Marion sometimes found herself fighting the urge to hug her.

As Cathy gathered her hat and bag, Marion opened the door for her. "Is there anything else you need? Will you be all right walking home?"

"No and yes, Dr. Bailey. Ian and I had a good day, despite the escape artist tomfoolery this evening. I'll look forward to tomorrow."

Marion nodded. She wanted to put off talking with Jeffrey, but she couldn't think of anything else to say. "Well." Awkward. "Good night, then."

Cathy looked past her toward the living room. "Don't let him get away with anything, Dr. Bailey. I know the type."

She turned and walked down the drive before Marion could reply. Once she was out of sight, Marion closed the door behind her. And then, reconciled to the fact that there was no use putting off the inevitable, she spun back and walked into the living room.

*J*EFFREY was sitting in the armchair that Ian had vacated, his ankle on his knee. Reading a novel that he had taken from one of the bookcases that lined the living room and the corridor leading toward the kitchen. Marion peeked at the book's cover before switching on a lamp and walking further into the room. Something by a Brontë. He wanted to annoy her. When he heard her moving, he set the book on a side table to his right and smiled up at her.

"It's a comfortable chair," he said. "I can see why he's appropriated it."

She sat on the edge of the sofa, which was equally worn and fragile from its use as Ian's trampoline when he had chosen to spare the chair for a few minutes. Didn't respond.

Jeffrey had left her Idrisi on the coffee table, a large, scuffed, square piece of wood, supported under one tottering leg by a thin volume of *usul al-fiqh*. The coffee table acted as a welcome barrier between them. He hadn't looked at the manuscript since he'd removed it from her office.

"He's self-possessed for his age," he continued. "I don't think I've ever been evaluated and found so terribly wanting."

"He's a good judge of character." She didn't like the direction the conversation was taking.

"Be grateful that at least one of you is." Jeffrey put his hand over the novel next to him on the table. "He's what? Six?"

"Five. He'll be six in November."

He tapped his fingers on the book. "Yes. Counting ahead from February, 1927. A delightful time—"

Marion jumped up from the sofa. "I don't ordinarily eat dinner. So I'm afraid I can't offer you food." She crossed to the other side of the room, searching for she wasn't certain what.

He watched her agitation. "Calm yourself, Marion. They eat late at Lambton. And they'll be certain to keep something for me even if I don't return on time."

She put her palm against her forehead, trying to relax. Then, coming to a decision, she walked, now with purpose, toward a cabinet placed low against the far wall. Opened it and retrieved a bottle of scotch and two tumblers. "I can offer you a drink, though. Would you like something?"

"Thank you. I will if you join me."

She poured two healthy measures of scotch into the glasses and set one on the table beside him. Took a few sips from her own, closed her eyes for a moment, and then returned to the sofa. Sat and held the drink in her lap, looking down. If she could keep from letting him anger her, he'd give up and leave. She simply must concentrate. Took another sip of her drink.

He observed her downcast eyes. Then, as though nothing had happened, he continued speaking. "He looks like a John. It's a good name for him."

She glanced up, confused. "A 'John?' Who—?"

"The boy. 'John' fits him."

"His name is Ian. Ian Bailey."

Jeffrey held up his drink and looked through it into the light from the lamp. "I think you'll find that it's John. John Willcox. Heir to my ill-gotten baronetcy, in fact."

"Don't be absurd. I registered him myself when we returned to England. Four years ago. In 1929. Ian Bailey. Mother: Marion Bailey. Father: Unknown."

He took a sip of his scotch. "Yes. You did. And then a week later, my solicitor brought our marriage certificate to the same office and explained your mistake—both with regard to the boy's parentage and with regard to his name. I swore to recognize him as my own, and the matter was resolved. John Willcox. Son of Sir Jeffrey and Lady Willcox." The corner of his mouth went down. "I realize you never officially took my name. But the sleight of hand on the birth certificate will make his succession infinitely easier when the time comes."

She was staring at him. "I don't believe you. They wouldn't change the document without my consent."

He set his glass on the table to his side. "Why not? With the marriage certificate in front of them, the only way that you could challenge his parentage would be by admitting to having committed adultery—"

"I *have* committed adultery!"

"With that damp Hegel scholar on the Philosophy faculty? I hardly think he merits yelling, do you? And unless he's more adventuresome than he seems, it's unlikely he was waiting in the wings in Bursa in 1927."

"You—"

"As a matter of fact, Marion, I've committed adultery as well. We're neither of us, sadly, the spotless domestic bliss type." He considered. "Although I do think that my discretion is more appropriate than your shouting it from the rooftops."

"You—"

"But the point is that in addition to having *committed* adultery, you'd also have had to take the extra step of going to the General Register Office and making an official statement documenting your misdeeds. Which, as I mentioned, is not a scenario that crosses most clerks' minds. Imagine the reprisals in store for a wife who made such a move."

"No reprisals are worse than this."

"It's hardly the end of the world, Marion. You can always continue to call him Ian Bailey at heritage festivals or when you teach him to play the bagpipes or whatever it was you were thinking you'd force on him when you saddled him with that monstrosity. Call him Angus, if it makes you happy."

"His *name*—"

"Is John Willcox," he continued lightly. "No son of mine is going to Eton with a name like 'Ian.'"

"He goes to Eton over my dead body."

"Given the information we've been receiving about your recent activities, I think it's entirely likely that he *will* go to Eton over your dead body. A sad fate. But the maternal tragedy will add color to his position there. It ought to balance out in the end."

She took another sip of her drink to hide her confusion. "My recent activities."

"Yes," he confirmed. "Your recent activities." He settled himself more comfortably into the chair and ran a fingertip along the edge of his glass. "You were wondering why I popped in for a visit after all this time—thoughtlessly ripping those dullards in your class away from any further opportunity to maim Rashid al-Din? Now you know."

She shook her head. "You're not making sense. I've been teaching. For the past three years."

"And during the holidays?" His voice was aggressive.

She recognized the tone and resented it. "Writing. Research. Scholarship. How dare you come in here—"

"And before?"

She exploded. "I had Ian! He was two. What do you *think* I was doing? If you'd leave me alone—"

He took a sip from his glass. "Impossible. If we left you alone, there's every chance that you'd bring down the Empire using nothing more than a homemade Mills bomb and a few rare manuscripts." Before she could respond, he held up a placating palm. "It's a compliment. Take it in the spirit in which it's offered."

She took another ragged breath and held her own glass tightly in her lap. "You're fishing. You have nothing. You *can't* have anything because there's nothing there."

"No. I'm not fishing." He stopped and let the silence fester. "But, it's true, I'm also not here to threaten you." He looked, interested, at her tense hands. "I've come in a conciliatory capacity."

"*Conciliatory? This* is conciliatory?"

"Of course it is. You've experienced the other. Surely you can spot the difference." He looked playfully under the coffee table. "No bodies strewn anywhere yet. Not even any body parts as far as I can tell."

"All right," she conceded. "This is you being—"

"Gentle."

"Fine. Gentle."

"And now I am *gently* advising you that it is in your interest to venture out into the field for a month or two, collect some information on our behalf, and provide us with unofficial guidance on a pressing issue of national import. Just this once."

Her eyes widened. "You want to *run* me?"

He burst into laughter. "God forbid." He started coughing and set his scotch on the side table. "Run you? Good lord, what a nightmare. *My* talent, Marion, is motivated by greed, fear, and heaven help us, if necessary, ideology. In that order." He tried and failed to keep a straight face. "*You*, contrarily, are motivated by some toxic witch's brew of unexamined impulses and desires that even the Viennese wouldn't touch with a barge pole. You don't even know yourself why you're acting the way you are half the time. No, thank you. I wouldn't run you if you were the last failed, damaged, easily manipulated linguist on the planet."

She placed her glass, now empty, on the coffee table. "*What* then?"

"Your advice. We'd simply like your thoughts."

"No." She leaned back and crossed her arms. "See you in six years."

"You haven't heard what the problem is."

"I don't need to. No. Never. Absolutely not."

He rested his hand on the novel and began tapping his fingers again. "Marion, I must tell you, you're in a spot of trouble just now. You really ought to listen."

She glared across at him. "I knew it. I *knew* that if I waited, the threats would start."

He stopped tapping his fingers. "I was hoping that perhaps, this once, I wouldn't need to threaten you. Clearly, though, my hopes were badly placed. So," he agreed, "yes. Now the threats begin." He paused, gathering his thoughts. "You've been under additional scrutiny the past six months." He faltered again, looking almost embarrassed. "And I'm afraid that this new attention is, at least in part, my own fault—"

"Fancy that."

"Will you shut up, Marion, so that I can finish?"

"Don't lose your snide equanimity, Jeffrey. It's all you have left, no?"

He frowned at her. Then, with an obvious effort, he schooled his features and smiled. "I'd forgotten what a joy it is to speak with you. Far too much time has passed since our last exchanges." He looked with renewed curiosity at the room. "And fear not. We'll revisit the question of what I 'have,' and what I do not 'have,' momentarily. But first, please, let me explain to you why—since you *have* been so very curious—I am here. Agreed, Marion?"

She swallowed. Despite the warmth from the June day that was still seeping from the walls of the house, she felt a chill. "Fine."

He took another breath and another sip of scotch. "You know that our people have been on you since Bursa, correct?"

She looked at her hands. "I had assumed—"

"It was a silly assumption."

"But when I left you in Bursa, you said that if you ever found me again, or that if I tried to cross a border and you were notified—"

"I'd have you arrested, yes." He examined his drink and set it on top of the novel. "I was angry." He toyed with the binding of the book and then caught himself in the nervous movement and stopped. "Upon reflection, I decided that I wasn't about to advertise my marital troubles to the world by dragging you back by your hair to your wifely duties." He half shrugged. "Besides, you're more fun to watch when you aren't fettered."

"Thanks." She felt ill.

"You're welcome. And indeed, I wasn't disappointed. We watched you in Eastern Anatolia. And in Isfahan. Where John was born."

"Ian."

"John. And then we watched you in Alamut. Interesting choice that." He shifted his gaze back to her hands, which were tightly clasped in her lap, turning white. "Incidentally," he remarked. "Nice ring."

Startled, she looked down at the antique gold band with the blue stones. She hadn't removed it since Jeffrey had given it to her in 1927. Another unexamined impulse. Horrified, she started pulling it off her finger. "It's yours. Take it. Please—"

"Nonsense. It's yours. Till death." His eyes travelled up to her neck. "And I'm more interested in that necklace anyway. Difficult to tell from here, but it looks awfully old. Eleventh-century Persian, perhaps?" He blinked when she backed further into the sofa. "You think I'll take it from you by force? Why bother? I can have you arrested on any number of minor charges the minute you step out of this house. Processed by the local constabulary. Hopefully you won't be too disappointed when any misappropriated bits of jewelry, product of rapacious looting—one would have thought so much better of Dr. Bailey—aren't returned with the rest of your belongings."

She stared at him. "Is this why—"

"No, not that. Passing remark." He put his elbow on the arm of the chair and rested his cheek against his fist. "So, we followed you to Alamut, to Dushanbe, on an interesting flyer through the Caucasus, and then back to Iraq." He looked up at the ceiling. "Can't keep away from Iraq, can you? Happy memories?"

"No."

"Whatever your reasons, you had us terribly excited when you chose to return. We were certain that we'd surprise you, somehow, in Baquba. We could almost taste that library—"

"What library?" she repeated mechanically.

"But—and I don't know how you did it, Marion. I admire you—*somehow*, with half the service on your heels, you still managed to keep its location secret."

"It doesn't exist."

"Hmm."

"Is that why—"

"No, Marion," he repeated, bored. "That is not why I'm here. Not even the library. But we're *just* about to the point." He lifted his chin. "Do you by any chance know Gilbert Clayton?"

"Who?" Off guard. "Gilbert Clayton? He was one of you, wasn't he?"

"One of us? Do you mean a diplomat? A statesman? An anonymous, self-effacing, and loyal functionary of the British Museum and Library?"

She threw him a pained look. "An occupier. A spy."

"Don't you think you're a touch old to be playing at passionate, extremist radicalism?" He looked down at his fingernails. "Be charitable and call him a diplomat, won't you?"

"You're the one who asked," she muttered, stung by his implication. "No. I didn't know him."

"You're speaking in the past tense. You knew he'd died."

"Yes."

"Do you know how he died?"

She considered his blank expression, mystified. "My understanding was that it was well-deserved heart failure. Why are you asking me these questions?"

"It wasn't heart failure." He watched for a reaction. "He was poisoned."

She looked him in the eye. "Good."

"We broadcast it as heart failure because his sudden death in the midst of negotiating the Anglo-Iraqi treaty—"

"Aren't treaties technically agreements between or among *sovereign* states?" she interrupted. "Whatever you were doing in Baghdad in 1929, it was *not* negotiating a 'treaty.'"

He lowered his eyes again. "I bow to your superior knowledge of international law." Then he looked up and continued, unperturbed. "At any rate, we broadcast it as heart failure because the last thing we needed was a further blow to our negotiations—" He held up a defensive hand. "You'll concede, at least, that they were *negotiations*, Dr. Bailey? As for the resulting document? Well, we'll leave that to future generations of legal historians." He paused again. "Put bluntly, the situation was explosive enough as it was without introducing a murder mystery into it."

"All right," she said. "Someone killed him. Four years ago. Good riddance. Why are you here, in my house, now?"

He was for a moment uncharacteristically at a loss. "I'm not certain how to proceed at this point." He looked at her with what almost seemed entreaty. She glared back at him. He schooled his features a second time. "Four years ago, in 1929, you were in Baghdad as well."

"A lot of people were in Baghdad in 1929. It's a large city."

"You were also watched. We thought you might make a move toward Baquba." He paused and pushed his hair off his forehead. "You'd be flattered. Your file now takes up an entire cabinet."

"Charming."

Ordinarily, Jeffrey would have replied with something snide. Instead, though, he pensively tapped his fingers a few more times on the arm of the chair. "This is where things become complicated. Unbeknownst to me—"

"Unbeknownst to *you*? Shocking!"

"Believe me, Marion, you won't be smug when you hear how this ends. Unbeknownst to me, others in the office had taken as much of an interest in your movements as I had. *Not*," he amended quickly, "because of any additional interest in your own case. This was an internal issue."

"Internal?"

He nodded. "There's something of a sea change taking place just now in the service. It's been infiltrated, you might say, by all manner of fresh-faced young novices who weren't old enough to fight in the last war and who are hoping that if they prove themselves indispensable as bureaucrats now, they'll avoid recruitment into the war that's brewing. They're nothing like us."

"Us?"

"Yes. Us. Again Marion, consider it a compliment. So, this new batch resembles, at the very best, and I'm being generous here, an appalling schoolroom full of frightened infants who resent and mistrust anyone with field experience." He looked bored again. "Moreover, despite the fact that my own operational expenses come from the Museum and Library rather than from their own obsessively guarded coffers, and also despite the fact that I have no power over—and indeed not the remotest interest in—their petty careers and promotions, they resent and mistrust *me* in particular."

"I can't imagine why they'd resent you, given your obvious openness to their methods."

He took another sip of his drink. "Quite."

"Do you know who you remind me of?"

"No."

"Langton. Wanting to punish and eliminate all the 'young asses' of your generation."

Jeffrey thought for a moment. Then he nodded. "Hmm. I suppose he had a point. His generation ruled with innocence. Mine has ruled with irony. We were incompatible. But Marion, these new brats don't want to rule at all. They're terrified that doing so will land them in a trench. They're cowards. I much prefer the Langtons of the world. At least he had the honor to try to kill me." He dismissed the memory with a quiet smile. "But let me proceed to the punchline." He rested his cheek against his fist again. "Unbeknownst to me, a cabal of the most contemptible of these halfwits—"

"Durham degrees?"

"Even worse. Unmentionable places."

"What about Nick? Isn't he one of them?"

"Trelawney's a field man. And properly educated. He's loyal."

"Are you certain?"

"We're spies, Marion. So no, I'm not certain. But I respect him. May I continue?" He didn't wait for her to reply. "So, a group of these tiresome children got it into their heads to read through the file on you. A vulnerability, you see. To me. And, my dear," weary, "the results were far from complimentary."

She began to interrupt, but he shook his head. "Wait. Don't say anything yet. It wasn't merely that you were in Baghdad at the time that Clayton drank his cup of poison. They also have sightings of you entering a notoriously effective apothecary's shop a few days before it happened. Not to mention that your movements in the hours leading up to his death are, frankly, damning." He smiled at her. "And then, of course, there are your political affiliations. You didn't even try to mask them when you were there the last time."

She was looking at her hands in her lap. "I went to the apothecary for—"

"Yes, for John."

"Ian."

"Really, Marion. All you need do is request a copy of the birth certificate to clear up this matter." He paused. "And no. That's not why you went. They checked out that story as well. It didn't hold up. Unless John—"

"Ian."

"—takes monkshood with his yogurt?" She didn't reply, and he nodded. "Perfect. So then they took the next step and asked their people in the field to bring in some of your recent associates for informal interviews."

She closed her hands into fists in her lap. "Oh."

"Look, Marion. This should hardly surprise you. If half of what they've put together on you is accurate—"

"You have no right to start this again. I am *not* involved."

"Haven't you heard what I've been telling you?" Angry now. "*I* didn't start it."

"*You* never ended it!"

"True," he admitted. "But let me finish. So, your associates were not in the best of shape by the end of the procedure, but without fail, and without undue pressure, they all pointed the finger at you." She looked up, and he held her eyes. "It was incontrovertible."

"I did *not*—"

"For heaven's sake, don't start denying it. I'm not remotely interested in tricking you into a confession. That's not why I'm here."

"Then why *are* you here?"

He looked angry still, but his voice, when he spoke, was calm. "I have no idea whether or not you poisoned Clayton. I admit it, yes, I've speculated. But I can't convince myself one way or the other. On the one hand, it seems reckless, suicidal, and pointless. The treaty was going into effect regardless of who signed it. So why bother, I thought to myself. She wouldn't have risked it just to make a stupid, hollow gesture." He finished his drink and placed the empty glass on the coffee table. "But, on the other hand—how shall I put it? It seems reckless, suicidal, and pointless. Just the sort of move that *would* appeal to an hysteric like you. So, who knows? I don't *want* to know. And, as I've said, that's not why I'm here. I'm not here to take you in," he repeated slowly. "I'm here to offer you a deal."

"I don't want a deal."

"When rumors of this escapade began circulating back at the office," he continued as though she hadn't spoken, "I took the precaution of approaching my—oblique—superiors and suggesting a means of controlling the fallout. No one, except the children, wants this public."

"I couldn't care less if it became public."

"The higher ups," he persisted, "agreed with me that before letting the children at you, you and I should, instead, have a quiet chat."

"Good." She said. "That's taken care of. We've had our chat. Now let them arrest me. If what you've said about them is true, I'll handle them."

"Marion," he said, "I will not have my wife arrested for murder and treason."

"Then divorce me."

"Never." Affectionate. "You see, I'm old fashioned. I believe that marital differences can always be resolved and worked through. Divorce is for the new generation."

"'Differences?' *Differences*? Jeffrey, you abducted me, imprisoned me in a consular building, and blackmailed me into marrying you. I think that type of difference counts as irreconcilable regardless of one's age or background."

He looked hurt. "You had the chance to withdraw your consent. In fact, I asked you explicitly whether you wanted to change your mind. You didn't. You responded with some typically convoluted logic about women's rights and equality and God knows what else—I wasn't listening all that closely—while I found myself pinned on my back, on the bed, in Bursa. Not that I'm complaining," he added. "It was, if memory serves, enjoyable for both of us." He glanced toward the stairs to Ian's bedroom. "And the outcome of it is acceptable. From what I've seen. Imagine the monster that it could have produced."

She put her palm on her forehead and closed her eyes. "If you won't divorce me, Jeffrey, then I'm sorry to say that you'll be forced to cope with the humiliation of watching your wife's political indiscretions being exposed. Because there is no way, ever, that I will help you find your murderer." She opened her eyes to look at him. "I am certain that your career will survive."

"You haven't understood, Marion. No one is arresting you. And no one will arrest you. At least not for this. They don't want you talking. Anywhere. To anyone. Not in a public trial. But also not extra-judicially to the children, some of whose loyalty to the Empire is, sadly, not what it might be." He looked at her, hard. "You will not be taken in for this."

She closed her eyes again. Exhausted. "Then why are you here?"

"That's what I've been trying to explain to you," he said. "They don't want you talking. But they also can't ignore this now that it's been opened up. So they've left you to me. To handle. A wayward wife, they've concluded—and we're talking now about men of Langton's generation, since you brought him up—is perhaps best controlled by her stern and loving husband."

"What possible influence could you have over me?" Her eyes were still closed. "You said yourself that you're not the type to drag me by the hair toward my—my wifely duties."

"You know, when *you* say it, it sounds—well, never mind. But yes, we've arrived at the crux of this conversation." He put his hand into an inside pocket of his jacket and retrieved a set of folded documents. "Open your eyes."

She opened her eyes. He handed her the papers, and she looked down at them, skimming the text. "What are they? I don't understand." Held the papers out to him and he took them back, folded them, and put them away in his pocket.

"They haven't been processed yet," he said.

"What are they?"

"Though times have changed over the past hundred years or so," he said in indirect answer to her question, "one of the benefits of being—in this case, in Durham—a Lambton is that you've always got a few docile judges and magistrates in your family's stable. To call on when delicate situations arise."

She waited. When he didn't continue, she prodded him. "So?"

He rested his cheek on his fist again. "So the first two pages of this document are a psychiatric evaluation. We completed that in-house. At the office. More than enough material to declare you incompetent." She stared at him, but before she could think of a reply, he continued. "The last page, signed by Lambton's tame judge, appoints me as your legal custodian, conservator, and guardian."

She continued to stare at him for a full thirty seconds. Then she pushed herself up from the sofa. "You can't. You can't do this to me." Started pacing the room. "You're not that squalid."

He watched her moving about the room for a few seconds. Then he spoke. "I've already done it, Marion. As I said, however, it hasn't been processed. Yet. That's up to you."

She stopped pacing and stalked to his chair. Stood over him, breathing hard. "Go to hell."

"Violent outbursts will hardly help your situation. Why not sit down again? If you lose control of yourself and attack me, who knows where we'll end up?"

She threw herself back on the sofa and put her face in her hands. "Why?" she spat through her fingers. "Why are you doing this? *Why?*"

"I've already told you why I'm doing this. The question is how you will react to it." He watched as she shook her head, her face still in her hands. When she didn't say anything, he persisted. "Would you like me to tell you more about how a relationship of custodial guardianship works?"

"No."

"I'll tell you about it anyway." Unemotional. "To start, we'd arrange a visiting schedule for you and John. He'd be removed from your care, of course. I'm thinking I'd have him stay with his aunt, uncle, and cousins—"

"He hasn't got an aunt, uncle, or cousins."

"My sister," he explained. "And her husband. Their children. It's a beautiful house with extensive grounds. He'd be happy there."

She rubbed her eyes and glared at him. "I've never even admitted that he's yours."

"Again, a visit to the General Register Office will cure you of this delusion about his parentage." She started to speak again, but he interrupted her. "And really, all you need do is look at the boy. He's absurdly like his father."

"He's *nothing* like—" She caught herself.

He smiled. "Oh dear. That was quite close to an admission of something or other, wasn't it?"

"Fuck you."

"Ah, Marion. I feel that we've finally found our conversational pace. I'd felt rusty after six years." He rested his hand, palm down, on the arm of the chair. "So, John will get to know his cousins. That's taken care of. Two, your finances would come under my control." He considered the scruffy living room. "It's a trivial income. Hardly worth my time. But I'm confident I could find something to do with it."

She was leaning forward on the sofa now, her elbows on her knees, her fingertips on her temples, staring at the ground. "Stop this."

"In a moment," he said. "I want you to make an informed decision. Look at me."

She ground her teeth and looked him in the eye.

"Good," he said. "And three, we'd put an end to your profession. Such as it is. Alfred, poor soul, seems not to have any compunction about maniacs and hysterics teaching in his Faculty. But I must consider the students as well my fragile wife. Poor dears might end—indoctrinated. Radical."

"I'm a medievalist. I don't indoctrinate."

"Never underestimate the power of historical allegory. Besides," he continued, "in order to teach, you'd be forced to leave our domicile. And in order to leave our domicile, you'd be required to secure my permission. And I'm afraid I'd feel uncomfortable granting blanket permission to someone with your symptom profile. Complete confinement is always best for a ward with your unfortunate mental problems."

She was looking back at the ground. "You've made your point, Jeffrey."

"Good," he repeated. "I was concerned that the message might have been too subtle for you."

"You win."

"Also good."

"But how can I be certain that you won't process the papers once you have what you want from me?"

"You can't be certain," he conceded. "But I can be honest with you, and you can decide whether or not you believe me. Here is the situation as I see it." He looked at the ceiling for a moment and then back at her. "First, yes, having a deranged traitor for a wife imprisoned in my attic is very slightly preferable to watching my deranged traitor of a wife publicly exposed. But Marion, the guardianship wouldn't do my career any great service either. I would very much like *not* to take this step—for purely professional reasons. In that sense, you are safe so long as you cooperate."

He watched her taking in what he had said. Then he continued. "And second, what I told you before still holds. I find you infinitely more interesting when you're at liberty to pursue your demented plots and stratagems. Your paper trails make for marvelous reading. They're more entertaining than most of the novels they put out these days. I'd miss them if you were immobilized. Besides," he added, "on occasion you even inadvertently send some useful information my way." He smiled at her unpleasantly. "In short, my dear, I don't want you locked up. Perhaps one day I'll change my mind. Hard to know."

"I think—I think I'm going to ignore all of that," she said still staring at the ground. "Instead, let me understand what I must do to make this stop. You want me to go to Baghdad to implicate someone? For Clayton's murder?"

"No."

"Oh, for God's sake," she shouted. "What then? What? Just tell me what I must do!"

"The *office* wants you to go to Baghdad to implicate someone," he said. "They don't care who it is. But they need a body. Everyone thinks you did it yourself anyway, so the choice of perpetrator is largely irrelevant."

"And you?"

"I vacillate."

"No, Jeffrey. I mean you say that the office wants me to do something about the Clayton murder. But *you* want me to do something different?"

"I think there's more to it than Clayton. And I think it has something to do with that." He nodded for the first time at the Idrisi on the coffee table. She looked up at him, startled. "Excellent. Thank you for that, Marion. Nearly ten years, and your tells are the same. I've missed you so very much."

Annoyed with herself, she tried to salvage the situation. "What possible connection could there be between *Kitab Rujar*—"

"It isn't Roger's Book."

"All right, then. Between Idrisi's twelfth-century collection of maps and apocrypha—"

"Is that what it is?"

"Yes," she said. "It's really nothing more than an elaborate version of the 'Little Idrisi,' the truncated *Kitab Rujar*. But this volume," she nodded at the manuscript on the coffee table, "has some—some extra embellishment."

"'Embellishment?'" he prompted.

"Yes."

"All right. We'll revisit the nature of the 'embellishment' later. Now, I want to be certain that I understand you. You're insisting that there's no relationship between—"

"Of course there's no relationship between this and Iraq! Between this twelfth-century North African manuscript," pointing at the volume on the coffee table, "and contemporary Iraqi politics? What possible connection *could* there be?"

"That's what I'm hoping you'll tell me."

She looked him in the eye. "I've nothing to say to you."

"You'd best come up with something to say to me, or you'll be spending a lot of time in the not so distant future communing with the Brontës here." He picked up the novel and tossed it across the table into her lap.

She grabbed it and slammed it down onto the coffee table. "Do you want me to fabricate a story for you? There's *no connection*. You're looking for something that's not there."

"Like the library?"

She put her head between her hands. "This again?"

"This *always*." He leaned back in the chair, reached into his jacket pocket and retrieved a cigarette case. "Do you mind if I smoke a cigarette?"

She shook her head and silently pushed a misshapen clay ashtray, one of Ian's efforts, across the coffee table. He looked at it, laughed shortly, and tapped a cigarette out of the case. Used a match to light it, inhaled, and blew the smoke up at the ceiling.

"All right, then. Let's try another angle. Why don't you tell me what you're doing with the Idrisi? What are you working on? This is a bit far afield from the Ilkhanids and Seljuks, no?"

"I'm not going to tell you anything."

He looked pensively at the end of his lit cigarette. "Don't make this difficult, Marion. If you won't even tell me about your research, apolitical as you insist that it is, then I'll know that my superiors at the office are correct. The guardianship will go into effect tomorrow afternoon." He took a drag from the cigarette, exhaled, set it still burning in the ashtray, and watched her. When she remained silent, he tried again. "Simple question, then. How did you get from the Turks, in Eastern Anatolia, to the Arabs in North Africa? And then to the Normans in Sicily?"

"All right," she said. "There's no reason to keep this from you. But you'll be bored to distraction before I'm halfway through."

"Try me."

"Fine." She rested her fingertips on her forehead. "I was working on Nizam al-Mulk, the Seljuk vizier. Assassinated in 1092." She looked up at him. "May I have one of those?"

He reached for his case. "Of course. Forgive me. Rude of me not to offer." He tapped a cigarette out of the case, held it out to her across the table, and leaned in to light it for her. He put the spent match in the ashtray beside his own cigarette.

She inhaled and then blew the smoke slowly down at the table. "Nizam al-Mulk was killed by the Assassins. The *Hashashin*. It's a well-known story, and there's a lot of fantasist speculation about who the Assassins were and what they were doing. People associate them with the Nizari Ismailis, and I hadn't questioned the association between the two." She tapped a bit of ash off the end of her cigarette. "To be honest, I wasn't very interested. I'd always found the European fascination with the Assassins embarrassing. Secrecy and terrorism and drugs—just the sort of absurdity to justify—"

"—a strong imperial presence in the region to nip in the bud any resurgence of that sort of 'tomfoolery,' I suspect Cathy would call it," he finished for her.

She looked at him, unimpressed. Then she put her cigarette next to his in the ashtray. "*But,* since I was in the area anyway, I thought I might visit Alamut, in Iran—the supposed 'Assassin stronghold' at the time that Nizam al-Mulk was killed. I had come across a—a suggestion, in a Seljuk text, that I might find evidence there that altered the ordinary interpretation of what the Assassins were doing."

"What luck." Nasty. "I wonder where you stumbled across that helpful bit of documentation?"

"I'm a good researcher," she said, equally snide. "And my hypothesis proved to be correct." She unconsciously moved her hand toward the necklace under her shirt, but when he followed her movement, she stopped herself and lifted the cigarette. Took a quick drag and returned it to the ashtray. "In fact, I found a fragment of a document in Alamut Castle itself that also called into question the usual scholarly identification of the Assassins over the next few centuries."

"A further stroke of luck," he said. "Amazing how all this material falls into place for you. Stumbling across lost books and documents right and left. Extraordinary, Dr. Bailey. Truly."

"Do you want me to tell you about this or not?"

"Please do. I'm fascinated."

She crushed the cigarette in the ashtray. "The fragment from the castle hinted at a more than incidental relationship between the Assassin Da'i, Kiya Buzurg-Ummid, the third commander of Alamut Castle, and the Norman King, Roger II, who was ruling Palermo and Sicily, not to mention parts of North Africa, at the same time. Twelfth century." She paused in thought for a moment. "At first, all I had was the fact that the fragment, which was attributed to Idrisi—odd in itself, given that it was hidden in Iran—drew a literary parallel between 'the gardens of humanity' and the so-called 'heavenly gardens' in Alamut.'"

She stopped again, thinking.

"But then," he prompted.

"But then, I—I found a more complete version of the same manuscript—"

"Did you really?" He was laughing. "Imagine that. Almost unbelievable good fortune. And where did you find this manuscript, Marion? Left behind in the second class compartment of a Turkish Railways train? Underneath a bench on the ferry from Calais? I must know."

"Yes," she said. "To both. That's where I found it."

He rested his cheek on his fist again. "I'll let that go for now. Continue."

She nodded at the Idrisi on the table. "It was *that* manuscript." She glanced up at him. "You know about Roger's court in Palermo, yes?"

"Vaguely. Remind me."

"Roger was nominally Christian. But his court, when he established it after the Normans took Sicily from the Muslims, was multi-confessional. And most of his governing apparatus looked Muslim. He simply left everything from the previous century in place. It had worked well. There was no reason to change it. In fact, there's an interesting theory that English common law, which developed under Henry II, also a Norman, was Sicilian Islamic law transplanted from Roger's court to Britain."

He raised his eyebrows. "Good lord. Don't tell the Prince of Wales. He's already confused enough about his cultural loyalties."

"Right. So Roger's court in Palermo in the twelfth century was multi-confessional, cosmopolitan, a meeting place of minds, all that sort of thing. He invited Idrisi—who had already been traveling, suspiciously now, I think, all over Central and West Asia—to compile the geography for him. Idrisi took up residence in Palermo in 1140. He finished King Roger's Book in 1154, the year Roger died." She reached out and put her hand on the manuscript. "But Idrisi also wrote this. The *Gardens of Humanity*. And although I'm still putting my translation together, it seems to me not just a collection of maps, but also a complete list, in the form of a kind of travelogue, of all the—the targets of the Assassins between the mid-eleventh century and the time Idrisi wrote. The geography and the history and—and the politics overlap with one another."

"It's a kill list?"

"*No*. That's what's interesting about it. It suggests that although the Assassins did, obviously, kill, they killed selectively. And their motives were complicated. And most interesting, at least for re-thinking their influence in the region, membership in the group was not dependent on Nizari Ismaili status." She opened the volume and turned a few pages. Then she ran her finger across a few lines of text. "The Assassins were, like Roger's court, cosmopolitan. They came from everywhere. Even Idrisi's medical texts—"

"Which are lost, of course. You're speculating here?"

"Yes," she said coldly. "I'm speculating. The medical texts are lost. But even the—*lost*—medical texts are more than a little concerned with poisons and toxic substances. They are, I suppose you might call them, manuals on conducting behind the scenes politics." Before he could interrupt with another sarcastic remark, she rushed to finish. "But the purpose of both sets of texts, and a purpose that comes through loud and clear in the prose, is to protect a—a particular interpretation of the world. Of what the world is. Or ought to be. The globe, as Idrisi and other Assassins—because I think he may have been one of them—understood it was being trampled by the geopolitics of the day. They thought it was their duty to halt the destruction of what they understood to be 'the earth.' As a whole. So the assassinations were—protective."

"Of course they were. Poor, misunderstood terrorists. No wonder you like them so much."

"You *asked*, Jeffrey. And I've answered. This is what I'm doing. Are you satisfied?"

"No. Not remotely. Because there's obviously more. The holes in your story are almost comically gaping." He noticed for the first time her drawn expression, and looked contrite. "But we'll work through the rest of it later. For now, I have only one further question."

She stared down at the table in front of her. "What is it?"

"You brought this manuscript all the way back *here* with you. You wanted it in England. Why?"

"Not necessarily England," she said. "It may be Wales or Ireland. Possibly France."

"Explain."

"In addition to this volume, Idrisi also commissioned a silver disk or globe to be made to accompany his work. His works. Both the geographical work and the—the political work. It's mentioned by commentators who visited Roger's court in Palermo. But the disk disappeared."

He nodded. "Yes. I think I remember hearing something about that. And?"

"And I have another hypothesis."

"Which is?"

"Roger II, in Sicily, and King Henry, in England, had something else in common besides an interest in Islamic law. They also both had an advisor, Master Thomas Brown. He was born in England in the 1120s, but he accompanied Henry on his campaigns throughout Ireland and Wales. He surfaced in Sicily, at Roger's court, between 1137 and 1150. By the mid-1150s he was back in England. It's about the time that Thomas leaves Palermo that the silver disk also disappears. Or, at least, no later than 1160. I think he either stole it from, or was entrusted with it by, Idrisi. And I think he brought it here."

"Ah. Things are starting to make more sense."

"But it's all centuries in the past," she insisted.

"Perhaps."

"And I must do more research. I can't be certain about any of it yet."

"I see."

"Please," she said. "I must go to Italy. To Sicily. I already have plans to travel there when my term ends. I can't help you unless I examine one more source. And then I'll come back here." She stopped. "Or to Baghdad. Wherever you want me."

He leaned back in the chair and put his ankle on his knee again. "Well this *is* lucky. Because, do you know? Three or four weeks ago, Italy popped up as a region of interest at the office as well. In fact, I was going to suggest that you begin your more mundane information gathering—on our behalf— in Rome." He smiled at her confusion. "It seems that our two projects may coincide. Such serendipity."

"I don't understand."

"Neither could we. All this useful, if alarming, information coming at us from what had been a geopolitical backwater. Practically volcanic. So much so that the children dismissed it as noise. Disinformation from a less than friendly former ally."

"Information from the *Italian* government?" she asked. "You're working with Mussolini? That's—that's—"

"Informally. Our people aren't bound by the same rules of etiquette that guide other parts of the service." He considered. "You don't find the Italian revolution attractive? An appealing ideological alternative to Great Britain's hypocritical liberalism?"

"Don't be revolting."

"Ah. I'd forgotten. You're not guided by anything so coherent as ideological commitment. Forgive me."

"Why Rome?" she persisted, genuinely curious.

"As I said, most of the office disregarded it. But I wasn't so certain. And now that I've spoken with you, I feel convinced that there's something there."

She felt her frustration rising. He was being deliberately opaque. And she could sense that he was trying to trick her. But she had no idea why. "Jeffrey, what is 'it?' I still can't understand what you're hinting at."

He held her eyes for an awkward moment, and then he nodded. "All right. Our Italian colleagues have asked, quietly and unofficially, for guidance on a matter having to do with their laughable attempts to establish an 'Empire' in Africa. It seems that the bureaucrats and functionaries they've charged with pacifying and governing Libya, Ethiopia, and Eritrea—'spies and occupiers,' I think you'd call them—keep turning up dead."

She tried to interrupt, but he continued before she could say anything. "Nothing spectacular. It could be coincidence. Ill health. Freak accidents. That sort of thing. But their reports got me thinking. Especially," he added, "when these same reports were sitting on my desk next to your most recent psychological profile and the damning descriptions of the unfortunate Clayton's last days."

She blinked at him. "Are you mad? So now I'm responsible for killing off Italy's imperial establishment as well? Well I do just have boundless energy, don't I? When was I supposed to be undertaking these operations, then? In between marking examinations and taking my son to piano lessons? This is lunatic even for you, Jeffrey."

"It's a bit early for piano lessons, don't you think?"

"What?"

"I merely think he might want to enjoy his childhood for a few more years before being subjected to the tyranny of some sadistic spinster with an upright Broadwood—"

"Jeffrey, I am not in the mood for this."

"All right," he yielded. "But you're deliberately misunderstanding me. I'm not accusing you of killing off Italy's comic imperialists. And, to repeat, I'm not even accusing you of killing Clayton— despite my intuitions to the contrary. I do, though, think that the two are not unrelated. In fact, I suspect there may be a recent history of quite a few more 'accidents' out there that wouldn't stand up to sustained scrutiny once we'd identified them as part of a pattern."

"What does this have to do with me?"

"Everything."

She put her face in her hands. "I'm so tired, Jeffrey. Please."

"Very well, Marion. Here is what I'm thinking. I'll be as clear as I know how. If you did kill Clayton, then you weren't working alone. There must have been an organization supporting you—an organization that, if the Italian reports aren't pure fabrication, operates across borders. If you *didn't* kill Clayton, then I suspect, along with the children, that at the very least you have an idea of who did. In either case, you can help us to map—and I use the term deliberately here—the contours of the organization that arranged his elimination. I also think," he added, "and this is purely my own speculation—nothing to do with the children and their vile accusations—that there's a more than chance connection between your interest in twelfth-century Sicilian Normans and what's going on in Italy and North Africa now. I don't know what it is, but it's there. You've been terrified and withholding ever since I introduced the Idrisi into the mix. That's more than enough evidence for me to want to push further."

He looked at her sitting hunched on the sofa with her face in her hands. "I haven't enough detail to force it out of you. But I'll say it one more time: that doesn't mean it's not there."

With an effort, she looked up into his eyes with something like calm. "I'll go to Italy as planned, then?" She wasn't going to dignify his other assertions with a reply.

He ran his hand through his hair and stood. "Yes. You'll go to Italy as planned."

She stood as well. "And—and what will you do?"

He bent and kissed her cheek. "I'll watch, Marion."

He walked past her toward the front door.

She spun back, taken off guard. A second later, she stalked after him. "That's it? Now you go?"

He was buttoning his jacket. "Unless there's anything more you'd care to discuss?" He waited. She didn't say anything. "I'm sorry not to invite you back to Lambton," he said. "They're keen to meet you."

She stared at him. "Me?"

"Yes. The family. My wife and child." His lips twitched in a smile. "But I've explained to them that you're likely to set the place on fire in a fit of rage. Or, at the very least, attempt to organize their servants." He considered. "Of course, that just makes them want to meet you more. Amusing people."

She continued watching him, speechless. Then she took refuge in awkward etiquette. "It's dark out. How—how will you—?"

"Find my way home?" His smile grew. "Such a touching regard for my welfare, Marion. Thank you."

"But—"

He eased the door open and looked out into the warm summer night. She heard crickets.

"I'll hitch a ride with Trelawney," he said. "I'm certain he's here somewhere. Under a bush. On the roof. It will be a relief to him to be back on reconnaissance. The postgrad bit was driving him to distraction. Trelawney," he called into the night air. "Would you or one of your people be good enough to drop me back at the Castle?"

She heard a rustling in the lilac bush a few feet up the drive. "Great," she muttered.

"There he is." Jeffrey smiled back at her. "And here *you* are, safe and surveilled." He looked as though he were about to say or do something more, but the moment passed. Instead, he glanced up the stairs. "Tell the boy that I was pleased finally to have met him, would you?"

And then he turned and walked up the drive.

Marion watched for a few seconds, but he didn't look back. Drained and exhausted she closed the door behind him. Leaned against the wood, her forehead pressed to the cool grain, for well over a minute. And then finally, with another effort, she pushed herself up and turned back toward the living room. Without bothering to pick up the glasses or clean the ashtray, she switched off the lamp. Dragged herself up the stairs to her bedroom. And, unconsciously gripping the pendant around her neck, she collapsed, fully dressed, onto her clean, solitary bed.

Rome and Messina, Italy
August, 1933

$\mathcal{A}$LMOST two months to the day later, Marion and Ian gathered their scant luggage—Marion the carpet bag that had served her since Bursa, and Ian a satchel that he took everywhere in preparation for "school"—and waited for their train to slow to a stop at Rome's Termini Station. Jeffrey hadn't spoken to Marion after he had left her house on the night he'd interrupted her teaching. He hadn't even protested when she'd resolutely finished her term, all momentum gone, and without Nick. In fact, he had kept palpably and mockingly out of her way.

But she had nonetheless come across unwelcome reminders of his surveillance every day, each of which made his message clear. Even if he wasn't running her, she was now, however tenuously, in his employ. The presence of the office had become invasive enough by the end of her time in Durham that she was jumping at every sound in the gallery that surrounded Alfred's workspace and ducking at every flicker in the summer light that crossed the walls of her house. Alfred's clock was the least of her worries. She was glad for the change of scene when June had passed.

Holding Ian's hand, Marion glanced one last time over the sleeping car they had boarded in Nice upon leaving the Blue Train that had brought them on their journey from Calais. Stared down at her feet for a moment as the porter opened the door to their carriage. Annoyed with herself for letting Jeffrey involve her in his world again. Then, with an effort, she quashed the emotion. Not useful.

Her musing was interrupted when Ian twisted his hand out of hers and jumped out to the platform before the train had stopped. Adhering to the habit he'd adopted since nearly falling into the gap between their car and the Dijon platform two weeks before. She chided herself for letting her attention wander now that they were in Rome. Then, shrugging half-apologetic at the porter, she shouldered her bag and jumped down after Ian. Tried to grab his hand before he could find his bearings in the station, but she was too late. He had spotted the arches at the other end of the ticketing area, and he was already running toward them.

She shouted his name as he sprinted across the station and out the doors leading to the square. But she knew it would make little difference to his flight. The ongoing humiliation of being Ian's ineffective mother did at least, she reminded herself as she apologized to two outraged tourists whose luggage was now toppled into a disorganized heap in his path, keep her from dwelling on her existential problems.

Marion caught up to him only because he was distracted by the sight of a woman he recognized walking toward the station. She watched as he halted and observed the woman across the square. Ian had been three when last he'd seen her, but Marion knew better than to be surprised by his recall. His memory of her friends was frighteningly accurate, and when she had arranged a meeting, he always spotted her contact before she did. Rather than heading out across the busy street separating the station from the overgrown park adjacent to the square, Ian turned and ran toward the woman.

"Claudia!" he shouted. "Claudia, Claudia! It's Ian! We're back!"

The woman, who had been threading her way through the traffic outside the station, stopped and turned at the sound of her name. When she spotted Ian, she ran toward him as well, scooping him up in her arms. "Look at you, monkey. Just look at you. If you hadn't been running from your mother, I wouldn't have recognized you, you've grown so big and strong." She was speaking Italian and hugging him.

"I'm strong enough to climb onto the roof of our house now. Mummy yells at me when I do it." Ian had also switched to Italian.

"Claudia." Marion, sweating, had reached them. "I'm sorry about this. I've told him repeatedly not to—"

"Nonsense," Claudia interrupted, speaking English. She was trying without success to disengage Ian's arms from around her neck. He was hanging off her small frame, unwilling to budge. "I wouldn't have expected anything else from monkey, here." She finally managed to set Ian on the ground. Watched, amused, as Marion grabbed his hand and held it hard. "How was your journey?"

Marion used a handkerchief to wipe the sweat from under the brim of her hat, still holding Ian with her other hand. She was wearing a lightweight suit, but it was still too hot for Termini Station in August. She regretted her choice. And looked enviously at Claudia's yellow silk dress, black pearls, and matching silk scarf holding back her bluish black hair. The outfit suited Claudia's childlike build beautifully. If Marion herself had worn it, she'd look like something out of a music hall.

She rearranged her hat. "Uneventful." Then she looked down at Ian and amended her statement. "Better than I would have expected. Although I think the Blue Train passenger list is composed now exclusively of American shoe manufacturers and the women who are trying to marry them. I miss the Russians."

"Not a lot to talk about, then?" Claudia asked, turning toward the road.

"No." Marion smiled, dragging Ian along behind them.

As they walked toward Claudia's blue Alfa 8C, custom built for her with back seats, and now wedged into a gap meant to hold a food cart, Ian chattered to Claudia in Italian. And Claudia held up her end of the conversation admirably for a woman who claimed to loathe children—which kept Ian placid as they moved toward the car. Marion remained silent, grateful for the opportunity to let her mind wander. She had noticed on more than one occasion Ian's facility with languages, and she'd been pleased to see it maturing.

As he spoke with Claudia, though, she felt the creeping anxiety that always afflicted her when traits he'd not inherited from her family presented themselves. Marion's linguistic skills were impeccable. But her abilities tended toward the careful deciphering of written dead languages rather than immediate fluency of conversation. She could speak several languages well enough. But communication was always secondary. Ian's facility with spoken languages—intuitive, unthinking and prodigious enough that she had once caught him conversing in some obscure Spanish dialect with one of the Blue Train porters—came from Jeffrey. She disliked the genetic link to his father.

But she pushed the thought away as Claudia opened the passenger side door of the car and stepped aside to let Ian scramble into the back seat. Then Claudia took Marion's bag and set it on the seat next to Ian, left the door open for Marion to lower herself into the front seat, and walked to the driver's side. She started the engine, backed cautiously into the traffic outside Termini Station, and launched them into the afternoon gridlock heading out of the city. Ian had grown quiet, kneeling on his seat, watching the cars, bicycles, animals, and pedestrians swarm behind and around them. Claudia was also quiet, concentrating on maneuvering the car toward Porta Pia and Via Nomentana beyond.

Marion, who was still enjoying the respite from cajoling or forcing Ian to take the next step in their journey, looked without curiosity at Porta Pia as they passed. Then she turned to Claudia. "You're certain we're not intruding? I can find us rooms in a hotel."

"What else am I supposed to do with the space? You and Ian will help fill the house." Claudia was smiling, but her tone was bitter, and she didn't meet Marion's eye. She shifted down and guided the car around a truck full of oranges.

Marion nodded and looked out the window. Knew better than to press. Claudia's father had been a surgeon with vague champagne-socialist leanings who had travelled to Libya in 1911 with the Italian Navy to liberate it, so he thought, from Ottoman misrule. What he had witnessed of the bombing of Tripoli and Benghazi had horrified, and then politicized, him—and by 1912, he had deserted the Italian military to commit himself to the Libyan Armed Opposition. He had married Claudia's mother, the daughter of a well-established Tripolitanian merchant, the same year, and Claudia had been born at the end of 1912. The family had traveled to Cyrenaica, in eastern Libya, to work at the center of the opposition movement, and by the time Claudia was six years old, she was trilingual and considered Cyrenaica her home.

In 1923, when Claudia was ten, and the year after Mussolini's march on Rome, the Italian military had launched its Pacification of Libya. When the aerial bombing had begun, Claudia's parents had sent her to Rome to live with her grandparents in the home they had built on Via Nomentana at the end of the previous century. In 1930, when Claudia was eighteen, her father had died in an Italian mustard gas attack on a Cyrenaican village. Two years later, she had learned from a message smuggled out of a Benghazi concentration camp that her mother had also died, of typhus, after a forced march across the desert. Her elderly grandparents had both given up—as Claudia put it—a few months later. Now, at twenty-one, Claudia had no family, an extensive portfolio of inherited properties and industries in Italy, and a political profile that would have made her father's look apathetic.

Marion glanced diffidently in Claudia's direction. She would never have had Claudia's resilience at twenty-one. Or, for that matter, now, at forty-one. The knowledge made her both respect Claudia and also shy away from talking with her. There was no social script for Claudia's situation, and without a script, Marion was lost even under the best of circumstances.

Cursing herself for her inhibited reticence, she tried again. "At least you can let me cook for you tonight? I'd be happy to make us all dinner."

This time Claudia's smile was genuine. "Absolutely not. I've seen you cook. Poor Ian deserves an amnesty from all that."

Marion looked out her window again. "He's been eating nothing but mushroom soufflés and chocolate pastry for a month. The Blue Train. I think he'll survive."

"Nonetheless. I forbid you to cook." Claudia slowed the car and turned it into a drive that wound behind a square stone building of four floors, built in the 1890s, painted dark orange with white marble trim. "And I've kept my grandparents' servants. They're ancient, but they want to help. Cook would be mortified if you got up to anything in her kitchen."

MARION observed the grounds behind the townhouse, curious, as Claudia parked the car in a garage at the edge of a narrow garden. Its layout had changed since her last visit, the topiary animals and rock walls replaced by serious beds of healthy, if unimpressive, greenery. Then she opened the door of the car and stepped out, followed by Ian, who ran toward the beds. "You've turned farmer, now? What happened to the zoo?"

Claudia shouted after Ian before answering Marion. "No, monkey. Don't touch the plants." She pointed to a shallow pool that kept the temperature of the garden bearable in the summer. "I think your frog still lives in the pond, there. Why don't you look for him?"

Ian stopped short and looked back at Claudia. "How big is he now?" He circled the pool, trying to surprise the frog.

Satisfied, Claudia put her arm through Marion's and walked with her toward the back door of the house. "Not farmer. You might say 'botanist?' I've been experimenting with the Idrisi manuscript you left me—his *Medicaments*. His advice on how to grow and distill the toxins is like nothing I've seen. His interest is untraceable poison, so the verses make almost no mention of the obvious culprits—monkshood, foxglove, hemlock, that sort of thing—beyond encouraging readers not to bother with them. Instead, he describes how the most innocuous plants can be transformed into—" She paused for a moment, looking both bereft and resolute. "Into something more useful. Via proper cultivation. It's an extraordinary document. I can't thank you enough for—"

Claudia stopped talking when she saw Ian racing toward them, waving a stunned, yet still living, frog over his head. He was drenched, and there was mill weed in his hair.

Marion glared at him. "Ian, how did this happen? There can't be more than five inches of water in that pool."

Ian held out the frog. "The frog did it."

Marion turned toward Claudia. "I'm sorry about this. We'll be tramping mud all over your floors now. I can—"

"Nonsense," Claudia repeated. "You'll want to wash after your journey anyway. Monkey simply started early." She bent over to talk with Ian. "Would you leave the frog in the grass? If you do, he'll find his way home, and he'll be waiting for you in the pond tomorrow morning."

Marion watched in disbelief as Ian obediently dropped the frog at the side of the path and fell into step behind Claudia. Then, smiling up at her confusion, he returned to Marion's side and held up his hand. As she took it in hers, the door to the house opened to reveal a woman even smaller than Claudia, wearing a black dress, string shoes, and a scarf covering her hair. The woman smiled and kissed Claudia's cheek as she passed through the door, bowed to Marion, and threw up her hands before patting Ian on the head.

"Monkey is back!" the woman said in a dialect that Marion could barely follow. "I've missed him!"

Ian grinned up at her and responded in a remarkable facsimile of the same language. "I've missed you too, Nonna. Do you have *mostaccioli*?"

"I have done nothing but bake *mostaccioli* cakes since I learned you were arriving." She turned toward the kitchen. "I'll bring them immediately."

"She mustn't exert herself. And Ian should have known better than to ask—"

"Will you stop apologizing?" Claudia dropped the keys in a ceramic jar on a side table in the entryway, which was lit by a muted roof-light four storeys above them. Then she looked down at Ian. "But it's true, monkey. You'll want a bath before the cakes. Mill weed and Nonna Antonia's *mostaccioli* don't mix."

As Claudia spoke, Marion considered the ascetic ground floor of Claudia's house. It hadn't changed since they had last visited. Yet somehow, Claudia kept the black and white tiled floor, the ornate interior windows, and the scrolled iron furniture immaculate. She suspected that Claudia didn't ask Nonna Antonia, Antonia's equally frail husband, or her cook to take care of the dust. And, once again, the respect, tempered by foreboding, that had silenced her in the car crept up on her. She wondered whether Claudia was equally adept at managing her father's industries and concluded that she likely was. But this isolated strength wasn't the sort that endured. Marion worried about her.

Blinking, she dismissed her apprehension as a symptom of too much train travel and settled her bag more securely over her shoulder. She was about to ask Claudia whether she needed help preparing the dining room, when Ian, pulling her hand, began dragging her up the circular staircase that led to the upper floors instead. And as she started up the steps, she gave up on trying to be helpful.

"The same rooms?" she asked.

"Yes. Third floor. The corner. Adjoining rooms. There are towels already in the bath, and the beds are made up. Do you think Ian will be ready for dinner in an hour? I imagine he's going to collapse soon, and it will be good to get food into him first. You and I will talk more about the Idrisi tonight after he goes to sleep."

Ian had already pulled Marion past the second-floor gallery. She shouted down into the hall. "Yes! See you in an hour, Claudia. And thank you."

Their rooms were more a suite than a pair of single chambers: two bedrooms, a dressing and sitting area that connected them, and a toilet and bath that Claudia's grandparents had installed in the mid-1920s. Marion's bedroom opened onto a balcony that overlooked the street, but she planned to keep the doors to the balcony locked, and the heavy curtains in place. Given the smallest provocation, Ian would use the balcony as a staging area for climbing down to the street or up to the roof, or both.

She dropped her bag onto the carpeted floor as Ian pulled her through the dressing area and into his own room. He threw his satchel on the double bed and began removing and tossing his damp clothes all over the carpet in preparation for his bath. Marion, who ordinarily would have made a halfhearted attempt to remonstrate with him, chose not to pick that fight. Silently, she gathered his clothing to wash later, walked into the uncompromisingly modern green glass bath, and filled the tub.

When the bath was ready, Ian slid down the side of the tub, creating a satisfying wave that flooded half the floor. Then he reached for the bar of soap and began cleaning himself. Marion clenched her teeth, turned, and left the bath. If he drowned, she'd hear him. She'd decide then whether to do anything about it.

She returned to her own bedroom and unpacked her bag, hanging her clothes and Ian's in the wardrobe on the far side of the room. Draped Ian's wet clothing over the arms of a purple streamline leather chair, in the not very optimistic hope that it might dry by morning. Removed her passport and her carefully wrapped *Gardens of Humanity*, and put them in the top drawer of a dressing table placed to the side of the wardrobe. Then she locked the drawer with a key that Claudia had left for that purpose and turned back to inspect the room.

Locking away the manuscript and her documents was more to protect them from Ian's curiosity than a serious security measure. Although all evidence of surveillance had disappeared with suspicious alacrity the moment she and Ian had set foot in Calais, Jeffrey was still tracking her progress. And the change in tactics worried Marion more than comforting her. It simply meant that his people had been issued a new brief, instructed to observe her rather than to harass her.

She listened for a moment to Ian splashing in the bathtub, and then she walked to the windows overlooking the balcony and street. Moving the curtain a few inches to the side, she looked out. Chaotic traffic. Anonymous facades of buildings across the way. They could be anywhere. And if they were competent, they'd be relieving one another with sufficient frequency to pre-empt any useful conclusion she might draw—even if she did suspect someone specific.

She drew an irritated breath and concentrated on something else. Glancing down, she noticed that the balcony was overgrown with potted plants. All out of season. Monkshood. Along with foxglove, hemlock, and a monstrous hellebore like something from an uncensored fairy story. She smiled to herself. Claudia was irrepressible. And, she reminded herself as she let the curtain fall into place, Ian was going nowhere near that doorway.

"Mummy! Mummy, there isn't any water left in the bath. I've finished."

Marion retrieved Ian's pyjamas from the wardrobe and returned to the room, hoping that his shouting meant that he had removed the plug and drained the bath. Although she wasn't surprised to find that he hadn't. The floor was flooded with an inch or two of water, while the bathtub, now almost dry, retained its plug. Ian was standing in the middle of the tub, looking pleased with himself. At least he was clean.

She waded through the puddles on the floor, grabbed a green towel from a gleaming rack, wrapped Ian in the towel, and lifted him bodily out of the tub. Carried him into his own bedroom, set him on the bed, put his pyjamas beside him, and opened his satchel. Pulled out a picture book that had, on occasion, occupied him for a few minutes, and placed that next to his pyjamas. Then she knelt in front of him. "Ian, I must wash as well, and I want to change my clothes before dinner. Would you please wait here while I do that?"

"Yes."

"And would you dry yourself off and put on your pyjamas? After dinner and dessert, we'll come back up here and try to sleep. All right?"

"Yes."

"Thank you."

Marion stood and returned to her own room to find some clothing to wear once she'd removed the grime from the train. On her way, she used three of the towels on the rack to mop up the water from Ian's bath. Glanced back toward his room but then gave up on controlling him and concentrated on getting through her bath quickly. She didn't trust him for a second.

She spread the towels back on the rack to dry, took a dry towel to use herself, and crossed to the wardrobe. Then she chose a linen dress and sandals, set them out on her bed, removed her filthy suit, and kept her pendant. She never removed the necklace. She wrapped the towel around herself and walked back through the door to start her bath. Peeked into Ian's room and saw that it was empty. She hadn't heard him sneak out. But then, she hadn't expected to. She noticed that his pyjamas were gone as well, and turned back to the bath, relieved. At least he wasn't wandering the house naked—a not unlikely scenario in her experience.

Dismissing Ian from her mind for ten minutes, she washed, drained the bath, dried herself, and combed her wet hair into a heavy chignon. In the hot weather, her damp hair felt refreshing, and she was grateful to Claudia for suggesting she change before dinner. With the towel wrapped around her in case Ian decided to return, she walked to her bedroom, stepped into the dress and buttoned it, slipped into the sandals, and left the room.

Winding back down the spiral stairs to the ground floor, she made her way to the breakfast room at the back of the house, an area surrounded on three sides with arched glass windows—now curtained—that looked onto the garden. When she entered, Ian was already sitting at the round walnut table, wearing his pyjamas, drinking a glass of orange juice, and making his way through an enormous plate of calamari and an equally enormous plate of Antonia's cakes. Claudia was sitting next to him, drinking Campari and soda. The table settings were already in place.

Marion crossed and sat in the chair opposite Claudia. "He said he'd wait before coming downstairs."

Claudia pushed back her own chair and walked to a side table to mix a drink for Marion. "Yes." She glanced in Ian's direction. "He mentioned that." She put the cold glass in front of Marion and sat again. "Drink."

"Thanks." Marion took a sip. Looked for a few moments at Ian's rapidly disappearing dinner. "Calamari?"

"For monkey. Antonia remembered it was his favorite." Claudia watched, bemused, as Ian finished the last fried tentacle, and then began to work again on the cakes. "Seems she was right." She peered through the doorway toward the kitchen. "Cook is making *caponata* and red snapper for us. She made a special stop at Galluzzi's this afternoon for the fish." She continued watching, her curiosity turning to amazement, as Ian ate the last cake and drank the remainder of his orange juice. "It will be ready when you've got monkey here into bed."

Marion smiled into her glass and drank more of her Campari. "Lovely thought." Then she addressed Ian. "What do you think, Ian? Are you full? Would you like to wish Claudia and Antonia good night?"

Ian looked for a split second as though he would argue, but then he yawned and nodded. Climbed out of his chair, walked around the table, and kissed Claudia's cheek. Then he ran through the doorway to the kitchen, returned a few seconds later with three more *mostaccioli* cakes in his hands, and dashed past Marion toward the hall and the spiral staircase.

Marion stood and ran after him. Turned back to Claudia as she was heading through the door. "He's exhausted. I'll be back in a half hour or less."

"Take your time," Claudia said. "I'll make you another drink."

BY the time Marion had caught up to Ian upstairs, he had stuffed the cakes into his mouth and eaten them. As she followed him into his bedroom, she stopped at the dressing table to retrieve his toothbrush and an unopened bottle of sparkling water. Found him already in the bed, pretending to sleep. When she put her hand on the edge of his pillow, he sat up, wide awake, and she opened and held out the bottle to him. He took it, drained it, and handed it back to her. She set his toothbrush on the side table and stood to take the bottle back into her bedroom.

"Are you going to clean your teeth?" she asked.

He thought for a moment, nodded, and then grabbed his toothbrush. She waited while he used the toilet, and then she followed him back into his room. He was lying in the bed again, this time with his eyes open. She leaned over to kiss his forehead, and he pressed his cheek against hers.

"Are you happy to be at Claudia's house again?"

"Yes. But I liked the train too."

"I'm pleased." She looked across the room, unseeing. "I like it here as well. I'm going downstairs now to talk more with Claudia. Is that all right?"

"Yes," he repeated. "I love you, Mummy."

"I love you too, Ian. Goodnight."

As she left his room and turned off the light, she heard him singing to himself, an odd habit he'd had since before he was speaking, but one that comforted her more than she liked to admit. She left the light on in her own room so that he wouldn't be frightened and descended the spiral stairs. Meditative.

The glow from the roof-light was almost gone, and she was forced to hold the railing to keep from tripping. But Claudia's house came into its own at night, and Marion let herself enjoy its tranquility. She knew that Via Nomentana was still hectic at this hour, but not a sound from the street penetrated the townhouse. She stopped on the stairs to appreciate the open lines of the gallery. Since Ian had been born, she'd rarely had the chance to feel spaces in the way she had when she was solitary—or in the brief years she'd had with Tariq before he died. She'd forgotten how she missed it.

When she returned to the breakfast room, Claudia had turned up the lights in the sconces along the wall that wasn't glass, and Antonia was waiting to bring out the *caponata*. Claudia had replaced the Campari with a jug of red table wine. She'd already drunk half a glass, and she poured Marion one as well.

"Thank you." Marion took the glass and sat at the table. "Don't worry. I'll catch up."

"Good," Claudia replied. "We'll want to be relaxed to have this conversation."

"We're already starting it? No small talk about the food?"

Antonia had spooned the *caponata* into ceramic bowls alongside chunks of olive bread and chopped hardboiled eggs. Claudia took a spoonful and spoke back across the table at Marion. "Antonia and Cook have heard me praising their food for more than twenty years now. If you'd like to send your respects to the chef, though, please do so."

"It's delicious," Marion said to Antonia in her faulty Italian. "You and Cook have outdone yourselves."

Antonia wiped her hands on her apron and turned toward the kitchen. "I'll bring out the snapper."

Marion colored. Antonia had no interest in praise from guests who knew nothing about food. But even so, she couldn't stifle her instinct to compliment it. Afflicted with what she recognized to be a politically awkward, middle-class need to placate people serving her. She hated herself for it, but it was ingrained too deeply for her to do much beyond feeling mortified when it backfired on her. As it always did. She blushed more deeply as she ate another bite. At least the food was, objectively, quite good. She finished her wine and ate a few more bites of the eggplant.

Claudia was laughing as she refilled Marion's glass. "I'd appreciate it if you'd refrain from disturbing my household any further. Things are difficult enough as it is."

"What am I supposed to say? It's good food. It's not my fault your 'household' is so touchy."

"Why say anything at all? Just be quiet and eat."

"Do you know? Perhaps I *would* rather have that serious conversation now. Small talk with you is dangerous." She schooled her expression into something solemn as Antonia reappeared with the fish.

"Thank you," Claudia said. "I knew you'd come around. But first, and equally serious, do you mind if we keep drinking the red? It's light. It will go with the snapper better than any of the whites I have chilled."

"Why ask me? I've no palate to speak of, have I?"

"Now who's touchy?"

Antonia was serving the fish and looking between the two of them. They were speaking English, which annoyed her further. And once she'd finished putting the plates on the table, she retreated to the kitchen to leave them alone.

Claudia watched her close the door behind her, trailing disapproval. She took a few bites of the snapper, nodded, and then set down her fork. "It's for the best. Even if we speak English, we ought to have this talk unobserved."

Marion moved some pieces of fish across her plate with her fork, her light mood gone. Forced herself to eat a small bite. The fish was as well prepared as the eggplant had been, but she was no longer hungry. She'd been dreading this moment and, despite dwelling on it throughout the train journey, she didn't know how she was going to navigate it.

"Claudia," she said finally. "There's been a complication."

Claudia sipped her wine. Unconcerned. "What complication?"

"I think it may be best to postpone the journey to Messina."

Claudia still seemed indifferent, but the taut stress that never completely left her reasserted itself. "Why?"

Marion looked down at her plate, thinking for a moment. "I had a visit," she began, choosing her words carefully. "From a contact. In the British government."

"I didn't know you had contacts in the British government."

"It's not a contact that I cultivate. But the information is usually good."

"And what was the information?"

"He said that the Italian security services, with the help of their British counterparts, had identified a pattern." Marion glanced up to see how Claudia was reacting, but she couldn't read her expression. Looked back down at her plate. "They're beginning to suspect that the deaths of their administrators are not innocent. Or accidental."

"'Suspect.'" Claudia pounced on the word. "Suspicion means nothing. What can they do? There's no evidence. No link to any perpetrators. They're not even certain that the pattern is a pattern, correct?" Claudia smiled, but her smile was brittle. "There's no need to postpone this," she insisted. "Don't get scared now, Marion."

Marion shook her head. "You don't understand. This contact. He's not sympathetic. He wouldn't have fed me the information if he hadn't expected it to affect my plans."

"But that makes it doubly imperative that we act now," Claudia countered. "He isn't sympathetic? Then his ploy is simple. He wants to worry you. He wants you to postpone the journey. Possibly so that the Italian government can make it more difficult later." She drank the rest of her wine. "Ignore him."

"No ploy is ever simple with him, Claudia." Marion was having more trouble than she had thought she would putting her concerns into words. "Here's what I think will happen if we continue. First, you and I are both being followed. You can be certain of that, regardless of whether you notice them or not. They're there and they're close." She paused and considered. "Second, you can be equally certain that the surveillance is a joint operation between the British and the Italians. I think the assumption is that we *won't* postpone Messina, and that we'll be observed in the act. That will give the Italian government the evidence it needs to arrest us, and the British government the opportunity to investigate their theory about the 'pattern.' I think my contact fed me the information as a sort of challenge. Or perhaps as a warning. Or perhaps both. I know that sounds contradictory but, for him, it's not."

She knew she wasn't making sense and tried again. "Claudia, listen. If you and I are both arrested, chances are that my passport will protect me from the worst of it. You, though—with your background—it's unthinkable. What they will do to you."

"I'm willing to take the chance."

"It's not a chance, it's a certainty."

Claudia raised her eyebrows. "And what makes it such a certainty? Isn't all of this conjecture on your part?"

"I told him that I was coming to Italy for research."

"And?"

Marion pressed the heels of her hands to her eyes. "And he believed me."

"Good," Claudia replied. "We've got cover. What's the problem?"

Marion shook her head, her hands still covering her eyes. "He never believes me. It was too easy. He's setting us up."

"You're paranoid."

"No." Marion rested her hands on either side of her plate and leaned back in the chair. "I'm not paranoid. I can't let you do this. We must postpone."

Claudia, who ordinarily struck Marion as her contemporary or even older than herself, now looked precisely her twenty-one years of age. Raw, vulnerable, and bereft. Like a child, she glared across the table at Marion and then spoke clearly, enunciating every word. "Petro Badoglio," she said, "the so-called Governor of Libya, and Rodolfo Graziani, the butcher whose camps killed my mother and everyone I loved as a child, will be together, three weeks from now, for one night, in Messina. Badoglio will be passing on the mantle of 'leadership' of the 'province' to Graziani. I will not miss this opportunity. I *will not*."

"It's not an opportunity," Marion said quietly. "It's a trap."

"My father died, choking on mustard gas. My uncle was hanged in a public square, for his family to watch. My mother was marched, starving, across a desert and left to die alone on the dirt floor of a camp. Every child I attended school with has been gassed, starved, bayonetted, raped, or interned behind fencing wire. Do you have *any* idea what that feels like?"

"No."

"Then you are *not*," Claudia said, "in a position to cancel this operation."

Marion hadn't thought that her arguments would persuade Claudia to alter their plans. But she had at least now flagged for her the dangers of continuing. She knew that there was nothing else to say—and that regardless of what she suggested, Claudia would go to Messina. She certainly wasn't going to alienate her by continuing to pressure her.

Tacitly conceding defeat, Marion nodded. If she went along, perhaps she could at least prevent her from taking any deliberately reckless action. Then she nodded again, with resolution. "All right. We won't postpone it." Looked, with what she hoped was a conciliatory expression, across the table at Claudia. "But might we at least reconsider our strategy? They'll be expecting us to use the same methods. It wouldn't hurt to try a different approach."

Claudia stood and dropped her napkin over her dinner plate. "I'd like to show you what I've been doing."

Marion pushed back her chair as well. She'd been curious about Claudia's work over the past two years. And she was more than glad to be moving away from the shaky personal ground they'd just traversed. With the same mixture of diffidence, respect, and premonition that had dogged her since they'd met at Termini Station, she followed Claudia out of the breakfast room and into the main hall of the house.

Claudia led her to a door embedded in the foundation of the spiral staircase, pushed it open, and pulled a string to illuminate a bulb hanging from the ceiling. A flight of wooden stairs led down to a flagstone floor, and Marion could make out a cavernous basement that extended to the far edge of the foundations of the townhouse. Claudia walked down the stairs, followed by Marion, and then flipped a switch that flooded the basement with a bright but chill bluish light.

Marion peered up at the tubes running along the ceiling. She'd never seen anything like them. "The lights—?"

"Metal vapor lamps," Claudia said. "Invented in Germany. They're glass tubes filled with illuminated gasses. They burn brighter and longer than ordinary lamps. And they're better for my work." She glanced up at them. "I've even been experimenting with growing seedlings under them. The results have been encouraging." Claudia took a few more steps into the room and looked up at the ceiling again. "I understand that a company in America is patenting something similar. They're calling it fluorescent light. But this," she waved her hand in the direction of the lights, "works fine for me."

She watched Marion observing the tubes for a few seconds longer. "Marion, I didn't bring you down here for the lamps. Besides, you'll blind yourself."

Embarrassed, Marion looked away from the ceiling and focused on the room itself. She was stunned by what Claudia had accomplished. In addition to the rows of seedlings flourishing under the lighted tubes, the room was packed with scientific equipment that rivaled what she had seen of the science facilities at Durham. She was afraid to touch any of it, but she walked carefully into its midst, examining the projects Claudia had started.

"It's extraordinary. Claudia, it's—"

Claudia picked up an empty test tube and eyed it. "It's a lab."

"But how did you manage it?"

"Money," Claudia said, putting the test tube back into its rack and walking toward the far end of the room. "I have a great deal of money." She crossed to a bench at which row after row of stoppered glass vials full of transparent liquid were displayed. "Come look at this. It's the reason I wanted you down here."

Marion followed Claudia. "What are they?"

"They look identical, but each is a different preparation. I'd been working toward this already, using what my father had taught me—" She faltered. Then resumed. "I wasn't making progress. Until I read the Idrisi." She smiled, wan and cold, at Marion. "What you see here is his *Medicaments*."

"You've reconstructed them?" Marion's eyes were wide. Claudia must have gone for weeks or months without sleep to produce this result.

"Every one," Claudia confirmed. "And they're like nothing you've ever seen. Most of them require ingestion to be effective. But there are a few that mimic extreme allergic reactions when they come into contact with the skin. And some work better after inhalation than they do after ingestion. Like mustard gas. Except subtler. Untraceable."

Marion was troubled by the direction Claudia was taking the conversation. Tried to bring her back to the realm of the professional. "Claudia, this is brilliant. Truly. You're a genius. Which, of course, I already knew. But we must talk strategy. Are you still willing to follow the orders we find in Messina?"

"Yes, of course. Provided that the orders aren't to postpone or abort." She fixed Marion's gaze. "I'm telling you that because I want to be honest with you. If the instructions are to abandon the kill, I'll ignore them and do it on my own."

"Not on your own."

Claudia watched her for a moment longer. "Thank you."

"Please." Marion disliked the feel of the room and tried for a teasing tone. "It has nothing to do with you. I have my own research to conduct. And I may come over apolitical when we reach Sicily and decide to read the *Gardens* as nothing more than a nice twelfth-century travelogue. But I also must be on-site to do so."

"Hmm. Travelogue and treasure map, perhaps."

"Perhaps. But that's my expertise. Not yours."

Claudia brushed by her, walking toward the stairs. She stopped at the bottom step and turned. "You're just jealous of my lab."

Marion followed. "Horribly jealous. In fact, I'm half inclined to spend all night working on my scholarship—my real scholarship—to overcome my feelings of inadequacy." They had reached the top of the stairs, and Claudia pulled the string, turning off the hanging bulb. Marion followed her through the door and shut it behind her. "But facing Ian while sleep deprived is too horrifying to contemplate."

"In that case, I'll wish you both good night." She kissed Marion's cheek. "That's for monkey."

"I'll be certain to pass it along," Marion said as she started up the staircase.

"Breakfast is at 8:30 sharp," Claudia called after her. "And try not to annoy Antonia when she brings out her customary feast for twelve. If you aren't more sparing with your uninvited praise, she'll punish you by serving you British food."

Marion was already up at the third floor. "I've told you," she shouted down into the hall. "I've no palate. I can't tell the difference. Immune to punishment."

Still smiling, and ignoring her dissatisfaction with the direction of their plans, she walked into the bedroom, checked that Ian was sleeping soundly, and stepped out of her dress. Then she crawled into bed and was asleep within minutes.

IAN and Marion stayed with Claudia at her Via Nomentana townhouse for the next five days. They ventured out into the city on occasion, but both Marion and Claudia disliked the urban atmosphere since Mussolini had stepped up his ideological campaigns in the early 1930s. And Ian preferred to play in Claudia's garden. So their days in Rome were leisurely. After lingering over breakfast on the lawn, Ian would entertain himself in the pond or among the plants that Claudia had indicated were his, while Marion and Claudia packed Claudia's Alfa.

They were bringing minimal clothing. Marion was content with her bag and Claudia was satisfied with three light dresses, which she claimed gave her greater freedom of movement than trousers. In addition, they strapped four Carcano M91 rifles, smuggled out of Libya the year before, under the car. And they stored emergency canisters of petrol, along with the entire liquid contents of Claudia's reading of the *Medicaments*, in the back seats.

Ian, they had decided, could ride in the front with them. He'd enjoy the view, and since they had scheduled twenty days for the drive between Rome and Messina, with no more than three hours spent on the roads at a time, they hoped that he wouldn't become restless sitting between them. There was also a small and implausible chance that Jeffrey's people would lose track of them on the meandering tracks between Rome and Naples—or between Naples and the crossing to Sicily. Evading the surveillance was unlikely, but they had a better chance of it playing feckless tourist in the car than they would have had by boarding the train and disembarking the next day in Messina or Palermo.

In mid-August, therefore—a wretched time to drive a car through the south of Italy—Claudia, Marion, and Ian started off for the city of Frosinone, and then toward a series of smaller, out of the way villages between there and Naples. They chose to ignore the coincidence of Frosinone as Graziani's birthplace. It was, to them, an unnecessary new provincial capital, and little else.

From Naples, they first went to Salerno and then took even less-travelled roads toward Messina. Marion doubted that they had shaken the surveillance, but they at least stayed well hidden. And Ian was pleased by the journey, at one point even joining in a semi-ironic saint's procession up a steep Neapolitan hill to the city's second largest cathedral. He also quite liked the array of livestock that blocked the car's progress as they made their slow way through Calabria.

Eventually, they reached their destination—a farmhouse perched on the shore across the peninsula from Messina proper, belonging to a cousin of Antonia's, and vacant during the sweltering summer months. They had chosen the farmhouse because they could stay in it and develop their strategy a safe twenty-minute drive from their target. If they'd tried to work from the center of the city, they would have been conspicuous even to the least curious of observers.

The sun was setting as the car and train ferry brought them across the strait from Calabria into Sicily, and it was dipping behind the mountains as they turned onto the dirt road leading to the stone farmhouse overlooking the Tyrrhenian Sea. Claudia parked the car to the side of the house, and before Marion had the chance to open the door, Ian had scrambled over her and out the window. By the time Claudia and Marion had dragged themselves out of their seats, he was at the top of one of the property's one hundred forty—according to Antonia—olive trees.

Marion shaded her eyes with her hand and squinted up at him. "Well, I suppose that's settled." Looked back at Claudia. "The orchard will occupy him while we unpack. Would you like to start now?" She didn't want to contemplate what he'd do when he discovered the fig trees at the edge of the stone pine forest.

Claudia stretched her back and nodded. "Yes. Best get it over with."

While Ian counted the olive trees, intent on proving Antonia wrong, Claudia and Marion moved Claudia's lab into a shed adjacent to the house. When they had finished and padlocked the door, they brought their two bags of clothing through the main entrance and dropped them on the floor of the low, stone living area. The rifles they left strapped under the car.

The farmhouse was small—two bedrooms, a living room, a kitchen, and an outhouse a few steps away. As Marion lit candles to stave off the encroaching twilight, Claudia disappeared into a back area of the kitchen, returning with eggs, herbs, tomatoes, white cheese, and an iron pan. She started a fire in the stove, disappeared once more, and reappeared with thick ceramic plates, wooden cups, and three sets of tarnished cutlery.

Marion finished lighting the bedrooms and living room and then discovered a clean pitcher to the side of the main door. She took the pitcher outside, found the well in the rapidly fading light, and drew some water. Shouted into the orchard for Ian to come inside for dinner, and when she was satisfied that the rustling among the trees was getting closer rather than further away, she brought the pitcher inside.

Ian burst through the door just as Claudia was transferring the omelette to their plates. He was carrying figs and oranges in his pockets and hands. Claudia glanced up at him briefly and then back down at the plates she was arranging on a squat wooden table in the middle of the living room, overlooking the sea. "Good," she said. "We'll have dessert as well."

Ian dumped the fruit on the table and climbed into a net chair in the corner of the room. "Antonia is wrong," he announced. "There aren't one hundred forty olive trees."

Marion poured three cups of water and brought one over to Ian. "How many are there, then?"

He drank all of the water, jumped up to get his slice of omelette, and coiled himself back into the chair. "I don't know. But not one hundred forty. Why did she say there were one hundred forty?"

"Hmm." Marion retrieved her own plate, sat cross-legged on the floor at the table, and began eating. After the long drive, she wasn't in the mood to gratify Ian's tendency toward interrogation. If she was lucky, he'd nod off rather than becoming more aggressive in his questions concerning Antonia's apparently deliberate dishonesty about the olive trees.

After he'd been quiet for a minute or two, she peeked behind her. She was lucky. He'd closed his eyes and was already beginning to breathe heavily. She put her empty plate on the table, exchanged a look with Claudia, and then stood. Lifted Ian, who was now deeply asleep, into her arms and walked the few steps into the bedroom she'd be sharing with him. Lowered him onto a down mattress, blew out the candle, and returned to the living room.

Claudia had removed their dinner plates while Marion was putting Ian into bed. When she returned, Claudia handed her another full cup of water. She sat on the floor across from Marion and stared out the window toward the dim, agitated water.

"You have the manuscript with you?" she asked Marion, not looking at her.

"Yes." Marion reached for her bag at the edge of the table and opened it. She removed the manuscript, set it on the table, and unwrapped its coverings. "We'll take it with us to the Cathedral in the city. They've dropped our instructions there." She thought for a moment. "There's also an interior wall of the church, the only remnant of the original structure. I'd like to examine it. I might be able to extricate some information on Idrisi's silver disk." A hint of a wry smile passed over her face. "My research, you know?"

Claudia wrinkled her forehead. "Wasn't the entire building destroyed in the earthquake? Rebuilt a few decades ago? How will you know which wall? And more important, how are we supposed to orient ourselves to find our instructions?"

"For our purposes," Marion answered, "the reconstruction doesn't matter. The drop is in the new astronomical clock—the one they've just finished building in the bell tower. A colleague who's friendly with the Ungerer brothers—the company contracted to build it—will see to it that it's waiting for us." She smiled to herself. "It's a perfect scenario, really. I can't think of anything better suited to distract Ian while we collect the brief than a belfry full of half-completed mechanical men attached to one another by clockwork. He'll be in heaven. And," she added, "as for my own research, the mosaics in the apse are new, but there's the possibility of an echo of something earlier there. I'll wait and see." Her hand traveled of its own accord to the pendant around her neck.

Claudia's eyes were leaden, but Marion knew that she'd internalized everything she'd said. Claudia would be prepared tomorrow morning, even if her thoughts were elsewhere now.

Claudia nodded slowly. Then, still looking out at the sea, she said: "and the day after tomorrow, Badoglio and Graziani will meet at the port. Aboard a naval ship. And after that, they will drive along the shore until they reach the offices of the War Ministry, where they will—" She waved her hand ambiguously in the air.

"Claudia," Marion said, "we do need to read what they leave for us in the drop. Can we at least *try* to play by their rules before we make up our own? Please?"

Claudia turned and sparkled dangerously at Marion. "Of course. Let's absolutely try. We'll *start* by playing by their rules. Who knows what will come next?" She stood and stretched again. "I'm exhausted, Marion. And so are you. We have a long day in store tomorrow. So—good night?"

Marion was still dissatisfied by their conversation, but she didn't know how to push Claudia in a different direction. She stood as well. "Yes. Good night. Sleep well, Claudia."

But Claudia had already lifted a candle and left the room.

THE next morning, Marion woke late, the sun already streaming through the window. Her first coherent thought was that Ian's bed was empty. After the initial jolt of irrational maternal fear had subsided, she reminded herself that it would have been more concerning to find him still asleep or, for that matter, awake and waiting compliantly for her to open her eyes. The empty bed and open window meant, in her household, that all was well. She closed her eyes again and steeled herself for the day.

Then she dragged herself into a sitting position, pulled on the linen trousers and cotton shirt she had set out the night before to play tourist, and slipped into her worn ghillies sandals. Ran her fingers through her hair and pinned it back into a knot at the nape of her neck. Finally, facing the inevitable, she peered out the window toward the orchard.

Ian was nowhere nearby. She wondered how long he'd been out, even while—glancing nervously at the window opposite—she pleaded silently that he hadn't climbed out over the sea cliff to pitch head first onto the beach below. She shouted his name across the one hundred forty—Antonia was rarely sloppy in her reckoning—olive trees.

She waited for a moment and thought she heard his response from the direction of the forest. Shouted again, telling him he'd miss breakfast if he didn't come back to the house soon.

"Figs." The word was almost lost in the breeze that was picking up off the sea.

"What?" she shouted back.

"Figs. I ate figs. I'm not coming back."

She looked down at the thick stone windowsill, mastering her annoyance. Then she shaded her eyes to try to pick him out from among the trees. Invisible. "All right," she said in a normal speaking voice. "But we're leaving in an hour, and if you're not ready, you won't see the clock." Turned away from the window and walked out into the living area. She didn't care whether he heard her or not.

Claudia was already awake, wearing a white cotton dress and drinking chamomile tea. She had moved the net chair so that it was facing the window overlooking the sea. Marion had the feeling that she'd been there, immobile, for most of the night. But she didn't comment.

Instead, walking into the kitchen, she found the kettle, poured her own cup of black tea, and took a fig from a bowl on the stone countertop. She returned to the living room, wandered toward Claudia, and leaned against the frame of the window. Set her cup on the sill and bit into the fig.

When she had finished it, she picked up her tea, took a few sips, and enjoyed the warm morning wind. In a few hours, it would be unbearable. They must remember to shutter the windows before they left to keep the house cool. She glanced down at Claudia, who had yet to speak.

Marion finished her tea and took the empty cup into the kitchen. Then she returned, walked to the doorway, retrieved the pitcher, and turned back to Claudia. "I'm going to draw more water to wash the dishes."

Claudia didn't move. "All right."

"After that, I'll try to trick Ian into the car."

"Good."

Marion paused. "Claudia, are you certain you can do this?"

Claudia stood and faced Marion with a lopsided smile. Anyone who didn't know her would have found her expression lighthearted or mischievous. But to Marion, who knew her, the look was ghastly.

"Claudia—" she started again.

"Yes," Claudia replied brightly. "I'll be ready when you are." She raised an eyebrow. "I'm looking forward to seeing the new belfry. Monkey and I will count the figurines."

Marion felt like crying, but she merely nodded and lifted the pitcher. "Very well. But let me know—"

"I will."

Marion nodded again and escaped into the orchard. Balanced the pitcher on the edge of the well, made quick use of the outhouse a few steps away, and then drew up the water. Ian was wandering in her direction, still wearing his pyjamas, and carrying a large branch, with which he was swatting the trunk of each olive tree as he passed.

"Ian," she called.

"Yes, Mummy?"

"We'll be leaving soon. Have you used the toilet?"

"I peed on an olive tree." Proud of himself.

Marion stared at a spot on the ground. Between Ian and Claudia—not to mention Jeffrey's people, who felt nearer this morning—she wasn't certain that she could maintain anything close to composure over the next few days. But, she continued to herself, turning back toward the house, most of the situation was of her own making. As much as she very much wanted to blame someone else for it.

Ian nearly knocked her over as he switched from his strolling pace to a run and sprinted past her into the house. And although she did remain standing, she also spilled half the water from the pitcher onto the dirt walkway. Grinding her teeth, she continued toward the doorway. What she had was sufficient. If Ian wanted more to clean his teeth, he could dive into the well himself.

When she returned to the living room, Claudia was back in the net chair, staring at the sea, and Ian—changed into clothing of a sort—was attempting a headstand on the living room table.

"I'll gather my things," Marion told them.

She took a canvas shopping bag from a hook on the wall, settled her wrapped manuscript at the bottom of it, secured a wad of lire with a string, and placed the money beside the manuscript. Selected three unopened bottles of mineral water that they had brought from Naples to cover the lire. And then, refusing to acknowledge the haunted atmosphere of the living room, she walked to her bedroom, cleaned her teeth, wrapped a light scarf over her head, and returned, shouldering the canvas bag. "Ian, would you like to clean your teeth?"

"No." He was still on his head, looking for a fight.

She nodded once, curtly. "Claudia, are you ready?"

Claudia stood and turned. "Yes."

After an awkward moment, the three of them walked out to the car, Claudia grabbing her keys from the hook next to the doorway. Marion let Ian into the empty back seat, sat in the passenger seat holding the bags in her lap, and Claudia started the car. She managed the journey across the peninsula to the city in less than fifteen minutes, driving with uncharacteristic irresponsibility, at the Alfa's top speed.

Marion pretended not to notice. And, aside from a startled goat, they met with nothing on the road that might have interrupted their progress. Ian asked Claudia to go faster on the way back.

"Absolutely. Anything for monkey." Claudia was backing the car into a space two streets away from the city's Cathedral—a building contemporary with Idrisi's time, but destroyed so often by armies and freak natural disasters that it was now an amalgam of unidentifiable periods and materials. The bell tower had been built less than thirty years before, at the beginning of the century. And the astronomical clock with the mechanical rotating figurines, where they hoped to pick up their instructions, was still not complete.

They left the car and wandered along with a host of other visitors in the direction of the Cathedral. It was the primary draw of the city's tourist trade and they easily blended into the crowd, especially with Ian chattering about the mechanics of the new clock. Once they'd entered the square surrounding the church, Marion made a show of admiring its fifteenth-century façade. Until her neck began to ache.

Then she turned to Claudia. "The clock hasn't been finished yet. Though they've attempted trial runs over the past few weeks." She grabbed Ian's hand to keep him from trailing off after a vendor selling shaved ice. "The Ungerers have left an area about the size of a broom cupboard at the foundation of the belfry where they keep the gears and figurines that haven't been prepared properly. They plan to clear out the recess and secure the wall when the project is complete and approved. Now, though, you can access it through a crawl space in the wall opposite the main door."

She reached into her pocket and held out a key. "There's no security. Just a little lock. It's a holding area for rubbish, and they don't expect anyone to break in." She let Ian go, took Claudia's hand and pressed the key into her palm. "There are two ways we can do this. Either we all go together, or you handle the drop, and I'll distract official attention with questions about the apse. I think it would be better to separate. But it's your decision. Always."

Claudia accepted the key and slipped it into a pocket of her dress. "We separate. What am I looking for?"

"A misshapen rooster's head." Marion smiled at Claudia. "It apparently fell and was dented during installation. They cast another one. But the dented one has a hinge where it's supposed to open its mouth to crow. Just reach in and pull out whatever you find there."

"Cute. And then we bring—whatever it is—back to the house?"

"Yes," Marion said. "I'll use the Idrisi to decode it."

Claudia's face clouded again. "But regardless—"

"Yes," Marion repeated. "Regardless of what it says, we'll be waiting for Badoglio and Graziani tomorrow. But let's at least see what they have to say first. All right?" She didn't trouble to apologize for her tone. Annoyed. And then quickly contrite.

But her contrition was as wasted as her annoyance. Claudia wasn't listening. Shading her eyes with her hand, she squinted up at the face of the clock. "It's 10:30 now. Let's meet here at 11:15. We'll stop by a grocer's for dinner provisions, wait until noon so that monkey can watch the procession of figurines, and be back in time for a nap at the house. What do you think?"

Marion took Ian's hand again. "Perfect. But wait for me to draw them toward the apse before you take the bell tower. Five minutes."

She didn't wait for Claudia to assent. Instead, strolling across the square, Ian in tow, attracting vendors like the tourist she was, she reached the façade of the older part of the building. Speaking English, she asked an official just inside the doorway whether it was true that the mosaics on the left apse were Norman. This question inaugurated an excited conversation among his colleagues, who were more than happy to bombard Marion with information about the few undamaged remains of the original building.

Ian she left to himself. Despite his destructive refusal to follow the mildest of instructions under ordinary circumstances, he was always well-behaved in historic buildings. She didn't know why. But she also didn't question it. It made her job easier. She didn't even look in his direction as he explored the reconstructed nave, unsupervised.

Her guides led her to the end of the left nave and pointed out the mosaic of Gabriel and St. Lucy. She looked closely at the gilt images, confused. "It's Norman?"

"No, fourteenth-century." A tall, older man in religious garb, their authority, spoke for the group.

"Oh." Disappointed.

"But." He held up a finger, delighted to have tricked her. "Along the bottom, here, there is an inscription. It is also fourteenth-century. Most agree, however, that it was transcribed, without error, from a twelfth-century original concerning the career of the bishop Richard Palmer."

94

"Oh." She brightened. "Do you mind?"

She knelt in front of the mosaic, knowing better than to try to touch it—although she was itching let her fingertip rest on the stone along the platform. Retrieved a pencil and her manuscript from her canvas bag, and looked up at the knot of officials watching her with curiosity. "I'd like to take notes on the inscription. Is that permitted?"

"Of course," the same man responded. "We're gratified by your interest. You are a devotee of Richard Palmer?"

She nodded slowly. "I knew that he was English. And that he was appointed archbishop of Messina in the 1180s. I had thought that the appointment was something of a banishment. From the English center of power. But this text suggests something different?"

"Indeed. Richard Palmer's concern with Sicily went back to the 1160s. Or even earlier." He shrugged elaborately. "They say that he was instrumental in the exchange of ideas—and other things—between Sicily and England. You can see here," he pointed to a line in the inscription, "a reference to his pivotal position in the relationship linking the two areas."

"And this?" She indicated markings at the extreme edge of the stone.

"Arabic." He lifted a palm. "But indecipherable. We've had experts examine it repeatedly. They all say the same thing. It's nonsense."

She took a quick breath to control her voice. "I—I'd very much like to take a rubbing of it. Would you allow me to do so? I'd be grateful."

"Of a series of Arabic characters with no meaning? I suppose. This once." His mouth moved in a smile that she couldn't analyze.

Rather than dwelling on his tone and expression, she made a careful rubbing of the small, marginal Arabic letters, folded the thin paper, placed it between the pages of her manuscript, and stood. "Thank you," she said, meaning it. "I can't thank you enough."

The group that had followed her had dispersed, and she was alone with her guide. He was older than she had thought. And he had a playful look in in his eye that unsettled her. He nodded toward Ian, who had become bored and reverted to type. Manifesting his annoyance at her lack of attention by attempting to climb one of the pillars lining the nave. "I believe that your son has finished his inspection of the building."

When she saw what Ian was doing, she blushed violently. "Oh no. Oh, I'm sorry—I'm so very sorry." She ran toward Ian to stop him. Looked over her shoulder. "And once more, thank you."

"You're quite welcome, Dr. Bailey."

She halted mid stride, and the color left her face. Turned. "How did you know my name?"

He nodded in the direction of the exit. "I believe that your friend, also, has finished her work. She's waiting outside. Impatiently, it seems."

Marion blanched further. She took a step back toward the man. "How—"

"Please do not distress yourself, Dr. Bailey. We're here to help. And we won't say a word about your research." He gestured vaguely about the nave. "We wish you the very best of luck in anything you might do to bring about the downfall of this ludicrous and embarrassing tyranny."

She held his gaze for a full ten seconds before nodding, turning back to Ian, taking his hand, and walking with a measured pace out of the building.

The man had been correct. Claudia was already in the square outside the Cathedral, pacing between the façade and the belfry, looking conspicuous. Marion felt her irritation well up again. She was beginning to wonder whether Claudia wanted to be apprehended. Why, she asked herself, couldn't Claudia have occupied herself with a newspaper and a cup of coffee?

She quashed her anger and walked as casually as anyone could walk toward a madly pacing, distraught young woman who had drawn every eye in the square to the spectacle she was making of herself. Before Marion could say anything, Claudia turned on them.

"Where were you?" she snapped.

Marion was astonished. It wasn't even 11:00. "I—"

Ian stared at Claudia in hurt bewilderment.

When Claudia saw his face, she closed her eyes. "I'm sorry, monkey. It's not you. It's the heat. The heat of this miserable city is getting to me." She took the empty canvas shopping bag from Marion, dropped a folded piece of paper into it, and took Ian's other hand. "Let's find food for dinner. And then we'll watch the clock chime, no?" She looked at Marion. "Mercato Zaera is about a mile away. Can we walk?"

Marion nodded. She took Ian's other hand, and they strolled out of the square and toward Viale Europa to buy meat, cheese, bread, and vegetables to supplement the oranges and figs that were overrunning and, Marion suspected, already rotting within, the farmhouse.

AFTER they had visited the market and let Ian observe the noon chiming of the clock, they had driven—sedately, to Ian's disappointment—back to the farm. Once out of the car, they had napped through the oppressively hot afternoon and eaten dinner. Ian, exhausted from the two-mile walk back and forth to the market, had not objected to an early evening, and Claudia had taken up her position in front of the window, watching the darkening sea.

Now, in unsteady candlelight, Marion was kneeling once more at the low living room table. The papers that Claudia had retrieved from the belfry were unfolded to her left, and her Idrisi was open and secured with a paperweight to her right. She was holding a pencil in her right hand and she had her forehead pressed against the palm of her left hand. After decoding it, she had checked and re-checked the note from the drop a dozen times. She hadn't made any mistakes.

Fortifying herself, she looked over at Claudia's back. "It's not good."

"I didn't expect it to be. What does it say?"

"It says," carefully neutral, "under no circumstances to proceed with the assignment. It says that Italian security has confirmed its suspicion of an operation in place. It says that they are expecting a move on Graziani—"

"But not Badoglio?"

"There's no mention of Badoglio. They're expecting a move on Graziani while he's in Messina. It says that the police have already arrested eight of our contacts. And it says that we'd have no backup. No cover. It also says that if we act on our own, they'll cut us loose."

Marion could sense Claudia smiling, though she'd kept her back to the room while Marion was talking. Rather than retorting immediately, Claudia removed her scarf and ran her hands through her long, black hair. "Could be worse."

"How?"

Claudia's smile had given way to laughter. "No. You're right. It couldn't be worse." She rose from the net chair, crossed to the table, sat on the ground beside Marion, and leaned her head against Marion's shoulder. "But we're still doing it."

Marion wrapped her arm around Claudia's shoulder. "Yes. We're still doing it. Plans?"

"Let's plan tomorrow morning before we leave. Keep chaos and spontaneity on our side." She was still laughing as she stood and dusted down the front of her white dress, wrinkled from the heat of the day. "Bastards," she said affectionately. "I hate them."

Marion stood as well. "Me too." Tried to think of anything more to say and couldn't. "Good night, Claudia."

"Good night."

THE same insistent sunlight that had invaded the room the day before woke Marion the next morning. It was always harsher here in the central Mediterranean than it was in the eastern Mediterranean cities where she spent most of her time. And she could never understand how her British acquaintances, who claimed that they were unable to stand what they called Middle Eastern climates, happily holidayed in Italy, or even in Greece. Marion found the light in this part of the sea unsettling at best. Mourned Turkey. Syria. Even Iraq. Glancing spitefully at the window, she covered her eyes with her arm for a few moments and then gave in to the fact of the unyielding Sicilian heat.

Remembering Ian, she glanced over at his bed. Empty. Sat up, pleased this time that he had ventured out. If he entertained himself in the orchard for an hour before breakfast, she and Claudia could develop a plan for the afternoon.

Not that Marion was optimistic. The foreboding that had descended on her when they had arrived in Rome had developed by now into a full-blown premonition. More than a premonition—a certainty. There was no way that any strategy she and Claudia cobbled together could end in anything but catastrophe. And Marion was becoming increasingly frustrated that she couldn't halt their inexorable slide into failure. Couldn't do more than try to control the damage.

She pulled on the linen trousers and cotton shirt she had worn the day before, plaited her hair, wrapped the plait into a tight knot, and slipped her feet into uncomfortably hot work boots. She would have preferred the sandals again, but she wanted to be able to climb and run should the quite likely worst case scenario occur. Once she had dressed, she tramped out into the living room. Saw that Claudia hadn't yet left her bedroom.

Taking advantage of Claudia's absence, she slipped out of the house, gazed across the orchard to see Ian trying unsuccessfully to ride a goat—hoped that no neighbor would accuse them of stealing it— used the outhouse, and drew up water from the well. When she returned to the house, Claudia was in the kitchen, boiling the leftover water for tea. Marion set the pitcher of new water on the kitchen table and leaned against the wall, her arms crossed. Claudia was wearing her third silk dress, dark purple, and boots like Marion's.

"Did you sleep?" Marion asked.

Claudia poured hot water into two cups. Handed one to Marion. "Yes. Better than last night."

She looked better. Less despairing. But at this point, Marion felt unable to read Claudia's moods at all. "You're certain you still want to—"

"Yes." Claudia walked to the living room and sat on the ground at the table.

Marion followed and sat across from her. "All right." Sipped her tea. It was too hot, and she put it back on the table to cool. "What are you thinking, then?"

"Graziani will be journeying to the Messina naval base by motorcade. His estimated arrival time is 10:30. Badoglio will come by ship, from Tripoli, at the same time. They will meet on the dock at 11:00. Badoglio will join Graziani in his armored vehicle. The motorcade is supposed to leave the naval base at 11:30 and travel along the shore to Largo San Giacomo, where the War Ministry keeps a secure building. When they exit their vehicle, they'll be exposed for two to three minutes before they enter the ministry offices." Claudia looked Marion in the eye. "Do you understand so far?"

"Yes."

Claudia took a breath. "There's an inn across the square. You'll be positioned in a room facing the square, at the window, with two M91s—"

"What? That's insane. How can I—"

"Wait until I've finished," Claudia persisted. "Please." When she saw that Marion wasn't going to interrupt again, she continued. "You'll be positioned in the building opposite. As cover. I'm not asking you to take any shots unless things go bad." She rubbed her eyes, looking like a child. "I have a distillation. Of a type of curare. But I've modified it so that it's a thousand times more potent than ordinary curare. Usually, D-tubocurarine is administered subcutaneously. You know—poison darts? But your Idrisi came up with a better recipe than that four centuries before anyone in Europe or Asia was supposed to have had heard of the stuff." She twinkled at Marion. "Your scholarly problem, not mine. At any rate, he included this recipe in the *Medicaments*. It's for a treatment that merely *touches* the skin. And then—respiratory failure and suffocation." Claudia picked up her cup of tea. "All I've got to do is touch them. I'll wear gloves. Like a lady. They'll be charmed by it."

"How will you extract yourself?"

"It will take two minutes for them to feel the effects of the toxin," Claudia replied. "That's more than enough time to apologize and disappear. We'll meet at the car—on the other side of the Cathedral, same spot—and be on the road before anyone has understood what happened."

Marion could list ten problems with Claudia's strategy. But one was so obvious that she couldn't help confronting her with it at once. "Claudia," she said. "I can't shoot."

"You know *how* to shoot. I've seen you."

Marion exhaled, half laughing. "Yes, I can assemble a rifle. And I know which bits do what. But I'm a terrible shot. From across a square? I'm not confident I could hit their car, much less one of them. I'd be useless cover."

"You needn't aim at anything," Claudia insisted. "Shooting into the air, even, would be enough of a distraction to get me out should something go wrong. And although you may not shoot, you're a master of the disappearing act. You'd be gone before anyone identified the hotel as the source of the commotion."

"Don't flatter me." She drank a few sips of her tea. "Or, at least, flatter me later. This is too important not to take seriously. Besides, you *are* a good shot. You have extraordinary accuracy. It seems to me that you've arranged this backward. Why not have me—and I can bring Ian along to make it real—stir up the confusion and plant your toxin while you cover us from the window across the square? That's a more effective use of the skills we have at our disposal."

"No." Claudia fixed Marion's gaze, cold. "I'll be in the square with them. No one else. I will do it."

Marion dropped her eyes. "Very well." Ran her fingertip along the rim of the cup of tea, which was now lukewarm. She wanted to discuss the myriad of other drawbacks to Claudia's plan, but she didn't feel energetic enough to present a list, only to have it rejected. Instead, she asked, "is there anything I can say to you to convince you to reconsider *any* part of this strategy? Can we have a conversation about it?"

Claudia shook her head and stood. "No. And it's time we got ready. We must get you and Ian settled in the hotel."

Marion stared at the table for a few seconds, sighed, and stood as well. Packed her canvas shopping bag with her manuscript, the lire, the bottles of water, and now her passport and two partially disassembled rifles that Claudia had retrieved from the car. Walked outside and called into the orchard for Ian.

He ran toward her immediately. Clearly the goat hadn't been as entertaining as he'd hoped. But he had changed into his clothing and was as prepared for travel as he ever was.

"Ian," she said, "we're getting back into the car to go to the city. Claudia thought it might be fun if you and I went to a hotel across the square from the clock. We'll watch it chime from up high this time."

Ian looked suspicious. "Must we stay in the hotel?"

"No, no. Of course not. We'll go over there now, find a room, watch the clock chime at noon, wave to Claudia down in the square, and then return here." Marion thought for a moment. "We'll buy you shaved ice afterward, if you'd like."

"Yes," Ian said, mollified, though not trusting her. "But I don't want to spend the night there. I want to be back here."

"We won't spend the night there," she promised.

"All right."

As they were talking, Claudia had loaded her own bag with her gloves and a stoppered, well-cushioned jar of what looked like gel into the car. She left it in the front seat for Marion to hold so that Ian wouldn't be curious about it. Then she walked back to the driver's side, opened the door, and smiled at Ian and Marion. As Claudia closed her door, Ian slid into the back seat, and Marion held the two canvas bags on her lap. Their journey across the peninsula was uneventful. No goats.

Registering at the inn at the edge of the square posed little problem for Marion and Ian once Marion had produced her British passport and her roll of lire. The innkeeper was enchanted to have them, even if for only one day. Marion suspected that the rate he asked her to pay for that day would ordinarily pay for a week's stay in the room, but being cheated as an ignorant tourist was not high on her list of worries at the moment.

Once she had given the room a cursory inspection, mostly to verify that the window did indeed provide a clear prospect of, for Claudia, the ministry building and, for Ian, the clock tower, she shouldered her canvas bags and took Ian back out to the street to explore. The motorcade wouldn't arrive for another hour, and Marion didn't want Ian becoming restless in the dingy hotel room. Better to tire him beforehand.

As far as Ian was concerned, their tour of the square was an enormous success. Obeying what was now a dismally familiar combined imperative of guilt and neglect, not wanting to think about him too carefully, Marion spent most of the hour buying Ian toys and food. By the time they had returned to their hotel room at 11:45, Ian was carrying a bag of hard candy, a box of chocolate, a wooden puppet, something that may have been a stuffed horse, but Marion wasn't certain, and three aggravating metal tops that were supposed to spin when their user dropped them from a string attached at their base—but never did.

Once they were through the door, Ian dumped his toys in the corner of the room and sorted them while chewing the hard candy. Marion walked to the other side of the room and sat on the floor under the window. Placed the canvas bag in front of her and extracted the components of the first of the rifles.

Then she looked over at Ian. "I must do some work now. Is it all right if I concentrate for a few minutes? No talking?"

Ian was examining the tops. Paying no attention to her. "Yes, Mummy."

She watched him a moment longer to see that he was well occupied and then turned her attention to the rifle. Resentful, she began snapping it together. She hated being asked to contribute what she knew would be, at best, mediocre results. And she hated the role of shooter. It was not her strength, and she didn't want to embarrass herself.

As she loaded the cartridge and shoved it into place, she thought wistfully of her manuscript in the bag. She *could* be helpful when given that sort of assignment. But, she reminded herself as she knelt and squinted over the windowsill into the square, the purpose of this operation wasn't to flatter her ego. She wasn't certain what its purpose was, exactly—but making her feel good about herself was certainly not it. And terminating it was also no longer an option.

Her thoughts were interrupted by the sound of the motorcade converging on the square. She lifted the rifle and took aim at the doors that opened into the ground floor of the anonymous building that the War Ministry kept for its use in the city. Claudia would be approaching within the next minute, and Marion had estimated Claudia's trajectory such that she'd meet Graziani and Badoglio just as they entered.

If she hadn't been sighting down the gun, she would have rolled her eyes again. "Estimated" was the correct word. The plan was nothing *but* estimates and optimism. A string of absurdities. But she quelled her annoyance before it blossomed into a silent rant and concentrated on the motorcade.

She watched as it halted, and as drivers from the navy base opened the doors to the armored vehicle that was its centerpiece. Flicked her eyes across the square, but Claudia hadn't made an appearance. Turned her attention back to the rifle. Badoglio, followed by Graziani, had stepped out of the car.

Then she saw Graziani look, confused, off to the side. Marion followed his glance and spotted Claudia. She was coming from the wrong direction. And she was walking with a purposeful, quick stride toward the knot of soldiers. Her posture was deliberate, angry, and aggressive. No gloves. Marion continued to watch as Claudia raised her arm, about to hurl the glass vial into their midst. The soldiers took up defensive positions.

Marion drew in her breath. "Oh Claudia," she muttered. "Oh Claudia, Claudia, please. Get hold of yourself."

"Mummy?" Ian's voice came to her from far away.

Without looking back, Marion replied. "It's all right, Ian. Claudia's gone off script. It will be fine."

"No, Mummy, please look."

Marion turned back toward Ian, about to tell him that now was not a good time, when she saw the open door. The innkeeper was standing to the side, the key to the room in his hand, a horrified expression transfiguring his smug face. Behind him were five Italian naval officers in full battle gear.

Marion dropped the rifle and stepped toward Ian. "Wait—"

Before she could say anything more, the soldiers had pushed the innkeeper to the ground and forced a hood over her face and head. She smelled the sweetish sickly odor of chloroform. And then she lost consciousness.

Undisclosed
September, 1933

HER first sensation upon waking was of movement; her second was of the sound of waves hitting the metal hull of a boat. When she opened her eyes, she could see almost nothing. A thin line of light flickered under what she took to be the door to her cabin and illuminated, grimly, large bolts joining the boat's hull around an otherwise empty expanse.

When she felt well enough to move, she crawled along the metal floor for a greater distance than she had expected, until she reached a curved barrier. Her hand also stumbled over a store of military rations—tinned meat, biscuits, and a puzzling collection of bottled juice—which she paused to eat and drink, if sparingly. She needed calories even if she felt no appetite.

Given the hollow sound of the waves and the expanse of her prison, she imagined that she was travelling in a military, or possibly cargo, vessel, likely in the forward hold. She refused to let herself imagine what the purpose of transporting her in this way might be. Besides, judging the passage of time was impossible given that she had no visitors and the light never changed. And so, she waited. After an endless seeming interval, somewhere between a day and three days, men entered the hold while she was sleeping, threw the hood over her face, and held the chloroform to her nose and mouth again.

When she next regained consciousness she was on a plane. Her wrists were manacled together behind her back, and the men hadn't removed the hood. They had, however, removed her necklace and boots. She was barefoot. She estimated that the plane was in the air for three hours before it dipped sharply and landed.

She was tensing for another application of the chloroform, but this time they simply held her by her upper arm and dragged her, unseeing, off the plane. They walked her across an outdoor area that she sensed was a camp or field, pushed her through the door to a building with echoing acoustics, half-dragged and half-helped her down a long flight of concrete steps, and then shoved her into a room. Before they shut the door, one of them unlocked her manacles and retreated.

She ripped the hood off her head and turned back to try to get a view of her jailors, but the door was already closed. Metal. A slit at the bottom for food, and a small window at the top, now shuttered from the other side, should anyone want to observe her. She dropped the hood and turned back to the cell to find clues to her whereabouts. The room consisted of a concrete floor and a bucket.

She sat on the floor, her back to the wall, and closed her eyes. She did have some guesses about where they had taken her. Although the combination of boat and plane had confused her. A boat alone would have suggested Libya. But the plane could have either flown back to the north, perhaps to Brescia, or to the south, to occupied Ethiopia or Eritrea. The feel of the air when she had exited the plane made her doubt she was in Europe. But in August—or September?—it was impossible to be certain.

Dropping her face into her hands, she told herself to stop analyzing her position. She would never reach a useful conclusion, and she must focus her energies on surviving her first few encounters with her jailors. Once she had met them, she'd develop a counter strategy. Until then, she'd keep her brain calm.

As it turned out, she needn't have worried about overthinking her situation. A few hours after she found herself in the cell, she felt a disquieting wave of nausea. An hour after that, she was in the grip of a vicious infection that left her vomiting repeatedly into the bucket and shivering with fever on the floor. When she wasn't vomiting or shivering, she was weeping, unable to stop herself. Her only thoughts were pleas to any divinity that might be listening that the sickness would pass. Analysis was off the table.

What felt like a day and a half later, she was no longer ill, but she was filthy and almost too weak to pull herself into a sitting position. In what she guessed arbitrarily to be the morning, the door to her cell opened for the first time since she'd been incarcerated. Two guards, dressed in uniforms she didn't recognize, entered. The first hauled her to her feet and locked her wrists loosely behind her back. Holding her by the arm, he walked her out into a corridor and then to the end of the hall. A third opened a door to an institutional toilet. They unlocked her wrists, pushed her into the room, and shut the door behind her.

Rubbing her wrists, she examined the room. A toilet, a shower, a sink, a towel, a prison uniform, and a toothbrush alongside a comforting tube of Pepsodent. She was half inclined to steal the toothpaste for moral support, but she didn't want to supply anyone an excuse for reprisals.

Instead, she cleaned her teeth four times, using nearly the entire tube. After that, she removed her vomit- and sweat-stained clothes, dropping them to the floor. Stepped into the shower and ran it cold, washing away the stench of her fever with the equally foul-smelling soap they had left for her. She washed her hair with the same soap, turned off the tap, and stepped out of the shower.

After drying herself, she turned to the dress hanging on the wall. Coarse grey cotton, buttoned down the front and gathered at the waist, it made her ponder the cross-cultural appeal of this sort of garb for women prisoners. When she had pulled it on and buttoned it, the skirt fell to just below her knees. She disliked the length, which made her feel vulnerable, especially without shoes. But such was the purpose. She ran her fingers through her damp hair to untangle it, and then she plaited it tightly before tying it off with a piece of linen that she ripped from her discarded shirt.

She felt better than she had when they had taken her from her cell, which made her, paradoxically, also anxious. The absence of bodily or physical discomfort opened up for her the luxury of worrying about Ian. But she stopped the thought before it formed. It would incapacitate her if she indulged it. In its place, she concentrated on the dehydration that was threatening to immobilize her again.

She re-examined the room, looking for a cup or a glass that she could fill with water from the sink. Nothing. Resigned, she cupped her hands under the tap and drank five handfuls of the water. It wasn't enough, but it would keep her functional. And she didn't want the guards outside the door to become impatient. She turned and knocked on the observation window to let them know that she had finished.

The shutter slid to the side, and a pair of eyes looked into the room. Then the shutter closed, and the door was unbarred and opened. She stepped through, obediently placing herself at their disposal. But rather than handcuffing her as a matter of procedure, they spun her violently, shoved her face against the wall, and shackled her hands behind her back in painfully tight manacles. Wrapped a blindfold around and over her eyes, and hauled her back down the corridor. She opened her mouth to protest, but a hand was clapped over it. She couldn't breathe, and her heart was racing, but her primary emotion was anger. She had been playing by their rules, and at the first opportunity, they had cheated. She fought the urge to bite into the hand covering her mouth.

Another door opened, and they dragged her through it, sat her in what felt like a wooden chair, and locked her cuffed wrists to it. When they had finished, she heard them leave the room, and the door slammed shut. She sat in the chair, trying to prepare herself for what would come next. The concrete floor felt damp to her bare feet, but otherwise she couldn't sense anything revealing about the room. After an interminable wait that she recognized in a corner of her mind to be no more than ten minutes, she heard solitary footsteps, masculine, in the corridor.

The footsteps stopped, and she heard the door to the cell open. It closed gently, with a click. She couldn't keep her heart from hammering in her chest as the steps approached her, casual, walked behind her, around her, and then returned, so that they were facing her, less than six inches away from her bare feet. She began shivering, and she tried, once again without success, to face the situation calmly.

She sensed him bending over her, and she flinched as his hand came under her chin and lifted her face. And then, to her astonishment, he was kissing her. She was so startled at first that she didn't react. By the time she realized what was happening, he had stopped and straightened up. But after a tense second, revulsion, horror, and above all recognition surged through her, as she nearly threw up again. Twisted against the manacles, which did nothing but abrade her already hurt wrists. Tried to wrench the blindfold off her eyes.

When that didn't work, she took a breath and shrieked at him with what she knew was ludicrously impotent rage. "You bastard! You obscene toad! I'll kill you! I'll *kill* you—" She choked and started coughing.

"Marion." Speaking English. "I'm flattered. Recognized on no more evidence than a single kiss. You were expecting Italians?"

She was trying to hold back tears. "How could you do this? Even you—"

"Ah, my dear." He had moved behind her while she was talking, and he seemed now to be sitting in a second chair, placed just to her back and side. His breath was close to her ear as he spoke, and his hand rested on her leg. She felt panicky. Tried and failed to move her head away.

"Forgive the lack of professionalism." He slid his hand off her thigh after patting it once or twice. "You see, I missed you so terribly while you were on holiday."

She heard him push his chair back and stand. His voice was now coming from the opposite wall of the room. "And if you had any idea how attractive you are just now, you'd understand the difficulties I'm facing in keeping this exchange within the bounds of propriety."

"Where's Ian?"

"We'll discuss that tomorrow." He was walking toward her again, and she recoiled, but all he did was brush her cheek with his fingertips as he continued to the other side of the room.

"*Where is Ian?*"

"In fact, my sole purpose in visiting you today was to pay my respects. Welcome you back." His voice was behind her.

She tried to turn, but it hurt her wrists. "Back? Where? What's that supposed to mean?"

"Think about it, Marion. Where do you think we'd bring you after all this time? I always knew we'd end where we started."

She heard him walking toward the door of the cell. Tapping to be let out. "Wait," she said. "Jeffrey—"

"Yes?"

"I—" She forced herself to speak. "I'm thirsty."

"I don't doubt that you are." She heard the door open, and his voice now came from the corridor. "Sleep well. I'm looking forward to our talk tomorrow morning."

She heard the footsteps retreating.

Within seconds of his departure, one of her original jailors was removing her blindfold, while the other unshackled her hands. She stood and blinked and saw that the cell was the same that she had occupied earlier. They had simply mopped it and replaced the bucket. She observed the guards— and their uniforms—with renewed interest. But before she had a chance to try to speak with them in English, they had gathered up the two chairs, left the room, and bolted the door.

She looked at the blank walls and the bucket. She had been wrong about the time. He had told her to sleep well. It was evening. And if it *was* evening, she did need to rest. But sleep wasn't possible after this. Instead, she sank down into a sitting position against the wall, hugged her knees to her chest, and squeezed her eyes shut. She must develop a strategy. She couldn't go into this situation without defenses. She shuddered, rested her forehead against her knees, and tried to shut her eyes even tighter.

SHE dozed intermittently throughout what she now took to be the night. And when the prison guards returned to her cell, they woke her out of a terror-inducing nightmare, which suggested that she had spent at least some time in a deep enough sleep to dream. But the dream, a discordant jumble of fear and hopelessness, was so enervating that when one of them nudged her with the toe of his boot to wake her, she was almost glad to see him. They also let her pick herself up off the floor, rather than dragging her up themselves. And they shackled her wrists in front of her rather than behind her. She chose to consider her situation improved. They used neither the hood nor the blindfold as she walked out of the cell, and she was grateful to enter the corridor without tripping and stumbling.

They brought her to the other end of the hall to a door that reminded her of hospital wards or of the doors she'd seen outside surgeries. It was painted a dull green and sported a handle rather than a knob, as well as a reinforced glass window. They opened it, walked her through, and sat her in a metal chair on one side of a metal desk. Locked her manacles through a loop bolt at the center of the desktop and left the room.

Marion looked about her. Aside from the desk, a standing lamp, her chair, and a chair opposite, the room showed every sign of having been designed as a surgery. There were medical tools stored in glass-fronted cabinets and left haphazardly on counters, a few curtains on rollers stowed in a far corner, and two gurneys with dangling straps on the other side of the room. There was also a glass pitcher of water and ice, as well as a tray of glasses, both arranged on a table with wheels at the far end of the room. She looked at the water, but she knew there was no way to reach it. Rather than torment herself by gazing at it, she examined the rest of the room. She was staring down at a discolored drain in the floor, a few feet away from her chair, when the door opened behind her.

"All the comforts of home, as you see." He walked toward the desk carrying a file folder and wearing the outfit she associated with him in Baghdad—quasi military trousers and a white cotton shirt with the sleeves rolled up. Unbuttoned collar. No tie. He was healthy and well rested, and when he bent over to kiss her cheek before she jerked her head away, his face felt cool. Her own was dry and hot, a vestige of her fever.

He put the file on the desk, sat in the chair opposite, and appraised her. "You look well."

When she didn't answer, he opened a drawer in the desk, retrieved a ring of keys, and detached her manacles from the loop. Set the keys on top of the file folder without removing the cuffs from her wrists. "A bit pale. That was a nasty virus you picked up. I'm pleased to see that you've recovered."

She put her hands in her lap and still didn't speak. He stood and walked to the pitcher of water. Poured a large glass. As he brought it back, he continued. "Although it's your own fault, you realize. You ought to have known better than to drink fruit juice of questionable provenance that you found stored in the hold of some dirty cargo vessel. You had no idea where it had been." He placed the glass of water on the desk in front of her, and sat. "You were lucky to have escaped with so little."

She stared at the glass. Then she looked back up at him. Felt a whisper of the nausea return. "You planted it?"

He looked at the glass as well. And then also back up at her. "As it happens, Marion, I've been thinking. Since Baghdad—since Cambridge even—I've been pulling my punches with you. I've never quite been able to do my job properly when faced with the prospect of your potential unhappiness. And the reasons for that, I fear, do me little credit." He beamed at her with an open, boyish expression that was almost charming. "Not anymore. From here on out, we're proper colleagues."

"And so you *infect* me with—with—"

"With a strain of gastroenteritis," he supplied. "As an opening gambit."

"What could that possibly do for you?"

"I've told you," he said. "It's a preliminary move. No point in strapping you to the rack or turning up the dials on some nefarious machine when a bit of mild discomfort or disorientation will do the trick just as well." He examined the ceiling. "And in your case, the rack would likely backfire. All that martyred moral superiority—you'd enjoy it. No one, however, feels superior after a day or two of purging into a bucket." He glanced over at her and then back at the ceiling. "Not that you didn't do it with style. I wouldn't want to be churlish or ungentlemanly by suggesting that you were anything but enchanting, huddled there on the floor covered in your own vomit."

She swallowed and tried without success to think of some reply.

He sat up straighter in the chair and nodded at the glass of water on the table between them. "You had mentioned that you were thirsty?"

She contemplated the glass in misery. She wasn't going to touch it.

"You don't want it?"

She shook her head.

He shrugged, picked up the glass, and took a sip. Then he set it at his elbow and busied himself opening the folder on the desk in front of him. "Your choice," he said, looking down at the papers in the file.

She wondered what he would do if she snatched the glass from across the table and drank its contents. Reading her thoughts, he smiled to himself as he flipped through the folder. "Changed your mind?"

"No."

He stood, walked to the counter, and poured another glass. "Viruses needn't be foodborne, you know. I could just as easily have someone walk into your cell with a needle and jab you while you were sleeping if it seemed productive of useful results." He placed the second glass in front of her. "I don't want you fainting. Drink."

She scowled at him as he sat down across from her. Then she grabbed the glass and drained it. Watching her, he continued talking. "But this, as I said, is a beginning. One of many. Now that you're a mother, there are any number of avenues to explore—"

"You will *not* use Ian as leverage."

"I don't see why not. It would be perverse for someone in my position not to take advantage of that time-honored vulnerability."

She laughed. "You don't see why not? Then I'll tell you why not. Because I know that you'd never harm him. What you have over me is the same as what I have over you. So by all means, you son of a bitch, infect me with leprosy if it makes you happy—"

"Leprosy is ugly," he interposed. "Tuberculosis, perhaps. A malarial mosquito introduced into your holding cell, maybe."

"—but you will *never* get anything from me by threatening my son."

"Who said anything about threats? You were curious about his whereabouts. If you cooperate, I can—"

"Where is he?"

"If you were willing to help us—"

"Stop it." She stared at him for a silent five seconds while he waited, politely attentive, for her to continue. Then she dropped her eyes. "What sort of cooperation?"

"This and that." He resumed his inspection of the ceiling. "I know that a number of years have passed since we did this last, but you must remember how it works. At this point, we're setting the groundwork for a productive conversation in the future. Developing a relationship of trust and mutual respect." He scratched his cheek, still talking to the ceiling. "I'm not asking you questions just yet. In fact, it could be that you'll require quite a few more days here before you come to appreciate the benefits of working with us rather than at cross purposes. A general statement from you now, though, that you'd consider cooperating, would do wonders in moving the process along. If you made such a statement, I might reciprocate by telling you about John's—"

"Ian's."

"—recent movements." He turned, put his chin on his fist, and gazed across the desk at her. "What do you say?"

She stared wretchedly at her manacled wrists resting in her lap. Uncertain that she could bring herself to assent. But she also couldn't summon up an alternative strategy.

"This, now," he said after close to a minute had passed, "is why I like you."

She looked up at him in sick bewilderment. Then down at her lap again. Silent.

"A liar," he explained in answer to her unasked question, "would have acquiesced at once, no thought involved. You, however, even here, even after all that has happened to you, still feel bound by your ascetic nineteenth-century honor. Was it too much Walter Scott in your childhood, I wonder? Because truly, Marion, I've never seen anyone outside of romantic fiction so capable of misleading like a professional, and yet never, *ever* breaking her word. It's breathtaking."

"I'll cooperate," she said, largely to stop him talking. She lifted her eyes to his. "Where is he?"

"In England. With his family."

"His family."

"Yes. My sister, his aunt Virginia, his uncle Teddy—"

"'Teddy?'" She wanted to cry.

"Eustace," he amended. "Virginia's husband. He goes by 'Teddy' for obvious reasons. His cousins, Charlotte, Paul, and Anne—"

"You've simply shipped him off to these—these *people* he's never seen before?"

"That was the original plan. But—and you would have been proud of him—John himself put an end to that. Refused to budge until he knew you were safe."

"He saw me? When I was here?"

"Good lord, no." Jeffrey looked genuinely shocked. "Not here. I wouldn't bring a child to this—to my place of work. He saw you on the boat."

"On that *boat?*" Feeling sick again.

"Let me start from the beginning," he said. "You'll enjoy the story. Lots of melodrama." He took a sip of his water. "The commander of the squad that picked you up—Pyneweck, he's a good man, I've worked with him before—wasn't expecting the boy to be in the room. He's a father himself, and although he hid it admirably, he was unhappy that he'd been forced to deal with the complication."

"Well, why didn't you tell him about the complication when you briefed him? Ian's existence could hardly have slipped your mind."

"Because, Marion, it honestly never occurred to me that you'd bring my five-year-old son along with you on one of your kills." His voice was still calm, but she sensed an underlying proprietary anger.

"He's not your son," she retorted. "And what else was I supposed to do with him?"

"Servants?" He asked. "Have you heard of servants? I understand that Sicilian women make excellent nannies. Discreet, you know."

"And once I've found one of these devoted nurses out of some pastiche of a Puccini libretto, how am I supposed to keep her? You see, Jeffrey, my son has an unfortunate habit of exploiting the vulnerabilities of every nanny who tries to care for him. Until she can't bear it anymore and leaves. I'm not certain where he inherited that trait. Perhaps you might shed light on it. But before you do that, please, I'd be grateful—you tell me where I can find one of these magical Sicilian servants impervious to the sadistic glee he takes in breaking them down."

"Sadistic glee? Are you confident that's what drives them off?" His anger was no longer in check. "Perhaps they simply can't stand his constant, maddening, bloody-minded contrariness. I imagine that would go a long way toward causing them to—"

104

"Oh? Is that what your sister is reporting to you? Model of caring motherhood that she is, she ought to know—"

He stood, put his palms down on the desk, and stared at her. She held his look, stony. "This," he said quietly, "is an unproductive conversation." He stood straighter and walked to the back of the room. Turned toward her, tossed his hair off his forehead, and crossed his arms, leaning against the counter. She felt her own immobility more keenly, which she knew was his purpose. She wanted to hurt him. An unhelpful emotion. She damped it down.

He continued evenly. "So, when Pyneweck's team entered the room, they took care of you, their target, straight away. You were easy. John, however, fought tooth and nail to protect you, and without any other option open to them, they bundled him into a blanket and brought him along with them. They worked quickly, before the Italians thought to search the building."

"They hooded him?" She was appalled. "He's a baby."

"They bundled him into a blanket. Not the same thing. They had no choice." He toyed with a scalpel that had been left behind on the counter. It looked deadly and none too clean, and it made her nervous. She didn't speak.

After a few seconds, he lifted his eyes again. "When they brought him to the boat, they kept him in the first officer's quarters. But he destroyed everything in the room." He half smiled. "I credit him for inventiveness—he wrecked things it never would have occurred to me could be wrecked. Eventually they asked me to speak with him."

"You were there?"

"A delicate operation. I wanted to be on site." He paused. "So, I spoke with him. And he was willing to listen to me. I think it was because he had met me before, however briefly, and he knew that you and I were acquainted. And," he added, "he may have sensed something else. I certainly did."

"Rubbish."

"If you'd like. It's possible that all I felt was pity. Because do you know what I told him, Marion? I told him that you were recovering from a difficult project, that you were fine, if sleepy, and that you must spend still a few more weeks away from him finishing your work. It was pitiful," he concluded coldly when she didn't respond, "how easily he accepted that explanation. 'Mummy's important work.' Can't get in the way of that, can we? So yes," he assented. "Perhaps you're correct and there was no connection between the two of us. It could be that what struck me was an impersonal desire to protect the boy from his mother's negligence."

"You have no right—"

"No, no. Of course not. Far be it from me to comment on the propriety of taking a five-year-old along to help assassinate Mummy's political enemies."

"Could be worse," she spat back at him. "I could be planning to ship him off to Eton. And I thought the problem was that I spent insufficient time with him. So which is it? Are you commenting on the fact that I bring him along with me when I have a job? Or is the problem that I don't? Please, Jeffrey, enlighten me on my proper maternal role. Because, to be perfectly frank, I suspect that your true criticism is that you think I ought to be back at home baking shortbread—"

"I don't believe in torturing children," he snapped back at her. "Besides, you'd likely mix up the anthrax with the icing sugar in your enthusiasm, and then your shortbread wouldn't set properly. Which would be a disappointment to the boy." He tilted his head. "And really Marion, is there no happy medium between sniping at Italian statesmen from the window of a bed and breakfast and baking biscuits for your child? Is your world truly too austere to handle that sort of nuance?"

"You *sent* me to Sicily!" she raged back at him. "You threatened me with—with—"

"With domesticity. Yes. A fate worse than death. But you were planning to go already," he corrected her. "And we're getting ahead of ourselves. I promised you news about John—"

"*Ian.*"

"Only to you, my dear. And I'm going to finish my report for you. In the interest of fair dealing. So, in short, he accepted that Mummy's work came first, as it always does. We cleaned you up while you were unconscious and left you in state in the Captain's quarters. John came to kiss you goodbye for now—"

"That's disgusting. You couldn't possibly have convinced him—"

"It did look a bit like kissing the corpse. But with his Gothic upbringing, perhaps it was normal to him. You would know better than I." He returned to the chair opposite her and sat. "After he saw that you were healthy, if sleepy, and after he had calmed himself, he became something of a mascot to the crew. Pyneweck taught him to play chess. Again, you'd be proud. Apparently he has an aptitude." He tapped his fingers on the desk a few times. "When we docked in Haifa—"

"Haifa?"

105

"Yes, Haifa. We put *you* on a plane here. I have a feeling you've got a good guess as to your general whereabouts. And John took a flight back to England."

"I don't believe you," she said shortly. "You're lying."

He sorted through the papers in the folder and extracted one. Placed it in front of her on the desk. "I thought you might need more than my word. Though I'm hurt that you don't trust me to keep my end of the bargain. So I had this flown back here. A few days after John had settled in with Virginia and the cousins."

"How long have I been here?" She had estimated two days, but Jeffrey was making it sound like over a week.

"You know better than that." He nodded at the paper between them. "Instead of asking unanswerable questions, evaluate the evidence of my good faith." When she didn't move, he leaned over and indicated figures in a drawing that, the moment she looked down at it, she knew could only have been Ian's work. "Here," he said, "you see the house—an ideal property for raising children. And there," he pointed, "in front of the house, that's Ginnie and Teddy. The blonde girl with the horse is Anne. Paul and Charlotte are the faces looking out the windows of the second floor. And oh—" He glanced up at her. "Look. This woman who's hidden herself at the top of the elm tree, with the hair and the rifle, that—let me see." He looked more closely at the drawing. "Yes. That's 'Mummy.'"

He examined the picture for a few more seconds. "He does your hair well. Artistic. Although the rifle could use some work." He considered, pointing again. "And then finally, I believe that *this* dashing figure on the boat off in the corner is meant to be me. But he hasn't labelled it. Confused about my role, I imagine, and he's wisely choosing not to commit himself." He pushed the drawing across the desk to her. "He *has*, though, signed it both 'John,' and 'Ian.' So he's learned something, at least, while he's been there. They've just about convinced him that 'Ian' is his mother's darling, if embarrassing, pet name for him, whereas his real name, obviously, is 'John.'"

She looked down at the drawing and felt tears welling up. Lifted her hand to take it, but he pulled it away and placed it back in the file. "I'll keep it safe for you. Those cells can get messy, and we wouldn't want to stain it."

"Why are you doing this?" she asked, her voice empty. "I've told you I would cooperate."

"I'm doing this because you didn't believe me when I informed you of his whereabouts. This is evidence of my honesty."

"I believe you now." She felt weak. Wondered when she'd last eaten. "So please—let me fulfill my part of the agreement. Tell me what you need from me so that we can get this over with, and I can rescue my son from your preposterous relatives."

"We're not even close to that stage of our conversation yet, Marion. As I said before, what we're doing now is preliminary. Reacquainting ourselves. Besides, there's no hurry. John is in good hands. And you and I have all the time in the world to discuss what you can do for me."

"We do *not* have all the time in the world," she shot back at him. "I want my son. And if I were you, Jeffrey, I'd take advantage of this atmosphere of compliance you've engineered. I give you my word—which you trust so implicitly—that if I become frustrated waiting for you to finish whatever it is you're doing here, that compliance will not last."

"Threatening me with some fantasy of future defiance," he replied, "simply reinforces my impression that you're not ready to cooperate. Verbal consent—and I do thank you for that—is a step in the right direction. But it's one step only. We must go quite a bit further before I'm convinced that a more focused conversation would be productive."

"So what are we doing here, then?" She pressed her hands to her eyes. "How long does it last?" Her weakness was giving way to faintness, and she pondered, in the abstract, how he would react if she lost consciousness before he'd finished with her. "Do we sit here exchanging insults in this—this—" She was at a loss.

"—hospital," he said. "We cure people here."

"—this dungeon until you've decided that I'm no longer likely to thwart you?"

"Yes. That would, in essence, describe the process."

She clenched her hands into fists in her lap. Felt as though she were losing her reason. "I want to cooperate with you, Jeffrey. I truly do. But I can't if you won't ask me any questions."

"Then the next few days will prove educational. Cooperation is a state of mind. If you're aware of a choice involved in whether or not you answer my questions, if you think to yourself, 'ah yes, now I'm cooperating,' then I haven't done my job. We can't talk usefully until you're beyond choice."

She stared bleakly at the desk in front of her. "Oh."

He took a sip from his water glass. "Speaking of doing one's job properly, how on earth did you end up as the shooter in that comic opera of an assassination attempt?"

She looked up at him, taken aback. Surprised by the non sequitur. "The shooter?"

"Yes. You know, Mummy at the window with the rifle? It's not your strong suit, is it?"

"It was Claudia's operation. She thought it best."

"Ah." He nodded slowly. "Claudia."

She shot him a look. Didn't trust herself to talk about Claudia. But she couldn't help it. She had to know. "Is she—"

He raised his eyebrows when she couldn't frame the question.

She didn't care. She would lose anyway. "Is she alive?"

"You know that asking me that places you in the weakest of weak positions. But you don't mind, do you? Loyalty triumphs over all." He reexamined the room. "In fact, I think you're correct to call it a dungeon. You belong in a dungeon. Fighting off dragons and making courageous escapes from dastardly enemies through secret passageways. How can you possibly survive in the fourth decade of the twentieth century?"

"Have you finished?" Cold.

"I haven't answered your question, have I?"

"No."

"Then I haven't finished. But since you've asked so nicely, I'll answer. Your suicidal friend committed suicide. What did you think would happen?"

Marion paled. "She wasn't suicidal."

"Of course she was. It's true that her method was elaborate. Would have been easier if she'd simply mixed one of the concoctions she had brewing in the basement of her Rome house into her morning coffee. But this way, at least, she could make a statement—if a garbled and quickly stifled one."

"She wasn't suicidal," Marion repeated. "They killed her. How?"

"Multiple bullet wounds fired at point blank range by a corps of confused and frightened soldiers. Works every time."

"They didn't try to stop her first?"

"They realized their mistake afterward," he replied. "They could have extracted quite a bit of useful information from her if they'd taken her alive. But they were new recruits. An honor guard. Partially trained. Eager to use their weapons." He shrugged. "I was disappointed as well. There was a chance early on, before she'd crossed the square, when Pyneweck's squad could have collected her. But we didn't want to risk losing you, and so we left her alone. A pity. I have a feeling I'd have enjoyed speaking with her. So committed."

Marion dropped her eyes.

Deliberately misunderstanding her look, he continued. "Not that she would have been much of a challenge, mind you. Wounded little girl, desperate for a father figure. Two minutes of pro forma pressure would have been enough to convince her that she'd resisted sufficiently to start talking. The real difficulty would have been shutting her up once she'd begun. Tiresome type." He re-crossed his legs. "But initially, yes, it might have been enjoyable. I could have used her to relax between sessions with you. Something straightforward when I'd had enough of the twisted emotional thickets you expect me to hack my way through whenever you and I have anything important to discuss."

She still couldn't think of anything to say to him. At this point, she was simply wishing for unconsciousness again. She hid her face in her hands.

"These organizations you join," he added, seeming not to notice her state, "ought to vet their people more effectively. It's a wonder they get anything accomplished at all."

"They warned us off," she said into her hands. "They didn't want her going through with it."

"Then I retract my criticism. They did know what they were doing." He thought for a moment. "And she obviously knew what she was doing. God only knows what you thought *you* were accomplishing."

"I didn't know she was so ready to die," she said, dropping her hands and looking back at him with bleary eyes.

"You don't get off that easily, Marion."

"What?"

"You knew perfectly well she was ready to die."

"*What?*"

"If the two of you had gone into the operation blind," he said, "if there had been no warnings, if there had been no indication that anything would go awry, *maybe* you could hold on to this fantasy that you had no idea that she was on the edge. But that wasn't what happened, was it? On the contrary, you knew with complete certainty that it *would* go wrong."

"Only because you set us up," she countered, anger lending her renewed energy.

"Yes," he said pleasantly. "We set you up. But, let me repeat, you *knew* we were setting you up. Claudia knew we were setting you up. And yet you walked into it anyway. Claudia's reasons for doing have become more than clear since then. Yours, however, remain, if I may say so, opaque. Let's probe them, shall we?"

She started to respond, but before she could do so, the edges of her vision darkened, and she began losing consciousness. Grabbed the edge of the desk with her manacled hands to try to keep from falling out of the chair, but she didn't think she could keep herself upright much longer. She heard Jeffrey curse, and then he was around the desk holding her up. He had a glass of water in his hand, and he was coaxing her to drink it, which she did. Her vision gradually cleared, and he sat her back in the chair. Then he walked to his side of the desk, opened the drawer, and found a package of Elkes malted milk biscuits. Ripped it open and tossed it in front of her.

On the desktop next to the loop bolt, out of place and redolent of Ian's teatime snacks in Durham, the biscuits felt sinister to her. She didn't want to eat them. Also, she reminded herself as her vision clouded again, if she fainted properly, Jeffrey wouldn't be able to talk with her anymore. She swallowed, but otherwise she didn't move.

"Eat them." His voice was dangerous.

She shook her head.

He sat. Rested his chin on his fist. "We have several well-tried methods for counteracting the tendency of hysterical female prisoners to refuse food. You see, we're not savages, and self-injury of the sort you're contemplating now is unacceptable. It's the duty of a civilized institution, such as this is, to take measures to prevent it. Believe me, Marion. You would not enjoy those measures."

When she still didn't move, he leaned back and crossed his arms. "I have no doubt that there are some hardened old suffragettes among your friends and acquaintances back home who were force-fed in prison two or three decades ago. You don't want to be in a position where you can share war stories with them. Truly you don't."

She closed her eyes and took a slow breath. Then she opened her eyes again and pulled the package toward her. She'd heard the stories. She didn't know whether she could keep food down, even if she wanted to, but she would try. Fortifying herself, she methodically consumed the entire contents of the package. Pushed the empty wrapper back across the desk toward Jeffrey. He took it and dropped it in a bin in the corner of the room. As he returned to the desk, the sugar hit her bloodstream, and she immediately felt less weak.

"We were talking about how you goaded your friend into suicide," he said.

"I can't do this."

"Of course you can. You've had your water. You've had your biscuits. You're good for another hour at least."

"I didn't know she would go off script," she said, deciding to follow his lead, trying to get it over with.

"But it wouldn't have mattered if she'd adhered scrupulously to the script," he countered. "You knew you were blown. The question is why you let her do it anyway."

"I couldn't stop her! What could I have done to stop her?"

"Really, Marion? Did you *really* try to stop her? Anything beyond a few weak protests before shrugging and going along with it?"

"What ought I have done? Disabled her car? Tied her up? You don't understand—"

"Why not?" he replied. "If it meant preventing her from throwing herself in front of an ad hoc firing squad?"

"You're doing this deliberately to undermine my confidence," she said, on the verge of tears. "You know perfectly well that—"

"Let me tell you what I know perfectly well," he interrupted. "As an impartial, if keen, observer, what I know perfectly well is the following. You were planning to travel to Sicily long before these complications arose. Possibly for scholarly reasons. Possibly for political reasons. Possibly for a little of both. Hard to know." He folded his hands together on top of the desk. "But then the situation unraveled. First, an old friend stopped by your classroom in Durham to let you know, purely for reasons of selfless altruism, that the journey you were contemplating would be more dangerous than it initially appeared to be. At the very least, you could be certain that you'd be watched." He paused. "You went anyway." He waited for her to respond, and when she didn't, he continued. "Second, your lovely colleague made it equally clear to you that she was, shall we say, none too stable. Short of telling you at dinner that she wanted to pop off into the kitchen and do away with herself, there's little more she could have done to telegraph to you her suicidal intentions." He paused again. "You went anyway. Third, a mysterious priest in the Cathedral—"

"He was yours?"

"He's nobody's. But he's sometimes willing to pass along a message. Anyhow, a mysterious priest in the Cathedral, like something out of Charles Maturin, hinted broadly to you that you were under constant and intense surveillance. And yet—you can see where I'm going with this—you went anyway. Fourth, your own organization told you to step away from the operation. They *ordered* you to drop it. But what do you think, Marion? Hmm?" He let the silence linger. "You went anyway." He unfolded his hands and set his chin on his fist again. "It seems to me that there's more going on in this story than egregiously faulty judgement."

She had her elbows on the edge of the desk, her forehead in her hands. "I made a mistake."

"I don't think so."

"Then what *do* you think?"

"Very well. I'll be blunt. Here is what I think. Claudia believed that you were using the research as cover for her kill. In fact, you were using Claudia and her kill as cover for your research. You *couldn't* postpone the assassination. You had to push it forward. Against all odds. In order to complete your research." He considered. "That trail you've been following must be important indeed for you to sacrifice your innocent little friend to it. Although I admit it, Marion. I'm shocked by your heartlessness. You're almost worse than I am."

She had sat bolt upright in the chair when he'd mentioned her research, her hands over her mouth, shaking her head. "You're insane. What you've suggested is reprehensible. Where do you even come up with this—"

"Your reaction is so telling," he said. "On the one hand, yes, I see that this version of the story has never crossed your mind. But on the other hand, your almost incapacitating horror at the thought of it makes it just as plain that you recognize its validity. What would you do without me, Marion? How would you ever understand your motivations?"

"You're insane," she repeated automatically.

"And so, the purpose of fumbling through this farce, it turns out, was never to assassinate a couple of Italian war criminals, despicable though they may be." He thought for a moment longer. "Incidentally, we'd appreciate it if you'd stay away from Badoglio. He may be a bastard, but he's a great friend to our intelligence services, and we expect to use him in the future. We'd very much prefer him alive, yes?"

She was staring, haggard, at the top of the desk.

He appreciated her expression for a few more seconds and then resumed. "Instead, it was cover for your true aim, which was collecting some additional bits of disconnected text from the decaying wall of a church to help you decipher your Idrisi. As I said, it must be quite the treasure you're after to risk not just your own life, but also Claudia's, for it. Would you like to tell me about it?"

She forced herself to look him in the eye. But she couldn't begin to frame an answer to his question.

When he saw her confusion, he held up his palm. "No, you're right. That's better left until tomorrow. For now, I suppose, you can simply thank me."

"*Thank* you?"

"Yes. Not only for helping you to work through your motives, always a tangled muddle, but also for the rescue."

"*Rescue?*"

He tapped his fingers on the table. "Are you going to sit there stupidly repeating everything that I say?"

"I—I don't even know how to respond to what you're saying."

"Then I'll explain." He leaned back in the chair and crossed his arms again. "Once the Italians realized that they'd gone off and killed their golden goose, they were desperate for another source. They knew you were travelling with her. You didn't do much to hide your connection. And, I must admire their quick recovery. Less than an hour after Pyneweck had whisked you off to the ship, they came looking for you at the hotel. Innkeeper was beside himself. They've been on us ever since to hand you over."

"But you haven't."

"The children want me to. Or, at the very least, they want you back in Britain. They've been applying the pressure as well."

"And you've been resisting?"

"Resistance isn't really my line, Marion. Besides, I needn't resist. The fact is, I have no idea where you are. You've slipped through our fingers once again. Master of the disappearing act I think someone once called it." He paused. "Although they've also made it laughably easy to feed them this story. You see, the children don't look past London because they're afraid of the Empire. And so, what they get from this particular corner of the field is no more and no less than what I send to them. The Italians, however, speak only to the children because they have a fetish for central authority. All of which means that what the Italians get, they get through London. And what London knows is that you're nowhere to be found. It's quite frustrating for everyone involved."

It took her a moment to understand. Then she looked about the room again. "This is all on your own initiative?"

"Yes. I appear to have gone rogue. Again. You bring it out in me. And," he continued, "as I said, I'm hurt that you haven't thanked me for it. Ordinarily when a loving husband saves his imperiled wife from the unwelcome attention of gangs of villainous Italians, she's at the very least blushingly grateful to him. A rose nearly crushed, but rescued at the final moment, and all that. Instead, you assail me with recriminations and insults. I feel that I've been cheated."

She rubbed her eyes, her manacled wrists now bothering her more than they had been. "I haven't read those stories for a while, Jeffrey, but I don't remember the bit where the heroic husband chains his grateful wife to a concrete floor, introduces an intestinal virus into her system, starves her, and then accuses her of driving her friends to suicide."

"It's implied," he said. "Why must you always be so literal? What else are they going to do with one another once they're out of Italy?"

She didn't know what to say to him. Couldn't understand what he wanted from her. Felt tears brimming up again. "How much longer?"

"You miss the bare cell and the bucket?"

She nodded. Silent.

"Then we're making progress. I may be ready to ask you some proper questions as early as tomorrow. First, though, I'd very much like to finish answering your questions. I'm anxious to have you satisfied that our agreement is properly executed."

She nodded again and stared at the desk in front of her.

"So," he continued, "with Claudia dead, and you disappeared, our Italian colleagues settled for third best. After cleaning out her Rome townhouse, they moved in on the farm in Sicily. And, for now, they're satisfied with what they've been getting out of her housekeeper's unfortunate cousin."

"Oh."

"They've updated us on the progress they've made with him. He's a strong man, apparently. Held out against surefire methods that would have killed a lesser subject. Not because he has the faintest interest in politics, of course. He may not even have been aware that Claudia had moved her household into his cottage." He lifted his glass of water and examined it. "Quite the pharmacy you left behind in the poor man's shed, by the way. Any professional would have seen at once that he was baffled by it."

He sipped the water. "Pity that Mussolini's men don't concern themselves with professionalism."

"Stop it."

"You know, I've always been perplexed, Marion, by your unwillingness to face the consequences of your behavior. Surely you must have realized that whatever it is you're doing—once more, we'll talk about that tomorrow—would entail innocent suffering."

She shook her head. "No."

"Still? You don't believe it? Impossible. Even you're not that delusional." He dismissed her stricken expression and continued his report. "So, as I said, he was bewildered by what had been going on in his house, but he held out as a matter of principle. Amazingly strong man. It seems that he said nothing—wouldn't even tell them his name—until one of his interlocutors hit on the idea of cutting down his olive trees."

"Stop it."

"They went through about a third of his orchard before he broke. Told them everything they wanted to hear. Useless information, of course, because he knows nothing. But it's an ingenious method for dealing with peasants." He drank the remainder of the water. "I must remember it."

"Have you finished?" she repeated.

"Not quite." He indicated her glass. "Would you like more?"

"No."

"Very well. We've discussed John, we've discussed Claudia, we've discussed Claudia's household. Now, I'd like to talk about you."

"And then I go?"

"Yes," he said. "And then you go. To think about our conversation. And prepare for tomorrow."

"Fine."

"Tomorrow," he explained, "I will ask you about your research. I'm entirely uninterested in your political goals. I don't find them interesting, and I don't want to know. Or perhaps I ought to say that I think anything politically useful you might offer me will be tangled up in your scholarship. As I said, in that sense, my approach to you as a problem is different from the approach you'd get from the children. Or from Mussolini's people." He watched her face as he spoke. "When I ask you about your work, you will be cooperative, compliant, and obliging. You will think of our discussion as a friendly exchange between two old colleagues. I would like you to spend the rest of today and this evening preparing yourself to play that collegial role. Do you understand?"

"Yes."

"I don't want to damage you."

He seemed to expect an answer, and so she nodded. "I—I understand."

"But I will if it's the only way. I want you to be aware that such a possibility is not out of the question. Do you still understand?"

"Yes."

He tidied up his folder. "Good. Put your hands on the desk."

Puzzled, she lifted her hands out of her lap and rested them on the desk in front of her. He ran her shackles through the loop bolt and used the key to lock them. Standing, he dropped the key into his trouser pocket. Walked around the desk and stood in front of her. "I've enjoyed hearing about your holiday. Wish I could have come along."

She stared at her hands on the table in front of her. Silent. Vowing to tell him nothing tomorrow.

"Brilliant, Marion." He turned toward the door. "And where do you think that will land you? Someone really ought to teach you to school your expressions. I've known children better able to disguise their thoughts."

She began to say something rude, but he was already gone. And so, instead, she waited, miserable, her wrists chained to the desk, for what felt like fifteen minutes. Eventually, jailors she hadn't seen entered the room, removed her cuffs from the loop bolt, and led her to her cell.

When they had pushed her in and closed the door, she saw that food had been left in the corner, beside the bucket. Military rations. Tinned meat, biscuits, a powdery square of chocolate, and bottled fruit juice. She felt her nausea rising. But before it overcame her, she sat back against the wall and took three or four deep breaths. Then she closed her eyes and surprised herself by dropping into a deep sleep.

SHE knew that she slept for several hours because when she woke, in the same position, her muscles were stiff enough to hurt. But she didn't know what time it was because the light hadn't changed. Pushing down her anxiety at the lost days and hours, she rubbed her eyes and looked dubiously at the rations of food in the corner of the room. Didn't want to go near them. But now, in addition to the fact that she needed calories to think effectively, there was the threat of force-feeding hanging over her. The necessity that she refrain from self-harm. A wintry smile passed over her face as she thought about what the phrase entailed.

She stood, stretched her arms, put her hand against the wall to steady herself as the blood rushed out of her head, and then, when her vision had cleared, she walked to the food. Sat cross-legged next to it and picked up the biscuits. Made her way through the package, ate the chocolate, and left the meat. They couldn't fault her for that. Then she spent a full minute looking with loathing at the juice. Eventually, she fortified herself, opened the bottle, and drank the entire contents. No choice.

When she had finished eating, she remained sitting on the floor and examined the bare cell. She considered trying to exercise, but she didn't want to deplete her stores of energy. Instead, she closed her eyes, still sitting, and tried to develop a strategy for her next encounter with Jeffrey.

He had said that he would ask her about her research. And it was only a short step from her research to her library. She was certain that he had brought her back to Iraq, and that any preliminary conversation about the Idrisi—which was explosive enough in its own right—would aim at tricking her, or forcing her, into revealing the location of her archive in Baquba. She must find a way to mislead him without him thinking that she was resisting him. She rubbed her eyes and considered what she knew of him.

To those few who were aware of it, Jeffrey had made a successful career out of the unlikely marriage of intelligence gathering and medieval Islamic literary scholarship. There were a number of spies who used scholarship as their cover. And there were a number of scholars who passed on helpful information to their diplomatic colleagues. But Jeffrey's contribution to imperial governance had been the selective removal of the artifacts of Britain's Middle Eastern possessions to London. Ransacking the library would be a highpoint in his career.

It seemed, though, from what he'd been saying since he'd turned up in Durham that the intelligence service to which he'd devoted at least the past fifteen years of his life was moving in a new direction—more professional and less enthusiastic about idiosyncratic refugees of the First World War who defied categories and refused to settle into the role of field agent, administrator, analyst, resource, or for that matter, interrogator. His position was more vulnerable than it had been before—weaker even than on those early occasions in his career when his loyalty to the Empire itself had been in question.

She felt the beginning of a counter strategy coalescing in her mind. If she fed him something political, but big, he might be tempted to take it and forget about the scholarship. If it were the sort of thing that would silence the opposition to his methods—that would quiet the children—he might be willing to direct his attention away from her library. He might even take her back to London for a proper debriefing. She winced at the thought of what would happen to her there. But her archive, at least, would be safe. And she would be closer to Ian.

As she fine-tuned her plan, she nodded to herself. She thought it would work. And, she told herself, opening her eyes and looking over the concrete floor and blank walls of the cell, there was no other option.

She was just beginning to wonder whether he meant to keep her isolated for another full day when the door opened. She stood quickly, before the jailors had a chance to touch her, and she lifted her wrists so that they could cuff them without hurting her. This time, though, one simply held her by the arm and led her into the corridor and to the toilet. She used it quickly, cleaning her teeth and washing her hands and face. When she tapped the door to be let out, they led her toward the surgery rather than back to her cell. Opened the door, escorted her through, and she saw that Jeffrey was already there. He was sitting at the desk, immersed in her Idrisi manuscript.

The two guards sat her in the chair on the other side of the desk. Jeffrey glanced up at them. "Thank you."

They nodded and left the room. He looked back down at the manuscript and continued reading. In addition to the Idrisi, he had brought her necklace. Twisting the chain through his fingers as he read. She waited for him to speak, but he was content to read. Turned a page, kept reading, and the silence in the room became heavy. She felt herself begin to fidget, but she caught it and stopped before it became noticeable. Just when she thought she couldn't bear it any longer and would speak herself if necessary, he closed the manuscript pages.

"Fascinating material."

"Yes."

He held the pendant by the chain and watched it twist a few times, two or three inches above the desktop. "And this, as I said in Durham, is lovely. Some of the markings are obscure—we'll discuss them in a moment—but as an object, beautiful." He set it down in a heap on the desk. "Not for daily wear, I would have thought."

"Jeffrey—" she started.

"Yes?"

"Before we talk about the Idrisi and the pendant, I want to ask you a question." She paused. Forced herself to look him in the eye. "If that's acceptable."

"You're going to try to deflect my attention, aren't you?" He rested his elbows on the desk, placed his chin in his hands, and looked across at her with what could have been boyish eagerness. "Let's hear what you've got, then."

He wasn't reacting in the way she'd anticipated, but she pushed forward anyway. "I think I know what day it is. I've calculated it from Messina."

"Interesting." He considered. "But a not unusual method to stave off the nightmares that go with isolation. Is there a reason you've told me this? I'll neither confirm nor deny your guess."

"I don't need your confirmation. I'm quite certain. It's the eighth of September."

"If you say so. Now that we've got that resolved, let's turn back to—"

"Jeffrey," she insisted. "I'm sorry to interrupt. But if it is the eighth of September, then I must ask you a question."

He looked at her with almost imperceptible suspicion. "I shouldn't indulge you in this. It will work contrary to our purposes. But all right, Marion. We do have the luxury of time. What is your question?"

"Where's King Faisal?"

"My compliments," he said after a short silence. "I wasn't expecting that one. But, very well. He's in Switzerland. Taking the mountain air."

"For his health?" She couldn't resist a smile.

"Indeed."

"If I were you, Jeffrey, and if I were at all concerned about the stability of this travesty of a government you've stitched together here—because, yes, I do have a very good guess as to where I am—I would get myself into communication with his handlers in Bern. I would ask them for a detailed report on his health." She looked him in the eye. "And I would do it *now*."

He held her gaze for ten long seconds. Then he stood, slipped her necklace into his pocket, and gathered up the Idrisi. "Stand up."

She stood. He walked around the desk, holding the Idrisi in his hand. Took her by the upper arm with his other hand and pulled her toward the door. It opened as they approached, and he shoved her toward the jailors. "Take her back to the cell."

They led her down the corridor, and as they pushed her into her bare room, Jeffrey passed behind her and up the stairs to the ground floor. He was almost running. She smiled to herself as the door shut. So far, her strategy was producing results.

AS hours passed and nothing happened, she felt less certain. She had no visitors and nothing to occupy herself. And, as a result, she brooded on the ways in which her situation could turn worse. By the time eight or nine hours, or so she estimated, had passed, she had almost convinced herself that she ought to have let him drag the information he wanted out of her. He could, and would, given the opportunity. But she hastily blocked that train of thought. She had to try to stop him. For reasons of self-respect if nothing else. And she also realized, as she retraced the contours of one of the worst of the hypothetical outcomes of her decision, she must sleep.

She was just settling herself onto the floor, when she heard footsteps in the corridor. She sensed that they were his, and when the door opened, her suspicions were confirmed. He entered the cell using his own key, slammed the door shut behind him, and glared down at her. He was in uniform, which she'd never seen, and haggard. He smelled strongly of cigarette smoke.

Warily, she stood to face him. "I—"

He walked a few steps further into the cell, raised his arm, and slapped her hard across the face. She crumpled and almost fell, but she regained her balance and turned to look up at him, astonished. Then she became angry with herself for her passive response. She was trained to fight, and she knew from previous experience that she was equally matched to him. But here in this prison, weak from illness and lack of food, all she could see was that he was healthy, fit, and bigger than she was, and that she had no defenses. She didn't even have shoes.

She did, though, manage to keep her voice cold. "So that's the next step in your vaunted 'process?' Hitting me?"

"If I wanted you beaten as part of my process, I'd have a team of professionals take care of it." He ran a hand through his hair. "No. That was to let you know that I'd received your message. Loud and clear."

She rubbed her cheek. "He's dead?"

"Heart attack."

"Good heavens." She raised her eyebrows. "So young. He couldn't have been more than forty-eight years old."

Jeffrey took a threatening step toward her, and she backed up against the wall. "The doctors attending him," he said, ignoring her defensive posture, "had never seen such a severe case of arsenic poisoning. We were forced to bribe three of them and blackmail the fourth with photographs of his visits to Bern's dreary red light district before we could persuade them to fill out the death certificate properly. What did you do, Marion? Shovel it down his throat with a trowel?"

"I? I was here in this cell. What could I possibly—"

"Although I suppose I ought to thank you," he interrupted. "I found out about it three hours before the children knew, which means that we got the body embalmed before all hell broke loose. No autopsy."

"It sounds like you'll have your work cut out for you in Baghdad," she said. "Setting his son on the throne. Attaching the strings to the new puppet and all—"

He walked across the cell and put his hands against the wall on either side of her head. She pressed herself further back, and he smiled down at her, his expression unpleasant. "I know what you're thinking, dear. You're thinking that because of this distraction that you've concocted—and I congratulate you, it's a decent one—I'm going to forget about the library. You think that I'll decide, after all, that the politics are more important than the scholarship."

He moved his face toward hers, stopping a fraction of an inch away. "You're wrong. In fact, the opposite is true. I want that library now more than ever." He pushed himself off the wall and walked toward the door of the cell. Turned and looked back at her, pulling a revolver out of its holster. "And we're going to go and get it right now." He opened the door and motioned courteously with the revolver for her to precede him through. "Welcome to RAF Hinaidi," he said as she passed. "We're going flying."

The guards from the first day had returned to duty, and they moved to escort her, but Jeffrey stopped them with a gesture. They stood back against the wall to let Jeffrey and Marion continue toward the stairs. Jeffrey held his gun down, but ready, as he walked behind her in the hall.

"I've left the escort behind," he said, "because we're going to go, as you like to say, off script, and the fewer witnesses to that the better." They had reached the stairs to the outside door, and he indicated to her that she ought to climb them. She did, and he continued talking. "Our history together, however, suggests that you'll take the brief absence of an army to keep you in place as an opportunity to try something daring and idiotic." At the door, he stopped her, moved in front of her, and faced her. "I'm going to give you a piece of advice: don't. I'm in a foul mood, and you do not want to provide me with an excuse to use this weapon. Do you understand?"

She nodded.

"Good," he said and opened the door for her.

What she saw when she exited the building stopped her in her tracks. The sun was going down over an endless series of barracks, hangars, and military structures. To the side was a field where close to thirty aircraft were tied down. And although it was evening, the base was busy with activity. No one paid them attention as they walked into the reddish sunlight.

She felt conspicuous in her prisoner's uniform and bare feet—the latter painful on the packed dirt that was ubiquitous throughout the camp. But her embarrassment was misplaced. No one noticed or cared.

Jeffrey watched her reaction with a trace of his usual amusement. "You're lucky to see it. In two years' time, we'll be returning it to its rightful owners, the Iraqi people. According to the terms of that treaty you tried to derail by eliminating the unfortunate Clayton." He squinted toward the reddish sun. "So we've built up another one, RAF Habbaniya, a few miles away. To house our orphaned aircraft once that glorious moment in Iraq's history of independent governance occurs."

"May I have some shoes?"

"No." He gestured with the gun toward a low institutional building at the end of an alley that ran between two sets of barracks.

She walked, annoyed, in front of him, trying to maintain a semblance of dignity as the soles of her feet burned in the dust and gravel. When they reached the door to the building, he used his keys to unlock it and pushed her through. She glanced about her, but she couldn't draw conclusions from what she saw. It reminded her of a school. Dingy corridor, linoleum floors, and three closed doors on each side. Jeffrey opened the first door on their left, and they walked into the room.

The room was as dull as the hall outside, but the space was also occupied by an ostentatious carved mahogany table, square, surrounded by equally incongruous mahogany chairs. The table was strewn with strategic maps, most of which were of Baquba and the Diyala district. She swallowed and pretended not to recognize the region. Instead, she focused on a tall, athletic man, also in uniform, who was standing with his back to the room, looking out a window. When he heard them enter, he turned and gave them a lazy half-wave, half-salute.

Jeffrey turned to Marion. "You remember Aldous."

She looked at Aldous in silence.

Aldous took in her prison dress and filthy bare feet. "Lady Willcox. Always a pleasure." He waited for her to respond. She remained mute. "Talkative as usual, I see." He exchanged a look with Jeffrey. Then he made himself comfortable in one of the chairs, put his hands behind his head, and waited for Jeffrey to take the lead.

Jeffrey closed the door behind them, holstered his revolver, and pulled out a chair for Marion, opposite Aldous. She held Jeffrey's eyes and sat. Jeffrey sat next to her and moved the largest of the maps toward them. Rather than referring to it, he tapped his fingers a few times on the table.

"Aldous is here should our conversation take a turn for the worse. I'm hoping we won't need to use him." He glanced at Aldous. "Forgive me, Parker."

"Always, Willcox."

Marion felt her stomach turning. She hated watching them interact with one another. Rather than responding, she concentrated on a spot on the table in front of her. Jeffrey waited for a moment, and when she still didn't speak, he continued. "I had hoped that you and I would initiate this part of our conversation later during your time here. After setting the proper groundwork for it. But unfortunately, your move this morning has made a leisurely approach impossible."

"Tragic."

Aldous sat up. Put his elbow on the table and leaned his cheek against his hand, looking like a bored schoolboy. "Willcox," he said. "Do you know who sent me a letter the other day? Daphne Blackham. William's little sister, you remember? Seems she's all grown up." He sat back in his chair. "She always liked you, Willcox. Nice girl." He shot a look at Marion. "Sane, you know."

"You're not helping."

Aldous held up his hands. "Sorry, sorry, old boy. Always blundering in where I'm not wanted. I'll be quiet as an inebriated mouse until you give me the say so." He made a show of putting his hands over his mouth.

"God help me," Marion muttered to the table.

Jeffrey turned back to her. "Nonetheless," he said as though he hadn't been interrupted, "I'd like to give you a chance to cooperate now. If you do, you'll avert a great deal of needless suffering."

She didn't speak. Didn't move.

The sun had set outside, and Jeffrey stood to turn on a light in the room. Then he moved two additional maps in front of her and placed a pencil next to them. "This is a map of Diyala," he said, standing over her, indicating the first map. "And this is a more detailed map of the city of Baquba, in Diyala. I would like you to use the pencil to mark on both maps the location of your former husband, Tariq's, library. And I would like you to write the name of the street and identifying marks on any building that might provide access to it."

At Jeffrey's mention of Tariq, Marion had looked up at him, surprised and angry. When he had finished speaking, she narrowed her eyes. "What library?"

He sat again and lifted the pencil. Examined it. Put it back on the table. Sighed. "I suppose, Parker, this is the point at which we must rely on your expertise."

"At your service, Willcox."

"Would you tell Marion, here, some of the relevant specifications of the Handley Page Hinaidi bomber? It was named after this base, no?"

"Delighted, Willcox." He nodded to Marion. "Lady Willcox." He sat up straighter in his chair. "They slapped her together when they needed more power in the air to quell the uprisings in the early twenties. First prototype, converted from the Hyderabad, came out in '23. But they also wanted a kite specific to Mesopotamia. Not something nabbed from India. So, they refitted her in '25, and then again in '27. Metal frame came out a few years ago. But," he beamed as though he were talking about a favorite pet, "the one we've got waiting outside is all new, fixed up last year. She's a heavy night bomber." He lifted his hand in front of him to demonstrate. "Bigger and stronger than the little fighters they were sending out before. Endurance, you see. Endurance. She flies steady up top at fifteen thousand feet. Carries three Lewis guns. Fifteen hundred pound bomb load. Can't maneuver worth a damn, and feels like a three-legged slug when you try to push her past one hundred miles per hour. But no one taking her up complains about that. She's got one purpose, and one purpose only. Scare the hell out of whatever's down below. And she does that admirably. Especially when they're all snuggled up tight in bed."

"Night bombing is Aldous's specialty," Jeffrey explained to Marion.

"Well," said Aldous, all modesty. "I do miss sometimes."

"Nonsense," Jeffrey replied. "How could you miss? The egg falls. It's bound to hit something. Total precision. Zero error."

"True." Aldous nodded sagely. "Very true."

Marion had watched their exchange with growing unease. "Why are you telling me this?"

"Ah yes," Jeffrey replied as though he had forgotten the purpose of their conversation. "Thank you for bringing us back to the point. So here," referring to the map, "we have Diyala. The library is somewhere in this region." He placed his hand, palm down, at the center of the paper. "You, we know, have visited it on multiple occasions since you discovered it eight years ago. And yet, you've always evaded our surveillance. Your success in doing so has been—and I say this with nothing more than admiration for your training—uncanny. But your success also," he persisted, "hints at a certain collusion on the part of the local population. You're very good. But you couldn't have gotten away with this for so long without a healthy bit of support from the villagers, peasants, and radicals in the area—in short, just the sort of people who've never appreciated all that British governance has done for them. Just the sort of people who must, it seems, be reminded of their place."

She shook her head, but otherwise she didn't try to speak. Didn't trust her voice.

Jeffrey continued, pedantic and inexorable. "Tonight, we'll fly a long overdue punitive mission. The villagers have been lending comfort to the enemy—"

"No—"

"—and they must be taught loyalty to their democratically installed government. There are," he consulted the map, "I believe twenty-two established towns, villages, and small to medium-sized cities in Diyala. Parker, how many could we hit in a single sortie?"

Aldous thought for a moment. "Using the guns as well? Two. At least if you want it done properly. Three if you want it slapdash."

"We'll say two, then—"

"Wait," Marion interjected. "Stop. I want to understand. You're saying that unless I make a mark on that map, you're going to start bombing—"

"No, Marion," Jeffrey said. "You misunderstand."

Marion relaxed. "Thank God."

"You still misunderstand," he said. "We're not going to start bombing unless you cooperate. We're going to start bombing regardless of whether you cooperate. And we're going to start now. Your actions are irrelevant."

"*What?*"

He looked at her as though confused by her inability to grasp the obvious. "They've undermined British authority in the region. They must be taught a lesson." He peered down at the map. "So why don't we start with—" he pointed. "Dwelah and Abu Saydah?" He looked a question at Aldous.

"Suits me," Aldous said. He stood. "I'll get the old girl into shape for us."

Marion watched as Aldous moved around the table to leave the room. Then she looked at Jeffrey. "Wait. Jeffrey. At least let me think about this. It's too fast."

Aldous had stopped. Jeffrey tilted his head toward the door, and Aldous half saluted again and left the room. Jeffrey addressed her. "There's no need for you to think about it. It's possible that you may feel, when we've returned, that you'd like to cooperate. And I imagine the inhabitants of the other twenty towns on that map would be grateful to you if you did. But that's an entirely different matter from what we're doing now. Now, you and I are going to admire, at close quarters, the demonstration of the new HP .36 bomber that Aldous has so kindly agreed to provide for us—"

"But you haven't even given me a chance to decide—"

"I've told you. Cooperation is a state of mind. Not a decision." He pushed back his chair and stood. "I have a hunch that you'll be close to that state of mind when we return from this sortie. If not—" He lifted his hands eloquently.

She stumbled as he led her into the alley, which was now dark, if still busy. The dirt had lost some of its daylight heat, and walking was easier, but she was hampered by the feeling that she could stop the nightmarish inevitability of the evening if she could only determine what he wanted to hear. Glanced at his profile as he led her toward the field, but it told her nothing. Looked hectically across the rest of the camp, but still no one was interested in their movement.

Eventually they reached the apron, where a four-seater plane was waiting for them. Aldous had already added gloves, a scarf, and goggles to his uniform. When Marion and Jeffrey approached, he handed a bundle of similar gear to Jeffrey. Jeffrey pulled on his gloves, and Aldous pointed to a pile of clothing resting on the lower wing of the biplane. Jeffrey walked over to it and lifted a leather trench coat and a pair of boots.

"Best I could do at short notice," Aldous said.

Jeffrey looked down at the boots. "Whose are they?"

"Bingley's."

Jeffrey snorted. "Well, at least he's clean. Will he notice?"

"Bingley wouldn't notice if I nicked them while he was still wearing them."

"Hmm." Jeffrey beckoned to Marion. "We've found you a uniform. You'll look charming."

Marion stared at him, hugging her waist. Didn't move.

Irritated, he walked over to her and shoved the trench coat at her. "Wear it. And put on the boots. You'll be frantic, or freeze to death, or both, if you go up in what you've got on."

She took the coat and slipped her arms through the sleeves. Then she walked slowly toward the plane, retrieved the boots, sat on the ground, and pulled them onto her sore feet. Jeffrey handed her goggles as well, which she slipped over her head once she'd stood.

"Why doesn't Bingley ever look like that?" Aldous asked. "Poor chap."

Jeffrey smiled at him and turned back to Marion. "Since our purpose this evening is effect rather than strategy, we'll do away with any attempt at surprise. At both Abu Saydah and Dwelah, Aldous will

116

begin by flying low so that you can see the village. After that, he'll bank back and let his load fall. Once the bombs have gone, we'll make one or two final passes to assess the damage and use the guns. I'll let you handle one of the guns if you'd like. It can be exhilarating."

She was standing with her arms around her waist again, looking at the ground. Didn't speak. He nodded to Aldous. "After you."

Once Aldous was in the cockpit of the plane, Jeffrey held Marion by the arm and walked her to the wing. "Up you go."

Numb, she climbed into the second seat. Jeffrey followed her, but before settling into his own seat, he leaned over and handcuffed her wrists to the harness. Aldous turned back, watched him for a few seconds, and then looked at him, perplexed.

"I don't want her trying to jump out when we're up there," Jeffrey explained.

Aldous shook his head. "Daphne Blackham," he shouted as he fired up the plane. "Really, Willcox. Beautiful eyes that girl has."

Jeffrey was laughing again as he lowered himself into his own seat and attached his harness. The plane moved off the apron and onto the well-used runway.

Marion had her eyes closed as they took off, but she forced herself to open them when they had levelled off. She had a faint hope that Jeffrey was bluffing, and that they'd bomb some unpopulated wilderness as a demonstration of what was possible. She could imagine him making his point in that way before bringing her back to Hinaidi to talk. Prayed that she was correct, and watched their progress to determine whether she was.

As the plane banked and headed toward the northeast, her optimism dissipated. They were on a precise course toward Abu Saydah. And when they lost altitude over a cluster of lighted buildings, she knew that the worst was about to happen. Aldous nosed the plane down and flew aggressively low over the main street of the town, low enough for her to see individual people looking up in alarm.

Then he regained his altitude and sketched a wide circle before letting the plane dive, nearly vertically, toward the largest group of houses. She felt the plane wobble as the bombs were released from the bay. After that, she closed her eyes. When they pulled up, banked again, flew low, and opened fire with the guns on what remained of the village, she couldn't watch.

She also kept her eyes shut as they performed the same maneuvers over what she assumed was Dwelah. Tried to look when they turned back toward Hinaidi, but the burning glow behind them, the remains of both towns, left her sick and scared. She was crying as Aldous landed them at the base. He let the plane roll to a stop on the apron, removed his goggles and gloves, and turned back to Marion and Jeffrey. Jeffrey was already leaning forward to unlock the cuffs from around her frozen wrists.

As he did so, he looked up at Aldous, exasperated. "I thought you said that the three-legged slug couldn't maneuver worth a damn. Were the dive bombing carnival tricks necessary?"

"You told me we were trying to impress a lady." Wounded. "It's the only way I know how."

"What do you think, Marion?" Jeffrey asked as he pulled her out of her seat. "Impressed?"

She dragged the goggles off her head, ripped off the trench coat, and staggered, tripping, out of the plane.

Jeffrey followed her and turned back to Aldous. "She seems impressed."

Aldous jumped from the cockpit to the ground. "I'll count the operation a success, then. True love is a beautiful thing." He looked about him, bright eyed and high on adrenaline. "What now?"

"Depends on Marion, here. But we may need you again." Jeffrey took Marion by the arm and began leading her back toward the building with the maps. "Do you mind?"

Aldous shook his head and followed them. As they walked, Jeffrey considered her feet. "And more important, will Bingley mind if she keeps his boots?"

Aldous was taking a pipe out of his pocket. He also looked down at her feet. "On the contrary. He'll be honored. Beautiful feet. Pity she's off her head."

They had reached the door to the building. Jeffrey unlocked it and pushed Marion through. Opened the door to the map room and switched on the light. "Not off her head, Parker," he said, primly. "Highly strung. Like a rare violin."

"Highly strung like a bloody gallows, Willcox, but if she makes you happy, I'll not comment." He sat in one of the mahogany chairs, lit his pipe, and blew out a cloud of acrid smoke. "Carry on. I've never seen you work before, you know."

Marion had sat in the same chair she'd occupied previously, her hands clasped tightly in her lap, staring into the middle distance. She had heard their conversation as though it were coming from miles away. When Jeffrey sat beside her and moved the map of Baquba in front of her again, she winced and came to herself. He placed the pencil in the middle of the map.

"Your move."

Without hesitation, she took the pencil and made a mark on the map. Next to it, she wrote a street name in both Arabic script and transliterated Latin script. Underneath that, she wrote a few more instructions on how to enter the vaults. Then she set the pencil down on the table and put her face in her hands.

Jeffrey, with a delighted smile, gathered up the map and stood. He turned to Aldous, who had raised his eyebrows. "I'll want to verify that this information is correct. It may take an hour or more. Would you wait here with her while I do that?"

"Willcox," he replied, "my hat's off to you. That display right there is why you're the one giving the orders. And yes, I'd be enchanted to entertain Lady Willcox while you're occupied. Give us an opportunity to get to know one another better."

Jeffrey glanced briefly at Marion, who didn't look up. Thought for a moment, and then retrieved the manacles from his pocket. She remained passive when he took hold of her wrists, moved them behind the chair, and locked them into the cuffs. He handed the keys to Aldous. "These are for use if the building burns down. Otherwise, under no circumstances, no matter what happens, and no matter what she says, let her out of the shackles."

Aldous took the keys. "Tea time must be a right barrel of laughs at home with the two of you."

"You have no idea," Jeffrey said. Then he left the room.

After he had gone, Aldous smoked his pipe for a few minutes, unhurried, watching Marion. She hoped he'd take pity on her and stay quiet, but eventually he spoke.

"You don't know him very well, do you?"

She looked him in the eye but didn't respond. He held her look. She could tell that he disliked her.

"I've known him all my life," he said. "I could tell you about him. Might help you to understand him. If you care to."

"I don't care to," she said.

He drew a few more puffs from his pipe. "His family is one of the oldest in East Anglia," he began, as though she hadn't spoken. "Established. No title, of course—" He caught himself. "Well, I suppose there *is* a title now, come to think of it. 'Sir Jeffrey Willcox, Bt.,' yes? But no one takes that seriously. The title's bosh compared to the rest. If they wanted to—which they don't, they've got other business to attend to—they could trace a direct line back to Ethelbert. Normans are a rabble of upstarts to them. And, Lady Willcox, you must understand, that ancient, aristocratic eccentricity, you might call it, it's there in all of them. In their blood."

He set his pipe on the table, put his hands behind his head, and stretched his legs out in front of him. "You should have seen his mother. Terrifying woman. Devoted. But terrifying. She'd have eaten you for breakfast, with your jumped up Edinburgh pretensions." He looked sidelong at her, disgusted. "I notice he gave you her ring. Besotted idiot."

"My family—" she started.

He waved his hand in the air. "Don't even try, Lady Willcox. Physicians, weren't they? Respectable and reeking of formaldehyde? You'll embarrass yourself." He paused for a moment. "Where was I? Oh yes. Old family. Been in the cloak and dagger business for centuries. Since the Hanovers at least, they've sent a son or a cousin or two into the breach—"

"Why are you telling me this?" she interrupted, rudely, hoping to stop him talking.

He turned toward the table and rested his cheek in his hand. "Conversation, Lady Willcox. Conversation. Awkward, you know, sitting and staring at one another." When she didn't reply, he resumed. "And, I suppose, I'm also trying to explain to you, as best I can, why you're going to lose. Whatever this game is that you think you're playing with him—you're going to lose badly. You're no match for him."

"It's not a game."

"Perhaps not to you. But to him, it is." He picked up his pipe and examined it. "That doesn't mean it isn't serious. But it *is* a game. And whereas he's been bred to it, for generations, you're just some mad Scottish witch with a grievance." His voice was level, unemotional, and he laughed in surprise when he saw her staring at him, wide eyed. "Time was, Lady Willcox, when people knew what to do with women like you. But he'll come round. You're not *that* interesting."

"You're a swine," she said. "I can see why the two of you get on. The air in Suffolk must be putrid indeed to produce specimens like you."

"Spoken like a true physician's daughter," he replied. Then he put the pipe in his mouth, drew another puff, and kept talking as though she hadn't insulted him. "He had a peregrine when he was seven or eight. His family goes in for that sort of thing. Raptors and riding and mews and all the Dark

Ages pageantry of it. Although, unlike the rest, they come by it honestly. Loved that bird. Called it 'Fluffy.' Romantic. Just as he is now."

"Romantic? Jeffrey Willcox?" She laughed. "And you think I'm unbalanced."

"Yes," he insisted. "A romantic. He was convinced, and no one could tell him otherwise, that if he let the blasted bird out of her jesses, even before she was fully trained, she would come back to him. True love."

"Then he was a stupid child. I'm not remotely surprised."

"So," he spoke over her, "he freed her. And off she flew. He was devastated. But he never let it show. Days passed. Weeks passed. And do you know what happened?"

"He took up torturing kittens in the cellar?"

"Fluffy returned. Perched outside his bedroom window looking for all the world as though she were contrite and missing him."

She raised her eyebrows. "Lovely story, Aldous. Thank you for that. And yes, I feel that I do know him so much better now. The love that he felt for his pet bird more than counterbalances the thousands of lives he's destroyed—"

"I haven't finished, Lady Willcox. So Fluffy returned. But that afternoon, she was nowhere to be found. Servants searched everywhere. No luck. Until eventually, days later, they found her in the rubbish behind the house. Seems someone had wrung her neck." He looked at his pipe again. "And Willcox appeared ever so pleased with himself—"

"Bollocks, Parker." Jeffrey had opened the door to the room and heard the last part of their conversation. "Why must you always bring up poor Fluffy's demise when you have a captive audience? You'll terrify her." He turned to Marion. "Fluffy was an utterly neurotic bird. We all assumed that she'd done herself in. Trick suicide. She was the type to annoy everyone with that sort of thing."

Aldous picked up the keys and tossed them back to Jeffrey. "Fluffy was a model of stability compared to—"

"*Thank you*, Parker," Jeffrey said.

Aldous stood and occupied himself in packing away his pipe. "If you'd leave us alone for a few more minutes, I could tell her about the appalling fate of Ginnie's Shetland." He looked up, teasing, under his eyebrows. "Ah, Willcox. Don't give me the death stare. I'll be a good little soldier and change the subject. Are we going back up?"

"No," Jeffrey replied, working to keep a straight face. "The information's good. Which means, Parker, that you're dismissed for the evening. Do everyone a favor, would you, and drink yourself into a stupor somewhere?"

Aldous walked toward the door and clapped Jeffrey on the shoulder, still grinning. "Spooky mind reader that you are, that's precisely what I was thinking of doing." He cast a careless glance at Marion. "A charming evening, Lady Willcox. I thank you for it."

She didn't reply.

When he'd left the room, Jeffrey removed the cuffs from her wrists, pulled out a chair, and sat next to her. She rubbed her wrists, but otherwise she didn't move. Didn't want to hear what he had to tell her.

"I've had a team secure the vaults," he said. "No one will enter them until I've had the chance to examine them tomorrow. After that, I'll grant access to a small committee of experts." He paused as though waiting for her to answer, but she just shook her head, trying to keep from crying. "I'm telling you this," he continued, "so that you won't worry. This is no free-for-all. No more than ten people will see the material before it's tagged, crated, and transferred to London."

She dug her fingernails into her palms to keep from screaming at him. He watched her clenched fists for a few seconds, thoughtful. And then he gave up and changed his tone. "I'll be leaving for Baquba tonight. In a few minutes. I'll arrive by morning, spend the day there, and return tomorrow evening. I'll want to compare notes with you once I've seen the collection. And we also must talk about the future."

She didn't speak, but at this point, he didn't expect her to. "You'll return to the holding cell," he told her, "for the remainder of the night. I've had bedding and a proper meal sent to you there. They'll also feed you regularly tomorrow. I'm sorry that I can't let you out until I've returned."

He stood and held her elbow to help her out of the chair. She shook off his hand and walked into the corridor in front of him. He hurried to catch up to her and opened the door to the alley himself. The jailors she associated with her first few days in Hinaidi were waiting for them there. Jeffrey returned their salute absentmindedly and then faced her. "It couldn't have happened any other way, Marion. You know that as well as I do."

And then he disappeared into the darkness of the camp.

THE soldiers escorted her back to the prison—or hospital—she still was uncertain as to the official purpose of the building—without the violence that had characterized their treatment of her before. If anything, they were attentive and considerate. In fact, if it weren't for her grimy uniform and the oversized boots, she might have imaged them as a sort of sheepish honor guard. She still wanted to kill them.

After they had led her down the stairs and helped her into the cell, she realized that her situation had indeed changed considerably. The room now contained a camp bed with a blanket and a pillow, a folding table, a small stool, and, in the corner, a neatly stacked pile of recent novels. On the table were a glass pitcher of water, a cup, a loaf of white bread, an orange, cutlery, and a china plate with roasted potatoes and half of a roasted chicken. She looked about the room, nonplussed. Then she sat on the stool, drank a glass of water, forced herself to consume a piece of bread, and picked for a while at the chicken. Despite her experiences of the past week, she had no appetite.

She gave up on eating and walked to the corner to examine the books. Discarded by departing officers, given their tone. Digging out *The Maltese Falcon*, she returned to the camp bed and curled onto her side to read. Two pages into the story, she was asleep.

But Jeffrey didn't return the next evening. In fact, three days and five novels passed before the guards tapped on the observation window of the cell to tell her that he'd given orders to move her. She felt a knot of fear in her stomach at the information, but her only response was to nod and follow them obediently to the toilet and shower.

When she entered the grim, damp room, she paused, nonplussed. A change of clothing was waiting there for her: a slim ivory day dress with muted but elaborate embroidery, square sleeves to the elbows, and a collar that stood out stiffly from a plunging neckline; women's shoes with higher heels than made her comfortable; linen; and a set of pins to put up her hair. She recognized Jeffrey's hand in the choice, and her anxiety rose. But she also knew that she couldn't continue to wear the prison uniform. It was on the verge of disintegrating altogether.

Ignoring her fear, she stepped into the shower, washed her hair, and toweled herself dry. Pulled her hair back into a tight chignon and used all the pins to keep it in place. Then she put on the linen, dress, and shoes. They fit perfectly, as though designed for her. Which annoyed her. She hated that he knew these intimate details about her, and that he had no qualms about making that knowledge understood. She felt less comfortable in the immaculate civilian clothes than she had in the prison dress. Refused to think about what the sartorial change signified.

When she tapped on the observation window to be let out, the door opened immediately. She stepped through, and then she stopped, startled, when she saw Jeffrey waiting for her in the corridor. The jailors had disappeared. He was also wearing civilian clothing. A brown three-piece travel suit, white shirt, and a dark red tie. His hair was brushed back, and he had a hat in his hand. He considered her dress, and then he held out his arm, which she took without thinking.

"The dress is by a Spanish couturier," he said as they walked toward the stairs. "I daresay he'll end in Paris. My sister thinks the world of him." He glanced down at her outfit. "And she's correct, of course. Though I'd never let her know it."

"Where are we going?" Marion was fighting back growing alarm.

"We'll talk on the plane."

"Plane?"

"Ah," he said, holding the door at the top of the stairs for her and settling his hat on his head. "I see we're back in mindless echo mode."

She stopped walking and faced him. "Where are we going, Jeffrey?"

"I've told you," he said, taking her elbow and pulling her alongside him. "We'll talk on the plane. We'll have hours to converse. I've borrowed a de Havilland Hercules from Imperial Airways, and although that will give us a fair amount of space to rest in the cabin, it also means that we'll be refueling with vexing frequency. The route, they insist, must be through Gaza, Cairo, Alexandria, Athens, Brindisi, and Paris before we finally wash up on our native shore."

"We're going to London?" She didn't know whether to be optimistic or terrified. Intuitively, her reaction was joy at the thought of being closer to Ian. But she didn't want to give Jeffrey an opportunity to hurt her again. She tried to school her features.

"Hmm." He looked sideways at her face. "Like an open book. But we'll discuss that as well."

They had reached the airfield, and a biplane was waiting for them, its engines already running. An anonymous civilian pilot in the cockpit. Jeffrey waited for her to climb the ladder into the cabin, and then he followed her up and shut the door himself.

The cabin looked like an exaggerated version of a first class railway carriage from the previous century. Enormous seats, bits of carved wood decorating every exposed surface of the interior, a galley and drinks cabinet secured to the tail end of the compartment, and periodicals that looked ripped from White's in London scattered with a deliberate lack of concern over a central dining table. An ashtray on a stand was bolted to the floor beside the table. Cautiously, she sat in a seat next to the large, square window.

Jeffrey sat across from her and examined the periodicals. There was a briefcase stored under his seat. "Comfortable?"

She nodded. The plane was already moving toward the runway. As they took off—serenely, compared to what Aldous had done to them—both Marion and Jeffrey looked out the windows without speaking. A few of the newspapers slid to the floor, and he bent to retrieve them, but he didn't try to talk to her. And eventually, when they had levelled off twenty or thirty minutes into the flight, he stood and walked to the rear of the cabin. Returned a few minutes later bearing a tray with two cups of tea and a plate of McVitie's digestives.

"They offered to supply us with a staff as well," he said, "but I told them we'd manage on our own." He set the plate on the table and sat back down in his chair. "I've taken the liberty of leaving the Elkes in the galley. But be warned, I can easily produce them should you become quarrelsome."

She looked at him under her brows and reached for the tea. Then, leaning back, she sipped from the cup, resolutely observing the view out the window.

He put his hand to the side of his chair and retrieved the briefcase. Opened the lid, extracted a sheet of paper, closed the lid, and spread the paper on top of the case as though about to read. Glanced at her averted face. "I found something of yours in the vault."

"I don't want to talk about this." She tried to drink more of the tea, but when she saw that her hand was shaking, she put the cup back in the saucer and left both on the table.

He cleared his throat and began reading from the paper. "'Marion: You are all that matters to me—'"

She twisted toward him in blind rage. "No! *No.* Don't you dare—"

"Granted my translation from the Arabic is a bit slipshod," he said. "But you knew him better than I did—at least, in some ways—and this was certainly not the sort of document he ever sent my way—"

"Shut up!" she shouted. "Don't say anything more! Not a single word, or—"

"Or what?" he asked. "I'm genuinely curious. What will you do if I continue to read this heart-wrenching final letter that your devoted late husband wrote to you?"

She was shaking all over. "Take your obscene hands off Tariq's—"

"'Just as I thought. 'Or nothing.'" He considered. "What would you have preferred, Marion? That I left it there for the philologists to pack up with the rest of the material? If they had filed it away, would that have kept your true love pure? Who knows? It may have ended up as a permanent part of the British Museum's collection. You know—an artifact?" Nasty emphasis on the last word.

"Please—" She didn't even know what she was asking for. Just that he would leave Tariq's memory out of whatever else he planned to do with the library. She tried to read his face and couldn't. His look was inscrutable. She tried again. "Please—"

"It's an interesting read. As a piece of literature, I mean." He perused the page. "So many layers. Because, although there are indeed all sorts of 'I cannot live without you's,' and 'you became my universe's' and 'my beloved, I long for you'—"

"Stop it!"

"Yes, you get the idea. There's just as much 'you will hear a squalid account of my behavior,' and 'I would never have made this bargain'—and, once again, you get the idea." Bright now with malice. "At least he was honest with himself in the end."

"Why are you doing this? He's dead. He's not relevant—"

"I'm doing it, Marion, because there's a problem with this note." She was shaking her head, but he refused to stop. "You see, despite its mostly formulaic tone, there are at least two passages in this cloying rubbish bin of music hall endearments that, to me, ring false—that are more than just the drivel of a love-struck traitor trying to whitewash himself now that he's been caught." He held the paper closer. "Let's see. And those two parts are—" he ran his finger down the page, scanning the text. "Ah yes. Here, when he refers to 'only you—your mind like my mind.' And then, here as well, when he asks you to 'sit beneath the broken arch and ponder' the meaning of, well, whatever it was the two of you used to do with one another. A bit obscure. Could you help me to understand? I imagine it would be cathartic for you to tell me all about how Tariq's mind was too sensitive for a monster like me to comprehend. So please, indulge me, Marion. What am I missing?"

"It means what it says," she snapped at him. "He and I were the same person. The same mind. When you killed him—"

"I didn't kill him."

"When you killed him—"

"Tariq killed himself, Marion. Suicide by elderly imperial enforcer." He slipped the paper back into the briefcase and put the briefcase under his chair again. "Come to think of it, he killed himself in much the same way that Claudia killed herself. Has it ever occurred to you that it may be your own malign influence that drives these friends and lovers of yours to—"

"Go to hell!"

He picked up his tea and took a sip. "What about the 'broken arch?' Any thoughts on that?"

She turned to the window and looked at the passing clouds. Her heart was thudding in her chest, but she ignored it. Took a few deep breaths.

"Hmm." He set his cup in the saucer on the table. "May I tell you why I'm pushing this conversation?"

She didn't move or speak. Sighing, he pulled a cigarette case out of his inside jacket pocket, tapped out a cigarette, and lit it with a match. Put the spent match in the ashtray next to the table. "I'm insisting on this because I have a sense—and at this point it is nothing more than a sense, although I suspect that will change—that the library is not what it appears to be." He took a drag from the cigarette and blew the smoke up toward the ceiling. "When it first came to my attention that it existed, and that it wasn't a sick joke perpetrated by that tiresome Vizier of yours, I had imagined one room. Perhaps two. A trove of maybe a hundred volumes. A rich archive, undoubtedly, but nothing like—"

He stopped himself, uncertain. Then he tried another tack. "Imagine it, Marion. There I was, arriving in Baquba at sunrise, making my way to that vermin infested orchard of date palms, dealing with that frenzied, halfwit peasant who protected it for you—he has a difficult couple of weeks in store for him, I can tell you—lowering myself into some sort of pit. And—" He examined his cigarette for a moment. Then he looked at her face, still turned away from his. "There must be thirty thousand manuscripts packed away in those caverns," he said shortly. "Perhaps forty thousand. It's the archaeological discovery of the century. Of a series of centuries."

She still didn't respond, which angered him. "And you kept it from me, you cold, withholding bitch."

At that she faced him. "It has nothing to do with—"

"And then," he interrupted her, "positioned precisely at the center of the first vault, in a place of honor, on a bloody *lectern*, what do I find? True love's testament. Tear stained—at least I hope those were tears—and awaiting the return of—"

"Stop it. I told you to stop it—"

"And not only that—and here we get to the crux of the matter—I also discovered, after only the most superficial of examinations, that not all of those volumes are medieval." He looked hard at her. "Are they? Some are recent. Some are quite recent." He took another drag from the cigarette and finished in a musing tone. "And so, I thought to myself, perhaps Tariq was doing a bit of contract work on the side." He tapped ash into the ashtray. "Perhaps you were too."

Suddenly the full value of what she had lost—of all that she had lost—hit her. Rather than answering him, she began to cry. Soon, she was sobbing more violently than she had since she was a child. She couldn't stop herself, and the more she cried, the more she wanted to cry. She put her face into her hands and leaned against the window of the plane, her entire body convulsing.

He watched her for a few moments, placidly smoking his cigarette. When she didn't stop, he reached into his pocket and retrieved a handkerchief, which he handed to her. "Calm yourself, Marion. It's not as though we're going to destroy it. We're not even going to hide it—as you were content to do. It will become part of the foremost scholarly collection in the world, protected and appreciated by the most—"

"All for the greater glory of England," she spat at him. She had stopped crying, but she was bereft, unable to comprehend her loss.

"For the greater glory of English *scholarship*," he corrected her. "That's hardly disgraceful. Think of what could be happening. Have you been paying any attention to what the Germans are up to? Thomas is beside himself." He crushed out his cigarette in the ashtray. "I was forced to find him a British passport to prevent him from attempting to take on the Reich single handedly. Your library," he told her, "will be put to its proper use. As for the material that doesn't quite fit, we'll have plenty of time to discuss it when we return to London." He took a digestive from the tray, looked at it, seemed to decide against it, and put it back down again. "Which brings us to the second topic we must cover before we land. What happens when we do return?"

122

"Short conversation," she said, wiping her eyes, and looking back out the window. "I collect Ian, return to Durham, and start Michaelmas Term. You go back to looting the colonies."

"Marion, if you set foot in Durham, you'll be abducted within the hour. Mussolini's people and our own—not to mention teams sent by God knows what other governments you've managed to outrage during your recent research excursions—will be crawling all over one another to drag you into one of their respective basements."

"I'll take my chances," she muttered to the window.

"I have no doubt. But unfortunately, and despite all that has passed, I feel a certain sense of responsibility for your well-being. And, ungentlemanly though it may sound, whereas rescuing my wife from marauding Italians once is a bit of a lark, doing so repeatedly can become tedious. So," he said, "no. You will not take your chances."

"What, then?" She closed her eyes and pressed her forehead against the glass.

"You have two options. The first is to return as a prisoner. I'll tell the office that after much sifting of intelligence, we finally located and apprehended you. It's not my favorite scenario—and I wouldn't envy you whatever the children have in store for you. But it does have two clear benefits." He crossed his ankle over his knee and folded his hands over his stomach. "The first is that you could be as uncooperative and bloody minded as you chose to be. It would be par for the course. Expected. You wouldn't be forced to try your hand at deception—never your strength. And the second benefit," he continued, "is that I would know where you were. As would John. We wouldn't worry. As much."

At the mention of Ian, she looked over at Jeffrey. Reading her expression, the corner of his mouth went down. "I think it highly unlikely that you'd be allowed to see him. But you can be certain that he'd figure prominently in your interrogation. As I mentioned before, it would be unprofessional, at best, not to take advantage of that opening. And the children are nothing if not professional."

"What's the second option?"

"The second option is for me to tell them that I've been running you. That you've been under wraps the entire time." He paused. "Since Cambridge, even, if it seems plausible."

"I thought I was too unstable for you to run." She had turned back to the window.

"You are. But they don't know that." He paused again. "And although they might not believe it entirely, they wouldn't be able to prove otherwise. You'd be cleared of any suspicion of involvement in the various ill-fated accidents to which you've been linked."

"Oh." She didn't know what else to say.

"There are, though, a few drawbacks to this option," he continued. "The most prominent being that you must play along. A fair amount of confusion over your loyalties would go unnoticed. A lot of people coming back from long stints in the field are a bit wobbly about their allegiances." He rubbed his cheek. "If, though, you forced me, say, to drag you back in chains, it might raise some suspicions. So, the question is, Marion, do you reckon you can manage not to shout, 'death to the empire,' or toss any bombs at members of parliament between disembarking the plane in Croydon and returning home to London?"

"Home?" she asked, her stomach dropping. An unwelcome echo of their conversation in Durham.

"Yes," he said. "That's the other potential drawback. If you choose the first option and hand yourself over to the children, they'll take you to one of their secure residences—indefinitely. But if you agree to pose as my talent, you still won't walk free. You'd remain under house arrest. It wouldn't be permanent," he assured her. "But I must have you available to answer questions about the material as it's transferred from Baquba to London." He continued to watch her profile. "And I also must convince myself that you aren't in danger. You'd have almost complete freedom of movement—I'd ask Lieutenant Trelawney to look out for you. And, of course, you'd be with John."

The plane shuddered and started losing altitude. Jeffrey peered out the window and then stood and retrieved the tray with the tea and biscuits. "I think the plane is about to land. You needn't make up your mind immediately."

But she knew already that she had no choice. She'd do anything she must to regain access to her son. She closed her eyes and rested her palm against her forehead. Thought she might begin weeping again.

London, England
September, 1933

THE flight to England took the better part of two days with repeated stops for refueling that turned, inexorably, into drawn-out meals. The Imperial Airways lounges in which Marion and Jeffrey waited seemed uncertain as to whether they wanted to reflect a fantasy of a luxurious nineteenth-century past or an equally hollow fantasy of a technological twentieth-century future. The conflicted atmosphere of the buildings gave Marion a headache. They entertained Jeffrey to no end.

Rather than fight the fixed schedule when darkness fell on the first day, they spent the night in a hotel in Brindisi, where Jeffrey politely insisted that she occupy the bedroom of their suite. He then stayed awake in the sitting room until morning, watching the door to prevent escape attempts during the night. Sleeplessness didn't affect him. He was as insufferably cheerful when they re-boarded the plane for Paris as he had been the day before, when they had first taken off in Hinaidi. Marion, despite her sleep, felt as though she were living in a fog.

Their plane finished its journey after nightfall on the second day when it landed in Croyden. Jeffrey opened the cabin door himself and waited for Marion to precede him down the steps. As she reached the ground, she looked up and saw a monstrous black Packard Twelve waiting for them on the apron. Stopped abruptly. "You can't be serious."

Jeffrey had climbed down behind her. "It's beautiful, isn't it?"

"Do you *want* to look like an American gangster?"

"You disapproved of the Bentley." Injured. "I thought you might prefer something less imperial. Packards are democratic."

He put his hand under her elbow and began guiding her toward the car. She stumbled and then caught her balance. "Democratic? *That?*"

"John will like it."

"Ian is going nowhere near that thing."

He opened the door for her. "Once he's seen it, you'll never get him out of it. Watch."

She balked at the door. Then, realizing yet again that she had no choice, she moved stiffly into the back seat. "I hate this."

"I know," he said sliding in next to her. He leaned forward to speak to the driver. She heard him say that he was pleased to be back as well, and then she looked stubbornly out the window and refused to be curious.

After an hour on the road, they reached the outskirts of London. Fifteen minutes later, they were driving along the ring road surrounding Regent's Park. The car slowed and turned into a garage in what she thought she recognized as Chester Terrace. The driver cut the engine, left the car, flipped a switch that flooded the garage with light, and opened the door for her. She stepped out of the car, followed by Jeffrey, and looked at the belligerently modern space.

Before she had a chance to form an impression, Jeffrey put his hand under her elbow again and pointed to a stairway at the far end of the room. She let him lead her up the stairs to the ground floor, where she saw a reception hall, the main entry, and, through a half-closed door, a formal dining room. Jeffrey turned up two cut glass lamps near the front door that illuminated parquet floors, Bukhara carpets, and radiators that, in this warm early September, were still inert.

He turned to her. "I daresay you're tired from the flight. I'll ring for Mrs. Bowen to show you to your room." He had set his hat on a console at the side of the hall. Ran a hand through his hair. "Before I do, though, I want to be certain that you and I understand one another. Tomorrow afternoon, I'll collect John from the train. I expect to bring him here directly. He'll be disappointed if you're not waiting to receive him."

She opened her mouth to reply, but he stopped her.

"All that means," he said, "is that I'd be grateful if you'd put off attempts to climb out the window and escape over the rooftops at least until tomorrow night. Agreed, Marion?" More weary than joking.

She nodded.

"Thank you, darling." He walked to an in-house telephone and pushed a button. "Mrs. Bowen? Yes, I've returned." He smiled with genuine warmth. "No, that won't be necessary. But if you would show Lady Willcox to—" He stopped speaking and looked down at the receiver. Then he replaced it and turned to Marion. "She's on her way. She won't approve. But then, she wouldn't approve if you were the Queen of Denmark. Less so then, I suspect—"

As he spoke, a caricature of a nineteenth-century housekeeper bustled up the stairs, wearing a complete uniform, including apron and cap. She stopped when she reached the top, actually bobbed a curtsy at them, and then unapologetically looked Marion up and down. "Hmm. Healthy, at any rate. If you'd care to follow me, Lady Willcox, I'll show you to your rooms." She walked toward the stairs, and Marion, mystified, followed her. "Shy, then, are you?" Mrs. Bowen continued as she climbed toward the first floor. "Choosing the third-floor bedroom rather than occupying the master suite? Not that I'm making a comment. A lady needs her privacy. As does a gentleman, for that matter. But it's old fashioned—"

She carried on talking as she moved further up the staircase. Marion threw a desperate look back at Jeffrey, but he merely grinned at her. "I'll be working late in the study, Mrs. Bowen," he called to her retreating back. "Would you tell Jenkins he needn't stay up?"

"I'll do no such thing," came the voice back down the stairs. "You need your sleep, and you'll go direct to bed once I have Lady Willcox comfortable."

"I won't stay up more than an hour, Mrs. Bowen. I promise."

"Hmph."

Marion hopelessly followed her up the stairs. On the first floor were a drawing room and the door to what she assumed was a study. The second-floor doors were all shut—the master bedroom, dressing room, and bath, she assumed. Finally, on the third floor, Mrs. Bowen opened the door to a large guest bedroom with new wallpaper, a scrolled sofa, pastel carpets over more parquet floors, a radiator as well as a fireplace, a dressing table, and windows overlooking the park. A second door led to a dressing room and a bath.

Mrs. Bowen busied herself turning down the bedclothes and fluffing up the pillows, pristine and white. She smoothed out a nightdress of the sort that Marion would never wear. "I understand that young John will be arriving tomorrow," she said. "It's short notice, but I've had the room across the hall made up for him. You'll be close. We're also turning the third guest bedroom into a nursery for the boy."

"That really isn't necessary—" Marion began.

"Nonsense." Mrs. Bowen glowered at her. Then she put her hands on her hips and looked about the room. "Now then, Lady Willcox. Will you be needing help undressing—"

"No!" Sharper than she had intended. "No. Thank you. I—it's a simple dress. I'll be fine."

"Very well, then." Mrs. Bowen nodded. "Ring downstairs if you require anything." She indicated a telephone resting adjacent to an alarm clock on a small table next to the bed. "I'll wish you a good night, Lady Willcox."

"Goodnight, Mrs. Bowen."

When the door to the room had shut, Marion walked over to it and locked it. Then she went to the windows and peeked between the heavy curtains at the dim outline of the park. Rubbing her eyes, she turned and made her way to the bath, where she found an array of toiletries, all ostentatiously Yardley. Bit her lip. Lavender bothered her. Nonetheless, she cleaned her teeth, washed her face and hands, and then wandered further into the dressing room.

She stopped when she flipped on the light. The room was stocked with sufficient clothing to last her, at least, a lifetime. She swallowed. She didn't know how long Jeffrey believed she would be staying in the house, but there was no way it would require this sort of wardrobe. The room made her uneasy. Choosing not to dwell on what it implied, she examined a looming and equally upsetting Eastlake wardrobe at the end of the dressing area and began opening drawers. Eventually, she found a collection of nightdresses—half frothy and half lacey—as well as one pair of almost acceptable dark blue pyjamas.

She removed her dress and hung it carefully among the others—an act that she knew would immediately telegraph to Mrs. Bowen what Aldous had described as her jumped up Edinburgh pretensions. She refused to care. She would not question her impulses in this house to ingratiate herself to Jeffrey's world. This aspect of his life was as off putting as the part she'd already encountered in the field. And she studiously chose not to notice that she was already analyzing her own behavior.

Pulling on the pyjamas, she returned to the bedroom and noticed for the first time that in addition to the bed, sofa, and dressing table, there was a solid and incongruous wooden work desk pushed up against the wall opposite the bed. It lurked under a window overlooking the street. There was nothing inherently suspicious about it. It was a desk like she'd seen in countless offices and bureaus—accompanied by an equally functional chair, banker's lamp, and six large drawers.

But it didn't belong to the room. She could tell that it had been placed there recently, and for a reason. She walked to the desk and opened each of the drawers. Empty. Meditative, she ran her hand over the desktop and then decided that she was too tired to speculate. Instead, she walked to the bed, switched off the lamp on the side table, slid herself under the covers, and slept.

SHE woke earlier in the morning than she ordinarily did—at least earlier than she did without Ian to manage. But the buzzing energy she felt had nothing to do with the two hour difference between Baghdad and London. After weeks of isolation and uncertainty about the day, to say nothing of the time, her mind was unable to remain at rest for more than a few hours consecutively. She found herself repeatedly starting up in a panic during the night, before reassuring herself and settling back into sleep. And having now woken yet again, she peered at the curtains and saw a sliver of sunshine making its way across the carpet. It was daylight. She looked at the alarm clock. 7:30. Decided against coaxing herself back to sleep.

She sat up, pushed her hair from her face, and considered the room. Then she got out of bed and pulled the curtains apart. Gazing across the park gilded in the early morning September light, she rebuked herself for being impressed by it. Resented Jeffrey for bringing her here rather than to a more neutral building. He was sending her a not very subtle message about what sort of institutions she'd be taking on if she chose her own line rather than letting him guide her. And she was determined to misunderstand that message. Pulling the curtains shut again, she went to the sink and cleaned her teeth. And after that, strengthening her resolve, she returned to the dressing room.

Upon discovering that there were no trousers and no flat shoes, she almost retreated back to the bedroom in defeat. Then, her dull loathing mounting, she stood in the middle of the dressing area in her pyjamas and wondered what would happen if she refused to emerge until they brought her clothes that didn't make her angry. Finally, after a last incensed moment, she accepted that she must choose her battles. Or prepare the battleground as responsibly as she could before Ian returned from Suffolk.

Pressing her lips together, she examined each of the dresses until she found one that was unobtrusive, if not to her taste. It was grey summer wool, buttoned high across the collar, and belted. When she had it on, she walked barefoot through the room until she found the lowest heels she could, oxfords with a tie. She didn't care whether they matched the dress or not.

She returned to the bedroom and sat at the dressing table to comb her hair and pin it back. Before venturing out the door, she stared hard at her face in the mirror. The glass was flattering, but she herself looked like someone who had spent the past week or more sleep deprived and starving on a bare concrete floor. She blinked and stood. If Jeffrey was unhappy with the effect, he'd know who ought to be blamed.

Then, dismissing her physical state, she opened the door slowly, feeling that she didn't belong, and peeked across the third-floor hall. It was empty. The small stairway to the servants' bedrooms above was also vacant. She left the room and made her way down the stairs.

When she reached the ground floor, the door to the dining room was open. She approached it. No notion of what she would meet on the other side, her heart thudding. The room, however, when she entered it, was pleasant and innocuous. Flooded with sunlight. At the center of an oval dining table was a flamboyant crystal vase of yellow freesias, but otherwise the space was furnished for comfort. Jeffrey was sitting at the end of the table reading the *Times*, a cup of tea and a plate of half-eaten toast in front of him.

When he heard her, he folded the paper and placed it next to his plate. "I knew you'd choose that one. I think you secretly miss the convict's uniform." Jeffrey himself was wearing a blue pinstriped suit with a light blue shirt and a pale yellow tie. His hair was brushed back again. He looked like a banker. "Breakfast, if you care for it." He gestured toward the sideboard.

Marion poured herself a cup of tea and put two pieces of toast on a plate. Brought them to the table and sat across from him. Took a sip of the tea and then smeared marmalade on the toast.

He watched her as she systematically applied the marmalade to every exposed surface of the toast. When she finally took a bite, he spoke. "You're like an eight year old."

"I have a process too," she said, chewing. Drank more of her tea.

He finished his own tea and looked at his watch. "I'll be at the office in the morning. John's train from Stowmarket reaches Liverpool Street Station at 2:30. I'll collect him and bring him here after that." He stood and folded the newspaper under his arm. "Lieutenant Trelawney will be arriving any moment—"

"I don't want to see Nick."

"He knows you. I haven't time to break in a new minder."

"*Minder?* How—"

"I haven't time for this either." He bent over and kissed her cheek. "If it makes you feel better, I've asked Mrs. Bowen to leave you to your own devices. She's agreed—but under protest. If you could show some interest in the house—redecorate a room or something like that—it would calm her immeasurably." He enjoyed her outraged expression and then walked to the reception hall. "I'll look forward to hearing about your day."

And then the door opened and clicked shut. She was alone in the room. After a few seconds, she looked down at her toast. She wasn't hungry. She also had no curiosity about the house. Her only interest was how to escape it. When Ian arrived, she'd find a way to take him back to Durham, or even Scotland, without Jeffrey's knowledge. She didn't believe that she was in danger from the Italian government. Or any government. All she had was Jeffrey's word that she was a target for abduction, and thus far, his was the only organization that had tried to harm her. It would be difficult eluding his people once she'd left Chester Terrace. But she'd done so before, and for five years she had done so while also caring for Ian. She was willing to take her chances.

She pushed out her chair and left the dining room. Cast a professional glance over the entryway and front door. No security at all. She and Ian would be able to walk to the street and make their way to a tube station within minutes.

She chewed her lip for a moment and then wandered up the stairs to the first floor. Pushed open the doors to the drawing room and examined the bright furniture, artfully placed side tables, and books of photographs. Too many lamps. She walked to an ebony armchair upholstered in immaculate green and white striped silk. Relaxing into it, she took up a catalogue of work by Paul Klee and began flipping through it. Thought that perhaps she would stay just long enough for Ian to claim this fragile and flawless room. Make it his own. Smiling to herself, she immersed herself in the book.

She almost didn't notice when the front door opened again. And it wasn't until she heard a murmured conversation in the reception hall and footsteps on the staircase that she remembered Nick was expected. She looked up when he paused on the threshold of the room. He was wearing a brown suit with a white cotton shirt, and no tie. Not a military uniform, but it might as well have been. He looked nothing like a student. But, she consoled herself, he also looked nothing like a banker.

"Good morning, Dr. Bailey."

She returned her attention to the book. "You needn't be here."

"I'm sorry, Dr. Bailey, but I do." He walked into the room, glanced about, and then peered into the study as well.

She snorted without turning away from the Klee. "You haven't checked behind the curtains. There may be some suspicious looking toes peeking out from under them." Turned another page. "Probably just Polonius."

He sighed and returned to the drawing room. Started to sit in the chair opposite her and then stopped himself. "Do you mind if I sit?"

"Suit yourself."

He sat. "It's my job, Dr. Bailey," he said. "I've been given an assignment, and I am completing it as capably as I know how."

"Your job?" She put the catalogue back on the table and stared at him. "This?"

"Yes. My job. This."

"May I ask you a question, Nick? Purely out of curiosity."

"Please do."

"You're an intelligent young man. In fact, you're more than intelligent. You're talented. Brilliant. You're remarkably well educated. You could do anything with your life. Take any job." She stopped.

He seemed nonplussed. "Thank you for saying so, Dr. Bailey."

"I haven't asked my question."

"I apologize."

His office persona was nearly as irritating as his postgraduate persona. But she pushed on nonetheless. "Here is my question. Even though you could have done anything with your life, turned your talents to any pursuit, you've decided, from what I can gather, to work as glorified jailor. And not even a proper jailor. Because, as I'm certain you're aware, this situation, in this ghastly house, is more than a little personal. It's corrupt. In fact, I might go so far as to say that, with all your talents and opportunities, you've settled on working as a two-bit pimp for your sadistic criminal of an employer. Any thoughts, Nick?"

She was pleased to see that he colored. By the time she had finished speaking, he was shaking. All he said to her, though, was: "may I speak freely with you, Dr. Bailey?"

"Always, Nick."

"Very well." He wiped his palms on the knees of his trousers. "Let me say this first. I feel nothing but admiration for your scholarship. You are, if you'll allow me the presumption of commenting, the most intelligent woman I've ever encountered." He paused. "Nonetheless, Dr. Bailey, I've also spent time gathering my own information about your history and, necessarily, about your relationship with Sir Jeffrey. I haven't come into this assignment blind.

"Here is what I've gleaned. You and Sir Jeffrey met at Cambridge, where you, Dr. Bailey, did all that you could to sabotage the research he was conducting with your mentor, Professor Dickinson. You were offered an opportunity to work in collaboration on their project, an opportunity, however, that you refused. Instead, you left Cambridge altogether, travelled to Turkey, and removed the only extant copy of the manuscript they were studying from the Istanbul archive in which it had been kept for centuries.

"After that, and after Sir Jeffrey began his work in the service, you spent years undermining his administration of the Iraq mandate. In the meantime, you made use of the manuscript you had stolen, but you never shared your results with him. Somehow, in the midst of all that, you married him. You then bore his child, whom you attempted to hide from him for five years. And now, most recently, you have been assassinating his friends and colleagues."

He looked at her, puzzled. "You ask me how I can be a party to an unofficial arrest that seems more than a little personal? An abduction that may even be corrupt? Here is my answer, Dr. Bailey: how could it *not* be personal? To be perfectly frank, had I been used by a woman in the way that Sir Jeffrey has been used by you, I am not certain that I would have shown his restraint. You ask why I would lower myself to the role of jailor in this scenario. The answer is simple. I hope to learn something of his self-control and wisdom."

Marion was stunned into silence. And after he'd finished speaking, she sat staring at him for nearly a full minute. "Self-control and wisdom?" she finally asked. "Did he ever tell you how that marriage came about?"

"I've heard something of it," he said. "But I've also seen your marriage certificate. Having some expertise in what documents signed under pressure look like, I must say, Dr. Bailey, if you'll forgive me, that the document doesn't support your implied claim that the marriage was irregular. Coerced writing always shows evidence of that coercion. There's no indication of duress in your signature on the certificate. Your hand is as steady as his. So, yes. I've heard the story. We all have. But no, I don't believe that you were forced to accept him. I think you had some other motive in agreeing to it. And I think he knew that as well."

He scratched his head. "I would like to learn how he identifies that sort of motive. If acting as his pimp, as you insist that I am—although what that makes you, Dr. Bailey, I'm not entirely certain—is the only way to educate myself, then so be it."

He hesitated. "Have I answered your question?"

"You have been utterly indoctrinated," she said.

"I have analyzed the information available to me, and I have drawn provisional conclusions," he corrected her. "You have done nothing in the time that I have known you to alter those conclusions. Sir Jeffrey thought you might like a walk in the park," he continued abruptly. "Would you care to accompany me?"

She stood. "I'm not his dog. So no. I needn't be exercised in the park." She walked to the door and toward the staircase. "I'll be in my rooms upstairs."

"Very well," he said, phlegmatic, to the empty furniture. She had already gone. He picked up the Paul Klee catalogue and began flipping through the pages.

Marion returned to her rooms and locked the door behind her. The lock made her feel safer, even though she knew that it was cosmetic and that it would never prevent a determined visitor from entering. She toyed with the idea of pushing furniture up against the door, but recognized, once again, that these impulses were counterproductive if she wanted access to Ian.

Thinking about his imminent arrival in London, she glanced at the clock. 10:15. If his train reached Liverpool Street Station at 2:30, the earliest she'd see him would be 3:00. She had five hours to occupy before she could take any sort of step toward escape. She clenched her fists and tried to quell her desire to hit something.

If Nick weren't waiting downstairs, she would have used the time to search Jeffrey's study. If she didn't find her Idrisi manuscript there, she'd at least find some clues as to where he'd taken it and what he knew about it. But she dismissed the thought. Nick would never let her wander into Jeffrey's workspace unaccompanied. She must use the time she had for a different purpose.

She threw herself onto her back on the bed and stared at the ceiling. Tastefully painted mouldings. Pink. They irritated her. She closed her eyes and considered her position for a few moments longer. It wouldn't hurt to look at the area immediately outside the front door. If she and Ian were hurrying, she wouldn't want to be casting about for a route. She sat up on the bed. And then she stood, smoothed down her dress, and left the room. Went down the stairs and marched into the study, where she found Nick still immersed in Paul Klee. "I've changed my mind. Let's go for a walk."

"Very well, Dr. Bailey." Nick set the book on the table and stood.

He waited for her to turn to leave the room, and then he followed her down the stairs. That he was walking behind her rather than next to her proved to Marion, if she'd ever been in doubt, that his role was guard rather than protector. She was certain that he was carrying a weapon. And she entertained herself as they passed through the front door with the prospect of forcing him to use it in Regent's Park. Speculated as to what his brief was should such an emergency arise.

They didn't speak as she wandered, aimless, across the street into the greenery. And anyone watching them, uninterested in one another, Nick a pace or two behind and to the side, would have wondered whether they were together or awkwardly spaced strangers. They were conspicuous, but neither was concerned with blending into the crowd. Continuing along at the same measured pace.

Once she'd found her bearings, she walked with more purpose in the direction of Marylebone. Without explaining herself to Nick. If he didn't ask, she wasn't going to make up a story, and she counted on him not to ask. As she moved, she marked the time until she caught site of Great Portland Street station. Where she paused, calculating. With Ian, she could make it from the front door of Jeffrey's house to the underground in ten minutes. A simple task. Smiling, she sat on a bench and allowed herself to feel a hint of optimism. Ignoring Nick at the other end of the same bench, stolid and expressionless.

Ten minutes later, she rose and strolled toward the center of the park. Aimless once again. Plodding. And by the time she'd finished dragging Nick around the pond twice, leading him past the zoo, and wound her way back toward Chester Terrace, they had passed more than two hours outdoors. Perfectly satisfied with her morning.

When they reached the front door, Nick rang the bell, and a maid let them into the house. She stood aside to allow them into the reception hall, and then she turned to Marion. "Lady Willcox, Mrs. Bowen wanted me to ask whether you'll be having lunch or tea this afternoon."

Marion shook her head. "No. Thank you. I'll be upstairs—"

"We'll wait until Sir Jeffrey returns," Nick supplied.

"Very good, Lady Willcox."

When she had left them alone, Nick waited for Marion to make the next move. She stared bleakly at the console for a moment, and then she came to herself. With a quick glance at Nick, she strode up to the first floor. Paused long enough in the drawing room to retrieve the Paul Klee catalogue from the table. And after that, she passed back out of the room, forcing Nick to step hastily to the side, before retreating upstairs to her bedroom. Where she locked the door again, sat on the sofa with the catalogue, and tried not to think about how slowly the time was passing.

*J*UST as she thought she would lose her mind if something didn't happen, she heard the door to the garage open and shut. She jumped off the sofa, jogged to the door, and then nearly tripped herself in her haste to get down the stairs. Nick emerged from the drawing room as she passed the first floor, but she didn't acknowledge him. He, however, did follow her, doggedly doing his job. She reached the ground floor as Ian, Jeffrey, and an exhausted looking young woman—the nanny, Marion assumed—surfaced from the garage.

Ian was carrying a small suitcase, but when he saw Marion, he placed it carefully on the ground against the wall and ran up to her. She lifted him into her arms, closed her eyes, and hugged him as tightly as she dared. "Ian, darling, I've missed you so much. I'm so happy you're here."

He pressed his cheek against hers. "I've missed you too, Mummy. Have you finished your work?"

"Yes." She nodded. She was having difficulty not crying. "I'm all finished."

She opened her eyes and saw that Nick, Jeffrey, the nanny, and Mrs. Bowen, who had also appeared from downstairs, were watching their display. She didn't mind. But she could tell that Ian did, and so she let him down. The nanny looked shell shocked. No more than a week before she gave notice, Marion predicted. Jeffrey, who was putting his hat on the side table, watched her with an indecipherable expression that made her nervous. She averted her eyes from him.

Before she could say anything more, Ian spotted Nick. "Mr. Nick! You're here!"

"Hullo, John. Pleased to see you again."

She stared at Ian and Nick grinning at one another. They had never met when Nick was at Durham. She looked a question at Ian.

"Mr. Nick was at Aunt Ginnie's," Ian explained. "He helped pick the tomatoes."

"Pick the tomatoes?" At a loss.

"Mr. Nick's a man of wide-ranging talents." There was malice under Jeffrey's tone. "But John, why not wait until dinner to tell Mummy about Aunt Ginnie and Uncle Teddy—"

"And cousin Charlotte," Ian added.

"—yes, and all of the cousins. She'll be pleased to hear about them, I'm sure. But we mustn't stand about talking in the hall."

"No." Ian agreed. His eye wandered to the nanny, who was hovering at the back of the group. He flashed a smile at her that Marion recognized all too well and that caused the nanny to shrink back against the wall.

Jeffrey, who had watched the exchange with an expression identical to Ian's, turned toward the stairs to hide his amusement.

Marion frowned. "Ian—"

Ian looked up at her, all innocence. But before he could say anything to her, his attention was drawn to Mrs. Bowen, whom he plainly identified as another potential source of inconvenience. He cast her an appraising glance, but she merely raised her eyebrows at him in return.

"And good afternoon to you, too, Mr. John," she said. "I know that face. But don't you think it frightens me the way it frightens this poor girl. I had him" nodding over at Jeffrey, "to handle for fifteen years. I think I can handle you."

Ian tilted his head, speculative, but otherwise he didn't reply. Intrigued by the challenge, if not all that worried by it. Rather than speaking to Mrs. Bowen, he turned to Marion with his angelic expression back in place. "When will we have dinner, Mummy?"

Marion looked a quick apology at Mrs. Bowen, and then she took Ian's hand and walked with him toward the stairs. No one stopped them, but when she began telling him that they'd take dinner in the nursery, Jeffrey interrupted. "Nonsense. The boy is old enough to dine downstairs. Shall we say 6:00, Mrs. Bowen? It's early, but John's had a long day."

"Of course, Sir Jeffrey." Mrs. Bowen turned to the girl who had arrived with Ian. "Come along, then," she said to her. "We'll get you some tea downstairs and then I'll see you settled into your room up above. You've had a long day as well, I imagine—"

She kept talking as she led the nanny into the sitting room, next to the kitchen, that she kept for herself.

Marion didn't wait to hear what Jeffrey would say to Nick. Instead, still holding Ian's hand, she continued up the stairs toward the bedrooms and nursery. Before she could go far, Jeffrey stopped her again. "Marion."

She didn't turn. "What?"

"We dress for dinner. Don't make me send you back to change this evening."

She didn't reply. Incensed, but trying to hide it for Ian's sake, she walked up the remainder of the stairs.

IAN was elated by the nursery that Mrs. Bowen had arranged for him, and Marion, though still uneasy about his attachment to Jeffrey's family, was content to watch him enjoying himself. She had been away from him for less than three weeks. But whenever she thought about what could have happened, her stomach dropped. She found herself fighting the urge to keep touching him. And she could have stayed in the nursery with him, satisfied, forever.

But the hours before dinner passed more quickly than she had expected, and soon she realized that she would need to find a dress to wear downstairs. She had no doubt that Jeffrey would make good on his threat to send her back to change if he thought she hadn't followed his instructions. Unwilling but resigned, she left Ian to his own devices and returned to the nightmarish dressing room.

Sorting through the dresses on the hangers, she tried to find anything that would satisfy Jeffrey without damaging her self-respect. Eventually, she came across a dark blackish-green silk frock, long sleeves, with a high neck. The material was light enough to wear in September—although she knew that he was expecting something more revealing. He could be disappointed.

She removed her grey day dress and pulled on the green silk. Then she returned to the dressing table and re-pinned her hair without bothering to examine herself in the mirror. Finally, feeling shy, she found Ian in the nursery. He looked up at her and smiled.

"You look pretty."

"Thank you, Ian."

He was still wearing the clothes he'd worn on the train, though he'd removed the jacket of the miniature Harris Tweed suit and flung it over a stuffed horse. But there was no way she was going to try to force him into dinner clothes. If Jeffrey was unhappy with Ian's outfit, he could ask Mrs. Bowen or the traumatized nanny to do something about it.

She held out her hand, and he ran over to take it. Together, they left the room and made their way down the stairs. On the second floor, they met Jeffrey emerging from his own rooms. He was wearing a white dinner jacket, and he was fixing a cufflink as he closed the door behind him. His expression didn't change when he saw them. "You aren't warm in that?"

"No."

"As you wish." He smiled down at Ian, gesturing toward the stairs. "And after you."

He followed Marion and Ian the rest of the way to the dining room, which was arranged for an extended dinner. Marion glanced down at Ian, uncertain as to how he would react, but he was untroubled. She herself, watching him sit in his chair and wait patiently for the first course, was sickened by the possibility that he had become used to this sort of meal in Suffolk. Nonetheless, she sat next to him quietly, trying to exude good humor, trying not to oppress him with her own anxiety. The freesias from the morning had been replaced by dark purple calla lilies.

As the food appeared—spinach salad and beets, roast duck with pomegranate sauce, apple cranberry stuffing, glazed brussels sprouts, and a treacle sponge pudding that dismayed her because it was Ian's favorite, and Jeffrey clearly knew that—she realized that she was meant to be anxious. With undisguised antipathy, Jeffrey led Ian to tell Marion all that he had done in East Anglia. And he watched, diverted, as she tried to respond with equanimity to Ian's repeated requests to see Aunt Ginnie and Uncle Teddy again soon. She ate almost nothing. And when the dessert had been removed, and Ian was nodding off, she jumped out of her chair to take him upstairs.

"Something else, Marion." Jeffrey was toying with a dessert fork that had been left in front of him on the table.

"What?" Ian was sleepy enough that she was lifting him up to carry to bed.

"When you've settled him for the night would you come to my study? To talk?"

She nodded. Then she rested Ian's head on her shoulder and walked with him to the stairs. As she trudged up the three flights, she thought to herself that he had gained weight. She also thought to herself that she wanted to hold him more tightly than she was. But she knew better than to wake him out of his early sleep.

She reached the third floor, pushed his bedroom door open with her shoulder, and saw both the nanny and Mrs. Bowen waiting to receive him. Mrs. Bowen was in a rocking chair, and the nanny was standing looking out the window into the dusk. Mrs. Bowen rose, smiling, when Marion entered the room. Put her hand on Marion's shoulder as Marion lowered Ian into the bed, pulled off his shoes, trousers, and shirt, and then tucked the blanket over him.

Marion found that she didn't mind Mrs. Bowen's touch. But the recognition of this sympathy with anyone in Jeffrey's household simply confused her further, and her disquiet grew. Damping down her apprehension, she smiled cautiously at Mrs. Bowen, exchanged an understanding look with the nanny, and then whispered that Jeffrey had asked her to speak with him downstairs. They nodded and shooed her out of the room.

When she was on the landing, she stopped and gripped the bannister for a full minute. Calming herself. Whatever he said, she couldn't give in to her fear. But even as she forced her pulse to slow, her mind refused to stop racing. And so, finally admitting defeat, she walked with incapacitating reluctance down the stairs.

The door to the study was closed. Uncertain as to whether he expected her to walk into the room, she paused for a few seconds. Then she knocked quietly.

"Yes?" Irritated.

"I—it's—"

The door opened and he looked at her, quizzical. "I thought it was Jenkins coming to reprimand me about the state of my shaving kit." He moved back. "Come in, then." She stepped warily into the room, and he closed the door. "Timidity doesn't become you, Marion. Especially when all that's preventing you from physically attacking me is uncertainty as to whether the time is right."

The room was furnished for work. The walls lined with rumpled books, the desk almost invisible under stacks of paper and files, the Samarkand carpet, though silk and tightly knotted, worn in places, and the leather sofa and armchairs well enough used to look comfortable. Jeffrey had closed the curtains over the tall windows. His dinner jacket and tie were draped over the chair behind the desk, and the top button of his shirt was unfastened. He ignored Marion, still standing in the middle of the room, and busied himself at a small cupboard in the corner. Eventually, he turned, holding two cut-glass tumblers of scotch. Nodded toward the sofa.

"Sit."

She sat, clasped her hands together in her lap, and looked up at him with what she hoped was a cold, polite lack of interest. He handed her a tumbler. She took it and held it in her lap while he sat in one of the armchairs across from her and set his own glass on a side table. He opened a box of cigarettes and looked at her enquiringly. She shook her head. He extracted one cigarette, lit it, and blew the smoke up at the ceiling.

He watched her tense posture for a few moments, and then he spoke. "I trust you've reconsidered your plan to make off with John at the first opportunity?"

She didn't reply.

He examined the end of the cigarette. "Trelawney said you made quite the elaborate reconnaissance of the area this morning."

"I didn't see any need to disguise from him what I was doing. And why wouldn't I take my son and leave as soon as I could?"

"Because you wouldn't make it past the front door before you were apprehended?" He was looking at her with affection, though his words were a threat. "Even if you don't believe me about the Italians or the children," he said, "credit me with enough foresight to have my own people watching the area. If you try to leave, you'll be caught. And imagine how embarrassing that will be."

"Not as embarrassing as having to admit to your colleagues at the office that your long-suffering wife and her five-year-old son have slipped away from you. Again." She took a sip of her scotch. "We'll see what happens."

"I'm pleased that you've overcome that timidity. Quick recovery. I like that." He took a drag from his cigarette and exhaled slowly. "But there is another obstacle facing you, you realize."

"Nothing I can't handle."

"Are you certain?" He put the cigarette in the ashtray on the side table. "Because the obstacle I'm thinking of is John."

"Ian—"

"How can you know he'll come quietly? Or even willingly? What if he insists on saying goodbye?" He watched her face closely. "It's possible—*possible*—that you could elude our people with a compliant, well behaved five-year-old in tow. With a five-year-old prattling on about how excited he is to see his cousin Anne compete in the pony trials? I think not." He smiled when she didn't reply. "I suppose you could drug him."

"Don't be an ass."

He shrugged. "I'm only trying to help."

She looked down at the glass resting in her lap. He was correct. She couldn't be certain of Ian's reaction to leaving, and if he balked at all, even if it was merely to assert his will, she'd never get him out of the house unnoticed. Ian had learned to keep quiet when he knew they were in danger. But she'd be hard pressed to convince him of any danger from Jeffrey's household. She raised the tumbler and drank a large part of the scotch. Then she lifted her eyes to his. "I want a timeline. How long do we stay here?"

"I can't give you a timeline. But I can assure you that it won't be permanent. And, let me repeat, that's a better deal than you'll get from any of the other interested parties."

She lowered her eyes, nodded, and then stood to leave.

"Wait a moment, Marion," he said. "We're not finished yet."

She sat back on the sofa and looked at him, exhausted. "What else?"

"I'd like to give you an idea of what I'm hoping to accomplish while you're here."

"I don't care what you're hoping to accomplish."

"Nonetheless," he said, "I'm going to tell you." He took a sip of his own scotch and set it back on the side table. "This morning, I examined the first few crates of material that arrived from Baquba. It was only a superficial read, and the majority of the volumes are still in transit, but I was able to get an idea of the breadth of the collection." He looked at her as though waiting for a response, and when she stared, stonily, into the middle distance, he seemed disappointed. "I've also been working my way through your Idrisi. I'm not as quick as you are, but I've made some progress." He tapped his finger a few times on the table. "I'm getting a feel for both. They're—odd—in surprisingly similar ways."

"I'm telling you this," he explained, when she still said nothing, "because I'll want to discuss the Idrisi and the collection as a whole with you when I'm more confident about my impressions of them."

She remained quiet, unmoved, the only evidence of her emotions her fingers gripping the nearly empty tumbler in her lap. He studied her taut hands for a moment longer. "I expect to be ready to have this conversation with you within the next two to three days," he finally said. "In the meantime, Marion, would you consider, please, playing at mother, if not at wife? Take the boy to Madame Tussaud's. Go to the zoo. I'll order Trelawney to remain as unobtrusive as possible." He ran his hand through his hair. "Three days is all I'm asking. I don't want to separate him from you again."

She flinched and glanced up at him before staring back down at her lap.

Seeing her reaction tired him. "Yes, Marion. That's the alternative. If you do something stupid, I'll be forced to move you. John will stay here."

She nodded. "I understand."

He stood. "Thank you."

She stood as well and faced him for a few seconds, uncertain.

"Goodnight," he said.

She turned and fled the room without replying.

SHE and Ian spent the next two days as Jeffrey had suggested. In the mornings, they ate breakfast in the dining room before Jeffrey left for the office. When Nick arrived, the three of them made leisurely visits to the zoo and to the nearby museums. They avoided the aggressive swans on the pond. After that, they returned each day for an elaborate tea that Mrs. Bowen set up for them in the drawing room. As Ian worked his way through four or five or sometimes six frosted cakes, Marion waited for him to begin destroying the furniture. But somehow, Mrs. Bowen and the nanny, operating together, limited the damage that he did to the house. Marion found herself admitting a grudging respect for them.

In the evenings, they ate dinner with Jeffrey, an activity that still filled Marion with dread as the hour approached. Jeffrey, though, was less inclined now to torment Marion with Ian's attachment to him and to his family. He contented himself with questions about how they had spent their days, and Marion did her best to play along. Their time should have been tranquil. But the enforced, and to Marion, sinister domesticity of the arrangement, along with the increasingly speculative glances that Jeffrey was casting at her, left her on edge.

It was almost a relief when, on the third morning, she and Ian walked into the dining room to find Nick already there. He and Jeffrey were sitting at the far end of the dining table, quietly conversing. They stopped and stood when she and Ian entered. Ian brightened at the site of Nick and smiled at Jeffrey. Then he took a plate from the sideboard and piled it with bacon and nothing else. He took his usual place at the table. Marion poured herself a cup of tea and sat next to him. Her stomach was churning, and she didn't trust herself to eat. She took a sip of her tea and watched warily over the top of the cup as Nick and Jeffrey sat down again.

Jeffrey spoke to Ian first. "Good morning, John."

"Good morning."

"Mr. Nick was telling me that Jasper Maskelyn's opened a new show. He has tickets to this afternoon's performance."

"The Magician?" Ian was bouncing up and down in his chair.

"The very one," Jeffrey said. "Would you like to see him?"

"I've always wanted to see him."

"Excellent. Mr. Nick will take you, then, while Mummy comes to the office with me today. Is that all right?"

Marion shot Jeffrey a look. He ignored her, still focused on Ian. Ian looked mildly disappointed, but it was clear that the thought of seeing Maskelyn perform made up for missing the day with Marion. He ate a meditative piece of bacon.

"Yes," he said. Then he turned to Marion. "I'll tell you about it at tea, Mummy."

She nodded, trying to look as though she'd been aware of Jeffrey's plans all along. "I can't wait to hear, Ian. You'll have a lovely time."

She lowered her eyes, flustered, to her cup and drank more of the tea. Lisianthus, she noticed. The lilies had been replaced by lisianthus. When she had drained her tea, she looked up again and saw that Jeffrey was waiting for her. He was wearing a subdued grey suit, white shirt, and darker grey tie. He looked at his watch. "Have you finished?"

She pushed back her chair and stood. "Yes."

She bent over and gave Ian and hug and a kiss. He smelled of soap and bacon. Then she looked hard at Nick, who lowered his eyes, and she left the room. Jeffrey followed her, gathered up his hat, and opened the front door for her. The Packard was waiting for them at the bottom of the steps.

"Ordinarily I walk," he said. "The Museum is less than two miles away, and this time of year it's a pleasant half hour outside." He opened the door to the car and waited for her to slide into the back seat. "But it looks as though it may rain today. And I don't want you to tire yourself."

She turned to the window as Jeffrey moved into the seat beside her. "The Museum?"

"Yes. My office. I want your advice."

She glanced at his face, but it was unreadable. Turned back to the window. "Oh."

It took fifteen minutes in the early morning traffic to reach what she still thought of as the new Edward VII galleries on the north front of the Museum. The driver opened Marion's door, and she exited while Jeffrey emerged from the other side. Jeffrey walked around the back of the car, took her arm and led her to a small side entrance to the building, at ground level, apart from the public hall. He used his keys to open the door and waited for her to precede him through it. As they walked down the modern, well-lit corridor, she examined the offices and the occasional laboratory. Glanced up at him again, hoping for some sort of explanation, but his expression was still blank.

Near the end of the corridor, he unlocked a second door. She walked through it as well, and then she stopped at the edge of what appeared to be a meeting room. The floor was carpeted in institutional beige, there was a long, rectangular conference table surrounded by comfortable if not ornate chairs, and pleasant light from two clerestory windows illuminated a chalkboard along one side of the room.

Jeffrey switched on a standing lamp at the other end of the room. When he did so, she saw that half of the table was covered with books and papers. A closer look confirmed for her that they were manuscript volumes from her library. Her Idrisi was there as well, open, the pages held in place by her necklace. Jeffrey had filled a writing pad with his notes. He had also numbered a series of file folders and stacked them into organized piles along the side of the table.

When Marion didn't move, Jeffrey walked back to her, took her arm again, and sat her in a chair at the end of the table. He sat across from her and pulled a pile of the folders toward him. "I'd much prefer to talk about the Idrisi," he said. "But I have a feeling you'll lie to me if I start with that." He rested his hand, palm down, on the folders. "So we'll start here instead."

He opened two folders and positioned them next to one another in front of him. "Not all of the material from Baquba has arrived yet," he told her. "In fact, most of it is still being crated and sent along. But I've asked the cataloguers to flag for me anything that looks out of place—anachronistic— when it comes in. They're estimating now that approximately ten percent of the material doesn't belong. It's a small amount, comparatively, but it's telling. It seems that this library of yours was never sealed up in the thirteenth century, only to be rediscovered once you, and you alone, had decoded that *qasida*. On the contrary, the papers here," he tapped his finger on the folders, "point to visitors popping in and out of it across centuries. With quite the uptick in recent years."

She swallowed and didn't say anything.

"No," he laughed, "I didn't think you'd have anything to say."

The smile left his face abruptly. "The pages I've found most interesting have been those with marginal markings that accumulate over the more recent years." He looked down at a sheet of vellum in the folder in front of him. "This leaf, for example, which is disconnected from any complete volume I've yet to find, has marginalia that my experts have identified as sixteenth-, seventeenth-, and eighteenth-century." He looked back up at her. "But your handwriting, twentieth-century, also appears near the bottom here." He pointed. "As does Tariq's." He pointed again. "There."

She shook her head. "No. You're incorrect. That's not his writing."

"He's been dead for nearly a decade, Marion, and you're still letting him manipulate you? You're still trying to protect him?" He raised his eyebrows. "I don't know whether to be angrier as your husband or your handler."

"You're neither," she said. "You never have been."

"Sadly, I'm both. Even if merely for show. Which is what makes this conversation so very difficult." He put his fingertips on his forehead and looked back down at the file. "This is not my strength, I admit it. I'm not a codebreaker. But unfortunately, the codebreakers we do have are weak in medieval Arabic and Turkish. So I've had a go at these pages myself. For lack of a better alternative." He glanced up at her. "Luckily, I do know Tariq's writing style."

He tapped the page with his finger. "If one reads this," he said, "alongside *this*," he extracted a thin volume from the second folder, "and if one then applies them, together, to this list of what turn out to be names, places, and dates—now in your handwriting—things—almost like magic," his voice was taunting, "fall into order. Despite my yeoman-like effort, however, I'm missing at least half to three quarters of the complete message. Still, though, let me tell you what I *have* managed to decode."

"No." She didn't want to hear it. She fought the impulse, childish, to cover her ears.

He was more tired than triumphant. "Item one," he read, "Henry Sinclair Horne, 1929, an attack of some sort while he was out shooting on his estate in Scotland; Item two, our friend Gilbert Clayton, 1930, heart attack, Iraq; Item three, Horace Smith-Dorrien, 1930, car accident, Wiltshire— ordered by the French?" He shook his head. "Item four, Henry Segrave, 1930, accident in a speedboat. Why on earth would the Germans want to get rid of a speedboat racer? Well, we'll have time for the details later. Item five, *against* the Soviets, support for Faizal Maksum and Ibrahim Bay fighting the occupation of Tajikistan in 1929; Item six, and now on *behalf* of the Soviets, Ibrahim Bay dies, 1931; Item seven, an attempt, unsuccessful, on Yakov Peters, *against* the Soviets, 1930, Tashkent; And then, item eight, as we already know, Badoglio, 1933, Messina—another botched attempt—and item nine, Faisal, 1933, Bern—a bit more successful. Heart attack."

He stopped speaking and looked up at her for a reaction. After a tense moment, she spoke. "You have no evidence of my involvement in this," she said. "You don't even have evidence that these deaths weren't accidents—except for Clayton's and, *you* say, but *I* would never admit it, Faisal's. You're speculating. The fact that you found that paper in the library doesn't mean that the library is related to it. Anyone could have left it there. The library has been open, if selectively, as you've said, for years now. The library is an archive—"

"An 'archive' is right," he interrupted. "I've never seen its match." He pushed his hair off his forehead and looked hard at her. "You'd like evidence? Very well." He pulled a third folder toward him and opened it. "That part was easy once I'd begun to decipher the list." He lifted a page out of the folder. "These are your travel itineraries between 1929 and 1933, generously provided by the Home Office." He set the page in front of her. "Are you going to claim that it's a coincidence that you were present, within a few miles, at every one of these tragic—"

"Not Faisal."

"No," he conceded. "Not Faisal. But that simply makes it more interesting, doesn't it? Who was Dr. Bailey's proxy while she was otherwise engaged? As I said, though, we'll discuss the details in a moment. For now, you might enjoy these photographs."

He tossed a folder across the table at her. She looked up at him suspiciously and opened it. Examined the glossy prints. Went through three before she didn't want to see any more and closed the folder.

"Our people were taking snaps of you in a routine manner the whole time. Nothing stood out as they sent the pictures home. But now that I know what to look for—"

"Yes," she said tersely. "All right."

"What the hell are you doing?" He still sounded tired. "There isn't even any ideological continuity here. Is it pure bloody-mindedness? Is that really all it is?"

She looked down at the table, silent.

"Of course you're not going to answer." He hadn't raised his voice. "I'm not even sure that you know the answer. But let me tell you, Marion, if I float this material on the market, you'll be dead within the week. You may not believe that the Italians want you for Badoglio and Graziani—after all, you failed. But I can promise you that when Stalin's people discover that you've been working against them as much as for them, when *our* people discover that you've let the damned French at one of our most respected and spotless war heroes, when, for all I know, the French discover that some particularly despicable branch of our own war service has been using you—"

She glanced up at him quickly and then back down at the table.

"Oh no," he said. "Oh, good lord, I don't even want to know." He collected himself. "The point, Marion, is that *now* you do need protection. And you and I are, once again, going to make a deal."

Her brows rushed together, and she began to say something, but he interrupted her. "No. You're going to listen to me. Because what I found *most* interesting as I made my way through this fetid swamp of medieval literature dressed up as kill lists, or kill lists dressed up as medieval literature—it's all so circular and twisted in on itself that I'm having difficulty understanding what is cause and what effect at this point." He placed his fingertips on his forehead again. "Which, granted, opens an interesting, if sickening, window onto *your* world—"

"You were saying?" His volatility was frightening her.

He took another breath. "Yes. Thank you." He looked back up at her. "I was saying that what I found interesting was that of all of these manuscripts, your Idrisi is the most—well used—of all. Centuries worth of notes and markings. All stacked up on top of one another."

She watched him carefully. She wasn't going to help him. But she was becoming frightened now that he no longer needed help. His lips twitched in something like a smile when he saw her altered expression.

"I've had the manuscript checked and re-checked," he said slowly. "It's twelfth-century. Original. Precisely what it purports to be—the lost *Gardens of Humanity*. But it's also more than that. It's a palimpsest. A palimpsest, however, that's not meant to be written over completely. Because all of the notes written across it—not just yours and Tariq's from the twentieth century—but markings from the thirteenth, fourteenth, fifteenth, sixteenth and so on centuries forward, refer to one another." He indicated a fourth set of files. "I've taken a log of their connections. This manuscript is a living text. Dynamic." He held her eyes, deliberately drawing out the moment. "The problem, Dr. Bailey, is that I can't quite determine what it's all in aid of. There's a power lurking beneath that writing. A power that cuts across nearly eight hundred years. But I don't know what it's for." He paused again. "Care to enlighten me?"

"You're doing so well on your own," she said. "I'd feel terrible stepping in and wrecking your well-deserved sense of accomplishment."

"I like you best when you're cornered."

"I'm not cornered," she said. "You've taken what look to be some impressive and thorough notes on the manuscript. Well done. I'm not certain what that has to do with me."

"You mentioned something in Durham about the Assassins," he said. "About how this manuscript challenges traditional interpretations of what they were doing?"

"Did I? I suppose I might have. So much has happened since then, it's difficult for me to remember."

"Marion," he said. "I'm enjoying this exchange. Truly I am. But surely you realize that your situation is no different to what it was before you walked into this room. In fact, it's worse. You're not in a position to play this sort of game."

She didn't reply.

He folded his hands together on top of the table. "I've decoded enough of this document now to have a feel for what it is hiding. But, and I acknowledge this freely, I'm not as good as you are. I can't read it well enough to take further steps. I need you for that."

"Well that's your own damned—"

"No," he interrupted. "It's your problem. But it's also your choice. If you cooperate, I'll destroy the evidence of your complicity in these various accidents. No one will know. I'll confirm to the office that you've always been my field agent. Just deep under wraps. They'll congratulate you on your service and think no more about you. And I'll release you from this marriage. You'll be free. No more attachments. No more surveillance. If John wants to visit, and if you're willing, I'll always be happy to have him. But there will be no pressure on you to comply." He looked down at his hands. "If you refuse to cooperate, you'll remain under my protection in London until you've had the opportunity to reconsider your choice. Mrs. Bowen will be delighted." He paused again. "And finally, if you run away, I'll shop the evidence of your betrayal of what looks to be nearly every Asian and European intelligence service in operation today to those who take an interest in such things. Of course, I'd also alert my own people beforehand—and I have no doubt that we would manage to collect you before the frenzy began. But once we did, you'd never be at liberty again. Permanent protection. Permanent house arrest. I have a property in the north that ought to suit your temperament well."

She was also looking at his folded hands. "There's a fourth option," she said.

"What is that?"

"I run away, you publish the documents, and you don't alert your people. I take my chances."

He shook his head. "Absolutely not."

"Why?"

"I don't want you dead."

"Why not?"

"Because you're the mother of my child. And I like you."

"*What?*"

"I like you." His smile hid a touch of remorse. "I'd be upset if they killed you."

"Oh, for God's sake, Jeffrey—"

"I've told you, it's not an option. And there's no way I'm letting you walk away free—if that's what you're thinking of asking next—without getting something in return." He unfolded his hands and began re-organizing the files. "So, which of the first three options do you choose?"

She knew there was only the one. "I was close to finishing my translation of the Idrisi that last night in Messina. I'll have results for you in less than a week."

"Thank you." He held her eyes for a moment longer. "I can tell that you'll try to mislead me. I would lose respect for you if you didn't. But please, Marion—don't push this too far."

"Is that all?"

"No. Before we go, I want you to answer a few questions about the manuscript for me." He watched her expression carefully. "I know the answers already to some of them. I don't know the answers to others. Your job will be not to trip up. Understood?"

She nodded.

"First," he said, "did Idrisi compose this text in the twelfth century to communicate with the Assassins?"

"Yes."

"Are the new markings in the text every century or so additional orders or commands?"

"No."

"What are they?"

"The manuscript is a key. Members use it to encrypt and decrypt instructions. Every half century, someone must re-set the key code and alert the members. The markings facilitate that."

"So the Assassins didn't disappear? They're still in operation?"

She looked down and didn't speak.

"Fair enough," he said. "Is the lost silver globe or disk the mechanism for resetting this code?"

She glanced up at him, sharply, and he smiled. "Perfect. Thank you. So that's our target. Where is it?"

"I don't know." All she felt was dull resentment.

"But you'll know within a week. Or, at least, so you claim." He stood. "We've made progress today."

She stood as well. "We're finished?"

"Yes." He walked to the door and held it open for her. "I'll have the manuscript and any reference material you might want sent to the house. It will be waiting for you in your room." He watched her profile as she passed him into the corridor. "Do you think John enjoyed the magic show?" he asked, taking his place beside her. As though their previous conversation had never happened.

She was hugging her waist, looking down. She nodded. He put his arm across her shoulders, affectionate, and she stiffened. Shivered when they reached the door to the outside and walked into the drizzle. Blamed it on the drop in temperature, hinting at autumn.

*W*HEN they returned to Chester Terrace, Ian and Nick were still out. Jeffrey retreated into his study to work, and Marion wandered, at loose ends, into the drawing room. Neither was interested in lunch or tea. Sometime in the early afternoon, the front door opened, and steps sounded on the stairway, entered her bedroom, and descended. Curious, she walked up, opened the door, and examined the room.

The work desk had now come into its own. Arranged on it with tidy regularity, were her Idrisi, an unnecessarily complete selection of dictionaries and reference volumes, a stack of loose blank paper, and a collection of sharpened pencils. She approached the desk and ran her fingertips over the manuscript. Then, still standing, as if only half-conscious of her movements, she turned a few pages of the book. Her tracing from the Messina Cathedral remained protected inside the volume.

She glanced at the window overlooking the park. Still light. Annoyed with herself for her addiction to this work, and yet unable to stop herself, she pulled back the chair and sat at the desk. With the manuscript in front of her again, the apprehension that had burdened her since she'd been picked up in Messina finally lifted. Smiling to herself, she selected a pencil and began working. Three hours later, when the unmistakable sound of Ian barreling into the reception hall floated up to the bedroom, she was confident that she'd have, at the very least, a location in which to begin her search for the disk. She set the pencil on the leaf of paper she'd been using for notes and walked down the stairs to greet Ian.

Ian was bursting with information about the magic show, but Mrs. Bowen and the nanny bundled him off to a bath before he could start his monologue, assuring him that he could tell Mummy about it at dinner. She hugged him and told him that she couldn't wait to hear. He left without protest, satisfied by the fact that he'd have two audiences if he told Mrs. Bowen about it now and Marion about it at dinner. Marion nodded to Nick, who had taken up his hat to leave. When he was out the door, she turned to Jeffrey. "I know where it is."

"Already? You couldn't have been working for more than three hours."

"Nonetheless. I'd like to finish this. So that I can—" She faltered.

"—be free." He half smiled. "Yes." He stood aside to let her precede him up the stairs to the study. "Do you know? I think you may be a witch after all. And I say that with complete seriousness."

When they reached the study, he closed the door, and they sat as they had three days before. She folded her hands on her lap. "Reading Abbey."

"That simplifies things. Not more than an hour's drive from here. Could you tell me why?"

"Yes." Wanting to get it over with. "I had already suspected the coincidence of the disk vanishing at the same time that Thomas Brown left Sicily for England. There were hints scattered throughout the first set of marginal notes on the manuscript—from the early 1200s—that Brown had taken it with him. The problem was that it didn't resurface. There was no mention of it appearing again—in England or Italy."

She looked at her hands in her lap. "But even odder to me was that none of the commentators from the 1200s, 1300s, 1400s, or onward, were bothered by its disappearance. In fact, their notes took as a tacit given its continuing presence. So I concluded that it couldn't have been lost completely. It must have been hidden—and its location must have been revealed only to a small group of initiates. People with access to the library. In Baquba." She paused. "Tariq understood that at once. The moment he found the manuscript."

"I don't doubt that he did." Jeffrey's voice was bland. Disdain beneath it.

"Do you want me to continue?"

"By all means."

She blinked, annoyed, and resumed. "There was mention, in a note from the 1400s that if the trail went cold, an initiate who knew what he or she was looking for could pick it up again in the Messina Cathedral. I decided that it would be worth investigating. And when I entered the Cathedral, it was laughably obvious. A lone, 'meaningless' string of Arabic characters, kept intact over the centuries even when the rest of the building had been destroyed, shouting out from the edge of the apse. I made a tracing of it. That evening, in Messina, I found that it was a message encrypted in the original code from the 1100s. A short cut that allowed a reader to start back at the beginning. And, this afternoon, I did."

"Once I'd re-translated the key," she continued when he didn't reply, "it flagged a second figure in the story. Richard Palmer."

He was nodding. "Not Thomas Brown."

"No," she confirmed. "Thomas Brown, as Henry II's almoner, remains obscure once he's returned to England. But Richard Palmer is extraordinarily flamboyant throughout the 1170s and 1180s. He's also something of a conduit between Sicily and England. For objects. And information. Once I'd worked my way back through the text with my reconfigured code, and once I had Palmer in mind, I found the connection."

"Which was?" Jeffrey was speaking to her with something like friendliness. He hadn't bothered to school his face into its customary detached expression.

"In 1185," she told him, "Henry II met with the Patriarch of Jerusalem in Reading Abbey. The purpose of the meeting was to discuss the succession crisis in the Holy Land and support for the crusades. But the Patriarch famously brought with him a collection of sacred objects—and not only from Palestine. Also from Italy. There's mention, in contemporary accounts, of him depositing a silver disk in the Abbey as part of his negotiations. No one thought twice about it. He was trying to muster as much support for his cause as he could, and leaving behind a few relics would have helped with that. But what's important is that there was no mention of the disk *before* he had reached the Abbey. Which means he hadn't brought it with him. Instead, he'd revealed something that was already there. And, even more important, Richard Palmer had been in Messina when the Patriarch had travelled through Italy."

She looked up at him. "I'm confident, based on the inscription in the Cathedral, that Palmer was an initiate. I believe that he signaled to the Patriarch that it was time to bring the disk, already hidden in the Abbey, into the open—at least for those who would be looking out for it. It was nearly 1200. Almost fifty years since Idrisi had completed the text. Time to shift the key code and alert the association that a new key was in place."

He shook his head. "I don't understand."

"The *Gardens of Humanity*," she explained, "is a key. Initiates with a mission refer to it to decipher their orders. But it is also nearly eight hundred years old. The association may be secretive, but it can't rely naively on the total discretion of its members. People break. Or are betrayed. And so, at intervals, every twenty-five to forty years, the key is shifted. Changed. That means that every forty years, at the outside, a member of the group must find the disk, activate it, determine the new code for the key, and disseminate that code throughout the network. When Henry II met the Patriarch of Jerusalem in Reading Abbey, it was a perfect cover for introducing the first shift. Since then, someone has visited a few times every century to activate it again. It's still there. Somewhere. And the broken arch—"

"This is from Tariq's letter to you?"

She felt her throat contract and nodded. "Yes. The broken arch is where we begin looking for it."

He didn't speak for a few seconds. Then he said: "I'm impressed, Marion. I never cease to marvel at your—quality of mind." He thought to himself. "That is, I never cease to marvel at it when it isn't landing you in some inane muddle."

She stood abruptly. "I've told you what you want to know. I'm—"

"Yes," he said. "And I'm grateful to you for that. But we still haven't finished." His blank look had returned. "Now we must find a way to retrieve this object without it leading to your arrest, execution, abduction, or God knows what else." Faintly exasperated, he watched her standing with her hands clasped in front of her, not speaking. "Would you wait a moment before fleeing the room, so that we can at least begin to develop a strategy?"

She nodded, but she didn't sit down. Instead, she walked, tense, to the window and looked out over the park. Jeffrey remained sitting. He spoke to her rigid back. "We'll go to Reading the day after tomorrow. But before we do that, I want to fulfill my end of this bargain. There's a crush at the Museum tomorrow night—drinks reception and dancing. Quite a few people from the office will be attending, and it will be an ideal place to debut you as triumphant talent back from the field. If we play it properly, they will congratulate you on your part in landing the material from Baquba—and that will be all. But Marion, to make this work, you must behave yourself with them. And you must be *happy*. Put away the gothic despair. Do you think you can handle that?"

She nodded again, still looking out the window.

"Good," he said. "You'll also keep up the act when we go to the Abbey the next day. We'll have an audience—small but observant. You *cannot* attempt any of your idiot ploys. These are professionals. And they will already smell a rat. If you raise their suspicions, I'll be unable to protect you." He looked dissatisfied, as though he were about to say more, but he didn't. All he asked was: "do you understand?"

"Yes."

He glanced at a clock set on the mantle above the fireplace. "Then I suppose that's the best we can do." He stood as well. "You'll want time to dress for dinner."

"I'm really not hungry, Jeffrey."

"John wants to tell you about the magic show." He was walking to the door to open it for her.

"Ian and I can eat in the nursery."

"We'll dine together as usual," he said inexorably. "As a family." Then he stood to the side to let her through the door.

She walked past him, her eyes downcast. Climbed the stairs and returned to the dressing room.

SHE maintained enough of a veneer of tranquility—or Ian was involved enough in his praise of Maskelyne's act—to make it through dinner without her disquiet showing. And the next day, she and Nick kept him occupied in the park with sailboats on the pond and pastries at tea rooms until well into the afternoon. When they returned to the house, and when Nick had taken his leave, Mrs. Bowen appeared to escort Ian to the nursery. Ian knew that Marion and Jeffrey would be out for the evening, and it was a commentary—to Marion, a dismal one—on Ian's comfort with their situation that he hardly objected at all. She could tell that he was looking forward to his night with Mrs. Bowen.

Jeffrey returned late from the office and walked straight up to his rooms to dress. And although Marion had disappeared into her own room when she heard him enter, she couldn't quite bring herself to find clothing for the reception. Instead, she shut the door and sat at the work desk. Her Idrisi was still on the desktop, and she idly turned a few pages, drawing comfort from its familiarity.

She was still perusing it, wearing the dress she had worn with Ian in the park, when Jeffrey knocked on her door and then entered without waiting for her to reply. He was wearing a black dinner jacket with wide collar wings, black tie, and a waistcoat. Frustrated when he saw that she hadn't changed. "Do you need help?" Deliberately obnoxious.

"No." She stood and tried unsuccessfully to smooth the wrinkled skirt of her day dress. "I lost track of the time."

He went into her dressing room. "Nonetheless, since I'm here—"

She followed him. "Jeffrey, I can choose something appropriate myself. I'm not that hopeless."

He was examining the dresses hanging from the rack. Without speaking, he turned and tossed her an expressive look. Then he resumed his search. "Ah," he said, finding what he was seeking. "This."

He held it out to her. It was something in white silk with wide black accents. She took it and looked at the label. Augustabernard. It meant nothing to her. He left the dressing room with exaggerated discretion, and she mechanically changed into the dress.

It was sleeveless and bias cut to the floor, which meant that it clung to her hips and legs. The neck and back were both low, with a small bow at the base of her spine, and she had to keep from moving her arm across her chest in an unconscious protective gesture. She wasn't certain she could wear it in a crowd without needing to escape. But she also didn't want to have an argument about it with Jeffrey. She found shoes that seemed to match it and that weren't impossible to wear, and she slipped her feet into them.

She walked into the bedroom to fix her hair and found him sitting on the bed, waiting for her. Stopped, surprised, but then mastered herself and continued to the dressing table to hide her confusion. She had expected him to meet her in the drawing room. Without speaking, she sat in front of the mirror and began brushing her hair into her usual chignon. He watched her for a few moments, and then he shook his head.

"No," he said. "Wear it up. In a twist. Like in Istanbul."

She turned to face him, holding her pins. "You remember that?"

"I'm trained to remember detail." He nodded at the mirror. "Wear it up."

She forced down her retort and did as he asked. She wasn't, she reminded herself, going to argue with him this evening. When she had finished, she stood, doubtful, waiting.

He stood as well and reached into the pocket of his jacket. "I have something for you."

He handed her a flat velvet box. She took it, her doubt blossoming into discomfort, and opened it. It was an elaborate antique necklace, dull gold, with large blue stones. She shut the box and tried to give it back to him. "I can't—"

"It's not a request. Wear it."

"But—"

"It complements the dress," he said. Then he looked pointedly at her hand. "And it matches the ring."

She also looked, reluctant, at her hand. She still hadn't removed his ring. She could never explain to herself why she wore it, and she was always weakly stupefied to see it on her finger. Without speaking, she opened the box again and began to extract the necklace.

"Here," he said taking it from her. "Let me help you."

She turned away from him, and he fastened it around her throat. After he had finished and stepped back from her, she could feel a trace memory of his fingertips against the back of her neck. Had to stop herself from rubbing the spot where he had touched her. When she faced him again, confused, she could tell from his expression that he knew what she was thinking. Irritated, but refusing to be baited, she walked out of the bedroom and down the stairs. He followed, and she could sense his complacent satisfaction all the way into the reception hall. Wondered when she'd be old enough, or confident enough, not to let that sort of moment fluster her.

The servant was waiting for them at the foot of the stairs, and she handed Marion a fur wrap, which Marion managed to take without more than a fraction of a second of hesitation. Then she handed Jeffrey an overcoat and his hat. He nodded at her as she opened the door for them, and he rested his hand on Marion's lower back and guided her down the stairs. The Packard was waiting for them again, but this time the driver was out and had the door open. She and Jeffrey sat in the back seat, the driver closed the door, and the car moved into the evening traffic toward Bloomsbury.

"Marion," he said, "to make this work, you must look less like you're being led to the dungeons to be shown the machines." He was examining his open cigarette case. Satisfied, he shut it, slipped it back into his jacket pocket, and looked at her.

"I feel ill," she said. She had no idea how she was going to be courteous to Jeffrey's colleagues. They were everything that she loathed. And despite Jeffrey's mocking praise of her field work, she was no operative. She couldn't dissemble.

"Yes, you would prefer Torquemada to the reprehensible architects of our own evil empire, wouldn't you?" His smile was lopsided. When she didn't say anything, he put his hand over hers and squeezed it. "They're benign as people, dear. They pride themselves on their civility."

"If you want me to survive this," she snapped back at him, "you can't take this tone. I'm not one of you. And if your only interest is in seeing me fail, then you might as well skip the intermediary steps and have me arrested straight away."

"Forgive me," he said, sounding almost contrite. "But surely you understand my giddiness. This is the first time—and, if all goes well, likely the last—that we'll appear in public together as husband and wife. I'm filled with a warm glow—"

"Stop it."

He was laughing in earnest now. "You have no sense of humor."

"No," she said. "I don't. I hate this."

He moved closer to her in the back seat and put his arm around her. "I adore that you hate it." He kissed her lightly, teasing, on the neck. "What am I going to do without you? But I give you my word—it will be over quickly. We'll do the rounds to have you seen by those who must see you, we'll dance once for the sake of appearances, and then I'll take you home. We have an early day tomorrow. They'll understand."

She nodded, and he removed his arm. A few minutes later, the car came to a stop at the foot of the brightly lit steps and pillars of the main entrance to the museum. The driver opened the door for them, and they left the car, walked up the steps, and then went briskly, uninterested in perusing the exhibits along the way, to the Reading Room. They left their coats just inside the door.

Drinks and food on ice had already been set with smug good humor on the catalogue desks. A band, in the center of the room, directly under the top of the dome, was playing dance music. The room was packed with philanthropists and celebrity scholars observing one another and beginning to venture out to the makeshift dance floor. When she passed through the swinging doors, Marion faltered and almost stumbled.

Jeffrey put a supportive hand under her elbow. Bending a touch, he whispered in her ear. "Into the belly of the beast, my beloved."

She turned to glare at him, but when she saw his teasing eyes, she realized that he was trying in his perverse way to comfort her. Gave him a weak smile instead and walked into the room. A waiter appeared out of nowhere, and they each took a flute of champagne. She drank a few grateful sips and tried to get a feel for the room. Eventually she gave up. She was out of her depth, and it was useless to try to read the situation. She'd be forced to rely on Jeffrey, which was not a prospect she relished.

He looked down at her, smiling, still reading her thoughts. "Are you ready?" he asked. "There are no more than two or three people you must meet in person. The rest will watch and draw the appropriate conclusions. If you'd like, we'll start with the easiest."

She nodded and drank more of her champagne. "Yes."

"Good girl."

She looked up at him, astonished, and he seemed abashed.

"I apologize," he said. "I enter a room like this and revert to type." He cleared his throat. "Very well, Dr. Bailey. First, then, let's meet Professor Richard Maugham. A member of the board of trustees. And director, informally, of my section."

They made their way to the other side of the reading room, where Jeffrey caught the eye of a short, bald man, almost completely round, wearing tails and a monocle. He was flushed with drink, but even from where they were standing, Marion could see that he was, for all professional purposes, completely sober. She was already afraid by the time he had beamed at Jeffrey and pushed his way toward them through the crowd.

Sober she could understand. Drunk she could also understand. But drunk and still cold and sharp made her nervous. She was also having difficulty not staring at his monocle. When he reached them, shook Jeffrey's hand, and bowed, correctly, in her direction, she looked instead at the top of his oddly shiny head.

"Willcox, my dear boy," he said, exuding nothing but childlike delight at encountering him. "You look more than well."

"As do you, Professor Maugham." He turned toward Marion. "I don't believe you've met my wife, Marion Bailey."

"Bailey?"

"Dr. Bailey," Jeffrey supplied.

"Ah." Maugham tapped his chin with his fingertip. Then he turned eyes as teasing as Jeffrey's in Marion's direction. "So difficult to choose, isn't it? Dr. Bailey or Lady Willcox? Titles can be terribly limiting. Those who don't face this problem rarely realize how troublesome it is."

Marion was shocked, if entertained, by his impropriety. "I hadn't ever considered it, to be honest. I've always simply felt myself more of a scholar than a—" She stopped, embarrassed.

"—than a lady," Maugham finished for her. "And good for you. Willcox here nearly bit their hand off when they dangled that baronetcy in front of him. Couldn't have cared less about the hard earned D.Phil. Such as it was."

"I protest." Jeffrey was laughing. "And have I not put both titles to good use? You do me an injustice."

"Hmph," Maugham grunted. "Yes, I suppose it's possible that I'm merely working through my jealousy. It's not every day that one of my people brings home the find of a lifetime without even alerting me that it's on its way. Didn't even give me a chance to take credit for it. Although," he turned back to Marion, "I understand that the real congratulations must go to you, Dr. Bailey. How many years did you spend in the field setting the groundwork for this? Eight? Nine?"

"Since Cambridge, really." Jeffrey wasn't going to let her say anything that might trap her later. She glanced at him, grateful, and he moved closer to her, protective. "We met at Cambridge."

"Ah yes." Maugham flagged a waiter for another flute of champagne. "You both worked with Ronny Dickinson, yes? Poor Ronny." He raised the glass into the middle distance and drained almost half of it. "May he Rest in Peace. We were contemporaries, you know. He got into a fistfight once on the Magdalene Bridge over some girl. They say he bit right through his rival's ear before falling into the river himself. Lucky he didn't drown. But it all came out in the end. The unfortunate boy with half an ear eventually took a Chichele chair at All Souls in Oxford. And, as you know, Ronny ruled Cambridge Oriental Studies with an iron fist until he finally keeled over at his desk. As he would have wanted it."

Marion, despite herself, was warming to Maugham. So much so that she had to remind herself that it was his job to trick people into precisely this sort of friendly feeling. He had a terrifying ability to open up cozy, confessional spaces in the midst of an anonymous crowd—an ability that was almost hypnotic. She took another quick sip of her champagne to keep from speaking. Jeffrey nodded to her, infinitesimally, in approval.

Before the lull in their conversation became awkward, another colleague of Jeffrey's appeared at Maugham's side. Nick's age, although without any of Nick's healthy, if repressed, strength. His complexion was sallow and pitted with acne that he tried to cover with unsuccessful facial hair. His dull, brownish hair was greasy, and his clothing—though obviously expensive—didn't fit. It bagged over his thin shoulders and then almost failed to button across his stomach. He smiled, disdainful, at Jeffrey.

"Willcox," he said. "I didn't think you'd make it."

"Wouldn't miss it for the world, Thacker."

They hated one another with an intensity that Marion could feel physically. She wanted to recoil. Risked a glance at Maugham to see how he was reacting, and then she felt alone in the room. In an unguarded second, the mask of genial donnish misbehavior had slipped. Maugham's expression was hard. And pleased. He enjoyed the fact that they disliked one another.

Maugham turned to Marion as though he had felt her watching him. And when their eyes met, he didn't alter his expression. Instead, he raised a malign eyebrow, no longer teasing. She dropped her own eyes and grabbed Jeffrey's arm. Jeffrey turned to her, perplexed, and then, smiling, looked back at Thacker. "Let me introduce my wife, Thacker. Dr. Marion Bailey."

Thacker turned his sneer in her direction. "A pleasure, Dr. Bailey."

"Mr. Thacker." Her voice was hoarse.

"Now, now." Maugham was all harmless joviality again. "Let's not have any fisticuffs in the Reading Room. Wouldn't do at all. Perhaps we ought to consider the sad story of Ronny Dickinson's dip in the River Cam as a cautionary tale."

Jeffrey was the first to recover. "And I, for one, have little interest in donating any part of my ear to the Museum's collection." He nodded to Thacker and smiled at Maugham. "If you'll excuse us, I haven't yet taken the opportunity to dance with my wife. It's rare that they allow this sort of exuberance under the dome. One feels obliged to take advantage of it."

"By all means, Willcox." Maugham was beaming again. "Dr. Bailey, I look forward to continuing our conversation tomorrow morning. Reading Abbey?"

She nodded, not knowing where to look. Maugham turned to Thacker. "You'll be coming along too, my boy? With the fair Lucy in tow?"

"Wouldn't miss it for the world." Thacker mimicked Jeffrey with narrowed eyes.

"Lucy?" Marion looked, bewildered, from Maugham to Jeffrey.

Jeffrey was already walking her, unhurried, toward the dance floor. "Miss Peters. Codebreaker. They thought she might help should we get stuck." He cast a quick, professional glance about the room. "You'll like her. She's got a brilliant way with crossword puzzles."

"Crossword puzzles?" They were out of earshot of Maugham and Thacker now.

"Yes," he said. "The new service. It's how they recruit nowadays. Makes one wonder what the world is coming to."

They had reached the dance floor, and Jeffrey put his hand on her lower back. She rested her own hand on his shoulder, and they made a pretense of enjoying themselves. The band was playing "I've Got the World on a String."

"Maugham doesn't like you," she said.

"Maugham doesn't like anyone. Occupational hazard. He wouldn't survive if he did."

She was silent for a few moments. Then she asked: "doesn't that scare you?"

"Of all the people he dislikes, he dislikes me the least. If that makes sense. He also appreciates my results. He has no reason to hurt me, and in this business, that's the best we can do."

"If it's so awful, why do you do it?"

"Why do you run about assassinating harmless old men?"

"I—it's—" She wavered.

He pulled her closer to him, enjoying her discomfort. "Ah Marion, you see? Ten years ago—five years ago, even—you wouldn't have hesitated. To bring down the system from within. To free the oppressed natives. To administer a good sharp kick in the shin to the colonial establishment. Now, though—" He shrugged. "One ages. One's certainties fall away. One continues out of habit. And, of course, one takes a bit of professional pride in doing an effective job. I think, in the end, that's all we have. If we're lucky. A small talent—at something—that we can continue to hone when the rest disappears. It's your misfortune that your talent happens to be illegal. And," he mused, "I suppose, it's my misfortune that mine happens to be unethical." He kissed her hand, which he had brought up to his chest. "But that doesn't mean we can't keep trying."

She had clenched the hand that he had kissed into a fist, but she didn't want to make a scene when they were being watched. Although, given the behavior of Maugham and Thacker, she wasn't certain what benefit there was in playing out this farce. Jeffrey's colleagues would undermine her, or Jeffrey, or both of them, regardless of whether they believed his story or not. She tried again. "Neither Maugham nor Thacker trust you. They don't believe you were running me."

"No," he agreed.

"Then what's the point of this?" She pulled away from him, but he drew her back toward him sharply.

"Careful, Marion. We'll wait until the song has finished, and then we'll go. Calmly. In no hurry." He looked over her head to see whether her movement had attracted attention. "Your world is so stark. I have no idea how you live in it. Let me explain the concept of nuance to you." He moved them slowly toward the edge of the throng of dancers. "No, they don't believe me," he said. "And yes, they know I wasn't running you. But they will be willing to accept that story if it supports their own aims. Eventually they will believe it. And then it will become true. Does that make sense?"

"No."

He sighed. "Well, trust me that it makes sense to normal people. To people who don't spend half their time deciphering crumbling manuscripts in obscure dead languages and the other half tossing petrol bombs at the politically impure. All right, my dear?"

She was suddenly overwhelmingly tired. The song was ending, and she looked at him, on the verge of tears. "Please. Can we go now?"

He kissed her forehead. "Poor Marion. Yes, we can go. You did very well."

He looked back and nodded at Maugham across the room, pulled her hand through his arm, and led her out of the Museum. She didn't speak in the car on the way back to Chester Terrace, and when she'd stumbled up the stairs to her bedroom, she only just managed to remove the necklace and peel off the dress. She left the dress in a heap on the floor and then crawled into the bed. Her dread of the next morning didn't interfere with her ability to drop into sleep.

SHE woke at dawn, unable to damp down her excitement. Her dread replaced by the edgy thrill she always felt when she was about to test her work. She drew the curtains from the windows and saw low pregnant rain clouds hanging, dull, over the park. Pleased by the sight.

Reading Abbey was a ruin, destroyed in the mid-sixteenth century by Henry VIII, and then subsequently pilfered for building material until fashionable aesthetes in the late eighteenth century, who had learned to appreciate historical detritus, put a stop to that. If it rained, the area would be a swamp. She blinked. And if her hypothesis about the location of the disk was correct, she'd be digging. Wet soil might help with that.

She turned back toward the room and halted in satisfied disbelief when she saw that she'd be dressed, at least, for the weather. Folded neatly, and resting on the arm of the sofa, were her own clothes. Wool trousers, a cotton shirt, and a light cardigan. Socks and work boots just beneath them on the floor.

Someone must have rifled through her house in Durham to retrieve them. But she was so grateful not to be wearing any of the hateful dresses from the next room that she chose not to dwell on the thought. Merely hoped that Cathy hadn't been frightened when the delegation had arrived at her front door.

Once she had pulled on her clothes, feeling comfortable for the first time since Messina, she walked quietly into the hall and opened the door to Ian's room. He was already awake, and the nanny had him dressed for an outing. She and Mrs. Bowen—the latter taking a rare leave from her duties in the house—had agreed to take him to see Maskelyne a second time.

Ian was thrilled even though it meant that Nick would be coming to Reading with Marion and Jeffrey rather than spending the day with him. He was jumping up and down on the bed, thoughtful despite the bouncing, as though only half conscious of what he was doing. When he saw Marion enter the room, he leapt off the bed into her arms. She stumbled backward.

"Mummy! Good morning. What's for breakfast?"

He slipped to the floor and bounded down the stairs. She turned, bemused, to follow him. "Bacon, I imagine."

"Good!" he called up from the ground floor.

When she entered the dining room, Ian was already sitting at the table, making his way through the pile of bacon. Jeffrey, wearing twill trousers, a white shirt without a tie, and a dark blue pullover, was hidden behind his copy of the *Times*. He folded the paper and put it beside his plate as Marion set her toast and tea next to Ian's. She pulled out a chair to sit.

Jeffrey was frowning and distracted, and his mood infected her. She concentrated on spreading marmalade on her toast. When she glanced up at him again, she noticed that there was now a tortured orchid, white, in the middle of the table. It saddened her, and she looked back down at her plate.

"Good morning," he finally said.

"Good morning." She tried to smile at him.

He turned to Ian. "I understand you're returning to the magic show today, John."

"Yes," Ian's mouth was full, and he was barely understandable. "Mummy read me a book about the rope trick. I'm going to catch him at it this time."

"Won't that ruin it?"

Ian swallowed. "No. It will make it better."

Jeffrey sipped his tea. "Undoubtedly. An unexposed secret is, at best, a provocation."

The atmosphere in the room was making Marion uncomfortable. "Will you tell me about it at tea, Ian?"

"Yes, Mummy. And then we'll read the book again."

The nanny appeared outside the door, and Jeffrey beckoned her into the room. He stood and looked at Marion. "Are you ready? We have a long drive ahead of us."

She nodded and stood as well. Then she bent to kiss Ian, cast another unhappy glance at the tormented orchid, and walked into the reception hall. The maid handed Marion a short tweed jacket—also her own, from Durham—and gave Jeffrey a grey trench coat. Neither wore hats. They walked down the front steps to the Packard, slid into the back seat, and looked out their respective windows. The drive to Reading Abbey would take more than an hour.

After ten minutes on the road, Jeffrey reached into the pocket of his coat and produced her necklace from Alamut. Without a word, he held it out to her. She took it, clasped it for a moment in her hand, and then put it over her head. Let the pendant fall under her cotton shirt.

"Thank you." Her voice was almost inaudible.

"Hmm."

Forty minutes later, as they wound their way toward the center of Reading, Jeffrey spoke to her, still looking out his window. "I have the manuscript itself in the front seat, if you need it."

"I don't," she said. "I know what I'm looking for. The pendant will be sufficient."

"Very well." He was silent for a full minute longer. Then he spoke again. "The office has seen to it that the Abbey will be closed to tourists. It's not an out of the way place. But we ought to have at least three hours to work uninterrupted."

"If my hypothesis is correct," she said, "it shouldn't take longer than fifteen minutes."

For the first time, a hint of a smile passed over his face. "And when have your hypotheses ever been incorrect?"

She wrinkled her forehead and looked back out the window. The car was turning into a drive fronting the Abbey gateway. Where two black government-issue Austin Sevens along with what looked to be a misplaced ambulance were waiting for them. As the car drew to a stop, Jeffrey took her hand. Startled, she blinked at him.

"Marion," he said. "Please. Understand that this is serious."

She pulled back her hand. "I do understand."

She opened her door and stepped out of the car, while Jeffrey did the same on the other side. As they walked toward the gateway, Nick and Maugham emerged from one of the Austins and Thacker and a woman Marion assumed to be Lucy Peters got out of the other. Lucy wasn't more than twenty-three years old. Wearing a red dress, lipstick to match, and a beret. With the look of a keen schoolgirl out on an adventure. Thacker hovered over her possessively, but she herself was casting bold looks at Nick.

Nick, unaware of Lucy, was admiring the architecture. Though his actual purpose was to confirm that the area was free of tourists. When he had finished, he caught Jeffrey's eye and nodded. Jeffrey took a breath and walked through the gate. "Let's get this over with."

Maugham, dressed in an Ulster coat with the cape attached, and looking like a rotund bat, trotted up to walk near Marion. "I understand that Jane Austen attended the Abbey School," he said, examining the picturesque ruins. "Famously unimpressed by the idea that anything of value could be hidden here, wasn't she?"

"Jane Austen didn't know where to look."

Maugham chuckled. "Ah, a fellow traveler. It's not often that one finds an intelligent woman, such as yourself, not soppy over Mr. Darcy." He gazed, worried, up at the gathering rain clouds. "I've always thought her something of a bitch, myself."

Marion stumbled and looked down at him in disbelief. "I'm sorry—I think I misheard—"

He smiled up at her. "No, you heard correctly. And admit it, you agree."

"Yes," Marion said. "She's awful."

"Then we shall be friends." The group had reached the chapter house, the most intact part of the ruin. He stopped and beamed at her. "I'd kiss your hand if I weren't worried about provoking Willcox into a jealous rage."

Jeffrey had seen them talking, and indeed a look somewhere between jealousy and concern had crossed his face. He stalked over to Marion and took her arm. "The broken arch?" he asked, gesturing about him. "There are a number of them—is this the correct one?"

She nodded. "Yes. It will be in the apse. In the same position as it was in the Messina Cathedral." She bit her lip. "I'll be looking for disguised Arabic script. If you could keep them away while I do—"

"We'll wait on the other side of the wall."

When she was certain that the group was out of direct sightline, Marion crossed to the center of the chapter house and tried to orient herself as she had in Messina. Once she was in position, she walked with confidence toward a corner of the ruin and knelt beside the wall, running her fingers along the pitted stone. Pulled the pendant out from inside her shirt and slipped it back over her head.

After a few minutes of work, she spotted a thin, but unmistakably alphabetic, scroll along the bottom of a large stone, and she began to dig into the floor with her hands, breaking her fingernails in the process. Less than three inches down, she found what she was looking for. A clean, functional, and—surprising given its age—well-used keyhole.

She slid her pendant into the slot, and it clicked easily, cleanly. Then she pushed the stone back, and an opening, six inches tall and a little more than six inches wide, appeared in the wall. She lay down on her stomach and peered into it.

The silver disk was there. Hanging upright, a circle, in a large enclosure twelve feet square. She could have shifted it a degree or two simply by reaching into the opening, but she didn't want to risk being caught.

Instead, she would show it as it hung to Jeffrey and Maugham to dispel any lingering suspicions they might have about her cooperation. She hated to let it fall into their hands, but she was confident they'd never know what to do with it. And her organization would have a good twenty-five years to develop a means of accessing it in the Museum. She knew her people. They'd find a way to do so.

More important to her now was a second object that had been left for her in a smaller recess at the base of the disk. She reached into the opening and pulled out a wrapped sheet of vellum. It was an encrypted list of the initiates that had been left in the Abbey when last the key code had shifted. Her task was to decode it and disseminate a message to those who were still alive. They in turn would alert their own recruits of a change in the code and in the location of the disk. She rolled the vellum into a tight cylinder to hide under her cardigan.

"Anything interesting?" It was Maugham.

Her heart began pounding against her chest before she even looked up at him. She jumped to her feet and brushed dirt off her trousers. "Yes." She swallowed. "It's there."

She tried to smile.

Maugham smiled back at her. Thacker was standing next to him with a similar expression on his face. Nick and Lucy were at the far end of the chapter house, pretending not to notice their exchange. Jeffrey had walked to the recess at the base of the wall. He bent over, shaded his eyes, and looked into the darkness.

"It's here," he said. "I can see it. We ought to have some experts with archaeological training get it out."

"I'm delighted, Willcox," Maugham said, still looking at Marion. "But at present, I'm more intrigued by the other part of the trove. Also 'archaeological' then, is it, Dr. Bailey?"

She looked down at the paper in her hand, which she hadn't had time to hide before they saw her. "It—it's a bit of wrapping. Used to protect the silver."

Maugham and Thacker looked at one another, entertained. Jeffrey straightened and was watching Marion with something like fear in his eyes. "Marion—" he started.

"Wrapping?" Maugham interrupted. He was laughing as though she had told him a joke. "Yes."

"May I see it?"

Silently, she held out the vellum. He took it from her and unrolled it. "Hmm," he said. "Miss Peters, would you come here, please?"

Lucy detached herself from Nick and walked, briskly confident, to Maugham. He handed her the sheet. She looked down at it and pursed her lips. "I've told you. I don't decode Mumbo Jumbo. English, German, French, Italian. Number strings. That's it for me."

"Yes, Miss Peters, I understand. But let me just ask you what it looks like. Is it scrap paper? Wrapping?"

She thrust the vellum back at him. "It's a list. You hardly need me to tell you that." She wandered back toward the crumbling arches.

Maugham returned his attention to Marion. "A list? What do you think?"

"I think this is absurd. I told you I'd find the disk. It's there. For you. What else do you want?"

"And I've told you, Dr. Bailey, I'd like to know more about this other artifact. Satisfy an old man's curiosity, would you?"

She stared back at him, angry, not speaking.

Jeffrey took a few more steps toward her. "Marion—" he repeated.

"Ah yes. Willcox." Maugham held the page out to him. "Forgot you were there for a moment. What do you think?"

Jeffrey took the page and scanned it. "It's Arabic script," he said. "Encrypted." He handed the page back to Maugham, but he was looking at Marion. "I'd guess names."

"That's at least some progress, then," Maugham replied. "Would you agree, Dr. Bailey? Is it a list of names?"

"Do you know?" she said, looking thoughtful. "I think I've done Jane Austen a terrible injustice. Looks for all the world like a laundry list to me." She cast him her sweetest smile and turned to leave. Nick was standing behind her. She glared at him and then faced Maugham again.

Maugham glanced over at Jeffrey, still chuckling. "Heavens, Willcox. Your Arabs must be dim indeed to have been fooled by this for ten years. Hardly subtle, is she? Has it occurred to you that she may, after all, not be on our side?"

Jeffrey stared at her, levelly. "Marion," he said, "now would be a good time to demonstrate to these gentlemen," he glanced over at Lucy, leaning bored against a wall at the far end of the ruin, "and lady, where your loyalties lie."

She held his eyes, but didn't speak.

"Why not just one name, Dr. Bailey?" Maugham had switched to his reasonable, rather than congenial, don voice. "As a gesture of good faith."

She turned on him. "So that you can 'collect' him and then torture the rest of the names out of him in one of your squalid cellars? Absolutely not."

Maugham and Thacker exchanged another look.

Then Maugham turned to Jeffrey. "Well, I suppose that settles things—"

Jeffrey stepped forward and took Marion's arm. "Would you give us a minute, Maugham? I want to speak with my wife."

"Five minutes, Willcox. But don't go far, hmm?"

Maugham, Thacker, Nick, and Lucy dispersed discreetly to the outside wall of the chapter house. Once they were gone, Jeffrey dragged Marion to the decaying wall at the other end of the building and pushed her violently against it. Stared down at her, breathing hard. "Marion," he said. "They will kill you. Here. Now. That ambulance outside is to carry away your body. Your dead body. Do you understand?"

She gazed up at him without speaking. He slammed his open hand against the wall next to her head, and she flinched. But she remained silent. "You *cannot* do this," he snarled at her. "You are not this cruel. All he wants is one name. If you give him one name, he'll know that he can work on you, and he'll leave you alive. At least for a few more weeks. You and I will have time to develop another strategy."

She felt tears welling up, but she still refused to talk. He put his hands on her shoulders and shook her. "Say something!"

When she remained silent, he calmed himself. "You can't do this to me." He spoke quietly, now. "You can't."

"To you?" She finally said with a bitter smile. "To *you?*" She felt the tear slide down her cheek. "So you enjoy power, do you, Jeffrey? Well how about this, then? You created me. You created this." She let her eyes wander over the walls of the Abbey. "All of it is your own doing. If you'd left me alone at Cambridge, I'd be a fat, content lecturer now. Two or three monographs on Ilkhanid taxation under my belt. Ten for my closest friends, the rest remaindered. Maybe I'd even have married. Eventually."

She swallowed. "Or later. In Baghdad. If you'd kept away from Tariq and me. Yes, we were dabbling in politics. In the wrong politics. But we were harmless. You knew that we were harmless. You knew that we weren't a threat to what you were doing. We would have grown up. Moved to Paris. Had a—"

She choked and swallowed a sob. "Or in Istanbul. I would have taken a flat in Galata. Lived quietly. Solved my little mysteries. Hovered about the edges of Turkish high society, where I like to be. But instead—" She shook her head quickly, dismissing the memory.

"Or even in Durham. You could have left me to my quaint job. And my boy—"

"You were *assassinating* people."

"Because you had driven me to it. And you needn't have set it up in the way that you did. Pushing me into—into this. But you couldn't resist—"

"Stop it," he ordered her. "This is self-indulgent. This isn't a question of what you or I want. Your son—*Ian*—will miss his mother."

"John," she said quietly, "will understand that his mother did what was necessary."

She lifted her head and kissed him gently on the mouth. Then she moved away from the wall and walked toward the group waiting outside the ruined building. Maugham, Thacker, Nick, and Lucy were filing back through the archway. Nick looked sick, but determined. Lucy looked excited. Thacker, who was carrying a pistol, looked bored. And Maugham looked like the pitiless bureaucrat that he was. The geniality had evaporated.

"All finished?" he asked.

Jeffrey pushed past Marion and stood in front of Maugham. "You can't do this, Maugham. She's mine."

"Your what, Willcox? Your wife? Your agent?"

"Your one true love?" Thacker interjected, smirking. Lucy giggled, and Jeffrey shot her a look as though marking her for future consumption. She paled, took a step back, and then hurried out toward the waiting cars.

"She is more useful alive than she is dead," Jeffrey persisted. "I can make her spill. Give me time."

"Willcox," Maugham said, tired now. "From what I've read of your reports, you've spent close on ten years making her spill, and all it's done is landed our policy in an increasingly chaotic mess."

"A mess? A *mess?* I've brought you forty thousand priceless, and in some cases, unique manuscripts for the library. We've found, less than a hundred miles outside of London, an artifact that scholars have been pursuing for close to a millennium. That list—once it's decoded—will point to an organization that is—"

"Yes, yes," Maugham interrupted. "And that's all very well. You'll get credit for it. I wouldn't be surprised if there's another title in the works for you. But the fact remains that your wife is a traitor. She always has been a traitor. She always will be a traitor. You appear to find that attractive. The office cannot."

"It's more complicated—"

"Dr. Bailey," Maugham said, turning to Marion, who was now flanked by Nick and Thacker. "Would you please give me one name from this list?" He held up the sheet of vellum.

Marion stared at the ground.

"Marion." Jeffrey's voice was cracking. "*Please.*"

She didn't move.

Maugham nodded at Nick and Thacker, who walked with her out through the arches and into the open space beyond. Jeffrey made a move as though to follow, but Maugham put out his hand.

"Jeffrey," he said. "Don't watch this."

Maugham left the ruin, and Jeffrey was alone. He looked blankly at the walls of the Abbey. Then he walked toward his car. When he heard the shot ring out, he winced, but he didn't stop. Asked the driver to take him to the office. He wanted time to come up with something to tell John when he returned from the magic show to tea.

London, England
January, 1934

A bright winter sun was shining through the tall windows when Ian entered the dining room. Jeffrey, dressed for the office, was reading the *Times*. Ian put toast and a slice of bacon on his plate and then slid into his usual seat. He looked at the back of the newspaper for a few seconds, nibbling his bacon. Then he spoke.

"I saw Mummy yesterday."

The paper didn't move, but Ian saw Jeffrey's fingers tighten over the edges. The silence continued for almost a full minute, and Ian wondered whether Jeffrey had heard.

Finally, without putting down the paper, Jeffrey said: "I killed your mother, John. It's a painful memory. I wish you wouldn't bring it up at breakfast."

"She told me that you'd say that," Ian said. "She said that if you did, I should ask you whether you fired the gun."

There was another drawn out silence, and then Jeffrey folded the paper and set it on the table. "No. I did not."

"She told me to ask whether you saw the body."

"John," he said, "this is ghoulish. Stop it." He picked up the paper again, unfolded it, and began to read.

"She said that if you still didn't believe me, I should give you this." Ian reached into his pocket and placed something in the center of the dining table.

Jeffrey let the moment drag before he lowered the paper and looked over top of it. An antique gold ring. Blue stones.

"Hmm," he said. He raised the paper again.

"She said that if you wanted to talk, she'd be waiting at the second bridge near the pond. At 2:30."

Jeffrey didn't lower the paper. "Typically overwrought," he finally muttered. "She could have simply come to the door and rung the bell."

Ian slipped out of his chair to go find Mrs. Bowen. He didn't see the smile that played across the corners of Jeffrey's mouth. Nor did he see Jeffrey put his hand over the ring, take it, and slip it into his pocket.

Bulgaria, 1934

London, England
January, 1934

*T*HE ten shilling note that she was smoothing flat into a respectable looking rectangle on the chipped marble tabletop was all the money she had in the world. The bill for her sandwich, uneaten and crumbled into pieces over the plate in front of her, and for her cup of tea, gratefully emptied, was five shillings and ninepence. She handed a passing waiter her note and stared down at the table, trying not to seem impatient for the change. She would need the money to make her way back from Regent's Park to the secure residence in Chelsea.

Marion had once had an income. Never questioning the ten shilling notes that had appeared like magic in her wallet. That had been before her informal incarceration in Chelsea in September of 1933. They had told her at the time that she was being kept at the house for her own protection. Not caring all that much whether she believed them. Now, though, more than four months later, they had still made no progress with her. When she had climbed over the wall yesterday morning, they were aware of what she was doing. But they had become as frustrated by the stalemate as she had. And they had looked the other way.

That didn't mean they had made her escape easy. She was wearing the only clothes they would allow her: the thin, almost transparent cotton dress and perforated t-strap shoes that were the unofficial uniform of the house—laughably inadequate for the frigid January temperatures. And, as a matter of course, they had frozen her income and bank accounts. She had been forced to steal what money she could from a kitchen drawer she had once seen the housekeeper use as temporary storage for change returned from the grocer's.

It wasn't much. But it was enough to survive for two days in the city. She had reminded herself with some bitterness, as she had pocketed the money, that she could have stretched it out over weeks in Istanbul or Baghdad. But then, she wouldn't have found herself under this sort of supervision in a city like Istanbul or Baghdad. She loathed London.

After scaling the conspicuously unsurveilled garden wall and disappearing into a Sloane Avenue construction site, she had walked for two hours, gradually losing feeling in her fingers and toes, toward Chester Terrace. She had avoided the tube, which was certain to be watched, and she had skirted the parks. She had also avoided contact with her acquaintances in London, not wanting to expose them to the attention of her jailors. Her walk had been both grueling and meandering, reinforcing her hatred of the city.

When she had finally reached Regent's Park, she had waited another two hours for Ian to leave the Chester Terrace house. She knew that he would slip away from his nanny once he was out—it was an inevitability that she didn't question, even after months away from him. And she wasn't disappointed. That afternoon, he chose to hide himself in a gigantic ash, giggling with manic cruelty at the frantic and traumatized nanny looking for him below. Before the nanny could track him, Marion had cajoled him down from the tree, hugged him, extracted a promise of silence, and sent him back to Jeffrey with her message.

Ian was now six years old, she reminded herself, tracing an invisible design on the marble tabletop with her fingertip. She had missed his birthday. The waiter brought back her change. He looked both repelled and relieved as she took the money, glanced up at the clock over the counter, saw that it was time, and made her way out of the restaurant.

She flushed as she pulled open the door, her cheeks burning even when the blast of cold, dirty air from the street hit her in the face. She had become used to feelings of alienation, rage, and, more recently, despair. Shame was new. Unpleasant. She shoved her hands into the thin pockets of her dress, hunched down, and trudged—the last of her money clenched in her fist—toward the other side of Regent's Park.

She couldn't blame the waiter. She had spent the previous night curled up in the corner of an empty garage that had been inexpertly secured with a cartridge padlock that couldn't have been manufactured after 1877. It had responded, theatrically and improbably, to pressure from a bobby pin. She had felt thankful, if also like a secondary character from an Inspector French novel, for the warmth and safety she had found. But the night hadn't helped her appearance. She was already wan and pinched from the months of protection in Chelsea. Now, after six hours on the floor of the garage, she looked desperate.

She slowed when she reached the second bridge at the edge of the pond. He was there waiting for her. Wearing a hat, scarf, gloves, and a heavy, dark grey double breasted wool coat. He was facing away from her, gazing out over the thin layer of ice that covered the turgid water. Calm and unconcerned. And warm. She shivered. And though she hadn't moved further toward him, he turned as if she had announced herself. He stood watching her, impassive. She took a few hesitant steps closer and then stopped again.

"They let you out." His expression hadn't changed.

She rubbed her arms with her hands to warm herself. "I escaped."

He didn't speak.

"They let me escape," she amended.

He unbuttoned his coat. Removed it. Held it out to her. "Wear this."

"No," she said. "Thank you. I'm fine."

He walked over to her, grabbed her shoulders, spun her away from him, and covered her with the coat. Before she could protest, he turned her back toward him. "Wear it. You're conspicuous dressed like that. People will think I'm hiring you."

"*What?*"

"What do you think you look like? I'm surprised you weren't arrested the moment you'd left that grim tea shop. Come to think of it, I'm surprised they let you into the shop to begin with."

"You were watching?"

"You ought to have felt it. You've gotten rusty stashed away in—" He paused, frustrated. "—in wherever they put you."

"Jeffrey—" She tried to collect herself. The conversation wasn't going at all the way she had planned. "Jeffrey, I thought—"

"What?" His voice was acid. "What did you think? That I'd spot you over the bridge, imagine that I was dreaming, eventually realize that, no, you were alive, *alive* all along, and run to you, clasping you to my chest in teary relief?"

"I sent Ian to tell you—"

"Ah yes," he said. "The boy. Pleased you could find another use for him. Never too early to begin training as a courier. There I was, innocuously finishing my breakfast this morning, when suddenly, out of nowhere: 'I saw Mummy yesterday. Turns out she's not dead after all. She told me to give you this.'" He took the gold ring with blue stones out of his breast pocket and held it up as though to admire it shining in the dull winter light. "I give him credit," he said, still biting. "He has impeccable timing."

A second passed in silence. And then, without warning, he caught her wrist and shoved the ring onto her finger. She winced, and when he released her, she stared at her hand, tears welling up. She fought them down. He was looking back out over the water again. Calm.

"Jeffrey," she tried again. "I came back for a reason."

"Of course you did."

"I must talk with you."

"Hmm."

Abruptly, she decided that she was angry. Angrier than she'd felt in all the time she'd spent detained. She saw no need to hide it from him. "How dare you? How *dare* you treat me this way? You did this to me. *You. You* wrecked everything. *Everything*. Systematically. You—"

He turned back to her. "So, let's call it even then. Have you any idea what *you've* done to me? These past four months have been hell. Torture." It was with an obvious effort that he was keeping his voice low. "You were dead."

"I thought you were trained to withstand torture."

"Don't provoke me." He turned back to the water. "It will only end badly for you."

"Badly?" She examined his once again bland profile in disbelief. "*Badly*? What else can happen? What could possibly be worse than where I am now?"

His lips twitched in the beginning of a smile. He didn't turn away from the water. "Let's go home."

"No. I must get back to Chelsea this evening."

"They took you to Chelsea?" He glanced over at her and then back out across the pond. "I retract what I said before. You look remarkably well for someone who's been locked up in the depot for four months. They must be beside themselves that you haven't broken." He watched a duck try to push through the layer of ice. Eventually it gave up and hopped awkwardly onto the bank. "You haven't, have you? No shadowy *hashashin* unmasked or medieval Islamic key codes compromised?"

She shook her head.

"And so," he mused, "they staunchly failed to notice as you vaulted over the wall yesterday. Knowing that you'd come straight to me."

"To Ian."

"To me," he corrected her. "And they believe that I might succeed with you where they've failed—?"

"That's not why I'm here."

"Yes, it is. They wouldn't have let you out otherwise. They wouldn't have shown their hand to me."

He turned toward her, leaned against the bridge, and crossed his arms. The cold didn't seem to bother him, even without an overcoat. He had kept his scarf wrapped over his black suit, waistcoat, and the subdued dark red tie that he was wearing with them. "But all right. I'm willing to listen to your own deluded explanation for this scenario as well. I'm all curiosity. Why do *you* think you've been allowed to rise from the dead, cross the city unmolested, and accost me looking like some redemptive whore out of a Russian novel? Will you absolve me of my sins, I wonder?"

She stared at him, increasingly confused by his unpredictable manner. "I want to ask—" she started.

"At home."

"No," she repeated, annoyed with him for failing to understand. "I can't stay. I must go back—"

"I want you home," he insisted. "The price of an audience with me." He took her arm and began walking her in the direction of Chester Terrace. "I have a feeling that Maugham won't protest all that much."

She shook off his hand. "*No.* I will not go back to that house. Ever." She removed his coat to hand back to him. "If you aren't interested in what I have to say to you, then there isn't anything more I can—"

"If you run off, I'll telephone them and tell them that I've seen you. They'll be waiting for you when you return."

"They know anyway. It won't matter." She held out his coat.

He didn't take it. "There's a difference between knowing and being informed. They know you've escaped, and they know where you are. But they can pretend that they don't—and didn't—if you're back in your room by this evening. If I inform them that I've seen you before you make it back, however, they'll be forced to act. Reprimand you for failing to follow house rules. Throw the book at you." He thought for a moment. "In Thacker's case, I daresay it will be an actual book."

"Stop it." She was shaking, and she wasn't certain that it was from the cold.

He took the coat from her still outstretched hand, draped it over her shoulders again, and led her toward the house. "But this is what you wanted, isn't it?" he said as they walked. "To force a move? After all these months of inaction?"

"Jeffrey—"

"And now I can play as well. I thank you for that. Although I do apologize for not following the rules you tried to peddle to me. One can only wonder what sequence of events you thought you were initiating."

She looked anxiously across the park, trying to summon a response. But she realized that she had no alternative plan in place. Shivering and desolate, she gave up, letting him lead her out toward the ring road. Consoled herself with the fact that she'd come to the end of her resources anyway. At least now, in this frigid park, something was happening. Even if it wasn't what she'd been predicting.

They walked for five further minutes in silence, and she saw the stairs leading up to the Chester Terrance entryway. Couldn't stop herself from shaking, now with violence. A physical reaction to what they had been doing to her in Chelsea. And to what she had just done—or failed to do—herself. Jeffrey wrapped his arm around her shoulders and held her closer to him. But his purpose wasn't to warm her.

JEFFREY used his latchkey to open the door and then waited for Marion to precede him through it into the house. The entry hall was what she remembered from the previous September, except that the radiators were now running at full blast, and the cut glass lamps were turned up against the winter light. Jeffrey removed his gloves, meditative, and set them alongside his hat on the console. A maid appeared as he unwrapped his scarf, and he handed it to her absentmindedly. She also took Jeffrey's coat from Marion, just as Mrs. Bowen emerged from her sitting room downstairs.

Mrs. Bowen lit up at the sight of Marion, and failed, with consummate professionalism, to notice the state of her clothing. "Lady Willcox, we're so very pleased to have you back from your retreat. I trust you've recuperated? Sir Jeffrey said you'd be returning to us this afternoon, and I've had your rooms made up for you."

"You knew that I'd—?"

"Lady Willcox has had a tiring journey." Jeffrey spoke across her to Mrs. Bowen. "Would you show her upstairs so that she can rest before we dine?"

"Of course, Sir Jeffrey." Mrs. Bowen turned to Marion. "If you'd care to follow—"

"Where's Ian?" Marion had no interest in playing along with the farce they were enacting. She stood rooted in the entryway, her clothes tattered, her arms hugging her waist.

Mrs. Bowen stole a glance at Jeffrey, who nodded, and then she turned back to Marion. "John is out with his tutor," she said. "They're visiting the National Gallery today, I believe. But he did look forward to your return, Lady Willcox. In fact, he drew a picture for you to have if you arrived home before he did. If you'd wait here, I'll bring it up to you."

Marion swallowed and nodded. When Mrs. Bowen disappeared back down the stairs, she turned on Jeffrey. "'*Retreat?*'"

"Mrs. Bowen knows perfectly well where you've been. But she takes pride in doing her job well. Discretion. You might learn something from her." A hint of some complex emotion passed over his face. "Besides, it was a retreat of sorts, wasn't it? Time to think. To assess one's situation. Though I concede that it's rare to return from the sort of rest you were taking. Rare, that is, outside of Virgil. And God knows I'm not the type to resist looking back."

Marion opened her mouth to respond, but Mrs. Bowen reappeared before she could speak, holding up a large piece of parchment paper. She handed it to Marion, who unrolled it and wrinkled her forehead. The drawing, unambiguously Ian's work, was labelled "to Mummy," and it was signed both "Ian" and "John." But the picture itself was obscure. She peered at it, and then she shook her head. Looked up at Mrs. Bowen for help.

"It's a drawing he made for his Modern History lessons," she explained to Marion. "He wanted to show you what he'd been studying. He's a bright boy. Eager." She paused. "If lively at times."

Marion smiled to herself. "A good way of putting it." She turned the paper to the side and looked again. "But I admit it. I'm at a loss. What is it?"

Jeffrey tilted his head and also looked down at the drawing. "Obvious, isn't it? The RAF air assault on Kabul. 1919. Third Afghan War." He pointed. "There's one of the first Handley Page bombers. Type O, I believe." He looked Marion full in the face. "John's fascinated by aerial bombing techniques these days. It's all he talks about. And we do like to encourage his enthusiasms. Within reason."

Marion blanched and thrust the paper back at Mrs. Bowen. Then she remembered herself and tried to school her expression. "Thank you for this, Mrs. Bowen. It—it's lovely work. I'm grateful to have seen it before—"

"Take it upstairs with you, Marion." Jeffrey was still watching her reaction, now with open malice. "He made it for you. You ought to keep it. He'll be happy to see that you appreciate it enough to have it close by."

She nodded, not trusting her voice, and rolled the paper into a cylinder that she reminded herself not to crush in her hand.

Mrs. Bowen, still smiling, still discreetly not noticing the taut atmosphere, put a gentle hand on Marion's shoulder. "Would you care to rest in your room now, Lady Willcox? You do seem wearied, if you'll forgive me for commenting."

Marion moved without speaking toward the spiral staircase that led to the third-floor bedroom and dressing room that she remembered with only a little less revulsion than her locked chamber in Chelsea. Mrs. Bowen preceded her, but Jeffrey stopped them before they made it to the first floor. "We'll dine early, at 6:00, Mrs. Bowen."

"Very good, Sir Jeffrey."

"And Marion?" he continued. "You mentioned in the park that you had wanted to speak with me. You'll find me in my study once John has settled for the night."

She clenched the fist that wasn't holding Ian's drawing, twisted back on the stairs, and glared down at him, enraged by his deliberately provocative domestic certainty. But she couldn't begin to articulate her feelings. Instead, as Mrs. Bowen continued to the third floor, she resolved to protect her son. "His name," she said to him levelly, "is Ian."

"In this household," Jeffrey replied in the same tone, "it's John." He was angry, or the anger that he'd been repressing since she'd met him was beginning to show again. But all he said was: "I'll look forward to having both you *and* John for dinner this evening. It's been far too long."

He held her eyes, challenging her to refuse, but she felt only exhaustion and defeat. Turned again without speaking and fled up the rest of the stairs.

MRS. Bowen had preceded her and opened the door to the familiar, suffocating room. When Marion entered, she was smoothing the white blankets on the bed and opening the curtains on the tall windows overlooking the park. "Would you like me to run a bath for you, Lady Willcox?"

"Yes, Mrs. Bowen. Thank you. And then I'd like to be alone, please." Marion had wandered, adrift now that her strategy had been shredded, over to the windows. She heard Mrs. Bowen open the taps on the tub and walk back to the bedroom. Marion turned to watch her go.

But rather than leaving, Mrs. Bowen paused at the door and took a cautious breath. "Lady Willcox," she finally ventured, "we are *truly* glad to have you home. Sir Jeffrey has been—not himself. And young John has missed you dreadfully."

"Thank you, Mrs. Bowen." Marion was having difficulty controlling her voice. She didn't want to initiate this conversation. She waited, now edgy, for Mrs. Bowen to leave.

But Mrs. Bowen remained standing, thoughtful, at the door. "It's not my place to say this," she continued. "But I'll take advantage of my age and my position to say it to you nonetheless. I believe that it may be of use to you in the coming months. And years." Mrs. Bowen paused again, looked at the floor, and chose her words carefully. "This family, Lady Willcox—" She glanced up at Marion. "I mean, Sir Jeffrey's family—" She dropped her eyes again. "They are committed to a service that those unfamiliar with their work might find objectionable. Or—or distasteful. My mother called it sinful. But it is a necessary service for all that, and honorable. There are sacrifices that must be made to it. That have always been made to it. Your son, Lady Willcox, is a member of this family. As, now, are you."

Marion had begun shaking again as Mrs. Bowen spoke. She couldn't stop herself. Wrapped her arms across her waist, self-protective. She replied, however, with something like calm. "My son is not a sacrifice, Mrs. Bowen. He never will be a sacrifice. And I despise the service to which you are referring."

Mrs. Bowen sighed. "Still, Lady Willcox, we *are* glad that you've returned. I myself have missed you very much. Will there be anything else?" she added, looking up, once again bright and professional, not missing a beat.

"No."

"Very well. Ring if you find you need anything." Mrs. Bowen closed the door quietly, without anger or resentment at Marion's rudeness.

Marion locked the door behind her and stalked into the bath to turn off the water that had now filled the tub. She realized that she was still holding Ian's drawing, rolled up tightly in her fist. She didn't want him to see it damaged. Looking about for somewhere to display it, she unrolled it and placed it on the shelf above her toothbrush. Then, averting her eyes from the violent scene it depicted, she looked down at her hands.

Her finger was abraded from where Jeffrey had jammed the ring over her knuckle. The cut bleeding slightly, smudging the antique gold. Biting her lip, she savagely twisted the taps on the sink to wash away the blood, and then, remembering the bathtub, she slammed the taps off again. Pressed her palms down on the counter, let her head drop, and tried to keep from sobbing. Finally, mastering herself, she turned away from the sink and stared, unseeing, at the bathtub.

She stripped off the dress she had worn for her escape from Chelsea, ran her fingers through her filthy hair, and stepped into the water. Before washing, she took three deep breaths. She wanted to scream, to throw something, to break something, to do anything to protest the turn her life had taken.

Instead, she fortified herself, took another deep breath, and sank further into the tub to wash her hair. When she had finished, she stepped out, drained the water, and wrapped herself in a towel. Walked back out to the bedroom and checked the clock on the bedside table. 4:30. She had no time to sleep if she also wanted to see Ian before dinner. Rubbing the palm of her hand across her forehead to stave off an incipient headache, she made her way to the dressing room.

The previous September, when first imprisoned in the house, she had found the dressing room, with its alien demands on her sense of self, upsetting. Now, after months in storage and after the catastrophe that she was gradually realizing she'd brought on herself this afternoon, she hardly gave the room a thought. She grabbed the first dinner dress she saw, rifled through the monstrous wardrobe for underwear, took a pair of shoes, and walked out to the bedroom. Pulled the dress over her head and buttoned it. Something in blue georgette with a plunging neckline and black embroidery at the waist. Jeffrey would like it. She didn't care.

She sat at the dressing table and combed her wet hair into a chignon, holding it back with pins she remembered leaving in the room four months earlier. No one had touched them. Had they known she was alive? Or had the pins been left undisturbed as a kind of mourning gesture? She shook her head. Didn't want to let her mind wander in that direction.

Rather, glancing at the clock—4:45—she decided to risk a short rest before Ian returned. She'd hear him bounding into the house from the outside. He was rarely furtive. And so, she rose from the dressing table and walked, nearly unconscious, to the bed. Without removing her shoes, she threw herself face down on the immaculate white blankets and pillows, rested her forehead on her arm, and fell asleep with tears seeping out of her eyes.

THE front door slammed an hour later, sending a tremor through what was, under ordinary circumstances, an ostentatiously well-built house. Marion, startled out of her sleep, lifted her head. Ian had returned. She jumped up from the bed, took a hurried look into the mirror, smoothed back her hair, peered at the clock—5:45—and ran out of the room and down the stairs. Jeffrey was already in the entry hall, dressed for dinner and speaking to a tall man in a tweed suit—the tutor she imagined. She gave him no more than a fleeting glance before descending on Ian, kneeling in front of him, and hugging him.

Ian pressed his cheek against hers, smiling, and then he pushed her back to look into her face. "I've missed you, Mummy. I'm glad you decided to come back."

He was wearing dark wool short trousers, a newsboy's cap, and a thick, belligerently expensive coat. He looked like he belonged in Regent's Park, which left her apprehensive. But she damped down her anxiety and smiled back at him. "I came as soon as I could, Ian. I wish I had been here even sooner."

He tilted his head, thoughtful and self-contained, the expression Jeffrey's. "You'll stay now?"

She swallowed, nodding. "Always. I promise. I'll never leave you alone again."

"Alone?" Jeffrey had turned away from the tutor and was looking down at Marion and Ian, an unkind smile on his face. "Nonsense. John and I had great fun together, didn't we John? While Mummy was away."

Ian grinned up at Jeffrey. "Yes, sir. We did."

Marion realized that she was holding Ian's arm in what was almost certainly a painful grip. Ian himself didn't seem to notice, but she dropped her hand anyway. Brushed back his hair with her fingertips, tucking it under the cap. "I'm pleased," she offered. "That—that you both enjoyed yourselves."

"But I do think," Jeffrey continued relentlessly, as though she hadn't spoken, "that Mummy ought to know better than to make promises she can't keep. Who knows when her work will call her away again? We both must be prepared for that, mustn't we, John? Mummy's absences?"

"Yes, sir."

Marion gaped up at Jeffrey, astonished by the open attack. Then she dropped her eyes, stood, and smoothed out her dress. Looked down at Ian. "I give you my word, Ian. I promise. I will never leave you alone here again."

Mrs. Bowen and the nanny emerged from downstairs before Jeffrey or Ian had a chance to say anything more. After looking a question at Jeffrey, the nanny asked Ian whether he was ready to change for dinner, and Ian, with relative docility, allowed them to lead him up the stairs. Marion moved to follow, but Jeffrey prevented her. "Marion, I'd like you to meet John's tutor."

She glanced back at the solid looking man, no more than thirty, still waiting by the front door. "There's no need," she said. "I'm not interested. And I want to speak to my son."

She turned again to leave, but Jeffrey reached out to stop her. "I really must insist," he said, pulling her by her upper arm toward the door. "I'd feel terrible if, as his mother, you disapproved of the educational arrangements I'd provided for him. Temple Grove is a fine preparation for Eton, but he'll be travelling a great deal as well, and a proper tutor is crucial." Still holding her by her arm, he addressed the tutor. "Mr. Gardiner, my wife, Lady Willcox. Or," he smiled, "if you prefer, Dr. Marion Bailey."

"Dr. Bailey." Gardiner inclined his head. "How do you do?"

Marion looked hard at the bland face and the relaxed, yet ready, posture of the young man standing in front of her. Then she turned, astonished, to Jeffrey. "He's one of you."

"Good." Jeffrey nodded. "You understand."

"Why?"

"Protection. Mostly from you and your unbalanced maternal instincts, it's true. But from others as well. Who knows when someone will target vulnerable members of the family? Gardiner has a unique array of talents." His voice was quiet. "I advise you not to force him to use them. No abductions, yes?"

She nodded.

"Fear not, though. He's also more than qualified to instruct the boy. Literature. Art. A bit of Latin." He paused. "Modern history."

Gardiner was watching their exchange with veiled, sleepy eyes that were nonetheless taking in every move that Marion made. After a beat, he addressed her again. "In fact, I've enjoyed teaching him, Dr. Bailey. More than I expected, to be honest. He's got a sharp mind. Curious. Complete lack of discipline, of course, but he'll learn the value of self-control eventually. Sport ought to help with that—"

"Thank you, Mr. Gardiner," Marion interjected, in a nightmare. "I understand. I needn't hear any more."

Gardiner raised an eyebrow at Jeffrey, who nodded. Then he inclined his head toward Marion a second time, made a move that could have been a salute in Jeffrey's direction, and walked out the door into the January night.

Marion turned to go upstairs, and this time Jeffrey didn't attempt to stop her. But before she'd reached the first floor, she met Ian and the nanny descending for dinner. Ian had washed and was wearing a child's suit that was as close to Jeffrey's as clothing for a six-year-old could be. Choosing to ignore it, Marion asked the nanny to wait upstairs, took Ian's hand, and walked with him to the dining room.

*J*EFFREY took pleasure, as he had the previous autumn, in making the dinner a torment for Marion. Any hope she had fostered that her reappearance in his life, alive and unharmed, would soften his feelings toward her evaporated as the evening continued. If anything, he was punishing her for tricking him into believing her gone. Trapping her, spitefully, into praising Ian's drawing of the Anglo-Afghan war, encouraging Ian to tell her all that he had learned of Britain's predominant place in the world, and acting all innocent, paternal pride when it transpired that the outing to the National Gallery that afternoon had been to view Turner's *Fighting Temeraire* and appreciate the evolution of British naval power.

The demonstration of Ian's political indoctrination ended only when Ian himself, sleepy and overwrought, nodded off over his pudding. Marion, tight lipped and exhausted herself, dragged him out of his chair, lifted him with difficulty into her arms, and carried him to his room, opposite hers, on the third floor. Jeffrey was evidently too satisfied with Ian's performance to assert any further paternal authority. Instead, he rose from the table along with Marion and walked up the stairs after them. Disappeared when he reached the first floor to wait for her in his study.

By the time she had reached the third floor, she was doubting her decision to involve Jeffrey in the problem that had presented itself in Chelsea. But, she reminded herself as she helped Ian into bed, pushed his hair off his forehead, kissed him, and nodded goodnight to the nanny, she had gambled a great deal on this opportunity to speak with him. She couldn't disregard the opening he had granted her.

She rubbed her eyes as she left Ian's room, wishing she had slept more soundly the night before. Thus far, she had failed spectacularly to predict Jeffrey's reactions to her overtures, and the conversation she was about to have was too important to spoil with sleep-deprived mistakes. She shook her head to clear it of her uncertainty. She had no choice. Or, she had made her choice when she went over the wall in Chelsea. It was imperative that she follow it through. She tapped her fingers on the bannister, thinking, and then gave up and walked down the stairs to Jeffrey's study.

When she knocked, he called from inside the room for her to enter. She pushed open the door and saw him standing at a window, gazing out over the nighttime park. He had removed his jacket and tie, rolled up his sleeves, and he was smoking a cigarette. He turned to her when she stepped through the door, but he didn't move away from the window. She shut the door, nervous, and crossed the room to stand next to him. She noticed for the first time that there were streaks of grey in his blond hair. Then she also looked, silent, at the darkness out the window.

"Would you like something to drink?" he asked.

"No," she said. "Thank you. This won't take long."

"Cigarette?"

"No. I just—"

"—clawed yourself out of a shallow, unmarked traitor's grave because you wanted to talk. Yes. I understand." He was still watching the black night beyond the glass. "Any particular subject?"

"Jeffrey, I'm sorry—"

"Except that one." He glanced at her. Back out the window. "If you apologize to me, I'm afraid I really will kill you. Properly this time."

She pressed her hands against her eyes. "You've made your unhappiness with my—my decision in September quite clear—"

"Why not tell me why you've come?" he interrupted her. "What happened in Chelsea that precipitated this? I'm uninterested in your other explanations."

She turned away from the window and wandered to a bookcase. Ran her finger along the spines of the books. Commentaries on Ibn Khaldun. Commentaries on Ibn Arabi. Commentaries on al-Farahidi's lost treatise on cryptographic messages. She paused, looked more closely, and resisted the urge to pull it off the shelf.

Then, still facing the bookcase, she spoke. "Maugham propositioned me. In September, behind the Abbey. I was kneeling on the ground, Thacker had the gun to my head, and Maugham told me that he could use me. He said that he'd keep me away from you. That you were a distraction—"

Jeffrey laughed shortly. "Prat."

She looked over at him. He hadn't moved from the window. She returned her attention to the books. "I refused. I told him to kill me instead. I told him I'd rather die than work for him." She paused again and leaned her forehead against the spines of the books. "Thacker cocked the gun. I waited. And then—"

She closed her eyes and stopped speaking.

Jeffrey turned back to the room, politely interested. "And then—? What then, Marion? I'm fascinated. You've got a gift for narrative. My compliments on painting such an evocative scene."

She didn't respond to his baiting tone. "And then, I woke up," she said simply. "In storage."

Jeffrey took a drag from his cigarette. Blew smoke up at the ceiling. "Typical Maugham. Brilliant man. But he underestimates everyone else. He never imagined that you'd call his bluff. That move wrecked the whole show for him, didn't it? Once they'd stashed you in the depot, you knew that they wouldn't kill you. Couldn't even hurt you all that badly, could they? Annoy you. Threaten you. But you had them on the back foot from day one." He looked down at his cigarette. "Maugham should have let me handle you."

She turned to face him. "They changed their message once they had me there. Said they were protecting me from you. That you'd shopped the evidence of my work against the Soviets. And the French. And the Italians—"

"Yes, yes. And the Turks and the Tajiks and us and anyone else with a military, a paramilitary, or an intelligence service that could be betrayed." Bored. "You weren't discriminating in the jobs you took on." He considered for a few seconds. "Did you believe them?"

"No."

"Why not?"

"I couldn't see what you'd gain from that."

"And of course I never act without some expectation of gain."

Marion shivered and looked blankly about the room. Walked over to his desk and began flipping through the papers scattered across it. He watched her, but he didn't try to stop her.

She looked up at him again. "Do you still have it? The decoded evidence, I mean. Of my assassinations?"

"What do you think?"

"Where is it?"

"Somewhere safe. Easily accessible. Should I find a use for it."

She was quiet for a moment. Then she said: "you wouldn't have kept it if you'd really believed I was dead. It wouldn't have had any value." She tried to read his face, but he was giving her nothing.

Then, gradually, his smile grew, slow and malevolent. "You cunt." He crossed to the desk and ground out his cigarette in an ashtray. He was standing over her, his anger once again overt. "So that's what this is about? That's why you showed up? You want to know whether I believed the performance you put on for me—"

"*They* put on for you—and no, that's not why I came. I—"

"Well how about this for an explanation, Marion? Those papers—the evidence of that 'work' you'd been doing—kept me sane. I combed through it for months, looking for any suggestion that things might not be as they appeared. *If*, I thought to myself, *if* she's capable of this, then perhaps—*perhaps* she's also capable of deceiving Maugham. Perhaps she's even escaped again. Who knows, she could be off teaching Ottoman paleography under an assumed name to third rate MPhil students in Canada. That—possibility—kept me from—from—"

She was still searching his face. "But you could have asked him," she said. "He would have told you. After a week or two. If you had started to suspect that I was alive, and if you'd offered him the papers in exchange for information about me, he would have been receptive. He needed—" She stopped herself. "He needs leverage. He would have let you see me if you'd given him the papers."

The corner of his mouth went down. "Don't think he didn't come round here sniffing after them. Dropping hints in that direction. But that only made me more determined. More hopeful. I was damned if I was going to satisfy him on his own sordid terms. And if you were alive, I wasn't about to let him threaten you with *that*."

"You were shielding me?"

"Don't flatter yourself. I'd simply rather break my toys than let others play with them."

She flushed and dropped her eyes back to the desktop. "So, I knew they weren't really protecting me," she said, returning to her theme rather than hearing any more from him about the files he'd hidden. "And to be honest, they didn't try all that hard to convince me that they were. It was a useful story. An easy threat to throw at me when they became frustrated."

"Which I expect they did become, rather quickly." He was standing uncomfortably close to her.

"Jeffrey." She looked up at him. "I never bargained with them. I never offered to help them. And I told them from the beginning that I never would help them. I was honest. Always. When they insisted that I was under protective supervision, rather than a—a prisoner, I told them to let me out. I said that I'd take my chances with the people they said wanted to eliminate me." She looked up at the ceiling. Gilded. Looked away. "And I told them if that wasn't an option, they ought to kill me themselves. If they preferred. But they didn't. They simply—waited. And kept working on me with the same tired tactics."

"What did they want from you?"

She rubbed her eyes again and looked about the room. "May I sit?"

"Please." He gestured toward the leather sofa.

She sat, her elbows on her knees and her chin in her hands. Jeffrey sat across from her in an armchair. He lit another cigarette, leaned back, and watched her.

"They gave me to Thacker first," she said.

"Ah." A flicker of something between amusement and embarrassment. "He has a vigorous style, yes?"

"I think he requested it. To get at you." She looked up at him and then quickly away. "I formed the impression, after a day or two, that Maugham wasn't expecting him to accomplish much."

Jeffrey laughed. "I imagine not."

"But Maugham let him continue anyway."

"Section morale. It isn't in Maugham's interest to tell Thacker outright that he's incompetent. He's useful in too many other ways. So Maugham does what he can to keep him pleased with himself. Letting him at you was a means of effecting that without doing any real harm to anyone."

She stared at the low table between them. "He kept shouting at me to confess my disloyalty. To Britain. To the Empire."

He was laughing in earnest now. "And you kept explaining to him that you needn't confess. That you were, and always have been, entirely disloyal to Britain. To the Empire. Must have enraged him."

"He hit me."

"Hmm." Jeffrey tapped a bit of ash off the end of his cigarette. "It's a pity Thacker wasn't born in Munich. His technique would see him promoted more quickly in Germany these days than here. But his time will come here as well, no doubt." He leaned back in his chair again. "I hope you hit him back. No? Ah well, lost opportunity. How long did he work on you?"

"Two weeks? Three maybe?"

"And then?"

"And then they sent a woman. Kind. Intelligent. I liked her."

Jeffrey nodded. "Margot Shields. Did she get anything out of you? She's very good."

Marion shook her head. "No. But the questions became less—bizarre."

"What did they want?"

"Names, contacts. Access to my—my organization. A gateway."

"Any pressure?"

"She hinted," Marion replied, "gently, and with great tact, that they would hurt me very badly if I didn't give them what they wanted. But I waited. And they didn't hurt me."

Jeffrey nodded. "It was a test. They don't want your contacts. At least not yet." He took a drag from the cigarette, exhaled, and watched her through the smoke. "If they'd truly wanted the names, they *would* have hurt you, and you'd have told them."

Marion swallowed. "Yes, I know."

"How long?"

"A month perhaps? It seemed endless."

"You should learn patience." He tapped more ash off the cigarette. "And then?"

"Maugham had Nick Trelawney take me to my library. To the collection that you looted from Baquba."

He raised his eyebrows. "Poor Lieutenant Trelawney. This explains his near inability to look me in the face over the past months. He'll be relieved to have this out in the open."

She stared at him. "He lied to you. For nearly half a year. Aren't you angry?"

"He followed his orders. I'd have been more disappointed in him if he'd cracked and spilled to me." He smiled at her. "And I think you'll find that the library belongs not to *you* but to the British people. To the scholars of the world—"

"Stop it."

"Very well." He lifted his chin. "But I suspect we're close to the turning point in your story."

She nodded, leaned back on the sofa, closed her eyes, and put her hand on her forehead. "Maugham was uncertain as to whether he ought to present the library to me as a reward or as a punishment. Whether to grant me access to it in return for—for compliance with his other requests. Or to force me to help him understand it."

"They can't make head or tail of it."

She smiled, her eyes still closed. "No."

"I've been making some progress with it."

She opened her eyes and her smile grew. "Have you really? Well, perhaps I've misinterpreted their demands. Surely they don't need me if they have you chipping away at it."

Jeffrey ground his second cigarette into the ashtray. "I think," he said, "that I understand why Thacker felt the need to hit you." He rested his elbow on the arm of the chair, his cheek on his fist. "Yes, Marion. I admit it. We all admit it. You and you alone are sufficiently deranged to appreciate that collection in all of its demented glory." He narrowed his eyes at her, spiteful. "But I can tell you something else as well."

"What's that?" She was still smiling.

"*You* may not have figured out Maugham's angle yet. But I have. And I wasn't even there."

"What do you mean?"

"You've let him seduce you."

She stared at him, bewildered, and he laughed when she failed to comprehend his meaning. "This entire, endless carnival was nothing more and nothing less than the prelude to a classic, textbook seduction. That's why he couldn't have me there. I *would* have ruined it. 'Distracted' you, precisely as he said. You're just so damned *easy*, aren't you Marion?"

She dropped her hand from her forehead and sat up straight on the sofa. "What on earth are you talking about?"

"'Dr. Bailey.'" He put his hand over his heart. "'My dear Dr. Bailey, you and your superb mind are simply too valuable for us ever to let you go. Your skills are indispensable. We need you. Desperately. What? Still you refuse? We don't want to coerce you. But we will, with the deepest regret, if necessary. Please believe that it is only your remarkable, extraordinary, unique intelligence that is forcing us to crush your equally remarkable, extraordinary, unique virtue. Perhaps a tiny bit of pressure— whoops, and *there* she is, on her back. Naked. Compliant.'" He held her eyes. "End of tiresome story."

The smile had left her face, but she was still staring at him, now in outraged disgust. "That is—"

"A metaphor. Obviously you didn't sleep with him." He raised an eyebrow. "Or did you?"

"*What?*"

"But you did work for him, didn't you? A bit of translation here. Perhaps some decoding there. Telling yourself it wasn't doing any harm."

"I was bored!"

"You were flattered."

"I—"

"And you were played."

"But you see, Jeffrey," she retorted before he could insult her any further, "I wasn't played, was I? Because I'm here. Now."

"They let you out."

"Why would they have let me out if I was doing what they wanted? There was something else, and I wasn't giving it to them."

He thought for a moment. "All right. I can believe that you kept something back from them. Something important. But Marion, what you're telling me still doesn't wash. You went straight from them to *me*. And you must forgive me for finding it a bit farfetched that you'd want to present whatever this morsel of crucial information is to me of all people. You see, I'm not quite as desperate for admiration as you are. As much as I'd adore to think of myself as your gallant savior in your time of need." He watched her reaction. When he saw that she had no rejoinder, he laughed at her again. "So tell me, Marion," he said sweetly, "why me? And why now?"

"I—" She squeezed her eyes shut. She didn't want to say this to him. "You're the only one who can protect me." She opened her eyes and looked at him with something like supplication. "And you have Ian."

"I don't believe you." His voice was cold. "But go on. That doesn't mean you shouldn't try to sell it to me. I'm curious to see how attractive you can make it."

"A week ago," she said, off balance and more than a little worried that she was doing her case more harm than good, "Maugham asked me to look over a new volume. A copy of Ibn Battuta's fourteenth-century *Rihla*. His *Travels*. Maugham was adamant that there was something unusual about it. Which was odd in itself, because before that, he'd never tried to guide my translations or interpretations."

"Was it unusual?"

"Yes."

"How?"

"It was bound together with another manuscript. Aşıkpaşazade's fifteenth-century history of the Ottoman dynasty."

"Did you tell Maugham?"

"No."

Jeffrey considered for a moment. "Why not? It's a strange juxtaposition of texts, but hardly relevant to anything happening now. They both—Ibn Battuta and Aşıkpaşazade—liked dervishes, no? But that's it. Not much there."

Marion looked down at her hands. "Maugham was too interested. It made me nervous. I didn't want to tell him."

Jeffrey examined her downcast face for five silent seconds. "No. You're lying. Why didn't you tell him?"

"I'm not lying. I—"

"And Maugham could tell that you were lying as well. You've never been a difficult read. So, he upped the pressure, didn't he?"

"No." Her mind was racing, trying to salvage the situation, but she felt paralyzed. She couldn't think of anything more to say.

He smiled at her, unpleasant. "You've come all this way to tell me. So what is it? What was in the manuscript? What makes it relevant to the sort of situations the office likes to monitor? You know—fragile economies, invisible diplomacy, the occasional geopolitically destabilizing kill? And why didn't you tell Maugham?"

Her eyes were wide. "I've told you the truth. He—"

"Oh, Good Lord." Jeffrey burst out laughing. "I don't believe it." He looked hard at her face. "The depot's porous, isn't it? Your own people got to you. They left you a message." He put his hand over his mouth like a little boy. "Thacker's going to go off his head when he finds out."

"No!" She was on her feet. "No, you're wrong. I—I just—"

Jeffrey stood as well. He moved, deliberately, between her and the door to the study. "Where are you going? Why not sit down again so that we can talk more about your manuscript? After all, if it's as important as you're hinting it is, I'm the only one who can protect you, no?" His voice was cutting. "And I do have John—"

"I was wrong to come here. I'm leaving." She looked hectically across the room. "Get out of my way."

He raised his eyebrows, still laughing. "You'd leave John? Broken promises to him again so soon?"

"I'll get him away from you somehow. But not now. Now, I'm going—"

"You thought you could manipulate me." He took a step toward her, and she backed into the coffee table. "You learned—whatever it was that you learned—from your *own* side and from that manuscript. And you thought that you could come back here, dazzle me with your return from the dead—your touching vulnerability to the cruel team that snatched you away from me—and trick me into telling you what *my* side knows. And then, you thought, you'd put the pieces together and escape back to the enemy. With your findings."

She shook her head. "No. And I'm leaving."

"You're not going anywhere."

"You can't—"

"Imprison you here? Why not? You're a valuable commodity, aren't you? Unique skill set. Consider it a compliment." He was ridiculing her.

"Maugham—" she started.

"Knows you're here. I telephoned him when you were upstairs. And do you know, Marion? He sounded relieved to have you off his hands. No idea what he had been getting himself into in September, had he? But if you do leave tonight, his people will collect you. They only let you alone during your tour of the city yesterday because they knew you were coming to me."

He took another step toward her, and she stumbled backward, sitting down hard on the sofa.

"He'll be here tomorrow morning to give us our brief," he said, smiling down at her.

"Us? Our brief?" She stared up at him. "I don't understand."

"What's not to understand? Your people were correct. Something *has* happened. And, Dr. Bailey, it's time for us to go to work." He sat next to her. "Together."

"Something's happened," she echoed. "That's why he had me reading the Ibn Battuta."

"Yes."

"What is it? Tell me."

"Absolutely not. Besides, you know some of it already, don't you? Shall we compare notes? Maugham gave me only a bare outline when we spoke on the telephone."

She stood again. "You can't keep me here."

He looked up at her. "It's January, Marion. You've nowhere to go. No money. You can't expose your friends by asking them for shelter. Where will you go if you leave? Where did you sleep last night?"

She stared at the floor. "A garage. In Kensington."

"That's where you plan to return tonight?"

"Yes." She twisted toward the door.

"If you play along with Maugham tomorrow, he'll give you the answers that you've failed so miserably to extract from me. Or, at least, he'll give you some half-truths with which to amuse yourself. Aren't you curious?"

"No."

"For the sake of your organization?"

She glanced sharply at him.

He laughed, stood, and kissed her cheek. "Such loyalty." Then he walked to the edge of the room and opened the door to let her out of the study. "Go up to bed, darling. You'll make yourself ill if you continue like this."

She started to say something more, but then she realized that she did feel sick. And weak. She wasn't certain she could survive another night in the cold. And she didn't trust her ability to elude Maugham's people in her present state. Nodding briefly, her eyes down, she passed into the hall.

Before she reached the staircase, he stopped her again. "I'll give you another piece of advice, Marion." Relaxed, happy for the first time since she'd returned to him. "If you're nice to Maugham, he may even let you have your bank account back. For what little that's worth."

She didn't bother to respond to his taunting tone, turned away from him, and dragged herself back to her room.

M ARION slept deeply, but she woke early in the morning, at the hour they ordinarily began working on her in Chelsea. The room was dark, and she switched on a bedside lamp that threw a yellow light over the smug, solid furniture. She sat up, blinked, and surprised herself by not weeping.

It had been months since her first reaction to waking in the morning hadn't been something between bleak acceptance and a violent, sickening despair. Not one to examine her own emotional state, however, she did no more than note the oddity of her changed psychological response to what could hardly be called an improvement in her circumstances. She didn't know why she wasn't crying. But she wasn't going to question it.

She pushed the covers off her legs, turned, and sat at the edge of the bed, her bare feet pressed to the carpet. Then she braced herself, stood, and walked toward the towering windows. The curtains were closed, and she knew that it was dark outside, but she pulled one to the side nonetheless and peeked out over the park.

When her hand touched the frozen windowpane, she recoiled. A faint, mostly repressed memory of waking yesterday at this time, her breath icy, on the floor of the garage. She looked down at her hand, let the curtain fall back into place, and retreated into the room with a wan smile. It would be entertaining if she broke now, just as they wanted her whole again. She turned and walked toward the bath. Not so entertaining, really.

After washing her face and cleaning her teeth, she returned to the dressing room. Refusing to let it bother her, she looked straight ahead, chose a day dress at random, and mechanically changed out of her pyjamas. After combing and pinning up her hair, she looked at herself in the mirror. Grey tweed to just below the knees, nipped at the waist, straight through the hips, wide white collar. A thin black patent leather belt that she buckled, staring into the middle distance. She bent over, tied her black oxfords, unlocked the bedroom door and stepped into the hall.

The door to Ian's bedroom was cracked an inch, and Marion took a few soft steps toward it. She pushed the door further open and peered into the room, wondering what Ian's morning routine had become. The nanny was awake and dressed, sitting in a rocking chair, reading a book.

She glanced up, surprised, when the door opened and then smiled at Marion, putting her finger to her lips. Marion looked over at the bed and saw that Ian was still deeply asleep, his mouth open, breathing slowly. He looked two years old. She watched him for close to a minute before casting a grateful look toward the nanny. She could only guess what her need to observe Ian must suggest. The nanny's decision not to pass judgement on it was one of the few comforting responses to her impulses that she'd encountered since returning to the house. She smiled again at the nanny, withdrew, and closed the door.

Steeling herself, she descended to the dining room on the ground floor. Hoping that Jeffrey wouldn't be awake yet. But when she pushed open the door to the dining room, he was already reading his *Times*, drinking his first cup of tea. He folded the paper when she entered the room. "You're up early."

She poured herself her own cup and sat. "You don't sleep at all."

"I find it interferes with my work."

She took a sip and considered the room. Massive vase of forced larkspur at the center of the table. Jeffrey watched her, uninterested in helping the conversation. She set down her cup. "When does Ian usually come down?"

She tried to hide her unhappiness at having to ask, but she could tell that he saw it. He was fighting a smile. All he said was: "in another hour. Sometimes a bit longer."

She nodded. Stared at the table. "Does he know—?" She faltered. Couldn't get the words out.

"Know what, Marion?" His voice was mild, but there was a cruelty underlying it that he was doing nothing to hide.

She looked up at him. "Does he know that you're his father?"

"No one has told him, as far as I'm aware." He drank more of his tea. "But he's not stupid. It couldn't have escaped his notice."

"Oh."

"*As* my son, he knows better than to ask about it. Or to insist on it. Keeps the knowledge close to his chest. I wouldn't be surprised if he's waiting until it's useful before tipping his hand."

"I—"

"He ordinarily calls me 'sir,'" he interrupted. "If you're wondering. 'Jeffrey' if it's absolutely necessary."

"Oh," she repeated. She couldn't think of any other response. Her head was buzzing, but she had no idea which of the shocks she'd experienced over the past day was causing it. A growing nausea kept her from taking any food. She sipped her tea again. "Will he be going out with Mr. Gardiner again today?"

Jeffrey shook his head. "No. I thought we might spend today as a family. A rare opportunity. Would be good for the boy."

She frowned. "I thought Maugham was coming over today."

"He is."

"Where will Ian be while he's here?"

"In and out."

She wondered whether, after all, they had damaged her mind—or at least broken her more effectively than she'd believed. She felt increasingly unable to follow the thread of a conversation.

"Jeffrey," she finally said, thinking she may not have understood, "he's six. He can't be here when Maugham gives you—us—our brief."

"Why not? He might learn something."

She stared at him. "Maugham has one mode," she explained, trying to sound reasonable rather than appalled. "Interrogation mode. Ian can't watch that. It—it's inappropriate."

"As I said, he might learn something. He might even find it interesting." He rose from the table, walked to the sideboard, and put a few pieces of toast on a plate. Brought them back to the table. Sat. "And his physical presence in the room will be an object lesson for you." He spread butter on his toast, lifted it, and looked at her. "He stays."

She shook her head. "No. That's—"

"For a woman who had no qualms about using her son as a decoy during God knows how many assassination attempts, you've certainly come over prudish and protective all of a sudden." He took a bite of his toast. Chewed. Sipped his tea. He hadn't raised his voice or changed its mild tone.

"How could you possibly think that this is the same as that?" She was trying with less success to keep her voice down. "I had no choice. What you're proposing to do now is wanton—"

"Nonsense," he said. "It's exactly the same." He raised his cup. "And I think the boy's lucky. He has Mummy to teach him the finer points of the kill. Father to teach him how to repurpose a field telephone." He considered. "And Mr. Gardiner to teach him Latin. And Ethics."

He sipped the tea. "A well-rounded education. Though I worry about him losing the languages you introduced to him as you dragged him all over Central and West Asia in his infancy. But that's easily remedied. Family holidays can be so invigorating, can't they?"

She pushed back her chair and stood. "I'm going back to my room. Tell me when Maugham arrives."

He lifted his paper and began reading again. "Very well. But I think I hear John coming. He'll be disappointed to have missed you."

She turned toward the doorway at the unmistakable sound of Ian hurtling down the staircase. Before she could move, he had crashed into the dining room, jumped onto a chair, and thrown himself into her arms. She staggered back against the table.

He kissed her cheek. "Good morning, Mummy."

She let him down, and he vaulted over to the sideboard for bacon and orange juice. "Good morning, Ian," she said to his back.

He turned and planted himself in the chair she had vacated, slamming his plate down on the table.

She stared for a moment at the back of Jeffrey's newspaper. Then she sat in the chair next to Ian's to watch him eat.

*A*FTER Ian had finished his breakfast, he grabbed Marion's hand to take her back upstairs to his nursery. It was as though the past months hadn't affected him at all. Aside from the fact that they were living in a sickeningly oppressive, alien household, there might have been no change in their relationship since leaving their cottage in Durham the previous summer. Except that Ian was both conscious of, and reticent about, Marion's antipathy toward Jeffrey.

Marion also suspected a shift in Ian's loyalty, but this was a suspicion that she stubbornly refused to acknowledge, even to herself. The past four months had left her interpretation of ordinary social interaction skewed at best. She wasn't about to poison her attitude toward her son with the wariness she had cultivated in storage. And so, she set out to enjoy his company. While she also set aside her misgivings.

As she let him show her his favorite toys and activities in the nursery, however, she did become convinced that one impression she had formed of him since returning was accurate. Ian had acquired a thorough knowledge of the professional workings of Jeffrey's home. He had met Maugham many times and, with a calculating innocence, he assured Marion—who was dutifully admiring a stuffed toy horse missing its head—that she, like he himself, would love "Uncle Richard" when she met him. The unspoken corollary to that statement was that she would love uncle Richard even though she disliked Jeffrey.

She chose to disregard as paranoia her suspicion of Ian's motives as he prattled on about the entertaining times he'd had with Maugham. She'd been away from him for four months. Four months was nothing compared to the five years she'd spent raising Ian on her own. He was still her little boy.

When they heard the downstairs door open, Ian jumped up from the line of wooden soldiers he'd been erecting with painstaking care, kicked them all over in destructive glee, thought for a moment, grabbed five or six to take with him, clasped Marion's hand, and dragged her back down the stairs.

Jeffrey had opened the door to Maugham himself, and the two were already engaged in a quiet, serious conversation. They broke off when they saw Marion and Ian descending, and Maugham focused instead on extricating his short, corpulent body from the convoluted winter coat, complete with fur collar and carved wooden buttons, that he had chosen to wear against the dropping January temperatures.

With the assistance of the maid, he escaped the coat and turned with genial helplessness to Marion and Ian. "Dr. Bailey," he effused. "Delighted to see you again. It's been far too long."

"It's been two days." Her voice was flat.

He wrinkled his forehead, still befuddled. "Two days? Is that all?" He considered. "Hard to believe, what with all that's happened." He turned his gaze, perturbed, to Jeffrey.

Jeffrey shrugged. Then he gestured up the stairs toward the drawing room. Before he could speak, Ian, who had been hiding in a parody of bashfulness behind Marion's legs, ran up to Maugham. "Uncle Richard!"

"John!" Maugham smiled at him. "You grow more like your father every day." He produced a Hamley's bag from his pocket, which Ian snatched away from him before sprinting back up the stairs.

Marion hadn't moved. She was watching Maugham with narrowed eyes. "His father?"

"One assumes," Maugham replied. "Be an odd state of affairs if he didn't grow more like his father every day. Whoever that might be." He wrestled with a handkerchief that had come out of his pocket along with the bag. "I hope you don't mind me spoiling the boy, Dr. Bailey. I can't resist. No children of my own, you see. My wife met with an accident before we had the opportunity. I still miss the treacherous bitch terribly. Almost wish she were alive." Finally succeeding in taming the handkerchief, he turned to Jeffrey. "Almost." He gazed up the stairs at Ian's retreating legs. "It's another wooden aeroplane. Unoriginal, I know. But I thought I might add to the collection Parker's been building up for him."

Marion, who had ignored Maugham's opening attack by climbing the stairs toward the drawing room, tripped at the mention of Parker. "Parker?" She turned back toward Maugham and Jeffrey. They had followed her up the stairs.

"You remember Aldous, Marion." Jeffrey's tone was all polite solicitude. "John met him when he came home on leave a few months ago. Negotiated himself some time off from Mesopotamia to marry Daphne Blackham. Gossip from Suffolk is that the next time he manages to escape his duties, he'll be returning to a new baby. Splendid to hear that he's settled down, isn't it?"

He climbed further up the stairs, put his hand on her back and, when she didn't move, pushed her ahead of him. "Where do you think John picked up his mania for aerial bombing? He's smitten. But then, Parker's always been the sort to collect admirers. All that bold, flying corps charm—"

"All right," she snapped. "I take your point. Since you dragged me here yesterday, you've not been subtle about your campaign to turn my son."

Maugham cast a mystified look at Jeffrey. "You dragged her here? And Regent's Park used to be so respectable. Sad sign of the times."

"Marion's strained." Jeffrey smiled back at him. "Long retreat. Difficult to find one's footing."

"Ah." Maugham pursed his lips. "I understand. Well, we'll go slowly this morning, then."

They had reached the drawing room, and Jeffrey pushed Marion through the door. Glanced back at Maugham. "Clarity is always best, I think."

When they entered, Ian had already colonized a corner of the room, overturning a chair, under which he had spread out his wooden soldiers. Marion peered at him for a moment until it became clear that he had decided to use the wooden aeroplane as a makeshift guillotine. He was hacking the heads off the soldiers with a placid, yet concentrated, savagery.

Maugham watched him for a few seconds and then turned, chuckling, to Jeffrey. "Wrong aircraft, I gather. Ah well."

Marion, mortified, tried one last time to assert a modicum of domestic authority. "Ian," she said, "why don't you take your soldiers and your—your aeroplane downstairs to Mrs. Bowen? She'd love to see the gift that Uncle Richard has brought you."

"No, Mummy. I'd rather stay here with you." He hadn't raised his eyes from the wooden carnage he'd created.

She looked to Jeffrey for help, but he simply smiled at her. Then she turned back to Ian, thoughtful. He *had* changed. Before, he'd been mischievous. And frequently disobedient. But there had also been an openness and a sort of saving happiness in his misbehavior.

Now, although he undoubtedly did want to stay with her, his insistence on doing so was angry. Calculated. She sensed more possessiveness than affection from him, and there was an unattractive adult quality to his cold certainty that she wouldn't thwart him. She realized that she didn't know him as well as she thought she had.

But there was no way she was going to let him challenge her without consequences. She was about to insist more vocally that Ian leave, or pick up the toys to take to Mrs. Bowen herself, when Maugham stopped her. "Why do you call him Ian?"

"Because his name is Ian."

As she spoke, Ian looked up at her, but with an expression that might almost have been scornful. Amused. She felt a familiar impotent rage building up. And controlled it, even as she recognized that she had no idea how to respond to his new attitude. She'd never encountered it in him before.

It was again Maugham who defused the situation. He looked over at Jeffrey, who had walked to a console where Mrs. Bowen had left a silver coffee service. "His name is Ian?"

Jeffrey poured a cup of coffee. Brought it to Maugham. "Only to Marion," he said, handing Maugham the cup. "Raised in Edinburgh."

"Oh dear." Maugham took the coffee and lowered himself onto a striped, green silk sofa. "Can't be helped, I suppose." He took a sip of the coffee and placed the cup on a table to his side.

Marion accepted, with a sharp increase in her nausea, that she couldn't fight all three of them at once. Stood in the center of the room for a few silent seconds longer. And then she stalked over to an armchair across from Maugham, sat in it, folded her hands, and stared down at her lap.

"Coffee?" Jeffrey was still busy at the console.

"No."

He glanced over at her and then poured himself a cup. Took a sip and walked to the armchair next to Marion's. Sat, set down his cup, and looked politely at Maugham.

Maugham himself turned to Marion. "You've purloined my manuscript," he said without preamble. "I'd very much like to have it back."

"*My* manuscript," she replied. She didn't look up from her lap.

Maugham watched her for a moment and then addressed Jeffrey. "Did she bring it here?"

"No." Jeffrey took another sip of coffee. "This is the first I've heard of it. Your people were on her, weren't they? They didn't see anything?"

Maugham shook his head. "They left her alone until she was out of Sloane Street. By the time we discovered she'd taken it, she'd already dropped it somewhere."

"The depot's leaky," Jeffrey offered. "She likely gave it to her contacts. Could have delivered it to them even before she went over the wall. They'd been in touch with her."

Maugham raised his eyebrows, a hint of donnish admiration. "Is it, now? And could she have?" He looked over at Marion again. "Well that saves time, at least."

Marion glanced up at him, confused.

"Something to contribute, Dr. Bailey?"

"No."

Maugham tapped his chin with his finger a few times, looking between Jeffrey and Marion. "Dr. Bailey," he finally said to her, "we've been getting to know one another now for four long months. Do you still have no notion what I'm asking you to do for me?"

"Professor Maugham," she replied, looking him square in the face, "I have not the slightest interest in what you're asking me to do for you."

Maugham leaned forward, his hands on his knees, conspiratorial. "What if you're already doing it?"

"I'm not."

"I believe, Dr. Bailey, that in fact you—"

"I'm not," she snarled.

Maugham turned a mystified face to Jeffrey. "And this is how you choose to spend your days?"

Jeffrey sipped his coffee. "You're mishandling her."

"Then you do it."

Jeffrey peered at Maugham over the top of his cup. "I'm not certain yet that I forgive you for staging her execution. And for letting Thacker at her in the depot. I'm feeling hurt and betrayed, Maugham."

"You're too hard on Thacker." Admonishing. "He didn't do any harm. And we all—higher ups as well—felt that you yourself could do with a lesson in humility. It's a fatal flaw, Willcox. This obnoxious, overbearing arrogance. We were only trying to help."

"And it's worked out so well, hasn't it?" Jeffrey set his coffee cup on the side table. "I certainly have less cause to be obnoxious now. Chastening to see how well you and the rest have managed this situation. You've made real progress with it. Impressive. I applaud you."

"I have a surprise for you," Maugham replied, obscurely. "You'll like it. But I'm saving it for the end." He turned his attention back to Marion, who had resumed her inspection of her lap. "For now, I'd simply like to apologize to Dr. Bailey."

Marion didn't move.

Maugham sighed and continued. "Dr. Bailey, I apologize for our treatment of you. And I congratulate you. You've defeated me. I've given up, and I'm leaving you now in the hands of your loving family. *But*, in the interest of clearing up what has become a truly exasperating muddle, I will also be passing along to Willcox a few significant points of the conversations that you and I have been having—and also the reasons I have had for belaboring those points. Those reasons, Dr. Bailey, might intrigue you. But I wouldn't dream of suggesting you'd be motivated to listen by anything so base as curiosity."

He leaned over and looked up at Marion's downcast face as though she were a pouting child. "And so, Dr. Bailey, you can continue to sit there," he pointed to her chair, "exhibiting your perfect lack of interest in anything I have to say. I will sit thus," he sat up straighter and turned so that he was facing away from her, toward Jeffrey, "addressing Willcox. And Willcox will listen. I beg of you, Dr. Bailey, pay no attention to our conversation. Ignore it. Expunge it from your mind. Heaven forfend that you should think that I'm attempting to recruit you. I would never, *ever* insult your honor so egregiously."

Jeffrey had been watching Maugham, his elbow on the arm of his chair, his fingertips on his forehead, laughing quietly. Marion wasn't going to give either the satisfaction of showing her anger. She continued to sit still in her own chair, staring down at her lap.

Maugham turned to Jeffrey and rolled his eyes. "All right, Willcox. Are you paying attention?"

Jeffrey nodded. "Yes."

"Very well. Our immediate aim this past week was for Dr. Bailey to pass along that manuscript to her colleagues. Put it into circulation."

"*What?*" Marion looked up at him in horror.

True to his word, Maugham ignored her. "Once that was accomplished, we could begin the operation."

"Why?" Jeffrey hadn't changed his position, but he was concentrating, internalizing everything that Maugham was telling him.

"Five months ago," Maugham said, "our influence in Bulgaria—Sofia more specifically— deteriorated. We'd been doing well with their Popular Bloc, playing the communists off the fascists, just as we do everywhere else these days. All we can do. But then our antiquities expert there—"

"Chris Archer, isn't it?"

"Well, 'Archer.' Yes."

"Wait," Jeffrey interrupted. "Before you go any further. Bulgaria's a bit far afield for me. Isn't this Grierson's area? Why not kidnap his wife instead?"

"You haven't let me finish, Willcox. You haven't even let me start." Maugham removed his spectacles and began cleaning them with the handkerchief that had caused him such difficulty upon his arrival. Jeffrey remained silent.

"So our man there," Maugham continued, looking through the glass, "Archer, went a bit, how shall I put it? Erratic." He settled the spectacles onto his nose. "Instead of lovely little trinkets spirited out of unwatched archaeological sites, he started sending us polluted information. Fantastic reports. Bizarre. Provocative. Consensus was he might be protecting someone near him. Someone who had been a ghost but was now visible. Vulnerable."

"You put him through the paces?" Jeffrey's voice was blank, professional.

"Oh so gently," Maugham replied. "From afar. We didn't want to spook him. He's been steady for well over a decade."

"And?"

"Two weeks ago, he vanished. Poof." Maugham stuffed the handkerchief back into his pocket. Unsuccessfully. "Couldn't even find the blasted rabbit hole, much less Archer. Pair of eyes thought she might have spotted him in Edirne a few days later, but she couldn't be certain."

"Hmm. Edirne is a *bit* closer to home." Jeffrey rested his cheek on his fist. "But it's still not my territory. Is that all?"

"Not remotely." Maugham lifted his coffee and tried another sip. Seemed unimpressed and put the cup down. "Domestics went to his flat in Sofia the day he disappeared. He'd been in a hurry and left it in state. They bagged it all. Sent it here."

"And?"

"Among other unexpected treasures, we found a trove of court documents. Seventeenth-century Ottoman, our experts said. From Sofia's Islamic Law Court when Bulgaria was a province of the Ottoman Empire. Common theme connecting the documents was that they all had to do with desecrated graves." He paused. "Or perhaps, more accurately, with unquiet graves."

"Unquiet graves." Jeffrey gazed up at the ceiling. "You mean vampires, Maugham? Are you telling me that you want me to go to Sofia to look into vampires?"

"Indeed. Exciting, isn't it?"

"All right." Jeffrey dropped his eyes back to Maugham. "But only if I get to be the big American Texan. That clerk with the diary is an embarrassment. What about you, Marion? Mina, do you reckon? Or perhaps you feel more of a connection to the misunderstood disciple unfairly imprisoned in the lunatic asylum?"

Maugham looked over at Marion, who was still staring down at her lap, trying to damp down her growing rage. Then he turned back to Jeffrey. "Leave her alone, Willcox. She doesn't want to play. Besides, you haven't let me finish."

"Very well, Maugham. Continue. You've got my attention."

"So, the experts did note one abnormality in the court documents. Aside from their ghoulish content. In the midst of the boilerplate—you know, the honorifics, name of the court, date of the trial, plaintiffs, and the rest—every one of them—" He turned to Marion. "In Turkish you call them *sicils*, yes?"

She stared back at him, stony.

He smiled, affectionate. "—in every one of the *sicils*, there was reference, first, and bizarrely, to passages from Ibn Battuta's *Rihla*, and second, to Aşıkpaşazade's history of the Ottoman dynasty. Nothing prominent. You'd miss it if you weren't looking. But strange for a collection of Bulgarian court documents from the 1600s."

"Hmm."

"And then, to top it all off, we stumbled across a disguised—hastily disguised, it is true, but disguised nonetheless—copy of the entire *Rihla* among Archer's papers. Same era as the one Dr. Bailey here pinched. But this one was covered, parts of it completely obliterated, by what looked to be *very* frustrated calculations and translations."

"He was trying to decode something." Jeffrey's tone was thoughtful.

"Yes. And failing, it seems, rather miserably."

"He didn't have the other half of the text. The Aşıkpaşazade."

"Apparently not."

"And so—?" Jeffrey prodded him.

"And so," Maugham obliged him, "we hoped that if we put the proper manuscript into circulation, the one that Archer obviously felt he needed, we might follow it on its travels. And it might lead us to Archer himself. We'd simply like to speak with him. No interest in reprimanding him, damaging him—"

"You put a tail on it?"

Maugham seemed embarrassed. "Well, to be honest, we didn't expect Dr. Bailey to be *quite* so motivated in taking that first step for us. And so—not to put too fine a point on it—no. We did not."

"What do you want me to do, then?" Annoyed.

Maugham leaned forward and spoke in a stage whisper: "I'd like you to release Dr. Bailey. Let her take a well-deserved holiday. She'll lead you straight to it."

"Maugham," Jeffrey said, matching his tone, "she's sitting right there. Do you really think she'd be that stupid?"

Maugham leaned back on the sofa. "You know her better than I do, Willcox. But, frankly, yes. I do. She won't be able to resist."

Jeffrey considered Marion, who was still looking down at her lap, now radiating as much incredulity as rage. She was becoming certain that she was losing her mind. Too long in storage. She shut her eyes.

"What do you say, Marion?" Jeffrey finally asked. "If Maugham gives you back your bank account, and I give you back your freedom of movement, would you like to take a journey to Sofia?"

"You are both," she said, her eyes still closed, "completely off your heads."

Jeffrey shrugged in Maugham's direction, but Maugham wasn't discouraged. He held up a finger. "Let me try." Turning to Marion, he spoke to her again. "Very well, Dr. Bailey. But may I ask you something else? You *are* acquainted with our man, aren't you? With Archer?"

She opened her eyes and looked at him, startled. Then she dropped her gaze to her lap again. Didn't reply.

Maugham exchanged an entertained glance with Jeffrey. "Let her go, Willcox. She'll lead you to him in a fortnight."

"This is where you keep tripping up," Jeffrey replied. "Yes, she's absurdly easy to read. It's embarrassing to watch. But she's next to impossible to push. You know that as well as I do."

"So work your magic, my boy."

"I'm still not certain that I want to, Maugham. You've given me very little. Thrace is not my field. Or, at least, it's scarcely my field. I can handle the *Rihla*. It's in a nice, civilized, classical Arabic. But my Ottoman Turkish is no more than serviceable. I'll be at a disadvantage compared to—to others. And the situation there is too fluid." Jeffrey thought for a moment. "What about her own organization? How do you know they'll let themselves be found? She's compromised. They may cut her loose."

"I've considered that," Maugham said. "But, first, as you pointed out, they've already opened a line of communication to her. And second, they need her. As much as we do. She's the only one who can piece together the manuscripts." He turned to Marion and put his hand over his heart. "Dr. Bailey, if you would only appreciate how valuable your unique talents are to—"

"Go to hell!"

Maugham, taken aback, glanced over at Jeffrey, who was projecting nothing but innocent surprise at Marion's outburst. Maugham tightened his lips. "You've tainted my well, Willcox."

"You abducted my wife, Maugham."

"And you're very welcome for that. You look much better for the rest. But don't you think it's time now to go back to work?"

When Jeffrey said nothing, Maugham made a face that could have been a pout. Then he brightened. "I haven't unveiled my surprise yet."

"No." Jeffrey's tone was hostile. "You haven't. What is it?"

"*You'll* be running her." Maugham beamed at him.

"Marion's right. You are off your head."

Maugham seemed bothered by his spectacles once again, and he removed them to examine their frames. As he concentrated on shifting the hinge back and forth, he spoke. "What's your formal role at the Museum and Library again, Willcox? I've forgotten. Cataloguer? Could use your expertise there as well. Numismatists are awfully backed up. They always welcome extra hands. Drowning in Syriac coins over there at the moment—"

"Or I could throw over the office altogether." Jeffrey reached across to Maugham, grabbed his spectacles, reattached the hinge, and returned them to him. "Grow some dahlias. Write my memoirs."

"Nonsense." Maugham resettled his spectacles with a satisfied grunt. "You won't quit any more than your lovely wife will. Besides, I had you hooked with the vampires. And Willcox," he persisted, "imagine what she'll retrieve for you this time. It's got to be good if it's destabilizing all of Thrace. Quite the coup for you."

Jeffrey was holding the bridge of his nose between two fingers, his eyes shut. "Let me understand then what you're trying to inflict on me." He opened his eyes, looking pained. "You want me to run a double who is not only contaminated, but actively working for the other side, in order to trace a second double, who is almost certainly also working for the other side, with the hope of tricking both of them into revealing the whereabouts of some as yet unidentified object that is of historical and geopolitical value to one of the most explosive regions in Europe at present? And you want me to do this after having kept the first double in the room, listening, for the entire brief?"

"Yes." Maugham looked pleased with himself.

"Novel."

"A challenge," Maugham corrected him. "Imagine how obnoxious and arrogant you can be after pulling off this one."

"There's an easier way to do this," Jeffrey suggested.

"Which is?"

"Let me finish what you interrupted in September." He glanced over at Marion, who had rested her elbow on the arm of her chair and covered her eyes with her hand. "I'll take her up north and talk with her. She's got an excellent memory, even if the manuscript itself is travelling. Let me have the *sicils*. Let me have whatever notes she kept on the manuscript. She'll read them and stitch them into the

Rihla they sent back from Sofia. She knows Archer. She likely even knows where he is. We'll resolve everything without letting her into the field."

"I want her in the field," Maugham insisted, petulant.

"*Why?*"

"The fluidity," he said. "To use your term. Yes, Willcox, this project is important. But I'm also interested in the future. I think her people will stay in touch with her regardless of what happens. She's their conduit to the collection you brought back from Iraq. And she's our conduit to them. It doesn't matter in the end where her loyalty lies. Information will reach her in any case. She can't ignore it. What's she going to do? Put her hands over her ears? So, she'll attract the information. And we'll access it. Terribly easy read, as we both know. I find myself increasingly fascinated by this organization of hers. I want to know more."

Maugham stood, patted the pockets of his bulging tweed suit, and fiddled with his spectacles again. "If we learn that she's channeling more to the other side than she is to us, you have those mysterious files you've decoded to keep her in line. Archive of her earlier missteps. Remind her of her interests."

Jeffrey, still sitting, opened his mouth to deny knowledge of the files, but Maugham interrupted him. "Don't bother, my boy. And don't worry. Waste of energy. I've been overseeing people like you and Dr. Bailey long enough to know better than to deprive you of your stockpiles of papers and passports and buttons and bits of string and the devil knows what else you idiots hoard for a rainy day."

He gave up on the spectacles and shoved them into his pocket with an ominous shattering sound. "Like hitching a tree full of rabid, suicidal squirrels to a locomotive and hoping it will go," he muttered. "Don't know why I bother sometimes."

Spotting Ian, who had sat, quietly fascinated, watching the conversation from the moment ghouls had entered the picture, Maugham beckoned to him. "John," he said. "Mummy and—" he waved a vague hand in Jeffrey's direction, "—whoever must speak together privately. I have another surprise for you downstairs. And, if I'm not mistaken, Mr. Nick may be here to take you out to the zoo. Would you like that?"

Ian crawled out from under the chair, leaving wooden body parts scattered across the floor in the corner of the room. He ran to Marion, draped himself over the back of the armchair, and kissed her cheek. His impulse, which ought to have warmed her, struck Marion yet again as more domineering than loving. But she pushed her reaction down, this time with some violence, and kissed his forehead in return.

"I'll tell Mr. Nick that you've come back, Mummy."

"Thank you, Ian. I'm looking forward to hearing about the zoo."

Ian ran over and grabbed Maugham's hand. Looked back toward Jeffrey. "And I'll see you at dinner, sir."

"Yes, John. Enjoy yourself."

At that, Ian dragged Maugham out of the room.

When the door had shut, Marion jumped up from her chair and began pacing. But before she could attach words to her revulsion at Maugham's proposal, Jeffrey, still sitting, spoke. "Don't say anything, Marion."

She spun back. "Why not? This—"

"We'll discuss it later. For now, simply think about it."

"What's there to think about?" She was close to yelling. "There's nothing to think about—"

Jeffrey rose from the chair and walked toward the door. Calm. "We'll discuss it later." He opened the door, but before he left the room, he turned back to Marion. "If you hurry, you'll catch up to John and Trelawney on their way to the zoo. You could use the fresh air."

"I will not see Nick."

"If you refuse to see Trelawney, not to mention Gardiner, you'll be seeing very little of John as well. Don't you think it's worth relenting? Just a touch?"

She stared at him for a few tense seconds. Then she pushed her way past him into the hall and down the stairs. Grabbed a winter coat from the entryway, not questioning how it had appeared there for her, wrenched open the door, and marched out into the park, buttoning it. When she saw Ian and Nick nearing the pond, she broke into a jog.

Jeffrey was correct. She did want to think about Maugham's proposal. And she relished the outdoor air. But there was no way she was going to let him or Maugham direct her moves. She took three or four stabilizing breaths as she caught up to Ian at the entrance to the zoo. Despite it all, she could make the situation work for her. She simply must plan it effectively.

MARION, Ian, and Nick returned from the park too late in the afternoon for tea. Jeffrey had maintained 6:00 as their dinner hour, and so rather than lingering, Marion and Ian went immediately upstairs to change. Dinner then passed quietly—Jeffrey too distracted to hurt her—and she took Ian to bed without mishap.

After that, she went back to the dining room and waited, resentful, for Jeffrey to ask her into his study. But he surprised her by wishing her good night and disappearing. Perplexed, but not questioning her good fortune, she took advantage of her rare evening of solitude by retreating to her room to take a bath.

She climbed the stairs and checked on Ian a final, obsessive, time. Then she crossed the hall, entered her own room, locked her door, and removed the frock she had worn for dinner. Not registering its color or style as she dropped it to the floor of the dressing room.

After wrapping herself in a clean towel, she went into the bath to fill the tub. Stepped into the water as it was still running, leaned back, let the warmth envelop her, and pinned up her hair to keep it dry. She stayed in the water for a long time, thinking, working through a strategy, until the bath became lukewarm. Then she stood, drained the tub, wrapped the towel around herself, and walked back out to the bedroom.

Jeffrey was sitting on the edge of her bed.

She stopped when she saw him, but she managed not to stumble or make a sound. Refused to acknowledge, even to herself, her panic at his appearance in her room. Instead, she observed him, letting the moment drag.

He was wearing his dinner clothing, absent the jacket and tie. He returned her look for a few seconds, and then he held up a set of picks. Tossed them to the bedside table. "Mrs. Bowen said that you locked the door. Did you think that would keep me out?"

She walked to the dressing table. Sat. Unpinned her hair. "No. It's psychological."

"Interesting psychology." He watched, blank, as she ran the brush through her hair. "Throwing up flimsy barriers that you know will fall to pieces at the slightest bit of pressure."

She put the brush back down on the table. Gently. Took another breath. She wanted to slam it through the glass in the mirror instead. Turned toward him. "Why are you here?"

"Have you thought about Maugham's proposal?"

"Yes."

"Will you do it?"

"Yes."

He nodded, thoughtful. "Well. That was easier than I thought it would be." He scratched his cheek. "You'll try to throw us off the trail? Follow it yourself?"

"Yes."

"Fair enough." He looked down at his fingernails. "Care to tell me anything about the three groups of documents? The *Rihla*, Aşıkpaşazade's history, and the court records?"

"No."

He nodded a second time. Looked back up at her. "Very well. I'll ask again when you've spent more time with them."

With some difficulty, she continued to hold his eyes, her expression cold. She didn't speak.

"Sofia, correct? You'll start in Sofia?"

"Yes." She dropped her challenging look. "I'll have Ian packed within the week. We'll travel by train from Paris—"

"John stays here."

"But I promised him—"

"The boy's used to your broken promises, Marion. He knows it's not your fault. Mummy's unreliable. A sad lesson, but we all must learn it one day."

"Jeffrey, please—"

"You could always stay here." Jeffrey smiled at her, unfriendly. "Take care of him. Be a mother. Maugham would understand. Fodder for the field—" He stopped himself. "Or perhaps I ought to say fertilizer for the field, is never in short supply. Maugham will find someone else. Not sure that John will."

She stared at him. "Jeffrey, I can't. I must—"

"I thought not." He laughed again. "Mummy's important work comes first. Always. But that's all right. It will teach the boy self-reliance—"

"This is despicable." She stood and strode to the bed to stand over him. Kept her hand on the towel. "What you're doing is reprehensible. Petty. Has anyone ever asked *you* to choose between your family and your—your duty? Has anyone forced you—"

"No." He was smiling up at her, enjoying her rage. "No one has. Terrible choice to be forced to make." He thought for a moment. "Although you certainly didn't spend all that much time on it. Split second decision that was, no?"

She spun away from him with a strangled noise, and paced to the windows. The curtains were closed, but she pressed her forehead against the heavy cloth, feeling the frozen glass beneath it.

He watched her. Still mild. Still sitting on the edge of the bed. "So that settles it, then," he finally said. "Sofia. And you'll leave next week. Excellent."

"Is that all?" She had closed her eyes.

"No."

She turned her head. "What, then?"

He looked down and smoothed an imaginary wrinkle out of the white blanket covering the bed. "I had a great deal of time to think. While you were in the underworld." He glanced up at her. Back down at the blanket. "I thought about a lot of things. But there was one reflection that recurred—kept pushing the others away, in fact. In seven years of marriage, I realized, I exercised my conjugal rights over you one time. Once." He laughed. Angry. "I feel, Marion, that that is sufficient respect and restraint for a lifetime."

He stood and looked at her with an expression that made her uncomfortably conscious of the fact that she was wearing only a towel. Her heart skipped a beat and then began thudding hard in her chest. All she could think to say was: "I see."

"Do you?" He took a step toward her.

"Yes." She swallowed. "Yes, Jeffrey. I do." She dropped her eyes to the floor, trying to collect herself. "All right."

"'All right?'" He looked at her in laughing incredulity. "Is that consent? Or shall I prepare myself for defensive maneuvers?"

She raised her eyes to him. "I'm your wife," she said. "You're my husband. You're not physically repulsive. And I refuse to gratify you by—by trying to fight back." She paused for a moment. "And to be perfectly honest, I think I prefer—that—to talking with you. So yes. 'All right.'"

"I'll consider all of that a compliment."

"Don't." She took an involuntary step backward, clenching the towel, and then caught herself. "But Jeffrey, consider the circumstances. I'm forty-one years old. I've spent the past four months under interrogation in your employer's prison. A month before that you had me starving and sleep-deprived in your own camp." She watched him as he walked toward her, an unreadable smile on his face. "I'm surprised that you're interested," she finished lamely. "Given what I am. Now."

He was standing close enough to her to look down into her face. "Nonsense." He brushed a strand of hair away from her cheek. "Stress becomes you. It brings out that misleading fragility that so maddens your admirers." He ran his lips along her temple and then kissed her ear. "Leaves half of them wanting to despoil you. The other half wanting to rescue you. And then, for those lucky few, those whom you've truly bewitched, an overwhelming, excruciating desire to do both at the same time." His eyes were warm. "And in my case, I can. All because, in a moment of typically deluded miscalculation, you signed over the rights to me and me alone—"

"This is not helping, Jeffrey." She ducked out from under him and walked to the other end of the room. "I told you. It will be infinitely easier if you stop talking."

He turned. "Who wants easy?"

"Are you certain there isn't someone else to assist you with this? Younger? Not broken and exhausted?"

"Of course there is." He crossed back to the bed and sat down again, grinning at her. "When I want something fresh-faced and silly, I sample from the office. They've got country houses full of little codebreakers, each and every one keen as hell to be the next Mata Hari. I let them think they're seducing me. Saves everyone from feeling resentful at the end."

With an effort, Marion pushed down her disgust. Then, coming to a decision, she nodded. "Do you know what? We're going to do this my way."

She walked to the bed, removed her towel, threw it to the side, toppled him onto his back, and straddled him. Then she leaned over and kissed him hard on the mouth as she began unbuttoning his trousers. She felt him smile as she kissed him, and she lifted her face from his, still working on his clothes.

He looked up at her, quizzical. "This again?"

"Yes. My way."

He reached down to help her remove his trousers, and then he let her unbutton his shirt. Watched her hands for a few seconds. "Do you think we'll have another child?"

She stopped and stared down at him. "*What?*"

In her confusion, he flipped her off him onto her side, pulled her wrists behind her back, held her down, and bent over to look her in the face. He was still wearing his unbuttoned dress shirt. "Unprofessional, Marion. Leaving yourself open like that."

"You son of a bitch." She moved her leg to kick him off of her, but he was prepared for it and used his own leg to push it down.

"I thought you said you weren't going to gratify me by fighting back. This doesn't feel passive, darling." He leaned over and brushed his lips along her exposed neck.

Then he released one of her wrists so that he could move his own hand over her left breast and down her navel. She felt her skin warming as his hand moved. Hated that he knew her so well. But, she consoled herself as the warmth spread, at least he wasn't talking. She closed her eyes and allowed herself to enjoy it. It was better than the alternative.

Istanbul, Turkey
February, 1934

*I*T was the second day of February, just before 2:00 in the afternoon, and Victoria Station was cold, damp, and wretched. Jeffrey and Ian had accompanied Marion alone to the station to catch the Golden Arrow train to Dover. The passengers were boarding, and Marion, clutching the carpet bag she had refused to relinquish to the porter, was kneeling and hugging Ian.

"I'll be back very soon, Ian. I promise."

Ian was pressing his nose to her cheek, making an effort not to cry. He collected himself, stepped back, and smiled at her. "What will you bring me?"

"What do you want?"

He didn't hesitate. "An aeroplane."

"All right," she conceded. "An aeroplane. I'll find you a Bulgarian one."

"I'll miss you Mummy."

Marion stood. "I'll be back very soon," she repeated.

Then she faced Jeffrey. He handed her an envelope containing her tickets. "Thank you."

She shoved the envelope into the pocket of the black Elsa Schiaparelli coat that Jeffrey had insisted she wear to blend in with the other Sofia-bound passengers. He looked pained at her treatment of the coat, but he didn't comment on it. Instead, he reminded her: "you'll board the ferry, the *Canterbury*, at Dover, rejoin the *Flèche d'Or* in Calais, and then in Paris, you'll switch to the *Simplon Orient Express*. Paris, Lausanne, Milan, Venice, Belgrade, Sofia. You'll be on your own in Sofia. We don't want to frighten your contacts."

"Yes," she said, annoyed. "I'm familiar with the route."

"The problem, Marion, isn't that you're unfamiliar with the route." Equally annoyed. He looked over at the clock to be certain she wouldn't miss her departure. "The problem is that you're too familiar with it. I know what you're going to do. At some point, you're going to bolt. Switch to a different line. It's tiresome."

"Your dilemma. Not mine."

"No. Your dilemma as well. Because I'll tell you now. I'm not stupid enough to reel you back in again when you jump out the window in some field outside of Zagreb. I'll simply watch. And you'll have no idea how I'm watching or what I'm seeing. So, go ahead, Marion. Run for it. As far as you're concerned, every passenger who gets on or off this train between here and Baghdad is working for us. Every one. Easily arranged when a matter of sufficient importance is at stake."

She smiled at him. "You think I'm such an easy read. But do you know, Jeffrey? So are you. I can tell when you're uncertain because you boast. Make empty threats. I'm better at this than you are. You know that I'm better at it. You just couldn't convince Maugham."

He kissed her cheek. "I'll miss you too, Marion." Glanced down the track at the locomotive. "Your train is about to leave. It's time."

She bent over to give Ian a last hug, gripped her carpet bag, and boarded the train. Waved out the window as it moved sluggishly from the station, and then she leaned back against her sofa when Ian and Jeffrey were no longer in sight. Exhaled.

Removing her gloves, she inspected the Pullman car, uninterested. Then, when she was certain she was alone, she opened her bag to examine its contents. A few changes of clothing, a pack of cards, a book she'd borrowed from Mrs. Bowen's library (*The Werewolf of Paris*), her passport—gratifyingly clean, pristine, and new—and, most important, the sheaf of Ottoman court records that, after extended and painful negotiations, Marion had convinced the office she needed with her to complete her assignment. Jeffrey had kept photographs of the records in a safe, but he had not been happy to lose the originals. It was another victory over him that she could attribute to Maugham.

She pulled an envelope out of the bag and turned it over in her hands. A less challenging task had been retrieving her income from them. Maugham had lost no time in allowing Marion access to her bank accounts again—supplementing them with an inappropriately generous and, she suspected, deliberately insulting contribution from the office. A backhanded act of good faith.

She, in turn, had respected the agreement by withdrawing sufficient money in London to pay for incidental expenses on the train and to help her find her bearings once she was in Sofia. They would expect her to take moderate funds, regularly, throughout her assignment—her second withdrawal from a bank in Bulgaria. It was a foregone conclusion that her accounts would be monitored, waiting for that second withdrawal to confirm that she was playing along with them.

She considered the envelop in her hands for two or three seconds longer and then placed it back in her bag. If all went according to plan, the first evidence they'd have that she'd gone under—at least the first evidence after Jeffrey's people reported her missing—would be when her second withdrawal was posted nowhere near Sofia. That would also be when, and where, they'd begin looking for her resurgence. She couldn't hold her breath forever, but she planned to take most of the account at that point anyway. Even if she'd already eluded them, they'd be forced to keep her account open, at least until the second transaction, to trace her. She was counting on that weakness in their position to keep her funded.

She stood, removed her coat, and hung it on a hook at the far end of the carriage. She had two days to rest before setting off their alarms. Two long days, during which she planned to bore Jeffrey's people to distraction. She knew they'd be eager at the beginning of the journey. And she knew equally well that they'd be feeling worn and careless after a night or two of monotonous inaction. She was looking forward to tormenting them.

As planned, Marion traveled from Calais to Paris, from Gare du Nord to Gare de Lyon, and waited there to board the *Simplon Orient Express*. The office would be expecting her to bolt early, in Paris, where the lines were confusing enough for anyone to lose an ordinary tail. But the functionaries following her were far from ordinary, and they would refrain from acting purely on expectation. She could feel them, at least fifteen, even as she used the toilet in the station and drank a cup of coffee. They hardly troubled to hide their presence.

After finishing her coffee, she resolved to oblige them and give them something satisfying. And so, she led them, first, to the ticket office. Once there, she bought herself space on the second of the three *Orient Express* lines—the *Arlberg*, which terminated in Athens, rather than in Istanbul, after stops in Zurich, Innsbruck, Vienna, Budapest, and Belgrade.

Having bought the tickets, her name was posted to the passenger lists of both it and the *Simplon*. As she folded her new tickets into her pocket, she could almost sense the triumph among Jeffrey's people. The clerk who sold her the space would be duly interrogated once she was out of sight. And the recommendation would go to the office that the *Arlberg* line be surveilled as well.

After leaving the ticket office, she made a show of taking her place in the empty *Simplon* sleeping car that Maugham had purchased for her sole occupancy. She knew better than to run for the *Arlberg* straight away. Doing so would look suspiciously stupid. They would be expecting her to challenge them, and she meant to give them their challenge.

To that end, she passed hour after hour on the *Simplon* torturing them with endless games of solitaire that she played on the small table in her compartment. She also wasted half a day on an appreciation of the scenery. They would be waiting for her to try to evade them at the Belgrade stop, where the *Simplon* and the *Arlberg* crossed paths. But by the time they reached Belgrade, Marion meant to leave them mad with boredom.

A day and a half later, as her train entered Belgrade for a thirty-minute stop, Marion collected herself and did as they anticipated. But not, she hoped, in the way that they anticipated. Her train arrived in Belgrade's main station at 7:15 in the morning, when the local Yugoslav State Railway trains were also starting their first runs. Counting on simplicity, Marion left the Schiaparelli coat in her carriage, draped herself in a shapeless trench coat, covered her hair with a kerchief, grabbed her carpet bag, and stepped off the train.

Rather than moving along the platform toward the station with the rest of the crowd, though, she used the crowd as cover to drop to the track, squeeze between the carriages with her bag, and board the local train that was waiting on an adjacent track. She never entered the main station, and she avoided the *Orient Express* waiting area altogether. She paid on board the local for a ticket to the terminus, and five minutes later she was on her way into the forests of Serbia.

She read her book. Didn't look up. When she reached Novi Sad, she left the train and drank a very slow cup of coffee at a kiosk. Later in the afternoon, she boarded a second local train, intermittently functional, on its way to Budapest. Eight hours later, after a sleepless night sitting guard over her carpet bag, she reached Budapest-Keleti Station.

She had bribed the officials at the Yugoslavia-Hungary border to ignore her passport, and she had made it clear that she was not an easy target for pickpocketing on the night train. Her passport was still clean, aside from the tags she'd picked up on the *Simplon*, when she reached the city. And her bag was intact.

In Budapest, where the *Arlberg* had long since gone through, she kept her head down and crossed the street to check into a dour railway inn. She was relatively certain that she'd lost the office, but she wasn't taking chances. After two wretched nights, bored and famished but unwilling to leave the building, she made her way to Budapest's *Nyugati* station.

There, she sat on a bench, unobtrusive if chilly, in the thin coat, and watched as the third of the *Orient Express* lines—the *Orient Express* proper, terminating in Istanbul after stops in Strasbourg, Munich, Vienna, Budapest, and Bucharest—drew into the station. A few minutes after the train had come to a stop, a woman from one of the sleeping cars stepped off of it and wandered through the station, in need of fresh air. She paused, looked across the room, and moved toward Marion's bench. Removed her 1920s Paul Poiret mink coat and her hat, cast Marion an inquiring glance, to which Marion replied with a nod, and sat beside her. After resting for a few minutes, the woman rose from the bench without her coat or hat and left the station.

Marion sat for five minutes longer. Her organization hadn't failed her. Then she stood, pulled the mink over her trench coat, adjusted the hat, and boarded the train, heading to Istanbul through Bucharest. Her carriage was identical to the one she had left in Belgrade. She half expected to find her Schiaparelli waiting for her where she'd left it. Exhausted by her sleepless journey from Yugoslavia into Hungary and the two alert nights at the inn, however, she didn't spend time amusing herself with comparisons. She simply pulled down her bed and collapsed onto it, waiting for the adrenaline to drain from her system.

As far as the porters were concerned, she'd been aboard this train, if quiet, in her very warm coat, since leaving France. And as far as Jeffrey's people were concerned—not to mention the office analysts when Maugham requested all three trains' passenger lists—she had switched from the *Simplon* to the *Arlberg* in Belgrade, but they had lost her in the process. She thought to herself that they might even be waiting for her at the end of the *Arlberg* line in Athens. And smiled.

She also congratulated herself, cautiously, on having put her plan into action. She knew better than to give in to complacency. Jeffrey's people were far from incompetent. And she rarely relied solely on what the office could supply. But she didn't feel them on her anymore, and she believed, at least, that she had a few days' respite from them. For the first time in nearly half a year, she felt safe.

She was also looking forward to returning to Istanbul. She'd visited the city with Ian many times. But it had been seven draining years since she'd been there alone. She surprised herself by feeling only a modicum of guilt for enjoying her solitude and her freedom from both Jeffrey and Ian.

THE train arrived at Sirkeci station in Istanbul early the next morning. Marion, now well rested, planned to begin work at once. Wanting to set the foundations for her strategy before, inevitably, the office picked up her trail. And so, as she stepped off the train, she kept the mink coat and the hat to throw off any stray observers who might be routinely posted to the station. It wouldn't occur to them that someone attempting to evade their surveillance would draw attention to herself so flamboyantly, and they'd give her no more than a quick glance.

If they did recognize her, though, she would draw them along for a few minutes before dropping the coat and losing them. Unless they were monstrously focused and well trained, they'd be following the outfit rather than the person. She had complete confidence in her ability to disappear among the Eminönü ferries waiting at the edge of the Golden Horn. She'd done it many times before.

Walking slowly from Sirkeci, making herself visible, she bought three tickets at the Eminönü ferry terminal and boarded a boat heading for the Üsküdar dock, on the Asian side of the Bosporus. A small man with a newspaper walked behind her. Preoccupied. And obvious. Which annoyed her. She'd grown attached to the coat and had hoped to keep it; now she'd be forced to sacrifice it to protocol.

Resigning herself, she sat on a wooden bench on the outside deck at the bow of the ferry, waited a moment, and then made a show of losing her hat to the wind. She rose, ran for the hat, stepped into the cabin, moved through a narrow corridor separating the bow from the aft seating area, and stuffed the coat into an engine room. Then she covered her hair with a scarf, jumped from the stern of the ferry to the dock just as it was leaving, and used a second ticket to board a boat heading for Kadiköy, also on the Asian side of the strait.

She rode to Kadiköy, uncovered her head, and used her third ticket to travel back across the Bosporus to Beşiktaş, on the European side. When she reached Beşiktaş, she paused in the terminal, felt the air, and satisfied herself that she had lost her tail. Then she left the terminal, crossed to an anonymous shop a few blocks away from the shore, bought a cheap but warm winter coat, and stepped, confident, onto the street. Flagged a waiting cab and asked the driver to take her up the hill to Taksim and İstiklal Avenue.

After leaving the cab, she walked for ten minutes back down the hill in the direction of Galata, and then she turned right into a side street. She stopped short at the familiar awnings of the café that she knew would be unchanged since her last visit there, seven years earlier. Gave herself time to appreciate the smudged windows, steamed up from the heat inside, and the unoccupied outdoor tables, placed optimistically along the street even in February.

She was surprised by her violently nostalgic reaction to it. Hadn't realized that she'd missed it so intensely. At 10:00 in the morning, it was opening to its first trickle of patrons. It came into its own in the evening, as a bar, but Marion had come to prefer the tranquility of the morning hours, when two or three artists or intellectuals lingered over their newspapers, pretentiously smoking Galoises—ironically conscious of their pretention—and drinking cappuccinos. It seemed very young to her now.

She clutched her carpet bag, walked to the façade, pulled open the swinging door, and nearly toppled over as the familiar smell of the place hit her. Shook her head. She'd have difficulty doing her job if she couldn't damp down these aggressively wistful memories. She took in the dark yellow wallpaper, the rickety wooden tables and chairs, the spiral staircase up to the second floor (unfashionable—only tourists sat up there), and then she peered at the bar. It was unchanged. She wandered toward it, sat on a stool, and held her carpet bag in her lap.

The bartender glanced over at her, uninterested, and busied himself with making a cup of espresso. When he had finished, he set the cup on a saucer next to a tiny, fanciful, tulip-shaped piece of chocolate, and then he placed the espresso in front of her. Before she could touch the cup, he looked more carefully into her face, shook his head, and turned back to the bottles behind the bar. He found a bottle of whisky, opened it, and poured a shot of it into the espresso. Replaced the bottle.

She sipped from the cup with a smile. "Hullo Chris."

"It's Dündar." He spoke in Turkish.

She wrinkled her forehead, trying to place his accent. Then she laughed. "What, you're Laz now?" She was speaking Turkish as well. "Drink. You look like you need it."

He nodded at the cup in front of her. "Drink. You look like you need it."

She finished the espresso and the piece of chocolate, and he took the cup. Put it in a sink behind the bar. Then he gestured over to a table at the corner of the room under a bend in the spiral staircase. She walked to the table and sat. Archer took a package wrapped in brown paper from under the bar, passed through a swinging, waist-high door, and sat across from her.

As he moved, Marion watched him, speculative. She envied him his ability to mold himself into each of his successive identities. He had been born Adnan Spahovic, in Livno, Bosnia, the descendent of a respected Muslim Ottoman governing family. His father had been a professor of German literature, his mother a concert pianist, and both had been—despite the Ottoman-Austrian alliance—killed as traitors to the Hapsburg Empire during the First World War. Adnan himself had wandered, a multilingual refugee among many post-War multilingual refugees, across Europe throughout the early 1920s, until he had made his way to London in 1928.

He had the double-edged good fortune of looking as though he'd been born in Cornwall. He was tall and graceful with reddish blond hair and large, light green eyes. If it weren't for a thin, middle European nose and the precise Slavic movements of his hands that, despite extensive training, he could never seem to tame, he'd be taken by anyone looking at him—or by anyone hearing his perfect accent—as an anonymous, hard-working, British civil servant. Which he had been, for a good ten years. As he pulled out the chair to sit, Marion concluded that he also passed superbly as Laz. She was having difficulty not laughing at the transformation.

He caught her mood and shrugged. "And what's wrong with being Laz?" he continued in Turkish. "Effective entrée into the darker sides of trafficking."

"Dündar," she reprimanded him. "You should know better than to denigrate your people in that way."

"You haven't let me tell you what sort of trafficking I've been involved with."

"Forgive me. I think your espresso may have been a bit too strong." She rested her chin on her fist. "I'm jumping to all sorts of conclusions."

"There's no such thing as espresso that's too strong." He lifted his package to the table and set it in front of her. "Here's a sample of my illegal, black market wares."

She lifted an eyebrow and then examined the package. Unwrapped it. It was the *Rihla* bound together with the Aşıkpaşazade. She grinned at him. "Dündar! So soon? Oh, I'm pleased. I can't tell you how happy I am to see this."

"The problem," he replied "is that I left Sofia in more of a hurry than I expected to. I lost the *sicil*."

Without answering, she opened her carpet bag, removed the sheaf of documents, and arranged them on top of the *Rihla*. "You mean these?"

"Marion." He held out his hand, palm up. "You're like some tortured fairy godmother. Amazing. Just amazing." He lifted the top page and gazed at it. Then he wrinkled his nose. "They smell of the office."

"They stink of the office," she agreed. "But they're here now. We'll air them out."

He perused the top page, nearsighted. Without looking at her, he said: "are you certain you're still working for us? Malicious gossip has you sleeping with the enemy."

"Sleeping with the enemy," she confirmed, "married to the enemy, raising a family with the enemy." She rubbed her eyes. "It's a long story. Dündar, I'm in the very strange position of being completely loyal to our side and yet also, at the same time, completely accessible to theirs. Malicious gossip is correct. It may be best to end my relationship with you. I'll understand. Our parting can be amicable."

"Hmm." He was still leafing through the documents. "I'll let the powers that be know your concerns. But I don't think they'll want to divorce you just yet. You have your uses."

"Fine," she said. "But please, Dündar. Tell them I can't know anything sensitive. *Anything* sensitive. I'll do piecemeal work, but I don't want to hear the tiniest bit of information that can be put together into a cohesive picture. Or portrait. Of anything."

He smiled up at her. "I'll tell them. Odd situations you create for yourself. But I'm the last person in the world to condemn a colleague's complicated identity." He stacked the documents into an organized pile. "So, what now?"

She blushed. "I haven't anywhere to stay. I must withdraw a large sum from my bank here, but once I do, they'll be on me within a day or two. I can't compromise my contacts."

"That," he said, "is easily fixed. Care to stay in my guestroom across the way in Cihangir? Top floor of the building. Nice view of the water."

"You've saved my life, Dündar. Thank you." She thought for a moment. "But are you certain you're willing to open yourself up to the scrutiny? It's dangerous."

He laughed. "I'm more worried about what that boy of yours will do to my furniture."

She dropped her eyes. "He's not here."

"Where is he?"

"They kept him." She grabbed her carpet bag and stood. "Insurance."

He stood as well and pulled a key ring out of his pocket. "Pigs," he offered, conversationally. She didn't say anything.

He detached a key and handed it to her. "The building is on Siraselviler street, first block, across from the grocer's. This opens the door to the building as well as the door to the flat. Utterly insecure, but the people who would come for me wouldn't be stopped by extravagant locks. Ground-floor neighbors keep a goat in the basement, but we all pretend not to notice. I'd advise you to do the same."

She took the key and smiled at him. "Thank you."

"Are you going straight there? If so, you might take those," nodding at the documents, "and start work on them."

She picked up the papers and the manuscript and arranged them in her bag. Then she shook her head. "I want to get this business with the bank sorted first. It makes me nervous. They may freeze my accounts again purely out of spite. They'll already know I've gone under. I don't want to think about the arguments they're having about it."

"Where are you going to put it all when you've withdrawn it?" Curious.

She laughed at herself. "Do you know? I hadn't even thought that far ahead. I suppose I can't wander through life carrying a canvas bag stuffed with cash, can I?" She shrugged. "Maybe I'll invest in bullion. My own small protest against Britain abandoning the gold standard." She paused. "Although then I'd be carrying great sacks of gold instead, wouldn't I?"

He was laughing as well, teasing. "I hear nothing but good things about Creditanstalt these days."

"Thanks, Dündar." Exasperated. "Perhaps I'll invest in gold jewelry after all." She considered. "But actually, you've given me an idea. I may put a chunk of it into Atatürk's experiment. İş Bankası. It's no less stable than anything else going at the moment. And better, the office couldn't access an account there."

She smiled to herself. "And then, with what's left, I think I will buy myself some gold bracelets to wear. Security is always better closer to home."

Archer was returning to his position behind the bar. "I've missed you, Marion. I'm looking forward to talking tonight."

"I've missed you too, Dündar." She pulled the swinging door, and made her way toward Galata, and her bank.

THE cobblestones of İstiklal Avenue were slick under her worn boots, but Marion reached her bankers' building without mishap. It was a few storefronts down from one of the rapidly proliferating İş Bankası branches, and if she did make good on her whim, physically moving the bulk of her account from one to the other would be a simple task. Simple, that is, if she were still undetected in the city. She decided to run another check before entering the bank.

Choosing her moment, she came to a leisurely stop outside the ornate green gates of Galatasaray lycée and leaned against the wall, watching the pedestrian traffic. She tried to get a feel for the atmosphere, even as a sleet-like drizzle forced most of the crowd into cafés and under awnings. After twenty minutes, she remained optimistic—thanks in part, she knew, to Archer's espresso—that she was still invisible. At the very least, the situation was conducive to taking the next step.

She rang the bell of the office that in some convoluted way eventually reached Midland Bank in London, and she waited to be let into the lobby of the building. The clerk who vetted her at the door used some telepathic extra sense to gauge her respectability and the authenticity of her business. He couldn't have been impressed by her clothing or by her lingering air of desperation. Without speaking, he led her up the cramped stairs to a first-floor bureau that tried and failed to exude wood-paneled confidence and security. Marion always felt as she entered this branch of the bank that she was being ushered into a disreputable surgeon's quarters.

Once up the stairs, the clerk showed Marion to a wooden desk at the center of the room. It was immaculate, clean, and completely empty. Sitting behind it, Marion was almost horrified to see, was the same banker she had dealt with seven years before. And on every visit prior to that. He looked as though he hadn't left the desk in all the time she'd been away. When she sat, he watched her silently, with a total lack of recognition or interest. Then he closed his eyes as though he had a migraine.

"Your business, Dr. Bailey?"

"I'd like to make a withdrawal."

"Very good, Dr. Bailey." He opened a drawer, extracted a small sheet of paper, a ledger, and an ink pencil. "In what amount?"

"All of it," she said. "Except for fifty pounds."

The banker's reaction to her request was to blink twice, slowly. Marion colored, even as she felt a sudden, overwhelming, and embarrassing affection for England and the English people generally. His phlegmatic lack of interest was unassailable. She had an involuntary image of herself poking him with a stick to see what he would do, which she violently damped down along with her inclination to giggle nervously.

He began writing in the ledger. "Very good, Dr. Bailey. In what currency?"

Marion considered. "One third in British pounds. Two thirds in American dollars, please."

"Very good, Dr. Bailey." He finished writing on the sheet of paper and looked up at a clerk, who rushed to the desk. He handed the clerk the paper. The clerk glanced at it, nodded, and moved to the back of the room. Disappeared behind a secure door.

Marion and the banker waited close to ten minutes for the clerk to reappear. Silent, they each stared at the top of the once again empty, immaculate desk. Marion remembered, as she did every time she visited this branch of the bank, how she liked her banker. She wished more of her acquaintances appreciated stillness in the way that he did. She would miss him. And she vowed never to poke him with a stick.

The clerk returned bearing a metal box full of notes. With reverence, he placed it on the desk in front of the banker. Without a word, the banker counted out the notes into neat stacks of twenty. He gave her, she was entertained to see, a canvas bag for her convenience, made brief eye contact to reassure himself that she was satisfied, and then filled the bag with the banknotes.

He pushed the bag across the desk toward Marion. "Any other business, Dr. Bailey?"

She stood and hefted the bag over her shoulder. "No. Thank you for your time."

"Good morning, Dr. Bailey." He looked back down at the desk. His notice of her had ended.

The clerk trotted along to see her to the stairs, and then she was out once more on İstiklal Avenue. After she walked the three storefronts to the İş Bankası branch, she entered the crowded, prosperous lobby convinced that she was still safe from surveillance. She knew that the clock on her invisibility was ticking, and that the office would know her whereabouts within the day. But unless they had someone hiding in the vault, she wouldn't have missed any observers stashed in the building. Anyone from the office would have stood out like children playing in a tomb. She gave herself between a day and a day and half before she must start looking in earnest for a tail.

The İş Bankası cashiers accepted her deposit readily, and they were more than willing to maintain it in the currencies she'd withdrawn from Midland. In what she knew was a financially suicidal moment of support for Turkey's economic experiment, she did convert a portion of her British pounds to Turkish lira. She rationalized her move by telling herself that doing so would make it easier to withdraw small amounts as she travelled throughout Istanbul. A less rational explanation, that she didn't acknowledge even to herself, was that she was still annoyed by Great Britain's willingness to subvert international economic interdependence by abandoning gold.

Balancing all of these whimsical financial decisions, however, was her hard-headed decision to keep sufficient American dollars out of the bank, as physical objects at the bottom of the canvas bag, to support her for at least a year at her ordinary level of consumption. Banks were fine. As was whimsy. But she didn't want to put all of her confidence in a system that would have been a comedy if it weren't destroying half the world.

After leaving the bank, she walked back up İstiklal Avenue for five minutes before turning right and taking side streets to Siraselviler. She thought she knew Archer's building already, even if she'd never been inside. It was prominent, perhaps fifty years old now. And the grocer's across from it was a local tradition. She stopped there to buy dinner to serve to Archer when he returned from the café. The job he had found for himself, she suspected, was exhausting.

At the same time, knowing well that any cooking she attempted would end badly, she limited herself to prepared dishes. A loaf of bread, fava bean salad, cold eggplant, yogurt, marinated green beans, red lentil balls, dolma, roasted red peppers, and cold roast chicken. She stacked her wrapped packages above the dollars in her bag, considered, added two bottles of mineral water, thanked the grocer and crossed the street.

When she opened the door to the building, the unmistakable stench of goat and, she thought, chickens or perhaps geese, hit her in the face like a physical blow. She stood motionless on the ground floor for a few seconds grinning to herself. There must be some municipal law in place now forbidding animal husbandry in urban flats. But obviously neighborly consideration overcame any modernist obsession with hygiene. She was still smiling when she reached the sixth floor of the building, where Archer had found a living space upon escaping Bulgaria.

The furniture in the flat was sparse. A tapestry sofa, two wooden chairs, a few large pillows in the living room, minimal cooking tools in the kitchen, and, in the dining area, an extendable enamel table that Archer had stretched to its longest position and that he seemed to use primarily as a work space. There were also two bedrooms. The bed in the guestroom was unmade, but Marion peeked into a trunk and found blankets for it. Her first move after unpacking the food and placing it into cold storage in the kitchen was to arrange the bed. Then she returned to the living room and stood at one of the long windows, looking down.

Archer hadn't exaggerated the view from the flat. Windows covered three of its walls, and she could see the Bosporus down the hill from Cihangir. She could also see some pushy seagulls nesting on the roof of the building adjacent, expecting her to feed them. She stepped away from the window.

Still well rested from the train, and eager to read the manuscripts and documents now that they were together, she lost no time in beginning her work. She made herself a pot of tea in a double kettle that Archer kept prepared on the stove, poured most of it into a large glass, and settled herself in front of his work table. Arranged the stack of Bulgarian court documents to her left and the *Rihla* and history to her right, readied a few sheets of writing paper, and rested her cheek on her hand, trying to determine an effective starting place.

She'd spent quite a bit of time with the Ibn Battuta and the Aşıkpaşazade whilst in storage in Chelsea. Enough to have begun to speculate on why her late-medieval librarians would have bound the two texts together in the fifteenth or sixteenth century. She'd also occupied herself in Budapest with skimming the *sicil*s, reading them with as much attention as her tense, uncertain state would allow her. At this point she had a feel for both, as well as an idea of how they were connected. But she wanted to run some more focused textual experiments on them to be certain that her intuitions were leading her in a useful direction. And then, she wanted to speak with Archer about what he'd discovered. He'd been on sight in Thrace for close to a decade. It was his project more than it was hers.

The tea in her glass had cooled, and she took a few absentminded sips of it. Then she opened the *Rihla* and began reading haphazardly to remind herself of the contours of this particular manuscript version of the text. The *Travels* was one of the most well-known classical Arabic works in the world, and the story was already more than familiar to her. Every manuscript, though, was different, and it wouldn't hurt to reacquaint herself with the idiosyncrasies of this one.

Ibn Battuta, she reminded herself as she skimmed, had left Morocco in the 1320s, ostensibly to go on a pilgrimage to Mecca. Rather than returning home to North Africa after completing his religious duty, however, he had continued his journey. Over the next thirty years he'd visited most of the Muslim world, including East Africa, Western China, South Asia, and Indonesia. The *Rihla* was a memoir of his journey. It was extensive, detailed, and on occasion fanciful and grotesque in a seductively medieval sort of way. Ibn Battuta was more than accurate. But his accuracy was the stuff of fourteenth-century story telling rather than nineteenth-century positivism.

The sections of the story documenting his travels in Anatolia in the 1330s were the most familiar to Marion in her academic capacity, as they were frequently—if critically—used by scholars of post-Seljuk rule at the time. And, she was pleased to note, it was the Anatolian sections of the manuscript in front of her that departed most significantly from other extant manuscript versions of Ibn Battuta's writing. Whereas much of the *Rihla* contained questionable content—few of its scholarly readers believing that Ibn Battuta had personally visited all the areas he described—the Anatolian sections were particularly baffling. The extant manuscripts all depicted a journey through Anatolia that skipped over hundreds or even thousands of miles in a single day or week—not to mention bizarre backtracking, circling, and repetition. As much as the rest of the story was fantastic, it didn't strain a reader's credulity quite so insistently as the Anatolian sections did.

But, Marion was smiling as she re-read the passages she had first translated in Chelsea, neither did this manuscript. This version of the text filled in the blanks of the Anatolian journey, as well as the visits to Seljuk and nascent Ottoman towns, with a remarkable attention to detail. And in some areas, Ibn Battuta's style in this variation on his travels would have pleased the most exacting of last century's social scientists. The manuscript she had here made Ibn Battuta an infinitely more reliable witness to fourteenth-century events in Anatolia than he had been before. And personalities. And objects.

It also took on additional—and fraught—meaning when read against the Aşıkpaşazade that had been bound together with it. Aşıkpaşazade's history of the Ottoman dynasty, compiled a little over a century after Ibn Battuta's *Rihla*, was also a well-studied text, by no means obscure. For the most part, though, it appealed only to historians of the early Ottoman Empire looking for source material on the first two to three hundred years of Ottoman expansion into the Balkans. It lacked the general appeal of Ibn Battuta's global travelogue.

Aşıkpaşazade had been born in Amasya, in Anatolia, just south of the Black Sea, in 1400, the descendent of a family of well-connected Sufi dervishes. He wrote his history of the Ottoman dynasty at the age of eighty-six, after witnessing—and in some cases joining—the Ottoman political expansion into the Balkans. Like Ibn Battuta, he had completed his pilgrimage at a young age, and he had then continued his travels, in this case as a soldier taking part in a series of Ottoman military campaigns in southeastern Europe throughout the 1440s and 1450s. After participating in the Sultan Mehmet II's conquest of Constantinople in 1453, Aşıkpaşazade had settled in the new capital city, now Istanbul, and had become an entrepreneur, buying up land, shops, houses, and businesses in his old age.

Aşıkpaşazade's history of the Ottoman state purported to be a tale of origins, but its primary goal was to legitimize the unification of the Balkans and Anatolia under a single Muslim ruler. Or, as some scholars were beginning to argue, to glorify early Ottoman military rule as a means of griping about the post-conquest bureaucratization and centralization that led to the taxation of Aşıkpaşazade's own urban property in the 1460s and 1470s.

What Marion found intriguing about reading the Aşıkpaşazade against her unusually complete Ibn Battuta, though, was his interest in the city of Edirne, the second Ottoman capital city, and "gateway" to the conquest of Thrace. And she was now re-reading a famous scene in Aşıkpaşazade's history—describing a banquet in Edirne celebrating the circumcision of Mehmet II's two sons—with more care. The details of this version of the chapter were strange. Worth reconsidering. At the very least, Aşıkpaşazade's style in the chapter suggested a common political goal driving the production of both this text and her apocryphal *Rihla*—a goal beyond travelogue and chronicle.

Not to mention that the overlaps she was sensing between the two manuscripts also threw her court records into striking relief. The Ottoman Islamic law courts in the Balkans—the *kadi* courts—had been overrun throughout the sixteenth, seventeenth, and even eighteenth centuries by repeated complaints of raided, desecrated, or unquiet graves. As many as one or two complaints every month.

The *kadi*s, or judges, uncertain how to deal with what they saw as disruptive local superstition, invariably wrote to their superiors in Istanbul asking for advice. And the head of the

Islamic legal bureaucracy in Istanbul equally invariably wrote back advising the *kadi*s to let the peasants have their superstitions. If villagers in Wallachia wanted to dig up a cemetery to prevent the spread of vampirism, Istanbul ordered, the provincial *kadi* should look the other way. It wasn't in the central government's interest to annoy their majority Christian populations by imposing restrictions on their mostly harmless practices.

These exchanges had become so widespread by the end of the seventeenth century that the documents were formulaic. And the paper trails produced by these complaints, requests for advice, and responses had become a favorite set of material for students of Ottoman and Balkan history in recent years. Commonplace.

The Bulgarian *sicil*s in front of Marion, however, were different. First, there was the repeated reference to the *Rihla* and to Aşıkpaşazade's history in the verbal testimony that the court scribe had ostensibly reproduced verbatim. And second, more mysterious, the plaintiffs claimed in *these* documents that the graves had been desecrated not to prevent something from rising up, but rather to remove something that was already buried. The complaints were not about destructive and superstitious vandalism, but about theft. Odd, to say the least. Marion was impatient to know what Archer had made of them.

REMEMBERING Archer, she looked over at a Telechron clock that he had improbably brought with him from Bulgaria and displayed on a windowsill of his new flat. It was 5:30. He'd be returning from the café soon.

Marion organized her papers into a neat pile at the edge of the table, took her cold tea into the kitchen, poured what was left in the pot down the sink, and brought plates and cutlery back out to the dining room. She arranged the food at the center of the table and returned to the kitchen for glasses and the bottles of mineral water. She was putting the bottles on the table when Archer opened the door and entered the flat. "Marion!" Removing his muffler and hat. "Darling, you've cooked." He was still speaking Turkish.

"Don't mock me. This is the best I do."

"I wouldn't dream of mocking you." He walked to the table and examined the dishes. "And I'm truly delighted. I keep my contact with the grocer limited nowadays. Made the mistake of referring to his meatballs as 'kufte' rather than 'köfte,' and he's been trying to trick me into further Bosnian slip-ups ever since. Intelligent man. I'm frightened of him."

She poured him a glass of mineral water and then poured herself one. They both sat and helped themselves to the food. "Why didn't you just resurface as Bosnian? Not that you don't make a wonderful Laz. But was the extra layer of obfuscation necessary?"

"Habit of dishonesty?" He shrugged, looking Slavic again. Sipped his water. "Although I suppose I also worried about that husband of yours poking about in my early papers, looking for a clue as to my whereabouts. I *think* that most of the material linking Christopher Archer to Adnan Spahovic has been scattered to the four winds. But winds can be tricky. A nasty one, some mischievous little *meltem* out to do harm, might blow my notorious past straight back to London. And so, for now, it's Dündar."

Marion nodded. "More than a sufficient explanation. I'll not question the decision again. Believe me, Dündar, I know what it's like to have that section of the office intent on tracking you. Leaves one jittery. At best."

"Jittery is a good way to put it." He dipped bread in yogurt and took a bite. Chewed thoughtfully. "So how shall we do this?"

"I was going to ask you the same thing. I'm happy to tell you what I've found. Or what I think I've found. If you'd like to start there. But I don't want to be pushy—it's your project."

He sighed. "My project. Yes. Eight years of my project up in smoke after one idiot mistake."

"What happened?" She wanted to comfort him, but she wasn't confident enough to force her sympathy on him. Dropped her eyes instead and concentrated on eating a few bites of the bean salad.

He was still thinking. Eating. And then, abruptly, he spoke: "let me tell you what I was supposed to be doing there—"

"No!" She raised her eyes to his, rattled. "I mustn't know. I can't know—"

"It's fallen to pieces anyway, Marion. Don't trouble yourself. And you'll need at least an outline of the operation to help me fix it." He drank another sip of his mineral water. "Besides, if Maugham's domestics went through my flat in Sofia, the office has this much already. Won't serve them any better than it served me." He held her eyes. "So I'll tell you. All right?"

She was still worried. But she nodded. Maybe one day she'd learn to keep herself closed off, or at least keep from being so easily tricked into talking. Her openness was becoming an increasingly severe liability to her work. Suppressing the further protests that were already forming at the front of her mind, she nodded again.

He rolled a dolma to one side of his plate with a fork. Considered. Rolled it back to the other side of the plate. Then he spoke again. "The assignment was simple. Straightforward. But it was also demanding. A lot of time and a lot of detailed work. My position at the Embassy in Sofia was ideal for it." He paused. Reflected again. And then he violently stabbed the dolma with his fork.

She jumped, startled, and he laughed at himself, surprised by his loss of control. He glanced up, embarrassed. "Oh dear. I'm sorry, Marion. I'm just so very angry with myself for having wrecked this. After so many years. I'm having difficulty being rational about it."

Marion stared at his plate, entertained, fighting a smile. "Don't apologize, Dündar. What you did there to that poor dolma? That's been the impulse I've been fighting for a good decade now. I understand. I empathize wholly and without reservation."

He handed the fork to her. "Here. Take this. Better that I don't have it while talking."

Still smiling, she set the fork next to her own on the table. "All right. Continue."

"So, my assignment," he said, "was to contact Kira Maria—"

"Kira Maria—?"

"Yes." He paused. "And yes. Precisely what you think. Kira Maria, the mysterious wife of the Bulgarian Emperor, Ivan Shishman."

"Ah." Marion replied. "The Kira Maria, then, who died in the 1380s."

"The same." He watched her for a reaction. When she didn't say anything, he lifted an eyebrow. "If you can believe it, this is the least bizarre aspect of the project."

"Sadly, I *can* believe it." She touched his fork with her fingertip. "Go on. So, eight years ago, you're asked to contact a Bulgarian Empress Consort who has been dead for half a millennium."

He lifted a hand. "Let me put it to you this way. In a romantically decrepit castle, a little over forty miles east of Sofia, lives a woman calling herself Kira Maria. Is she a descendent of the original Kira Maria? Who knows? Is she Kira Maria herself, preserved, immortal, and feasting on the local villagers? Possibly. Is she some crazed peasant woman with a rich fantasy life and a talent for breaking into medieval fortresses? Irrelevant, as far as our superiors are concerned. What she does have—and this is irrefutable—is an object, or, I suppose 'tool,' for pacifying Thrace. Which is—desirable? Yes? At present? You've been following recent regional events, I trust?"

"Yes."

"The British position on this 'tool,' and on the pacification of the region more generally, is at best equivocal. A bit of instability, they've decided, a bit of religious tension, a few massacres here and there never did anyone any harm as far as the office, especially, is concerned. More so if the instability keeps British industry ahead of anything developing in Central or Eastern Europe. Maugham and the rest don't like antiquities that might dispel regional tensions. Particularly when those antiquities remain outside of their control." He paused. "Our people, however, do go in for stability. For the most part. Yes, they like their assassinations. But mass killing and amorphous hatred? That sort of thing makes them nervous."

"Hmm." She nodded. "I'm getting an idea of what you're working on. Sounds familiar even. But why would it take close to a decade to speak to this woman? If she does have the—the secret to Balkan stability?"

He stood and walked into the kitchen. Flipped on a light against the gathering darkness outside the windows. Returned with a package of clove cigarettes and an ashtray. He placed the ashtray on the table between them and held out the package to her. She took a cigarette and waited. He took one as well, lit hers and his with the same match, and then he relaxed back into the chair opposite her.

He held the cigarette between his thumb and index finger, the rest of his fingers curved around its end. Took a drag and blew the smoke down. Marion smiled to herself. Another refugee habit. Hiding the burning tip from the eyes of any local police or patrols. She wondered whether he smoked that way in Sofia's Embassy building. And if so, what his colleagues made of it.

"I'll tell you a bit more about Kira Maria. That will help you to understand." He set the smoldering cigarette in an ashtray next to the match and gathered his thoughts. "As a historical figure, almost nothing is known of her. Whereas her husband, Ivan Shishman, has become the stuff of legend. Basic story is that Ivan was an incompetent, selfish, and eventually frantic ruler. He was going to lose out to the Ottomans anyway. There was a certain inevitability to their incorporation of Thrace into the Empire. But he certainly did nothing to halt their advance. Routed at the Battle of Kosovo in 1389. Refused to take part altogether in the Battle of Chernomen in 1371. At one point he tried to buy time by offering the Sultan Murad his sister in marriage. But then, in 1396, he lost Bulgaria in its entirety, at Nicopolis. Executed."

"Yes," she said. "It's not my field, but I know the general outline of the story. He's something of a folk hero now, isn't he?"

He laughed. "They all are. These doomed fourteenth- and fifteenth-century tyrants. They could lose every battle, convert between Christianity and Islam eighteen times for convenience's sake, rape their allies' daughters, rape their own daughters for that matter, and they'd still, now, be the intrepid crusaders holding the thin line of civilization against the barbarian Turk."

He lifted his hands again, palms up. Bosnian amusement at five hundred years' worth of peasant absurdity. "But two things make Ivan Shishman a bit more interesting than the others. The first is his family. Two sons. The eldest, Alexander/Iskender, converted to Islam and became a successful Ottoman governor. I went to school with a boy who claimed to be a descendant of an illegitimate heir to that branch of the family. Living mostly in Izmir now. The younger son, Fruzhin, remained Christian, continued fighting the Ottomans, and died a glorious martyr's death."

"Romantic."

"Not all that uncommon at the time." He picked up the cigarette. "Very concrete interpretation of the 'heir and spare' idea in the fourteenth- and fifteenth-century Balkans. I myself am a direct product of it."

"What *is* interesting about the family, then?" she asked.

"The mother," he replied. "Kira Maria. Remarkably—invisible—for an Empress Consort. Difficult to establish that she was even the mother of the two boys. Or if she was Ivan Shishman's only wife. *But*—and this is where the story becomes relevant—she *is* prominent in one of the more apocryphal accounts of the Emperor's last days."

"In what way?"

He smiled. "So, Ivan was an embarrassment as a military commander, an awful brother, a useless diplomat, likely a usurper in the first place, and yet—a great hero. Do you know what for?"

"No."

"Just before the Ottomans overran his territory, he successfully buried the legendary and sacred 'Treasure of Bulgaria' out of their reach. Somewhere along the Maritsa river. And Kira Maria, it seems, vanished along with it."

"Oh, I see. So our people believe—"

"Exactly."

"And you were supposed to—what? Just go and ask her for it?"

He lifted the cigarette from the ashtray and took an agitated drag. Then he ground it out. "No. And that's where I ruined it. Kira Maria refuses to speak to anyone who doesn't first give her 'the sign.' And when I say, 'the sign,' I'm not talking about a secret signal or code or anything so prosaic as that. My contact explained to me that there is a specific, physical *sign*, a 'key,' that her interlocutors must present to her before she'll acknowledge them. That 'sign' or 'key' has been lost for centuries." He stopped speaking. Thought for a moment. "They did, however, pick up a trace of it in the library in Baquba—"

"Oh God." Marion put her hand over her mouth. "But then I compromised the collection. Oh Dündar. I'm so sorry. I'm so very, very sorry."

"Marion, no one blames you for that." Embarrassed. It was clear that he'd worried she would react in this way to his information. He looked her hard in the eyes. "What were you supposed to do? Let them slaughter the entire population of Diyala? They would have. And they would have destroyed the library in the process. It wasn't your fault."

She couldn't face him. Averted her eyes to the table. "But it made your job impossible. You couldn't put the pieces together."

"They told me that they could get the manuscript to me anyway. Ordered me to wait. And stall." He put his hand over hers. She noted in a wry part of her mind that, unlike she herself, he had no difficulty comforting a colleague. She was annoyed with herself for her earlier self-consciousness.

"And you tried," she supplied. "But as time passed, the office got suspicious."

"I'd gathered together the court documents," he said. "Every *sicil* I needed. And I'd mapped them. It had taken seven years, but I had the archive together in one place. I was ready to take the next step. All that was left was the manuscript." He took his hand off hers and leaned back in his chair. "When they were slow about producing it, I even tried to use a different copy of Ibn Battuta. Contemporary to the one from the library, but—"

"Yes," she said. "They found it in your flat."

"Useless."

"So what did you do?"

"I approached Kira Maria without the key. To explain the situation."

"And?"

"Dear God." He shuddered. "The woman nearly killed me. I thought she was going to set her wolves on me or throw me off a parapet."

"Picturesque."

"Not at the time." He smiled at her. "But I'm here, so no harm done."

She blinked, thinking. "All right. Your immediate goal, then, is to find this 'sign' or 'key' so that you can approach Kira Maria. Once you find it, you go to Sofia, present it to her, and she—well, for now, let's say she speaks with you."

"You make it sound so easy." He was lighting another cigarette.

Marion realized she hadn't smoked any of her own. It was all ash. She crushed it out in the ashtray. "I can help you find the sign."

"After one day of research?"

"Not one day," she corrected him. "I was incarcerated for weeks with nothing to occupy myself but that manuscript. And then I spent a good five days hopping between trains with your *sicils*. I merely needed to compare my impressions of them. With both in the same room. I have. Or, I did. This afternoon. I think I know what you ought to do. Or, at least, where you'll want to start."

"Very well, then. Let's have it."

"Did you find time to read through this version of the *Rihla*?"

He shook his head. "No."

"It's an extraordinary manuscript. More than extraordinary. Priceless. One of a kind. Because do you know what it does?" She didn't give him the chance to answer. "It fills in the blanks of Ibn Battuta's journey through Anatolia in the 1330s. No more magical transportation between Konya and Van in a single day. No more painful, pointless backtracking along the Black Sea coast. It describes the journey as a rational, straightforward trek. And it's detailed."

"Half the faculty of Cambridge Oriental Studies would commit murder for access to it," he suggested.

"Half the faculty of Cambridge Oriental Studies would commit murder anyway," she said. "For fun. But yes. For this especially? They would." She glanced over at the papers she'd stacked at the end of the table. "For our purposes, the important bit is the description of Ibn Battuta's visit to the Sufi dervish, Ashiq Pasha's, tomb, his türbe, in Kırşehir. Halfway between Konya and the Black Sea coast."

"I already know where you're going." Suddenly full of energy. "Ashiq Pasha, obviously, being Aşıkpaşazade's progenitor."

"You're quick for a Laz. And yes. Aşıkpaşazade mentions only about eight hundred times in his history that he's descended from the great Sufi dervish, Ashiq Pasha. It's embarrassing at times. But it certainly makes identifying the connection easier." She paused. "So, in this version of the *Rihla*, Ibn Battuta visited the resting place of Aşıkpaşazade's ancestor—or, to be more accurate, Ibn Battuta visited the ancestor himself—*before* Ashiq Pasha died, in 1333. And, according to the manuscript, Ashiq Pasha showed Ibn Battuta a 'treasure' kept by his sect. It was an odd treasure for a Sufi sect to honor. The text refers to it as a *sicil*."

"A register?" Confused. "What does that have to do with dervishes?"

"That took me a while to understand as well. Made no sense at all. But then, I wondered, what would happen if I read the word not as the Turkish or Arabic *sicil* but as a transliteration of the Thracian Latin *sigil*. When I did, things fell into place."

"Because in Latin," he said, "a sigil isn't a register or a document—"

"It's a talisman. An object. A magic key," she finished for him.

"So the *Rihla*," he said, "or at least *this Rihla*, has identified the provenance of the 'key' we're looking for. Aşıkpaşazade's family kept it."

"And then Aşıkpaşazade's history itself," she added, "taken along with your Bulgarian court documents, tells us where he put it. After it had been passed along to him. Those graves that were desecrated in the seventeenth century were desecrated by someone, or by some group, out to find the 'sign' or 'key' that would allow them to access Kira Maria and the rest of the 'treasure.'"

"And you know where Aşıkpaşazade left it—?"

"I have an idea," she said. "I think you'll want to start in Edirne. I also have a more tenuous hypothesis about what will happen when you get to Edirne, given how the manuscripts fit together as a whole. If you'd like to hear it? It may not be relevant."

"Let's hear it."

"All right," she said, trying to present her ideas as coherently to him as she could. "The second Sultan of the Ottoman Empire, Orhan, had a son, Süleyman Pasha. Aşıkpaşazade goes into raptures about Süleyman Pasha's conquest of Thrace in the 1340s. He also praises, extensively, Lala Shahin's conquest of Edirne for the next Sultan, Murad, less than twenty years later. What's interesting about these passages is their description of the *speed* of the conquest. The Ottoman expansion into the Balkans went remarkably fast once Lala Shahin got to work. Too fast. In some cases, the leaders of the cities the Ottomans were approaching simply opened the gates and welcomed them."

"The Ottomans were nice people," Archer said. "Pleasant to know. Why doubt the hospitality of those well-defended fortresses?"

"Right," she smiled. "An alternative interpretation is that the Ottoman dynasty had some—some sort of object—that leant them legitimacy. That helped those gates to swing open. That helped them to expand. And Dündar, if you read Aşıkpaşazade's history with that in mind, there are hints about this object all over the place. For example, there's a repeated reference, as each Sultan dies, to the fact that these early Sultans had *no* legacy, nothing to inherit, *except* their 'legitimacy to conquer.' Given what we've been reading, I'm beginning to think that the 'legitimacy' that Aşıkpaşazade keeps invoking is less rhetorical than it is physical. I think it was an object."

"The 'treasure' or 'key,'" Archer said.

"Yes," she repeated. "But then 1402 happened. The Ottoman state collapsed when the Sultan Bayezid was captured by Timur. Tamerlane. The Ottomans lost most of their land during the civil war that followed. And I think that they also lost the 'treasure,' somewhere in the Balkans. Likely Bulgaria since you've mapped those court documents. But although they lost the treasure itself, they kept the sign or the key that granted them access to it. And that also granted Aşıkpaşazade's family the access to the dynasty that he emphasizes so often in his history."

"He could have simply been a snob." Archer was grinning too.

"Stop it," she laughed. "I'm proud of myself. Let me finish. *I* think that the 'treasure' or '*sicil*' that the Sufi dervish, Ashiq Pasha, showed to Ibn Battuta in Kırşehir in the 1330s was the object that was about to help the Ottomans move into Thrace and the Balkans. I think that Aşıkpaşazade's family retained and then hid the 'key' that would lead to this 'treasure' even after the treasure itself was lost in 1402. I think that your Kira Maria, or her post-1380s descendants, retained the 'treasure,' but not the key. And I think that those Sharia court documents of the seventeenth century are documenting a renewed search for the key. Someone, or some group, in the seventeenth century thought they had an idea of where to find the key. And they thought that, with it, they might access Kira Maria and the treasure."

"But they were digging up the graves in Sofia," he reminded her. "Not Edirne."

"Yes," she conceded. "My only response to that is that they may have been misled. I'm not sure why they believed it was in Sofia. I'm convinced it's in Edirne. There's a passage from Aşıkpaşazade's history that appears in every one of those *sicil*s of yours. Every one. It isn't attributed to him, but it's unquestionably from his history. When Aşıkpaşazade describes the celebration of the circumcisions at the palace in Edirne, he mentions that Mehmet II rewarded the dervishes for coming. He says, specifically, that the dervishes 'came poor, and left rich.' And in every document from your collection, at some point, one of the plaintiffs says the same thing. Identical formulation. It can't be an accident. So, my guess is that you're looking for something in Edirne, close to the palace, likely a tomb, and likely a particular type of tomb—a Sufi's or a Janissary's—"

"*Hurufi*s." Archer interrupted her.

"What?"

"*Hurufi*s," he repeated. "A Sufi sect. Came out of Azerbaijan. Huge influence among the early Janissaries, the Ottoman soldiers. Edirne became a central city in the spread of *Hurufi* spiritualism throughout the Empire—despite the orthodox religious establishment trying to stamp it out. Mehmet II was even suspected of being a follower. *Hurufi*s believe—believed," he corrected himself, "that alphabetic characters or signs carried mystical meaning. In and of themselves. As a result, they left behind quite a bit of—writing—I suppose you might call it. If we're looking for a Janissary's tomb with a connection to Anatolian Sufism, to Aşıkpaşazade's family, to talismanic *sigil*s, *and* to the conquest of the Balkans, it will be a *Hurufi* tomb." He looked sly. "We'll simply look for one with the proper set of signs."

Marion stood and stretched. Gathered the dishes to take to the kitchen to wash. "I'm feeling optimistic."

"Leave them," he replied, referring to the dishes. "We'll deal with our mess tomorrow. My life's philosophy."

Marion took the dishes she already had in her hands to the kitchen and placed them in the sink. Walked back out to the living room and kissed Archer's cheek. "I like you a lot, Dündar. I'm glad they didn't collect you."

He kissed her forehead. "I'm glad they didn't collect me too."

She laughed. Then she crossed to the other end of the flat, used the toilet, cleaned her teeth, and returned to her bedroom. Archer was in the kitchen washing the dishes when she left the toilet. Which annoyed her. Rather than chastising him for his exaggerated hospitality, she slipped quietly into the guestroom, pushed herself under the covers of her bed and fell asleep.

$\int$HE woke the next morning to the smell of coffee and pastry. Excited about continuing their work, she rose hastily from the bed, pulled on her trousers and jumper from the previous day, and walked barefoot into the bath to wash her face. She pinned back her hair and followed the smell of Archer's cooking into the kitchen.

He had heard her moving about the living room, and he was pouring coffee out of a copper *cezve* into two small cups when she entered the kitchen. He had already divided a heap of warm *kifle* between two plates and arranged jam and honey on the counter. He handed her a plate and a cup of coffee. They ate standing in the kitchen. He was already dressed for a journey in thick tweed trousers, a cotton shirt and a wool cardigan. He looked like he'd stepped out of a Charles James Lee story of the Cornish seaside.

She spread jam on a piece of *kifla* and took a bite. "I think you protest too much about people spotting your Bosnian slip-ups." Chewing the ostentatiously Slavic pastry. "You want to be caught. Excessive national pride."

He sipped his coffee. "And I think you're the last person in this business to fault me for my self-sabotaging tendencies. My desire to get caught? Really, Marion?"

She laughed, stung. "Fine. I can tell already that I'll be the loser in this conversation. So I'll simply compliment you on this beautifully prepared breakfast, *Dündar*. What *do* you call these in Laz, then?"

"*Kifle,*" he said. "We call them *kifle* in Laz. I understand they call them the same thing in Sarajevo. Although I wouldn't know from personal experience."

"Very well. I concede to your superior ability to fit in." She drank a large portion of her coffee and enjoyed the feeling of the caffeine hitting her bloodstream. Finished her *kifla*. Licked the jam off her fingers. "Do you have any thoughts on next steps?"

"We go to Edirne, no?"

"Are you certain you want to travel with me? Or that you want me to be there at all? I've told you all I know. You have both sets of documents. And I have a feeling I'll be more of a liability than a help from now on. The office will know I'm in Istanbul at this point. They'll be looking for me."

"All the more reason to go to Edirne, then." He was washing their coffee cups.

"Dündar," she reasoned with him. "Don't take unnecessary risks out of some misplaced protective sensibility. At some point I'm going to let myself be picked up anyway. I can't leave my son with them."

He finished washing the cups and turned to her. "So, what's your plan then? Wander Sirkeci station looking suspicious until they figure it out and grab you?"

"Why not?"

He put the jam and the honey into a cupboard. He wasn't looking at her. "Why bother moving your money?"

"I don't know." Her excitement was dissipating. Replaced by the more familiar dull hopelessness that ordinarily dogged her. "A pointless little rebellion? To make myself feel less implicated? I try not to examine my impulses too carefully."

He smiled to himself. "Very well. You've said several times that this is my project. My operation. That means I'm in charge."

"Yes."

"So you'll follow my orders."

"Yes." Suspicious.

"Good. I think you'll be helpful in Edirne. I do have a general idea now of how the documents fit together. But you're the mastermind when it comes to this sort of enterprise. I'd like you to assist me in identifying the proper tomb."

She dropped her eyes. "Thank you, Dündar."

"Good," he said again.

"The stations will be watched." She was tracing a pattern on the kitchen countertop with her fingertip.

He wiped his hands on a kitchen towel. "No worries. We'll take my vehicle."

"You *drive?*" She was startled into raising her eyes to his again.

"In a manner of speaking." He turned and left the kitchen. "Pack your things. It's a four-hour journey and we'll need a place to stay once we arrive."

She went into the toilet for her toothbrush, wrapped it and put it in her carpet bag, pulled on her socks and boots, grabbed the canvas sack full of her American dollars, and walked to the dining table to settle the manuscript and documents on top of the dollars. "Ready."

"Me too." He'd put on a hat and a canvas coat.

Laughing quietly, she slipped into her own winter coat. "I just know we're forgetting something."

"We aren't." He opened the door and stepped to the side to let her precede him. "And if we are, Kira Maria will be more than happy to lend us what we need."

The smell of the goat reached the top of the building. Still smiling, followed by Archer, she trudged down the narrow spiral staircase toward Siraselviler street. Her excitement had returned. She was grateful to Archer for allowing her to stay with him. At least for a few days longer.

When they were out on the street, Archer pointed further down the hill, and they walked for three or four minutes until he stopped and opened the unlocked passenger door of a mid-sized, industrial panel lorry, an ugly light blue.

"This?" She stared at him.

"I stole it. In Burgas. When I was leaving Bulgaria." Pleased with himself.

"You can drive it?"

"Get in and see. I learned quickly."

She climbed into the passenger seat, metal with a small, red pillow, embroidered implausibly with yellow flowers. Someone had worked on it. Which left her saddened for whoever had missed it once Archer had appropriated it. Necessity, she told herself, not very convincingly.

Archer had moved around the back and was climbing into the driver's seat. "I *think*," he said as he turned the ignition, "that it was built in the Polski-Fiat plant. In Warsaw. Papers were in the back."

There was a painted, wooden crucifix hanging from the mirror. She touched it with her fingertip, and it wobbled.

He glanced over at her and then maneuvered, jerking, into the light morning traffic. "I had the chance to get to know it well on my travels. Slept in it a few times." He patted the dashboard, affectionate, and then remembered himself and swerved out of the way of an angry *simit* seller. "And it was more than up for the job. Handled rough roads. Roads that scarcely deserved to be called roads. Even if it seems constitutionally unable to go faster than forty miles per hour."

Marion was enjoying herself, despite the mind-numbing vibration of the vehicle as it picked up speed. "You're certain it will make it?"

"Not remotely." He pushed the accelerator pedal all the way to the floor. Which did nothing. "But *inşallah.*"

"*İnşallah,*" she agreed. Then she looked out the window to appreciate the passing, if jumbled, scenery.

And less than four hours later, against all odds, they reached the outskirts of Edirne. Archer was guiding the lorry along the main road into the southeast section of the city, when Marion turned to him. "Stop."

"What's wrong?" He slowed the lorry and eased it onto the grassy shoulder. "Did you see something? I can try to lose them."

"No." She shook her head. "It's not that. Or, at least, I haven't noticed a tail." She pulled her canvas bag into her lap and removed the manuscript. Smoothed open the crumbling pages and ran her finger along the lines of the *Rihla*. "I had a thought." She flipped forward to the Aşıkpaşazade. Concentrated on the passage in front of her. Squeezed her eyes shut. Then she opened her eyes and smiled. "Circle the city," she said to him. "We'll go in from the northwest."

"Why?" Archer was smiling as well, picking up her mood. "What just clicked?"

She turned to him, pushing the manuscript back into the canvas bag. "I had been dissatisfied with the tenuous connection between Sofia and Edirne. I couldn't figure out how the defendants in those trials, if they *were* members of our organization circa the 1600s, could have been so clumsy. Digging up the wrong graves. Getting themselves arrested. Finding nothing. Especially when all along the *sigil*, or the 'key,' they were supposed to be locating was two hundred miles away from Sofia. Here, in Edirne. It seemed—ineffective. Incompetent. Not like our people."

"True." He thought for a moment. "But I can attest, personally, to the clumsiness that comes of desperation. I fell prey to it myself, Marion."

She shook her head. "No. This was nothing like what happened to you. It was too haphazard. And it was extended. Lasted for months." She paused. "But then, I thought, what *wasn't* haphazard in those documents were the references to the two manuscripts. Those sections were deliberate. Like clockwork. In every record, in every *sicil*, references to the same two manuscripts. To the same two passages in both manuscripts. Ibn Battuta and Aşıkpaşazade. Ibn Battuta and Aşıkpaşazade. Over and over and over again. It belied the randomness of the cases themselves."

"Hmm."

"So what if it wasn't the defendants who were working for the organization, Dündar? What if it was the court scribe?" She paused again. "Here's what I think. I think the facts of the cases were real. I think that they *were* commonplace vampire registers. The defendants, in good faith, were desecrating graves to halt the spread of supernatural monsters. Like the good peasants they were. But the scribe was one of us. He simply used the vampire panic in Sofia to pass along a message to his contacts in Istanbul. And the message was from Kira Maria herself. Or, at least, it was a message from the Kira Maria of the 1600s. Who knows? Perhaps she even whipped up the frenzy in the first place to give him the opportunity to make his point. Left a few picturesquely mauled bodies here and there. Accidentally let the wolf out at night—"

"But," she interrupted herself, "even more important than the possibility that the scribe was passing along a message, was that the message wasn't a plea to help her *find* the sign or the key. She already knew where it was. She was asking him to tell his people to relocate it. For whatever reason, she was unhappy with the *sigil*'s location. It *was* in Sofia. But she wanted it better hidden. Maybe she felt it had been compromised. So the references to the manuscripts in those *sicils* were a means of telling the scribe's contacts, further south, where to move the key. Where to hide it."

"And you know where they moved it."

"Yes," she said. "I think you were correct about the *Hurufi* connection. But we're not looking for a tomb with Sufi alphabetic characters. We're looking for a bridge with Sufi alphabetic characters."

"A bridge?"

"Easier, no?" She smiled at him. "Not so many of them in the city. I had been focusing on the references to the circumcision ceremony in the Aşıkpaşazade. But the court scribe kept coming back to two distinct passages in the *Rihla* as well. Both were depictions of Kırşehir. I think the scribe wanted to draw a parallel between Ibn Battuta's visit to Kırşehir and Aşıkpaşazade's residence in Edirne."

Archer thought for a moment. "This is dubious, Marion."

"But there's more." She put her hand on the manuscript resting in her lap. "I couldn't understand why the version of the *Rihla* that we received was so different from other extant copies, whereas the Aşıkpaşazade, although old, is no different from a handful of other manuscripts. But then I realized, there's one—*one*—passage in the Aşıkpaşazade that is altered. Deliberately changed."

"Which is?"

She ran her finger along the text. "This bit. This poetry—very bad poetry, incidentally—that surrounds Chapter 101. In every other version of the text, the couplet reads: 'Aşıkpaşazade has written these stories as a warning; when has a bird alighted on a branch and not flown away?' But in *this* version, in our version, the word 'bird,' '*kuş*' has been replaced by the word 'bridge,' '*köprü*.'"

"I don't believe it."

"It doesn't alter the meter all that much," she said. "And Aşıkpaşazade is never very concerned with adhering to classical poetic form in any case. To the say the least. His poetry is, to put it kindly, awkward. But in every other version of this chapter—the Istanbul manuscript, the Upsala manuscript, you name it—the line reads '*kaçan kondu budağa uçmadı kuş*.' In this one, it reads '*kaçan kondu budağa uçmadı köprü*.'"

He laughed. "That's slippery language, even for old Ottoman. Every one of those words has about twelve contradictory meanings. Except for 'bird' and 'bridge.'"

"Yes," she agreed. "Or, you might say 'flexible meanings?' Open to interpretation? Maybe he wasn't the terrible poet everyone faults him for being."

"I'm already imagining some evocative alternative translations of that last line." He tapped his fingers on the wheel of the car. "How about he's 'written these stories as a warning: consider a bridge set on—knotted branches? that nonetheless never falls?' Although, do you know, Marion? That translation sounds more like our people than it does like Aşıkpaşazade. I worry," he mused, "that our organization may have done violence to his text."

"They've improved it," she said. "And yes. I like your translation. We're looking for a bridge. We're looking for a bridge that has been built up a number of times. On knotted foundations or frames. And ideally with some connection to Ashiq Pasha in Kırşehir."

"Do you have an idea of which bridge?"

"I have more than an idea," she said. "Because Dündar, a million years ago, in my long-suffering scholarly capacity, I visited Kırşehir's beautiful thirteen-arch Seljuk bridge, Kesikköprü, built sometime near 1270—its intricate, if baffling inscription, full of mystical Sufi letters, still intact. I also visited the *han*, the caravanserai, adjacent to that bridge. There's a lovely portal to that building. Covered, if you can believe it, by a motif of repeated keys. Carved into the stone. A good eighteen of them."

She leaned back against the seat of the lorry. "And," she continued, "I also visited, more recently, although as nothing more than a fascinated tourist, the beautiful eleven-arch Byzantine bridge, Gazi Mihal köprüsü, built sometime near 1270, right here in Edirne—its intricate, if baffling inscription, full of mystical, if well hidden, Sufi letters, still intact. Both bridges were repurposed by the Ottomans in the fifteenth, sixteenth, and seventeenth centuries. Both reflect the key motif. It's prominent on the *han* attached to Kesikköprü. It's hidden near the foundations, more often than not under water, on Gazi Mihal köprüsü. But it's there on both. Keys."

"Same keys?"

"Same keys," she confirmed. "At least if you're looking for them. Which, it seems, our scribe has suggested that we try doing. *Hurufis* like that, don't they? Letters as 'keys' that work in secret, and in the process open or reveal the world?"

Archer started the lorry and maneuvered it back onto the road. "I'm not sure their interpretation of the power of letters is quite so concrete. They prefer their messages in smoke and water. But yes. I believe they do enjoy that sort of thing."

She looked sidelong at him as he drove, bearing off onto a smaller side road that would skirt the city and take them northwest. "And *Bektaşis*?" she persisted. "Sufi scourge of the Balkans? Dirty secret of every Ottoman ruling family between the gates of Vienna and the wilds of Moldavia? *Bektaşis* aren't all that different from *Hurufis*, are they? Do they also like that sort of thing?"

"How would I know?" He was blushing. "I'm Laz. I work hard and keep my head down." He tried to accelerate. Little happened. "And Christopher Archer wouldn't have the faintest idea what you're talking about."

"No," she agreed. "He wouldn't."

Fifteen minutes later, Archer was slowing to a stop alongside Gazi Mihal mosque, on the banks of the Tunca river. He and Marion sat in the lorry and looked out over the bridge, which was part of the same complex.

"How will this work?" he asked.

She peered across the street at a muddy field, a few leafless trees scattered throughout it. Clumps of dirty snow. Then she gazed back at the bridge. "We'll do it at night."

"Do what?"

"I'll want to remove one of the stones at the base of the central arch. Under a key. See what I can find."

"That water's freezing, Marion." He tapped the wheel of the lorry with his index finger. "It's dangerous. I'll do it. My project."

"Dündar, this is one of the few aspects of my work that I do with confidence. Please. Besides, you're stronger than I am. I'll need you to pull me back up again."

"Hmm." He backed the lorry into a circle and drove for a few minutes in the direction they had come. "Agreed, then. You'll go over the side. At night." He sighed. "But in the meantime, I must eat something. I'm famished. And I think I saw a hovel back there selling Edirne's notorious liver. Are you willing? It's not for the faint of heart."

"More than willing." She turned to her window. "And more than used to you Balkan types trying to shock me by presenting me with plates of the curious bits of the animals you slaughter. I'm not some southern pansy, Dündar. No one does offal like my people."

He was smiling slightly as he pulled up alongside a small wooden structure with a hand-painted sign hammered into the ground in front of it. The sign had a single word—"liver"—written in large, capital letters in the new Latin alphabet.

"If I'm not mistaken," he said, "weren't last century's ethnographers convinced that 'your people' and the people holed up in the chilly fortresses of the Carpathians, doing unspeakable things to English solicitors, the degenerate product of one and the same stock?"

"Yes," she said climbing down from the lorry with her canvas bag. "So watch out."

He opened the door to the building and a hot blast of liver and peppers hit them in the face. They closed the door quickly against the cold and looked for a table to wait out the afternoon and evening.

MARION had a weakness for Edirne's traditional dish, and the hovel that Archer had spotted didn't disappoint. The building was a single room with a single window, at the center of which stood a fire pit with a cast iron cauldron of oil, already steaming. It was plain that the fire was never completely banked. Thinly sliced liver was waiting, prepared, on a wooden block to the left of the fire pit, and when Marion and Archer entered the room, a huge man—like a caricature of a Thracian oil wrestler, with shaved head and cartoonish biceps—welcomed them and shouted at them to sit anywhere.

They chose seats at the end of an empty communal table on the other side of the room, and a woman entered from a door leading to an enclosure outside the building. She carried two glasses of *ayran* and two sets of forks and knives. She placed the glasses in front of them, arranged the cutlery, and repeated that they were welcome. Archer, taking the lead, thanked her and said in broken Turkish that they were French tourists. Asked her for recommendations on parts of the city to visit.

Hospitable, the woman accepted his story, but there was a hesitation in her manner. She also shot a quick, split-second look at the man—presumably her husband—before giving them advice about popular tourist sites in Edirne. Marion sipped her *ayran* and reminded herself to keep alert. She thought, if anything, that they might try to steal something from them, either by stealth or by force. Kept her canvas bag in her lap.

They didn't have to keep up their conversation for long before the man behind the fire transferred fried liver, a raw onion, and a fried hot pepper to each of two plates and held the plates out to the woman to bring to them. When Marion tried the food, she preemptively forgave the proprietors for whatever they were planning. The meal was precisely what she needed. She felt less weak than she had for months.

As she ate, she became convinced that Archer had also sensed something wrong with the atmosphere of the room. But she knew better than to exchange the sort of glance that had given away the woman. As the afternoon and evening wore on, and as more patrons arrived and the restaurant grew lively, she and Archer played their roles, practicing their Turkish and showing their gratitude for the hospitality. At one point, the man slipped outside and left his cauldron unattended for close to twenty minutes. Marion didn't comment. But a half hour later, she signaled to Archer that it might be time to leave.

Archer understood at once, payed their bill, thanked the proprietor and the remaining guests, and followed Marion out of the building. She felt almost more nervous when they left without incident than she would have if someone had, at the very least, tried to extort additional money from them. She hugged her waist as they made their way to the lorry. When Archer had climbed into the driver's seat and turned the ignition, she looked over at him. "You felt it?"

"Yes," he replied. "Something was off."

"I thought they'd try to rob us."

"I was hoping they would."

"Me too." She was silent for a few minutes as Archer drove them back toward the bridge. "What do you think it was?"

"It might have been nothing more than a healthy suspicion of strangers turning up at what was an outlandishly local business." He glanced over at her. Back at the road. "The region isn't what you'd call peaceful now. And they can't encounter French tourists all that often."

"Do you believe that?"

"No."

"I could use a cigarette."

"There are some cloves in the pocket of my coat. And matches. Light one for me as well." Not confident enough in his driving to take his hands off the wheel.

She reached into his coat pocket, extracted the cigarettes, Indonesian, unfiltered, lit two, and handed one to Archer. He took a grateful drag. "Thanks."

Marion smoked, thoughtful, for a few moments. Then she said: "Maugham told Jeffrey that a pair of eyes thought she'd seen you in Edirne. When you first went under."

"Damn."

"But she wasn't certain."

"Would the office have saturated the city on the basis of so little?" he asked, more to himself than to Marion. "It seems excessive, doesn't it?" He blew smoke down and to the side, remembered himself as the lorry drifted off the road, and then righted the wheel. "If they've bribed or threatened even the likes of that establishment, they've spent an enormous amount of time and energy on this. After one unconfirmed sighting?"

"I think," she said, "that they're angry. At their loss of control."

"Damn," he repeated.

She decided that she was finished with the cigarette, rolled down the window, and tossed it out onto the road. Rolled up the window again. "Let's do this quickly," she suggested. "If my hypothesis about the *sigil* is correct, we can locate it and continue up toward Sofia tonight. The border into Bulgaria is easy. I know at least three crossing points, and I'll wager you know more. We'll be at Kira Maria's by morning." She rubbed her eyes. "And if I'm incorrect, and there's nothing at the bridge, we'll drive at least to Hıdırağa. I have a friend in town there who will let us stay for the night. Then we'll regroup. Rethink." She looked over at him. "Does that work?"

"Better than anything I have."

He was slowing the lorry to rest next to the field they'd seen earlier in the day. The bridge looked ominous now, in the moonlight. And the river did seem unpleasantly cold. She jumped down from the lorry almost before Archer had brought it to a stop and walked to the back. He shut the driver's door and followed her.

"Any rope?" she asked.

He pulled open the back doors. "Rope. Tools. I think he was a mechanic."

She felt guilty again. Pushed the feeling down. "Rope," she said, grabbing a coil, "and—hammer, I think." She pulled a hammer out of a box of what looked to be carpentry implements. Necessity, she reminded herself. She had a fantasy of returning the lorry to its owner and chided herself for her lack of professionalism.

The cold night was empty. As they walked toward the bridge, still trying, absurdly, to exude touristic keenness, they watched the bleak road that stretched away to the north and west. Nothing. But they must nonetheless work quickly. A wind was blowing dirt and gritty snow from the field into their faces. If it picked up further, she'd have difficulty examining the stonework.

They reached the edge of the bridge and then walked, still with purpose, to the central arch. Marion cast a quick look about, secured an end of the rope to a makeshift cleat on the top rail, handed a loop to Archer, wrapped a second loop around her wrist, shoved the hammer into the waistband of her trousers, and then lowered herself over the side. The wind was, if anything, stronger as it passed under the arches of the bridge. Biting. She focused her energy, ignoring the air, and peered at the underside of the arch. Concentrating, she lowered herself further. Then she stopped, looked more closely under the curve of the arch, smiled to herself, and began to swing.

Less than three minutes later, she tugged the rope to signal Archer to help her back up. When she was over the rail, landing with a graceless stumble, Archer looked disappointed. "Nothing?" He was untying the line, coiling it, and watching the road.

"Got it." She held up a small, black object. Triumphant. She thought it might be the fastest job she'd finished yet.

He stared at her. "You were over the side for less than five minutes."

"Let's get back to the lorry."

"What is it?" He was trotting after her.

"I'll tell you when we're on the road." She glanced about again. "The atmosphere here is worse. They're on us. I want out."

He nodded.

Without speaking further, they climbed into the lorry, and Archer maneuvered them onto the highway, such as it was, that would take them to the Bulgarian border. He pressed the accelerator to the floor. No acceleration. They continued at a sedate forty miles per hour, no more and no less, to the north and to the west. The mechanic's revenge.

When they'd left the outskirts of Edirne behind them, Marion turned to Archer, forgetting her anxiety and smiling. "It's a cauldron," she said, holding up the black object. "A miniature *bektaşi* cauldron—"

"Would you stop hinting at the Sufi connection?" He was laughing again, but he sounded annoyed.

"No, really!" She couldn't help laughing as well. "That's what it is. I could see it as soon as I cleared the top of the bridge. The original arch frame, the falsework Gazi Mihal used to strengthen the building? It was there. It was nearly all rotted away, but it was there. The 'complicated, knotty foundation.'" She was pleased with herself. "And obviously, that was wrong. A clue. They should have removed the frame when they'd finished the bridge. Instead, not only hadn't they removed it, but someone had even patched it over a century or two later. The timber from the patch was also old. Very old. Seventeenth-century, maybe. So, I swung myself over to have a look." She grinned. "Peeled off the patch, and there it was waiting for us. A lovely, miniature version of a *bektaşi* cauldron. The kind the Janissaries liked to overturn when they felt badly used, you know?"

"Hmm. I still think you're trying to trick me into an admission of something. Won't work."

"Not me. Blame your court scribe." She began easing the iron lid off the base of the cauldron, which she held tightly in her lap, between her legs. "I'm certain that we'll find something talismanic and mystical hidden in here. It's just the place a Sufi in league with a vampire to pacify a notoriously volatile region would hide something important. Nod to his Janissary compatriots, no?"

She had rubbed away the accumulated grime that had kept the lid of the cauldron sealed to the body, and then, using a fingernail, she pried it open. There was an ancient popping sound, and the lid was free. She placed the lid gently on her lap next to the base of the cauldron. Noticed in passing that there was an engraved poem or inscription on the underside of it. Reminded herself to read it later.

Inside the cauldron itself was a ball of densely packed sheep's wool. She extracted the wool from the cauldron and could tell by its weight that it was protecting something. Using her fingertips, she probed the wool until she touched a smooth object. Cool even under its coverings. She moved the wool away from it until she could see what it was. Then she drew in her breath.

"It's glass," she said, more to herself than to Archer. "Dear God, if I'd known it was glass, I would have moved more slowly." Her hand was shaking. "I was certain it was metal. If I had broken it—"

"You didn't break it," he said, watching the road. "But what is it?"

She lifted the object in the palm of her hand. It was between five and six inches long, a delicately blown glass sculpture, gilded and decorated with thin lines of enamel. But its beauty came not from the gilding as much as from the structure of the glass itself, almost completely transparent with a few strands of red twined inside of it.

"It's a key," she told him. "A glass key. With a flower embedded in it." She peered at it, turning it in the minimal light from the road. "I think the flower is a geranium."

"Health," he said. "Geraniums are for health. Health of the territory in this case, I'd guess."

He turned off the main road and onto a forest track that Marion assumed led to one of his crossing points. She didn't know it. But they had already tacitly agreed not to pass the border officially.

He squinted at the black trees outside the windshield. A blurry sleet had begun to fall, obscuring their way. "I hope Kira Maria appreciates it. I know I'll feel more like a proper guest presenting it to her."

Marion settled the key into the wool, wrapped it, placed the wool in the cauldron, and secured the lid on top. Leaned back and closed her eyes. Said nothing. It was a long drive to Sofia.

Sofia, Bulgaria
February, 1934

THEY reached the town of Etropole, fifty miles east of Sofia, just as the sun was rising behind them. Marion had slept intermittently throughout the drive, but Archer looked spent and pale, his eyes rimmed in red. Without speaking, he stopped the lorry at the first roadside inn they encountered. Leaned back and rested his head against the seat, his eyes closed.

"Kira Maria's castle is just above the village of Lopyan," he said. "A little less than ten miles from here."

"It might be wise to ask for a room," Marion suggested. "You can sleep for a few hours and then we can discuss how best to approach it. Or her."

Archer shook his head, his eyes still closed. "No. I'll be fine once I've had a cup of coffee." He opened his eyes and shot her a bleary smile. "I wouldn't sleep anyway. Too excited. Too excitable."

"You look as though you'd sleep through another Balkan War. But you're the one making the decisions." She opened her door. "Coffee, at least, is a good idea."

They walked toward the entrance, slipping on a trace of snow that had fallen during the night. The inn was two storeys, built of white painted wood surrounded by dark red latticed trim. It looked bright and welcoming after their drive through the forest tracks during the night. More encouraging, before they had even reached the door, the innkeeper, equally bright and neat, had opened it and welcomed them to his establishment.

Marion and Archer continued to play at French tourists, a role that served them better here in Etropole than it had in Edirne. The innkeeper's daughter, he was eager to tell them, was studying political economy at the Sorbonne. And when they let drop that they were Parisians, he did all he could to demonstrate to them his cultured cosmopolitanism.

The most concrete benefit that accrued from this most fortunate choice of camouflage was the best café au lait Marion had encountered anywhere, ever, including Paris. The collection of pastries that the innkeeper brought to them was also more than she would have expected from a suburban inn in Bulgaria. She was delighted. Sneaking a glance at Archer, she was pleased to see that he also looked less like he was going to collapse at the slightest pressure. He was even enjoying his conversation with the innkeeper about France's historical commitment to Bulgarian sovereignty. She smiled into her coffee.

When they had finished their breakfast and promised the innkeeper to make themselves known to his daughter on their return to Paris—a promise that Marion, guilt-ridden yet again, vowed to keep—they returned, optimistic, to the lorry. The village of Lopyan, evocative of wolves to Marion—though Archer insisted that the lupine sound of the town's name was accidental—sat on the slope of a large mountain that dominated much of east-central Bulgaria. Kira Maria's castle, further up the slope, built on Roman foundations, and embedded on three sides in the near-solid rock of a cliff side, hovered over the village, both menacing and fragile. From below, it looked about to topple off its precipice. But it had clung to that slope for at least seven hundred years. Its architects must have had some idea of what they were doing.

As he maneuvered the lorry up a dizzying, narrow track that hugged the side of the cliff, Archer explained to Marion that Kira Maria, or her family, had made efforts in recent decades to become, or to appear, at least, more accessible to the outside. Bourgeois. Open to a rapidly changing, differently violent, world. Impenetrable fortresses, the family had apparently determined, were no longer insurance against the wars that states had taken to waging nowadays, and Kira Maria wasn't about to be left behind or vulnerable.

One of these efforts, Archer said, was the road that they were now traversing. A concession to availability. But the family had also modernized sections of the castle, much to the disappointment of the villagers who were beginning to thrive on the nascent tourist industry that had accompanied the global violence, and that very much preferred its decayed Balkan families properly decayed.

The road ended abruptly at two solid iron gates, unembellished, mute, and well over twenty feet tall. They were open, and Archer drove the lorry through them slowly, without stopping. Marion, looking out the window behind her as they passed, decided that if this was what Kira Maria imagined to be accessible, she didn't want to know what inaccessible looked like. Had looked like. And she must stop picturing the courtyard when those doors were locked shut. The space would be a killing field. Which had undoubtedly been its purpose when it was first built, before the new warfare had left the space anachronistic.

Archer let the lorry roll to a stop in front of a curved wooden door, as menacing in its blank, solid simplicity as the gates had been. Marion would have enjoyed at least a bit of scrolled ironwork—something, anything, that hinted at decoration rather than defensive function—but she was disappointed in her hopes. The door was flanked by unadorned sconces, empty now, meant to hold torches, and it was embedded in a stone wall that shot upward to turrets four or five ordinary storeys above them. Wings of the castle did extend outward and back from the prominent entry before encountering the stone cliff face. But the effect of the structure as a whole was pure verticality. Daunting, dizzying, unwelcoming verticality.

Nervous, she clutched her canvas bag and climbed down from the lorry. Locked eyes with Archer, who had also stepped out onto the flagstones. He shrugged, trying for irony, and she lowered her eyes to remove the cauldron from her bag. Handed it to him. "So—we ring the bell then?"

"I don't know," he admitted. "The last time I was here, her servants hit me over the head with a cudgel before I got this far."

She peered at the empty courtyard. "Then, we've made progress?"

"It appears so." He smiled at her, also uneasy, dropping the irony.

Marion was fortifying herself to walk toward the door when, to her astonishment, the door itself opened from the inside. A tall, thin woman, mid-fifties, wearing a tailored dark wool outfit that even Marion could identify as Marcel Rochas, and professionally waved black hair, emerged and stood on the threshold. Without speaking, she turned and closed the door to the castle. Quietly. Sedately. The move evoked latchkeys and semi-detached houses in Blackheath. Out of place. Marion shook her head to clear it of the dissonance.

"Good lord," Archer whispered before she could speak. "That's Kira Maria herself. She's come out alone."

"Why?" Marion, flummoxed, hadn't moved beyond the front of the lorry.

"I don't know," he repeated. "This isn't right."

Kira Maria turned from the shut door, unperturbed, stepped off the worn stone stair, careful not to soil her shoes, and approached Marion and Archer. She looked like an American film actress. Marion searched her memory, irrelevantly, trying to put the name to the face. Norma Shearer. She looked like Norma Shearer. She bore not the remotest resemblance to whatever medieval fantasy of an undead chatelaine that Marion had unconsciously been harboring—although Marion herself was having difficulty now remembering what she'd expected, as this calm, benign, ludicrously modern woman stood in front of her. She felt paralyzed. And stupid. Archer, equally paralyzed, equally stupid, simply stood next to her.

Kira Maria smiled at them and held out her hand to Marion. Marion took it automatically. Felt an urge to curtsey, fought it down, inclined her head and let the woman's hand go. Kira Maria turned to Archer next, and he did bow, just a touch, correctly, Slavic again. Something remembered from his childhood.

"Dr. Bailey," she said. "And Mr. Archer. I'm pleased that you've arrived. I've been awaiting you." She spoke to them in English with a delicate Bulgarian accent.

Archer, coloring but doing an admirable job of maintaining his composure, held out the cauldron. "We thank you for your welcome, madam," he murmured. "We've brought you—"

Kira Maria held up her hand, elegant yet imperious, and Archer stopped speaking. "This is not a welcome, Mr. Archer. You have not entered my home. And," including Marion now in her speech, "you will not pass over its threshold this morning. I *am* pleased that you've arrived. Now you will leave."

Archer looked stricken. He began to explain himself, but Kira Maria stopped him again, this time with a look. "Mr. Archer, please be patient. You are not at fault. Nor is Dr. Bailey. Circumstances in our village have become complicated in recent days. Quite suddenly—and intriguingly—complicated. It would be unwise to initiate a relationship, such as I hope that ours will become, in an atmosphere of uncertainty."

She lifted her head and looked out over the mountains, as though hearing something. "I expect to resolve these complications at a gathering that I will host this evening. We'll drink at 8:00. Dine afterward. Would you both be good enough to attend? I'll have rooms made up for you to occupy until the morning. And we three, then, will have ample opportunity to discuss our mutual interests. I would also be pleased, *then*, to accept your guest gift." She let her eyes settle on the cauldron briefly, as though by accident, and then she gazed back at Archer.

Archer was at a loss. He stood silent, looking at the cauldron in his hands. After an awkward moment, Marion spoke instead. "We're honored, madam," she said hastily. "And we thank you for your invitation. We'll return at 8:00."

"I'll look forward to that return." Then, with a smile that might have been roguish, if she weren't so insolently chilly, she tossed a few quick sentences in Bosnian inflected Serbo-Croatian at Archer.

He stared at her, but before he had a chance to reply, and without any further acknowledgment of their presence, she turned away from them, walked back to the door, entered it, and closed it behind her. A suburban matron preparing for her dinner party.

Archer, incredulous, raised his eyebrows and handed Marion the cauldron. She placed it in her canvas bag, and they both returned to the lorry.

"What did she say to you?" Marion asked when they'd reached their seats.

He laughed as he started the engine and eased the lorry toward the terrifying, yet still gratifyingly open, gates. "She begged my pardon for trying to kill me. Before. Said she had mistakenly believed that I was 'attached to the other side.'"

"Attached to the other side?"

"Yes," he answered, slowing to negotiate a near vertical hairpin turn on the downward slope. "I'll be curious to hear more about that 'other side' this evening."

He squinted down the track, slowed the lorry further, and eased it back in the opposite direction. Took the next hairpin turn. "Although, to be honest," he continued, "I'm more astonished that she admitted her mistake in the first place than that she's aware of the various—sides—involved in this situation. If she's even close to what she claims to be, that admission, not to mention the apology, is akin to handing over the keys to the castle and giving up. Self-annihilation."

He slowed the lorry to let a work vehicle pass in the opposite direction. "One or two generations ago," he mused, "anyone of the sort of blood she has running in her veins would have died before admitting that an attempted murder was the result of a misunderstanding. And they'd have taken the whole family with them before *apologizing* for it. Something must be very, very wrong up there."

He had reached the level road at the base of the mountain, and they both unconsciously exhaled as the lorry accelerated—to forty miles per hour—on the smooth, paved, main highway. "Sometimes I hate the twentieth century," he muttered. "Degrading era." He turned on the near useless wipers against an accumulating sleet. "She ought to have finished what she started with me. Even if it was a mistake."

Marion gazed out the window for a few minutes and then turned to him. "Where are we going?"

"Sofia, I thought," he said. "An hour away at this pace. We must buy something to wear to dinner. On Vitosha Boulevard, perhaps? It's the only shopping district I know."

She nodded. "Your city. I'll follow your lead."

"And then," he admitted, "I would like to find somewhere to sleep for a few hours. I'll be able to now."

"Good." She gazed at the forest, dark and cold, passing the window of the lorry. "I'm unhappy about those 'intriguing complications' plaguing the village."

"As am I. But I trust Kira Maria."

She nodded. "She seems—not easily fooled."

"And honorable."

"Hmm." Marion's experience with honor had never been positive. Or straightforward. But she didn't say that to Archer. He wasn't troubling to fit in anymore. His central European mannerisms, which he'd been disciplined into subduing, were on the surface. And though she understood his inclination, she didn't think it would serve either of them well in the coming days. Hoped that she was wrong.

ARCHER brought Marion to a small shop just off Vitosha Boulevard that specialized in serving minor Embassy functionaries who had been caught off guard by sudden invitations that they couldn't avoid. It was a risk for both of them to be seen in the neighborhood. But Archer had no other suggestions about where to purchase an appropriate outfit. He, like Marion, didn't want to endanger his colleagues or contacts in the city by approaching them for advice. Or for clothing.

They spent a half hour watching the entrance to the shop for unusual activity before Archer entered first and emerged a few minutes later with a serviceable dinner jacket. He confirmed that the proprietors were happy to accept Marion's American dollars as payment. While Archer was inside, Marion observed the area from a café, taking her time over a second, welcome, cup of coffee. When nothing suspicious surfaced after Archer's visit to the shop, Marion left him at the café and bought her own outfit. She chose the first dress she located in her size—something in dark brown velvet with a high neck. She also purchased a pair of shoes.

She didn't trouble to fit the dress before buying it because she knew from the material that it would stretch or cling to her regardless of its tailoring. More or less. Her primary consideration was the ability to move freely should she need to run or climb over anything when Kira Maria failed to resolve the complications that she had mentioned to them in her courtyard. And that aspect of it couldn't be tested until the inevitable crisis erupted.

As she left the shop, Marion's anxiety about the direction their strategy was taking them sharpened. The situation was not what they'd thought it was. At this point, it was more likely to go wrong than it was to reach a satisfying conclusion. But, she reminded herself as she sat in the seat across from Archer, picking at the baklava he wasn't eating, this was his project. She was there to help. To follow instructions. And she didn't want to know anything anyway, should she find herself in a position where people might ask her questions.

He smiled and pushed the plate across the table to her. "Take it," he said. "I ate the first portion when you were in the shop."

She didn't need further encouragement. Lifted the last piece and finished it whole. "Thank you."

"We ought to leave the city before we find a room for the afternoon," he continued. "Something closer to Etropole."

She stood. "I agree. Perhaps a house further into the forest?"

He stood as well and walked to the door, opening it for her. Then he paused, thinking, as she passed. "Actually, I know just the place," he said, catching up to walk beside her. "It's quiet. And secure."

They returned to the lorry, and Archer drove them east, out of the city for a little over half an hour before turning onto a track that led up a forested hill. At the top of the hill, they reached a dilapidated and uninhabited eighteenth-century house with stone walls, traces of whitewashing, and wooden balconies. As Archer brought the lorry to a stop in front of the stone walkway, smothered and invisible under last year's pine needles, Marion looked at him, puzzled.

"Trust me," he told her. "It's perfectly livable inside. Belongs to a friend of mine, ambiguously connected to the Embassy. But he never uses it. He was a widower, married a second wife, and she told him the place spooks her. Too isolated. I used it when I was going under, and it was the safest place I slept before I reached Istanbul."

"It looks ideal to me," she assured him. "To be honest, I was worried you were going to suggest sleeping in the lorry."

They gathered their bags and walked to the house. Archer pushed open the door, which was unlocked, and they entered a stone entry hall, colder than the outside. "This way," he said, leading Marion straight through the house to a ground-floor drawing room. He closed the door to the room behind them.

The drawing room stretched along the entire side of the house and was lined with windows overlooking a slope. The slope had once, even recently, been a grass lawn. But now, in February, it was fighting a losing battle against the encroaching forest. Trees were sprouting up everywhere, looking creepily deliberate in their violation of the mansion's domestic boundaries. The growth seemed animated. She didn't like it. It left the drawing room dark and pinched.

But the curtains hadn't been drawn, and the light in the room, though brittle and wintry, was strong. Archer removed cloth covers from two sofas that were facing one another across an Isfahan carpet, showing signs of mold. The sofas were more than long enough to use as beds, and Marion lowered her bags onto the one closest to her.

Archer walked to a brick fireplace, next to which a stack of firewood and implements waited. He knelt in front of it. "I stockpiled the wood the last time I was here," he explained. "In case the border was tight, and I was forced to backtrack."

Marion sank onto the sofa and pulled off her boots. "Let me make the fire," she said. "You're exhausted."

He turned back to her on his heels, grateful. "Thank you, Marion." Rubbed his eyes, and smudged ash across his temple. "I forget sometimes what it's like to have a partner."

She stood and walked to the fireplace. "So do I."

Without replying, he dragged himself to the second sofa and reclined onto his back, closing his eyes. He was already sleeping when she had the fire burning and beginning to heat the room.

THEY woke simultaneously, six hours later, long after the sun had set. The room was dark aside from the red glow of the fireplace, and they were both disoriented. Archer collected himself before Marion did, peered at his wristwatch, which he had kept wound, and then sat up on the sofa. "7:00. Perfect timing."

She sat up as well, stretched, and looked about the room. "Does the plumbing work?"

"Yes. Just off the main hall. Can you manage in the dark?"

"After all that early training with the blindfold? Easily. Who knew it would be so useful?" She felt her way to the toilet, used it, splashed water on her face, and returned to the drawing room. Archer had built up the fire, and the room was almost cheerful. But Marion nonetheless empathized with the second wife. The place was spooky. She'd be glad to leave it.

Archer took the bag with his dinner jacket in the direction of the toilet. "I can get most of this put on in the dark. Do you want to change here?"

"I'm not bashful. We can both change here."

"I *am* bashful. I need my privacy." He turned and walked toward the hall. "Besides, I don't want to see something I'm not supposed to see and give Sir Jeffrey an excuse to hurt me more than he already plans to."

She gaped at him for a silent second and then started laughing. "That was utterly unprovoked. What on earth have I done to deserve that?"

"You married him, Marion." His voice was muffled in the hall.

Peeved, she remained silent as she heard him close the door. Then she removed the dress from its bag, pulled off her jumper, and draped the dress over her shoulders. Folded the jumper, stepped out of her trousers, folded those as well, and shoved both into the canvas bag, over her American dollars. After reaching behind her to fasten the back of the dress, she picked up her boots and placed them beside her bags. Finally, meditative, she banked the fire.

When Archer returned to the drawing room, she was ready to leave. He was wearing serviceable, but not ostentatiously well tailored trousers, a dinner jacket, a dress shirt, and a tie, unfastened, hanging over his neck. "I'll finish dressing when we reach Lopyan," he said.

"You look nice."

"As do you," he replied. "Though I have a feeling we'll be outclassed by Kira Maria's more complicated guests."

She handed Archer his bag and gathered up her own. "And I have a feeling that we're meant to observe rather than take part in the action. Unimpressive clothing will facilitate that." She paused. "At least I think that's the plan. Her plan. I'm not yet certain what our plan is."

Archer didn't reply, but Marion was sufficiently pleased to be abandoning the close, heavy atmosphere of the house to question his silence. They climbed into the lorry, and forty minutes later they were ascending the hairpin turns to Kira Maria's castle above Lopyan.

When they reached the courtyard, it was transformed, bustling with servants welcoming guests, the sconces next to the door and along the outside wall decorated by massive, roaring torches. The atmosphere was celebratory, but Marion still disliked the ugly, intimidating gate—the only entrance or exit to the castle—the solid cliff face behind it, and the narrow exposed track leading down to the village. She chided herself for her inability to set her twentieth-century scruples to rest in order to enjoy the thirteenth-century architecture. But she couldn't damp down her anxiety. Her heart was beating rapidly by the time Archer had inched the lorry forward and brought it to an idling stop in front of the entry to the house.

Servants helped them to step down from the vehicle before driving it to a makeshift car park in front of the longer east wing of the castle. She had left her carpet bag with the manuscripts and taken the canvas bag with her. As she glanced behind her, the light blue Polski-Fiat, squeezed into place among the conspicuously expensive automobiles left by Kira Maria's guests, went a long way toward lifting her mood. The lorry occupied a place of distinction between a Bugatti Type 57 in red and black and a Mercedes-Benz 500K painted a shocking bright green. There was a streak of rust just above its wheel well that she hadn't noticed before. She hoped that the mechanic from Burgas, whatever he was driving now, would have appreciated the honor.

Taking the arm that Archer held out for her, she walked with him into the castle. Over the threshold. A servant just inside the door recognized them, bowed to them, and offered to take Marion's canvas bag as though it were the most natural impulse in the world for her to carry it into a reception of this sort. She paused, considering, and then she removed the cauldron. Handed the servant the sack, absent the cauldron, assuming that it would find its way to her rooms in the castle.

The servant bowed a second time and gave the sack to a liveried boy, no more than ten years old, who disappeared into a side corridor. After that, he led Archer and Marion into a central hall, soaring, intimidating, and gothic enough to be a parody of itself. The hall, despite its classic construction, however, was disordered, a chaotic riot of long mullioned windows, flagstone floors, and hanging scrolled lamps that were lit with electric bulbs rather than with candles. The space was also crowded, suffocating, and warm already. Diplomatic. A backdrop to the scads of Embassy minions out on an excursion from Sofia, circulating across the flagstones, confused, but still doing their jobs.

Marion threw a surreptitious look at Archer and concluded that he'd formed the same impression. His expression hovered between apprehension and contempt. "I didn't know there would be so many people," he said.

"I'm surprised that she knows so many people."

"Curiosity?" he suggested. "She doesn't entertain very often. They probably see this as an opportunity to extend their spheres of influence."

Marion frowned. "How do we—?" And then she stopped. She felt uncomfortably visible holding the cauldron. It was just large enough to be drawing intrigued attention.

"She'll make herself known to us when she's ready." He glanced down at it. "Would you like me to hold it for you?"

"Thank you." She handed it to him.

"You ought to concern yourself less with appearances. So British and middle class. Why not simply let them wonder and be damned?"

She flushed. "I *am* British and middle class, *Chris*. So are you."

"You'll be the death of me, Marion. I'm Laz. And anything and everything except middle class." He was laughing as he scanned the room.

"I don't know what you are sometimes." She wanted a drink. A drink, and then she'd worry about their next move.

"I'm not so certain myself these days," he countered. "Awfully disconcerting to have a crisis of the subject when for well over a decade there's been no subject to throw into crisis." He squinted and looked to the opposite wall. "Paralyzing."

"Perfect," she said, spotting a waiter with a tray of martinis. "Now you're Kierkegaard. That will serve us beautifully this evening."

He followed her, holding the cauldron, still smiling. "After you've taken that cocktail, Marion, let's make our way to the other end of the hall. I think we've received our signal."

She retrieved a glass from the tray, nodding her thanks to the waiter. Then, drinking a few sips and eating the olive, she followed him across the room. She already felt better.

A servant, the same who had taken Marion's canvas bag, was waiting for them to approach. When they did, he bowed a third time and opened a small door just behind him, secured with a single slab of wood, that exposed a low-ceilinged corridor stretching away from the central hall. He stood to the side, and Marion and Archer, ducking, passed under the archway. Marion drank the rest of her martini and left the empty glass on a ledge inside the door.

This area of the castle was lit with torches. Blueish and sullen. And the air was heavy and oppressive once the servant closed the door behind them. But they walked briskly enough to the end of the hallway, toward a second door, wooden, splintered with some centuries-old gash, and cracked open. The servant knocked, and Kira Maria's voice ordered them to enter. He stepped to the side, and Marion and Archer walked into the room.

The space was unexpectedly large and bright after the airless corridor that led to it. A tower room, octagonal, taller than it was wide, and affixed precipitously to the side of the castle. Its windows looked out over a sheer cliff face with the hint of a stream or river running hundreds of feet below. A second, smaller door, adjacent to the windows, was closed and partially covered by a tapestry.

Kira Maria, wearing a floor-length, long-sleeved dress in a heavy metallic silk that looked black, grey, and bronze simultaneously, was sitting, magisterial, in an oak chair that was carved into an exaggerated serpent motif. The chair's carving, as chaotic as the central hall, made Marion dizzy. She looked at the wall above it. Kira Maria remained motionless, sitting, facing the door.

This time, it was Marion who was at a loss. Their reception was so artificial, so staged, that she couldn't imagine how she was supposed to respond to it. But Archer remained composed. He bowed, deeply, and spoke to Kira Maria in Bulgarian. Then he held out the cauldron to her. Kira Maria nodded, let her eyes rest on Marion for a moment, and smiled faintly. She took the cauldron and set it in her lap.

"I am pleased to accept your gift, Mr. Archer," she said in English. "And I welcome you to my home. Find pleasure here."

"We've found it," Archer replied in English.

"And you, Dr. Bailey?" She turned to Marion.

"I'm grateful to you for—for your welcome," she said. Irritated. The theatricality of the scene was forced. And purposeless.

As though sensing Marion's annoyance, and entertained by it, Kira Maria smiled more broadly. She rested her hands over top of the cauldron. She hadn't opened it, or even shown curiosity about its contents. "Then please, both of you, enjoy your time here. I'll be dining in an hour with a small group of friends who, like you, will be staying the night. You'll join us upstairs, in the small dining room. Dimitar will show you." She paused and looked down at her ring. A large, sickeningly green stone, almost organic, caught the light and then dimmed again.

"And once we've dined, we will discuss how to proceed with your *sigil*." She enjoyed, with overt hostility, Marion's surprise at her use of the term. "I find that I think more clearly at night. Don't you, Dr. Bailey?"

"Yes, madam." Marion was having difficulty keeping her voice neutral. Something was wrong. And she couldn't understand what it was. She ventured a look at Archer, but he was wearing his professional face. His neck, however, was taut. He was as nervous as she was. "Is that all, madam?" She heard the belligerence in her voice and cursed herself. Anger wasn't going to help the situation.

"Yes, Dr. Bailey." Kira Maria hadn't moved from the chair. "Mr. Archer. That is all. You may leave me. Dimitar will collect you in an hour for dinner upstairs." She glanced behind her at the half-covered door. "I have business in my study. Below."

Marion, incensed, didn't respond. As she turned toward the door, Archer was bowing a final time before following her into the corridor. He caught up to her and walked alongside her toward the central hall.

"That," Marion fumed, "was a nightmare. A circus act. Madame Tussaud's Chamber of Horrors. Her 'study below.' How absurd. Who does she think she is?"

"She thinks she's the Empress Consort of Ivan Shishman," Archer replied.

Marion laughed. "And you? Who do you think she is?"

"I'm satisfied with her being the Empress Consort of Ivan Shishman,"

"The one who died in 1380." She couldn't believe he was willing to let the woman playact in that way.

"Why not?" He held the door to the hall for her. "Marion, our people made it clear that I wasn't supposed to question her identity. Give her the sign. Wait for her to make the next move. That's it."

She stopped and turned to him before stepping into the hall. "But Dündar," she said, "you gave her the sign and she's given you nothing in return. Nothing. You're empty handed now."

"She'll tell us more tonight. She must find the right moment."

"She's a lonely madwoman living on the edge of a cliff, desperate for relevance," Marion explained, patiently. "The 'right moment' for her will be when she's kept you here flattering her and entertaining her for the rest of your natural life."

"Or my unnatural life," he smiled. "Balkan nobility. They have all the time in the world. Proverbially."

She allowed herself to smile back at him. "Fine, Dündar. It's your eternity." Deciding to be entertained rather than angry. She looked back at him as she returned to the crowded hall. "But if I were in your position—"

"What would you do, Marion? If you were in Mr. Archer's position?"

She whipped her head around at the voice, and then she stumbled backward against the door. Dimitar had already closed it behind them. She gripped Archer's arm, involuntarily, steadying herself. "Oh God."

"Good evening, Mr. Archer," he said. He was wearing a white dinner jacket, black tie, his hair brushed back. "Delighted to see you again. Although I'd thank you to unhand my wife."

Marion released Archer's arm.

Archer was unsurprised to see Jeffrey. But he was also unambiguously ill-disposed toward him. "Sir Jeffrey," he said. "So far from London? Or Baghdad? It's an unexpected pleasure."

Jeffrey reached out, took Marion's arm, and pulled her over to stand next to him. "You know how Maugham can be. Sends us out on the strangest journeys. Frustrating. Almost enough to drive one into the embrace of the enemy."

"Jeffrey—" Marion interposed.

"But if you'll excuse us," he spoke over her. "My wife will want to look in on our son. He's sleeping upstairs. She's missed him during her travels." He caught Marion's eye. "Haven't you, dear?"

"Ian's *here?*"

"As I said." He began half walking, half dragging her to a stairway that led to an upper gallery.

"Wait," she said.

He didn't wait. Kept walking.

She looked back at Archer, shaken, as she stumbled after him. Archer held her eyes, passing her a message, reassuring her. At which point she dropped her gaze and turned, allowing Jeffrey to lead her to the stairway. Her heart pounding unevenly once again.

As they walked, she tried to calm herself. Let her thoughts wander to the lorry, squeezed between the Bugatti and the Mercedes-Benz. Which almost worked. But not entirely. She'd already forgotten the tricks she'd learned in storage. Shutting down. She must remember how to shut down.

JEFFREY, silent, holding her upper arm, walked her up a flight of stairs and then along the gallery that surrounded the central hall. She could see the guests moving about on the floor below, but she and Jeffrey were walking too quickly for her to spot Archer again. She prayed that he hadn't already been picked up. That he'd disappeared once he'd been recognized.

A moment or two later, Jeffrey stepped into a smaller side corridor, off the gallery. Escorted her to a thick, arched door near its end, pushed the door open, and gestured her into the room. Then he followed her and shut the door. Watching her.

Marion stood at the center of the room and looked about her. It was massive, the size of Archer's flat in Istanbul, with three windows overlooking the same river that Kira Maria could see from her tower chamber. The floors were covered with five or six layers of carpets, and a tapestry obscured almost the entire west wall. She peered at it. The assassination of the Sultan Murad I at Kosovo. Graphic depiction of his internal organs being buried, with reverence, on the battlefield in 1389.

She swallowed and looked away from the tapestry. A dark, wooden bed, seventeenth-century, with curtains drawn around it took up a large part of the same side of the room. The rest of the furniture was equally dense, ancient, unyielding.

She noticed that her canvas bag had been placed, respectfully, on a stand to the side of the bed. Jeffrey's three Goyard suitcases were also there, positioned next to it. She was relieved that she had left her carpet bag with the manuscripts and *sicil*s in the lorry. Hoped once again that Archer had had the presence of mind to secure it. Or simply to take the lorry and drive away. He'd completed his assignment. He would know to leave.

Jeffrey followed her gaze to the bag. "You've taken up robbing banks now?"

She closed her eyes. "You said that Ian was here?"

He nodded and walked to a door on the other side of the room. Put his finger to his lips and then opened it for her. A short hall led to a second room, smaller than the first, but still overwhelming. Ian was sleeping soundly in a bed that would have fit ten children of his size. He was holding a wooden aeroplane in one hand.

She walked toward him, to kiss him, but she stopped short when she saw that both Nick Trelawney and Gardiner were also in the room. Nick was sitting in a window seat, his knees up, reading a book. The irrelevant part of her mind noted that it was the new edition of Ibrahim al-Mazini's *Ibrahim al-Katib*. He almost looked like a student again.

Gardiner was standing with his back to the room, observing the view out a window, hands clasped behind him. Military. They both looked at the door when it opened and then relaxed when they recognized Jeffrey. Nodded, cool and polite, at Marion. She would have found their identical reaction to her presence humorous, as humorous as their identical outfits—twill trousers and closely fit pullovers—if she weren't so unsettled to see them there at all.

She blinked, nonplussed, and then decided to ignore them. Walked to the bed, bent over Ian, and kissed him on the cheek. Kept her face pressed to his for a few seconds longer than she needed to, smelling his hair, and then straightened and left the room without acknowledging Nick or Gardiner. Jeffrey followed her, closing the door.

She noticed a spray of what could only have been bullet holes, recent, along the wall of the short hall connecting the two rooms. Decided to ignore that as well. If she internalized everything that she'd seen over the past ten minutes, she'd be unable to think straight. And she must keep her mind clear. She'd been dreading this encounter, even when she had imagined it would take place weeks or months in the future. Reminded herself, yet again, to shut down.

When she reached the bedroom, she walked to one of the windows and stared out over the black cliff face. Remained silent for a full minute. Then she spoke: "what are you doing here?"

"My job." He removed his jacket, hung it over a chair, walked to the bed, and drew the curtains from around it. Sat and leaned back against the pillows at the colossal wooden headboard, his feet up, ankles crossed, his hands behind his head. Relaxed.

She sighed and turned toward the room. "Your job."

"Yes," he confirmed, gazing up at the canopy nine feet above him. "My job. As your runner. Unwilling though I may be. Always helpful, I find, to contact my talent in the field every now and then. Ask them in person whether they have messages to pass along home. Any confusion about the brief." He glanced over at her. "Any confusion about the brief, Marion?"

"No." She didn't want to let him drag her into one of these hellish conversations. She vowed not to say anything more. Even though she knew that he'd easily trick or provoke her into speaking again when he felt it served his purposes.

"I also have something to show you," he continued. Looked at his watch. Put his hands back behind his head. "But it won't be ready for another twenty minutes. I thought we might discuss your holiday in the meantime."

"I don't want to discuss it." She turned back to the window.

"Very well. I'll discuss it. You listen."

She squeezed her eyes shut. Steadied herself. Forced herself to keep from retorting. Didn't look back at the room.

"You mustn't fault yourself for being caught off guard here," he told her. "You did very well up till this evening. Made my people look utter fools on the train. And Maugham has nothing but respect for you now. Fell for you completely, in fact—true love—when he tried to freeze your bank account a second time and nothing was there. Or, at least, nothing but that fifty pounds. Taunting him, were you?"

He considered. "Better you than me, I must say. You'll never get rid of him now. Like the monkey riding that poor chap with the green tea habit." He smiled to himself. "Enjoy it, Marion."

He waited for her to respond, and when she didn't, he kept speaking. Tranquil. Unhurried. "We knew from what we'd picked up in Archer's flat that you'd end here. But we'd hoped to intercept you both before you made contact with the lady of the house. Follow *you* to Archer, collect the two of you together, and be home before any mysterious objects fell into the hands of any equally mysterious undead empresses. Keystone cops on the Simplon, however, put an end to that. Incidentally," he looked over at her mute back, "where did you resurface? Bucharest?"

"Istanbul," she said.

"I guessed as much." He turned his attention back to the canopy. "Pair of eyes spotted you in Sirkeci. But he's seen better days, and most of what he sends us is rubbish. Couldn't track a twenty-foot wallaby painted orange through Trafalgar Square. Unless it was transporting a stash of opiates in its pouch, of course. He had you in an expensive fur coat and a hat, running for the ferry, looking confused and disheveled. We assumed he'd been hitting the *nargile* a trifle early that day."

She laughed, but didn't speak.

"You dropped the coat?"

She nodded, still facing the window.

"Such dedication," he commended her. "I'm not sure I would have had the stomach for that." He thought for a few seconds. "Which means they really did almost grab you in Edirne. Damn."

"Why are you telling me this?" She left the window and sat in a carved chair facing the bed. An intimate version of the serpent seat from Kira Maria's tower. Curled her feet up underneath her and rested her elbow on the arm of the chair.

Jeffrey remained leaning against the pillows at the headboard, his hands behind his head. "I'm complimenting you," he said. "My wife. On her skilled work." He looked over at her again. "Heaven knows I can't compliment you on your dress. It's very brown, isn't it?"

"That isn't why you're telling me," she said levelly, ignoring his comment on her outfit. "You're telling me because you want me confused." She watched him, trying to read his expression. But she knew it was useless.

"Indeed, I do want you confused," he agreed after a moment. "But also flattered. Nothing wrong with both. Confused *and* flattered. I've taken a leaf from Maugham's book."

"You're misinforming me."

"I've told you. I'm doing my job." He checked his watch. "And I'm also passing the time. We have ten minutes until my surprise for you is ready. Shall I tell you more about why I'm here? Why

202

Maugham wants me out of the way for the next few weeks? Gossip from the office, now that you're one of us?"

"I'm not—"

"Yes, yes," he interrupted. "We'll take the indignant protest as read. But you are, you know. Up to your neck in it. And sinking."

He paused.

She didn't reply. She still couldn't understand his reasons for speaking to her about these things. And the disturbing collegiality was more ominous to her than outright aggression would have been. His style reminded her of the depot. She didn't like it. And she had less of a feel for his aims now than she'd had when he'd confronted her downstairs. She felt light headed. Ineffective.

"It seems," he said, returning to his subject, ignoring her silence, "that I'm making a nuisance of myself. At the office, that is. Minor kerfuffle in progress, and I'm not helping." He observed her confusion. The wariness. Waited for her to respond. And when she didn't, he answered her unspoken question: "yes, a kerfuffle."

She blinked, but didn't speak.

"You remember Gertrude Bell's factotum in the Arabian Peninsula?" he persisted. "Adequate languages and a mania for fancy dress? Robes, camels, beads, the whole lot—"

"If I recall," she interjected, unable to help herself, "you're not averse to Arab house slippers yourself."

"Yes," he rejoined. "In the *house*. Because they're comfortable. I don't wear them to visit the Cabinet Office." He lifted his chin. "Anyhow, the point is that now that Miss Bell has met with her tragic end, and now that her boy in the desert has lost what little sanity he had left and begun confusing his Sheik of Araby fantasies with reality, the office has begun salivating over junior. He's just finished at Trinity, and they're champing at the bit to sign him up."

"So? He sounds like your type."

"Trelawney's met him. Says he's neurotic and unreliable. Narcissist in all the wrong ways."

"You like neurotic and unreliable." Bewildered again. Uncertain as to why he was treating her like some sort of equal. She wanted another drink.

"He also can't pick up a language to save his life," he added. "Or to order a cup of coffee, for that matter. His father's a git, but at least he can read a document."

"Why do they want him then?"

"Continuity? Family business?"

She thought for a moment, trying to remember what she'd heard of recent British policy in the Peninsula. "I think you're jealous," she finally hazarded. "Philby—that's his name, isn't it?—backed the winning side. Abdulaziz ibn Saud made quite the travesty of your Hashemites when the pressure built up."

"They're not my Hashemites." He was fighting back a smile. "They're the Hashemites of the Iraqi people." He moved a hand from behind his head and looked down at his fingernails. "The issue, though, is that the office, just now, is tense. To put it nicely. They have no notion what they're doing, and even Maugham would rather hum quietly to himself in a corner than push the situation in the proper direction."

She looked hard at him. "You're trying to recruit me. That's why you're here. Why you're telling me this. Cozy. You're Maugham's emissary. And you really think that I'd—"

"You've already signed on, Marion. I've no need to recruit you. Ask Maugham if you don't believe me." He laughed up at the canopy. "I'm here to tell you that we're *pleased* that you've chosen to join us. To thank you for your service. You're an infinitely better resource than some whinging Oedipal failure nicknamed after a Dickensian waif transplanted to the sub-continent by a writer of music hall doggerel. '*Kim*.' For Heaven's sake." He recited, still smiling up at the canopy:

> "We've spat on you and shat on you
> We've taken all of Sindh
> Dialectical Materialism
> Attractive, Gunga Din?
> You've lied to us, you've spied on us
> Been to bed with Kalinin
> Yet we'll never doubt your loyalty
> Let's promote you, Gunga Din!"

She stared at him, astonished. If he weren't so obviously in control of himself, she'd suspect he'd been drinking excessively. Then she considered. "I don't think you've got the meter right. That sounds more like Tennyson. *The Lady of Shalott?*"

He sat up, put his feet over the side of the bed, and cast her an injured look. "Are you never satisfied? *Never?* You're relentless. What if I translated it into Latin? Would that impress you?"

"'Been to bed with Kalinin?' Good luck."

"All right, Marion. You're looking for a meter that matches? How about this?" He put his hand over his heart and in a willfully offensive parody of her accent, he recited:

> "Wha, for Scotland's king and law
> Freedom's sword will strongly draw
> Free-man stand, or free-man fa'
> Let him follow me!
> By oppression's woes and pains
> By your sons in servile chains
> We will drain our dearest veins
> But they shall be free!"

"You're an idiot." Her voice was cool.

"But I've got you talking, haven't I? That's all I wanted. The silent anguish was tiring me."

She narrowed her eyes at him,

"In my day," he continued, pursuing his earlier subject, "we learned useful things at Trinity. Now, from what I can tell, they spend all of their time testing one another's ideological purity. Although," he conceded, "even with my impeccable training, I wouldn't know where to begin translating that mess into Latin. Or any other remotely organized language. Perhaps it works in Turkish. You'd know better than I."

She was silent for a minute longer, and then, eventually, she spoke again. "Whatever it is that you're doing, Jeffrey. It's not working." She closed her eyes. "I admit it. I'm baffled. Your approach is— is disconcerting. Makes me miss the coercion. But I'm not giving you anything." She opened her eyes. "*Anything.*"

"Ah well," he continued as though she hadn't spoken, "so they'll recruit the boy, and I'll stop the Cassandra act. It's not my section anyway. According to Trelawney, he wouldn't recognize the Museum if it fell on him. So, at worst, they'll be mildly disappointed when there's no blood on the bedclothes the morning after the nuptials. And as long as they don't let him near anything sensitive, he won't do them harm. They'll only be able to post him to regions where everyone speaks English, so there can't be too many opportunities for him to act out."

He stood, walked to the chair, retrieved his jacket, and put it on. "The way things are going, of course, he'll end up head of intelligence in America or somewhere. But even that will be satisfying in its way. Watching the Yanks rage when it all explodes in their faces." He buttoned his jacket. "Odd world."

He turned to Marion, who had remained sitting, her forehead wrinkled, listening to his monologue. "Get up, my dear. It's time."

She stood, suspicious. "Where are we going?"

"I want to show you my surprise. It ought to be ready now."

He held out his arm, and she took it. Telling herself to play along, not to provoke him, not to push him into hurting Archer. When Gardiner appeared a moment later, also looking at his watch, her suspicion blossomed into fear. But she reminded herself that Archer was a professional. He would have disappeared. He wouldn't have waited for Kira Maria. And she herself was precisely where she ought to be. A few weeks early was all. She tripped as they left the room, but she steadied herself again in the corridor. The situation was as it should be.

THE sound of the reception floated up to the gallery as they entered it from the small corridor. The hall was, if possible, more crowded than it had been a half hour earlier, guests packed together, talking, drinking, failing to drain the endless supply of alcohol. Marion expected Jeffrey to take her back to the staircase and down to the ground floor. But instead, he and Gardiner brought her to the far end of the gallery, beneath a tall pointed arch, with a view of the reception in its entirety.

Once there, Jeffrey stood at the parapet and surveyed the scene. Beckoned to Marion to stand next to him. Fighting to remain composed, she stepped forward, gripped the rail, and looked down. She recognized no one in the crowd and relaxed, convinced that Archer had been prudent after all.

But then, she spotted him. He was emerging a second time, alone, from the corridor to the right of the room, ducking under the low arch leading to Kira Maria's tower. Dimitar shut the door behind him. She glanced over at Jeffrey, who was studying his wristwatch. He looked up and caught her eye. "Right on time."

She stared back down at the hall. Archer appeared harassed. But he was moving with purpose toward something or someone she couldn't identify at the other end of the room. Kept finding his way blocked by knots of intoxicated diplomats, circling back, trying to clear a path for himself. It seemed that his target was also moving. Eventually he stopped, a wry expression on his face, and pulled the clove cigarettes out of his pocket. He lit one and scrutinized the crowd. Marion bit her lip, nervous, and then looked at Jeffrey.

Jeffrey laughed. "A man after my own heart. I'd have done the same in his situation."

She found her voice. "What is this, Jeffrey?"

"Let me narrate," he said. "I've arranged a pantomime for you. Pity John isn't awake to watch it as well. I'm quite proud of it." He observed Archer for a few seconds longer, and then he spoke again. "Here we have Mr. Spahovic, having lost his lovely partner, nonetheless pursuing his duty, little knowing—"

Marion's hands tightened over the rail at Jeffrey's use of the Bosnian name. Once her shock had passed, though, she resolved to act. She took a tentative step back, planning somehow to lose Jeffrey and warn Archer that he'd been compromised. But she felt Gardiner behind her, blocking escape, and she stopped. Jeffrey, who had broken off at Marion's movement, put his arm around her waist and pulled her toward him.

"You're surprised that we've identified him?" He patted her hand. "You of all people know that old files never die. Consider your scholarship. And besides, look at the way he's smoking that cigarette. If he's not direct from a ruined Mitteleuropa, then he's been a dockhand at the Port of London since childhood. I think even Chris would have difficulty making that role work for him."

She opened her mouth to reply, cautiously, but he interrupted her. "Yet observe!" He pointed toward the other end of the hall. "Entering at the left of the scene are Dimitar, the treacherous valet, and what appear to be—oh dear." He looked at her in mock consternation. "A gang of villainous brutes. What will our hero do? He seems not even to be aware—"

Marion didn't wait any longer. Using the parapet for balance, she kicked back at Gardiner with all her force. A part of her mind registered a satisfying grunt of pain from him, even as she concentrated on wrenching Jeffrey's hand from her waist. Before Jeffrey could pull away from her, she twisted his arm behind him, hoping to dislocate it, and tried to slam his face into the rail. She missed her aim, and he fell to the side instead, but his collapse gave her time to run toward the staircase. She caught a glimpse of Gardiner, doubled over but regaining his breath, as she made her way back through the series of pointed arches that supported the roof of the gallery.

When she reached the last arch before the stairs, she stumbled to a stop. A gate had been lowered across it. Metal. It was crumbling and medieval, but it was substantial enough to keep her from passing. She looked behind her and saw Jeffrey closing in on her, followed by Gardiner, who was murderous. She examined the gate and saw that it fit only the inside of the arch. If she climbed over the rail and skirted the outside, keeping a grip on the external ornamentation of the parapet, she could make her way past the arch and find her footing on the other side. She swallowed and reminded herself not to look down.

Scaling a pillar, she stood on the top of the rail, balancing, looking for a handhold in the smooth stone of the arch in front of her. Spotted a promising lip and reached for it, but before her fingers made contact, Jeffrey was on her, grabbing at her leg. She held the pillar and kicked out at him, but he was expecting the move, and he ducked. Then he lunged for her waist, caught it, and dragged her from the parapet, throwing her face down on the floor of the gallery.

"Come over suicidal again, darling?" He sounded as angry as Gardiner had looked.

Without speaking, she rolled onto her side to try to trip him. And she did force him to stumble. But before she could press her advantage, Gardiner had straddled her and shoved her face back into the floor. He yanked her arms behind her with enough force to cause her to cry out. Then he dragged her up into a standing position, lifting her bodily to face Jeffrey. She wondered, abstractly, through the pain, if he meant to break her arms. She couldn't slow her breathing.

Jeffrey, who was also breathing hard, pushed his hair off his forehead. "I think you've angered Gardiner. Unwise."

She was too concerned about Archer to let him bait her. Twisting against Gardiner's hands, she tried to locate Archer in the crowd below.

Jeffrey followed her look. "You know, if you're that interested in the story, Marion, perhaps you shouldn't attempt to break the narrator's nose. Would have been difficult to describe to you the subtler plot points with blood streaming down my face."

"Next time," she spat at him, "I'll buy the libretto and break your fucking neck instead."

Gardiner, still holding her, began laughing, quiet and astonished. Jeffrey caught his eye. "Something on your mind, Gardiner?"

"Forgive me, sir. I can't believe she's your wife." He paused. "And John's mother."

"Not even John's mother?"

Gardiner considered. "John," he conceded, "does make more sense now, come to think of it—"

Marion tried to break his grip while he was talking, but he was ready for her, and he wrenched her arms more securely behind her back. She felt tears well up from the pain. But there was no way she'd make another sound for them.

Jeffrey glanced, indifferent, over the side of the rail. "You needn't worry," he told her. "You aren't missing anything. In fact, you might consider this an intermission. Kira Maria's people want time to cover the exits to the hall properly before they can make their next move. And Mr. Spahovic still has no idea what's waiting for him. I believe he's expecting to cross a courier." He shaded his eyes with his hand. "Though he does seem to have finished his cigarette. Calm before the storm."

He straightened and leaned against the parapet, facing her, his arms crossed. "Actually, this might be a good time for me to tell you the other reason that Maugham exiled me to this dreary village. I fear I neglected to do so when we were passing the time before. Slipped my mind in the midst of all that absorbing office gossip."

She glared at him, silent.

"When it became clear from Mr. Spahovic's papers that Kira Maria was the lynchpin of this operation," he explained, "—and apparently has been, in a ghostly sort of way, for centuries—the office thought it might be worth testing her receptivity to a deal. A small deal. Nothing earth-shattering. But enough to make her feel influential. Relevant. Meaningful in this hectic modern world."

He frowned down at a cufflink that had become crooked when Marion had twisted his arm. Fixed it. Looked back up at her. "So, Maugham sounded out his contacts in the Foreign Office, and they thought we might give it a try. Creative approach. Nothing else seems to be helping our cause in the region." He tilted his head. "My entirely genuine concerns about Gunga Din, therefore, were an excellent excuse to spirit me out of London. And once I was out, I made—in my capacity as humble travelling salesman—the Empress Consort our offer.

"Would she be interested in trading up, we asked her. Would she like to set aside her outdated, medieval Assassins or *fida'i*—or whatever you people like to call yourselves these days—and try some corporate solvency instead? A bit of geopolitical prestige? We paid for tonight's party to show her what was possible. A small, yet demonstrative example of what was possible. She'd never have been able to put it together, or likely even have produced a guest list, without, believe me, a great deal of help."

He paused, enjoying Marion's reaction. "And do you know? It seems that Milady loathes this moldering heap of rock as much as we moderns do. Wouldn't be surprised to see her living in Finland in a glass box designed by Alvar Aalto once this comes off." He considered the gothic arches. "Nor would I blame her. This place would drive anyone mad after a century or two."

"We did, though," he said, returning to his theme, "request two favors of her before we *made* it come off. First, we asked her to eliminate our Spahovic problem—simply to prove her willingness to play along, of course. Initiation rites and all that. We're not so different from your own former organization, you realize, when it comes to demonstrations of loyalty. Aside from the sovereignty and the very large navy."

He paused again. "And second, we told her she must deliver that 'treasure' of yours to the grateful curators of the British Museum. The first part of the contract will be easy for her to perform—ethically, that is. Because Marion, you ought to have seen her stunned reaction to the information that Mr. Spahovic had abducted you, my wife, and threatened you with all sorts of unmentionable violence if you refused to work with him."

"She's met him," Marion said. "She knows that I wasn't—"

"You put a good face on it," he interrupted. "I wouldn't have married you if you weren't courageous. Stoic. But anyone looking closely would have seen the duress. She certainly did. Horrifying to watch. You do get yourself into trouble, don't you, dear?"

Marion decided that if she couldn't reach Archer physically, she'd try one last time to warn him. With a painful pitch toward the rail, dragging Gardiner with her, she shouted down into the hall. Managed to call his name once, loud, before Gardiner clapped his hand over her mouth. Struggled to free her face, to shout a second time, but Gardiner was pressing her head against his shoulder, and she was losing consciousness. She stopped moving, and he relaxed his grip. He didn't move his hand away from her mouth.

Archer had started and looked up, confused, when she had called his name. But her voice had been submerged in the sound of the crowd. Her scream had, though, alerted Dimitar that he ought to take action. His people began to move in on Archer.

Jeffrey observed the scene in the hall. "I think you may have started something, Marion." He raised his eyes to Gardiner. "Let her watch."

Gardiner pushed her forward against the rail, still holding her arms behind her back, keeping his hand over her mouth. She watched as Archer realized that he was being stalked and maneuvered himself into a defensive position. His evasion was classic, elegant, and it would have worked if the crowd weren't constantly blocking his exits and his lines of sight.

Eventually, and inevitably given the terrain, he was backed into a wall that turned out, typically for the chaotic architecture of the building, to have an invisible door embedded in it. His stalkers pushed him through the door, Dimitar closed and locked it, and the crowd registered nothing. It was as though Archer had never been in the room at all.

As she watched the scene unfold, Marion did all she could to free herself, twisting against both Gardiner's hands and the parapet, but Gardiner was holding her too securely. Jeffrey followed the action with professional detachment, occasionally glancing back at Marion to see how she was reacting. When it had finished, he looked at her for a few seconds longer, impassively registering her inability to keep the tears of something between pain and panic from streaming down her face. Then he addressed Gardiner again. "You needn't hold her any longer."

Gardiner released her and stepped back. She held the rail with one hand to keep herself upright, and she covered her mouth with the other. Forced herself, gradually, to stop crying. She wanted to kill them. To do something destructive. Self-destructive if necessary. But she damped down her rage and closed her eyes instead. She couldn't indulge herself in this way. Clear headedness, she told herself. And shutting down. She must shut down.

As she was composing herself, the gate on the other side of the arch slid up to reveal Dimitar, unruffled and attentive. "Would you follow me upstairs?" he asked, in English. "Dinner will be served in thirty minutes."

Jeffrey turned to Gardiner. "Would you look in on Lieutenant Trelawney and John for us, please? While we dine?"

"Of course, sir." Calm, self-possessed, his eyes sleepy once again, he half saluted and retreated toward the bedroom. He didn't acknowledge Marion at all.

Jeffrey, however, turned to her and offered her his arm. Still holding the parapet, she stared at it with revulsion. But, remembering her promise to herself, she pushed down her visceral antipathy, stepped forward, and took it. Walked beside him, following Dimitar. Playing along was more strategic.

As they walked, Jeffrey leaned over and spoke to her. "You'll want to fix your hair."

"Yes," she said, mechanically.

She disengaged her hand and pinned her hair into a knot at the nape of her neck. Her dress, its material as forgiving as she'd hoped it would be, hadn't sustained damage. She knew that she looked presentable. If haggard. But despite her calm appearance, her world was a nightmare. Again. It had taken so little time for her to forget this cold feeling, the despair, once she'd escaped London. Now, though, here, in this preposterous castle, it had returned. With a vengeance. And she was already forgetting the freedom she had felt in Istanbul.

But she had her work, she told herself. She could focus on her work. She would do her job. Just as Jeffrey was doing his.

KIRA Maria's small dining room on the third floor of the castle was octagonal, much like her tower room, but elongated and set back into the cliff face. The flagstones covering the floor were unadorned with carpet, and the room was spare aside from a rectangular table covered in damask cloth and prepared for thirteen—with Kira Maria herself at the head. There were no large windows as there were in the east-facing chambers. Instead, slits positioned near the ceiling would let light into the room during the day. Now, late at night, a wrought-iron chandelier, six feet in diameter and lit with at least two hundred candles had been lowered over the table. It illuminated the room remarkably well.

Marion and Jeffrey were the last guests Dimitar escorted to the gathering. When they arrived, ten others, including an emissary from the British Minister to Bulgaria, were standing in small groups, making practiced conversation. Marion recognized at least two faces from the financial sections of the newspapers she purchased to wrap her manuscripts when she wanted to protect them from wear. But she couldn't attach names to their faces. She rarely did more than skim the headlines before putting the papers to what she felt was their more appropriate use.

Her quick evaluation of the women in the room led her to conclude, first, that they were all professional wives, and second, that her dress was a disaster. She didn't mind. Her single, and single-minded, purpose in allowing Jeffrey to bring her here was to discover Archer's whereabouts. She meant to be direct. Rude, if necessary. And her inexpensive, badly cut dress might help her with that.

A few minutes after Dimitar had ushered Marion and Jeffrey into the room, Kira Maria herself emerged from a separate door and gestured her guests to the table. Jeffrey was placed to her left, presumably as the facilitator of the evening, and the Minister's emissary was placed to her right. Marion sat beside the emissary, and the industrialists, their wives, and an aged Bulgarian naval hero from the First Balkan War sat in the remaining chairs. The Battle of Kaliakra, Marion thought. More than twenty years ago, but he was still spry. He sat at the far end of the table, ignored even by his wife, which appeared to suit him perfectly.

Servants produced the first course, a clear soup, less than a minute after the guests were seated. Kira Maria had made no attempt to speak to anyone, and the appearance of the food was abrupt. Contemptuous. Even the diplomatic wives were briefly at a loss as to how to initiate a conversation. But there was wine, a great deal of it, and the table was grateful for it.

Marion decided to use the awkward silence as an opportunity. The situation would become substantially more awkward once she'd spoken, but she had little interest in observing the rules of polite decorum after what she'd experienced in the past hour. And if her insistence on locating Archer wrecked Jeffrey's salesmanship, as he put it, all the better. She set her spoon delicately next to her soup bowl. She hadn't used it.

"Madam," she said to Kira Maria, "I'm honored to be dining with you this evening."

Kira Maria inclined her head, gracious, but didn't respond.

"Will Mr. Archer be joining us?" Marion persisted.

Kira Maria sipped her soup. Observed the guests. "Who?" she asked, not looking at Marion.

"Mr. Archer," Marion repeated.

"I do not know a Mr. Archer." Her accent was heavier, her English less fluent than it had been when she'd spoken to Marion and Archer earlier. Marion suspected the change in her speech was deliberate. And dishonest. But she wasn't going to be put off.

"Mr. Spahovic, then," she said. "Will he be joining us."

"Is this a different person?" Kira Maria was still gazing, vaguely, across the table.

"No."

"Is it Mr. Archer or is it Mr. Spahovic? You confuse me. It could be that my English is not good."

Marion stole a glance at Jeffrey. He was looking down at his soup, eating, repressing a smile. He acted as though he'd expected Marion to open the conversation in this way, and he was enjoying her discomfiture.

Marion took a breath. "Madam, Mr. Archer and I spoke with you earlier in the evening. Mr. Archer brought you an artifact. You accepted it. Less than an hour later, I witnessed Mr. Archer forced by your servants into a passageway adjoining your grand hall. I would like your assurance that Mr. Archer, as your guest, has not met with any harm."

The silence at the table shifted from awkward to stunned. Marion saw one of the diplomatic wives mouth the word "retreat" across the table to a second, and the second cast a compassionate look at Jeffrey sitting diagonally from her. The first smirked, unkind, over at her husband. He made a show of impatiently looking at his watch. But Marion wasn't going to be bullied any more than she'd be put off. She gazed, cold and level, at Kira Maria.

Eventually, letting the moment draw out many seconds longer than it should have, Kira Maria turned to Marion. "People see many things in my house, Lady Willcox." She looked down at the ugly green ring on her hand. "It is an old house. It plays tricks on those who allow it to. Do you know," she spoke slowly, "there was a rumor in the village, oh, three, four centuries ago, that this house consumed people. Ate them. Not many. No—gluttony. But a few people. Sometimes. Girls come up to work the kitchens at feast time. Little boys trained as pages. The villagers told their stories. Brought witnesses."

She shifted her attention from her ring to her spoon, heavy gold, the serpent motif repeated. Lifted it and looked at it as she spoke. "But these were peasants, Lady Willcox. Peasant minds. Undisciplined. Frightened. No listening to reason." Pausing, she put the spoon down on the table and fixed Marion's eyes. "If you discipline your mind, Lady Willcox, you will not see these things. The house will be—" she shrugged, evoking Archer, "simply a house."

"And a beautiful house it is, Madam. Beautiful *as* it is. No need to slander it with children's ghost stories." The first diplomatic wife had regained her command of the conversation and her authority. She smiled across the table after she'd spoken.

Kira Maria might not have heard her. She nodded at Marion's untouched soup. "You do not like your soup, Lady Willcox?"

"I'm not hungry," Marion said, hostile.

"You must eat." Kira Maria signaled to Dimitar. "The next dish."

The servants removed the soup bowls from the table and returned seconds later with small plates, eighteenth-century Meissen, on which a round of raw meat and thin slices of toast were arranged alongside a sprig of mint.

"Lamb tartare," Kira Maria said quietly. "A family recipe."

She lifted a fork and ate a small bite. Her guests followed suit, complimenting her on the preparation.

"There is a secret to the preparation, Lady Willcox." Kira Maria still spoke to Marion, who continued to eat nothing. "I will tell you what it is?"

"Please do." One of the industrialists down the table had finished off his entire portion. The soup had evidently been insufficient for him, and he was hunting about the table for additional food.

Kira Maria watched Marion's face. "The secret, Lady Willcox, is fresh meat. The lamb must be slaughtered no more and no less than thirty minutes before its loin is ground and combined with the shallots, lemon, and mint. Thirty minutes," she repeated. "No more. No less. Always. For centuries."

"The dish is matchless, Madam." The diplomatic wife had found her stride. She was doing her job, just as Marion was doing hers. Well, if thanklessly.

"It is interesting about lambs," Kira Maria continued. "There is a myth, an incorrect belief, that they don't struggle. That they meekly submit to the slaughter." She took another small bite of her dish. "But it is not true. They fight." She paused again, holding Marion's eyes. "This one fought."

"And the meat is better for it, Madam." Jeffrey had joined the conversation. Eating the tartare, deliberately, provocatively, he smiled across the table at Marion. "Do try a bite, dear. It will invigorate you. You need your strength after your recent—" he allowed himself to seem concerned, "—your recent troubles."

The second diplomatic wife sent him an encouraging glance, and he dropped his eyes, flustered, to his plate. Marion glared at his downcast face and the slight smile that only she could see. She pushed the plate away.

The rest of the table had finished eating, and the servants removed the small plates. They brought large dishes of rice mixed with meat and spices to the table. Kira Maria didn't have to encourage her guests. They began eating the pilaf with relish as soon as it was in front of them. Marion stared down at her own plate, nauseated. Paid no attention to the conversation that had finally begun, haltingly, to develop.

Kira Maria, speaking now only to the four guests closest to her, described the dish. "It is a folk recipe," she said. "Pilaf with the organs of the lamb. The chef cuts away the fat from the heart, kidneys, liver, and lungs of the animal, chops the meat into small pieces, and then boils these pieces with salt, pepper, and a minced onion. As the meat becomes tender, he adds the rice, and then bakes the platter in a large oven. It is served, in my family, always as the third plate. An hour or more after the slaughter. We use, as much as we can, the whole animal. No waste."

"And no evidence," Jeffrey added, delighted. He had eaten a substantial portion of his dish, and he was fighting laughter, sipping his wine. Marion's anger had turned to horror. She gaped across at him, and he lifted his glass in a mock salute.

Kira Maria, also smiling now, addressed Marion directly once again. "Lady Willcox," she encouraged her, "please try the dish. We have added a new spice to it. One that we haven't used before. I believe it has improved the taste."

Marion was staring down at her plate. She didn't respond.

"Cloves," Kira Maria said. "We have added cloves this time."

Marion put her hand over her mouth and pushed back her chair. She stood, looked frantically about the room, and then ran for the door. It was shut, and she tried to pull it open. Unsuccessfully.

The conversation, never robust to begin with, faltered again. The first diplomatic wife raised her eyebrows, a delicate sneer. She looked over at Jeffrey.

"Poor dear," he said. "Marion, are you feeling unwell? Shall I take you back to our chamber?" He stood and nodded, courteous, to Kira Maria. Raised her hand and kissed the grotesque ring. The gesture seemed to please and flatter her. "Madam," he said. "I regret that I shall miss further examples of your chef's culinary mastery. But my wife—"

"Go to her, Sir Jeffrey," Kira Maria said. "She needs you."

He bowed. "Madam."

He dropped his napkin on the table beside his plate, walked across the room to Marion, opened the door with ease, and helped her out to the corridor.

When they were through the door, Dimitar was waiting for them. They weren't to wander the castle unescorted. "Allow me to show you back to your chamber, Lady Willcox." Dimitar inclined his head to Marion. "Sir Jeffrey."

Jeffrey slipped Marion's hand through his arm. "Thank you, Dimitar."

They followed Dimitar to their rooms on the first floor, off the gallery, and then waited for Dimitar to withdraw, closing the door behind him. When he'd left, Marion lowered herself into the armchair and stared, unseeing, at the carpet. Jeffrey crossed the room to his suitcases, opened one, busied himself with toiletries and pyjamas, and then glanced back at Marion. "We're in the modern wing of the building, I believe," he said, as though the previous half hour hadn't happened. "Water closet tucked away behind Sultan Murad there. I won't be a moment."

She watched with raw eyes as he left the room, and then she dropped her face into her hands. He returned a few minutes later wearing striped pyjamas and a dressing gown. Sat on the edge of the bed and observed her, his lips twitching in a smile.

"We'll begin our return journey to London tomorrow morning," he told her. "Kira Maria is on schedule now to cooperate. She'd been hesitating, uncertain, but now that you, as the sole remaining representative of the competition, have so gloriously humiliated yourself in front of these important people she's desperate to impress, she'll know where her interests lie. Thank you, Marion," he added, "for acting your part to such perfection."

After waiting a moment for her to reply, he continued. "So, tomorrow morning, she'll hand over your—key, is it?"

She lifted her eyes to him, dull. Didn't speak.

"—your key," he confirmed, "and whatever 'treasure' it whimsically unlocks. And we'll be on our way. I'm curious to see what her unhinged family's been hiding away under the mattress all these centuries. Aren't you?"

She stood and walked to the window. Stared out at the darkness.

"Do you have anything to wear?" he asked after a moment.

"I brought a cardigan and trousers. In my bag."

"I mean tonight."

She turned to face him, incredulous. "You're not serious."

"Oh, Good Lord, Marion. If I'd been moving in that direction, I wouldn't have asked you if you'd anything to *wear*." He was laughing at her. "You and your chastity. Even Milady was provoked into prodding about for an opening—"

"Stop it—"

"Metaphorical, of course," he said. "I suppose. Though I must admit to a certain husbandly concern at this collection of gallants you can't seem to keep from gathering about you. Maugham. Archer. The Mad Cannibal Queen—"

"I said, stop it!"

"Food not to your liking, dear?"

She covered her mouth with her hand and turned to the window. After a silent minute, she collected herself, walked back to the chair, and sat. Held his eyes, cold. "I don't need anything else to wear tonight."

"So what's your plan, then?" he asked. "Sitting up till morning in that morbid chair, wearing Mrs. Bowen's housecoat?"

She stood again. "I'll sleep with Ian."

He raised his eyebrows. "And Gardiner and Trelawney?" He considered. "Although, if I'm not mistaken, even Gardiner is smitten at this point. They'd likely welcome you. If they didn't know I'd feed them to Kira Maria the moment they looked at you wrong."

"Why are you doing this?" She was close to shouting, her fists pressed against her eyes. Her voice, she knew, was verging on the hysterical. And she was having difficulty not bursting into tears.

"Marion," he said. "Must everything, *always*, be so difficult? I'm simply asking you," he spoke patiently, "whether you would like to borrow pyjamas for the night. That's all. It's late. We're both tired. You've brought, in your usual, inimitable fashion, what looks to be a mid-sized feed sack as your luggage. You've nothing to wear to sleep. Would you like me to give you something?"

She was standing, now, in the middle of the room, trembling, her arms hugging her waist. She stared at him for a few seconds. Then she nodded.

"Thank God that's settled," he said, rising and walking to his suitcases. "I can only imagine the crisis I'd have precipitated if I'd offered you a spare toothbrush." He was bending over the suitcase, extracting pyjamas. Glanced back at her. "You don't need a toothbrush, do you—"

"No!"

"Very well."

He handed her pyjamas, dark blue, and she grabbed them and walked toward the tapestry. Lifted a corner of it, entered the tiny water closet, used the toilet, changed, and returned to the room.

He was lying back on the bed, his hands behind his head again, contemplating the canopy. He looked over at her, wearing his pyjamas, holding the dress in her hand. "Toss it out the window, would you?"

She folded it, walked to her sack, and tucked it underneath her day clothes, over the American dollars. Then she turned back to the bed.

"I give you my word of honor—" he started.

"I know," she said, walking to the other side of the bed. "You've had your fun for the evening. Feeling replete now, are you?"

Something like surprise flickered over his face, and then he smiled quietly and slipped under the covers. "I like you because you know me so well."

She pulled the covers over her shoulders at the other end of the absurdly expansive bed. "I don't think you do like me. Because of that."

He laughed, but he didn't respond. And they both were sleeping soon after.

MARION awoke, confused and unrested, in the darkness. She thought for a moment that she'd been shaken out of her sleep by one of the nightmares that regularly afflicted her since Jeffrey had reappeared in her life. Couldn't have slept for more than an hour. Too exhausted. Turning onto her side, she tried to slip back into unconsciousness.

But then, through half-closed eyes, she noticed a lighted candle sitting on the table to the side of the serpent chair. Even in her sleep-deprived fog, she knew that the presence of the candle was wrong. The room was lit electrically. And there had been no candle on the table before. She blinked and peered into the dimly lit room. Someone was sitting in the chair. As her eyes adjusted, she recognized him. Dimitar.

She sat bolt upright in the bed and reached over to shake Jeffrey. He wasn't there. The bed was empty. She was on her feet seconds later, facing the chair, prepared to defend herself.

Dimitar stood and put his finger to his lips. Then he spoke to her in a whisper. "Do not alarm yourself, Dr. Bailey."

A part of her mind registered that he had switched back to her professional name. She shook her head slightly, to clear it. "What do you want?" Flat. Aggressive.

He held up a folded slip of paper. Then he put it on the table, next to the candle. "I have brought a message from Mr. Spahovic."

"Chris—"

"Read the message please, Dr. Bailey." He lifted the candle. "I also bring you the respects of the house. The gate will remain open and unlocked until sunrise. Two hours. We hope that you and your child will find this ample time to collect your belongings and descend to Lopyan."

She was holding the top of Jeffrey's pyjamas closed over her neck. "Sir Jeffrey—?"

"Sir Jeffrey, Mr. Gardiner, and Mr. Trelawney are speaking with Madam in her study." Dimitar walked toward the door of the chamber. He continued, without turning back to her: "it will be an extended conversation, Dr. Bailey. They have much to discuss. Do not concern yourself with it. Or with them." He opened the door, quietly, discreetly. And he closed it, equally quietly, once he was in the corridor.

Marion stared at the door for ten long seconds. Then she walked to the end of the room and switched on the lights. Returned to the chair and unfolded the note.

"Dear Marion," Archer had written in Turkish, "I've salvaged the project. And I'm grateful to you for your assistance. I'm also deeply sorry for any distress my necessary deception has caused you.

Kira Maria told me when we conversed in the courtyard this morning that the office had saturated the village and her house. She had no choice but to feign collaboration until they were off-guard. She's neutralized the threat, however, and she and I will be collecting the artifacts tonight. I'm optimistic, Marion. These objects, if they are anything like what she says they are, will do much to stabilize the region. To quell the fighting. The higher ups will be more than pleased. I must sign off soon, but first: Kira Maria has asked me to send you her sincere apologies for her treatment of you. She's told me that if you ever choose to return to Lopyan, she'll show you the hospitality you deserve. Likewise, if you ever meet Dündar on İstiklal Avenue again, he'll skip the espresso and serve you straight whisky. You deserve it with what you've endured. With my deepest respects, Adnan Spahovic. P.S. I thought no one did offal like your people. Such squeamishness tonight…"

Marion sat in the chair, smiling to herself. Then she re-folded the note. Walked to the luggage stand and noticed, with a pang of treacherous concern, that Jeffrey's suitcases were gone. She pushed down her confused feelings and rifled through her canvas bag for her day clothes. When she found them, she removed Jeffrey's pyjamas and held them in her hands, looking at them. Told herself to remember her loyalties and folded them carefully. Left them on the side of the bed.

She pulled on her cardigan, trousers, and work boots and pushed the note from Chris into her pocket. Then she made her way to Ian's room. Nick and Gardiner were, as Dimitar had said, gone. But Ian was still sleeping in the enormous bed, gripping the wooden aeroplane. Marion found his small suitcase, removed clothing for him, set it on a chair, and approached the bed. She leaned over and kissed his cheek.

He opened his eyes, and when he recognized her, he smiled, put his arms over her neck, pulled her down and hugged her. She let him hug her, awkwardly bent over the bed, for a full minute. Then she disengaged his arms, and lifted him out of the covers. He sat on her lap for a few seconds, still sleepy, before he stood and looked about the room. "Where are Mr. Nick and Mr. Gardiner?" he asked.

She retrieved his clothing and held it out to him. "They've left. For work."

Even she could hear the dishonesty in her voice, and she wasn't surprised when Ian peered at her face, silent, suspicious, for a few seconds. He didn't take his clothes. "Where are we going?"

"Home, Ian." She arranged the clothing on the bed next to him.

"With Jeffrey?"

"No," she said. "Jeffrey must also work. He won't be coming with us."

He looked mutinous. "He'll meet us later?"

She sighed. She didn't want to lie to him. She never had before, and she wasn't about to start now. "No, Ian. Jeffrey won't meet us later." She smoothed out the clothes on the bed. "It will be like before. Mummy and Ian."

"And Mr. Nick?"

"No," she said.

As he watched her, silent once again, she felt a new panic rising in her chest. Ian wasn't angry. He was frightened. Which terrified her in turn. She could have managed petulance. Or even rage. But his fear left her paralyzed. She'd never explained herself to him, and she didn't' know how to do so now. Nonetheless, controlling herself, she damped down her anxiety. Viciously. She must be patient with him. Cajole him out of the building. "It will be all right, Ian—" she started.

"You're leaving him here, Mummy? In this castle?"

"No, Ian—"

"You are!"

"Ian." She picked up his clothes again. Held them out to him. "It's dangerous here. We must leave. Now."

"If it's dangerous, we can't leave Jeffrey. Or Mr. Nick. Or Mr. Gardiner."

"They're grown men, Ian. They can protect themselves."

"If they could protect themselves, they'd be here. They wouldn't leave me."

"I—"

He stared at her, wide-eyed, petrified. "Mummy, I can't leave Jeffrey. He's my father. I can't leave my father."

And to her horror, he started crying.

She knelt in front of him, gathered him into her arms, and hugged him. He sobbed against her shoulder, holding her, but she knew that he wouldn't let her take him away, even in his distress. "Ian—" she tried again.

"No!"

She released him from her arms, stood, and walked to the window. Facing away from him, she looked out. The darkness had taken on the pregnant look that precedes dawn. She turned back to him. "Ian," she said, "if I agree to find Jeffrey, will you put on your clothes?"

He'd stopped crying. Grinned at her, knowing he'd won the argument. "Yes, Mummy."

"And will you do everything—*everything*—I tell you to do? Without arguing?"

"Yes, Mummy."

She sighed again. "Very well."

She held out his clothes, and this time he took them. As he was dressing, she placed his wooden aeroplane in her canvas sack and snapped together his small suitcase. Less than a minute later, he was fully dressed, eager for the adventure. It was as though his tears had never happened. Marion held out her hand, he took it, and they left the room.

They walked along the dimly lit gallery to the staircase and made their way to the central hall. Detritus from the party covered the floor and the occasional table, and they skirted more than one puddle of broken glass and alcohol. But the hall was empty. Kira Maria didn't bother with guards. Her reputation was sufficient protection. Or, Marion thought wryly, her reputation had been sufficient protection. Not anymore.

They reached the arched doorway that opened into the corridor leading to Kira Maria's study. She lifted the wooden slab that secured the door from the outside and pushed. It swung open. No lock—only the slabs on either side.

The corridor was barely visible by the guttering candles left from the night before. No one had snuffed them, but they were almost burned down. Ian, after his fear in the bedroom, was now more than willing to accompany Marion anywhere. He was in high spirits. Compliant. And all in aid, Marion reminded herself acidly, of finding Jeffrey. She felt ill again. Still in a nightmare. Only it was now a substantially more bizarre nightmare than it had been before.

They reached the end of the corridor and pushed open the door to the tower room. Marion half hoped to find Kira Maria sitting there, waiting to receive them. She, Marion, would come up with some excuse for seeking the woman, say her farewells, and then be on her way.

She chewed her lip and looked into the dark room. Empty. Holding Ian tightly by the hand, she walked to the sinister door at the edge of the window. A key ring hung on a hook to its side. Resting on the floor were Jeffrey's suitcases.

Marion stared at the keys before venturing to touch them. They bothered her. Too prominent. Too available. Was basic security really so alien to this house, she wondered? Six-foot-thick walls and a staff of rabidly loyal minions only went so far.

And then the reality of the situation hit her. She had been sent to this room, presented deliberately with these keys. Kira Maria, for reasons she couldn't understand, was making the rescue easy for her. Sending Dimitar to her chamber to tell her where she'd taken Jeffrey, leaving all the intervening doors open, making the keys available. Had she been ordered to clear the way for her? Marion blinked. Best not speculate.

Taking refuge, instead, in action, she put Ian's suitcase and her canvas bag next to Jeffrey's luggage, grabbed the keys from their hook near the door, and began testing the lock. After two tries, she found a key that fit and pushed open the door. Decrepit stone stairs, spiral, covered in damp bacterial life, sputtering torches in ancient sconces—she almost laughed.

For Ian's sake, she didn't. Rather, gripping his hand, she led him to the bottom of the stairs. The scene was what she would have imagined. Four massive, iron-studded wooden doors with barred windows at the top encircling a small room adorned by an ominous platform hanging with manacles. She risked a look down at Ian and allowed herself to smile. He was thrilled.

Two of the doors were open. She peeked into them and saw that the rooms, dungeons direct from American stage sets, were empty. She walked to the first closed door, experimented with her keys, and then used all her strength to pull it open once it was unlocked. Ian, to her annoyance, ran into the room before she had the chance to enter it herself. She followed him and then stopped abruptly.

Nick and Gardiner, shirtless, were chained standing to the walls of the room, facing one another, their arms outstretched, wrists secured with medieval iron cuffs. They were both looking down, puzzled, at Ian. Nick seeming weak and unwell. When Marion examined him more closely in the gloom, she could see why: most of his little finger was gone, and he was losing blood from the wound.

"Mr. Nick!" Ian whispered, playing his role to the hilt. "Mr. Gardiner! Mummy's come to rescue you!"

Nick and Gardiner shifted their bemused look from Ian to each other and then, uncertain, toward Marion.

She returned their gaze, cold, and then addressed Nick, ignoring Ian for the moment. "Nick," she said, "we'll pretend now that we're back at Durham. I'll tell you what to do. You'll do it. Understand?"

"Yes, Dr. Bailey."

"Good." She walked over to him and began unlocking his wrists. "Take Ian upstairs and wait in the courtyard while Gardiner and I see about Jeffrey. If we aren't there to meet you in twenty minutes, you and Ian leave without us."

Nick and Gardiner exchanged another silent message before he nodded his agreement. But she ignored their interaction. Lowered the keys and watched as Nick let his arms drop to his sides. "Are you strong enough to make it on your own?"

"Yes, Dr. Bailey."

Ian was staring at Nick's hand. "Mr. Nick, your finger's off."

"Just a scratch, Ian. It's nothing."

"But it's off."

"Flesh wound."

Gardiner lifted an eyebrow across at Nick as Marion began unlocking his wrists as well. "Could have been a lot worse too, if Himself hadn't drawn her off. She was working up to taking a lot more than your finger, Trelawney."

Nick had torn fabric from his pyjama trousers, which he was wrapping around his hand. "I'll have my future wife thank him when the time comes." He secured the bandage and pulled it tight. "I still don't understand how he infuriated her so. What *was* that?"

Gardiner watched as Marion worked on his other wrist. She refused to acknowledge his almost imperceptible smile as she leaned across him to reach the cuff.

"I think you'd call it calculated, magisterial twattery," he said as she worked on the lock. "Pure, undiluted insult. The man is a demented genius." He paused. "And you are one very lucky boy."

Marion succeeded in unlocking Gardiner's second manacle, and he dropped his hands, rubbing his wrists. Grinned at Nick. "Though it *is* a shame. Marring the perfect specimen and all. Office will be forced to give you different assignments. No more batting those big brown eyes at teacher—"

"Sod off, Gardiner." Nick had taken Ian's hand in his own uninjured hand, and he was leading him toward the stairs.

Ian appeared satisfied that Marion and Gardiner would succeed in releasing Jeffrey, and he didn't protest at being led back up to the tower room. He did, though, begin questioning Nick. "But what's worse than losing a finger, Mr. Nick?"

"A toe, of course." Nick's voice was becoming fainter as they climbed the stairs. "Imagine if I'd lost a toe. I'd never dance again."

"But without a finger, you'll not be able to play the piano."

"I never liked the piano, John—"

Marion turned to Gardiner. "Is he alive?"

"I think he is. But he may not be pretty. Trelawney and I heard her working on him. Are you prepared for it?"

She nodded. Then she followed Gardiner out of the cell and concentrated on unlocking the door to Jeffrey's dungeon. After a long minute, she found the proper key, and Gardiner pulled open the door. The room was identical to the others she had seen, but Jeffrey wasn't chained to the wall as Nick and Gardiner had been. Instead, he was stretched out on a low table, also wearing only his pyjama trousers, eyes closed, his wrists secured above his head.

Strips of flesh, four to five inches long, had been pulled from his chest, his left shoulder, and both of his arms. The pincers, iron, a foot long, and still warm from the furnace, were set carelessly at his side. Whoever had done it clearly intended to continue upon his or her return. The wounds were raw, untreated, and bleeding heavily. There was a smell, or a parody of a smell, of burnt meat in the room.

Jeffrey turned his head when the door opened, and he smiled at the sight of Marion and Gardiner. Then he closed his eyes again. "At last," he said. "I kept asking the daft bint when the fair one with the mouth would appear. She's in all the stories. I was feeling cheated at being deprived of her." He opened his eyes and looked over at Marion. "And finally, here she is. Late but radiant. Now that I'm weak, defeated, and at your mercy, will you rob me of my vital fluids?" He gazed up at the ceiling. "I hope so."

Marion walked toward the table, gripping the keys in her hand. She stood over him and looked down at his face. "I'm here because of Ian."

"You're here because you like me too much to see me served up as an uninspired second course." He smirked up at her. "Just can't keep away from me, can you, darling?"

Without pausing to think about it, she slammed her fist into the wound on his chest. He screamed and arched his back in pain, which gratified her more than she'd have expected it to. She managed to slap him across the face as well, brutal, before Gardiner pulled her off him and began wrenching the keys from her hand.

Jeffrey, once he'd recovered, started laughing. "Stop," he said. "Gardiner, please. Forgive my wife. She forgets herself in front of the staff." He shut his eyes, trying to control the pain. "Marion," he eventually said, calmly, "would you please release me from this unbelievably embarrassing predicament? We'll continue this exchange when we've returned home."

She thought about Ian waiting for her in the courtyard and, with an effort, controlled herself. Without acknowledging Gardiner, who had let her go on Jeffrey's order, she took the keys and unlocked the cuffs around his wrists and ankles. He pulled himself up into a sitting position, and then he eased his feet onto the ground. Gardiner made a move to support him, but he shook his head.

"I'll manage." He looked down, annoyed, at his tattered pyjama trousers. "Provided Lady Willcox doesn't attempt to break my arm again. Watch my back for me, would you, Gardiner?"

"Yes, sir." Gardiner moved to the door of the cell, propping it open. He waited for both Jeffrey and Marion to precede him before following them out and up the stairs.

When Jeffrey spotted his suitcases beneath the window, he exhaled, relieved. "Thank God. I'd never live it down if Maugham learned I'd been forced to flee, barefoot and half-naked, from this wretched assignment." He opened a case, retrieved a shirt, and tossed it to Gardiner. "It'll be snug, but it will cover you."

"Thank you, sir." Gardiner buttoned the shirt over his pyjama trousers as Jeffrey also handed him socks and a pair of shoes. A moment later he passed him a pistol as well.

Jeffrey found a second shirt. "This for Trelawney, do you think?"

"But Trelawney looks so nice without any shirt at all, sir." Gardiner had finished buttoning his collar. He pulled on the socks, and slid his feet into the shoes.

"Envy doesn't become you, Gardiner." Setting aside the shirt and a pair of shoes for Nick, he turned to Marion. "If you don't mind? It won't take long."

He stripped out of his bloodied pyjamas and found a dark shirt that wouldn't show the new blood stains that would inevitably form on his chest and arms. He pulled on wool trousers, socks and shoes, and then rummaged in the case for a tweed jacket and, Marion noticed unhappily, his Webley revolver. He put the jacket on over his shirt, secured the revolver, snapped the case shut, and lifted it to take with him. Marion lifted her canvas sack and Ian's small suitcase.

"Let's see what John and Trelawney have found for us to drive," Jeffrey said, bright, animated, driven by the same edgy high spirits that had motivated Ian.

Marion remained silent. She abhorred the growing similarities that she was noticing between the two of them, but she forced herself not to dwell on them. Her job, she reminded herself. She must do her job.

They made their way through the corridor, across the cold, grey hall, and to the courtyard. The sun had just started rising over the mountains to the east.

*I*AN and Nick were sitting on the bonnet of a 1933 Pierce Silver Arrow, Ian trying to twist and remove the ornament. When Marion, Jeffrey, and Gardiner emerged from the castle, Ian lit up, jumped from the car, and barreled into Jeffrey, hugging him. Jeffrey paled at the impact, but he stayed upright, patting Ian wanly on the head.

Ian looked up at him. "Mummy rescued you, sir! From the dungeon."

Jeffrey smiled, unpleasant, at Marion, who was trying to extricate Ian from his legs. "Indeed, she did, John. Bad habit of Mummy's. Never ends well for her."

She decided that Jeffrey could detach Ian himself. Straightened and walked toward the eight or nine vehicles that remained parked in the courtyard from the previous evening. Jeffrey firmly removed Ian's arms from around his leg, held his hand, and followed Marion, examining the cars. "I had hoped to take Mummy's lorry, given that our own vehicles appear to have been appropriated. But it seems that someone has made off with the lorry as well." He spoke to Marion's angry back. "I wonder who that could have been, Marion. Any thoughts?"

She turned to face him. "My thought is that we ought to get ourselves down off this mountain before Dimitar's patience wears thin."

Jeffrey looked down at Ian. "Mummy always has the best ideas, hasn't she? Let's do get ourselves down off this mountain. Care to choose our transport, John?"

Marion stared at him. "What?"

"We'll need a vehicle. How do you propose we choose?"

Ian had already begun inspecting the possibilities scattered across the courtyard, taking his assignment as seriously as a six-year-old could. Eventually, he made his decision and pointed to a car. "This," he announced.

It was a stretch, six-seat Mercedes-Benz 770 in silver. Marion thought she remembered the exiled Kaiser owning something similar. She looked at it more closely. Or perhaps it was this very car. She was about to suggest that they look for something less stupidly visible, but Gardiner was already working on the locked doors. Thirty seconds later, all four doors, along with the bonnet, were open.

Jeffrey, handing Nick the shirt, told him to sit in the front passenger seat and try to keep from losing any more blood. He gestured Marion into the back seat, and, resigned, she slid into the car. The seat smelled of cheap scent. She cracked the window a few inches. Walking to the open bonnet to examine the ignition coil, Jeffrey turned back to Ian and Gardiner. "Care to drive, John?"

"Yes, sir."

"Gardiner?"

"Of course."

Gardiner slid into the driver's seat and positioned Ian in his lap. He waited for Jeffrey to bypass the interlock, and when the engine came to life, he let Ian grip the steering wheel along with him. Jeffrey jogged back and sat beside Marion. Slammed the door. "Drive, Gardiner."

Gardiner accelerated past the looming gates and took the first hairpin turn at a rate that left Marion clenching her fists in her lap. She glanced over at Jeffrey, but his eyes were closed, a crease of pain knotting his forehead. As Gardiner continued careering down the mountain, however, Jeffrey opened his eyes and looked out the window.

"We're going to Sofia?" she asked.

"Eventually," he said. "Yes."

Gardiner screeched around another turn, and Jeffrey peered at the passing road. The sun was hovering over the edge of the mountains, but the shadows on the ground and in the forest were still dark. A deceptive mist obscured the tops of the trees.

"Let's pause here, Gardiner," he said. He turned to Marion. "Lovely view. I'd like to admire it in a more leisurely manner."

Gardiner brought the car to a halt at a bulge in the road that gave way to a rough track leading further into the forest. When Marion opened the door and left the car, she examined the path. Then she put her hand over her mouth, her eyes wide. Further along the track, superficially hidden by tree branches, was Archer's lorry.

"Oh," she said.

Jeffrey, who had also left the car, smiled at her. "What luck."

"For God's sake, Jeffrey, would you just let it alone? Please, let's go to Sofia." She felt more tired than angry or frightened. "I can't do this."

He didn't reply. Opened the front passenger door to speak with Nick. "Trelawney," he said, "would you retrieve Dr. Bailey's remaining luggage from the lorry? See to it that the manuscript and *sicils* are intact. Then wait for us here. Shouldn't be more than a half hour."

"Yes, sir."

Gardiner and Ian had disentangled themselves from the driver's seat and were standing alongside the car as well. Marion knelt in front of Ian. "Ian," she said, "I'd like you to stay here with Mr. Nick. I'll be back—"

"John," Jeffrey interrupted, "would you like to see a real vampire?"

"Yes!" Ian ran over to take his hand. Then he considered. "The sun is up. Will it be sleeping?"

"Not yet. Still a few more hours yet. Come along."

"Jeffrey—" Marion started.

"Too late, Marion." He looked back at her over his shoulder as he started out on the track. "He's coming with us."

She stood, rooted to the ground, watching Jeffrey, Ian, and Gardiner disappear around a bend in the track. She was obscurely aware of Nick leaving the Mercedes and making his way to the lorry. Didn't bother to watch him. Instead, staring at the ground, still resigned, she followed Jeffrey. This was her responsibility. Everything that happened next would be her own doing. She tried to swallow, but her mouth was dry. She thought she might be sick.

The track ended abruptly at a clearing after a steep ten-minute hike up a cleft in the mountain. Two sides of the clearing were blocked by the cliff, but a third side, opposite, gave way to a steeper track that led to the river valley a mile below, on the far side of Kira Maria's castle. The edge of this second track, after a small lip, became a sheer drop of three or four hundred feet.

The space felt simultaneously suffocating and precarious. Like the castle itself, Marion thought. Pointlessly. She identified her disconnected musing as the now familiar work of her brain not wanting to process. Not wanting to see. She forced herself to look up.

Archer and Kira Maria were exposed, unprotected, and without cover, using shovels to dig a pit in the corner of the clearing where the sides of the cliff met. Jeffrey and Gardiner, having reached the edge of the clearing, had pulled out their weapons and aimed them, almost casually, at both. The four appeared oddly frozen. But the illusion lasted only a fraction of a second.

Archer was the first to move. He spotted Jeffrey and Gardiner, straightened, and wiped away the sweat that had formed on his forehead despite the frost on the ground.

"Don't let us stop you," Jeffrey said to him, still training his revolver. "Please continue, Mr. Archer."

Kira Maria had stopped digging as well. She was wearing jodhpurs, boots, a white blouse, and a tie. Her matching jacket and hat, equestrian, were resting on a rock at the base of the cliff. The cauldron and key sat next to them.

Archer spotted Marion and smiled, crooked. Unsurprised. "They said you'd free him if you were given the opportunity," he said to her, speaking English. "I didn't believe it. Told them they'd misread the situation entirely."

"Chris." Her voice was hoarse. She was mortified. "I—my son—" She stopped. There was nothing she could say.

Archer leaned over and peered at Ian, hiding behind Gardiner's legs. "I'm glad you brought him. I was curious about the boy. Ian, isn't it?"

Ian was disappointed. He moved out from under Gardiner and looked up at Jeffrey. "Is that the vampire?"

"No."

Ian turned to Kira Maria. "Is she?"

"We'll find out."

Jeffrey waved his gun at the pit and spoke to Kira Maria. "As I said, don't let us interrupt. Carry on. Pretend we're not here."

Kira Maria straightened and sneered at Jeffrey, projecting in a single glance six hundred years of aristocratic contempt. "Never."

Jeffrey pointed his revolver at her face and smiled back at her, malicious, enjoying the moment. "Dig."

"Death first."

He shot her.

The bullet ripped through her face. Blood, brain, and bits of skull drenched the cliff behind her. She remained upright for three or four seconds too long before collapsing into a heap over her shovel.

Marion cried out when Jeffrey pulled the trigger, but her first move was toward Ian. She lunged for him and hugged him, burying his face in her chest, wishing that he had never seen it, that she could undo the moment. She was shaking, squeezing her own eyes shut.

Ian pushed her away from him, annoyed. He looked up at Jeffrey again. "She was the vampire?"

"Looks like it," Jeffrey confirmed.

Ian considered. "Golly." Then he turned to Marion, who was still kneeling on the ground, shaking. "It's ok, Mummy. She was a vampire."

Marion stood and stared, trembling, at Jeffrey. "That was—"

"Marion," he said. "The lunatic harpy *ate* Trelawney's finger. I don't care what sort of noble cause she thought she was serving, she got what was coming to her. And speaking of noble causes," he added, turning to Archer and pointing his gun at the pit again. "If you don't mind?"

"Oh hell, Willcox." Archer dropped his shovel. "Shoot me too. I know your reputation well enough not to let you coerce me. If nothing else, I've seen what you've done to Marion. Look at her. She's demolished."

"Maugham will never let me hear the end of it if I kill you, Mr. Archer." There was a trace of respect in his voice. "He's looking forward too much to his conversation with you. So if you won't dig, would you sit there against the wall, please? Hands where I can see them?"

Archer threw an irritated glance at Marion, and then he walked to the far end of the clearing. Sat on the ground against the wall, his knees up, his hands folded over them.

Jeffrey turned to Gardiner. "I would do it myself, Gardiner, but—"

"Understood, sir."

Gardiner handed Jeffrey his pistol, took the shovel, and began digging. A few minutes later, his shovel hit the top of a wooden box. He used his hands to disengage the box from the surrounding dirt, and then he lifted it out of the pit.

Jeffrey gave him back his weapon. "Watch Mr. Archer."

Gardiner nodded, and Jeffrey approached the box. It was unornamented, old, a little more than a foot square, hinged in well-preserved iron. No latch. Jeffrey squatted in front of it. Opened the lid and drew out an object wrapped in rotting green silk. Set the object on the ground in front of him and gently pulled the silk off of it. He wrinkled his forehead, stood, and stepped back from it.

It was a plain, solid, transparent glass cube. Roughly the size of the box that had held it. He looked at Marion. "What is it?"

She shook her head. Baffled.

He nodded. And then, briskly, he spoke. "Ah well. Whatever it is, it's glass. Will make the job easier."

"The—job?"

Jeffrey was backing away from the cube, raising his revolver. "Did I neglect to mention that as well?" He wasn't looking at her. Aiming the gun at the cube. "So much excitement at the castle, Marion. Must have slipped my mind. My brief, you see, wasn't to retrieve whatever Kira Maria brought to us. It was to destroy it. Nullify it. The last thing the office, or for that matter the government, needs at the moment is some charismatic leader with the fabled 'Treasure of Thrace,' or whatever the propagandists would brand it, uniting this bedeviled part of the continent into something coherent. We already have more than enough of that going on in Southern and Central Europe. The Balkans are, and always have been, bickering, bloody, and provincial. Satellites. We'd very much like to keep them that way. This—object—whatever it is—is a threat to our policy. Sadly."

He paused. "At least it's not all that aesthetically pleasing." Without further warning, he pulled the trigger and shot the cube.

Marion tensed, expecting the sound of shattering glass. Instead, she heard a dull thud. The cube was undamaged. Jeffrey frowned, confused. Fired another bullet. Nothing happened. He turned to Gardiner. "Care to try?"

Gardiner stepped toward the cube, held his gun in two hands, feet stable, and squeezed the trigger of his pistol. The bullet hit the center of the cube and ricocheted off of it. The cube itself was pristine. Not even a dent.

As Marion watched, a peculiar but insistent thought formed at the edges of her mind. Gradually, she recognized what had been bothering her, if unconsciously, about both the key and the cauldron ever since she and Archer had found them in Edirne. Neither was extraordinary or fantastic enough to merit the awed praise that surrounded them in the Aşıkpaşazade or Ibn Battuta manuscripts. Yes, they were novel. Interesting. But they weren't the stuff of conquering armies or rapidly expanding empires. They'd seemed paltry to her. But she hadn't let herself follow that impression to its logical conclusion.

Now, though, that she'd seen the "treasure"—similarly novel but also by no means a marvel—she allowed herself to reconsider her feelings about Archer's assignment. Since London, she'd been misinterpreting the passages in the manuscripts that described the *sigil*s. Even after she had shifted from Arabic and Ottoman Turkish to Latin, she had still been looking for "signs" or "talismans." But *sigil*s in the medieval Balkans, in Thracian Latin, also referred to pure magic. Beyond simple signs. They invoked forces that did things without human input. They were what in 1934 she'd call "technology." The treasure wasn't an object. It was a technology. An industry. And she had a good idea now of what that technology was.

She stole a glance at Jeffrey and Gardiner, who were still frowning, frustrated, down at the cube. Ian had joined them, mimicking their concentration. They were preoccupied, but they weren't going to let her wander across the clearing to speak with Archer. Her vexation at being unable to pass along her message lifted, however, when Jeffrey himself addressed Archer.

"It's your project, Mr. Archer," he said. "Would you be good enough to lend us your expertise?"

Archer shrugged, rose, and crossed to the cube. Looked down at it, indifferent.

"Well?" Jeffrey asked.

"I have no idea what it is." Archer didn't trouble to hide the boredom in his voice.

Marion took a breath. "I know what it is."

They all looked over at her. She also crossed the clearing and stood next to them, gazing down at the cube.

Jeffrey raised his eyebrows, skeptical. "Do you now, Marion? I should have guessed. And you're going to share your theory with us in the spirit of—what? Collegial, scholarly exchange?"

"Yes," she said. "To get this over with." She forced herself not to make eye contact with Archer. Knew that he'd understand her purpose in talking, and she didn't want to raise Jeffrey's suspicions more than they already were raised. "It's spinel," she told him.

"Spinel?"

"There's a vein of spinel—ferrospinel—running through this part of Bulgaria and into Turkish Thrace. The Ottomans considered mining it in the nineteenth century. But there wasn't any practical use for it. Without knowing how to treat it, that is. Legend has it, however, that if you *do* know how to treat it, it can be melted, sintered, into transparent, indestructible sheets. For armor. It's an old legend. Centuries old. Goes with the glass-making secrets that you find all over the region."

Jeffrey looked thoughtful. He nudged the transparent cube with his shoe. "But obviously no one ever produced this armor. They couldn't have. As a military technology, it would have been devastating. Even today it would be devastating. Could be used for a lot more than armor. Optics. Aircraft."

She ignored him. "In Aşıkpaşazade's description of the ceremony in Edirne, when the dervishes leave 'rich,' the word he uses for 'rich' is '*gani*.' You could translate it as 'in abundance.' It usually is. But there's a strong suggestion of 'with an abundance of *plunder*.' It sounds odd in the text. Jarring. Why would dervishes, Sufis, leave a circumcision celebration carrying 'plunder?' But the term does make sense if the purpose of the passage isn't only to describe Mehmet's generosity to the dervishes, but also to connect Edirne back to the detailed, painstaking descriptions of each and every earlier Sultan passing along his armor and thus his ability to extract 'plunder,' as a legacy, to his sons. Then the passages harmonize beautifully." She shot Jeffrey a look. "Aesthetically. A technological secret like this would be quite the treasure," she continued "—quite the legacy. And it would explain why all of those supposedly invincible Byzantine fortresses toppled without a single battle being fought in the fourteenth and fifteenth centuries."

"Then the late Kira Maria," Jeffrey concluded for her, "wasn't trying to unearth an artifact. She was trying to bring this vein of spinel, which runs through her land, together with the lost instructions on how to treat it. The instructions that you and Mr. Archer brought to her. 'Treasure of Thrace,' indeed. No wonder she wasn't impressed by our appeal to her greed. She didn't need a bribe. If she'd succeeded, she'd have monopolized a technology that would have brought every military in the world to her feet." He thought for a moment. "But we still don't know where the instructions are. A pretty glass key doesn't help us much."

"On the contrary," Marion said, switching from English to the medieval Ottoman that she knew Jeffrey couldn't follow, but Archer could. "We know where the instructions are. Dündar," she spoke quickly, before Jeffrey could stop her, "there's an inscription on the lid of the cauldron. I hadn't understood it before, but I know what it is now. It's the recipe. The technology. The key and the cube are unimportant. They're samples. In thirty seconds, I'm going to cause some chaos. Take the cauldron and get yourself out of here."

Archer blinked, acknowledging her instructions.

Jeffrey, however, was entertained rather than angered by her shift from English to Ottoman. Which made her nervous. She had expected violence. But she continued counting down, nonetheless, preparing her distraction, even as her throat contracted in anxiety.

"John," Jeffrey said, smiling at Marion rather than at Ian. "What did Mummy say to Mr. Archer?"

Ian looked up from the cube, distracted, uninterested. "Mummy told Mr. Archer to steal the cooking pot and run away." He glanced at Marion. "Sorry, Mummy." Went back to examining the cube.

Marion gaped at Ian, stunned.

Archer swore and dove toward the cauldron, instantly followed by Gardiner. He grabbed it, but his path to the track down the mountain was blocked. Gardiner raised his pistol, more to halt Archer than to shoot him. He knew that Jeffrey wanted Archer alive, in London, and he couldn't kill or injure him too severely.

Marion, also knowing that Gardiner would hesitate to pull the trigger, lost no time. She threw herself at him and propelled him against the wall of the cliff. Archer, his way clear, sprinted toward the track, dropping a small square of paper near Marion's foot. But before he could take cover around a bend in the mountain, Jeffrey raised his Webley and fired.

Marion, struggling with Gardiner, tensed. Jeffrey's target, though, wasn't Archer himself. He had aimed at Archer's hand, and he had shot the cauldron squarely at its center. Archer let the cauldron go, and it skidded along the track, teetered, and then plummeted over the drop.

They all froze, watching it fall for a slow split second.

Then Marion shouted at him: "run!"

Archer confirmed that she had pocketed the square of paper before sliding down the track, trying to keep the trajectory of the cauldron in view. He'd be forced to spend a lot of time in the trees below to track it. But there was a possibility, at least, that he'd succeed. A very slight possibility.

Gardiner used Marion's momentary lack of attention to slam her into the ground at the base of the wall and follow Archer down the trail. But Jeffrey stopped him. "It isn't worth it. Let him go. He'll never find it in the forest." He walked over to Marion to help her up. "We'll call this a qualified success. There wasn't much more Maugham could have extracted from Mr. Archer anyway."

She shook Jeffrey's hand off her arm and stood on her own. Briefly considered hitting him again. Couldn't decide between his shoulder or his chest. When she saw that he had read her thoughts, amused if wary, she gazed desolate, at the cliff edge instead. Ian was standing close to the drop, peering over the precipice.

Jeffrey followed her look. "You can't seriously have thought that I'd let you deceive me with that a second time."

"But Ian—"

"Gyula Germanus," he said. "Worth every farthing."

She turned to him. "Vambery's protégé? You had Gyula Germanus teaching him Ottoman? That's—it's perverse, Jeffrey."

"He was passing through London." He returned her look, innocent. "When you were dead. And he owed me a favor. So, I thought, why not? As you see, John was a more than adept pupil."

She watched as Gardiner led Ian away from the cliff. He paused at the cube of spinel and looked a question at Jeffrey. Jeffrey nodded, and Gardiner wrapped the cube, fit it back into the box, and held it under one arm. Then he collected the key, which was still resting next to Kira Maria's forgotten hat and jacket. Skirting her prone, disfigured body, he brought the key to Jeffrey.

Jeffrey turned it over a few times in his hands and then slipped it into his trouser pocket. "It's beautiful," he said. "Unlike the rest of the material. Will make a nice exhibit for the Museum, I think." He turned toward the track leading back to the main road. "Though obviously we'll label it 'medieval glass' rather than 'military grade spinel.' Don't want anyone getting ideas, do we?"

Ian ran up to take Jeffrey's hand, and they half-walked, half-slid down the hill toward the Mercedes. Gardiner, not taking any chances, walked behind Marion. She was still dumbfounded by what she had seen. Still shaking from the violence. But she clutched the square of paper in her pocket. And she reminded herself, repeatedly, insistently, that Archer hadn't been harmed. He was free. And he would file a report. And perhaps he would even find the lid of the cauldron. As Jeffrey had said, it was a qualified success. She would call it a qualified success. She wanted to cry.

MAUGHAM had secured them three private carriages on the Simplon Orient Express, leaving Sofia the following afternoon at 2:40. Jeffrey and Nick had spent the evening in the Aleksandrovska Hospital having their wounds treated, and both were less fragile when they boarded the train next day. Ian, who had shared a carriage with Jeffrey on the way down, was excited to sleep with Marion on the return journey to Paris. He was already explaining to her, as they boarded, how he could dive head-first from the top bunk to the bottom without the use of the ladder. He said he'd demonstrate the trick to her as soon as she'd gone to sleep that night.

The activity of the previous days, however, defeated him, and he was unconscious before Marion even considered trying to sleep herself. As the train passed through, and then gained speed out of, Belgrade, she sat on the small sofa in her sitting area, watching the twilight from her window. She could hear Ian breathing heavily in the upper bunk.

Darkness fell a few minutes later, and she considered changing out of the loose wool jumper and trousers she had worn to the station in Sofia. She had marshalled just sufficient energy to find her pyjamas, when she heard a quiet knock on her door. She stepped across the carriage and opened it.

Jeffrey, wearing a blue suit, striped yellow shirt, and paisley tie, held up a bottle of scotch and two tumblers. He looked as though he were returning from a beach holiday. If it weren't February. In the Balkans. As she stepped to the side to let him enter, she decided that she missed the blood stains.

He relaxed into the chair facing the sofa, placed the tumblers on the mahogany tabletop, and poured the scotch. She sat on the sofa and took her glass, looking down at it rather than at him. He raised his glass. "To a job well done."

She stared at him, blank. He shrugged, drank, and then set the glass on the arm of his chair. Watched her.

"Jeffrey," she finally said. "What you did back there. In Lopyan. It was worse than looting. It wasn't just—just the destruction of an artifact. It was irresponsible. Immoral."

She waited for him to reply, but he didn't. Continued to watch her. Interested.

She wrinkled her forehead and drank a large swallow of her scotch. Then she looked at him again. "There was a possibility—" She stopped. She couldn't think of how to phrase her horrified disbelief at what he had done. Gathered her thoughts. Tried to sound reasonable. "If Chris had passed the instructions for that technology to the proper people," she said to him, wanting him to understand. "I mean, to people who appreciated its value—it might have redirected the hatred that's been building up in the region. It might even have quelled it."

She stared down at her lap. "Now, though, there's nothing to stop the rage. It's inescapable. There was hope. You interfered. It's gone."

"Indeed, it is gone," Jeffrey agreed. "Never to be resurrected, I daresay. In fact, with all of their recent 'resettlement' laws and their ethnic purity manias and the frantic shoring up of their borders, our analysts are predicting at least ten thousand people massacred by June. Perhaps twenty thousand. Likely more. And that's only in Thrace."

She lifted her eyes to his, appalled. "And you consider that acceptable?"

He sipped his scotch, fighting a smile. "If the rest of the world is committing suicide, perhaps it won't notice that the British Empire is dead as well. The new service. Wrecking everything else in the hope that it will forestall the inevitable. Worth a try."

"'*Worth a try*?' That's—"

"Have you considered your own recent activities? The ethics of them, I mean." He was still watching her, now unambiguously entertained. "My dear, in your ongoing, decade-long search for a virtuous employer, you have turned not only terrorist and assassin but now, it seems, also arms trafficker. You're *running weapons*, Marion. You know—weapons? Tools for killing, hurting, and maiming people? And there's no way you're stupid enough to think that doing so is innocent. That there's some 'good' government out there, better than the others, that would use that—that cooking pot—solely in the name of peace and freedom. Innocence doesn't exist. As you know perfectly well. Cross a border and the ones who were being slaughtered become the ones organizing the slaughter. It's universal."

He was still smiling. "And your recent assignment, darling, wasn't to *stop* that process. It was to facilitate it. To make it easier. To pass along a mechanism for making the massacre that much more efficient. You consider *that* acceptable?"

"I do what's necessary."

"You do what you're told," he said. "Just as I do."

"But I don't—"

"What? Enjoy it? Of course you do. That's why you're not nearly as upset at being obliged to switch sides as you ought to be. Although I warn you, Marion, when you work for the office, the office wins. Not you. Never you."

"I don't work for the office," she shot back at him. "And it hasn't won."

"This looks like winning to me," he said, glancing about the carriage. "And if you think that your personal loyalty to your organization has any bearing at all on your professional contribution to our section's work, you truly are deluded. You can scream your hatred of all things British from the rooftops if you'd like—take out a few troupes of Morris Dancers if it makes you feel better—but it won't alter your relationship to His Majesty's Government in the slightest. You're ours. And there's nothing you can do to escape it."

"I can die."

"Again? I suppose. You don't choose this business if clinging to life is a high priority. But I don't think you will die." He sipped his scotch. "Leaving aside your tormented attachment to poor John, there's also your resilience. It's a paradoxical weakness, you realize. This refusal *ever* to accept defeat. And, as your handler, I'll cultivate that. Give you the occasional taste of your manuscripts. Let you convince yourself that, on balance, you're fighting the good fight on behalf of your own people rather than allowing yourself to become ever more sullied by mine. But, my dear, you must forgive me if, on occasion, I feel moved to puncture that vanity of yours."

He smiled at her, affectionate. "I can't help myself, you see. It's just so fun." He stood, collected his glass, and stepped to the door. "That's all I wanted to say, Dr. Bailey. In the interest of furthering our professional relationship. Thank you ever so much for your assistance in this recent matter. We look forward to working with you in the future."

He glanced back at her as he passed through the door.

"I'll leave the bottle."
The door slid shut.

Simplon Orient Express
February, 1934

MARION had finished more than half of the scotch that Jeffrey had left for her on the table. After changing into her pyjamas, she had stared at her own reflection in the dark window of the carriage, drinking glass after glass of the alcohol. Eventually, dizzy and ill, she had closed the curtains and checked on Ian. He was still deeply asleep, breathing slowly. She calculated that they were approaching the outskirts of Trieste.

Pushing down her nausea, she retrieved the square of paper that Archer had passed to her. She also extracted from her bed the manuscript that she had stolen from the depot what now felt like a lifetime ago. Pilfering it from Nick that morning had been child's play, given his bleary reaction to the analgesics from the hospital. She had considered making off with her luggage in its entirety, but she didn't want to alert Gardiner to her plan. So she had done no more than slip the manuscript under her mattress once she'd entered her carriage.

Now, with the manuscript open to the third page of the *Rihla*, and the note unfolded next to it on the tabletop, she felt prepared to read the message from her organization. The note was composed in the simplest encryption her people used, and it took less than five minutes, checking it against the Ibn Battuta, to decode it.

> Supplementary instructions: Remain embedded. Maintain your link to the
> collection. Remain open to Willcox and Maugham. Follow their orders. Allow
> them to use you. Do not, repeat, do not disengage. Await further instructions.
> Contact will come as usual. Thank you for your service.

Marion stared down at the frayed note, unseeing, for close to five minutes. Then she pressed her fists into her eyes and forced herself to keep from screaming. She didn't want to wake Ian.

She considered crying. She could cry.

Or, she could drink. She gazed, unfocused, at the half-empty bottle of scotch resting on the table beside the manuscript. Lifted it and poured an unsteady three fingers into the tumbler. Leaned back on the sofa. If she drank enough, perhaps she wouldn't dream.

Azerbaijan, 1935

Suffolk, England
December, 1934

THE small man sitting in the corner of their carriage was wedged, cringing, into his dark purple, velvet seat. Visibly terrified. Marion had cast him no more than a quick, embarrassed glance when he had opened their door—enough to register oddly light blue eyes, what she refused to believe was a wig, and an air of delicate, child-like misconduct. Then she had turned to examine the passing, twilit scenery out her window. Studious. Uninterested.

She had been surprised by the man's winded and flustered appearance at their door, ten minutes into their journey from Liverpool Street Station. Jeffrey had reserved their first-class compartment in its entirety for the rail journey from London to Stowmarket. And Ian, now seven years old, exhausted from his first term at school, was stretched out asleep, his head in her lap. He hadn't noticed the intrusion. She followed Ian's lead. Forced herself not to notice.

As darkness fell outside the window, Marion realized that she couldn't keep up the pretense of interest in the view. She tried focusing instead on Jeffrey's reflection in the dark glass. He was sitting across from her, tranquil and absorbed, reading the *Daily Worker*.

His hair was brushed back, and he was wearing a brown suit with a double breasted waistcoat and a heavy silk tie. Yellow. His Vacheron Constantin wristwatch was just visible under his French cuff. She wrinkled her forehead, confused by his choice of reading material.

Then she turned once again, trying to appear benign, toward the man who had occupied their compartment. She observed, inconsequentially, that although his suit was new and well-tailored, the soles of his shoes had been repaired with badly cut pieces of leather. They were already fraying.

When he caught her eye, the man reacted as though Marion had hit him. His jaw dropped, and he fidgeted about in his pockets, searching for something apparently vital. Eventually, retrieving a handkerchief, he dabbed sweat from his forehead. Then he nodded, brief and mortified, in Marion's direction. She flushed and stared back out, or at, the opaque glass. Noticed that Jeffrey, still reflected in the window, concentrating on his newspaper, had a smile playing across his lips.

She rested her cheek against the frame of the window. If Ian hadn't been so deeply asleep, she would have moved his head off her lap and taken her own book from her carpet bag. As it was, she began instead to pick at the hem of the tailored tweed suit, Edward Molyneux, that Jeffrey had insisted she wear to meet his sister. She hated both the jacket and the skirt, and she hoped, half consciously, that she'd unravel the lining before they reached Stowmarket. She'd agreed, for Ian's sake, to pass the Christmas holiday with Jeffrey's family in Suffolk. That didn't mean she must make a favorable impression on them.

Jeffrey sighed and folded his *Daily Worker*. He watched her tugging at the thread along the hem of her suitcoat for a few seconds, and then he looked up and held her eyes. She glared back at him, but she did move her hand. Let it rest on Ian's inert shoulder. Jeffrey removed a cigarette case from his breast pocket and a lighter from his waistcoat. Then, as though initiating a distasteful but necessary chore, he addressed the man in the corner of their compartment. "I wonder, sir, do you mind if I smoke a cigarette?"

The man, who had been immersed in, and apparently fascinated by, his rail and bus schedule, stared at Jeffrey in what looked now to be abject horror. "No! No, sir. Not at all. Please do."

Jeffrey opened his cigarette case and held it out diagonally across the compartment. The man curled, startled, into his seat before collecting himself and nodding again. He took a cigarette between the tips of his thumb and index finger, still cowering and frail. Marion noticed that his hands were shaking. She cast an astonished glance at Jeffrey, but Jeffrey was enjoying himself too much to notice her. She tightened her lips and stared down at Ian's head in her lap.

She assumed that Jeffrey managed to light the man's cigarette without further commotion because they were soon both smoking, silent, in their opposing corners of the compartment. After a few more tense minutes had passed, Jeffrey addressed the man a second time. "Do you know what time we arrive at Ipswich?"

Marion kept her eyes down, averted from the scene. They had passed Ipswich fifteen minutes before. He was toying with the man. She couldn't tell whether it was for professional reasons or to amuse himself to pass the time. Didn't know which would be worse.

"Ipswich?" The man's voice was hoarse. A whisper.

"Yes. Ipswich. Do you know when we arrive?"

"Are you travelling to Ipswich?"

"No." Jeffrey's voice was subdued, but Marion could easily sense the amusement underlying it.

She looked sidelong at the man. He was staring across at Jeffrey's wristwatch, manifestly unable to formulate a reply. Finally, he swallowed. "I'm afraid I can't say, sir. But Ipswich is, in fact, my destination. It can't be more than—than—" He faltered.

"You wouldn't want to miss your stop." Jeffrey made a move as though to retrieve his folded paper.

The man jumped from his seat, stinking of fear and sweat, and collected his hat and holdall. He nodded a last time in Marion's direction, fumbled with the door, and disappeared. He kept the cigarette.

Marion stared at Jeffrey, who was turning back to his *Daily Worker*. He crushed his cigarette in an ashtray and unfolded the paper. "Wrong train, I gather."

She looked down at Ian to be certain his sleep hadn't been disturbed. Then she examined the back of Jeffrey's paper for three or four seconds. "Jeffrey," she finally said. "What was that?"

"Greetings from Maugham, if I were forced to guess."

"Why?" Careful and patient. She didn't know whether she wanted an answer.

"Office slows down at Christmastime. He gets bored." Jeffrey was still hidden behind the paper.

She considered pushing the conversation further, but then concluded she'd never learn anything intelligible from Jeffrey by asking direct questions. If it was important, she'd figure it out in time. Deciding on a different tack, she braced herself for what she knew would be an unpleasant, but more important, exchange. "Jeffrey," she repeated.

He folded his paper and placed it beside him on the seat. "Yes, Marion?"

"Ian is unhappy at Temple Grove."

"Nonsense. He adores it."

"He's attended for one term, and he's run away four times."

"High spirits." He reached for his paper again.

Marion leaned across the compartment and took the paper before he could open it. "They found him," she said, tossing the *Daily Worker* into the seat vacated by their visitor, "hiding in the Martello tower, at two in the morning, trying to befriend a rodent."

"I understand they're moving to Heron's Ghyll in the coming year. Fewer fortifications. He'll have a grand time."

"Jeffrey—"

"Marion, we've already had this conversation. The matter is settled. The boy attends Temple Grove." He leaned across the compartment to retrieve his paper. "And I think you ought to treat the People's Revolution with a bit more respect—"

"He doesn't attend it," she interrupted. "He escapes from it. He's spent more time scaling the walls than taking lessons."

"Yes. An inherited predisposition. This tendency to bolt at the first sign of pressure. He'll learn to control it. Even if you never have."

"I'm not faulting him for his—his tendencies." She glanced down at Ian's face, worried he was sensing the tension mounting in the compartment. But he was still deeply asleep. "I'm faulting the school. He hates it."

"You hate it. That's not the same thing."

She narrowed her eyes but kept from satisfying herself with an angry retort. Instead, steeling herself, she made a last effort. "All right, Jeffrey. I can't prevent you from sending my son—"

"—our son."

"—to that—that barracks. But I can refuse to play along. If he returns to Temple Grove in January, you'll have nothing to keep me in London. I leave. You and Ian will see me again during the Easter holiday."

"Where will you go?"

"Durham?" she offered. "Edinburgh? Istanbul, perhaps? Irrelevant."

"You'll have difficulty keeping tabs on me if you're living in Istanbul."

"What do you mean?"

"Your orders? Your brief? To report back to your people on my work for our failing, yet still nefarious, empire? I daresay your superiors will be far from pleased if all that effort they took embedding you came to naught. And on a selfish personal whim, no less."

"I have no idea what—"

"Don't you?" Puzzled. "It's obvious, isn't it? Even without decoding those messages that come to you in the park." He looked down at the folded paper in his lap. "Although I do read those as well. I wondered how far you'd be willing to go in the name duty. Pleasant conjectures to enjoy when I had a few moments free. I'm disappointed that you've proved yourself so easily discouraged from completing your assignment."

She leaned back against the velvet seat and closed her eyes. "This isn't an assignment, Jeffrey. It's an eternity."

"You'll stay, then?" He smiled. "Eternally?"

She shook her head, her eyes still closed. "No. I can't do it anymore. They must find another—" She stopped. Opened her eyes. "—another way. If Ian returns to Temple Grove, I'll be gone that evening."

The train was slowing into Stowmarket station. Jeffrey stood and began gathering their belongings. "I'll consider myself warned. But this changes nothing. The boy, as a Willcox, will be properly educated. If you feel he isn't learning enough, Dr. Bailey, in the way of medieval Turkish or paramilitary organizational strategy, you can supplement his lessons during the holidays. I shan't stand in your way."

He was holding Marion's coat. Blue wool with a wide brown mink collar. He watched as she woke Ian and helped him, still drowsy, into his own coat. She hadn't spoken further.

"Are you looking forward to seeing Aunt Ginnie and Uncle Teddy again, John?" Jeffrey had helped Marion into her coat, and he was pulling on his gloves.

Ian nodded, sleepy but grinning. He held Marion's hand as they left the carriage and stepped out onto the Stowmarket platform.

The air was sharp with frost as the porters moved their luggage into the waiting car. Marion stifled an annoyed comment when she saw it in the glacial light of a gibbous moon. A stretch Voisin C25 Aerodyne. Dark red. She stuffed her fists into the pockets of her coat as she walked toward the open door. She dreaded meeting Jeffrey's family.

THE drive to the house from the station took no longer than a half hour. But it was more than sufficient time for Ian to pounce on, and empty, the hamper waiting for them in the wide back seat. Grey leather and polished wood. It made Marion tired.

But Ian was elated, and before they had left Stowmarket behind them, he had finished the container of gingerbread and begun on the fudge. Jeffrey had also been searching the car, and at length he found a bottle of port and two glasses in a box beneath his own seat. He held them up for Marion, lifting an inquiring eyebrow.

She shook her head.

He secured the bottle back in its box. "For the best. You'll want your wits about you."

She watched as Ian made his way through the fudge. Didn't reply.

"Later, then," Jeffrey said.

"Unquestionably." Her stomach was churning. She had no idea how she was going to endure the coming two weeks.

Sooner than she would have liked, the car turned into an avenue of yew trees before rolling to a gentle stop in front of a long—and old—half-timbered house. As she exited the car, she looked up at the brick façade. There were too many chimneys.

She squinted, confused, trying to get an idea of the dimensions of the building, but the view made her dizzy. And yet fascinated. She couldn't look away.

Jeffrey, following her gaze, put his arm around her waist. She shook her head, startled out of her inspection of the roofs and gables. Then she pushed her hands back into the pockets of her coat again. Stared at the frozen ground instead.

"Stop trying to analyze it, Marion. It's an old house. Every century or so they knock something over or add a new wing. The result? Chimneys. Everywhere." He smiled to himself. "Entertaining for the children. Though I think you may be the first visitor over the age of twelve who's given them more than a passing nod. I've told you how I like you, no?"

Ian had already run toward the now open front door, arched and oak with medieval-looking nails and hinges. Jeffrey and Marion strode after him. Marion still silent. Tense.

As they walked, Jeffrey smiled down at Marion's taut face. "Fair warning," he said. "There's a scorpion motif carved into the older beams of the original building. But don't let it spook you. I give you my word of honor that they stay put. Provided, of course, that you don't anger the family."

She was staring at a huge letter carved over the door. An ornate "W?" For "Willcox?" She was vaguely embarrassed for them.

"No, no," he continued, reading her thoughts. "Not a 'W.' It's 'VV,' '*Virgo Virginum.*' For Queen Elizabeth? Piety and patriotism? I'm surprised you haven't noticed how the two run so clear and strong in our blood. Or in John's blood and mine. Not certain what yours is made of." He brought her to the threshold of the house. "But that doesn't mean we shouldn't get you warm."

When she entered the wood-paneled entry hall, Ian was already chattering to a girl of eleven or twelve. Describing, in obsessive detail, his rail journey. His cousin Anne, Marion supposed. Charlotte and Paul, his other cousins, were older.

Behind Anne, a tall woman, blonde, graceful, and disconcertingly similar to Jeffrey in manner and expression, stood beside an open, kind-looking man, also tall, but disheveled and slightly overweight, wearing a threadbare smoking jacket. Virginia and her husband, Teddy.

Marion swallowed, ordering herself to keep composed.

But before she or Jeffrey could speak, Virginia stepped forward and took Marion's hand. She kissed her cheek, and said: "Marion, we're pleased that you've come. Ian missed you terribly when he was visiting this past year. He spoke about you so constantly that I feel I already know you. But I also hope to know you better. Welcome."

"Ian?" Marion gaped at Virginia. "You—you called him Ian."

Virginia laughed. Without malice. "You named him Ian, didn't you? Typical Jeffie to try to force you to change it to suit some juvenile caprice. So yes. Of course I call him 'Ian.' In this house, he's 'Ian.'" She looked over Marion's shoulder at Jeffrey. Malice now in place. "Obviously I can't comment on what happens in London."

Marion's head felt foggy. She'd never expected this sort of greeting. "I'm pleased to be here as well, Virginia," she ventured. "Thank you."

Jeffrey was matching Virginia's look. Smiling and sardonic. "You're looking dazzling as ever, Ginnie." Before she could reply, he turned a less lopsided smile toward Teddy. "Happy Christmas, Teddy."

"To you too, Jeffrey." Teddy had taken Jeffrey's coat. "Jenkins and your Mrs. Bowen arrived yesterday afternoon. They've settled in well, as far as we can see. But do let us know whether you need anything?"

Virginia let Marion's hand go and addressed Ian. "Ian, darling. I understand that your nanny is recuperating with her people in Cornwall for the holiday. Do you mind sharing Constance with Anne and Paul while you're here?"

Ian grinned up at her. "I like Constance."

"Hmm." The corner of Virginia's mouth went down. A feminine echo of Jeffrey's customary expression. "And I suppose Constance has no choice but to like you as well. Be aware, though, Ian: she does have a protector in Paul. He *truly* likes her. So keep the torment to a minimum, yes?" She bent down and whispered something into Anne's ear. Then she straightened and smiled back at Ian. "I think Anne has something to show you in the library. Would you like to see?"

Anne took Ian's hand and led him further into the house.

Marion scarcely registered their departure. Trying to distract herself from her social confusion, she was gazing now at the riot of marginal carving along the exposed beams of the entry hall. But it was a futile effort. The carving was as baffling to her as Virginia's greeting had been.

She focused on a sinister Green Man glaring down from a rafter. Absorbed. The house kept drawing her eye up to roofs and ceilings. Mouldings. She couldn't help herself. Even though the detail was making her ill.

She forced herself back into awareness when Virginia stepped toward Jeffrey and hugged him. "I *am* pleased to see you, Jeffie. Despite all." She was laughing quietly. At herself. She had pulled her midnight blue embroidered silk shawl, an endless-seeming length of material, more tightly across her shoulders.

"And I'm glad," he replied, "that you're still your old, schizoid, exhibitionist self. Are you *really* pleased to see me, Ginnie? Or is this merely some fanciful new defense mechanism you've trotted out for the holidays?"

"Darling! And how *is* Dr. Fairbairn? I've missed him." She paused, amused. "Speaking of mental illness, Richard Maugham stole a march on you. He arrived early yesterday morning. Have no idea what train he took. Perhaps he dropped from the sky."

Marion turned to Jeffrey, horrified. "Maugham is *here*?"

Virginia answered for him. Rolling her eyes. "I feel, sometimes, that he's never anywhere else." She exchanged an understanding look with Marion and then addressed Jeffrey again. "I've put him in the tapestried chamber in the east wing."

"With the undead nun? In the sackcloth and plague doctor mask? A bit cruel, don't you think?"

"He likes it there. Says he gets on with her." She shrugged. "Apparently she keeps him from feeling lonely in the night."

Jeffrey considered. "Fair enough. Can I speak with him—"

"No." She had taken Marion's arm and was leading her toward the staircase to the first-floor bedrooms. "No office tonight." She paused at the foot of the stairs. "And really, Jeffie. It would be nice, for once, not to have Mephistopheles join us for Christmas dinner."

Jeffrey shook Teddy's hand and clapped him on the shoulder, after which Teddy wandered toward what Marion assumed was the library. Jeffrey followed Virginia and Marion to the foot of the stairs. "It's tradition, Ginnie. Like the pudding."

"Ah well." She stood to the side to let them pass. "At least the children like him. Little savages. It's your usual room," she added. "And Marion, I'll ask Constance to bring Ian to you before he collapses into sleep tonight."

"Thank you, Virginia." Marion hesitated. "Really. I'm grateful."

Virginia smiled and turned to leave, but Jeffrey stopped her. "Ginnie," he asked, almost shy. "Is George here?"

"He wanted to be," she said after a moment that lasted a touch too long. "But he had some ministerial matter come up at the last second." She began to smirk again. "He's displeased with you, Jeffie."

"He's always displeased with me." Annoyed now. "What is it this time?"

"Oh, I don't know. Something about being dead tired of always cleaning up after his little brother's war crimes. Diyala? Baquba? I can't remember, honestly."

Jeffrey looked more pleased than chastened. The vulnerability was gone. And he smiled in return, nasty, but at Marion rather than at Virginia. "I was frustrated."

Virginia, taking in Marion's blanched face, glared at Jeffrey. "Well stop it, Jeffie. It plays merry hell with Christmas." She spoke deliberately to Marion: "I'll look forward to speaking further with you at breakfast, Marion. Goodnight."

*J*EFFREY led Marion up the stairs and along a paneled corridor to another large, arched, wooden door. He pushed it open and stood to the side to let her through. The room was low-ceilinged but extensive, with mullioned windows in two walls, and antique carpets covering the floors. The ceiling was covered with intricately designed plaster that she had to compel herself not to examine too minutely.

A fireplace with a dark, heavy wooden mantel took up a section of the third wall. The fire was lit and roaring, leaving the room almost uncomfortably warm, dry, and hot. Their trunks were already waiting for them alongside a huge, functional wardrobe.

The bed was a simple wooden four-poster. Its tester was also carved wood, scorpions hidden in the fleurs-de-lis at each corner. The blankets of the bed were heavy and dark red. Round tables on spiral wooden stands stood to either side of it. Crystal carafes of water alongside clean glasses.

Marion smiled wanly. Wondering whether they had Robert Browning bricked up somewhere in the fourth, disconcertingly blank, wall of the room. So many references to references to references to the original Tudor design of the room—it made her light-headed. She chose to focus on the practical instead. A small door at the edge of the last wall led, she supposed, to the toilet.

Jeffrey closed the door behind him and flopped into a scrolled wing chair, dark red cushions matching the blankets on the bed. It flanked the fireplace, and he held out his hands, unnecessarily, to warm them. He looked up at Marion, quizzical, but said nothing.

"Your usual room?" she finally asked.

"You were expecting something different?"

She examined the fireplace. Ironwork scorpions escaping from the flames at the edge of the hearth. "No," she said carefully. "Or—" She paused. "I suppose it was either this or something white and blank. Clinical. Hint of scalpels." She let herself examine the ceiling again and then quickly looked away. "I suppose I prefer this. Is there a painting behind a curtain you'd like to show me?"

He laughed. "Don't let Ginnie fool you, Marion. She's my sister, remember."

"I liked Teddy." Deliberately oblique.

He rose from the chair and kissed her cheek. "Yes. A good man." Then he walked to their trunks and opened one. Found his pyjamas. "Constance will be by soon with John. To say goodnight. And, after that—if you don't mind—?"

She shook her head. "No. I'm exhausted as well. We'll go to bed."

She found her own pyjamas and pulled open the door to the toilet. It was modern, no more than a few years old. Sink, toilet, tub. Clean checkered tiles on the floor. A medicine cabinet to the side of the room.

Curious, she opened the cabinet. It was empty, aside from an anachronistic glass bottle of Macfarlan Smith laudanum. Intrigued, she took it from the cabinet and examined it. A good twenty-five years old. If not more.

She pursed her lips and uncorked it. The acrid smell hit her before she even brought the bottle up to her face. Coughing, she replaced the lid and put the bottle back on its shelf. Stared at the sink for a few seconds. The bottle bothered her. Then, shrugging, she cleaned her teeth and changed into her pyjamas. She was pulling on a dressing gown when she heard Ian calling to her from the bedroom.

She hurried back out to see him and found him bouncing on the bed, trying to reach the carved scorpions at the edges of the tester. Constance was at the door, looking apologetic, and Marion threw her a sympathetic look, hoping to convey understanding. Then she reached out and caught Ian mid-bounce. At least she could be certain this bed would never collapse under his weight. "You're happy to be back, Ian?"

He hugged her before hanging, heavy, from her neck. "Yes, Mummy. I share a room with Paul."

"Good." She glanced over at Jeffrey, leaning against the mantle. Then she disengaged Ian from her neck and let him drop to the floor. "I'm looking forward to tomorrow." She kissed his temple. "Goodnight, Ian."

He pressed his cheek against hers and ran back toward Constance. "Goodnight, Mummy. I love you."

When Constance had led Ian out of the room, Marion turned back to Jeffrey. He was watching her with a look that she knew well. But he didn't speak. Also silent, she dropped her gaze and walked toward the bed. She slid under the covers and closed her eyes. Her head was spinning.

THE next day was pleasant. Surprisingly so. In fact, the hours she spent at the house were so far from what even her most optimistic expectations had been that, despite herself, she felt suspicious. She chided herself for failing to appreciate what she ought simply to have called her good fortune. But the combination of the temporally chaotic design of the house and the comfortable, undemanding time she was passing in it, left her off guard. She couldn't trust her reactions.

After a late breakfast on their first day, neighbors from the surrounding countryside began to arrive for an extended visit with Virginia and Teddy. Marion, watching out the bedroom window as the stream of smug, ostentatiously engineered automobiles emerged from the yews, was prepared for the worst. And indeed, in addition to Maugham, she saw that she'd be forced into contact with Aldous Parker.

But even on this score, she was surprised. Virginia and Teddy, working discreetly, protected her from sustained contact with either Maugham or Aldous. Even Marion, rarely a clever or successful observer of social interaction, could recognize the extraordinary, if circumspect, effort they were putting into keeping Jeffrey's contacts from hurting her.

They were also, she noticed with a colder eye, preventing Jeffrey from having private or meaningful conversation with Maugham. For which she was grateful. But she was also doubtful. She couldn't believe that they were cosseting her for altruistic reasons. She was a stranger to them. And, as Jeffrey enjoyed pointing out, she was alien to their world.

Nonetheless, Ian was giddy with the excitement of spending his holiday here, which alone was sufficient reason to push down the amorphous, unfounded suspicions that were crowding at the corners of her mind. Like the strange, small man on the train, Virginia's behavior would be explained in time. If it must be explained. Perhaps she simply knew her little brother's proclivities too well to let him loose, unsupervised, on her guests.

As the day wound to a close, and as the children, sated and drowsy, were put to bed, the party moved into the music room. Teddy, wearing black tie, and yet rumpled, as though he were still in a dressing gown, was sitting at the piano. He was playing jazz one-handed while sipping brandy from a snifter. Flushed, but not otherwise obviously intoxicated. Virginia's guests were scattered in groups throughout the room, talking together or watching Teddy. His playing was deceptively casual. Marion was struck by his skill.

Virginia was wearing a fitted, floor-length, dark green velvet dress with a low back and a hint of a gathered train. Also Edward Molyneux, Marion thought. She was holding Marion by the elbow, guiding her into the room, smiling and chatting.

After spending a full day with her, Marion remained astonished and somewhat awed by Virginia's calm—and calming—presence. She knew that as Jeffrey's older sister, Virginia must be close to fifty. Yet her hair and eyes were bright, her face was unlined, and her bearing was strong. Playful. Graceful. And Virginia was soothing. Marion found herself, despite herself, becoming increasingly partial to her.

As she brought Marion to a chair between the piano and the fireplace, Marion was also grateful, for the first time, to Jeffrey for his domineering control over her sartorial existence. She was wearing a dark and muted, yet shimmering, grey silk dress designed by the Spanish couturier Jeffrey forced her to patronize. It had a lighter grey spray of flowers winding up and around the waist and bust, but the appliqué vine was visible only under certain lights. She felt, almost, as though she fit in with Virginia's other guests.

When she sat in the chair Virginia had found for her, Teddy smiled and raised his glass in her direction. She returned his smile and leaned back, content to enjoy his playing. She tried to place the song, but couldn't.

Virginia, sitting next to her, answered her unasked question. "Johnny Mercer," she supplied. "Some frightful American. Teddy's entranced by him."

Teddy, as though overhearing Virginia's comment, threw her a teasing glance, placed his glass beside the empty music rack, and played a more complicated, two-handed, ragged version of the song. Virginia pouted at him, also teasing, but then spotted Jeffrey across the room. Her eyes hardened. "Damn it. The loathsome little brat."

Marion, following Virginia's look, caught sight of Jeffrey as well. He was engaged in a quiet, serious conversation with Maugham. Ignoring everyone else. Maugham, short, and if possible even rounder than he had been the last time Marion had seen him, was wearing tails and a monocle. His usual, if bizarre, formal wear.

Maugham felt Virginia's eyes on them before Jeffrey did, and he twisted and looked toward them. He twinkled at Marion. Then he turned a calculating and contemptuous smile on Virginia.

Virginia pressed her lips together before turning back to Marion. "If you'll forgive me, Marion?" She rose, put on a deliberately false hostess smile, and sailed across the room toward Jeffrey and Maugham.

Jeffrey, prepared for her approach, made eye contact with Aldous, who was in the midst of playing a loud and aggressive game of chess with a florid neighbor of Virginia's and Teddy's. The neighbor, looking wrong, somehow, not astride a horse, didn't notice their interaction. Aldous lifted his eyebrows when Jeffrey tilted his head in Marion's direction, and then abandoned the chess game, throwing Jeffrey a mock salute. Once Aldous had stood, Jeffrey turned, impish, back toward Virginia. Fighting laughter.

Marion chose to ignore the exchange. Focused, deliberately, on Teddy's now virtuoso performance at the piano. She didn't want to know.

To cover the incident unfolding as Virginia spoke, low and angry, to Jeffrey and Maugham, Teddy began singing as well as playing. Ironic.

> Napoleon, at Waterloo,
> Writing Josephine a billet doux
> Josie, I've got to close this epistle
> There goes the whistle
> Here come the British! Bang, Bang…

Soon, most of the guests in the room were singing along, drunk but happy and more or less in tune. Marion, bemused, watched them. She'd never heard the song they were singing, but she was entertained.

As Teddy launched into a new verse, however, her equanimity shattered. Aldous, standing over her, bowed, sarcastic, and took her hand. "Hullo, Lady Willcox." Enjoying her shock. "Splendid to see you again. Let's dance."

He jerked her up out of the chair before she could reply. He was tall, too athletic, and she felt physically repelled by his close presence. "What—?" Aldous hated her. She couldn't imagine why he was doing this.

The other guests in the room, jovial and tipsy, clapped good naturedly. A few joined Aldous and Marion in their dancing. Teddy, trying to draw Virginia's attention, kept playing:

> …all at once, the subs got skittish,
> Here come the British! Bang, Bang!"

He played a long interlude, drawing unexpected big band exuberance out of the piano. And then he continued with another verse:

> In the air, the same applied.
> Jerry looked all set to ride.
> But just when things were Messerschmittish,
> Here come the British! Bang, Bang!"

Aldous, still bullying, was laughing down at Marion. "Ripping song, isn't it? And so true. Leave it to the Yanks to strip things down to their essentials."

He wrenched her hand up to his chest when she tried to slip it out of his grip. Then he kept talking at her: "that M37 that Willy Messerschmitt knocked together in Augsburg this past spring, to take an example. Huns are calling it recreational. Though why any recreational flyer would want that sort of climb rate is more than I'll ever know. 'Bang, Bang!'" He laughed again. "Reminds me of that romantic night Willcox arranged for you over Diyala last year—"

Marion, not responding, was still trying to disengage herself from Aldous without making a scene. If he continued, there was every possibility she'd be sick. But he was holding her too tightly. As though sensing her discomfort, Virginia turned and saw Marion's face. Cold, she directed her attention back to Jeffrey, who grinned. Boyish. Delighted by the situation.

Without speaking further to Jeffrey, she walked, still wearing her hostess face, over to a group of young men who looked just out of university. She whispered into the ear of one, who brightened and made his way to the piano. The boy sat next to Teddy, and they played a four-handed version of the Johnny Mercer.

Languid, Teddy left the piano to the boy and wandered over to Aldous and Marion. He tapped Aldous on the shoulder. "I know you won't mind. I've had so little chance to speak with Marion since she's arrived."

Aldous released Marion's hand. "She's all yours, Teddy." He didn't bother to say anything further to Marion as he walked away.

Teddy examined Marion's face. Unthreatening. Apologetic. "You're popular tonight," he said to her after a moment. "But unless I'm mistaken, that's not your preferred role?"

"No." After a few more seconds of perfunctory dancing, she looked about the room. "Could we get some air?"

He nodded and led Marion to the door. When they reached the corridor, Marion stopped to gather herself. She continued to fear she'd be sick before she reached a sink or toilet. Took a few deep breaths, hugging her waist and staring at the floor.

Teddy looked about to say something as she calmed herself. But then he decided against it. Instead, he watched her for a minute, and only when she had regained some of her color, did he speak. "Do you need anything?"

She shook her head. Then, considering, she looked up at him. "Actually, yes." She paused. "It's a bit strange. But do you think I could have some salad oil, or—or olive oil? From the kitchen?"

After a moment of confusion, quickly veiled, Teddy smiled at her. "Quite the dark horse, aren't you? But yes. Easily accomplished. Wait here, would you?"

Marion smiled back at him, grateful. "Thank you."

"Not at all. It'll be just a moment." Teddy walked to a door at the edge of the hall, leading, she imagined, to the servants' wing of the building. When he was out of sight, she leaned against the wall, breathing deeply again, trying to remain calm. She still didn't know what was happening in the house. But whatever it was, it had started. And she planned to protect herself.

Teddy returned a few minutes later, carrying a small stoppered glass bottle. He handed it to her. "We're proud of the olive oil. Import it from Spain, just as we always have. Despite the mounting excitement there." The corner of his mouth went down. "At least there's no armada this time."

She examined the bottle. "It's perfect. Thank you."

"Not at all," he repeated. "Enjoy." Then he paused. "I imagine you'd rather not return to the entertainment this evening. Shall I wish you a good night?"

She nodded. "Yes. Thank you, Teddy." She blushed. "And would you thank Virginia for me as well?"

"Of course. Sleep well." He turned and walked back in the direction of the music. It hadn't escaped Marion's notice that Teddy had avoided questioning her about what any impartial observer would have identified as, at best, an extreme overreaction to the events of the evening. Almost excessive discretion on his part.

She forced herself to be grateful. Rather than suspicious.

MARION hid the bottle of olive oil behind a leg of the bathtub when she returned to her room. Then she changed into her pyjamas and slipped under the covers of the bed. She wanted Jeffrey to think she was sleeping when he returned. Although she suspected that such an easy strategy would never succeed.

And, as she had expected, he appeared too soon for her to play that role, walking through the door just as she was putting her head on the pillow. He had plainly left the gathering immediately after her own departure. Planned. Her anxiety rose, but she kept her breathing in check. Sat up in bed, wrapping her arms around her waist, looking at him.

Jeffrey watched her for a few seconds before closing the door gently, without speaking. He removed his jacket and tie and hung them over the back of one of the wing chairs. Taking off his cufflinks and rolling up his sleeves, he walked over to her side of the bed. Sat down on the edge next to her, crossed his legs, and looked into her face. His cufflinks in his hand. She curled her knees up under the covers, but otherwise she didn't move.

"I'm sorry that you were taken ill this evening," he said. "It was a pleasant gathering until your lightheadedness got the better of you."

"I'll be fine." She swallowed. "All I need is sleep."

"Excellent." He stood, put his cufflinks in his trouser pocket, collected the water glass from her bedside table, and walked toward the toilet. "I know just the remedy for that."

She heard him busying himself with the sink. Then he emerged once again, carrying the full glass. She could smell the laudanum he'd mixed with the water before he was halfway across the room. He sat next to her on the edge of the bed again and offered her the glass. She took it mechanically, holding it in two hands, staring at him in disbelief.

He smiled, unpleasant, challenging her to refuse it. "It will do you good, my dear. Always so overwrought."

She considered trying to argue, but thought better of it. Instead, she let her eyes register defeat and dropped her gaze to the glass. Dull. "I want to use the toilet first."

He took the glass and set it on the side table. "Good idea." He shifted position so that she could move the covers off her legs, and watched as she walked, subdued, in the direction of the toilet. "If you're thinking of squeezing through the window and climbing down the exterior wall, Marion, do keep in mind that it opens into a locked courtyard. And it's supposed to snow tonight."

She closed the door quietly, composed, without answering. Then she knelt on the floor and found the stoppered bottle of olive oil. Still kneeling, she forced herself to drink, slowly, measured, the bottle's entire contents. When she had finished, she kept still, willing herself not to throw it up again.

After a few seconds, confident she was keeping it down, she replaced the bottle, stood, flushed the toilet to prevent Jeffrey from wondering, and crossed to the sink. She worried for a moment that the oil would come back up after all, but she managed to keep from gagging before cleaning her teeth. Finally, she returned to the bedroom.

Holding Jeffrey's eyes, level and hostile, she got back into bed. He placed the glass in her hand. "Bottoms up."

Still glaring at him, she raised the glass to her lips and drank. Then she shoved it, empty, in his direction. He took it and replaced it on the bedside table. But he didn't move from the bed. For five minutes, he watched her face. Intent. Neither spoke.

Eventually, she sighed and leaned back. Rested her head on the pillow. Closed her eyes. He leaned over and kissed her forehead. "Thank you for doing this the easy way, Marion. I was dreading having to incapacitate you by force. He smoothed her hair over the pillow. "I'll be back before you know it."

She waited, her eyes closed, for him to leave the room and close the door. Then, to be certain, she waited for a further two minutes. Finally, as confident as she could be that he wouldn't return to check on her, and not willing risk waiting any longer, she threw off the covers and ran into the toilet.

The olive oil would delay her digestion of the alcohol and opium, but it wouldn't prevent it forever. She must get it out of her stomach before it hit her bloodstream. Steeling herself, she knelt in front of the toilet and forced herself to vomit. When she had thrown up as much as she could, she pulled the chain to flush the toilet, trembling, her eyes watering. Then she stood, drank water from the tap, and knelt in front of the toilet again.

Her rage at Jeffrey for doing this to her almost taking her mind off the pain in her throat, she vomited twice more. After that, she pressed her sweating forehead against the cool tiles of the floor, convinced she had purged all she could. Some of the drug would have escaped her precautions. But if she was lucky, it wouldn't be enough to interfere with her ability to find Jeffrey or to follow whatever conversation he was having with Maugham.

She stood, staggered, cleaned her teeth again, and retrieved her dressing gown from a hook near the door. Wrapping the heavy silk around her shoulders, she walked into the bedroom, pushed her feet into slippers, and opened the door to the corridor. Peeked out. Empty. The sound of the party still floated up, distant and cheerful, from the floor below. She closed the bedroom door behind her and walked toward the stairs leading down to the central rooms of the house.

If Jeffrey and Maugham planned to speak in one of the empty bedrooms, she knew she'd never find them. She had a feeling, though, that they'd keep up at least a pretense of social, rather than professional, interaction. Which meant they'd use a public room. Marion guessed the library.

She hurried down the stairs, still hugging her dressing gown tightly around her body, trying to push away the dizziness that she knew was the effect of the laudanum. Then she walked toward the low, oak door at the far end of the hall. She had spent much of the morning in the library with Virginia, and she felt she already knew it.

The door to the library was half open, low firelight filtering through it into the corridor. Quiet voices coming from the far end of the room. Marion moved to the door and peeked into the room. Jeffrey and Maugham were sitting facing the fire, their backs to her, drinking brandy. The bottle rested between them on a table. Jeffrey had lit a cigarette.

She slipped through the gap, not touching the doorframe, and crouched behind a tapestried sofa. Held still, waiting for any indication in the air that they had sensed her presence. Nothing came. Remaining in the shadows, she crept closer to the fireplace. When she found an alcove to the side of a bookcase where she could hear their conversation and also see their profiles unobstructed, she stopped. Dropped into a squat, prepared to move if they seemed to feel her in the room watching them.

Maugham was gazing into the fire, sipping his drink. He'd removed his monocle. "You're certain we won't be interrupted?"

"She's chasing the dragon." Jeffrey blew smoke up at the ceiling. "Not the first time. She'll be out till morning."

"Ah." Maugham chuckled. "Feminine ailments. The time-honored solutions are always best."

Jeffrey laughed, but otherwise he didn't reply.

"Your sister is taken with her." Hint of a threat.

Jeffrey lifted an eyebrow. Still didn't speak.

"I can't help but notice," Maugham persisted, "how you surround yourself with these disloyal women. Dangerous predilection."

"Ginnie simply likes to steal my things." Jeffrey was also gazing, annoyed, into the fireplace. "Always has. And we can't all make conquests of other people's family ghosts. Sleep well last night?"

Maugham began searching through the pockets of his waistcoat. "Yes. Thank you. I slept beautifully. Mother Superior sends her regards." He found what he was looking for and held it up in the glow. "She left this behind. Not sure how to return it to her."

"Oh, for God's sake." Jeffrey had looked at Maugham's find and then turned back to the fire. It was a decaying finger bone.

"It's your house." Injured. "I was merely trying to keep things in their proper place." He returned the finger bone to his waistcoat. "Or, at least, it's your family's house. Strange how it ended with Virginia rather than with George. Convoluted set of legacies your family has."

"Quite." Jeffrey took a drag of his cigarette. "Though they've served you well enough. Especially when George came over fastidious in his youth and refused to cooperate. You had your pick of the spares, hadn't you?"

"You haven't started regretting it now, Willcox? I'd feel just awful—"

"No." Jeffrey's voice was short.

"I thought not. You're so good at it."

"You sent me Mr. Hamilton? On the train?"

"Ah yes. Best get to the assignment. Then back to the festivities."

"Was there a reason for Mr. Hamilton?" Jeffrey blew smoke slowly out toward the fireplace. "He was in Berlin, wasn't he? Or Mexico? He's difficult to follow."

"Well. Not Berlin anymore, at any rate. Had a spot of trouble." Maugham took another sip of his brandy.

"I'm not surprised." Tired. "His training's abysmal. You couldn't have found another intermediary?"

"He likes you. And I believe his people live round here."

"He likes muscular Aryans, Maugham. Explanation?"

"We wanted to pique your wife's interest as well. This project will require Dr. Bailey's distinctive talents too."

"And Mr. Hamilton would help with that how?"

"Dr. Bailey poses an interesting problem."

"Yes." Jeffrey examined the end of his cigarette. "It hasn't escaped my notice."

"Unmoved by loyalty to King and Country," Maugham said. "Or wifely duty."

"Hmm."

"Coercion doesn't work."

Jeffrey smiled. "But it can be fun sometimes."

"This is serious, my boy." Maugham was smiling as well. "What *has* been effective, however, is confusion. A nice, sustained, low level of confusion keeps her active. Forthcoming. Mr. Hamilton was our initiating effort in that direction. He's so very obvious. Such a sinister, yet despicable, type. Raises everyone's hackles. We've used him in that way before, with remarkable success."

Jeffrey continued to listen. Quiet.

"And it does appear to have worked," Maugham added. "Perhaps too well. She fled poor Teddy's performance tonight as though she were being pursued by all the demons of hell. Although, it's true, that was only after you'd set Parker on her." Maugham peered into his brandy. Dissatisfied. "That was unkind, Willcox. And unnecessary."

"Ginnie was bothering me." He tossed his cigarette into the fire. Then he considered. "Very well. So you want Marion. And you sent Hamilton to disturb her equilibrium. Such as it is. What's the next step? You can confuse her all you like, she'll never speak with you."

Maugham rearranged himself in his chair and drank more of his brandy. "Let me tell you about the situation that's arisen at the office. After that, we'll discuss how Dr. Bailey might contribute."

"Very well," Jeffrey repeated.

Maugham raised his glass and looked through it into the firelight. Then he finished off the drink and placed the glass to his side. "Petroleum," he said.

Jeffrey lifted the bottle and poured another large shot into Maugham's snifter. "Petroleum bores me." He lit another cigarette. Slipped his lighter back into his trouser pocket.

"It's more than just petroleum," Maugham said. "Let me explain the problem that we've encountered. I think you'll find it worth your while. And Dr. Bailey's."

Jeffrey exhaled smoke. Waiting.

Maugham continued. "You're familiar with the Mosul-Haifa pipeline?"

"Are you joking?"

"I merely want to be certain that we're starting on the same page." Maugham paused. "Chaps over at the Iraq Petroleum Company are terribly excited. Construction completed this past month. Grand opening early in the coming year. Fields in Kirkuk producing like a warren of abnormally fertile rabbits. All is success and triumph."

Jeffrey laughed. "Have they also constructed the large 'Imperial Vulnerability' sign with the arrow? 'Attack Here to Cripple Great Britain's Military?'"

"Yes," Maugham smiled. "There is that too. Not even operational yet, and already the Palestinians have been sniping at the Haifa end of it. And," he added, "of course Dr. Bailey's friends have been going after the other end, in Kirkuk."

Maugham considered. "Not only Dr. Bailey's friends, to be fair. The French are not entirely free of blame." He lifted his glass. "Though one can't fault them. We've been going after their bit in Tripoli as well. To keep everything equitable."

"So what's the problem, then?" Jeffrey asked. "It sounds precisely as we predicted."

"Indeed," Maugham agreed. "And, as I'm sure you know, in the midst of the fanfare and ceremony surrounding the Mosul-Haifa line, we've also spent the past few years quietly, carefully, and oh so painstakingly, setting the groundwork for a more promising energy source. Five hundred or so miles to the northeast. On the Caspian. Half of it piped out toward the Gulf. The other half toward the Black Sea."

"I've told you," Jeffrey repeated, petulant, "petroleum doesn't interest me." He put his elbow on the arm of his chair and rested his cheek on his fist. "It doesn't interest you either, Maugham. What does this have to do with the Museum? Can't you leave the endless squabbling over petroleum and pipelines to the people with the Patek Philippe timepieces and the conspicuous personal security arrangements?"

"Patience, my boy. Let me finish."

Jeffrey took an irritated drag from his cigarette. "Very well. Continue."

"Willcox, I'm beginning to fear that if I give you any further detail, you'll stalk off in an affronted rage. I hadn't realized you were a snob."

"I'm not a snob. I specialize." Jeffrey hadn't moved his cheek from his fist. "This isn't my field. Nor is it yours. Nor, for that matter, is it Marion's. At this point, I'm feeling a pang of conscience for sending her off to commune with Kubla Khan to listen to this twaddle."

"Why don't we go about things in a different way, then?" Pleased to have annoyed him. "We'll end—I give you my word—with something interesting. In Baku, no less. The geographical shift must intrigue you, at least? A pleasant change of scene?" Maugham raised his glass, hint of a salute toward Jeffrey, and took a sip. "So, tell me what you *do* know about petroleum. In the Caucasus, that is. Or Azerbaijan. Or, more specifically, Baku. If you do it well, I'll consider you briefed. After that, we'll get to the surprise at the end."

Jeffrey tossed his second cigarette into the fireplace. "Petroleum in the Caucasus." He sounded as though he were reciting a tedious lesson. "Not much to say anymore, is there? From the 1890s through the War, Shell—our chaps—fought madly with Standard Oil—Yanks—for control over Baku's fields. The Americans repeatedly outmaneuvered us, so we partnered with Royal Dutch. Partnership worked as well as one could expect. By 1917, Royal Dutch Shell was pumping twelve million tons out of the fields near Baku, on the Caspian, in Azerbaijan. Piping it all to Batumi, on the Black Sea coast, in Georgia. Loaded onto tankers. Distributed to our various," Jeffrey took a sip of his brandy, "industries."

"I applaud you. Well summarized."

"But irrelevant." Still bored. "Historical materialism put an end to all that. By 1920, Azerbaijan's petroleum belonged to the great Soviet people. Or, more narrowly, to Stalin. Last I paid attention to conversations in that direction, our sole interest in tracking the fields and pipelines in the region was to determine where we ought to bomb them should we find ourselves displeased with the Soviets in the coming war."

"Then the Board of Trade people have been acting with a bit of discretion. For once." Maugham stretched out his legs in front of him toward the fire. "I'll send my counterpart your compliments. Because, Willcox, you see, we've been doing quite a bit more than identifying potential targets for Parker's colleagues to hit. Though obviously should it come to that, we'll be prepared for the military option as well."

Maugham tucked his fingers into his waistcoat. "But in fact, we'd rather *not* send in the cavalry. Especially now that we've found the weaknesses in the existing pipes. Weaknesses such that we might, in the not so distant future, siphon off a modest bit of our own. Stalin won't notice. Far too wrapped up in eliminating poets and playwrights critical of his Leninist theory." He closed his eyes. Pleased with himself. "There's such a great amount there, you realize. A few trucks and weapons to a few disgruntled peasants in the mountains surrounding Baku, and we'd have as much coming to us informally through Georgia and the Black Sea as we'd have flowing through what will almost certainly be a beleaguered and sadly-abused Mosul-Haifa line."

"Do you know?" Jeffrey was looking at Maugham's complacent, corpulent form in the chair. "It's extraordinary. I'm still entirely uninterested in what you're telling me." He rose, as though to leave.

Maugham opened one eye. Looked up at Jeffrey. "Do sit down, Willcox. We're almost there. Haven't I given you my word?"

Jeffrey smiled down at him. Affectionate. "Forgive me." He sat and ran a hand through his hair. "Mr. Hamilton must have gotten to me too. I feel unsettled. Continue."

Maugham closed his eye. "As you say, all of this was of negligible interest to our section. I was aware, vaguely, of the enthusiasm surrounding it. But unless someone stumbled across a cache of Sassanian coins while establishing an unofficial well somewhere, I couldn't see it affecting our work. I paid it the attention it deserved. Which was very little."

"And then?" Jeffrey leaned forward, took a poker, and stirred up the fire.

"And then we received an anonymous note." Maugham opened his eyes again and twinkled at Jeffrey. Childlike.

"Ah." Jeffrey replaced the poker and leaned back in his chair. "Best look after your chastity. Was there a bottle of scent to go with it?"

"No. Just the note."

"Any idea who slipped it to you?"

"We believe," Maugham answered, obliging, "that it was from Dr. Bailey's organization. Your Assassins. Still mourning that library you brought back to us from Baquba."

"It was a threat? Revenge?"

"Quite the opposite. It offered us some well-intentioned advice."

"Hmm. About?"

"The note suggested," Maugham said, "that we examine three manuscripts from the collection we'd acquired. Given that they themselves were unable to do so on their own. Collegial of them, no?"

"Yes. They've always struck me as remarkably accommodating. Did you follow their instructions? Locate the manuscripts?"

"How could we resist?"

"And?"

"The first was an Ottoman social satire—a collection of jokes and stories—that looks more or less identical to a similar manuscript a contact of ours has seen in the Topkapı library in Istanbul. Circa the seventeenth century. The second was a copy of Evliya Çelebi's *Seyahatname*, his *Book of Travels*, also seventeenth-century. Ottoman. And the third was one that the cataloguers missed when you sent the material to us from Baquba. A fascinating fragment of the *Codex Cumanicus*, that half-Latin, half-medieval Turkish—Kipchak, I think it is—linguistic manual that made its way from the Caspian to Italy in the fourteenth century? Your Vambery was always taken with the Venetian version of that text, if I recall—"

"Hardly 'my Vambery,'" Jeffrey interrupted. "I was eighteen years old."

"At any rate," Maugham continued, placid, "it was the second part of the text. The riddles. Thirteenth- or fourteenth-century."

"All three manuscripts were there? Where the note said they'd be?" Thoughtful.

"Yes." Maugham paused. "There were actually six different copies of the *Seyahatname* in the collection. We examined them all."

"And?"

"Simple task identifying which they meant. It contained a map."

"Of Evliya Çelebi's itinerary? The path of his 'travels?'"

"No." Maugham repositioned himself in his chair. "The map appended to it was a detailed diagram of the informal pipeline our people have been working to establish in the Caucasus. An exact copy of the routes they'll be using to move the petroleum they plan to skim off the top."

"Oh dear." Jeffrey lit a third cigarette. Replaced the lighter. "What about the *Codex Cumanicus* and the Ottoman satire?"

"Same map."

"Heavens. That must have raised some eyebrows."

"It gets worse." Maugham was enjoying himself.

"How could it get worse?"

"The maps are contemporary with the manuscripts. Two are sixteenth- or seventeenth-century. One is fourteenth-century. No mistake about it. Our experts tested the ink and parchment repeatedly."

"Oh *dear*."

"The minister's involved now," Maugham said. "He'd very much like to know how a seventeenth-century geographer, a likewise sixteenth- or seventeenth-century composer of dirty limericks—and they do raise a blush, I must admit; make Petronius look like a priggish moralist—and a linguistically inclined fourteenth-century monk all became privy to an excruciatingly secret plan to exploit the Soviet petroleum industry in preparation for the coming war."

"I daresay he does."

"But there's more."

Jeffrey took a drag from his cigarette. "You win. I'm pleased I stayed." He watched Maugham. Intent. "Yes?"

"The maps also hint at a fourth diagram. Or possibly an object. On site somewhere in Baku." Maugham looked Jeffrey in the eye. "That fourth—object—it seems, can explain to us how the first three diagrams reached our library. And attached themselves to those manuscripts."

Jeffrey didn't respond for several seconds. Then he took another agitated drag of his cigarette. "You can't be serious."

"I'm always serious."

"It's a trap."

"Indeed."

"Maugham," Jeffrey said, exhaling smoke, "You will not send Marion into this mess."

"I wanted to."

"Absolutely not—"

"Calm down, Willcox. The petroleum people have already quashed that idea. They don't want me complicating their important negotiations with my pet projects. Not that they could stop me if I were truly interested in sending her—"

"Maugham—"

"But I'm not," he repeated. "They're correct. I do want her in the field. At some point. Worth it to draw out her people a bit further. But that can wait. For this, we'll want someone less prone to running off and disappearing for months on end. And, obviously, treason."

"Good." Jeffrey tapped ash from the end of his cigarette. "What is your plan, then?"

"We'll still use Dr. Bailey. She's the only resource we have who can read the manuscripts properly. The maps were a provocation. A beginning. But there's more contained in those texts than a simple diagram. And thus far, my experts have given me nothing but a cursory reading. I'd like to see what she can do with them. But she can accomplish that as well here as anywhere else."

Jeffrey was quiet for a few seconds. "That will be a challenge." He smoked, pensive. Then he said: "I'll give it some thought. But let's say we're successful with that first step. What next?"

"I'd like you to send some specialists into Baku for the fourth diagram. Object." Maugham waved a vague hand. "Whatever it is. Once she's given us an idea of where to find it. Also, if possible, I'd like you to have them bring us a visual, from the ground, of some of the points indicated on those maps. See whether they can determine anything unusual about those areas."

"Is their ultimate objective to stop the spread of the Marxist infection or to contain the barking mad despot who's overrun Germany? I'm still not quite clear on our ideological motivation."

"Does it matter?" Maugham looked, interested, at Jeffrey's face.

"It will help me to identify potential volunteers."

"Why not a few of each?" Maugham leaned back in his chair again. Closed his eyes. "It can't have escaped your notice that our foreign policy isn't what one would call consistent these days. Perhaps we'll want to prop up Stalin's ailing economy in the coming years as a bulwark against Hitler. Or perhaps Stalin and Hitler will decide that they're fellow travelers in a cruel and hostile world. Cozy up to one another. In which case, boom goes Baku. Either way, it has nothing to do with our section. We're interested in the artifacts. You know that, Willcox."

"Forgive me," Jeffrey said again. He inhaled slowly, and then exhaled smoke toward the fireplace. "I'll visit Baku myself for a report once they've found their footing. We'll work primarily in Azeri Turkish and Farsi, I think." He paused. "But I'll brush up on my Russian as well. Just in case."

Maugham nodded. "Good. And then when you've secured whatever this fourth item is, we'll involve Dr. Bailey once again. She'll be delighted to lend us her expertise a second time."

Jeffrey made a sound that could have been a laugh. "There is one potential obstacle." He glanced over at Maugham. "I ought to tell you this before we go any further. Marion's threatened to go under again after the holiday. And I'm not certain that I can stop her. So long as John's in school, I have no leverage to keep her with me in London. She'll bolt."

"I'm surprised by you, Willcox." Entertained. "This is hardly beyond your resources. You'll discover a solution to this problem if you put your mind to it."

"You're continuing to underestimate her." Jeffrey crushed out his cigarette in an ashtray on the side table. Annoyed. "And if I recall, your people had no better luck tracking her than mine had once you let her loose in the Balkans this past February. 'Putting all of your minds to it.' Don't forget, she still has that money you threw at her stashed somewhere. Untraceable."

Maugham smiled. "Yes. Captivating creature. I can see why you're smitten by her."

"Maugham—"

"The key, my boy, is not to let her loose to begin with. As I said, we won't put her in the field this time."

"It's not simply a question of keeping her out of the field." Jeffrey's voice was still irritated. Verging on angry. "I can't do what—what's necessary—in London. This isn't Iraq. And to be perfectly frank, I'm not certain that I'd have the stomach to do it again anyway. Even in Iraq."

"I think you'll find that anything you can do in Iraq we can also do here. Use your imagination." Maugham was still laughing. "You've never struck me as squeamish."

Jeffrey was examining the fire, his face now blank. He'd pushed back the anger. But he didn't respond.

"What about your house up north?" Maugham suggested. "Wedding gift from your uncle? We all knew it would come into its own. And she'll enjoy it," he added. "A sort of homecoming for her. Isn't there a view of sheep or a distillery or something similar from the tower? Ought to be ideal."

"I think we should reconsider our strategy," Jeffrey said, his voice unemotional.

"I could always have Thacker collect her if you feel unable to complete this assignment effectively."

The corner of Jeffrey's mouth went down. A hint of what might have been amusement. "Yes. That worked brilliantly for you the last time."

"I concede, Willcox, that Thacker lacks your precision. But he does get results. In his own way. A lot messier and less pleasant for the subject, obviously—"

"All right," Jeffrey snapped. "You've made your point. I'll begin setting the groundwork for this tomorrow." He stood. "But I warn you, Maugham. If you continue to provoke my family in this way, your serving of Christmas pudding will be conspicuously absent silver coins this year."

Maugham stood as well, chuckling. "It's your own fault, dear boy. You should have married someone less agonizingly useful." He patted down the pockets of his waistcoat. "Though to be fair, I'd not have resisted it, either. In your place. Unusual type."

MARION, who had been watching and listening, professionally attuned to both the atmosphere in the room and the conversation, chose that moment to escape back to her bedroom. The laudanum had left no more than a light, pure, floating feeling. She had to remind herself that a loud or sudden movement would alert listeners to her presence. But she also knew that her faculties were unimpaired.

And although she had forced herself not to react to, or try to process, what she had heard until she'd thought through it more carefully, she was prepared to act. She refused to wait for Jeffrey or Maugham to use her. As she crept through the door of the library and ran rapidly, silently, up the now dark stairs, the contours of a strategy were already coalescing in her mind. She had been revolted by their conversation. But she was pleased to be returning to her work.

She slipped into bed and closed her eyes a good three minutes before Jeffrey himself returned to the room. Heard him walk through the door, close it behind him, remove his dress shirt and trousers, and change into his pyjamas. He then spent a few minutes in the toilet and slid under the covers of the bed.

Rather than resting his head on his pillow to sleep, however, he remained on his side, propping his cheek on his hand, looking down at her. Even through her closed eyes, she could sense him examining her face. She compelled herself to be still, breathing deeply, regularly. Prayed that he would lose interest and turn over to go to sleep.

But instead, he lowered his face to hers and kissed her on the mouth. He took his time, enjoying himself, while she struggled to remain inert. Drugged. After what felt like an eternity, he stopped. Raised his head again. Then he lowered his lips to her ear. "Learn anything interesting?"

Her eyes flew open, and she moved to push him away, but he instantly had her wrists in his hand. Laughing down at her, teasing. "I've been using that alcove for games of hide-and-go-seek since I was eight."

She stared up at him. "You knew?"

"That you had a tolerance to opium? No."

She tried to free her wrists, but the attempt was feeble. Perfunctory. She stopped. "I'll never, *ever* cooperate with—"

"Nor would I expect you to, darling." He released her wrists and brushed her hair off her forehead. Soothing.

She couldn't think of a response. She was horrified. And so, with no other option presenting itself, she turned away from him and curled up in the bed. Shaking. He laughed and put his arm across her waist. Pulled her close to him. She considered pushing him away. But he was warm. And perversely comforting.

Deciding to let him hold her, she allowed herself, acknowledging the residual laudanum, to float into sleep. At least she was beginning to understand what was happening in the house. And she wasn't remotely overreacting.

Caithness, Scotland
January, 1935

*T*HE remainder of their holiday with Virginia and Teddy was uneventful. Ian, spending his second Christmas in Suffolk, explained to Marion in careful and possessive detail the traditions he'd adopted as his own. And Marion, grateful to, as well as enthralled by, Virginia and her husband, found herself encouraging his sense of belonging. In her most extravagant fancies, she'd never have imagined herself nurturing Ian's attachment to Jeffrey's family. But she felt devoted to Virginia in her own right. Virginia calmed her.

Nonetheless, when the time came to return to London to prepare Ian for his upcoming term at Temple Grove, Marion was ready. She considered, as they packed Ian's trunk and prepared for the journey to Eastbourne, returning a few days later to remove him from the school on her own. Perhaps bring him along with her to Azerbaijan, where she planned to escape once Jeffrey had let down his guard.

But such an arrangement was impracticable. Her days of travelling freely with Ian were over. Her son was still attached to her. And loyal. But he was also fascinated by his father. Marion could no longer rely on Ian's cooperation. And uncooperative, he would be better than any tail Jeffrey affixed to her. He'd have them identified and detained before they left Calais.

Marion was still pursuing this unproductive train of thought on the tenth of January, a damp Thursday, as she watched the school gate close on her son. Small and brave. She felt that she was watching him enter a prison, and her rage toward Jeffrey surged. But even in the midst of her anger, she knew better than to provoke him. And so she sat, silent, in the passenger seat of his Duesenberg Model SJ, black, silver, and obnoxious, clenching her fists in her lap. He had insisted on driving the three of them to Temple Grove himself, and he was now pulling on his gloves in preparation for their return journey.

Jeffrey had also refrained from speaking once they had hugged Ian and watched him disappear into the school. As he maneuvered the car onto the road, Marion looked steadily in front of her. Bleak, monotonous landscape out the windscreen. Low clouds. She meant to remain mute throughout the three-hour drive back to London. She'd spend one night in Chester Terrace planning her departure. And she'd be gone by morning.

She didn't know how she'd access the manuscript material once she'd gone under. But she trusted her organization to have a plan in place once she'd contacted them in Baku. And, she vowed, she'd finish the project by April. In time to welcome Ian home for his holiday.

Jeffrey, his profile blank, his gloved hands gripping the wheel, was clearly thinking along similar lines. Planning. Aware as he was of her intentions, he'd have a strategy in place to thwart them. But now that he no longer had Ian in his household to maintain his advantage, she was confident that she could outmaneuver him. Jeffrey worked by changing the field to suit his tactics. On an even field, she could easily elude him. In fact, she was looking forward to it.

The two and a half hours that brought them to the outskirts of London passed more quickly than she had expected them to, occupied as she was by mentally working through her itineraries. She barely noticed him turning onto a side road and then slowing toward an aerodrome. Coming to herself, she blinked and looked about her. Croydon. She recognized it from her last, traumatic, flight to London from Baghdad. Her heart jumped and began beating hard in her chest.

Jeffrey, still not speaking, still blank, brought the car to a halt at the edge of the apron. He let his hands drop from the wheel and continued gazing out the windscreen for a few seconds. Then he turned to Marion, an apologetic half smile on his face. She opened her mouth to say something to him, to ask him why he'd brought her here. But before she could speak, he reached into a pocket on the driver's side of the car, retrieved a six-inch hypodermic syringe, pushed her skirt up over her leg, and rammed the needle into her thigh.

The site of the injection burned as he introduced the drug into her muscle, and she gasped, hurt as well as shocked. He finished his work cleanly, professionally, and then he returned the empty syringe to the side pocket. As he turned away from her, Marion fumbled for the door handle with her fingertips, trying to drag herself out of the car. But she could already feel the effects of the sedative.

Jeffrey faced her again, pulled her back into her seat, and held her in place. Still calm. Still professional. As she stopped struggling, he released her and watched her eyes.

"Something more up to date this time, I thought." He had removed a glove and was holding his fingertips against the underside of her wrist. Checking her pulse. "Although if you prove yourself impervious to paraldehyde as well, I'll consider myself defeated. Be forced to use a truncheon, I suppose."

Satisfied that she was losing consciousness, he dropped her wrist, pulled on his glove, opened his door, and got out. He walked to her side of the car, and opened her door as well. Leaning over, he lifted her up and out of her seat, smoothing her skirt back over her legs as he did so.

"Ordinarily I would wait fifteen minutes for you to black out completely." He spoke as he carried her toward a waiting plane that she registered, hazily, as military. A large bomber. "But we're in a bit of a hurry, so I'll risk you attempting your customary break for freedom once we're underway." He smiled down at her. "Fear not, though. I'm certain the crew will understand your lack of social graces."

Marion, struggling to keep her eyes open, looked up into Jeffrey's face. "Please—" she started.

He bent over and kissed her cheek. "Shh. You'll be asleep in three minutes. Don't fight it."

As the edges of her vision turned black, she felt Jeffrey lift her toward the door of the plane. Waiting hands pulled her up and positioned her in a makeshift seat near the tail. A harness across her chest. Her wrists secured behind her, unnecessarily, to the chair. And then she lost consciousness.

She had a nightmarish memory of the plane landing, a second painful injection, and then being carried to another car. A salty wind. Cold. Mention of Wick Aerodrome. Then blackness. She opened her eyes again as the car seemed to be passing through a medieval gate. And then over a moat? A single tower silhouetted against the night sky. Waves crashing. Something out of legends and fairy stories from her childhood.

She shook her head. Groaned. "Oh God. Stop it—"

Jeffrey's hand smoothing her hair from her forehead again. "Almost there, darling."

SHE woke in a room that would have made her laugh under any other circumstances. A classic medieval keep. Round. Four arched windows set into six-foot-thick stone walls. One facing each compass point. Heavy iron bars over each, but also glass to keep out the weather. Flagstone floors. A solid wooden door, reinforced with iron bands, and a stone fireplace, lit and heating the room, alongside a pile of extra logs to use as fuel. A long oak table on a trestle with a carved oak chair at each end occupied the center of the room. Empty for now.

She herself had been placed on a straw pallet against a curved wall. Chamber pot discreetly positioned at the end. A pitcher of water, a basin, and a ceramic cup at the other end. Heavy wool blankets covered her. As the wind picked up outside the tower and screeched through the glass windows—ineffective as they turned out to be—she wondered whether Jeffrey was deliberately insulting her. A safe conclusion.

She pushed down the blankets and sat up on the pallet, testing her body's reaction to the previous night. She was wearing the same dress she'd worn to take Ian to Temple Grove, but her coat was gone. Her shoes were arranged neatly to the side of the chamber pot. After she had established that she felt no more than a dull headache and a dry mouth, she brought her fingertips to the hem of her skirt, cautious, and pulled it up to examine her thigh. An ugly bruise spread out from the point where the needle had broken her skin. She prodded it experimentally and then winced. Pushed the skirt back down over her legs.

She didn't feel brave enough to attempt standing quite yet, and so she twisted back and poured herself a cup of water. Drank. Poured another. Looked up at the ceiling. Bare, solid beams. More stone. Glanced over at the fireplace and noticed for the first time a large oil painting, the work of a master, out of place in the austere room. It was hanging above the vestigial mantel.

A supercilious woman, eighteenth-century, Marion would have guessed. The woman's hand was holding a fan. Marion peered more closely at the painting, and then down at her own finger. She and the woman were wearing the same wedding ring. Marion decided not to internalize that piece of information. Pushed it to the side. Told herself to move. Be active.

She put the cup on the ground next to the pallet, fortified herself, and rose to her feet. Pain shot up her leg, as she'd expected, but it wasn't as debilitating as she'd feared it would be. She walked, with a limp, toward the door. Pulled it halfheartedly. It didn't move, and she hadn't expected it to, but she would have felt a fool if it were unlocked and she hadn't tried it.

She walked the circumference of the room, slowly, testing walls, peering out of windows, until she'd convinced herself that there weren't any obvious escape routes. Late afternoon, she noted in passing. Then she wandered back to the first window, climbed into the embrasure until she was up against the bars and the glass, and wrapped her arms around her knees. Gazed down the sheer drop at the waves crashing against the rocks. Pulled back her hair with her fingers and plaited it. And waited for Jeffrey. Defeated.

He appeared sooner than she had expected, before the stone against her back had become uncomfortable. But she didn't move when she heard the door to the room opening. Instead, she continued looking down at the foaming water. Heard him close the door, move further into the room, add a log to the fire, and then stand at the window, watching her. "Welcome home."

She looked over at him. "I'm from Edinburgh."

He let his gaze wander over the walls. Perplexed. Took in the chamber pot and the straw pallet. "There's a difference?"

"Fuck you."

He smiled. "We haven't quite worked through the plumbing arrangements in this part of the house, I'm afraid. But there's a water closet at the base of the stairs. I'll take you, if you'd like."

She crawled back out of the embrasure, stood, smoothed down her skirt, and limped to a chair. Noticed that he had brought her a tray of food. Cheese and pickle sandwiches, a sliced pear, and a bottle of cider. She sat at the table and prodded the pear with her fingertip. Didn't eat. "Later."

"Very well." He nodded toward a carpet bag, her own, that he had placed to the side of the door. "I've brought you clothing as well. From Durham. To keep out the chill."

She kept her eyes on the plate of food. "How long?"

She pulled out the other chair and sat. Crossed his ankles in front of him and pushed his hair off his forehead. He looked comfortable. Brown corduroy trousers and a dark red V-neck over a white shirt and a striped tie. "I'll bring you the manuscript material now."

She laughed. Didn't reply.

"Think of it this way, Marion. You need access to it in any case. You can't take your next step any better than we can without reading it." He examined her downcast eyes. "Why not look it over, form a few impressions, and then decide whether or not to speak to us about it? You can always refuse. Who knows? You may even manage to escape before Maugham boosts the pressure."

"I'm not stupid."

"You are far from stupid."

"You think you can trick it out of me. Once I've looked over the manuscripts." She raised her eyes to the painting above the fireplace. Frowned.

"Yes, that would be the basic strategy. But you needn't be bound by it." He nodded up at the portrait. "She wasn't."

"She—?"

"The closest I have to a painting behind a curtain." He was still focused on the picture. "My great- great-grandmother. She was an actress. My great- great-grandfather picked her up at the Comédie-Française. On assignment. Perfect combination of Republican intelligence and Royalist loyalties."

He smiled fondly at the painting. "Or, so he thought. It soon transpired that she was one of the most notorious Jacobin agitators of her generation." He glanced over at Marion, and then back up at the painting. "Whoops. But my great- great-grandfather couldn't bear to dispose of her. So, he brought her up here instead. The impenetrable fortress." His tone was irreverent. "They had eight children together. Including my great-grandfather."

He turned to the table and took a slice of pear from Marion's plate. Ate it. "Family lore has it that she never stopped working. Somehow or other, despite the state-of-the art security surrounding this pile of rock, she continued to get messages out to her contacts. And then later, God help us, to Napoleon."

He leaned back in his chair again, stretched out his legs, re-crossed his ankles, and put his hands behind his head. Examined the ceiling. "Entailment on this bit of the inheritance is a trifle obscure. Bounces about quite a bit. But when my uncle, its most recent proprietor, learned of my marriage to you, he signed the building over to me." He crossed his arms over his chest and grinned at Marion. "Can't imagine why he'd do that."

She let her eyes fall from the painting back to the fire. "Bring the material to me tonight."

Jeffrey stood and walked to the door. "I can do better than that." He pulled open the door and stepped out into what Marion assumed was the keep's staircase. Returned a few seconds later carrying a stack of vellum and paper. Arranged it on the table, away from the plate of food. Four piles.

"Evliya Çelebi's *Seyahatname*," he pointed to the first set of volumes. "The *Codex Cumanicus*, or at least the collection of riddles at the end of it, and," indicating the third set of pages, "the seventeenth-century 'satire.'" He paused. "I've skimmed that last selection myself. Out of curiosity. Are you certain you won't be offended? The language is far from modest."

"I'll be fine."

"This last pile," he continued, "is reference material, blank sheets of paper, and pencils." He looked about the room. "Candles are on the mantle. Is there anything else you'll need?"

She stood and walked to the embrasure, curled up next to the window, and looked out over the water. Night was already falling. "No. Go away."

"One more question, Marion."

She was silent.

"You haven't any Russian, have you?"

She was sufficiently surprised by the non-sequitur to glance back at him, standing by the door. "No. Why?"

Jeffrey had pulled open the door. "Maugham underestimates you. I've learned not to."

He closed the door. It was substantial enough that she couldn't hear him walking down the stairs. When he was gone, she dropped her face to her knees.

SHE kept her eyes squeezed shut and her face against her knees for more than an hour after Jeffrey had left the room. Long enough for the extended twilight outside the window to turn black and leave the room dim and red from the fire. Eventually, she lifted her head, pushed back her shoulders, and crawled out of the embrasure. Stood and looked vacantly about her. Then she walked to her carpet bag to see what he had brought her to wear.

She dug through the familiar clothing until she found thick warm socks and flannel pyjamas. Grateful to him for not providing her with something more appropriate to the setting. White lace nightdress. Prone to shredding. She had no doubt that the thought had crossed his mind.

Standing near the fire to keep warm, she removed her dress, folded it, and placed it to the side of the hearth. Then she pulled on her socks and pyjamas and examined the candles he had left her. They were large and solid. They'd illuminate the room well.

After adding a few more pieces of wood to the fire, she took two candles, lit them, and brought them to the oak table. Arranged them next to her plate of food. Then she drew one of the chairs up to the table, sat, lifted a sandwich, and examined the material in front of her. She took a bite and chewed, thinking.

She had initially thought she'd start with Evliya Çelebi's travel account. It was the most familiar to her, and the most well-known generally. Evliya Çelebi had been born in 1611 in Istanbul, the capital of the Ottoman Empire. His father had been chief jeweler to the Sultan and the descendent of a well-connected, governing family. His mother and uncle had come to the Sultan's court from the Caucasus. Near Azerbaijan.

Evliya himself had spent most of his life, close to forty years, travelling, visiting much of Europe, including Sweden and Russia, the Crimea, Iran, the Arabic speaking provinces of the Ottoman Empire, Sudan, and most of the Caucasus. He had returned repeatedly to Baku. His *Seyahatname*, written in Ottoman Turkish in the 1670s and 1680s, was a detailed, sometimes painfully so, account of his journeys.

Although only pieces of it had been translated into European languages, a number of accessible manuscripts or photographs of manuscripts of Evliya's travelogue were available to interested scholars. And the un-translated bits were a common assignment for early post-graduate students studying variations on Ottoman Turkish. Marion herself had completed more than her share during her truncated career at Cambridge. She suspected that the manuscript on the table in front of her, from the Baquba library, was unusual in some way. But even so, it wouldn't be difficult to get a feel for the writing and language.

At the same time, the *Seyahatname* was ten volumes in length. And, taking another bite of her sandwich, Marion could see from where she was sitting that the copy of it Jeffrey had provided her included every last one of those ten volumes. The pile of vellum was close to toppling over. She set down her sandwich and drank some cider from the bottle.

Her immediate reaction to hearing Evliya Çelebi's name linked to some ongoing political complication in Azerbaijan had been that whatever clue she might find in the text would be hidden in the second, seventh, or possibly the fourth volume—one of those concerned with his time in the Caucasus. Potentially, there might be something in his personal biography as well. Something having to do with his mother's family.

Thinking about the situation more carefully, though, she felt less certain. Maugham had already had his pet scholars read through the material. And his experts were more than competent enough to deal with Evliya's prose. In fact, they were likely more confident with it than she was, given that her specialty was pre-Ottoman, rather than Ottoman, Turkish literature. The seventeenth century counted as excessively modern to her. Not her field. She let her eyes rest briefly on the fourteenth-century *Codex Cumanicus*.

Then she shook her head and forced herself to ruminate further on the travelogue. Maugham's experts would have gone over the second, seventh, and fourth volumes with painstaking care. If they hadn't found anything, then her initial thought on where to look was flawed as well. She sat still, thinking, considering a quicker and more effective approach.

Then she realized that she was famished and finished her sandwich. Drank the rest of the bottle of cider. She wouldn't start with the *Seyahatname* tonight.

Quietly relieved, she mentally set it aside. If her intuition was correct, the other two manuscripts would yield up sufficient information to point her to a specific section of Evliya's account. She'd be able to avoid slogging through all ten volumes, looking for discrepancies or re-formulations of what was to her, in any case, only a half-remembered text.

She picked up a slice of pear with one hand and reached over to the much thinner volume of satirical stories—*latife*s or *letaif*—that were apparently also seventeenth-century. She was less familiar with this genre, but she'd read a few similar short collections. The idea on the part of the writer was to demonstrate linguistic flexibility and wit by describing, and satirizing, prominent people or professions, often in short rhymed couplets.

It was the sort of literature that Jeffrey had enjoyed as a student, although his specialty had been the classical Arabic, rather than the Ottoman Turkish, variation on the theme. She herself disliked the style. Not, as Jeffrey had insinuated, because of prudishness on her part. She simply felt uncomfortable with the aggression underlying the insulting, supposedly humorous, language. Even separated by three hundred years.

She frowned as she read a few introductory lines. Not three hundred years. Four hundred. She skimmed a bit further. Even a shallow reading told her that the stories couldn't have been written later than the 1530s. The references, necessarily contemporary to their composition for the satire to hit home, were all to sixteenth-century rather than to seventeenth-century figures. She ate another slice of pear and kept reading. Why would Maugham have presented them to Jeffrey as seventeenth-century?

She flipped to the end of the collection, counting each individual satire or *latife*. Thirty-five. She could read it all in a few hours. But she was still uncertain as to what she was trying to find, and she didn't want to begin haphazardly. She went back to the first few passages and translated more carefully. Then she paused, surprised. For a collection of cosmopolitan jokes meant for an appreciative, courtly Istanbul audience, there were a surprising number of references to places and incidents in the far from urbane fields and mountains of the Caucasus.

She slowed down and began reading for detail. Then, annoyed, she pushed the pages away and finished her pear, gazing into the fire. She'd come across the fourth reference to sexual impotence in as many pages. She wasn't a puritan, she insisted to herself. She just couldn't evade the image of some privileged, self-satisfied courtier smirking over the humiliation of some equally privileged, self-satisfied rival. Didn't want to start with that either.

That left the *Codex Cumanicus* or the "Cuman Book." She ran a fingertip over the thin volume, no more than six pages. Wry. She'd known from the moment she'd heard Maugham mention it in Suffolk, that this was the material she wanted to study. Its period—the eleventh through fourteenth centuries—coincided precisely with her period of specialization. And the language, the Kipchak dialect of Turkish, would come to her more easily even than Ottoman.

Kipchak was spoken by the nomadic Turkic Cumans, who in the thirteenth century had extended their informal rule across Central Asia, the Caucasus, and southeastern Europe, eventually settling in Hungary and other parts of the Balkans. Hence the "Cuman Book." She hadn't read anything in the dialect before. But she was confident that she could familiarize herself with it quickly.

Moreover, the text wasn't completely new to her. She'd been aware of its existence for many years, and had frequently been tempted to travel to St. Mark's library in Venice to examine the one extant manuscript of it. But she'd never found herself with the time or the freedom to do so.

If she'd known that there had been a copy of it in the library in Baquba, she'd have made the time to read it when she had visited on her own. But she hadn't known. And now it was too late. She pushed away the irritation that mounted as she wondered what other material she'd failed to study before Jeffrey had looted the library. It was an unproductive train of thought. Instead, she pressed her fingertip against the first page of what she had in front of her.

The *Codex Cumanicus* was, at least at its core, a lexicon. It had been written to assist medieval European missionaries and merchants travelling through the Caucasus and Central Asia, especially those who had wanted to access the silk road without employing costly, and sometimes dishonest, interpreters. The manuscript in Venice had been divided into two sections. The first was a dictionary in three languages: Italian inflected Latin, Kipchak Turkish, and the common language of the region at that time, Farsi.

The second part, more curious and ordinarily of more interest to scholars, was quite different. Composed in Latin, Kipchak, and medieval German, this second part consisted, oddly, of a combination of religious tracts and folk-riddles. What she had in front of her were the riddles. But she could already tell that the pages she was examining weren't a facsimile of the last part of Venice manuscript. On the contrary, they were as old as, if not older than, the Venetian *Codex Cumanicus* in St. Mark's.

She remembered having read that the Venice copy contained errors that suggested it had been hand-copied from an earlier manuscript. The copy that Jeffrey had brought her was clean. She knew, even if she couldn't verify it, that it was the original. The Venice text was the copy.

She positioned the pages in front of her and read a riddle she had chosen at random from the list. Then she smiled, entertained.

When one departs from the left, and the other departs from the right, what remains are thirty specks of thirty fires. Answer: the sun, the moon, dawn, and the stars.

She relaxed and appreciated the deceptive simplicity of the first line, starting with *onlu solulu*, and the final answer, echoing the initiating line with *yulduz*. She found this writing far more evocative than the tortured, spiteful verses that were coming out of Istanbul three hundred years later. But she also knew that she was in the minority. Jeffrey would deride her if he suspected her partiality to this sort of "peasant" writing.

She turned her attention back to the pages in front of her and counted the riddles. Forty-six, just as in the Venice manuscript. Decided that she would devote the remainder of the evening to a quick, schematic translation of the more straightforward passages. After that, once she was better rested, she'd address the lines that were obscure or difficult to decode. If she was lucky, a complete reading of the riddles would give her an idea of where to start reading the Evliya Çelebi. And, she sighed, it would also give her a clue as to the relevance of the satirical *letaif.* Resting her fingertips against her temples, she began making her way through the first set of lines.

SHE had difficulty convincing herself to stop once she'd begun. But she also knew that she wouldn't make any progress at all without sleeping for a few hours every night. Eventually, therefore, she dropped the pencil she'd been using to take cryptic notes on the riddles and rose from the chair. Blew out the candles, added a few more logs to the fire to keep the chamber from becoming too cold in the night, and walked to the pallet. Her head was buzzing as she slipped under the woolen blankets, but she fell asleep easily and quickly. No dreams.

She woke to the sound of Jeffrey moving about in the room. He had built up the fire and replenished her wood while she was sleeping, and he had left breakfast, including a pot of strong tea, on the table. When she opened her eyes, he was standing over her notes, reading what little she had written the night before. She sat up on the pallet, wrapped the blanket around herself, and looked at him, hostile.

"Keeping it all in your head, then, are you?" He put the paper back on the table.

"Yes."

"Understandable." He smiled down at her. "Surely you'll let me take you downstairs now. Unless you prefer the chamber pot?"

She nodded and stood. Kept the blanket wrapped over her shoulders. The room, despite the fire, was cold.

He walked behind her out the door and down a fortified stone staircase. Arrowslits in the walls. No glass. Keening wind and hailstones outside. At the bottom of the stairs, he indicated a small door, recently built into the stone wall.

She handed him the blanket and walked through it. The toilet and sink were minimal, but clean and apparently attached to some sort of pipe or sewer. She used the toilet and washed her face in the sink. Saw that he had also brought her toothbrush from Durham and left it for her on the sink. She used it and set it back in place. Then she pushed open the door again.

As he handed her the blanket, she looked about the empty tower. "No guards?"

"Maugham doesn't want you talking to anyone." He was following her back up the stairs.

"What if I kill you?" She pushed open the door to the keep.

He followed her into the room, shut the door, and leaned against it with crossed arms. Slight smile. "You won't."

She gazed back at him, level. Didn't say anything.

His smile became apologetic again. Hint of what he'd done to her in Croydon. "This—situation," he said, looking about the room, "has become rather serious. I've never seen Maugham in this state before. If you do clear the defensive walls and the moat, you'll be faced with what looks to be, though I haven't inspected them too closely, a hastily reassembled war-era Machine Gun Corps." He glanced up at the ceiling, thinking. "All sorts of happy memories for me, I must admit. Even if they do look a trifle out of place not covered in French mud."

"Oh." She walked to the table to examine the breakfast he'd brought to her. A boiled egg and toast in addition to the tea. She poured herself a cup of the tea and looked up at him. "Go away."

He turned, obliging, and opened the door. "I'll return in a few hours with your lunch," he said as he closed it on her. She didn't bother to respond.

After she'd finished the tea and toast, leaving the egg, she built up the fire and retrieved clothing from her carpet bag. Then, wearing tweed trousers and her favorite wool sweater with the hole in the elbow, she returned to the Cuman riddles. Devoted the entire day to the short text, increasingly impressed by both its skillful simplicity and what she was coming to realize was its astonishing significance. Initially, she refused to accept the conclusions that she was drawing from the document. Pushed them aside as fanciful or exaggerated. As she checked and re-checked her work, however, and especially as she turned to the sixteenth-century satire for corroboration of her hypothesis, she became convinced that her interpretation was correct.

But what she was learning, though riveting, was also disturbing. As the days passed, she became more anxious than satisfied with the work. Found herself repeatedly stopping, rising from her chair, pacing the room to clear her head, and only then returning to her reading.

By the fifth day, when she felt confident enough to turn back to Evliya Çelebi's *Seyahatname*, she half hoped that it would fail to support her conclusions. In that, however, she was disappointed. Turning to the tenth and final volume of Evliya's travelogue, recounting the years he had spent in Egypt, rather than in Azerbaijan, she found the information she was seeking. And she knew that her reading of all three manuscripts had been correct.

She also knew that Maugham had misinformed Jeffrey about the problem that had arisen in Baku. And this knowledge, more than anything else, left her hesitant. Uncertain.

Under ordinary circumstances, she would have let Jeffrey continue in ignorance while she did all she could to mislead both. She would have enjoyed the fact that Maugham distrusted Jeffrey enough to hold back pieces of the puzzle. But what she had discovered was sufficiently horrific that she felt a creeping obligation to inform him. To convince him to work against Maugham.

She might, she rationalized to herself, even push Jeffrey in the proper direction without giving him everything she knew. Just enough for him to realize that he'd been used—or misused—and must act. She stopped work in the afternoon of the fifth day to think through a potential strategy.

Throughout the five days she'd been reading, Jeffrey had been in and out of the room, bringing her food and accompanying her to the foot of the tower when she wanted to use the toilet. She saw no one else, and she spoke as little as possible, but he was content with the situation and never pressured her to talk. If she could pique his interest by speaking with him, though, she might convince him that Maugham's goals were questionable. It was worth an attempt.

On the evening of the fifth day, therefore, when he arrived with her dinner—cold sliced roast, Roquefort cheese, a half loaf of brown bread, and another bottle of cider—she changed her approach to him. As he walked into the room, she watched him from the embrasure. Speculative. He set the tray on the table and held her look, still almost imperceptibly entertained.

"Do you need anything?" he finally asked.

"Yes." She crawled away from the window and stood. "Can you bring me something else to drink? And take away this foul cider?"

"Forgive me. I wish I'd known sooner it wasn't to your taste."

She sat heavily in the oak chair. "You knew perfectly well it wasn't to my taste." She looked up at him. "And when you come back, bring two glasses."

"Delighted." He took the bottle and walked to the door. "I won't be more than five minutes."

After he'd left, Marion stared unseeing at the food on the table in front of her. She was unconvinced that she was making the right decision. But she couldn't think of any alternative. She picked absentmindedly at the cheese as she waited.

By the time he'd returned, the cheese was a crumbled mess on the plate. He cast it an eloquent look as he walked through the door, but he didn't comment. He was wearing a pullover, shirt, and tie similar to those she'd seen before, but there was a distinct air of golf about this new variation. She suspected that he was making fun of her again. Asked herself whether it was truly necessary to confide in him and concluded glumly that, yes, it was.

He pulled the second oak chair toward the table, sat across from her, placed a bottle of scotch between them, and produced two tumblers. He poured a substantial measure into both glasses, and then looked at her in inquiry. "Are we talking or just getting tight?"

She took her glass and drank a large swallow before answering. She couldn't speak to him until the alcohol had deadened her anxiety. Waited for a few seconds and then looked up at him as she felt the flat warmth begin to spread from her stomach. He watched her. Not speaking. Deliberately unhelpful.

"Maugham's lying to you," she finally said to him.

Jeffrey took a small sip from his glass. "Maugham lies to everyone. That's his job."

"This isn't an insignificant lie. He's using you. For—for something immoral."

"Good heavens." Jeffrey raised his eyebrows. "For something immoral no less? I must look to the state of my soul."

"Jeffrey, this is important—"

He pushed back the chair and stood. "If I need to know, he'll tell me."

She watched him walking toward the door. Stupefied by his reaction. "Wait." She stood as well. "Jeffrey, wait. This situation in Baku. It has nothing to do with petroleum. The petroleum is a distraction."

He was at the door, opening it and about to go through without responding. But then he relented, paused, and turned back to her. "Good," he said. "I can think of little more tedious than petroleum. You'll tell us both more about it tomorrow—"

"I'll tell *you* about it. Now."

"No."

"No?" She stared at him in disbelief. "*No?* What do you mean 'no?' Wasn't the purpose of storing me here to get me talking? Well, I'm talking now. To you."

"And I'm overjoyed by your compliance, Marion. Truly. It's an attractive facet of your personality that I rarely have the opportunity to enjoy. I do hope to see more of it in the coming years." He opened the door further. "But anything you have to say to me you can also say to Maugham. If, as you insist, he's been using me inappropriately, you can confront him in person with the evidence of his nefarious plotting against your beloved husband." There was a smile in his voice. "And imagine how satisfying that will be."

"Jeffrey—"

"Tomorrow."

He shut the door.

She stood facing the closed door for a good thirty seconds. Couldn't understand what had just happened. Then she returned to the table. Finished her tumbler of scotch in a single swallow, built up the fire, and collapsed, without changing into her pyjamas, onto the pallet. She left the food.

SHE woke the next morning before Jeffrey had brought her breakfast. Stared, from her reclined position on the pallet, at the muted light playing over the keep's ceiling. Then she closed her eyes, tense, and forced herself to sit up. She would put on unwrinkled clothing before her visitors arrived. She had no interest in pleasing Maugham. But she also didn't want to give him more conversational ammunition than he already possessed. Appearing disheveled and upset would only weaken her position.

She considered changing back into the dress she'd worn to take Ian to school. It was the only professional outfit she had with her in the tower. But, glancing at it with revulsion, folded next to the fireplace, she decided against it. She'd wear the shoes along with her ordinary working uniform of wool trousers, cotton shirt, and heavy jumper. It was the best she could do.

Compelling herself into activity, she stood, fed the fire, retrieved clean clothing from her carpet bag, and changed. She let her eye wander, with a trace of regret, toward the bottle of scotch waiting on the table. Resolved against it. She'd have a drink afterward. A series of drinks. She'd need them.

As she was pulling her hair back into a knot at the nape of her neck, the door opened. Jeffrey entered, followed by Maugham, who was out of breath from climbing the stairs. Wearing plus fours and a jacket in Prince of Wales check, argyle socks, and a cap.

Maugham nodded in Marion's direction and then gazed up at the painting above the fireplace. "Milady is looking ravishing today. More so every time I visit." He turned to Jeffrey. "How is that possible, Willcox?"

Jeffrey shrugged. He was clearing away Marion's dinner tray. Placing it outside the door on the staircase. He hadn't brought breakfast or tea for her. No caffeine. A deliberate omission.

Maugham settled himself into one of the chairs, and then looked, confused, about the room. "Only two chairs?"

"I'll stand." Jeffrey had returned to the room and was closing the door. He pointed to the chair across the table, facing Maugham. Addressed Marion: "sit."

She crossed the room and sat in the chair. She didn't want Jeffrey standing. She wouldn't be able to watch his reactions. And she particularly didn't want to be facing Maugham for this conversation. She knew, again, that the arrangement was intentional, and her disquiet grew.

Reading her thoughts, Jeffrey smiled faintly and wandered over to the window behind her. Looked out at the opaque light reflected from invisible water. The skin on the back of her neck was crawling, but she didn't turn. She wouldn't gratify him by reacting.

Maugham was also smiling, more broadly, looking genial and mischievous. He folded his hands together in front of him on the table and observed Marion. Waited a few seconds. And then, his eyes wide, he spoke to her: "I understand, Dr. Bailey, that our interest in Azerbaijan is not, in fact, petroleum."

"No."

"Fascinating." He leaned toward her, conspiratorial. "And what is our objective, then? I hope it's something equally remunerative, or the minister will be terribly disappointed."

She already felt the beginning of a headache. A combination of caffeine withdrawal and what she knew was going to be a surreal nightmare of an exchange with both Maugham and Jeffrey. She closed her eyes.

"Professor Maugham," she began. "Under any other conditions, I would keep my information to myself. Let your tame academics beat themselves up trying to interpret this material. But I think what you're doing with it—" she opened her eyes, held his look, "—what you're doing with it is terrifying. It scares me. And I don't think you've told Jeffrey everything. And I think—" she dropped her gaze, "—I hope—that when he hears what's at stake, he'll be in a position to stop you. Or at least in a position to help me stop you. Because there's no way that anyone with a modicum of decency could hear about this without taking action against it. Even Jeffrey isn't base enough to make allowances for what you're putting into motion."

Maugham looked over Marion's shoulder at Jeffrey, who was still standing behind her, his back to the room, peering out the window. "Hear that, Willcox? I believe your lady wife has just invited you to deliver her from her confinement in the castle keep. Went about it in a circuitous sort of way. As is her wont. But that was, if I'm not mistaken, a quite definite and unalloyed appeal for rescue. Are you feeling a warm, uxorious glow?"

Jeffrey didn't turn. "Marion has that effect. Though I must admit, the glow was equally pronounced when I shut her up here in the first place."

Maugham resumed his examination of Marion. "He seems unconvinced. Why not answer my question? What are we looking for, if not petroleum?"

She remained quiet for a moment. Then she fortified herself and continued. "Fine. I'll answer your question. But not straight away. I'm going to tell you how I got there first."

"Even better." Maugham leaned back in the chair. "Continue."

She rested her elbows on the table and put her fingertips to her temples. Stared down at the tabletop. "I'll start with the Evliya Çelebi."

"Very well. Which volume?"

"The tenth."

Jeffrey turned, interested. "The tenth? Isn't that the description of Egypt and Sudan?"

"You wouldn't be trying to mislead us now, would you, Dr. Bailey?" Maugham's voice was still entertained.

She looked up at him. "No. The map was appended to the tenth volume. Why not start with the tenth?"

"The map was appended to the tenth volume," Maugham said, "because it was the last volume. Your seventeenth-century librarians simply tacked it onto the end. My people were adamant that the description of Egypt couldn't have anything to do with—"

"Your people were wrong." She dropped her eyes back to the tabletop. "In fact, the description of Egypt is the *only* relevant part of the manuscript."

"Is it indeed?"

"Yes," she answered, shortly. "There's a section in the tenth volume that describes medicine. In Egypt. It's a peculiar set of passages even without the map because both the illnesses and the cures that Evliya describes are next to impossible to identify. The rest of the *Seyahatname*, every volume, is meticulously detailed. Notoriously so. But these parts of the tenth volume are convoluted. Vague. In the past, commentators have dismissed the apparent ignorance underlying them as just that—ignorance. Evliya wasn't an expert. A physician. Yes, he observed. But he didn't understand what he was seeing. And so, his descriptions were flawed."

She hesitated. "Another possible explanation for the discrepancies in that section is that they're the result of copyists' errors. Either way, the descriptions of the illnesses and cures in the Egyptian hospitals are ordinarily rejected. No one has paid them much attention over the centuries." She considered her next step. Then she spoke again. "But given what I've extracted from the other two documents—"

"And what have you extracted from the other two documents, Dr. Bailey?" Maugham had picked up on her hesitation. He was trying to exploit it. Instinctively. The move annoyed her.

"I'll get to the other two documents," she snapped, "when I'm ready, Professor Maugham."

Maugham exchanged a pained look with Jeffrey, who was still standing behind her. "Very well," he repeated. "Continue."

She nodded. "Given what I had extracted from the other two documents, I thought it was worth revisiting the medical passages in the travelogue. I'm not going to tell you my process," she added hastily. "But I drew two conclusions from that method." She paused again. "First, I discovered that Evliya's descriptions of the medical practices were as accurate as the other passages in the *Seyahatname*. He was obsessed with detail. As a writer. Recorded how many steps it took to reach each stall in the Damascus markets. How many trees grew in the gardens surrounding Tabriz. That sort of thing. His writing is the same in volume ten. Precise. Excessively so. And therefore, second," she continued, "I concluded that the usual scholarly identification of the diseases and cures that he discusses in Egypt is incorrect."

"In what way?"

"Ordinarily, commentators assume that his more lurid descriptions, even though they're difficult to parse, are of syphilis. The 'French disease.' A new problem in Cairo at the time. A destructive one." She thought for a moment. "But if you read the passages in light of—of what I read in the other two documents—you find instead references to a type of swelling. A different type of swelling."

She stopped to think. Then, confident, she spoke again. "They're descriptions of tumors. At one point, he even says that afflicted women look pregnant. But the word he uses in the 'pregnant' comparison is *gebe* rather than the more medical *hamile*. It's an evocative word. Suggestive more of—of excessive organic growth than of a specific symptom of a disease like syphilis. But even more important than the descriptions of the illnesses," she persisted before Maugham could interrupt, "are the descriptions of the cures. Evliya Çelebi is fascinated by the use of theriac—"

"Theriac? The Greek medicine?" Jeffrey stopped her. "The concoction that Galen popularized in the second century? It was supposed to be a cure-all, no? All sorts of rare and secret ingredients, gallstones taken from criminals, the skin of abnormally large frogs, brewed in cauldrons for years at a time, set out under the full moon, that kind of thing." He considered. "I do remember something about the Egyptians being adept at mixing it. A key ingredient was snake venom, if I'm not mistaken. And Egyptian snakes were notoriously venomous." He paused again. "Not sure what any of this has to do with our pipelines in the Caucasus."

"Let me try, Willcox." Maugham was chuckling. "So, unless I'm misunderstanding you, Dr. Bailey, you're telling us that we ought to be concentrating our attention—along with our considerable political and financial resources—on snake venom in Egypt rather than on petroleum in Azerbaijan. Hence your concern about the ethics of our ongoing fact-finding mission on the shores of the Caspian." Maugham raised his eyebrows at her. "I fear that we'll have difficulty convincing the powers that be to redirect their—"

"Wait," she told him. Her voice hard.

"Very well," he said a third time. Slight sigh.

"Evliya Çelebi," she continued, "devotes an extended collection of passages to how the Egyptians brewed their theriac. Which is unusual because it was a secret process. It's surprising he would have been allowed to see it, much less record it. Unless," she emphasized, "knowing the process was less important than gaining access to the ingredients. Which appears to have been the case." She stopped again, choosing her words carefully. "The ingredients were scarce. Close to nonexistent. Even in Egypt. Evliya wasn't exposing any secrets because even those who knew the recipe couldn't locate the raw material."

"Snakes aren't rare," Jeffrey said. "Even highly venomous ones."

"Evliya Çelebi's snakes were," she replied. "Because when he identifies the snakes used to make the Egyptian theriac—which, as you said, was unique in the world—he describes them as, first, 'horned' and second, 'lizard-like.' He could be referring to Egyptian 'horned vipers,' but the details are off. The attribution doesn't work all that well—and in fact, this is the point at which most readers decide he's simply misinformed. Especially when he then goes on to say that the snakes are not only horned and possibly also lizards, but additionally both '*musk*' and '*safi*'—words that are usually left untranslated, as errors. Both strike a strange note in the text against the 'horned lizard' references. Or they do if you're thinking of classical theriac brewed from Egyptian snake venom.

"*But*," she said, "in the version of the text you gave me to read, the descriptive terms do work. *Musk*, he explains in a marginal note, is a sort of talisman or stone amulet. And in fact, *musk* is a common word for a stone talisman, a word you see frequently in other medical texts of that period. It just never made sense in the *Seyahatname*. *Safi* is more difficult. But the *safi* here, in this manuscript, is actually *safir*, "sapphire." There's an extra 'r' at the end of the word. He's not talking about an actual sapphire, it's true. The word was used at the time as a catch-all term for any stone or rock with unusual energy or curative power."

Maugham was rubbing his cheek with his hand. "So this panacea he's describing, then, is—"

"It's a talisman they used to treat tumors. A talisman related to 'horned snakes' or 'lizards.' But these 'snakes' weren't animals. The word 'snake' was shorthand for some sort of mineral." She watched Maugham's reaction, wondering whether she had made her point. "Evliya Çelebi," she elaborated when he was unmoved, "was describing the use of a rare, curative *mineral* that was brought to these seventeenth-century hospitals—at least according to your map—not from the Egyptian desert but from the Caspian Sea. Just outside of Baku."

"I'm still not certain what this has to do with our petroleum problem," Jeffrey said. He had moved closer to her. Close enough for her to feel him behind her. It made her uncomfortable.

"I'm getting to that," she said, irritated. "I'm going to tell you about the Cuman riddles now."

"They're riveting, I have no doubt." Maugham was occupied with a loose button on his jacket.

Marion's eyes wandered, of their own accord, to the bottle of scotch, just out of reach on the table. She caught herself and changed her expression before her interest in it became too obvious. But not before Maugham had looked up at her and lifted an inquisitive eyebrow. She squeezed her eyes shut again and continued speaking. "The second part of the *Codex Cumanicus*," she said, "the section including the so-called 'Cuman riddles,' hasn't been as well studied as Evliya Çelebi's *Seyahatname*. But at the end of the last century, it did receive a bit of attention. Count Geza Kuun, a Hungarian interested in the Cuman migration into Hungary in the thirteenth and fourteenth centuries, published an analysis. And a facsimile of the manuscript circulated a few years ago. I looked at it when it appeared in print."

She opened her eyes, but didn't raise them. Continued to focus on the tabletop. "The preservation of the manuscript in Venice has been regarded by most of the people who've read it as a happy accident. It's extraordinary that a fourteenth-century missionary's or merchant's lexicon of an obscure language like Kipchak should have survived. But no one is going to question the amazing luck that preserved it for the people who research this sort of thing. Now that I've read this copy, though, I don't think that its survival was an accident. This text was vital. It *remains* vital. And its content is extraordinarily important. Relevant. Even today."

"One hopes that its importance lies in more than the secret curative powers of wool of bat and tongue of dog," Maugham contributed helpfully.

Marion put her hands in her lap under the table to keep from trying to hit him. Took a steadying breath. "The first line of the first riddle," she continued, as though he hadn't spoken, "is in the imperative. It's a command. And do you know what it's commanding the reader to do?" She didn't wait for Maugham or Jeffrey to reply with something snide. "Let me just give you a quick translation," she offered. "It reads, in its entirety: 'Find it, find it; a dripping drop; a dripping drop of fire; a burning flash of fire; the answer—'"

"Petroleum!" Maugham had held up a delighted finger.

"The answer," she said, keeping her tone level, "is a butterfly."

"Well that makes no sense at all." Jeffrey wandered over to the fireplace. Threw a few more logs onto the fire and stirred up the flames.

"I'll explain the 'butterfly' answer in a moment," she said. "Although, it's true. Ordinarily, the answer to this sort of riddle in Turkic languages is—"

"Petroleum!"

"A mirror." She didn't bother to look up at Maugham.

"The point," she explained, "is that it's in the imperative mood. The first riddle tells us to find something. Something both liquid and fire. And the word that it uses for the burning flash of fire at the end, *göyedirgan*, is related to all sorts of organic and inorganic processes, not just burning, but also ripening, decaying, and—and desiring. It's a brilliant use of—"

"Thank you, Dr. Bailey." Maugham interrupted. "But in fact that's not the point. The point would be the bit where you explain to us what this has to do with our pipelines in the Caucasus. Or even—although I feel this will end in an equally arcane muddle—what it has to do with your analysis of Evliya Çelebi and his syphilitic Egyptians."

Jeffrey, smirking but silent, had returned to his position behind her. He was turned away again, looking out the window.

She rubbed her eyes. Considered refusing to speak any further. Then, resigned, she concluded that the consequences of remaining silent were too potentially catastrophic for her to indulge herself in that way. She forced herself to look up and hold Maugham's gaze. "I'll summarize."

"Good."

"There are a number of themes that appear in these riddles. And they're *all* relevant to—to your situation. But three are telling. The first has to do with a 'greasy,' or 'oily' snake—or sometimes a lizard or salamander—usually *yağlı yılan*—that hides under the ground. The 'greasy' in this formulation also suggests 'profit-making,' for what it's worth. And this snake or lizard, when it emerges from the ground, does so most often in a dull yellow color. Understand?"

"No," Maugham said. "But continue."

"The second theme has to do with the 'stinking' or sometimes 'smoking' lake into which the fire or dripping drops descend. Or from which they sometimes ascend." She stopped, but they remained silent. "And the third theme," she resumed, "has to do with a series of pits, or sometimes cauldrons, into which the drips and the fire and sometimes other objects are dropped. After which they're retrieved. And then dropped and burned again."

"Remarkable, Dr. Bailey." Maugham was smiling past her at Jeffrey again. "What you've said is still entirely incomprehensible. Care to try again?"

"The riddles," she explained, speaking slowly, as though to a stupid child, "are *riddles*, and hence every word and every formulation of words contains multiple meanings. They're effective *because* they're incomprehensible. But, nonetheless, let me put this to you in the simplest and stupidest of language, so that you can—"

"Now, now, Dr. Bailey."

"I know," she said sweetly, "how very valuable your time is."

"Indeed."

"As a set," she told him, "the riddles command us, first, to find something. Then they tell us *how* to find it. And then finally, they tell us *what* it is that we've found."

She paused. "The 'how' is straightforward. It involves digging under the ground for that snake. Or, to put this in terms that will perhaps, *finally*, begin to make some sense to you, it involves a mining operation. For something that, upon treatment, becomes a dullish yellow color. Someone in the thirteenth century discovered that if one digs for that 'snake'—the same 'snake' that we see in Evliya Çelebi's theriac—one can treat it such that its energy is released and what's left is a kind of yellowish product. Or by-product."

"Are you certain this isn't about petroleum, Marion?" Jeffrey's tone was no more than interested. He was willing, at least, to give her the benefit of the doubt.

"No," she said. "The material *is* fuel-like. But it's also solid. And the treatment process described in these riddles has nothing to do with the way that petroleum was treated in the medieval period. For lamps and the like. There are countless of descriptions of Caspian petroleum in medieval and modern sources—from Marco Polo to, in fact, Evliya Çelebi. These riddles are distinct from that genre."

She gathered her thoughts. "Here, the treatment is more an extended, repetitive sequence of burning, dripping, and scattering, burning, dripping, and scattering, over and over again, until there's both a 'red' product and a 'dull yellow' product. After which, the process begins again. Until those who are mining it release what the riddles describe as the 'living rock.' This 'living rock' they then also associate with 'bird's milk,' *kuşsüt*."

She resisted turning to speak to Jeffrey instead of to Maugham. "That phrase, bird's milk, is a common cipher in Turkic folklore for something that doesn't exist or is impossible. But its role in these riddles is the opposite of its role in other folklore. The riddles want to demonstrate that what doesn't exist—" She paused, trying to express her meaning properly. "—actually does. And then, also," she added, "there are the butterflies from the first riddle. It seems that the butterfly becomes—different, a skewed mirror image of itself—when it's flying near the pits where this metal is worked. Something happens to it during the mining and treatment process. It—changes, maybe? But these—altered— butterflies are also a clue. A means, in fact, of locating what was apparently a very secret mining and treatment process."

"'A very secret mining and treatment process.'" Maugham's tone was less playful than it had been before.

"Yes," she said.

"But not for petroleum."

"No."

"Some sort of mineral, you say."

"Yes."

"With—curative properties?" Wanting to lead her.

"Yes," she ventured. "But that's confusing too. There's a definite sense that the rock or the fire or the energy that's released after the mining and treatment is medicinal. But wrapped up in its medicinal qualities is a kind of decay. An illness. In fact, at least two of the riddles state explicitly that 'death has no cure.' Despite that, though," she stressed, "I'm confident that the 'snake' that the riddles command one to seek underground is the same 'snake' that Evliya Çelebi associates with Egyptian theriac." She fixed her eyes on him. "This theriac, you understand, that they were using to treat tumors."

Maugham pursed his lips. "What about the seventeenth-century pornographic vignettes?" he asked, ignoring her look. "Contemporary with the *Seyahatname*, weren't they?"

"Sixteenth-century pornographic vignettes," she corrected him. "Not contemporary with the *Seyahatname*. And yes. They were easy once I'd deciphered the riddles."

"Were they now?" Maugham's voice was acid. He was no longer entertained.

"Yes," she repeated, equally hostile. "Whereas Evliya Çelebi's travelogue describes the use of this—stone—in Egyptian medicine, and whereas the Cuman riddles describe how to extract it from the ground and treat it—"

She stopped. Considered. And then she pressed on. She must let Jeffrey know what she'd discovered. "The satires tell us where to mine it. Your maps do indicate a few small, paltry mines. To whet the appetite. The *letaif*, however, although referencing the maps, take you instead to an enormous, and uniquely rich, lode. Near Baku, it appears to be."

"Does it, Dr. Bailey?"

"Yes."

"Care to elaborate?"

"I wouldn't want to bore you. With excessive eye of newt and toe of frog."

"On the contrary." Maugham had folded his hands on the table in front of him again. "I'm transfixed."

"I thought you might be." She traced a design on the table with her fingertip. "First, there are several unexpected geographical reference points in the collection. Surprising to find in a satirical composition that was intended for a hothouse urban audience."

"For example?"

She pulled the sheaf of papers toward her. "This bit, to start with. Where Mount Elbrus, in the Caucasus—" she glanced up at him, "—although closer to the Black Sea than to the Caspian—is described as a tiny speck or grain of opium poppy in the shadow of the poet Ahmed Pasha's nose—"

"His 'nose?'" Jeffrey had walked up behind her and was reading over her shoulder. Laughing. "Are you certain you've translated that correctly?"

"The word is *burun*, Jeffrey." Waspish. "It also means empty, conceited arrogance."

"Dr. Bailey is the expert, Willcox." Maugham was chuckling as well. "Please continue, Dr. Bailey."

"This is one example of many," she said shortly. Then she paused and added, pleasantly: "but I've realized, Professor Maugham, that we may remain in disagreement about what we're seeking in the Caucasus. Or on the shores of the Caspian. Are you still convinced that these maps and manuscripts point to petroleum fields? To pipelines?"

Maugham's smile grew. Then he peered up at Jeffrey. "Oh dear, Willcox." Parody of regret. "I do believe we've been found out. She's so frightfully intelligent, isn't she?" He lowered his eyes to

Marion, who was watching him. Suspicious. "I confess it, Dr. Bailey." He put his hand over his heart. "The petroleum is, as you've deduced, no more than a cover. Although, as far as most of the people involved in this project are aware, our objective is an exploitation and informal extension of the existing Azeri pipelines. They needn't be told otherwise." He leaned forward again. "You, however, are now one of the initiated few. Once again, I commend you."

"You're not going after petroleum."

"No."

"What, then?"

"Why, the theriac, of course." He beamed at Marion. "Nothing wrong with seeking out a new medical technology, is there? Especially in the face of what looks to be a quite destructive coming war."

She narrowed her eyes at him.

"You don't believe me?" He was on the verge of laughter.

"I had a friend," she said. "During my last year at Cambridge. In 1921. He was considering sitting for a scholarship at St. Johns. Couldn't afford to study there otherwise."

"I had no idea that you had a friend at Cambridge," Maugham replied. "Willcox has always described your self-imposed isolation during your time there as a kind of deranged mania. I congratulate you on your acquisition of a social connection."

"We got on," she explained calmly, "because he was also excluded from the inner circle of Etonian, Pitt Club, toff—"

"Really, Marion." Jeffrey's voice was mild. "Why must you persist with this fantasy that you're some persecuted serving wench or milkmaid I abducted from her mud hut on the moor? Your father was a Professor of Mathematics at the University of Edinburgh. Your mother was a physician. You were no more 'excluded from the inner circle' at Cambridge than—than Maugham was in his time."

"Touched a nerve, Sir Jeffrey?" Maugham was laughing openly now. "And I'd thank you to take care with your comparisons. My people have always been but simple merchants."

"Yes," Jeffrey said patiently. "With the East India Company."

"Merchants nonetheless." Maugham returned to Marion. "You were saying?"

"My friend received the scholarship," she said shortly. "He became a research student in physics. At the Cavendish Laboratory. We've continued to communicate with one another, informally. *As* friends." She met Maugham's gaze. "His work is beyond my understanding, I must admit. I want to make that clear from the outset. But he's patient, and he explains things well, and I think I do have a grasp of its implications."

The smile had left Maugham's face. He was watching Marion carefully. Jeffrey had moved closer to her and put his hand on the back of her chair. She fought down the urge to push back the chair and stand.

"It seems that a great deal of progress has been made over the past two or three years in the field of atomic physics," she told them. "I think that's what they call it? Splitting the atom?" She held Maugham's eyes. "The work that he's been doing has obvious military implications. But the problem is that he and his colleagues haven't found an element that lends itself to the chain reaction necessary to move the energy that's released during their experiments from the laboratory to the battlefield."

She looked up at the ceiling. "But there are a few likely candidates. Some of the best are those that Becquerel and then the Curies isolated a few decades ago." She let her glance wander toward the bizarre painting above the fireplace. Rubbed her eyes again. She felt numb. "I read an article about their work. When it became popular. And do you know, Professor Maugham? What struck me about the processes that the Cuman riddles describe was how closely they echo the processes that Marie Curie perfected. When she worked with those—elements. Or, I suppose, speaking metaphorically, when she found the key to that living rock that cures and kills."

She stopped speaking and glared at Maugham. Deciding, finally, to make her accusation. "So, you want to know how it is that your 'pipelines' were sketched into maps that were drawn a good three to six hundred years before your minister began concerning himself with Caspian petroleum?" She paused, still fixing his eyes. "Well, there's only one possible explanation, as far as I can tell."

Maugham said nothing.

After waiting for a few seconds longer, she continued: "you have people on the ground there. Now. They're asking the local peasants where to find pockets of that rock. Not petroleum. Rock. I wouldn't be surprised if they're also asking about its treatment. Or about its tradition of treatment. And the peasants there, drawing on the same historical knowledge that's been warehoused in these manuscripts, are telling you what they know. What you want to know. In fact, helping you to draw new, up-to-date versions of those same maps."

She smiled at him. Scornful. "But they're not telling you everything now, are they? Because they don't trust you. Any more than I do. They know perfectly well that your goal in the Caucasus has nothing to do with *medicine*."

There was a tense silence in the room after she'd finished speaking, which lasted close to thirty seconds. Marion and Maugham sat across from one another, holding one another's eyes. And it was Jeffrey who defused the situation. "Do you know, Maugham," he said, breaking the atmosphere. "Despite the fact that I have now, categorically, won our wager, I'm finding myself less triumphant feeling than I imagined I'd be." He tapped his fingers a few times on the back of Marion's chair. "Are you convinced now that letting her at this material was a mistake?"

Marion twisted back to look at him. Her face fell as she saw his eyes and understood the implications of what he'd said. The half-apologetic smile was back.

"This isn't a shock to you." She thought she might cry. "You knew about it all along." She turned back to the table and dropped her face into her hands. "Oh God."

Jeffrey straightened. "Well, not the physics of it obviously. But I have read the H.G. Wells story." He paused. "I'd have thought you'd find it heartening, Marion. Yes, of course, the bomb itself is a shame. But its aftermath ushers in all that glorious internationalism. Isn't that what you're always claiming to be working toward? At least, when you're pressed to identify some coherent goal toward which you're directing your various indiscriminate acts of violence?"

Maugham wasn't listening to Jeffrey. Instead, he was continuing, impassive, to watch Marion as she pressed her fists to her eyes. His face was blank. All expression gone.

After a few seconds, he stood and brushed down his suit. "She stays here, Willcox, do you understand? Chain her to the floor if necessary. I'll have another battalion sent up here if you feel you need it." His eyes were hard. "She does not leave this room. She does not speak to anyone. No exceptions."

Maugham walked to the door and opened it. But he stopped before going through it. Looked back at Jeffrey, who had left Marion in her chair and was adding another log to the fire. "I want the location of that uranium."

Marion moved her hands from her face and looked at Maugham. Spoke before Jeffrey could reply. "You think that stashing me here will keep this a secret?"

Maugham didn't respond.

"Why do you think my organization sent you that note? Pointed you like well-trained little terriers toward those manuscripts? They know why you're there. They've known the whole time. And they wanted to you to be fully aware of that fact." She collected herself and smiled at him again. Bitter. "I wouldn't be surprised if the people you sent in there have already vanished." She paused. "They have, haven't they? They're gone." She laughed shortly when he still didn't speak. "And you have nothing."

Maugham turned to Jeffrey again. "Use the electricity if it takes more than a day."

He left the room.

$\mathcal{A}$FTER Maugham had closed the door, Marion covered her face with her hands again. She didn't want to see anything. To interact with anyone. Jeffrey, having built up the fire, turned back to her. He watched her for a few seconds, and then he said: "I'll bring your tea now." When she didn't answer, he glanced over at the table. "Unless you'd prefer the scotch."

"Tea." She hadn't changed her position.

"Very well."

While she waited for Jeffrey to return, she mentally explored methods of escape. She couldn't wait, passive, for him to elicit what he wanted from her. But one by one, she dismissed each of her ideas as ineffective. The tower, anachronistic caricature though it was, served its purpose remarkably well. It was solid. Impenetrable.

She also suspected that neither Jeffrey nor Maugham had exaggerated the military presence they said they'd established beyond its walls. Even if she made it out, she'd never reach a road or a railway station without someone stopping her. She let her hands fall to the table. Curled her fingers into fists. Tried to keep from crying.

Jeffrey returned with a tray containing a large pot of tea, two cups, milk, sugar, and a plate of Jaffa Cakes. He closed the door, placed the tray on the table, and occupied the chair Maugham had used. He poured Marion a cup of tea and handed it to her. She splashed milk into it as he poured his own cup, and then she looked across at him.

"We needn't begin immediately," he said, sipping his tea, watching her over his cup. "Maugham won't start pressing for another week or so. Tantrum aside, he knows I need at minimum three or four days to get him useful results."

She couldn't think of a reply. Swallowed. Nodded.

"I really would advise you, though, Marion, to stop provoking him so brazenly. There will come a time when he no longer finds it diverting." He set down his tea. "You don't want to see him angry. Truly you don't. Someday, I'll tell you what happened to his wife. Horrifying story. Even to me."

"Maugham," she said, incensed, "is a—"

"Very bad man." He picked up a Jaffa Cake. Considered it. "Yes. But you must simply accept that fact. Without reacting to it. If you want to survive."

"Maybe I don't want to—"

"Yes, you do." He broke off a small piece of the cake and popped it into his mouth. "For the sake of your son. We've already been through this."

"Not on your terms, I don't. We've also been through *that*." She drank more of her tea. Wished she could eat but recognized it as unwise in her current state.

"Perhaps." He thought for a moment. Changed the subject. "May I ask you a question?"

"No."

He smiled. "If we ignore," he began, "the personal considerations—your aversion to Maugham, your refusal, ever, to give me the slightest quarter—what really is so wrong with providing a little boost to our nuclear physics program? I imagine it would even help your friend's career."

"Are you insane?"

"That isn't an answer."

"I never promised you an answer."

He watched her, affectionate, for a few seconds longer. Then he said: "someone is going to develop the technology, Marion. It's inevitable. Who would you choose? If not us?"

"Not you."

"Who, then? The Americans?" He examined her face, interested. "The Germans?"

"Not. You."

"Most of the Caspian is Soviet territory now." He lifted his chin. "In a manner of speaking. Would you prefer the Russians develop it first?"

She pushed back her chair and stood. Glared down at him. "*Not. You.*"

He looked disappointed. "Ah well. It isn't all that relevant to what you and I will be discussing. I was merely curious." He stood as well. "I'll leave you to your own devices now. We'll start work tomorrow morning after you've had some time to think." The corner of his mouth went down. "And I'll hold off on preparing the electricity for the moment."

She walked to the fireplace and stared down at the fire, hugging her waist. Didn't watch as he opened the door. And then closed it, gently, behind him.

Instead of returning to the manuscripts, which she knew would agitate her, she made another tour of the tower. Testing the walls. Looking for any way out. Useless. Then she walked back to the table and forced herself, standing, to eat a Jaffa Cake. Surprised herself by keeping it down. Ate a second one. Finished the tea.

Motivated by the artificial optimism that came from the caffeine rather than from any plan she had formulated to resist Jeffrey's questioning, she turned back to the sixteenth-century satires. Thus far, she hadn't revealed anything to Jeffrey or Maugham about the location of the uranium. They knew it was there. And they knew that the *letaif* concealed instructions on accessing it. But they didn't know how to consult those instructions.

She rubbed her cheek, thinking. Then she came to a decision. Rather than returning to the text, she'd pack away the manuscripts in her carpet bag. If an opportunity to extricate herself from her situation presented itself, she'd take at the very least the satires with her. At best, she'd make off with all three manuscripts. Whatever happened, though, she'd have difficulty moving quickly with pages scattered all over the table. Organizing them would be a useful occupation.

Pleased by her targeted activity, she gathered the leaves of vellum and paper together into a single pile, wrapped them in the dress that she knew she'd never wear again, and slid them into her bag. If Jeffrey wanted to consult them tomorrow, she could retrieve them. And if not, she had them all in one, accessible place.

After she'd finished, she ate another Jaffa Cake. Then, reconciled to a dreary and anxious afternoon, she curled herself up next to the window. Watched the pallid water streaming over the rocks.

SHE slept better during the night than she had expected to, but she was shaky and restless when she woke. And she opened her eyes earlier in the morning than she had previously, the dawn light just illuminating the ceiling. She sat up, left the pallet, and fed the fire. Then she plaited her hair and drank a cup of water. Looking about the room, at loose ends, uncertain of what she ought to do, she wandered over to her carpet bag. More to draw comfort from the manuscript pages than to dress or prepare herself.

Squatting in front of it, she unbuckled it, and peered at her rumpled clothing, trying to decide what to wear for the day. Then, shocked, she sat back on her heels. After a few seconds of stunned disbelief, she laughed, reached into her bag, and pulled out a small pistol with a tiny barrel and wooden grip. Attached to a note. Encoded. From her organization.

The pistol was obviously not meant for use on a battlefield. But Marion, never confident with weaponry, was delighted by it. Her talents ran toward invisibility and disengagement rather than shooting or combat, anyway. The little gun would serve her needs perfectly. And far more important to her than the weapon was the note. It was not only evidence that her superiors hadn't discarded her, but a strategy for getting her out of, and away from, the tower. Full of energy, she re-secured the manuscript pages in her bag, changed into the warmest clothing she had, and hid the pistol at her waist under a thick, woolen jumper. Then she paced the room, impatient, waiting for Jeffrey. Wished she had any other shoes than her useless strapped high heels.

As she should have expected, he took his time. Giving her a chance to dwell on what he planned to do to her. When the room was as bright as it ever got—a watery sunbeam, even, illuminating part of the table—the door finally opened. Jeffrey entered, without food or tea, but carrying a file folder. He was wearing dark wool trousers in a grey check, and a white shirt. No tie, the top button unfastened.

He looked surprised to see her standing near the table, where she'd stopped mid-stride upon hearing him at the door. Apparently expecting to find her curled up against the window. Nonetheless, he didn't speak as he shut the door behind him. Instead, after a few seconds of silence, he nodded in the direction of the table.

He looked about to tell her to sit, but before he got the word out, she pulled the gun from under her jumper, held it in two hands, aimed at his left foot, and squeezed the trigger. When the bullet hit, he exhaled sharply, paled, and dropped the folder. Then, making an effort to push down the pain, he looked up at her under a lock of hair that had fallen over his forehead. "Damn it, Marion." More annoyed than hurt. "That was my toe."

She gestured with the gun toward the table. "Sit. Hands flat on the table."

He stayed where he was. "*That's* what they got to you?" He was peering at the pistol. "A pre-War baby Nambu? What will you do? Use it as an auxiliary measure when your samurai longbow lets you down?"

"Sit," she repeated, angry. "Or I'll shoot your other foot as well."

He limped to the table, sat, and folded his hands. There was a spot of blood on the floor where she'd hit him. "Only," he said to her, "because I fear that the combination of your hopeless marksmanship and the notorious inaccuracy of that museum piece will leave me with a hole in the head if you do try for my other foot."

She backed toward her carpet bag, keeping the pistol aimed at his leg, preparing herself for any move he might make against her. Then she leaned over and reached for the bag's handles. When he kept still, she straightened, moved in the direction of the door, and pulled it open. "I'll be back in April. For Ian's Easter Holiday."

"You'll be back," he said, "in twenty minutes. Accompanied by a battalion of soldiers." He still sounded no more than irritated. "At least, I hope you'll be back. Those men have been out there bored and freezing for a week now, with nothing to do but snipe at pine marten. They may be resentful enough at this point to forget that their orders are to immobilize rather than to kill you." He watched as she moved through the door, the gun still trained on him. "When they do bring you back," he said, angry now, "the gloves are coming off."

She smiled at him. "You'll want to see about that wound first, Jeffrey."

She slipped out the door and ran down the stone stairs until she reached, as her message had instructed her, the third arrowslit. Her orders were to avoid the landward side of the castle altogether. If she could make it out on the seaward side, there would be a boat waiting for her behind one of the jagged rocks at the base of the bluff. And the soldiers, if they were indeed waiting for her beyond the tower's gates, would never see her.

At the third arrowslit, she let down her bag, shoved the pistol into the waistband of her trousers, and crawled into the embrasure. Holding her breath, she pushed at one of the large stones that surrounded the slit. Then she exhaled. Her instructions had been good. The stone had been loosened for her, and it slipped out of place before crashing into the surf below. She pushed out a second and third stone, taking no more than thirty seconds altogether, until the opening in the wall of the tower was wide enough to accommodate her.

Knowing that it was a matter of minutes, if not seconds, before Jeffrey followed her, she worked rapidly. Extended her arm through the opening she'd made, feeling for the climbing rope that had been left in a depression in the exterior stone. Found it, secured the hook to a sturdy part of the arrowslit, lifted her carpet bag, and crammed herself through the opening in the wall. Then she lowered herself toward the beach and foaming water below.

Before she had reached her mark—a flat, circular crack in one of the rocks—she heard a bullet slice through the water. She looked up and cursed silently. A soldier, calm and precise, was taking careful aim at her.

She knew that his orders must be to harass her rather than to kill or hurt her because he hadn't shot through her rope. A conclusion that comforted her. But she also didn't want to give him a chance to block her path. She looked down and saw that she had no more than five feet left to drop. Steeling herself, she slid from the rope toward the tide pool.

She hit the pool, stumbling. Enraging a gannet. She also ripped up one leg of her trousers as she lurched against a thin outcropping of stone. She felt a sharp pain and a wave of nausea when a spray of salt water hit the gash that had opened in her calf.

Instinctively she crouched, waiting for a second bullet. Nothing came. She looked up at the tower. The soldier had disappeared. They were undoubtedly spreading out toward the beach as a unit. She didn't know whether Jeffrey and Maugham had also organized security on the water, but she suspected they hadn't. Without help from the outside, she'd never have been able to escape by sea. And they wouldn't have expected her organization to contact her in the tower. Nonetheless, she didn't want to test her hypothesis.

Instead, sliding down the rock into the hectic water, she waded toward her encounter point. The water, close to freezing, with a strong undertow, reached her knees. And she was grateful when her feet and legs went numb.

She felt less so when she saw nothing but water, spray, and foam at her rendezvous. But then, looking more closely, she spotted the bow of a tiny wooden boat lift on a roller and smash down behind the rock. She frowned, confused, and pushed toward it through the water.

It was an open, two-seat, inboard wooden racing boat, low in the water, no more than thirteen feet long. A woman, tall with loose brown hair and a Scandinavian-looking oilskin coat and rubber boots, was holding it in place on the surf. She nodded, dour, at Marion, took her bag to shove into a storage area in the bow, and then helped her into the red leather seat. The seat, which was drenched, left Marion colder than she had felt in the sea.

Once Marion was seated, the woman launched herself into the boat, causing it to dip precipitously. She pushed them away from the rock with one hand whilst simultaneously starting the motor with the other. Then she picked up speed, sliced between two jagged rocks, and headed out into the open water. After they'd cleared the rocks, the waves became rollers, and the boat, planing, crashed hard into the top of every one it hit. Marion looked behind her for pursuing vessels. She couldn't see anything, but she thought she ought to warn the woman.

"They saw me leave the tower," she shouted over the wind and motor. "They may attempt to follow us."

The woman snorted. "They're welcome to." She had a Swedish accent. "Crandall's never built a flyer faster than this one. She reaches thirty-five miles per hour even in crap like this. We could circle back, let you say your goodbyes, and still be out of sight of their sluggard assault boats five minutes later."

Marion smiled. "Let's not do that."

The woman, who didn't seem entertained, grunted.

Marion looked back again and peered out over the leaden, rolling sea. No one was behind them. She was convinced. She faced forward and relaxed into the seat, enjoying the ride.

Fifteen minutes later, an industrial icebreaker, close to two-hundred-sixty feet in length, appeared off their bow. The woman pulled back on the throttle of the flyer and slowed into a wide arc around the ship before reversing against the steel hull. The smell of the engines hit Marion like a physical blow, but before she registered more than the stench and the substantial size of the boat, two hooks came down from a hoist on the deck.

The woman secured the hooks to loops at the bow and stern of the flyer and shouted up to invisible crew on the deck. The flyer lifted out of the water, and a few minutes later hands were guiding Marion onto the wooden deck of the ship. She looked about her, saw that the boat was flying Japanese flags, which surprised her, but not unduly, and then turned to thank the woman for transporting her away from Caithness.

But the woman had already disappeared. Instead, a member of the crew, polite and speaking Azeri Turkish, asked Marion whether she wanted to warm herself and rest. She thanked him, accepting his offer as well as the carpet bag he'd retrieved from the flyer's bow. Paid little attention to the details of the ship as he led her below to a spartan cabin with a private bunk, toilet, and sink.

He asked her whether she needed anything, and when she saw the apples and water that had been left on a stool bolted to the floor, she shook her head. He left her alone, and she attacked the apples. When she'd finished, she pulled the little pistol from her waistband and placed it in her carpet bag. Then she removed her shredded trousers and examined her lacerated leg. The sea water had cleaned away the blood, and the gash was less serious than she had feared it would be.

She ripped a few strips of cloth from her trousers to wrap over the wound and then put on new, dry clothing from her bag. After that, pausing and considering the wood and metal cabin, painted a bright white, she concluded that she couldn't be faulted for crawling into the bunk to sleep. Yes, it was four in the afternoon. But darkness was falling outside. And she'd worry about where the boat was taking her tomorrow.

Satisfied by her decision, she flipped over onto her back, pulled a rough, green blanket over her chest, and let the sound of the boat's engines put her to sleep.

The Soviet Union
February, 1935

MARION woke to the vibration of the icebreaker making energetic and unobstructed headway through the Norwegian Sea. She slid out of the bunk, folded the blanket, and straightened her jumper and trousers. Decided not to change into new clothing. But she did waver, doubtful, over her shoes. Not only were they inappropriate—feminine, heeled, and meant for the dress she'd worn to Temple Grove—but they were also sodden and disintegrating from wading through the Caithness surf. After an annoyed moment, she sat on the bunk and strapped them over her feet. The only other option was wandering the passageways of the boat in her socks.

Following another split-second of uncertainty, she also grabbed her carpet bag containing the gun and the manuscripts. She had complete trust in the ship and the crew. But it would have been stupid to leave her material unwatched in a makeshift visitor's cabin. She ducked through the oval door into the passage and made her way forward toward the upper decks of the ship.

The boat's motion gave her an idea of its design, and after a few wrong turns, she was climbing the ladder to the bridge. The crew had made no effort to question her or to stop her progress. If anything, they showed deference.

When she entered the room, the pilot, concentrating on the view from the helm, was speaking to a slim man wearing a fisherman's sweater, oilskin coat, and boots. Recognizing him, she lit up. "Mr. Hashimoto!"

The man turned and bowed. Smiled as well. "Dr. Bailey. I'm pleased to see you looking refreshed."

They had both instinctively fallen into speaking Istanbul Turkish, although Kingoro Hashimoto could converse in a number of European languages as well as in Japanese. And she was looking forward to speaking further with him. But even so, she felt shy. Despite having seen the boat's flags the previous afternoon, she'd never have guessed that he was her contact. His career had been as fraught as hers had been over the past decade, possibly more so, and he looked duly aged. She wasn't certain what she ought to mention and what she ought to pretend she didn't know.

Sensing her embarrassment, Hashimoto held out a hand, gesturing her back out the door. "Shall we walk to the galley? We'll speak more while you eat."

She nodded, turned, and climbed down the ladder, clutching her carpet bag. He followed, and then he pointed her to the deck below, where a few members of the crew, coming off a watch, were drinking coffee. He indicated a square table with two chairs, secured to the floor, in the corner of the room. Once they'd sat, and once Marion had set her carpet bag beside her, a sailor brought Marion her own cup of coffee and a sweet roll topped with coconut.

Hashimoto saw her examining the roll and laughed. "Skolebrød, I think? We took on provisions in Alesund." He watched her take an experimental bite. "I don't think the Norwegians eat these for breakfast. But try telling that to an Azeri chief steward."

She swallowed. "It's good." Took a sip of her coffee. "Your crew is from Azerbaijan?"

"Most of them are Azeri and Georgian. There are also a few dissatisfied and patriotic Poles and Ukrainians."

"Under Japanese flags?"

He smiled again and didn't speak.

"Mr. Hashimoto," she said, unable to control her curiosity. "What is this? I'm delighted to see you again. More than delighted. But the last time we spoke was in 1929, in Istanbul. You were working as a military attaché," she grinned at him, "to your consulate in Turkey. Sending out all those feelers to Trotsky, hidden away on his island in the Marmara Sea. Weren't you going to use him as a flashpoint to bring down the new Russian menace before it established a foothold?"

"Not new to us, Dr. Bailey. Our disagreements with Russia reached a crisis point in 1905."

"Yes," she replied, taking another bite of pastry. "And you won that war. Everything was resolved."

"But they never accepted that," he countered. "And now we're dealing with an entirely changed entity. This Soviet Union that's 'never been defeated.' Different psychology. Same problem."

"Wait," she said. "You're distracting me. I assure you, I'm interested in the geopolitics. But before that, I'd much rather hear about you. Gossip. After that, I give you my word, you can deflect my attention back to the job."

He was entertained. "Only if you'll reciprocate with the story of your own tribulations. Since Istanbul."

"Agreed." She considered for a few seconds. "Although I'm quite certain that my tribulations haven't been as politically interesting as yours have." She swallowed more of the coffee. "So, you were in Turkey until 1930, correct? Then you went home?"

"Yes."

"Big promotion. 'Head of the Russia Section of the Second Intelligence Department of the General Staff?' Impressive."

"Indeed," he said. "If also disagreeably prominent."

"And then—" She watched him, doubtful whether to laugh. Forced herself to keep a straight face. "And then you tried to bring down the government?" She paused. "Twice?"

Catching her mood, he laughed himself. "I had my orders."

"Your orders."

"I had to get myself out of the Intelligence Department hierarchy," he said. "Back into the field. Otherwise our people couldn't do anything with me. A couple of failed coup attempts are an extraordinarily efficient means of effecting a quick removal from the corridors of power."

She stared at him. "Either a quick removal from the corridors of power or an equally quick secret execution. You were lucky."

He made brief eye contact with the sailor who had brought Marion her coffee, and a second cup appeared at his elbow a few seconds later. He took a sip. "I'm too useful to Japan's war effort to be executed."

"But you did disappear." She ate another piece of the pastry. "To be honest, I feared you'd been eliminated."

"I was demoted. To the Reserves." Mild regret. "Same effect. Personal disgrace is a good cover for what we're doing, Dr. Bailey. Haven't you learned a similar lesson over the past ten years?"

She felt herself blush. Didn't answer.

He nodded. "I can see that you have. And gossip from your direction reaches me as well. But the fact that you're here now also suggests that our superiors have found your adversity as productive, and even as profitable, as my own." He sipped his coffee, watching her. "Mine has allowed me a free hand in the Caucasus that I would never have had as 'Head of the Russia Section of the Second Intelligence Department of the General Staff.' And yours," he nodded in her direction, "has granted you access not only to that collection of manuscript material that the British plundered from Iraq, but also to the inner workings of a less than well-studied branch of their service."

"Mr. Hashimoto—" she began in protest. Uncomfortable.

"Forgive me." He smiled again. "Perhaps I feel a pang of envy. Your situation is, I'm aware, painful. But it's also hidden. Mine, I fear, will become only more public in the coming years." The same fleeting look of regret. "But we have our work to comfort us."

"I congratulate you," she said. "You've left me thoroughly morose. I regret goading you into gossip. Fascinating though it was to hear."

"You *should* be morose," he replied with the same hint of humor. "This is serious business."

She finished her pastry and drank another swallow of the coffee. "As I've gathered. Could you explain to me the next step? I was forced to make educated guesses while they had me walled up in Scotland."

"Yes." He paused. "I'll outline the next few steps for you. I want to be certain first, though, that you've had sufficient time and access to the material to locate our target. Have you?"

"Is it our target? Or are we simply sending a message to the British that their interest in it is no longer secret?" A trace memory of the panic she had been feeling in the tower came back to her. "I can locate it, I'm certain. But what happens then? Our people can't be interested in initiating a mining operation."

"Correct," he said. "I believe our intention is to obscure it." He nodded to her bag on the floor. "And your next move is to access the fourth map, in Baku, containing the instructions on identifying the lode. Having accessed that map—"

"It isn't a map. It's—"

He held up a hand. "I needn't know what it is. Better that I don't."

She nodded, silent.

"So, having accessed that—we'll call it a map—you'll drop it with a dispatcher who will contact you in the usual way. The dispatcher will have his own instructions."

She nodded again. Still nervous. Then she took psychological refuge in detail. "How will I travel to Baku?"

"By train." Cryptic. "But before I describe to you your itinerary, let me give you additional background on the connection you'll be making in Azerbaijan."

"All right. I'm listening."

"His name," Hashimoto said, "is Dr. Polat."

She couldn't help raising her eyebrows. Refrained from commenting.

"Yes. I know," he agreed. "But rest assured. He is a quite straightforward Azeri intellectual working with the resistance against Soviet rule. He was cultivated in the early 1930s by my successor in Turkey, Masatane Kanda. Mr. Kanda has a fanciful streak."

"I understand," she said, still fighting a smile.

"In broad terms," he continued, "our work in the Caucasus—as well as in Ukraine and other recently Soviet territories—has been to fund and promote local anti-communist nationalist movements. We've subsidized a revolutionary publication, *Kavkaz*, that's helped us to identify potential resources in that regard. Dr. Polat is one such resource."

She spent a few seconds processing what he had told her. Then she considered. "'Our work?' Do you mean the work you do for Japan? This doesn't sound like our superiors."

"Yes," he replied. Innocent. "The work that I do for Japan. Much like the work that you do for Great Britain."

She blushed again and looked down. "No," she elaborated. "I mean, is Mr. Kanda—"

"Mr. Kanda is not one of us," he said. "And the Soviets have already lifted his cipher. He's unaware, but everything he communicates to Tokyo goes direct to Moscow. Sometimes only to Moscow."

"But 'Dr. Polat'—"

"Is one of us," Hashimoto said.

"I understand," she repeated. "So I'll travel—by train—to Baku and make quiet contact with Dr. Polat. At the journal's offices—?"

"No," he said. "We want you visible. To attract the attention of the other interested parties in the area. The British have already shown their hand. Or," he nodded at her, "thanks to your work, their hand has been exposed. But there are indications that one, or even two, additional organizations are also watching this situation. We'd like to know who they are. You'll leave a few false trails. Before you secure the fourth—map."

"If the British catch up to me there," she said, "they'll collect me. Immediately. Extreme visibility doesn't seem an effective means of counteracting that."

"We don't think they will," he told her. "They want this uranium very badly. We think, now that you've gone under, they'll watch you instead. It's no longer in their interest to stop your progress. If they collect you, they'll be forced to start from the beginning again."

A familiar dull resentfulness coalesced at the edges of her mind. She pushed it away. But not before she succumbed to a sick inward protest at the fact that her primary skill—disappearing—was increasingly irrelevant to the work she was doing for her organization. Hashimoto, watching her expression, met her eyes, understanding. "Invisibility is a luxury, Dr. Bailey."

"Yes," she said shortly. "I'll stop interrupting you. Tell me how I'm to contact Dr. Polat."

"You'll be travelling as a British leftist. A Turkologist attending a symposium in Baku on Marxist ethnography. It's a painfully inadequate veneer, but that's the point." He drank the remainder of his coffee. "The symposium's participants will be staying at the Intourist Hotel. Construction on the building completed last year—a demonstration of Soviet prosperity and engineering. Dr. Polat will cross you there. The hotel is entirely porous. If you do find yourself harassed, you'll have little difficulty making use of its idiosyncratic architectural features."

"I understand."

"But first," he continued, "I'll explain to you how you'll enter the city."

"Thank you."

"It will take this ship nine more days, without excessive ice, to reach the port of Murmansk, on Russia's north coast. We'll dock at night, without flags. While we deal with the inevitable questions surrounding our visit there, Inger will take you to shore in the flyer. We'll be certain to dock with enough force to break up any ice that would obstruct her boat."

When she nodded her comprehension, he continued. "There will be a sled waiting to transport you to the railway station. From there, you'll travel by rail to Leningrad, Moscow, and then south through the Caucasus. You ought to reach Azerbaijan by the beginning of next month. The symposium begins on the seventh of February."

"I haven't any Slavic languages," she said, coming to terms with her unexpected itinerary. "I have Turkish, Farsi, Arabic, and a few romance languages. But I can't speak a word of Russian."

"Shame on you." He smiled. "But, in fact, Dr. Bailey, it's better that way. We're hoping to keep you unobtrusive until we unveil you in Baku. You'd be suspicious speaking non-native Russian on the train. Or even inadvertently signaling an understanding of some stray conversation. So, on your way down, you're a keen, scholarly tourist to any Russians you might meet. Meanwhile, the British won't expect you to travel from the north at all. Knowing your background, they'll be watching the lines through Turkey and Iran. In this one case, ignorance is beneficial."

"Very well," she said, still uncertain. Then she thought further. "In fact, I'm looking forward to it. I've never moved in Russia before. Always on the fringes, you know."

He held her gaze for a moment longer, companionable, and then stood. She stood as well, clutching her carpet bag. "We'll have the opportunity to speak again, won't we, Mr. Hashimoto? I've missed the conversations we used to have in Istanbul."

"I'll look forward to it, Dr. Bailey." He bowed again, slight, correct. "I'm pleased that this situation has brought us together another time."

They left through opposite doors of the galley. Marion to return to her cabin, and Hashimoto to return to the bridge. She felt buoyant. The energy that animated her when she had a job, away from Jeffrey, was now back in full force. She had to resist running back along the passageways to her door.

*W*HEN she reached her cabin, moving at a deliberately sedate pace, she was pleased to discover a new plate of apples and a pitcher of water waiting for her. More welcome were a heavy wool fisherman's sweater similar to Hashimoto's, a shearling trench coat, double breasted and waterproof, wool gloves and hat, and a pair of felt valenki boots with dark green galoshes to wear over them.

She wasted no time in pulling on the warm clothing. Eager to watch the icebreaker's progress from the outside, she knew that as they entered the arctic circle, she'd need proper protection from the weather to do so. The clothing the crew had found for her was ideal. Taking a few bites of apple, and then dropping the hateful shoes she had brought from Scotland into a rubbish bin on her way out, she hurried back up to the deck.

As the boat crossed from the Norwegian Sea into the Barents Sea, Marion spent most of her time standing at the stern, watching the waves and weather. The short to non-existent daylight hours didn't bother her, accustomed as she was to childhood winters spent in Scotland. And the accumulated layers of ice over every exposed bit of metal on the ship, from stanchions to hidden guns, intrigued her, protected as she was in her heavy clothing.

She went inside only to sleep and to drink an occasional cup of coffee with Hashimoto. Reliving with him the time she had spent in Istanbul just before returning to England with her son left her wistful. And angry. Although she and Hashimoto had been no more than friendly acquaintances in 1929—part of the same world and therefore companionably and instinctively aware of what could and could not become conversational fodder—being in contact with him again reminded her of how drastically her situation had changed, disintegrated, over the past five years.

At the time, a foreigner alone with a toddler, never knowing when or whether she'd be picked up by someone sent by the British authorities, she had felt scared and confined. But her restricted freedom of movement then was nothing compared to what she would experience once Jeffrey had re-entered her life. Hashimoto, a fragment of her existence from before Jeffrey's renewed interest in her, brought home to her the mistakes she'd made since her return. Nonetheless, she couldn't keep from seeking out free moments with Hashimoto. To remember those few months with Ian in Istanbul. She liked him too much.

The nine days to Murmansk, however, passed quickly. And aside from an unpleasant few hours during which they did encounter fast ice, riding up on top of it, ramming and cracking it with their bow, it was an uneventful journey. They reached the port of Murmansk on the twenty-eighth of January, late in the evening, in thick darkness. The crew lowered Inger and Marion over the side before the icebreaker had been secured to the dock.

Under the sound of the ship's engine, Inger brought the flyer toward an unused pier at the edge of the port, and Marion crawled out of her seat, which was now slick with ice. After that, she climbed the three rungs of an equally treacherous ladder hanging down toward the water. Inger, still not speaking, tossed Marion's bag up to the dock beside her. Then she sped away, back toward the icebreaker.

Once on the dock, Marion pulled her hat further down over her ears and pushed a gloved hand into the interior of her coat to reassure herself that her clean passport and her railway tickets to Baku were still in place. A stupid move. Signaling to potential eyes where she kept her valuables. But she couldn't help herself. Being unable to communicate in the local language made her feel nervous. Amateur.

Having satisfied herself that the tickets and papers were where they ought to be, she lifted her carpet bag and walked, resolute, down the pier and toward the road skirting the waterfront. She knew that the sleigh was supposed to meet her as she walked, but she didn't have a specific crossing point. She tried to project conviction as she trudged, sliding occasionally, along the deserted road. And before she had gone more than ten minutes, she heard a horse, moving at a walk, pulling up behind her.

She stopped, stepped back from the road, and looked at the sleigh—agricultural, made of rotting wood—drawing to a halt. A figure covered beyond recognition in layers of winter clothing gestured her into the back. Bundles of firewood frozen into a solid heap. She climbed over the brittle cargo and wedged herself into a depression between two bundles.

The figure turned back to her as the sleigh lurched into motion. "We'll reach the station in a half hour, Dr. Bailey." Azeri Turkish. A male voice. Marion settled back against the wood and silently thanked Hashimoto.

After thirty minutes of ragged motion, during which she registered little beyond her frozen breath on the air and a complete absence of stars in the night sky, the sleigh drew to an irresolute stop. They were in a side alley, but Marion could see the top of the station building a few streets over. The man jumped from the sleigh, spent a few seconds calming the horse, and then walked back to help Marion down to the icy mud.

When she was standing, clutching her carpet bag and about to thank him, he stopped her with a gesture and reached under a second bundle of wood. Retrieved a cloth sack and presented it to her. "Food."

She took it in the hand that wasn't holding her bag. "Thank you."

"There's a night train twice every week. It leaves in an hour. If there are no delays, it will take you three days to reach Leningrad." A hint of a smile that Marion could somehow sense through the clothing. "With delays—" a movement that could have been a shrug. "You'll want to stay on the train. Whatever the situation."

"Thank you," she repeated.

"In Leningrad, you'll switch to the Moscow line. Seven hours. And then from Moscow to Baku. Four days. With luck."

"Thank you," she said a third time.

Then she turned and walked, carrying both the sack and her carpet bag, in the direction of the station. When she entered and oriented herself, her train was already waiting at the platform. It looked no different from countless trains she'd boarded in other parts of Europe and Asia. And so, showing a not entirely feigned touristic eagerness—out of place as the act was in the middle of the night, in Murmansk—she approached a passenger carriage.

No one stopped her as she climbed up into the aisle and chose an empty bench seat. She looked at the other passengers scattered throughout the carriage, but they were uninterested in her. Pleased to find herself the object of so little curiosity, she opened the sack she had taken from the sleigh and smiled to herself. Even with an extended delay, she needn't worry about provisions. It was packed with food. Heavy emphasis on cured meat.

She pulled out a bottle of cold black tea and took a few swallows. Replaced it. Looked about her a few more times. Just as she was wondering whether or not the train would move, the carriage jerked into motion, pulling them out of the station. There had been no indication that they would be leaving. No announcement. The train simply started.

Nonplussed, she peered out the window into the blackness. Nothing identifiable. And then, after waiting for a conductor or ticket taker who never appeared, she rested. Leaned against her window, closed her eyes, and forced herself not to dwell on what she would meet in Baku.

I N fact, her trains kept to a precise schedule. She had no difficulty switching to the Derbent line in Moscow, and aside from a mild bewilderment that no one, at any point, ever bothered to check her tickets or papers, her impressions of Soviet rail travel were benign. She stepped, blinking, into Baku's railway station, late nineteenth-century imperial glory still intact, on the morning of the fifth of February. Clutching her carpet bag and her now near-empty sack of food.

If any eyes were in attendance, her rumpled, unbuttoned shearling and visible backache from days of semi-reclined travel would have convinced them that she was precisely what she purported to be: a leftist academic. Keen enough to suffer through extended austere rail travel to reach a meeting of the minds. But then, her goal wasn't to convince the eyes. It was to excite their attention.

Stifling a sigh, she walked toward the building's exit, intending to find someone willing to drive her to the Intourist Hotel. A line of vehicles, set in motion by a dizzying array of propulsion methods, was waiting outside the station. They were all private. Entrepreneurial citizens boosting their minimal salaries with a bit of work on the side.

Standing on the pavement, she considered. She could easily protect herself should a driver try to extort money from her once she was in a vehicle. But she didn't want to have to do that. She was tired. And so, coming to a decision, she walked toward a very small man who was manifestly proud of his very large 1933 GAZ-A. Painted a bright, almost painful, pale blue.

When the man saw her approaching, he walked toward her, efficient and non-threatening, and held out his hand for her bag. Said something to her in tentative Russian.

"I'm sorry," she said, embarrassed, speaking Azeri Turkish. "I don't understand Russian." After a fraction of a second of surprise, the man grinned. "Good. Russian's an ugly language. But how—?" Realization. "The symposium. Intourist Hotel, then?"

She nodded, kept her bag, and slid into the back of the car. Before he closed the door, she settled on a fare. Then she let him shut the door on her, and she relaxed into the abnormally soft, cushioned seat. He walked to the driver's seat, started the engine, and pulled out into traffic.

"You're German?" he asked as he moved slowly yet inexorably through gridlocked streets.

"No," she said. "I teach in England."

"England." He nodded a few times, unable to find a suitable comment to make to her about Britain, its policies, or its people. She was grateful.

After an intricate maneuver around a bit of wall from the old city, the driver changed the subject. "You'll enjoy the Intourist Hotel. It's brand new. Same architect built Lenin's mausoleum in Moscow."

"Wonderful."

The driver had a more nuanced grasp of tone than she would have thought. He made amused eye contact with her in the mirror. "You don't sound like a Marxist intellectual."

"I'll work harder on it." Annoyed with herself for the transparency.

But then, she wasn't supposed to be effective. Incompetence was what they wanted from her. She shifted uncomfortably in her seat. Being detected by a taxi driver five minutes off her train, however, was galling. If not her fault. His intuition about her was undoubtedly a by-product of Darwinian survival in the new Soviet system.

A few minutes later, when he pulled up in front of the extravagantly clean, modernist building, she gave him his fare in silence. But he couldn't resist one final swipe as he opened the door for her. "Long live the Revolution."

She stared at him, exasperated. Then she couldn't help laughing as well. "Thank you," she said firmly.

After that, she turned and walked into the hotel. Now that she knew of its connection to Lenin's tomb, the lobby did strike her as elegiac. Although what it was mourning, she wasn't entirely certain. And the hint of the funereal was more than counterbalanced by optimistic pillars and plants— not to mention a serpentine grand staircase leading to the rooms above.

As she moved toward the reception desk, her glance fell on a professorial type she recognized from her time as a postgraduate student at Cambridge. Wandering the lobby. Looking for a conversational victim. Horrified by the prospect of exchanging awkward greetings with him, she dropped her eyes to the floor and walked rapidly to the desk. Thought nostalgically of the sleep-deprived week she'd spent on the train. Already resenting the role she'd be playing in the hotel. She hated this sort of gathering.

The receptionist greeted her in Russian.

Marion hesitated again, surprised by the prevalence of the language in Azerbaijan. She'd travelled through much of the Caucasus and Central Asia in the early years of Soviet rule, and rarely had anyone spoken anything to her but variations on Turkish and, in Tajikistan, Persian. She was having difficulty processing the changes that had apparently occurred in the region over the past five years.

And the new atmosphere left her apprehensive. Uncertain. A taxi driver, used to collecting Russian tourists at the railway station, was one thing. A hotel worker welcoming participants to an event specifically about Turkic languages and cultures was a symptom of something more. She reminded herself to remain opaque. Not to speak unnecessarily.

After responding in Azeri Turkish to the receptionist with the same apology she had made to the taxi driver, she mentioned her reserved room. Unmoved by Marion's embarrassment, the receptionist nodded once, handed her a key, and explained to her, now in Azerbaijani, how to find her quarters. Marion thanked her, flustered despite her decision to remain blank, and hurried to the stairway. She dreaded being waylaid in the lobby now that her identity was public knowledge.

Her room on the third floor of the hotel was less imposing than the lobby had been. In fact, it might have been taken from one of last century's lodging houses. Thin rugs over wooden floors, old cigarette smoke hanging in the air, two narrow beds with likewise thin brown blankets, and a stray wooden chair with no desk or table to go with it. But there was a private toilet with a shower, which was a pleasant surprise.

And, better, there was a view of the water, whitish green even under the February clouds. When she opened the door to the balcony, the air's maritime smell was almost a burlesque of itself. Too salty. Or too mineral. Letting it hit her in the face for a long minute, she concluded that she liked it. She'd always prefer the Marmara. But the Caspian had much to recommend it.

She closed the balcony door, stripped off her shearling, and hung it in a wardrobe positioned at a haphazard angle in the corner of the room. Then, shedding the rest of her filthy clothing, she moved toward the shower. Secured the chain over the door, pulled off her wool jumper and trousers, and tried the faucet.

It worked. The water was clean. And they had left her a towel. The same brown as the blankets on the bed. A deliberate design effect? She chose not to wonder and stepped into the shower, ridding herself of the scent of the train. As much as she had enjoyed the cured meat.

It was an easy decision to change into pyjamas and climb into bed rather than venture into the lobby. She knew that she'd be expected to spend at least a few hours playing at academic intercourse in order to make her presence known to Dr. Polat. And to attract the other interested parties, as Hashimoto had termed them. But she had time. Her trains had run with admirable efficiency, and she wanted to make up for lost sleep.

In fact, Marion slept throughout the afternoon, evening, and night, waking only at dawn the next day as the sunlight hit her, vivid and insistent, in the face. She had neglected to close the curtains. But then, she hadn't expected such bright sunlight in February. Squinting, she rolled over, collected herself, and pushed herself out of the bed. Walked barefoot across the unpleasant rug to the balcony. She looked out over the water before turning, moving into the room, and rummaging through her bag for appropriate clothing. The day was bright, but it was also chilly. Not as frigid as Murmansk. But then, little was.

She located a pair of wool trousers that hadn't been too wrinkled and damaged in their travels from Scotland, and a heavy silk shirt. Hardly fashionable, but that was part of her leftist academic identity, which in this case was not all that difficult to simulate. She put on her clothes, used the toilet, cleaned her teeth, brushed and pinned back her hair, and then prepared to do her scholarly duty. Loathing every minute of it.

Trudging down the stairs toward the breakfast room, she examined the off-putting efforts that had been made to combine modernist design, Soviet optimism for the future, and a carefully curated, non-threatening nostalgia for Azerbaijan's Turkic heritage. It wasn't worse than what she'd experienced of British and French presentations of their own empires, of the populations they had variously assimilated and sought to civilize. But whereas she'd learned to block out the British and French references to their Orients, the Soviet variation on the theme was just eccentric enough to her expectations to draw her eye.

When she found herself tripping over the carpet as she stared at a photograph of an ancient, beaming peasant woman, toothless, wearing an elaborate headscarf and holding up a small sheep against the backdrop of an exploding petroleum well, she forced herself to focus on the stairs. She couldn't read the rousing caption explaining the photograph in any case. Written in Russian.

The breakfast room was already busy by the time she entered it. She did, though, manage to find an empty table near a window overlooking the street, and she arranged her carpet bag on the chair next to hers with the hope of projecting what she knew was a futile air of antisocial misanthropy. Aware from sad experience that something about her bearing attracted vocal male academics like a beacon.

And so, she was pleased when it was a server rather than a colleague—a young woman who looked more angry than sullen—who first approached her. The woman stalked toward her, set down a pot of tea, produced a plate of bread, white cheese, honey, and butter to go with it, and then, as a kind of afterthought, tossed two hard-boiled eggs onto the table. After that, without speaking, she walked away.

Marion approved of the service. And, as she poured a glass of tea and began drinking, she thought she might spend more time in the Soviet Caucasus and Central Asia. Fantasized for a few minutes about bringing Ian along with her. A period of readjustment for him. Excellent antidote to the narrative of the devoted family servant that Jeffrey and his relations had persuaded him to swallow. Alongside the brutal and ascetic schooling that apparently went with that narrative.

Then she pushed away the thought of Ian. Drank more tea. If she weren't careful, she'd miss her cues from Dr. Polat whilst silently haranguing herself.

As she looked away from the window, her chest contracted in dismay. Moving with purpose across the room was the man she'd seen the day before. Affable smile on his face. Closing in on her table. She remembered vaguely that he was affiliated now with Magdalen College at Oxford. Wasn't certain that she could make the required conversation, but she hastily drank more tea to hide her confusion. Caffeine would help.

Resisting the urge to jump from the chair and retreat to her room, she prepared herself for the pity that would accompany his formulaic curiosity about her career. Unconsciously squared her shoulders. But then, to her surprise, his face fell, and he readjusted his trajectory toward another table. Skillful. As though he had always been aiming away from her.

She looked about her, curious as to who or what had liberated her, when a harassed looking man, heavy, older than she was, full beard, wire glasses, and a carefully tailored suit, eased himself into the chair across from her. The server appeared at once and proffered a second pot of tea. A hint of deference this time. Though, again, she left without speaking.

The man poured himself some tea, took a sip, and re-settled his glasses on the bridge of his nose. "I apologize, Dr. Bailey, for interrupting what would have been a pleasant and productive exchange with Professor—?" He paused, uncertain as to the name. He was speaking French with a thick Azeri accent.

"We can speak Azerbaijani, if you'd like—" she began in Turkish.

"No, no," he said, still in French. "Better to converse in a language not known to those in attendance. Although obviously doing so is hardly a deterrent to particularly curious listeners."

"French is fine," she replied in French.

She found the man aggressive. As much as she appreciated him rescuing her from a traumatic return to her days at Cambridge. Surprised herself by thinking that she didn't want to give him more information than necessary. Waited for him to speak further.

"My name," he said, "is Dr. Polat."

"How do you do?"

She wondered whether Mr. Kanda was in fact to blame for Dr. Polat's working identity. There was little the man could do to appear more suspicious. But then if, as the behavior of the taxi driver suggested, everyone in Baku these days assumed that everyone else was a spy, perhaps acting and dressing like a caricature of one was a smart move. Confuse the opposition. She smiled into her tea. Drank more. "I had thought, Dr. Polat, that you and I were to cross a bit later during my time here. After I'd remained visible for a day or two?"

"Ah yes, Dr. Bailey. That was the original strategy. But you see," he raised a bushy and diabolical eyebrow, "the situation has matured."

"Has it really?" She was having difficulty not laughing. This was unquestionably better than listening to academic one-upmanship. But she still missed her manuscripts. Being away from people.

"It has." His voice was grave. "We've received information that a number of other parties, who have their own interest in the map, have increased their presence in the old city—"

"It isn't a map. And it isn't in the old city—"

"Don't tell me what it is." Echoing Hashimoto. "Or where it is. We've agreed to call it a 'map.' And if it isn't in the old city, so much the better. They've been searching in the wrong place."

"Very well." Tired now for some reason.

"So, these—other parties," lift of the same eyebrow, "have intensified their efforts. We have reason to believe they will make a move against you. Rather than watching. Your brief now is to retrieve the map immediately. Tonight. A dispatcher will be waiting in your room to collect it when you return." He paused. "Don't kill him."

"Well, obviously I won't—"

"I say this only because you might, quite reasonably, be startled to find a stranger in your room so late at night." He peered at her. "You have a reputation."

"That is," she began, irritated by his implication, "the most ridiculous—"

Dr. Polat stood before she had finished. "That is all Dr. Bailey."

"Wait," she said. "If I'm going after it tonight, I'll need transportation. To the south of the city."

"A truck will be waiting for you. Mention my name."

She watched as he strode, still harassed, out of the breakfast room. Then, annoyed, she finished her tea and ate a few pieces of bread and honey. But upon reflection, her predominant emotion was gratitude. Given her new brief, she needn't attend the symposium at all.

And as she stood, took up her carpet bag, and wandered back to her room to re-read her manuscripts, she decided she'd take unfriendly, uranium-obsessed government agents out to kill her over academic symposium participants any day. Even the bizarre photograph in the corridor didn't bother her. She felt nothing but comradery for the peasant woman with her sheep and her gushing petroleum.

By the time she'd lowered herself onto her narrow bed, her back against the headboard, her *letaif* in her lap, she was more than relieved. She was elated. She knew without a doubt where she wanted to go that evening to look for the 'map.'

To comfort herself and to distract from the slowly passing time, she retraced her path through the text. Reaffirming what had become, in Scotland, a certainty. She also ventured out into the city for a few hours, eating some *döner* before returning to her room. But mostly, she marked time. Waiting with mounting impatience for sunset. And then for twilight.

When it was finally evening, she rose from the bed, stretched, and changed into dark wool trousers, a dark shirt, her boots, and, for lack of a better alternative, her shearling. She also covered her hair with the wool hat. She left her manuscripts under the mattress of the second bed. Any serious thieves would find them at once, but casual visitors to her room would be dissuaded from making off with them. She couldn't bring them with her on this assignment.

She locked her room and walked down the staircase, noting in passing the sound of drunken scholars floating from the direction of the ballroom. Silently thankful, once more, that she wasn't in the midst of them. Then she passed through the front doors of the hotel to come face to face with a monstrous, green ZIS-5 military truck blocking traffic in the street outside. She stopped and stared. Dr. Polat couldn't possibly have been so incompetent.

Then, blinking, she decided that he could have been precisely so incompetent. She walked to the driver's side of the truck, stood on her tiptoes, and looked into the open window. "Dr. Polat sent me," she said in Azeri Turkish.

"Hop in." The driver was speaking French.

Stifling her continued annoyance, she walked to the passenger's side of the truck, stood on the running board, and climbed into the seat. Pulled the door shut. "I'm going to Kobustan. The side nearest Alat."

The driver brought the truck into traffic without paying attention to the angry drivers slamming on brakes and sounding their horns. "We'll be there in an hour," he told her.

"Fine." She sat back in the seat. Closed her eyes.

True to his word, the driver brought her through the dry, caked scrub to the south of the city in less than fifty minutes. Eventually, he stopped the truck in the middle of the road, uncertain as to her exact destination. A small footpath to their right led up toward a collection of alien-looking rocks and hills spreading out inland, away from the sea.

He pointed behind him, toward the sea and city. "Alat." Then he gestured up the hill. "Kobustan."

"Thank you. Would you wait here for me?"

He nodded. "Yes. Anything else you need?"

"A torch would be helpful. And a hammer."

He left the cab of the truck and walked to the back. Marion, following him, saw him moving equipment until he retrieved a miner's lamp and a hammer. He held them out to her. "This is what I have."

"They're perfect." She took the lamp and the hammer from him and walked in the direction of the rocks. Turned back briefly. "Thank you again."

He shrugged, lit a cigarette, and returned to the cab of the truck. Marion walked up the footpath until she reached a series of petroglyphs etched into an overhanging stone. They weren't her target, but she examined them, curious, before moving between two hills and into the barren landscape.

After an hour of walking, she found what she was seeking. A small stylized flower, twelfth- or thirteenth-century, carved into a stone that might have been natural or, if one were looking carefully, might also have been placed there deliberately. From elsewhere.

She made note of the flower, tracing it with her fingertip. Then she knelt in front of the stone, raised the hammer, and hit it hard at its base. A chunk of the stone fell to the ground, and she picked it up, stood, and pocketed it. Clutching the piece of rock in her pocket, she looked for the next flower. If she had read the manuscript properly, there would be a trail of them leading to one of the mud volcanoes scattered throughout the area. Except, in this case, it wasn't a volcano.

She found her next flower and smiled. Walking slowly now, she wound her way up a tall hill, absent vegetation, caked mud and stagnant air, until she reached a seething mud pool. Flower motif pale and faded on a flattish stone to the side, but visible to anyone looking for it.

Confident that she had reached her destination, she squatted in front of the pit and watched in the light of her lamp as the mud bubbled out of the hole in the ground and seeped over the side of the mound. She removed the rock from her pocket, squeezed it for a moment, and then tossed it into the center of the mud pool. At first, nothing happened. But then, with a deep sucking sound, the mud drained out of the pit in a powerful whirlpool. She watched, still squatting, but didn't move. After thirty seconds of inactivity, a low boom precipitated a tower of flame—burning gas from under the mud—shooting out from around the edges of the hole. Still she didn't move. The flame dissipated. And the hole remained empty.

She stood and walked to the edge. Looked down. On a stone platform that never would have been a part of an ordinary mud volcano, sat a snake of worked bitumen. Coiled and not much larger than a closed fist. It had been cast and hardened such that a series of diagrams and instructions wound over and across it. Even in the dim light of her lamp, Marion could see that the diagrams were more than detailed.

"Apparently it's about petroleum after all," she muttered to herself.

Then she balanced the lamp on the edge of the pit, lowered herself to her stomach, and prepared to reach down and retrieve the snake. As she stretched her hand toward the bitumen, she felt, more than saw, a figure emerging from behind the rock to her side. She was immediately on her feet, the hammer in her hand, waiting for the next move. She didn't wait long. With a ferocity she wasn't expecting, the figure launched itself bodily in Marion's direction, shoving her onto her back.

Marion curled and rolled to the side, her wool hat sliding off. As she recovered, she thought to herself, first, that she was too old to be doing this, and second, that her attacker was a child. Or at most, a slim adolescent. Tiny. Light. Marion had easily thrown him off of her. But, also like an adolescent, he wasn't injured, and he was already coming at her again.

Rather than trying to subdue her opponent, Marion turned toward the pit to retrieve the bitumen. She dodged a flying kick from her attacker and crawled toward the hole. But she was too late. It was already filling with mud again. The snake had been submerged. Cursing to herself, she considered wading into the rising mud to find the bitumen by feel. As she hesitated, pondering her best approach, a bullet hit the clay to her right. Dull thud.

She looked behind her and saw that the figure—wearing some sort of robe?—was taking careful aim at her from a serious looking pistol. Cursing again, louder, Marion ducked and ran for the footpath. Slipping against the scrub and abrading her palm as she steadied herself against an ancient rock, she sprinted back toward the truck. Prayed that the driver was awake and ready.

She wasn't disappointed. The driver, having seen her running, without the hammer or lamp, had already started the engine. She dragged herself into the passenger seat and worked to control her breathing. "Go."

He lost no time in getting the truck onto the road. Didn't comment on her patently failed excursion. After twenty minutes of driving, during which Marion calmed herself, she turned to him. "Would you tell Dr. Polat that I'll want the truck again tomorrow night?" She looked behind them and saw nothing but empty road. They weren't being followed. "I'll come prepared next time."

The driver nodded. Still didn't speak. Marion leaned her head back against the seat and closed her eyes. Grateful, again, for the silence.

THE driver brought the truck to the same position in front of the hotel. Prominent. Visible. Embarrassing. Marion, still humiliated by her unsuccessful effort in Kobustan, blushed and pushed open her door. The driver hadn't spoken throughout their return, for which Marion remained appreciative. But she nonetheless felt a fool. She closed the door quietly and walked, inwardly raging, toward the hotel's entrance.

When she entered the lobby, the drunken reception following the symposium's opening was still rowdy and boisterous. But its volume dropped noticeably when Marion, her hair caked with mud, her hands bleeding, and her trousers ripped at the knees, limped through the door. One by one, conversations faltered as the occupants of the lobby noticed her condition.

Preoccupied by her own thoughts, Marion didn't register the attention until she was halfway across the room. When she did finally detect the impression she was making, she looked up, confused, only to make eye contact with her former Cambridge colleague. He was staring at her, astonished, and making no effort to hide it. She stopped and glared at him. When he dropped his eyes, mortified, she ignored the rest of the looks and made her way across the remainder of the room, toward the stairway, and up to her floor.

By the time she had reached her room, the adrenaline as well as the humiliation was beginning to ebb. She felt only exhaustion. Along with a hint of optimism. Yes, she was a perfectionist. And she suffered her failure almost physically. But she also recognized that she had a more than satisfactory chance of success tomorrow evening. Her hypothesis had proved correct, and her only task now was to divert the eyes on the scene before she re-activated the "volcano." Somewhat comforted, she unlocked and pushed open the door to her room.

Everything was as she had left it. Except that there was now a bearded, hirsute man in a badly tailored pinkish suit lying on his back on her bed with a gunshot wound in the middle of his forehead. Bleeding onto her blanket. The dispatcher.

She stared at the man for a few seconds in shock. Then she pressed her fists into her eyes. "Oh no."

Before she had the chance to formulate a plan to deal with the body, the child from the mud volcano launched himself at Marion from behind the second bed, pushed her to the floor, and slammed her head back against the wardrobe. Less prepared to defend herself this time, Marion felt her head crack against the wood. And then she lost consciousness.

She woke to smelling salts held under her nose. Secured to the wooden chair, her wrists tied tightly behind her with twisted fencing wire. As her vision cleared, she saw a tall, irregularly proportioned man standing in front of her. Thin shoulders, flabby stomach, flaking skin, no more than thirty years old, wearing a greenish twill belted trench coat. The belt carefully secured and buckled. He also wore a hat. Eric Thacker.

She noticed, irrelevantly, that he had shaved off his ill-fated attempt at facial hair. Then she shut her eyes. Willing him to disappear. "Oh *no*."

Without speaking, Thacker stepped across the room and rammed his fist into her stomach. She doubled over in the chair, retching, gasping for breath, as the wire cut into her wrists. Before she had managed to draw in air, a third figure entered the room. Shutting the door to the balcony.

"That wasn't your brief, Thacker."

"The lines are blurry, Willcox." Thacker was examining the hand he'd used to hit her. "Hard to know where your job ends and mine begins."

"Ah." Jeffrey glanced briefly at Marion, who was still frantically sucking in air. Back at Thacker. "Let me elucidate, then. To allay further confusion. If you touch my wife again, in any way, without my express permission, I'll skin you alive." He took a step toward Thacker, who moved, instinctively, backward. "I'll do it, too. You know that I will."

Thacker, regaining his snide equanimity, snorted. Nodded in Marion's direction. "She's upright again. Your turn."

Jeffrey lifted his chin and watched Marion for a few seconds. She had forced herself to sit up in the chair. Breathing heavily. Staring, horrified, at Jeffrey. He was wearing an anonymous charcoal grey wool overcoat, dark trousers, and a lighter grey shirt. But that was all she could read from him. His face was blank. Practiced. She couldn't begin to speak.

"There's someone I'd like you to see, Marion." Jeffrey stepped behind her and led the child, now docile, toward the chair.

Except that it wasn't a child. Her attacker was indeed as small and lithe as a ten- or eleven-year-old boy. But she was also wearing her usual uniform of shirtwaist silk dress, black now for work, and heavy boots. Her blue-black hair was secured in a long plait down to her waist. She'd be twenty-three years old now. But her eyes didn't look like the eyes of a twenty-three-year-old. They were ancient. And tortured.

"Claudia?" Marion felt her own eyes begin to well up with tears. "You were dead."

"I wasn't dead." Claudia's voice was flat.

"How—?"

"How not? You didn't question it." Claudia took a step toward the chair. Curious. But restive. "You believed it the moment you were told. Maybe you hoped it was true? That I was gone?"

"How could I have hoped it was true?" Marion was having difficulty processing Claudia's existence, much less her altered, empty, affect. "Claudia, I was devastated. I—"

"They used me." Claudia was leaning over now, her hands on Marion's shoulders. Staring down at her. Angry.

"They—?"

"Your people."

An unexpected trace of the exasperation that used to dog her when she was on assignment with Claudia crept up on her. Incongruous, but impossible to ignore. She held Claudia's look. "Of course they used you. That's what they do. They use people. You. Me. They want skills, Claudia. Not relationships. What do you think—"

Claudia slapped her hard across the face, slamming her back against the chair. A wave of nausea hit Marion as she shook her head to clear her vision.

"*You* used me." Claudia had her hands on Marion's shoulders again. Her face inches away.

"I—?" A sick realization came over her. She looked past Claudia at Jeffrey. Standing behind her. Watching the exchange with no more than concentrated, professional interest. He held her eyes. Didn't speak.

"I—"

"But I forgive you," Claudia interrupted her.

"You *forgive* me?" Marion stared at her. "Claudia, listen to me—"

"I deliberately aimed wide," Claudia said, releasing Marion's shoulders and straightening. Hint of a smile. "In the mud. I could have killed you."

"I know you could have."

"And even if I had missed," she said, extracting two stoppered jars from the pockets of her dress, "I have these as well."

"Claudia—"

"Dinitrogen tetroxide," she nodded at the jar on the left, "and hydrazine." Nodded at the jar on the right. "Although I've altered each. In small, but chemically significant, ways. I haven't quite figured out the percentages yet, but what I do know is that regardless of how you mix them, they make a very, very big boom."

Marion was feeling panicky. Claudia, her psyche always brittle, had shattered. She wasn't right in the mind. But Marion was damned if she was going to dismiss her now that she had reappeared, alive, after two years. "Claudia—"

"I think that's enough nostalgia for the time being." Jeffrey, satisfied with the effect he had brought about, took Claudia by the arm and led her away from Marion. "You'll want to go with Mr. Thacker now, Claudia."

"Yes, Sir Jeffrey." Claudia, biddable again, moved toward the door.

Marion stared, her stomach turning at the paternalistic certainty with which Jeffrey handled her. And at the readiness with which Claudia obeyed him. "Claudia—" she tried a third time, on the verge of tears.

Claudia glanced back at her, mild. "Give my regards to Monkey."

"Monkey? Ian—oh God, Claudia, wait—" Marion was crying freely now.

"Best not tell him what they did to Antonia." Claudia spun away from her and left the room.

Thacker, following, raised his eyebrows at Jeffrey. After Claudia was safely in the corridor, he spoke. "I'm nothing if not fair, Willcox. That was a masterfully arranged scene." He glanced over at Marion, still crying. "But really, if you'd simply use the shower, we'd have what we need from her in fifteen minutes. Likely sooner. This is all so unnecessarily baroque."

"We'd have something out of her." Jeffrey was concentrating on Marion, paying only half attention to Thacker. "Nothing close to what we need."

"Perhaps." Thacker was shutting the door. "But do try not to let her 'overpower' you this time, hmm, Willcox? Or if you and Lady Willcox could limit that sort of thing to your own time? I know that everyone at the office would breathe a sigh of relief."

He slammed the door before Jeffrey could reply.

JEFFREY watched Marion crying in the chair for a few seconds longer. Then he walked, still favoring his right foot, back across the room. Sat on the edge of the bed nearest her. The one without the body. Continued to watch her. He didn't remove his overcoat. "Maugham made me bring Thacker," he eventually said. "He doesn't trust me with you."

"You told me she was dead!"

"Hmm." Jeffrey scratched his cheek. "Yes, I did tell you that. But as you can see—" He waved a vague hand toward the closed door. "In fact, she was in a cell on the other side of the camp. In Hinaidi. Complicated situation."

"That isn't possible." Marion had stopped crying. But she was still having difficulty breathing normally. "It isn't *possible*."

"Why not?"

"*Why not?*"

"Not to belabor the obvious," he said, "but did you witness the event I described? Did I provide you with evidence?" He smiled at her. Vindictive. "Did you see the body?"

"That is grotesque—"

"Is it?" He considered. "You'd know better than I. But Claudia's correct. You did accept my story rather quickly. One wonders why you didn't press. *Did* you want to see her gone?"

"I will not let you do this to me." Marion looked him in the eye, stony. "Not a second time."

"Very well. It's irrelevant anyway." He crossed his legs. "She's proved tractable without any excessive psychological pressure, for what it's worth. Wants desperately to be a good girl, and all that—"

"Stop it!"

"And she has a skill set as distinctive and almost as useful as yours." He examined his foot. "Not to mention she's an infinitely better shot."

Marion decided that the only way to derail Jeffrey's complacency was to move toward the concrete. She didn't want to hear about his work on Claudia. "Why is she here? Why is Thacker here?"

"I've told you why Thacker is here. To prevent you from leading me astray." He looked up at her under a lock of hair that had fallen over his forehead. Flirtatious. "You ought to be flattered."

She swallowed to keep herself from throwing up. "Is that all?"

"No," he told her. "Thacker is also here to do what must be done." He paused. "Should it need to be done."

"What must be done."

"Yes. This is Maugham's arrangement." He sighed, pushed back his shoulders, and ran a hand through his hair. "A not very subtle reprimand for having cocked up in Caithness. Thank you for that, incidentally."

"Fuck you."

"You see, I'd been pleased with Claudia. Enjoyed working with her. As I said, she's more than malleable. She's also intelligent. Competent. I've run her a few times with excellent results. And until Caithness, as far as I was concerned, we could have kept her from you indefinitely. Good talent isn't so easy to find these days."

"You're a—"

"Yes, yes, Marion. I know. But believe me, the value that Maugham's decided to attach to her is far more disturbing than anything I've done with her. Although, and I admit it freely, it's also effective. He's a force of nature when he chooses to be."

"I don't understand."

"Maugham, trusting to your unhinged sense of loyalty, believes that you'll spill if the alternative is, this time, a genuinely dead Claudia."

"I don't understand," she repeated. Though she did. She didn't want to understand.

"Thacker has taken her back to Kobustan. They're waiting for us there now. If we don't arrive in three hours, amenable, collegial, and free with our information, he'll kill her." Jeffrey turned his gaze to the ceiling. "At least, his orders are to kill her. Knowing Thacker, he'll probably incapacitate her first, and—"

"Stop."

Jeffrey, accommodating, stopped. Examined her face. When she didn't say anything further, he resumed. "This is your game, Marion. I've no control over it. None. Although, if it means anything, I can tell you that if I were you, I'd let her die. She's working for us. We've flipped her. Completely. Irrevocably." He examined his fingernails. "Your superiors would likely thank you."

She narrowed her eyes at him. "Why are you saying that?"

"Because I'm just enough of a bastard to prefer watching Thacker and Maugham bollocks up this time to watching yet another assignment completed to flawless perfection?" A smile played across his lips. "I also dislike their contemptuous attitude toward our idiosyncratic, yet always rewarding, marriage. And," he added, "I particularly dislike the direction our section has been taking in recent years. As a matter of principle. All of this petroleum and uranium and haggling over pipelines and technology. It's demeaning. Very little in the way of lost artifacts for us to liberate these days."

"Why must it be Thacker?" She chose to ignore his advice for the moment. "Why is it *always* Thacker? He's not even a specialist in this region. What's his field anyway—"

"He read classics." Jeffrey was now laughing quietly. "Initially. Never quite finished the D.Phil." He uncrossed his legs. "The story is that he tried to slip a dish of poison mushrooms to a rival who caught him in a spot of plagiarism. Fancied himself something of an Agrippina, I suppose. His family covered it up, but that was the end of the scholarly career. Until Maugham got hold of him. Saw something in him. And so, Dr. Bailey, here we are. With Thacker. A classicist in Azerbaijan. A very angry classicist in Azerbaijan."

"Untie my wrists."

"Are you going to attack me?"

"No." She closed her eyes. "I'm going to prevent that violent halfwit from killing my friend."

Jeffrey stood and walked behind her chair. Started work on the wire. "You're being stupid, Marion."

She winced as the wire dug into her skin. Didn't respond.

"Not that I'm not gratified," he added. "I'm curious, obviously, to know how this ends." He twisted again, and she gasped, but he continued to work. "As one professional to another, however, I must say, this is a fatal liability on your part. Your demented steadfastness."

He finished and straightened up. She stayed in the chair, rubbing her wrists. Watched as he returned to the edge of the bed. "Not steadfast to you."

"I'm special." He moved the manuscripts he had retrieved from under the mattress onto his lap. "So where do we begin?"

"I'll show you," she said, "when we get there. Can we leave now? I don't want Claudia alone with Thacker."

He shook his head, apologetic. "Unfortunately, I must have an idea of your logic. Before we leave. Should you mislead us once we've reached the target area." He brushed nonexistent dust off the pages in his lap. "Shocking though the thought of your duplicity may be."

She considered for a few seconds. "Fine. But I want to use the toilet first."

"Oh, for heaven's sake, Marion. Are you really going to try—"

"No, you idiot. Look at me." She stood and let him see her wrecked state. "I want to wash my face, brush my hair, and change into clothing that isn't in tatters. Do I have your permission?"

He put the manuscript pages beside him on the bed, stood as well, and removed a revolver from a holster under his coat. Gestured toward the toilet. "I think you look fetching. But I suppose female vanity must always prevail. So yes, you do have my permission. Keep in mind, however, that I'll be watching. And I'm still feeling resentful about my toe."

Without speaking, she walked to the wardrobe, ignoring the body on her bed, and retrieved trousers and a sweater. She changed her clothes, crossed back to the toilet, splashed water on her face, and brushed as much of the mud out of her hair as she could. Then she pulled her hair into a tight knot on the nape of her neck. Using the remaining mud to set it. For lack of a better alternative. Fetching.

She stared blankly at the mirror for a few seconds before walking out to the chair in the bedroom. Sat. Held out her hand. "Give me the *letaif*."

He handed the manuscript to her, and she arranged the pages in her lap. Thought for a few seconds longer. Then she looked up at him. "There was a system, centuries old, for transporting the—the mineral—that was the key ingredient in Egyptian theriac out of the Caucasus. Primarily to Egypt. But elsewhere too. The three manuscripts that you found in the library are examples of this system's uninterrupted use. Its efficiency. Fourteenth, sixteenth, and seventeenth centuries. Same mineral or 'magic.' Same journey from Azerbaijan. Over four hundred years."

She let her eyes drop to the pages in her lap. "My impression is that my organization has always kept track of it. Since its inception. Whenever there was a stray mention in a text of the mineral—or of its processing, export, or use—the librarians noted it. Appended the map. A kind of cataloguing system. I suspect that if you were to look carefully, you'd find more examples of it in the collection. Beyond the three they told you to locate."

"I'll let Maugham know." Jeffrey had returned the revolver to his holster and sat on the edge of the bed again. He looked academic.

"Do, will you?" Waspish. Then she sighed. Continued. "But some of the references to it are more targeted than others. Or, I suppose you might say, some of the references to it are instructions rather than descriptions. So, for example, whereas Evliya Çelebi was writing about it as nothing more than a keen observer—not part of the trade—the people for whom the Cuman riddles, in the fourteenth century and, more so, these," resting her palms on the *letaif*, "in the sixteenth century, were written, were expected to act. Upon being made aware of a new vein or lode, I think."

"Riddles and dirty jokes? A strange delivery method."

"Is it?" She looked up at him. "It doesn't seem all that different to what you do. Hide the message in Marmite advertisements that run in the *Daily Telegraph*. That sort of thing."

"Oh dear. You realize now that I must kill you? Nobody can know about the Marmite and live."

"You get the idea."

"Yes. Continue."

"These sixteenth-century *letaif* are—are extraordinary. First," she said, "there's the writer. This set of satires is usually attributed to a minor sixteenth-century poet, Faqiri. A pen name. There's nothing wrong with that attribution except that Faqiri wrote almost nothing else similar to this. In fact, he wrote very little at all. Aside from these. So there's a possibility that 'Faqiri' was the pen name of another, perhaps more well-known, poet who didn't want to be associated with these."

"I'm not sure I'd want my name associated with—"

"Thank you," she interrupted. "I haven't finished."

She dreaded Jeffrey's sardonic commentary slowing down their progress toward Claudia. When she was certain he wouldn't speak again, she continued. "There are a few candidates for the 'other' poet. One is Hayali. Another pen name. But that seems unlikely because he's insulted several times in this text, and I can't imagine he'd go so far simply to disguise his identity. Hayali himself, however, does mention in a different composition that he met, during his lifetime, an even more famous poet, Fuzuli. Also a pen name."

"All right."

"Fuzuli," she explained, "brings us closer to home. He was Azeri, but he lived primarily in Iraq, which had only recently come under Ottoman control. Iraq had been a battleground between the Ottoman Empire and the Iranian Safavid Empire throughout much of the early sixteenth century. Despite that, Fuzuli managed, in the midst of the wartime atmosphere of the 1530s, to secure the patronage of the Ottoman court almost immediately upon the Ottoman conquest of Baghdad."

"Lucky fellow."

"The problem was, what with the war between the Ottomans and Safavids raging, his salary never materialized."

"Must have annoyed him."

"Yes," she said. "He wrote a long poem complaining about it."

"Quite the epic subject."

"Not epic," she replied, ignoring his tone. "His style sounds more like what I have in my lap. Light. Lots of wordplay. Even more interesting," she added quickly, before Jeffrey could interrupt again, "he had a notoriously difficult time choosing a pen name and sticking to it. He didn't want to be tied to a single identity. He wrote a poem about that as well."

"So?"

"So, I think Fuzuli was sufficiently annoyed by his absent stipend in Iraq to journey to Istanbul in the late 1530s to try to get his hands on it. As 'Faqiri,' though. The impoverished one. And I also think, perhaps to fund his travels, he conducted some business on the side—bringing a message from his connections in Azerbaijan to interested readers in the Ottoman capital. Concerning a newly discovered lode of—of the primary ingredient in Egyptian theriac."

Jeffrey put his palms on the bed to either side of him and nodded. "This is all very interesting, Marion. But awfully speculative. Would you like to tell me how we use it now, four hundred years later, to rescue little Claudia? Because I'm at a loss."

She blanched at the mention of Claudia, fought down her reaction, and then nodded in turn. "Yes. Fine." She closed her eyes for a few seconds. Opened them and continued: "the relevant passages in the manuscript are embedded in the second *latife*. I'll read you a superficial translation, if you'd like. Although I know you've already seen it. And then I'll explain how 'Faqiri' pointed his more careful readers toward the mineral deposit. Instead."

"Very well."

She gazed down at the pages in her lap. Bit her lip. Then began. "It reads: 'this is a story about the highest judge in Istanbul. It seems that a bloke—'"

"A—'bloke?'" Jeffrey raised his eyebrows.

She felt herself coloring. "*Herif*," she said. "It means, as you know perfectly well, a fellow. A—a guy. Informal. Perhaps derogatory." She glared up at him. "I'm trying to translate this in a way that makes sense to you. *I'd* say something like 'scunner.'"

"Ah." He was fighting back a smile. "That sounds inappropriate. Let's go with scunner."

"Fine," she repeated. "'So this—scunner—was stopped in front of the courthouse because he seemed drunk. He denied it. And when they tested his breath, there was no trace of a smell. But the judge told them to look for a—a drinking instrument—on him—'" She paused. "The word for 'drinking instrument' is *alet-i şürb*."

"Is it now? '*Alet*.' Hmm." He crossed his legs again.

"Yes," she answered tersely, daring him to say more. When he remained silent, she resumed speaking: "it continues, 'so they searched him, and they found a cup—*kadeh*—in his clothing. The judge said his culpability had been established, and because they had found the—the instrument for drinking—'"

"This would be *alet-i şürb* again?"

"Yes." She didn't look up at him. "'Because they had found it, they should punish him—'" She flicked her eyes up at him, "'the punishment the judge orders is discretionary—*tazir*—rather than religious. Less serious." She looked down at the text. "But then the 'scunner,'" she couldn't damp down her growing rage at Jeffrey, entertained, sitting on the bed, "'took his—his own instrument—'"

"I don't think 'instrument' is the proper translation for *alet* in this context, Marion."

"His—tool—"

"Try again." He was grinning at her.

She drew a breath and held his eyes. Cool. "Very well. 'He took his penis in his hand and he said: and this, my lord, is my instrument for fucking—*alet-i zina*—so go ahead and give me the religious—*had*—punishment instead.'"

"Ah Marion." Jeffrey's voice was delighted. "That was exquisite. Superlative work. Truly."

She looked back down at the page in front of her. "I'm not finished yet," she muttered.

"There's more?"

"Yes. A moral. In poetic form."

He burst out laughing. "A moral? Well thank goodness the educational potential of that little parable wasn't lost on the writer. Do tell."

"It reads," she said, "'Come, diver in the sea of meanings, value the jewels of speech in their proper place, take careful heed at the beginning of every undertaking, so that you won't feel regret at the end.'"

"Sage words." Jeffrey was nodding, thoughtful.

"That," she said to him, "is the superficial translation of the passage. And it makes perfect sense. For the genre. There's no reason to look for anything else unless you're aware that something else might be—be hidden there."

He continued nodding, slowly. "But you're saying that there is something else hidden there."

"I know there's something else there because I tested it tonight. And it worked."

"Explain."

She rubbed her eyes. "First, and I think this is important: my method of interpretation will work only for someone who has access to the original manuscript." She rested her hand on the pages. "This. There are markings on it that appear to be errors—and that wouldn't have been reproduced in later copies. But they're not errors. They're key to deciphering the instructions on reaching the—the diagram—of the mine."

"I understand. Continue."

"I must show you the writing." She held up the top folio of the manuscript. "Can I bring this page to you? To see?"

He moved over on the bed. Gestured to the space beside him. "Please."

She stood, walked to the bed, sat next to him, and placed the page between them. Then she pointed. "Here, for example. 'Diver in the sea of meanings,' should be *gavvas-i derya-yı maani*. But it isn't. There's a 'd' in front of the 'n' in *maani*. It's quite clear. Separate from the 'i' and no dot. So the word, *maani*, 'meanings,' is actually *maadin*, metals. Or, it can sometimes refer to mines. Ores. *Gavvas* also means student or seeker as well as diver. So, if we read the line with the errors intact, it goes: 'come, seeker of the sea of metals—or mines.'"

Jeffrey, leaning over to look at the writing, nodded again. "Interesting. Is that all?"

She shook her head. "No. Look. Here too. At—" she felt herself blushing, "—at *alet-i zina*." She could sense him smirking, but she didn't look up. "*Alet* has an extra 'a.' It's not *alet*, singular, 'tool;' it's *alat*, plural, 'tools.'"

"Goodness. He had more than one of them?" Jeffrey raised his eyebrows. "This is even more depraved than it first appeared to be."

Marion clenched her hands into fists, sat up straight, and looked him in the eye. "Would you please, please stop this, Jeffrey? This situation is atrocious enough as it stands without—without—"

He leaned over and kissed her cheek. "For you, my dear, anything." The corner of his mouth went down. "But only if you promise to translate some Nafzawi with me when we return home." He looked back down at the pages between them. "This sort of thing is better in Arabic than in Ottoman anyway. I keep worrying the Turks are going introduce a steppe horse into the picture somehow, or—"

"Fine," she interrupted him again. She was increasingly troubled about Claudia alone with Thacker, and Jeffrey's attitude was driving her to distraction. "So let me just explain this quickly. Here," she pointed, "*alet-i zina dir*, meaning 'it's a tool of fornication,' is actually written *alat-i zinad dir*. Which means, instead, 'these are the instruments for striking fire.' *Alat* can also be a place name. 'Alat, the place for striking fire.' It's a play on words.

"And then here," pointing again, "where it says 'a drinking instrument was found,' the words 'drinking' and 'found' run together. Into *şerbetli*. It's an uncommon word. But it has to do with people or things that have an immunity to snakebite. Which was an important attribute of theriac. So basically, what you have in this section is a juxtaposition of the 'tool for making fire,' below, and the key ingredient in theriac, above. Same wordplay as in the Cuman riddles. Identical.

"And then finally," she concluded, "the *had* as it appears in the manuscript, here, doesn't refer to a legal or religious-legal punishment. Instead, *had* retains its root meaning of border or spatial limit. It's another bit of textual flexibility to bring the reader back to *Alat*. The proper place. The reader is to go to the border of Alat, where fire strikes. That's the edge of Kobustan."

Jeffrey, carefully scanning the page on the bed between them, nodded once more. Then he smiled up at her. "I must say, Marion. Watching you do this is almost as enjoyable as watching you read the—what did you call it?—the 'superficial' interpretation of these passages." He paused. "Almost. Not quite."

"Most important, though," she said, ignoring him, "is *kadeh*, 'cup,' or 'drinking glass.' Here. The poet deliberately switches from the pornographic pun at the beginning to the more straightforward 'cup' in the middle. It's unexpected. But *kadeh* also refers to the sepals of a flower. Which becomes relevant when we associate them with Alat. And Kobustan.

"So in sum," she said, rubbing her eyes a second time, "this short passage has explained to its reader, first, where to go for the map of the new mine, second, the device to look for upon arriving there, third, what to do when he's found this device, and fourth, what will happen once this—this device is activated. In the space of twelve lines. It is, as I said, extraordinary." She paused. "And, as I saw tonight, it's also accurate."

"*You're* extraordinary." Jeffrey stood and buttoned his overcoat. "If also unbalanced. But one grows accustomed to that in time."

She stood as well, subdued, and picked up the shearling that had fallen to the floor when Claudia had attacked her. Put it on, still avoiding looking at the body on her bed.

Jeffrey walked to the door, entertained by her averted eyes. "Domestics are waiting in the wings for us to exit the scene," he said as he opened the door and waited for her to precede him through it. "They'll tidy up your room once we've gone." He took her arm as they walked down the corridor. "It will be like it never happened."

When they reached the lobby, he looked across at the still lively reception. "Shall we join the festivities when we've returned, do you think? They appear to be having a splendid time. And I think I may see some old acquaintances of ours. Shall I draw their attention—?"

She ignored him.

THE car, parked across the road from the hotel entrance, wasn't as prominent as Dr. Polat's military truck. But nor was it unobtrusive. It was a Riley Imp roadster, green with a cloth top, right hand drive, that Jeffrey had apparently imported to Baku solely for this assignment. Though why he would want an open-top rally car in the middle of winter, in the Caucasus, was something she couldn't fathom. To spite her, she imagined. She marveled at his talent for acquisition even as her irritation hit a new high.

"Its twin is in the garage back in London," he told her after they'd settled into the seats and he'd pulled the car into the still gridlocked traffic. "Lest you miss it when we return."

"I won't be returning—"

"Speaking of which," he interrupted, swerving around a 1918 Russo-Balt truck and moving onto the open road, "and given that we do have some time before we reach Kobustan, I ought to tell you. John's been having a bit of difficulty at Temple Grove."

She stared out the windscreen and waited for a few seconds before responding. Told herself to remain rational. Then she gave up and turned on him. "Well what did you expect to happen? What were you thinking, insisting that he attend that—that—hateful—"

"I'm confident that it can be smoothed over." Bland. Ignoring her reaction.

"Who wants it smoothed over?" She was yelling now. "What happened? What did they do to him?"

Jeffrey checked the mirror and then sped out onto the sea road. Shifted up and leaned back in his seat, relaxed. "Seems he's developed a new strategy for evading his lessons there. Started from the moment he returned."

"Which is?" She had her arms crossed. Looking away from him out her window.

"He's refusing to speak anything but Arabic."

She felt herself smiling. A touch proud. Kept it in check. "And?"

"Well, it took them a few days to understand what he was doing. At first, they thought it was nonsense. But then another boy there, some al-Nahyan or other, tipped them off. Didn't help, though. He wouldn't stop."

"Good," she said.

"So they telephoned me. While you and I were in Caithness." He glanced over at her averted profile. Back at the road. "Perhaps you noticed my absence? A little over a day? While you were working."

"I didn't."

"Hmm." He slowed and maneuvered around an abandoned cart. Accelerated again. "I flew down to have a word with him."

"What did he say?"

"He wouldn't speak anything but Arabic to me either."

"Good," she repeated. Giving in to her smile.

"So, I told him, in Arabic, to stop being a whingeing little toad and to do what he's asked." The smile left her face. She didn't respond.

"It worked, in the sense that he did begin speaking English again." He peered through the windscreen at the dark road and then reclined back into his seat. "Along with a bit of French, when he was feeling troublesome."

Still she said nothing.

"But then," he continued, "some other boy apparently made disparaging remarks about our allies in the desert." He spoke slowly, choosing his words. "All seemed calm at the time. But in fact, it wasn't. It appears that rather than retaliating immediately, John resolved to choose his moment. Waited for the other boy behind the playing fields. And then attacked him." He was quiet for a few seconds longer. "They say he nearly broke the boy's arm." He looked at Marion again. "Not sure where he learned that one."

"A child must know how to defend himself," she said to the window.

"Undoubtedly," he agreed.

He was quiet again. For a full minute. "The headmaster was fair about it," he eventually continued. "He ordered canings for both of them, despite the fact that John was clearly at fault—"

"*Ian* was at fault?" She turned to stare at him. "What utter rot—"

"And the other boy, from what I understand, took it like a gentleman."

"Took what like a gentleman?"

"Six strokes, I believe it was."

"Like a gentleman?" She was raging. Consumed by hatred for Jeffrey and everything that he represented. "Like a *gentleman*? And tell me, Jeffrey, how does a gentleman 'take' that?"

"Cheerfully," he said. "And without flinching."

"Are you mad?"

"Well educated."

She dropped her face into her hands. "Oh God."

"John, however, failed to appreciate the lesson. Wouldn't keep still. In the end, four of the older boys held him down while the headmaster completed his task."

"How can you possibly talk about this as if it were normal?" she spat, her face still in her hands. "How can you—"

"Afterward," he said as though he hadn't heard her, "he appeared to be settling in. But instead, he was biding his time. Waiting again. For an opportunity. Likely also waiting for the cuts to heal—"

"Oh, dear God."

"He made it out, despite a special watch, on the third night after the caning." He wrinkled his forehead. "Before he left, he scrawled insults, in Arabic, all over the walls of the headmaster's study. They have no idea how he got in and out without detection. And they searched the countryside for two days before they telephoned me a second time to report his disappearance."

She lifted her face out of her hands. "They let him wander alone in the countryside for two days before they thought to contact you? Two days?" She was gaping at him. More astonished than angry. "He's seven. He's—"

"Yes. It was an eventful morning. They telephoned on the same day that you decamped from my tower." He flipped his hair off his forehead. "Planned it together, then, did you?"

"Where is he?" Her voice was hard.

"I was on the verge of flying down a second time. Which, to be honest, would have been much preferable to calming the angry Machine Gun Corps you left in your wake." Wry. "Maugham was unhappy about that, of course. But then I heard from Ginnie. She and Teddy had found him asleep in one of their stables the previous afternoon. No harm done."

"*No harm done*—"

"He had a feral cat with him. Wouldn't let him go." He considered. "At least, he wouldn't let him go until Anne and Charlotte agreed to take him in hand. The cat, that is. Not John." He glanced at the mirror again. "He won't tell them how he got there."

"Suffolk," she said, "is 150 miles away. He could have been killed. He could have been—"

"Most likely he took the train."

"Took the train?" She was pressing the heels of her hands to her eyes. "How? How does a seven-year-old with no money, no map, and no one to care for him take the train? You tell me—"

"I daresay he hid." Jeffrey was slowing to a stop at the base of the footpath leading up to the rock formations in Kobustan. He cut the engine. "I thought you'd want to know. Though obviously the situation will be resolved when we return. They'll simply watch him more carefully. I'll dispatch them help if they feel they need it."

"If you send him back there," she growled, "I will kill you. And then I will remove him myself."

"You won't kill me," he replied, mild, turning toward her in his seat. "And he must face up to his responsibilities."

"What responsibilities?" She was beginning to shout again. "*What* responsibilities? He has no responsibilities. No duty. He owes nothing to that—"

"In fact, that's precisely what he has. A duty." He held her eyes. "He'll learn to perform it."

"That is the most asinine, Victorian rubbish I have ever—"

"Perhaps. But it's served us well."

"Us?" Spluttering. "*Us?*"

"Indeed."

"It's served you well, then, has it?" She wanted to hit him. "Served you well? Has it really? *Look* at you. Look at how you've just passed your evening!" She shoved open the door, and got out of the car. He did the same, watching her. Pushing down a smile.

"You've strapped your wife to a chair with razor wire," she shouted at him over the cloth top, "stood by and supervised as your colleague assaulted her, and then forced her to read you foul, four-hundred-year-old pornography in some arcane dead language."

She turned away and stalked up the footpath. "And you've *enjoyed* it. *That's* what 'taking it' cheerfully and without flinching does to a person. You fucking get! Served you well, my arse—"

He watched her walking away from him for a few seconds and then hurried to catch up to her. Pulled her hand through his arm. "I'm confused. You consider that an unusual or inappropriate way to pass the time?" When she didn't say anything, he continued: "I did suggest that we join the reception at the hotel, but you were unenthusiastic." He sighed. "I'm not sure what else I can offer you as holiday entertainment."

"If you send him back there," she repeated, her voice level. "I will kill you. I will make it *hurt*. And then I will remove him myself."

"I'll consider myself duly warned."

SHE wrenched her hand away from him when they reached the standing rock decorated with the first etched flower. Faced him and crossed her arms. "I'll need a hammer."

He reached into his overcoat and retrieved the revolver. "Will this do?"

She nodded and held out her hand for it. He gave her an expressive look. "I think not." Nodded toward the stone. "Indicate where I ought to aim."

Her brows rushed together, but she didn't speak. Instead, she crouched at the base of the rock and pointed. When he nodded again, she stood and stepped back. He stepped back as well, took careful, two-handed aim, and squeezed the trigger. A substantial fragment cracked and fell to the ground. Marion moved forward, took the piece of stone, and pocketed it. Jeffrey didn't stop her.

Then, silent, they made their way, following the etched flowers, to the mud volcano. Claudia and Thacker were, as Jeffrey had promised, waiting for them there. Thacker leaning, bored, against a stone. Claudia pacing between the stone and the pit with her usual frenetic intensity. Perhaps ratcheted up a few more notches. Marion could feel her almost before she caught sight of her.

Thacker pushed himself up from the rock when Jeffrey and Marion appeared. Still contemptuous. Uninterested. "Thought you'd be truant." He pursed his lips, watching Claudia pacing. "Hoped you'd be."

"And jeopardize the success of our assignment?" Jeffrey was taking in the outlandish environment of caked mud and bubbling volcanoes with open interest. "You ought to know me better than that, Thacker."

"I already know you better than I want to, Willcox." He examined the side of his muddy boot. Disgusted. "Now what?"

Jeffrey turned to Marion. "Still your show, Marion."

Since they'd arrived at the site, Marion hadn't taken her eyes off Claudia. Who had finally stopped pacing. She was now standing at the edge of the pit, staring into the slowly building mud, paying no attention to them. But even standing still, the impression of edgy movement hovered over her. Marion wanted to touch her. To calm her. She shoved the thought down.

Forcing herself to remain blank, she approached the edge of the hole as well. Stood slightly apart from Claudia. After risking a sidelong glance at her, which Claudia ignored, she spoke. "I'm going to activate it now."

Claudia nodded once. Cold. "Good."

"You remember what happens?"

"Of course." Claudia hadn't altered her position or her gaze.

"Be careful of the flame." Marion caught the hint of pleading in her own voice. Followed by embarrassment. "All right?"

Claudia, surprisingly, laughed. Finally made scornful eye contact. "Yes, Marion. I'll be careful."

Marion took the rock in her hand and tossed it into the center of the mud. Stepped back in preparation for the heat. Just as before, the mud drained, turgid, out of the hole. And then the gas flames shot up around its circumference. Claudia hadn't moved. And although she was safe standing where she was, she seemed unnecessarily close. Marion fought her inclination to reach out and pull her back a few steps. Closed her eyes instead.

Once the flames had burned down, Marion opened her eyes and turned to Jeffrey. He and Thacker, intrigued, had moved closer to the volcano as well, but they were still far behind Marion and Claudia.

"I must work quickly," she said to Jeffrey. "Before the pit fills again. May I continue?"

When Jeffrey said nothing, merely widened his eyes, surprised and entertained, she frowned. Confused. Thacker had begun searching the pockets of his trench coat.

Jeffrey lifted his hands, palms up, hint of surrender. "It's not there, Thacker."

Marion was bewildered. "Not there—?"

"No, Mr. Thacker," Claudia said. "It's here."

Marion twisted back. Claudia was standing, her feet apart, shoulders squared, training a .357 Smith and Wesson Magnum at Jeffrey.

Jeffrey, his hands a bit higher, still looked more entertained than worried. He scrutinized the revolver Claudia was aiming at him. Glanced over at Thacker, who had finally given up searching his trench coat. "Really, Thacker." He nodded in the direction of the gun. "You're Al Capone now?"

"Willcox," Thacker started, "you are a—"

"Marion," Claudia interrupted. "Go over to Sir Jeffrey and relieve him of his weapon. Walk slowly. Keep your hands in view. Do you understand?"

Marion nodded and did as Claudia asked.

"Bring the weapon here and leave it on the ground beside me." Claudia hadn't changed her stance or her tone. Marion knew that she could easily kill all three of them. Without a thought. Or, she corrected herself, without a thought beyond whatever broken logic was now motivating her.

Marion set Jeffrey's revolver on the ground at Claudia's feet. Backed away from her and stood, uncertain. The volcano had begun filling with mud again. The snake was submerged. Claudia turned toward Marion, aiming now at her head. "Come here."

Marion, walking forward, wondered whether Claudia meant to kill her. Or only to hurt her. And either way, what her exit strategy would be. Claudia had never been one to keep a back door open. When she was no more than a foot away, close enough that Claudia was pointing the gun up at her to threaten her face, she swallowed. Stopped.

Claudia took the last step forward and held the barrel of the gun against Marion's temple. Marion closed her eyes, waiting. But instead of squeezing the trigger, Claudia stood up on her toes and hugged her. Slipped something heavy into the pocket of Marion's shearling. "I'm glad they used me," she whispered. Then she stepped back, kept the gun on Marion, and narrowed her eyes at Jeffrey. "Now go stand with Sir Jeffrey."

Marion, obedient, backed up until she was next to Jeffrey, whose primary emotion remained glee at the turn the situation had taken. Claudia reached into her pocket with the hand not holding the gun and pulled out another piece of the standing stone. Tossed it behind her into the mud, which reversed motion, draining away. Rather than waiting for the flame to flare up and disperse, however, she stepped lightly, still childlike, over the lip of the pit and waded into what was left of the mud.

Marion, refusing to believe what she was seeing, shook her head. "Claudia!" she shouted. "Claudia, stop. It hasn't finished."

Claudia dropped the gun in the mud and held up her two jars. Dinitrogen tetroxide and hydrazine. Her altered recipe. "This time, Marion, it has."

Then, as the natural gas flames shot up, Claudia smashed her jars together. Marion made to run toward her, but Jeffrey grabbed her arm, pulled her back, and held her underneath him as the gas in the pit ignited, surging upward rather than out. When the flames subsided, the pit had been erased. As had Claudia.

Marion pushed Jeffrey off of her and ran, tripping, to where Claudia had stood. But all that was left was blackened clay and a few scattered stray fires. Flickering in the remaining gas. Whatever mechanism had controlled the pit was also gone. No mud was seeping over the remnants of the volcano. It was inert.

Jeffrey walked up behind her and let his eyes wander over the scene with muted shock. He didn't speak.

A few seconds later, Thacker, pulling the belt of his coat tight and shoving his hands into his pockets, followed. Bored again. He made a cursory inspection of the scene and then turned away. "That's the last of my Magnum, I suppose." Mumbling. He made his way back down the path. Toward whatever transportation he and Claudia had brought to Kobustan. "Tiresome business."

Jeffrey moved to put his arm around Marion's shoulders, to comfort her. But she shrugged him off and stalked after Thacker. Violently wiping a tear out of her eye with the heel of her hand. She didn't want to talk about it. Didn't want to think about it. She wished she could simply keep walking, without stopping, over the barren landscape and into the sea.

She felt Jeffrey behind her, but he kept his distance.

Suffolk, England
April, 1935

M ARION awoke alone in the bed. Wooden tester and carved fleurs-de-lis with scorpions hanging above her. After a few confused seconds, she remembered that she was in Suffolk—and that Jeffrey had already dressed and gone to breakfast. It was late in the morning. But Ginnie and Teddy had insisted on celebrating the night before, into the night, and she was exhausted.

After her return from Baku, Marion had forced all thoughts of Claudia from her consciousness. She couldn't acknowledge what had happened and remain functional. Instead, and in their place, she had turned her energies to rescuing Ian. Floating every argument she could muster against his returning to Temple Grove.

But Jeffrey had remained adamant. They'd been back less than a week before Jeffrey had placated Ian's headmaster and brought Ian, already planning his next escape, through the school's gate. Marion didn't know what additional security Jeffrey had installed in the surrounding countryside, but whatever it was, it had worked. Ian had stayed put.

Marion, however, had not. True to her word, the moment Ian had returned to school, she'd gone under. And she'd taken precautions. As a matter of professionalism. But Jeffrey hadn't made much of an effort to track her. He knew better.

Two months later, and four days before the start of Ian's Easter holiday, she had returned to Chester Terrace. Jeffrey had welcomed her without comment, and a week later, they had all boarded the train to Suffolk. No one mentioning Ian's term.

Marion rolled over in the bed, squeezed her eyes shut, and then sat up. She had a job to do. Throwing off the covers, she moved her legs, pushed her feet into slippers, and walked to the toilet. Emerged a few minutes later dressed in her usual uniform of tweed trousers and wool cardigan. Pulled on work boots.

Then, taking a cursory look about the room to be certain she was alone, she returned to her trunk. Opened it, felt for the corner, extracted a wool sock, unrolled the sock, and pulled out a coiled snake. Cast bitumen. Instructions and diagrams etched, tiny, across its surface. She'd carried it with her since Claudia had slipped it into the pocket of her coat in Baku. Having retrieved it herself earlier that evening. Marion hated the thing.

And, as she was well aware, her trunk was an entirely insecure place to store it. But she was out of ideas about what to do with it. The dispatcher was dead, she hadn't crossed another one, and despite keeping herself conspicuously open to approaches during her time away from Jeffrey, she hadn't heard from her organization. After what they'd done to Claudia, she wasn't certain she'd respond to them even if they did contact her.

But she also couldn't let Jeffrey or, worse, Maugham near it. She straightened and dropped it into her trouser pocket. Whatever happened, she'd get rid of it today. It represented nothing but pain and failure to her.

She left the bedroom, descended to the ground floor, walked down the corridor, and then peeked into the library. It was empty. She slipped through the door and explored the room, looking for an unused book behind which to store the snake. Ideally forever.

After several false starts, she singled out a leather-bound volume of seventeenth- and eighteenth-century labyrinths and hedge mazes. Placed at the bottom of a shelf in an out-of-the-way corner. Then she knelt and pulled the snake from her pocket.

"That book isn't nearly as neglected as it appears to be."

Marion looked up, startled. Virginia was sitting in an armchair, wearing a silk dressing gown, resting her chin on her fist, watching.

Marion stood abruptly. "I—"

"Maugham's fascinated by eighteenth-century labyrinths. Especially the haunted ones." Virginia stood as well. Beckoned to Marion. "He'd ferret out that little serpent of yours in a matter of minutes."

Marion looked stupidly at the bitumen snake in her hand. "It's not that. I—I just—"

Virginia tilted her head with a faint smirk. Jeffrey's. "Oh, good heavens, Marion. Don't try to explain." She rested a thoughtful finger on her chin. "But let me see. Ah, I know—"

She crossed to the fireplace, twisted a knob on the mantle, knelt, and used her fingertips to remove an otherwise solid-looking stone from the hearth. Revealed a cavity underneath. Then she held out her hand, still kneeling.

Marion, in a daze, handed her the snake. Virginia set it in the cavity, replaced the stone, stood, and retied her dressing gown. Returned the knob to its previous position. "Jeffie has no idea it's there. I give you my word. Drives him batty."

She put her arm through Marion's and walked with her out of the library. "I think it's beastly that he's sent poor Ian off to that prison again. But Teddy and I will be certain to keep a lookout. Should he turn up here again." She lifted a delicate eyebrow. "Next time, we'll forget to inform the father."

"Virginia—" Marion began, wanting to explain to her the seriousness of the snake. What it represented. How it was more than a game. But she couldn't finish her thought. And so, she stayed mute.

When Marion didn't finish her sentence, Virginia nodded, and then let her smile turn into a grin. "Would you like to make him *really* angry, Marion? I've got some ideas."

Marion found her voice. "Yes."

Yemen, 1935

London and Brighton, England
May, 1935

*T*HE heavy curtains shut against the midmorning sun left the room, despite its vaulted ceilings, oppressive. The atmosphere thick and hot. Not for the first time that day, Marion toyed with the idea of ripping them all open. Letting in the light. Perhaps even a bit of air.

Then, obedient, she fought down her impulse. The doctor would have to grant her permission first. She felt a stranger in the room in any case, not having entered it more than twice in all the time she'd spent in the Chester Terrace house. When she stayed in London, Jeffrey visited her room. She pretended that his didn't exist.

She shifted uncomfortably in the armchair she'd occupied since before dawn. Tried to read a sentence of the book she held in her lap. She'd bought it from a bookseller at the railway station, Graham Greene's *It's a Battlefield*. Couldn't concentrate on the jumpy prose.

Tentative, she lifted her eyes to Jeffrey's bed. He hadn't moved, and he was deeply asleep now that the fever had broken. After gazing at his tranquil form for a few seconds, she turned her attention to the carved serpent, cast bitumen with elaborate engraving, resting on his bedside table, against the ceramic pitcher of water. It was supposed to be there, she told herself. Pushing away her aversion to it.

As she forced herself to return to the book, Jeffrey stirred under his bedclothes. She waited for him to move further, apprehensive, but he didn't wake. Still asleep.

And so, she stared back down at the lines running over the pages in her lap. Communism, she reminded herself. Agitators. Brutal metropolitan police force. Willfully stupid journalists.

Then she gave up and let herself silently rant. She wasn't supposed to be here—in this city or in this room. Ian was at his hateful school. Against her wishes. And Jeffrey had tacitly accepted her refusal to remain in London so long as Ian wasn't home.

She had been content with the situation. Buried and invisible in a cheap hotel at the end of an unfashionable street in Geneva, reading a new study of Chinese motifs in Ilkhanid architecture. She had even been taking a sickly pleasure in the leisurely, tortured thoughts of her lost academic career.

But then, her peace had been shattered, along with any fantasy she'd harbored that her movements weren't monitored. A telegram from Mrs. Bowen had reached her, forwarded with infallible accuracy to her hotel, pleading with her to return to London. Jeffrey was gravely ill. He might recover with his wife at his side. He might recover *only* with his wife at his side. Marion had sensed the desperation underlying the three short lines, and she had been sufficiently shaken to take them seriously. Mrs. Bowen was not prone to exaggeration.

Even so, she hadn't been shocked by the summons, sensing as she had in its circumstances the machinations of her organization. Or of Jeffrey's. Or, quite possibly—and distressingly—of both. Jeffrey, as Mrs. Bowen enjoyed pointing out, hadn't been ill a day in his life.

Frustrated yet resigned, Marion had done her duty. Packing her carpet bag and her book, she'd left Geneva, a vacuous city, the economy of which was entirely dependent on people like her passing along messages to one another while other people like her watched and paid. And she'd dragged herself back to London. Inwardly protesting all the way.

Sitting now in Jeffrey's room, she wondered how the city—Geneva—had survived before last century's advent of inviolate borders and the despotic guards who policed them. Surely not solely on timepieces and chocolate. And banking. She rubbed her eyes. Not her problem.

Her problem, instead, was how at age forty-two, and Jeffrey four years older, she could maintain her enthusiasm for following orders. She gazed, unseeing, at the book. Ideological commitment had always eluded her. She lacked Jeffrey's joy in the absurd. And she felt increasingly disinclined to obey the bewildering instructions that reached her from her superiors these days.

She was, however, more than adept at ignoring her contradictory motivations and impulses. Which she did now. Not the time for soul searching.

"I know his sister."

Marion, startled out of her unhealthy train of thought, raised her eyes. Jeffrey had pulled himself up in bed and was leaning against the headboard, his arms crossed, the blankets over his waist. Dark purple pyjamas. Despite his pallor and the shadows under his eyes, he looked younger, somehow. More like Ian than ever. His tousled blond hair, Marion concluded, before pushing the uncomfortable and disloyal thought away. She didn't like finding similarities between them. Ordinarily, she kept herself convinced that Ian resembled her family alone.

Jeffrey nodded toward the book in her lap. "Elisabeth Greene. She's more intelligent than Henry—'Graham'—is. Keeps her counsel. Big brother never shuts up."

He pushed his hair off his forehead and re-crossed his arms. "Maugham's branch has already made a play for her, if you can believe it. Poor child. But they'll almost certainly lose her to a less arcane section when they've finished grooming her. Which," he added, "is for the best. Be some space then to bring the literary siblings into the fold once they've given up trying to sell themselves to the more dashing services out there." He considered for a moment. Irritated. "Why is it that everyone wants to join the Soviets these days? *Everyone.*"

Marion said nothing.

After a few further seconds, he closed his eyes, pained, although she couldn't tell whether his distress arose from the vestiges of his illness or from the educated, middle-class vogue for being seduced by Russian intelligence services.

"So vulgar."

She shut the book. "Do you know, Jeffrey? Even at the height of your fever, at death's door, out of your mind and delirious, you never stopped talking. Never. Don't you think you ought to rest? Let the office alone for a few weeks?"

"If I stop talking," he said, opening his eyes again, "it will give you an opportunity to blame me for wrecking your Swiss holiday. And I don't feel strong enough for that yet."

She looked at him under her brows, not speaking.

"Bring back any souvenirs?" he prodded. A trace of quiet mockery.

"No."

"Yes you did." He leaned over and reached for the pitcher of water and a glass. Seemed not to notice the sculpted snake. "But you can discuss them with Maugham."

She stood. "Later. You seem quite recovered. I'll leave you now to your—"

"He's downstairs." Jeffrey poured water into the glass and took a sip.

"He's not downstairs." Marion hadn't moved. She was standing, her book in her hand, watching him drink his water.

He finished swallowing. "He is. I asked Mrs. Bowen to send for him last night. Once I'd regained my senses." Marion started to say something snide, but he interrupted her. "Don't, Marion. It's too easy."

He set the glass on the bedside table, still ignoring the serpent. "She felt much the same way that you do about the invitation. For different reasons, I daresay. But, just this once, I refused to let her bully me. Maugham, she assured me, would be here by ten. And," checking the clock on the other bedside table, "that means we've kept him waiting for fifteen minutes."

He pushed the blankets off his legs, got out of bed, and stood. Grabbed a bedpost to steady himself as the blood rushed from his face, leaving him deathly pale. "Be a dear, would you, Marion, and entertain him until I can make myself presentable?"

"Jeffrey," she began, uncertain as to whether she felt more concerned or enraged. "You can't—"

"I already have." He had released the bedpost and wrapped a dressing gown around himself. Tying the belt, he glanced up at her. "I'm utterly exhausted, Marion. Please—relent. Don't make me send someone out to drag you back at gunpoint to speak with him. He's in the drawing room."

She stood still, silent, for a few seconds. Let her eyes travel of their own accord to the bitumen snake. Then she nodded, turned, and left the room.

MRS. Bowen was outside the door. Neatly dressed in her anachronistic uniform, but more drawn than Marion had ever seen her. She didn't bother to pretend she was doing anything other than waiting and worrying. Marion nearly stumbled into her before recovering herself. "He'll be out in a few minutes," she said, pushing back a strand of hair. "He's much improved. Back to himself."

Mrs. Bowen nodded. "Thank you, Lady Willcox, for returning. And—for sitting with him. It was an imposition, I know, but it made all the difference."

"I did it for you, Mrs. Bowen."

Mrs. Bowen, professional, failed to understand the implication. "Professor Maugham is waiting in the drawing room," she said instead. "I've brought him coffee, but if there's anything else—"

"No." Marion closed her eyes. Took a breath. Opened them again. "No. Thank you. I'll go down to him now."

"Professor Maugham is well occupied," Mrs. Bowen ventured. "If you'd like to refresh yourself first?"

Marion looked down at the wrinkled cotton men's shirt and the tweed trousers she'd been wearing now for two days. Then she cast Mrs. Bowen a quick, wry smile. "The last thing I'm going to do is dress for him."

"Professor Maugham," Mrs. Bowen said a third time, stopping her again, "if you'll forgive me for commenting, may be an unhealthy visitor for Sir Jeffrey to entertain just now. Lady Willcox."

"He's an unhealthy visitor for anyone to entertain. At any time." Marion turned to walk down the stairs. "But Jeffrey's made his wishes clear. God alone knows why."

Mrs. Bowen hesitated. Then she nodded a second time. "Do let me know whether there's anything more I can do, Lady Willcox."

"I will, Mrs. Bowen. Thank you." Fortifying herself, she made her way to the first floor and opened both doors to the drawing room. Then she stopped short.

Maugham—short, round, and malevolent—was lying on the ground. On his stomach. Reaching under a striped silk sofa. Unable to process the scene, she simply stood and stared.

When he saw Marion immobile in the doorway, Maugham jumped up from behind the sofa, brandishing a pen knife. "Dr. Bailey! Overjoyed to see you again."

Marion, not speaking, dropped her eyes to his hand and took a step backward. Maugham frowned and then noticed the knife as though for the first time. Lowered it. "Blasted thing has a mind of its own. Couldn't for the life of me get that—" nodding at a pink paper baker's box on the console next to the coffee service, "open. And then when I brought in reinforcements," holding up the knife, "chaos ensued."

He turned away from Marion, crossed to the box, cut the string surrounding it, closed the knife, and slipped it into the breast pocket of his jacket. Wide lime green and pale blue stripes. He had it buttoned tightly across his protruding middle.

Marion stepped into the room and closed the doors—gently, patiently—behind her. Tried to think of something innocuous to say to him, but Maugham was paying no attention to her now. As he shoved the knife into place in his jacket, he smashed down a white silk handkerchief that had been peeking jauntily out of its pocket.

He looked puzzled at the fate of the handkerchief, but then he pursed his lips, ignored it, and busied himself arranging the pastries on a spare plate. Brought the plate to the coffee table, returned to the console for a cup of coffee, and then lowered himself, satisfied, onto the sofa. "I walked with them all the way from Soho," he told her unnecessarily. "A convalescence gift for young Willcox. Be damned if I wasn't going to have them out and waiting for him when he finally made his appearance." He looked about the room, confused. "He is coming, isn't he?"

"Yes." Marion, choosing to disregard the rest of Maugham's speech, walked to the console herself, poured her own cup of coffee, added milk and sugar, and then sat, cautious, in an armchair across from him. Maugham was well into hapless mode. Which meant menace. She didn't want to say anything damaging.

Maugham sipped his coffee, fully aware of her thoughts. A glint of entertained malice flickered behind the befuddlement. He set the cup and saucer on the table, inadvertently tipping over a vase of cornflowers. Then he reached for his pocket handkerchief to wipe up the pool of water, but he upset the pen knife instead, which fell back to the floor. Slid partially under the sofa.

When he bent over to retrieve the knife a second time, Marion clenched her fists to keep from yelling at him. Knelt on the ground to find it herself. She wasn't about to let him continue the pantomime.

"You see what I mean, Dr. Bailey?" He was leaning over, red faced, watching Marion's progress as she reached under the sofa. "I believe it may be possessed. But those lovely flowers weren't there before, were they?" He straightened, considered the room again, and then bent back over to speak to Marion, who had felt the edge of the knife behind a leg of the sofa. "Ah yes. I see. They're here because young John—Ian—whoever—is away at school? No one to knock them over? I thought it felt quiet—"

"Here." Marion straightened and handed Maugham the knife.

As he accepted it and was slipping it, unfolded now, back into his pocket, Jeffrey opened one of the doors to the room. He took in Marion, kneeling in front of the sofa, and Maugham, flushed, handkerchief in hand, knife blade protruding from the bottom of his jacket's breast pocket, and he sighed. Closed the door. "That bad?"

"Willcox. You look ghastly." Maugham sounded delighted.

Marion looked up at Jeffrey, colored, and stood. Returned to the chair, sat, and armed herself with her cup of coffee. She promised herself not to speak any further. Jeffrey wanted her in the room for this meeting. He was ill. She'd do him that favor. But the minute it was over, she would return to Switzerland.

Jeffrey was wearing a loose, knit V-neck, white and navy blue, a white cotton shirt, and summer wool trousers. His hair was damp from washing, he'd shaved, and he seemed more than able to handle a conversation. But she'd never seen him so pale or weak. She realized, with some surprise, that he recovered from gunshot wounds more readily than he did from a few days' fever. She felt obscurely guilty. Sipped her coffee again.

Before he poured himself his own cup, Jeffrey walked to the coffee table, reached into his trouser pocket, and pulled out the black snake sculpture. Left it beside the now upright vase of cornflowers. Neither he nor Maugham commented on it as he went to the console and busied himself with the coffee service. Marion, uneasy, ignored it as well.

Jeffrey lowered himself into the armchair next to Marion's, placed his cup on the coffee table without drinking, and observed Maugham, who now looked more mischievous than bewildered. After a few seconds, he spoke: "you've overturned a vase of flowers, irrevocably water-stained that beautiful silk handkerchief there, ripped a hole in the pocket of Oscar Wilde's boating jacket there, left Marion on the verge nervous collapse, and," he peered across the room at an offensive gold Chinese ormolu clock, "it's not yet 10:30." He paused. Glanced at the plate on the coffee table. "You've also brought pastry."

Maugham was beaming, but he didn't speak.

"What is it?" Jeffrey looked at his coffee cup, but didn't seem ready to drink from it. "Has someone abducted the King? Eradicated our navy? Please just tell me so that we can get past the bit where you set fire to the drawing room."

"It was you who sent for me, dear boy, not the other way round." Maugham was holding his handkerchief up to the sunlight shining through the tall windows. Examining the damp spots spreading across it. Puzzled again. "I had planned to give you a few days to recuperate before presenting this one to you." He crumpled up the handkerchief and stuffed it into his trouser pocket. "Or a few hours. Oh," he added as an afterthought, reaching into his other trouser pocket. "I forgot. There's this too."

He pulled out a black snake sculpture, identical to Jeffrey's, and put it on the coffee table. Marion, despite herself, stiffened. They both looked at her.

"Thoughts, Marion?" Jeffrey still seemed no more than drained.

She shook her head. Silent. She had no incentive to speak.

"I have a thought—" Maugham started.

"Wait," Jeffrey interrupted him. "Before we do anything at all, I want one straightforward answer. To one simple question. Yes?"

No one spoke.

He looked hard at Maugham. "Here it is: I don't fall ill. Ever. It doesn't happen." He hesitated, choosing his next words. "And my understanding is that what appeared at first to be pneumonia these past weeks has turned out, now that the physicians have finished with me, to have been—something else. Unidentifiable. Still no one knows what."

Maugham raised concerned and derisive eyebrows. "Dear boy. How simply awful for you."

"Maugham," Jeffrey continued, cold. "Did you do this to me?"

Maugham held his eyes, entertained. "No," he finally relented. Disappointed. "I wish I could claim responsibility, but I much prefer you lucid." He sipped his coffee. "I did visit, you know. The sick bed. All I can say is thank the gods you're back. Keats, I am sorry to report, you are not. Never witnessed such an unromantic spot of debilitation."

Jeffrey watched him for a few seconds and then nodded. He turned to Marion. "Did you do it?"

"I—?" Marion stared back at him, wide-eyed. "I—I was in Switzerland."

Maugham, after a split second of disbelief at her response, began chuckling. Drank more coffee. Jeffrey glared at her, half angry and half astonished. Then he let the bland, professional mask slip over his features. "We'll discuss this, Marion, when I feel strong enough to address it. At length. Don't think I'm going to forget it."

She glared back at him. Pure anger. "*I was in Switzerland.*"

"I have a feeling," Maugham supplied, "that one of you is not long for this world. The way you two go at each other. Not that it isn't a joy to watch. Reminds me of my own sadly truncated period of domestic bliss."

Jeffrey stood, walked to the fireplace, and opened a box of cigarettes resting on the mantel. Turned back toward Marion and Maugham. "Would either of you care for a cigarette?"

When neither accepted, he chose one, lit it, and blew smoke up at the ceiling. Returned with the box to the chair next to Marion's and moved an ashtray on the coffee table closer to him. Put the box beside the ashtray. Inhaled slowly and then exhaled—thinking—gathering his strength. "So, what is it then?"

"Tell me what you remember of your delirium first," Maugham replied. "I believe that your unfortunate illness," twinkling appreciative at Marion, "has a singular bearing on the events the office is hoping you'll look into. Once you've recuperated, of course."

"There isn't a lot that can be put into words."

"There must be something." Still entertained by Jeffrey's discomfiture. "Anything at all that you remember? At the time, you were quite communicative. It grew tiresome."

Jeffrey tried again. "Very well. Mostly there was water. A great deal of water. Everywhere. Suffocating." He took another drag of the cigarette. "But the fear—" he looked up at Maugham, "—and I've never felt such fear, even as a child—it wasn't a fear of suffocation. It was of something else. Something terrible—living—under the water." He laughed. Uneasy. "Alienists would pounce on that one posthaste, I have no doubt."

Maugham widened his eyes, childlike. "Something under the water? Goodness, Willcox. Could it have been sea serpents, do you think? Monsters?"

"If you'd like." Jeffrey was avoiding Maugham's gaze. "Fine. Let's call them sea serpents."

"Anything else?"

"No." Jeffrey tapped ash off the end of his cigarette into the ashtray. "And this is embarrassing."

"Hmm." Maugham considered for a moment. Then he lifted the plate of pastries. "Madeleine cake? Jog the memory?"

Jeffrey snorted. Inhaled more smoke. "Subtle. Planning that since Soho, were you?" He exhaled. "I'm surprised you held back for so long."

"I make no claims to subtlety." Maugham was still smiling broadly. He held out the plate to Marion. "Dr. Bailey?"

"I wouldn't, Marion." Jeffrey crushed out his cigarette in the ashtray. "Maugham uses the wrong kind of almonds."

"Not on you, my boy." Hurt. "Never on you. Frightful thought."

Marion took a madeleine from the plate and bit into it. Still not speaking. She was famished. "Brave."

She shrugged, chewing. "I see it as an easy way out of this already interminable conversation."

"Oh dear," Maugham said, returning the plate to the coffee table. "Dr. Bailey is less than diverted. Let's move the conversation in a direction closer to her interests, shall we?"

"Yes." Jeffrey took a second cigarette from the box, lit it, and blew smoke up at the ceiling. Then he set the burning cigarette in the ashtray, rested his elbow on the arm of the chair, and leaned his cheek against his fist. Weary. "Let's."

Maugham nodded at the bitumen snakes in front of them. "What about those? Do you remember how yours found its way to your bedside two weeks ago?"

"I have an idea." Jeffrey closed his eyes. "I remember needing Nick Trelawney. Sending for him. I wanted him to go and find it." He opened his eyes, reached for his cigarette, and took a restless drag. "The sculpture was at Ginnie's. I don't know how I knew it was there, but I did. I also knew where she'd hidden it, though I'd never seen it before. I was terrified nonetheless, all the time that Trelawney was away. Not that I'd been incorrect about its whereabouts—but that he wouldn't retrieve it."

Maugham, who had been watching Marion, not Jeffrey, as Jeffrey spoke, let the silence in the room hang for a few seconds before smiling again. Nodding briefly. "Yes," he confirmed. "Trelawney was good enough to invite me to accompany him to Suffolk when he visited. Virginia was outraged when he led us directly to her most confidential of childhood hiding places, revealed your serpent to all and sundry, and then spirited it back to London that same afternoon. Wouldn't even stay for tea and interrogation."

Maugham was still observing Marion's face as he spoke. "She thought at first that Dr. Bailey had something to do with the betrayal." His voice was both ironic and intrigued. "But when Trelawney, honest schoolboy that he is, was genuinely bewildered by the notion that Dr. Bailey—paddling by the Alpine lakeside as *she* currently was—had any idea what was transpiring at your sickbed, she dropped that idea. Not the anger, mind. The anger, I regret to say, is still very much in place." Maugham finished his coffee. "I must warn you, Willcox. Virginia is girding herself for battle. She won't let this one go."

Jeffrey looked up at the ceiling. Sighed again. "Brilliant. Charming turn of events. Anything else you'd care to tell me?"

Maugham picked up the snake he'd brought with him. Examined it in the light. Then he turned back to Jeffrey. "I can tell you how I came across mine. Would you like to hear?"

"Not particularly."

Maugham turned to Marion. "Would you, Dr. Bailey?"

"No."

"Excellent." Maugham relaxed into his chair. "The story begins in Aden."

"Professor Maugham," Marion began, feeling that the conversation had crossed a line from unpleasant into gruesome, "now is not a good time. If you'd return in a week or—or three—Jeffrey would be more receptive to—"

"Get it over with, Maugham. Tell me." Jeffrey turned a pale, yet sardonic face to Marion. "He's not the one who poisoned me, you know." Closed his eyes again. "At least not this time."

"I've told you, Willcox." Maugham held Marion's look as he spoke, spiteful and triumphant. "You're entirely uninteresting when you're raving. If ever I poison you, it will be a quick and permanent state of affairs. No wasting illness. You have my word."

"Comforting." Jeffrey's eyes were still closed. "I know how you always keep your word."

"Quite." Maugham put the snake back on the coffee table. Then he reached into an inside pocket of his boating jacket and withdrew a sheaf of newspaper clippings. Placing the clippings next to the snake, he fished a satin sack out of another pocket and set it beside the clippings. "Best begin with Theodore Bent."

He paused, waiting for a reply. No one spoke.

"Bent," Jeffrey finally said after a confused minute. "Intrepid Victorian Explorer of darkest Italy, wasn't he? Long before my time?"

"You're being unfair." Hurt again. "Intrepid Victorian Explorer of all sorts of out of the way places. For the era. Including much of the Arabian Peninsula. And some interesting bits and pieces of the Red Sea."

"Hmm."

"He died," Maugham supplied.

"Yes," Jeffrey agreed. "Forty years ago."

"Do you know how?"

"One of those diseases that always used to take off Intrepid Victorian Explorers? Dysentery? Malaria?"

"Malaria," Maugham confirmed.

"All right."

"In London," Maugham continued. "A few days after he'd returned from Aden." He paused. "Or, at least they called it malaria, though the symptoms didn't fit. An unusual strain, they said. We had a few witnesses from the office taking notes in his sickroom as he faded away. It wasn't your run of the mill Death of the Explorer, Willcox."

"I'm very tired," Jeffrey said. "I know how you enjoy building up to the thrilling shock at the end. But could you please, for me, just this once, make it short?"

"No," Maugham said. "Patience, Willcox. Smoke your cigarette."

Jeffrey, obliging, lifted his cigarette from the ashtray and took a long drag. Remained silent.

Maugham considered for a moment. "So, Theodore Bent died of something that almost certainly wasn't malaria forty years ago. Something that came on him quite quickly, according to our reports, after he was 'jostled'—observer's term—by a Somali sailor disembarking a boat in Aden harbor. Natives, you know." He twinkled at Marion again. "No decorum."

She remained silent as well. Didn't rise to the bait.

"And?" Jeffrey hadn't opened his eyes.

"And so, from the moment he was—bumped—he began to fail. Seemed to expect it, too. As a result, he kept two objects remarkably well-hidden, even as his faculties deserted him. Embarrassingly well hidden." Maugham lifted the snake sculpture and examined it again. "Given that he was an Intrepid Victorian Explorer, and all that."

"I needn't actually know where he hid them."

"Very well." Disappointed by Jeffrey's lack of enthusiasm. "I'll skip over that bit. Move on to the fact that they are now, owing to Bent, here in front of us. This little sculpture." He set down the snake. Then he nodded at the satin sack. "And this little bag of coins. Hadn't thought much about them. For years, no one had. But then," smiling again, "you—or whatever it was that installed itself in your unconscious three weeks ago—sent Trelawney off to ransack Virginia's buried treasure. The moment I saw what your sister had tucked away under the floorboards, memories flooded back."

He took a madeleine and popped it whole into his mouth. Chewed. "Memories of those bits and bobs hidden away for forty years in the mountains of unused office files that no one's ever tamed. We never could figure out what was so fatally special about poor Bent's finds. A little black serpent. Some old coins. Fatimid maybe." He shrugged. "Who cares? Why 'jostle' him simply for shining the light of civilization on them?"

"How old *are* you?" Marion finally interjected, unable to contain herself. As Maugham spoke, she felt increasingly as though she were talking to some immortal, malign personification of centuries of European Empire. He never aged or weakened.

Maugham laughed, jovial. "You wouldn't believe me if I told you, Dr. Bailey." Then he turned back to Jeffrey. "But there is one more bit of information about Bent's final days that might interest you, Willcox." He paused, drawing out the moment. "The delirium, you see. Once he was back in London. It was unusual, to say the least. He raved and raved—so the notes tell us—about—and you'll enjoy this—sea serpents. Oddest idée fixe. Something was living under the water, he kept shouting. Under the Red Sea. Living, and about to surface." He chuckled to himself. "Suffocating, he insisted. The monster was suffocating him—"

"Yes," Jeffrey interrupted him, opening his eyes. "Thank you. I take your point."

"You seem," Maugham said mildly, "to have developed an aversion to your own serpent. Gone clean off the poor thing now that you've liberated it from Suffolk." He waited for Jeffrey to reply. And then, in the silence that followed, he continued: "and so, I won't ask you to speak further about it. Nor," smiling at Marion, "will I encourage Dr. Bailey to edify us with her own thoughts. Instructive though I have no doubt they'd be."

He paused again. "I would, though, like you to listen to the end of my story. About Aden. The Indian Ocean. And the Red Sea. We needn't disturb Theodore Bent's memory any longer." He kept his eyes on Jeffrey. "But you really must be made aware of this situation, Willcox."

Jeffrey crushed out his cigarette in the ashtray. "Very well. Continue."

Maugham held up his sheaf of newspaper clippings. "You haven't been keeping up with your *Times*, I imagine. What with being otherwise occupied?"

Jeffrey shook his head.

"No time like the present to bring you up to date on world events. So. Let me see—" Maugham shuffled through the clippings, held one up to his face, nearsighted, and nodded. "Yes. We'll begin here. The 29th of April. Two days after you fell ill. French merchant ship limped into the port of Aden. All but two crew missing. The two who remained were out of their minds, claiming that the others had been attacked and pulled into the sea by an enormous fish or monster. Frenzied. Couldn't get anything further out of them." Maugham glanced up. Then back down at the clipping. "French. Excitable."

He turned to another clipping. Nodded again. "Yes. And here we have two further reports on the 2nd and 3rd of May, one from an Italian smuggler who—let me be clear about this—had no interest whatsoever in making a spectacle of himself. The other from the imbecile we had embedded with him. Talking to reporters, no less. End of his short-lived career, I can tell you. But," Maugham returned to the point, "relevant to our situation, we hear the same story from both. This time, they claimed, there was also an odd current, a whirlpool maybe, accompanying the appearance of the 'serpent.' Neither, from what we understand, is willing to go anywhere near the sea again. The smuggler hasn't stopped weeping since he washed up in the harbor."

Maugham looked up at Jeffrey, inviting comment. When Jeffrey still remained silent, he sighed and shuffled through more of his clippings. "There are one or two of these reports—of the serpent, that is—appearing in the newspapers every day between the 29th of April and the 11th of May. All from boats entering Aden, having left the Red Sea."

He set half of the clippings on the table and turned his attention to the remainder. "And then, there is the local reaction. To the tales from the sea, you know." He perused the first clipping. "I believe, to invoke dear, departed Theodore Bent and his ilk, that their attitude to the situation might best be termed 'native unrest.'" Maugham pursed his lips again as he found the stories he was seeking. "Yes." He held them up one by one. "30th April, native unrest, 2nd May, native unrest, 4th May, native unrest, 7th, 8th, and 9th May—"

"Are you certain," Marion interrupted, unable once again to keep quiet, "that your natives are restless because a parade of French pirates, off their heads on hashish, have chosen to blame their inability to navigate the Red Sea on attacks by magical sea dragons?" She watched him, cool. "Could it possibly be, instead, that they're unhappy because you've been dropping bombs and gas on them since you established your air command there in 1928? And that you just gave away a large portion of the northern part of their state to the Saudis?"

"Ah. Pleased you've joined the conversation, Dr. Bailey." Maugham beamed at her. Then he considered for a moment. "And, in answer to your questions, no, I think it's almost certainly the magical dragons infesting the Red Sea that are spooking the natives."

He remained silent for few seconds of further thought. His eyes on the ceiling. Then he looked at her again. "What gas? I believe you're confusing our brave lads engaged in peaceful reconnaissance with the shameful Italians eradicating the African populations they've taken it upon themselves to rule." Gently reproving. "No notion of how to run an empire, the Italians. One almost prefers the excitable French."

"Dr. Bailey, however," Maugham continued, turning to Jeffrey before Marion could react to his answer, "does raise an interesting point. Your see, our position in Aden just now—not least because of the Italians and their unethical and illegal expansion along the East African shore—is delicate. We've always needed the port, as you know, to supervise traffic between Suez and India. And now, given the increasing prominence of our petroleum indust—"

"I don't want to hear about petroleum." Jeffrey's tone was adamant. And the shadows under his eyes had deepened.

Marion glanced over at his taut features. "Professor Maugham—"

"I'll come to the point soon," Maugham insisted. Then he turned his attention to Jeffrey. Irritated. "Time was, Willcox, I could brief you while you were bleeding out from three bullet holes and hadn't eaten solid food for two weeks. Surely you're not going to let a touch of grippe defeat you now?"

"I've told you," Jeffrey said, "I'm tired. That's all. If you'd simply continue—quickly—I'll be perfectly capable of taking it all in. Leave out the petroleum."

"Very well." Maugham thought for a few seconds longer. Then he resumed: "so our position in Aden is delicate. Our nine treaties with the local rulers are worth less than the paper—"

"Nine tribes," Jeffrey interrupted again. Still tired. "Well over twenty treaties with them, I believe."

"Anyhow." Gratified to have provoked Jeffrey into a reply. "Our—numerous—treaties with the—equally numerous—leaders in the region are, shall we say, no longer carrying the portentous weight that one might hope a serious document of that sort ought to carry. Increasingly open to unfortunate misinterpretation these days."

He nodded, encouraging, at Marion. "Hence, you see, Dr. Bailey, the importance of the airborne cartographic work that Aden Command have been undertaking. Local leaders in the hinterland are infinitely more inclined to recognize the moral authority of the treaties they've signed when the geographical arguments underlying them are reinterpreted from the air. On occasion, sadly, our lads do become exuberant with their aircraft."

Marion dropped her eyes. Forced herself not to retort.

"More than that, though," Maugham continued, "changes are afoot across the Empire. Not only in Yemen. The endless fight between the India and Cairo offices, for example, is finally—well—nearing an end. To the detriment of India, I fear. But much to the gratification of those of us who prefer our Orient rationally organized."

Maugham took another madeleine from the plate and bit into it. "Aden, after close to a hundred years, will be detached from India's administrative orbit and made, officially, part of 'Arabia.' A Crown Colony. Which," he said, "although a great relief to those who take an interest in the proper order of things, will also demand a new set of treaties, a reassertion of local influence, a series of renegotiations with our French and Italian colleagues—you understand."

"Hmm." Jeffrey looked revolted by the sight of Maugham eating the madeleine.

"We do not," Maugham continued, finally showing his hand, "need predatory snake-like monsters rising up out of the Red Sea and making a nuisance of themselves. These are intricate talks. Sea serpents will not help them."

"I see," Jeffrey said. His pallor increasing. "So you'd like me, then, to travel to the Arabian Peninsula to tell the magical dragons infesting the Red Sea to stop it until we've re-established our presence in Aden on new footing? That's the assignment?"

"You have a remarkable knack for getting to the core of a matter." Maugham, affectionate, watched Jeffrey fighting down his weakness. "Indeed. That's what I'd like you to do."

"Send Philby." Jeffrey's tone hadn't changed. He seemed to be sitting upright now solely by force of will. "It's his territory. I'd be stepping on toes if I went."

"Philby doesn't like boats," Maugham replied. "In fact, these days, he refuses to travel by any means but camel. Or car. Or, according to some of the more outlandish reports we've been receiving, a camel sort of—stuffed—into a car. I fear he may not be all—"

"Nonetheless," Jeffrey said. "This isn't my field. Irrelevant to the Museum."

"But you see, Willcox, it is your field. And it is entirely relevant to the Museum. You forget your mysterious carved serpents there." He nodded toward the snakes resting on the table.

Jeffrey, with an obvious effort, considered the snakes. Then he shook his head. Looked at Maugham. "Insufficient. All I have is your speculation that Theodore Bent, stumbling out of the desert forty years ago, draped in all of last century's melodrama, was describing the same sea serpents that are plaguing your smugglers now. And your insistence that there's some slight similarity between his sculpture and the one that Virginia had hidden—"

"Slight similarity? My boy, they're indistinguishable. This is beneath you."

"I'm ill, Maugham—"

"And then," Maugham continued, relentless, "there are also these." He opened the sack and spilled the coins onto the coffee table. "Eleventh-century Fatimid, I understand. Or Sulayhid? I've asked our colleagues at the Museum about them, and they insist that you're the acknowledged expert on this sort of thing."

Jeffrey leaned forward and picked up one of the coins. "Bloody numismatists. Do they hate me?"

"Yes," Maugham assured him. "They do hate you. But that isn't why they've named you as a source on this."

Jeffrey set the coin with the others on the table and leaned back in his chair. Closed his eyes again. "Still insufficient, Maugham." He opened his eyes. "And incidentally, Philby may be a twat, but he's not stupid. This is the very worst time of the year to venture out onto the Red Sea or Indian Ocean. Wouldn't need sea monsters to wreck an untried navigator given the seasonal winds. I'd like to state now, and for the record, that I don't like boats either."

"And then finally," Maugham persisted, still ignoring Jeffrey, "there's the book that Dr. Bailey brought back with her from Geneva."

"The Graham Greene?" Jeffrey began smiling. Despite himself.

Maugham raised his eyebrows. "Henry? He's got another one out already? Heavens. The boy does have a great deal to say, hasn't he?"

Marion, at the mention of Switzerland, had looked hard at Maugham. Then she turned to Jeffrey. "I—"

"Not the Graham Greene, then." Jeffrey spoke over her.

"No." Maugham tapped his chin with his fingertip. "But I must purchase a copy of it for myself. 'Gritty and modern,' they're calling him, no?" He paused, unimpressed. "Much prefer his glossy and traditional sister." He dismissed the novel with a regretful shake of his head. "No. I was referring to the collection of eleventh-century maps—Fatimid as well, I believe—that Dr. Bailey's charming Turkish paramour—no jealousy now, Willcox, our people have assured us that it was all above board—slipped to her in the café she was frequenting—"

Marion stood. "I'm leaving."

Maugham looked up at her, unperturbed. "You haven't heard the best part yet."

She spoke to Jeffrey: "I'll return at the end of the month. For Ian's holiday."

"Dr. Bailey." Maugham was watching her with nothing more than amiable regret. "If you leave this house before I've finished speaking, I'll be forced to have the remainder of this conversation with you in Chelsea. And I assure you, you'll never see that book of yours again."

"I'll buy a new copy of it at the railway station," she said. "I like 'gritty and modern.'"

"Dr. Bailey," Maugham repeated as she turned to open the door, "I really do think—"

"Stop." Jeffrey looked as though he were about to lose consciousness. He was keeping his face studiously relaxed, but he was also gripping the arms of the chair to remain upright. His fingers were white. Marion turned back and took a step toward him, wanting, ambiguously, to help him. Then she faltered.

"Maugham," he said. "I'm not going to take this assignment. I apologize."

Maugham pouted, petulant, and began to speak, but Jeffrey interrupted him: "and I would consider it a personal favor if you would leave Marion to her own devices for the time being. Go ahead and have one of your people lift the manuscript she picked up in Geneva—it sounds like an excellent addition to the Library—"

Marion glowered at him. "If you think for one minute—"

"I wish you the best of luck, Marion, in keeping it away from them." Jeffrey threw her a smile. "I have no doubt you'll pose them an interesting challenge. But," his tone was absolute, "I am not going to be a part of this. I can't."

Maugham stood and brushed crumbs from his jacket. "As you wish, Willcox. I can't force you."

"You can easily force me. But I'd thank you not to this time."

Maugham smiled at him. Fatherly. Chillingly so. "You're correct. I can force you. But I'll refrain from doing so just now. You need your rest." He patted down the pockets of his jacket. "But do take some well-intended advice, my boy: if your lovely wife offers you a cup of cocoa to ease the chill tonight—refuse." He turned to Marion. "Dr. Bailey, I look forward with eager anticipation to our next encounter. You terrify me. My compliments."

Marion couldn't help letting a trace of smug satisfaction creep over her face. She nodded at him. "Professor Maugham."

He ignored her and spoke to Jeffrey again. "I'll leave the coins. You may find something to do with them during your convalescence." Without speaking further, he opened one of the doors and left the room.

Marion, confused by his sudden departure, stood in the middle of the room. Doubtful. She watched Jeffrey, who had closed his eyes again and was taking a series of deep, steadying breaths. Finally, she spoke: "I'll bring Mrs. Bowen to—"

"Wait, Marion." He opened his eyes. "Don't bolt yet." He examined her face, weak and amused. "Maugham doesn't give up that easily."

"I know." She hugged her waist with her arms. Didn't want to talk any further with Jeffrey about Maugham's assignment.

"He has all the money and all the manpower in the world to devote to this," Jeffrey said to her. "If you take him on alone, he'll crush you." He laughed quietly when she said nothing. "Yes, yes, but you're not alone, you're thinking. You have your always mysterious organization backing you. And," he rubbed his cheek, "you've already so efficiently removed *me* from the equation—what could possibly go wrong?"

"I've told you," she said, angry. "I was in Switzerland. I didn't—"

"And *I've* told you, more times than I can count, you are an abysmal liar."

"I didn't—"

"Marion, I am too weak to do this now."

She turned toward the doors. "I'll bring Mrs. Bowen—"

Jeffrey stood, gripped the back of the armchair to steady himself, and walked to the door to hold it open for her. When she went through it, he closed it and walked beside her up the stairs. He stopped at his bedroom. "All I ask, Marion, is that you don't provoke him into doing something that will make us all sorry." He leaned over and kissed her lightly on the cheek. "That's all."

He straightened. "I suppose it says something unfortunate about my upbringing that I like you even better now that you've tried to poison me. And you've been an excellent nurse." He retreated into his bedroom and shut the door before she could reply.

She stared, nonplussed, at the blank, closed door for a few seconds. Then she spun on her heel and walked to her own bedroom on the floor above. Without wasting time to change her clothing, she packed the carpet bag she had brought with her from Switzerland, reassured herself that her passport was secured in an inside pocket, and trudged back down the stairs. Left the house quickly, pausing only briefly in the drawing room to pocket the sack of coins and the two serpent sculptures. She'd be a fool to leave them behind.

SHE exited via the front door, pleased to be free of the stifling house. Then she crossed the street into Regent's Park. By the time she had oriented herself toward Marylebone, she could feel three of Maugham's people on her. There were likely more. But she wasn't overly concerned by their presence. She had left her manuscript—the collection of Fatimid maps—in a drop before she'd made her way to Chester Terrace the week before. And there wasn't anything else of importance that they would take from her.

True, they could easily deprive her of the serpents and the coins—at least they could if they all attacked her simultaneously. But she was certain that they wouldn't. Maugham had left the coins in Jeffrey's drawing room deliberately. He wanted her to take them. Which meant that his people would be forced to track her, rather than confront her, to bring him useful information about what she planned to do with them

As she appreciated the budding trees and groggy insects making their appearance in the park, she was surprised by the hardened pleasure she felt at the thought of losing Maugham's people. Ordinarily, she approached these situations as abstract, if absorbing, puzzles to solve. Problems of space rather than of relationships. Now, though, her feelings were different; she was only just realizing how violently she hated them—and him.

But her personal feelings wouldn't interfere with her ability to elude them. Trained and professional though they were, previous experience had taught her that they went to pieces when faced with superficially irrational targets. They couldn't respond effectively to her method. She gripped the handle of her carpet bag and strode, fighting a smile, through the park. She meant to lead them on a chase that defied even the most basic principles of logic or self-preservation. They'd be baffled.

Once she reached the Marylebone tube station, she began putting her plan into effect. She'd had ample time, sitting in Jeffrey's dark bedroom, to consider the best means of disappearing from London once her duty there had been completed. And as she'd watched over his troubled sleep, thinking through her itinerary, she'd decided that using the office's advantages—its money and its manpower, as Jeffrey had termed them—against it would be her best course. Her strategy would fail if Maugham put a single skilled operative with an eye for detail on her. She'd never lose a tail, alone and clever, concentrating on her alone.

But she knew that Maugham, despite the blundering-don persona he adopted for interrogation purposes, couldn't resist an aggressive show of strength on the ground. He'd have an army of eyes, each equipped with the latest tracking technologies, covering any conceivable route she might take out of the city. He would try to scare her. And she would respond by turning their saturation of the area back on itself. It would be simple.

Taking a cursory glance about for the sake of appearances—etiquette to let them know she was attuned to their presence—Marion descended into Marylebone station. Her first step would be textbook, in part to lull them into complacency and in part to make her subsequent moves more confusing to them. Even more than that, though, she wanted to establish that they were as dependent on their technology—two-way radios and access to the telephone network at the very least—as she believed them to be. A classic test run would help with that.

Their radios, she knew, were recent acquisitions, installed in unmarked vehicles that would patrol the street surface. These vehicles could relay messages back to a fixed station in a building held by the office, which could in turn contact other vehicles on the network. But individual vehicles couldn't communicate directly with one another. And extended radio communication would drain the cars' batteries entirely.

Also, so long as she was underground, the radio operators in the vehicles would rely on a runner, on foot, to take information back up to the surface. Which meant that the effectiveness of the radios was as dependent on the mobility of the runners as it was on the vehicles sending messages back to the fixed station. It was a system that demanded seamless cooperation among operatives who were at least moderately aware of how the technology worked.

But the office had good reason to depend on its well-trained, highly orchestrated, coordinated functionaries. The sophisticated surveillance system that its technological branch had erected throughout the city and Empire was unparalleled. As far as its intelligence officers were concerned, there was only one way to evade it: to spend as much time as possible underground, ducking and hiding, trying to elude the exchange of information that would happen at the street surface. And a sufficient stable of runners moving between the surface and the underground would see to it that such a tactic would eventually fail.

Marion, however, knew better than to try to escape detection. Her plan was to do the opposite: to turn the communication network into a liability by ascending and descending with such frequency and such visibility that it would be glutted by the deluge of messages sent to and from the fixed station. She would give them all the information they wanted, and more. Refrain from hiding altogether. And if all went well, the vehicles sending and receiving the messages would drain their batteries that much faster—any drivers who were unaware of the dangers of excessive radio operation left immobilized. Their cars dead.

She'd used the tactic before with satisfying and often entertaining results in colonial cities run by governments that also prided themselves on their technological superiority. But she hadn't tried it in a metropolis like London. And rarely with British operators. She was looking forward to the challenge. Not to mention having mounting difficulty keeping the grin off her face.

As she rode the new escalator down toward the platform, she noticed the first of the runners returning to the surface. A woman of approximately her age. Carrying shopping bags. She'd been a few yards ahead of Marion going down, and it made little sense for her to be ascending now without having boarded a train. Marion felt a flicker of recognition pass between the woman and an earnest University student riding down behind her. He'd be entering the train with her.

She reached the platform just as the train was arriving, walked into the carriage, and remained standing. The young man followed her and sat down. At the next stop, Oxford Circus, she left the train and surfaced. The man followed her up and then walked south toward Piccadilly. Marion lingered, bought a copy of the *Daily Sketch* from a news stall, and watched as a new tail, another clean, nicely dressed young man, took the place of the University student.

After a few seconds, a bright, laughing woman, no more than twenty-two years old, walked up to him, kissed his cheek, and they chatted on the corner, animated, engrossed in one another's company. Marion smiled to herself, but she didn't move. Waiting for her cue. Less than a minute later, it arrived—a dark green Vauxhall 10-4 operated by a man who had apparently decided to drive his family of five through central London in the middle of the day on a Tuesday. Children not in school. Marion had seen it idling at Marylebone. The message had been sent, received, and relayed.

Having confirmed her hypothesis concerning the radio network, Marion tossed the *Daily Sketch* into a rubbish bin, unable to damp down her distaste at having purchased it. Began walking again. Straight back to Marylebone. She sensed the startled confusion from the couple at the street corner, and smiled more broadly.

On her way, she stopped at every telephone box she encountered and rang up a tea shop she quite liked. Then she observed, amused, as one after the other, the eyes fell by the wayside as they also stopped to collect the details of her communications. Using their remarkable technology. They would know by the second call that her messages were meaningless. But they couldn't—or wouldn't, devoted as they were to protocol—risk the possibility that she was contacting her people. They'd painstakingly review every call she made. At least it would keep them busy.

When she reached the tube stop, she descended again, rode back to Oxford Circus, and surfaced a second time. Waited for one of their vehicles to appear—or now two—and then descended back into the station. She boarded a train for Piccadilly, surfaced, waited, and then walked back toward Marylebone. Noticed out of a corner of her eye that one of the vehicles tailing her—an MG M-type driven by a frustrated socialite in a very large hat—nearly hit a pedestrian in reversing direction to follow her. After which it stalled, and its battery died.

This time, she descended into Oxford Circus rather than Marylebone. There was one runner ascending from the platform, and three more eyes on the street surface assessing telephone boxes. But no suspect vehicles. The radio network had already been overwhelmed. The fixed station could no longer communicate with its vehicles. She hoped, in addition, that at least a few more of the mobile units, beyond the MG, had lost their batteries.

More gratifying, as she rode the escalator down, she noticed that the runner, a middle-aged office worker who wasn't even bothering to pretend to read his newspaper, looked panicky. His brief, she knew, was to report on her movements in the tube to a vehicle at the surface, while a colleague, following her, boarded the train behind her. But there was no vehicle for him to contact, and the eyes were all still above ground in telephone boxes. No one was tailing her. She felt almost sorry for him as he squared his shoulders and prepared to pursue her himself. Which meant that he'd need to get himself off the up escalator pretty quickly.

He did manage to do so, scrambling back through the turnstile and drawing annoyed looks from the other passengers—and, just barely, he made it into her carriage as the train left the platform. But Marion, reading the advertisements on the wall across from her seat, felt little concern. He was clearly not their best man.

She left the train at Tottenham Court Road station, and walked in the direction of the escalators. The new escalators. But, to the confusion of her tail, she ignored them. The shafts from the recently removed lifts were an equally effective means of reaching the surface. They were also more private—the ladders along their sides still quietly in place, absent the lifts themselves, and awaiting the renovation of the building.

Allowing the miserable runner to keep up with her, and feeling ashamed of her good humor, she reached a shaft and slipped through a gap toward a ladder. When the runner squeezed himself through the same gap, she turned, slammed the heel of her hand against his temple, and eased him to the ground when he lost consciousness.

As she climbed the ladder toward the street, she told herself that she had done him a favor. He was not the type to be climbing three storeys up to the surface on what was becoming a remarkably hot spring day. He could regain consciousness in the knowledge that he had accomplished far more than the office could have expected him to. Certainly more than his colleagues had. At this point, they had likely regrouped and were attempting to triangulate her movements among the tube stations—and her telephone calls to the tea shop—into some coherent, deeply encoded, message. She hoped, spitefully, that their radios were all permanently damaged from overuse.

When she reached the surface, she unsuccessfully wiped the grime from her face, hair, and clothes, and exited onto Charing Cross Road. She felt a vague gratitude to English social blindness as no one noticed that she was covered in filth from the shaft—and she felt a far more concrete gratitude when the ticket taker at the Astoria Theatre allowed her to enter the cinema despite her wrecked clothing. As though he expected that sort of thing. Radically uninterested in what she was doing there or why. She reminded herself to smile at him on the way out.

She found a toilet in the basement, locked the door, turned on a light, and removed her grime-covered shirt and trousers. After stuffing them into a rubbish bin, she cleaned herself with water from the sink, and then she dug through her carpet bag for the change of clothing she had planned for her departure from London. A cheap cotton dress with a bright flower print, strapped shoes, a white hat with a yellow and red scarf tied over the brim, and a green and pink striped linen tote bag. She pulled on the clothing, brushed her hair, arranged the hat, and looked at herself in the mirror as she applied lipstick. Wry.

She was going to the beach. She held open the tote bag and settled her carpet bag inside of it. Then she tossed the lipstick into it as well, sighed, and snapped it closed. She hated the beach.

As she left the theatre, she nodded, pleasant, to the ticket taker, who didn't notice her. Then she walked back to Tottenham Court Road station, the tote over her shoulder, descended—using the escalators this time—and boarded a train toward Embankment and then Victoria Station. She reached into the carpet bag, hidden under the brightly colored linen, as the train left the platform, and pulled out *It's a Battlefield*. Entertained herself with the self-destructive drama until she reached her stop.

THERE was every possibility that the office had flooded Victoria Station as well, simply as a precautionary measure. But Maugham's people, if they were paying any attention at all, would be scrutinizing the boat trains and the trains to Dover. They would expect her to head back toward Geneva, or even direct to Aden, having no reason to waste time in England now that the material was in her possession. It would never occur to them that—resigned and dreading it though she was—Marion was heading to Brighton instead. Aboard the Brighton Belle, no less.

But not quite yet. Before finding the Brighton platform, she had a final task to complete in London. And so, she wandered—preoccupied—toward a newsstand, waited for two customers in front of her to purchase their newspapers, and then placed a coin on the counter. Asked the proprietor for a copy of yesterday's *Evening Standard*. He nodded, took the coin, rummaged in the back of the stand, and pushed a thin package, wrapped in the *Evening Standard*, across the counter at her.

She took it and slipped it into her bag. "Thanks."

The proprietor, ignoring her, was already addressing the man behind her. She turned away and walked toward the cheerfully painted Pullman cars of the Brighton Belle. Feeling vulnerable now that the Fatimid maps, wrapped in their newspaper, were back in her possession. But as she pulled the brim of her hat lower over her face and occupied her seat for the hour-long express journey to the shore, she sensed nothing in the atmosphere of the carriage that suggested professional attention. Her habitually morose expression did draw a few compassionate looks. But she could easily be the sort who travelled to Brighton to take her mind off some personal tragedy. Interesting, perhaps. Hardly suspicious. It was a complicated town.

Looking out the window as the train left the London suburbs behind, she worked through her next few steps. She had little interest in enjoying the seaside, even if she had been inclined to do so under other circumstances. Her days would now be tightly scheduled, and she must work with precision to prepare for her escape from Britain.

Also, her next move would be nerve-racking. Before she crossed her contact, she must protect her son from Maugham and from the office. Having received information from her own organization that Ian was at risk, that Maugham had floated the possibility, in-house, of using him to control her movements. But even if she hadn't known of Maugham's plans, she would have taken precautionary measures. She wasn't about to let Jeffrey complicate her assignment by producing Ian at some awkward moment. This time, she would take Ian with her. She couldn't trust him to anyone else.

She let her eyes drop from the view out the window to the colorful linen bag at her side. After deliberating for a moment, she unbuckled it and reached inside. It took a few seconds for her to decide to leave the maps—the Brighton Belle not an ideal place in which to reacquaint herself with them—and to pull out the novel instead. She wouldn't read. But having the book in her lap would help her to formulate her strategy.

As she stared down at the pages, she tried to decide whether to switch immediately to the Buxted line at Brighton station or to find a hotel first, rest, and return to the station the next morning. Ian's school had recently moved to Heron's Ghyll, a four-mile walk from Buxted. Marion planned to speak with him there privately, and then to arrange with him an effective way to return with her to Brighton. She was confident that she and Ian could disappear before the school's security learned that she had visited. She simply didn't know whether it would be better to work in the evening or in the morning.

Irritated by her indecision, she continued to focus on the pages in her lap. It was a source of mild embarrassment to her that she was more frightened of provoking Temple Grove's headmaster than she had been of provoking Maugham and his surveillance apparatus. She couldn't imagine how Ian survived there day after day. Her throat tightened at the thought of it.

Frowning, she shook her head to clear it of the unpleasant image. Rubbed her eyes. She loathed Ian's school. She hoped its headmaster would be humiliated by Ian's successful escape. But she must keep a clear head. Resentfulness was not useful.

Dropping her hands to her lap, she admitted to herself that she was in no condition to continue on to Buxted that afternoon. The journey from Brighton to Buxted was over an hour, and a four mile walk on top of that would be more than she could handle after the morning she had spent at Chester Terrace, not to mention the afternoon she had spent evading Maugham's people. The creeping exhaustion from her sleepless nights was beginning to take its toll. And the motion of the train was giving her a headache. She would find a hotel near the station once the train had reached Brighton. Satisfied, she slipped the book into her bag and waited for the train to slow and then stop.

The inn that Marion chose was pink, floral, and packed with Dresden porcelain. The woman who greeted her at the door, fluttering, fragile, and batty. It smacked to Marion of popular legends from her childhood—tales of charming old ladies poisoning or imprisoning their healthy, young male lodgers. Concentrating on other things, however, she failed to appreciate the atmosphere. Didn't even register the taxidermy cat behind the reception desk until a few days later.

Instead, she took her room key, looked, perfunctory, about the white and pink bedroom the woman showed her, reassured herself that there were two single beds in it, decided that she could tolerate the stench of synthetic gardenia, and then accepted the offer of an early supper. Descending to the dining room, she thanked the innkeeper for her recommendation that she try the Regent Dance Hall, and allowed her to think that, yes, personal tragedy had brought her to the beach. To recover. She certainly looked haggard enough at this point to lend credence to that idea.

Her meal finished, and incurious about what had been in the meat pie, Marion thanked her hostess and walked back up the stairs to her room. She closed and locked the door, sat on the bed, opened her bag, and removed the package she'd retrieved from the newsstand in Victoria Station. Unwrapping the pages of the *Evening Standard*, she exposed her bound collection of eleventh-century Fatimid maps. She didn't intend to examine them here. But she wanted to reassure herself that they hadn't been damaged. Otherwise, she'd never get to sleep.

At ease for the first time that day, she ran her finger over a page at random and worked through a few of the images and lines of text. Then, content that all was as it should be, she re-wrapped the volume and slipped it back into her linen bag. Lowered the bag to the floor. After that, she changed into her pyjamas, threw back the quilt covering the bed—hand made, blue dolphins leaping out of a pinkish surf—and slid between the starched, faintly salty sheets. She was looking forward to seeing Ian tomorrow.

THE next morning, Marion woke early. She pulled on a second floral dress, green, arranged her hat, grabbed the linen bag with her manuscript, novel, and passport, and made her way down the stairs. To the innkeeper's dismay, she also skipped breakfast. Rather than sitting at the fussily set table, she said a quick good morning, pushed through the front door, and stepped out into the unseasonably humid weather that had settled over the back street leading to the railway station.

Ten minutes later, she was sitting in a carriage, looking out her window, and eating the rock cake that the innkeeper had thrust on her as she was leaving—while her train, the first of the morning, eased out of the station. She forced herself to damp down her giddiness. She couldn't wait to see her son.

By the time she reached Buxted an hour later, the weather was indecently clear and bright, the sky pale blue, the countryside innocent. She didn't trust it. And she herself was more than giddy now. Jittery. But at least the journey to Temple Grove would be pleasant. She inhaled deeply as she turned onto a footpath that wound alongside the road.

She wasn't worried about being questioned or stopped as she closed in on Heron's Ghyll, but she kept quiet and invisible nonetheless. And once she'd entered the school's grounds, she moved with purpose toward the field. When she knew with certainty that she was unwatched, she paused and slipped behind a stand of thin maple trees just beginning to show their leaves. Then she waited, watching.

She spotted Ian almost immediately. He hadn't yet changed out of his uniform, and he was walking, solitary, at the edge of the grass, avoiding eye contact with the other boys. She was horrified by his demeanor, by the misery that couldn't have been more pronounced if he'd been weeping. But frustration wasn't going to help her extract her son any better than resentfulness had. She must concentrate on her task.

As she returned her focus to Ian, trying to determine the best way of drawing his attention, he solved her problem for her. Sensing her scrutiny, he stopped and looked up. Wrinkled his forehead as though someone were calling to him. And then, once his eyes had picked out the figure beyond the trees, he recognized her.

To her pride, he kept his face blank, changed direction casually, and walked toward her as though he'd been moving that way all along. His technique was flawless. No one noticed that he had a specific goal in mind. No one paid him the slightest attention as he walked, with intent, toward the edge of the field. She hadn't realized until now how well he had internalized her largely unspoken lessons about how to disappear and deflect observation.

Three minutes later, he was behind the stand of trees, smiling up at her. A bit shy. "Why are you here, Mummy?"

Unable to stop herself now, Marion bent over and hugged him. He hugged her back, less moved than she was. After a few seconds too long, she released him. "Ian," she said, "I'm on holiday in Brighton. Do you want to join me?"

He frowned. Didn't speak.

She noticed that he had a smear of blue ink along the side of his chin, although his tie was neatly knotted and his jacket carefully buttoned. He didn't affect the sloppiness of the more confident boys. She fought down the urge to rub away the ink.

"Why are you in Brighton?" he finally asked.

"I won't be staying in Brighton," she replied, not answering his question. "I'll be leaving for Aden in a few weeks. And I might spend some time in Lisbon before that. We'd be in Brighton for only two or three days."

"Oh." He brightened. "Yes, then. I'd like to come."

He didn't press her further as to why she was on the coast, seeking him out. Though she knew he had caught her evasion. He had learned not to pry when she didn't want to offer information, unless he had some motive of his own. When he did have a motive, he was relentless.

She peered over the field to reassure herself that no one was watching them. Then she spoke again: "good. We'll leave now. Unless there's anything you want from your trunk?"

He followed her gaze across the school grounds. His eyes settled on a boy tripping over a small heap of mud. A group of larger boys pointing and laughing. "Does the headmaster know?"

She shook her head. "No."

"Oh." He considered again. "Good." Then he turned his attention back to her face. Suspicious. "What about Jeffrey?"

"Jeffrey doesn't know either."

A mutinous expression came into his eyes. "Jeffrey," he told her, "says I must stay here. For my education. He says it's cowardly to leave." Annoyed with her for putting him in a position in which he must lie to his father.

She took a quick breath and pushed down her own, equal, annoyance. "Jeffrey isn't always correct, Ian." She held his eyes. "Do *you* think he's correct? That it would be cowardly to leave?"

He shook his head slowly. Thinking. "No," he finally admitted. Then he hesitated. "But my education?"

"What did you learn today?" She knew that she was being manipulative, but she didn't want to risk their being seen or Ian being missed before they were well away. She wanted him moving. Quickly.

"Divorced, beheaded, died," he recited, as she ran her eyes, quick and professional, across the grounds again. "Divorced, beheaded, survived."

"What?" She looked back at him, briefly puzzled.

"Oh, and in Latin we read Livy. On the Sabine Women. Livy says that if you're kind to a woman after you've been unkind to her, she won't remember that you weren't kind to begin with, and she'll respect you." He paused. "I got bored and re-translated the passage into Urdu, but Spode took my exercise book and threw it into the rubbish bin before I'd finished."

"And do you feel well educated today? After that?"

"No." His tone was becoming more confident.

"So would you like to come to Brighton with me?"

He nodded, this time without pausing. "Yes." He took her hand and walked with her back into the woods. Toward Buxted. Remembering her earlier question, he looked up at her. "I don't want anything from my trunk, Mummy."

"Good," she repeated. "I've brought a change of clothing for you. It's at the hotel."

"Can I have some rock candy at the beach?"

"Yes, Ian." She looked down at him as they walked. "I've missed you."

He smiled up at her.

They sat across from one another on the train, companionable but quiet. Marion didn't want to force him to talk about what she knew was a woefully unsuccessful term at Temple Grove. And she wasn't certain that she wanted to hear about it. Aware though she was that she ought to let him confide in her, her response to any detail he supplied about his pitiless education would be anger. Or violent rage. Which would leave Ian only more uncomfortable and reticent.

She never thought she'd miss the wayward, rebellious, and ungovernable boy he'd been two years before. The one who had gleefully driven off every nanny who'd ever cared for him and who had made every passing second of her life an obstacle to surmount. But seeing him now, chastened and uncertain, with the ink stain across his chin, she did miss that boy. She hated what had happened to him at Temple Grove.

"Mummy?" Ian was staring at her, appalled. "Are you crying?"

"No." She forced herself to smile, and then she opened her linen bag. "It's a warm day already. Would you like me to carry your tie and your jacket in here? I don't think you'll need them."

"Yes, Mummy." Ian dutifully removed his jacket and loosened his tie. Handed them to her to place in the bag next to the Fatimid maps. Her chest contracted when she saw his easy submission to her request. The previous year, he would have turned her question into an extended, excruciating negotiation. After which he'd have lost both the tie and the jacket in some roadside gully.

By the time the train reached Brighton Station, however, he was reverting to type. Bouncing up and down on the seat and peering out the window at the rush of brightly dressed holiday makers streaming off the express from London. When he jumped to the platform before their own train had come to a stop, she knew that the school hadn't hurt him in any permanent way. He was still her disobedient boy. She enjoyed the silent gratitude that flooded through her even as she leapt down after him and shouted at his retreating back to wait for her before running into the street.

Catching up to him seconds before he disappeared into the crowd, she grabbed his hand. She meant to pass most of the day entertaining him at the piers and the beachfront. Observing the people asleep in their deck-chairs or buying toys and candy from the stalls. But she did have one job to do later in the evening, and she wanted him to understand that it was important. It would take only a few minutes, but she must visit an antiques shop a few streets away from the front to retrieve a message from her superiors.

As she held his hand, following the crowd toward the water, she reviewed her instructions. The message would be simple—nothing more than two or three lines about how she would be crossing back through Europe before continuing on to Yemen. But she did need the information. She couldn't leave England formally, and if she weren't provided with a back door, she'd be immobilized in Brighton indefinitely. London, she knew very well, was not an option for her at the moment.

She pulled the brim of her hat further over her eyes and looked down at Ian. Most likely they would land a boat for her somewhere on the beach. Perhaps something large enough to take them directly to Calais. She squeezed Ian's hand in hers. He'd enjoy the voyage. Boats brought out his reckless side. And she'd always been proud of his fearless attitude toward wind and water.

"Mummy, can I have an ice now?"

They were nearing the pier, the tide high, crashing against the pilings and almost but not quite drowning out the sound of the people selling ices and cakes. "Let's have some proper food first. Fish and chips? And tea?" She pointed at the end of the pier.

He nodded, and she walked toward the turnstiles. But before she reached the boards, the back of her neck prickled, and her head went up. Not breaking her stride, she looked about. Behind her. Something was off. But she couldn't identify it, and she wasn't going to stop and reveal her concern. Instead, she schooled her face and kept walking. Testing the atmosphere. Forcing herself to project oblivious pleasure in the moment.

Then she saw it. A woman, eighteen or nineteen. Wearing a tight pink dress. Manicured fingernails. Dead eyes. Marion had noticed her walking in front of them out of the railway station. Now she was behind them. Unconvincingly enjoying herself.

Marion meditated as she led Ian along the pier. She knew that the woman was out of place, but she also knew that she herself was running on adrenaline from her work in London the day before. She was over-analyzing the crowd. And even if she wasn't, she refused to wreck Ian's afternoon.

They found a table at the edge of the terrace, overlooking the water streaming under the pier, and a waitress appeared a few seconds later. Ian, shy again, ordered fish and chips and a lemon squash. He colored violently and stared at the table when the waitress winked and told him after writing down his order that he could take her out to Sherry's any time he pleased. He had no idea what it meant, but he recognized the tone and couldn't respond coherently to it.

Marion, equally inhibited, quietly ordered fish and chips and a pot of tea. If they hadn't been obvious before, they certainly were now. She and Ian were ludicrously out of their element in Brighton. Nonetheless, when the food came, they both ate ravenously. The sea air.

As they ate, Marion took stock of the other tables on the terrace, and her anxiety rose. Now that she was looking for it, there were at least two other parties that didn't belong. An older man who was wearing his holiday clothing as if he hadn't been out of a suit and waistcoat for decades, and a mother leaning over a pram that she had no notion of how to maneuver. Marion forced herself to eat a few more pieces of the fish. Ignored the crowd.

Then she finished her tea and told herself not to panic. If Maugham's people had followed her here, she'd simply lose them again. And if it was someone else tailing her, she would observe them to form an impression of what they were after. She did, though, need now more than ever to retrieve the message from her superiors. It might shed light on the attention she and Ian were drawing. She kept her foot firmly on the linen bag she had placed in front of her under the table.

Once they'd paid for the food, and Ian had eaten two ices from a stall, Marion decided to visit the shop straight away. And so, taking a few precautionary measures, she led him up toward the quieter back streets of the city, lined with gifts and antiques shops. Glancing behind her as they entered a narrow road, more an alley than a proper street, she smiled. They were alone now. Their tail gone.

Losing the eyes had been laughably easy. Like a training exercise. Which made Marion even more nervous—curious to know who was giving them their orders. But rather than dwelling on the anomaly, she forced herself to concentrate on the task in front of her. She'd worry about the tail and what it meant later.

At an unprepossessing, warped wooden door, she stopped, checked the hanging sign, and walked with Ian into a dim, cramped interior. Mildly relieved. Although it was as hot as the outside, the dark shop felt restful after the hectic streets and their carnival atmosphere. She didn't even redirect Ian as he turned his attention toward a fragile mahogany table heaped with blown glass paperweights. The fact that she was in the shop meant that she was nearly out of Brighton.

At the sound of the bell above the door, a wizened old man wearing a striped shirt with the sleeves rolled up, a waistcoat, and a green eyeshade emerged from a back room. He smiled, benign and vague, at Marion. Then he turned the same absentminded smile on Ian. "You have excellent taste, young man. Those are beautiful examples of the type." He reached under the counter and produced an illustrated copy of Edward Lear's *Nonsense Songs*. "You might enjoy these as well. If you haven't read them already?"

Ian, withholding judgement, took the volume from the man. Then, turning the pages, he concluded that the book was acceptable. Looked up, smiled his thanks, and perused a few more pages.

The man turned back to Marion. "Are you searching for anything in particular, Madam?"

"Yes," she said, "*Madame Bovary*. A first edition. Do you have it?"

He nodded. "Indeed. In the back, if you'd care to follow me?"

Marion glanced over at Ian to be certain he was well occupied, and then she walked behind the counter and into the back room. The room was even smaller than the shop, windowless, packed with broken bits of furniture and heaps of paper. There was a desk wedged into it, against a wall, but it wasn't discernible under the debris. As soon as she had entered, she was itching to leave. She could scarcely breathe. But, gathering herself, she remained detached. Waiting.

The man, stepping over a collection of disused parts of a clock, reached the back corner of the room, bent down, and tugged at a book that was shelved between a brass umbrella stand and a yellow ceramic elephant. When he succeeded in extracting it, he exhaled with satisfaction, stood, and brought it to Marion. "I believe," he said, "that Madam will find page forty-three to be of particular interest."

She took the book from him. "Thank you. How much?"

He shook his head and walked past her toward the front of the shop. "Nothing. I'm pleased to have it off my hands."

She followed him, stuffing the book into her linen bag. "Thank you," she repeated.

Passing the counter, she began to tell Ian that it was time to return to their hotel. Then she stopped short, her stomach in her throat. The shop was empty. Ian wasn't there.

Not quite processing what she was seeing, she looked about the tiny room. There wasn't anywhere he could be hidden. No adjoining doors. He was gone. She turned back to the shopkeeper, but he had disappeared into the room beyond the counter.

Then she shook her head, rebuking herself. She knew Ian. He'd gotten bored and was exploring the street. Edward Lear could keep him entertained for only so long. She resettled her hat on her head and walked out of the shop, prepared to tell him in angry and painful detail what she thought of him for terrifying her.

But the street, quiet and sinister, was empty. Oppressive. Hot. A cat slunk along the gutter and disappeared into a crack between two buildings. There was no sign of Ian.

She ran to the end of the street and looked up the hill. Nothing. Then, breathing heavily, she ran back to the shop. The front was still empty, but she went through it, wrenched open the door behind the counter, and stalked into the back room. The man was sitting at his desk, going over a sheet of figures, his face hidden by the eyeshade.

She slammed her hands down on the desk. "Where is he?"

A few sheets of paper floated to the ground, and the man looked up. "Madam?"

"My son. The boy. *Where is he?*"

"Madam," he said, "will find page forty-three to be of particular interest." Then, dismissing her, he returned his attention to his sheet of figures.

"I will *kill* you, you despicable old man, if you don't tell me, *now*, where he is." When he failed to respond, she reached across the desk and grabbed him by the throat.

"Madam," he said, unperturbed, "how will this help you?"

She took a ragged breath and let him down again. He straightened his shirt and waistcoat. A fleeting look of understanding, which evaporated almost as soon as it had appeared. "Page forty-three," he emphasized. "Madam will find it to be of particular interest." He held her eyes. Challenging.

She swallowed, nodded, and left the back room. On her way out, she paused at the display of glass paperweights, glared down at it, and then shoved the table over. The sound of the glass shattering stayed with her all the way back to her hotel.

By the time she walked into the musty entryway of the inn, she was shaking, unable to control her shock. The old woman, knitting something pink at the reception desk, took in Marion's state with a serene lack of understanding. Then, confused, she let her eyes wander toward the doorway. "You had said there would be a boy?" She shook her head. "I fear I misheard. So silly. And I bought him rock candy." The woman held up a paper bag. Also pink. Tied with a ribbon.

Marion pushed down a sob and walked up the stairs without speaking. Personal tragedy, she raged to herself. The innkeeper would understand. When she reached her room, she sat on her bed, willing herself not to throw up the food she had eaten on the pier. Then she poured herself a glass of water, drank a few sips, set the glass on the bedside table, and opened her bag. She removed the copy of *Madame Bovary*, a pencil, and a spare sheet of paper.

Her fingers were trembling so severely that she had difficulty turning the pages of the book to forty-three. When she finally found her place, she traced the lines of text with her fingertip until, in the middle of the second paragraph, the letters scrambled. Same font. You'd need to be looking for the change. The encoded message from her organization.

She smoothed out the page of the book, still feeling ill, took up the pencil, and began decoding. She made so many mistakes and had to re-start so many times that it took her nearly an hour before she had the short message in its entirety spelled out on the paper in front of her: "the child is safe. Remain in your current location. Contact will come as usual."

She crumpled up the sheet of paper and tossed it into the bin next to the bed. Then she stared, unseeing, at the wall across from her. She'd been so stupid. So very, very stupid.

MARION stayed in Brighton for two further days, not in obedience to her orders but because she had a frail hope that she would find clues in the city as to what had happened to her son. As she plodded through the streets and along the shore, sweating in the still unseasonably hot weather, she enumerated to herself all the places they could have taken him. Where she could go to find him. But the list was endless. Global. He might be anywhere in the world.

She noticed, dully, that the eyes remained on her as she retraced her route throughout the city. Without variation. Three, four, or five times every hour. She didn't bother to vanish. Though in a moment of desperation, she did consider speaking to one of them. Asking whether he'd seen anything at the time that Ian had disappeared. Begging him to answer.

But she prevented herself before she took the humiliating step. She knew very well that he'd respond with blank, embarrassed confusion. As he'd been trained to do. And anyway, she'd lost them before contacting the antiques dealer. Disdainful of their inferior skills. Proud of her impressive work.

On the evening of the second day, she resolved to stop. Her obsessive rounds of the city were making her weak. And the walking was doing nothing to help her find Ian. She was using the search—wearing the same soiled cotton dress, eating nothing, suffering in the oppressive heat—as a penance. Because she was afraid to do what must be done.

And so, on the morning of the third day, she came to a decision. Packing her carpet bag, leaving the empty linen bag and *It's a Battlefield*—which left her now feeling sick—on the bed, and taking leave of the kind, distracted, and useless innkeeper, she walked to the railway station. Boarded the first express to London. Stared into the middle distance throughout the journey. This time, she looked worse than morose and picturesque. The other passengers, returning holiday-makers, gave her wide berth. The social quarantine surrounding those in grief.

When she reached Victoria Station, she took a taxi straight to Chester Terrace. Revolted by the thought of the tube. After paying the driver, she clenched her carpet bag, walked up the steps to the front door, and rang. The maid looked surprised to see her, but covered it admirably and smiled, letting her into the house. "Good morning, Lady Willcox. We hadn't expected you." She took Marion's carpet bag and hat. "Sir Jeffrey, I'm afraid, has already left for the office."

Marion tried to smile. "It's Saturday. He's recovered already?"

"Mrs. Bowen wanted him to stay home for a few days longer. But Sir Jeffrey—"

"—insisted." Marion rubbed her eyes. She hadn't slept since Ian had disappeared. "Yes. He would." She looked at the maid with something like entreaty. "Is my room made up? I don't want to trouble you."

"It is." She stood to the side. "Is there anything else you need?"

"No. Thank you. But would you have someone ring the office to let him know that I've returned?"

"Yes, Lady Willcox. Immediately."

"Thank you," she repeated.

Then, unable to remain upright, she took her bag from the maid, and trudged up the spiral stairs to her room. When she opened the door, she was surprised by the comfort she felt. Ordinarily, the room left her at best apprehensive.

She shut the door, locked it, lowered her bag, and peeled off the sticky floral dress. Wadded it up and stuffed it behind the bag. She had intended to collapse immediately into bed, but the thought of dirtying the immaculate bedclothes with the stench of desperation she had brought back from Brighton depressed her. So instead, she ran a bath for herself, washed quickly and without enjoyment, rinsed her hair three times, trying unsuccessfully to rid it of the smell of the seaside, and then stood, dripping, and drained the tub.

She wrapped a towel around herself, returned to the bedroom, and crawled into the bed without troubling to find pyjamas. She slept for eight hours. When she woke, she was disconcerted by the changed light in the room. She had planned to be up and dressed after a short nap. But when she rolled over and peered at the clock on the bedside table, she sat up, shaken. It was nearly seven in the evening. If they had contacted Jeffrey when she had asked them to, he would have been home hours ago.

She pressed her clenched fists against her eyes for a few seconds, and then she threw off the covers and walked to the dressing room. She had avoided contemplating the conversation she would initiate with Jeffrey when she returned to London. She couldn't begin to predict his reaction to Ian's disappearance—and she didn't try—but whatever that reaction was, she'd be forced to endure it. Swallow his anger. Or his mockery. Possibly both. This was her mistake, and she needed his help to clear it up.

Wearing the sort of dinner dress he liked wouldn't hurt, she told herself. Unconvincingly. Unhappily. Running her fingers through her still damp hair, she examined her options. Eventually, she settled on a wine-red, draped Chéruit cocktail dress that evoked—ironically, she supposed, although the joke was lost on her—the 1920s. She chose shoes that were a little higher than she preferred, found new stockings, and then brought them out to the bedroom.

She dressed carefully, walked to the dressing table, sat, and brushed her hair. Twisting it back and up. He liked her to show her neck. Then, pensive, the palm of her hand against the side of her neck, she stood, walked to her carpet bag, and dug through it looking for the lipstick she'd worn for her cover. When she found it, she brought the tube to the dressing table, sat again, paused, and colored her lips. Resigned. He'd laugh at her. But, she reminded herself as she stood, dropped the lipstick onto the table, and walked to the door, he'd laugh at her anyway.

She pulled open the door and peeked into the corridor. Empty. She walked down the stairs toward his study. And she was about to knock on the closed door when Mrs. Bowen stopped her. "Sir Jeffrey is in his bedroom, Lady Willcox. He asked that I send you to him when you'd dressed."

"His bedroom? I thought he'd recovered."

"He has." Mrs. Bowen smiled. Proud of his constitution. Hint of the nursery. "He's dressing now. For dinner."

"Oh." Marion looked down at her own dress. "Oh. I see. I'll—I'll find him there, then." She turned and walked back up the stairs before Mrs. Bowen could tell her how pleased they were to see her returned to Chester Terrace. Her anxiety at the thought of the coming conversation was bothering her stomach.

She stopped in front of the door to his bedroom, fortified herself, and knocked. When she heard him shout from inside to enter, she pushed open the door, walked into the room, and shut the door behind her. The curtains were now open in the fading sunlight, and the room had lost the close, heavy atmosphere of the infirmary. It was bright and pleasant. Also alien. She wrapped her arms around her waist, looking at him.

Jeffrey was sitting on a sofa, slipping his feet into shoes. He had washed and brushed back his hair, and he was wearing black trousers and a starched white shirt. His dinner jacket and tie were hanging over the back of an armchair near the window. There was a pallor to his complexion, but otherwise he looked healthy. The repressed energy was back.

The corner of his mouth went down when he saw her outfit. "Marion. You look lovely."

"Thank you." Ignoring his tone.

He finished lacing his shoes and straightened. Let his arm rest over the back of the sofa. Enjoyed her discomfort at standing in the middle of the room in front of him. "I left the office the moment I received news that you'd arrived. But by the time I made it back here, you were already asleep. I felt it would be unkind to wake you. And," he continued, standing and walking toward his jacket and tie, "of course, you lock the door."

As he knotted his tie, looking in a mirror, she examined his reflection, trying to read his mood. There was an emotion lurking beneath his light tone, but she couldn't tell whether it was contempt or triumph. And Jeffrey knew as well as she did that he could easily enter her room regardless of whether she locked the door.

She remained quiet, watching as he buttoned his jacket and fixed his cuff links. When he had finished dressing, he held out his arm. She didn't take it. "Jeffrey—" she started.

He stepped toward her and took her elbow in his hand. Propelled her toward the door. "Let's talk at dinner," he said. "I'm eager to hear how you found Brighton." He brought her out into the corridor. "How you both found Brighton."

She looked up at him, startled. But she didn't say anything. Instead, she swallowed, dropped her eyes, and let him lead her down the stairs. When they entered the dining room, she saw that the table had been set for three. But she didn't comment. Sat in her usual chair and waited.

Neither said anything as the soup arrived. Asparagus. Three bowls. Marion forced herself to eat a few bites, still waiting. But Jeffrey remained silent. Eating. Placid. As minutes passed.

It was only after the atmosphere in the room had become unbearable that he finally chose to initiate a conversation. Taking a sip of wine, he considered the empty seat next to hers. "Oh dear. Someone appears to be missing."

Marion, frightened now, dropped her spoon. Stared at his bland face. And then, realizing that Jeffrey had no intention of helping her, she could no longer hold in her misery. She put her face into her hands and sobbed.

Jeffrey relinquished his wine glass and returned to his soup. "Is something the matter, Marion?"

She choked back her tears and balled her hands into fists over her mouth. Her eyes now wide. "This is monstrous. It's grotesque. Why are you—?"

"Yes," he agreed, still eating. "Monstrous is a good word for it. Guilt is an ogre of an emotion, isn't it?"

"Guilt?" She gaped at him. "*Guilt*? What are you talking about—"

"Noble soul that you are, perhaps it's unfamiliar to you." He lowered his soup spoon. "So, let me help you to identify it. Do you know that pain that's knifing through the pit of your stomach just now? Feel it?" He paused, waiting for a reaction. "Guilt."

He nodded at the servant who removed the soup bowls and replaced them with poached salmon. Dill sauce. Peas. Three plates. Then he turned back to Marion. She had taken a fork and was trying to eat a bite of salmon. Her hand was shaking furiously.

"Guilt," he continued, "because, at long last, it's happened, hasn't it?" He watched her hand, coolly interested, as he cut into his own fish. "The boy—your decoy—went the way of all decoys. You were given a choice between your son and your work, and—" He shrugged. Eloquent.

She stared at him in horrified disbelief. And then, before she knew what she was doing, she threw her fork at him. He ducked as it clattered against the wall, and then he glanced at the floor behind him. He turned back to her, astonished. "Did you just throw a fork across my dining room?"

She pushed back her chair and stood. "You're a pig."

When she turned to leave, he started laughing. Breaking the atmosphere he had engineered. "Marion," he said. "Darling, wait." He stood as well and spoke to the servant. "Please tell Louise that the food was delicious. Unfortunately, Lady Willcox is feeling unwell."

She was already out the door as he strode to catch up to her. When he reached her, he took her arm again and walked her up the stairs toward his study. Then he opened the door and pushed her into the room. "Will be an interesting conversation downstairs tonight."

She shook her head, still weeping. Walked to the window and looked out into the darkness. He went to a cabinet in the corner of the room, found two tumblers, poured a measure of scotch into each, and brought one to her. Stood beside her at the window. "Perhaps it's not guilt after all," he said when a few more seconds had passed. "Is it humiliation, I wonder? You don't fail very often, do you?"

She took the glass of scotch, but she didn't drink any of it. "Stop it."

His reaction was worse than anything she'd predicted. She felt annihilated. Closing her eyes and taking a sip of her drink, she made herself stop crying. At least he already knew. She wouldn't be forced to tell him. But then, when her mind returned to the image of Ian, terrified and alone somewhere, her tears brimmed up. She choked and returned to the sofa. Put the scotch on the side table, her face in her hands, and began sobbing again.

Jeffrey followed her, set down his own glass, and sat next to her. He wrapped his arm around her shoulders and pulled her closer to him. "Marion," he said. "He'll be fine. It isn't in anyone's interest to hurt him."

She rubbed her eyes and looked up at him, suspicious. When he saw her expression, he smiled again, faintly sardonic. "They told you the same thing, did they? Your people?" His smile grew. "So you see? All is well. You needn't bother yourself."

"When did you find out?" She straightened and reached for her drink.

He loosened his tie, removed it, and draped it over the arm of the sofa. Then he unfastened the top button of his shirt. Stood and walked to a box of cigarettes on his desk. He spoke as he chose one: "his headmaster at Temple Grove telephoned me on Wednesday when he didn't appear on the field. It wasn't difficult to connect the dots." He lit the cigarette and inhaled. "I sent a few of my people to the station directly. Had them in the area anyway to look after the boy. Keep him on the straight and narrow."

He walked to an armchair and sat across from her. Relaxed and let his hand, holding the cigarette, hang down toward the ground. Vestiges of his illness catching up to him. Despite his flippant attitude, he was tired. "They saw the two of you board at Buxted. And so, in the interest of professional courtesy, I informed Maugham. He was more than happy to send his own people down on the next express from London."

He rubbed his temple with the back of his thumbnail, still holding the cigarette. "I fear they weren't his best. Forced to make do with what was immediately available." His lips twitched in the beginning of another smile. "His *very* best, or so gossip has it, were in disgrace, having recently allowed a shockingly expensive surveillance apparatus to go up in smoke with not the tiniest bit of intelligence to show for it."

Marion wasn't in the mood to let him lead her. She stared across at him, hollow eyed. "What am I going to do?"

"I've told you, Marion, you needn't worry. Your people have no interest in harming the boy. Your guess is better than mine as to why they felt they must collect him." He took another lazy drag of his cigarette. "But they will contact you. When they do, you'll have your location." He raised a wicked eyebrow, teasing. "As, of course, will we."

"No, I won't." She dropped her eyes. "They told me to stay in Brighton. I left."

"Well, that was a stupid thing to do."

"They lied to me. They kidnapped my son. I wasn't about to sit there, obedient, waiting on their word." When he didn't respond, she stood and stalked over to the box of cigarettes. Took one and lit it with Jeffrey's lighter. Inhaled, tense. Paced back to the window. Stood with her back to him, looking out.

Jeffrey watched her from his chair. "You know," he finally said, "if I were running you—and thank God I'm not this time—I'd leave you hanging for a few more weeks merely to make it clear what a pest you're being. Has it occurred to you that by stomping off in an affronted rage—not to mention bringing that manuscript you were so keen to protect straight back here to me—you've jeopardized what is almost certainly a larger and more important project?" Exasperated, he kept his eyes on her angry back. "I find it bizarre to be admitting this, but I feel a certain sympathy for your handlers. Might like to sit down with them someday to share a drink and commiseration. A few drinks."

She turned back toward him and glared. Didn't say anything. He took another drag of his cigarette. "You aren't frightened of them?"

"No." Sullen.

"Then they haven't done their job." He considered for a few seconds. "But you've piqued my curiosity. What do *you* think you're going to do? Now that you've disobeyed your orders?"

She looked down at the cigarette in her hand. Took another quick drag. Cursed the fact that her fingers were still trembling. "I thought perhaps that Maugham—"

Jeffrey burst out laughing. "*Maugham?*" He ground out his cigarette in an ashtray. "Marion, if Maugham does know anything—and yes, it's entirely possible that he does—it will give him nothing but the greatest pleasure to keep it from you. He'll watch you grovel. And then he'll go into bureaucrat mode. Torture you with irrelevancies. If nothing else, it will be an opportunity for him to avenge his honor now that you've demonstrated to his minister the utter waste of the tens of thousands of pounds they spent on that radio web."

"I wouldn't go into it with nothing," she replied, cool now. "I could offer him something in return. A trade."

"What could you possibly give us that we don't already have?" He lifted his scotch and took a sip. Watched her over the rim of the glass.

She returned to the sofa and sat across from him. Held his eyes. Hopeful. "Cooperation. I could cooperate."

"Darling." His voice was warm. "I thought you knew. You're more useful to us when you don't cooperate." He set down his drink. "Not to mention entertaining."

"If you're saying that to insult me, I—I understand. But I'm serious, Jeffrey. I could—"

"I'm saying that because it's true." He tapped his fingers a few times on the arm of the chair. "When you 'cooperate,' you do so under duress, no matter how forthcoming you think you're being. And the message gets muddied. But when you're coerced, seduced, or tricked, your tells are so classic you might as well be typing up the reports yourself."

She stared at him, uncomprehending. Ground out her cigarette in the ashtray. "But—but surely—"

He shook his head. "No. The office is quite satisfied with your work as it is." He smiled. Impudent. "I'm pleased that we've had this opportunity to discuss your progress."

"But—" Her voice was weak. Desperate.

"It isn't only that, Marion." Relenting. "As much as Maugham is a pragmatist—always willing to negotiate if he thinks it will further his aims—beneath all the layers of cold utilitarianism, he's also human. You've mortified him more than once now. He'll leap at the chance to do the same to you."

"Ian is my *son*." She felt the tears coming again and pushed them back. "I can handle a bit of mortification."

"It will be a great deal more than a bit. And it will do nothing to help you find your son."

"Our son," she corrected him, quietly.

"Indeed." He continued to watch her, inscrutable now. "Our son. And you're my wife. I won't be a party to this punishment you've chosen to arrange for yourself. I refuse to let you debase yourself for no reason."

She couldn't understand what he was saying. Shook her head to clear it of the confusion. Then she stood and looked down at him. "Jeffrey, if you won't come with me, I'll go and see him myself."

He stood as well. "I can't change your mind?"

She shook her head.

He sighed. Stoic. "Then I suppose I must back down. Having no honor of my own to besmirch." He held her look. "I'll go with you." For a split second, he was angry. But the expression evaporated almost before she registered it. "God knows I don't want to hear about this second hand."

"Thank you."

The smile was playing about his mouth again. "Tomorrow morning, then?"

She frowned. "Tomorrow is Sunday. Will he be there?"

His smile grew as he walked toward the door. Opened it for her and stood to the side. "He's always there. Where else is he going to be? Visiting the vicar?"

"I—I just thought—"

"I have a feeling he'll be expecting you, Marion."

THE weather was still warmer than usual for May, the cherry trees in tyrannical bloom, the late tulips looking artificial in the beds lining the park. Neither Jeffrey nor Marion paid them any attention as they walked to the Museum. They also didn't speak. Nor did they hurry. But both had tacitly concluded that an hour outdoors would help them prepare for the bleak conversation ahead of them. Neither had eaten much breakfast.

When they reached the Edward VII galleries, Jeffrey used his key to let them into the belowground offices. Then he led Marion up through the main wings of the museum to the Library. Maugham's office, he told her as they bypassed the dome, was in the stacks. Which surprised her. Given that Maugham's official role was "trustee," she had assumed that his professional space would be imposing. Potentially daunting. At the very least, she would have expected the office to contribute to the upkeep of a room in keeping with his status.

Jeffrey, reading her thoughts, smiled. "It keeps visitors off-guard," he explained. "The dust." He unlocked another door and walked them further into the stacks. "And the squalor."

"Oh." She looked at the metal shelves of books stretching into the dim interior of the building. "I didn't know there were offices back here."

"Most people don't." Jeffrey pushed aside a moving shelf and gestured toward a blank, wooden door. Round doorknob. "Here we are."

He knocked. There was the sound of movement, rustling, rodent-like, in the room, and then the door cracked open. When Maugham saw Jeffrey, he lit up and opened the door wider. Stepped back and threw a nasty smile at Marion. Then he returned to the functional oak chair behind the bureaucratic desk, resettled his spectacles on his nose, and marked his place in the book he'd been reading. *Allan Quatermain* by H. Rider Haggard. She decided not to notice his choice of reading material.

Instead, she focused on the fact that there was, at least, a window in the room. A large one in fact, wider than she had expected, and looking down, in a disconcerting manner, onto the courtyard. Maugham could see everyone who entered the Museum. She frowned. Couldn't understand how the room could be positioned in the stacks to provide that view.

Jeffrey had already lowered himself into an unstable oak chair on casters and placed his briefcase beside him on the floor. He was fighting down a smile as he watched Marion fail to interpret the space. It was a room that left one on edge. Increasingly disconcerted as bits and pieces of it intruded themselves into the consciousness. There was an ancient stuffed bird of some sort perched atop a teetering set of wooden bookshelves. Complete works of Haggard occupying a place of honor just below it. She sat carefully in a second chair, the twin of the one that Jeffrey had taken.

"Willcox," Maugham effused. "Dr. Bailey. What a pleasant surprise."

Jeffrey nodded at a blank, nearly empty file folder left carelessly at the corner of the desk. "Working on Syria today, are you?"

Maugham raised his eyebrows. "Is that why you've come to visit?"

"No," Jeffrey replied. "Passing remark."

Maugham took the folder and dropped it into an open drawer in the desk. Rolled the drawer shut. "Best remove temptation."

"We're looking," Jeffrey said without further preamble, "for our son."

Maugham bent over in his chair and peered under his desk for a few seconds. Then he straightened. "I don't think he's here." He paused. "Is that all?"

"He disappeared in Brighton."

"Good heavens." Maugham looked at Marion. "Have you checked the trunks at the railway station's left-luggage office?"

Marion stared at him, lost for words. Prayed she wouldn't begin crying again. Maugham turned back to Jeffrey. "Isn't this the bit where she storms out of the room? Refuses to talk anymore?"

"Not this time." Jeffrey, idle, reached for a second thin, unmarked folder on the desk, but Maugham grabbed it before he could touch it.

Dropped it into the drawer with the first. "What, then?" Irritated. He nodded at *Allan Quatermain* in front of him on the desk. "You know how busy I am, Willcox."

"Marion," Jeffrey said, "wants to open negotiations."

Maugham removed his spectacles and peered down at the lenses. Replaced them on his nose. "Can she speak for herself?"

Marion nodded. Cleared her throat. "Yes."

"Your superiors abducted your son," Maugham said to her. "From what I understand." "Yes."

"And so, in exchange for information we may have gathered concerning his whereabouts— gathered, that is, in the course of our more general investigation into your organization—you'd like now to work for us?"

"No." Marion felt her stomach tightening. "No. I—"

"Work *with* us, then?"

"No." She shook her head. "But I can—"

"—leave me in peace to my research," he finished for her. "Dr. Bailey, you seem not to understand the nature of 'negotiations'—"

"I can tell you what I know about the Red Sea." Her voice was level. "I think you'll be interested."

"Hmm." Maugham pursed his lips. "Very well. You have a bargain. Proceed."

"Thank you, Professor Maugham." Relief flooded through her. "*Thank you.*" She'd expected him to torment her a great deal longer before agreeing to her offer. And she felt a certain satisfaction that her estimation of Maugham as someone who valued outcome over personal considerations had been correct. She glanced at Jeffrey. Projecting gratitude to him as well. Failed to register the fleeting look of pity that crossed his face.

Then she spoke: "my instructions were to bring an object to Yemen. It's either a piece of inscribed rock crystal or a 'great pearl'—the *Durrah*—"

Jeffrey interrupted her before she could finish her second sentence. "The *Durrah*? You can't mean the Umayyad 'great pearl.'" He stared at her. "It was cut in two in the eighth century by the Abbasid Caliph al-Mahdi's slave girl. To use to play backgammon. Or, if not that, it was certainly lost by the eleventh century. Even if it was a piece of rock crystal instead, its value would be—" He stopped himself. Pushed down his excitement and nodded. "Interesting."

She dropped her gaze to her hands, tightly clasped in her lap. Then she looked up, speaking to Maugham again. "It was hidden. Not lost. Not cut in half. Initially, it was kept in the Fatimid treasury, in Cairo. Ibn al-Tuwayr mentions that it was—or had been—there in his twelfth-century *History of the Two Dynasties*—"

"His lost *History of the Two Dynasties*, you mean—"

"But then the treasury was looted in 1067," she spoke over him, "when the Fatimid government failed to pay its troops properly. Although there's a suggestion that it was already gone a few decades before. After that, it was kept in a separate location. Under guard. Because it was of too much political value to leave vulnerable again."

"Explain." Maugham's voice was as flat as Marion's.

"This piece of crystal or, if it's a pearl, this '*Durrah*,' is a dynastic piece. It's a source not only of legitimacy, but of—of a unifying 'eloquence.' Speech that consolidates. Or—calls. When the regional leaders of the southern Arabian Peninsula must unite against an outside aggressor, they do so—and have always done so—under the family with access to this, I suppose, 'clarity.' But the family is unknown. Quiet. Certainly not one of your nine tribes."

"It's true that the fault lines among the factions remain. Between the Sunnis and the Shia, and between the Zaydi Shia and the Ismaili Shia. But despite that, under this—object—the southern peninsula comes together. To expel invaders from the territory surrounding the Red Sea. It worked against the crusaders, against the Portuguese, against the Ottomans, and against—" She stopped.

Jeffrey was smiling. "And now against others. Of course. But even so, I find it difficult to believe that any family, however quiet, could heal the rifts you've mentioned. Are they Zaydi?"

"No. Not Zaydi. Ismaili. Sulayhid."

He raised his eyebrows. "You don't say. Hence, I suppose, your own organization's interest in the situation. But Marion," he continued, his voice smooth, "didn't you say that your Assassins were, how did you put it? Cosmopolitan? Multi-confessional? A meeting place of—"

"That doesn't mean that they aren't also—"

"—attentive to Ismaili affairs. Yes. I understand. But there's an additional problem." He scratched his cheek. "The Sulayhid family died out in the twelfth century. They've been a lot more than 'quiet' since then."

She raised her eyes to his. "I'm telling you what my instructions were."

"Let Dr. Bailey continue her explanation, Willcox." Maugham was holding the bridge of his nose between two fingers. "We'll test for weaknesses later. Incidentally," he asked dropping his hand, "did you draw any conclusions about the provenance of those coins I brought to you? In the brief time you saw them before Dr. Bailey made off with them? *Were* they Fatimid? My experts were uncertain."

"Sulayhid," Jeffrey replied. "Without a doubt."

"Hmm." Maugham nodded again.

Jeffrey, not speaking further, leaned back in his chair. Gestured for Marion to continue.

"So, I'm to bring this piece of crystal, or, again, if it's a pearl, this *Durrah*, to the Sulayhid family. In Yemen." She turned to Jeffrey. "My understanding, if it helps, is that the unity of the peninsula under their family isn't necessarily geopolitical. Though it can be. It's deeper than that. It's a sort of intense and personal refusal on the part of those who follow them to accept the divisions fostered by external power."

"A bit sinister."

"It isn't—" she began. Then she stopped herself again. They wanted information, not exegesis. "So the jewel," she continued, keeping her voice calm, "remains in hiding until it's needed against a new threat. But when it *is* needed, there are clues embedded in two or three Fatimid texts that the family uses to reach it. My—my specialty—" She colored and dropped her eyes. "I mean, my—job—for my organization—has been to decode that sort of text. They had the first manuscript delivered to me in Geneva, from Istanbul, where it had been kept—to see whether I could draw anything out of it."

"And?"

"And I did."

Jeffrey ran his hand through his hair. "Of course you did."

"No jealousy now, Willcox." Maugham was smiling. "What then?"

"Well, I would have taken the next step," she replied. "But they—"

"Filched your boy." Maugham was silent for a few seconds. "Odd move on their part, don't you think?"

"I don't know what to think." She heard her voice rising again. Tried to control it.

"So, you came to us instead—"

"I can tell you what's happening in the Red Sea," she repeated doggedly. She didn't want to talk about her motivations.

They waited, polite. But she hesitated before making her next statement. Unable to formulate the words. In the end, it was only the image of Ian, frightened and isolated, that forced her to plunge forward: "I can assure you, Professor Maugham, that if I don't locate their object for them, you'll have nothing to worry about in Aden. Your bickering regional governments will continue to bicker. Indefinitely. Your position there will be secure."

"Surely, your organization has someone else working on this." Interested notwithstanding the spite.

"I'm confident that they do," she said. "But they can't do anything without the material. And I have it all. Here." Pointing to Jeffrey's briefcase.

"Actually," Jeffrey interrupted, sitting straighter in his chair, "*I* have it all. At home. Not here. The briefcase is empty."

Maugham tightened his lips but otherwise he didn't show his annoyance. "She thought she was bringing it along today?" he asked Jeffrey. "Part of the negotiation?"

"Hmm." Jeffrey leaned back and held Maugham's eyes.

"And you've done a switch on her?"

"Indeed."

"Do you know, Willcox? You and I will be having a long talk, sometime very soon, about your loyalties."

"Electricity or water?" Jeffrey was grinning.

"Both, if you'd like."

Marion was looking back and forth between the two of them, not understanding the intensity of their exchange. Certainly not understanding why Jeffrey had chosen to keep back her evidence. But she didn't want to follow that train of thought. It wasn't important.

Important was finding something else to give Maugham to prompt him to share his file on Ian. And so, ignoring the charged atmosphere, she pushed forward: "I can tell you," she repeated for a third time, "what's happening in the Red Sea."

"Very well, Dr. Bailey." Maugham had turned away from Jeffrey. Still incensed, but keeping his voice in check. "Tell me, then. How *do* we rid ourselves of these vexing sea serpents?"

"There aren't any sea serpents. That's how. There's nothing there at all." She closed her eyes and compelled herself to continue. "The crystal or pearl is hidden on an island in the Red Sea. I haven't yet identified which island it is, but when it comes time to transport it, its guardians set up a series of blockades across it. One of the most effective is a—a sort of drug. Those who get too close to it breathe it in, and—and they see terrible things. You can track the movement of this object, historically, by collecting reports of these disruptions in the Red Sea. Clusters of accounts of the serpent, of 'marvelous sea creatures,' or even of unusual currents—and you see these accounts all over the place, in Portuguese, French, Mughal, Ottoman, even Chinese documents—indicate that the crystal, or if it's a pearl, the *Durrah*, is on the move. And then the stories die down." She paused. "And the peninsula is protected for a few more decades."

Maugham remained quiet for close to a minute. Thinking. Ignoring both Marion and Jeffrey. Then, coming to himself, he nodded at her. Satisfied and authoritative. "I thank you for your explanation, Dr. Bailey. Sir Bernard will be most gratified to learn that it was all done with smoke and mirrors."

"Sir—Bernard—?"

"Chief Commissioner of Aden," Jeffrey supplied.

"Oh." She hesitated again. Then she looked back at him. "I've given you all I know. What do you have on Ian?"

"Ah yes." Maugham, reassuming his addled air, opened a second drawer in his desk and rifled through a series of files. "Of course, of course." He peered, nearsighted, through his spectacles. "Hmm. Yes, here it is." He pulled out a folder and pushed it across the desk at her. "Our reports indicate that the boy is currently in Yemen."

She grabbed the folder and opened it. Then she stared up at him. "It's empty."

He looked down at the folder. Back up at her. "Yes," he confirmed. "It is. Indeed. Empty." He leaned back in his chair, resettled his spectacles, and watched her face as he spoke. "You see, Dr. Bailey, the office is stretched so very thin at the moment. All manner of unforeseen crises have arisen over the past weeks and months. Drawing away our best people. The people, you understand, who would be working on your project."

He gazed up at the ceiling. "If you have the time, I'd be happy to enumerate a few of these complications for you." When she said nothing, he let his eyes drop back to her face. Vindictive. "First, if you can believe it, a number of our resources went missing in Azerbaijan at the end of last year. Poof. Disappeared completely. Poor souls. And *then* the team we sent in after them made an even bigger mess of things trying to find them. Catastrophic situation." Morose. "We have yet to clean that one up."

He scratched his bald head, pensive. "And *then*, a most delicate surveillance system that we had *just* put into place right here at home went—what's the term again?—ah yes, 'haywire.' Noise everywhere, according to our technical people. Not certain what that means entirely, but I do know that we've been forced to redirect yet another portion of our limited resources toward that as well." He thought for a few seconds longer. "Not to mention that we're still trying to reel in Chris Archer, lost somewhere in the Balkans. No idea what's become of him. And so," letting the malice back into his voice, "as a result, we've been obliged to make cuts, Dr. Bailey. Across the board. Most regrettable. But, as I'm confident you'll understand, there's simply no time or money to devote to this matter of your son. More pressing matters are bedeviling our sadly understaffed bureaucracy." He shrugged. "As I said, however, we have received information that he's in Yemen."

She continued to stare at him. "What am I supposed to do?"

"My advice, Dr. Bailey, is—if I may offer you this suggestion—to search. Yemen."

"Search—Yemen—?" She leapt across the desk at him. "You fucking—"

Jeffrey was out of his chair, pulling her back, before she could get to Maugham. "Marion," he said. "You can't possibly be surprised by this."

She raised her eyes to his face. "He—he's a—"

"Which, my dear, you already knew." Jeffrey, confident that she wouldn't move now, sat again. "At least the guilt has gone." He watched her. "It has, hasn't it? Not certain how your organization is going to react to the extreme method you used to expunge it, but it must feel better to have a clean conscience. I'm here as your witness. You've sacrificed all that you could." He glanced over at Maugham. "Thank you for that."

"Always glad to be of service." Maugham had removed his spectacles again, and he was cleaning the lenses with a handkerchief. He peered up at Jeffrey. "I do have a favor to ask of you in return, Willcox."

Jeffrey looked at Marion for a few seconds, reassured himself that she was too shocked to react, and then relaxed into his chair. "What is it?"

"Care to take a journey to Baghdad?"

"What for?"

"Shia revolt in the countryside is well underway." Maugham was still fiddling with his spectacles. "Third one this year. The government's finally identified a few of the ringleaders, but every time they get one into custody, he dies off before telling them anything useful." He folded the hinge back and forth. "Unhealthy atmosphere, I gather. Miasmas." He popped his spectacles into the breast pocket of his tweed jacket. "The king—Faisal's boy—has asked for you personally. They could use your expertise."

Jeffrey examined his fingernails. "My expertise in twelfth-century Fatimid coinage?"

"What else?"

Jeffrey sighed and stood up. "Send the file to the house. I'll look it over this evening."

"Excellent." Maugham reached for his *Allan Quatermain*. "And if you'll forgive me, I really must get back to work."

"Thank you again, Maugham." Jeffrey's voice was amused.

"Hmph."

Jeffrey turned to Marion and held out his hand. She took it, numb, and let him pull her up. Noticed stupidly that she was still holding the empty folder in her other hand. Maugham, following her gaze, gave her a kindly smile. "Please, Dr. Bailey. Take it with you. You may find it useful to you in your search."

He opened his novel and began reading. "Terrible business," he muttered. "The loss of a child. Ghastly."

*J*EFFREY took her back to the park. Sat her down next to him on a bench overlooking the pond. Cherry blossoms floating on the surface of the water. Swans. Servants tending to clean, well behaved children.

"I detest London." It was the first thing she'd said since they'd left Maugham's office.

Jeffrey looked sidelong at her. "I know."

"I need your help."

He watched the sunlight playing over the rippled water. "I know."

She faced him on the bench. "Will you help me?"

"I haven't decided yet." He didn't alter his expression. "You held back quite a bit of information from Maugham."

"Of course I did." She wrinkled her forehead and turned back to the water. "I'm not a complete fool."

"No," he agreed. "Just mind-bogglingly innocent."

She checked her angry retort. "What did you make of the coins that Maugham left you?" she asked instead. "I know you didn't get to see them for long."

"I had the chance to examine them more closely while you were sleeping yesterday." He crossed his legs.

She turned back to him. "They were in my room. In my bag—"

He was smiling again, still watching the pond. "Yes, Marion. In your locked room. In your bag. Are you shocked?" He turned to her as well. "I also looked over the manuscript. Out of curiosity."

"Yes, all right." Tired. "Did you draw any conclusions? Coins aren't my strength."

"They're interesting," he began slowly. "Early twelfth-century. Minted in Aden. For Queen Arwa bint Asma al-Sulayhi. The Queen of Yemen between 1067 and 1138."

"Is that what makes them interesting?" she asked. "She would have had her own coins minted, wouldn't she? Once she took power?"

"Yes," he said. "But they're geopolitically wrong." He gazed out at the water. "You know the story. The Sulayhids were an Ismaili dynasty in Yemen attempting to govern a largely Zaydi population. Difficult in its own right. But then, when their most able ruler was Arwa rather than any of her male relatives, they faced a legitimacy crisis. So Arwa secured the support of one of the two Great Powers of the day—the Fatimid dynasty, also Ismaili Shia, ruling from Egypt."

He paused and then continued: "the Fatimids had already set themselves up as quite the rivals to the other Great Power in the region, the Sunni Abbasids, ruling from Baghdad. It certainly didn't hurt to add another state in the Arabian Peninsula to their stable of tributaries. In fact, once Arwa had proved her staying power, they also granted her the highest rank in the Ismaili religious hierarchy—*hujja*, proof of God. An unusual move."

He squinted toward the bright light, reflected now almost painfully off the pond. "And Arwa's loyalty became only more useful as time passed. In 1094, the great Ismaili schism divided Egypt. Typical story: two brothers, each with a claim to rule the dynasty. The one who lost out—or perhaps his son—" He hesitated. "It's a bit fuzzy—took himself off to Iran. Established himself in Alamut of all places. And hence was born the Nizari Ismaili sect. 'Assassins,' I believe the people of the time used to call them once they started terrorizing their former friends and neighbors." He turned teasing eyes on her. "You may be familiar with that branch—?"

"Why are the coins significant?"

He smiled more broadly and turned back to the pond. "So, the relationship between the Fatimid Ismailis and Queen Arwa's Sulayhid Ismailis was, to all appearances, solid. Based on the strongest of foundations—mutual self-interest. Now that the Fatimids were facing a challenge not only from the Abbasids, but also from this new sect, she was a vital prop to their authority. In fact, she was one of the few leaders in the post-1094 Ismaili Shia world who didn't at least flirt with the possibility that the Nizari claim to rule was, *perhaps*, just a bit more authentic than what remained of the Fatimid claim."

"But?"

"But the coins that Theodore Bent brought back forty years ago, minted after the schism—all in Arwa's name—make no mention of the Fatimid ruler. Not the slightest gesture, even, toward Fatimid sovereignty. It's as though the Fatimids, to Arwa, were already dust and gone."

He rubbed his cheek with his hand. "At the time, if a dependent—which Arwa, despite her title and her ruling capabilities, was—minted that sort of coin, it would have been tantamount to an act of treason. States went to war for less."

Marion nodded. What he had told her didn't surprise her. But it did make her confident that her hypothesis about the location and character of the object she was seeking was correct.

"There's something else," Jeffrey said, reaching into his trouser pocket and withdrawing a coin. He held it in his palm and pointed. "Recognize that?"

She looked down at the coin and nodded again. She'd seen it in Brighton. A tiny snake. Identical to the serpent sculptures that Maugham had brought from the office and that Jeffrey had sent Nick Trelawney to retrieve from Suffolk.

"Yes," she said.

"So," he continued, returning the coin to his pocket, "I admit it. I'm intrigued. Casts the Sulayhids, at least, in a new light."

"Then you'll help me?"

"I don't know that I'm so intrigued that I'd bring down Maugham's wrath on my head." He laughed. "This all happened nearly nine hundred years ago, after all. And he does want me in Baghdad."

"For Ian, then?"

"Really, Marion." Annoyed. No longer laughing. "If you stay put, they'll bring him back. They're not going to keep him from you out of spite."

"Jeffrey," she said, her voice, to her dismay, shaking with tears again, "I can't just sit and wait. I *can't.*"

"What 'help' do you want, then? Precisely?" He was watching the water now with cold eyes. "I must say, this is becoming exhausting."

"I need you to get a manuscript for me out of the Library. From the Baquba collection." She wiped her eyes with the heels of her hands. Avoided the embarrassed glances of the people walking past the bench.

A few seconds passed in silence.

Then he turned to her in quiet disbelief. "What sort of an idiot do you take me for?" he finally asked. "Do you really think that after a lifetime in the service, I'm going to be influenced by a pretty girl crying at me?"

"I—" She shook her head. "No! He's your son too! What if they don't bring him back? What if—"

"Do you know, Marion?" He was still watching her, thoughtful now. "I wouldn't be surprised if this is their strategy." He nodded to himself. "In fact, I'm quite certain that it is. All that remains to be seen is whether you're a willing party to it." He looked carefully at her face. "I think not. This seems genuine. And God knows you haven't the skill to simulate this display. But that's hardly relevant, is it?" he continued when she didn't respond. "They know you. They know the distorted morass that is your ethical code. And they knew that when they took him from you, you would disobey your orders and come back here. Make this request of me." He laughed shortly. "Despite myself, I'm beginning to respect them."

"But if that *is* what they've done," she said, "they *won't* bring him back. Not until I've convinced you to help."

He sat, reflective, for thirty seconds. And then, eventually, he spoke. "Damn."

"Jeffrey—"

"Wait." He considered for a few more seconds. Sighed. Faint irony. "I wasn't looking forward to Baghdad anyway. Unfortunate peasants." He stood and held out his arm. "Let's discuss this as we walk."

She stood as well. Took his arm, her hand cold despite the abnormal heat in the air. "You said that you'd looked over the manuscript I brought from Geneva?" she asked.

"Yes." He led them toward the bridge. "It was curious as well. Unattributed? A collection of maps?"

She nodded. "Yes. On the surface. It's an unusual, but not shockingly so, geography. Annotated maps. The markings suggest that it's Fatimid. The writer Ismaili. Likely eleventh-century. But, as you saw, anonymous." She looked across the grass at a boy flying a kite. Looked away. "The compiler had a fair interest in the Byzantine Mediterranean. Could have been commissioned as a military work."

"Hmm."

"But there are three sections of it that are more than just unusual. A careful reader, interested in—in Red Sea jewels, might find those three sections—important."

"Which are they?"

"The first is the chapter on what the writer calls 'bizarre things that grow in the water among the fish and savage animals of the sea'—*fi 'aja'ib nabat al-ma' min al-sumuk wa-al-wuhush al-bahriya*."

He nodded, but he didn't reply.

"The second," she continued, "is a detailed, *incorrect* map of the Arabian Peninsula and the Red Sea. All the place names are off. Well known cities, mountains, everything really, is placed in an inaccurate position."

"I hadn't noticed." Tiring again.

"You must look closely," she said, trying to keep him interested. "It's—significant."

"Hmm."

"And the third part," she rushed to finish, "that—that makes one wonder—is a rectangular, rather than round, map of the known world. I've never seen a rectangular map from that era before. It's striking."

"You appear to have all that you need, then." He gazed across the water at a small girl crying in terror at an approaching swan. "Why risk pilfering the Library?"

She shook her head. "No. I haven't got everything. There's something else." She stood beside him and watched as the girl was scooped up and out of the way of the swan. Wondered what she'd done to provoke it. Then she focused. "The writer cites a separate treatise in the manuscript. Something he'd written earlier. He calls it *al-Kitab al-Muhit*. Which is difficult to translate. Sort of his 'all encompassing' or 'all surrounding' book? The book that covers everything else?"

"Yes," he smiled, "I can manage *'muhit.'*"

She blushed, but otherwise didn't react. Instead, she kept talking, trying to convince him to help her. "He says he goes into more detail about the seas in that other book—the one that covers 'everything else.' And," she added, "he also says that he defends an argument that he only summarizes in the pages we have. *That* argument," she spoke carefully, "is that coastlines aren't worth mapping because they keep changing anyway." She looked up at his profile. "That's the key. I want to know why he's so adamant about the changing coastlines. It's a strange thing for a geographer—a military geographer—to belabor. The coasts ought to be the most important part of his analysis. Even if they do occasionally shift."

"And this—other work—then, is in the Baquba collection." Resigned.

"Yes." They were walking again. As they approached the bridge, she thought further. "There's also a copy of Qutb al-Din al-Nahrawali's account of the sixteenth-century Ottoman conquest of Yemen. *Al-Barq al-Yamani*. It's uniquely annotated. I need that too. Oh," she rushed on, before he could refuse, "and also, from the Library's regular collections—not from the Baquba material—it will be available in the stacks—I'll need Carsten Niebuhr's eighteenth-century *Flora Aegyptiaco-Arabica*. About the plants of southern Arabia." She paused again. "And, if you could find it, there's a seventeenth-century Portuguese chronicle on Ethiopia and the African Red Sea coast by João dos Santos. Perhaps among the rare books. That would be helpful as well."

He looked sideways at her. "Anything else?"

She didn't notice his tone. "No. I think that's all."

"Very well." He stopped her and looked her in the face. They were standing in the middle of the bridge. "But here's how this is going to work, Marion. Yes. I'll steal your manuscripts for you. And, as an upstanding patron of the library, I'll make what I think will be a convincing case for bending the rules to remove the Niebuhr and the dos Santos." He shook his head, smiling at his predicament. "But you'll never be alone with them. Not for a second. I will stay in the room, watching, as you work on them. And when you've finished each day, I will take them, and I will lock them away from you."

She opened her mouth to protest, but he stopped her. "When you're ready to test your hypotheses in the field, I will go with you. You will not leave my presence. You will not speak to anyone without my permission." He looked hard at her. "If you take your own line at any point in this project, I'll rescue the manuscripts, and I'll return, repentant, to Maugham. You know that he'll have people on us. I've seen one or two already. You may have spotted more."

He lifted his chin. "But I have a feeling that, despite the eyes, he'll give us a long string. He wants to see what you can unearth for him. So we shouldn't have difficulty crossing borders. At least, not yet." Turning, he began walking with her toward Chester Terrace. "If, however, I go to him with the news that you've become unmanageable, he'll scrap the whole thing. They'll grab you before you've even considered an evasive strategy. They're getting to know you now. And they do have a reputation to protect."

He put his hand against the small of her back as she climbed the stairs toward the front door of the house. "And heaven knows what will become of the boy should that occur." He unlocked and opened the door. "Attractive situation you've created for us, dear."

THE next morning, Marion waited anxious in the drawing room for Jeffrey to return from the Museum. He had left shortly after breakfast, dressed for the office. Promising to be back in the house before noon.

Since then, she had wandered aimlessly up and down the stairs, unable to occupy herself. She had tried reading his *Times*, which he had left on the dining table, but it had made her angry. So she'd tossed it, disassembled and badly folded, on the console in the entryway as she'd walked up the stairs to the drawing room. After that, she'd stood for close to an hour, staring out the window, refusing to admit to herself that she was watching for his return.

When she finally saw him, walking brisk and youthful toward the front door, she turned away from the window and sat in an armchair. Took up the first magazine she encountered on the side table. *The Tatler*. Stared at the lead story and waited.

She heard him come through the door, speak to the maid, and walk, still brisk, up the stairs. Then he pushed open the doors to the drawing room and looked down at her. "Catching up on the latest gossip?"

She raised her eyes. Noticed that he had his battered *Times* under his arm as well as his briefcase in his hand. He looked pleased with himself.

"Did you get the material?" She dropped *The Tatler* on the table and stood.

"Thank you, Marion. Yes, I did have a pleasant morning at the office. How was your day?"

She held his eyes. Didn't reply.

"I got the material," he relented. "No alerts. Which means that unless he changes his mind, Maugham will let us over the border when the time comes. He'll want to watch." He stood to the side of the door and gestured her out into the hall. "I thought we might work in my study. Unless you'd rather eat first?"

She shook her head and walked past him. Clasping her hands together in front of her to keep from trying, absurdly, to turn and snatch his briefcase. When he opened the door to the study, she saw that he had organized it for them both to use. His own desk, a substantial piece of George III mahogany, was clear of files and papers aside from the manuscript she'd brought with her from Geneva. It was the first time she'd seen the desk's surface. Unexpected rosewood inlay. The coffee table between the sofa and armchairs was also clear. Ready for work.

"Would you like to use the desk?" he asked, closing the door.

She nodded, cautious, and walked to the chair behind it. Leather and mahogany. Also George III. She sat. He watched her, an unreadable expression on his face. "Suits you," he said after a second too long.

She frowned. "You said—"

"Quite." He brought the briefcase to the desk and opened it. Placed his *Times* next to it. The first volume he removed was nothing more than a bundle of parchment, secured with a frayed silk ribbon. "Our anonymous author's book of 'everything else.' More maps. No binding. But we'd catalogued it, so it wasn't difficult to find." He set it on the desktop in front of her beside the original manuscript.

Then he produced a book bound in elaborately embossed blue leather. "Chronicle of the sixteenth-century Ottoman conquest of Yemen. Eighteenth-century binding, but the pages are original."

She nodded, and he smiled. Placed it above the loose folios. "Next," he continued, "and easier to pilfer, your Niebuhr, in Latin." He arranged another bound volume in front of her. "And finally, your dos Santos. Portuguese." He paused again. "I didn't know you had Portuguese."

"I don't," she said, resting her fingertip against the edges of the unbound pages. "But I know what I'm looking for. I think I can muddle through it."

"Very well." He snapped the lid of the briefcase shut, left it on the floor to the side of the desk, and took up his *Times*. Then he moved behind her and opened a safe in the wall. Pulled out a thick file folder and shut the door to the safe. "I'll leave you to it, then. Let me know whether you need anything."

She looked, worried, at the folder he held in his hand. He glanced at it as well, and then grinned back at her. "From Maugham. On the rebellion in Iraq." He turned and walked toward the sofa. "No harm in acquainting myself with the situation." He sat and unbuttoned his jacket. "I had, it's true, meant to start with something lighter, but—" He lifted his badly used *Times* and examined the wrinkled pages. "Best keep up with one's work."

She watched as he opened the file and spread its contents on the coffee table. Typed reports, clippings, and a series of photographs. One of the photographs, from where she sat, appeared to depict a bloodied dead body. As he took up the first of the reports, leaned back on the sofa, and began reading, she decided not to think about what he was doing. What they were doing.

Instead, she turned her attention to her anonymous author's treatise on "everything else." Untied the silk ribbon. It was a short work, despite its title, only forty-two pages compared to the ninety-six pages of the manuscript she had received in Geneva. But, she concluded as she skimmed the introductory chapters, it was more useful than the first collection of maps had been. Noting the author's now detailed argument against identifying coastlines, she wondered whether the original manuscript had been produced as a calculated invitation to those of his compatriots who were aware of the fate of the *Durrah*. A call to arms.

It seemed to her that the author had inserted ambiguous clues into the first work that would lead an interested reader to the more concrete instructions hidden in this chronologically earlier, but perhaps deliberately "lost," second work. The assumption underlying it—that the reader was pursuing the same religious and geopolitical goals as the author—was pronounced. And it nagged at Marion as she read.

When she reached the fifteenth folio, her guess as to the intent of the author became a certainty. This folio reproduced an astrological map and itinerary that a boat might use on a voyage along the western, African, side of the Red Sea. Each point at which this boat might meet "monstrous" aquatic representatives of constellations or star groups was carefully and vividly marked. There were also several references in this folio to the *nazm*, or string of pearls, that made up the constellation Orion's belt, where these pearls or crystalline stars might be found in the sea, and what strange creatures to avoid while seeking them. A more detailed annotation alongside the most elaborate of these references informed the reader that a skilled navigator could follow these strings toward a forest of African frankincense trees with "unique and marvelous" properties. Marion made her own note on the connections the text had drawn among Red Sea pearls, crystalline stars, and Red Sea frankincense.

But she was still unable to draw geographically specific conclusions from the page. Both the images and the annotations remained frustratingly absent relevant coastlines or mention of coastlines. Or, for that matter, meaningful place names. And in that sense, they were no more useful than the maps in the collection she'd secured in Geneva had been.

Uncertain of how to proceed, she let her hand rest to the side of the page, just over the most prominent of Orion's "pearls." Then, surprised, she lifted her fingertip. Pressed more deliberately against the spot. The paper was bumpy. Thicker than she was used to encountering in manuscripts of that era.

She lifted the page and peered at the edge. It wasn't hollow. There wasn't anything hidden inside of it. Then she ran her finger over the map again. Pressed against Orion's belt. The page, she determined, had been treated. Covered with some substance that had thickened it over the centuries. Something applied with care and meant to last a very long time.

She leaned back in the chair and smiled. She knew now what she wanted to find in the other volumes that Jeffrey had brought to her. Reassembling the leaves of the anonymous manuscript—the book of "everything else"—she set them to the side. Then she turned her attention to the eighteenth-century botanical work, *Flora Aegyptiaco-Arabica.*

This book, a description in Latin of plant specimens collected in the Arabian Peninsula by an ill-fated Danish expedition, wouldn't ordinarily have interested her. But when Maugham had described Theodore Bent's condition as he had brought the serpent and coins out of Yemen a half century ago, she'd remembered what she'd read of Carsten Niebuhr's research. There were parallels between his experience and Bent's that she felt she ought to examine.

The story began in 1761, when a royal Danish expedition left Copenhagen for the Arabian Peninsula with the goal of identifying and providing a scientific basis for the plants and animals mentioned in the Bible. Five scholars—Pehr Forsskal, a botanist, Carsten Niebuhr, an astronomer, Frederik Christian von Haven, a linguist, George Wilhem Bauerenfeind, an illustrator and artist, and Christian Carl Kramer, a physician—had joined the team.

They had travelled without difficulty, taking notes and sending these notes home, until they had reached the Red Sea area. At that point, the updates on their progress had thinned. And it was only six years later, in 1767, that Niebuhr, the sole survivor, had returned to Denmark. Ill and chastened.

Niebuhr had diligently published the results of the expedition, and he had even preserved the botanical specimens and descriptions that Forsskal had collected before dying of an unspecified illness in the southern part of the peninsula. The illness had taken him just outside the town of Jibla—Queen Arwa's family stronghold seven hundred years earlier. She paused, thinking.

Then she forced herself to focus on the fate of the specimens. Niebuhr had donated the seeds and dried plants to the University of Copenhagen. But these seeds had remained hidden and unstudied for a century or more after their donation to the University. And the sole scientific publication that Niebuhr had produced, the *Flora Aegyptiaco-Arabica,* was notoriously incoherent.

Even when it was rediscovered at the end of the nineteenth century by British botanists keen to rehabilitate the royal Danish expedition, it was difficult to describe as a work of organized taxonomic description. It was by no means fanciful. But it was—oddly—jumbled.

She opened the volume on the desk in front of her. She knew which bit she wanted to read. Even without an index or remotely meaningful pagination. And so, she turned the pages mechanically, scanning each one, until she found it. The botanical description of the nettle to which Forsskal had posthumously given his name. She read the two-paragraph description carefully. Then she re-read. And then she smiled again, marked the page, and turned to the chronicle of the sixteenth-century Ottoman conquest of Yemen.

She knew that she already had what she wanted, and that she needn't plod through the less than literary Arabic describing the Ottoman military's quasi-successful attempt to incorporate, or re-incorporate, Yemen into their Empire. The account read like Caesar punishing and plundering Gaul. Not her favorite genre. But, meticulous, she also wanted to confirm—and re-confirm—her suspicions.

She flipped to the two chapters that interested her—the conquest of the town of Jibla, where Arwa had ruled four hundred years earlier, and the description of the naval forces that had supported the hero of the story, the Ottoman commander, Sinan Pasha. Skimming them, she smiled a last time, marked those pages as well, and then turned her attention to the Portuguese chronicle—recounting an Indian Ocean battle just ten years after the 1571 incorporation of Yemen into the Ottoman state.

It hardly mattered that she was trying to translate the Portuguese text via her knowledge of Latin, French, and Italian. She already knew what the short passage was going to tell her. And, having read it, satisfied, she closed the book and looked up at Jeffrey. Through the windows behind him, she could see that the sun was setting. The light was warm. Yellow.

"We can leave tomorrow," she said.

He raised his eyes to her. He'd spent most of the time she'd been working sitting on the sofa, taking the occasional note on Maugham's file. Twice he had smoked a cigarette. But he had kept on his jacket and tie, and he still looked like a banker. "If you'd like." He organized the pages on the coffee table and slipped them back into the folder. "Where?"

"Copenhagen."

"I suppose the Niebuhr should have warned me," he said after a short pause. "But before I make the arrangements, I'd like to know what we'll be doing there. Not that Denmark isn't lovely in its own right this time of year."

She stood. "I can tell you on the way."

He didn't move. "You can sit, and you can tell me now. I like seeing you in that chair for some reason."

"I'm tired, Jeffrey—"

"You're excited. And we have a good hour before it's time to dress for dinner. Sit."

She sat.

"But before you tell me what you've discovered in those documents," he said to her, preempting further protest, "there are some other, more mundane questions I'd like you to answer for me."

"What are they?" She clasped her hands tightly together in her lap. Remaining in the room when she could be packing and moving a step closer to Ian was upsetting her equilibrium. She'd never wanted so badly to escape Jeffrey's relentless conversation.

Reading her mood, he laughed, quietly exasperated. "Would you like a drink?"

"No." She clenched her fists tighter. "What are your questions?"

"Very well." He moved his file folder to the corner of the coffee table. "You were, as you say, in Switzerland this past month. Nowhere near London. How did you poison me?"

"I didn't—"

"All right, then. How did you drug me?"

"Jeffrey—"

"This will go faster," he said, "if you'll simply satisfy my curiosity."

She stared down at the top of the desk. Then, deciding it was no longer relevant or important, she looked back up at him. "They gave me a powder," she said. "In Suffolk. In April. I slipped it to you there. It takes three weeks to go into effect. By the time you fell ill, I was gone."

"Lovely."

"Oh, I'm so sorry," she shot back at him. "I hadn't realized that you're perfectly free to drug or infect me any time you'd like, provided it serves your purposes, whereas I ought to shrink from doing the same to you. Obviously, I—"

"Marion," he interrupted her. "Have I rebuked you? Have I found fault? No, I have not. I was about to say that it was lovely work. I applaud you."

"Good." She glowered at him. "Can we talk about Denmark now?"

"No," he said. "There's a second question. You drugged me and disappeared. But the purpose of doing so, so far as I can tell, was to induce me to reveal the location of that serpent. Presumably to provoke Maugham into digging up its twin. I gather you need both for this project?"

She held his eyes. Silent.

He nodded, satisfied. "So, here's my question. You were, as we've established, in Switzerland. How did you plant the location of the serpent in my—my head? It couldn't have been three weeks earlier. I wasn't delirious then."

"They sent someone else," she said. "Once you'd weakened."

"Another member of your organization?"

She nodded.

"In this house?" Uncharacteristically shocked. "In my bedroom?"

She nodded again.

"Hmm." Mildly diverted. "At least I'm in good historical company. Pity he didn't leave a threatening note and a poisoned dagger near my pillow."

"She."

"I'm sorry?"

"Pity that *she* didn't leave a threatening note and a poisoned dagger. Near your pillow."

"Ah well." He was laughing now. "Lost opportunity. On both sides." But he didn't drop his eyes from hers. "Third question, then."

She let her own gaze fall. "What?"

"So, you infected me. Your colleague persuaded me to order Trelawney up to Suffolk. How did the serpent find its way into Ginnie's house in the first place?"

She started to speak, but he stopped her. "Before you say anything, Marion, I must warn you that I've spoken with Ginnie already. It was a typical ordeal of a conversation, and at first, she didn't want to tell me anything. But I did eventually trip her up. She let slip that you had brought the serpent with you. That she'd helped you to hide it. In April."

"Yes." She hated handing him this information. But it was outdated. And if it moved her closer to Denmark, and to Ian, it was worth appeasing him.

"You brought it from Azerbaijan?" Mystified.

She nodded again. Didn't speak.

"I don't understand." He watched her face. "Your target there was a map—or a diagram—some object—that could reveal the location of uranium in the area. Nothing about this. About Yemen, or rock crystal, or pearls, or—or Fatimids."

She traced a design on the desktop with her fingertip. "I think the object—the map—that was supposed to point to the uranium had already been removed before I arrived. Long before I arrived. Perhaps centuries before." She lifted her eyes to his and then looked back down at the desk. "And I think my organization used the uranium to prompt Maugham into action. Remember, they were the ones who pointed him toward those maps in the first place. They knew that the serpent was already planted. Waiting. They needed it out of the ground—again—to take their next step.

"They never sent me another dispatcher," she explained after a few seconds, when he didn't say anything. "To relieve me of the sculpture." She hesitated. And then plunged forward: "I kept waiting, you see. Leaving myself open to contact, wanting to get it off my hands. But I heard nothing from them. I had to do something with it. I'd been carrying it with me for weeks. So, finally, I dropped it in Suffolk.

She shrugged. "It seemed as good a place as any. But," rubbing her eyes, "that was when they finally reopened communication. With the aim, I'm now confident, of removing this," resting her hand on the loose pages of the manuscript, "from your control. They wanted to get it away from the Museum so that they could locate the *Durrah*."

He sat up on the sofa and pushed back his shoulders. "Well, we wouldn't want to disappoint them, would we? So what, then, will be bringing us to Denmark?"

"Look at this," she said, pushing the pages of the fifteenth folio across the desktop toward him.

He stood, walked to the desk, and bent over the pages. Scanned them quickly. "Hmm. Yes, he does have an eccentric horror of coastlines. I like this bit where he argues that if you draw a coast properly, you'll never position the cities accurately. And," he furrowed his brow and read a few more lines, "vice versa."

"Yes," she said, impatient. "But look at the paper itself. Feel it."

He ran a finger over the map and its annotations. "A shame. It's been damaged. But the ink is still clear enough, I think—"

"It hasn't been damaged," she interrupted, now more than impatient. "It's been treated."

"Oh, Marion." He straightened and laughed down at her. "You can't mean—"

"Yes, I'm certain—"

"Disappearing ink?" He raised his eyebrows. "How embarrassing. Shall we hold it over a candle? Do you think they used lemon juice?"

"No," she said, annoyed. "It's more complicated than that."

"I should hope so," he said, turning on a lamp in the failing light and returning to the sofa. "Otherwise, I shall be forced to conclude that the reason they've made off with the boy is to help them frustrate the plans of the other seven-year-olds who have infiltrated their secret organization. If so, we'll never get him back."

"Jeffrey—" She thought she might start crying again.

"Very well. Tell me how you've drawn this entertaining conclusion."

"In the Niebuhr," she told him. "When he wrote up the results of the expedition, he included a new kind of nettle. Discovered in the peninsula. He named it after the botanist, Forsskal, who had died collecting and describing it. Forsskal—"

She stopped. Thought for a moment. Jeffrey needn't know about the connection to Jibla. That Forsskal had fallen ill at the foot of Queen Arwa's castle.

He watched her, cold, noting her hesitation. Didn't speak.

"—Niebuhr," she amended, "wrote at some length on the attributes of this plant. And most of the description is straightforward—structure of the roots, the leaves, the flowers, the stems, the sepals, and the rest. He does add an interesting note in his description of the leaves—talking about the roughest parts of the plant, which are attached to the underside of the leaves. In Latin, that passage reads *folia…subtus scaberrima adhaerentia*. Of course, under ordinary circumstances, I'd pass over that description without a second thought. It makes perfect sense in its context. But now that I have this—this folio, with its very rough underside, in front of me on the desk, I'm not so certain."

"Hmm." Noncommittal.

"But there's more," she said. "He goes on in the next paragraph to discuss the plant's reputation among the local population in Yemen. And that second passage *is* unusual. Effusive for a botanical description." She scanned the page. "After writing that this nettle grows most commonly in the valleys of desert mountains," she began, "he remarks on its 'marvelous gripping quality'—*plantam mirae indolis*—which leads it to stick not only to clothing, by means of hooks, but also to smooth surfaces. He says that it's so adhesive, in fact, that it can't be removed except by ripping apart or destroying whatever it's managed to hold."

She glanced up at him. "Literally, the passage reads that the nettle 'isn't torn from the fellowship—or partnership—'" She paused. "That is, the 'partnership' with whatever it has gripped, 'except via tearing or mutilation': *a qua societate non avellitur, nisi discerpta.*"

She looked up at him again, and when he remained silent, she continued. "Even an enthusiastic botanist would avoid describing a plant's attributes as 'marvelous'—or 'miraculous'— wouldn't he? Unless there *was* something miraculous about this particular plant's adhesive quality." She considered. "I'm also intrigued by his use of *societas*—companionship, confederacy, fellowship, and the like—to describe what the nettle brings together. When it grips."

"I see." Jeffrey was holding back comment.

"And then, there's his discussion of the plant's local reputation. It's—evocative. At first, he simply writes that the Arabic term for the plant, which he transliterates as *lussaq*, is the same as what he's reproduced in Latin: *adhaerens.* Sticky or clinging." She blinked and gathered her thoughts. "But *then,* he continues that there's also a 'less common' term for the plant. He transliterates that word as *hadie.*"

Jeffrey raised his eyebrows. "'*hadie*?'"

"Yes. From *hidayah.* Guidance. The thing that shows a seeker the proper way." She glanced up at him again. "So apparently, the local population understood this plant to be 'that which points one in the right direction.'"

"Interesting."

"There's a second word also used to denote it, which he implies is Arabic, but he doesn't provide an Arabic spelling for it. He does transliterate it, however. As *hamsched.* I had a difficult time figuring out what to do with that. There are some possibilities that work in Arabic. But they were unsatisfying. Then, though, I realized that if the plant had some meaning to our anonymous cartographer, he wouldn't have been working solely in Arabic. He might have been fluent in Persian as well—"

"The 'curve-straightener.'" He grinned. "*Hamsched.* Inelegant, and something of a stretch, but it works."

She nodded. "Yes. That's what I thought. The people growing, or guarding, the plant in Yemen—and this is now a good seven hundred years after our manuscript appeared—didn't know Persian. But they might have offered Forsskal the word that had been associated with the plant. Or a facsimile of that word. Altered a bit after a few centuries of oral transmission. But even that isn't really convincing. At least, it isn't until one arrives at his description of the daisies."

"Not the nettles?"

"No," she said. "Daisy—*margarita*—means 'pearl' in Latin, right? But the daisies in the Arabian Peninsula weren't a new species, so Niebuhr—or Forsskal—didn't go into as much detail about them." She looked past him out the window. Darkness had fallen. She couldn't see the park. "In fact, he says nothing at all about them. Under '*margarita*,' he simply writes '*vide urtica.*' See nettle."

"So," Jeffrey concluded, "if you're interested in a pearl, a *margarita*, Niebuhr wants you to look for a nettle."

"Yes." She pushed the original collection of maps toward him. "Now read this passage again. In the manuscript they brought me in Geneva from Istanbul."

He rose, walked to the desk, and lifted the book. "Roughly," he began, "our anonymous geographer says, yet again, that cartographers shouldn't map seas. When a cartographer does attempt to map a sea, the sea forms coastal curves, gulfs, and headlands. But these curving lines can't be represented accurately on the map, which means that if the cartographer then tries to locate—or 'build' is the term he uses—cities or important places in the midst of these coasts and gulfs, it all ends in chaotic misery. Or something like that. I'm translating loosely." He looked up at her.

"So, the only way to find, or build, the place or the city that one might be seeking," she said, "is to straighten the curves. With a 'curve-straightener' that then points one in the proper direction."

He looked back down at the pages. "Hence the importance of this miraculously adherent nettle. Which provides guidance. And fixes curving lines. Yes—I see.'" He placed the book on the desk and returned to the sofa.

"Niebuhr was doing more than describing botanical specimens," she said as he leaned back and continued watching her. "He was passing along a bit of knowledge from the peninsula. He was saying that if one 'applies' Forsskal's nettle to—to the roughest part of the page—one in turn can make or build the place one seeks. And then, having built that place, one can discover the 'pearl.' To locate the *Durrah,* one must look for the nettle."

"I find it difficult to believe that an upstanding Danish astronomer was party to this thousand-year-old conspiracy to which you've attached yourself, Marion." Jeffrey was leaning his cheek on his fist, his elbow on the arm of the sofa.

"He wasn't," she said. "He was simply doing everything he could to reproduce his dead botanist friend's notes. But," she continued, hurried, "I don't think Forsskal knew anything about it either. I think he discovered something in Yemen. Just as Theodore Bent did. He tried to describe it. But he fell ill before he could do so."

"Ah." Dry. "Then I'll count myself fortunate to have suffered no more than a bit of delirium."

"I also think that if I find that specimen," she ignored him, "I mean a specimen of the original nettle—I can use it to reveal the coastline on this map. The itinerary toward this—this hidden source of eloquence." She rested her hand on the folio.

He still looked noncommittal. Didn't reply.

"They stored the royal expedition's specimens at the herbarium in the University of Copenhagen's botanical garden," she said, trying to persuade him. "Almost no one has examined them since the end of the eighteenth century."

"Interesting." He thought for a few moments. "But we're only halfway through. What about the Portuguese manuscript? And the chronicle of the Ottoman conquest?"

"Please, Jeffrey. Can I tell you about them on the way? They won't become important until we go to Lisbon."

"Lisbon as well?" He hadn't moved. "Heavens. Quite the tour of the continent you're planning for us."

"Yes."

"Very well. But don't think I missed your evasion before. When you were describing Forsskal's death. You were about to add a detail—no doubt an important one—and you decided it would be better that I didn't know it." He stood, walked to the door, and opened it. "I'll agree to discuss the remainder of this material with you in Copenhagen. Or even Lisbon. But at some point, I will become curious about the fate of our unfortunate botanist. You'd do well to satisfy my curiosity when that time comes."

Marion stood as well, unhappy, leaving the material on Jeffrey's desk. "Fine," she said as she passed him into the corridor. "I understand."

Copenhagen, Denmark
Lisbon, Portugal
May, 1935

I know where we can stay."

Marion was clutching her carpet bag. Walking hurriedly beside Jeffrey, who was signaling a waiting taxi. Their Imperial Airways flight had just landed in Kastrup, Denmark. Five miles outside of Copenhagen.

Marion stole a quick glance back at the sheep industriously trimming the grass runway now that the plane had reached the terminal. Then she strode to keep up with him. "It's a small hotel. In Nørrebro. It isn't picturesque, but it's quiet. And it will be easy for us to go under if we—"

"I've had our trunks sent ahead to the Hotel d'Angleterre." He held open the taxi door for her.

She stopped and looked, confused, at his briefcase. All he was carrying. "But—"

"Marion," he said, "the fact that I'm tagging along with you doesn't mean that I've also agreed to play fugitive extremist. I take my shaving regimen seriously."

"The Hotel d'Angleterre," she replied, still standing fixed outside the taxi, "is an insane place for us to stay. We'll be spotted before we're halfway across the lobby."

"Good." Peering up at the morning drizzle. "Then we needn't worry about when or where it will happen. Once they're on us, we'll keep track of them as well."

"Jeffrey—"

"If you'd prefer, Marion, you can stay in Nørrebro." He held up his briefcase. "Your manuscripts will be waiting for you at the Hotel d'Angleterre."

She stood silent for a few seconds longer. Then she climbed into the back of the taxi. Jeffrey slid in next to her and leaned forward to speak to the driver. Marion turned to him, surprised, when the car began moving. "Danish?"

"My mother brought me here to summer a few times. Years ago. But it comes back quickly." He half smiled at her. "You'll enjoy the hotel. If you manage to put away the asceticism for a few days."

She looked out the window. Didn't reply.

But it wasn't a long silence. Fifteen minutes later, the taxi reached the wide cobblestone street outside the hotel entrance. Tables under the awnings packed already, even in the damp, cloudy weather. Drab if expensively dressed patrons avoiding eye contact with one another. Church bells.

When the car rolled to a stop, the doorman—the first of a parade of functionaries, every one of whom could be bribed or threatened into passing along information about their movements—helped them into the lobby. Obsequious. Watchful. Also dowdy, despite his cross-cultural uniform.

Her impressions of hotel's atmosphere didn't change once they'd entered the lobby. There was a continuing fight throughout the building between the sort of ostentation that international guests expected and an underlying local aversion to display. It played out with particular violence in the lighting and flooring. She would have smiled if she weren't so bewildered by Jeffrey's insistence that they stay there at all.

Watching, suspicious, as he spoke with the concierge, she concluded that he'd simply lost his senses. She'd rarely been in a space more conducive to surveillance and less likely to offer a quiet escape. The bright, vaulted, and embarrassed room left her claustrophobic. She had to force herself not to flee back out into the street.

Jeffrey felt her panic and smiled at her. Teasing. Then he followed the hotel page up the stairs and toward their first-floor suite. Marion, resigned and refusing to relinquish her carpet bag, followed as well. She trusted Jeffrey not to be falling stupidly into some ambush. Whether he was setting her up for failure was another matter.

The suite—bedroom, living room, dining room, toilet, and balcony, the first three with parquet floors and dangerous looking chandeliers hanging low from painted ceilings—faced Kongens Nytorv Square. When Marion, still silently trailing Jeffrey, stepped through the glass doors out to the balcony, she stopped short. Astonished.

The balcony was less than thirty feet above the square. Low enough to be watched from any prospect without putting effort into it. Someone with the proper equipment could potentially sit at a table in the café beneath them and hear every word. She rested her hand on one of the white marble sculptures—self-satisfied cornucopia—surmounting the balustrade. At least the balcony supplied a shield should someone decide to snipe at them, she told herself. Acidly.

Then she turned toward Jeffrey, allowing anger to replace her mounting anxiety. "Are you out of your mind?"

He was leaning against a baluster, watching the movement in the square below. The mist had given way to a watery, almost warm, sunshine. "You don't like it?" He was still laughing at her.

"Jeffrey," she said, "you could have simply told me in London that you wouldn't help me. Why go to the trouble to—to accompany me here if you're going to make it impossible to do my job?"

"I stole your manuscripts for you," he replied, obscurely.

"Yes. Thank you for that." Uncertain. "But—how—" She paused. "Jeffrey, the whole city, should it choose to, can watch us here. I can't even begin to do what I must do—"

"Have we ever had a proper holiday, darling?" He straightened and looked at her. Beginning to smile again.

"You're not serious."

"No," he admitted. "I'm not." He turned and walked back through the glass doors into the dining room. "But think about it. *Have* we ever had a proper holiday?"

She followed him and shut the glass doors behind her. More violently than necessary. "Why are you doing this?"

He went through the living room and into the bedroom. Checked the wardrobe. Their clothing had been unpacked. Nearly ran into her, still doggedly following him, as he returned to the living room. Eventually, he sat on one of two facing sofas. Low table in between. Poured himself a glass of water from a carafe.

"Marion," he said. "You know that I adore you. More than anything or anyone else in the world. You are all that matters to me." He paused. "But you do have an unfortunate habit of almost trying to kill me." He thought. "Or is it trying almost to kill me?"

He shrugged and sipped his water. "You understand. Since the day we met, you've wanted me almost dead. And—and I say this with nothing but the deepest respect—you're quite good at getting what you want. Even if you decide later that you didn't want it after all. All of which means that I have spent more than a fair amount of time in your company almost dead." He considered again. "Not that I'm complaining. Pleasant memories."

She sat on the sofa opposite him. Stared at him. "What?"

"Quite simply, I'm protecting myself."

"But—"

"Yes, yes," he said. "I know. I've locked away your manuscripts. Should you almost kill me again, you'll be unable to follow your trail. You'll be stuck." He set down his water glass and pushed his hair off his forehead. "Experience, however, has taught that precautions of that sort are often insufficient in your company. So, I've added an additional layer of security this time."

He gestured at the room. "Our movements are, as you've seen, entirely open. There's no going under in this place. A mortifyingly exposed arrangement. But our situation does have this one advantage: should I fail to appear to our audience for two or three consecutive days, someone will come to investigate." He stood and returned to the bedroom. "Maugham may be cross with me, but he won't hesitate to extract me if I seem genuinely threatened. He needs me at the office. Bores himself otherwise."

She stood as well and followed him. He had removed his jacket and tie, and he was unbuttoning his shirt. Changing before going down to lunch. She watched him for a few seconds. Then she shook her head. Put what he'd said out of her mind. "How will I get Forsskål's nettle specimen?" Returning to their target. "How will I make it to the botanical garden without bringing a swarm of eyes along with me?"

He opened the wardrobe to choose a clean shirt. "We'll go after it tomorrow."

"How?"

He brought the shirt to the bed. Returned to the wardrobe for a jacket. "You'll follow my instructions."

She watched, silent, as he set a tie alongside the shirt and jacket. "Fine." Waiting for him to elaborate.

But he didn't. Instead, he went into the toilet. Shut the door behind him. "You may want to change as well, Marion," he said over the sound of running water. "The chef here is a genius. But they won't let you into the restaurant looking like an exile from Nørrebro. And I don't want to eat alone."

She shut her eyes for a few seconds. And then she walked toward the wardrobe to find a dress to wear downstairs. She would suffer through the afternoon and evening. But after that, she'd complete her task regardless of what sort of hindrances Jeffrey decided to throw in front of her. She had only so much patience.

$\mathcal{S}$HE woke the next morning before dawn. Her head on Jeffrey's shoulder. The chandelier suspended above the bed making her nervous. He was still asleep.

Edgy, she slid out from under the bedclothes, pushed her feet into slippers, and used the toilet. Then, wrapping a dressing gown over her pyjamas, she walked through the living room doors and out onto the balcony. The sky was turning from black to dark blue as the sun rose behind the hotel.

Enjoying the clean smell of the sky, she peered into the square. Just made out a figure opposite, male, lighting his first cigarette of the morning in the new French Embassy. Then she shivered, tied the dressing gown more tightly, and retreated indoors. Chilled. She had felt eyes on her movements. Idle early morning curiosity, no doubt—no different from her own. But the exposure left her unhappy. Mourning Nørrebro.

She closed the door behind her and turned toward the living room. Pushing away the thoughts of Ian that always assailed her when the world was quiet. Stopped short. Jeffrey was now awake, wearing a dressing gown, and sitting on the closer of the two sofas. Watching her. She hesitated, blinked back at him, and then crossed, silent, to the seat opposite him. Sat.

"I've sent down for breakfast," he said.

"Thank you."

Her nervous energy was mounting again, feeding on the knowledge that they'd be waiting at least two hours before making their way to the University. She didn't know whether she'd be able to eat given the state of her stomach. And she had no idea how she'd survive the empty time stretching out in front of her.

He looked through the glass door she'd closed behind her. The sun had risen past the top of the hotel, and the light in the square was now a cheerful yellow. "Splendid morning. Shall we breakfast on the balcony?"

She shot him a look.

He laughed, stood, and kissed her cheek. "The dining room, then. You and your modesty." There was a knock at the door, and he straightened to open it. "There's time for you to hide yourself away in the wardrobe if you feel that your dignity will be damaged by the impure gaze of the hotel staff."

She held his eyes, level, and then turned, still without speaking, to retreat into the bedroom. Uninterested in watching his practiced interactions with the servants. Doing so always left her embarrassed—although she was never certain why, or for whom.

When she heard the door to the suite close again, she returned to the dining room. "I only wanted a cup of coffee," she said, letting her eye wander, irritated, over the banquet that Jeffrey had ordered for them.

He was already tapping the top off an egg in an eggcup. "If you'd like. But you may surprise yourself. The croissants are quite well done. As, it goes without saying, is the salmon."

She sat at the table, reached for the silver coffee pot, and poured herself a cup. Decided she'd drink it black. Took a few sips. And then, when the caffeine had begun to work on her mood, she looked with renewed interest at the table. Spotted profiteroles at the center of the elaborate array.

As she reached for them, pleased, Jeffrey smiled into his eggcup. "I wish I'd known you as a child."

She spooned three profiteroles with chocolate onto her plate. Then she looked up at him. "I would have frightened you."

"I would have let you frighten me," he responded, still smiling at his egg. "If it gave you pleasure."

She ate a few bites. "When can we leave?"

"An hour, I thought?"

She nodded. Then she finished off the profiteroles and coffee in silence, stood, and started back toward the bedroom. "I'll get dressed."

"Wait," he said, standing as well and dropping his napkin onto the table. "We ought to dress the part."

She turned on him. "Look, Jeffrey. All I need do is get a feel for the building and its surroundings. Once I've established one or two vulnerabilities, I'll talk my way into the—"

"This is Denmark, Marion." He had followed her into the bedroom. "People here are unimpressed by strangers appealing to their vulnerabilities. They will, however, go out of their way to help those of us who follow the rules and to whom they've been properly introduced. It's an orderly nation, darling. Didn't you notice the military precision with which our breakfast was arranged?"

"Yes. I did notice. It nearly put me off my food."

"Which means," he continued, walking to the wardrobe, "we must play—and dress—our parts."

"I don't see how fancy dress is going to get us any closer to the locked sections of the herbarium," she replied, crossing her arms and watching him remove clothing from the wardrobe. "And we can follow the rules all we want; we'll still not have an introduction to anyone who can get us close to the specimens."

"But we will," he said, placing a shirt on the bed.

"How?"

He walked to a wall safe installed to the side of the wardrobe, opened it, and pulled out an envelope. She had a brief view of the two serpent sculptures and her manuscripts, neatly stacked, before he closed it again. He handed her the envelope.

She pushed it back at him without opening it. "What is it?"

He set it on top of the dark brown tweed jacket he'd selected from the wardrobe. "A letter of introduction to the retired director of the University's botanical museum and seed bank. From Professor Hans Krebs."

She considered for a few seconds. "I've heard that name before."

He nodded. "He's more a chemist than a botanist, but his recommendation carries weight in the natural sciences generally. He was at the University of Freiburg until two years ago. Making quite the reputation for himself. Sadly, being of impure blood, he was booted out by the Nazi academic establishment in 1933. He landed softly, though, at Cambridge, a few months later. He's at Sheffield now. Always willing to do a favor."

He slipped out of his dressing gown, removed the top of his pyjamas, and pushed his arms through the sleeves of an inexpensive looking light brown cotton shirt. "If you'd care to read the letter, you'll see that I, Dr. Willcox, research botanical references in medieval Islamic poetry. For the British Museum, obviously." He looked up at her as he buttoned his shirt. "And you, Miss Bailey, are my always able assistant."

"Pig."

"Better that than my always incompetent assistant, I would have thought." He flipped up his collar and knotted an ugly brown and green striped necktie over the shirt. "At any rate," he continued, "I've taken it into my head that Forsskal's eighteenth-century specimens from South Arabia might help me to solve a tricky puzzle involving the attribution of an influential, yet anonymous, Abbasid *ghazal* fragment. Professor Krebs has suggested to the staff of the University of Copenhagen's seed bank that they do everything in their power to aid me in my extraordinarily—harmless—project."

He picked up the tweed jacket and pulled it on over his shirt and tie. "Now don't you think this is a better strategy than sending you off to seduce some hapless groundskeeper before shattering all the windows in their Palm House during a midnight raid?"

She stared at the ground for a few seconds. Then she looked back up at him. "What am I wearing?"

"Marvelous." He brightened and pointed toward a green plaid skirt, light wool, and a white cotton shirt with short puffed sleeves that he had arranged on the bed. "That." He held up a pair of black, patent-leather heels with straps. "And these."

"Fine."

She took the clothing and the shoes and disappeared into the toilet. Dressed herself, leaving the top button of the shirt unfastened. Combed her hair back into a chignon. Shrugged at her reflection and returned to the bedroom.

Jeffrey had pulled on the trousers of his tweed suit and buttoned the jacket. He was also now wearing spectacles, clear glass, with prominent black frames. His hair falling over his forehead. He looked shy. She tilted her head and took in the effect. When he smiled, impudent, at her surprise, the illusion dissolved. She flushed and walked toward the door.

"You *prefer* me this way." He was following her, laughing.

"It's a low bar, Jeffrey." She opened the door leading to the hotel corridor.

"You have no taste." He took up his empty briefcase, waiting beside the door, locked the suite behind them and hurried to catch up to her as she strode toward the wide stairway leading to the lobby. "Wait," he said, stopping her as she reached the gallery that was exposed to public view.

Before she could question him, he turned her, set his briefcase to the side, and fastened the top button of her shirt. "Modesty." Then, preventing her from turning away again, he held her shoulders and looked down into her face. "Once we've made contact with the staff of the herbarium, you're to keep quiet. You'll say nothing. Do you understand?"

"Why?" Cold.

"Because doing so runs us an unnecessary risk?" Impatient. "Why provoke their curiosity? Simply don't initiate conversation. And if they talk to you, smile back at them. Polite." He lifted his eyebrows when she grew mutinous. "For the boy, Marion?"

She narrowed her eyes, but she didn't argue. Instead, nodding, curt, she turned back toward the staircase. She'd be relieved to escape the building. But when they'd passed the doorman—the same dully sinister man who had greeted them the previous morning—the move outdoors did nothing to minimize her sense of vulnerability. As they oriented themselves on Gothersgade street, walking in the direction of the botanical gardens, Maugham's people were already in place. Almost smug.

"Jeffrey," she said, alarmed, staring at the ground, "they're everywhere. We'll never lose them."

"Good," he repeated, echoing his attitude of the day before. "Something to entertain ourselves as we walk." He looked up at the sky, checking the weather. Turned his gaze back to her and pushed his spectacles into place on the bridge of his nose. "I count three. What about you?"

They continued to walk, leisurely, out of the square and along the street. Marion glanced up at his profile. He was trying to comfort her by turning it into a game. She half smiled. "Four."

"Four?" He let his eyes wander over the street. Past a few shop windows. "No. Not four. There are three."

She smiled more broadly, despite herself. "Four."

"Very well. Let's compare notes."

"All right. First, the fat boy on the bench, wearing the leftist cap but reading the nationalist newspaper. He's been on the same page since we left the building, and his eyes haven't moved."

He smiled as well, nodding. "Yes. He's terrible. I ought to report him to Maugham, but he's so young. Likely needs the money for his family. And perhaps he'll learn in time."

He stopped her at a shop window. They stood side by side, considering the reflection of a woman across the street. She had stopped as well, tending to a child in a pram. "Why does he do that?" Marion asked, still facing the glass.

"Do what?"

"Field all of these women with babies?" She lifted her eyes to his again. "It's morbid."

"Maugham likes babies." They resumed walking. "They distract people. So innocent. And who could suspect a young mother?"

"Anyone with experience as a mother. That one," nodding at the woman who kept pace just ahead of them on the other side of the street, "is dividing her attention between her baby and her surroundings entirely incorrectly. To me, she's even more prominent than the boy reading the wrong newspaper."

"Very well, then," Jeffrey said. "That's two. Three, of course, is the old chap doddering along behind us with the walking stick, limping on the perfectly healthy foot."

"Yes," she agreed. "That's three."

Jeffrey furrowed his brow and took in the street again. Shook his head. "There isn't a fourth. You're being dramatic."

She laughed. "There is. The man on the bicycle. He's been with us since the square."

"Nonsense," Jeffrey said without turning. "I saw him, of course. But he's neutral. A nice, strapping Danish lad enjoying Gothersgade street. Pleasant May morning."

"Look at his shoes."

"Really, Marion. You take things too far."

Humoring her, however, Jeffrey stopped them at an intersection and glanced both ways down the boulevard. Then, startled, but covering it, he pushed down a smile. Took her arm and strolled with her, relaxed, further toward the gardens. "I stand corrected." He adjusted his spectacles again. "And yes, you do frighten me sometimes."

By the time they reached the botanical museum, Marion's nerves were almost settled. She and Jeffrey, together, had spotted three more of Maugham's people in the forty-five-minute walk through the crowd to the end of Gothersgade street. And though she suspected there were more, she was no longer worried. If she and Jeffrey followed the rules, as he had suggested they do, the observers wouldn't be able to track their progress inside the museum building. Without an introduction, they'd be forced to wait outside.

Still, she would have preferred moving invisibly from Nørrebro. At night. She could easily have evaded the mild security protecting the specimens. And she'd have been out of Copenhagen before anyone at the office had realized she was there to begin with. Infinitely easier than Jeffrey's elaborate, if superficially respectable, approach. She remained irritated with him for keeping them both on display. And her irritation only grew as she obediently followed him through the red door of the brick building that housed the older botanical material.

Once inside, Jeffrey found a neat, organized reception area overseen by a seated and severe woman, late-twenties, wearing a tailored blue suit. The woman looked up from her work when she heard them enter, but she didn't welcome them or make a move to speak to them until Jeffrey had reached her desk. She kept her attention firmly on a book open in front of her on a green blotter.

When Jeffrey did near her desk, he put down his briefcase, retrieved his envelope from an inside pocket of his jacket, and spoke to her in Danish. Even with no understanding of their conversation, Marion could tell that he was playing up his British accent. Emphasizing that he was a foreigner who had taken the trouble to learn the language. His speech was as painfully accented as it was painfully correct.

Simple maneuver. And it worked beautifully. The woman, against her inclinations, began to smile, amused and almost friendly, before asking him a few questions. Then she took the letter from him, scanned it, and raised her eyebrows. Impressed. She looked with renewed curiosity at him, asked a few more questions, and turned, equally warm, to Marion. Before she could speak, however, Jeffrey interrupted with a short explanation. Presumably telling her that Marion couldn't speak Danish.

Closing up again, the woman nodded. Addressed Marion in cold, proper English: "I was informing Dr. Willcox, Miss Bailey, that unfortunately Professor Raunkiær—to whom his letter of introduction has been addressed—is in the field. He spends little time in Copenhagen since he's retired. But—" looking with increasing cordiality at Jeffrey, "I can grant Dr. Willcox access to the specimens he seeks to examine. Your project is fascinating. I do hope to read your results when you've published them." At which point, to Marion's annoyance, the woman actually blushed. "I'm completing my own doctorate this year," she offered. "On the nitrate content of Anemone Nemorosa."

Jeffrey, still shy, and deliberately letting his hair fall further over his forehead, said something to her in Danish. The woman blushed more violently, looked grateful, and stood. "Let me take you to the herbarium." As she walked out the door and into the hallway, she turned back to Marion. "Do you also have a project you're researching?"

Jeffrey, who was walking alongside her, shot Marion a warning look. After a split second of inward protest, she checked the moderately intelligent answer she had prepared. Instead, she smiled, shrugged inanely, and looked at the ground. Hating herself.

The woman paused for a moment, confused. Then she dismissed Marion and turned her attention to the stairs leading down to the historical specimens. Marion just caught the look of contempt on her face as she turned away. As well as Jeffrey's small smile. Not remotely shy.

When they reached the herbarium, the woman walked, confident, down an aisle between a row of metal stacks. Near the end of the row, she stopped, shifted a metal shelf, bent down, and carefully—reverently—removed a thick sheaf of loose pages protecting preserved dry samples. Crumbling with age.

She brought the pages to an exhibit table, waist high. Set them down, and then asked Jeffrey a question in Danish. He responded, and she slowly turned the pages until she reached the sample she wanted. She looked a question at Jeffrey, and he nodded. Before examining the page, however, he let himself color a touch and asked the woman a different question. Marion thought she heard "Anemone Nemorosa."

The woman brightened and replied quickly. Eagerly. Jeffrey nodded again and rested his hand on the exhibit table, a trifle closer to the woman than was strictly professional. The woman pretended, badly, to not notice his hand, and gestured Jeffrey toward a different part of the herbarium—leaving the pages she had retrieved from the stacks open on the table. Jeffrey, careless and following her lead, left his briefcase to the side of the exhibit table. Intrigued by her research.

Before they'd gone more than a few steps, the woman hesitated. Looked back at Marion and bit her bottom lip, thoughtful. Marion, who had been examining the device that moved the metal shelf forward and backward, gave her another vague smile. The woman stared, astonished, smiled back at her, and visibly decided that she was too stupid to do any harm. Dismissing her a second time, she spoke, more than animated now, to Jeffrey—drawing him further into the stacks.

Once they were out of sight, Marion turned to the pages open on the exhibit table. Ran her fingertip over the short Latin description. Looked closely at the dried leaves, flowers, and seeds that had been protected by the paper. Then, with a pang of guilt, she took up Jeffrey's empty briefcase, opened it, and slipped the page inside of it. Shut it and put it beside the table again.

After that, she closed up and rearranged the remainder of the pages, tidy, just as they had been when the woman had removed them from the shelf. And waited. She heard Jeffrey's laugh from somewhere in the stacks. Echoed by the woman. Rolled her eyes. Waited further. When they returned, companionable, Marion spoke before the woman could see that she had already re-secured the pages of specimens.

"Dr. Willcox," she said, looking at a clock embedded in the wall above the nearest shelf, "I'm afraid we've run out of time here. You'll be late to your meeting with Dr. Sørensen if we don't leave now. Perhaps we might return tomorrow? Now that you know you can conduct your research here?"

Jeffrey looked, dismayed, at the clock. Then he took up his briefcase and spoke in Danish to the woman again. Glanced sidelong at Marion. The woman, laughing, nodded as she retrieved the pages Marion had rearranged. Placed them, without checking their condition, back on the shelf before she and Jeffrey walked, still chatting, back up the stairs.

Marion, trailing them, fought down her irritation. She needn't understand Danish to know that Jeffrey had said something about his assistant at least having some uses. Without her, he'd never keep his appointments. Focused as he was on higher things.

WHEN they had extricated themselves from the museum and from the woman's repeated offers to help them navigate academic Copenhagen, Jeffrey grew subdued, throwing off the role he'd been playing. And by the time they were walking down Gothersgade street, he was almost pensive. Worried. Eventually, he turned to her. "You found what you need?"

"Yes." She looked up at him. Back at the crowded street.

"Will you use it this afternoon?" He was paying her only half attention.

She shook her head. "No. I need a sample from Lisbon as well. I'll mix the two before I apply them to the treated pages of the map."

"Hmm." He cast another practiced glance over the crowd. Maugham's eyes were still very much in attendance. "I suppose, then, that now would be a good time for you to tell me what you drew out of that Portuguese chronicle. We can't speak in the hotel, obviously. And I have a feeling that cafés are out at the moment as well."

She frowned, feeling tired. Surprised by the vehemence with which she balked at telling him her findings, especially now that he'd humiliated her at the botanical museum and left them wantonly open to surveillance in the city. She didn't trust him. And she disliked him even more having witnessed his fieldwork. The tactics he'd used in the herbarium had been upsetting—more upsetting, irrationally, than they would have been had they failed.

Not, it was true, that she hadn't seen hints of that persona before, when he was conducting formal interrogations. And not that his approach was any worse than the tactics she herself adopted when such work was necessary. She was in no position to pass judgement. But being in a room with him while he worked on someone else, even if in this case his technique was far from coercive, was a different matter. She felt ill.

Nonetheless, he'd never take her to Lisbon if she didn't give him something to demonstrate her willingness to cooperate. And if she provoked him, he'd have little compunction about simply leaving her in Denmark, without Danish, without her manuscripts, and unable to cross a border. An easy target for Maugham's network. He'd enjoy it. Which meant she couldn't work alone just yet, as much as she wanted to.

She ran a fingernail along her temple, thinking. She could, she told herself, continue to hold back from him the connection between Forsskal and the town of Jibla. If she kept that, he wouldn't know where in Yemen she was expected to deliver the *Durrah*, even if he'd have an idea by the time they were finished of where she'd be going to collect it. He'd be stuck, as he put it, as well. She nodded to herself. Imperceptibly.

Remaining silent on Jibla was the best she could do under the circumstances. She was convinced. And besides, she was uncertain even now as to whether she was pursuing her project solely to rescue Ian or whether she was still, grudgingly, working for her organization. If the former, she would open up to Jeffrey eventually. And if the latter, she could always lose him later. Before moving toward Jibla. It needn't happen immediately.

"Well?" He'd been watching her as she walked, working through her options. Undoubtedly picking up bits and pieces of her thought process. He sounded entertained.

"Let me start with the Ottoman chronicle," she said, ignoring his smile. "The account of Sinan Pasha's conquest of Yemen between 1569 and 1571."

"As good a place as any."

"There's only one part that's relevant to our map."

"Only one?" Still amused. He'd already sensed an evasion. "Out of the entire chronicle?"

"Yes," she said. "One part. Out of the entire chronicle." When he didn't reply, she continued: "you know the background. The Ottomans had sent a series of incompetent governors to rule the province throughout the mid-sixteenth century. Thereby exacerbating the inclination for independence that's always typified the southern peninsula. Eventually, the Zaydis—the majority of the population—revolted. Not unexpectedly. The chronicle is an account, heavy on the hagiography, of the Ottoman response to that revolt. Each and every battle over each and every hill and town is recounted in glorified detail. And the hero of the story is Sinan Pasha, the land commander. The one who did, eventually, restore partial Ottoman sovereignty to the territory."

"All right."

"But the Ottomans also sent a fleet, under the command of admiral Khayr al-Din—'Hayreddin' or 'Hayrettin' in the Ottoman Turkish accounts—to support the conquest. The admiral and his fleet get almost no mention in the chronicle. If the history is to be believed, they were next to useless to the military effort. Might not have been there at all."

"That's hardly unusual," he said. "The purpose of the work was to emphasize Sinan Pasha's role. He commissioned it himself, didn't he? Wouldn't do for his chronicler to portion out the glory."

"Yes," she said. "But it's not only that the fleet was, according to the chronicle, unhelpful. It was also—most of the time, at least—pursuing some entirely other goal. Its activities are completely disconnected from the suppression of the Zaydis."

"In what way?"

"So, the first mention of Khayr al-Din," she said, "is when he leaves the port of Mocha, on the Red Sea Coast, with twelve ships armed and prepared to take Aden from the rebels. His orders are to secure the port city from the sea prior to Sinan Pasha's more difficult approach from the land."

She paused. "So, off he goes. But then, when he reaches Aden, he doesn't bother to attack it. Spotting a fleet of Portuguese ships entering the Gulf of Aden, he sails after them instead. To the southwest. Toward Africa. For days. And it's only once they've dispersed that he returns to the city of Aden and, with help now from the land troops who have already arrived, takes the city."

"And then?"

"And then, the next time he appears, he's been given a land command—"

"Where?"

"I—I can't remember." Feeling foolish. "It's unimportant—"

"Where was his command?" Jeffrey's tone was impatient.

"I've told you," she insisted, stubborn, "it's unimportant. What's relevant," she rushed on before he could ask again, "is that this command is disastrous. He's crushed by the Zaydi guerillas. Killed in battle."

"I see." He didn't push her any further on the location of Khayr al-Din's final command. "So what, then, do you conclude from that?"

"I conclude that his orders, from Istanbul, weren't to support Sinan Pasha's campaign at all. Someone in Istanbul knew that no matter how powerful the Ottoman military was, they'd never hold Yemen—and in fact they didn't; they were driven out again by 1636—without an additional source of legitimacy. They sent Khayr al-Din after that source of legitimacy. But he failed. Perhaps owing to the Portuguese. And so, as a result, they gave him a command entirely alien to him that could end only in his death. They didn't want him talking."

She stared down at the ground as they walked. "The manuscript—the original collection of maps, I mean—that I received in Geneva. It came from Istanbul. The binding was sixteenth-century Ottoman. Holding together eleventh-century Fatimid pages. I'm certain that it was accessed, there in the Ottoman capital, at the time of the Yemen campaign. There's even an illegible note—possibly encoded—in Ottoman Turkish rather than in Arabic, on the inside of the binding. In sixteenth-century writing."

She glanced up at him. "Someone in Istanbul, I'm confident, already knew about the *Durrah*. They also knew about its link to Yemeni unity. And they wanted to locate it. Using the cartographical—and botanical—information stored in that manuscript. Whoever that person or group was, they sent Khayr al-Din to find the plant, or mixture of plants, that could reveal the coastlines hidden on the second map. But he couldn't find it."

She dropped her eyes again. "I suspect that the Portuguese also had some idea of what he was pursuing. There were rumors of a—a politically important—Red Sea or Indian Ocean treasure everywhere at the time. Rumors that something was amiss. Because the Red Sea was—troubled—in those years." She spoke carefully. "All of which meant that Khayr al-Din had no choice once he'd reached Aden. He *had* to go after the Portuguese. Drive them off. Doing so was far more important to his assignment than waiting to take the city."

Jeffrey nodded, intrigued. But then he hesitated. Considered further. "Would the powers that be in Istanbul have risked weakening their campaign like that? For nothing more than a few provocative hints in a Fatimid-era manuscript?"

"There were all sorts of factions within the Ottoman government at the time," she answered. "Some were traditionalists, yes. They wouldn't have been interested. They would have done all they could to run a straightforward campaign. In which case the admiral's behavior would have been suspicious at best. Treason at worst."

She continued to examine the ground as they walked. Didn't want to catch accidental sight of any of Maugham's eyes. "But others in the government had ambitious ideas about expanding the Empire's sea power. A group of ministers even floated a quite serious proposal a few years later, in 1579, to dig a waterway from the Mediterranean to Suez—connecting the Mediterranean Sea to the Red Sea. The only reason it fell through was that the group's leader, the Ottoman Grand Vizier Sokollu Mehmet Pasha, died before they could garner sufficient imperial support to begin the project."

"Killed by an Assassin's blade, wasn't he?"

"Yes," she said, ignoring his implication. "So they say. But, of course, the other problem with the plan for the—the canal was that they could never subdue the southern part of the peninsula. Without controlling Yemen's Red Sea and Indian Ocean coasts, digging a passage through to the Mediterranean wouldn't have done much for them. And the Portuguese kept getting in their way. So it was dropped by the turn of the seventeenth century."

"Let's leave the Suez project, then," he said, "to the side for the moment. Tell me again why this group of ambitious ministers would bother themselves with searching for a single jewel—fabled thought it might have been—at the risk of weakening what was an already challenging military campaign." His tone was mild. Not challenging. Simply seeking information. "It still seems an unnecessary risk. Sending the fleet off in the opposite direction just as the army was making headway from the north."

"They ran the risk," she explained patiently, "because their goal—that is, the goal of the people running Khayr al-Din in the 1570s—*wasn't* a pearl or a piece of rock crystal. It was more than that. They wanted to take advantage of what was, in hindsight, a turning point in—in the nature of imperial governance. The shift toward the sea."

She peered into a shop window. Reflected observers. Then she sighed and continued: "to secure their place in the changing maritime balance of power, they needed a unified, peaceful, and compliant Arabian Peninsula and Red Sea coast. The *Durrah*, regardless of whether it was actually a 'pearl,' could have helped them to achieve that goal. As it happened, they never found it. And they also never secured Yemen. From the seventeenth century onward, Ottoman control of the Red Sea and Indian Ocean diminished."

"As did that of the Portuguese," he reminded her, brisk now. He had noticed the reflections in the shop window as well. "Which, of course, leads me to wonder how it is that the Dos Santos account—product of another empire at a tipping point—can tell you anything about Khayr al-Din's unofficial instructions to head in the wrong direction once he'd left Mocha. Why not another Ottoman document?"

"The Ottomans never admitted that the second part of this story happened," she told him. "There's no mention of it in the Ottoman material at all."

They had reached Kongens Nytorv Square. Choosing a quiet bench with evacuation routes on either side and the prospect of the crowd in front of them, they sat. They'd move if their pursuers came within listening distance.

"So how do *you* know about it, then?" Jeffrey had placed the briefcase on his knees. Prim. Enjoying the effect.

She herself felt preposterous in the plaid skirt, girlish white shirt, and patent-leather shoes. "Actually, it's a relatively well-known story." Ignoring his pose. Shifting awkwardly on the bench. "The Ottomans denied knowledge of it because it was an embarrassment to them." She paused. "And also— probably more so—they had to pretend not to know about it because admitting to it would have left them open to accusations of impropriety. Violations of the period's already relaxed maritime law."

She avoided eye contact with a passing functionary from the French Embassy. "But it *is* recounted in several Portuguese, Spanish, Dutch, and even Austrian chronicles. I asked you to bring me the Dos Santos version because he places it in the context of what he sees as a wider story of Portugal's occupation of the African Coast. Which is helpful. To us."

"I see."

"So, it begins in 1588, a little less than twenty years after Khayr al-Din chased the Portuguese away from the Gulf of Aden in supposed aid of Sinan Pasha's campaign." She watched a bicyclist, this one unquestionably neutral, circle the square and then disappear behind the tram making its way past Gothersgade street. "By now, the internationalist faction in Istanbul had found a more likely instrument for their purposes. Mir Ali Bey. A pirate—or, I suppose, a 'corsair'—rather than a respectable admiral like Khayr al-Din." She glanced up at him. "Lots of dashing escapades to his name already. Most of them ordered informally by officials in Istanbul wanting to make a case for a stronger Ottoman presence in the Red Sea and Indian Ocean. None acknowledged."

"Hmm," Jeffrey said, resting his arm on the bench and enjoying the spring air. "But what could have happened in 1588 to convince his superiors at the capital to forget that he existed? If what you've said of him is correct, it must have taken more than a single failed assignment to persuade them to cut him loose. Good talent, and all that."

"It's an odd story," she answered, indirectly. "You see, he'd been ordered to drive the Portuguese out of Mombasa. In East Africa. To gain control the naval traffic heading northeast from the Indian Ocean toward the Gulf of Aden and then into the mouth of the Red Sea." She lifted her eyes to his again. "This, now, is according to the Portuguese chronicles remember, because the Ottomans claimed no knowledge of it."

She looked down again and resumed: "he was well equipped to complete his task. Or at the very least to cause some damage. And, in fact, he had no difficulty establishing himself in the port and setting up an artillery presence that ought to have destroyed any Portuguese boats that arrived to dislodge him."

"But?"

"But then something strange happened," she said. Smiling slightly. "So the Portuguese arrived and engaged him. Mir Ali was certain to win. The Portuguese boats were on the verge of flight." She looked at him. "At which point, so the accounts say, tens of thousands of 'Zimba'—a sort of derogatory, all-purpose term for people coming from the African interior—descended on Mir Ali's forces. They gathered on the landward side of the harbor and wrecked the Ottoman position. These 'Zimba' also attacked the Portuguese—but their primary interest was the Ottoman military. Mir Ali escaped and surrendered to the Portuguese. Riding his horse into the sea toward the Portuguese boats."

She pushed her skirt down further over her knees. Wished yet again that she weren't sitting in full view on the bench. Then she finished the story. "The Portuguese pulled him aboard. And, according to the chronicles, Mir Ali converted to Christianity. Lived the rest of his life in Lisbon. But—and this is important—after they had rescued Mir Ali, the Portuguese weren't finished. Their fleet then sailed up and down the coast, destroying the towns and cities. Burning the forests inland. That sort of thing."

"Ah."

"But Jeffrey," she said, "this story doesn't make sense. None of it. There's no logic to it. No reason for the punitive expedition. No careful consideration of moral cause and effect of the sort one ordinarily finds in these accounts. And the only explanation that the chronicle provides for the attack from the interior is that the 'Zimba' were enraged cannibals bent on indiscriminate violence. No goal. No strategy." She paused. "Which is silly."

"Is it?" He smiled sideways at her.

"Yes," she said. "It is. So the question then becomes what did Mir Ali do earlier, before reaching Mombasa, that provoked the people inland to follow him and to attack? And also—and I think this is related—what were Mir Ali's orders? Istanbul would have known that a single corsair, no matter how—dashing—couldn't have driven the Portuguese out of a position they'd held for a good century or more. Caused some damage, yes. But eliminate their presence in Mombasa altogether? Absolutely not. Even if that's what the Portuguese chronicles insist he was trying to do."

"I have a feeling you're going to float a hypothesis now." Jeffrey resettled his spectacles. Still enjoying the fact that he could.

"Here's what I think," she said. "This collection of ministers in Istanbul had been aware, at least since the 1560s, of the *Durrah* and its potential usefulness. They had at least one of the Fatimid manuscripts that hinted at its location. I wouldn't be surprised if they had access to the other as well. Before it reached the Baquba library." She looked down at her hands clasped in her lap. Strange looking against the plaid skirt. "They had almost succeeded in securing what they needed during Sinan Pasha's campaign. And if Khayr al-Din hadn't failed and died—"

"Wherever it was that he did fail and die," Jeffrey contributed.

"Yes," she said shortly. "If he hadn't failed, chances are that they would have had it by the mid-1570s. As it was, Mir Ali came quite close in the late-1580s as well. I think his orders were to go inland to find the second ingredient that was needed to—to expose the hidden coastlines on that map." She kept her eyes down. "And I have a notion of what that ingredient was."

"Yes?"

"Yes. It was frankincense. The anonymous author isn't even all that subtle about it. Not only does he dwell on the usefulness of the three 'crystalline' stars in the constellation Orion's belt—the *nazm*, or string of pearls—to those navigating the 'secret parts' of the Red Sea—"

"Ah," he said, slowing her down. "And those three stars, of course, have always been associated with the magi. At least, among those inclined to Sufism. And the magi in turn—"

"Bring frankincense," she finished for him. "But the manuscript also states baldly, I suppose for those who can't take the hint, that the constellation discloses the location of forests that produce a 'marvelous' frankincense. Even during those months when it isn't visible in the sky. There's also something in the margin about how a navigator seeking this frankincense needn't wait for the resin to mature. One can take it immediately after slashing the bark."

"So, you think—"

"Yes," she interrupted again. "I think that Mir Ali had been sent to secure the frankincense. The second ingredient."

"Why not buy it?' Jeffrey asked. "This group in Istanbul couldn't have lacked the funds."

"There are countless varieties of the tree—*boswellia*—that produces frankincense. Maydi Frankincense is the purest. I read up on it before we left for Copenhagen. But there's a subtype even of that strain that's unique to Somalia." She prayed that they were out of listening distance, sitting as they were on the bench. "When Mir Ali sailed, he stopped, first, at the island of Socotra, off Yemen. And then he turned back, went up through the Mandeb Strait, and made a series of additional stops along the African coast of the Red Sea and the Gulf of Aden. By the time he'd reached Mombasa, south of Somalia, I think he had what he wanted. But he'd taken it in bad faith. Hence the 'Zimba' coming at him from the northwest, trying to retrieve it."

"But you believe they failed as well." Jeffrey's tone was thoughtful.

"Yes," she said. "When Mir Ali surrendered to the Portuguese, many of his sailors surrendered as well. Many of them were as rich as he was. Well born. Certainly willing to convert. But every one of them was either killed or sent to the galleys. No mercy."

"Not Mir Ali himself, however," Jeffrey supplied. "Because he had something to offer them. More than a ransom or a name. Something that bought him a relatively comfortable retirement in Portugal."

"He offered them the trees," she said. "The resin. I'm certain. And he likely hinted to them that they could use the trees or the resin to find the fabled piece of crystal. Quite the jewel for their King—"

"Or," Jeffrey interrupted, grinning, "their King could have passed it along to the Spanish instead. Consolation for having lost the Armada a month or two earlier."

"But," ignoring him, "Mir Ali also covered himself. He would have had to work on—on solving the mystery—in peace once he'd settled in Lisbon. Which meant they'd leave him alone. He never did work on it, of course. But I'm certain the trees he carried with him in his saddle bags were well cared for." She considered. "That also explains the strange course the Portuguese punitive mission took afterward. Yes, they would have made an example of the leaders along the Swahili and Somali coast who had gone over to Mir Ali. Execute them in unpleasant and public ways. Level their towns."

She watched the tram. Returning now from the opposite direction. "But why go inland and destroy the forests?" She paused. "I think they razed them because they wanted a monopoly on the resin. They wanted to be certain that the only trees producing it were in Lisbon. Inaccessible, at any rate, to their Ottoman rivals."

Noticing a harried office worker wandering a touch too close to their bench, Marion and Jeffrey both stood. Walked in the direction of the hotel. Leisurely.

"And in fact, it remained inaccessible," Marion concluded as Jeffrey slipped her hand through his arm. "The group in Istanbul that had fielded both Khayr al-Din and, twenty years later, Mir Ali, dwindled and disappeared." She peered up at the self-satisfied façade of the Hotel d'Angleterre. Nodded to the doorman as she and Jeffrey entered the lobby. "As did any chance of Ottoman supremacy in the Red Sea and Indian Ocean. They'd made their attempt. And it hadn't succeeded."

"And so, three centuries later, we travel to Lisbon," he said as they climbed the stairs.

"Yes," she replied. "We travel to Lisbon. We'll begin by looking in the botanical garden at the Ajuda Palace. That seems the most likely place for the trees they'd have cultivated from Mir Ali's saplings."

His face was dissatisfied as he opened the door to their suite. "There is one other problem, Marion. The Lisbon earthquake. In 1755? It destroyed the city. Are you certain the trees survived?"

"The Portuguese royal family," she said as she passed him into the suite, "took very good care of their plants after the earthquake. Proud of their gardens, you know. Proverbially."

He followed her and shut the door. Removed his spectacles. Watched her, quizzical.

"Very good care," she repeated. Then she went into the bedroom to change out of her odious clothing.

THEY flew to Lisbon the next morning. Jeffrey, delighted by his luck, had found them spaces on a dirigible travelling to Portugal via Germany. A special flight. But when Marion had refused to go anywhere near it, he hadn't argued all that forcefully in favor of his plan. Let it go with nothing more than mild disappointment—leading her to suspect that he'd used the suggestion as a tactic to keep her from protesting too vocally his second recommendation: a Farman F.220 bomber flown by a silent French pilot who took them from Kastrup to Alverca airbase, thirty miles outside of Lisbon. Brief stop in an anonymous French field where an equally silent peasant provided them, improbably, with fuel. She had no idea where Jeffrey had secured their transportation. Didn't ask.

When the taxi they'd found in Alverca entered the outskirts of Lisbon, however, she did ask where they'd be staying. His response, more than she wanted to know, was that their unusual flight plan wouldn't have thwarted Maugham's people. The office knew where they were. He could sense it. And so, they were staying at the central, easily surveilled Avenida Palace Hotel. Even more stupidly visible than the Hotel d'Angleterre had been.

Annoyed as she was, she wasn't as mystified by Jeffrey's choice in Portugal as she had been in Denmark. Neither of them knew Lisbon professionally—and touristic prominence was preferable to drawing the attention of Salazar's police by acting furtive. Better to be sightseers.

It was with equanimity, therefore, that she entered the suite that Jeffrey had secured for them on the top floor of the hotel. Hiding her astonishment when she entered the bedroom—optimistic blue and yellow striped paper on the walls, and a gold chaise longue facing the window—to discover that their trunks and clothing had reached the hotel before they had. Cleaned, unpacked, and hung in the wardrobe, the result of Jeffrey's monstrous organizational capacity.

But, after staring at it for a few seconds, she shrugged inwardly, turned away from the wardrobe, and walked back to the living room. Distracted momentarily by a painting, primitivist in a gilded frame, of a bowl of indecent looking fruit. Perhaps their clothing had arrived via the dirigible. She hoped it had enjoyed itself.

When she reached the living room, Jeffrey was already sitting in an armchair, gold as well, and reading a copy of the *Times*. Delivered to their rooms along with the trunks. He looked pleased with himself. Relaxed. There was a glass of Cointreau with ice resting on the table next to him. Half empty.

He looked up at her when she appeared and stood, hesitant, in the middle of the room. Folded his paper and set it beside the glass. "You want to go out straight away, don't you?" He lifted his glass and took a sip.

"Yes. I'll change my clothes, and we'll—"

"I need rest." His voice had an edge that she couldn't identify. "For a few hours. And after that, I thought we might enjoy a ride on the tram." He smiled, malicious. "It's famous, you know."

She sat heavily on the sofa opposite him. "*Why*? Jeffrey, Ian is—"

"Perfectly fine. Enjoying himself, I daresay. Relieved to be free of the Livy."

"We're so close," she insisted. "This is perverse. We can't sit in this hotel, doing nothing."

"We're not doing nothing. I've told you. We'll experience the historic tram." He gazed at his glass. "And then, this evening, I thought we might try the theatre."

"*Why*?"

"Do you know, Marion? It's strange. I've been feeling a touch weak the past day or two. It's by no means severe. But I can say now with some confidence that I'm not, at the moment, entirely healthy."

She forced herself to keep her voice steady. "I'm sorry to hear that, Jeffrey. But don't you think that's even more reason to go out *now*? In case—"

"I'm confident it's nothing. Two or three days and I'll feel right as rain. And so," he picked up his newspaper again, "we'll wait. For it to pass."

"No." She stood and paced to the window. Looked out onto the traffic moving through the square. "I'll go on my own, if necessary. I'll bring the resin back here—"

"You'll bring it back here to an empty room." He spoke over her, perusing his *Times*. "And to no manuscript. You remember the bargain, surely?" He looked at her over the top of the paper. "You retain access to your material only so long as I watch you. I'm afraid I can't watch you if I'm too ill to move."

She turned back to him. "Please."

"Tomorrow morning, then," he said, standing and folding the paper. "A compromise. We'll simply hope that I'm not—yet—confined to bed at that point." He walked toward the bedroom with the newspaper. "And meantime, I think your idea is excellent. I'll change out of these clothes. Before venturing out to explore this charming neighborhood."

She watched him retreat into the corridor, and then she crossed the room. Sat in a second armchair and stared, anxious, at the coffee table. Then, steeling herself, she rose again and followed him. She wanted to change her clothing as well.

JEFFREY did precisely as he had threatened, and after dragging her through the city on the glacially slow tram, he brought her, hours later, to the hotel. After that, they changed into evening clothes and made their way to the Teatro Eden, which, implausibly, was showing *Drake of England*. With Henry Mollison, whom Jeffrey claimed to adore.

By the time they'd returned to the hotel, Marion was close to snapping. She kept her anger in check, however, and silently changed into her pyjamas. Crawled into the smug gilded bed and willed herself to relax into sleep. She hadn't spoken to Jeffrey since they'd left for their tour of the city that afternoon. But, slipping into the bed beside her, he seemed not to expect her to. The animosity hadn't left his bearing since he'd told her he was feeling unwell. He was as angry as she was.

She woke the next morning before he did. But instead of escaping immediately to the living room, she peered down into his sleeping face. He looked well enough, she thought. Normal color.

Then she pushed the covers off her legs and stood. Went into the toilet to clean her teeth. He'd be strong enough to visit the botanical gardens today. He must be. When she left the toilet, he was already sitting up in the bed. Running a hand through his hair. "I appear to be conscious."

"Yes." She pulled on a dressing gown. "We can leave immediately."

"Breakfast—"

"*No*," she nearly shouted back at him. Hint of hysteria. "No." Calmer. "Let's eat on the way." She hugged her waist. "All right?"

He got out of bed, his face unreadable. "Very well."

She walked to the wardrobe and chose serviceable clothing to wear while they searched the gardens. Blue linen trousers and a white silk shirt. A functional white hat. Low heeled, brown oxfords. She also slid a pen knife and a small stoppered jar into the pocket of her trousers. For the resin.

As he used the toilet, she changed out of her dressing gown and pyjamas and went to the living room to wait for him. Sat, tense, on the sofa. Staring into the middle distance. Ignoring his folded *Times* on the side table.

When he emerged from the bedroom, her anxiety shifted to annoyance. He was wearing a pale camel sport coat, white trousers, and a yellow dotted tie with a matching pocket handkerchief. Brown and white wingtips, insufferably well-made. Holding a white panama hat. He was also pallid. But she set aside that observation. Nervous. Didn't want to think about it.

Instead, she stood abruptly. "Shall we go? That is, if you feel able to miss your rendezvous with the syndicate in Havana."

"Goodness. You're keyed up this morning, aren't you?" He examined his cigarette case, snapped it shut, and slid it into the inside pocket of his jacket. "Guilty conscience? Again?"

"Only about ransacking centuries-old botanical collections," she said shortly. "But I'll get past it. Let's go."

He opened the door. "I telephoned down from the bedroom. The car is waiting for us." He stood to the side to let her through. "Shouldn't take more than twenty minutes in the morning traffic."

She followed him to the lift, forced a smile at the genial old man operating it, and then let Jeffrey guide her through the lobby. Potted palm trees. Marble statues. Inexplicable sound of water from some invisible source. Identical to hotels of its sort the world over. She barely noticed. She was merely glad to be out of the building.

That is, she was pleased to be leaving the building until she saw the car that was waiting for them. A spotless, dark green Mercedes-Benz 500. Idling just outside the front entrance to the hotel. Patient, discreet driver. "I borrowed it from the Embassy," Jeffrey said as he opened the door for her.

She stared at him, more overwrought than amazed by this point. "Why are you *doing* this?" Feeling, foolishly, on the verge of tears again. When he didn't speak, she obediently slid into the rear seat of the car and tried again. "*Why?* Why provoke them? Why provoke Maugham?"

"I've told you," he said, sitting next to her and shutting the door. Nodding at the driver to go. "For protection. Mostly from you, it's true—"

"Jeffrey—" Her voice was unnaturally tight.

"But also from unforeseen trouble. I've never worked in Lisbon before. It's an opaque city to me, and I have no back doors available should difficulties arise. I suspect you haven't either." He paused, inviting her to reply. When she didn't, he elaborated. "If we're caught misbehaving in that garden, do you know what will happen to us?"

She turned stubbornly to the window.

"We'll find ourselves in a Portuguese prison cell. Waiting for the local constabulary to decide what to do with us." He examined her profile. "Should that unfortunate eventuality arise, Marion, I intend to have sufficient influence available to me on the outside to see to it that the constabulary decides intelligently. So yes, two or three efficient but unassuming members of the Embassy's staff know that we're in the city. It would have been reckless not to let them know."

He looked out his own window. "And now that they're aware of our presence, they will do everything in their power to avoid an embarrassing situation. One in which, say, I—or even you—despair, having languished forgotten in prison for a few days, and begin spilling bits and pieces of information to the Portuguese authorities. If we draw unwelcome attention from the gendarmes—unfamiliar as we are with the local customs—the Embassy will extract us. It's in their interest to do so."

"How do you know they won't just kill you?" She was still watching the city passing out her window. "Quietly."

He laughed. Put his hand over hers. "As I said, Maugham would miss me if they killed me." He patted her hand a few times and then withdrew his own. "Same reason that you've never quite done away with me."

"Not yet." She turned back to him. "And, to be perfectly honest with you, Jeffrey, I don't think there's much to choose between attention from your efficient, unassuming Embassy functionaries and attention from Salazar's police. I, for one, would rather take my chances in a Portuguese prison cell."

"Only because you enjoy that sort of thing, dear." The car was slowing to a stop in front of the bright white neoclassical façade of the palace. "I prefer to take my pleasure elsewhere."

The car rolled to a stop, and Jeffrey thanked the driver before opening the rear door himself. Stood to the side as Marion stepped, blinking, into the sunlight. He closed the door and looked up at the building as the driver maneuvered the car to the edge of the car park to wait for them. "It's very tall, isn't it?"

She exhaled, annoyed, and moved toward the entrance. "I think we go through the ground floor to reach the gardens."

Smiling and adjusting his panama hat, he followed her. They entered the formal garden spread out behind the palace and walked between low box hedges for several minutes. Brightly tiled pools of water, a pleasant breeze off the Tagus river below them, massive, unmistakably ancient palm trees.

Eventually, as they circled back to their starting point, Jeffrey took her arm and stopped her. "This is lovely, Marion." He contemplated, mildly disturbed, a white peacock that had kept pace with them throughout their walk. "I may even prefer it to the tram. But do we have an itinerary? A strategy?"

She sat on a stone bench, looked up at him, and nodded. "Yes."

"Care to divulge it?"

She didn't want to. But she nodded again. "Yes. The royal family commissioned this garden in 1755, after the earthquake. To house new specimens and to rejuvenate what had been saved from the destruction. They had thousands of species of plants flourishing here by the turn of the nineteenth century. But then, in 1808, when Napoleon invaded, the French removed most of them. Took them back to Paris."

He sat beside her on the bench. "But not the one that interests us."

"No. I think it was too old. Too big to steal."

"Learned their lesson with Ramesses II, no doubt." He grinned at her.

She didn't reply.

He sighed. "This tree then, you think, is from Mir Ali's time?"

"One of the most celebrated specimens in the collection," she said instead of answering his question, "is an ancient African elemi tree. A *canarium*. It was one of the symbols of Portuguese colonial power. Their sailors transported and transplanted them all over Southeast Asia and East Africa. The one here is supposed to be four hundred years old. Which is possibly a bit of an exaggeration."

"All right." He used his toe to encourage the peacock to move in a different direction. But it stayed put, complacent, gazing at him.

"The *canarium*," she continued, "is related to *boswellia*, the plant that's tapped for frankincense. They're both from the *burseraceae* family. Variations on resinous trees. And, over the centuries, merchants and pirates with all sorts of backing—not just the Portuguese, but the Mughals, the Chinese, the Arabs, even the Safavids and the Ottomans—tried to mix them, to grow them together. *Boswellia*, from what I read back in London, is difficult to root, whereas the African elemi takes root easily, just about anywhere. Mixing them wouldn't have been easy—they're from the same family, but different genera. But it also wouldn't have been impossible. And people kept trying."

"You think the *canarium* they have here is an attempt at that mixture?" he asked.

"I think," she said, "that if Mir Ali was collecting a uniquely valuable strain of *boswellia* for his superiors, he would have covered his tracks. And he did make several stops, including at ports in Ethiopia and Somalia, before he entered Mombasa. Given his route, he could have hidden the *boswellia* specimens he'd been sent to collect from Somalia among a few other, less valuable, *boswellia* variants from Socotra off Yemen. Maybe a couple of *canarium* samples from further up the East African coast. That sort of thing. Doing so wouldn't have been suspicious. Other pirates were doing the same."

She stood and moved with more purpose toward a corner of the garden. "The royal family would also have wanted to obscure the value of the *boswellia* specimens once they'd arrived in Lisbon. Doing so wouldn't have been much of a sacrifice. Unlike the *canarium*, the *boswellia* isn't a display tree. It isn't striking in appearance." Pausing at a split in their path, she nodded to herself and turned to the left. "And the best way to hide a plant—I mean *really* hide it—is to allow it to grow or melt into something else. Something showier. Something like a tall, dramatic *canarium* with bright leaves and clusters of white flowers or purple berries. But," she slowed as they reached a twisted, ungainly tree with small, spiked white May flowers, "if that specimen failed, which it would do after a century or so, and if they were looking for something similar to support it, why not hide it in another *canarium* in their collection? Repeat the process?"

Jeffrey was peering up at the tree in front of them. "If what you've hypothesized is correct," he said, "—and this process would have demanded unprecedented horticultural skill for the time—then the *boswellia* that Mir Ali transported would have been hidden, swallowed up, by this *canarium* centuries ago." He nodded up at the tree. "Even if it's in there, how do you access the resin? You'll tap the wrong sample. African elemi resin is used for making paint and treating roundworm, yes? So at least we'll come away with something."

"I want to look at the bark."

After a quick glance about to be certain they were alone, she approached the tree. Placed her palm on the trunk and examined it closely. She thought she could just make out the outline of a thin second trunk that had melted into the larger *canarium*'s trunk. Something not quite natural. But the bark at the base was uniform. It reminded her of thick, darkish maple. Unusual, but not what she wanted.

She stood on her toes, reached up, and ran her finger along one of the higher branches. After that, she tried a second. Then a third. Finally, feeling a patch of bark that crumbled and peeled, paper-like, against her fingertips, she stopped. Squinted up at it and reached into her pocket for the pen knife. She looked over at Jeffrey, who was watching the path for tourists or groundskeepers, and then she turned her attention back to the branch. Using her other hand to mark the place she'd strike, she drove the pen knife into the thick wood. Withdrew it and waited. A clear, yellowish excretion. Liquid. Not what she wanted.

Irritated, she ran her fingers further along the base of the branch. Stopped at a more prominently abnormal patch of bark. Like layers of parchment pasted onto the base of the tree. She struck it with her knife a second time. Waited for a few seconds, and when it came, she smiled. The resin was milky white. More viscous than she had expected, but certainly not liquid. It was the resin that preceded the orange-ish fluid that would seep from the cut a week or two later and could be hardened into frankincense.

She removed the stoppered jar from her pocket and let the resin pool at the bottom of it. The "navigator," according to her manuscript, needn't wait for the orange. What the *boswellia*, hidden from view since the sixteenth century, was giving to her now would serve equally well, if not better, as a treatment for her map. Once she'd collected two inches of resin at the bottom of her jar, she stoppered it, rose, and slipped it and the pen knife into her pocket. Then she and Jeffrey left the garden. Avoiding the inquisitive peacocks.

BY the time they'd returned to the hotel, Jeffrey was decidedly ill. Although he made it up to their rooms without help from the hotel staff, he was too weak to do more than collapse into the armchair once the door had shut. His eyes closed. His breathing shallow.

Marion, after leaving her jar of resin on a desk in the bedroom, telephoned down for food to be brought to their room. They'd eaten nothing all day, and it was possible that a meal would restore his strength. Then, walking back to the living room, she looked at him. "Do you feel well enough to open the safe so that I can begin work on the map?"

He opened his eyes and gazed back at her. Sardonic. "Relentless, aren't you?"

"Yes." She sat on the sofa. "You've mentioned that before."

"Did you do this to me?" He pushed himself up straighter in the chair. "*Again*?"

She didn't respond.

"Marion, I'm beginning to find this tedious." He closed his eyes. Swallowed. "And I warn you, if it happens a third time, I'll reacquaint you with that strain of gastroenteritis from Hinaidi. A pretty pair we'll be then."

She still didn't speak.

"Oh, very well." He rose from the chair and walked, carefully steady, to the bedroom.

She heard him opening the safe and moving papers. A pause. No sound of the safe closing. But before she had the chance to investigate, there was a knock at the door. Their food had arrived. She opened the door, still listening for the click from the bedroom that would indicate the safe closing, and stood to the side to let the waiters bring their dinner into the dining room. Chicken soup—*canja de galinha*—rice with duck meat, a salad, a bowl of oranges, and a basket of bread rolls. She had also ordered two bottles of mineral water. Thinking they might settle his stomach.

He looked in on the dining room as the waiters were leaving the suite. Poured himself a glass of mineral water, but otherwise was unenthusiastic about the food. He lifted his glass to Marion and gave her a wan smile. "Perhaps later."

"An orange might help to—"

"As I said," he interrupted her, moving away, "later. And weren't you eager to begin work?"

She blinked, uncertain as to whether she ought to pressure him to eat. Decided against it and followed him into the living room. She hadn't heard the door to the safe close. But she forced herself not to peek into the bedroom to check on it.

He had arranged the two serpent sculptures, the page from the Copenhagen herbarium, her stoppered jar of resin, and the single treated folio on the coffee table. The rest of the material—the manuscripts, the Ottoman chronicle, the Portuguese chronicle, and Niebuhr's botany—weren't there.

She looked at him, sitting languid in the armchair. "What about the rest of it?"

"You don't need the rest of it."

"But—"

"What do you need it for, Marion?"

"To—check my work—"

"You see? You don't need the rest of it. You want the rest of it. To take with you when I'm well and truly incapacitated. Won't happen."

She turned her attention to the folio on the coffee table. Considered for a few seconds. Then she addressed Jeffrey again. "I'm tired as well. In fact, I fear I'll make a mistake." She paused. "I don't want to ruin the only plant samples we have. I'll go to sleep and work on it tomorrow."

"Damn it. Now you're going to try something."

"No," she said. "I'm going to sleep. Do whatever you'd like with that material."

"If I'm delirious tomorrow morning," he told her, "you'll be forced to wait until this—malady—has passed."

"I'm willing to wait," she said. "If necessary."

Then she turned and walked back into the bedroom. Smiled when she went through the door. It was as she'd hoped. He'd neglected to close the safe. His condition was worse than he'd let on. She wondered how much longer he'd remain lucid.

But still, she knew better than to remove the manuscripts that were still stacked at the back of the metal shelf. He was failing fast, but he'd notice that the safe was empty. And so instead, working quickly, she went into the toilet, wadded up some paper, returned to the bedroom, and crammed the paper up against the two pins—a simple locking mechanism of the sort she'd seen in countless other wall safes—to keep them from sliding back into place. They'd click against the paper. But she could use a screwdriver to pry them back once he was asleep. It was an obvious ploy, and it would never have worked if he were clearheaded. But she was counting on his illness to keep him disoriented.

After that, she walked to the wardrobe, found her pyjamas, and returned to the toilet. She heard Jeffrey coming through the door just as she had finished changing. A short, annoyed laugh. "Thank you, Marion," he said through the door, "for not doing the painfully obvious."

She opened the door and looked out at him. "I told you. I'm tired." She watched as he replaced the sculptures, the bottle, and the two sets of pages on the metal shelves. "I'm going to sleep." She walked across the room and got into bed. Waited for him to join her.

He shut the safe, was momentarily puzzled by its feel, but dismissed it, too tired to speculate, and went to the wardrobe. "My only regret," he said as he rummaged through his clothing, "is that I won't be conscious to enjoy whatever it is you'll be attempting tonight." Changing into his own pyjamas, he slipped into the bed next to her. Switched off the lamp.

Marion expected him to slide immediately into sleep, and so she waited, patient, lying on her side. Keeping her breathing as steady as possible. In his weak state, it wouldn't take long for him to fade. But, to her annoyance, he didn't relax. Instead, he seemed increasingly, if half-consciously, concerned. Alert. Likely about the feel of the safe when he'd closed it. He kept initiating a move and then hesitating, apparently thinking better of it.

When she sensed that he was on the verge of leaving the bed to investigate, she knew that she couldn't wait. Taking a resolute breath, she curled up against him and ran her hand up under his pyjama top. Over his chest. He rolled over and faced her, smiling. "You're trying to distract me from something."

She smiled back at him. "Is that a problem?"

"No." He brushed her cheekbone with his fingertip. "I don't want you under the illusion that you're misleading me."

"I have no illusions about you." She sat up, straddled him, and pulled the top of her pyjamas over her head. Then she began unbuttoning his pyjamas as well. Bent over him and kissed him on the mouth. Gently. She was taken aback by the feverish feel of his skin. Surprised by how ill he already was. Setting the thought aside, she leaned closer to him and removed the rest of his clothing. Kissing him harder.

"So is this the secret, then?" He was laughing. "Enervated and depleted is all it takes to interest you?"

"I like you this way." She had shifted her hand further down under the bedclothes.

"Pity," he said, grabbing her other wrist and trying to flip her over.

But he was too weak to lift her. She disengaged her wrist, took his hand, and pushed it up over his head. Held it there and smiled down at him. Then she whispered into his ear. "I can't stop thinking about you in those spectacles."

He laughed again and tried to move out from under her. Before relaxing back into the pillows. Defeated. "Witch."

"So you say."

After that, he let her take her time. And when she'd finished, she was pleased to see that he did slip into sleep. He was breathing deeply, entirely unconscious, when she got out of bed, went to the toilet to wash, and changed into comfortable travel clothing.

She retrieved her carpet bag from the wardrobe, packed one additional change of clothing, secured her passport—although she knew she wouldn't be using it any time soon—and walked to the safe. She worked on it for five minutes with a screwdriver from her bag, prying back both pins. Then she pulled open the door and packed the safe's contents on top of her clothing and passport.

She glanced, irritated, at Jeffrey's prone form when she discovered that he hadn't stored the Ottoman chronicle in the safe with the other material. An added precaution on his part. But leaving the hotel immediately, before his fever woke him, was preferable to searching his things haphazardly for the chronicle. As he'd said, she wouldn't need it to complete her assignment. It was reference material at this point.

Resisting the urge to kiss him a last time, she walked out of the bedroom and into the dining room. Wrapped two oranges and three bread rolls in a napkin and placed them at the top of her bag. Then, still standing, she ate a few bites of the duck. Poured herself a glass of mineral water, and drank most of it. Finally, gazing one last time about the suite, she grabbed her hat and left. She took the stairs two at a time to the ground floor. Didn't want to force a smile at the lift operator.

SHE was heading toward Cabo Ruivo. The floatplane base. And when she exited the hotel, it was a simple matter to find a taxi willing to take her. Although she couldn't speak Portuguese, she managed to communicate her destination as well as the specific street to which she'd been directed, and they left the hotel behind a few seconds later.

The driver took her inland for ten minutes before turning back toward the water and heading north. She was certain that she still had a tail. Following her would be easy in the light traffic. But she had decided not to go under in Lisbon. Jeffrey had been correct about their vulnerability in the city, and whoever the office put on her would be familiar with the terrain. She'd be foolish to try to outmaneuver them.

Instead, she counted on their confusion over her split from Jeffrey to keep them at a distance. They'd need new orders if they were going to apprehend her, and by the time they'd communicated with their superiors, she'd have boarded her plane. To Marseille. A city that had been built, she always imagined, to provide places in which people like her could hide. She would easily elude them there.

As the taxi turned off the boulevard that had brought them toward the shore and entered a warren of dark, twisting alleys, Marion peered out the window. Trying to get a feel for the atmosphere of the place. After a few moments of observation, she appreciated it. And she enjoyed the quiet. But she'd be pleased to be back in familiar surroundings. She felt no need to return to Lisbon.

At an abrupt dead end, the driver brought the taxi to a stop. He turned back to her and pointed toward a wooden dock that extended into the Tagus river. The river, which was narrower and deeper further south, was wide and smooth here. But as Marion paid the driver and thanked him, she saw that there was no plane. Nothing but moonlight reflected off the water.

Nervous, she gripped her bag, left the taxi, and shut the door. As the taxi reversed down the alley, she told herself to remain composed. She'd received her instructions in Copenhagen. There would be transportation. She merely needed to find it.

Taking a breath, she walked, more quickly than she wanted to—betraying her anxiety— toward a squat, ancient, stone building at the edge of the dock. She could see a lone lightbulb through an open window, yellow, hanging by a rope from the ceiling. When she reached the door, thick wood, cracked a few inches, she stopped. Knocked timidly. The floatplane base was nothing like what she had expected.

She heard footsteps cross the room, and the door opened. An old woman, bent but alert and wiry, eyed Marion. Then her face wrinkled into a contemptuous echo of a smile. "Marselha?"

Marion nodded. "Marseille. Yes."

The woman turned back into the building and shouted at a boy, no more than fourteen, who was sitting in a wooden chair dangling a piece of string over a sleepy cat. He looked up, sleepy as well, and nodded. Rubbed his eyes and walked out the door past Marion. Toward the end of the dock.

The woman pointed at the boy's retreating back. "Marselha."

Then she shut the door. Marion thanked the blank wood in front of her, turned, and followed the boy. When she reached the end of the dock, she saw a small rowboat tied up to the float. The boy jumped into it and held up his hand to help her. Not wanting to offend him by refusing, she took his hand and let him guide her. Once she'd settled herself, she looked further up the river and laughed in astonishment.

The largest and most awkward looking float plane she'd ever witnessed was idling beyond a bend, unmoored, pushing against the current, and apparently waiting for her. Instead of two floats, it had a single hull, low in the water, on top of which was a rectangular box which served, she supposed, as the cockpit. Or bridge. She wasn't certain what terminology its pilot, or captain, would prefer. The wing, with three large propellers, rested above the rectangular box.

Admiring the boy's endurance as he rowed upriver, vigorous, toward the massive plane, she prepared to pull herself up onto the hull. Neither the rowboat nor the plane was secure, and she'd want to time her jump from one to the other carefully. The boy, however, rowed them just beyond what she took to be his contact point and then skillfully let the boat drift back against its hull.

Marion stepped out of the boat and smiled, shy, back down at the boy. She was impressed. He smiled back at her, bright and smug, and then pushed the rowboat away from the plane's hull. After that, he brought the oars up, leaned back against the transom, and gazed up at the night sky. Letting the current take him back downriver. In no hurry to return to the woman and the cat in the terminal. If that's what they called the solid, chilling building standing guard over the dock.

The door to the bridge opened a few seconds after Marion climbed onto the hull. She looked up, and reached, again, for the proffered hand. A man in his early thirties, wearing an Aéropostale uniform, complete with grease spots, pulled her into the cockpit. Exposed metal, packed with instruments, strong smell of cigarette smoke and, after a moment's confusion, sandwiches. There were two other men waiting inside—the remainder of the crew—and one empty seat.

The man who had helped her up gestured gallantly for her to occupy the empty seat, while the other two prepared the plane to take off. Marion sat, held her carpet bag in her lap, and looked, interested, about the cockpit. "Thank you," she ventured. Deciding on French.

"You're quite welcome." The man had settled himself into the seat opposite her. Definitely French.

"And you are—?"

"Jean," he said, grinning. He pointed toward the pilot and co-pilot. "They're Jean too. Would you like to be Marie?"

She laughed. "Yes. Marie is fine." She raised her voice over the revving engines as the plane picked up speed along the smooth water of the Tagus, lifting with a wobble into the air. "I needn't speak at all, if you'd rather."

"It will be a boring three hours to Marseille if you sit there silent," he said.

"True." She looked at the cockpit again, bemused but entertained. She had no idea what to make of the transport her people had arranged. Beginning to wonder whether they'd been talking with Jeffrey. "You're delivering the mail?" she finally asked.

"Indeed we are," he said, still smiling. A bit manic. He patted the plane's fuselage. "Blériot 5190. Nothing but the best for Aéropostale."

She was quiet for a few seconds. But then she couldn't control her curiosity, even if she risked offending Jean. "Didn't Aéropostale break up two years ago? I thought you were all Air France now."

"In name," he said, putting his hand over his heart. "But not in spirit."

"I see." She thought she was beginning to understand his casually roguish demeanor. "So—"

"So," he said, "on occasion, we have some mechanical trouble as we begin our trans-Atlantic route. We must put down. Perhaps on a Swiss lake. Perhaps on a Portuguese river. Wherever we can, no?"

She felt herself smiling almost as widely as he had been. They were doing this, she realized, for fun.

"The tool we require to fix this mechanical trouble," he continued, offering her a cigarette, which she refused, "is, however, in Marseille. We've managed temporary repairs to get us from Lisbon. But before crossing the ocean, alas, we must land for a few hours at Marignane as well." He shrugged. "Unavoidable."

"And then?"

"And then we'll deliver the mail," he said, lighting his own cigarette. "A few days late. But who expects a flight like ours always to keep to schedule? Impossible."

He took a drag off his cigarette, but after that, he smoked almost none of it. Preferring it as a prop to help him talk. And he did talk. Throughout the entire flight over Spain and the south of France, he never stopped.

Not that Marion minded. His experience delivering the mail—an activity which he defined broadly as everything from transporting a bag of, in fact, mail to arming revolutionary guerilla movements throughout Africa and Latin America—made her own desultory fall into militancy seem mundane. She concluded that she very much liked Jean. All of them. And she was disappointed when they began losing altitude over the Marseille-Marignane airport and float plane base.

As they circled toward the port, Jean stood and stepped forward to speak to the co-pilot. Then he returned to his seat and strapped the harness over his chest. "The weather's bad down below. Four to five foot swell. But we can land her in a trough."

She nodded, not entirely understanding what he meant.

He grinned at her again. "Just don't let go of your suitcase."

"I won't." She wrapped her arms around her carpet bag and waited for them to hit the waves of the lagoon.

When they did hit, their landing remained smooth for fifteen seconds, as the plane slid along a trough between two waves. Then, with a shift in the wind, they tilted sickeningly up the side of a roller and, gaining speed again, descended into another trough.

A few repetitions of the maneuver, and Marion was more than ready to be out of the metal box set atop the single hull of the plane. But she didn't wait long. Ten minutes later, they were tied securely to a dock dedicated to postal boats and planes, separate from the public terminal. She unstrapped her harness, stood, and thanked Jean for the lift.

As she looked a last time at the cabin, she considered her next move. She wasn't certain how she'd travel the fifteen miles from Marignane to the center of Marseille. The city would be among the first places that the office would resume a search for her. In fact, it was probable that they'd already alerted Marignane that she might be passing through.

But it was unlikely that anyone would be watching the mail carriers, leaving her confident that, with the proper precautions, she could travel unobtrusively. If she remained outside the public areas of the airport, she could enter the city quietly. And if she were lucky, she wouldn't even be forced to go through the tedious routine of losing a tail on the city streets. She hoped she wouldn't have to. She was tired. She simply wanted to get to the boat that was waiting to move her to Port Said. Go to sleep.

As though reading her thoughts, Jean, lighting another cigarette that wouldn't be smoked, nodded in the direction of the pilot. A large man, middle forties perhaps, stretching after having unstrapped himself from his seat. "Jean," he said, nodding at the pilot, "is driving into the city. For the tool we need. He'd be glad of the company, if you'd like to join him."

Marion turned to the pilot, who shrugged, taciturn, and beckoned to her to follow him out the door and onto the dock. She looked back at Jean, and he gave her friendly salute. Then he leaned forward and kissed her on both cheeks. "A pleasure to have met you, Marie."

"And you, Jean." She took up her carpet bag, climbed to the dock, and trotted to keep up with the pilot—a dark hulk, walking with a gait that reminded her more of sailors than of pilots.

He stopped at a rusted 1924 Citroën B10 that looked abandoned at the edge of the crowded car park. Then he walked to the passenger door and hit it hard with the flat of his hand. It popped open and, without speaking, he went to the driver's side and performed the same maneuver on his own door. Marion pulled the door further open and sat on the seat. What was left of the seat. A metal frame and no cushion. She placed the carpet bag in her lap.

The pilot then lowered himself into the driver's seat, which drew ominous, metallic squeaks from the car's chassis. After that, he hit the dash with his fist, and the motor came to life. Marion glanced over at him, feeling a twinge of respect. If she ever learned to drive, she liked to think she'd drive a car like this one.

Without speaking or looking at her, Jean brought the car out onto the road. It was only after they'd travelled in silence for ten minutes that he cleared his throat. "Where are you going?"

"Hangar J1," she said. "Place de la Joliette. The port. The new one."

The man didn't respond.

And Marion, content, leaned back against the metal seat. Closed her eyes.

Mocha and Jibla, Yemen
June, 1935

Marion squinted up at the paraffin lamp, burning low, suspended from a loop bolt in the ceiling. She was three days out of Marseille and another four to Port Said, if all went well. Travelling in the hold of a small cargo ship. The ship was just over two hundred feet, flying Norwegian flags, and the captain, Algerian, had pointedly failed to notice as his boatswain, Somali and speaking Arabic, had smuggled Marion from the hangar to the second hold on the third deck of the ship.

The boat was empty, floating high in the water, and it was unlikely that any Egyptian or British official would give it more than a glance as they passed Port Said before entering the Suez Canal. Even so, should someone in Egypt become curious, there was a container full of automotive tools in the otherwise vacant hold. Just under six feet cubed and with a false bottom, she could squeeze herself into it for an hour or two should it become necessary. She hoped she wouldn't be forced to take that step.

Otherwise, aside from the fact that she couldn't leave the third deck—preserving the Captain's studied ignorance of what he was transporting—her situation wasn't uncomfortable. The area was cavernous, the boatswain brought her more than sufficient food during his twice daily inspections of the boat, and a makeshift head installed in a corner, with a pump toilet and a sink, suggested that she wasn't the first invisible passenger the ship had taken on. There were even clean blankets on the mattress she was using and a tattered, overstuffed brown armchair positioned under the swinging lamp. She'd experienced worse.

Her only complaint was that the voyage was slow. After the seven days from Marseille to Port Said, and the twenty hours through the canal, it would be another week down the Red Sea until they crossed the boat in which she'd travel toward the *Durrah*. From the bits and pieces of information that the boatswain had let drop, she understood that the cargo ship wouldn't be docking. Instead, idling a mile off the port of Mocha, in Yemen, they'd meet her contact. She'd disembark there.

And so, she passed her time by checking the work that had occupied her from the moment she'd boarded the ship. After the first night, during which she'd slept, deeply and gratefully, on the mattress, she had unpacked her carpet bag. Then, under the light of the paraffin lamp, she had smoothed out the treated eleventh-century map of the Red Sea, and she had placed the two serpent sculptures into position at either end of it. Satisfied with their placement, she had opened her jar of resin and, with a pang of conscience, she had crumbled and emptied the dried eighteenth-century samples from Copenhagen into it.

After stirring the mixture with a paintbrush she'd bought for the purpose, she had knelt on the metal floor in front of the map and had calculated from the position of the serpents where she ought to begin applying the paste. Once she was certain, she had dabbed the brush in a line between the two sculptures. The effect had been immediate. Stunning.

What had begun as a schematic diagram, absent useful or even interesting detail, of the sea's simplest contours became a breathtakingly exhaustive—almost multi-dimensional—illustration of not only the coasts, but the tides, the islands, and even, remarkably, the ocean floor. Marion, neither a cartographer nor a geographer, didn't know whether the seabed mapping was accurate. But from the perspective of an amateur, it looked suspiciously precise to her.

More important than the imaging, however, were the annotations. They were almost too detailed. Distracting. But as she accustomed herself to her cartographer's writing style, she developed a feel for his instructions. One by one, based on what were frequently arch or poetic hints, she eliminated likely spots in which the *Durrah* might be hidden. Until eventually, she settled with confidence on the Hanish Islands, in the middle of the Red Sea.

These were positioned on the map—in a geopolitically provocative way, even for the eleventh century—at the apex of a nearly equilateral triangle joining the Islands in the north to Mocha, in Yemen, to the southeast, and Beylul, in Eritrea, to the southwest. Geometrically satisfying. Strategically, a bit more complicated.

And indeed, the "unity" promised by the *Durrah*, starting as it did with the Hanish Islands, would have troubled certain segments of both Arab and African populations even a millennium earlier.

Marion had been mildly entertained by her cartographer's assumptions. But her confidence that she was making the proper decision wasn't shaken. She was pleased by her progress.

Having narrowed her search to the Hanish Islands, though, she had met a new obstacle. As she read the annotations and notes surrounding that part of the map, the writing became elusive, obscure, and even nonsensical. She simply couldn't understand the instructions provided to the "navigator" once the archipelago was in sight. It had taken her the entire third day—and only after consuming a bottle and a half of the Fix Hellas lager provided by the boatswain—to take her next step.

The note closest to her target directed those seeking the island that housed the jewel to follow the lines of what it called the "floods, torrents, and salts" that afflicted the Hanish archipelago. But the islands, arid, volcanic, and barely supporting vegetation, had no floods. They barely had water. Salt, perhaps, but not in any distinctive way. Marion had stared at the passage for hours, until realization had hit her.

Suyul, "torrents," and *mamalih,* "salts," referred instead, via a cutely deliberate misspelling, to Suyul-Hanish island, little more than a rock in the archipelago, two miles long, with a peak of perhaps four hundred feet, and, according to the map, an anchorage on the eastern side. The annotation assured her that should she scale the peak and follow the torrents, now re-framed in the text as *eabab,* "swirls" or "billows," she would find the *Durrah.*

She had known, once she'd pinpointed Suyul-Hanish island, that she'd be forced to wait until she was at the site to determine what "swirls" meant in practice. But she had entertained herself, as the days had passed, and as the cargo ship had crept across the Mediterranean, by speculating on the nature of the *eabab,* and by trying to develop a more targeted approach. Her experience with these puzzles in the past suggested that the solution would be both unpredictable and, once she'd seen it, obvious.

She'd also spent hours reading through the additional notes and annotations scattered over the map, astonished by her anonymous author's disconcertingly prescient interpretations of how the world's seas flowed into, and affected, one another. The title of this second (or first) work, *al-Kitab al-Muhit* was itself, even, a nod at the mysterious totality of the seas, evoking less a discrete, strategic Red Sea, belonging to this or that land power, and more *al-bahr al-muhit,* the "surrounding ocean" or the Atlantic, which belonged to no one.

Occupied as she was by these thoughts, she failed to notice when they passed through Port Said, mooring at the customs dock for less than an hour before moving on again. No need to make use of the container with the false bottom. And though she was pleased when, five days later, the boatswain told her that they'd spotted her contact off Mocha, she didn't feel that she'd wasted the previous two weeks. She'd found her time in the hold an unexpectedly enjoyable means of clearing her mind. Preparing for her next step.

A half hour after the boatswain had notified her that her boat was on the horizon, the captain had slowed the cargo ship and begun to idle in neutral, still entirely unconscious, as far as the rest of the crew was concerned, of what was happening on his third deck. And once the engines settled, the boatswain led Marion from the hold to a hatch opening onto a ladder near the stern. When he opened the hatch for her, she looked down toward the water and saw that a wooden sloop, sails furled and perhaps forty feet long, had rafted onto the ship.

She smiled at the boatswain and thanked him. He wished her a good voyage and then hesitated, peering worried at a reddish haze that had begun to obscure the late afternoon sunlight. He nodded in the direction of the haze. "Khamsin's coming. Be careful."

She had already started down the ladder to the sailboat, but she stopped and looked up at him. "We'll be all right. Thank you again."

He smiled before he closed the hatch. "Good luck."

*W*HEN she had landed safely on the foredeck of the boat, she saw more clearly that it was a meticulously varnished teak racing sloop reminiscent of some of the American imports she'd encountered in Istanbul. Although the sails were furled, it was obvious from the position of the mast that the boat privileged the jib over the mainsail, perhaps to help it beat closer upwind when the weather on the Red Sea chose not to cooperate. It made objective sense, but she'd rarely seen that sort of arrangement on anything but a pleasure craft. It smacked of short, recreational races undertaken by bankers and businessmen on holiday.

Also, although the boat was long—closer to forty-five feet than to forty—its captain, a tall Yemeni woman dressed like a nineteenth-century smuggler, was holding a tiller rather than a wheel. The boat was an odd choice for their assignment. But thus far, her organization had moved her toward her goal with admirable efficiency. Marion wasn't going to question their decisions now.

Instead, she made her way to the cockpit, skirting the dinghy that was tied down to the deck, still clutching her carpet bag. When she was close enough, the captain, speaking Arabic, shouted at her that she'd be in the forepeak. Looking about, Marion counted a crew of six, in addition to the captain and herself. She felt guilty for taking more than a single bunk, but she didn't protest. Better to be grateful for the hospitality.

Nodding, she lowered herself into the cabin and walked toward the bow, noting in passing the immaculate teak, also varnished, throughout the interior, as well as the neatly made bunks and carefully stored charts. She threw her carpet bag onto the triangular cushion in the forepeak and turned to go back up again. The captain, she deduced from the state of the cabin, was someone whose orders weren't to be questioned.

When she reached the cockpit again, the captain pointed Marion to a seat. Then she squinted toward a mountain of black clouds that were massing over the Arab coast above a sinister reddish fog. "Khamsin," she said, echoing the boatswain.

Marion watched the clouds rolling toward the water. Uncertain what to say in response. The cargo ship had already disappeared into the distance. Moving fast into Mocha. And the crew of the sloop, apprehensive, were raising a small heavy-weather sail.

Despite the palpable anxiety coming from the crew, the water beneath them was flat and calm. Ominously so. And the air, smelling metallic, was growing hotter than anything Marion had ever experienced. It was as though the clouds, still more than a mile away, had sucked every bit of moisture out of the atmosphere. Marion peered at the single, limp sail as she forced herself to breathe the withering air normally.

"We've got to raise something," the captain told her, following her look, "to keep the boat stable. And to stay on top of the waves. But too much, and we'll have a broken mast. Fucking khamsin." She removed a purplish cotton scarf from her neck and tossed it at Marion. "Wear this when it hits us. I'm Yasmin."

"Marion," Marion said, catching the scarf as she attempted to follow the disconnected conversation. "I'm Marion."

"Where are we headed, Marion?"

"Hanish Islands."

Yasmin laughed. "You'll want to hang on then, Marion."

After that, they were both silent. As was the crew. Leaning against the rigging, watching the clouds and the red haze moving toward them over the water. The wind would be coming up on them from the south and the east, which meant that it would be behind them, pushing them up toward the Islands.

At first, all that announced the wind's arrival was an insectoid humming sound that gradually replaced the eerie, silent calm. But then, a violent gust, thick with dust and sand, struck them with more physical force than Marion had ever felt in a wind. And yet, when it hit, it also did so without warning. Even though they'd all been watching it as it crept toward them.

Once it was on them, Yasmin moved quickly. Pulled her own scarf up and over her nose and mouth and shouted at the crew to let the sail out gradually, collecting the wind even as they did all they could to prevent the wooden mast from snapping. Marion, following Yasmin's example, wrapped the purple scarf over her head and mouth, silently thanking her for the protection. In the few seconds before she had gathered her wits about her, she had taken a breath full of sand, and she was coughing, her throat burning and abraded. She watched the crew as they handled the sail, not by any stretch of the imagination controlling it, but managing at least to keep it in one piece.

Then she turned back to Yasmin, who was concentrating on the sail and the tiller to keep the boat's stern from turning through the wind. If the wind shifted and they accidentally gybed, the best-case scenario would be broken rigging. At worst, the boat would be wrecked. As she moved her eyes away from Yasmin and watched the water passing underneath them, she couldn't believe their speed under the single, small sail. It was stupefying.

And, as much as she knew that the crew were cursing the wind—and that they would be exhausted if not entirely demoralized before it had blown itself out—Marion couldn't help feeling an irrational thrill at the violence of the weather. The black clouds, with their outline of glowing red were like nothing she'd seen. And the boat, travelling nearly as fast as the swells, balanced completely flat as it fled downwind, felt, despite its screeching speed, as though it were gliding and hovering a few feet above the waves. Against her inclination, she found herself smiling.

Curious, Marion glanced back again at Yasmin. And smiled more broadly. Although she could see nothing more than the captain's eyes above the scarf, there was something in her stance as she gripped the tiller that suggested she was enjoying herself as well. And though the rest of the crew relaxed when, three hours later, the wind, still murderous, shifted incrementally into a southwesterly, and then finally a westerly—losing the sand along the way—there was also a disappointment lurking behind their return to normal operation. They'd never admit it, but they'd miss its ferocity as well. Even though they were almost shaky in their relief that it had passed.

Soon after the khamsin dissipated, night fell and, free of the haze, a few stars and a half-moon appeared. Yasmin had the crew raise a jib and set the sails for a beam reach toward the islands. Then she loosened the scarf from her nose and mouth and relaxed, sitting back in the cockpit, one hand on the tiller, the other resting on the lifelines.

She shook some sand out of her hair, chestnut brown and fashionably cut, and then grinned at Marion. "Welcome. Go below and get some sleep, if you can. We won't reach the Islands for another three hours."

"I'd rather stay here." Marion was also unwrapping the scarf from her hair and face. She held it out to Yasmin. "If I'm not in the way, that is. I don't think I could sleep."

"Keep it." Yasmin waved away the scarf. "You may need it." Then she looked up at the sail and adjusted the tiller. "You aren't in the way."

"Thank you." Marion watched the water, still choppy, especially as the wind continued to veer toward its normal northwesterly direction. She'd be happy sitting just as she was for longer than three hours.

"Which island?" Yasmin asked after ten minutes of silence.

"Suyul-Hanish."

"We'll anchor to the east?"

"Yes." Marion looked back at her, but she couldn't read her face in the darkness.

A few minutes later, Yasmin spoke again. "We'll keep the engine cut. Sail into the anchorage. Motors trigger the defensive barriers. The old devices." She paused. "Or at least so I've been instructed. I didn't know it would be the Islands until you told me."

"I understand," Marion said. "Once we're there, I'll go inland on my own. It won't take more than a few hours."

Yasmin didn't answer. Instead, she watched the sails, meditative. Marion, in a similar mood, closed her eyes and enjoyed the feel of the boat. Although the air was still sweltering, it was refreshing compared to what it had been when the wind and sand were blowing from the south. There was even the tiniest hint of moisture in it. A proper sea breeze. It felt healthy again.

Just over two hours later, Marion opened her eyes to a changed scene. The sky was still dark, although the stars were visible. But what drew her attention was the water. The phosphorescent ripples at the surface of the sea were so bright that she could see Yasmin's face as distinctly as if it were day. And the wake from the boat was blindingly green. Peering ahead, she could also see the Islands materializing in front of them. Not because the land was prominent; the rocks were as dark as the sky behind them. Rather, the streams of phosphorescent water outlined each contour of each jagged rock like a photographic negative. The effect was unsettling. Uncanny. But Marion was seduced by it. She couldn't stop staring.

Distracted as she was by the atmosphere, she almost didn't notice when the phosphorescent water off their starboard side bulged up, thick and unnatural, before subsiding into a quiet splash. Catching it out of the corner of her eye, she attributed the abnormal effect to her suggestibility after having stared at the bright green water for too long. Put it out of her mind.

A few minutes later, however, when a similar effect—something arching out of the water and then sinking down with a slapping noise—appeared first on one side of the bow and then, thirty seconds later, on the other side, she did pay attention. It reminded her of dolphins playing with the boat. But it couldn't be dolphins at this time of night. Or this near the Islands.

She glanced back at Yasmin, wondering whether she'd noticed the same disturbance. But Yasmin was watching her sails. Avoiding Marion's look. Before Marion could make a more deliberate attempt to speak to her, the boat shuddered, lifted a few inches off the surface of the sea, and dropped back down. It wasn't a significant bump, but it also wasn't something that could have been caused by wind or water.

Marion turned quickly to catch whatever it was that had moved the boat. But she needn't have hurried. Completely visible now, a thick, scaled tail—organic and yet with a metallic sheen—the diameter of a large oak tree, lifted out of the water behind them, coiled, and sank into the phosphorescence. Almost simultaneously, a different part of it surfaced at their bow, surged, and went under. All part of the same creature. Coiling and uncoiling around them.

Telling herself that she was letting the grotesque effects of the phosphorescence get to her, she continued to watch the surface. Now that she was awake and focused, she'd be immune to the tricks of her imagination. But then, and somehow half expecting it, she saw what she dreaded most. An eye—dull, ancient and enormous—moved up toward the surface, just off the cockpit, and hovered less than a foot under the clear, brightly lit water. It kept pace with them for a few seconds and then disappeared downward again in a swirl of phosphorescence.

At that point, Marion couldn't keep quiet anymore. "Yasmin," she said, more tersely than she wanted to. "What is that?"

Yasmin kept her eyes on the sails. "What do you think it is?"

Marion stared at her for a few seconds. Then she collected herself. "I think it's a trick of the phosphorescence."

Yasmin laughed. Looked away from the sail and smiled at her. "If you'd like." She peeked over the side, but the water, apart from their wake, was undisturbed now. "Either way, you needn't worry. It's on our side."

There was another slapping sound behind them. An eddy of phosphorescence that could have been something abnormally large sinking into the water. Or it could have been an effect of the odd currents surrounding the Islands. Marion watched it growing smaller in their wake. Playful. Indeed, like dolphins. Cute. But then, despite the almost incapacitating heat that rose as they made their way toward the calm weather on the eastern side of Suyul-Hanish Island, she shuddered. She'd be content to forget that she'd ever seen that elongated pupil gliding alongside their hull. Didn't want to know that that sort of thing existed. Even if, for now, it was well disposed to them.

Yasmin maneuvered the boat with remarkable skill through the rocks littering the anchorage, using little more than the phosphorescence to guide her. She and the crew then secured it, dragging and repositioning the anchor until they were confident it wouldn't drift during the night. And once the boat was anchored, she posted a watch before ordering the rest of the crew to sleep.

Marion, moving toward the unendurable heat of the forepeak, noticed that Yasmin and the others were settling themselves on the deck outside rather than using their bunks below. She knew that she'd been offered the large bunk in the bow because they believed she'd be more comfortable there. But the thought of descending into the baking torment of the cabin was more than she could bear. Shy, she approached Yasmin, who was already stretched out and closing her eyes in the cockpit. "Do you mind if I sleep out here as well?"

"Please do." Yasmin's sleeping position behind the tiller was not noticeably different from the position she took while at the helm. "Anywhere that strikes your fancy." She opened one eye. "You aren't what I thought you'd be."

Marion half-smiled down at her. "You're exactly what I thought you'd be."

Yasmin chuckled but didn't respond. And Marion, finding space for herself in front of the mast, drifted into sleep.

*T*HEY woke the next morning to what was already paralyzing heat assaulting them in waves from the barren, dark soil of the island. No one was in the mood to spend more time than necessary in the anchorage, and so Marion drank three cups of water and ate a handful of raisins as soon as she was awake. Then, steeling herself, she descended below into the airless cabin to rifle through her carpet bag.

She pulled out the two serpent sculptures and secured them in a sling over her shoulder and waist. Then she arranged a light brown linen scarf over her head to protect herself from the sun and returned to the deck. She was sweating uncomfortably by the time she'd climbed the ladder back into the cockpit.

But Yasmin, she was pleased to see, already had the boat's dinghy lowered into the water. Two members of her crew were sitting in it, holding the oars, waiting for Marion. Stuffing an additional few handfuls of raisins and a canteen of water into her sling, Marion climbed down to a platform at the base of the transom and stepped into the dinghy.

They pushed away from the boat once she was balanced, the splashing of the oars drawing the attention of a manta ray that had been hidden in the sand twelve feet below them. A silvertip shark also surged up in the wake of the dinghy, aggressive and curious, before turning away, uninterested after all. She watched, unseeing, as it disappeared into the deeper water beyond the bay. Then, coming to herself, she squinted at the shore to determine the best route for ascending the brownish hill that rose from the mud of the beach.

After she'd jumped from the dinghy and waded through the last few feet of water toward the shore, holding her linen trousers above her knees, the crew maneuvered it toward a rocky overhang to wait for her in an approximation of shade. Uncertain as to what she would encounter on the island, she had also pulled on her working boots. Sodden, muddy and hot after their submersion in the sea water, they revolted her. But she didn't want to be in a position in which she couldn't run or climb if necessary.

The island, nearly devoid of vegetation and covered with dark brown mud that gave way, at higher elevations to exposed rock, was an unpromising site for seeking something like the *Durrah*. But she knew that the islands of the Hanish archipelago had always been used by smugglers. She trusted there to be hidden and protected rocks or caves where such an object might be concealed.

Wiping sweat from her cheeks as she trudged toward the summit of the unimpressive hill that was the island's only noteworthy feature, she tried to convince herself that the view from the top would provide her with insight into which "torrents" or "billows" she was meant to follow to her target. But the more she got to know the island, the less optimistic she felt. The land was dispiriting. Its atmosphere peculiarly closed. Inhospitable.

When she reached the peak, scrambling over brownish-black rock formations and once or twice pulling herself up with her hands, her mood failed to improve. The landscape at the top was less forthcoming than the beach and the slope had been. Unhappy, she sat in the partial shade of a boulder, pulled out her water, and drank. Ate a few raisins. Took in the unprepossessing rock and dirt about her.

After five or six minutes, feeling recovered if not cheerful, she sighed, stood, and crossed the flat, high ground. When she reached the slope leading down the other side, she stopped and surveyed the view. More rocks. A bit of scrub. And then, the water of the Red Sea.

She drew another frustrated breath. She couldn't simply scramble down the other side and keep looking. There must be some pattern she was missing. Something having to do with swirls, floods, torrents, salts, or even serpents. Something that would evoke her map or her manuscript.

Staring down the hill, she let her mind wander. Knowing at this point that forcing herself to think about it would be counterproductive. Especially in the growing heat. Taking a few more deep breaths of the unpleasant air, she reconsidered the landscape.

And then it occurred to her that the scrub was wrong. Something about it, embedded in her subconscious, nagged at her. But she couldn't bring it to the surface of her mind. She narrowed her eyes, focusing carefully and rationally on the vegetation. It was certainly more prolific here than it was on the other side of the island. But that could simply be a trick of the climate. And even so, one could hardly call the dry, minimal bush flourishing.

She titled her head. And then smiled. The scrub had been planted. Tended. Someone had put it there. She reached into her sling and pulled out one of her serpent sculptures. Held it in front of her as she looked down on the volcanic landscape. The lines of withered bushes followed, precisely, the contours of the sculpture. Just like another botanical garden, she thought to herself, grim, as she returned the serpent to her sling and slid down the side of the hill toward the end of the display.

When she reached the bottom, she dusted down her trousers, now caked with the volcanic dirt, and then, bemused, followed the spiraling line of plants. She wasn't certain what she'd do when she reached the end. But she was confident that it would be obvious when she reached it.

It wasn't obvious. The trail of scrub bushes ended in a rock wall. Solid. No markings. A rise toward a second hilltop to her right. A rocky platform and then a drop into the sea, two or three feet down, to her left. She removed the serpent sculptures from her sling, held one in each hand, and stared at the wall. Disheartened. Not to mention filthy and sweating. She couldn't quite believe the utter impenetrability of the wall. It was almost mocking her.

Unable to accept that she'd been incorrect, she let her gaze wander, frustrated, across the rock. Looking for anything abnormal. But there was nothing. A greenish crab scuttled along the ground to her left and dropped toward the water. A school of tiny red fish also materialized at the surface and darted away. At which point, accepting that she'd been wrong, a hint of nausea spread up toward her throat from her stomach. She swallowed it down. And then, leaning forward, she pressed her forehead against the painfully hot rock in front of her. Squeezed her eyes shut. Miserable.

"You've got to swim, I'm afraid."

Marion's eyes flew open, and she spun back. The voice had come from the water. Astonished, rubbing her burning forehead, she stared down to her left. A girl, perhaps nine years old, was treading water where the red fish had been. Calm. As though the situation were perfectly ordinary. A part of Marion's brain noted that the dialect of Arabic she was speaking sounded like what classically educated jurists she knew had spent a lifetime cultivating. Only in the girl's case, it also sounded natural.

Gaping at the water, Marion wondered whether the heat had gone to her head. And, if so, how she'd ever get back to the boat.

"I'll carry the serpents for you." The girl, still treading water, held up both hands. When Marion simply stared, foolish, at the sculptures she was holding, the girl smiled, a trifle shy, but also authoritative. "Don't worry. If I miss, and they sink, I'll go down and find them." She waited. "But I won't miss."

Marion swallowed. "Let me take off my boots first."

"All right."

Marion sat, fumbled with her laces, and then, with an effort, pulled the repellent boots off her feet. Set them comically side by side on the rock. Then she knelt and handed the girl the two sculptures. She didn't doubt the girl's ability to dive down to retrieve them. But she also didn't want to test her skills. Finally, removing the scarf from her head and confirming that her sling was secure, she slid into the water.

Without speaking further, the girl dove under the surface and swam for a few yards along the edge of the island. The sculptures didn't cause her any difficulty as she moved, confident, toward an outcropping, vibrant with anemones and brightly colored fish. Where she slowed and began feeling her way.

Marion, still bewildered by the turn her search had taken, was nonetheless sufficiently aware of her surroundings to note the startling opposition between the dingy surface of the island and the blindingly colorful scene it presented underwater. She was almost disappointed when the girl, with a few final strong strokes, led her through an invisible fissure that ended, unsurprisingly somehow, in a circular cave, half full of air. A thin ledge protruded above the surface along the back wall.

The girl pulled herself up onto the ledge and then moved over so that Marion could follow her example. When Marion, breathing heavily, was sitting cross-legged next to her, the girl handed her the sculptures. Silent, Marion returned them to her sling. Looked about her.

Light evidently entered the cave from somewhere because she could see the greenish waves reflected over its walls, and she could also make out the features of the girl sitting beside her. Regular and regal. But she quickly dismissed the thought as she wondered instead what they were meant to do next. The ledge was just wide enough to fit the two of them sitting side by side.

"This way," the girl said, kneeling and facing the solid wall at the back of the cave.

Marion, dubious, turned as well. Crouching under an overhang. The girl pushed aside a rock to expose a tunnel, little more than three feet in diameter, tilted upward. Without explaining herself, she climbed on her hands and knees up the shaft.

Marion, unhappy, but not knowing what else to do, followed her. She hoped that the passage through the tunnel wouldn't last long. She hated caves with something close to a phobic terror. Had to work to take normal, deep breaths as she crawled behind the girl. Force herself to keep her eyes open.

But they weren't in the shaft for more than five minutes. Soon, the girl dropped to the floor of a vaulted cavern. It was also lit from some hidden source. If dimly. And it was pleasantly cool. And, curiously, it was furnished like an eighteenth-century palace. Carpets, furniture, plates of fresh food, books, toys even. Which meant, more practically, that there must be another entrance. The rococo armchairs wouldn't have been delivered via the fissure in the reef. Perhaps the girl would allow her to leave less picturesquely than she had arrived.

As, still dripping sea water, Marion came to terms with the cavern, the girl dried herself, slipped into a long, purple sheath, and coiled her black hair into an elaborate pile at the back of her head. After securing her hair with a gold pin, she settled a turquoise silk scarf over it. Then she pulled on three gold bracelets and slipped her feet into gold sandals.

Neither had spoken since they'd left the tunnel. Eventually, though, Marion's awe at the beauty of the cavern gave way to a creeping horror at its implications. She turned to the girl, who was standing, silent and patient, watching Marion. "You can't possibly—" She faltered, not wanting to know the answer to her question. But then she forced herself to ask it. "Do you live here?"

"No." Self-possessed.

"But—you're here now. All alone." Impressed as she was by the girl's adult dignity, she wasn't fooled. A child was a child. "Is there—" She stopped herself again. "Do you have a guardian?"

"I did. Tutors." The girl was examining Marion's face, intelligent, drawing information out of it. Her eyes, dark brown with green flecks, flickered as she processed. Disturbing in their detachment. "They left. It was time."

"Time—?"

"You're seeking something?" The girl was still reading Marion. Drawing conclusions. Smiling.

"It's unimportant," Marion said, off-balance. She couldn't set aside the fact that this vulnerable nine-year-old was alone, surrounded by bizarre French furniture, in an underwater cave in the middle of the Red Sea. Even if she did have the *Durrah*, and even if she wanted to part with it, Marion couldn't simply take it and leave.

The girl, however, raised her eyebrows. Entertained. "I hardly think it's unimportant. It's the most important thing in the world."

Marion shook her head. Couldn't think of any reply.

"Tell me what you're seeking," the girl repeated in a tone that made it difficult to refuse.

"It's a—an inscribed piece of rock crystal. Or a pearl." She felt degraded asking for it under these grotesque circumstances. "I'm expected to bring it back with me to—"

The girl shook her head. "That isn't what you're seeking."

Marion narrowed her eyes. Sensing a cruel streak underneath the innocent poise. Something old. Aristocratic. More than adult. "I don't understand." Sullen. More childish than the girl.

"He's in Jibla." The girl smiled again. "Waiting for you."

Marion kept completely still. Trying unsuccessfully to read the girl as the girl had read her. Then she spoke: "if I go there now, will they give him back to me?"

"Yes. But they're hoping you'll complete your assignment first. Bring them what's required."

"Do you have it?" Unemotional, now. The brief maternal sympathy she had felt for the girl was gone. There was something inhuman about her. Trying to protect or save her would be like trying to protect or save a natural disaster. She would, Marion decided, be perfectly fine all on her own.

"Yes." Unhelpful.

"It's a source of unity," Marion prodded. "Or—of eloquence. Clarity. A sort of call."

The girl continued to stand in the center of the room. Unspeaking. Watching Marion.

Marion, unwilling to be outdone, stood across from her. Compelling herself not to fidget. She held the girl's eyes, uncomfortable, while seconds, and then close to a minute passed. Eventually, however, a glimmer of a thought formed in a corner of her mind. Coalesced. And became a certainty. "Oh. Oh, I see."

"Good," the girl said. "You can call me Arwa."

"Will you bring anything?" Marion looked, mystified, about the richly furnished cavern. Wondering whether there was some object she'd want to use to identify herself.

"No. Nothing." Still wearing her inhuman smile, Arwa walked through an arched door leading to a second cavern. Glanced back at Marion, who was following her. "I believe this way is faster."

Once they'd passed through the second cavern, equally packed with palatial furnishings, Arwa opened a square door that revealed a winding corridor dug out beneath the island's summit. She lit a torch and entered the tunnel, which was wide, tempered by a breeze that hinted at the surface, and thus didn't provoke any further claustrophobic panic on Marion's part. The floor was smooth and even under her bare feet.

Twenty minutes later, they reached another door. Arwa pulled it open and stepped through it onto the mud beach. Marion followed, winced as her feet hit the hot sand, and saw that they were only a few hundred yards from where she had landed that morning. Yasmin's boat was visible anchored out in the bay.

But she hesitated before making for the dinghy. Curious as to how she had missed the door on her way up the hill. When she turned back to internalize its location, though, it was gone. Entirely obscured, as though it had been swallowed up by the rock. Marion wouldn't have been able to find it again if she had tried.

Still not quite believing her situation, she turned away from the hill. Walked with Arwa across the beach and then helped her into the dinghy. The crew, working the oars, didn't comment on the unexpected passenger. Quietly obedient, as always, to their captain.

When they reached the boat, however, Yasmin raised her eyebrows as nine-year-old Arwa climbed up the transom and jumped, light yet still imperious, into the cockpit. Supervising the dinghy's placement on the deck in preparation for raising the anchor, she turned to Marion. "The *Durrah*—?" Then she stopped, struck by the same thought that had taken Marion. Laughed. "Oh, I see. Of course."

She watched, mildly astonished, as Arwa made herself comfortable in the cockpit. Shook her head as she maneuvered the boat between the rocks scattered throughout the archipelago. But after that, she put the girl out of her mind, telling the crew to let out their sails in preparation for their return to Mocha. Running downwind in front of the peaceful northerly that was supposed to blow over the Red Sea. No visits from dolphins.

YASMIN offered to accompany them once they'd docked in Mocha. She was unhappy about the thought of Marion and Arwa journeying the one hundred fifty miles inland to Jibla on their own. And although she hadn't spoken to Arwa since they'd left the Hanish Islands, she'd grown attached to the girl. There was something fragile about her, despite the aloof self-assurance. People wanted to protect her.

Marion, less romantic, recognized the usefulness of projecting vulnerability of that sort, even as her respect for Arwa increased by the minute. Not that the girl was manipulative. Everything about her was honest, and it was quite clear that she considered artifice demeaning. Below her station. But Arwa was also the sort to whom misfortune simply didn't happen. She could afford to be fragile. And she could, as a result, make good use of the protective instincts that her fragility aroused in others.

But more to the point, Marion had already received instructions on her approach to Jibla. As much as she would have enjoyed spending more time with Yasmin, therefore, she declined the offer of an escort. Contented herself with the prospect of working with her on a different project. Later. And feeling a half-pleasurable twinge of regret as she left the beautiful boat.

When their transportation—two Zündapp K500 motorcycles with open sidecars—met them off the dock, she bracketed her thoughts of Yasmin altogether. Shifted her attention to the future. The motorcycles, likely stolen, were far from unobtrusive in Mocha's old port, and she and Arwa would want to move quickly.

Even so, she was pleased that they wouldn't be attempting the ride inland in the back of a truck. She'd used trucks the last time she'd been in Yemen, and the clumsy, interminable journeys she'd endured had been more than enough for a lifetime. The motorcycles, prominent though they were, would be a different prospect: fast, agile through the mountains, and, should she and Arwa face trouble, easily hidden. They were also more fun.

As she lowered herself into her sidecar, stuffed her carpet bag into an open space at her feet, and re-secured her linen scarf over her hair, she sensed that Arwa felt the same. The girl—whose rider had unceremoniously lifted her up and into her seat—was radiating genuine, nine-year-old excitement at the prospect of the journey. Showing signs that she could, under the proper circumstances, enjoy her childhood.

Once they'd left Mocha behind, their ride through the dry mountains was uneventful. They stopped three times to hydrate themselves, but otherwise they kept moving. Intending to reach Jibla before dark. And indeed, a little less than five hours after leaving Yasmin's boat in Mocha, the city of Jibla—spread out over two high peaks, a ravine in the center, green slopes in the background—came into view. The sun hanging low behind it.

Marion had expected their riders to leave them at the foot of the first hill, after which she and Arwa would walk up to the house she knew from previous visits to the city. But the motorcycles didn't slow as they passed the first of the three- and four-storey brick and stone buildings that lined the entrance to the city. Fishtailing as they took the first curve.

They didn't even stop when, higher up, the road gave way to crumbling alleys. Moving along the near-empty ridge road, they circled up through the main streets of the city. Aside from a few incurious looks from people conducting early evening business in the narrow passageways off of these streets, no one paid them attention. Expecting the intrusion. Ignoring the motorbikes speeding and skidding toward the top of the hill.

It was only when they reached the crest, where Queen Arwa's empty castle—eleventh-century and well preserved, if partially ruined—sat overlooking the ravine, that the motorcycles slowed and stopped. Marion pulled herself out of her sidecar, stood, and adjusted her tunic and scarf. Then she reached for her bag and watched in the last light of dusk as Arwa's rider—more courteous this time—lifted the girl to the ground. After that, without speaking, the riders jumped onto their bikes and disappeared down the other side of the mountain. Dim and shadowed.

By the time Marion had found her bearings, the sun had set completely. But the waxing moon that had lit their way through the Red Sea illuminated the area well. And Queen Arwa's castle was even more imposing in the moonlight than it had been in the dusk. The stone whiter—ghostly—and its edifice looming larger over them. Formidable. Sovereign despite the gaping, empty, black windows and the crumbling defensive wall.

The castle was, however, not their target. Instead, to its side, an almost equally imposing four-storey tower house was waiting for them. Square and brick with arched windows decorated with visible tracery, and a white fretwork door—intricate and mesmerizing. Their secure location.

As Marion led Arwa to the door, it opened of its own accord. An adolescent boy in a *thobe*, holding a lantern, stood to the side to let them through it into the building. After that, and without speaking, he brought them up the building's central staircase to the first-floor reception room. There, they removed their shoes and sat on a cushioned seat against a colored glass window, through which a few rays of moonlight filtered. Otherwise, the space was lit by lamps on shelves higher up in the wall. The boy indicated a tray of fruit and honey cake on a table in front of them. Then he began pouring them both glasses of mint tea.

But Marion wasn't going to let herself be thwarted by etiquette—by the boy's careful and deliberately obstructive hospitality. She had finished her assignment. She now meant to find her son and leave. Even if it shocked the sensibilities of her host. Looking at the boy, she put her hand over her tea glass. "Where's Samir?"

The boy, surprised, replaced the teapot. But he answered readily enough. "He's upstairs. Working."

"I'm going to see him."

"Please, Dr. Bailey," the boy replied. "If you'd rather not eat, I'll show you to your room—" She stood. "Immediately."

The boy shot a worried glance at Arwa, who was sipping her tea. Demure. Her eyes lowered, failing to notice the exchange. She set down her glass and ate a small bite of honey cake.

Marion, looking between Arwa and the boy, lifted a spiteful eyebrow at him. "Don't worry. You're safe with her."

She was pleased to see that the boy blushed, his veneer of serenity shattered. Then she turned and started up the staircase to the top floor, where she imagined Samir was waiting for her. She left her carpet bag in the reception room. The boy tried halfheartedly to move ahead of her, but she stopped him. "Go back and watch Arwa. She's too important to leave alone."

The boy hesitated, uncomfortable. Then he nodded and retreated down the stairs. She would have moved him out of her way by force if necessary. And she knew that he appreciated her mood. Retreat was his only option.

When she reached the fourth-floor sitting room, dominated by a *takhrim* stained glass window in a geometric floral design that was picked up by, and echoed in, the tile and plaster along the floor and ceiling, she didn't appreciate it as she ordinarily did when visiting the building. Instead, wishing her house slippers made a more imposing sound as she walked, she marched across the tiles and the threadbare yet minutely wrought carpet toward the alcove where she knew she'd find Samir. Her superior. Many times over. A figure in her organization who filled her with, at the best of times, timidity. Now, she was ready to assault him.

He was a slim, ironic looking man, Syrian or Lebanese, depending on where the French were drawing the borders at the moment, in his mid-fifties. Playful grey eyes and a closely trimmed black beard and mustache. Here in Jibla he was wearing a *thobe* like the boy's, but Marion knew that he preferred American sportswear. He looked at his most comfortable dressed for a game of tennis. Now, he was half reclined on a couch, marking up what appeared to be a tactical map of Algiers.

When he saw her, he sat up straighter, folded the map and smiled. "Marion. You look like you could do with a good night's rest. Shall we catch up tomorrow?" He was speaking English.

"I can speak Arabic," she said, in Arabic.

"So can I," he replied, still in English. "But I like to practice my English."

His English, leaving aside the American accent he had picked up at Columbia University, was identical to her own. He was deflecting her. Which only made her angrier.

"Where's Ian?" she asked. Abrupt. Rude, she hoped.

"Sleeping."

She turned to leave the room. To go and find her son. But he stopped her. "Marion, let him sleep. He's worn out. He's finally convinced Alain to teach him to abseil, and they've spent the entire day jumping off cliffs. The boy's implacable." He smiled at her. "I won't continue with the obvious corollary."

She stared at him. Cold. Not about to let him jolly her out of her anger. "You told me," she said, "that I was to extract him from his school because he was vulnerable there." She took a menacing step closer to him. "You *told* me he'd be safe once I got him out."

"He was safe."

"You kidnapped him." She couldn't keep her voice from rising. "You took him and—and you left me—" She choked on the words. Unable to articulate the memory.

"Marion," he said. "Will you sit down?"

She sat on a cushioned seat across from him. Unable to communicate her outrage.

"You wouldn't have agreed to it if you'd known the details," he explained when she was quiet for a few seconds longer.

"Of course I wouldn't have agreed to do it!" Feeling the sick rage that had driven her in Brighton. "Of course I'd have refused—"

"But, nonetheless, we had to get him sheltered before you began your assignment." He watched her. Kind. Yet neutral. "We couldn't let your husband use him against you this time. It was too important. Your family is a weakness—"

"Well, why not tap someone without a family, then?" She was shouting again. "Without the liabilities? I didn't ask for this job. I was perfectly content taking a bit of time off. I—"

"You're good at it," he said, smiling again. "You're the best we have at following this sort of trail. And—so that the compliment doesn't go to your head—we did also need that map from the library. If you hadn't convinced your husband to remove it for you, we'd have been nowhere. Sailing blindly around the Red Sea looking for a clue as to the girl's whereabouts."

She dropped her eyes to the tile floor. "That's what he said you were doing. When I went back to him."

Samir stood. Looked down at her. "He has his intuitions as well. Evidently." A trace of a French accent. Despite Columbia.

"You think I'm working for him?"

"I think you have conflicting obligations." He held out his hand to her. She took it, and he helped her up. "As do we all. But Marion, if we don't want to use you, we won't use you. It's as simple as that. You're strained enough without worrying about how to prove your loyalty to us. Not to mention about whether we believe the evidence."

She rubbed her eyes. "I want to see him before I go to sleep."

"We've put him in your room."

"Good." She turned away from him without wishing him goodnight.

Although what he'd told her was rational and even comforting—the best that Samir could give her—she was still horrified, terrified, that he'd taken the step of abducting her son. If he'd done it once, he could do it a second time. Easily. And she couldn't think of any argument that would convince him to do otherwise. Regardless of whether they believed her to be loyal.

Yet her angry reaction to the revelation was in large part shock rather than dismay. She'd already come to terms with the fact that her son was vulnerable to Jeffrey and the office. She'd even decided that she could survive and work despite that disadvantage. Somehow, though, she'd never realized that Ian was equally exposed to her own people. And now that the realization had been brought, with some force, to her attention, she shuddered at its implications.

She felt tears coming again. Which, once more, she pushed down. And then, chiding herself for trying to think through a situation over which she had no control, she blocked any further analysis of it. Descended the stairs to the bedrooms on the third floor of the house. Surprised by her utter lack of curiosity as to what had happened to Arwa. Who would, Marion sighed as she reached her room, be perfectly fine.

T HE bedroom that Marion used when she stayed in Jibla hadn't changed since she'd last visited. Two low mattresses on either side of a tiled room, clean cotton bedclothes, tall colored glass windows in three of the bright white walls, filigree lamps hanging by metal chains from a high ceiling—even the clothing she had left two years earlier was waiting for her in the wardrobe. Her carpet bag had been placed to the side.

And, to her harassed relief, Ian was asleep on the mattress against the far wall of the room, his thin blanket thrown off, his pillow on the floor, one hand splayed above his head. Wearing pyjama trousers she'd never seen before and nothing on top. His hair was longer than it had been. And there was a smile on his face. A trace of whatever it was he was dreaming.

She fought down the urge to touch him and arranged the blanket on her own bed instead. Still watching him. Enjoying the smile. Then she pulled her own pyjamas out of her carpet bag and changed. Grabbed her toothbrush and walked barefoot out to the gallery toward one of the two water closets on this floor. Used the toilet and padded back to the bedroom.

Ian was now lying on his stomach. His face pressed against the cotton sheet covering the mattress. Breathing deeply. She risked kissing the top of his head, which elicited no response from him, and then she dimmed the lamps in the room. Crawled under the blanket of her bed and slipped into a sleep almost as deep as his.

As tired as she was, she woke early the next morning, before the sunlight hit the bedroom windows. Her first waking move was to turn her head and look over at Ian on his mattress. Then, reassured, she sat up. Pushed her hair out of her face and stood. She changed into sandals, a clean tunic and trousers of dark blue and white linen, and used her fingers to pull her hair into a knot at the back of her head. Rifled through the wardrobe for a blue scarf to settle around her neck and shoulders. She'd pull it over her hair when she left the house.

Glancing over at Ian, she saw that he was unlikely to awaken any time soon. But she didn't want to leave the room until she'd spoken with him. Unoccupied, she wandered to one of the windows and peeked through the yellow and blue glass. View of Queen Arwa's palace. Still looming, if less menacing in what was now sunlight. Then she walked to the door of the bedroom and pulled it open a crack. Saw that the boy had left her a platter of breakfast. *Khameer*s, a pot of cardamom tea, and a glass of mango juice, presumably for Ian.

She told herself to be nicer to the poor child when next she encountered him—thirteen or fourteen was at best a confusing age. She already felt guilty for having humiliated him in front of Arwa. But, she rationalized as she brought the tray into the bedroom and put it on a low table under a window, she had humiliated herself just as thoroughly. Perhaps they could both forget it. Or bond over it. She poured herself a glass of tea, took up a piece of *khameer*, and watched Ian. Ate a few bites as he shifted in the bed, about to come to himself.

When he opened his eyes and saw her sitting across from him, he smiled. Gentle. Then, noticing the platter of food, his brows rushed together, aggrieved instead. "Don't eat them all, Mummy."

She stood and brushed a few crumbs off her tunic. Bent over to leave the glass of tea on the table. "I won't, Ian. The rest are yours."

He sat up. Rubbed his eyes. "Good."

She sat next to him on the mattress and put her arm around him. He leaned into her and wrapped his own arms around her waist. She kissed his head again, took a deep breath, smelling his hair, and then she shifted back to look at him. Not certain what to say.

Ian himself broke the silence. "You should have told me that Alain was collecting me in Brighton, Mummy." He looked up at her. "I almost didn't let him take me. And I did want to say goodbye, you know."

To hide her troubled reaction to his misunderstanding of how and why he'd travelled to Yemen, she stood, crossed the room, and retrieved the platter of food and glass of mango juice. Handed him the juice, which he drank in its entirety, and then set the tray between them on the bed. "I'm sorry, Ian," she eventually said. "I'll tell you the next time."

He picked up a *khameer* and ate it. Pensive. Not responding. As she watched him, a new variation on the habitual shame she felt at her maternal incompetence crept up on her. She had expected joy—or, if she'd been unlucky, anger or recrimination—from him when they were reunited. But these had been misguided expectations.

In fact, her son's easy acceptance of her disappearance—not to mention his assumption that she had simply handed him off to her organization in Brighton—was more in keeping with the life she'd built for him. The older he grew, the less he looked for consistency from her. He anticipated her absences. And they no longer bothered him. She stood again and walked over to the window. Observed the glass. Didn't notice the view.

"Don't be angry, Mummy." Anxious. "You needn't tell me next time if you don't want to."

"I'm not angry. I'm very happy to see you again. I was worried." She turned and smiled at him. Bright and, she suspected, ghastly. Making the situation worse. "Why not get dressed so that we can go downstairs? You can meet Arwa. I brought her with me when I came."

"A girl?" Unenthusiastic.

"Yes," Marion said. "A few years older than you are. You'll like her."

"All right, Mummy." He stood, obedient, and went to the wardrobe. Still wearing nothing but pyjama trousers.

As she watched him, she realized that she didn't know what they'd have given him as clothing. Surely not his uniform from Temple Grove. When he pulled khaki short trousers, a white cotton shirt, braces, hiking boots, and a khaki cap out of a drawer, she smiled to herself. Dressing him like the invader. But they must have their reasons. And he did look the part.

Once he'd dressed, they walked to the door and out onto the third-floor gallery. Took the central staircase down to the large reception room. Samir, Arwa, and two women Marion didn't know—dressed expensively and entirely occupied with Arwa—were already there, eating breakfast. Three other men she also didn't recognize were speaking in a corner. Engrossed.

And, of course, Alain. Dressed in an outfit identical to Ian's, except that Alain was well over six feet tall, reddish-blond, fifty-eight years old, and built like an advertisement for a chest expander. When Marion saw him, she burst out laughing. "Alain, you look like an idiot." She was speaking French.

"Two years, and that's all you have to say to me?" He was pouting down at his hairy legs sticking out of the short trousers.

"No," she said, less friendly. "In fact, I have a great deal more to say to you. But not in front of my son."

Alain, sheepish, turned his eyes toward Samir who was speaking with Arwa and pretending not to hear them. "Orders, Marion. What would you have me do?"

She held his look, not responding. Playing large and stupid was his working strategy. She'd seen it before, and she wasn't fooled. Before the silence became awkward, he grinned over at Ian instead. Protecting himself. "And you should see the child on the mountain. It's good he came. You'd be proud." He clapped Ian on the shoulder with an enormous hand. "He's a natural. Likes to go head first."

"Thanks, Alain," Marion said. Yielding. "That's more than I want to know."

"You used to go head first too—" he began.

"I'm old now," she interrupted. "And it's time for us to leave. To go home. I promise that I'll find him ample opportunity to practice when we've returned."

"Really, Mummy?" Ian looked pleased. "I'd like that."

She nodded and then gazed across the room to catch Samir's eye. When he responded to her look and disengaged himself from his conversation, she left Ian with Alain. Smiled at Arwa as she walked toward him.

Samir gestured her toward a cushion against a window, and she sat. Lifted the glass of tea he offered her. "You don't want anything else from me, do you?" She looked at him over her glass.

"No. Arwa will be meeting delegates from the regional governments this afternoon. Those further afield tomorrow. They'll begin arriving within the next hour or two." He glanced over at Alain and Ian, absorbed in animated conversation. Lots of hand gestures. "We'll have a car ready to take you and your son back to Mocha this evening. Is that acceptable?"

"Yes. Thank you."

"Good." He paused. "In the meantime, would you walk me through the manuscript material? I'd like to familiarize myself with it, in case any problems arise."

She nodded. "Easily. It's straightforward once you get a feel for the style."

He laughed. "To some, perhaps. Thank you for this one, Marion. I know it was difficult for you." She made as though to stand to go back to Ian, but he held out his hand, preventing her. "Alain would be happy to take Ian back up the mountain today. With your permission, of course." He paused. "You and I might get through the material more quickly without him underfoot."

She sat back down on the cushion. Weary. Looked, wistful and depressed, over at Ian. He was paying no attention to her. Captivated by Alain. Then she turned her attention back to Samir, pushing down her annoyance that he believed she'd be mollified by his asking her permission. They both knew that her wishes were irrelevant to the situation. She'd rather he hadn't tried. Disliked what she thought of as his French deference to purposeless etiquette.

Instead of trusting herself to speak, she simply nodded again, rose, and returned to Ian. "Samir has told me that our car won't be ready until this evening. Which means you've got another day to go out hiking with Alain. If you'd like to go," she added, hating herself for hoping he'd choose to stay in the house.

Ian lit up. "Oh, I am glad. Thank you, Mummy." He hugged her, quick and embarrassed, and then ran out of the room toward the stairs. Looked back at Alain. "We'll leave now, won't we?"

"Yes." Alain bent over and gave Marion a quick kiss on the cheek before he turned to follow Ian. "It'll be all right, Marion. He adores you, you know."

He left before she could think of a response. And, a few seconds later, she retreated as well. Walked up to her room to grab her carpet bag. Climbed to the top floor of the house and arranged the manuscripts, maps, and sculptures on a work table in a second alcove off the sitting room. Waiting for Samir to extract himself from the interactions downstairs and join her.

As she sat and reacquainted herself with the maps and annotations, she allowed herself to appreciate the room. It was best in the morning. The sunlight shining through the multicolored glass. The tracery over the windows. The calligraphy hung high on the walls. Leaning forward, her fingertips against her temples, reading through the sly prose and verse, she heard the call to prayer float up from the mosque further down the hill.

And relaxed a bit more. She had, despite her best efforts, very little religious feeling of any kind. But she was nonetheless glad to be out of Copenhagen and Lisbon, with their ceaseless church bells. The bells always left her on edge, whereas the call to prayer helped her to concentrate. Jeffrey, she knew, would have something to say about that. But she would never make a confession of that sort to him. Or even acknowledge it to herself. And so, instead, she willed herself simply to enjoy the atmosphere. To try not to analyze it.

Twenty minutes later, Samir emerged from the stairwell, carrying a file folder and a pencil. He sat next to her, opened the folder, readied a blank sheet of paper to take notes, and invited her to begin. And, pleased to be doing the one thing that didn't leave her anxious, she did. Relaxing further.

More than three hours later, he was still debriefing her, asking her to repeat and explain the more complicated steps she had taken, questioning aspects of her translations and interpretations, as well as—she could tell—drawing conclusions of his own that he wasn't sharing with her. She didn't mind. She was merely relieved that this project was ending. She would take a very long holiday indeed once she and Ian were back in Britain.

When eventually he set down his pencil, satisfied, it was well past noon. They both stood, stretched, and moved toward the stairway. "Would you care for lunch?" Samir was walking beside her. Preoccupied by what she had told him.

"Yes," she began. "Thank—"

She stopped as the house, centuries old and rock-solid, shuddered. Wondered whether it was a mild earthquake and hesitated in the corridor, waiting for aftershocks. But nothing came. And in any event, the initial jolt had felt wrong. Not like an earthquake at all.

After a long moment of silence, she heard a different sound—the dull booming of thunder, perhaps, from a few miles away. Confused she looked up at the light streaming in from the windows along the ceiling and walls. The day was clear and bright. Not the weather for thunder.

The next sound was unmistakable. First a low rumbling. And then a whining screech from just above them, followed by a flat thud. Another screech and the thudding was closer. The house shaking in earnest. She turned to look at Samir. Wide-eyed.

"Bombs," he said.

"Oh God."

He took her arm. "Get to the ground floor. Wait there for Alain and Ian. I'll see about moving Arwa."

She turned away from him and fled down the staircase. Praying that Ian had already returned. When she reached the bottom, she saw that he had. He and Alain were crouching down against sacks of grain. Both smiling and excited—though both, shamefaced, knew that they weren't supposed to be. She ran across the floor and squatted next to them.

Alain spoke to her across Ian. "We saw them coming. It's more than planes. They've got three trucks, and it looked like two armored cars moving up the ridge road." He stood and moved toward the stairs. "I must tell Samir."

"Wait." She looked up at him. "What were they? Could you tell?"

"Crossley. d2e2. British." He turned and strode up the steps toward the first floor.

She leaned back against the canvas. Her arm around Ian. Eyes closed. "Fuck."

Inwardly, she scolded herself for using profanity in front of her child. Then she said it again. "*Fuck.*"

DO you think it's Aldous?" Ian sounded at most curious. Mildly thrilled.

She turned to him. "What?"

"Aldous Parker," he said. "Flying one of the aeroplanes. They were Hawker Harts. I saw them. Though Aldous says he prefers the Hawker Audax. Maneuvers better and can carry a bigger load, even if it's got a bit less speed."

She stared at him, not quite believing that his reaction to the situation was to provide her with trivia about the specifications of the aircraft that had come to kill them. Then, as the house shook again, she collected herself. The whistling in the air above them was closer.

"If it is Aldous," she said, "I'll kill him."

"How?" Intrigued.

"So that he never sees it coming." She peered toward the staircase, wondering whether she ought to help Alain and Samir move Arwa to safety. She hoped the delegates coming to meet her hadn't been caught in the attack. "I believe he's still in Iraq now."

"Oh." Disappointed.

She crept, crouching, toward the base of the stairs. Using her hand to steady herself against the near constant shaking of the ground. Then she reached the first step and looked up just as Alain was returning, descending through swirling dust from the floor above. Harried. A few pieces of plaster in his hair.

"We're evacuating," he said. "There's an escape tunnel from Queen Arwa's time connecting the palace to the base of the hill. It bypasses the main roads into the city. When we get to the bottom, you and Ian will go to Mocha. The road ought to be safe—heading away from the assault." He began pushing aside the sacks of grain. Grunted his thanks as Marion stood to help him. "I'll take Samir's boy and one of the Zündapps back up and along the ridge road. Warn away the delegates."

"What about Arwa?" Marion was pulling the last sack away from the wall.

"Samir's taking care of it. Best not to know." He moved aside a dirty canvas sheet to reveal what looked like a solid brick floor. Pried up a single large brick, and then six more, to expose a wooden trap door. He took a key from his pocket, unlocked the trap door, and pulled it open.

Ian, who had been watching, fascinated, as Alain worked, crept closer and peered down into the hole. A brick staircase descended into the darkness. He grinned up at Alain. "A secret passageway."

"To the palace, even." Alain, boyish, was smiling back at him. "But it can't be your first, can it?"

"Maybe." Ian didn't want to admit his inexperience with tunneling between buildings. Even so, he went down on his hands and knees and stared into the darkness.

"This will help." Alain walked to a corner of the room, pulled a lamp off a hook, and lit it with a match. Returned to the trap door and held it above the gap in the floor for Ian to see.

Before Ian could comment again, Samir, Arwa, and the rest of the people Marion had seen in the reception room descended to the ground floor. They were dressed for travel.

Alain looked up at them, serious again. "News?"

"The trucks are more than halfway up the hill." Samir's voice was impassive. "We've got people on the streets, acting confused, making the ascent difficult. But I don't want anyone shot. They're giving way when they have to."

"How long?"

"Five minutes." Samir moved toward the gap in the floor. "Three perhaps."

"Samir," Alain, speaking quietly, switched from Arabic to French. His Swiss accent more pronounced. "That isn't enough time. They'll see the floor. And they already have a view of the street. Anyone who stays to clean up will be trapped in the house."

"It's the time we have."

"I'll stay behind." Marion was still holding a small sack of grain. She put it on the ground. "Ian and I will arrange the floor. Delay them when they arrive."

Samir paused, considering. Before he replied, she spoke again, more confident: "if Alain doesn't get out onto the road, they'll set up camp here and detain every person who visits this house. Every one. The regional governments will think it was deliberate."

Samir nodded. "Very well. Do whatever it takes." He turned to Alain. "Give her the key."

She took the key from Alain, who kissed her on both cheeks. Then she waited while Alain, followed by Arwa, the five people Marion assumed were some sort of entourage, the boy, who cast her a quick—forgiving, she decided—smile, and Samir lowered themselves into the tunnel. Once they were gone, she closed the trap door and locked it.

Slipped the key into her pocket and turned to Ian. "Help me replace the bricks?"

He nodded, eager to be of assistance, and they began placing the bricks back into order. Then they both spread the sheet over the floor and moved the sacks of grain into place. Tried to smooth the dust in such a way that it didn't look suspiciously trampled.

When they had finished, Marion heard the rumble of military trucks slowing on the stone street outside. The bombers had moved off. Their aim, presumably, had been to terrorize the countryside sufficiently that no one thought to obstruct the progress of the vehicles on the ground. Which they had accomplished admirably.

Marion pushed a stray strand of hair out of her face. Looked about, determining where she ought to wait. Not on the ground floor. Upstairs. And so, unlocking the front door—no use providing them with an excuse to splinter the fretwork—she smiled, a little ashamed, at Ian and pointed toward the stairs. "I think it's better to receive them on the first floor."

"All right." He climbed the stairs in front of her. Twisted back to talk to her. "Are you certain it isn't Aldous?"

"Yes," she said. She hoped.

When they reached the reception area, she saw that the boy had left it as clean and organized as he could in the short time he had before Samir had brought him to the tunnel. The breakfast food had been cleared away, but he had had missed a plate of *halwa* and a pitcher of water with clean glasses. Someone had placed them at the far end of the room, opposite the door. A tall window to the side.

Trying to ignore the sound of the trucks, she sat next to the pitcher and poured a glass of water. Thought for a moment and slipped the key to the trap door under a cushion. Then she gazed through the colored glass of the window and saw that Alain had accurately assessed the vehicles. Three trucks and two armored cars, all of them Crossley. They were positioned now at haphazard angles in front of the house, blocking the street. Between twenty-five and thirty soldiers, she estimated, were emerging from them. Armed and alert.

"Ian," she asked. "Would you like a glass of water?"

"No, thank you." He was kneeling on the cushion, peering down into the street. Watching the soldiers.

She sipped from the glass she had poured. Heard the front door crashing open. Boots on the brick floor. Spreading upward. Aggressive rather than cautious. Thirty seconds later, two entered the reception area, wearing dismally familiar khaki drill. They stopped at the door and trained rifles on her. Two others followed with revolvers. She sat still on the window seat, holding her glass with both hands, wishing her heart weren't beating as fast as it was. Didn't move.

She heard others spreading further up into the house. Bedrooms. Library. Kitchen. And then Samir's sitting room on the top floor. She knew he'd taken the manuscript material with him. But she hoped nonetheless that they weren't causing too much damage. A stupid hope.

A few seconds after the sound of the boots had stopped, she heard them shouting to one another from room to room that the house was clear. She remained sitting on the window seat. Quiet. Observing the soldiers at the door who were, in turn, observing her. Ian, picking up her mood, sat beside her, equally subdued.

Less than two minutes later, she heard slower footsteps on the stairs. Three people. Pausing in the gallery for several seconds—to inspect the area, she imagined. And then they were in the room. Two of the soldiers stood back and at attention, while the other two kept their weapons on her.

The first to enter was a gaunt, affronted looking man with his eyes placed too closely together. An officer of some sort. In his late fifties, she guessed. Followed by Jeffrey and Nick Trelawney. All in uniform. She suppressed a sigh, even while Ian brightened. He looked about to run across the room to them until a slight shake of the head from Nick, a step behind and to the side of the officer, warned him not to.

When they entered the room, Marion didn't move. Watched all three of them. Neutral.

Eventually the man addressed Marion. "Well?" Bad tempered. "And who are you, then?"

Marion remained sitting. Holding her glass of water in her lap to keep her hands from shaking. Didn't speak.

"This is the one Richard Maugham wants extracted?" He was talking to Jeffrey now. "Yes?"

"Yes, sir." Jeffrey's voice was respectful. Polite. But there was something in it—something that even Marion could sense—that mocked the officer. Made it clear that Jeffrey's orders were coming from elsewhere.

The officer looked about to say something to Jeffrey, perhaps about insubordination. But he stopped himself and thought better of it. Considered the room instead. "What about the rest? Weren't there supposed to be others?"

It was unclear to whom he was speaking, and so no one answered.

"You." Addressing Marion again. "Where are the others?"

She returned the officer's look, perplexed. Ignoring Jeffrey's lips twitching in a smile and the expression of weary resignation that passed over Nick's face.

Then, she spoke. "What others?" When no one responded, she continued. "*Oh.* Oh, I see. You mean the others who moved to a less visible house in the city when you announced your imminent arrival with all that commotion in the air. Yes. They did want me to thank you for that. Advanced warning. Very sporting of you." She paused. "Those are indeed some large and impressive aircraft you've got. I'm afraid I don't know where the house is."

"They aren't that large, Mummy." Ian, missing Marion's tone, wasn't about to have his knowledge of aerial bombing techniques questioned. "Hawker Harts. I told you. They're *light* bombers. Not much heavier than a fighter."

He was disappointed when Marion didn't reply. But he also didn't insist. Recalled to the atmosphere in the room, which had taken a decided turn for the worse.

The officer had gone silent again. Looking between Marion and Ian. Ruminating. Not, it seemed, given to excessive speech. There was, however, anger building slowly behind his otherwise lifeless eyes.

Close to a minute after the silence had become unpleasant, Jeffrey finally interjected. "May I propose a way forward, Colonel Griffith?" Quiet and civil. And yet also a continuing mild caricature.

"What is it?"

"We ought to begin searching for this 'less visible house,' sir. If for no other reason than to establish that the residence we're in isn't vulnerable to counter attack. The others are certain to be nearby. We've covered the roads leading out of the city. It's simply a matter of finding them."

Griffith didn't respond.

"And then," Jeffrey continued, "if you'd lend me Trelawney and a guard of five or six men, I'll speak with Dr. Bailey. While your soldiers see to the street. I may be able to help her remember where that second location is." He paused, his face blank despite the hint of amusement that had hovered over it since he had entered the room. "It's a disordered town, but I'm confident that, with assistance, she'll find her bearings."

Griffith remained quiet, if still indefinably harassed. Then, amenable as he seemed capable of being, he spoke: "very well, Major Willcox. Do whatever it is you do, then. Your bloody debacle." He turned and walked back out the door. "You and you," to the soldiers with the rifles, "follow me. You," to the two with the revolvers, "stay here."

When Griffith had left, Jeffrey let himself smile in earnest. But he didn't speak to Marion. Instead, benign and paternal, he turned to Ian. "Enjoying your holiday, John?"

"Yes, sir." Ian, responding to Jeffrey's smile, opened up again. "Alain taught me abseiling."

"Did he, now?" Jeffrey glanced over at Marion, malicious. "You must tell us all about 'Alain.' Mr. Nick, you know, is not such a bad hand with a rope himself. Perhaps they could compare notes."

Ian jumped up from the cushion, relieved that the oppressive atmosphere in the room had evaporated, and ran over to Jeffrey and Nick. He looked up at them. "I can go head first, Mr. Nick. All the way down."

Nick, following Jeffrey's lead, was also smiling down at Ian. "Truly, John? I can't believe it."

"No, really. I can."

"You learned it from Alain?"

"Yes, Alain says—"

"Ian," Marion interrupted. Silently berating herself for not having instructed Ian to keep quiet about what he'd seen. "Ian, wait—"

"Now, now, Marion." Jeffrey walked toward her across the room. "You can't keep the boy all to yourself. Let him tell Mr. Nick about the fun he's been having. John," turning back to Ian, "would you like to help the soldiers secure the house? It's an important job. They must make absolutely certain that not a single hiding place is—"

"Ian." Marion stood and started after him. "Ian, don't go yet—"

Jeffrey caught her by the arm before she reached him and turned her, leading her in the opposite direction, back toward the window seat. "This way, Marion. John really must concentrate on his duties now. Mr. Nick," glancing back at Nick, "why not start at the top floor and move down?"

"Yes, sir." Nick bent over to speak to Ian. "What do you reckon, John? Shall we begin at the top of the house?"

Ian nodded seriously. "Yes, Mr. Nick. That would be best, I think."

"Ian—" Marion shook her arm out of Jeffrey's hand and turned back toward the door. He pushed her down onto the cushions. "Go, Trelawney."

"Yes, sir." Nick, preceded by Ian, left the room.

Once he was gone, the two soldiers moved into place in front of the door. Sitting incensed on the cushion, Marion curled her hands into fists in her lap. But she didn't bother to say any more. There wasn't any point.

When he was certain that Nick and Ian were safely away, Jeffrey sat next to her, exhaled in relief, and removed his peaked cap. Placing the cap beside him on the cushion, he poured himself a glass of water. Took a piece of *halwa* from the plate and shrugged at her look of disgust as he ate it. "Privilege of the conquering army. Plunder." He chewed. "That drive from Aden is brutal, and I'm famished." He looked about the room. "Anything else to eat, I wonder?"

He was, to her annoyance, entirely healthy. No trace of illness. Picking up on her thoughts, he smiled again. "I recovered quite a bit more quickly this time. Who can tell? Perhaps I'm developing an immunity. If so, you'll want to inform your superiors." He ate another piece of *halwa*. "Speaking of which, thank you for leaving me that soup in Lisbon. I was in dire need of nourishment the next morning, as I'm sure you can imagine."

She looked out the window. Unresponsive. Praying without a great deal of confidence that Ian would show some sense and stop chattering to Nick.

"You're wondering how I knew you'd surface in Jibla?" He lifted his glass and drank some water.

"No."

"I'll tell you anyway. Advice from your handler. For the sake of your future work for us." He set down his glass. "Surely you realize, Marion, that your silences are as telling as your always diverting attempts to lie. Really, darling. You must find another strategy."

"I don't work for you."

"Going mute at any mention of where Forsskal succumbed to his tragic illness. Forgetting where Admiral Khayr al-Din got himself betrayed and overrun by rebels. Neglecting to point out where the Sulayhids built their stronghold." He relaxed further and stretched his arm across the back of the cushions. "All it took was a quick perusal of your reference material. Jibla, Jibla, and—oh yes—Jibla."

She stood and walked to the other side of the room. Looked out a different window. "How long do we stay here?"

"Obviously, that's up to you." He hadn't changed his position. "Though you don't seem all that averse to prolonging the ordeal. Quite cold blooded of you, I thought, sending Colonel Griffith and his men on a useless rampage across the city. Ripping apart the houses of God knows how many blameless townspeople who, I have a feeling, haven't the slightest notion what a 'less visible location' even is."

He paused. "Well. Not entirely blameless. That impromptu street market that our vehicles met—repeatedly—on the way up the hill was suspiciously attuned to the finer points of urban combat theory."

"There's nothing here, Jeffrey." She didn't turn away from the window. "You're too late."

"Eyes reported a couple of stolen German motorcycles leaving Mocha yesterday morning," he said. "We aren't too late."

She faced him. "A day and a half. Ample time to—"

She stopped speaking when Nick walked back through the door. He cast her a quick, embarrassed glance and then moved across the room toward Jeffrey. "I've left John upstairs with Corporal Williamson," he said. "They're disassembling a wardrobe."

Jeffrey frowned. "A suspicious wardrobe?"

"No, sir." Nick kept his face blank. Soldierly. "But destroying it ought to keep the boy occupied for a few minutes."

"Not to mention Corporal Williamson. Very well. Any progress?"

"Yes." Nick avoided looking in Marion's direction now. "There were nine people in the house in addition to John and Dr. Bailey. All nine left together five minutes before we arrived."

"Excellent. Identities?"

"Yes, sir. The house belongs to a man called Samir. Syrian. Between twenty-five and seventy—"

"Between twenty-five and seventy?" Exasperated.

"John said he was 'old,'" Nick explained. "The best I could get out of him was between twenty-five and seventy."

"Very well. Continue."

"Samir, I believe, is their—their commander."

"Good. Anyone else?"

"There was also a boy, Hasan, fourteen or fifteen years old. A servant, I think." Nick hesitated. "And a girl, Arwa, nine or ten years old."

"Also a servant?"

Nick looked embarrassed. "John said she was a princess, sir."

"Then she must have made an impression." The corner of Jeffrey's mouth went down. "Ordinarily, he's not so fanciful."

"Yes, sir." Struggling to keep his voice empty. "There were also five adults attending, he said, the girl. Two women and three men. He couldn't give me details about them."

"Hmm." Jeffrey was thinking. "And 'Alain?'"

"A Swiss national, sir. Tall. Red hair. Fit." Nick paused. "Alain Vaucher, John said."

Jeffrey's eyebrows went up. "Alain Vaucher, no less." He laughed quietly. "Well, I'll take comfort from the fact that he's learning from the best." A thought occurred to him and he looked over at Marion. "Vaucher didn't teach you as well, did he?" He paused, musing. "That would explain quite a lot."

She remained silent and rigid in front of the window. Cold. Unwilling to hear what else Ian had spilled. Unfair though it was to blame a seven-year-old, she felt ashamed that he hadn't had the presence of mind to keep quiet. He wasn't that naïve.

"Very good work, Trelawney." Jeffrey stood and resettled his cap on his head. "And did John mention where Mummy's nine friends were all going in such a hurry five minutes before we arrived?"

There was a split second of what might have been apologetic silence. And then Nick, still expressionless, replied: "he said, sir, that he didn't want to say anything more until he knew that his mother—Dr. Bailey, that is—approved of him talking with us." Nick caught Jeffrey's eye. "I'm sorry, sir."

Jeffrey, annoyed, but also imperceptibly proud, nodded. "Ah well. So the boy has a contrary streak. We can work through that."

He glanced over at Marion, who was now smiling, challenging Jeffrey and Nick to find a way forward. Silently apologizing to Ian for having doubted him. Then he turned back to Nick. "You're certain he said they left five minutes before we arrived, Trelawney?" Rubbing his cheek with his hand. "All nine of them?"

"Yes, sir. He was definite on that point. He said that Samir had given them five minutes to get out, and that he and Dr. Bailey had only just walked up to the first floor when—"

"Walked up, he said?" Jeffrey looked out the window, still thoughtful. "They were on the ground floor before that?"

"Yes—I imagine so, sir."

Jeffrey nodded slowly. Then he said: "I don't think that nine people could have left the house, moved through the streets, and secreted themselves in a new building less than five minutes before we arrived. We were already at the top of the crest. We would have seen them."

After considering for several seconds longer, he spoke, confident now, to Nick: "would you tell Corporal Williamson to let the wardrobe recover for a few minutes? Tell him to go find Colonel Griffith, convince him to stop demolishing whatever coffee house he's decided is at fault for his disappointing life, and bring him back here. We'll want all of his men working downstairs." He gazed over at Marion's face, examined her expression, and then smiled, satisfied. "Tell them to move fast, Trelawney. We're racing against the clock."

"Yes, sir."

Once Nick had left the room, Jeffrey went to Marion, who had returned her attention to the window. Stood beside her, also looking out. Complacent. She wanted to hit him.

"I'm afraid I must leave you now," he told her. "Oversee our work downstairs."

"Good. Go away."

"I'll be certain to inform you immediately should we discover anything."

"You're still here, Jeffrey."

"Do you know," he said to her after a gratified moment, "I was desolate upon waking alone in Lisbon. If unsurprised."

Then he turned and left the room.

SHE spent the next hour sitting in the corner of the room, finishing the plate of *halwa*. After a surreptitious inspection of the two soldiers Jeffrey had left guarding the door, she decided against escape. She didn't want to leave Ian. And she was tired of this project. It wasn't worth going under again.

So instead, she waited. Listening first to the sound of Colonel Griffith's men returning to the house, and then to the sound of them destroying the floor and the walls below her. She tried, stubbornly, to keep from flinching whenever she heard a particularly damaging sounding crash.

Forty minutes later, Jeffrey returned. Looking pleased with himself. He sat, playful, next to her on the cushion. Dust and a few pieces of grain on his uniform. "Guess what we found tucked away in a corner of the cellar."

"You're still too late."

"A secret passage!" He ignored her, his expression unpleasantly similar to what Ian's had been. "Imagine that. Everyone is quite excited. Runs straight over to the picturesque ruin of the castle next door. And then, it seems, bang down through the middle of the mountain." He sighed. "Makes a frightful mockery of all that surveillance we set up along the roads. But I suppose we'll learn in time."

"It doesn't matter."

"Colonel Griffith has sent a troop down after Mummy's friends." He stood. "And he's also established a temporary base of operations on the top floor here. He's unhappy about the calligraphy and the *takhrim*, but he says it's the only room in the building with a proper table, so he's making do."

"I don't care."

"He wants you up there too." Entertained. "To help when the troop returns. He's ordered them to kill on sight whoever or whatever they meet when they emerge from the tunnel. Hoping, I daresay, to make it all go away. But he's got a sense that things won't end quite that cleanly." He paused. "I've got a similar sense. Secret passageways do that to a person. So, we may want your advice when the time comes."

She stood as well. Refusing to give him a chance to coerce her. "Fine. But this is pointless."

"Hmm." He removed his revolver from its holster and stood to the side to let her pass. Waited for her to precede him out the door and up the stairs.

When she reached Samir's sitting room, it had been rearranged to accommodate Colonel Griffith and his staff. The work table had been dragged from the alcove to the center of the floor, leaving the carpet wrinkled in places. Which bothered her. And armchairs that had been scattered throughout the house had been gathered together and placed around the table. Incongruous.

Griffith himself was standing at a window looking out over the city and the mountains. He was drinking a glass of tea. He turned when Marion and Jeffrey entered the room. Looked harassed, again, to see them. "Sit if you care to, Major Willcox."

"Thank you, sir." Jeffrey sat in one of the armchairs. Poured himself a glass of tea from a pot in the middle of the table. The pot that Samir used to entertain. It made her unhappy to see it in Jeffrey's hand.

Griffith looked at Marion for three or four seconds. "You may sit as well, Dr. Bailey."

She sat across from Jeffrey. Decided that caffeine was more important than her offended sensibilities, and poured her own tea. Didn't speak.

And for the next ten minutes, all three remained silent. Marion, who had expected Griffith to interrogate her, was nonplussed. But she wasn't displeased. Awkward silence was always preferable to Jeffrey's professional conversational mode. She glanced across at him to see how he was reacting to the standstill. But he seemed content. Calm. Which, predictably, made her nervous.

She had nearly finished her second glass of tea when she heard heavy footsteps climbing the stairs. Boots. The troop that Griffith had sent down the trap door.

And when they arrived, she closed her eyes. Crestfallen. Three heavily armed soldiers had entered the room. Sweating. A hint baffled, but hiding it behind impassive faces. Followed by Nick, unruffled, carrying a clipboard and a pen. And Arwa. Looking no less composed than she had when she'd entered the house the evening before. Her dress clean and smooth. Her face detached.

But when Griffith, who had taken a seat at the head of the table, saw her, he stared at her for a good fifteen seconds, incredulous and horrified. And then—the incredulity turning to anger—he glared at his soldiers. "Your order, Sergeant, was to eliminate the problem."

"Yes, sir." The largest of the three soldiers was standing at attention. Uncertain. "We have eliminated the problem, sir."

"Then what is *that*?" Griffith pointed, livid, at Arwa.

"It's a little girl, sir."

"Yes?" Griffith waited a few seconds for an explanation. When it didn't come, he snorted, annoyed. "Very well, Sergeant. Report?"

When the sergeant began to speak, Griffith interrupted. "And don't stand like that. Just tell me what happened."

The three soldiers relaxed. Then the sergeant, collecting himself, spoke again: "they were well away when we reached the bottom of the hill, sir. Almost out of sight. But Private Henderson noticed a cloud of dust at the base of a second hill. Two motorcycles and a truck. We lost the motorcycles, sir. But we disabled the truck." The sergeant was unable to continue. He looked, nervous, at Nick, who was taking notes on the clipboard.

"Yes?" Griffith was still glowering at the sergeant. "And then?"

"There were six people in the truck, sir. Five adults and—and this girl. There were also provisions and a box of valuables. The box is outside, sir, if—"

"No, Sergeant." Unwilling to let the soldier distract him with the box. "What happened then?"

"Sir, we—we eliminated the problem. As we'd been ordered to do." The sergeant swallowed. "They were unarmed, sir."

"Hmph." Unimpressed.

"Were any of them," Jeffrey asked, bored, "between twenty-five and seventy years of age, I wonder?"

The sergeant turned to him, bewildered. "Yes—yes, sir. I believe they were all between those ages, sir."

Jeffrey sipped his tea. "Well, that's all right then. Continue, Sergeant."

But the sergeant was now entirely unable to continue. He was looking, almost frightened, at Griffith.

"What *then*, Sergeant?" Griffith's voice was waspish.

The sergeant gazed into the middle distance. His voice wooden. At attention, even if his posture was relaxed. "And then, sir, we brought the girl and the box back up the hill. To await your orders. Sir."

"My orders," Griffith said, "were to eliminate the problem. *Did* you eliminate the problem, Sergeant?"

"No, sir." Still wooden.

"Oh, for God's sake." Griffith pushed back the chair and stood. "Get out."

"The—the little girl, sir?"

"Leave her here."

The soldiers left the room, and Griffith, baleful, stared at Arwa. She stood at the other end of the table, holding his look. Poised and unconcerned. Eventually she spoke. "I shall understand, Colonel Griffith, if your government finds it necessary to execute me." Her tone suggested she was doing him a favor. "I'm prepared."

Marion was mildly, if inappropriately, entertained to note that Arwa's accent when speaking English was as patrician as her accent when speaking Arabic. She made Griffith sound like a country squire. But Griffith himself was taken aback. As she spoke, he narrowed his eyes. Astonished that she had addressed him at all.

Finally, however, after longer than it should have taken, he did reply. "My government isn't in the habit of executing children."

Arwa looked amused. "Eliminating me, then."

Griffith turned stiffly to Nick. "Get the girl something to eat, Trelawney."

Nick stood. "Yes, sir." He slipped the clipboard under his arm and walked across the room toward Arwa. Gestured to the door. "I understand that you're a princess," he said to her in Arabic. She smiled at him. But she didn't speak as he ushered her out of the room.

When they were alone, Griffith turned on Jeffrey. "Now what? What the blazes am I supposed to do with—with *that*?"

"I'd like to see what's in the box," Jeffrey said.

Griffith laughed shortly. "Nor am I surprised."

He shouted out the door for a private. When a soldier appeared, he ordered him to bring the box into the room. The soldier nodded and returned a few minutes later with a flat, wooden container, three feet square, two feet high, closed with a latch.

After he'd set the box on the table, Jeffrey stood and lifted the lid. Examined the contents, and then began removing them and placing them on the table. A series of rock crystal chess pieces and goblets. A menagerie of solid gold animals with jeweled eyes. Gold and silver knives and plates. A large rock crystal chest containing what looked to be one or two thousand gold dinar coins. And then, protected at the bottom of the box, a folded silk map of the world, square, woven in gold and colored silk thread, depicting land, water, climates, cities, and mythical creatures.

Jeffrey laughed, disbelieving, when he came to the map. "Fatimid, I believe." He looked at Griffith. "All of it. From the looted treasury. Curators at the Museum are going to have a fit when they see this last piece."

"And you?" Griffith was uninterested in the artifacts. Soldierly. Though he seemed mollified that he could at least bring something back with him from the expedition.

Jeffrey closed the lid of the box. "There should have been a jewel. A large pearl or a uniquely worked piece of inscribed rock crystal." He glanced over at Marion. "It wasn't there."

"What about the girl?" Griffith returned to his problem. "None of this helps with this—this stray child."

Jeffrey half shrugged. "If you'll forgive me, Colonel Griffith, I think you're making too much of the girl. Why not simply have her adopted by a family back in England? People interested in collecting curios from the Orient. She's an orphan, after all—or, if she wasn't before, she certainly is now—"

He stopped short. Caught himself. And then thought for a moment. After that, he smiled, slow and wicked, at Marion. "An 'orphan.'" His smile grew. "Of course."

He turned back to Griffith. His smile gone and his tone serious. "On second thought, let me retract what I've just said. You're correct, sir. We can't have any loose ends. It's a bad business, but we ought to erase this problem before it grows into something bigger. The girl must be dispatched."

Griffith nodded in agreement. Grim and curt. "Best get it done quickly, then. I'll order Sergeant—"

"Colonel Griffith," Marion interrupted, finally processing the drift of their conversation. "If I understand what you're about to do—and I hope to God that I do not—I want to make it absolutely clear that there will be consequences. I'm a witness. I've heard this entire exchange. And I will tell every reporter between here and Manchester *exactly* what has happened. Think very carefully before you—"

"No one will believe you, Dr. Bailey." Griffith rose from his chair. About to call back his private.

"Jeffrey." She stared, aghast, across the table at him. "She's *nine*. You can't—"

"It's war, Marion. Have you any idea what the Italians are doing on the other side of the Red Sea? This is nothing."

She pushed back her chair and stalked over to him. "You can't do this."

"Care to convince me otherwise? Anything, for example, that you'd like to share about the location of the *Durrah*? Something, perhaps, to convince Colonel Griffith that he's quite correct to bring the girl back to his superiors? Along with the rest of the 'treasure?' Rather than eliminating her?"

She glowered at him. Unable to believe he'd jeopardize a nine-year-old girl's life to verify a hypothesis. Then she dropped her eyes. "You're repellent."

He didn't reply.

She swallowed. "Where can we talk?"

ONCE Jeffrey had convinced Griffith to postpone giving the order to dispatch Arwa, he escorted Marion downstairs. Samir had installed both a large library and a smaller, intimate library on the third floor. Each was well insulated from curious listeners. Meant for study and quiet conversation.

Jeffrey took her to the small library, where he sat in an armchair that Griffith's soldiers had missed. He set his cap on a table to his side, found a small ceramic vase, empty of flowers, to use as an ashtray, and lit a cigarette. Pointed Marion to the window seat across from him. Between two tall bookcases. "Tell me about the *Durrah*."

She sat on the window seat. Curled her feet up under her and looked through the glass for a few seconds. A view of the castle. "Arwa's the *Durrah*."

"So I gathered." He inhaled smoke. Blew it pensively in front of him. "It makes superficial sense. The crystal or pearl unmatched in clarity, radiance, and eloquence. The peninsula's legendary unifying force. It was certain to be more than a piece of jewelry. And she undoubtedly acts the part." He watched the smoke unfurling. "But—historically? There are too many discrepancies."

"No." Marion shook her head. "It works. I re-read the passages about it—about her—in the manuscript you retrieved from the library. Once I'd located her. It all fits."

"Is the manuscript here?"

"Samir took it."

"Ah." He considered. "And then fled our pursuing soldiers on his motorcycle. Leaving the girl to us. Hardly chivalrous."

She didn't say anything. She was having difficulty understanding Samir's decision to leave Arwa to the British as well. But she wasn't going to admit that to Jeffrey.

He laughed. "Loyalty. Faith. Dear God, Marion, you are terrifying in your irrational belief in your superiors sometimes."

Still she didn't speak.

He sighed and took another drag of the cigarette. "Tell me why I shouldn't allow Colonel Griffith to get rid of this girl now. As the youngest member of a sad little extremist group that got beyond itself. Provoked the wrath of Yemen's legitimate government." He looked at the end of his cigarette. "If her claim can be established, you know, we may find we can use her. In which case she'll stay alive for at least a few more years."

"Isn't it enough, Jeffrey, that she's nine years old?" Marion still couldn't quite bring herself to believe he'd let the girl die if he didn't get what he wanted. "Isn't that sufficient reason for her to 'stay alive for at least a few more years?'"

"No." When she didn't reply immediately, he tapped ash from the end of the cigarette into the vase. "She's Sulayhid?"

"Yes."

"The family didn't die out?"

"No." She turned back to the window. Let her eyes run over the blank façade of the castle. Empty. Gaping windows.

"Ismaili?"

She turned back to him. "That's complicated."

"Explain it to me, then." He watched her averted profile. "We haven't a lot of time."

"The Queen," she said, "Arwa al-Sulayhi, was born in 1048. In Yemen. She became sole ruler in 1067." She glanced at him. Back out the window. "A little less than thirty years later, in 1094, the Nizari schism, in Egypt, split the Ismaili community. Two sons of the Caliph-Imam, both claiming leadership of the Fatimid Ismaili population, challenged one another. The loser, Nizar, disappeared."

Possibly executed in Alexandria in 1094. Possibly imprisoned indefinitely. Possibly off to Alamut, in Iran." She hesitated. "Possibly something else."

"Yes," Jeffrey said, bland. "A turbulent period."

"Nizar also had three sons," Marion continued, ignoring his tone. "One, Imam Hadi, almost certainly went to Alamut. Became a rallying point for the Assassins."

"All right."

"It's unclear what happened to the other two."

"Isn't that always the case?" Smiling. "Royal pretenders. Troublesome."

"So there were," she said, "in fact three members of the Fatimid family—potentially designated imams—who were untraceable after 1094." She paused. "Except, you see, that they weren't untraceable. As it turns out. That manuscript—'everything else'—tracks them in painstaking detail. And the central map in it depicts, clear as day, the itinerary of Nizar himself." She caught herself again. "It may not have been Nizar, it's true. That's the only bit of the annotation that's opaque. It could have been one of the sons instead."

"I have a feeling I know where you're going with this." Jeffrey blew smoke up at the ceiling.

"Yes," she said. "So Nizar—or possibly his son—came to Yemen. To Arwa." She faced him. "Arwa was claiming at the time—at least overtly—to support the Caliph-Imam al-Musta'li. The winner following the schism. The brother who actually took power."

"But—"

"But, as those coins that Theodore Bent brought with him out of Aden indicate, things— covertly—were more complex. Her support of the Fatimid state wasn't as absolute as it appeared to be." She looked down at her hands. "At best, she recognized the Fatimid Caliph's temporal authority. Never, though, his right to—to unite the community." She lifted her eyes to his. "She couldn't have. Because she'd already married Nizar. Possibly his son."

Jeffrey shook his head. Skeptical. "No. That can't be right. She was already married. Fatimids pushed her into it. To her late husband's cousin, wasn't it?"

"Never consummated," Marion replied. "Notoriously so. She wouldn't even let the cousin into her palace."

"Poor man. So—"

"So Arwa married. Let's say it was Nizar. And then, shortly afterward, she had a daughter. Also Arwa—"

"Marion," he said. "She would have been fifty years old. A little late for that, don't you think?"

"She would have been forty-four," she corrected him. "Still quite possible."

"Is it, now?"

"Yes," she said shortly. "Physiologically. It was possible." She didn't like the expression on his face and pushed forward. "So, she had a daughter, Arwa. Whom she designated as her successor. Who, in turn, designated *her* daughter as successor. And—so on. They were all the *Durrah*. Think about it, Jeffrey. How do you think this region, geopolitically one of the most important in the world, has remained independent over the past millennium? *Always* independent. Despite the story of 'tribal infighting' that should have left it weak and open to any larger state with an interest in controlling the Red Sea? Which, of course, every large state has."

She looked hard at him. "There's no infighting. No 'nine tribes.' And no one from the outside, ever, has controlled this part of the Arabian Peninsula for more than a few decades. Even," she continued, snide, "when fielding some *very* impressive weapons. Arwa needn't make an overt claim," she continued when he looked unconvinced. "She simply makes herself known, periodically, and the invaders are repelled. Every time."

"Very well, Marion." Jeffrey dropped the end of his cigarette into the vase. "So perhaps Queen Arwa's line didn't die out. Perhaps there was a daughter. And perhaps this daughter designated her own daughter as the next leader. And perhaps they've even managed, on occasion, to act as a focal point for regional unification." He thought for a moment. "But why call her the *Durrah*? This jewel— whether it was actually a pearl or, instead, a piece of rock crystal—was legendary long before the Sulayhids had staked a claim in Yemen. Its first mention is in an account of al-Mahdi's court in the eighth century. Al-Mahdi's Sunni Abbasid court, that is. Not Shia. Not Fatimid. And a good three hundred years prior to Arwa's reign."

"But," she said to him, "that eighth-century origin myth is strange in and of itself, if you analyze it. It makes little sense given what was already a well-established 'precious gemstones' genre in Islamic literature. The *Durrah* gets no mythical back story. No tie to pre-Islamic or pre-historical origins, as there is with every other legendary jewel. Instead, its origin is quite the opposite. This—object—

simply appears, suddenly, at the court of al-Mahdi. The Caliph Harun al-Rashid's father. And then it's quickly, and clumsily, associated with an earlier Umayyad jewel of similar 'unmatched radiance.' Investing it with a bit of political legitimacy." She paused. "How does the tale go? When the Umayyads transferred their rule to the Abbasids, they also transferred the *Durrah*. After which, al-Mahdi gave it to his slave girl, who cut it in half to play backgammon."

"Something like that." He lifted his chin. "So?"

"When was Harun al-Rashid born?"

"Approximately 765, according to most of the chronicles." He lit another cigarette. Inhaled. Blew out smoke.

"When did the Ismailis coalesce as a separate Shia branch?"

"Same time. 765."

"Who was Harun al-Rashid's mother?"

He wrinkled his forehead. Not expecting the question. "Al-Khayzuran bint Atta. A former slave. From—" He took another drag of the cigarette. "Ah. Yes. She was a slave from Yemen. Kidnapped and brought to Baghdad. Influential in the Abbasid court for decades, through both her husband and her sons. *Not* the slave who was supposed to have cut the *Durrah* in half, it's true—but it's evocative. Two sons. Both future caliphs. The jewel cut in two pieces. Used to play a game of chance and strategy."

"Her religious practices were heterodox," Marion said. "Or, at least, so her enemies claimed."

"Hmm." Thoughtful. "Yes, I see. The timing is intriguing. The *Durrah* appears in the Abbasid Court just as a Yemeni slave girl—who shouldn't have been enslaved to begin with, given that she was Muslim, unless, of course, she wasn't quite properly Sunni Muslim—starts amassing huge influence there. Her religious beliefs are murky. And, over the same years, the Ismaili sect begins to practice in earnest. If in secret. Laying the foundation for what would, a hundred or so years later become the Fatimid dynasty in Egypt."

"And the *Durrah*," she added, "then starts appearing with some regularity in the chronicles. As well as in the 'precious gemstones' literature. After it stays with the Abbasids, in Baghdad, for a little over a century, it resurfaces as a symbol of sovereignty to the Fatimids. In Cairo. Strange jump, if you think about it. But the Caliph-Imams there begin displaying it every year during their New Year ceremonies. As a token of their right to rule. Wouldn't it be difficult, though, to 'display' an actual pearl in that way—no matter how large it was supposed to have been? Difficult even to display a piece of rock crystal. But—" She stopped and rubbed her eyes. Realized she was tired. "But then, it disappears again. In 1048. When Queen Arwa was born."

Jeffrey smoked quietly for another minute or two. Thinking about what she had told him. "That was quite the collection of treasure she had with her in the truck. Any more where that came from, do you think?"

"For God's sake, Jeffrey." Her stomach was starting to churn. "Let the poor girl alone. *Please.*"

He dropped his second cigarette into the vase and stood. Retrieved his cap. "She's anything but a poor girl, Marion. I'd back her against Colonel Griffith any day. But," he settled his cap on his head, "you've convinced me. We'll call her an exiled government and bring her home. Install her at Claridge's. See what happens when we put her in a room with our always temperamental nine tribes. Will be an interesting experiment, at any rate."

Marion stood as well. "I'll take her back to—"

"You're going nowhere near her." He took her by the arm and led her out the door. "This project of yours quite nearly ended in catastrophe. The only reason I'm not more put out about it is that I'm looking forward to seeing the numismatists' faces when I present them with that hoard of dinars." He pushed down a smile. "To catalogue."

Then, considering, he scratched his cheek. "And Maugham will like the menagerie. Probably keep one or two for himself." He smiled more broadly. "I'm betting on the rabbits." As he walked with her toward the bedrooms, he continued speaking: "so yes, the loose ends are taken care of. But I will not stand by and let you unravel them again. You'll stay in your room until this evening. Colonel Griffith will take Arwa and his men back to Aden. Calling the soldiers an honor guard."

He pushed her into the bedroom. "And after he's gone, we'll travel, as a family, to Aden as well. Giving Griffith ample time to forget that he ever met us. Find ourselves some space on the P&O. John will enjoy it. A leisurely and triumphant return to our native shores."

She started to say something in reply, but he shook his head and turned away. Found a soldier to watch the door. And then disappeared.

*F*OR the next three hours, she lay on her back, on the bed. Her eyes closed. Not sleeping. She had packed her bag in preparation for departure as soon as Jeffrey had left her alone. But she had nothing to occupy herself after that. No manuscripts. No books. Not even Graham Greene. Even so, she didn't mind terribly. She welcomed the opportunity to put her thoughts into order.

At one point, Nick appeared outside the door and spoke to the soldier, who saluted and disappeared down the stairs. Nick himself then stayed behind, watching the door. But he wasn't intrusive. Neither of them wanted a confrontation. And a few minutes after that, she heard the soldiers leaving the house. The vehicles withdrawing. Moving down the hill.

Finally, as dusk was falling, Jeffrey returned to the room. He looked tired, but he was buoyed up by the energy that always pushed him when he had work to do. Although this time the energy had an edge to it. She sat up on the bed when he walked through the door. Watched him, cautious. Silent.

Uncharacteristically, he didn't speak when he saw her. Instead, standing in front of her, he held out a scrap of vellum. Old. Crumbling. Smelling of ancient schools and libraries. She frowned and took it. Looked up at him, questioning, rather than down at the writing.

"From Arwa," he said shortly.

"You read it?"

"Of course I read it." His voice was hovering somewhere between entertained and enraged.

She observed his face for a few more seconds. And then she smoothed the scrap out on her lap. After a few lines, she thought she recognized it. A passage from Al-Biruni's eleventh-century treatise on "precious stones." She couldn't fathom why Arwa would have wanted her to have it. But, with an inward shrug, she kept reading.

Then, nearing the end, her eyes widened, and she laughed. Read a bit further and put her hand over her mouth. Looked back up at Jeffrey.

"Diverting," he said acidly. "Isn't it?"

"Biruni," she summarized for him, unnecessarily, still laughing, "says here that pearls of extraordinary size and radiance are priceless. *But*, citing Ubaydallah?" She flicked her eyes up to his and then back down to the lines in front of her. "Citing someone at any rate, he goes on to say that should a pearl of that sort have a 'twin' from the same shell, then the pair are *beyond* priceless."

She shook her head, reconsidering. "No, a better translation is that if there's a sister, then the value of one—of either one—is beyond measure, while the value of the other is nothing. Worth less than the shell."

"Indeed." He snatched back the vellum.

"She's got a sister," she said slowly, working it out. "The *Durrah* was cut in half. And Samir—Samir had a sidecar on his motorcycle. He wasn't alone."

She put her hand over her mouth again. Couldn't keep from laughing. "Alain took Hasan," she told him. "The boy. And Samir took—someone else."

"Stop laughing, Marion."

"I can't." She tried and failed to keep a straight face. "I'm sorry. I can't. It's too funny."

London, England
July, 1935

LONDON was sweltering when Jeffrey, Marion, and Ian returned three weeks later. And though Jeffrey had kept his word to find them a stateroom on the next P&O that docked at Aden, Marion quietly missed her space in the hold of the Norwegian cargo ship. When they passed the Hanish Islands, she looked in the opposite direction. Unable to analyze her abnormally strong reaction to the brownish lumps rising out of the sea. Otherwise, the voyage was uneventful.

Once in London, she had planned leave as soon as she could. To wait until Ian had returned to school—not fighting it this time—and then go to Switzerland. Finish reading the study of Ilkhanid architecture. Paddle, as Maugham had put it, on the lake.

But, to Ian's joy, Jeffrey had decided that it wasn't worthwhile to take him back to Temple Grove for such a brief stay before the end of his term. And Marion, at first unwilling to admit it, gradually concluded that she was feeling too unwell to travel. Unable to keep down food. Out of sorts. Frail.

Initially, she blamed Jeffrey. Assuming that he was engaged in some childish revenge to punish her for the past few months. He certainly had the resources to do so, and it was the sort of pastime he'd invent for himself now that he was at loose ends, his project finished.

But when he adamantly, if gleefully, denied that he had anything to do with it, she believed him. He would have told her outright if he'd been responsible for infecting her. He'd have been proud of it.

And so, concluding that it was nothing more than a summer virus, she waited for it to pass. But it hadn't passed. And now, three weeks since their return, with Jeffrey at the office torturing the numismatists, Marion was sitting in the drawing room failing to read the magazines she'd been unable to read two months before. Waiting again. This time for word from the physician. She'd visited his consulting room three days earlier, and he had promised her results this afternoon.

When she heard the front door open, she stood, doubtful, listening. And then she sat back down in the chair. Footsteps on the stairway. Which meant it wasn't the post. The door opened and she looked up. Jeffrey. Back early. She dropped her eyes to the magazine again.

"It's outdated gossip, Marion. They're all embroiled in different scandals now." He was wearing a light grey pinstriped suit. Pale blue tie and pocket handkerchief. Unaffected by the heat.

She placed the magazine on the table beside her. Didn't speak.

"There was an envelope waiting for you downstairs." He reached into the inside pocket of his jacket and held it up. Thin and beige. "You must not have heard the post."

She leapt from the chair and grabbed for it. "Thank you—"

He held it away from her. "Let me, darling. You've been unwell."

"No—"

But he already had it open. Skimmed the page. Unpleasant smile on his face as he handed it to her. She snatched it from him and read it, still standing. Then she sat stunned on the sofa. "No." She shook her head, refusing to believe it. "*No.*"

He sat next to her. Prim. "I know it's not very modern of me, but I feel sorry for the rabbit."

"It isn't possible."

"Quite possible," he replied. "Physiologically."

For a split second she couldn't answer. Then she turned on him. "You pig! You vile swine! You *did* this to me! You—"

"*I?*" He raised his eyebrows, laughing, unable to maintain his demure composure. "Marion, you know perfectly well when this happened. I was unconscious at the time. This, my dear, is fate, getting its own back—"

"*No!*" She dropped her face into her hands and began sobbing. Violently.

She had vowed it would never happen again. Never. The havoc it had wreaked on her body had been only a prelude to the havoc it had wreaked on her life. It had ruined her, and she had told herself she would do everything in her power to protect herself from letting it hurt her again. But now, just when she thought she was safe, it was starting over. She'd be doubly vulnerable. For years to come.

He put his arm around her as she continued to weep. "It won't be like before, darling. You'll be here. I'll take care of you."

There was something in his tone that made her look up. Catch the hint of malice in his eyes. "Oh God."

"I hope it's a girl," he continued in the same tone. "Sweetly docile, just like her mother."

She shook her head. Tears welling up again. "I can't do this, Jeffrey. I can't. I *can't.*"

"Nonsense." He smoothed her hair. "You're agitated. It's your condition. You're not yourself. Shall I buy you something to read? Pass the time? I believe Graham Greene has a new novel in print."

She narrowed her eyes at him. Anger replacing her despair. He was gloating. Not even troubling to hide it. She shook off his arm and stood. "I'm leaving. I'm going to Switzerland. I'll go under. You won't find me."

He burst out laughing. "In this state? I'll find you anywhere. One of my favorite snaps of you, you know—I keep it on my desk—is when you were hiding out in Dushanbe, seven months gone with John. Colleague took it as you were walking—very, very slowly—through the Monday market."

He wiped a tear from his eye, still chuckling. "And if I have any difficulty, I'll set Mrs. Bowen on the trail. You think she'll let you out of her sight once she finds out? She's got better skills than all of Maugham's people put together—and she will use manacles if necessary." He was still laughing, unable to stop himself.

She stared down at him. Watching him. Hating him. "Stop it," she finally said.

"Stop what?"

"Stop laughing."

He shook his head. His hand over his mouth. "Darling, I can't. It's too funny."

England, 1935-1936

London and Suffolk, England
October, 1935

FORTY-two years old and five months pregnant, Marion left the Chester Terrace house nominally to visit the chemist. She took a grateful breath of fresh air as she let the door, solid and hateful, shut behind her. Glanced across the street at the sodden leaves beginning to blanket the park. She was, she had decided, in need of something to alleviate her morning sickness.

In fact, her nausea had evaporated weeks before. But she had cultivated its appearance, even after it had gone, should an opportunity arise to evade the household's constant, oppressive, and maddeningly well-intentioned scrutiny. This morning, her chance had come. Taking advantage of a commotion in the kitchen, she had dressed quickly for the leaden autumn weather, made her way down the stairs—her training to silence still, if only just, counterbalancing her clumsy gait—and she had escaped the house.

She had told no one that she was leaving. But if they were waiting for her return, and insisted or asked, she'd be certain to bring back an innocuous package to present to them. Mint. Raspberry leaves. Some placebo. Women in her condition, as they'd told her more than once when she'd unsuccessfully sought solitude, get ideas into their heads.

Her idea now was to move herself to Soho. Two miles, and under ordinary circumstances, an undemanding walk. But now, reacting more violently than she had expected to the musty smell of the wet street, she wanted nothing more than to give herself over to her lethargy and return home. She hesitated in the midst of the crowd hurrying toward Oxford Circus. There was no need to take on a new project in her current state. No one could fault her for passivity. This one time.

Then, irritated by her momentary weakness, she collected herself and resumed walking. Tightened the belt of the polo coat she'd taken to wearing once she could no longer button her favorite tweed overcoat across her middle. When a few drops of mud splattered against her ankle and the hem of the shapeless dress she wore under the coat, she cursed the fact that she could also no longer fit into any of her trousers. But she didn't pause. She'd reach the shop in less than an hour if she kept up her pace. Staring at the pavement in front of her, she continued walking.

When she reached Great Windmill Street, she glanced at the façade of the Lyric Theatre. Then she let her gaze drop to her feet again before she made accidental eye contact with the men loitering outside of it. And, less than two minutes later, she arrived at her target: a grubby, resolutely disreputable storefront. Loud, jarring bell as she pushed through the door. Scent of dead mice on the disagreeably warm, dry air that hit her face as she entered.

When her eyes adjusted to the dim interior, she saw that a young man, frail and shy, sat behind the counter, half hidden behind an Edwardian till. He was organizing three-decade-old editions of *Photo Bits* by date, and he paid her no attention. Instead, bothered by the gaps he was finding in the sequence of the magazines, he ordered and reordered the display. Uninterested in the content. Engrossed.

Marion began to move toward him, but she halted, startled by a movement in a dark corner of the room. Then she relaxed and stifled a smile as a boy of eighteen or nineteen, having already noticed her presence in the shop, registered—horrified—her condition as well. He dropped the postcards of half-naked dancers he'd been perusing and fled to the street, activating the unpleasant bell again.

Once the door had swung shut, she moved with more confidence toward the counter. The young man, nervous now, but still obstinately sequencing *Photo Bits*, didn't acknowledge her. After waiting for a few seconds, running her fingertip over a display of innocuous, at least as far as she could tell, ink bottles, she spoke. "Hullo, Stephen."

He lifted his eyes, but directed his gaze over her shoulder. Then he reconsidered the till. "They said you couldn't come," he said to the counter.

His tone was accusatory. But she knew that he was annoyed more by the ambiguity of his instructions than by her, personally. "I had a spot of luck today. I'll return another time, if you don't yet have them ready—"

They both cringed as the bell clattered, and a man with his hat pulled low over his eyes, entered the shop. Upon noticing Marion, he flushed, turned on his heel, and retreated into the street. He'd scarcely crossed the threshold of the building.

Stephen reached under the counter. "No. They're ready—"

The bell over the door rang again. This time, a florid, heavyset, older man walked with confidence toward a short bookshelf to the side of the shop. He ignored the counter altogether and picked up a volume wrapped in brown paper. Unlike the others, he knew what he was seeking, and he was unmoved by Marion's anomalous presence.

Stephen placed an envelope on the counter and, still avoiding Marion's eyes, pushed it toward her. They jumped as the bell announced another customer. Two young men, encouraging one another, made their way, furtive, to a rack of postcards at the back of the room.

She took the envelope and secured it under her polo coat. Then she squinted, irritated, up at the bell. "How do you stand it?"

"Duty." There was a hint of self-mockery in his voice. Older than his twenty years.

She let herself smile and tried to catch his eye, but he'd returned to his careful organization of *Photo Bits*. "It would drive me mad," she said.

"I'm already mad." Same nearly imperceptible irony. "Degenerate."

"Stephen, don't—" She caught herself. "How's your sister?" she asked instead. Wanting to draw him into conversation, though she knew that doing so was unnecessary. Dangerous even.

He took so long to answer, that Marion thought he wasn't going to speak. As she was turning toward the door to leave, he rubbed his nose with the palm of his hand and looked over her shoulder again. "She's well. Sacrificing herself."

"Oh." Marion had turned back to the counter. She didn't know how to reply.

"I wish she'd stop," he said.

"Have you asked her?"

"Yes. I've asked her. But I'm mad. Degenerate. She doesn't listen. Comforts me instead. Keeps me afloat."

"Stephen," Marion repeated, "you're not mad."

"Sensitive—"

The bell above the door clattered again, and Marion clenched her fists. Stephen made a sound that might have been a groan. Then, almost making eye contact, they smiled.

"Fine," Marion said. "I'll give you sensitive." She paused. "Which has its uses as well as its torments."

"I wish she'd stop," he said in the same level, almost toneless voice. "She's unhappy. I want her happy. And I don't want her help."

Marion considered for a few seconds, staring down at the top of the counter. Then, shifting her attention to the ink bottles, she spoke again: "I think—" She stopped. "I think that some people become attached to their encumbrances. Even when they're imagined encumbrances." She pushed one of the ink bottles a fraction of an inch to the left. Nodded, satisfied. "Especially when they're imagined."

"I don't know what that means." Stephen had returned his attention to *Photo Bits*.

"Oh." Marion thought for a moment longer and then walked toward the door. She knew better than to try to explain to him.

When she reached it, she bent over and pulled a small stool into place just under the frame. Then, holding a protective hand over her belly, she climbed onto the stool, reached up, tore the bell off the wire, and threw it out into the street, where it was crushed by a passing automobile. Stepped down from the stool and moved it away from the door frame.

"Sorry," she said. "It was an accident."

Stephen peered up at the wire hanging loose from the ceiling. "You're a degenerate too." Surprised, but not unhappy about it.

"Sensitive," she corrected him. She started out toward the street, but then stopped herself again, remembering something. Turned back. "Do you know of a chemist nearby? I must buy some raspberry leaf tea."

THE low clouds had given way to a sharp drizzle by the time she returned to Chester Terrace. And once she had unlocked and pushed open the door, the brown paper bag holding her tea had begun to disintegrate. She set it, a sodden mess, on the console at the side of the entryway. Then she removed her dripping, ruined hat. Closed her eyes. Allowed herself to feel her fatigue.

"You could at least have found a taxi."

Taken aback, she opened her eyes and caught her reflection in the mirror above the console. Drenched hair plastered to her forehead. Drained, pale face. Shadows under her eyes. And, behind her, Jeffrey. Looking healthy, comfortable, and dry. He was wearing the same suit he had worn to the office that morning.

Too tired to be annoyed, she faced him. "I fancied a walk."

She heard movement on the spiral staircase and looked up. Mrs. Bowen was standing halfway down, sympathetic as well as embarrassed. She opened her mouth to say something, but Jeffrey spoke over her. "Thank you, Mrs. Bowen." Short. "That will be all. Lady Willcox will call if she needs anything."

Marion turned, astonished, back to Jeffrey. She'd never heard him speak to Mrs. Bowen with anything but measured good humor. And she certainly had never imagined that he'd take out whatever anger he felt at her escape from the house on his housekeeper. He knew better than to use her as a jailor.

Marion raised her eyes, apologetic, to the staircase. And although Mrs. Bowen was too professional to acknowledge the look, Marion knew she'd received the message. She nodded toward both Marion and Jeffrey, composed now, and retreated up the stairs.

When she had disappeared, Jeffrey returned his attention to Marion. "You fancied a walk."

"Yes." She wrapped her arms around her stomach.

"To Soho."

"Yes." Holding his eyes. Her own anger, despite the exhaustion, growing.

"For?"

She pointed at the sodden bag on the console. "Tea."

He flicked his eyes to the package and then back to her face. Didn't bother to respond to the obvious lie. After a moment, he stepped toward her. "May I help you with your coat?"

She sighed, unable to muster the energy to thwart him, and worked on the damp, knotted belt. Eventually, she loosened it and let Jeffrey take the coat from her. He caught the envelope as it fell to the floor and tossed the coat over a polished wooden chair positioned next to an umbrella stand.

Without speaking, he opened the envelope and extracted a sheaf of papers. Kept his expression blank as he examined each leaf in turn. Then he returned the papers to the envelope and looked back at Marion. "Circles. Page after page of circles."

"Yes." Terse. "May I have them back?"

"No."

He was about to say more, but before he could speak, she felt a drop in her blood pressure. She put a hand to the wall to steady herself, took a breath, and pushed her wet hair out of her face. Then she forced herself to look, as calmly as she could, at Jeffrey.

He held her eyes, tired as well. Then he ran a hand through his own hair. "Go upstairs, Marion. Get yourself warm and dry. Commiserate with Mrs. Bowen about your tyrannical husband. And, when you feel ready, we'll talk further." He waited for her to begin climbing the stairs. "I'll be waiting in my study," he said to her slowly retreating back.

When she reached her room, Mrs. Bowen was already filling the bathtub for her.

CIRCLES."

Jeffrey tapped his fingers, irritated, on the sheaf of papers. He'd organized them into a neat pile in front of him on his desk, and he was gazing across at Marion. She had changed into another shapeless frock, brushed her hair into a chignon, and reconciled herself to an evening of deflecting Jeffrey's curiosity. Now, sitting on a sofa across the room from him, holding a cup of lukewarm raspberry tea in her lap, she willed her sluggish mind to respond to his questioning. She sipped her tea and nodded.

"You walked for two hours in the cold and rain for circles." He rested his hand, flat, on the pages.

"Yes."

"They're very precise."

"He uses a compass."

"He?" Jeffrey stood, walked to the other side of the room, and drew the curtains over the tall windows. Night had already fallen.

She swallowed more tea and spoke again. "Stephen. My friend." She didn't trouble to turn and face him. She could hear the rain spattering against the glass outside.

"This would be the Stephen whose sister and brother-in-law, from what my people have just told me, sell smutty photographs of dancers and prostitutes in Soho?" His voice was mild.

"I don't know his sister or brother-in-law."

"Marion, whatever project you've agreed to take on, you can drop it. I won't have you endangering yourself or the—"

"No. No, you stop right there." She stood and turned on him, still holding her tea. "You will *not* use my—my situation—as an excuse to doubt my—"

"Would you rather I accepted your story at face value?" He took a few steps toward her, angry now. "Fair enough. Far be it from me to doubt your word. You're not working. You have no orders. Instead, you've lost your reason completely, and you've chosen to spend your afternoons walking to Soho because you've come over curious about what the Windmill Girls are up to. And then, obviously, you popped in on your friend Stephen with the circles as a social call."

He paused, glaring at her. "Shall we consult Dr. Chapman about appropriate measures to take in the face of this now truly worrisome collection of symptoms? Take his advice on how best to keep you and the baby safe? As you know very well, he's already confided to me several concerns about your emotional state. The strain, you know. Your age." Snide. "And type."

When she didn't reply, he continued across the room to stand in front of her. He put his hands on her shoulders and looked down into her face. "No assassinations until after the baby is born, Marion. No treason. Leave the Empire alone for a few months. Understood?"

She scowled up at him. "I—"

"You haven't the time for a new project anyway." He let his hands drop from her shoulders and pushed them into his trouser pockets. "We're leaving London tomorrow. Unhealthy atmosphere in the city just now."

Shaken by his abrupt announcement, her anger evaporated. More frightened than enraged, she sat back down on the sofa. Looked up at him. "But—" Stopped. "Where?"

"I must admit," he said. "After this most recent exploit, I was tempted to stage your confinement in Caithness. Especially now that you're unlikely to fit through any of the arrowslits in my tower."

"But—"

"But it's cold there in the autumn. And my conscience would bother me, inflicting that sort of environment on Gardiner and Trelawney."

"*Where?*" Her anger mounting again.

"We'll stay with Ginnie and Teddy in Suffolk."

She considered for a few seconds. Then she nodded. "Fine."

He laughed, affectionate despite his irritation. "You'll tell your people to send the courier there instead."

She held his eyes and didn't respond.

"Of course you will." He walked back around the desk and sat. Rested his chin in his hands, looking across at her. "Very well, Marion. I can't keep you from contacting them. And I certainly can't keep them from tracking your movements. But I do have your circles now, whatever they're worth. And when the next bit of material comes to you, I'll collect that as well. Along with each scrap of paper that follows. I know your methods now. I know the terrain. And you're far from agile at the moment. So, go ahead and alert them that I'm on to you. Every piece of information that reaches you, reaches me as well. And then gets put somewhere safe, out of harm's way."

He leaned back in the chair and crossed his arms. "I'll look forward to examining what will likely be a series of valuable contributions to the Museum and Library."

She set her tea, now cold, on a table to the side of the sofa and stood. "Is that all?"

"Yes dear, that's all." He stood too, walked around the desk, and kissed her cheek. "Sleep well. We have an early train tomorrow."

VIRGINIA and Teddy were standing in front of the ancient oak door of the house, waiting for them. As their car from the station passed through the avenue of yew trees to glide to a stop in the circular drive, Marion noted that they both appeared pleased rather than inconvenienced by their arrival. And after Jeffrey had unnecessarily helped her from her seat, Virginia stepped forward and smiled at her with genuine warmth.

Disconcerted as she always was by the age of the house, its illogical plan, and its profusion of chimneys, she was grateful for her stabilizing calm. She threw a shy smile at Teddy, reassuringly unkempt in his wool cardigan, as they all left the chill of the October afternoon for the warm entry hall. Of the various places Jeffrey could have chosen for, as he liked to put it, her confinement, Suffolk was the least demoralizing. And she could work here. Easily. Perhaps even more easily than in London.

When they'd removed their coats, Marion cast a worried look over the familiar, if still grotesque, carved ceiling of the entrance—avoiding the malicious looking Green Man hidden behind the beam. There was now a small bundle of straw and acorns hanging beside him. She had no interest in whatever arcane family reason they had for the addition to the ceiling. But she also couldn't stop staring.

Rapt, she scarcely noticed as Virginia—tall, graceful, and wearing a tailored skirt that made Marion feel her own shapelessness more keenly—turned to Jeffrey. "Shall I have a room made up for Ian as well?" Lightly mocking.

"The boy's at school, Ginnie." Jeffrey gave Virginia a brotherly kiss on the cheek.

"Hmm." Virginia examined her manicured fingernails. "At school in our stables? Like the last time?"

"The last time, his escape was encouraged and abetted from the outside." Jeffrey put his arm around Marion's shoulders, startling her out of her uneasy observation of the room. "This term, his co-conspirator is considerably less active. He knows better than to take on Temple Grove's security alone, now that his mother can no longer move nimbly enough to divert their attention." Feeling Marion stiffen under his arm, he smiled more broadly. "Who knows? Perhaps he'll complete a full year this time around."

Virginia exchanged a quick, sympathetic look with Marion before returning her attention, still delicately malignant, to Jeffrey. "Nonetheless, Jeffie, I'll ask Charlotte and Anne to keep watch for him. They've missed their wayward cousin. And we don't want him spooking the horses, do we?"

"Ah, Ginnie." Jeffrey let his arm fall from Marion's shoulders. "You make it a joy to return home." He turned to Teddy, who had been busying himself with their coats, studiously uninterested in the exchange. Now, sensing a shift in the atmosphere he tactfully reinserted himself into the conversation. "You look well, Teddy."

"As do you Jeffrey." Teddy put his hands into the pockets of his cardigan. "I hope you like beetroot. We've produced more than we expected this year. And if we don't lift them now, the slugs will be at them."

"No sprouts?"

Teddy grinned at him, walking him toward the stairs that led to their bedroom, as Virginia and Marion followed. "Sprouts too. Goes without saying."

At the base of the stairway, Virginia kissed Marion's cheek. "We're pleased that you're both here, Marion. Settle in, and we'll talk further during dinner, yes?"

Marion nodded and let Jeffrey help her, once more unnecessarily, up the long staircase. She just managed to keep from shrugging off his arm.

THEIR customary room, still off-putting to Marion in its self-satisfied Elizabethan abundance, was nonetheless restful over the next few days. And unenthusiastic as she had initially been about the idea of an unusually large harvest of beetroot and brussels sprouts, she found herself eating ravenously, uncertain as to whether her appetite was prompted by the food itself or by her condition. Her irrational craving for radishes—also easily procured, without comment, in a way that would have been impossible in London—she grudgingly acknowledged to be the result of her pregnancy. She refused to return Jeffrey's expressive look as they appeared, sliced and undressed, beside her plate at every meal.

She also refused to confront him with the palpable fact that he was keeping her under acute surveillance both inside and outside the house. He rarely forced his company on her as she wandered the grounds in the brittle autumn air. But whereas Teddy and Virginia were scrupulous about preserving her privacy, Jeffrey made clear, via sardonic and often invasive questioning, that he knew precisely how and where she had spent her days.

He needn't have belabored the point; she could feel his people on her even in the emptiest and most abandoned of fields or woods. After three days, she was chafing at his overbearing presence, at a loss as to how she would take her next step. And once a week had passed, she came to the glum conclusion that she had either to move forward, evading Jeffrey's scrutiny, or abandon her project altogether. His invisible observers had become more than a nuisance. At this point, given their increasingly close interest in her movements, the only safe time to cross her contact or retrieve instructions would be after dark. Soon it would be too late even for that.

At least she had insisted that he occupy a different bedroom throughout the remainder of her pregnancy.

AND so, on the last Thursday of the month, under a thin, white crescent of a waxing moon, she prepared to go to work. The family had dispersed early for the night, and Marion had followed, changing into a nightdress and slipping under her blankets. Once in bed, she remained still, trying to relax, until she heard the muffled sound of the clock downstairs chime midnight. Then, pleased to be moving, she sat up, pushed the heavy, embroidered blankets off her legs, and eased herself out of bed. The embers from the fire that had heated her room earlier in the evening threw a reddish glow over the furniture—more than enough to see.

Catching a glimpse of herself in a mirror on the other side of the room, she stifled an irritated oath. She could see too well. Her white nightdress shone like a beacon in the dim light, and the only outdoor coat that now fit her was equally bright. An ivory wool cape. Even under the small sliver of moon, she'd be absurdly visible.

Swearing more audibly, she walked to the wardrobe next to the mirror and felt inside for something—anything—that would keep her both hidden and warm. She had remembered seeing clothing from earlier occupants of the house hanging behind that which she and Jeffrey had brought from London. There must be something that would cover her. She leaned further in, running her fingers over the closely packed fabric.

Eventually, and keenly aware of the passing time, she pulled out a hooded, dark blue, velvet cloak that smelt of thirty-year-old Edwardian dissipation. Black braided cords hung from the edge of the hood. It would do, although she'd never have chosen it herself. A touch embarrassed, she wrapped it over her nightdress and then pulled on a pair of waterproof boots.

When she stood and drew the hood up over her hair, she saw that the cloak was meant for a shorter woman. At least five inches of white showed beneath its hem. It was also, however, made for a wider woman than she ordinarily was, covering her bulging stomach more than adequately. In a hurry at this point, she simply noted that the ghostly reflection in the mirror looked more confused than romantic, and then slipped from the room.

The corridor was black, but Marion was used to its contours, and she made her way to the stairway and front door without mishap. Squeezing through the door, she kept close to the wall of the house before orienting herself toward the churchyard. There was, she noted, frost in the air for the first time that autumn. Then, dismissing the sharp wind that hit her as she left the protected lee of the house, she concentrated on her objective.

The church and graveyard, where she'd cross her contact, were a half mile from the house, separated by a stretch of barren scrub, occasionally overgrown by what were now damp, rotting brambles. A smell of the sea, a few miles to the east, also permeated the open area. Not being religious, Virginia and Teddy maintained the church because doing so was their family's responsibility. But the footpath leading in its direction had disappeared years earlier, and the walk was far from easy. Marion didn't mind. Bent over against the wind, her hand across her belly, she counted on the inhospitable terrain to put off Jeffrey's people. She herself felt exhilarated.

Her high spirits dampened when she approached the gate surrounding the burial-ground. She knew from previous observation that it was unlocked—perhaps not cable of being locked. And she almost managed to summon up her earlier, daylit ironic response to the twisted yew tree and bent, stunted cypresses that overshadowed the graves themselves. But somehow, what had been disarmingly trite during the day had become forbidding and hostile under the bleak, October night sky. She shivered as a gust of wind whistled through the scrub and hit her, forcefully, in the back. Then she took a determined breath and pushed through the gate.

The interior felt darker, even, than the black waste outside. And she stood still for a few seconds, letting her eyes adjust to the nearly absent light cast over the scattered stones and monuments, tilting at haphazard angles throughout the grounds. Then, reassured, she focused on a white marble vault—"Willcox" engraved across the top—placed at their center. Took a few tentative steps toward it, and then stopped, startled, when something disturbed the dry leaves behind her.

She felt the air, quiet and receptive. But when the sound didn't recur, she chided herself for her nerves and walked with more confidence in the direction of the tomb. Wrinkling her forehead, she peered at its façade. Someone had wiped away a few inches of grime from a spray of sculpted oak leaves at its top left corner.

Smiling to herself, she stood on her toes and reached behind the sculpture. This was her target. The grime had been smeared away deliberately. Unable to see the area, however, and in no condition to climb the façade, she used her fingertips, blindly, to search the cavity. When she failed to encounter any papers or package, she grunted in frustration and stretched her arm further back, her stomach now pressed hard against the cold marble.

Finally, just as she felt she couldn't hold her position any longer, her fingers brushed something other than wet stone. She grabbed the object. But what she was holding wasn't papers or anything resembling instructions; it was a damp female hand. Which squeezed her own fingers in turn.

Without thinking about the consequences, she cried out, pulled back her arm, and toppled onto the frost-hardened ground. Put her other hand over her mouth and backed further up against a stone cross half buried in the dirt. Her mind racing. Paralyzed.

"Dr. Bailey." A lithe figure, wearing sensible black winter clothing, leapt silently, efficiently from the top of the stone. "Forgive me, Dr. Bailey. I had to be certain it was you."

Marion stared up at the woman approaching her. Her heart was hammering in her chest. "I—?"

"Your ring."

Marion looked hectically down at her finger.

The woman offered Marion her hand and pulled her into a standing position. "Are you all right?" When Marion nodded, still breathless, she continued whispering. "I couldn't leave the material. His people would have lifted it. The place is flooded." She handed Marion a package, which Marion secured under her cloak.

"I was expecting Robert." Her heart still hadn't settled.

"Robert's dead." The woman cast a practiced glance about the churchyard before continuing. "The Germans picked him up outside the museum in Dresden. But he dropped your material for us before they got to him."

"Oh." Unconsciously hugging her belly again.

"He didn't have time to take his capsule." The woman's voice was unemotional.

"Oh."

"They kept him alive for eighteen hours before he provoked them into ending it."

"Oh." She felt ill, fingering the papers under her cloak. She didn't know what else to say.

"So you must work quickly," the woman prodded as she edged backward toward the wall. "Robert was good, but they'll have extracted at least some of the story from him. Eighteen hours. It was too long."

"Wait." Marion took a step toward the woman's retreating figure. "I won't be able to keep these papers from my husband. He already has Stephen's calculations. And I'm not—" She stopped. "In my condition, I can't do what—what I ordinarily—" Faltered again.

"The remainder of the material will be sent via the usual channels." Businesslike. "They've asked me to thank you. There's some urgency involved, as you know, and you're the acknowledged expert in these matters. They'd like you to locate and analyze the target quickly."

"But if he appropriates everything that you send—"

"You'll retrieve it from him." There was now a subdued smile in her voice. "From what I understand, you always have."

"It's different now—"

Before she could finish her sentence, a shot ripped through the air, and a bullet hit a second headstone, newer, less than six inches away from the woman's leg.

"Shite." Looking down, more surprised than shocked. Sounding suddenly Irish. Then, without another word, she disappeared, still supple and graceful, over the church wall.

Marion, with fewer options, took three uncertain steps toward the gate. When she saw Jeffrey, wearing the trench coat she associated with his worst moods, giving orders to Nick Trelawney and Arthur Gardiner, she stopped. Cursing, she turned back to the wall and looked for a way up and over.

Behind her, she heard Jeffrey saying to Gardiner, "track her, find her, and bring her back to the house. Shoot if you must, but don't kill her."

"Yes, sir." Gardiner melted back into the scrub.

As Jeffrey and Nick made their way further into the burial ground, Marion held her breath and pulled herself up onto a square stone marker just under the wall. She had a small hope that she could find a handhold that would support the short climb to the top. But the stone, ancient, crumbling, and unable to bear her weight, broke in half, and she fell hard on her ankle. She kept from crying out, but her cloak flew open, and the white nightdress made her position excruciatingly obvious.

"Oh, for God's sake." Jeffrey stalked over to the marker, followed by Nick, who looked uncertain. Jeffrey peered down at her. "Is there a reason for Aunt Euphemia's cloak? Or did you simply feel it worked with the atmosphere?"

She felt herself coloring, but she didn't speak. Instead, she tried to stand. But when she felt the pain rip up her leg from her ankle, she gasped and began to topple over again.

Jeffrey threw out his arm to steady her and then turned to Nick. "Would you go to the house and tell Teddy to call a doctor? Marion's had herself an adventure this evening."

"I'm fine." She pushed away Jeffrey's arm.

"I think I can carry her back." He was still speaking to Nick, holding her upright.

"Yes, sir." Nick looked quickly at Marion, blushed, and strode back through the gate.

"I'm fine." She repeated, darkly, once Nick had disappeared.

"You aren't fine. You can't walk."

"I can walk."

Jeffrey stood back. "All right then, Marion. Walk."

Unprepared for his sudden movement, she stepped hard on her hurt foot, cried out, and crumpled to the ground. Then, to her mortification, she began weeping.

Jeffrey looked down at her for a few seconds, on the verge of what seemed to be laughter. Then, collecting himself, he gave a short sigh, squatted in front of her, and opened the cloak. "Since you're down here, we may as well take care of business."

He felt about the lining of the cloak, fastidiously avoiding her skin or her nightdress, until he found the package. Pulling it out, he stood, secured it inside his trench coat, and then watched her, still crying, for a second or two longer. Finally, taking another breath, he leaned over and picked her up off the ground, one arm under her knees, the other under her shoulders, the cloak now billowing out behind them.

As he passed the church gates, he was laughing again. "If you'd known Aunt Euphemia, Marion, you'd realize how comic this situation is." When she didn't reply he continued, still entertained. "And really, I ought to thank you." He gazed up at the clouds skidding over the thin moon and at the icy wind whipping up the scrub. "For the first time, ever, I feel myself a proper baronet. Until now, the title never quite sat right."

He considered for a minute or two as he pushed through the rotting brambles. "But I must say, I firmly believe now that we baronets, as a class, have been sorely misrepresented. Here I am, the victim of circumstance, carrying an incapacitated woman in a delicate condition and a flimsy white dress, weeping, against her will, to an isolated country house on All Hallows Eve. Anyone seeing us would think that I was bringing some devious and ignoble intrigue to its dastardly conclusion. Yet I certainly never imagined my evening would develop in this way. I was looking forward to a bit of reading, a cigarette, and a good night's sleep. And so, I repeat, we've been maligned. An entirely unjust situation."

He looked down at her again. "You did know that it was Halloween, dear, didn't you?"

"Fuck you, Jeffrey." Her voice was muffled against his sleeve.

"Oh, for heaven's sake." He was laughing more audibly now. "What did you expect, Marion, disturbing my ancestors? There's always a price to pay for that sort of thing. You know there is."

She refused to say any more to him.

*W*HEN they reached the house, it was close to three in the morning, the moon had set, and the countryside was silent. The ground floor of the building, however, was brightly lit. And when Jeffrey carried Marion into the music room—ignoring her insistence that she could now limp perfectly well on her own—it was crowded.

Nick, wearing the dark jumper and corduroy trousers he had worn in the burial ground, was curled up in an armchair, drinking a cup of cocoa. Teddy, in a worn green cashmere dressing gown over pyjamas, was sitting at the piano, picking out a Chopin nocturn with one hand. Virginia, in a dark blue silk kimono with peonies embroidered at the hem, was smoking a cigarette next to him on the bench. And there was also a man Marion took to be the doctor, professionally dressed but quite obviously recently out of bed, pacing the room.

Jeffrey crossed the room and lowered Marion lengthwise onto a sofa, adjusting a pillow under her head. She immediately sat up, humiliated, and turned to Virginia and Teddy. But before she could speak, Virginia smiled at her, half delighted, half apologetic. "Oh, Marion. You've found Aunt Euphemia's cloak."

Marion felt herself coloring violently. She had never been so ashamed. "I'm so very, very sorry about this," she said to Virginia. Then, glancing over at the doctor as well: "you needn't have concerned yourselves. I thought I could—" She paused. "I thought I could do with some night air. But I'm not at my best now, and—and—"

"And you had no other option. Under the circumstances." Virginia, her voice still light, but now also softly dangerous, was looking at Jeffrey, rather than at Marion.

Marion, confused by the shift in Virginia's tone, didn't answer. Instead, she looked, bewildered, over at Jeffrey as well. He was removing his trench coat and rolling back his shoulders to stretch them after his exertion. The clothing he wore underneath was similar to Nick's. As he draped the coat over a polished, carved chair, the corner of his mouth went down in a provocative smile, and he held Virginia's look. Equally playful and equally dangerous. "Marion tried to break into the family vault."

Virginia rose abruptly from the piano bench, left her cigarette in an ashtray, crossed the room, and gathered his coat off the chair. "It's staining the finish. I'll hang it up."

"Really, Ginnie." Jeffrey had sprawled out in an armchair near Nick's. "There are eight more of them in the house somewhere or other. Don't you think we ought to see to Marion's ankle first?"

"Dr. Gaunt." Virginia smiled sweetly as she left the music room, ignoring Jeffrey. "Would you? Now that we've dragged you out of bed, perhaps it might be best—?"

The doctor, coming to himself, nodded and approached Marion. As he removed her boot and felt her ankle, Marion glanced back at Virginia in the next room. And it was only her years of training that kept her from staring as she saw Virginia, through a gap in the door, deftly lift the papers from the inside pocket of Jeffrey's trench coat and slip them under a pile of Teddy's sheet music before hanging the coat itself on a hook to dry.

Jeffrey was busy lighting his own cigarette and hadn't noticed. Nick's view of the next room was blocked by a music stand. And Teddy, who had seen everything, hadn't interrupted his lazy Chopin. When Virginia returned to the music room and sat next to him on the piano bench, he turned to her and kissed her hair. Not missing a beat.

"You were lucky, Lady Willcox." The doctor rose to his feet and brushed down his trousers, also unaware of what had transpired as he'd felt the bones of her ankle. "It's a mild sprain. You'll feel completely recovered in two or three weeks. In the meantime, keep off of it as much as you can. I'd recommend a comfrey compress and perhaps some tea, but in your condition, it may not be advisable."

Marion smiled up at him. "My mother used to give me comfrey when I'd had a tumble."

"Intelligent woman." He snapped his medical bag closed. "I can't imagine it would do any harm. But it's best to be cautious."

"I understand, doctor."

"Would you care for a whiskey before you set off, Edward?" Teddy had stopped playing and was moving around the piano toward the doctor.

"Not this time, Teddy. They'll be missing me at home."

"Fair enough." Teddy walked the doctor through the door, discussing recent changes in the weather and the remainder of the harvest.

Once they were safely out of the room, Virginia stood as well. "Jeffie, darling, don't you think you ought to help Marion back to bed? It's close to dawn, and she'll want to sleep."

After a suspicious silence, Jeffrey crushed out his cigarette. Then he rose from his chair, made brief eye contact with Nick, and walked to Marion. "Shall I carry you?"

"I could use an arm," she said, understanding that Virginia had a reason for wanting Jeffrey upstairs.

"Hmm." Cold. "All right, Marion. Let's take Ginnie's advice, then. She always knows best."

He didn't speak to her as he helped her up the stairs and into bed. And after a quick kiss, he left her alone. No gloating. Which left Marion more nervous than she had been throughout the entire ordeal of the evening.

*W*HEN she woke the next morning, earlier than she had expected, she tried, against the doctor's advice, to move about on her own. Pushing off her covers, she sat up and lowered both of her bare feet to the silk carpet under the bed. As she stood, she felt a dull pain in her foot and leg, but it was less severe than it had been the night before. Gratified, she limped to the wardrobe, pushed her feet into slippers, and wrapped a dressing gown over her nightdress.

After using the toilet, she hobbled out the door and down the stairs to the dining room. Ordinarily, breakfast was waiting on a sideboard for the family as they woke at different times and descended to the ground floor. When she reached the dining room this morning, however, the door was closed, and Teddy—wearing the same green dressing gown he'd worn the night before—was sitting on a cushioned window seat across from it. He was drinking a cup of coffee.

When he saw Marion, he brightened and gestured her to the seat beside him. "I'd do the same in your situation," he said. "Doctors' orders are made to be broken, aren't they?"

She smiled and sat next to him. "I'd lose my mind if I spent any more time in bed."

"I'll bring you a cup of coffee if you'd—"

He was interrupted by raised voices behind the door to the dining room. "I won't ask you again, Ginnie. Where *are* they?"

"Ask me a million times over, you little brat, it'll do you no good. I won't tell you."

"You won't leave this room until you do—"

There was a loud crash and the sound of a chair toppling over. "Let *go.*"

"I've told you, you aren't going anywhere until—"

Marion looked, astonished, at Teddy. He rubbed his cheek. "It used to make me jealous, if you can believe it."

"That can't be Virginia and—" She faltered, in disbelief.

"She's so calm otherwise." Teddy sipped his coffee. "Jeffrey's the only one who can whip her into this state. Even George—" He paused and looked at her. "Have you met George? Their older brother?"

"No," she said. "I—I'm a bit—disreputable. I think."

Teddy laughed. "Who isn't?"

"I mean—"

"I know what you mean. And I meant what I said." He leaned against the side of the window seat. "Who isn't disreputable in this world? Well—except for George, perhaps. George is respectability incarnate. He's ten years older than Jeffrey. Eight years older than Ginnie. And scarcely human. A 'confirmed bachelor' I think they call it. The family never quite knew what to do with him."

She frowned across at the door. "You knew the family well?"

"We're neighbors," he said. "I've adored Ginnie for as long as I can remember. It took her some time to notice, of course." He smiled to himself for a few seconds, then looked back at Marion. "Jeffrey was considered something of a local catch as well, you know. But, despite that, no one was surprised when he turned up with you."

She blushed. "Our marriage isn't—" She paused again, searching for the right words. "It isn't regular, Teddy. He and I—we—"

He laughed. "Once again, Marion. Whose is? Especially in this family."

She was about to reply, when the door to the dining room shook as though something—or someone—had fallen against it. "You will lose this baby, not to mention your wife, if you continue to push her like this." Virginia's voice was vicious. "It isn't a game, Jeffie. Leave her alone."

"I think I can gauge her resilience a little bit better than you can. After all, I'm her husband. Not you. You just want her for—"

"For God's sake, Jeffie. Let her do her work. Is your pitiful career so important to you that you're willing to risk—"

"Oh, do shut up, Ginnie." Jeffrey was shouting. Marion had never heard him so incensed. "And stop flaunting the altruism. You've no audience now. Except for me, of course, and I know perfectly well that your motives are as—*professional*—as mine are. More so. It would do you nothing but good to have her move forward with this initiative she's started."

"It would do *her* nothing but good to—"

"*Where* are the papers you lifted, Ginnie? I'm warning you. You will regret it if—" There was another loud crash, and the sound of what might have been running, before another chair toppled.

Marion cringed and stood. "Do they know we can hear them?"

Teddy, who had finished his cup of coffee, set the cup and saucer on the window seat and stood as well. "I don't think they care. Old family. A trifle mad." He adjusted the belt of his dressing gown. "This could go on for hours. May I take you to the kitchen for some breakfast?"

He held out his arm, and she took it, hobbling beside him down the corridor. As they descended into the kitchen, she looked up at him. "Will he get the material from her, do you think?"

"Sometimes he does, sometimes he doesn't." Teddy shrugged. "I've found that it rarely makes any difference."

"Hmm."

Marion hoped they had fresh apples in the kitchen. She'd been enjoying the end of the harvest.

*A*FTER a companionable morning outdoors with Teddy, Marion decided that she did want to rest for a few hours. Her ankle was bothering her more than it had earlier on, and she was feeling the edges of the buzzing headache that had afflicted her periodically since the second month of her pregnancy. Once she'd taken leave of Teddy, she made her way into the house.

Climbing the stairs to her first-floor bedroom, she paused at a small painting she hadn't noticed before: a pleased looking Jacobean magistrate who bore more than a passing resemblance to Virginia and Jeffrey. He was seated before the backdrop of a weakly discernible woman being burned alive. He had also recently finished a meal of wine, pears, and venison. Old family, Marion reminded herself as she continued up the stairs. Mad.

When she entered her room, Jeffrey was waiting for her, sitting in one of the scrolled armchairs that flanked the fireplace. He'd had a fire lit, and the room was warm. Despite her displeasure at seeing him there, she wasn't surprised. Expecting him to seek her out after the conversation she'd overheard in the dining room. Stifling a sigh, she walked to the second armchair and lowered herself into it.

"Do you have them?" he asked without preamble. "Did she give them to you?"

"No."

"You'll tell me if she does?"

"Of course not." She looked at him, bewildered.

"She is not a friend to your organization, Marion."

"Neither are you."

"I do, though, have a personal interest in your well-being. Selfish though that interest may be." He stood, selected a cigarette from a box on the mantle, lit it with a match, and sat again. Tossed the match into the fire. "She hasn't."

Marion felt her headache reassert itself, and she pressed her fists against her eyes. Without moving them, she spoke again. "Jeffrey, the last time I gave birth, I was alone, with a midwife, in Isfahan. After that, I spent two years, still alone, travelling with Ian through Iran and Turkey. Protecting my son. I do not need your personal interest."

"No, darling." He took a drag of his cigarette. "No, you're incorrect. The last time you gave birth, you were indeed in Isfahan. But make no mistake: you weren't alone. You were as closely monitored then as you are now."

She dropped her hands from her eyes and stared at the fire. "Would you please just tell me what you want?"

"I want you to drop this project. It's dangerous. There's more to it than you're aware of, and—forgive the ungentlemanly remark—you're not in your best form at the moment." He stood once more, found an ashtray on the mantle, and tapped ash off the end of the cigarette. "You'll get hurt. And I don't like you hurt when you can't fight back. It's no fun."

"How do *you* know there's more to it than I'm aware of?" She pushed herself up out of the chair and scowled at him. "If you're trying to trick me into telling you something, it won't work."

"You're not the only one with organizational backing, Marion. And if your mind were working as it ought to be, you'd know that." He gazed at the burning tip of the cigarette and then back at her. "And do give the office a bit of credit for moderately competent information gathering. It's true, we're not the millennium-old cabal to which you've attached yourself. But we are capable of overhearing a bit of gossip here and there. From Turkey. Iran." He paused. "Germany."

"Germany," she repeated, stupidly.

"Hmm." He inhaled more of his cigarette and exhaled slowly. "The Germans would like nothing better than to collect someone like you just now. An opportunity to test some new techniques." He ground out his cigarette in the ashtray. "I would like that not to happen."

"You can't scare me away from this."

"Yes, dear. You've made that quite clear." He leaned against the side of the mantle and crossed his arms. "Would logic work, I wonder? Unlikely, I realize, but I've exhausted every other channel, and I'm finding myself feeling desperate." He lifted his chin. "So, let's try logic, shall we?"

She frowned and limped without speaking to the window overlooking the yew avenue and the drive. Kept her back to him. Willing him to leave.

"Here is the situation as I see it. From a position of pure, rational objectivity." He hadn't moved from the mantle. "Your people, my people, and the Germans are all, at present, racing after something. It's unclear what that something is, but I'm guessing that it's of more than simple historical significance."

He paused, waiting for her to reply. When she didn't, he pressed on. "But things have become complicated recently, not least of which because both your people and my people have tapped you as a resource. Which, obviously, is awkward." He ran his hand through his hair. "Your people, as usual, are relying on your demented loyalty to whatever cause it is they claim to be serving to keep you moving forward. Fair and reasonable. And my people—" He faltered again. "Well, ordinarily my people would rely on me to guide you in the proper direction. As your handler."

She made an irritated movement, but she didn't bother to contradict him. She felt too tired.

He resumed speaking. "Strange to say, however, I've been balking—terribly unlike me— which has thrown a spanner into the works. And my people are consequently off to a slow start." The corner of his mouth went down. "Not as slow as the Germans, granted. From what we can tell, they've been attempting to run your dead colleague. Typical German strategy. Bizarre."

When he paused again, waiting for a rejoinder, she remained silent. She had nothing to say. In fact, as he had been speaking, she'd been only half listening, staring through the glass at the yews, watching but not registering the approach of an incongruous, shuddering, five-year-old Austin 7, wheezing to a halt in the drive. Flaking black and red paint.

Wanting to put off responding to Jeffrey's conversation as long as possible, she continued watching, only half focusing on the action, as a tall, fit driver emerged and then stood to the side to allow a passenger to climb, clumsily, out of the back seat. When she saw the passenger—short, round, flustered, and wearing an ulster coat from the previous century—she gasped. Forgetting everything he had said to her, she turned on Jeffrey with blind rage.

"You bastard!" She felt her heart jump once and start racing unhealthily, but she didn't care. "You pig! So you don't want me exerting myself? You want to protect the baby? Then why did you drag that—that obscene lunatic into this? How dare you? How *dare* you?"

Jeffrey blinked at her, astonished. Then, suspicion flickering over his features, he crossed the room in four strides and stood at the window, looking down. After a few further seconds of disbelief, he laughed quietly. "That bitch."

"What are you talking about?"

"Ginnie sent for him."

"You're lying. Virginia hates him."

He was still smiling down at the figure approaching the door. "Bureaucratic infighting," he said. "Worse than hate. But in this one case, they're on the same side." He turned back to her, his smile now lopsided. "Your side."

"My—?" She stared at him, uncomprehending.

"Yes, darling." There was a hint of anger under his tone now. "You want to complete your project then, do you? You want your papers and your manuscripts?" He paused, still angry. "Well, I congratulate you. You've got your wish." He laughed in disgust. "And I give up. I can't fight you all."

When she merely gaped at him, his demeanor changed, the professional mask slipping over his features. Then he grabbed her upper arm, spinning her toward the door. "So, let's go to work, dear, shall we? Perhaps I'll begin applying pressure by withholding the radishes? Proceed from there?"

She shrugged off his hand and held her ground. "I will not speak to that—that—"

"Of course you will." He took her arm again and began walking her out of the room. "How else will you access the remainder of your material? What do you think your superiors expected you to do?"

"No!" She wrenched her arm away, but before she could stop herself, she stumbled onto her hurt ankle and crumpled again.

Jeffrey caught her before she hit the floor, but she was breathing too hard to balance immediately. He held her for a minute until her breathing regulated. Then looked down into her face. "Shall I carry you?"

"Leave me alone."

"Too late for that now, I'm afraid. Perhaps next time you'll listen to reason." He let her lean against him as they made their way to the stairs.

BY the time they had descended into the entry hall, the visitor had wrestled his befuddled way out of his coat, removed his hat, and was gazing up at the carving that covered the ceiling. He appeared to have an affinity with the Green Man. Smiling up at it, delighted. Wearing maroon plus fours and a matching belted jacket with a hint of a bright pink silk lining.

Virginia, who was closing the door, a grim look on her face, turned to Jeffrey and Marion once they had reached the bottom of the stairs. Ignoring Jeffrey, she spoke to Marion: "forgive me for taking the initiative, Marion, but I do believe this is the lesser of two evils." She laughed quietly, echoing Jeffrey's earlier tone. "By the smallest of margins, of course. You'll let me know whether things become unmanageable?"

Marion swallowed and nodded. She didn't trust her voice.

"I'll leave you to reacquaint yourselves then." Without troubling to acknowledge Jeffrey or her visitor, she passed them and walked back up the stairs.

"Maugham." Jeffrey nodded at him. "I trust your drive was comfortable."

"More than comfortable, dear boy." Maugham was beaming at him. "Invigorating. We lost the heater manifold halfway here. Reminded me of the old days. Should have brought a hot brick." He wrinkled his bald forehead and considered the now empty staircase. "I wouldn't say no to a warm Atholl Brose, but my hostess appears to have absented herself. Odd given her eagerness to have me here. Couldn't leave London quickly enough for her."

"There are coffee and brandy in the library," Jeffrey said, gesturing toward the hall. "I hope that will suffice."

"I suppose it must," Maugham replied, grunting, and walking in the direction of the library. When Marion and Jeffrey didn't match his pace, he paused and looked back. "Dr. Bailey! Forgive me. I ought to have paid my respects before. I understand that we're to expect an interesting event sometime soon. My congratulations to you and your family."

He peered at her foot as she limped painfully down the corridor, leaning on Jeffrey. "Strange symptom, that. Not that I'm an expert of course. But have you considered consulting a physician?"

"Marion fell off a gravestone," Jeffrey said to him, his voice bland.

"Ah." Maugham turned back to the library. "That would explain it. Say no more."

A fire had been lit in the library as well, and they arranged themselves in front of the hearth, Jeffrey and Marion on a tapestry sofa, Maugham in an armchair to the side. As Jeffrey busied himself at an end table pouring coffee and brandy into two glasses, looking a question at Marion, who shook her head, Maugham began chatting again. "And how is your boy? Still at large?"

"He turned up in Yemen," Jeffrey said, handing Maugham his glass. "Just as you predicted. He's at school now."

"Excellent. Glad to have assisted in the matter." Maugham took a sip of his coffee and leaned back, corpulent and satisfied, in his chair. In no mood to help the conversation further.

Marion was looking down at her hands folded in her lap, straining to keep from shouting or throwing something.

After a long minute of tense silence, Jeffrey sighed and spoke. "You have an assignment for me?"

"For both of you, in fact." Maugham watched, entertained, as Marion kept her eyes averted, her hands clasped.

"Marion's listening as well," Jeffrey said to him after a few more awkward seconds had passed. "With her usual enthusiasm."

"Excellent," Maugham repeated, dismissing Marion for the moment. He cogitated, admiring the fire. Then, abruptly, he asked: "any information from the courier?"

Jeffrey took a sip of his coffee, set the glass on the table to his side, and lit a cigarette. Tossed the match into the fire and then looked, perplexed, at Maugham. "Which courier?"

"We had word of an Irish agitator in the area. Stirring up discontent. Desecrating churchyards. That sort of thing." Maugham stretched out his legs in front of him toward the fire. "Thought you might have caught up to her."

"Oh. That courier." Jeffrey blew smoke up at the ceiling. "I sent Gardiner after her, but she had a head start. He lost her."

"Gardiner fails to exert himself."

"Gardiner is the best we have," Jeffrey countered. "He only let it go because I ordered him to do so. He'd be out there now if I hadn't told him to leave it and get some rest."

Without replying, Maugham unbuttoned one of the two rectangular pockets on the outside of his belted jacket. Then, pursing his lips as he tugged unsuccessfully for a few seconds, he pulled out a package of papers. Held the papers in his lap. It was the material Virginia had taken from Jeffrey's trench coat.

Still muddled, he rested his hands on the package and looked back at Jeffrey. "Courier might have had something to say about these papers, Willcox. An entry point into your upcoming conversation with Dr. Bailey, perhaps?"

Marion raised her eyes to Maugham's, held his look for three seconds, and then returned her attention to her hands. A wave of nausea, worse than she'd experienced since her morning sickness, swept over her. She swallowed again.

"So that's why Ginnie invited you here?" Jeffrey was also watching Maugham, but unlike Marion's, his expression was bemused. "This scenario is even more convoluted than what she ordinarily inflicts on us. She could have simply handed them to me herself."

"I believe that Virginia wanted all of the material in one place," Maugham said. "Before Dr. Bailey goes to work."

"All of the material?" Intrigued. "There's more?"

"Dear boy, if you'd been paying any attention at all to the instructions we've been sending you, you'd realize that this scenario, as you put it, is more than convoluted. It's a glorious time bomb, just about to go boom." Maugham folded his hands over the package on his stomach, pleased with himself. "Yes, there's more."

"Your instructions to me," Jeffrey said, "were to watch Marion. Which I've done." He took a drag of his cigarette. Exhaled. "You've felt well watched, haven't you, Marion?"

They both looked at her, waited, and then when she didn't speak, exchanged a glance. A second or two later, Maugham continued. "There was also the Greenwich Observatory. You were supposed to watch that as well. And you've sadly failed in that endeavor."

"I'd assumed that bit was a joke," Jeffrey replied. "Cryptographers enjoying themselves."

"The cryptographers are incapable of enjoying themselves, Willcox." Maugham reached for his cooling cup of coffee and took another drink. "You know that. And you've missed an opportunity. They tried to blow it up again yesterday."

"Who? The cryptographers?"

"A profound and abiding hatred of the place they seem to have," Maugham said, ignoring him. "This is what, the third time over the past half century that some radical group has attempted to set it ablaze? What's the Greenwich Observatory ever done to them? How could gazing at the stars halt the inevitable triumph of their revolutionary cause?" He sniffed. "It's become tiresome."

"Even more important than that, though, Maugham, is what the Greenwich Observatory has to do with us." Jeffrey was refusing to be drawn. "I feel for the astronomers. I do. But our section of the Museum and Library concerns itself with other branches of letters and learning. Astronomy is not my field. Nor is it Marion's, polymath though she may be."

"True," Maugham said, unbuttoning the other pocket of his jacket. "But astronomical expertise is not what's needed in this case."

He withdrew from his second pocket a collection of manuscript pages wrapped in protective paper and put it on the table next to Jeffrey's coffee. Then he found a further eight or nine scraps, similarly wrapped. Placed them beside the first. "These are, in order, the second part of the *Chronica Majora* by Matthew Paris, a thirteenth-century Benedictine monk." Pointing at the first set of folios. "The pages we have here are his thoughts on Mongol and Ilkhanid habits and learning. The remainder of the pages come from a copy of an Arabic astronomical text. Muayyad al-Din al-Urdi, from what I understand."

Jeffrey peered at the papers on the table next to him. "Hmm. You've got my attention." Glanced over at Marion, who had remained motionless, but also tense and waiting. "Marion's too, though she's doing a good job of hiding it. The best she can, at least." He waited. "So where did you find them, then?"

"I thought I'd made that clear." Annoyed. "I found them at the Greenwich Observatory. Where you would have found them yourself if you'd been doing your job properly. Though they're both from the British Library originally."

"I don't understand." Jeffrey scratched his temple with a thumbnail. "You found them at the Observatory—but they're from the Library?"

"Really, Willcox—I've never seen you quite so slow. The expectant state, it pains me to say, does not become you." He grunted. "I'll be forced to spell it out for you, I see." Resettling himself, he folded his hands over his belly again. "So here it is: two weeks ago, these manuscripts went missing from the Library. We kept it quiet because we wanted to follow them. Curious as to whether the thief had an interest in them aside from their literary value. But nothing emerged. They were simply—gone. One week ago, the police—" He glanced over at Jeffrey. "Yes, dear boy. I've been interacting these past days with the constabulary. And all because you were too busy mooning about after your—"

"Yes, Maugham. Point taken. I feel well and truly chastised. Continue."

"Very well. So Scotland Yard, God help us, received a tip that the Greenwich Observatory was under threat. Again. And, in typical Scotland Yard fashion, they failed utterly to neutralize that threat, even though they had all the intelligence in the world pointing them toward the likely perpetrator." He chuckled to himself. "Some mentally incompetent shopkeeper from Soho, from what I understand. Outwitting The Yard. I must admit I wish I'd been there to see that bit of the story."

Marion had raised her eyes at the mention of Soho, but Jeffrey cast her a warning look before she could speak. He tossed his cigarette into the fireplace. "I still don't see the connection. What does this have to do with the Library?"

"Patience, Willcox." Maugham closed his eyes, complacent now. "The lad from Soho had a mishap. Instead of blowing up the Observatory, he ignited the bomb outside of the building. Yesterday afternoon, it was. Ripped himself to pieces. All that was left was a bloodied scrap of an old coat with his address helpfully inscribed to identify him. And a convenient witness who saw the entire event."

Jeffrey, who was lighting a second cigarette, looked up, entertained, at Maugham. "His address? And a witness? Surely they couldn't have been convinced by that."

"It's Scotland Yard."

"But you—"

"The degenerate boy from Soho was nowhere near the Observatory," Maugham said. "That much is obvious from the evidence left at the scene. But there's more to it than that. Enough, in fact, to make it worth tracing the perpetrator ourselves. Informally."

"Yes?" Jeffrey inhaled smoke and blew it up at the ceiling.

"The reason that The Yard called me in—unwilling as they ordinarily are to cede territory— is that one more bit of material was left, provocatively, at the scene of the crime. And they had no notion of what to do with it."

"The manuscripts," Jeffrey supplied.

"Correct." Peeved that it had taken Jeffrey so long to make the connection. "From what I can gather, this group—organization—whatever—undoubtedly aligned with Dr. Bailey's people— purloined the manuscripts from the Library merely to leave them for us at the Observatory." He sat up and peered again at Marion. "Why do you think they would do that, Dr. Bailey? Any thoughts?"

"It was Halloween, Professor Maugham. Perhaps they were feeling prankish." She hadn't raised her eyes from her lap.

He relaxed back into the chair. "Thank you, Dr. Bailey. Very helpful." Looked back over at Jeffrey. "But there's more."

"Oh dear." Jeffrey watched the smoke curling up from his cigarette. "Yes?"

"In the midst of fending off the increasingly persistent demands made on me by the Halfwits of The Yard, I received sudden word from your brother, George. Just hours after Virginia had extended her kind invitation to me." When Jeffrey didn't reply, he continued. "I found this surprising, Willcox, because, as you know, George and Virginia both have a lamentable aversion to my conversation and company. Strange to say, but I believe they disapprove of our methods."

"Hmm."

"And yet, all at once, here they are, seeking me out. Most gratifying." He put his hand over his heart. "It makes one feel that one's unappreciated labor is finally—"

"What did George say to you?" Jeffrey asked shortly.

"Apparently," Maugham said, dropping his exegesis, "the ministry—George's ministry, that is—have been watching the mentally incompetent boy from Soho as well. Popular lad. One wonders if perhaps he's not quite the degenerate everyone makes him out to be." Maugham paused, musing. "In George's case, however, he's a person of interest for different reasons. Nothing to do with the radicals and their all-consuming antipathy for accurate timekeeping."

He closed his eyes again, smiling. "George said to me that the boy from Soho has also been mixed up in an ongoing investigation into the growing Italian submarine presence in the Mediterranean. Since Abyssinia, you know. Everyone's jumpy."

"Hmm," Jeffrey repeated, unhelpful.

"They would very much like to know, Willcox, what these thirteenth-century manuscripts have to do with Italian naval maneuvers in the Mediterranean and Red Sea." Maugham chuckled again. "George was irritated. He dislikes academic mysteries sneaking into his geopolitical calculations."

"George is always irritated." Jeffrey was gazing at the fire, tired. "He's been irritated since he was born."

"This was something more than the usual," Maugham said. "You wouldn't believe it, but I detected some faint emotion in his voice as he was haranguing me. It was extraordinary."

He opened his eyes and looked sidelong at Jeffrey. "You'd earn some well-deserved praise from your older brother if you could aid him in this matter. It's not often we can say that, now, is it? In fact, from what I understand, he's particularly displeased by the thought of Dr. Bailey's shadowy organization involving itself in the affair. He likes invisible partners even less than he does academic mysteries. He wants them brought into the open. And you are, you realize, uniquely qualified to help him in that regard."

"And Marion?" Jeffrey's tone remained noncommittal.

"Dr. Bailey can do her work." Prim. "As always."

Jeffrey made a sound that might have been a laugh. Then he turned to Marion. "Satisfied, dear? Is this what you wanted?"

She shook her head, horrified. "No." Swallowed down her nausea, waited a few seconds, and then spoke again. "I'll stop. They'll give it to someone else." Held Jeffrey's eyes. "They'll understand."

"Will they?" Jeffrey, unhelpful, was wearing his professional face again.

She didn't respond.

"I thought not." He tossed his second cigarette into the fireplace.

Maugham, his cup of coffee and brandy finished, rose from his chair and patted down the pockets of his jacket. "All settled, then. I'll leave the pages to you, Willcox. And, of course, you already have the degenerate boy's—?" He paused, at a loss again.

"His circles," Jeffrey supplied, standing as well.

"Circles?"

"Yes."

"Heavens, Dr. Bailey." Maugham was trying without success to re-button his pockets. "You do keep unusual company." Defeated by the buttons, he cast a mournful look at Jeffrey. "Do you think Virginia would consent to my staying the night? My Austin could do with the rest. If I attempt to force it back to London, I fear it will kick over its traces and canter off onto your moor."

Jeffrey, who had gathered up the material, held out his arm to help Marion from the sofa. She was silent, shocked by the turn the conversation had taken. But she held his elbow.

"She'll be delighted to have you," Jeffrey said as Marion steadied herself. "Especially if we don't tell her. You prefer the East Wing, if I recall? Tapestried Chamber?"

"Is it prepared?"

"It's as you left it, Maugham. No one else is willing to go near it."

"Excellent," said Maugham for the third time that evening. Then, stopping and shooing Marion and Jeffrey away with a pudgy hand, he continued. "I'll find my own way, Willcox, thank you. Dr. Bailey mustn't exert herself. Complete rest is always the best policy." He beamed at Marion. "A pleasure as always, Dr. Bailey. And once more: my congratulations."

At that, he disappeared down the corridor into the unused, haunted part of the house.

*W*HERE would you like to work?" Jeffrey asked, the manuscript pages in one hand, his other hand on the small of her back as they climbed the stairs.

"I'll use the bedroom," she answered dully.

She knew that Jeffrey was correct about her superiors' reaction to her abandoning the project. As the courier had told her, the situation was urgent, and they needed her work. But they must also know that she was in no state to go under and bring her conclusions to their attention once she'd examined the manuscripts. She could scarcely move from one room to another.

And even when her ankle had healed, the strategies she ordinarily used when counteracting the attentions of the office would be impractical. Every step she took would be watched and recorded by Jeffrey and his associates—and every bit of material she discovered would be collected by them. Her only course of action was to go on as she had been before, hoping that at the critical moment she'd manage to elude them and pass along her findings. It was a demoralizing realization after an upsetting day.

She examined the painting of the magistrate as they passed. He looked silly and smug. Unworthy of his office. Jeffrey, following her look, smiled. "Dangerous times," he said. "Witches and traitors everywhere. One understands that he would have appreciated a good meal."

She stared down at the floor and continued walking toward her bedroom. When they entered, he looked a question at her, and she pointed toward the dressing table. "Leave it there. If I need more room, I'll use the bed."

"Very well." He put the package on the table. "I'll bring you the papers from Soho too. Won't be a moment."

When he left the room, Marion sat at the dressing table and idly turned the pages of the *Chronica Majora*. Medieval Latin wasn't her specialty, but she'd read Matthew Paris on the Mongols before, as background for her research into Ilkhanid statecraft and diplomacy. The text in front of her was familiar.

As she reached the fourth set of pages in the collection, however, she paused, surprised. Although she was paying only half-attention, skimming, something felt wrong. Turning back to the beginning, she read through the folios again, this time with greater focus. Then she compared the pages. Finally, shaking her head to clear it of confusion, she read through the passages a third time.

She was still staring, baffled, at the pages when Jeffrey returned with Stephen's circles. His lips twitched, entertained that she was already at work.

"This isn't right," she said abruptly.

He placed the papers next to the other material. "Already?"

"I've read Matthew Paris on the Ilkhanids before. This isn't it." She'd had her fingers to her temples, gazing down at the manuscript. Now she looked up at him. "The first two folios are correct. After that, it becomes something different. Even the script is different. I'm guessing it's the *Life and*

Customs of the Mongols—de vita et moribus Tartarorum—which Paris and his contemporaries did reference. But which was lost." She paused. "Is lost."

Jeffrey sat on the edge of the bed. "So, your people—"

"It wasn't my people—"

"Do you really want to begin this way, Marion?"

"No."

She stayed quiet and let him speak.

"So, your people removed the Paris manuscript from the Library, inserted these alien—lost—pages into it, and then returned it to us two weeks later via a botched terrorist attack on the Greenwich Observatory." He considered. "An awful lot of trouble. Why not send them by post?"

"I don't know."

"Yes, you do," he said. "They wanted Maugham—and presumably Scotland Yard and a few quiet civil servants in George's ministry—to pay attention to them."

He looked down at his fingernails. "And they wanted slightly less attention paid to your friend Stephen's circles and the pages that Gardiner's courier—he can't stop thinking of her, you know; I think he may be in love—dropped you. Although they would have known that I'd take those pages too, and that they'd go into circulation. Just a bit more quietly." He looked up at her again. "There's a method here. I'm not certain what it is, but it's by no means random."

She didn't speak. This was not the exchange she wanted to have with him.

"Oh, very well, Marion." Annoyed, after a few seconds of silence had passed. "We'll postpone this part of the conversation. I'd rather you devote your energy to deciphering these texts anyway. But, make no mistake, we will return to it. Otherwise, how will I ever impress my stern older brother?" He nodded at the pages on the dressing table. "Also, before you go any further, I'd like you to supply me with a bit of context. Lie to me if it makes you feel better."

"What context?"

"Observatories," he said, "tossed together with Mongols makes me think of Maragha. In northwestern Iran. What about you?"

"You don't need me to tell you about it, then." Sullen. "You already know."

"True," he agreed. "I don't need you to tell me about it. But I'd like you tell me about it nonetheless. See what I pick up from what you emphasize and what you omit, yes?"

She considered the tabletop. Then, with an irritated movement, she began: "fine. Context. Hulagu Khan, the leader of the Ilkhanid dynasty, founded an observatory in Maragha—in northwestern Iran—in 1259. The year after he sacked Baghdad and ended the Abbasid Caliphate. Three years after his armies had taken Alamut and obliterated the regional influence of the Nizari Ismailis, the Assassins.

"Maragha was the most sophisticated observatory in the world at the time. It operated for close to sixty years, until 1316, longer than almost any other before it. Long enough to complete a series of unprecedented observations. Some of the most celebrated astronomers and mathematicians in Asia and Europe—from China to the western Mediterranean—were attached to Maragha. They transformed the study of star and planet movement."

"Who worked there?" His voice was blank.

"Nasir al-Din al-Tusi was the most famous," she said. "He was the motivating force behind the observatory's construction. Hulagu left most of the decisions to him."

"And?"

"Hundreds of people worked and studied there," she retorted, annoyed. "I can't name them all."

"Name some."

"Muayyad al-Din al-Urdi," she muttered. "Syrian."

"Ah," he brightened. "Responsible for the second collection of pages that turned up in Greenwich, correct?"

"Yes."

"Good. Interesting. I have a feeling there will be one or two others who become relevant. But let's leave them for now. What about the building itself? Any thoughts?"

"Work began on the wall and the main structures in 1259," she said. "They were situated on a hill, and Muayyad al-Din al-Urdi devised a set of wheels to bring water up to the equipment. He also designed many of the instruments that were used there."

"This would be the same al-Urdi—"

"Yes," she said shortly. "There was a dome, a tower, and a library—according to contemporary observers—of approximately 400,000 mathematical and scientific treatises."

"Is that all?"

"No. By 1261, a series of uniquely precise instruments—armillary spheres, astronomical clocks, an azimuth ring, and the like—had also been constructed. They were unmatched in their accuracy."

"Is that all?" he repeated.

She sensed that he was waiting for her to mention a specific item from Maragha, and her distrust grew. "No."

"Care to elaborate?"

She didn't speak.

"Anything that, say, found its way to Germany?"

"If you know already," she exploded, "why bother asking me? This is demeaning. Why not let me work? You'll be watching anyway. You can read these texts as well as I can. I'm not hiding anything from you. At least, not—" She caught herself.

"At least, not yet," he said laughing. "I've told you, Marion, I merely want to hear your version. Your interpretation of events is often edifying."

"I'm finished. I don't want to do this."

"Very well. Then I'll take the material from you now." He stood. "And I'll also begin withholding the radishes. As a start."

"Al-Urdi," she said, "also—"

"Same one?" he asked, sitting down again.

"His son."

"Continue."

"Al-Urdi also constructed a special, small armillary sphere, a bronze celestial globe, in 1279 or 1289. It's approximately eight inches in diameter, and includes, among other things, the constellations, the equator, the horizon, and the meridian, all inlaid in gold and silver. It turned up in Dresden in 1562, and it's been there ever since." She felt disgusted.

"It's still there," Jeffrey said. "At least according to our sources. Your colleague failed to lift it."

"He wasn't supposed to take it," she said.

"Then why bother getting himself tortured and killed?"

"He made a rubbing."

"There are a number of good photographs of the globe in circulation," he said. "A bit of a waste."

"Of the inside."

"Ah." He paused to consider. "That makes more sense. And so, what Gardiner's paramour brought to you is—"

"The inside." She rubbed her eyes with her fists. "Of the globe. He knew how to open it. There was a trick."

"Very well. Let me summarize then," he said. "You'll be working over the next few weeks on these thirteenth-century pages from Matthew Paris that are not really by Matthew Paris; a section of Muayyad al-Din al-Urdi's likewise thirteenth-century astronomical treatise, written while in residence at Maragha; a rubbing of the *inside* of the also thirteenth-century celestial globe constructed by al-Urdi minor; and—a collection of circles?"

She nodded, not wanting to give him any more.

"Am I correct in thinking that your friend Stephen's circles will guide your reading of—I would guess the inside of the globe?" Interested. No longer aggressive.

"Yes," she said. Tired.

He ran his hand through his hair and stood. Crossed the room and kissed her cheek. "A good start, dear. I feel invigorated. Pleased to be working with you again."

She continued staring at the tabletop in front of her and didn't reply. As he left the room, he paused and looked back at her. "Any thoughts about Italian submarine movements in the Mediterranean?"

She raised her eyes and glared at him, silent.

He smiled, turning back to the door. "I thought not."

SHE devoted her afternoons to work. Under ordinary circumstances, she would have spent every waking moment reading and analyzing the material she'd collected. Going without sleep as well. But as she passed through her sixth month of pregnancy, she found herself increasingly lethargic. Unable to summon the intellectual or physical energy she needed to make creditable connections among the texts.

She was still perfectly capable of completing this sort of assignment, she insisted to herself. She simply wasn't confident about it. And so, she spent her morning hours walking outdoors, mentally buttressing the conclusions she'd drawn the afternoons before—conclusions that, under previous conditions, she'd have trusted immediately. It was better to take rests, she told herself. More responsible. As time grew more pressing, however, her inner monologue became less and less persuasive.

The first afternoon she devoted to the folios from the *Chronica Majora* by Matthew Paris. Paris was an English Benedictine monk of St. Albans who wrote and illustrated historical works, culminating in the *Chronica*, a grand study of world history from creation until his death in 1259. The fact that Paris died in the same year that Hulagu Khan endowed the Maragha Observatory meant that he wasn't a helpful source on what Marion suspected was her primary concern: technological advancement under the Mongols. But if her organization wanted her reading these pages alongside the astronomer, Muayyad al-Din al-Urdi, she wasn't going to question their logic. Something must be there for her. Especially given that the folios they had sent her were not by Paris, but rather from an as-yet unstudied section of the more targeted *de vita et moribus Tartarorum* or *Life and Customs of the Mongols*.

This hitherto lost manuscript would have been written a year or two before the *Chronica*. Otherwise, Paris and his contemporaries wouldn't have been able to cite it. Also, it was almost certainly more detailed and accurate than the later chronicles—concerned with passing along precise and useful information about the Mongol Ilkhanid state in Iran to worldly readers invested in the ongoing Crusade against the Mamluks in Egypt. It was a work meant to inform rather than to entertain. And Marion had always been curious to know what its well-cited, yet elusive, author had to say about her field.

She was disappointed, in fact, that all she had in front of her were a few disconnected pieces of the text—no more than eight pages. She would gladly have read a complete version of the manuscript. But, smiling to herself as she translated, what little she had was already going a long way toward satisfying her curiosity.

Indeed, she was so surprised by the account—a short description of the fall of Alamut, the Nizari Ismaili or Assassin stronghold, to the Mongol armies in 1256—that once she had finished translating it, she sat, dumbfounded, at the dressing table, unable to process what she had drawn from it. She then spent the remainder of the afternoon and evening preoccupied, slept fitfully, failed to reassure herself during her morning walk the next day, and re-read the entire collection of pages that afternoon.

The next day she read it again. The day after, she repeated the process. And it was only on the third day, when she had finally accepted that her interpretation was correct, that she moved on to Muayyad al-Din al-Urdi's treatise on astronomical instrument-making. Still dissatisfied, but uncertain as to what to do but press forward.

She had never read al-Urdi's writing on what he cumbersomely called "Techniques of Astronomical Observations and the Necessary Theories and Practices for Making Them, and How to Understand the Periodicity of the Stars," or, in its even more extended title, *Risala fi kayfiyya al-arsad wa ma yukhtaj ila 'ilmihi wa 'amalihi min al-turuq al-muwaddiya ila ma'rifa 'awdat al-kawakib*. But she had seen two separate manuscripts in Istanbul libraries, and she had heard of two more in Iran and France. She didn't know where Maugham's version had originated; though she suspected that when he had said "the Library," he had meant the library that Jeffrey had moved to London from Baquba.

If it *was* a fifth version from that collection, she was pleased that her people had managed to access it before having it brought to her. Having done it once, they could do so again—which meant that the Baquba material wasn't as lost to them as she had feared it was. But her pleasure ended there. As she skimmed a few preliminary pages of the text, she felt a growing dread of pushing through what would be a highly technical discussion of astronomical instruments and their use. Her scientific vocabulary was as limited in Arabic as it was in English.

But as she familiarized herself with the pages that Maugham had collected, she discovered that she wouldn't be forced to attempt a complete reconstruction of al-Urdi's study. Two miscellaneous scraps—inserted into the manuscript in the same way that *de vita* had been inserted into the *Chronica*—pointed her toward an unavoidable conclusion: this fifth copy of the manuscript differed from the other extant versions. The incongruous pages wouldn't have been attached to it with such care and purpose if it did not.

The first of these scraps was an anomalous section of a Greek rendition of a Persian *Zij*, or astronomical table, translated from the Persian and Arabic by Gregory Choniades. Choniades had studied and worked at the Maragha Observatory in the 1280s and 1290s before returning to his home in Constantinople. He was a moderately significant philosopher and astronomer during his lifetime, but not one of the most prominent who had resided at Maragha. There was no obvious reason to insert into the manuscript a page from his *Zij*, completed thirty years after al-Urdi wrote.

386

The second scrap, unattributed and impossible to date, was a peculiar discussion in heavily Turkic-inflected Persian of the importance of falconry to Ilkhanid statecraft and diplomacy. The scrap emphasized the virtues of the gyrfalcon especially, noting that messengers bearing these falcons also bore powers and privileges that their common counterparts did not. When Marion had finished translating the page, she sat back in her chair, musing. Its very lack of relevance must be important.

And so, taking a determined breath, she skimmed al-Urdi's treatise from the beginning, praying that she would find the reference or textual anomaly she was seeking. Something must be there that would connect his writing to Choniades and, even stranger, falconry. Otherwise, the two scraps were purposeless. Forcing herself to concentrate, she read and re-read every word of every page, from beginning to end.

She had almost given up, rubbing her eyes in frustration, when, on the second to last page of the manuscript, she identified the passage she knew she wanted. She then re-read the lines. Squeezed her eyes shut, opened them, and re-read them one last time. Then, satisfied, she pushed herself out of her chair, left the room, and went for a very long walk in the limp, damp, nearly freezing air outside.

After finishing her analysis of al-Urdi, she needed only two days of testing her work, pacing the house, venturing into the sodden outdoors, and re-checking her translations, before she felt confident in her findings. She knew that she had identified the connection she was meant to identify. And she also knew what her next step would be. She must, and quickly, make use of the celestial globe.

Applying Stephen's calculations to the interior of the globe, however, was simple now. In part this was because Stephen himself had done all the work—first, calibrating his circles to the star and planet positions as they existed in southern England in October of 1935, and second, thereby providing Marion with perfect overlays for the rubbing Robert had taken in Dresden. But she also knew *what* she expected to see in the schematic map she would be constructing. All she must do was to take both sets of papers outdoors under the full moon to find the coordinates she sought.

The next full moon would fall on Sunday, the 10th of November. It was now Thursday, the 7th. She became restless at the thought of the wait, but at least the moon was days, rather than weeks, away. In the meantime, she maintained an appearance of calm, checking her translations a fifth, sixth, and anxious seventh time. And on the night of the 10th, when she left the house, unmolested by any aggressive eyes, optimism had replaced her anxiety. She was itching to test her hypothesis.

Two hours later, as the light of the moon fell in the spot she had predicted, the optimism turned to satisfaction. She'd been correct. And so, after marking Robert's rubbing with a pencil, she rolled it and Stephen's calculations into a careful cylinder and walked back to the house. Although she wasn't alone under the bright, cold moon, she was grateful to Jeffrey for ordering his people to keep their distance.

She was more than grateful to Teddy and Virginia for their virtuoso display of discretion over the past week. Throughout the ten days she'd been working, they had both nearly convinced her that they had forgotten her project altogether. Their skill at dissimulation left her almost frightened. But, she reminded herself as she walked, her labored breath distinct in the air, they were an old family. Good at that sort of display. Mad.

When she reached her room, her clothing damp, clutching the cylinder of papers, Jeffrey was sitting in front of the fire again, waiting for her. She was unsurprised, but she nonetheless set the papers on the dressing table and removed her wet overcoat before letting herself notice him. It was only after she felt moderately dry and prepared that she walked to the armchair and lowered herself into it. "We need to go to Istanbul."

"Now?" He kept his features blank, but he was clearly displeased by the announcement.

"Soon," she said, rubbing her hands over her arms to warm them. "Before Ian's holiday, I think."

"Very well." He stood, bent over her, and kissed her temple. "They tell me one ought to humor the whims of women in your condition." When she frowned at him, he straightened, smiling. "We'll talk further tomorrow?"

"If we must." She was still staring at the fire.

"Sleep well then, darling." And he was gone.

*W*HEN she woke the next morning, Jeffrey was already back in the room, sitting at the dressing table, reading through her material. He had also brought her breakfast on a tray, which he had placed on a stand to the side of the bed.

"I thought we'd get an early start," he said.

"I'm not going to stay in bed for it." She sat up and looked, bewildered, at the tray.

"As you wish." He reorganized the pages he'd been skimming. "Provided you're comfortable."

"Idiot."

She pushed the blankets off her legs, got out of bed, and covered herself as effectively as she could with her dressing gown. Then she used the toilet and returned to the bedroom. He'd moved the tray of food to the side of one of the armchairs at the fireplace. She walked to the chair, sat, and looked at what he'd brought her. Toast, marmalade, an egg in an egg cup, a pitcher of milk, and a pot of tea with two cups. Along with a bowl of radishes.

Choosing not to comment on the radishes, she spread marmalade on a piece of toast and bit into it, watching as he walked to the other armchair. He brought her material with him and smoothed it in his lap when he sat. "Why Istanbul?"

"Let me start with the *Chronica Majora*." She poured tea into the two cups, handed one to him, splashed milk into the other, and took a sip from it.

"Which isn't in fact the *Chronica Majora*." He set his teacup on a low table to the side of his own chair. "Even I caught the change in the script. I don't imagine it was meant to fool anyone. Do you think it's really from *de vita et moribus Tartarorum*?"

"I don't know. I think it might be. It's certainly genuine. Thirteenth-century." She finished her toast and glanced at the egg. Decided against it. "I wish they'd sent the rest of the volume."

"It could be that this is all there is left," he said. "Interesting interpretation of the fall of Alamut, at any rate. From what I was able to skim. Although Matthew Paris himself writes no more than a sentence about it before it gives way to our other, anonymous, author's description."

He opened the second folio of the monk's manuscript and ran his finger over the lines. "Yes, here it is: '*Circulo eiusdem anni Tartari detestabiles Assessinos detestabiliores, quos cultelli feros appellamus, destruxerunt. Ipsorum Tartarorum immunditias, vitam, et mores si quis audire desiderat, necnon et Assessinorum furorem et superstitionem, apud Sanctum Albanum diligens indagator poterit reperire.*' 'The abhorrent Mongols destroyed the abhorrent Assassins about the same year as'—presumably the things he'd been discussing before. 'If you want to know more about either of them—and by the way, have I mentioned how abhorrent they are?—go do your own research.'"

He closed the pages again. "Helpful man, Matthew Paris of Saint Albans. I must say I'm relieved that someone saw fit to append these additional folios. I certainly wouldn't have wanted to begin this project on the basis of a few vague, pious sentences." He retrieved his cup from the table and took a sip of tea. "All the same, Marion, I can't see the relevance to our Maragha problem of even this more detailed description of the fall of the vile Assassins to the equally vile Mongols. Aside, obviously from the prominence of Nasir al-Din al-Tusi in the tale. And the fact that Alamut was the original home of your—"

"Fine," she interrupted him. "Let me help you, then."

"Very well." He smiled, pleased to have provoked her. "Enlighten me."

"When the Mongol armies surrounded Alamut," she started, wanting to forestall further comment from him, "the governor of the fortress temporized for as long as he could. He'd already been ordered by the imam to surrender. The fall of the castle was inevitable. But still, he waited. The question is why. He wouldn't have been shoring up the castle's defenses or preparing a counter attack. Nizari Ismaili soldiers, even highly placed ones, didn't disobey their orders. So why stall? Contemporary sources suggest that he was hiding something before he surrendered. From the Mongols. I think, now, that those sources were accurate. He was."

He nodded and took another sip of tea.

She continued. "But the Mongol leader, Hulagu's deputy, refused to let him wait. And so, the governor opened Alamut to him at once, and the Mongols entered the same day." She paused. "There are several accounts of what they found there, what they looted, and what they destroyed. For example, they likely removed, but preserved, the famous library."

"And who would blame them?"

She ignored him. "But, contrarily, if the legendary gardens there did exist, they certainly ceased to do so after Hulagu's armies had finished with them."

"Hmm."

"They also found, according to at least a few sources, evidence of an observatory there. Astrolabes, an armillary sphere, a triquetrum, a few celestial globes. Sort of scattered about in an open area."

"'Evidence.'" He picked up on her term. "No functional observatory."

"Yes," she said. "That's what's strange. It was as though an observatory *had* been operative. And quite recently. But it had been dismantled and partially hidden—ineffectively hidden—when the Mongol armies surrounded the fortress."

"Why dismantle the observatory?" He set down his cup. "They would have had more pressing issues to address, surely?"

"I think that's what these pages are trying to tell us." She finished her own tea and placed the cup on the tray.

"If so," he replied, "they go about it in an indirect way." He peered down at the pages in his lap. Thoughtful. Then he handed them to her and gestured for her to continue.

She put the folios on the tray next to her breakfast. Didn't need them to explain her reasoning. "Their author would have wanted to be indirect. You can tell from his tone that this wasn't written for a general audience. And I have a sense, from the terse style of the pages we have, that the purpose of the work was military rather than—touristic. The author was making an argument to a few key leaders in favor of an alliance between the Mongol Ilkhanids and the English Crusaders against the Mamluks."

She considered again. "And the crux of this alliance would have been some sort of technological advantage that had presumably been acquired by Hulagu. But the author couldn't spell out in detail what that technology was. If he had done, its value on the battlefield would have been lost. So he hints at it instead." She paused. "When you read it alongside al-Urdi, you can see that he's hinting at it pretty strongly."

"Go on."

"When the Mongols took Alamut, they found more than just physical evidence of an observatory. They also found Nasir al-Din al-Tusi. He'd been a guest there—"

Jeffrey grinned. "A 'guest?'"

"My impression," she said primly, "of Nasir al-Din's career is that he worked as the 'guest' of a number of similarly inclined rulers in the region. If he'd wanted to preserve his freedom of movement, he might have been a bit less vocal about his remarkably useful collection of skills and talents. You can hardly blame the governments of the time for taking an interest in him."

"An important lesson." He was still smiling at her. "Although one always learns it too late, doesn't one?"

She stood, irritated, and walked to the window. Then she looked out on the wind stirring the bare branches of an elm tree beyond the yews. "When the Mongol military leaders found Nasir al-Din at Alamut, they didn't know what to do with him. But they knew they couldn't simply let him wander off. So they sent him to Hulagu, who immediately recognized his value."

She paused again. "The problem was that Hulagu's brother, Möngke, who was the nominal ruler of the Mongol State—Hulagu's superior—had already heard about him as well. He wanted Nasir al-Din sent to China to work under him instead."

She closed her eyes, willing the caffeine she'd drunk to do its work on her mind. She felt sluggish again. "Hulagu played for time, and Möngke died a few months later. He was succeeded by Kublai, who also wanted Nasir al-Din in China. But Kublai had less clout, and Hulagu ignored his orders. Instead, Nasir al-Din began work on the Maragha Observatory in Iran. In 1259."

Jeffrey had turned his chair to face her as she was speaking, though she was still looking away from him. Now he lit a cigarette and watched her. "You're saying that the infighting among the khans for Nasir al-Din's services was about more than his astronomical expertise."

"Yes." Her back to him. "It says as much in those pages from *de vita et moribus*."

He frowned and took a drag of his cigarette. "I didn't see anything like that when I read it."

"You didn't read it properly."

"I rarely do when I'm in your company." Friendly rather than offended. "So where have I gone wrong, then?"

"This set of pages describes the discovery of Nasir al-Din hiding in the fortress of Alamut. It also lists the various observational tools that the 'Assassins' left behind when they surrendered. And then it goes on to describe the pleasure with which Hulagu Khan greeted the arrival of Nasir al-Din in his court. After that—and this is interesting, in that this would have been written before Matthew Paris died in 1259—it describes the plans that were made for the complex that would eventually become the Maragha Observatory. An oddly up-to-date catalogue of information. I'm surprised that the manuscript made it back to England in time for Paris to cite it."

"Yes," he said. "I noticed that as well."

"It also describes the expertise and tools that Nasir al-Din brought with him. Not only what was found at Alamut. To 'amaze and delight' the Khan."

"Yes, I remember."

"But it then goes on," she said, "to discuss where Nasir al-Din put these tools once he was at Maragha, and what he planned to do with them."

"Yes." His voice was mild.

"He put them, the author says, in the network of caves that underlay the flat hill on which the observatory was eventually built." She paused. "Remember, this manuscript would have been written before the observatory was completed. Or even started. So all the author could describe were the plans and the landscape. But the caves, he makes clear, were already being put to good use before the observatory was even erected." She stopped speaking again. Then she asked: "why put observational instruments in a cave?"

"For alchemical research, he says." Jeffrey tapped ash off the end of his cigarette. "That wasn't unusual. Most leaders patronized astronomers for their astrological rather than astronomical expertise. Alchemy frequently went with astrology. Doesn't Rashid al-Din even write a bit guiltily about Hulagu's obsession with astrology and alchemy? It was an embarrassment to proper scientists and philosophers. But not surprising or out of the ordinary for military leaders. And the caves under the observatory buildings weren't a secret. They're evident even now."

"The extent of the alchemical research—*before* even the construction of the observatory— and the fact that the tools were housed in the caves, though, does make this passage unusual," she insisted. "I think. Especially in light of what al-Urdi writes later."

"I'll withhold further judgement then." He put down his cigarette and took a sip of tea. "Continue."

"There's also the description of the most impressive tool that Nasir al-Din set up for Hulagu. Later in the text." She turned from the window, crossed the room, and sat in the chair again. "The author of *de vita et moribus* writes that Nasir al-Din brought many observational instruments with him from Alamut, and that he also planned to build tools at Maragha. But, most 'fabulous,' he writes, is that he presented Hulagu Khan with plans for the 'perfect tool' for observation."

"Ah yes," he said. "I do remember that bit. But then he fails to explain what the 'perfect tool' is, or would be. Frustrating."

"The omission is telling," she replied. "He must make clear to his readers that the Mongols have something of significance. But he can't say more, or he'll show his hand. His phrasing, though, certainly hints at something with value beyond a variation on an astrolabe."

"Does it?" He frowned again.

"Do you remember the phrase he uses for 'perfect instrument'?"

"*Telum perfectum*, wasn't it?" Before she could speak, he smiled. "I know what you're going to say. *Telum* is more 'weapon' than 'tool.' But it works as 'tool' as well. Given the context."

"No." She paused. "I mean, yes, *telum* means 'weapon.' But more important, *telum* also means a shaft of light. And *perfectum* need not be 'perfect' in our sense of the word, right? It could be 'completed' or 'executed.' So, another translation would be that Nasir al-Din brought Hulagu not only his expertise, but some sort of weapon that was a completed shaft or ray of light. One that related to the alchemical work undertaken in the caves."

"You can't have drawn these conclusions based solely on the word play. It's too fanciful." He picked up his cigarette and took another quick drag. "Where's the rest of it?"

"In al-Urdi."

"Good." He handed her the pages from al-Urdi. "I feel more confident about the treatise on observation. He writes a nice Arabic. And I must admit I'm grateful this time that we're not plowing through the irrational Turkish you enjoy so much. There's just that one scrap. And it can't be all that important."

"Wait." Her voice was grim.

"Hmm."

She set al-Urdi on the Paris and rested her hand on top of both. "You've read the treatise. Al-Urdi describes in some detail the tools and instruments that he made or modelled for use at the Maragha Observatory."

He nodded. "Yes."

"There's a mural quadrant, an armillary sphere, a solstitial armilla, an equinoctial armilla—"

He lifted an amused eyebrow. "You know what all of these do?"

"I used a dictionary." Annoyed.

"Forgive me." He took a drag from his cigarette. Exhaled. "Curiosity. One never knows where your mind will go next. Continue."

"There was also an azimuth ring, a triquetrum or parallactic ruler, and—"

"Yes," he interrupted again. "I know where you're heading. And finally, there was what he, also, called 'the perfect tool,' or 'complete instrument,' '*al-ala al-kamila*.' Evocative in light of the passage from *de vita et moribus*. But unlike our anonymous author, al-Urdi does describe this tool—which he says he'd already constructed in Syria for al-Mansur, so it couldn't have been all that secret. It's just another version of a—parallactic ruler? Is that what it's called in English?"

"I think the term is important," she insisted. "And it's *not* the same thing as a parallactic ruler. He says you use it by spinning it or revolving it. And he also says that one can—or maybe should—use it in a deep well. Also intriguing. Perhaps he even means in a cave—"

"'Perhaps,'" he said. "Conjecture. If this is all you've got, I may come over protective and decide a jaunt to Turkey is not the healthiest of options for our family at the moment—"

"Did you notice his slip? Or the scribe's slip? Fifteen lines after he mentions the 'perfect tool?' Where the unattributed scrap was appended?"

He gave her pained look, and then stood, stepped across to her breakfast tray, and retrieved the al-Urdi pages. "I didn't read the scrap," he said, sitting again. "I've told you. I refuse to concern myself with your illiterate Turkish barbarians."

"It's in Persian."

"Barely." He turned to the page she had mentioned of al-Urdi's astronomical treatise. Then he skimmed the scrap, his forehead wrinkled. "Something about falconry. Obscure."

"Now read al-Urdi's discussion of the perfect tool. Slowly," she added before he could say something snide.

He acquiesced quietly enough and began reading. Then he nodded and looked up. "I think I see it. But it's not much. Here, yes, where he talks about dividing the meridian into smaller parts to make the azimuth horizon. And how the center column of this tool he's constructing will then spin in place over a circle at the center. He's put an extra dot, or an 'n,' and an extra loop, or a 'u' in 'smallness,' *sigar*. An error."

"Not an error." She poured herself more tea and took a sip. "He didn't mean *sigar*. He meant *sungur*. Falcon."

"*Sungur* isn't the word for 'falcon' in Arabic. Only in Persian and Turkish. And Al-Urdi wouldn't have used a Persian or Turkish word for that." He ground out his cigarette. "He was educated."

"But Hulagu wasn't, was he?" She frowned down at her tea. "And what does that scrap say in its entirety? That the Ilkhanids made a habit of bestowing the 'falcon' or '*sungur*' class on those who had achieved the highest honor. And that upon attaining this honor, those who possessed it would be given a gold tablet on which gyrfalcons were inscribed—a tablet that would allow them to 'see' further than anyone else in the Empire. Why attach that particular scrap to that particular error in the text if it the changed term weren't meaningful?"

"I still don't see how altering a single word changes the general sense of the manuscript. It simply turns the passage into nonsense. Turkish nonsense."

"No," she insisted. "What it does is prompt a reinterpretation of every word surrounding it. What does al-Urdi say just after the error? He says, 'we call this the azimuth horizon.' One could certainly translate that short sentence in a purely technical way. But both 'horizon' and 'azimuth' are words with countless meanings in Arabic if we leave aside the scientific focus."

She paused, thinking. "'Horizon,' for example, *al-afaq* might just as well be 'field of vision.' Or even 'range' or 'region' of vision. And 'azimuth' in English and Latin famously comes from the Arabic *al-samt*, 'way,' or 'manner,' or 'mode.' So, one could conceivably read al-Urdi to be saying that one constructs the 'perfect tool' with reference to a 'falcon' that can radically change one's mode of vision—or even that it alters the way one understands one's field of vision."

"It certainly alters the meaning of the treatise's title. 'Techniques' or perhaps 'modes' of observation," Jeffrey allowed, though still not convinced.

"Yes," she said. "More poetic. But also telling—for those who are looking for it. I think, having read these pages alongside one another, that al-Urdi's perfect tool, like Nasir al-Din's, was something more than astronomical. I think it had some immediate, concrete value to Hulagu—something to do with seeing or optics on the battlefield as well as in the sky. And I think a large part of its construction took place in the caves *under* the Observatory. Among the alchemists."

She considered again. "Perhaps he started work on it in Syria. But I don't believe he was able to complete it until he was talking with Nasir al-Din in Maragha. And I think the anonymous author of *de vita et moribus Tartarorum* learned enough about it to want, imperatively, to get word of it to England."

He lit another cigarette and smoked meditatively for a few moments. Then he spoke again. "Why falcons?"

"I'm not certain yet," she admitted. "It could be metaphorical. Falcons, gyrfalcons in particular, have proverbially acute vision. But I wouldn't be surprised if there's more to it than that. I'll know when we reach Istanbul."

He exhaled smoke, displeased again. "Yes. Istanbul." He looked sidelong at her. "That bit has to do with the pages from the Greek astronomical table?"

She nodded. "It's from a work translated by Gregory Choniades. He was at Maragha a few decades after Nasir al-Din and al-Urdi conducted research there. And then, once he'd finished his project, in the 1290s, he travelled back and forth between the Byzantine and Ilkhanid Empires until he died in 1320. He also worked for the Byzantine Emperor, Andronikos II Palaiologos."

"Is that all?"

"There's a story that he was part of the entourage that brought Andronikos's illegitimate daughter, who was later called Despina Khatun, to marry Öljeitü Khan, Hulagu's great-grandson. Approximately 1305." She drank more tea. "In return, Öljeitü promised Andronikos military support against the emergent Ottoman state and the Mamluks. And he made good on his promise. His armies kept the Ottomans busy for years. But more important, between 1312 and 1316, when Öljeitü died— and, importantly, I think, when the Maragha Observatory ceased operation—he made all sorts of overtures to Byzantine and European rulers to form an alliance against the Mamluks and, incidentally, the Ottomans."

She peered into her cup and set it to her side again. "The exchange of falcons was a consistent theme in those talks. And they were certainly part of another gift that Öljeitü sent to Andronikos in Constantinople in 1315—accompanied, these same sources say, by Choniades."

"Yes?" he prodded her.

"It was a defensive weapon. Without equal. Secret."

"Well, it obviously didn't work all that well. Over the next century and a half, the Ottomans overran the Byzantine Empire. Until they destroyed it." He took a quick drag of his cigarette. "And the Ilkhanid Empire hardly fared better."

"I don't think Andronikos used it properly."

"Why on earth not?"

"He was busy with his family." She rubbed her eyes. She already felt tired, although it wasn't even noon. "He had disowned his heir, who was a drunkard, and that prompted a civil war, which lasted nearly a decade. Once the war had wound down, he was forced to abdicate, and he became a monk. This—gift—from the Mongols was lost. Or forgotten. Andronikos never had the chance to erect it or make use of it."

"But now you—or your people—have remembered it," he said. "Via Stephen's circles and the globe from Dresden. And what with the growing Italian submarine presence in—"

"We must go to Istanbul," she interrupted him, stubbornly.

He crushed out his second cigarette and stood. "I'll think about it." Then he collected the papers they'd been reading. "May I take these with me? I'd like to read them more carefully on my own."

She nodded and finished her tea. She was looking forward to being in Turkey again.

Istanbul, Turkey
November, 1935

THE plane they took from Croydon to Istanbul's Yeşilköy aerodrome on the 13th of November was an Imperial Airways Avro 652. Its interior was smaller than many of the aircraft in which Marion had flown to and from the Eastern Mediterranean, but she appreciated its solid feel. She also appreciated the fact that the designers of airline passenger compartments had finally given up on trying to replicate the atmosphere of nineteenth-century railway carriages—a style choice that had always left her with cultural and temporal vertigo.

The cabin was simple, functional, and comfortable. Four wide leather seats that could be swiveled to face one another. Small round windows. A low table with an ashtray bolted to the floor. A door leading to the cockpit, and a galley near the tail. She lowered herself, gratefully, into one of the capacious leather seats.

Once Jeffrey had closed and secured the outside door, he sat in the seat across the aisle from her. Then he swiveled his chair toward her. Boyishly entertained. "I believe they plan to replace these seats with rows of stationary, forward-facing chairs in the coming month or two. Before they make these aircraft available to commercial travelers." He sighed. "A shame. I daresay these will be a source of great entertainment should we encounter inclement weather."

She felt the plane begin to move off the apron and toward the runway. Didn't reply.

As they gathered speed and lifted into the air, Jeffrey continued talking. "Maugham has called in a favor owed him by the powers that be at Imperial Airways." He moved his chair into its forward position and looked out the window. "Or, at least, by the wife, Gwendolen, of the powers that be. Sir Eric is a bit—eccentric."

He moved a curtain across the window and reached into the inside pocket of his jacket for a cigarette case. "And so, as a result, we'll be following their usual Croydon-Cairo route. Croydon-Paris-Lyons-Rome-Brindisi-Athens. But then we'll go north rather than south from Athens, arriving in Istanbul tomorrow afternoon. The crew and the Avro will wait for us there. So we shan't be delayed once we've collected what we need."

He chose a cigarette, shut the lid, and returned the case to his pocket. Then he lit the cigarette with a match that he put in the ashtray. "It shouldn't take more than two weeks, I imagine?"

"One week," she said to the window. "Or less. I know what I'm looking for now."

"Good." He inhaled smoke and blew it thoughtfully up at the ceiling. "I have an idea as well. But care to update me? Gregory Choniades brought this—instrument—to Constantinople in the early fourteenth century. Andronikos II failed to use it. It was lost or forgotten. And then—?"

She closed her eyes. Tired again. "And then—"

"Wait," he interrupted. He set his cigarette in the ashtray and stood. The plane had leveled off and was flying smoothly. "Would you like something to eat or drink? A glass of water? Some tea? Or I could probably find you—"

"Don't say 'radishes,'" she muttered, her eyes still closed.

"Tea, then."

"Yes, fine."

He walked to the tail of the plane and spent a few minutes making a pot of tea. Then he bent over, looked into a cupboard and found a package of digestives. He arranged the digestives on a plate and brought both it and the pot of tea to the table. Returned to the galley, found two cups, and put those down as well. Poured tea into both cups and handed one to her. "I couldn't find milk."

"I don't need milk." She took the cup and sipped the steaming tea. It was too hot, but she didn't care. She took another sip.

Jeffrey sat and lifted his cigarette again. "What happened between the 1320s and—I'm suspecting the Ottoman conquest of the city?"

"It remained lost," she said. "Or I assume it did. Otherwise, the celestial globe wouldn't have pointed me where it did."

"Where did it point you?"

"To the Istanbul Observatory. Overseen by Taqi al-Din Muhammad al-Rashid ibn Ma'ruf in the mid-sixteenth century. A scientist as talented as—if not more so than—Nasir al-Din al-Tusi."

He shook his head. "That doesn't work. Al-Urdi's son constructed the celestial globe in the 1290s. The Istanbul Observatory operated in the 1570s. How could an object made three hundred years before he was born point you toward Taqi al-Din's life and work?"

"The celestial globe isn't a static object." She took another sip of her tea. "It's a tool. It can be set. Provided you know how to open it and correct for the star and planet positions of wherever— and whenever—you happen to be using it. It's an active map. And someone set it, with these coordinates, in the mid-sixteenth century. Then, to be certain it wouldn't be discovered by the wrong people, that person dropped it. Quickly. How else do you think it ended up in Dresden, of all places, in 1562? The same year that Taqi al-Din decided he no longer wanted to be a judge in Egypt, and instead began to write scientific treatises on clocks, light, vision, and the stars?"

"Hmm." He ground out his cigarette in the ashtray. "Perhaps. Remind me, then, of what Taqi a-Din was doing in Istanbul."

"The Istanbul Observatory was an odd institution," she ventured. "You know the story, correct? Taqi al-Din came to Istanbul from Egypt sometime before 1570. By 1571, he was appointed the Sultan's head astronomer. In 1575, with support from the Grand Vizier, Mehmet Sokollu Pasha, he persuaded the Sultan to found an observatory. The Sultan was enthusiastic, and construction started at once. The building project was, according to sources at the time, lavish—you know, gold coins were 'spent like sand,' that sort of thing. Prominent scholars from all over the region came to work under Taqi al-Din. He was making a variety of 'marvelous' discoveries."

She paused. "And then, less than five years later, at the beginning of 1580, the Sultan ordered the Observatory demolished." She considered. "That's important, I think. He didn't simply disband the research staff or stop funding their work. He didn't order it abandoned. He wanted it destroyed." She took a sip of her tea. "And it was."

"I do remember the story," he said. "It was because of the comet, wasn't it? It appeared in 1577, portending doom and disaster. The Sultan asked Taqi al-Din to interpret it. Taqi al-Din tried to put a positive spin on it—as who wouldn't when asked by a monarch to prognosticate? But then— plague, military defeat, natural disaster. Whoops. He should have known his comets better."

"That's one story," she conceded. "Another is that the Sultan, who had been more than a little bit taken by astrology and astrological prediction, came over religious. His clerics convinced him that astrology—and hence astronomy—was immoral. And *therefore* he ordered the observatory destroyed. It didn't help that the Grand Vizier who had supported the project—again, Mehmet Sokollu Pasha—had been killed a few months earlier, in October of 1579."

"By the Assassins, they say."

"Hmm." She looked into her tea cup. He'd prodded her about that before. "But there's more than that. I mean more than that to make the conventional interpretations of why the Sultan destroyed the Observatory unconvincing."

"Such as?"

"Taqi al-Din's reaction to the order," she said, finishing her tea and putting the cup on the table. "Without exception, the accounts all declare that Taqi al-Din wasn't disappointed by it. Or even resentful."

"That's surely to keep, even obliquely, from questioning the Sultan's decision-making capacity?" He pulled the curtain back from his window and looked down. The plane was pushing through a cloud formation. The cabin felt bumpy.

"No. It's something else." She looked out her own window as her cup began to rattle on the table. Glad she'd finished her tea. "Some of them even say that Taqi al-Din himself recommended that the Observatory be demolished. Because his work was 'complete.' He didn't have any more to do, and so he advised the Sultan to tear it all down."

She pulled the curtain over her window and swallowed. Wished the pilot would take them higher or lower to get them out of the cloud. "But how could the work of an astronomical observatory be 'complete' in less than five years? The usual number given for even a basic *zij* was thirty years—the orbit of Saturn around the sun."

"So perhaps Mehmet Sokollu Pasha was alone—and misguided—in wanting the work of astronomical observation to continue?" Jeffrey mused. "And hence his attention from the Assassins?"

She didn't answer his questions. Instead, she said, "I do think that we ought to take Taqi al-Din at his word. He had finished what he'd set out to do. Which, given the timing, couldn't have been astronomy. I believe it was something to do with optics. Vision. Perhaps light. His preferred research topics. The observation of the stars and planets was always of secondary interest to him. And he was entirely uninterested in astrology."

She rubbed her eyes. "But there's something else."

"What?"

"Before—" She stopped. Then resumed. "Before we went to Suffolk. When I was—was starting work, I wrote to Max Krause. In Berlin. He's been investigating medieval Arab mathematics and astronomy. He'll be publishing an article next year, but he told me that most of the more famous manuscripts on optics—in Arabic as well as in Persian—made their way to Istanbul sometime in the sixteenth century. Ibn al-Haytham's *Kitab al-Manaẓir*, others like it. All collected in a single library in the Ottoman metropole. I don't think that was a coincidence either."

Jeffrey nodded. The plane had ceased shuddering, and they were gently losing altitude. "I think we're landing." He relaxed into his seat and swiveled forward. "And, for the time being, you've convinced me. We'll start with the grounds of the Observatory. It was located somewhere on the hills above Tophane, yes? You'll be able to find it?"

"Yes." She closed her eyes again. "I have the coordinates."

Then she leaned back in her seat and tried to relax as well. Paris would be the first stop on a painfully long journey.

$\mathcal{S}$HE was unable to stand upright when they reached Yeşilköy, in Istanbul, the next day. Jeffrey, concerned about her condition, had suggested—this time without mockery—that they rest and spend a night in Brindisi or Athens. But Marion had obstinately insisted that they press forward. She didn't want his concern.

She soon realized that her attitude had been a mistake. By the time the plane landed, she couldn't feel her feet, and she was forced to lean heavily on his arm as they descended the stairway. But at least the temperature in Istanbul was a good twenty degrees warmer than it had been in Suffolk. It felt almost like summer.

Relying on Maugham's continuing influence, they evaded the interest of customs officials, and made their way directly from the plane to a car that was waiting for them at the edge of the apron—a 4 ½ litre Derby Bentley in two-tone black and grey, with a grey interior. A driver was waiting to load their minimal luggage into the boot, and he greeted Jeffrey with pleased, but subdued, recognition.

Marion thought, suspiciously, that she knew him from nearly a decade before as well. But the driver's affect was bland, and he failed to remember her. Nonetheless, she fought down a moment of inner protest, laced with an echo of early trauma, before she reconciled herself to the situation and slid into the back seat of the car. She was in no state to comment on Jeffrey's obnoxious choice of vehicle.

Jeffrey sat in the seat beside her, and the driver brought the car into the traffic heading toward the city. The Marmara Sea, to their right, was looking light green under the low clouds and the humid, choppy wind. Mischievous. Sinister.

"I've borrowed transportation from the Consulate," he said, watching her watch the water. "I felt it would be the easiest. Though, fear not, I do remain aware of your unfortunate aversion to the works of the Bentley brothers." He looked past her at the waves breaking on the surface of the sea. "They're owned by Rolls Royce now. Does that make it more acceptable?"

She wrapped her arms over her belly and closed her eyes. Didn't respond.

"Do you know?" Teasing now. "I believe when last we were in Istanbul together, we were married. Perhaps we ought to consider this an anniversary of sorts."

"Stop it." She didn't open her eyes.

"Would you like to stay in your old room at the Consulate, I wonder?"

"I said, stop it." She was beginning to feel sick. And he was taking advantage of her. After her reaction to the day and a half of air travel, she was unable to protect herself against this sort of conversation. She felt vulnerable, and she resented him for taking advantage of her situation. Though she wasn't surprised by it.

After a few minutes of silence had passed, and they were circling down into the more closely packed residential neighborhoods of the city, she spoke again. "Where are we staying?"

"Beyoğlu."

Her eyes flew open. "Absolutely not. I will not go near the Consulate. You will not—"

"I own a flat," he said, his voice no longer mocking. "In Galata, really. I have since before the War. Where do you think I was staying all those months and years you were rampaging and intriguing throughout the Near East?"

She relaxed. "Fine." Then she considered. "Above Tophane?"

"Close enough," he said. "Midway between the Consulate and the likely grounds of the observatory. We'll be well-situated."

She nodded and closed her eyes again. And she didn't open them until the car was winding down past Taksim square and into the narrow, twisting streets below Galatasaray Lycée. She paid more attention when it slowed to a stop in a narrow alley that was never meant for automotive traffic, and the driver, brisk, exited and opened her door for her.

She pushed herself out of her seat and looked up at the façade of the building across from them, bemused. It was late seventeenth-century. A good hundred years earlier than most in the neighborhood. And flanked on either side by modern residential buildings that couldn't have been built before the 1920s. Its entryway was modest, a low, stone archway, with a dark green wooden door embedded in it. But the stones were carefully carved and thick. And the two stairs leading up to it were smooth marble. Not what she had been expecting.

Jeffrey watched her reaction to it. "My father bought the building from the Camondo family forty years ago, after they relocated to Paris. It's less grand than the Camondo Palace, and less useful than the two complexes of flats they were also selling, but my father had always liked it. I don't use the top floors."

He unlocked the door and stood to the side while the driver brought their luggage inside. Then, after thanking the driver, who disappeared into the street, closing the door behind him, Jeffrey turned on a lamp resting on a table in the small foyer. He slipped off his shoes and positioned them under a carved mahogany bench to the side of the room. Marion did the same and looked about her. The floor of the interior of the building was also green marble, covered by a very old carpet. The lamp was a Louis Tiffany lotus lamp. Scuffed.

He waited for her to precede him into the living room. "I've met Beatrice a few times," he said, turning on a second lamp.

This room was also tiled in green marble, but the stones were themselves covered by two or three additional layers of carpets, repeating the lotus pattern. A low sofa and two armchairs took up the center of the room, brought together by another table, also mahogany. Bookcases covered two of the walls. And when he pulled aside a heavy curtain covering a set of three stone mullioned windows, she assumed there must be a courtyard beyond.

"Beatrice?" She walked, cautious, toward the windows. Surprised that he used the lower floors of the building rather than the top floor, which must have an impressive view of the Golden Horn and Bosporus.

"The daughter." He pulled open what turned out to be a door, rather than a window, at the edge of the wall giving onto the courtyard. "She's converted from Judaism to Catholicism. Trying to fit into French society." He paused. "I'm not sure that doing so will bring her what she wants. Given the state of the world. The family, perhaps, should have remained in Turkey."

He looked troubled for a few seconds and then masked his discomfort. Gestured for her to walk into the courtyard. She did so and then stumbled to a stop, astonished by what she saw. The sun was sinking, but there was still more than enough light to illuminate the area. The courtyard was an ancient garden.

At each of the four corners were pomegranate trees, trained to single trunks, gnarled and thick enough to be one or two centuries old. In the center was a quince tree, also trained to a single trunk, and equally old. All five trees were heavy still with ripe fruit. The quince had dropped a few smaller specimens, but the bright yellow windfall were by no means littering the ground. They'd been gathered recently. Two pear trees, espaliered against opposing walls, had already been harvested. Finally, an old, thick grave vine twisted across a trellis along the top of all four walls. It still bore ripe bunches of dark purple grapes. Corsican mint formed a green carpet over the octagonal paving stones.

To the side of the quince tree, a green fountain, also marble, was trickling into a pool that disappeared into a gutter beyond the far wall. Against the pool was a stone table surrounded by four cushioned chairs. It had been set for dinner.

"I asked my housekeeper here to prepare the flat for our arrival," he said. "She lives further down the hill. I hope you don't mind."

She shook her head, unable to speak, still stupefied by what she was seeing.

"It's an old building," he continued unnecessarily, walking toward the table and sitting. "Looks inward rather than outward. You recognize the style, yes? There aren't many of these left in the city. I think the trees are contemporary with the house."

She walked to the table and sat across from him. Although it was twilight, the air felt warm. No longer like summer, but by no means uncomfortable. He poured them both glasses of wine, and then he arranged poached sea bass, which had been waiting under a silver dome, and a shepherd's salad on a plate for her. He handed the plate to her, prepared the same for himself, and began eating.

"Ayşe Hanım—my housekeeper—prepares a brilliant candied quince," he said, taking a sip of wine. "I imagine that's what's under the last plate, there." Indicating a smaller dish hidden by another silver dome that he hadn't disturbed. "You ought to eat, Marion."

She nodded, took a sip of her wine, and then ate a small bite of fish. It was expertly prepared. She ate more, wishing she weren't so impressed by his, to her, always terrifying domestic efficiency. She hated that she was softening under his attention—aware from experience that she was more susceptible to the confusion prompted by this sort of arrangement than she was by his more coercive techniques. She told herself to keep closed. Not to tell him more than he needed to know.

The corner of his mouth went down, watching the play of what she knew were excruciatingly obvious emotions behind her eyes. "You'll be tired after the journey. Shall we go to sleep straight away?"

"Yes," she said, trying to keep her expression blank. "Thank you."

"There's only the one bedroom on this floor," he continued, refusing to relent in the face of her discomfort. "I can make up a second room for you upstairs, but I thought now that you're no longer raiding churchyards under a chill full moon, you might not object to sharing—"

"Yes," she repeated, interrupting him. "That's fine. If you'd like, that is. I don't sleep soundly these days. You may find it—"

"On the contrary," he said. "I've missed you."

She dropped her eyes and ate more of the fish. Violently pushing down her politically disloyal feelings. Then, to defuse the situation with civility, she looked up at him. "Jeffrey, thank you for bringing me here. This is—it's—" She let her eyes wander over the fruit trees and the ancient stone walls. Uncertain of how to make clear what she was thinking.

"I know, darling." His smile was still lopsided. "I'm pleased that you approve of it. The harvest may not be as extensive as Ginnie's and Teddy's. But we do what we can."

THEY ate breakfast in the courtyard late in the morning, after sleeping longer than Marion had for weeks. And the bright, clear weather, a few degrees warm for early November in Istanbul, looked as though it would hold for at least another two or three days. She was in no hurry to leave the calm light of the courtyard, her cup of coffee, or the second chocolate croissant from the French patisserie across the alley. She was disappointed to be keeping to such a tight schedule. Feeling sleepy and content. Didn't want to ruin the quality of the morning.

"You sighed?" Jeffrey, sitting across from her, a hint of a smile, set his book face-down on the table. It was something old, in Arabic, and looking like poetry. He'd been smoking all morning as he read, and he now dropped his spent cigarette into his empty coffee cup. He hadn't eaten anything.

"No," she said. She pushed away the remains of her croissant. "It's late. We ought to start."

"As you wish. Where?"

She thought for a few seconds, and then spoke, slowly, not wanting to turn her attention to her work. "The Observatory," she said carefully, "was built somewhere on the hill—this hill—overlooking Tophane, near where we are now. Before the area had grown into a residential center." She stopped, considered what to say next, and then resumed. "At the time of its founding, what residential construction that existed was sparse—although there were a few scattered, mostly non-Muslim neighborhoods along with some impressive gardens, schools and, later, fountains."

She paused, thinking again. "A century or so later, after the Observatory had been demolished, the area began to draw the international diplomatic community. As it does now. Tradition has it that when the Sultan ordered the destruction of Taqi al-Din's complex in 1680, he gave the land to the French. To build their Embassy. It was the first permanent diplomatic residence in the Ottoman Empire. Others followed."

She sipped the dregs of her coffee. "A little over a hundred years ago, the original French Embassy buildings burned down. They rebuilt them in the 1830s in an even grander style. The 'French Palace.' Just south of Galatasaray Square—a few streets over." She faltered again. "That's where we ought to begin."

When she'd finished, Jeffrey remained quiet for a few seconds. Then, irritated, he spoke: "you could have told me this before we left London. We would have avoided a great deal of unnecessary trouble."

When she didn't reply, he continued, more than irritated, as though he were speaking to a slow pupil. "Perhaps, Marion, under the most ideal of circumstances, when you and I were in top form, we could carry this off. But now? As we are?" He laughed. "I forbid it. You will not pilfer the French Consulate. You will not *approach* the French Consulate. Can you imagine the embarrassment if you were caught? I don't think even Maugham could extricate us from that one. Not that he'd likely want to."

He lit another cigarette, flattening out his anger. "So here is our new plan: we'll enjoy a pleasant holiday in the lovely city where we wed, see the sights, return to London next week, and then make our apologies to Maugham. He can fend off the Italian submarines on his own. We've finished with this."

She pushed her fists against her eyes and took a deep breath. She hated the charged atmosphere. Even the light had changed. Dropping her hands, she looked at him. "I said that *tradition* has it that the Sultan gave the grounds of the Observatory to the French. That we *ought* to begin there." She scowled down at the table. "Tradition is incorrect. And we won't. The coordinates that I gathered from the celestial globe place the complex about half a mile further up the hill."

"Where?" His voice still hard.

"The area is entirely built up," she said. "It's all blocks of flats and mansions constructed over the past seventy-five years or so."

"Where?"

"If I'm not mistaken," she said, raising her eyes again and coloring, "the area of the Observatory that interests us is now occupied by a nightclub. On the ground floor of a nineteenth-century block of flats." She let her eyes drop back to her belly. "At least, it was a nightclub fifteen years ago. I haven't, obviously, been there for—for a while."

"You've visited it?" His anger was gone. Replaced by the beginning of another smile, delighted and incredulous.

"I used to go there frequently." She toyed with a butter knife on the table. "Before. I recognized the coordinates as soon as I'd derived them. It's—a coincidence, I suppose."

He grinned. "When I knew you then, you didn't strike me as the sort who—"

"When you knew me then," she spat, her embarrassment turning to anger, "you were corrupting and killing my husband, ruining my career, and interrogating my friends and colleagues. I was rarely in a mood to go out for a night of dancing and entertainment when our paths crossed."

"Which career? Foot soldier or hired killer?"

"Fuck you." She was torn now between useless rage and an increasing desire to finish her second croissant—which she knew would only entertain him further. She hated her condition.

"What was it called?" he asked, his lips still twitching in the repressed smile.

"What?"

"The nightclub. What was it called? Fifteen years ago."

She gave up and reached for the croissant. "The Jazz Vampire." She tore off a piece of the pastry and put it in her mouth.

"Oh Marion." Charmed. "Really? If only I had known you better—"

"You wouldn't have been welcome." She finished the croissant, giving up on her self-respect.

"And now?" He lit another cigarette.

"Neither of us would be welcome now," she said. "New generation. If it's still there, that is."

"How shall we approach it, then?" He inhaled and blew smoke slowly up toward the sky. "I feel more confident about this than I do about the French Palace. It may even be a lark to be found out and exposed. One wonders what they would do to us—"

"If it is still there," she said, "its proprietor will also be the same. I knew him relatively well. At the time. He may understand our situation."

"What was his name?"

"Nuh Efendi."

"Ah." He considered. "Not his real name, then."

"I don't know." She was still irritated. To sidetrack him, she said: "we could walk up there today to determine whether it's still operational. If it is, we'll go back this evening and try talking with him. If that doesn't work, then tomorrow we'll identify vulnerabilities in the building's security. It won't be difficult to access, even as—as we are."

"I'm not lifting you over any walls." He was still smiling to himself.

She stood. "I'll get myself ready. Let me know when you'd like to leave."

She walked from the courtyard to their bedroom, which was as immaculate as the rest of the house. Then, dejected at the thought that she'd be wearing the same draped, beige silk dress and embroidered ivory overcoat that she'd been wearing the day before—all that fit her as she was nearing her seventh month—she changed as quickly as she could for the street.

On her way out to the corridor, she saw that Jeffrey was already settling a hat onto his head. He was wearing light brown wool trousers and a tweed sport jacket with a dark brown striped tie. Perfectly fit and perfectly tailored. The contrast between her heavy, disheveled clumsiness and his light, clean energy made her recoil at the thought of leaving the house with him. But then, steeling herself, she took the arm he had held out to her and stepped into the alley. She would focus on her work.

They walked slowly, but with purpose, up the hill in the direction of Taksim Square. Jeffrey's alley connected first to Tomtom Kaptan Street, which passed between the Italian and French Consulate complexes. Ignoring both, they walked along the south edge of Galatasaray Lycée, before taking a series of small side streets to their right, until they intersected Siraselviler Avenue.

Once on the main street, Marion walked—memories now flooding back to her—to another alley off to the right. There they found a building into which an unprepossessing door, wooden, protected by thin iron bars, half at street level and half seemingly buried in the ground, was embedded. To the side of the door was an unembellished plaque attached to the concrete foundation of the building. "Jazz Vampire." In both Latin and Ottoman script.

She half smiled. "I think it's the same place."

"Is that man selling disconnected bits of exhaust manifolds?" Jeffrey hadn't heard her. Instead, he was looking, perplexed, at a storefront across the alley. Having lifted the wood and wire grating over the entry, the owner was displaying row upon row of metal tubes and coils afflicted by varying degrees of rust and decay.

She turned and looked as well. "I think so. Why?"

He took her arm and they began to walk back down the hill. "Maugham is in the market for one. I'll pass him the information."

They stopped and bought *dürüm* and *döner* kebab from a vender on the street, eating as they retraced their steps. Considered leaving the paper wrappers on the grounds of the French Consulate, but decided against drawing attention to themselves. Instead, once they reached Jeffrey's building, they dropped the greasy paper into a bin and, without needing to talk about it, agreed to rest until dinner and their return to the Jazz Vampire.

*T*HE sun had long set, and they were drinking coffee in the living room after dinner, when Jeffrey suggested that they dress for their evening out. Refusing to allow Marion to walk back up the hill after dark, he had contacted the Consulate and confirmed that the driver would be waiting for them outside their door at 11:00. It was now 10:30.

Marion wanted nothing more than to lie in bed and read one of Jeffrey's books, but she nodded morosely as he left the room. She felt not simply ungainly, but old. Unable to summon even a trace memory of the excitement she used to feel at this time of night when she expected to go out dancing. If she weren't careful about her mood, she'd be in irrational tears soon.

She reached across the sofa for Jeffrey's book of poetry, wanting to deflect her dismal train of thought. But before she had read more than a few lines, he reappeared in the doorway of the living room. Wearing a white shirt and dress trousers, with a black dinner jacket hanging over his arm.

"White tie or black tie?" He had one in each hand.

"I really don't think it matters." She stood and smoothed down her beige dress.

"Of course it matters." He considered, and then draped the black tie around his neck. "If we fail to observe basic sartorial conventions, we may as well bow down and submit to the barbarian." He let his eyes drift over her own outfit. "What will you wear?"

"This." Her voice, she knew, was shrill, and she willed herself to control it. "And the coat. Jeffrey, it's all I can wear."

"You didn't fancy Nuh Efendi by any chance? Fifteen years ago?"

She stared at him, astonished by his sudden question. Then she felt herself blushing. "I was married to Tariq." She dropped her gaze to the ground. "Nuh was interesting. That's all."

"You don't want him to see you like this." He had turned to the wall and was bending toward a mirror hanging between two bookcases, fixing his tie.

"Married to you, you mean?" Glaring at his complacent reflection in the mirror. She might as well blame him for her mood. He was, fundamentally, responsible for it. For everything. For her life. And she already hated him. "Yes, well that is quite the come down, isn't it? Humiliating. But a job is a job, and that's what we're here to do. So let's do it then, shall we?"

"I'm pleased to see you energized again." He moved away from the mirror and put on his dinner jacket. "You've been less than enthusiastic over the past few days." He held out his arm. "So yes. Let's do complete our job, darling. It's what we're here for."

She narrowed her eyes at him for a few seconds, then turned away without taking his arm and walked down the corridor. Shoved her feet into shoes and left the house. The driver already had the door to the Bentley open for her.

It took them less than ten minutes, winding through the streets, pushing through occasional high spirited groups of young—to Marion, very young—men and women flowing in and out of unmarked bars and nightclubs, to reach the Jazz Vampire. The driver let them out two streets away, and they walked along the cobbled alleys, past stray dogs and bits of waste paper, until they stopped a few yards from the entrance.

The wooden door was now partially open, revealing a narrow staircase to the cellar of the building, from which the sound of a full band and clouds of cigarette smoke floated into the street. At the top of the stairs, just inside the door, was a fashionable looking woman, wearing sequins and a diamond bracelet, sitting behind a counter. Outside the door were two large bouncers in the customary ill-fitting suits.

A small crowd had gathered in the alley, and the woman and the bouncers were indicating couples who could enter, blocking the way of those who would wait. There was a mathematical precision to their decision-making process, but Marion was too old to recognize the code any longer. She felt her anxiety mounting, uncertain that she could get them into the building, much less into an audience with Nuh.

Jeffrey, never anxious, was eyeing the crowd with tolerant good humor. He seemed already to be enjoying himself, though he was four years older even than she was. "How much?" he asked her.

She thought for a moment. "Two lira?" Guessing, not wanting to insult the bouncers in either direction.

He raised his eyebrows as he reached into his jacket for a wallet. "Steep."

"They give you a free drink once you're inside," she said lamely. She wanted to go home. Read a book. Stop what she was confident could only be a mortifyingly humiliating experience.

"Oh." He returned the wallet to his jacket, the cash folded between his fingers. "That's all right then."

He put his other hand to the small of her back and led her into the crowd. "Shall we, then?"

The crowd gave way as they approached, showing a confused deference to their age and to her obvious condition. She stared down at her feet as they passed the bouncers, Jeffrey slipping the two bills to the larger one, on his left. The bouncer handed the money, in turn, to the woman sitting inside, who—far from discreet—spread it on the table in front of her, her hand, manicured and glittering, palm down on top of it.

"Are you certain you've come to the right place?" she asked in English, looking at Marion rather than at Jeffrey. Her tone was concerned—no hint of derision or contempt. Worried about Marion's health.

Marion took a breath and addressed the woman in Turkish. "Would you please tell Nuh Efendi that I'd like to see him? My name is Marion Bailey. I used to know him when he wanted to be a novelist. Tell him I'm looking forward to the sequel."

The woman pushed the money back across the table toward them, but they didn't touch it. "Wait here a moment," she said, also now in Turkish.

Then she leaned across the counter and gestured down the stairs to a waiter, wearing white tie and tails, who hurried up to speak to her. He leaned over her, and she whispered something in his ear. He glanced, nervous, at Marion, and then disappeared into the smoke and music again.

As they waited, the woman allowed two additional couples to enter, and then smiled as a girl, no more than eighteen years old, wearing a nearly transparent glittering red sheath emerged from a taxi. The crowd parted for the girl, who ignored them, ran up to the woman at the counter, kissed her on both cheeks, and descended into the cellar. Marion hugged her belly. Jeffrey looked bored.

After what felt like ten minutes, the waiter returned, bent over, and whispered to the woman. She lifted an eyebrow, impressed. Then, standing, she gestured them toward the stairway. As they passed, she tried to give the two bills back to Jeffrey.

He shook his head. "Would you buy the bouncers a drink for me?" he asked in Turkish. She smiled and nodded, tossing the money onto the table as she returned to her seat.

In addition to the smoke and music, the heat grew as they made their way into the club. Marion wanted to remove her coat, but in a rare moment of vanity, she forced herself to keep covered. She didn't want to expose her belly any more than she must.

By the time they'd reached the floor—half taken up by couples dancing, half by high, round tables, crowded and nearly invisible under cocktail glasses—she was sweating uncomfortably. But there was no way she was going to make her situation any more obvious than it was. Even under the low lights.

She flinched as the music, which had stopped for a few seconds once they'd left the staircase, swelled again, reverberating across the domed, wooden ceiling. Glanced over at the stage. The woman in the red dress was standing at a microphone, in front of a complete big band ensemble, singing "You Do Something to Me." She looked casual and aloof. Unaffected by the gelatinous air in the room.

At the same moment, a tall, thin man, sitting alone, but drawing the muted respect of everyone in the room, raised his hand in greeting. Marion raised her hand as well, and let Jeffrey escort her through the dancing couples toward the table. When they reached it, the man stood, shook Jeffrey's hand, and then kissed Marion on both cheeks. He was wearing a white dinner jacket with a dark green tie. The edge of a tattoo, some sort of aquatic animal, was just visible on his wrist, under his cuff. He also wore a complicated signet ring on his little finger.

He stood back, holding Marion by the shoulders, and looked her up and down. "You've changed, Marion."

"I'm pregnant, Nuh."

"Oh, thank God." He dropped his hands from her shoulders. "I thought you were—simply—" He held up his hands, expressive.

They'd fallen into Turkish, and Marion continued speaking as she looked about her, appreciating the room. "I like the changes. The band is good. And the girl is extraordinary."

He pulled out a chair for her. "I can have them play 'Wild Cat Blues.'"

"Oh Nuh." She sat, pushing her sweaty hair off her forehead. "That girl wasn't even born when Sidney Bechet was in Paris."

"Of course she was." Nuh gestured Jeffrey into a chair and sat as well. "I attended her eighth birthday party." He opened a bottle of champagne and poured glasses for them. "But it's for the best, I suppose. If they started in on Bechet, I'd force you to dance with me, and that might perturb your—husband?"

She nodded. "Yes. My husband. I'm sorry. I should have introduced you. It's Jeffrey. Jeffrey Willcox."

He tapped the rim of his champagne glass. "I was sorry to hear about Tariq."

"We were all sorry about Tariq." Jeffrey sipped his champagne and spoke to Nuh for the first time that evening. "A terrible accident."

If Nuh was surprised that Jeffrey understood Turkish, he hid it. But, having survived twenty years in the cutthroat Ottoman and Turkish demimonde, he easily picked up on the quiet threat under Jeffrey's banal tone. It appeared to interest him. He nodded and lifted his glass. "A good man. An excellent husband."

Jeffrey raised his own glass. "And so much more."

Marion, watching the two of them, felt her nausea returning. She swallowed and took a sip of her champagne. Then she held the cold glass against her cheek. If Jeffrey thought that he could bully Nuh into helping them, he was mistaken. Nuh didn't buckle. And she frantically wanted to move the conversation away from Tariq. She tried to signal to Jeffrey that he was handling the situation badly, but he was deliberately ignoring her. Still holding Nuh's gaze.

"I congratulate you," he said. "This is lovely little club."

"And what do you do?" Nuh appeared to find Jeffrey's aggression entertaining. He was enjoying himself.

"I work for the British Museum and Library," Jeffrey said, sipping more champagne. "As a cataloguer."

"Fascinating work."

"Indeed. I specialize in the medieval Orient." He paused. "Marion and I were at Cambridge together."

"Before Tariq, then." Nuh waved away a waiter who had been cautiously approaching them.

"Indeed," Jeffrey repeated. "Before Tariq. Marion and I have worked together a great deal. We're here together now researching a new project."

"This would be for the Library? Or the Museum?" Nuh, no longer able to control his expression, had broken into an appreciative smile. Marion had the impression that he was bored much of the time, and that he was grateful for the diversion they were supplying him this evening. But the direction the conversation was taking was by no means helpful to their work. She was beginning to worry.

"Both, really—" Jeffrey started.

"Oh, for Heaven's sake, Jeffrey," Marion said in English. "Why are you doing this? He knows perfectly well—"

Nuh held up his hand. "No, no, Marion." He had also switched to English. "Better to keep the conversation as it is. God forbid your colleagues at the British Museum and Library should decide that I know too much and set out to silence me."

"They can be a ferocious bunch," Jeffrey agreed, his voice mild.

Nuh lifted his glass again in a half salute to Jeffrey and drained it. He poured more champagne for Jeffrey and himself. Marion hadn't had any since her first, nauseated sip.

"How can I help you both, then?" He had switched back to Turkish.

"Do you know anything about the history of this building?" Marion asked, deciding to be as forthright as possible. "Or of what existed here before?"

Nuh thought for a few seconds, surprised by the question. "I believe," he finally said, "that it was empty ground before construction began on the block of flats. But there's a local legend that a hundred or so years before that, there was a warehouse owned by a famous apothecary. Or alchemist. That building burned down at the end of the eighteenth century. We even considered calling the first club 'The Apothecary.'"

"Jazz Vampire is better," Jeffrey said helpfully.

"Thank you." Nuh was clearly still more interested than annoyed by Jeffrey's conversation, but the balance looked about to tip in favor of the latter.

Jeffrey smiled into his glass.

Before he could say anything more, Marion moved closer to Nuh. She spoke quietly. "Are you certain they say it could have been an alchemist's?"

"Yes. There are many colorful stories about him," Nuh was smiling again. "They say that's why the place is haunted." His eyes twinkled. "Good for business."

"Do you know whether any of the original foundations of that building—whatever it was— are still in place?" Pushing down her growing excitement.

He nodded. "Yes. All of them—they continue into, or under, the building next door. Only the above-ground parts of the old construction burned. There's a stone cellar that's original. We keep the wine there."

"Nuh," she said, "could we look at it? I know it's asking a lot—"

He stood. "Shall we go now?"

She was startled by both his easy acquiescence and his quick decision-making. She'd forgotten his impulsive streak—the quality that kept his competitors off-guard. But she also didn't want to take advantage of him.

"We can return tomorrow during the day," she offered. Looking at the packed room, the tipsy dancers, the still cool singer, she thought it was inappropriate to use them as cover for their job. And Nuh worked hard during the evening to see to it that the club ran properly. She didn't want to distract him unnecessarily.

"Better to do it now," he reassured her. "Less curiosity. I'm rarely awake before two in the afternoon anyway."

"Lucky fellow." Jeffrey had stood as well. He drained the last of his champagne and left the glass on the table.

Nuh turned to him, astonished now by his brazenly obnoxious conversation. He blinked, looked at Marion, shook his head, and then indicated that they should follow him.

Marion rose from her chair, stifling a sigh. Jeffrey, she had finally realized, was doing his job as well—and doing it quite successfully. He had read and analyzed Nuh's personality within minutes of meeting him and had determined that his current act—insufferable—was the most likely to yield quick results. But the fact that she understood Jeffrey's motives didn't make them more palatable to her. She loathed his working persona. And she had to keep herself from shrugging off his hand as he guided her past the stage and toward another narrow staircase, a contemptuous smile on his face.

Nuh preceded them down the staircase, which was hidden behind a curtain to the side of the bar, until they reached a locked wooden door. He unlocked the door, stood to the side, and let them enter the cellar in front of him. As they did so, Nuh turned a switch on the wall that operated an electric light bulb dangling from the ceiling. The bulb threw a greenish light over the ancient stone floor, the wooden casks, and the racks of bottles arranged along the walls. A large grey rat disappeared into a hole in the corner of the room when Nuh turned on the light.

"Is there anything I can do to help you?" he asked as they considered the room. "I can bring someone down to move the heavier casks, if you'd like."

She shook her head, still looking thoughtfully about her. "No. If we're lucky, that won't be necessary. I have a feeling it will be under one of the stones on the floor." She stepped further into the room and ran a finger along part of the wall. It was damp. She could also sense the hollow area behind it.

Deciding again on forthrightness, she turned back to Nuh. "Are there any birds?"

"Birds?"

"Yes. Have you seen any carvings or sculptures or—or diagrams of anything that looks like a bird?"

He grinned. "You mean Doğan?"

"Doğan? A falcon? You've seen one here?"

"Of course," Nuh crossed briskly to the edge of the cellar. "He's our mascot. Been here since we bought the building."

He shifted an empty barrel and pointed to a rectangular stone at the base of the back wall. It was only an eye and beak, and faded to a thin scrawl, but it was unmistakably a falcon's head carved with care into the surface of the rock. There was also a large mouse or rat hole at the corner of the stone. She tried to squat to get a better look, but couldn't. Frustrated, she lowered herself to her hands and knees and peered into the hole.

"Good God, Marion, don't do that." Nuh was bending over, helping her up. "There are rats everywhere. We can't get rid of them. That's the last place you want to be putting your face."

"I can reach in with my hand—"

"You want to shift the stone?" he asked, pulling her up.

She nodded. Embarrassed. "Could we? I don't think it will weaken the wall. With—with what the rats have already done."

He nodded, walked back up the stairs, and returned less than a minute later with a two-foot-long pipe. "Sinem keeps it upstairs with her. At the door. Should the bouncers fail to do their job effectively."

He squatted and inserted the pipe into the hole at the edge of the stone. Wary. As soon as he'd done so, a sickening scrabbling sound grew to a crescendo behind the wall. Ignoring the sound, he leaned against the pipe and shifted the stone. The stone moved easily, and he stumbled as the cavity opened. But he righted himself quickly, upset and drawing in his breath, as eight rats sprang from the hole and scattered across the floor of the cellar.

Marion squeezed her eyes shut, squeamish despite herself. Then, forcing open her eyes, she approached the gap in the wall herself. Tried to bend over again, but once she was close to the cavity, she toppled over, and had to catch herself. Irritated, she began to lower herself to the ground, but Jeffrey prevented her, equally exasperated.

"Stop it, Marion." He'd dropped his snide voice. His face was now blank and professional. "I'll do it."

He squatted in front of the wall and reached into the cavity with both hands. Flinched as the scuttering sound recommenced and a single large brown rat emerged from the hole, dropping to the ground and running in the direction of the others. But he didn't remove his arms until he'd found what he wanted: a lead box, undecorated, eighteen inches long and a little over a foot wide, caked with dust and rodent droppings. Satisfied, he straightened.

Nuh peered at the box, impressed. "That was there all along?"

Marion nodded. "It may be best if you don't tell anyone about it yet. Hide it somewhere safe in the club and then decide what you'd like to do with it. It may be valuable. But, Nuh, if you'd let me examine it when you're ready to open it, I'd be—?"

"Examine what? I haven't seen anything here. Other than far too many rats for one night." He turned to Jeffrey. "That," nodding at the box, "is precisely the sort of bother I avoid like the plague. Whatever is in there, I don't need it in my life."

Marion, who would never have expected such a reaction from a businessman who had discovered buried treasure in his wall, gaped at him. Then, without thinking, she threw her arms around him. She had also forgotten his generosity. "Thank you, Nuh. *Thank you* for this."

He hugged her back and kissed her hair. "You feel the same as you always did, Marion."

She disengaged herself, flustered. "Really, Nuh. I'm grateful. We're grateful. Thank you. But if you change your mind, it belongs to you. I don't want you to regret—"

"I never regret my decisions. And I've learned not to court unnecessary trouble." He stood to the side of the stairs to let them pass.

Jeffrey, the box under one arm, took Marion's elbow with his other hand to help her up the stairs. As they walked, he turned, smiling, back to Nuh. "I myself like trouble."

"You're a real cunt, aren't you?" Nuh was smiling as well. Almost as taken by Jeffrey as he was by Marion.

THEY left the box on the living room table when they returned to Jeffrey's flat. Neither was in any state to investigate its contents that evening, and so—without discussing the matter—they both went to bed. Marion would be happy never to see another nightclub again. Jeffrey, she suspected, felt the same, though he wouldn't have admitted it to her, or to anyone else.

When they woke the next morning, they also avoided mention of the box until they'd eaten breakfast. It sat, silent and ominous, on the table in the living room, and they scrupulously avoided looking at it as they passed in and out of the courtyard. When Marion felt she'd drunk sufficient coffee, and Jeffrey had smoked two cigarettes, they made shamefaced eye contact and rose together from their seats outside to return to the living room. Then they sat, side by side, on the sofa in front of the low table. Both still in their dressing gowns.

"Would you like to open it, or shall I?" Jeffrey was lighting a third cigarette. He inhaled and set the match in an ashtray well to the edge of the table.

She ran her fingertip along the top of the box, sending up a small plume of dust. Then she leaned forward to examine its hinge and the clasp. It was remarkably unembellished for its time and apparent importance.

"Look," she said, pointing to the clasp, "it was meant to be locked."

"But it wasn't."

"Perhaps they were in a hurry."

"Perhaps." He blew smoke up at the ceiling. "Are you going to open it?" he repeated.

She said nothing for a few seconds, and then she nodded. Taking a breath and lifting the clasp, she eased the box open. When the interior was exposed, she let out her breath. Nothing horrible had leapt from it to skitter across the room and hide itself in the walls of the building. She had half expected a repetition of their experience of the previous night.

Instead, the next few steps were familiar to her. After removing the disintegrating linen sheet covering the contents of the box, she withdrew a tall, metallic, cylindrical cup. Beside it was a tightly stoppered green glass bottle. She placed both on the table next to the linen sheet. Underneath, she found three crumbling pieces of vellum or cotton.

The first two were pages of tightly spaced script taken from a manuscript or collection of manuscripts. The third was an illuminated Persian or Ottoman miniature depicting a number of scholars or scientists that, even as she lifted it delicately out of the box to place on the table, she thought she recognized. She'd be more certain once she'd examined it in detail.

When the box was empty, she leaned back against the sofa. Jeffrey, having left his cigarette in the ashtray, was walking to the other side of the table, the better to read the two manuscript pages. He bent over the first, his forehead wrinkled. Then he scanned the second as well.

"Part of a poem," he said. "And a scientific text. I'd guess the scientific study is by Taqi al-Din, but that's only because of how and where we found it." He returned his attention to the poem. "The verses are certainly *about* him." He pointed. "Look. Here—the observatory is mentioned prominently. Complimentary. But also a bit backhanded." He smiled. "I like it. Whoever it is, he's a good poet. Unlikely to get himself caught out."

She pushed herself into an upright position and walked around the table to stand behind him. Then she lowered herself into another chair and leaned forward to skim the pages. "I think the poem is by 'Ala' al-Din al-Mansur. His description of the comet—or, yes, here, the 'fiery stellar body'—usually attached to a longer poem about the reign of Sultan Murad III. He's always been a useful source on Taqi al-Din and the Observatory. And, obviously, on the Sultan's generosity to both, even though he tore the whole thing down after five years."

She read a few more lines. "I agree. It is an unusual poem. Complicated. But I have a feeling that this page is different from the other extant versions. Otherwise, why preserve it here?" She tilted her head. "This looks like the list of the Observatory's 'instruments of great perfection.'"

Jeffrey returned to the sofa. Reached for the cylinder—or cup—but before he could say anything, Marion spoke again. "Yes." Nodding to herself. "And this other folio is by Taqi al-Din himself. It's from his study of light and vision. Not his work on astronomy. I think it's called something like *The Book of Light and the Pupil's Vision and the Truth of Perspectives—Kitab Nur hadaqat al-ibsar wa nur haqiqat al-anzar.* This folio here is another list of tools. Interesting."

Jeffrey opened his mouth again to comment, but she spoke over him a third time. "And I've seen this miniature before, attached to one of the early versions of al-Mansur's poem." Running her finger over the illuminated page. "The manuscript is in the city. At Istanbul University." She peered down at it. "It's famous. A sort of real-time pictorial record of the astronomers at work in the Observatory."

She paused again, thinking. "But this one *is* different. Instead of a terrestrial—rather than celestial—globe at the center of the image—which has always already confused people—it looks like he's using—" She raised her eyes. "—that. That—cup? Odd."

Jeffrey had started laughing.

"What?" Annoyed that he hadn't been listening.

"I'm allowed to speak now?" He reached for his cigarette again.

"I'd rather you didn't." Embarrassed now.

"Don't be stroppy," he said. "I enjoy you like this."

"I don't do it to please you."

"As I've learned," he said, blowing smoke up at the ceiling. "To my desolation."

"What did you want to say?" she repeated doggedly.

Although, even as she prodded him, she remained more than half focused on the pages on the table in front of her. Ready to go back to work. Excited. Energetic. But previous experience had taught her that Jeffrey frequently held her back at precisely these moments. He didn't want to be excluded from her thought processes when she was on the verge of learning something important. And so, he kept her anxious—as a working strategy.

Knowing that it was a strategy, she tried to summon up the strength to respond to it—shaking her head, irritated, as he began to ask his question one more time. An idea—she wasn't certain what—was beginning to coalesce just beneath her consciousness. Indulging Jeffrey in his desire for endless, torturous conversation would kill it before she could consider its implications. She silently implored him to give up and leave her alone to her work.

He smiled at her, a touch malign. He knew what she was feeling. But his question was innocuous enough. "What do you think this is?" He was holding up the cylinder, turning it in the light, examining its markings.

"I think I'll have a better idea once I've read the manuscript pages." Belligerent and evasive.

"It looks like an antimonial cup," he said, ignoring her tone and placing it back on the table.

"A what?" Not listening, still itching to read the pages in front of her with proper care. She'd already dropped her eyes back to the poem.

"An antimonial cup," he repeated. "Ginnie's got one in the house somewhere. People used them in the seventeenth century to help them purge after an excessive meal."

That caught her attention. She looked up. "What?"

He shrugged. "You saw the painting. The man ate too much. Gout. When the alchemists of the sixteenth century discovered the secret to isolating antimony—"

"Antimony?" She felt her idea growing clearer.

"Yes," he said. "Kohl. The crystalline metal used to darken the eye. It also worked well as an emetic. And for vision—"

"For vision?"

He nodded, suspicious now. "Yes." He paused. "Anyhow, the secret to isolating it as a malleable metal was revealed—to use alchemical language—sometime in the sixteenth century. By the seventeenth and eighteenth centuries, fashionable households all had an antimonial cup for their more exuberant entertainments. You'd let wine sit in it overnight, drink the wine the next morning, and—enjoy the purge. No gout."

"And you think that's what this is? An antimonial cup?" She was still chasing the edges of her idea.

"No," he said. "I think it *looks* like an antimonial cup. Same—texture. But it's more complicated than that. And a bit too long."

He picked it up again and held it lengthwise. "It's almost more a tube. And it's got these glass—or maybe crystal?—pieces at each end. You can look through them to see inside. But not through it." He held his eye to one end. "Yes, a third of the way down, on both sides, there's an opaque metal plate."

He put it back on the table and considered it. "And then there's this ceramic compartment at the base where the handle should be." He peered into the compartment. "It's got a sort of crumbled sheet of copper surrounding a rusted stick of iron inside."

He leaned back against the sofa. "But it's the same shape as a longish goblet. And it feels like antimony. I used to switch Ginnie's breakfast cup for the household antimonial cup when I was six or seven years old. I remember the texture well." He took a morose drag from his cigarette. "I only ever fooled her once. And she was already ill that day. Likely would have been vomiting for the rest of the afternoon regardless."

She blinked, uncertain as to how to respond. Then, her mind still racing, she indicated the stoppered bottle. "What about that?"

"Shall I open it?" He lifted the bottle and examined it in the same way he'd examined the tube. "I'm not sure I ought to. In the stories, it always ends badly."

"I can do it," she said, reaching across the table.

"No," he said. "One unbalanced child is enough. I want this one sane. God knows what you were inhaling when you were carrying the boy."

"And yet you claim to have been watching the entire time?" Spiteful. "You ought to field more competent thugs."

"Hmm." He began to work the stopper out of the bottle. "The problem, darling, is that whenever I field anyone with anything close to your tolerance for alcohol and opiates, they vanish into the ghastly world of Edwin Drood, never to be seen again. You appreciate the difficulty, surely?" He broke the seal of the bottle and set the stopper on the table. After a second or two of silence, he smiled. "We appear still to be conscious."

Lifting the bottle closer to his face, he took a wary sniff. Then he squinted into it, shaking the contents. It sounded to Marion like fine sand.

"What is it?"

He held the bottle out to her, and she took it.

"It looks like salt to me," he said.

"Salt." She arranged the bottle on the table next to the manuscript pages. Then she closed her eyes for a few seconds, thinking. Her idea had taken shape. And, to her annoyance, she'd need his help to finish putting the pieces together. But she couldn't tell him very much more or he'd begin drawing conclusions himself. She remained silent, considering her next move.

"Jeffrey," she eventually said. "In that miniature of the scholars in the Observatory, the central figure is holding that tube up to his eye. Like a telescope."

He shook his head. "No. Not possible. The telescope was invented in the Netherlands. Muslim scientists notoriously failed to produce one—though they invented just about every other astronomical technology of the time. Rather than telescopic lenses, they used more and more elaborate pinnules. It's a famous problem."

He crushed out his cigarette. "Granted, it looks a bit like a telescope. And the pieces of glass at each end could be lenses. But those metal circles in the middle of the tube block light from entering. It's opaque. You can't look through it." He paused. "Taqi al-Din couldn't have invented the telescope. It's a dead end to consider it."

"I think he may have skipped it," she said, half to herself.

"I'm sorry?"

She looked up at him. "No, you're correct. And I didn't say it was a telescope. It's like a telescope. But he's using it incorrectly. Pointing it into a corner of the room rather than up at the sky. Peculiar way to use an astronomical instrument." She ran her finger over a few lines of the scientific treatise. "And he makes no claims about inventing telescopic lenses."

She gazed down at the page for a moment longer. "Instead, he says here that he used a crystal—*billawr*, or it would be *billur* in Turkish, a kind of rock-crystal lens, though he's writing in Arabic—to make the details of—of murky objects—clear. Then he goes on to say that this instrument he's created is the same as what the ancient Greeks placed at the top of the Tower of Alexandria. Not a telescope, obviously. But—something 'wonderous.' The Tower of Alexandria supposedly lit up the whole Mediterranean. Until it was dismantled. Destroyed. Like the Observatory. And then," she continued when he didn't reply, "look at this section of al-Mansur's poem. I haven't seen it for years, but I know this can't be how the original reads. It doesn't even scan."

Jeffrey, obliging, stood again and walked around to her side of the table. He bent over her as she read.

"He's talking," she said to him, "about how the tools and instruments of 'great perfection' were all built and installed in the Observatory. He goes into a lot of detail—even describing the raw materials that were used to construct them. I remember having seen this section of the manuscript before. But in the extant versions of this poem, he mentions brass, copper, and maybe bronze, wood, and iron as the building materials. Typical for creating instruments and tools at the time? Look at what he lists here instead."

Jeffrey leaned over further and read in turn: "'the tools were all prepared, and they were of great perfection, with sections of—' hmm. He says, 'with sections made of *ithmid*, antimony, and *suda*—' a headache?"

"Yes." Annoyed. "But *suda* is also—"

"Ah yes," he continued. "Salt. Used to treat a headache."

"Perhaps 'sodium,'" she suggested. "To go with the antimony."

"Very well." He turned his attention back to the poem. "And *al-qaliya*—' ashes? Or alkaline materials? Burnt alkaline material?" He brightened. "He's talking about potassium. The original *kali*. 'Element K.' He hasn't got a specific word for it."

He straightened and took his place on the sofa again. "So, he's saying that these observational tools were made of antimony, sodium, and potassium." Smiled to himself. "I can see why the Sultan was disappointed."

"But he insists," she said, "that these—these chemicals—were assembled into tools to help him *see*. Or, more accurately, to reproduce things seen. He even calls one of the instruments *al-mushabbaha bi'l manatiq*, which suggests that its function was to re-create a region or zone of vision within a similar or parallel—but not identical—other region or zone. Everything happening at the Observatory had to do with vision."

She stopped again, uncertain as to whether to tell him more. Then, recognizing that she must to keep them moving in the proper direction, she pressed forward. "This sounds to me quite a bit like the experiments that Nasir al-Din and al-Urdi were undertaking in the cave network under Maragha." She rested her finger on the page and turned it to face Jeffrey. "And look here—at this sketch in the margin."

He peered down at it. "A little tower. And, yes, I believe that's a falcon circling it."

"I think it's the tower of Alexandria," she said. "Which connects it back to Taqi al-Din's *Book of Light*."

He nodded, rose, and moved toward the courtyard. "Excellent. So, we'll bring this material back with us to London, and you'll complete your analysis there. You'll likely have something to satisfy Maugham before the boy returns for the holiday—"

"No," she said, also standing. "We can't leave yet. I need—I mean—" She paused. "It would be helpful if we also went to Gallipoli tomorrow. The Dardanelles. To the town of Bolayır." She rubbed her eyes. "I—I want to confirm that I'm on the right track."

The corner of his mouth went up. He wasn't looking at her. Instead, he was gazing through the window at the courtyard. "I wouldn't want you to tire yourself."

"Jeffrey," she said. "Please. Don't do this. I can't help Maugham, or—or your people—any better than I can help my own without—"

"But you'll still pass a bit more to them than to us," he replied, not moving. "I caught the change in your tone."

"Of course I'll try to pass along the better part of the material to my people," she said. "It would be stupid of me to attempt to convince you otherwise. And you'll try to stop me. I expect that as well. But neither of us can take any further steps unless I finish my work in Turkey. You'll be undermining your own project if you stop me now. You know that."

"Marion," he said, "has it ever occurred to you that you could simply fail? Just this once? Or leave, perhaps, a few loose ends for others to tie up?"

"*No*," she said, feeling desperate. She couldn't leave her work now that it was coalescing into something satisfying. She'd never stop thinking about it.

"Of course not." He turned to her. "Stopping short isn't your style. But let me warn you now. Maugham won't accept anything but a complete story. You know as well as I do that he enjoys nothing more than spotting evasion. And if he asks me to interview you formally about your findings, I'll do so. As a professional. You'll be utterly vulnerable. Think about your condition."

She merely stared at him, without speaking.

"I think you're making a mistake," he said.

"I'm not." She returned to her chair and began reading the manuscript material again.

He stayed at the window, looking out. "Then I'll ask the Consulate to send the car for us tomorrow morning. It ought to take between four and five hours to get there. We'll stay the night and return the day after.

She didn't reply. She was immersed in the poetry.

EARLY the next morning, before the sun had illuminated the courtyard, they met the car that would take them to the village of Bolayır, on the Dardanelles Strait. Marion was pleased not to delay their departure; but when they stepped out into the alley, there was a wet chill in the air. And Jeffrey grabbed her arm to steady her as, still mortifyingly off-balance, she slipped on the slick cobblestones. As they slid into the rear seat of the Bentley, a stray dog was nosing through a sodden pile of damp paper and food scraps that had accumulated in a corner of the building next door. The dog looked cold.

Once the driver had edged the car down the hill, he turned right and made his way to the coastal road leading out of the city. Along the Marmara, in the direction of the Aegean. When they passed the old Byzantine wall, Marion gazed at the water to her left. It was calm this morning. But leaden. The changed autumn air had affected the sea as well.

She shifted uncomfortably in her seat. Pleased that Jeffrey had agreed to take her to Bolayır, but uneasy nonetheless, picking up the oppressive atmosphere of the sea and the city. She closed her eyes.

"Are you going to tell me anything at all?" Jeffrey was looking out his own window at the less picturesque construction scattered along the right side of the road.

"No." She opened her eyes again and stared at the water.

"Let me put the question in a different way," he said after a few seconds of vexed silence. "We are now driving five hours to Bolayır, on the Dardanelles. Unless you give me something marginally satisfactory on the way, I'll tell the driver to circle the village and bring us straight back here tonight. We'll find petrol elsewhere. We'll tell Maugham that we lost our trail."

When she simply frowned and continued looking out the window, he ran a hand through his hair and asked, patiently: "what's in Bolayır?"

"Falcons," she said shortly.

"I think," he said, watching her face, "that it's falcons and submarines. Given the geography."

Startled, she turned to him. Didn't know what to say.

"Thank you, darling, for the confirmation." He resumed his observation of his window. "Begin with the submarines."

"I'll begin with the falcons," she said, turning back to the sea.

"And then the submarines."

"The tomb of Gazi Süleyman Pasha, the son of Orhan, the first Sultan of the Ottoman Empire, is in Bolayır," she said, ignoring him. "Süleyman Pasha died there in 1357 while out hunting. He was known for his skill at falconry. He was flying his gyrfalcons when he fell from his horse. He was the initiating force behind the Ottoman love of—obsession with—falconry. In the 1390s, the Sultan Bayezid used to ransom his European prisoners for falcons and skilled falconers. Gyrfalcons in particular."

She stopped speaking, and he was quiet for a few seconds longer. "Is that all?" he finally prodded.

"Yes." Sullen. "We haven't explored the references to falconry sufficiently. I want to be certain that we aren't missing something."

"And the submarines?"

"I don't know anything about submarines." She balled her hands into fists in her lap.

He observed her hands for a moment, and then he spoke: "I do. Shall I tell you about it?"

"I'd rather rest. It's a long journey."

"The importance of the submarine support during the Gallipoli Campaign," he began, ignoring her in turn, "has always, I feel, been underestimated. I wasn't there, mind you. In March of 1915, I was taking the air at Neuve-Chapelle. But I've maintained an interest. Especially as my early days in France and Belgium gave way to a fascinating grand tour through Mesopotamia and other equally interesting former Ottoman holdings."

"I don't want to hear about the mud and gas," she said. "You've mentioned them before. They bore me."

"You're a dreadful helpmeet, dear. Thank heaven I married you for your bad temper rather than for companionship and sympathy."

She stared out the window, silent.

"Let me get to the submarines."

"If you must."

"The Gallipoli Campaign," he said, "didn't go as planned."

"Yes, I recall."

"The unfortunate Winston's original idea—"

"He seems to be doing all right now," she interjected.

He turned to her. "Does he? Raising a fuss, yes. But a following? I'm not so certain."

She didn't reply.

"Anyhow," he resumed, "the original idea, once the Navy had begun bombarding Ottoman fortifications on the Dardanelles in November of 1914—"

"Begun illegally bombarding Ottoman fortifications," she corrected him. "Britain hadn't yet declared war on the Ottoman Empire."

"Weren't you going to sit there in hostile silence? Refusing to hear a word I said concerning this nonsense about the submarines?"

She stared out the window.

"Good," he nodded. "That's more like it. So, once the bombardment began in November of 1914—three days before we declared war—the need for a more detailed plan of attack became apparent. So, in early January of 1915, the War Council approved the proposed strategy for forcing the Dardanelles. Great rejoicing. We'll be through the straits and dining in Constantinople—" He looked at her in mock concern. "You don't mind if I call it 'Constantinople,' do you, dear? Excellent. So we'll be in Constantinople by the beginning of February. Then onward to the Balkans, up into Austria, and—you know the rest."

She still didn't speak.

"Things didn't go as strategized."

"Your Admiral had a nervous breakdown," she said to the window.

He smiled. "True. But that was a few months later. And, I think, not explanatory."

When she didn't say any more, he continued. "So, warships bombarded positions on both sides of the water, but January passed, February passed, and the straits failed to fall. The shelling continued into the end of March and beginning of April 1915. No luck. Finally, in April, the powers that be took the brilliant decision to land an amphibious force on the Gallipoli peninsula and entrench. And so, between the end of April 1915 and the beginning of January 1916, the land on either side of the Dardanelles looked eerily like France and Belgium. 9 January 1916: Winston's forces depart for good."

"Fine." Hoping that he had now finished. "Is that all?"

"I haven't mentioned the submarines."

She sighed. The road had turned inland, and she could no longer see the water. But she wasn't about to look away from the window.

"Before I get to the submarines, though," he said, choosing his words carefully now, "I would like to return briefly to Süleyman Pasha's tomb."

"Fine."

"In March of 1915, before the land forces arrived, the *HMS Queen Elizabeth*—a dreadnaught battleship with long range bombardment capabilities—started shelling fortified positions along the Dardanelles." He paused. "Which makes good sense. Between 25 March and 29 March, however, her targeting decisions became a bit less—rational."

He waited for a few seconds longer and then continued. "Because you see, Marion, at the end of March, she initiated a concerted, calculated, and frankly bizarre attack on the tomb of Gazi Süleyman Pasha. Shelling it repeatedly until most of it—but particularly the minaret on the mosque attached to it—was a wreck. The Flying Corps chaps on reconnaissance at the end of April double checked on that."

She continued to stare out the window. But she was aware that he could easily read the tension in her neck. She tried, unsuccessfully, to remain opaque.

"It made very little sense," he mused, watching her taut profile. "The tomb was of no military value. A cultural edifice. Why would they shell it?"

"Because they're war criminals?"

He smiled. "Who isn't? But that's not the point."

"I fail to see the point."

"Let me return to the submarines, then," he said. "So, the fate of the submarine battle was nearly the inverse of the campaign as a whole. At the start, it was a catastrophe. Nothing got through. French boats, Australian boats, British boats, it didn't matter—they were an embarrassment. Running aground. Getting captured. Surfacing at awkward moments. Not to mention that our nighttime operations were, to be generous, a farce."

He watched the passing scenery for a full minute before he continued. "But that all changed in April, when the first submarine—Australian—made it through the Dardanelles and into the Sea of Marmara." He paused. "And after that, it was something of a free-for-all. The campaign itself foundered, but the submarines had a ripping time. As though, somehow, some sort of obstacle had been removed at the beginning of April. By the end of May, a few of them even made it into the Bosporus. Causing all sorts of chaos in Constantinople itself."

"I wonder what could have changed at the end of March and beginning of April?" he asked when still she didn't reply. "Could the crew of the *HMS Queen Elizabeth*, do you think, have received intelligence that—"

"I'm hungry," she said. "Can we stop somewhere?"

"That's beneath you, Marion. Using your condition as a—"

"I think we're coming up on Tekirdağ," she persisted. "Perhaps we'll find some *köfte*. And I'd like to walk a bit. Before we continue. My legs are cramped."

"Very well," he said. "I've made my point. I know you'll want to think on it for an hour or two before coming up with what I'm confident will be a creative and entertaining response to it."

He leaned forward and spoke to the driver. Five minutes later, they were entering the suburbs of the city. And fifteen minutes after that, Marion was devouring a plate of meatballs and drinking a glass of *ayran*. Jeffrey was smoking a cigarette, watching the crowds passing the tall windows of their café. Oblivious to the changed weather. Or, perhaps—indomitable—they simply refused to acknowledge the encroaching cold and mist.

Thirty minutes later, they were back on the road. The driver had found petrol for the car, which meant that they wouldn't stop again before entering the village of Bolayır. And, in just under two hours, they were slowing to halt in the green area that surrounded the mausoleum. Well-tended. Flourishing. In the twenty years since the village had been shelled, the population had more than rebuilt, and neither the mosque nor the tomb bore marks of the damage they had suffered.

Reassured by the prosperous and open feel of the town, Marion and Jeffrey left the car, wandered through the decade-old plantings, and climbed the stairs to the monument. There was no caretaker, and so they entered without explaining themselves. The building was deserted.

But once inside, Marion was nonplussed, uncertain how to proceed. The building was new. Nothing remained of the original construction. And she was at a loss as to how to gather the information she needed. Walking pensively through the space, all she could do was take note of its layout and hope that it echoed, if it didn't replicate, the original complex. But internalizing the layout wouldn't be sufficient for her purposes.

Squinting up at the ceiling of the room, she spoke to Jeffrey. "I want to see the exterior of the mosque as well. I needn't enter it. I'd just like an idea of its position."

"Very well."

They left the tomb and walked the perimeter of the adjacent mosque. It was equally new. Well cared for. But lacking any historical feel. She scrutinized the likewise new minaret. Then, smiling, she exhaled. The fencing surrounding the balcony was a dullish grey metal mesh. Old. She hadn't realized she'd been holding her breath.

"I've finished." She began retracing their steps toward the car. "That's all I need. Thank you."

He trotted to catch up to her and then slipped her hand through his arm. "That's it?"

"That's it. I've told you. I found what I needed."

"Which is?"

They reached the car, she opened the door before the driver had a chance to emerge, and she slid into the back seat. "Nothing about submarines."

He opened the door opposite and sat next to her. "I think it's in your interest to tell me why we drove here."

"We needn't stay the night, need we?" She looked at him with an apologetic smile. "I know it's a long drive back, but I'd rather not talk with innkeepers just now. I'm tired."

A flicker of something between frustration and affection passed over his face. "Oh, very well."

He leaned forward and spoke to the driver again. His tone also sounded apologetic as they conversed through the screen, but then he nodded and laughed, looking, amused, at Marion.

As the Bentley picked up speed leaving the town, he leaned back in the seat, relaxed. "We'll talk later, then."

London, England
January, 1936

THEIR plane returned to Croydon on the 21st of November, a day later than planned because Jeffrey had insisted that they rest for the night in Brindisi. He was worried about Marion's simultaneously haggard and charged affect, and he wouldn't accept her insistence that her work was more important than perfect sleep. Her brittle enthusiasm, she knew as well as he did, was unhealthy. But she couldn't damp it down. And, spiteful, she didn't want to. She resented Jeffrey's unspoken concern for her emotional state. His wary attention to her moods echoed too closely his familiar mocking interest in her mental equilibrium. It left her both cross and frightened.

Not that she regretted the night in Brindisi. By the time they'd reached Chester Terrace, she was on the verge of disintegrating. And her only conscious act before climbing the stairs to her room and giving herself over to sleep was to watch where Jeffrey left her material. His study, she confirmed. On the desk rather than in the safe. If she woke early enough tomorrow morning, she'd be able to work with it before breakfast. Perhaps even before Jeffrey returned to it.

Pleased with herself and comforted by her knowledge of her project's whereabouts, she slept well and woke before dawn. And once she'd pulled on a dressing gown, she wasted no time in walking down the stairs to his study. But when she pushed open the door, the desk was empty. The manuscript pages, the rubbing of the celestial globe, Stephen's circles, the metal tube, and the bottle were all gone. Frowning, she stepped further into the room and shut the door.

She walked past the desk and stood in front of the wall safe adjacent to the bookcase, considering. He'd known she would come looking for her manuscripts, she told herself. He'd moved them to the safe. Which was an annoyance, but not an insurmountable obstacle. He'd grant her access to the material at some point. Otherwise he'd be unable to deliver to Maugham the information he'd demanded. And if he insisted on watching her, she would simply hold back her conclusions—as she'd already been doing now for two months.

Rubbing her lower back with the flat of her hand, she turned and left the room. She saw no one, and no one spoke to her, as she reached the ground floor of the house—which pleased her, but also left her uneasy. Unnerved by the quiet, she moved in the direction of the dining room. It was unlikely that they'd have prepared breakfast so early, but she could forage. She also wanted to be there when Jeffrey appeared. Go on the offensive and ask him directly where he'd put her papers.

The radiator hissed as she crossed the hall, but otherwise, the ground floor was silent. She was just beginning to feel a nervous chill on the back of her neck, wondering where the usual morning bustle of Jeffrey's household was, when the door to the kitchen stairs opened. Mrs. Bowen, dressed in her uniform and uncharacteristically preoccupied, emerged and then started upon seeing Marion standing in the hall.

Recovering herself almost before Marion had perceived her surprise, she smiled. "Lady Willcox. You're up early this morning."

Marion threw her a wry smile. "I don't sleep very well these days."

"Nonsense." Mrs. Bowen stepped toward the door to the dining room to open it for her. "You look beautifully rested, if you'll forgive the comment. I've rarely seen such a glow on an expectant mother. But you'll want to eat something to keep up your energy."

Marion blinked, quizzical, before continuing toward the dining room. She couldn't quite accept Mrs. Bowen's endless fascination with her pregnancy. Not that she had any reason to doubt her honesty. Mrs. Bowen was integrity personified. But she also wasn't a stupid woman, and Marion had difficulty believing that her attitude toward childbirth wasn't more complicated than she let on. Professionalism, she concluded as she passed Mrs. Bowen into the dining room. Mrs. Bowen's profession was the family. Or so she supposed. It was the best she could do.

She was surprised when she saw that the sideboard had already been prepared for breakfast. She'd expected to ask for a piece of toast from the kitchen while she waited for Jeffrey to appear. As she took up a plate, she turned to Mrs. Bowen, who was disappearing through the door. "It's not yet dawn. You can't do this every morning. I would have noticed."

"Sir Jeffrey had an early start to the day. He asked last night that we prepare breakfast for him." She paused. "He also asked me to pass along his apologies. He'll be late at the office and will miss dinner."

"Oh." Marion felt a stab of apprehension, but she ignored it. Instead of asking further questions, she nodded. "Thank you, Mrs. Bowen."

"Do you have plans for the day, Lady Willcox?" Mrs. Bowen had remained in the door.

"I had thought—" She considered. "A walk in the park. Perhaps." She smiled slightly. "If that's all right. I don't want to leave you open to reproach a second time."

"I'm certain the park will be acceptable, Lady Willcox." Mrs. Bowen smiled as well. "If you find yourself needing raspberry tea from Soho, though, perhaps we ought to send one of the boys?"

Marion dropped her eyes to the sideboard and put two pieces of toast on her plate. "Yes. Agreed."

"Thank you, Lady Willcox."

Once Mrs. Bowen had left the room, Marion sat at the empty table with her plate of toast and a cup of tea. She was unhappy with the direction the morning had taken. And she had no confidence in Jeffrey's sudden desire to spend the first day of their return at the office. Something was wrong.

She sipped her tea and gazed in front of her. A large blue vase of purple Michaelmas Daisies took up much of the center of the table. Well over a hundred stems. It was too bright for the morning, and she blinked and looked away from it. Then she considered her options.

After a few minutes of silent thought, recognizing that she in fact had no options, she scowled and stood up. She finished her tea, standing, and took her plate with her out of the room. She'd eat upstairs in her bedroom. Take a bath. And then, when she was feeling more energetic, she'd cross the street into the park. She wanted to investigate convergence points anyway. When—inevitably, she insisted to herself—she had finished her work, she'd want to pass her conclusions along to the courier quickly. Reacquainting herself with her drops would help with that.

Somewhat, but not entirely, mollified, she spent the morning as she'd planned—and the hours outdoors in the park did clear her mind. It was true that the air was biting, the clouds low, and most of the leaves had fallen from the trees. But the paths were dry, and she was able to rest under a stand of snake bark maples that hadn't yet dropped all of their brilliant red foliage. As she watched the thin leaves drifting to the ground, she forced herself to push away what had now become rage at Jeffrey's disappearance. Rage was unhelpful. And, worse, he'd enjoy it.

When she returned to Chester Terrace, she took her tea and her dinner in her room. And then, as the brown afternoon gave way to twilight and darkness, she changed into her shapeless cotton nightdress and pulled a dressing gown over her shoulders. Its belt, to her frustration, hardly tied now—and only when the knot rested on top of her belly.

After she'd changed, she glanced at the clock on her bedside table and lowered herself into an armchair near the window. She would read a novel. *Right Ho, Jeeves*. Mrs. Bowen had left it for her, and she'd been disappointed that Marion hadn't begun reading it. It was 9:00. He couldn't stay out much longer.

Just after 10:15, she heard him walk through the door. She knew that he'd stay long enough in the entry hall to remove his hat, overcoat, and gloves, and so she left her room at once to begin walking down the stairs. She'd intercept him before he reached his study. Insist that he explain the delay in her work.

She reached him just as he was opening the door to the study. His hair was brushed back, he was carrying a briefcase, and he was wearing a black suit and waistcoat with a muted blue tie. He looked tired. But she didn't care.

She was just about to ask him what he thought he was doing when he caught sight of the book she'd kept in her hand as she left her room. "Ah," he said, opening the door. "Mrs. Bowen's influence. She has a stalwart belief in the benefit of the comic novel to ladies in a delicate condition. Poor Ginnie used to have to pretend to enjoy Anita Loos."

She followed him as he walked into his study, still trying to talk to him. But he spoke over her. "In your case, I imagine it's counterproductive." He unbuttoned his jacket and sat in one of the armchairs, gesturing Marion to the sofa across from him. "Bertie Wooster must enrage you. All of that effete passivity masking the brutal hand of colonial exploitation." He considered. "Though I personally enjoy Aunt Dahlia."

She looked, confused, at the book in her hand, and then, remembering her purpose, walked to the sofa. Set the book on the coffee table between them. "Where is my material?"

He reached for a box of cigarettes on the table, opened the lid, and chose a cigarette. "At the office."

She stared at him as he lit it. "When will you bring it back?"

"I won't."

"I don't understand. How am I going to complete my—" She paused, annoyed. "—our assignment without the manuscripts?"

"You won't be completing it."

She narrowed her eyes at him. Then she went on the offensive. "Maugham couldn't possibly have given up on this. He wouldn't have let you stop me just as I was drawing useful conclusions for him." She held his eyes, cold. "I'll go to him if I must. I'll make a deal with him."

He smiled. "Darling. Maugham will be delighted to know that you trust him so implicitly. I'll bring your offer to him myself, if you'd like. But it won't alter the situation."

"I don't believe you."

"When I delivered the material to the office this morning, I explained to Maugham that although you've done effective work thus far, at this point you're no longer thinking as clearly as you ought to be." He inhaled and blew smoke up at the ceiling. "Maugham is a man of a certain generation. He understood immediately."

"That's absurd." She felt her rage from the park reasserting itself, but this time she didn't bother to push it down. "He wouldn't have believed you. And who else can finish this for him? He's got nothing at this point. Nothing."

"He hasn't got nothing." Jeffrey set his cigarette in the ashtray. "He's got the pages and artifacts we collected in Istanbul, he's got the information from the celestial globe, he's got your colleague Stephen's circles, he's got the manuscripts he collected at the Greenwich Observatory, and he's got my report on your movements and conversation in Suffolk as well as in Turkey. It's a start."

"He's got nothing," she insisted.

He threw her an affectionate glance and retrieved his cigarette. "Look, Marion. Your deranged intelligence is, I grant you, unmatched. You are the very, very best at this sort of thing. We are all in awe of you. Happy?" He took a drag from his cigarette. "But, first, you wouldn't be working *for* him. You'd be working for the competition. And he'd be forced, as he always is, to try to trip you up before—if he's lucky—collecting sufficient scraps of information to cobble together a workable picture. An entertaining process, yes, but not ideal when time is of the essence."

He considered the burning tip of the cigarette. "And second, we do have a number of people of at least some minimal talent working in-house. We are, you may be shocked to hear, not entirely without our own resources. And, as we speak, his three best are looking through our material. Maugham has given them a month and a half to produce results before we re-think our strategy."

"A month and a half?" She was gaping at him. "*A month and a half?* Are you mad? Do you know what can happen in a month and a half?"

"A happy event, if I'm not mistaken." He inhaled again.

"You—you—cretinous—" She took a wild breath.

"Ah. You're rightly annoyed by your absent-minded husband's sloppy calculations. The happy event is more likely to happen in a little over two months."

She sat back against the cushions of the sofa, eyeing him suspiciously. "I don't understand."

"Maugham is hedging his bets. He's allowed his people six weeks to work, under the conviction that if they *don't* satisfy him, you'll still be available. For at least a week or two." He laughed shortly. "I couldn't convince him otherwise."

"So—" She looked at him, a glimmer of fear behind her eyes.

"So I've bought you breathing room." He crushed out his cigarette.

"I don't want breathing room."

"I want breathing room for you." He pushed back his hair, which was falling over his forehead. "I tried to persuade him to let you off the hook entirely. To trust his own bloody specialists for once. But he likes you too much. He wants to see what you can do. Even now."

She felt ill. "So why not let me work on it now?"

"For the reasons I've told you," he said. "And also, though I'm loath to wound your vanity, you are, at the moment, less acute than you usually are. One can tell. I can tell. I don't like taking advantage of you. I think you might make mistakes. And I convinced him of that likelihood as well."

"You had *no right*—"

"Nonsense, Marion." Irritated. "I did exactly as you should have expected me to do. And under ordinary circumstances, you would have taken precautionary measures beforehand. But now, as your mind is going ever more soft and sentimental, all you can feel is outrage at the personal betrayal."

He shook his head, almost disgusted. "'No right.' For Heaven's sake. If you can't even remember that I'm the enemy, how on earth will you put together a coherent report for *anyone*?"

She felt, to her horror, on the verge of tears. Pushed them away. Violently. "But what I am going to do?"

"You and I are going to enjoy the holiday. As a family. John—"

"Ian," she corrected him automatically.

He sighed. "John will join us in Suffolk when his term has finished. As usual. Ginnie will be pleased, one hopes, that Christmas isn't ruined by interlopers from the office. And I will be damned relieved that no one will be asking me to debrief you over Boxing Day. We'll have a respite. For a month and a half. Maugham usually keeps his word about this sort of thing."

"But then?" She still felt tears welling up. Clenched her fists to keep them from showing.

"I'll be honest, darling," he said. "My fondest hope is that you deliver early. It happens. Especially when the mother is of advanced years."

He smiled at her, still tired, when she glared weakly at him. "Should that occur, we'll be released from our obligations. Even if you decide, in your typically unhinged way, that you want to complete your work, say, in the midst of labor, Maugham will never make it past Mrs. Bowen's security cordon. He'll be forced to leave you alone." He paused. "And your people will be obliged to find another conduit to your material."

"And if not?" She wiped her eyes with the sleeve of her dressing gown.

"We must trust Maugham's specialists to do their job. Perhaps they'll manage to gather something useful from what they have." He considered. "Otherwise, the first person our child encounters in this world could very well be a fat, diabolical imp shrieking at its mother to confess."

He stood. "Which is fitting, perhaps. John's—"

"—Ian's." She stood as well.

"—early childhood was far too lacking in paternal authority. He questions where he ought to obey. And he fails utterly to appreciate the responsibilities of his class and country."

"Piffle."

"As you say, dear." He leaned across the table and kissed her cheek. "Good night."

She still wanted to cry, but she kept her emotions in check until she left his study. Then, when she reached her bedroom and realized that she'd left her book behind, she crumpled into her chair and wept. After that, crawling into the bed, lying uncomfortably on her side, her back against a pillow, she wept herself to sleep.

T HEY drove to Temple Grove to collect Ian from his first term at school on Wednesday the 11th of December. Three days later, on Saturday the 14th, they all boarded the train to Suffolk to spend the remainder of the holiday with Virginia and Teddy. Ian, to her annoyance, mimicked Jeffrey's paternalistic concern for her welfare from the moment he saw her changed state. Trying to help her up and down steps. Refusing to let her carry anything. Worrying about her moods.

He had turned eight years old the previous month, and he was missing a front tooth, which should have softened her to his antics. But instead, she was having difficulty keeping from snapping at him. She was comforted, at least, that he was eager for, rather than inimical to, the imminent addition to the family. He'd spent too many years alone with her, half-hiding, itinerant and on the run, not to welcome an increase in the size and stability of his household. If anything, he was aggrieved that she hadn't provided him with a sibling earlier. Not having understood that doing so was an option.

"Did you keep the tooth?" Jeffrey asked as their evening train gained speed out of Liverpool Street Station.

Ian, sitting across the compartment next to Marion, nodded. He pulled a folded handkerchief out of the pocket of his trousers and carefully exposed its contents in the palm of his hand. Then he extended his hand out toward Jeffrey.

Jeffrey leaned forward, examined the handkerchief, and nodded. "Good. You can throw it into the fire to keep it from the witches the moment we arrive. We'll ask Uncle Teddy to build a hot one in the library."

Marion frowned as Ian returned the handkerchief to his pocket. "Throw it into the fire?"

"Yes," Jeffrey said patiently. "To keep it from the witches. What did you do with your teeth?"

"We left them for the rat," she retorted, irked, before she realized how odd it sounded. "The rat."

"Yes." Embarrassed now. "The fairy rat." She flushed and looked down at her hands. "It left us a coin in return."

"Let me guess," he continued for her. "And then you all used the rat's coins to pay off the devil before transforming yourselves into hares and whistling up a little something to put King James I off his seaside honeymoon."

"James VI," she muttered.

"I'll leave the next one for the rat, Mummy," Ian interjected, sensing the tension, but unable to identify its source.

"The rat may leave you a coin tonight anyway," she said. "It will understand that you wanted to protect your tooth."

"And that's why the rat will never establish an empire," Jeffrey said, opening the evening edition of the *Times* that he had purchased at the station. "Weak will."

Marion stared for a few seconds at the back of his newspaper and then reached into the carpet bag she had placed on the unoccupied seat to her left. She extracted an illustrated edition of *A Christmas Carol* and opened it, balancing it precariously on her belly.

"Would you like to read more, Ian?" She put her arm around his shoulders. "I think the ghost of Christmas Past had just appeared."

He nodded and leaned against her as she began reading. He'd be sleeping, she calculated, within the next fifteen minutes. And indeed, by the time the young Scrooge's fiancée had emerged, dejected, onto the scene, Ian's eyes were closed, and he was breathing deeply. She closed the book and put it back into her bag.

"Thank God," Jeffrey said from behind his paper. "I've always felt he had a narrow escape with that Belle business."

When she didn't respond, he remained silent as well. And, following Ian's lead, she leaned back, closed her eyes, and tried to sleep.

THEIR return to Suffolk for Christmas was as cheerful and chaotic as it had been the year before. And Marion, having experienced it once already, felt less adrift than she had previously. She even responded with composure when Maugham, per tradition, appeared on Christmas Eve. In fact, loitering at the top of the stairs when he entered, she felt a spark of pleasure as she overheard Jeffrey greeting him.

"Any progress?"

"An utter fiasco, dear boy. They're hopeless."

Smiling, she returned to the bedroom as Virginia stepped in to separate them.

She also paid more attention to Virginia's and Jeffrey's efforts to involve Ian in their family's traditions. Ordinarily, she ignored what she considered their off-putting indoctrination of her son into a world for which she felt little but contempt. Not trying to stop them—knowing that she couldn't in any case. But also not encouraging it. This time, however, she wanted to learn more. They were all surprised, therefore, when at dinner on the 27th of December—an evening when Teddy's and Virginia's three children were visiting neighbors—she offered to accompany Ian to the mews to see the peregrine he had received for Christmas.

"You'll like her, Mummy," he said as he ate the last of his treacle tart. "She's beautiful. And fast. Wait till you see her fly."

"I'm looking forward to it." She had long since finished her own dessert and was drinking the dregs of a glass of wine.

"You haven't given her a name yet, John." Jeffrey was also finishing his wine.

Virginia smiled, bright and malicious, across at Jeffrey. "He should call her Fluffy, Jeffie. After your first peregrine."

"Fluffy had a troubled life, Ginnie. And a difficult death. Hardly a fitting namesake."

"Poor Fluffy." Virginia's voice was light. "You drove her to it. We were all witnesses."

"I don't want to call her Fluffy," Ian said, finishing his tart.

"What do you plan to call her then?" Teddy had spent dinner, as he usually did, watching the interplay between Virginia and Jeffrey. He now took up Ian's gambit to bring an end to the bickering.

"Dido."

There was a moment of silence around the table before all four of them looked, perplexed, at Ian.

"Why Dido?" Marion asked after a few more seconds had passed. Slightly worried about him.

"Because Dido turned and walked away from Aeneas in the underworld. And she wouldn't change her expression for him," Ian said. "When he tried to explain himself, I mean. We read the passage at school. I liked it better than the story of the Sabine women. Not as silly."

Jeffrey ran a fingertip along the edge of his empty wineglass. "Aeneas had a duty to perform," he eventually said.

"Dido had honor." Ian yawned, pushing away his plate.

"He's right you know, Jeffie." Virginia stood, signaling that dinner was over. "Aeneas mistook ambition for duty. And it was cheap of him to beg her forgiveness."

Teddy, standing as well, leaned over and put his hand on Ian's shoulder. "I think 'Dido' is a marvelous name for a falcon."

As Marion walked with Ian toward his bedroom, she bent over and kissed the top of his head. "I can't wait to see you fly her tomorrow."

The next morning, Marion, Jeffrey, and Ian tramped across the frozen mud outside the stable yard to the mews. Marion had seen the wooden structure before on her walks, but she had never examined it closely. Now, she saw that it housed eight peregrines on perches. Their falconer took the birds out every day, so the mews was enclosed by a grille—aimed at keeping the birds from feeling stress when they'd returned from flying rather than at leaving them space to move. Ian's bird was hooded, waiting for him at the end of the building.

Since he and Jeffrey were already each wearing a leather glove, the falconer brought them their hooded birds as soon as they'd arrived. They thanked him and then, walking to an open field beyond the stables, they stood several paces apart. Ordinarily they'd be riding as well, and Marion was grateful to them for understanding that she was in no state to try to follow them on horseback. She pushed her hands into the pockets of her winter coat, waiting for them to begin.

Looking up at the sky, she thought to herself that their prospects weren't promising. Although there hadn't been snow, the dirty white clouds and greyish meadow had merged into a flat, blind landscape. She couldn't pick out the most obvious stones and clumps of damp vegetation, much less the grouse that had been stocked there. She pulled the woolen coat more tightly around her shoulders, shivering.

At a signal from Jeffrey, the falconer released two hunting dogs that sprinted into the field, startling three grouse into the air. He and Ian then removed the hoods and jesses from their birds with a practiced motion and held up their arms as the birds rose toward the sky. Marion watched the falcons climb until they were dots in the clouds. She felt a small stab of concern as Dido appeared to be flying away. But then Ian's falcon turned back, circled, and targeted one of the grouse.

A few seconds later, Dido was plummeting toward the ground, her wings folded behind her. Before taking the grouse with her talons, she unfolded her wings, slowing her descent. Then, grabbing the flying grouse by the back, Dido rose into the air for a few moments longer before bringing the bird to the ground. Thirty seconds later, Jeffrey's bird also brought down its quarry.

After that, Jeffrey, Ian, the falconer, and the dogs approached the birds and their prey. Jeffrey let the falconer collect the grouse and leash the dogs while he made certain that Ian was hooding Dido properly. Then they walked back toward the mews, each carrying a bird on his glove. When they reached Marion, she turned to follow them, impressed in spite of herself.

"She's magnificent, John." Jeffrey had returned his bird to her perch and was smiling as Ian reluctantly took leave of Dido.

"She is, isn't she?" Ian was grinning. Then, unwilling to keep to Marion's slow walking pace, but also not wanting to "upset" her, he bounced ahead, turning back to face them. "I'll run to the house to tell Uncle Teddy and Aunt Ginnie how it went, Mummy. All right?"

"Yes, Ian. Good idea." She watched him dart back across the stable yard and disappear around a corner of the house.

Jeffrey held her arm as they walked, slowly, after him. "Your maternal enthusiasm for our son's sporting interests is touching, darling. But you had ulterior motives for wanting to see the demonstration today?"

"Your outfit is absurd." She glanced down at his hunting boots. He looked like one of the more parodic paintings of their ancestors in Virginia's dining room.

"You're hardly in a position to comment on appearances, Marion." He adjusted the leather bag holding the dead grouse. "And what ought I wear to the mews? Socialist overalls?"

"How do they target their prey?" She'd rather have the conversation he knew she wanted to have than snipe at him. "Especially in weather like this. When everything is flat."

"Good eyesight." Deliberately uninformative.

"And why do they circle up?" She pulled the woolen hat she was wearing further over her ears. "I mean, before they attack. Is there some use to the preliminary sweep of the area?"

"Peregrines don't hunt in the same way that gyrfalcons do," he said, still avoiding her question. "I'm assuming you're more interested in the latter."

"Jeffrey, stop it." They were nearing the house, and she slowed further. "I need everything you can tell me. I don't think Maugham's people have found anything. You would have—shown it. Somehow. And I can tell that you're worried."

"You've been listening at doors," he said. "You don't pick up on social cues."

"Jeffrey—"

"Oh, very well." He stopped walking and looked down at her. "There are some who argue that the circling is psychological. To convince the target that the hunter is flying away. Uninterested."

"Oh." It wasn't the answer she wanted.

"And there are others," he continued, taking her arm and walking again, "who've drawn different conclusions. They believe that raptors like peregrines and gyrfalcons can pick up on light beyond what humans consider the visible spectrum. When they're high up and circling, they see not only their prey, but also the trail their prey has made. In non-visible light."

"I see." She nodded, thinking.

"But they can't," he added.

"Can't what?"

"Raptors don't see beyond the visible spectrum. I've watched them. It's not what they're doing." They had reached the door to the house, and he opened it. "They can see very far, but the circling is psychological. The older theories are correct. They can't track non-visible light."

"But it's a common theory that they can," she said as she walked through the door. "Among falconers?"

"Yes." He removed the bag of grouse from his shoulder and lowered it to the ground. "A recent theory, obviously. Since the discovery of light beyond the visible spectrum."

"Oh." She was standing still in the entry hall. Thinking harder.

"Marion," he said. "Maugham's people have two weeks left to complete their work. They're making progress. Let it go."

She came to herself and smiled at him. "If I said I would, you'd know I was lying."

Then, without speaking further, she turned away from him and struggled out of the layers of winter clothing she had worn to watch Dido fly.

THEY drove Ian back to Temple Grove on Monday, the 6th of January. Marion was both reassured and vexed that he showed almost none of the reluctance to return to school that he had in previous terms. She was pleased that he was less miserable there than he had been. But she herself detested the education he was receiving, and she was unsettled by the idea that once he became comfortable with the institutional ritual, he would also start to believe in it. Watching from the car as he disappeared through the gate, she accepted, once more, that there was little she could do to block his indoctrination. She simply must trust to his strength of character.

Once Ian had vanished from view, Jeffrey maneuvered the car out of the school grounds and joined the afternoon traffic heading northward toward London. He didn't speak to her as they drove, but she could sense that he was troubled. Angry. And his demeanor baffled her because nothing in their situation had changed. Nonetheless, she didn't try to draw him out. She knew better.

It was only when they'd returned to Chester Terrace and walked up the stairs from the garage that she understood what had happened. Waiting on the console in the entry hall was her material. All of it. Neatly wrapped and organized. When she saw it, she smiled at him, delighted.

"Time's up," he said, removing his hat and gloves and tossing them on the console next to the manuscripts. "You've got your material. Where would you like to work?"

"My bedroom." She didn't like his tone.

"Marion," he said, resting his hand on the pile of papers. "I'll say this one last time. You're making a mistake."

"I'm not."

She turned and walked up the stairs. Elated. Itching to finish her project. He followed her without additional protest, carrying the material. Acquiescent. When they entered her bedroom, she stood to the side to let him place the manuscripts, the notes, and the artifacts on the work desk she still kept under a window overlooking a side street. He arranged them on the desktop, held her eyes for a moment, and then left the room, closing the door quietly behind him.

Before she approached the desk, she made a show to herself of looking out the other, larger, windows facing the drizzle over the darkening park. Then she wandered into the dressing room to change out of the uncomfortable clothing she had worn not to embarrass Ian at Temple Grove. She didn't want to return to her project with too much eagerness. She must pace herself. And she dreaded making errors in her haste.

Eventually accepting that she wasn't calming herself, she returned to the desk, pulled out its practical wooden chair, sat, and reorganized the pages in front of her in a useful order. Wrinkling her forehead, she reacquainted herself with the conclusions she'd drawn in Istanbul. And then, relaxing, she took pleasure in the feel of the objects and in the rhythm of her now familiar texts.

Two hours later, she sent word to Mrs. Bowen that she was feeling unwell and wouldn't be down to dinner. Then she waited, nervous, for ten minutes. Under ordinary circumstances, Jeffrey wouldn't let such an obvious lie pass without appearing in her bedroom to taunt her with a demonstration of false concern. But fifteen minutes later, he hadn't materialized, and so she turned back to her desk. He was working as diligently as she was. Organizing a strategy to support Maugham's new policy. He'd let her finish her project now even if she became ill in the process.

Six hours later, she glanced at the clock on her bedside table and saw with shock that it was nearing midnight. Morose, she left off memorizing the final lines of the report that she'd spent the evening drafting and encoding. She must stop. Unwilling as she'd been to accept Jeffrey's judgement of her mental acuity, he was correct about her increased tendency toward error. Her mind needed sleep in a way that it hadn't before. And she couldn't jeopardize her organization's project by gratifying her edgy excitement.

Rubbing her eyes, she rose from the desk, gathered the loose pages of her report, and walked to the toilet. She'd changed into a nightdress earlier in the evening, and so she simply splashed water on her face, brushed her hair, and cleaned her teeth. Then she submerged the papers on which she'd written her report in a sink full of water, watching them disintegrate. Finally, satisfied, she returned to the bedroom and crawled into bed, her body drifting into sleep even as her mind, unwilling to rest, worked through the lines that she'd written, internalized, and destroyed. She'd flush the pulp down the toilet tomorrow morning.

She woke late in the morning to the same optimism that had driven her the night before. She was confident now that her interpretation of the material was accurate. She knew what Nasir al-Din and Taqi al-Din had discovered at the Maragha and Istanbul Observatories, and she knew its contemporary relevance. She also knew how her organization could make use of it. All that remained for her to do was pass her verbal report, along with the artifacts, the rubbing of the celestial globe, and the manuscript pages, to the courier. The courier would forward it to Stephen, and he would draw his map and report to their organization.

Her one concern was that Stephen needed a full moon to finish his work. And tonight, Tuesday, the 7th of January, was the first of three when the moon would be sufficiently visible for him to make his calculations. If he didn't have her information by Wednesday or Thursday at the latest, when the moon would be at one hundred percent, he'd be forced to wait another month. Time they didn't have.

Shifting uncomfortably as she sat up in bed and her abdomen tightened, she admitted that she also didn't have a month to spare. She'd been bothered all night by spasms passing across her belly. Having given birth before, she knew they weren't contractions—she had no fear that she'd go into labor any time soon. They were, however, annoyances, each hardening of her stomach a reminder that she must work quickly.

Her primary obstacle at this point was evading the concern and attention of Jeffrey's household. Her standing arrangement with the courier—an arrangement of which she hadn't taken advantage in months—was to meet at 10:00 at night at a pre-determined convergence point in the park. This evening, the courier would be waiting just beyond the gate to the zoo. But she couldn't slip out of the house to make the drop as she would have before her pregnancy. If she tried to move after dark, they'd stop her before she reached the door. Likely before she'd left her bedroom.

As she rose with difficulty from the bed, used the toilet, and flushed away the remains of her written report, she evaluated her options. The only feasible one was to leave the house during the day and then fail to return until after she'd met the courier. If she could hide in the city until after dark, she could make her way back to the zoo—and then, her job finished, into the building. Jeffrey's household would be turned inside out. And Mrs. Bowen would be beside herself with fear. But she couldn't think of any other solution to her problem. She'd apologize once it was over. Both Jeffrey and Mrs. Bowen would, in their own ways, understand.

Clenching her fists as another spasm passed over her belly, she walked into the dressing room, pulled a day dress over her head—the only one that now fit—pushed her feet into shoes, and found a shopping bag in which to transport the material. Then she brought the bag—Hamley's, preserved from one of Ian's expeditions to the toy store—to her work desk. The artifacts, the manuscript pages, and the rubbing fit easily. And there would be more than enough room for the bag itself under her tent-like winter coat. Her only task now was leaving the house without raising alarms.

Pensive, she buttoned her coat, pushed the Hamley's bag up underneath it, held it in place with the hand supporting her belly, and left her bedroom. It was nearly 11:00 when she opened the front door. Another grey, soggy morning, a degree or two above freezing. On her way out, she asked one of Mrs. Bowen's maids to tell Mrs. Bowen that she was going for a walk, that she'd breakfast in a tea room, and that she'd return before lunch. The maid nodded, shut the door behind her, and she was out. The maneuver was easier than she'd expected.

Once across the street and out of view of the house, she sat on a park bench and removed the Hamley's bag from under her coat. Then, breathing in the smell of the damp, rotting leaves surrounding her bench, she considered her next move—finding a place to hide herself for the day. But she didn't stay long. Embarrassed by the concerned looks she was drawing from passersby, she rose and walked the park for a few minutes longer, still thinking.

She knew that the office had eyes on her. Even now, Jeffrey wouldn't risk leaving her to her own devices. But she trusted them not to be paying excessive attention to her movements. She was hardly at risk of flight. She stopped short, her hand over her stomach, as her abdomen tightened again. Irritated this time. And then, ignoring the worried look of a passing bicyclist, she continued her slow walk.

If she could get herself into a tube station without his people noticing, she could hide herself anywhere in the city. A cinema, she supposed, would be the most effective. Although the thought of sitting in the dark for eight or nine hours was distasteful. For some reason, she felt an urge to walk. She wasn't certain why. Perhaps the exercise would simply do her good.

As she pondered her sudden burst of energy—building inside of her like something apart from herself—a strategy formed itself in her mind. She *could* walk a little bit, perhaps leading the eyes into thinking she was heading for Soho again. Stephen had long ago hidden himself elsewhere. But they didn't know that. And if she put the idea into their heads that he had remained in the neighborhood, they might outwit themselves. Stay ahead of her, as they'd been trained to do. Fail to notice when she descended into a tube station, behind them, on the way.

Inwardly nodding again, and projecting the vague purpose that any trained tail would suspect, she began walking more quickly, south, toward Madame Tussaud's. She felt interest behind her, and slowed, trying to look frustrated. Then, rubbing her lower back, she crossed out of the park and picked her way along side streets in the direction of Stephen's Soho shop.

Before she had gone far, she sensed her followers spreading out in front of her. Satisfied, she walked even more slowly and then paused and felt the air again. It was clean for the moment. And so, taking her chance, she circled back to Regent Street and descended into Oxford Street Station, calmed, immediately, by the crowd.

In addition to hiding her, the mass of people was busy enough with its own concerns not to notice, or care about, her condition. A comfort after the park. Also, the train was arriving just as she reached the platform, and so she could allow herself to be pushed by the crowd into the carriage, grateful for the empty seat that a young woman—politely not noticing her state—vacated across from her.

She sat, waited for any indication of a tail, and then relaxed into the seat when the train began moving. She was alone. And she could ride all the way to its terminus at Elephant & Castle. She'd try the Trocadero Cinema. It was large. She could lose herself in it. And it was notoriously showing films all day.

Once she'd entered the cinema, she lowered herself into a cushioned seat in the half-empty theatre. *The Last Days of Pompeii* had just begun, and she prepared herself for an extended viewing. As her abdomen cramped again, she wished once more that she could be walking. But, steeling herself, she reminded herself that she had a job to do. And in any case, the parks and the streets were no longer available to her. Mrs. Bowen would have already reported to Jeffrey that she hadn't returned to the house; his own people would have told him that they'd lost her; by now, he would have sent his entire network out to saturate every neighborhood in the city. Watching films all day was her only alternative.

The Last Days of Pompeii was followed by *Mutiny on the Bounty*, *Captain Blood*, a short interlude on the cinema's organ, and then *The Raven* with Boris Karloff and Béla Lugosi. Unable to stay in her seat for more than a half hour at a time, Marion stood and wandered the theatre, making frequent use of the toilets, as the films succeeded one another. The first three, especially, left her edgy and unable to remain in one place.

But *The Raven*, despite her smothered energy, held her attention by virtue of its pure peculiarity. She watched Karloff and Lugosi, fascinated, for over an hour without leaving her seat. She also watched them a bit shamefaced, knowing that Mrs. Bowen would have been driven to distraction to see her immersed in horror rather than in Wodehouse so close to her happy event. Nonetheless, she couldn't look away, until the grisly end.

As the theatre emptied into the dark streets after *The Raven*, she followed the crowds, trying without success to keep from looking prominent. It was 9:15, and she was well on track to crossing the courier at the zoo. She also suspected that none of Jeffrey's people would be targeting the Trocadero's showing of *The Raven*. She certainly didn't feel any of them on her. Her choice of burrow had been too outlandish for even them to consider.

Nonetheless, as she hailed a taxi and asked the driver to take her, slowly, in the direction of the zoo, she remained on guard. Although they likely weren't anywhere near Elephant & Castle, they would be watching Regent's Park. She couldn't make mistakes at this point.

She stayed in the taxi for over a half hour, harassing the driver by directing him aimlessly around the perimeter of the park, until she feared he'd simply leave her somewhere. Finally, when he looked to be near a breaking point, she asked him to drop her on Delancey Street, a few blocks from the zoo. After she'd paid him and left the car, she retraced her steps to the zoo's gates, still trying to fit into the thinning late-night crowd. It was only when she saw her mark on one side of the gate that she silently thanked the courier and approached with confidence, stopping, annoyed, to grip her stomach as a spasm stronger than those she'd yet experienced passed over it.

When the courier saw her, she also detached herself from the crowd and moved toward a stand of trees near the gate. It was the same woman who had followed her to Suffolk. Dressed now for the street, should she want to blend, but also in black, should she be forced to disappear into a green area. Marion contrary to her training, was walking straight toward her, holding out the shopping bag, willing her to take it from her.

When they were within speaking distance, Marion began to pass along her verbal report at once, trying to get through it quickly, before her stomach tightened again. But before she could finish the first sentence, she doubled over, gasping at what she knew was a true contraction.

"Dr. Bailey." The woman put her hand on Marion's shoulder, concerned. "Are you all right?"

"Here." Marion held out the shopping bag. "Take this. I'm fine. I've still got a while to go."

"Where am I delivering it?" The woman, sensing Marion's mood, relapsed into professional decorum.

"Stephen." She took a few deep breaths. "He's all right, isn't he? He can work?"

The woman looked uncertain. "He's poorly, to be honest. His sister threw herself off the Channel Boat. Killed herself when he went under after Greenwich. She thought he was dead. He isn't taking it well."

"Oh." She wished she could say more. "Poor Stephen. I—"

"He can work, though." The woman was securing the shopping bag to her wrist. Invisibly. To keep from accidentally letting it go. "In fact, he wants to work. Can you repeat the message?"

"Yes." Marion felt weak. She'd eaten very little in the Trocadero. But she was nearly finished. And the trees were hiding their odd behavior from observation. "Tell him that the number is 621. And that he must read the margins—"

"Understood."

"No. There's more." Marion was about to continue, when she cried out and doubled over in pain.

The woman took a step toward her, but Marion shook her head. "Go. That's going to draw attention. He'll decipher it with what's in the bag and what I've told you." As the woman turned, Marion heard running from a second stand of trees behind them. "Fuck."

She watched desperately as the woman began running as well. Prayed that she had a sufficient head start. But to her dismay, a figure, twice the woman's size, converged on her from the opposite direction. The figure tackled her out of sight of the street and drew one of her arms behind her back.

"Gardiner!" The voice, a harsh whisper, came from another figure, running toward them on the other side. It sounded to Marion like Nick Trelawney. "Look out. She's put something in her mouth. Make her spit it out."

"Oh, bloody hell." Definitely Gardiner. But more frightened than he usually was. "Don't do that, you stupid—" He scuffled with the woman, and then sat up, holding her in what looked more like an embrace than a restraint. "Why would you do that? You don't want to die. For God's sake—"

"She's fine, Gardiner." Nick again, but with a trace of amusement under the whisper. "She's got rid of it. Worried about losing the intelligence then, are you?"

Before Gardiner could retort, she heard Jeffrey. Standing above both of them. "Get her to the car, take her to the depot, and give her to Margot. Tell her to work quickly. We need this 'Stephen's' location."

"Sir—?" Gardiner was standing, pulling the woman to her feet, but sounding uncertain.

"Margot's gentle, Gardiner." Jeffrey's voice was also entertained, but there was an irritation underlying it. "Though I should hardly have to reassure you about that sort of thing." He was walking in Marion's direction. "God knows how I work under these conditions."

Marion, who had watched the entire episode half bent over, her hand flat against the trunk of a tree, looked up at Jeffrey as he approached. He gazed down at her, livid. Outraged.

"Pleased with yourself?" He didn't move to help her as she gasped at another contraction and pressed her other hand against her abdomen. "You and your work. Is there anything you won't do—anyone you won't betray for—"

"I thought that concerning oneself with personal betrayal was a symptom of a compromised intellect." She half smiled up at him. Contrite. Trying to apologize. She found to her surprise that she didn't care about the botched drop. And she knew that her people would easily extract the courier.

When he simply watched her, icy, she gave up and decided to be more direct. "I'm sorry, Jeffrey. But it's over now, and—"

He stepped toward her and helped her to stand upright. "It isn't over."

She let him walk with her past the trees, past the gates to the zoo, and toward the road. Squeezed her eyes shut as another contraction, less severe than the others, shot through her. "What do you mean?"

"Loose ends, darling." He was leading her toward a waiting ambulance. "Can't have any loose ends."

The ambulance, which at first had comforted her, on second thought looked wrong. Blank. There weren't any insignia on it. She tried to read his neutral profile. "Are we going to Dr. Chapman?"

He didn't respond as the rear doors of the ambulance were opened by two large orderlies. They didn't look right either. Too military.

"Jeffrey," she said, as the orderlies unbuttoned and removed her coat before half-helping and half-pushing her into the vehicle, "we are going to Dr. Chapman, aren't we?"

As they forced her to lie back on a reclined stretcher and removed her shoes, she saw the full moon out the doors of the ambulance. Then the doors shut on her. Also blank.

Jeffrey, who had climbed in after her, and was holding her hand, husbandly now, still hadn't spoken. But he did follow her gaze. As the doors shut, he looked down into her face. "Mrs. Bowen has great faith in the notion that labor always starts on the full moon. She'd been looking forward to this week."

She tried to struggle into a more upright position, but he put his hand on her shoulder and, none too gently, pushed her back.

"Jeffrey," she said. "Please. Whatever you're feeling now, this isn't the moment to indulge it. It's time. The baby's coming." When he didn't respond, she became afraid. "Please."

He laughed. Angry. "I told you that you were making a mistake. You refused to listen." Smiled down at her, malicious. "And I can do my job too."

*T*HEIR journey in the ambulance was brief, and Marion felt a faint relief when it rolled to a stop. At least they weren't taking her out of the city. But when the doors opened, and the orderlies removed her from the vehicle, still on the stretcher, she panicked. They'd driven to Chelsea. To the secure house kept by the office for informal incarceration and interrogation. The moment she understood where she was, she tried to lift herself off the stretcher, which caused the orderlies carrying her to stumble and nearly fall.

Jeffrey, walking beside her, pushed her, violently now, back into a reclined position. Then he spoke to the orderlies. "Ground floor. Use the restraints if you must."

He strode away from her toward the main entrance to the house as the orderlies brought her to a service entrance below. She felt another contraction gathering momentum, but before it hit, she shouted at his retreating back. "Jeffrey! Stop this! I'll tell you everything afterward. I can't—" She stopped speaking as the pain crested and she clenched her fists against it.

He ceased walking, stood still for a few seconds, and then turned back to her. Relaxed. "You've started it, Marion. I think you ought to finish it. No more delays. You'll hold up."

Then he disappeared into the house. When the orderlies reached the service entrance, the door was already open, and they lifted her onto a wheeled stretcher. She tried to sit up again, but she was pushed back into place, this time by a serious female nurse. They wheeled her along a basement corridor until they reached the doors to a makeshift surgery.

Although the surgery was brightly lit by a hanging overhead lamp, the room was large enough that Marion couldn't see into its darker corners. It held only a single hospital bed, onto which the nurse and the orderlies moved Marion just as she felt another wave of pain building. The air smelt of congealed sweat, fear, iodine, and decaying metal. The floor was of concrete. She tried to curl forward, but they held her flat on her back until she cried out.

Once the contraction had weakened, they released her, and she looked, vaguely, about her. Approaching her, jovial and dressed for surgery, was a doctor. She couldn't understand why he was familiar until a largely blocked memory intruded itself on her mind. He was the doctor who had attended her during her first incarceration in the house. His job was to see to it that she wasn't hurt so badly that she couldn't cooperate with their process. At the time, she had held him in contempt. Now he terrified her.

He observed her for a few seconds and then turned to speak to two men standing in the shadows behind him. "Already? I had understood that we'd keep her here for a few days before it started."

"It was a surprise to us as well." Jeffrey's voice. Though his face was hidden in the shadow. "The walk this morning may have brought it on."

"Ah well. A unique opportunity. Best not waste it." Maugham. But she couldn't see him either. "Are you game, doctor?"

The doctor, whom she could see, pulled on a pair of surgical gloves, smiling, a bit abashed. "I confess, Professor Maugham, this is not my area of expertise. But she's in better shape that many of the patients you bring me. I'll do my best." He returned to the bed and spoke to Marion in a jolly, bantering tone. "So how are we feeling Dr. Bailey? Excited about the imminent event?"

Before they could push her down again, Marion raised herself onto her elbows and shouted into the recesses of the room. "Jeffrey, get this daft wankstain away from me, and bring me Dr. Chapman! And God help me, if that heinous, unspeakable bodach is still in here five minutes from now, I'll—"

The doctor put his gloved hand over her mouth and pushed her back on the bed just as the pain of another contraction started building. Only half intentionally, she bit down, tearing the rubber of his glove. She tasted blood.

"Fuck." The doctor pulled back his hand.

"Agitated." Maugham stepped into the circle of light. "I understand they get this way." He peered down at her, interested. "Am I the heinous, unspeakable bodach?"

"I'm leaving." She began lifting herself off the bed again.

Jeffrey, emerging from the shadow, pushed her back. "If you bite me, you'll regret it." Then he addressed the doctor. "If we do this without her cooperation, will the baby be hurt?"

"Well, she certainly can't prevent the process from happening." The doctor had draped a stethoscope around his neck and replaced his glove. A few seconds earlier, he had been speaking quietly to the nurse, who had disappeared into a corner of the room. "But it may not serve your purposes if she remains in her current unaccommodating humor. I do have ether—"

"We need her awake." Maugham was still looking down at her face, intrigued by her reactions to the situation.

"I've asked my nurse to prepare an injection of scopes and morphine." The doctor walked into the shadows and then returned with a large hypodermic syringe. "She'll remain conscious. And I believe it will make her a tad more sympathetic to your objectives. Better to do it sooner than—"

"Jeffrey." Marion had grabbed his wrist with her hand. "'Scopes' is scopolamine. From scopolia. Carpathian nightshade. You *cannot* let this butcher—" She cried out as another contraction, worse than any she'd yet experienced, flooded her with pain.

He twisted his wrist out of her grasp and spoke to the doctor. "Is it dangerous?"

"Not at all. My colleagues use it for all of their society deliveries." He glanced down at Marion. "Twilight sleep. Most women adore it. Say they can't remember a thing afterward."

Maugham lit up in recognition. "Twilight sleep? Yes, I know it."

"Jeffrey, *please*." Marion was staring up at him, wide-eyed in terror. "Please don't do this."

"Regretfully, I must concur with Dr. Bailey," Maugham unexpectedly intervened. "Thacker's already tried the morphine-scopolamine cocktail on a few volunteers. Obviously not under these precise conditions—but close enough. It's true they remembered nothing afterward." He pursed his lips. "Unfortunately, all he could get out of them while they were under was a flow of highly poetic gibberish.

And then, when he became frustrated and threatened them with actual pain, they laughed at him. Poor Thacker. Margot was obliged to sit up with him for three days and nights to restore his confidence."

The doctor looked disappointed. Returned the syringe to the nurse. "Then I suppose we must trust nature to run its course. As the moment draws nearer, she may become more cooperative." He brightened again. "I could force dilation. That might—"

"We're in no hurry." Maugham had wandered over to the nurse's tray to examine her tools. "Let's be leisurely."

"What about the baby?" Jeffrey asked as Marion twisted through another contraction.

"I'll check its position," the doctor replied, unenthusiastic now. "The orderlies will assist me."

While the two men and the nurse approached the bed and held Marion's ankles and wrists apart and in place, the doctor tested his stethoscope. He waited for Jeffrey and Maugham to move to a corner of the room, outside the light, and then he lifted Marion's dress and cut away her underwear. Pressed his fingertips against her abdomen, checked her dilation, and held the stethoscope against her belly for thirty seconds. After that, he signaled to the orderlies and nurse to release her arms and legs. She pushed her dress back down over her legs, weeping.

"Did your water break?" He had dropped the jovial tone.

"What?" She couldn't look him in the face.

"Your clothing is dry. Has your water broken?"

She shook her head. "I don't think so."

He nodded. "Thank you."

He returned to the shadows, and she heard him speaking to Jeffrey. "The baby is in a good position, and its heartbeat is steady. It's still in its sac, which will give it an extra layer of protection should she remain recalcitrant. I'd estimate you have an hour to talk to her before she'll start pushing."

She felt another contraction starting and turned her head to the side, crying in misery rather than pain. "No. No, no, no." As the pain built, she screamed.

Jeffrey returned to the bed, waited for her scream to subside, and then spoke down at her. "We have Stephen's location. Margot tripped up your courier. A team is out collecting him now. If you can't tell us what you have on the Observatory, he will."

He squinted across the room, spotted a metal chair on wheels, and brought it to the side of the bed. Then he sat down in such a way that his face was less than a foot above hers. She couldn't see his expression with the bright light behind his head.

"Stephen is—fragile—from what I've been informed," he continued. "It won't take Thacker long to break him."

"Thacker will demolish him," she said weakly. "But he'll get nothing out of him. Stephen doesn't understand—" She paused. "He doesn't follow the give-and-take of a relationship—its logic— all of it eludes him. He'll die before he speaks. But he won't understand why he's dying." She turned her head away from him. "Letting Thacker interrogate Stephen is purposeless sadism."

"You, however, do understand the give-and-take of a relationship, don't you, Marion?" He held her chin with his hand and moved her face back into the light. "Let's talk, darling, hmm?"

Before she could respond, another contraction swept over her, and she gasped in pain. He waited, irritated, for it to pass, and then stood and crossed the room to Maugham. She heard them speaking in low tones, but she couldn't pick up what they were saying. A few minutes later, Jeffrey returned and sat in the chair again.

"Maugham would like to know when your people first approached you about working with Stephen on this project." He waited for three or four seconds. "That's hardly sensitive information, is it? And once we're through it, you can concentrate on more important things."

"June," she said.

"On our return from Yemen?"

"Yes."

"Why?" He reached over to a rolling table at the end of the bed and pulled it toward him. Took his cigarette case out of his jacket pocket, chose a cigarette, and lit it. Set it, burning, on a small tray embedded in the table.

"You signed the Naval Agreement with Germany," she said, turning her head to the side and coughing.

"I?"

"Your government."

"I believe this is George's area," Maugham shouted helpfully from the shadows. "Balancing interests and all that. German re-armament. Their navy is tiresome, of course, but what were we supposed to do? Declare war over it?"

"You'll declare war anyway." She felt a contraction coming and decided, this time, to welcome it. The way the midwife in Isfahan had taught her. She breathed through it, grunting, while Jeffrey looked on in mild distaste.

"That's what Winston says, anyway," Maugham shouted further. "But you know Winston—anything for attention. By the way, bravo, Dr. Bailey. That's the spirit!"

"Jeffrey," she growled, "get him out of here."

"Not my call." He inhaled, but thoughtfully turned his head and blew the smoke behind him. "So why were your people unhappy with the naval agreement?"

"The Mediterranean was threatened. And the Black Sea. In a way they hadn't been for centuries." She closed her eyes and breathed out.

"By the Germans?" Mystified.

"By everyone. The Naval Agreement created an imbalance." She started pushing herself up again, trying to find a more comfortable position. "It had to be rectified."

He put his cigarette in the tray and pushed her back into place. "Not yet, Marion."

"What's the Greenwich Observatory got to do with it?" Maugham contributed from the edge of the room.

"There's an ancient machinery," she said, her eyes still closed. "To protect the Mediterranean. But it's massive, and it must be rebuilt on an international scale. Quickly. They wanted you and the Germans preoccupied while they initiated that. But they also wanted you both interested enough to cooperate when it was time. The attacks in Greenwich and Dresden were meant to get you thinking—but in the wrong direction. About astronomy rather than—than about optics."

"Dresden was deliberate? A provocation like Greenwich?" Jeffrey's voice was blank. Professional.

"Robert," she said, "I mean my colleague—he could have been in and out of that museum without anyone ever knowing he'd been near it. But that wasn't his brief. He was ordered to leave a trail. A few hints. Raise some hackles." She felt another contraction coming and concentrated. "Someone exposed him. So they collected him instead. He told them more than they were supposed to know." The contraction swept over her, and she almost managed to breathe through it, only letting out a groan when it reached its most intense point.

"Meaning?" Annoyed, again, by the delay.

"May I have a glass of water?" She pushed her sweaty hair off her forehead.

"Answer my question first."

She swallowed. "The Germans are ahead of you. By a good six weeks now because of your idiot decision to keep the material from me. And they're uninterested in international cooperation." She took a deep breath and then exhaled slowly. "But they haven't got everything. They're missing key information. And what they have got is narrative rather than technical."

He stood, walked to the nurse's table, and poured a glass of water. When he brought it back, he put it on the rolling table rather than giving it to her. "One more question."

She turned her head away from him. Desperately thirsty.

"What is the nature of this 'machinery?'" He sat back down in the metal chair.

"If I tell you without context, you won't understand. Or believe me."

He considered, and then he helped her to sit up. Handed her the water. "Very well. Start at the beginning."

She drank the entire glass in four swallows and handed it back to him. "Thank you." She remained sitting upright. "May I walk?"

"No." He watched her coldly. "You may sit up for now. Tell me about the machinery."

"No one has ever understood," she started, "why Muslim astronomers like Nasir al-Din and Taqi al-Din, whose theories of optics rivaled their eighteenth- and nineteenth-century peers in sophistication, never invented the telescope." She swallowed again. "But the answer is simple. They were uninterested in what the telescope could do for them because they'd already invented—or re-discovered—something more effective."

"Which was?"

She opened her mouth to respond, but she sensed that another wave of pain was gaining traction. She also suddenly wanted to bear down. Urgently. "Jeffrey," she said, panting, "I can't. I truly can't now. I need to push."

He swore, stood up, and beckoned to the doctor. Both the doctor and the nurse crossed the room and watched her for a few seconds as, instinctively, she began to push. Then, ignoring her grunting, the doctor lifted her dress and checked her dilation.

"Too early." He pulled the dress back over her legs.

"Fuck you, arsepiece." She continued to push.

As Jeffrey turned away to force down an unprofessional smile at her response, the nurse acknowledged Marion for the first time. "Dr. Bailey," she said. "If you bear down before you're fully dilated, it will be counterproductive. It will also hurt more and take longer."

Marion, who had pushed through the contraction and was now panting from her exertion narrowed her eyes at the nurse. She could see that the nurse disliked her. But the nurse also seemed intelligent. Marion was uncertain whether or not to believe her. "You'll tell me when it's time?" she eventually asked. Wary.

"Yes." The nurse turned away from her and retreated into the shadows.

"Wait," Jeffrey said to the doctor as he began to follow her. He had recovered his cold demeanor. "You said before that you could force dilation."

The doctor nodded. Unhappy with his role in the scenario.

"Can you do the opposite? Slow it down? We need time."

The doctor considered the question, intrigued. "I suppose it's possible. Interesting. Yes—let me see what I can do." He returned to the nurse's table to take stock of his drugs.

"Jeffrey." Marion was clawing at his sleeve. "Jeffrey, you can't let him experiment on me. The man is a buffoon."

"Nonsense." He pulled her hand off his sleeve and sat back down in the metal chair. "He's the best in his field. Extraordinarily good at his job." He took up his cigarette again. "This simply happens not to be his job."

"Jeffrey, don't let him touch me." She thought she might begin weeping again.

"My advice, Marion, is to start talking instead of pushing. Quickly." He took a drag of his cigarette and didn't bother to blow the smoke away from her. "It will take him a fair amount of time to mix up something suitable. If we're lucky, you'll have satisfied me before that happens."

She shook her head, crying in earnest now.

"You're wasting time." He watched her face, unmoved. "What did Taqi al-Din discover?"

"How to see in the dark," she said abruptly, forcing herself to focus.

"He was an astronomer," Jeffrey replied. "He could already do that."

"No." She pushed herself into a sitting position, praying that he wouldn't force her down again. "I mean he developed a way to see in almost complete darkness. Anywhere." She shook her head, clearing it. "He didn't develop it. He rediscovered it. It was already centuries old. But he perfected it." She felt tears coming again. Knew she wasn't making sense.

"I don't understand."

"I'll tell you how he used the objects that we found in Istanbul," she said, trying to create a coherent picture for him. "And then I'll tell you where they were used."

"And the submarines?" Mollified by her cooperation.

"Yes. At the end. It won't be consistent otherwise."

"Very well. Continue."

"The tube," she said, "is a tool for turning low or no light into daylight. It works by transforming very low visible light, or even invisible infrared light—" She paused. "You know what infrared light is? Its applications?"

"Yes," he said. "The RAF use it. Continue."

"It turns that light, which the viewer can't see, into light that he or she can see."

"How?" he asked, still neutral.

"The tube," she continued, breathing hard, "consists of a lens at one end, through which very low or infrared light passes. This nearly non-existent light then hits that first metal plate. You remember you saw it in Istanbul? It's opaque?"

"Yes. Continue."

"That plate is made of antimony, potassium, and sodium. Just as al-Mansur described Taqi al-Din's 'instruments' in the poem. When the light hits the plate, the metals release electrons. I think the process is called the photoelectric effect." She pushed back her hair. "Though Taqi al-Din and his astronomers wouldn't have known that."

"Obviously not." Skeptical. And impatient.

"Jeffrey," she said, willing him to believe her, "they wouldn't have known the physics of it—or, if somehow they did know how it worked, they wouldn't have explained it in nineteenth- and twentieth-century terms. But they did conduct alchemical experiments. You saw the description of them. In the caves under Maragha. In the Istanbul Observatory. It's not beyond the realm of reason that scholars who were specialists in both optics and chemistry, with extensive royal patronage, would have noticed that light hitting certain combinations of alkali metals produced another sort of energy."

"I haven't asked for a defense of their technique." He crushed out his cigarette. "Tell me more about the tube."

She felt another contraction building, forced herself not to push, and panted through it. Proud of herself for not crying out. When she'd finished and was recovering, he lit another cigarette. Blew smoke up at the ceiling. "Tell me more about the tube," he repeated.

"So, the nearly invisible light hits the first plate, which emits electrons. Those electrons then move through a second plate—which we can't see, but I know it must be there from the diagrams in the manuscript scraps. The second plate, from what Taqi al-Din indicated, increases the energy, until it—or, if you're thinking in our terms, they? the electrons?—hit the third plate. You did see the third plate, remember? Through the lens at the other end of the tube. That third plate is supposed to be coated with the dust, from the bottle."

"It wasn't salt?"

She shook her head. "It's zinc and copper. Easily acquired metals at the time. Al-Urdi and Taqi al-Din both mention their usefulness. And in Maragha and Istanbul, they used dust from both to coat the surfaces of tools they were using in their optics experiments. The dust coats the last plate of the tube," she repeated.

"Why?"

"When the electrons—I'm using modern terminology now; Taqi al-Din generally calls them 'rays'—which have been increased or multiplied by the second plate, hit the powder, the powder becomes luminescent. The 'rays' hitting it cause it to emit light in the same pattern as the invisible light that entered the original lens. But the pattern is visible to the viewer now, whereas it wasn't before, because so many more electrons—our term, not his—are leaving than have entered the second plate. When you look through the viewing lens, you see the invisible infrared or low-light image that entered the tube 'recreated'—now using Taqi al-Din's language—in visible light on the third plate."

She clenched her fists and breathed through another contraction. They were coming faster now, and she felt panicky. She also frantically wanted to push. When the wave of pain had subsided, she leaned forward to peer into the shadows, looking for a sign from the nurse. But the nurse didn't acknowledge her. And Jeffrey, sighing, took her chin in his hand and twisted her face toward his again. "This way, Marion. Concentrate. What next?"

"That effect," she said, trying to get through it before the next contraction, "is what Al-Mansur and Taqi al-Din were describing when they talked about transferring an image from one field of vision to another. It was the same image, but it had left the realm of the 'murky' and been reassembled in a visible field. The tube is the instrument that makes that possible. That's also why the astronomer in the miniature was pointing it into a dark corner, rather than up at the sky. He was looking at invisible light. The stars and planets were of only incidental interest."

Jeffrey smoked, contemplative, for a few moments. Then he shook his head. "All of this would have required a power source. Which they didn't have."

"They used a battery," she said. "The ceramic container with the copper and the iron at the bottom."

"In the seventeenth century?" He laughed. "In the *thirteenth* century at Maragha? I think not."

Her brows rushed together, and she would have said something snide to him if another contraction hadn't shot through her—short, but excruciating. When it had subsided, she glared at him. "Batteries are everywhere in the ancient and medieval world, Jeffrey. They aren't difficult to manufacture. And there are descriptions of their operation in countless manuscripts. You've got one in your own Museum, you twit."

"The Parthian Battery, Willcox," Maugham shouted from the shadows. "Unearthed in Mesopotamia, on your watch. Shame on you for failing to pay attention to it."

"I specialize in coins and poetry," he muttered. "Very well. So it was powered by a battery." He considered. "The Parthian Battery has been dated—questionably, from what I understand, but let's leave that—to approximately 250 BC. A date that evokes to me, under the current circumstances, the Lighthouse at Alexandria. Is that a coincidence? Why did Taqi al-Din say that this device he'd created was similar to the one used in the Lighthouse? Why not claim he'd invented it?"

"Because he hadn't," she said. "He'd perfected it. It *had* already been used—and on a grand scale—hundreds of years before, most famously at the Lighthouse. But its operation at the Lighthouse of Alexandria was dependent on an infrared light source—"

"In the third century BC?" He peered into the dim edge of the room. "Maugham, if you're going to tell me that we've also got an ancient infrared bulb hidden away in storage somewhere, I'm giving up."

"No, my boy." Maugham was chuckling. "Dr. Bailey is on her own here."

"They used tungsten," she said.

"Tungsten was isolated from wolframite in the eighteenth century, Marion." He took another drag from his cigarette. "And Wolframite is rare. I know that because George is always going on about the Germans buying up all the most productive mines. It's wearisome."

"The alchemists—" she started.

"—had discovered that as well," he finished for her. "Of course they had. Evidence?"

"They heated cubes and mesh nets of tungsten to incandescence. And then those nets lit up the Lighthouse. As well as other beacons. But tungsten doesn't produce only visible light. When it's filtered, it emits infrared light." She wanted more water, but she couldn't ask him for it. She swallowed instead.

"Conjecture. Not evidence."

"They didn't call it infrared light," she said. "It wasn't part of their vocabulary. But they did know that lenses of the sort that Taqi al-Din left under the Observatory, and that were used in Alexandria in the ancient period, responded to it. It was a simple test. Flood the area with a filtered dark light. Without the tube, you can't see anything. With the tube, everything is visible."

"Evidence?"

"The mesh balcony around the minaret in Bolayır," she said. "It's tungsten. And it's fourteenth-century."

"What?"

"I was looking for it when we visited. There was a hint in al-Mansur's poem. And, when I saw it, it was obvious. The mesh net was the only part of the building that hadn't been demolished by your shells. Because it couldn't be destroyed." She wet her lips with her tongue. Didn't know whether she could cope with another contraction without more water. "Tungsten doesn't melt."

"Let me understand, then." He set his cigarette in the tray and held the bridge of his nose between his thumb and forefinger. "These—tubes—for seeing in the dark have been periodically re-invented over—centuries? Millenia?"

She nodded. Then, as another wave of pain began, she held his eyes. "Jeffrey, please, may I have another glass of water?"

He watched her face for a few seconds and then acquiesced. Continued speaking as he walked over to the nurse's table to re-fill her glass. "But the tubes work effectively only when the area has been flooded with non-visible, infrared light. So, when that sort of visual information acquisition becomes necessary, towers—the Lighthouse at Alexandria, minarets on the Dardanelles, presumably others as well, if the *Life and Customs of the Mongols* is any indication—shine these invisible spotlights on key positions. And those with access to the instruments—" He paused as he handed her the water. "Well, they have an advantage. The 'perfect weapon,' to quote our Benedictine monk."

She nodded again and took the water. Then she drank a quick swallow before shoving the glass at him and screaming in pain. She hadn't been prepared this time. When it was over, she dropped her face into her knees, breathing heavily for a few seconds. After that, giving up, she raised her head and shouted into the darkness. "Can I push now?"

"No." It was the doctor's voice. Preoccupied.

"Not yet, Marion." Jeffrey sat back down in the metal chair. "Soon. We've almost finished." He took up his cigarette and inhaled. "I want you to tell me how your people became involved. And what they're doing now."

The contractions were coming so quickly that she scarcely had time to recover her breath between them. But unwilling to give the doctor an excuse to experiment on her, she forced herself to continue talking. Gasping and clenching her fists throughout. But talking.

"Fine," she grunted. "As you say, this device for seeing in the dark was an old one. Ancient. It had appeared and reappeared from the third or fourth century BC onward. But the earlier versions all needed the invisible spotlight to be useful."

She took another breath and closed her eyes. "Then things changed. By the time Nasir al-Din was working in Alamut, people were wondering whether it might be possible to—to recreate the image on that third plate without flooding the area in infrared."

She decided she would push regardless of the nurse's advice. Couldn't stop herself. Bearing down, she continued talking. "Nasir al-Din had begun work on that when the Mongols took Alamut. But he kept it from them when they moved him to Maragha. They knew only about the original mechanism. From Alexandria."

Pushing was an agonizing pleasure. She took a deep breath and continued. "This is important, Jeffrey, because it means that the Germans also know only the first part of the story. From Robert and the celestial sphere. They don't know that it might be possible to develop a device that doesn't need the spotlight. They also haven't got Taqi al-Din's model. We have that—from Istanbul."

Jeffrey frowned. "But they do have quite a lot."

"Yes," she said, panting. "They've got—"

"Vampir!" Maugham shouted from the edge of the room.

"I'm sorry?" Jeffrey squinted into the darkness.

"Gossip from Berlin," Maugham said. "They've started work on something called 'Vampir.' It's not my branch, but I do overhear the odd conversation. No one could figure out what it meant. Something about 'night vision.' Now we know."

"What about your own people, Marion? I did notice the omission." He titled his head, watching, as she half-grunted and half-screamed through another contraction. "You're not at your most subtle. Not that you're ever adept at evasion."

"My people," she gasped, "want the towers and the instruments reconstructed along the Dardanelles and on the shores of the Mediterranean. The foundations and materials are already in place. They've always been there. If you'll let Stephen work with my material, he'll find the coordinates. I've already found Taqi al-Din's model."

She clenched her fists and pushed again. "But nothing can be done so long as the Dardanelles remain in limbo. As they are now. Your agreement with the Germans and the increased Italian submarine presence in the Mediterranean has left it and the straits vulnerable. Unworkable. They must be protected. And then the towers must be rebuilt."

She grabbed his wrist again. "Jeffrey, listen to me. You can't hide that tube away in your collections as an artifact. And you also can't pass it along to your technicians to develop secretly in the name of national interest. The Germans have already started on that. It's a mistake."

He crushed out his cigarette, stood, and beckoned to the doctor. She waited for him to answer, still breathing heavily. When he didn't, she glowered at him. "You do *not* want my people actively working against you."

He laughed down at her. "Are you threatening me?" Delighted. "Darling, I'm flattered. But don't you think you ought to be focusing on more important matters? The baby's coming." He looked, grave, at the doctor and nurse, who had converged on the hospital bed. "I think it may be time."

As the nurse wiped the sweat from her forehead with a cloth, the doctor moved the chair on wheels around to the end of the bed. He pushed back Marion's dress and sat on the chair, checking her progress. "I can see the head, Dr. Bailey. You'll want to push hard now."

Marion looked about, wildly, for Jeffrey, but he'd disappeared into the shadows to speak with Maugham. Squeezing her eyes shut, she pushed. As she did so, she heard them conversing.

"I took the liberty of sending for George, Willcox." Maugham's voice carried in the odd acoustics of the room. "I hope you won't think me forward. He heard the last part of the conversation."

"Hmm."

"I believe he was pleased." There was a smile in Maugham's voice. "His facial expression changed."

"Dr. Bailey." The doctor's tone was stern. "You must concentrate now. One more push will do it."

She pushed, clenching her fists until her fingers were white, and then she felt it pass out of her. As she cried weakly in relief, she heard the conversation continuing.

"And so?" Jeffrey sounded tired.

"I believe he intends to take up Dr. Bailey's proposal. He'll contact his counterpart in the Turkish government tonight—" Maugham stopped short as the sound of a newborn wail pierced the air.

"It's a girl, Dr. Bailey. Born with a caul." The doctor sounded relieved. "You must push just one more time to deliver the placenta."

"Is he still here?" Jeffrey's voice was cool. "Would he like to meet his niece?"

"Good God, Willcox. George? Interacting with our talent?" Maugham laughed outright. "You know how he feels about our methods." He paused. "I wouldn't mind meeting her, though. I feel almost part of the family, having attended the happy event."

"By all means."

The nurse had washed the baby, wrapped her in a blanket, and given her to Marion. Marion pressed her face against the top of the baby's head, breathing in, ignoring Jeffrey's and Maugham's approach.

"Would you like to keep the caul, Sir Jeffrey?" The doctor was standing, removing his gloves.

Jeffrey considered. "Yes, actually. Thank you. Who knows when it may become useful?" He turned and looked down at Marion and the baby. Then he started laughing. "Oh no. Oh, Marion. Her hair."

Marion hugged the baby closer. Her copious hair was a violent, bright red. She looked up at Jeffrey. "My mother's hair."

Maugham, who had been watching, detached, turned to the doctor. "Dr. Bailey will want to rest now. After her exertions. Don't you think, doctor?"

"Of course, Professor Maugham."

And before she could move or protest, the doctor had jammed a hypodermic syringe into her arm. She only had time to note the nurse taking the baby, and the doctor turning with an entertained smile to Jeffery, before the edges of her vision went black.

"Morphine," the doctor said as she fell back against the bed. "Something traditional. Given her distaste for modern procedures."

*London, England
Sometime in 1936*

MARION woke in her bedroom in Jeffrey's Chester Terrace house. She didn't know how she'd been moved there or how long she'd been unconscious. When she sat up in bed, nauseated, her head thick and heavy, her body ripped to pieces inside, she was almost afraid of what she might see. But when her eyes rested on an elaborate white cot placed against the far wall, festooned with ribbons and carving, she relaxed.

Mrs. Bowen was sitting next to the cot in a rocking chair that was also new, sewing something complicated. Behind Mrs. Bowen, a young girl—a nurse of some sort—was standing and looking down into the blankets.

The girl turned as Marion sat up, smiled, and put her finger to her lips. "She's just settled, Lady Willcox."

Mrs. Bowen, her brow furrowed, made a complicated knot in her sewing, put it in her lap, and smiled at Marion as well. "She's a lovely girl, Lady Willcox. With very interesting hair."

Marion started struggling out of bed, just as something between a mew and a cry wafted up from the cot. The nurse sighed, frustrated, and exchanged a look with Mrs. Bowen. "At least I thought she had settled. She does go on, doesn't she?"

Mrs. Bowen rose from the rocking chair, leaving her sewing behind her on the seat. "Just this once, it's for the best. Lady Willcox will want to hold her."

She bent over the cot and lifted the baby, which was dressed, Marion thought, in too many layers of white cotton and lace. Then, with a practiced movement, she wrapped the trailing material around the baby's legs and brought her to Marion.

Marion, who had leaned back against the headboard of her bed, took her from Mrs. Bowen. The baby, satisfied, nuzzled against her and became quiet.

After watching, indulgent, for a few seconds, Mrs. Bowen spoke again. "Sir Jeffrey asked that I inform him when you woke."

Marion blinked at her, uncertain as to how to respond. Her tone was complicated. Hovering between dictatorial and apologetic. She couldn't decide whether it was an obscure manifestation of reproach for her walk through the city before she went into labor or something deeper. But she also felt too tired to wonder about it. She shifted the baby into a more comfortable position. "Thank you, Mrs. Bowen. I understand."

When Mrs. Bowen left, followed by the nurse, she continued to gaze down at the baby. Feeling that she could watch her sleeping forever.

But less than five minutes later, the door opened, and Jeffrey appeared, dressed for the office. He closed the door behind him and sat on the edge of the bed, a sardonic smile on his face. She instinctively held the baby closer to her, but otherwise she didn't move or speak.

"She hasn't got a name yet, Marion."

"You aren't going to apologize?"

"I don't apologize."

She swallowed and looked down at the baby. Didn't want to transfer the revulsion she was feeling to her child. Jeffrey seemed content to sit in silence, and he simply watched her for more than a minute. Still with the lopsided smile.

Eventually, looking down at his fingernails, he spoke again. "You said that the hair, God help us, is your mother's?"

She nodded, but she didn't raise her eyes.

"Your mother was called Elizabeth, no?"

She shook her head. "Marion."

"We do have a file, Marion. She was Elizabeth."

"Marion Elizabeth," she corrected him. "We're all Marion. My mother, my grandmother, my great-grandmother—" She fell silent again.

"And you call my family mad."

She flicked her eyes up to his and then dropped her gaze. Didn't want to give him an opportunity to hurt her. She wouldn't ask.

He laughed, fully aware of what she wanted. "'Marion' it is, then. And my mother was Lydia. Is Marion Lydia Willcox acceptable? 'Lydia' in practice to avoid confusion?"

She nodded, grateful despite herself.

"I'll have the papers completed at the office." He stood and began walking to the door. "Mrs. Bowen and Alicia, the nurse, will be here if you need anything. I'll return before—"

"Jeffrey," she interrupted him.

"Yes?" His voice was smooth. Baiting. She didn't care.

"What about—" She stopped, uncertain how to ask.

He waited, obliging, without speaking.

"The Dardanelles," she finally said, hating herself. "Will there be—any—any change?"

He let his gaze fall on Lydia, sleeping now in her arms. Then, his eyes hardening, he held her look. "My understanding is that the Foreign Office has been communicating unofficially with the Turkish Embassy in London about changing the status of the straits. The negotiations will take quite a while. No one will like it, and we imagine that the Italians and possibly the Soviets will refuse to accept it altogether."

"Oh."

"Those who make predictions about such things," he continued, "are saying that a more formal arrangement might be negotiated sometime in May or June. There's been talk of a conference in Switzerland. Montreux, perhaps."

"Oh," she repeated.

"Fancy a family holiday in Switzerland?" He was turning back to the door, his tone biting now. "You'll be recovered by then, I daresay."

"Jeffrey," she said. "I'm sorry—"

He looked back at her. "No, you're not."

He pulled open the door, but before he walked through it, she stopped him again. "Jeffrey, wait."

"Yes?"

"I—I don't know how long I've been unconscious." She looked about the room, uncertain even as to the time of day. "What's the date?"

He smiled at her, warm now. "You know better than to ask me that, darling."

And he was gone.

Morocco, 1936

London, England
July, 1936

THE candles had burned down, and they were consuming the dregs of their coffee, summoning sufficient energy to leave the restaurant. It was 10:30 in the evening. Most of the tables were vacant. But they still had another half hour before the customary ill-natured spleen of the restaurant's staff turned to overt belligerence. They could linger.

Simpson's had been Aldous's idea. He was recently returned from his RAF posting in Iraq, his wife Daphne was visiting London from the countryside, they were both staying at the Savoy Hotel, which housed Simpson's, and Jeffrey hadn't felt inclined to argue with their proposal. Marion alone had felt a nauseated dismay at the idea of the restaurant—a reaction that had only sharpened as she'd watched Aldous attack his pile of sliced, bloody meat while Jeffrey basked privileged and boyish in the ill-concealed contempt of the supercilious man who had carved it at their table. Jeffrey enjoyed specialists who served him despite hating him. The restaurant catered to his type.

Even Daphne, whose early worship of Aldous as Flying Corps Hero had dwindled to nothing after producing two children for him, appeared content. She was smoking a cigarette, her enormous, fashionable blue eyes gazing into the flickering light of the candle. Unaffected by Aldous's possessive arm around her waist.

Marion took a sip of her cold coffee. She hadn't been out in the evening since her daughter had been born six months earlier, and she was determined, despite the dismal company, to enjoy herself. She let her attention wander from Aldous—large, healthy, and sated, his black hair shiny, his excessive muscle on the cusp of turning to fat—toward Daphne. Daphne was inoffensive. She'd focus on her instead.

"Yes, I was there," Aldous said in response to a question Jeffrey had asked a few moments earlier. "Amarah. Southern Mesopotamia. On the marshes. We captured it in June of 1915, I think it was. No. 30 Squadron and the Australian Half Flight chaps moved straight in."

He leaned back in his chair, reached into his pocket, and extracted a pipe. Nodding his thanks to a waiter who scuttled over to light it for him, he inhaled smoke, preparing to reminisce. Taking up more space even than he ordinarily did. Marion, watching him in horror, tried to catch Jeffrey's eye. She'd snap if she was forced to listen to him glorying in his decades of bombing Iraq.

Jeffrey deliberately avoided her look. "But then Kut fell."

"Indeed." Aldous looked down at his pipe. "We did attempt to drop them supplies during the last part of the siege. But we hadn't perfected the technique at that point. My own lads eventually gave up and took bets instead on who could hit the most enemy camels." He chuckled to himself. "I think it was Bobby Cuthbert who—"

"Cuthbert?" Jeffrey interrupted, although without seeming to. "Cuthbert, whose political reputation rests solidly on that series of dashing relief flights? Cuthbert, responding with all alacrity to General Townshend's anxious wireless messages concerning the likely fate of Spot, his dog, at the hands of his besieged and starving soldiers?" He paused. "Although, I grant you they could be dangerous. The enemy camels."

Marion sighed and stared down at the tablecloth. She recognized Jeffrey's professional interest in Aldous's answers. He wouldn't stop until he had what he wanted.

Aldous, however, unaware that Jeffrey was doing anything other than providing him a platform on which to parade his heroics, grinned. "You'll never prove it, Willcox. And Cuthbert is now, as we speak, involved in some hush hush affair with the Empire's gold bullion. You divulge to the world his camel-crunching record of 1916, and he will respond in kind."

He drew a few more puffs from his pipe. "Cuthbert can be spiteful. You wouldn't want to find yourself on the outs with him. In fact, we all wondered at the time whether Fergus didn't hand him the record voluntarily to preserve harmony in the ranks."

He winked at Jeffrey. "Don't tell Cuthbert, but the honest to God truth is that the camels had more to fear from Fergus than they had from the rest of us combined." Wrinkling his forehead, he considered. "I think he even managed to lob a parcel or two of food into Kut itself. More than Cuthbert ever did. Pity about the fold up over Kurdistan."

Aldous looked thoughtful for a few seconds. Then he brightened. "Incidentally, Willcox, you should see how Habbaniya Station is shaping up these days. You wouldn't recognize it—"

"But surely that wasn't Fergus's error." Jeffrey redirected him again. "The aircraft they'd supplied you in 1915 and 1916 weren't fit to fly. They couldn't handle the heat."

"Bollocks." Decisive. "That merely made things more interesting. Give me a mechanical cow to jolly into the desert air any day. The Farman Shorthorn was one of kind. A man was obliged to take care of her if he wanted her to perform for him. As it should be."

He pulled Daphne closer to him, and Marion's respect for her grew. The grimace of distaste lasted no more than a split second before her face resumed its ordinary expression of placid satisfaction. Daphne, she noted with a touch of envy, had a great deal of self-control.

"But they gave the Australians Caudrons, didn't they?" Jeffrey continued, still showing only a friendly interest. "Not Farmans."

"And that just goes to show you." Aldous pounced on the example. "Superior machines, they said. Safer for the tots. Better in the East than the cows. And what happened? The Caudrons arrived in early July. And then, less than three weeks later, they were all going tits up in the desert, the crew fighting back irate natives hurling stones and spears and dead sheep and bits of glass and God knows what else at them. Chaps just trying to do their jobs, right? Bloody savages."

Marion put her elbows on the table, her chin in her hands, and examined a spot of gravy on the tablecloth. She wasn't going to react, she told herself. Soon, if she was lucky, the restaurant's staff would forcibly eject them. The room was empty now aside from the four of them.

"What were their names?" Jeffrey asked. "The first Australians who went down?"

"Merz and Burn," Aldous said without hesitation. "Pleasant lads. A pity," he repeated.

"Those Caudrons could hold more than two, though, couldn't they?" Jeffrey was watching Aldous's face carefully. "There was a rumor floating about at the time, I remember—and also a few years later—that Merz and Burn weren't alone? That there was a third? A ghost. He disappeared too, they said—"

"Willcox." Aldous stopped him, exasperated, as realization finally dawned that Jeffrey was taking more than a passing interest in the story. "You twat."

He had taken his pipe out of his mouth and was laughing across the table at Jeffrey. His cheeks were bright red and his teeth almost artificially white. His good health was almost indecent. Grotesque. He was also, unlike Jeffrey, more than a little intoxicated.

"So this is how you treat the returning war hero looking to do nothing more than spend a precious night of his leave over a meal with his childhood compatriot, enjoying the candlelight, the memories, the meat, and—and whatnot?" He waved his pipe in the direction of the empty tables lined up throughout the room. "Pumping him for information to aid you in your infernal craft?" He eyed Jeffrey, still laughing. "I feel used."

"Rubbish, Parker. You enjoy being used. It makes you feel relevant." Jeffrey smiled back at him. "Was there a third?"

Now that he understood more was at stake than his memories of the War, Aldous made an effort to regain a modicum of sobriety. Sitting up straighter in his chair, he narrowed his eyes at Marion, considering. His face, which was rapidly shifting between calculating and guileless, looked like that of a seven-year-old playing at law enforcement.

"Fear not, Parker," Jeffrey said, enjoying Aldous's transparent inability to decide whether keeping or divulging his information would make him seem more important. He put his arm around Marion's waist, breaking her focus on the gravy droplets. "Marion and I have no secrets. Speak freely."

Unlike Daphne, Marion was unable to keep her annoyance from showing. But still, she didn't say anything. Instead, she cast an appealing look at the waiter who had lit Aldous's pipe. The waiter, staring into the middle distance, didn't acknowledge her. He was waiting for word from Jeffrey that they had finished. Recognizing that she was alone, she stifled another sigh and redirected her attention to the table.

"Been at work on each other, have you?" Aldous's attempt at stealth gave way to the dislike that better suited his features. "My condolences."

"Basil Kingsbury."

"Well, if you already knew, Willcox—"

"Did you know him?"

"Know him? How could I know him? He was one of you, wasn't he? None of us 'knew' him." He paused, still thoughtful. "But yes. He did go up with Merz and Burn that day. On the strict

Q.T., you understand?" He puffed a few more times on his pipe. Then he looked back over at Marion. "Really, Willcox. Are you certain that we ought to—"

"Powers that be have given me explicit permission, Parker. No one will come round to slap your wrist. I give you my word of honor." Jeffrey removed his arm from her waist. "Besides, it was twenty years ago. How hot could it be?"

Marion covered her eyes with her hands. Going out had been a mistake. She missed Lydia. And Ian—now eight years old, home from school, and asleep. She wouldn't see him until the morning. And she'd exchanged the time she could have spent with them for this circus that, she finally appreciated, Jeffrey had arranged days beforehand.

She fantasized about simply getting up from the table and leaving the restaurant. Finding a taxi to take her home. But then, resolved to see it through, she let her hands drop into her lap and looked across at Aldous. The smell of his pipe was giving her a headache.

"No one knew what he was doing there," Aldous was saying. "But what's even odder is that although he went up with Merz and Burn, the witnesses who saw the two of them fighting off the villagers once the kite had crashed couldn't account for Basil at all. He wasn't there. He'd vanished."

He looked down at the stem of his pipe. "So obviously there were stories that he'd survived. In fact, a few months later, after Kut had fallen and the Turks had marched their prisoners off to the Taurus mountains, there were even sightings of him. The three Australian Half Flight chaps who survived the forced labor in Anatolia said afterward that he would show up periodically to help them, feed them, that sort of thing. A kind of mascot. But you've got to keep in mind, Willcox, most of them were starving and hallucinating at that point. And once they'd recovered, they wouldn't swear to it."

"The Taurus Mountains?" Jeffrey asked. "In Anatolia? Not the marshes in Iraq?"

Aldous nodded. "Anatolia. Turkey. Not Iraq. But only over the next year or so. By 1918, he was gone again. This time for good. No more sightings."

Jeffrey made eye contact with the waiter, who nodded and began preparing their bill. Then he turned back to Aldous. "Until now. He's turned up."

"Basil Kingsbury?" Aldous stared at him. "'Turned up?' What does that mean? 'Turned up?'"

"Just as I've said." Jeffrey took the bill from the waiter and paid, shaking his head when Aldous reached for his own wallet. "A bit worse for wear, unfortunately."

He stood and slipped his hand under Marion's elbow when she rose from her own chair as well. Turned back to speak to Aldous as they all left the table. "I don't suppose you'd be willing to talk with him? He's mentioned you."

"Basil. Back after all these years." Aldous was shaking his head. Then, as they left the restaurant and a driver appeared with Jeffrey's car, he nodded. "Of course I'll see him. Be good to remember old times."

"I ought to warn you, Parker, he's changed. The conversation will be awkward." Jeffrey held open the passenger side door for Marion and closed it on her when, silent and obedient, she sat. She lowered the window a fraction of an inch so that she could listen.

Jeffrey leaned against the side of the car, still speaking to Aldous. "Nick Trelawney will be there to translate. But that may not be sufficient to get you as involved as you ought to be."

"Translate?" Aldous laughed. "I grant you Basil could be puzzling at times. He cultivated it. But I'll stay sober long enough to follow. No excessive celebration of the glories of Kut."

"It's not only that." Jeffrey ruminated for a second longer. "But better to explain everything tomorrow morning. Would 10:00 be convenient?" He turned to Daphne. "And will you forgive me for depriving you of your criminally absent husband's company for a few hours?"

She smiled, wry. "I'll find something to do with myself, Jeffrey. Though of course I'll miss him dreadfully."

"No doubt." Jeffrey kissed her quickly on the cheek and then shook hands with Aldous, clapping him on the shoulder. Although he was nearly as large as Aldous, his movements suggested energy rather than Aldous's threatening bulk. Instead of occupying space, he disappeared from it.

Taking the key from the driver who had vacated the car, he walked around to the driver's door and opened it. "They're keeping him at Norfolk House," he said, before he lowered himself into his seat. "St. James's Square."

"Why Norfolk House?" Reluctant now to retreat back into the Savoy.

"Lots of room?"

"Does he need room?"

"Everything will become clear tomorrow, Parker. Just be there, all right?"

"Oh, very well." Aldous had begun laughing again. "One more question, though, Willcox. What is this crate you're driving?"

"Lagonda. V12."

Aldous shook his head. "They don't make a V12."

"They're introducing it this coming October."

"Prat." Aldous draped his arm around Daphne's shoulders to lead her back into the hotel.

"Play nicely tomorrow, Parker, and they may find one for you as well." Jeffrey was still laughing as he closed the door. Once he'd started the engine, he glanced at Marion. "Something for Daphne to enjoy, at least, while he's stumbling about after the mirage of his youth in Habbaniya."

She stared out the windscreen. "I don't want to do this."

"There's a draft, dear. Would you close the window?"

Scowling, she raised the window. "I'm not coming tomorrow."

"Nonsense," he said. "You'll like it there. Lots of rotting gold leaf. Just your sort of place."

When she didn't respond, he continued driving for a few minutes, until he'd reached the edge of Regent's Park. Then he looked over at her again. "This is pure pique, Marion. You wouldn't miss the opportunity. And your people wouldn't let you miss it."

"Why do you want me there?" Toneless.

Before answering, he maneuvered the car into the garage under his Chester Terrace townhouse. Then, switching off the engine, he turned to her. "You can ask Maugham tomorrow. But surely you've got an idea. It seems that your people have struck again. Obliquely this time. But nonetheless—struck." He opened his door and stood. "It's an interesting problem. You'll enjoy it."

She also got out of the car. Without speaking, she walked toward the stairway leading to the ground floor of the house. The garage was stuffy, having retained the day's summer heat. He closed his own door and followed.

"You showed remarkable restraint tonight." He had his hand on the small of her back as they climbed the stairs. "There was a moment early on when I feared that Aldous would be decorated with potted shrimps before the main course had arrived."

"I was hungry. He wasn't worth it."

He kissed the back of her neck. "You'll see Lydia and the boy before going to sleep?"

She nodded. They'd reached the ground floor, and he took her wrap from her. Then, as he removed his hat and coat, he tilted his head. "May I visit you tonight?"

She turned away from him and walked up the spiral stairs toward the bedrooms. "If you must."

THEY were eating breakfast late the next morning in Jeffrey's dining room, where pink Arrillaga roses in a glass vase took up much of the center of the table. The flowers bothered Marion, who always smelled death and decay under strongly scented roses—though she never knew whether the hint of mortality she detected in them was a psychological effect or present in their actual smell. It didn't matter. The result was that she was yearning to leave the room even before Jeffrey had begun speaking. Something of a record.

She had spent the early part of the morning feeding and playing with Lydia. Then, when Ian had wandered, rumpled and still warm from his bed, into the nursery, she had let him sit in her lap while they both watched the baby sitting up, clapping, and making sounds that were almost speech. Ian continued these days to watch Lydia with mild suspicion, not quite believing that the incomprehensible yet lively thing that was taking shape in the nursery would become his sister. But he was also withholding judgement—willing to see what transpired.

He also enjoyed his role as protector, and so when his nanny and Lydia's nurse appeared to take them both into the park, he left without protest to change into outdoor clothing. Then, returning briefly to hug Marion, he hurtled down the stairs. They were going to the zoo.

Once they'd left, Marion changed into black summer wool trousers and a matching coat nipped at the waist—still close enough to her pregnancy to feel gratified that the tailored clothing fit her. Then, after slipping her feet into a pair of flat oxfords, she descended to the dining room. Resigned and—refusing to admit it to herself—curious.

Jeffrey was already there, drinking tea and reading his *Times*. She poured her own cup, spread marmalade on two pieces of toast, and observed the back of his paper, trying to ignore the sickening rose scent that was coming at her in waves. But she didn't suffer long. After two or three minutes, he looked at his wristwatch before folding and setting down the paper. "It's 9:30. Shall we leave?"

"We'll drive?" She stood.

"It's two miles, and the weather is oppressive." He stood as well. "Best arrive unruffled."

She nodded and followed him out of the house to a car that was waiting for them on the street. Jeffrey wouldn't be driving this morning. And he also, it appeared, wouldn't be speaking to her.

When he slid into the back seat beside her and closed the door, he remained preoccupied and silent—until eventually they reached Norfolk House, and he turned to her. "No questions?"

"Useless to ask." She pushed open the door and left the car before he could help her. Peered up at the building's portico and at the two rows of nine windows spread out above it. "This is bizarre."

"It's a perfectly ordinary building, dear." He held her elbow as he led her toward the entry.

"Why store him here?"

"As I told Aldous, lots of room." When she wasn't drawn, he smiled. "They couldn't keep him at the depot, obviously. Despairing outbursts on the part of the other guests there would have spooked him."

He nodded a greeting at the blank porter who admitted them to the building and not only closed, but locked, the door behind them. There was a wooden chair with a bottle of whiskey hidden behind one leg—the porter's office, she supposed—just to the side of the door frame. She remained silent.

"A hotel was out of the question for reasons that needn't be elaborated." Leading her across the geometric black and white floor of the hall and to the right, toward what she would later hear called the morning room, he continued speaking. "But here, we have an ideal shelter in which to soothe, comfort, contain, and exercise dear, delusional Basil. The Duke of Norfolk has been trying to sell this property since 1928. Since 1930, the poor man has even engaged estate agents. Chilling for a figure of his type. And yet, despite his efforts, here the albatross sits—languishing."

He reached the door to the morning room and paused. "You can imagine his subdued and noble delight when the office approached him with an offer. Not for the purchase of the place, of course. But to make use of it—with suitable cash remuneration—off and on when potential buyers didn't materialize. Empty aristocratic homes unlikely ever to be sold," he explained further, when she simply stared at him, "are Maugham's specialty. Since the crash, he's strung together a constellation of them, all across the country."

He blinked when she still had nothing to say in response. "Surely you didn't imagine that Chelsea and the Museum were his sole bases of operation? Someday, in fact, if you prove yourself a trifle less ungovernable, you might find yourself stashed in a lovely little drawing room in the Lake District rather than strapped to a hospital bed in dreary London. If you play along, that is." After waiting for a reply for a few seconds, he shrugged and opened the door. "Or not. Your preference." Escorted her into the room.

Aldous and Maugham were already there, waiting for them. Aldous, awkwardly, had chosen to wear his uniform—complete with the no. 30 Squadron palm tree badge. Any excuse, she imagined, as she dropped her eyes to the floor to avoid making eye contact.

Maugham—also awkward, although she had expected it of him—was wearing a billowing white shirt tucked into what she couldn't quite accept were leather trousers, high boots, and a large brimmed hat that he had apparently refused to relinquish to the porter upon entering. He looked like a very short, very round variation on the hero of a Louis Boussenard novel—the sort who is shown on the frontispiece half-conscious and alone in the middle of some alien continent, being dragged through the sand by a desperate horse.

She distracted herself by examining the room. But Norfolk House defeated her. The morning room was a rococo nightmare—plasterwork across the ceiling, massive marble fireplace, cherubs, vines, gilt, mahogany, and an overwhelming painted panel of what looked to be chickens. Thee large windows also let the July sunlight into the building to illuminate an almost complete absence of furniture. The room was empty aside from an incoherent contribution from the office: five wooden chairs on casters, an oak desk in a color that clashed with the mahogany, and a badly varnished table in the same wood, on which stood a pitcher of water, glasses, three ashtrays, and a mismatched selection of pencils and writing paper.

Maugham had positioned himself in a chair behind the desk, and Aldous was standing, his back to the door, looking out a window. When Aldous heard Jeffrey and Marion enter, he turned, smiled at Jeffrey, and raised the glass of water he'd been drinking. Maugham, who had been examining a tarnished metal bottle on the desk in front of him, looked up and raised that instead. He was sweating under his hat.

"Dr. Bailey! Willcox! So pleased you've come." He pointed the end of the bottle at the unsteady table and the remaining wooden chairs. "Make yourselves comfortable."

Jeffrey walked to the table, poured two glasses of water, handed one to Marion, and then moved an ashtray over to Maugham's desk. He sat and looked about the room. "Is Trelawney here yet?"

"He's entertaining Mr. Kingsbury in the study," Maugham said. "We'll join him later."

Marion sat in the chair next to Jeffrey's, holding the glass of water in her lap. Aldous, she noted, had decided to remain standing, leaning against one of the trumeau mirrors that flanked the windows. He'd left his now empty glass on the sill.

Maugham placed the metal bottle on the desk in front of him and regarded Jeffrey and Marion, pleased with himself. "Mr. Kingsbury," he said, "is talkative this morning. You've come at a good time."

"You'd like us to speak with him straight away?" Jeffrey had been reaching into his jacket pocket for his cigarettes. Now he stopped. Unlike Aldous, he was wearing a muted grey civilian suit.

"No, Willcox. Stay here for a few minutes. Smoke your cigarette." Maugham removed his hat and fanned himself with it. "Better you're familiar with his history before descending on him. Although forthcoming," he continued, "Mr. Kingsbury is something of an erratic conversational partner. We four must remain unified and focused on our target."

Jeffrey removed the case, chose a cigarette, and lit it. "Very well. I've already heard most of it. But Marion and Parker haven't. From the beginning, then?"

"And I'll go on till I come to the end," Maugham said, replacing his hat, "then stop."

He examined the chandelier hanging from the plasterwork ceiling for a few seconds, and then, without lowering his eyes, he began to talk. "Mr. Kingsbury went up with two Australians in July of 1915. Unlike the Australians, he failed to come down. It's true that they didn't find the Australians' bodies either—just the wrecked aeroplane. But witnesses watched them as they were overtaken by the marsh Arabs. Mr. Kingsbury was not with them. Two soldiers met their fate that day. Not three."

He tipped the metal bottle onto its side. It was a little over a foot long and of very old, very badly tarnished bronze or copper. Furrowing his brow in concentration, Maugham used his thumb and index finger to spin it on the desk in front of him. "After that, there were a few unverified sightings of him in the Taurus Mountains of Turkey. Doing good deeds. Possessed of a sanctified glow. Nothing wrong with that—keeping up morale among the prisoners."

He stopped the spinning bottle with his hand. "But then, he vanished again. Such that no one, anywhere, saw him for—well on twenty years. Remarkably well-trained boy, it seems. Would have made Captain Sir Mansfield George, etc. etc. with the artificial leg proud. Good for him. Although the twenty years, I do regret to say, haven't treated him as well as they might have. I'll let him provide you the details of his adventures himself. He's more than willing to rant about them."

He blinked and gave a slight sigh. "At any rate, five months ago, he chose to come out of occultation. A collection of French missionaries—or perhaps they were sexually promiscuous, drug addled utopians? I find it difficult on occasion to differentiate between the two—in Abalessa—"

"Abalessa?" Aldous, who had been struggling to follow the first part of Maugham's disquisition, interrupted him. "What's Abalessa?"

"A town in southern Algeria," Marion said without turning to face him. "At the base of the Hoggar Mountains. On the edge of the Sahara."

"Thank you, Dr. Bailey." Maugham smiled across at Aldous. "Satisfied?"

"No," Aldous said. "But continue."

"So, Mr. Kingsbury stumbled into Abalessa, wearing very little and raving in Darija—"

"Darija?" Marion interrupted this time. "Moroccan Arabic? Are you certain? Why not Algerian dialect?"

"Trelawney's the expert, Dr. Bailey." Maugham folded his hands in front of him on the desk. "He insists that it's Darija. Oldish Darija, apparently, though it's difficult to date it given that Darija isn't written. But I myself am convinced by Trelawney's analysis. You'll draw your own conclusions when you see him."

"You mean to say that he's still using Darija?" she asked, beginning to feel uncomfortable. "Why isn't Nick speaking with him in English?"

"As I was saying to you, Dr. Bailey," mildly irritated, "he stumbled naked into Abalessa, raving in Darija." He observed his folded hands. "And nothing else. No French. No English. Nothing."

"No Iraqi Arabic?" she persisted. "You'd dropped him in Amarah. Surely his field languages were—"

"*I* did no such thing, Dr. Bailey." Hurt. "As I said, it was Captain Sir Mansfield George—"

"He can't understand English?" She stared at him. "Even now? Nick's been communicating with him *only* in Darija?" She shook her head, shocked. "That's—he should be in hospital—he—"

"He's undergone a spot of stress, Dr. Bailey." Maugham's voice was punctilious. "As he was trained to do. He'll shake it off. And meantime, it isn't as though we're unable to debrief him. Trelawney is more than capable of—"

"I can't do this." She turned to Jeffrey. "I won't do it. And even if I were willing, I'm the wrong person. My Moroccan Arabic is scanty. I've got Iraqi, Egyptian, and Classical. That's it. I won't be useful."

"You'll be better prepared than Aldous, Marion." Jeffrey took a sip of water and placed his glass on the desk next to the ashtray. "All he's got is a bit of dirty Latin. And my North African dialects are serviceable. I'll help you if you get stuck—"

"*Profert Oenothea scorteum fascinum,*" Aldous began declaiming from across the room, his hand on his chest, "*quod ut oleo et minuto pipere atque urticae trito circumdedit semine, paulatim coepit inserere ano meo. Hoc crudelissima anus spargit subinde umore femina mea. Nasturcii sucum cum habrontono miscet, perfusisque...*"

"Thank you, Parker," Maugham said, stern, "that's quite sufficient."

"Oh, for God's sake." Marion turned back to Jeffrey. "I'm going home to Lydia and Ian."

"At least stay to hear the end, Marion." Jeffrey smirked over at Aldous. "I'll answer for him. He'll remain on his *very* best behavior from now on. Keeping in mind that there are ladies present."

"I can't see any," Aldous drawled.

"That's beneath you, Parker." Maugham's voice was now that of a schoolmaster. "Easy mark." He turned to Marion. "I, too, will answer for Group Captain Parker."

"Comforting." Marion took a sip of her own water. "Fine. Continue. Make it fast."

"Where was I?" Maugham scratched the top of his head through his floppy hat. "Ah yes. So, the French saw him—briefly—in Abalessa. Long enough to establish who he was—or claimed to be— and to send a message along to those who take an interest. But he disappeared again before they thought to restrict his movements." He tapped the side of the bottle. "Oh yes. And I forgot to mention, although he was far from respectable in his sartorial choices, he did have luggage with him."

"Luggage?" This from Aldous.

"Indeed." Maugham lifted the bottle. "This jar." He paused. "And a table leg."

"A table leg?" Marion glanced about the room. "Where is it?"

"He refuses to be parted with it," Maugham said. "You'll see it when we walk through to the study. It's an attractive table leg. One understands that he wants to keep it with him." He waited for further questions, and when there weren't any, he pushed on. "We haven't examined the table leg in any detail because he won't let anyone near it—and we haven't yet found it advantageous to remove it from him by force. But we have had a few of our experts look over the bottle."

"And?" Aldous sounded interested, eager in a childish sort of way.

"It's copper," Maugham said. "And old. With an unidentifiable residue inside."

"How old?" Marion asked.

"Twenty-five hundred years? Perhaps three thousand?" Maugham set it spinning on the desk again. "They were surprised."

"Do they know what it is?" Marion was peering at it, but she couldn't see it well, rotating as quickly as it was.

"Only what Mr. Kingsbury has told them." Maugham stopped it spinning.

"Which is?"

"I'll let you tell you himself," Maugham repeated. "I mustn't prejudice you." He leaned back in his chair and folded his hands over his belly. "Let me tell you, instead, how he found himself here, now, in the Duke of Norfolk's well-appointed London townhouse."

She nodded and took another sip of her water.

"So, he vanished from Abalessa sometime at the beginning of March," Maugham resumed. "And he was gone for another three months. Until, yet again, he became—active. Walther Wever, for example."

"The Luftwaffe General?" Aldous ventured when Maugham didn't elaborate. "He died last month. The Heinkel he was flying went down over Dresden. It hadn't been properly inspected."

"Sabotage," Maugham said.

"You don't say." Shocked. "Wever was—not stupid. A good strategist. I'm surprised he would have let that happen."

"The Germans were surprised too. They didn't want to advertise the fact that their security was vulnerable." Maugham's voice was bland. "So they called it an accident. But they were also, if quietly, unhappy about the situation. You'll never guess whom they blamed for the attack."

"*Basil?*" Aldous was staring at him now. "They're barking mad."

"They are indeed barking mad," Maugham said. "But in this one case, they have more than enough evidence to support their accusations. They wanted us to hand him over to them, but by the time they'd made their unofficial complaint, he'd disappeared again. Not that we had any control over his movements. We'd only just confirmed that he was still alive." He frowned. "So that was on the third of June. I'll bet you can't guess what he did in Abyssinia three weeks later, on the 27th?"

"Antonio Locatelli was ambushed in Boneya on the 27th of June," Aldous said, without waiting this time. "But he's on our side. We flew together during the War. He was the best pilot the Italians had. Basil wouldn't have gone after him."

"Locatelli was indeed on our side," Maugham said. "Was. Not anymore. He's been more than supportive of the Italian occupation of—"

"Rubbish." Aldous's face was flushed. And stubbornly set. "Locatelli was a hero. He didn't deserve to die that way. Attacked by a mob of half-dressed natives in that backwater African village—"

"Then it will please you to know, Parker, that whereas his fellow travelers—the officers, the second in command of their Air Force, and the journalists—were shot by natives, Locatelli himself, at least according to the information we've received, was shot by Mr. Kingsbury." Maugham paused. "I don't know what he was wearing at the time."

Aldous was glowering at him, bullying now, but Maugham held his look, provocatively gentle. "Have you anything further to contribute, Parker?"

"No, sir."

"Very good." Maugham took off his hat and began fanning himself again. His bald head was damp with sweat. "So now we jump ahead a few more weeks. To the 20th of this month. July."

"Jose Sanjurjo." Aldous laughed shortly. "He served in Morocco before lending a hand to Franco's coup. A prominent fascist. His biplane went down over Portugal last week. An accident. And you're saying—"

"Mr. Kingsbury overreached himself this time," Maugham confirmed. "By now, he had the Germans, the Italians, *and* the Spanish—such as they are—on his heels. If it weren't for some quick work on the part of our unofficial partners in Portugal, he'd never have made it out. But our acquaintances spirited him into France. And then the French—wanting nothing at all to do with him—passed him along to us."

Maugham stood abruptly, before any of them could reply, and replaced his hat. "He's in the study."

When no one moved, he looked across the table at Marion. "Have you relented, Dr. Bailey? Will you speak with him? Throughout his ordeal, remarkable though it is to narrate, he kept hold of both his table leg and his bottle—if not, one fears, the better part of his sanity. They're worth investigating at the very least, wouldn't you agree?"

She stood as well. "This is reprehensible. But yes. I'll see him."

Maugham turned to Aldous. "And you, Parker? Yours is the only name from his previous life that he's mentioned at all. Despite an array of leading questions."

"You're certain that it's my name?" Aldous was straightening his tunic.

"Trelawney rarely makes errors."

"All right, then." Aldous glanced, baffled, at Jeffrey. "I'll do my best."

"Excellent." Maugham pushed up the sleeves of his white shirt and led them all through the door. "I have great hopes for a profitable conversation. In Darija."

MARION took the opportunity to examine the entry hall as they crossed back toward the Duke's study. Then, thinking better of her curiosity, she focused on her feet. Someone had chosen to decorate the area surrounding the main staircase as though it were the exterior of a late eighteenth-century palazzo. Iron scrollwork on the bannisters. Bewildering iron lanterns hanging from the ceiling and in place above the doors. All on top of the ubiquitous cupids, grapevines, and plasterwork she'd already seen in the morning room. It made her feel dizzy. Ill.

She was comforted by the relative normality of the study. The plaster ceiling was muted, and the chandelier looked no more than functional. And aside from a carpet and two sets of glass fronted bookcases without books, the furniture resembled what she'd seen before. Here, the office had supplied seven upholstered arm chairs in clashing, mismatched patterns. These were arranged haphazardly around a square coffee table, also oak, on which were scattered another ashtray, two tea pots, several cups and saucers, and a pile of thirty or forty Cadbury Flake bars.

When they entered, Nick Trelawney, who had been sitting, rose and crossed the room to meet them at the door. He looked back at Basil, who was still seated, content it appeared to concentrate on the chocolate he was consuming. Two empty Flake wrappers were on the ground at his feet. Nick nodded at Marion and then spoke in a low voice to Jeffrey.

"I've put him through the paces, sir, and he's yet to trip up." He ran a hand through his brown hair, looking worried and even younger than his just thirty years. "We've been at it now for three hours, and if I hadn't seen it myself, I wouldn't have believed it. He's entirely consistent."

He paused. "If it makes a difference, I'm convinced that he thinks he's telling the truth. I've also tried every which way to trick him into revealing an understanding of English, French, German, or Iraqi Arabic, but not a flicker. He seems to *want* to understand. But he can't. And he certainly isn't holding anything back when we converse in Darija."

Jeffrey nodded slowly. "What about the Darija? You said that it was unusual?"

"Yes," Nick said. "Initially, I thought it was a regional variation—one I'd not encountered. But now—especially given the story he's been telling—I have a feeling that it's what one would have heard in the south of the country, at the edge of the Sahara, a thousand years ago. The vocabulary and syntax feel archaic. But obviously that's impossible to test. The language has never been written."

"*Can* he write?" Marion asked. "If you could convince him to put his thoughts on paper, it would indicate that he was at least aware of a standard form."

Nick shook his head. "No. We've tried. Again, he wants to. But he can't. And then, when he realizes that he can't, he becomes agitated."

"Hmm." Jeffrey addressed Maugham, who had moved to the edge of the room and was looking out a window. "Shall we introduce Parker?"

"By all means." Maugham didn't turn from the window.

Jeffrey stepped to the side to let Aldous into the room. "Are you ready, Parker?"

"What shall I do?" Nervous.

"I'll introduce you," Jeffrey said. "After that, we'll extemporize."

But as they crossed the room, Basil himself stood, staring at Aldous, eager, uncertain, and a touch flustered. As he took a few faltering steps toward them, Marion was able to examine him more closely. Under ordinary circumstances, he'd be a nondescript man of medium height with unremarkable brownish hair—an appearance perfect for his job.

But now, with dark circles under his eyes, thin and near starvation, a livid scar running under his chin, he was horrifying. He also appeared younger than he ought to be, given his experiences—no more than Nick's age. But then, his type wasn't the sort to show age. Aldous stopped mid-step when he got a better look at him. Then, taking a breath, he opened his mouth to speak.

"Flight Lieutenant Parker." Basil almost smiled as he preempted him.

Aldous lit up. Relieved that he wouldn't be forced to initiate the exchange. "It's Group Captain now, Kingsbury."

Basil's face fell. He didn't say anything more.

"No matter, Basil." Aldous closed the gap between them and clapped him on the shoulder. "You look as though you've been in the wars, old boy."

Basil shook his head, and Marion thought she saw something like tears well up in his eyes. But she didn't look for long. Humiliated to be a part of the scene, she walked to the table to pour herself a cup of tea. She'd never forgive Jeffrey for involving her in the interrogation of this broken person. Sitting in one of the chairs surrounding the coffee table, she stared down at her teacup, trying to remain invisible.

"Please. Ask him to stay. It doesn't matter that he can't understand." Shocked, Marion looked up. Basil had been addressing Nick in what sounded to her like native Darija.

"Of course, Mr. Kingsbury." Nick turned to Aldous and switched from Darija back to English. "He'd like you to remain here, sir. If you're willing."

Aldous smiled at Basil and slapped him on the shoulder again. "Wouldn't miss it, Basil. I'll stay as long as you can put up with me. Perhaps longer. But I warn you now, I'm giving you a run for your money on those Flake bars." He settled into one of the armchairs and, grinning provocatively at Basil, appropriated five or six Flakes, which he began unwrapping. "We can't get these at Habbaniya. God knows why."

Marion stared at Aldous. His heartiness didn't even sound forced. Then she dropped her eyes down to her teacup. She'd lose her mind if she had to start respecting him.

Basil, genuinely smiling now—but thin lipped and disdainful, a hint of the spy he'd been— turned back to Nick. "No need to translate," he said still in Darija. "I think I followed."

"Very well." Nick addressed Aldous in English again. "We'll conduct the remainder of our conversation in Darija, sir, if you'll forgive us."

"Whatever gives you the greatest pleasure, Trelawney." Aldous's mouth was full. "I'm well occupied."

"Thank you, sir." Nick, still quiet and serious, sat in the chair beside Marion's.

Jeffrey sat next to Nick and reached for his cigarette case. Before opening it, he looked up at Basil. "Do you mind if I smoke a cigarette, Mr. Kingsbury?" he asked in Darija.

"Not at all—" Basil, still standing, paused, uncertain as to how to address Jeffrey.

But Jeffrey didn't help him. Less convinced than Nick was about Basil's honesty. And he already had Aldous in place to represent comfort. Soothing him wasn't his role.

Marion, who had seen Jeffrey use social awkwardness before to keep his interlocutors off guard, frowned. Still looking down at her lap. It was a cruel tactic to use on someone so obviously on the edge of incoherence.

Jeffrey held out his cigarette case. "Would you care for one, Mr. Kingsbury?"

Basil considered the question with more seriousness than it deserved. Then, coming to a decision, he shook his head. "No. But thank you."

He sat carefully in his original seat without further comment. After that, still without speaking, he reached under the chair and withdrew a thick bat-like object, approximately four feet long. This he placed across his lap before turning back to Nick, polite and waiting.

The object, Marion saw as she sipped her tea, was unquestionably a table leg. But it was a table leg made of solid gold, and encrusted with spirals of rubies, sapphires, and pearls. The foot was a slab of emerald. Her eyes widened when she saw it, and she glanced over at Jeffrey. Maugham was still looking out the window, his back to the room. Paying no attention.

"That's a nice piece," Jeffrey commented.

"Thank you," Basil replied as though Jeffrey had complimented him on his choice of tailor. "It belonged to King Solomon."

"Did it?" Nothing more than polite.

Marion, however, turned, increasingly uncomfortable, to Nick. But Nick's face was also blank, reflecting Jeffrey's. Finally, she glanced at Aldous who, understanding nothing of what was going on, was well into his fifth Cadbury Flake. When he felt her attention, he looked up, crossed his eyes at her, and grinned like some halfwit schoolboy. Annoyed, she returned her attention to Basil.

"And where did you get it?" Jeffrey tapped the end of his unlit cigarette on the flat part of the case.

"St. George gave it to me." Basil leaned toward the table and poured himself a cup of tea. He put the cup on a saucer and then balanced both on the table leg in his lap.

"The St. George who kills dragons?"

"Yes." Basil sipped his tea.

"And the bottle?"

"There are a lot of those," Basil said. "The one I brought back and gave to Professor Maugham is a sample."

"And they're for?"

"Imprisoning demons." Basil paused. "Jinn too."

"Hmm." Jeffrey lit the cigarette. Blew smoke up at the ceiling. "Could you tell us again how and when you encountered St. George? And the jinn?"

"Yes," Basil replied, unruffled. "Merz and Burn dropped me in the marsh. I saw their plane go down. Then I saw them fighting off the villagers. I didn't stay to watch. I went under, as I'd been ordered. But when the Turks took Kut, I lost my network. I could have run home, but I thought that since I was there anyway, I'd continue collecting information. My idea was to follow the prisoners. I thought I might even get a few out. I have—"

He stopped, confused. "I used to have—that is, I believe I could speak Turkish. Which would have helped." He drank more of his tea and set the cup and saucer on the table. "As it was, by the time I reached the Taurus Mountains, they weren't in any physical condition to escape. So I stayed there, living in the caves, doing what I could."

"Which caves?" Jeffrey tapped ash off the end of his cigarette into an ashtray.

"Near Sagalassos, mostly."

"The ruined, ancient Pisidian city of Sagalassos?" Jeffrey inhaled smoke again.

Basil looked confused. "Is it ruined?" He shook his head. "It was empty. Very black. I met St. George there. Or, in a cave nearby. A big cave."

"What did St. George look like?" Jeffrey, who was holding his cigarette between two fingers of one hand, now leant toward the table to examine the Cadbury Flakes. Not acknowledging Basil, he left his cigarette in an ashtray, took a chocolate bar, and unwrapped it.

"He wore a lot of green," Basil said. "And he was two thousand years old. Or more. Transparent expression. Not a liar." He directed his thin-lipped smile at Jeffrey. "I was once trained to detect artifice as well."

"Hmm." Jeffrey had taken a bite of the Flake. "Group Captain Parker is correct. These are delicious."

Aldous looked up. "Was that my name I heard, Willcox? You'd best not be spreading malicious gossip about me when I'm in no position to defend myself."

"You're in no position to defend yourself, Parker, because you're the one who starts the rumors." Jeffrey had switched back to English.

Aldous considered. "Fair enough." Then he ripped open another Flake bar. "Do you think your people could have a crate of these sent to the Savoy?"

Jeffrey returned his attention to Basil without responding to Aldous. "What did St. George do when you met him?"

Basil tapped the table leg with his fingertip. "He gave me this."

"Ah yes." Jeffrey put the chocolate on the table and retrieved his cigarette. "And the bottle that once housed the jinn."

"No," Basil said. "The bottle came from the Sea of al-Karkar. I've already told you that."

"Forgive me," Jeffrey said. "I'd forgotten."

Basil held his look, his gaze untroubled. But he didn't speak further.

"And then," Jeffrey prompted. "Did St. George do anything else? In the cave?"

"Yes," Basil said. "He taught me to fly."

Marion, who had been sipping her tea, choked and began coughing. She stopped soon after, but not before Jeffrey had shot her an irritated look for interrupting the rhythm of his questioning. She closed her eyes. The man was out of his mind. She couldn't understand why Jeffrey was pushing him in this way. He needed care.

"In an aeroplane?"

"No," Basil said. Confused again. "Or perhaps, yes. It was difficult to tell in the dark. He set me down in the desert. And then I couldn't go any further."

"Why not?"

"The Assassins." Basil's hands tightened around the table leg in his lap. "I lived there. In the dead city—"

"The dead city?" Jeffrey's tone hadn't changed, despite Basil's anxiety. "Was this city also in the dark? In the desert?"

"Yes," Basil repeated, though it wasn't clear which of the questions he was answering. "There was nothing to eat. They had all died."

"What about St. George?"

"He'd left me." Basil started blinking quickly, his hands trembling. "I didn't know what to do. I was—"

"But you made it out," Jeffrey said, calming him. "Because you're resilient. Just a few more questions, Mr. Kingsbury. Yes?"

Basil nodded. "Yes. I made it out. There was a mechanical horse. It helped."

"In the desert."

Basil nodded again. "But mostly I swam."

"Swam?"

"Yes. Until I'd reached the Sea of al-Karkar."

Jeffrey took another drag from his cigarette. "Were you alone there as well?"

"No," Basil said, recovering now. "It's a well populated area. Prosperous citizens."

"Were the citizens living or were they dead?"

"They weren't dead."

"Could you find this sea on a map for us?"

"No." Basil thought for a few seconds. "It's too dark."

"Hmm." Jeffrey paused as well. "Let's say that the government of Great Britain had an interest in opening negotiations with the people of this region. Could we find them? Could you find them?"

"St. George found me again once I'd made it to the Sea," Basil said, unhelpful. "He showed me the way out. But only on the condition that I perform three tasks. And he also cursed me. With this malady. My speech." He paused. "And I was forced to swim again."

"Did you offend him?" Jeffrey asked.

"No."

"Did you perform your tasks?"

"Yes."

"Walther Wever, Antonio Locatelli, and Jose Sanjurjo."

"Yes." Basil shuddered.

"Did St. George explain to you why you were charged with those three tasks?" Jeffrey crushed out his cigarette in the ashtray. "They were both dangerous and—if you'll forgive me for saying so, Mr. Kingsbury—trivial."

"No more dangerous and trivial than the tasks I was asked to perform by 'the government of Great Britain' before St. George found me," Basil said in an echo of what might once have been intelligent asperity. "I didn't question then either."

Jeffrey's lips twitched. "Was that a pleasantry, Mr. Kingsbury?"

"I don't know." Basil swallowed. "If it was a pleasantry. The point is that one doesn't question, does one?"

"Hmm," Jeffrey said again. "You mentioned before that the 'Assassins' were responsible for your time in the desert. Could you elaborate?"

"They drew him off," Basil said, beginning to shake again. "And I was alone."

"Any idea why?"

"I think," Basil said, his voice also shaking now, "that St. George had made a mistake in the cave. He expected to meet someone else. But he'd already given me this," still gripping the table leg, "and so they were obliged to see what I could do. But I failed. Before I'd even started."

"Does St. George make mistakes, I wonder?" Jeffrey, finishing the remainder of his Flake, seemed surprised.

"He's not God," Basil said. Confusingly.

Jeffrey was quietly thoughtful for a few seconds. "Indeed not." Then, nodding, he stood. "Well, I think that clears up any confusion we may have had concerning your experiences. Thank you once again, Mr. Kingsbury. You've been more than helpful."

Aldous, seeing that the conversation was ending, stood as well. He looked, uncertain once again, at Jeffrey. "I'm more than happy to stay here, Willcox, if you think it would help the poor chap."

"Would you, Parker? I'd be grateful." Jeffrey glanced over at Maugham, who hadn't moved from the window. "We could use Trelawney in the morning room with Marion just now. The four of us must discuss Mr. Kingsbury's statement." He considered Basil. "It won't be much of a reunion for you, I'm afraid."

"On the contrary." Aldous sat and spread himself out in the chair again. Then, with a silly smile, he waved his arms above his head. "We'll use hand gestures. And I may summon up a bit more Latin. We'll have a ripping time. As I said, he rarely made sense to me when he was speaking English twenty years ago. This might be the beginning of a far more satisfying relationship."

"Thank you again, Parker." Jeffrey was opening the door for Maugham, who had left his position at the window. "You're not nearly the bastard you think you are."

He's mad."

They'd returned to the morning room, and Jeffrey was sitting in the chair he'd occupied earlier, sipping from a fresh glass of water.

Marion, next to him, rubbed her eyes with her fists. Although she'd said nothing, the conversation in the study had exhausted her. She saw no reason to conduct a post mortem on it.

"We'd very much like to open a line of communication to this 'St. George' and his people. On the Sea of al-Karkar, that is." Maugham, tapping the copper bottle with his fingertips, smiled across at Jeffrey. "They might prove useful allies to us in Northwest Africa. Our presence in the region, as it stands, is an embarrassment."

"The Sea of al-Karkar," Jeffrey said patiently, "is from a fairy story in *One Thousand and One Nights*. As you well know, Maugham. A late fairy story. Not even from the original manuscripts. St. George is—St. George. Next you'll be wanting to set up Telex machines in Valhalla."

"When one of my people returns from the dead after two decades bearing a golden leg from Odin's dining table and the severed head of a Valkyrie preserved in a three-thousand-year-old bottle, Willcox, I'll consider that." Maugham leaned back in his chair and folded his hands over his middle. "For now, all we have is Mr. Kingsbury, his lost city, and St. George, his extremely aged guide."

Jeffrey blinked. "I don't remember a severed head."

"One can hope, can't one?" Irked by Jeffrey's lack of enthusiasm.

"Shall we give him to the Tibet people, do you think? This seems more in their line."

"No." Decisive. "I'm convinced by Mr. Kingsbury's story. You'll pursue it."

Marion rose abruptly from her chair and walked to the window. Looked out at the hot street, keeping her back to the room. She was having difficulty forgetting the discomfort and pity she had felt as Basil was speaking. Maugham's callous excitement bothered her.

Jeffrey glanced over at Marion's back and then returned his attention to Maugham. "You say that you're hoping to boost our presence in Northwest Africa, Maugham. But Mr. Kingsbury never mentioned Africa. He said he'd been flown from the Taurus mountains in Turkey to a 'desert.' And that he'd then found the sea. No geographical reference points for either."

"Traditionally, the Sea of al-Karkar is in West Africa," Maugham said. "And the desert must be the Sahara. What else could it be?"

Jeffrey laughed. "It could be any desert near any sea in the world. Jinn travel fast. Ibn Khaldun mocked people for trying to find it. A level-headed person, Ibn Khaldun."

Maugham held Jeffrey's eyes for a few seconds. Then he spoke carefully, his voice dangerous. "We'll pretend now, Willcox, that you, too, are delighted and intrigued by Mr. Kingsbury's story. We'll also pretend that Mr. Kingsbury is undamaged—trusted and dependable talent back from a jaunt in the field. And finally, we'll pretend that you and I are of one mind concerning this project. Do you understand, my boy?"

He directed his gaze toward the ceiling and dropped the threatening tone. "Or, if you feel inclined to take on a less whimsical assignment, you'll go to Palestine to help Thacker interview prisoners in the camp we've set up at Auja al-Hafir. He's extracting all sorts of useful information from the Jewish communists and Palestinian nationalists we've collected there. And, indeed, whom we continue to collect. The place is bulging at the seams. You'll enjoy it. Challenging work."

The corner of Jeffrey's mouth went down. "Goodness. That was disproportionate. You aren't going to threaten me with the numismatists first?"

"I'm in a hurry," Maugham replied, petulant, lowering his gaze from the ceiling. "You've read the story. Over and over again, I would imagine, as a child. You must have had some guesses over the years as to where the 'Sea of al-Karkar' was. Let's go back over the pertinent information, shall we?"

Jeffrey sighed. Then, folding his hands on his crossed knee, demure, he spoke: "in the tale of the 'City of Brass,' in *One Thousand and One Nights*, our hero, Musa, who—in the story—governed North Africa for the late seventh- and early eighth-century Caliph, Abd al-Malik ibn Marwan, decides to go in search of the bottles in which King Solomon imprisoned the demons and jinn who displeased him. The bottles, he and the Caliph have learned, are available and accessible, floating about in the Sea of al-Karkar, in the far west.

"After various, mostly depressing, adventures, helped by a series of robotic horsemen and remarkably forthcoming demons half buried in the sand, Musa, his worrisomely elderly guide, and his impetuous and often stupid companions reach the City of Brass. Which, though implicitly—or, explicitly, if you're Tabari—constructed by King Solomon, is now dead. Populated by dead bodies.

"They loot the city—while also thinking sadly and soberly on the tragic brevity of life. Then, once they've loaded up their plunder, they march for another month or so along the seashore until they reach a range of mountains and caves inhabited by a population of tall black people who are vaguely Muslim, but only because a saint or prophet—al-Khidr—appears to them every now and then to tell them how and when to worship. The leader of the blacks, who helpfully speaks Arabic, sends his divers out to bring the bottles back to Musa. They do so—while also collecting a few mermaids as a novelty.

"Musa thanks them, returns to the Caliph in Damascus, and the Caliph, delighted, removes the seals holding in the demons in order to watch the bottles go pop. The mermaids, unfortunately, die in the heat. Musa himself gives up the treasure he took from the City of Brass to spend the remainder of his days in the ascetic contemplation of God."

Jeffrey paused. "Historically—or, at least, more historically than in *One Thousand and One Nights*—Musa is supposed to have taken dishonest credit for the discovery of King Solomon's table during the eighth-century conquest of Spain. According to the story, his general, Tariq ibn Ziyad, a Berber from North Africa, discovered the table himself in the treasury of the Visigoth Spanish King Roderic, whose ancestors had looted it from Rome. Tariq, suspecting Musa's dishonesty, however, removed a leg from the table and replaced it with an inferior one before Musa could present it to the Caliph, al-Walid. When the Caliph asked Musa why one of the legs was not as it should be—well, he was found out. The table went into the Caliph's treasury, but then disappeared. No further information has since surfaced about it."

"Thank you, Willcox," said Maugham, not having missed the sarcasm underlying Jeffrey's summary. "But you've said nothing about the sea's location."

"When I was fourteen years old or so," Jeffrey replied, annoyed as well now, "and I devoted my energy to such things, I thought that it must be on the Niger river. The black population suggested a sub-Saharan city. And Suetonius mentions a river, almost certainly the Niger, that he calls 'Gir,' which is a word sounding somewhat close to 'Kar.' Also, my father once gave me an excessively detailed atlas that noted that the Berber term for the Niger was 'Ger-n-ger.' Even closer.

"I decided, in my adolescent wisdom, that the 'Sea of al-Karkar' must not be a 'sea,' but instead a wide part of the Niger that the medieval compilers of *One Thousand and One Nights* hadn't understood was a river. Al-Masudi puts it somewhere in that location as well. Burton disagrees. He says in a footnote that it's from *Cercar*, an ancient Roman fortress in Libya, near the city of Leptis Magna. Or, perhaps, from the Greek and Latin, *carcer*, incarceration, etc. Though, modestly, he finishes that footnote with a question mark." He held Maugham's eyes. "Happy?"

"And you, Trelawney?" Maugham didn't bother to answer Jeffrey. "Did you ever speculate?"

Nick thought for a few seconds. "Yes, sir. I suppose I always associated it, at least phonetically, with the word for snarling or snoring in Arabic. *Kharkhar*. Perhaps the water was so called because of the sound it made? That ominous feeling—*kharkhar*—would also link the water back to the hint of 'misfortune,' *nuhus*, that permeated the 'city of brass'—*madinat al-nuhas*."

"Hmm," Maugham said. "Immoderate snoring can indeed be a misfortune. Those not troubled by it rarely understand the torment its victims suffer."

"The word," Nick continued, unaffected by Maugham's comment, "might also come from the Greek. I seem to remember that the wall- and tablet-inscriptions that Musa encounters on his journey in the story are written in Greek. He asks his guide to translate them for him. And there is an Indo-European root, *karkar*, meaning 'very hard,' that enters classical Greek early on. Herodotus, for example, uses the single, rather than doubled, form when he's comparing the Thracian and Scythian treatment of cannabis. The Thracians, he says, pounded cannabis into a cloth 'very like linen.' The 'very' in that formulation is καρ—"

"But the Scythians inhaled it, didn't they?" Maugham interrupted, chuckling. "Yes, I remember that bit. Wouldn't be surprised if Parker did as well."

"Yes, sir." Quiet and unruffled.

"Trelawney." Maugham beamed at him, indulgent. "You are a marvel. You and Dr. Bailey together must have been the terror of Durham's Oriental Studies Faculty. I regret that I was never there to watch you guiding and mentoring her appalled students."

Marion, annoyed herself now, turned back toward the room. She didn't want to be reminded of Nick's spell impersonating her research assistant.

"Dr. Bailey!" Maugham beckoned her with one finger toward the desk. "Please do join us."

She stayed where she was.

"Any thoughts?" he pressed.

"I think," she said, "that Mr. Kingsbury needs a doctor. I think that when the aeroplane went down in Amarah, he lost his reason." She narrowed her eyes at Maugham. "It must have been a shock to all three of them—Merz and Burn as well as Kingsbury. Set upon by the very Arab villagers they were out to protect. The ones—at least according to T.E. Lawrence and the rest of your propaganda officers—who were so desperate to throw off the Turkish yoke that they'd join forces even with the likes of you. One understands that they would have been left—off-balance."

"Really, Marion." Jeffrey's voice was subdued. "Two men died. You might relent."

She turned on him. "But they never found the bodies, did they? So perhaps they didn't die. Perhaps all three had the presence of mind to sew themselves up into animal skins for a giant Roc to spirit them away to a magical palace perched on an inaccessible mountain beyond the edge of the world. Who knows? The other two may still be enjoying the company of a flock of women with faces like moons and a way with pomegranate seeds."

She faced the window again. "I wouldn't be remotely shocked to discover that Mr. Kingsbury's true mishap was entering the forbidden room and getting himself ejected by the fantastic flying horse. I've forgotten. Is he missing an eye? We must check on that."

"I'll make a note to do so, Dr. Bailey. Thank you." Maugham turned to Jeffrey. "You'll discuss this with her later, Willcox."

"Discuss *what*?" Jeffrey's exasperation was mounting again. "Forgive me, but this is an impossible assignment."

"Which is what makes it so very interesting." Maugham looked up at the ceiling again. "What about St. George?"

Marion, preempting any answer from Jeffrey or Nick, spoke tonelessly, without turning away from the window. "In Anatolia," she said, "and especially in the Taurus Mountains, St. George and Hızır or Khidr—the al-Khidr who taught the people on the Sea of al-Karkar about Islam—are identified with one another. Together, they're a composite Green Man, dragon-slayer, spiritual guide, and immortal shaykh. Mr. Kingsbury likely encountered variations on the story of St. George-Hızır during his time there."

Maugham, Jeffrey, and Nick all looked, surprised, at her irritated back. Then Maugham prodded the bottle in front of him with his fingertip. "I think, Dr. Bailey, that this may be the first time, since I've had the pleasure of your acquaintance, that you've willingly offered up information without someone, somewhere having to be hurt." He cocked his head, his eyes still on the bottle. "A momentous occasion. But is there a reason for the concession? I feel a trifle nervous."

She spun back toward the room. "I'm going to the toilet."

Then, trying to substitute an air of conviction for her fear that they would stop her, she crossed the room. They didn't stop her. As she left, she heard Maugham ask Jeffrey and Nick about her assessment of the story.

"I've heard something similar to it before," Jeffrey was saying as she closed the door behind her. "And yes, in Anatolia, Hızır—al-Khidr—shares characteristics with the Green Man, St. George, and also the prophet Elijah. Even if they aren't identical figures."

When she reached the hall, the porter stopped her, asking whether he could provide assistance. His expression, a deliberately unconvincing burlesque of deference, made clear that his job was to prevent visitors from wandering the building unattended. She understood now why Maugham had so readily let her leave the room.

"I'm looking for the toilet," she said shortly.

"I'll take you to it," he replied in the same tone. Then he led her, mimicking the stately pace of a house servant, across the hall, past the study, and toward a water closet in a corner of the ground floor.

"Thank you," she said, closing the door to the tiny room in his face.

When she turned, she smiled to herself. There was a window, locked by nothing more than an elaborate, yet flimsy, latch. She stepped toward it, stood precariously on the toilet, and pushed it open. Looking down, she saw that its ledge was five feet above the alley outside. It wouldn't be an easy climb, but with a box or a crate on which to stand, she could make it. The alley was deserted and would likely remain so at night as well. And she could certainly squeeze through the window with room to spare.

Considering for a few further seconds, she resolved to break the latch. It was embedded in soft wood, and it would take only a few seconds to twist it off the window. The porter might notice the change, but chances were he'd simply check to be certain the window remained closed before continuing what she suspected was a bored and superficial nightly inspection of the house. And if she left enough paint around the scar on the wood, it would scarcely be visible. Satisfied, she bent the latch back and off the window before dropping it into a pile of rubbish in the alley below. Then she drew the window shut, stepped down from the toilet, and pulled the flush.

As she glanced about the small room to be certain she hadn't left signs of her activity aside from the broken latch, she pushed down her concern that she was inviting trouble for no good reason. She didn't know why the feeling had crept over her that she'd want or need access to the building. As it stood, she had no curiosity whatsoever about the problem that Maugham had presented to them that morning. But she also knew better than to ignore the promptings of her intuition when they were as insistent as this one had been. Something had lodged itself in her subconscious as Maugham had been speaking, and she'd regret not giving it free rein. She felt an irrational sense of security at the thought of the vulnerable window.

When she opened the door, the porter was standing outside. Nodding to him without speaking, she let him lead her back to the morning room. Upon entering, it was as though she had never left. Maugham, Jeffrey, and Nick didn't acknowledge her return even by a look, engrossed as they were in conversation. Pouring herself another glass of water, she sat next to Jeffrey.

"And the residue in the bottle?" he was asking Maugham. "They can't make at least a guess as to what it is?"

"They refuse to try." Maugham was leaning back in the chair with his hands over his belly again. "They can't even determine whether or not it's organic."

"Is it possible that whatever destabilized Mr. Kingsbury came from there?" Jeffrey was leaning back as well, his legs still crossed.

"Was he possessed by the jinn that the bottle disgorged, do you mean?" Maugham leaned forward, conspiratorial and entertained. "*Majnun?*"

"Why not?" Jeffrey rubbed his cheek with his hand. Still aggrieved.

"He said that St. George cursed him." Determined to defend Basil's story to the last detail.

Jeffrey gazed across at him, impassive, for a few seconds. Then, just before the silence became uncomfortable, he said: "I would consider it a great favor, Maugham, if you would ask one of your technicians to spare a drop or two of whatever they've isolated from that bottle to test on, say, a rat." He paused. "If the rat begins to speak Darija and consume Cadbury's products, we'll have our answer."

"Hypnosis works wonders on men of Mr. Kingsbury's temperament," Maugham offered.

"Hypnosis and drugs work better," Jeffrey replied.

Maugham pursed his lips. Then, after three or four silent seconds more had passed, he straightened and stood. "Well. This has been a more than edifying morning. I thank you all for your cooperation. And I'll look forward, Willcox, to perusing the reports on your progress."

Jeffrey stood as well, keeping a blank mask in place over what was now wrath. "And I'll work diligently," he snapped, "to write them in such a way that you're well diverted."

"Keeping in mind, of course, that you'll have stiff competition, my boy." Maugham, smiling again, replaced his hat and hitched up his leather trousers. "Thacker's updates from Auja have kept the office in hysterics these past weeks. You'll want to be sharp to top them." Bowing slightly toward Marion, and casting a last provocative smile at Jeffrey, he turned and left the room.

Marion, confused by the abrupt end to the meeting, remained seated for a few seconds longer. Then, slowly, she rose to her feet too. She considered the closed door. "Did I miss something when I was gone?"

"Were they lederhosen?" Jeffrey was also looking at the door.

"Technically, I suppose." She wrapped her arms around her waist. "I think he was aiming more for American cowboy."

"Ah." He pushed down his anger and addressed Nick, who was now also standing. "You'll be minding Mr. Kingsbury for the remainder of the day, won't you, Trelawney?"

"Yes, sir."

"And Parker?"

"I'll mind him as well, sir." Nearly imperceptible smile.

"Thank you, Trelawney."

Jeffrey put his hand on the small of Marion's back, preparatory to leaving the building. Then, pausing as a thought struck him, he spoke to Nick again. "Is Muriel here somewhere? Invisible? Under the desk, perhaps?"

"She's in the next room, sir."

"Would you ask her to have a box of Flake bars sent to Parker's suite at the Savoy?"

"Yes, sir." Nick nearly smiled again. "I expect she's already on it."

"Thank you again, Trelawney."

And then, without speaking, Marion and Jeffrey left Norfolk House.

*W*HEN they returned to Chester Terrace, Jeffrey disappeared into his own study. To sulk rather than to work, Marion suspected, but she wasn't about to interrupt him. Given that it was early afternoon, Ian and Lydia were also still in the park. Deciding that she might as well use the brief period to herself to deliver a report to her people on the farcical events of the morning, she climbed the stairs to her room and wrote and encoded a summary. Then, changing into a lighter linen jacket, she descended to the ground floor and left the house.

Her report was perfunctory. Her superiors wouldn't be interested in Maugham's bizarre new obsession. But they expected her to keep them informed on the activities of the office, and she'd be remiss letting more than a day or two pass before filing her impressions. She walked briskly toward the newsstand across from Marylebone, chose a bus map from the wire display on the pavement, slipped her report between the pages, and then walked to the counter.

"Excuse me," she asked. "How much for the London Transport map?"

"Issued free." The man behind the counter was cleaning the side of his till with a handkerchief.

"This one is ripped," she said, sliding it across the counter. "May I have a different one?"

He took the map and tossed it under the counter. Then, without speaking, he handed her a new map.

"Thank you," she said, pushing it into the pocket of her jacket.

"You're welcome, Madam." The man hadn't looked up from the till.

Marion left the newsstand and wandered into the park. Then, finding a vacant bench next to a stand of delphiniums—and well away from the roses—she opened her map. A small pinhole in the paper indicated her next drop. Great Portland Street. She'd go there to collect a response—also perfunctory, she was confident—tomorrow. As she tore the map into pieces, certain to obliterate the original hole, she resolved to bring Ian and Lydia along with her. She'd spent too little time with them recently, and the walk there and back would be entertaining.

After throwing the remains of the bus map into a bin, she took a meandering route toward Chester Terrace—still avoiding the roses. By the time she'd returned home, Ian and Lydia were back—and Ian monopolized her until dinner, telling her in manic detail about how Lydia had touched Percy the Penguin without crying or any apparent fear. Proud of her. Ian had himself nurtured a terror of the penguins in the zoo until he was well over seven years old. She was pleased that he'd chosen to be impressed by, rather than jealous of, his sister.

The next morning, Jeffrey left early for the office, still bad-tempered and preoccupied. Marion avoided him, staying with Lydia again until Ian woke. Then, following an extended negotiation with him about getting himself dressed, she took Lydia down the stairs to her pram. After settling her into the blankets, she hooked a soft giraffe onto the sunshade above her head. Waited for Ian to join them on the pavement.

When he finally emerged, wearing tattered shoes that were a size too small for him and that he must have dug out of the rubbish—unwilling to part with them—they walked south through the park. After a leisurely and meandering half hour, they crossed out of the green area onto Great Portland Street. Then they walked through the busy streets until they reached a newsstand at the intersection of Great Portland and Weymouth. Marion let Ian choose a chocolate bar—Rowntree's Chocolate Crisp—took another bus map, and maneuvered Lydia's pram toward the counter.

Once she'd paid for Ian's chocolate and retrieved a new map—noting in passing from the newspaper headlines that the Berlin Olympics would be starting in a few days—she walked with Ian and Lydia back toward the park. When they'd retraced their steps into the greenery, they turned left and continued on until they found a vacant bench near the pond. Marion sat, positioned Lydia's pram next to her, and suggested to Ian that he might explore the water—provided he wasn't put off by the carpet of goose droppings on the grass. He made his way, gingerly, toward the shore, and she unfolded her map.

When she saw the message that it contained, she blinked and stared at it, aghast. Told herself that it must be a mistake. There was no other explanation. She couldn't have misread it—encoded as the lines were, they were sufficiently short, and in a sufficiently old cipher, that she could understand them immediately: "locate and remove St. George. Exit scheme, Wednesday, 5 August, will come via the usual channels."

Feeling cold, despite the rising late-July temperatures, she squeezed her eyes shut, unwilling to comprehend. But her interior revolt against her situation didn't last long. Lydia, sensing her divided attention, began to squirm in her pram. Then, when Marion failed to comfort her after three or four seconds had passed, she let out a piercing wail. Startled, Marion slipped the page into the map, stuffed the map into her pocket, and lifted Lydia out of the pram, holding her and bouncing her, still preoccupied, in her lap.

Ian, who had felt a similar change in the atmosphere, picked his way back toward the bench. "There's too much goose stuff," he said to her. "I got some on my shoe." Persecuted. Wanting to blame Marion for her suggestion that he explore the water. Also wanting to force her out of her newly tense mood.

But try as she might, she couldn't push down her creeping fear. Instead, she rose from the bench, holding Lydia, and began pushing the pram in front of her with one hand. "I'm sorry, Ian. Perhaps we ought to continue walking."

He remained rooted on the path, looking up at her. "You're not happy." It was an accusation rather than an expression of sympathy.

"I'm fine, Ian. Really." She tried pushing the pram more quickly, awkwardly, as Lydia worked up to another cry.

Ian remained immobile. "I want to hold your hand." Sullen. Looking for a fight.

"Ian," she said, her voice rising. "Look at me. How am I supposed to—" She stopped, embarrassed, as a young couple walked by in the other direction, observing her agitation with disapproval. Ian was attractive, even when petulant. She was haggard, bitter, and unsympathetic.

Lydia was now crying in earnest, drawing more looks from passersby. They must get out of the park. Keeping Lydia in her left arm, she turned away from Ian and began pushing the empty pram with her right hand. The soft giraffe swaying violently from its hook. If he refused to follow, he could find his way back to the house on his own. He wasn't an infant. And she couldn't let the situation spiral any further downward than it already had. She'd be inviting the intervention of strangers soon.

As she walked, she heard Ian running to catch up to them. Let her breath go, relieved, but she didn't turn to acknowledge him. Given the chance, he would reopen his grievances concerning his shoe and the fact that she no longer was happy. Repeating the altercation from a few minutes before. Her best strategy was to watch him out of the corner of her eye without speaking to him.

Half-jogging across the park past a bed of allium she hadn't seen before, they made it to the house in five, humiliating minutes. When they climbed the stairs and opened the door, she stopped short. Jeffrey was in the entry hall, removing his hat. He'd returned early from the office. Having failed once again, if his expression was any indication, to convince Maugham to reconsider his strategy.

Turning now, surprised by the sound of Lydia wailing in anger, he raised his eyebrows. Then he flicked his eyes from Marion and Lydia to Ian, who had resumed his affronted questioning as to why she wasn't happy, why she'd allowed him to dirty his shoe, and why, presently, she wasn't talking to him or answering him. At which point, he began laughing.

After scowling at him, she turned her attention to the stairs, where Ian's nanny and Mrs. Bowen were standing, not quite disguising their embarrassment. "I'm going to feed Lydia," she announced to the room at large, daring any of them to comment.

Then, leaving Ian to them to handle, she carried Lydia up the stairs to her own bedroom. Closed the door, lowered herself into the rocking chair near the window, and held Lydia against her. As she did so, she felt the transport map, badly folded, crumple further in her pocket. She'd forgotten to drop it in the park. She silently cursed and then forced herself to pretend, at least, to relax.

But even as Lydia calmed, Marion's agitation mounted. It was shocking enough that her superiors wanted her to locate Basil's imaginary travel companion. That they wanted her to kill him as well was incomprehensible. It must be an error. A mistaken interpretation of her own message to them. But Wednesday, the fifth of August—the day they wanted to move her out of the country—was a week away. If she didn't ask for and receive a confirmation of their order within the next day or two, she'd be prompting a great deal of confusion and, potentially, violence.

She shifted Lydia into a more comfortable position. She also must destroy the transport map she'd stupidly kept in her pocket. Although the message was encoded, the cipher was by no means unbreakable. It was the simplest code her organization used, meant for immediate comprehension and destruction rather than for extended transmission and potential interception.

Whatever the situation, though, she couldn't worry further about it today. Surrounded by Ian and Lydia, as well as Jeffrey and his household, she had no chance of taking any steps to contact her people. Determined to relax, she leaned further back into the rocking chair and concentrated on Lydia.

As she rocked, Lydia's now placid content began to infect her. And her last thought before pushing away all consideration of her organization was that she might at least work on probable locations for Basil's "St. George," if not on a means of destroying him. None would be anything other than fantastic. But if she cooperated with the first part of their instructions, they might reconsider the more preposterous second part. She nodded to herself as Lydia drifted into sleep. Cooperating was better than provoking them into obstinacy. The search might even prove interesting in an academic sort of way. Something literary to occupy herself during the many hours she was still spending feeding and soothing the baby.

Once Lydia's breathing had slowed and steadied, she rose from the rocking chair and lowered the baby into the cot she kept in her room. Then, when she was confident that Lydia would remain asleep, she smoothed out her wrinkled coat and trousers and left the room to find Ian. To prove to him before dinner that she was, indeed, as happy as she'd ever been. And also to convince him to part with his awful shoes.

IAN, politic, failed to remember that the visit to the park had been anything but idyllic—which made Marion's task of performing sufficiently believable happiness for him easier. And by the time they'd parted to change for dinner, there was little trace of the tension that had dogged them that morning. Meaning that the only interrogation she'd endure that evening would be Jeffrey's. And perhaps not even his, she thought, as she entered her dressing room to examine her dinner dresses. His antipathy toward Maugham's project might very well leave him taciturn and distant this evening—as he had been throughout the day and the night before.

She, however, wanted to draw him out of his silence. As she'd been entertaining Ian that afternoon, a part of her mind—the same restive part that had led her to chop the window at Norfolk House—had been mulling over the whereabouts of St. George. And despite herself, an idea that attracted her had begun to form at the edges of her consciousness. Something she hadn't considered before. Something interesting. But she'd need Jeffrey's help to test her theory, which would in turn mean provoking him into speech, if not cooperation.

She stopped and stood in front of an ivory satin sheath she'd not yet had the courage to wear. It was sleeveless and bias cut—a fashion far beyond her comfort level. Determined to initiate her plan, however, she removed it from its hanger and brought it out to arrange on the bed. Then she rolled on stockings, pulled the dress over her head, slipped her feet into the matching shoes she'd also never worn and sat in front of her dressing table.

As she ran a brush through her hair, she viciously shoved down the guilt she was feeling for letting her mind dwell on Maugham's preposterous project. She couldn't spend every waking moment caring for her children. She had other interests as well. She'd go mad if she didn't pursue them.

She winced as she inadvertently jabbed a hair pin into her scalp. Then, resigned, she decided that she might as well stop haranguing herself. Her conscience remained stubbornly unconvinced, and if she kept it up, she'd be bleeding. Letting her mind go blank, she finished putting up her hair. And after that, prepared as she'd ever be for dinner, she stood and left the room. Her eyes averted from Lydia's cot.

When she reached the dining room, Jeffrey and Ian were already waiting for her. As was a vase of dark purple delphiniums—in place of the roses. Pleased by the absence of the overpowering rose scent, but also quizzical, she sat beside Ian. Refused to acknowledge her paranoid suspicion that the new flowers were a reference to her route through the park the previous day. Although they did remind her that she'd not yet destroyed the transport map and message in the pocket of her linen jacket. She'd do it the moment she returned to her room.

Ian lit up when he saw her. He liked it when she made an effort with her dress. "You look pretty, Mummy."

"Thank you, Ian." She sat.

Jeffrey sat as well, preoccupied, and then let Ian monopolize the conversation throughout the meal. Ian, pleased to be the center of attention, played his role admirably—describing an outing to the park that bore no relation to what Marion remembered of it—until exhaustion got the better of him. As dinner was ending, he yawned, and Marion rose from her chair to help him up to bed. Leaving the dining room, she turned back to Jeffrey. "Do you have a moment this evening?"

He pushed back his chair and stood. "Yes. In my study."

Surprised by his continuing ill-humor, she nodded, quiet, and then took Ian's hand to walk him up to his room. When he'd settled into bed, she kissed his forehead and descended to the floor below. The door to Jeffrey's study was closed. Misanthropic in its blank lack of communication. Obstructive. Annoyed, she didn't trouble to knock. Instead, she pushed open the door and entered, the palm of her hand resting nervously against her bare neck. Then, taken aback, she stopped.

Jeffrey was lying full-length on his back on the leather sofa, reading a novel and smoking a cigarette. His crossed ankles were propped up on a pillow. His dinner jacket was thrown over a chair on the other side of the coffee table. Marion blinked, astonished. She'd never seen him do anything other than work—extravagantly—in his study. He was more upset by his conflict with Maugham than she'd imagined.

When he saw her, he placed the book, pages downward, on the coffee table beside him. *Eyeless in Gaza* by Aldous Huxley. Noting her confused interest, he smiled and took a drag from the cigarette before blowing smoke slowly up at the ceiling. "I thought it might be useful should Maugham decide to send me to Palestine. A gift for Thacker." He sat upright and rested his elbow on the arm of the sofa, his cheek on his fist. "But he'll be disappointed. The story fails utterly to live up to the title."

He let his other hand, holding the cigarette, rest along the back of the sofa. "Though I may not be giving it a chance. Perhaps it picks up in the second half."

"Have you been drinking?" She hadn't moved from her position just inside the door. Now she closed the door behind her and took a few more steps toward him.

"No," he said. "Good idea. Care to join me?"

"No." She stopped him as he made a move to pour them drinks. "I only wanted to ask you a question. Or—or make a request."

The corner of his mouth went down, and he gestured her toward the chair across from him. The one not occupied by his jacket. She crossed the rest of the room and sat, her hands folded on her knees. "Would you take me to the Museum tomorrow? I'd like to look at the tablets from the Ashurbanipal Library. With a curator who can decipher cuneiform if possible."

"Oh damn." He closed his eyes. "You can't mean that the prodigal spook has convinced your people as well. God help us."

"I didn't say that."

"Yes, you did." He opened his eyes and took another drag of his cigarette. "And what are they planning to do to you when you refuse? If they send you to Auja to eliminate a few camp guards, we'll make a family holiday of it."

She frowned at him. Silent.

"Ah. Not an issue. Because you won't refuse." He laughed. "Toady."

451

She stood. "I see that now is an inconvenient time to discuss this. There's no hurry. But if you would simply ask whether—"

"Oh, sit down, Marion." He crushed out his cigarette in an ashtray on the coffee table. "You want to see the tablets they dug up in Mesopotamia? Assyrian? Seventh century BC? Not the first place one would look for clues to a North African mystery that couldn't have occurred before the eighth century AD, is it?"

She remained silent.

"There are thirty thousand of them in storage, Marion. Any thoughts on which you'd like to view? Or do you plan, with your customary hysterical thoroughness, to examine every one of them?"

"I remember reading an article about the Anu Enlil Series. There was a titular litany—" She paused. "There's something I'd like to check. To see whether I'm remembering accurately."

"You needn't check," he said with quiet mockery. "Your memory is alarming. If you've recalled it, it must be accurate."

She fell silent again. Didn't like his tone.

He watched her for a few seconds and then relaxed and nodded. "Very well. We'll go tomorrow morning. You're in luck. Leonard is recently back from Ur. Planning now for his jaunt to Syria. Raising public interest. And money. It's not often one is guided by the very best."

"Leonard?" Nervous. Distrusting his easy acquiescence.

He took another cigarette from the box on the coffee table and lit it. "'Sir' Leonard now, I suppose." He exhaled. "Sir Charles Leonard."

"Have I met him?"

"Not that I know of," he said, his lips twitching. "But I'm certain you'll adore him, Marion. He's excavated all of the very best sites. T.E. Lawrence and Gertrude Bell had nothing but glowing things to say about him. And the people who concern themselves with such things agree that the archaeological research he conducted for Naval Intelligence during and after the War was instrumental in the eventual, long overdue dismantling of the Ottoman stranglehold on the Near East." He paused. "I believe he also seduced and married the wife of his expedition artist."

"Leonard Woolley."

"Perhaps you encountered him during your time in Turkey?"

"Jeffrey," she said. "All I want is someone who can decipher cuneiform. This is unnecessary."

"True. But I want to see you and Leonard in a room together."

"*Why?*"

"In part, because I deserve to enjoy myself after being saddled by this calamity of a project. Watching the two of you interact will go a long way toward restoring my good humor." He observed the smoke from the end of his cigarette curl up toward the ceiling. "But also, in part, because I'm curious to see how eager you are to access the tablets. If you keep from throttling him during the twenty minutes or so he'll be able to devote to us, I'll know that you think you're on to something important. Which will be a great relief, because I certainly have bugger all."

She stared down at her folded hands for a moment and then stood. "Fine. Tomorrow morning, then?"

He stood as well. Almost happy. "I'll telephone him straight away. He'll be pleased to be able to do Maugham a favor. The scent of money, if not of fame. The tablets will be ready when we arrive."

She nodded and turned to leave the room.

"The boy is correct," he said to her back. "The dress becomes you, darling."

She frowned and looked around at him, but he was already sitting at his desk, reaching for the telephone.

JEFFREY had arranged for nine tablet fragments from the Anu Enlil Series to be brought to one of the Museum's conference rooms. Although the room was a flight of stairs below ground level, July sunlight was already streaming in through clerestory windows by the time they'd arrived, illuminating dust motes, an institutional carpet, and a long, equally institutional, table. The clay tablets were placed with regularity across the table.

Sir Leonard, accompanied by a heavy-set, balding young man wearing thick spectacles, was waiting for them when they entered the room. He turned away from his slightly theatrical inspection of the tablets as the door opened, and then he held out a cordial hand to Jeffrey. His carefully rumpled suit, Marion thought, was too warm for the July weather. And she suspected that he shaped his dark eyebrows. But perhaps he found London chilly after his many years in the desert. Or affected to do so.

"Jeffrey. Delighted to see you again."

Jeffrey shook his hand, equally friendly. "And I you, Leonard. Thank you for finding time to meet with us. I know you're overwhelmed by invitations."

Leonard laughed. "I owe Maugham a favor."

"The whole world owes Maugham a favor," Jeffrey replied. "He wouldn't have it any other way." He turned to Marion. "Dr. Marion Bailey, Sir Leonard Woolley."

"How do you do, Dr. Bailey?" Leonard smiled at her, charming and interested. Then he held out his hand, inviting her to shake it. As a colleague.

"How do you do." She shook his hand, unhappy, while struggling to maintain eye contact with him. The deliberately penetrating intensity of his gaze raised her hackles. But she forced herself to remain outwardly calm. Desperate not to antagonize him.

"You're an expert on the Ilkhanids," he said, intrigued, as he walked with her toward the table. "An engrossing area of study." He smiled at her again, facing her, his hands on the edge of the table, his back to the tablets. Soliciting a response.

But Marion, never socially adept under the best of circumstances, was at a loss. The Ilkhanids were irrelevant to their meeting today. And although she knew intellectually that he expected her to be complimented by the attention he was paying to her as a scholarly equal, she didn't know how to mimic a flattered reaction to it. She wanted to do so, if only to move them closer to answering her questions. But she couldn't force herself to overcome her utter indifference to his opinion of her—or to engage in the ritual he'd initiated. She'd seen it enacted many times before, and she'd always failed.

Panicky, and unable to summon up the response she knew he wanted, she stared at him for three or four confused seconds. Then, pointing to the clay tablets behind him, she said bluntly: "can you translate these for me?"

When he was surprised by her blank reaction to his interest in her, she attempted to explain further. "That is, could you read them phonetically first? And then translate them? I—I'd be very grateful to you for your time, sir," she continued feebly, when his eyes went cold and insulted for a split second before he resumed his smiling, charismatic demeanor.

"Of course, Dr. Bailey." Urbane now. "We ought to begin. I'm afraid I have a busy schedule to keep during my time in London, and I can't stay long." His smile deepened. "Though of course I wish I could."

She waited for a few seconds longer, uncertain as to whether he wanted her to exhibit regret that he couldn't spend more time with her. When he made no move to turn and examine the tablets, she tried for something more direct. Leaning across him, she indicated the first tablet in the series. "Perhaps you would start *here*, Sir Leonard?"

"Ah. Well, in fact I've brought my assistant, Mr. Atkins, to complete the translation for you. The spadework, as it were." Leonard nodded across at the man in the spectacles. "He's the expert, after all." Jovial and chuckling.

"He is?" Catching the subjunctive, but missing his tone, she turned to Mr. Atkins. "Would you start here, Mr. Atkins? I'll tell you when I'd like you to repeat or re-translate a line."

"My role," Leonard continued, as Mr. Atkins crossed the room to stand beside Marion at the table, "will be to provide assistance on the important process of synthesis and interpretation, Dr. Bailey."

"Oh." She blinked at him. "Thank you, Sir Leonard."

Then she faced Mr. Atkins, who resettled his spectacles and peered down at the first clay tablet. She noticed out of the corner of her eye that Jeffrey, stifling laughter, had turned away from them and wandered toward the other end of the table. She ignored him. Whatever it was that was entertaining him, it wouldn't interfere with collecting the information she needed.

Once Mr. Atkins began reading, she waited, listening, until he reached the middle of the ninth fragment. Then she stopped him and asked him to repeat a line. Nodding, he retraced the line with his fingertip and re-read it: "u-mu-un si ka-na-am-ma si kur-kur-ra. 'lord of the life of Sumer, of the life of the lands.'"

"Is that sign the 'kur'?" she asked, pointing at a symbol on the tablet. "The little mountain?"

He nodded again, still looking down at the tablet. "Yes. 'Kur-kur-ra' here is 'sovereign of the lands,' with 'kur' meaning 'land' or 'lands.'" He raised his eyes to her face, shy. "But 'kur' is a complex concept, Dr. Bailey. It can also, as you see, mean mountain. Additionally, it can refer to the netherworld or the land of the dead. And some have argued—convincingly, I think—that it is a term for what the ancient Mesopotamians believed was a great freshwater river that flowed under the desert in the far west of northern Africa." He returned his attention to the tablet. "And finally, others—less convincingly, in my opinion—have identified the symbol with the dragon that inhabits the waters of the netherworld—"

"The dragon?" Jeffrey turned back toward the table. "A dragon of the sort that St. George is supposed to have slain?"

"Quite so," Leonard answered him, too loudly. "Indeed, we see here a fascinating antecedent or archetype for any number of ancient dragon-slaying myths—particularly those associated with a descent into the underworld. Heracles. Perseus. St. George, of course. But in our case, the hero who rescues his fair maiden from the clutches of the beast is Enki, god of water and wisdom."

Marion looked at him for a moment or two. Then she addressed Mr. Atkins. "You said that you found that translation of the term unconvincing?"

"It's important," Mr. Atkins said, frightened now, "to remember that 'kur' is a broad idea in Mesopotamian culture. I myself haven't found sufficient evidence to conclude that it can be used as a name for the dragon slain by Enki. But it's certainly associated with the dragon. So—so it needn't be discounted altogether."

He took a breath, palpably deciding that if he'd already provoked Leonard, he may as well say his piece in its entirety. "But, Dr. Bailey, I would also caution against using the terms 'netherworld' and 'underworld' interchangeably in this context. 'Kur' does mean both 'netherworld' and the 'land of the dead.' But it's dangerous to draw too close a connection between the Sumerian or Assyrian netherworld—the area between the surface of the earth and the freshwater river or sea underneath it— and, for example, the classical Greek underworld. They have distinct geographies."

Marion nodded slowly. "Thank you, Mr. Atkins." Then she thought further. "But you would be confident identifying this region with northwestern Africa, with a desert, with a mountain, and with a waterway beneath the desert or mountain?"

"Yes." His tone was quietly certain.

"Is there an entrance?" she asked.

"Seven gates, traditionally."

She considered again. "Do the inhabitants of the netherworld eat?"

"Dust," he said. "They're famished. Unless their descendants set out food and drink for them."

"What about—" she began.

But Leonard interrupted her, looking pointedly at his wristwatch. "Well, Dr. Bailey," he said. "This has been a profoundly engaging conversation. We are never more grateful than when an intelligent amateur prompts us to re-think our work. Sadly, though, I have a luncheon engagement with the Museum's trustees, and I'd be remiss to keep them waiting." He aimed his smile at her again, now a touch forced, before crossing the room to shake Jeffrey's hand. "Pity you won't be joining us, Jeffrey. I'll pass along your regrets to Maugham."

"He'll know you're lying," Jeffrey said, smiling in turn. "But do try nonetheless." Then, unable to resist a final shot as Leonard and his assistant went through the door, he continued: "thank you ever so much, Mr. Atkins, for your thoughts as well. I'm confident that Dr. Bailey found them useful and edifying."

Mr. Atkins, trailing Leonard and attuned to mockery, turned back briefly to glare at Jeffrey from behind his spectacles. But neither he nor Leonard said a word as they left the room.

When the door had shut on them, Jeffrey walked around the table to join Marion, who was still gazing, perplexed, at the ninth clay fragment. "I wanted to ask him whether there were any colors associated with 'kur,'" she said. "Or even with Enki."

"Enki is their Green Man, I believe," he replied. "Which fits. Al-Khidr. Hızır. St. George. Slaying the dragon and all."

She rubbed her eyes. "It's too vague. The associations are all superficial."

He walked to the door to open it again. "You think Basil escaped from the Sumerian netherworld? That's where the Sea of al-Karkar is? And that's what you're going to tell your superiors?"

"I think Basil lost his mind in Amarah," she said, walking into the corridor. "But they don't want to hear that."

"Neither does Maugham."

"I'd like to examine the table leg," she continued after a few seconds.

"That shouldn't be difficult to arrange," he said as they exited the corridor, moving from the quiet of the Museum to the heat and chaos of late-July London. "I'll pinch it for you. And Basil should know, even if only in Darija, that he can't keep it forever."

"Thank you, Jeffrey."

He settled his summer hat on his head. "Shall we walk?"

MAUGHAM claimed to be unhappy about letting it out of the building," he said, unwrapping the cloth and arranging the golden column on the coffee table between them.

It was the last night of July, they'd finished dinner an hour earlier, and both Ian and Lydia were asleep. Jeffrey had brought the leg from Norfolk House that afternoon. But they'd tacitly agreed to wait until evening to examine it, so that they wouldn't be interrupted. Now, it was resting on the coffee table in his study, ancient and uncommunicative.

Marion, sitting on the sofa, ran her fingertip along the gemstones arrayed across its edge. Tried to recognize a pattern in them, any message that might be embedded in the object. But it remained mute. She turned it so that the emerald at its base was facing her. "This bit—the foot—was supposed to have been removed at one point?" She looked up at Jeffrey for confirmation.

He nodded. "But I'd rather ask Maugham before testing that ourselves. Or at least have an expert on hand who can confidently put it back together again."

She leaned back against the sofa, thinking. Then, feeling uncomfortable in her dinner dress, she stood. "I'm going to change. I'll be back down in five minutes."

She left the room and climbed the stairs, still thinking. She planned simply to change into pyjamas before returning to Jeffrey's study. But as she tied the belt of her dressing gown, she remembered that she still hadn't disposed of the message she'd left in the pocket of her jacket. Deciding to take advantage of her solitude, she retreated into her dressing room, rifled through the jacket, found the crumpled map, and brought it out to her bedroom to rip into pieces before flushing down the toilet.

But when she returned to the bedroom, Jeffrey was walking through the door, carrying the column. He smiled at her, apologetic. "Honestly, Marion. I can do nothing with this. Useless leaving it in my study. Keep it here instead. Do whatever it is you do with this sort of thing." Then, teasing: "whilst keeping in mind that if you make off with it, Maugham will have the hounds of hell dogging your every move. And absconding with it is precisely what he wants you to do."

She knew better than to draw attention to the paper she held in her hand by hiding it or stuffing it into her pocket. Instead, tossing it absentmindedly on the work desk to the side of the room, she walked toward him and took the column from him. Praying that he'd turn and leave. But he didn't. Instead, he wandered over to the windows, still uncovered by curtains, and looked out onto the black park.

Marion, keeping well away from the desk, sat on the edge of her bed and made a show of examining the gemstones. Her mind racing. Willing him to leave the room. As though sensing her growing fixation on it, however, he turned and drifted toward the desk. She took a quiet breath, her eyes still down.

"You had said something about removing the emerald foot at the base," he said as he idly examined the papers scattered across the desktop. "I suspect—"

She looked up. He had fallen silent and was holding the map in his hand, concentrating. After a few seconds, he raised his eyes to hers. The code was facile. He'd read and understood the message.

Letting her training take over, she rose from the bed, crossed the room, and hit him—hard—over the head with the column. Leaving him no time to react. But she also aimed for his forehead rather than for a more fragile part of his skull, hoping to incapacitate him without killing him. Ian would never forgive her if he died.

When he collapsed, she knew that she'd targeted well. He'd have a bump. A large bump. But he wouldn't be permanently damaged. Squatting in front of his prone body, she watched his breathing for a few seconds. Then she felt his pulse with her fingertips. It was strong. She predicted he'd be out for five minutes. Perhaps longer. Long enough, at least, for her to go into action.

First, she wrapped the column in one of her pillow cases, obscuring the brilliant gold exterior. Then, moving quickly to her dressing room, she stripped off her dressing gown and pyjamas, and pulled on brown linen trousers and a matching tunic, a wide linen scarf that she could pull over her head, socks, and work boots. Grabbing a canvas sack that she'd used before on assignments for which she didn't have a set itinerary, she filled it halfway with Lydia's nappies and four baby blankets.

After that, she went to the toilet and rifled through a drawer beside the bathtub until she found her toothbrush and two bottles—unused: Lydia refused to take a bottle—and filled the bottles with water from the sink. She must keep from becoming dehydrated herself while feeding the baby. Finally, returning to the bedroom, she added the wrapped table leg to the sack and stuffed a passport and cash—neither of which she planned to use—into the empty spaces surrounding the nappies. After a quick look back at Jeffrey—still breathing regularly—she left her own bedroom and crossed to Ian's.

When she pushed open the door, Ian was deeply asleep, his legs uncovered, one hand gripping the soft toy cat he kept hidden under his pillow. She left her sack on the ground just inside the door, walked quietly toward his bed, and knelt down next to him. Then she brushed his blond hair—understated compared to Lydia's violent red—off his forehead with her hand and kissed him. His eyelids fluttered, and he put his arms around her neck, pulling her toward him.

"Is it morning?" He was only half awake.

"No, Ian," she said, disengaging her neck from his arms. "I came to tell you that I must go away for work tonight. I'm bringing Lydia with me because she's too small to leave. But I want you to be a big boy and wait for me here. I'll be back before you return to school."

"Oh." Sleepy though he was, he was trying not to show his disappointment. "Will you bring me another toy aeroplane?"

"Yes," she said. "The best one yet."

"Where are you going?"

"Turkey and Morocco, I think." She swept back his hair again.

"I've never been to Morocco, Mummy. I want to come too."

"I promise to take you soon, Ian. On a proper holiday." She kissed his cheek. "You wouldn't enjoy this one."

"Oh." He put his arms around her waist and squeezed. "I'll miss you, Mummy."

"I love you, Ian."

"I love you too." He released her waist and watched as she took up her sack and left the room. Then he pressed his face into the pillow, squeezed his eyes shut, and gripped the cat under his pillowcase. Marion didn't see his tears.

She walked further along the corridor until she reached Lydia's nursery. Leaving her sack outside the door, she entered and spoke to the nurse, who was sitting beside Lydia's cot, rocking and reading a book. "Alicia, Jeffrey's hit his head rather badly. I'm certain he'll recover, but we ought to call a doctor. Would you ask Mrs. Bowen to look in on him? He's in my bedroom."

If Alicia thought it strange that Marion had come to her rather than calling a doctor herself or going directly to Mrs. Bowen, she didn't say anything. Instead, young and biddable, she looked concerned and rose from the rocking chair. "Certainly, Lady Willcox. Immediately."

When Alicia had left the room, Marion gathered Lydia up from her cot and wrapped a blanket around her. Then she unhooked the soft giraffe from the cot's frame and pushed it into her trouser pocket. Lydia, in her first deep sleep of the night, didn't make a sound.

Holding Lydia tight against her chest, Marion left the room, grabbed her sack, and descended toward the first floor. When she heard Alicia and Mrs. Bowen climbing the stairs toward her room, she slipped into Jeffrey's study. Then, in the midst of the commotion surrounding their discovery of Jeffrey prone near the desk, she walked to the ground floor, left the house, and crossed into the park.

Not having planned to leave London until the fifth of August—and, she had hoped, not even then—Marion wasn't certain where she would spend the night. She knew that Jeffrey hadn't been exaggerating Maugham's interest in following her should she retrace Basil's steps. But she didn't know whether that strategy would change when it emerged that she had attacked Jeffrey on her way out.

She couldn't imagine that it would—Maugham would find her exit entertaining. But, nonetheless, she wanted assurance that he still meant to follow, rather than to collect, her before she crossed her people on the fifth. Also, her options were limited with Lydia in tow. She wouldn't be sleeping in any abandoned garages tonight.

As she walked, thinking, enjoying the breeze that was stirring the hot evening air, she realized that her choice of shelter was obvious. She'd return to Norfolk House. They wouldn't think to look for her there. She'd be able to listen to their conversations. And, as Jeffrey had said, there was a great deal of room. She'd use the servants' quarters in the attic, where the porter was unlikely to reconnoiter, and where Lydia could make a bit of noise without being heard. Pleased by her decision, she pushed the straps of her sack up over her shoulder and held Lydia closer as she left the park and made her way toward St. James's square.

But when she reached the alley outside the house and pulled open the window she had prepared, she paused, momentarily at a loss. Alone, she could easily have lifted herself up and through the opening. Carrying Lydia up with her, however, using only one hand, would be an impossibility. Frustrated, she examined the window and the ledge for close to three minutes, defeated by it.

Then, without any better option presenting itself, she put her sack on the ground, pushed down the nappies and blankets, and settled Lydia on top of them. After that, she removed the soft giraffe from her trouser pocket and hooked it to one of the sack's straps. Lydia stirred, but she didn't wake. Lifting the sack back to her shoulder and securing it as tightly as she could, Marion then turned to the wall.

Taking a deep breath, she gripped the ledge and pulled herself up until she was leaning painfully on her waist, halfway through the window. Then, after testing her balance, she moved the sack around to her side, squeezed it through the small space between her body and the edge of the window, and placed it on the toilet. Finally, exhaling, she dragged her hips and legs through the window, lowered herself to the ground, and pulled the window shut. A trace of adrenaline pounding in her temples.

The fact that she had nearly been vanquished by an easily navigated open window left her more frightened than she wanted to admit about her ability to complete the remainder of her assignment. Forcing herself to concentrate on the present, however, she looked down at Lydia sleeping in the sack and decided to continue using it as a cot. Better than risk waking her as she lifted her out again. And so, after hitching the straps of the sack over her shoulder, she pulled open the door to the toilet an inch or two and peered into the main hall of the house.

The exterior room was dark and—testing the air—empty. She slipped out of the small room and made her way to the Duke's study. Moving silently, she entered it, letting her eyes adjust to the light shining in from the street. The curtains over the windows had been removed, which made her squint, but also made her next step easier. Examining the well-illuminated coffee table, she smiled to herself. In addition to the Flake bars, there was a basket of fruit—about to go off—and a plate of stale pastries.

Not wanting to raise suspicions by taking too much, Marion chose two apples and three Flake bars, which she stuffed into her trouser pockets, and a concrete-hard blackberry scone, which she carried in her hand. She planned to return every evening to replenish her stores, living easily on what they left behind after their interminable meetings. Although she did wish that Basil's food preferences were a trifle less heavy on snacks for twelve-year-olds.

Grateful now for how the evening had progressed, she climbed the empty, haunted stairway until she reached a near pitch black corridor of small bedrooms on the top floor. Feeling her way, she chose a room at the end with a steep, sloped ceiling and a view over the city. The lights from the street below, turning the room a greenish-yellow, raised her spirits after the black corridor, and she spent a moment or two looking down from the window.

Then, as Lydia began waking, expecting to be fed, she turned and spread out blankets on the floor, positioning her sack to use as a pillow. Finally, after taking two or three minutes to change Lydia's nappy, she lay down on her side, set Lydia next to her, and drifted into sleep. Her last impression as she lost consciousness was of the baby eating.

THE next day, she fed and changed Lydia early, ate the crumbling scone, drank half a bottle of water, and emerged silently from her perch in the attic to observe Nick and Basil interacting. After an hour of listening to their disjointed conversation, she concluded that neither Maugham nor Jeffrey would be visiting Norfolk House that day. And so, moving back toward her room, she risked opening each of the doors along the attic corridor in daylight until she discovered, to her pleased surprise, a tiny water closet with a sink and toilet.

She wouldn't use either until the empty hours of the very early morning. But she was relieved to find that she'd be able to wash Lydia's nappies—not to mention avoid accumulating chamber pots for herself. Her shelter was more luxurious than many in which she'd found herself. She was even developing a taste for Flake bars.

And Lydia was becoming increasingly engrossed by the gemstones scattered along the golden column, their appeal rivalling even that of the soft giraffe. As she watched Lydia grabbing and trying to manipulate the rubies and emeralds on the shining edges of the table leg, concentrating and serious, she thought to herself that the three additional days she'd stay in the house until her people could move her out of London might prove a pleasant holiday. In a sheepish way, she was looking forward to it.

That night, once she was certain that the porter had retired to his wooden chair and his whisky, she hummed to herself as she arranged Lydia in her blankets. Then, making her way to the ground floor, she slipped into the study and collected two more Flake bars, an orange, and a desiccated piece of sponge cake. She also refilled one of her bottles with water from a warmish pitcher, not entirely trusting what came from the tap of the attic's water closet. Finally, she retreated upstairs, collected the washed nappies that had dried throughout the day on a line she'd strung in an adjacent room, and lowered herself to her side to sleep next to Lydia.

On the second morning, she expected to repeat her routine. But instead of waking to the noise of the street, she woke to an agitated discussion between Nick and Basil, floating up from the ground floor. Without leaving the room, sitting on the floor and feeding Lydia, she strained to hear. Then, satisfied, she relaxed against the wall. Maugham, Jeffrey, and Aldous would be arriving together that afternoon. She even had an estimated time for their appearance: 1:00. If she planned well, she'd have Lydia fed and well into a two- to three-hour nap by the time they'd begun their conversation.

After spending the morning trying without success to coax Lydia into crawling or pulling herself across the floor of the room, she wrapped the baby in her blankets, gave her the table leg to hold—the soft giraffe now entirely supplanted as a comfort object—and crept out of the room. Then she waited at the top of the stairs until she heard the front door open, followed by the sound of conversation moving through the entry hall. They'd arrived.

When she was certain that they'd be returning to the morning room on the ground floor, she descended to the first floor and slipped into the room above it—a drawing room, if the red silk damask wall-hangings, enormous pier glasses, and plasterwork palm fronds were any indication. Either that or a brothel. Ignoring the bellicose opulence of the room, she positioned herself to the side of a white marble fireplace that connected to the fireplace in the morning room below. Then she squatted to listen.

"Are you certain you're well enough for this? You look frightful." There was laughter in Maugham's voice.

"It can't wait, Maugham. The project is coming off the rails. Has already come off the rails."

"Nonsense." The sound of Maugham lowering himself into a chair. "She's done just as we hoped she'd do. Leaving aside that ghastly lump. And the missing child. I admit I feared this time that she wouldn't take the bait. So repetitive. But you did your part well, Willcox—"

"She didn't take the bait." Jeffrey's voice was tense. "Her people pushed her under. And she went too soon."

"Even better." Entertained. "If she's following orders, then she won't have second thoughts." He paused. "As for the accelerated schedule, it's a nuisance, but she'll surface at some point. And she's certain to leave a trail."

"A trail of dead bodies." The smell of Jeffrey's cigarette smoke wafted up from the floor below.

"She does tend to leave the odd corpse bobbing in her wake. But that can't be helped, can it? Far be it from me to question her methods."

"They will be the bodies of people you'd prefer to keep alive, Maugham. Believe me, you will not be happy with the results of this assignment." Jeffrey's voice was rising and falling in volume, as though he were pacing the room, toward and away from the fireplace.

"Provided she locates this mysterious shaykh and his followers," Maugham replied, "I'm willing to sacrifice one or two expendable—"

"Read this." She heard Jeffrey slam what sounded like a paper down on what had to be the desktop.

"Really, Willcox." Mild. "So dramatic. This is unlike you. Are you certain that the blow to the head hasn't—"

"Read it, Maugham." Calm and blank now.

There was a pause. "I can't read it, obviously. It's encoded—"

"Muriel?" Jeffrey striding across the room again. Knocking on the wall. "Damn it, Muriel! Would you get in here, please?"

"Yes, Sir Jeffrey?" The tapping of heels. A woman's controlled voice.

"Would you please read these lines to Professor Maugham?"

"Of course, Sir Jeffrey." A pause. "'Locate and remove St. George. Exit scheme, Wednesday, 5 August, will come via the usual channels.'"

A longer pause. Then Maugham said, "are you certain the word is 'remove,' Muriel?"

"Yes, Professor Maugham. 'Locate and remove St. George.'"

Silence for more than ten seconds. Then, Maugham's voice again: "thank you, Muriel. We'll call should we require anything more."

The sound of heels tapping and a door shutting.

"Her orders aren't to contact him." Jeffrey's voice was now much clearer. She thought he might be leaning against the mantle. "They aren't to communicate with him. They're to kill him." Another silence. Then more cigarette smoke rising through the chimney. "You said you wanted a severed head, Maugham. It appears you've got one."

She thought she heard Maugham blowing his nose, loudly. Then: "keep in mind, Willcox, that the assignment in Auja is still very much on the table. Indeed, I'm wondering now whether it might not be salutary to store her there herself for a few months. Let Thacker practice on someone less prone to whimpering than the prisoners he's interviewing now. *Why* won't she—"

"Kill her." Aldous was speaking for the first time. His tone brutal.

"Oh, for heaven's sake, Parker—"

"Look, Willcox. I'm not one to judge another man's pleasures. But I'm beginning to worry about you. And truly, if you enjoy this sort of thing, I can easily acquaint you with a lovely girl in Holborn who'd be pleased to leave you bruised and bleeding any time the fancy takes you, and all for pin money and perhaps a small investment in a shop when you tire of her." Aldous's voice was entirely serious. "And then you can rid yourself of that mad, treasonous bitch—"

"That mad, treasonous bitch is my wife, remember." Gentle.

"Your *wife*, Willcox, just concussed you with King Solomon's magical table, snatched your infant daughter, abandoned your terrified son, and is now out to assassinate the patron saint of England." Aldous's voice was rising. "Any court would consider that more than reasonable grounds for divorce."

"I don't think the St. George she's after is the one who protects the Order of the Garter." Jeffrey had moved away from the mantle. His voice was less distinct. "England is safe. And it was just the leg. Not the entire table."

"You couldn't at least have injured her? Defended yourself?" Aldous was ranting. "She's more than lost any claim on your chivalry. Why didn't you stop her?"

"She's quick, Parker."

"Oh, for fuck's—"

"Does this girl in Holborn have any languages?" Maugham sounded intrigued.

"French, I think." Confused by Maugham's intervention.

"Oh." Disappointment. "Ah well. Always looking out for new talent."

There was another pause, and then Aldous returned with renewed vigor to his theme: "what is wrong with you both? She's a criminal. She's a traitor. She is working against the nation's interests. *Kill* her."

"She's useful." Maugham's voice was tired.

"Christ," Aldous said disgusted. "No wonder Basil went off his head. And speaking of Basil, don't forget what she's done to him. He's desolate without his table leg."

"But," Maugham continued as though Aldous hadn't spoken, "in this one instance, Parker is not entirely incorrect. We mustn't have her rampaging about off her lead. Reel her in, Willcox. Now."

"How?"

"She can't have gone far," Maugham said, testy. "Her organization won't be extracting her until the fifth. Wednesday. She's still in the city. And with an infant? Surely your people can't be that incompetent."

"Your own people have had a day and a half already," Jeffrey replied, a smile in his voice. "While I was recovering from my unfortunate injury. Any luck?"

"I can recall Thacker—"

"Yes, yes." Jeffrey was still audibly smiling. "I understand, Maugham. I'll do my best. But you know that I can't make promises."

There was a thoughtful silence for a few seconds. Then Maugham spoke again. "Have you any idea why her people would want this figure dead to begin with? It's an odd directive on their part."

"God knows," Jeffrey said, sounding weary himself now. "Jealousy? They're displeased by the thought of competition from a second shadowy, millennia-old, occult conspiracy?"

Maugham made cogitating sounds. "Hmm. Yes. Most likely." Then he paused. "Tedious."

She heard them making what might be moves to leave the room. And so, quietly, before they reached the main hall, she stole back up the stairs to the attic, where Lydia was still sleeping. She had what she needed from them. And she knew now that she must stay out of their way—she couldn't count on them simply to let her go and watch. But she also felt safe in Norfolk House. They didn't know where she was. And she had complete trust in her organization's capacity to extract her when the time came.

Sitting on the floor of the attic room, eyeing the dry sponge cake with distaste, and unwrapping a Flake bar, she watched Lydia sleeping on her blankets. She'd never travelled with her daughter before, and she was beginning to feel excited about it. If nothing else, she'd see whether the baby enjoyed it. Ian, she thought with a pang of guilt that she immediately squashed, always had. And he'd never been terrified of anything, except penguins, in his life.

THE next two days were placid and even relaxing, as Marion became accustomed to the routine of the house. But she was also more than ready to leave as the sun set on Wednesday the fifth. Eating the last of her Flake bars at 10:00 in the evening, arranging her canvas sack, and settling Lydia—deeply asleep once more—on top of the blankets, she risked descending to the ground floor before her usual hour. The porter would still be prowling—he didn't usually start drinking until 11:30 or midnight.

459

But the only dangerous part of her exit would be crossing the main hall toward the water closet. Once there, she'd lower herself and Lydia into the alley at her leisure.

After timing the porter's bored rounds for fifteen minutes, she easily reached the tiny room without attracting his notice. More confident now about the sack's effectiveness as a cot, she also pushed open the window without having to consider the process, sat on the ledge, and descended to the ground without hesitation. After that, the ten-minute walk to Embankment Pier—her crossing point— was simple. The neighborhood was still crowded with couples emerging from restaurants or enjoying the warm evening air, and she almost fit in with them. No one thought to examine the contents of her sack.

Once she'd reached the water, she leaned against a stone balustrade, watching the night-time river traffic. The air was heavy and warm, and the water smelt of rapidly reproducing plant life. But she didn't have long to enjoy it. After waiting for less than five minutes, a boy wearing short trousers and a cap—no more than Ian's age—approached her. "Looking for a tour, madam?"

Half entertained and half concerned about him working at this hour of the night, she almost didn't answer. Then, collecting herself, she nodded. "But I've got only four shillings."

"That will do, madam."

She gave him the coins, and he led her toward a ramp attached to a disused part of the wooden dock below the balustrade. Then, helping her into a wooden rowboat equipped with a tiny outboard motor, he pushed them out into the river without drawing the attention of the interested people strolling above them. The boy had a talent for invisibility.

After ten minutes of quiet puttering on the dark water, the hull of a flat-bottomed barge came into view. It was also equipped with an engine, idling, though it had once, and recently, sported masts as well. The barge, even before they'd reached it, gave off an overpowering smell of damp sawdust.

As they approached, one of the crew threw a ladder over the side. Thanking the boy, still impressed by his age and his excruciatingly competent work, she climbed to the deck, taking care to keep her sack from swinging precariously. Her hand just above Lydia's head.

Despite her efforts, however, by the time she'd reached the top of the ladder, Lydia was moving on top of the folded blankets, beginning to wake and demand food. And as a wiry man in an outfit similar to the boy's walked toward her from the cockpit, about to speak, an angry wail floated up from the bag. The man stopped mid-stride and stared at the sack.

Marion, blushing, placed the sack on the deck and clumsily extracted Lydia, holding her against her chest. "I'll feed her," she said, apologetic.

The man—the boat's owner, she assumed—gaped at the baby in her arms. "That's coming with us?"

"Yes. That is—'she.' Lydia. It's a girl." Marion was bouncing Lydia in her arms, failing to calm her. "She's—"

"No," the man said. "Stop. I don't want to know. Can you keep her quiet when we reach Gravesend?"

"Yes."

"A little under four hours all told."

"All right." Tense. She wanted to find a place to settle and feed Lydia. "I'll sit on the foredeck to keep out of your way. That is, if you don't use sails."

"Suit yourself."

Marion turned to make her way toward the bow of the boat, but as she walked, the man stopped her again, wanting in an obscure way, it seemed, to apologize for his brusque greeting. "If you need anything for—" He paused, at a loss. "Well, just let me know," he finished gruffly.

"Thank you." She tried to smile at him through Lydia's yelling. Then she turned again, found an open, flat area at the bow, sat, and quieted the baby. By the time the boat was moving forward past the Tower, Lydia was quiet, on the verge of sleep again.

The man's prediction as to the time it would take them to reach Gravesend was remarkably accurate. And although it was still long before the sun would rise when they passed the pier—the water lit solely by the lights of the boats anchored and bobbing off the shore—there was a hint of dawn in the air. Marion didn't know what her next step would be, but she was feeling optimistic—both from the expectant atmosphere of the water at the end of the river and from the simple joy of being out of London. As much as she had improbably enjoyed Norfolk House.

Holding Lydia against her chest and shouldering her canvas sack, she felt her way back to the barge's cockpit. The boat's owner was waiting there, peering into the darkness, smoking a cheroot.

When he saw her, he cocked his head toward the dark water. After a few seconds, the sound of another tiny outboard motor spluttered toward the hull.

"That'll be for you," he said.

"Thank you." She moved in the direction of the ladder.

"Wait," he said. He followed her to the ladder and lowered it over the side for her himself. Then, seemingly annoyed by his impulse, he held out a tiny, carved wooden dolphin. "For the little one." Sullen. "She's got teeth coming in. This will help."

She smiled, took the dolphin, and secured it in her sack. "Thank you."

"Boat's here," he replied. Then he stalked back to the cockpit.

She climbed down the ladder into a dinghy operated by another taciturn, nearly invisible man. Without saying a word, he shoved them away from the barge and brought them out into the open water. After close to twenty-five minutes of forcing the boat through choppy, if insignificant, waves, the man pointed ahead of him. Waiting—looming—in the sea was a massive biplane flying boat. With RAF markings on it.

The markings set her heart racing, and she instinctively held her sack closer to her. But knowing that there was little she could do to protect herself, sitting with Lydia in a dinghy off the coast of Great Britain, she remained still, waiting to see what would happen. What did happen was nothing that she'd have expected.

As the dinghy approached, a man and a woman, wearing strangely visible bohemian clothing, helped it to raft alongside the aircraft. Then, without speaking, they led Marion, carrying Lydia in the sack, into a spacious, if unfurnished, cabin—metal floors, metal fuselage, huge metal bolts, and an assortment of bedroom pillows, tinned meat, and bottles of beer fastened with adhesive tape to the exposed framework.

She wanted to ask a question, even if only about the tinned meat. But before she could gather her thoughts—as she was crouching down into something like a sitting position on one of the pillows—the flying boat picked up speed, preparing to lift into the air. "Hold on to something," the woman said in native English. "It'll be bumpy."

Clutching Lydia with one arm, she grabbed a pillow with the other, and wedged herself into a secure corner of the fuselage. After twenty minutes of nausea-inducing climb, the plane levelled off, and Marion relaxed. Lydia, in her deepest sleep of the night, hadn't moved.

"Look love." The woman addressed her companion. "Darling little baby."

"Thank you," Marion said. Perplexed.

The woman was clearly British. English. In her thirties. Fashionable hair, and an intelligent, if chatty, air about her. Wearing an indefinite number of multicolored floating scarves. The man, although he hadn't spoken yet, was a male twin of the woman. Thin, bald, and sporting unusual facial hair along with a jumper she suspected had been knitted by the woman. She had no idea who the pilot was. What was apparent, however, was that none of the three was an RAF officer.

"What's her name?" the woman asked, crawling across the pillows on the floor of the plane to look more closely at the baby.

"Lydia," Marion said. "She's—"

"Seven months old," the woman announced. Then she peered more closely into Lydia's face. "No. Six months. Look at her beautiful auburn hair." She smiled up at Marion. "She's a good traveler. Tranquil."

"At some point," Marion said, trying not to seem rude, "I hope to be in the Taurus Mountains. In Turkey."

"And that's precisely where we're taking you, love." The woman had leaned against her side of the cabin again and was detaching a bottle of beer from the fuselage.

"It's a floatplane," Marion countered. "The Taurus Mountains are—mountains."

"Lots of lakes where you want to be. We'll be fine." The woman opened the bottle of beer and handed it to the man. Then she began working on a second bottle. "And it's not just any floatplane. It's a Blackburn Perth. Thousand-mile range. Hundred and thirty mile per hour top speed—or a hundred and fifty if Nigel up there is pushing it. We'll have a marvelous time."

"Were those RAF markings on the side?" Marion asked, taking the bottle of beer the woman offered her.

"We nicked it," the man said with a sly smile. Drinking his beer.

"You nicked it." Marion blinked across at him. "And—and they haven't—?"

"They'll be wanting it back," the woman offered, opening a third bottle for herself. "Only four of them built. Can't go losing twenty-five percent of their fleet, can they?"

"But—"

"They've got no notion where it is," the man said, answering the question she hadn't formulated. "But they also don't want to make a fuss about it. Too embarrassing. So, we've got time. They'll track it quietly."

"This time," the woman continued, smug, "we thought we might leave it floating in Lake Sevan. In Armenia. Make the recovery interesting for them. We may even watch from the woods."

"'This time?'" Marion drank a sip of beer. "Do you mean you've done this before?"

"All the time." The woman put her head on the man's shoulder. "We always give them back."

"For—?"

"Laughs?" The woman ran her hand up under the man's sweater. "Though a baby might change all that."

"You'd bring the baby along with us," the man said. "Like Lydia here." He paused and addressed Marion. "We'll land three times for fuel. But we don't plan to linger. Should take forty hours total. Will she manage that? Lydia, that is?"

"I don't know," Marion said. "But I suppose she must."

"Of course she will." The woman smiled in turn. "Darling little girl."

After that, they relaxed further against the pillows, finishing their bottles of beer. It would be a long journey.

Taurus Mountains, Turkey
Sahara Desert, Morocco
August, 1936

*T*HE flying boat landed, first, in the Mediterranean off Marseille, next, off the Dalmatian Coast of Croatia, a third time in the Aegean near Thessaloniki, and then finally—with great care—on Lake Burdur in the Taurus Mountains of Turkey. At least, so her companions told Marion. Her own impressions were of little more than stomach churning descents into uncooperative, anonymous seas followed by screeching ascents back into bumpy clouds. And they never stayed on the water for longer than a half hour—time enough to empty the waste they'd accumulated in the cabin and for the ever-present outboard-equipped dinghy to appear out of the darkness or mist, provide them with fuel, and disappear.

Lydia, satisfied by her immediate access to food, her golden table leg, and her wooden dolphin—and delighted by the woman's collection of scarves—remained manageable throughout the journey. A large part of her unusually tractable behavior undoubtedly had to do with the fact that all Marion drank whilst in the air were bottles of beer—which relaxed Lydia, eating like clockwork, as effectively as it did Marion. But Marion certainly wasn't displeased by the result. In fact, she made a note to herself to remember it in the future. Next time, she'd try scotch.

When they finally landed on the green, salty waters of the lake, night had fallen once again. According to the now malodorous—but nonetheless cheery and helpful—man, it was just after 10:00 pm on the 7th of August, local time. Moving quickly, not wanting to delay their exit, Marion gathered her belongings, collected Lydia's soiled nappies, took a tin of meat and a bottle of beer for emergencies, and settled Lydia—awake but calm—into her canvas sack. She then turned to the bewildering couple, who were even more involved with one another now that they'd completed the first part of their assignment.

"Thank you again," she said, embarrassed, as they wrapped themselves around one another.

The woman, detaching herself with palpable regret from the man's pungent jumper, opened the hatch for Marion. "Nonsense, dear. It was a pleasure. We'd stay longer except that dumping the kite in Armenia demands our immediate departure." Then she wriggled a finger at the baby, who grabbed it, smiling. "Doesn't it, Lydia? Yes, it does. We don't want the bogies after us, do we? They can just bogie off, they can—"

"Nonetheless," Marion said, uncertain whether to smile as well. "I'm grateful." She climbed out of the hatch as Lydia gurgled at the woman. "Good luck to you both."

"And to you," the man replied as she disappeared through the hatch.

Once she was free of the hull, she waded toward the shore, holding the canvas bag well above the water. And long before she had reached the beach, she could hear the flying boat picking up speed to lift off again. By the time she had made her way to the dry grass at the edge of the hard, flat sand, wet to her waist, she could no longer see it in the water or in the sky. The Blackburn was gone.

After checking to be certain that Lydia was comfortable, she hefted the straps of the canvas sack over her shoulder and trudged further up through the grass until she reached a stand of twisted pine trees. Sitting beneath the largest of them, looking unruffled in the dark night, alone, counting prayer beads on his *tespih*, was a young, round man in a cloth cap and a voluminous brown moustache. She approached him slowly, diffident in the face of his calm.

"Necmettin Aksu?" she finally ventured in Turkish. "I believe you have a car for me?"

He stood, dusted his knees, and crinkled his eyes in a smile at Marion. "This way, Dr. Bailey."

She followed him along a dusty path, past the occasional mound of scrub or pine trees, until they reached a clearing. Waiting for them was a compact, armored, open-top rough terrain vehicle with two seats in front and one, larger seat, in the back. Right hand drive. Mr. Aksu climbed into the driver's seat and gestured to Marion to sit beside him. Taking care not to jolt Lydia, who had fallen asleep again, she climbed into the black leather passenger seat, sliding involuntarily on the colorful beaded seat cover that Mr. Aksu could only have added to the décor on his own initiative.

"Kurogane Type 95," he said, proud, as he started the engine. "From Japan. Nothing else like it in Turkey."

He maneuvered the vehicle onto a track that was difficult to distinguish from the footpath they'd followed up from the beach. Then, enjoying himself, he accelerated with a jerk over a hillock of scrub grass, the wheels bouncing and jarring as they continued not to meet anything resembling a road. Lydia, shaken out of her new sleep, wailed, angry rather than hungry or tired.

At the sound of Lydia's cry, Mr. Aksu slowed the vehicle—though only marginally—and peered into the sack while Marion gathered the baby into her arms. "Forgive me. I didn't know you had a baby with you." He accelerated again.

"Please don't worry." Marion held Lydia against her chest, uncertain as to how to calm her. Bouncing her, she suspected, wouldn't be all that effective. But Lydia quickly calmed herself, inclined to sleep at that hour in any case. Soon, mollified by Marion's tight grip, she closed her eyes and was breathing heavily again.

Mr. Aksu glanced over at Marion as he turned the vehicle onto a very slightly wider, smoother track. "Is it a boy or a girl?"

"A girl," she said. "Lydia."

"She's very pretty," he commented. Then, furrowing his brow: "where's her father?"

"He had work to do." Blushing. But at least she was telling mostly the truth.

"Stupid man." His moustache smiled, gallant. "Leaving such a beautiful girl to fend for herself."

Marion smiled as well. "I have a feeling he'll be joining us soon." Which was also, if dishearteningly, most likely the truth.

"He's still a stupid man," Mr. Aksu replied impassively.

"I agree," she conceded. "At times."

He continued smiling for a few seconds. Then, becoming serious, he gazed back at the track that remained not quite a road. "Where are we going?"

"Are you from the area?" she asked in turn. "That is, you know the local geography well?"

"My family," he said, "has lived on the shores of that lake for a thousand years. Or more. Yes. I'm from the area."

She nodded. Then, feeling her way along, she spoke: "I'm hoping to find a cave—or, or perhaps a tunnel—associated with Hızır. Al-Khidr." She paused. "Do you know of anything like that near the lake? Or in the region?"

Mr. Aksu drove silently for over a minute, his forehead still wrinkled. Then he laughed quietly. "So, it's started."

"I'm sorry?"

"We all knew you'd come looking for him eventually." He was laughing more audibly now. "That he'd make himself known. And, of course, there was that forerunner during the War."

She remained quiet, polite, hoping that he'd continue. And he did. Cautioning her. "But Dr. Bailey, you don't want to end the way he did. The poor man was already half gone already. Crazy Englishman speaking bad Arabic, starving himself on the shores of the lake. We left him alone, except to try every now and then to convince him to eat."

He was thoughtful for a few seconds longer. "And he did comfort the prisoners. The ones they were working to death over in the valley. A brave man, if not quite sane. The rest of us just kept our heads down, trying not to draw their attention." He stopped speaking again, troubled. "I was eight years old at the time. And if you can believe it, they were so desperate by the end they nearly drafted me as well. My mother put me in a dress. In the grand tradition."

The 'they' to whom he was referring, she realized, was not the prisoners, but the provincial Ottoman government. She'd heard stories. And she eyed him now with new respect. But, as much as he was warning her off, she couldn't drop the project.

Taking a breath, she prodded him. "So there is a local story, then? A place where Hızır is supposed to—to return? To reside?"

He drove, silent, for another thirty seconds. "I'll take you there," he eventually said. "To the cave. Wouldn't want them taking away my Type 95." He looked sidelong at her. "But take my advice, Dr. Bailey. Don't offend him. The crazy Englishman, he—" Mr. Aksu considered his choice of words. "Well, he failed to amuse. And he found himself hurt quite badly. I suppose if you're here, he must have found his way home in the end. But you don't want to go through that man's troubles. *I* don't want you to go through his troubles, and I don't even know you."

"I—I think I understand," she said.

"I can see that you don't," Mr. Aksu countered, stolid. "But you will. All I can say is that things as old as Hızır is—two thousand, three thousand, five thousand years, God alone knows—those things have a rotten sense of humor. Inhuman. You can't expect—honor—from them."

He turned off onto another narrow, crumbling track. "That sounds disrespectful. But it isn't meant to be—as Hızır himself would know. It's a conclusion based on fact. Drawn from what I've seen here. And what my family has always seen here. Over the past thousand years." He brought the vehicle to a stop in the midst of a semicircle of unhealthy conifers that were lit into unexpected clarity by a bright gibbous moon. A rocky hill rose up to their right. "This is as close as I can get."

She thought for a moment before climbing out of the passenger seat. "Have you been into the cave?"

"Once," he said, laconic.

"Can you tell me anything about it?" She shivered, despite the warm air. "Or about its history? Do you have advice—aside from what you've already said—about any physical obstacles I ought to avoid?"

He smoothed his moustache with two fingers. Then he nodded. "My village," he began, "has been inhabited for five thousand years. The legend is that the Sumerians settled it as a mining outpost. The bronze weapons they used required a great deal of copper—which was easy for them to acquire—and also a great deal of tin, which was rare to the point of nonexistence. They started by importing the tin from Afghanistan. Very expensive. But eventually, four thousand years ago, they discovered tin deposits here too. There are ancient tin mines all over the place. The children make a game of finding them."

He paused again. "Now, the demand for tin waned three thousand years ago, when metal workers learned to smelt iron. But this area kept its reputation as a center of metallurgy in spite of that. We've even got a few old men in the village who claim to have heard—from others—who heard from others—the lost secret to producing Damascus steel."

His moustache twitched, entertained. "But you know old men. They've also got a rotten, inhuman sense of humor." He eyed her. "The point is that there's a five-thousand-year-old tradition of mining and secret metal work in and around that cave that can't be ignored. Or escaped."

She nodded, slowly. "So you're saying that the cave is a mine?"

"No, no," he said. "Nothing like that. The cave is natural. It's as old as the earth."

"Then I don't understand." She rubbed her cheek with her hand. "What is it that I must remember?"

"People here say that the cave is endless. Infinite," he replied, not quite answering her question. "That's not the case—though no one I know has found any back wall. They also say that some of the ancient mines lead into obscure parts of the cave." He shrugged. "That may be true—but I've also seen no evidence of that."

He tapped his fingertips against the wheel of the vehicle. "But what *is* true, Dr. Bailey, and what you must remember, is that the stone in the cave, and its water, they're—not dead. Whatever living spirit those ancient metal workers drew out of the rock—it's still there. And it is badly disposed to visitors. When we pray to Hızır—when he's resident in the cave, that is—we ask him first, before even mentioning the crops, to bind the rock and the water. Because the rock and water in there," nodding up at the cave, "they have no sense of human time. Or of human cares. We need an intermediary with them."

He shrugged again, breaking the atmosphere. "Or it may simply be that thousands of years of children dying in mine shafts creates an uncanny fog about a place." He started up the vehicle again. "Whichever it is, you'll want to be careful about what you initiate in there. That's all."

Disturbed by the tenor of the conversation, but uncertain what else to say, she climbed out of the vehicle, holding the canvas sack close to her waist. "Thank you, Necmettin Bey."

He reached into his trouser pocket and pulled out a silver cigarette lighter. "Take this."

"I can't take this from you," she said, astonished. "It's too valuable. Really. I'm grateful. But—"

He pushed it into her palm. "There's a torch at the entrance to the cave. For supplicants. Use this to light it." When he saw her close her fingers around it, he nodded. "There are additional torches along the gallery. Up to the edge of the first lake. Be sure that you always have at least three burning. Whatever happens, you must not lose your light while you're inside."

She pushed the lighter into her own trouser pocket. "Thank you," she repeated.

"There's a second cave," he continued over the idling engine of his Type 59. "I've never seen it, but I understand it's covered in crystal formations. And then, beyond that, there's a fissure in the wall, which leads to the cave of the dead."

"The dead?"

"Yes," he said. "No one I know has seen it. But the legend goes that if you make it past the animals guarding it, there's a pit at the center that you can ignite with your torch. It will give you light for your work."

She nodded again. "Thank you. I'm—"

He shook his head. "Don't thank me. If I had any integrity at all, I'd never have brought you here. And remember—he's nearly omnipotent, almost omniscient, close to immortal, and revered by millions of monotheists who ought to know better. But he's a son of a bitch."

"Thank you—" she started to say a fourth time, but he sped away down the track before she could get the words out, skidding in his haste.

*H*ER first task, before exploring or sleeping, was to wash Lydia's nappies at the edge of the underground lake. She'd been through nearly all of them during the journey from London, and she wasn't about to take on Hızır's lair carrying a wet and angry infant. The labor involved in cleaning the absorbent cloth also kept her mind off her persistent and phobic horror of caves. Although she had reached the entrance, lit the torch, and climbed down into the first gallery, driven by a numb perseverance, she knew in a corner of her mind that, given a chance to think, her psyche would revolt. Keeping busy was her only defense against the silent, not quite conscious screaming that she couldn't quell. It also warmed her in the frigid, flat subterranean air.

Once she'd rinsed the nappies and set them out to dry on the smaller of the many stalagmites, she climbed through the gallery, trying to find any torches she'd failed to light. When she was confident that she'd made the area as bright as she could, she returned to Lydia, who was beginning to wake, wanting to be fed. Holding the baby against her chest, wrapped against the cold in all four of the blankets, she willed Lydia's feeding to calm her own mind. She would sleep for a few hours. And then, when she saw daylight through the small opening she could just perceive above her, she'd find the cave of the dead. As much as she dreaded it, she knew that the third gallery must be her staging area.

The next morning, she ate the tin of meat she had taken from the flying boat and experimented with the lake water—cleaning her teeth and drinking a few swallows. It tasted potable, but she didn't want to take too much before knowing its effects on her digestion. Then she fed Lydia, placed the baby on a blanket—the golden column to amuse her and a flickering torch to light her—and rewrapped the standing torches that had gone out during the night. Excess cloth had been left there for that purpose by previous visitors. A number of years before, if the dirt coating them was any indication.

She felt guilty that she couldn't leave anything herself. But then, remembering Lydia's nappies, she brightened. Gathering three of the more tattered ones, she unfolded them near the sconces for future supplicants to use. An odd offering, but she had never been religious. Even when forcing herself to crawl into an alien deity's hostile tomb.

After she'd tidied the torches closer to the cave entrance, she packed her canvas sack, arranged Lydia at the top, lifted the straps over her shoulders, grabbed one lit, and two unlit, torches for emergencies, and climbed further down toward, she hoped, a tunnel that would bring her to the second gallery. But when she reached the lowest part of the cave floor, hunching over to keep from hitting her head on the low-hanging rocks, she stopped, nonplussed. The lake stretched out in front of her into the darkness. She had no idea how deep it was. Or what lived there.

Lowering herself into a squat on the cold, damp rock, the sack beside her, the lit torch in her hand, she frowned, both irritated and on the edge of panic. She didn't know how she'd compel her increasingly terrorized mind to move her body into that darkness, even if she could discover a means of doing so. And when she noticed a sizeable wooden raft, beached on a rock to her side, clearly meant for those in her situation, her reaction was less satisfaction than it was something that she refused to accept were tears.

Angry with herself now, she shut down her unhelpful conscious mind and forced herself to go through the motions of dragging the raft into place, resting her unlit torches on top of it, moving the raft into the water, shouldering her sack, and pushing herself out onto the underground lake. She ignored the tears that were streaming down her cheeks. Tears of abject fear.

Once she was away from the shore, she detected an unexpected—and disturbing—current that moved the raft toward the back wall of the cave. And when she reached that wall twenty minutes later, she was able, with her lit torch, to push herself along the edge until she came to an opening, leading further down. The opening was wide—at least four feet across. The raft would fit. But there was little more than a foot of air between the water streaming into it and its rock ceiling. She would be forced to lie flat on her stomach on the raft, clutching her sack, and holding her torch behind her to navigate it. She also had no way of knowing whether the air pocket continued all the way through. If it diminished or disappeared, she'd lose the raft in the current and have to swim, up-current, back to the lake. Carrying Lydia.

Crying more freely now, she flattened herself against the raft, held the sack close to her face—noticing in passing that Lydia, cooing, giggling, and clapping her hands, was delighted by the situation—extinguished her torch, and let the raft drift into the fissure before picking up speed and being swept, three or four minutes later, into an area that once again felt open and cavernous. She couldn't tell whether that feeling was correct because it was pitch black.

Warily lifting her head, she sat upright. Then, reaching into her trouser pocket, she found Mr. Aksu's lighter, and failed twice to produce a flame—whimpering—before re-igniting her torch. When she looked about, the walls were glittering with flashes of wet crystal. The water also extended over the entire floor of the gallery—reflecting the sparkling light. Lydia was laughing, her eyes bright in the glimmer of the torch.

Giving Lydia no more than a quick, frightened glance, reassured that she wasn't screaming in terror as Marion herself wanted to be, she held the torch higher. Though she couldn't see a back section of the cave, the raft continued to move of its own accord in that direction. Gravity, she concluded, sickened by the recognition that she was moving downward, away from the surface and light. She was both surprised and gratified when the raft beached itself on a stretch of dry dirt at the base of a cliff-like face rather than being sucked into another underground river.

Even more surprising was her discovery of a torch—decades old, but usable—left to the side of a fissure in the wall. She lit the torch with the guttering flame of her own torch, nearly extinguished now, and peered into the fissure. At which point, she sat on the damp ground, pushed her face into her knees, and sobbed.

The fissure had no end. It was no more than two feet high. And it was narrow enough that she'd be squeezing herself through it, holding her breath in places. She couldn't continue. She couldn't force herself to crawl into that shaft. She'd come to the end of her resources. For close to three minutes, she pushed her fists against her eyes, taking shallow, panicky breaths.

Then, taking a deeper breath, she decided to resolve the situation by drinking a beer. Laughing shakily, she propped up the lit torch, lifted Lydia out of the sack to enjoy the sparkling crystals stretched out across the gallery, and clawed through the sack until she found the bottle of beer she'd taken from the flying boat. Then she hit the neck of the bottle against the rock until the cap flew off. Finally, she leaned against the cliff face and drank its entire contents in five swallows.

After that, she leaned back, dropping the empty bottle, staring out at the black water, waiting for the alcohol to do its work. It wasn't as strong as she wanted it to be. But it was better than nothing. As she felt it dulling her racing mind, she gathered up Lydia and held the baby against her chest. She didn't know where the fissure would lead, but it would be best that Lydia was fed and sated when they arrived. Perhaps a trifle intoxicated as well.

Once Lydia was satisfied and becoming sleepy, Marion rearranged her canvas sack, stored one dry torch to the side of the golden table leg, placed the baby on top of the blankets, and positioned herself in front of the fissure. Then she extinguished the lit torch. She couldn't bring it with her through the narrow shaft, and she didn't want to leave it, lit, behind her. She suspected that nothing in the gallery could ignite. But the thought of a flame shooting into the fissure as she was squeezing through it was paralyzing. She wouldn't run the risk.

When the gallery fell into darkness, she felt for the shaft's opening and lifted her sack through it in front of her. Then she pushed the sack along the bottom of the shaft with the palms of her hands, while she crawled, and occasionally slid on her stomach, along a mostly horizontal tunnel. Every few minutes, the tunnel would dip or turn sharply. At one point, she squeezed herself down at an angle, dirt from the ceiling less than an inch above her head falling into her face and bringing the tears back to her eyes.

But eventually, after close to an hour, during which she prayed that the effects of the alcohol wouldn't wane sufficiently to allow her to think about her situation, she felt a skeletal air current reach her from the other side of the sack. And then she found herself crawling into another open-feeling area. Reaching into her trouser pocket, she found the lighter, lit it on the first try, pulled out the dry torch, and ignited it.

When she held the torch above her head to get a better view of the cave, she nearly dropped it again. The walls were crawling with millipedes. A foot long or more. Flat. Writhing. And she also sensed something larger scuttle off and glide into the water of the lake that occupied most of the floor of this cave as well. She scrambled up into a standing position, lifted the sack off the floor and kept it securely hoisted over her shoulder. She didn't know whether Lydia would find the fauna in the caves as entertaining as she'd found the close air, the black water, and the darkness. But she didn't want to find out.

She peered into the now dimly lit gallery, holding the torch higher, and saw emerging from the water, a small, circular edifice that didn't look natural. It was too symmetrical. And the stone covering it was greenish—not the pale grey and brown that she'd encountered throughout the rest of the cave. She moved closer to the edge of the water and tried to examine it more closely. But to her dismay, the only way to reach it would be to wade. There was no raft here. And her torch was already starting to dim in the close air.

Clenching the fist that wasn't holding the torch, she stepped into the cold water, grateful, at least, that she was wearing her work boots. When she wasn't swarmed by anything more alarming than what was already surrounding her, she took two additional steps, which brought the water to just under her knees. Then, determined, she waded the rest of the distance and tossed her torch into the center of the circle of green stone. If nothing happened, she'd lose her light anyway—better simply to know.

The moment the flame of the torch hit the stone, it lit up, burning with a blinding intensity, illuminating every wall of the gallery. Many of the millipedes—but certainly not all—disappeared into invisible cracks when the light reached them. But the water was as well populated as the walls—inhabited by a mass of rodent-like creatures, which were excited by the changed environment. The water had begun churning under their movement the moment the light had exploded.

She drew in her breath and stumbled backward, holding the sack against her stomach. Then, squeezing her eyes shut as she reached the narrow beach, she whimpered again. After which, she observed the water, nervous, until she'd convinced herself that whatever was thrashing about in it was uninterested in returning to the strip of dry rock along the edge of the wall. Finally, steadying herself, she turned to examine the cavern. Looking for any hint of what she must do to follow in Basil's footsteps.

The light was intense enough for her to see the wall with some clarity, and so she took her time, peering at the brownish rock, flicking away the occasional stray millipede when she thought it might be obscuring something useful. It took her well over an hour, but she eventually found a square slab that looked unnatural in much the same way that the circle of green stone had. It was the same brown-grey as the rest of the wall. But it had been smoothed and flattened. The markings on it also resembled cuneiform rather than the random scars she'd seen in other parts of the cave. It was nothing so uniform as a tablet. But it struck Marion as not geological.

When she saw, repeated, what looked like the symbol for "kur," she became more convinced that this was the area in which she ought to work. After a great deal of manipulation of the panel, however, she accomplished nothing. Nothing was hidden behind it. And it was unwilling to shift or move. It was simply a part of the stone wall, re-fashioned.

Nonetheless, knowing that abandoning her search wasn't an option, she knelt in front of the panel, brushing aside the millipedes with irritation, and felt all about it with her fingertips, looking for some hint as to its purpose. When still nothing emerged, she sat back on her heels, frustrated, shifting debris from the area just underneath it. Then, intrigued, she looked at the ground more carefully. There was an indentation, perfectly circular, unquestionably also made by hand, situated directly below the "kur" symbol in the panel.

She dusted away the area surrounding the indentation more deliberately and felt along the circle. A metal ring was embedded inside of it. The ring looked like the top of a cylinder buried in the ground, but she couldn't dig enough dirt from around it to test that theory. She could, though, see that the circle's measurements matched the measurements of the emerald at the base of her golden table leg. As though the emerald were meant to be attached to the ring.

It wouldn't hurt to try. And so, withdrawing the golden column from her canvas sack—gently, so as not to disturb Lydia—she positioned it on top of the circular indentation in the ground. For three seconds nothing happened. And then, without warning, a deafening humming sound shattered the silence of the cave. After which, the light was sucked into the water. The cave was pitch black. And the things that had been in the water began climbing out of it. Moving toward her.

Frantic, she tried pulling the column out of the ground. Which was easy. It popped out of the circle with little more than a light tug. But the darkness remained. And she could now smell the rodents and feel the millipedes as they emerged from the cracks in the cave wall. One fell into her hair, and it took all of her presence of mind to pluck it out with her fingers rather than to scream into the darkness. Holding the table leg in one hand and pulling the sack over her shoulder with the other, she straightened into a standing position, her eyes wide, seeing nothing. She felt something wet, with matted fur, investigating her boot, and she kicked out wildly, nearly losing her balance.

Then, gathering what remained of her rational mind, she began feeling her way toward the fissure. She could squeeze back into it, she told herself. Climb up and out into the second gallery. The raft was still there. She had one dry torch. Not to mention Mr. Aksu's lighter. She'd move the raft upstream. She'd find the exit. She simply must keep from panicking, she silently screamed to herself. Whimpering again as she stumbled over the swarming bodies of the rodents, her hand crawling with millipedes as she traced her way back along the wall, she thought she found the edge of the opening.

But then, shocked, she stopped. Felt the air. She could see. Or, to be more accurate, she had a sense that the blackness wasn't as complete as it had been. The light wasn't from a torch. Or from the source at the center of the lake. And she certainly couldn't distinguish shapes or objects. But the intensity of the darkness was not what it had been before.

Suspicious, she twisted in the direction of the panel, expecting something even worse than what she'd already experienced. But instead, far above her head, was a sliver of white. The sky. Not light, but daylight. Making an inarticulate noise, she turned and felt her way back toward the area in which she'd seen the panel. Unwilling to hope, but irrationally grateful for the reprieve from returning to the shaft.

When her hand brushed something that wasn't alive—but also wasn't stone—she allowed herself to acknowledge a small tinge of optimism. It felt like a rope. And when she'd run her hands over it more thoroughly, she discovered that it wasn't just a rope, but a rope ladder. Kicking aside another rodent, she settled the table leg in her canvas sack, hoping that Lydia was still well asleep, and ascended the ladder. It took more than two hours and all of her remaining energy, but eventually, nearing the top, she could see landmarks. And, when she had only a few hundred yards to climb, she could make out the ground.

Finally, sweating and struggling, she pulled herself up and out of a hole in the surface of a flat-topped, square-shaped mountain. After sucking in multiple breaths of fresh air, sitting on the grass, her hands around her knees, the sack beside her, she pushed herself up into a standing position. The mountain was empty. Isolated. And on every side of it was a cliff that looked unscalable. But the ground, aside from the occasional tuft of grass, was smooth. Unnaturally so. More than one person had been there, working it.

Most bewildering of all, though, and what she hadn't quite been able to accept when she'd first dragged herself from the hole, was an aeroplane—civilian, with a passenger cabin—waiting at the edge of the mountaintop. The door to the plane's cabin was open, and there was another ladder dangling down from it, waiting for her to climb. And yet, not a single living person appeared from within or outside the plane to explain its presence or purpose to her. The pilots, invisible behind the cockpit's windows, had no interest in introducing themselves.

Marion spent more than ten minutes standing apart from the plane, watching it, severely mistrusting its menacing presence. But then, after examining the edges of the mountain cliffs and determining that there was no way down or up, she accepted that she had no choice but to take up the silent offer. The plane was the only way off the mountain.

Sighing inwardly, she approached the ladder, secured her canvas sack, and climbed into the passenger cabin. Then she pulled up the ladder, closed the cabin door, and sat in one of the comfortable seats arranged in six rows along either side of the interior. Before she'd lifted Lydia out of the sack to hold in her lap and comfort, the plane was moving, picking up speed, and lifting into the air.

More concerned with seeing to Lydia's needs than useless speculation as to where the plane was taking her, she didn't pay attention to the view out the window. After twenty minutes, however, when they continued to climb without any hint of levelling off, she glanced down, surprised. She'd never been on an aircraft that flew as high as this one did. And when, fifteen minutes later, they were still climbing, she began to feel concerned. Her ears were bothering her, and Lydia had begun to squirm.

Five minutes later, Lydia let out a cry, her face red, angry, and pained. Marion's head was also aching, and she peered, frightened, out the window. She could see nothing but clouds. But even as she wondered when they'd level off, she felt a disturbing change in the cabin's pressure. The air was becoming thinner. Holding Lydia, wailing, in her arms, she forced herself not to pursue the implications of that thought. She needn't have bothered. Less than a minute later, the edges of her vision went black and, holding Lydia against her chest, she lost consciousness.

SHE woke, still sitting in the aeroplane's cabin, still holding Lydia—who had, on her own initiative, begun feeding. But they were now in a steep descent, screeching out of the sky. She didn't know how long they'd been in the air, or whether they had landed to refuel—but as she became aware of her surroundings and looked out the window, she realized that the passage of time was the least of her worries. They weren't simply descending. They were crashing. The ground, nothing like the Taurus

Mountains, was coming at them too fast, and their angle was vertical. Bending over Lydia, cradling the baby in her arms, she shut her eyes, waiting.

Just before they hit, the pilot or pilots brought the plane's nose up. But the sand into which they were plowing bore no resemblance to an airstrip, and the plane skidded at a diagonal before slamming down hard on one wing, which cracked and sent up a cloud of sparks. After that, the cabin spun three or four times before crunching to a halt against what Marion later discovered to be a towering dune of yellowish sand.

Once they'd ceased moving, she remained bent over Lydia, breathing hard, for more than a minute. Then, deciding that the plane was as inert as it would ever be, she straightened, testing her body for injuries. She felt undamaged. Lydia also was unhurt. Angry and wet, but unhurt.

Marion pushed a shaking hand into her canvas sack and found a clean nappy. She would change Lydia before venturing out of the cabin to assess her situation. Take care of immediate requirements. Put off knowing the extent of her predicament for as long as she could.

But by the time she had pinned the nappy around Lydia, the metal cabin of the plane was sweltering. Wherever they were, it was both bright and hot, and she couldn't stay inside much longer without suffocating herself and the baby. Pausing for a moment, she looked first at the door out of the passenger cabin and then at the door leading to the cockpit. That the pilots hadn't emerged while she was changing Lydia suggested that they were injured or needed help. She couldn't leave them without checking on them.

And so, retrieving her linen scarf to protect her head from the heat, shouldering the sack, and holding Lydia in one arm, she walked to the cockpit door. When she tried it, it opened easily. But once she'd pushed it open, she cringed backward, her free hand over her mouth. There was only the one pilot. And he was dead—though the smell from the cockpit suggested that he'd been dead for longer than made any sense. Even more than from the smell, though, Marion recoiled from the swarm of ants, each as large as her hand, that were crawling over his decomposing body.

Clenching her teeth together, she pulled the door to the cockpit shut, turned to the cabin door, wrenched it open, and half-fell, half-slid into the sand that had partially buried the wrecked plane. Put as much distance between herself and the twisted metal, shimmering in the heat, as she could before stopping and assessing her situation. What she saw made her little more optimistic than the scene in the cockpit had. Stretched out before her was an endless ocean of sand—blown into dunes to her left and flatter to her right. No hint of habitation in any direction.

For over a minute, she simply stared at it. Immobile. Then, determined not to give in to her fear, she attended to Lydia again. It was obvious that the baby couldn't be exposed to this sun for more than a few minutes at a time. And so, creating an indentation in the interior of the canvas sack, she placed the baby back into it, gave her the wooden dolphin to hold, and stretched the lightest blanket she had over the opening, as a sunshade.

After that, she walked in the direction of the flatter sand. Although she didn't trust her senses in the notoriously mystifying environment, she thought she saw something on the horizon that might be a structure. A goal, at any rate. And working toward an objective, rather than wandering aimlessly, would keep her alive for a few more hours, if not likely for a full day.

Also, she reasoned to herself as she trudged, at least she knew where she was. The only sand she'd encountered that was as relentless as the sand surrounding her was in the Sahara. The pressing question, therefore, was where in the three and a half million square miles of the Sahara the plane had left them. Perhaps when she reached the horizon, someone would tell her. She pulled the linen scarf further over her forehead and face and continued walking.

After an hour, Lydia began to squirm and lift herself out of the sack. Resigned, Marion sat cross-legged in the burning sand—no hint of shade anywhere—and pulled Lydia out of the sack to feed. When the baby was sated and beginning to sleep, she settled her back into the blankets and stood, wobbling. She was monstrously thirsty and certain that she'd be able to feed Lydia only once or twice more before her body shut down. Glancing up at the horizon, failing now to see the shape that had initially attracted her, but refusing to acknowledge to herself that it had probably been her imagination in the first place, she continued walking.

She wondered whether Hızır's—St. George's—or, she supposed, now that she was in North Africa, al-Khidr's purpose all along had been to kill her. From the moment she'd entered his cave. He would have known her assignment if his reputation was remotely close to the reality. And he'd done an effective job on Walther Wever, Antonio Locatelli, and Jose Sanjurjo. But not on Basil, she mused to herself. She'd found Basil both pathetic and supercilious when they were in London. Now, she grudgingly respected him. He'd survived.

"Would you like a glass of water?"

Marion stopped walking, raised her eyes, and saw a tall, slim woman, wrapped in light green silk, holding out a glass of cold water. Speaking English. Condensation on the exterior of the glass dripping over her slender fingers. Then, annoyed, she stared back at the sand. She was already hallucinating. Perhaps the few hours she'd estimated she could endure the heat was an optimistic miscalculation. Keeping her eyes down, she continued walking and ran into the woman.

"Whoops." The woman laughed and stepped backward. "It's all right. It hasn't spilled." She held out the glass. "I'm Hakimah."

Marion scowled down at the sand. She refused to give this bizarre emanation of her dying brain the satisfaction of interacting with it. Though she wanted to hit it for toying with her in this unacceptable way. She took a few calming breaths of the searing air. Then, still looking down, she thought about her situation. There was no need to die resentful. Why not accept the "water" and convince herself that she was refreshed and hydrated before she lost consciousness? She held out her hand.

Hakimah handed her the glass, which felt solid, cool, and quite real. Marion lifted it to her lips and drank. When she'd finished, she let her hand drop to her side, holding the empty glass, and looked up, expecting to see empty space and sand.

Hakimah was still there. When Marion didn't speak, she leaned forward. "Dr. Bailey, isn't it? Or Lady Willcox?"

Marion began walking again. "Call me Marion."

"Very well, Marion." Hakimah fell into step beside her and looked surreptitiously down at the bag. Lydia was toying with the sunshade, her fingers grabbing at the stray threads hanging over her. "You've brought your baby?"

"Yes," Marion said. "Lydia."

"Unusual."

"Isn't it?" Marion retorted acidly. She wished her mind would conjure up something less self-assured and socially intimidating. Though she admitted that the imaginary water had done wonders for her system. She felt almost able to tolerate the heat. And the glass still felt delightfully cold in her hand.

After a few more minutes of walking, Marion looked sidelong at her companion. She was still there, cool and unaffected by the environment. Then she peered at the horizon and thought she saw the shapes that had attracted her notice when she'd left the plane. She pointed in front of her. "What's that?"

"Sijilmasa," Hakimah replied.

"The ancient ruined city at the edge of Morocco? In the Tafilalt oasis?"

"Yes," Hakimah said. "Not all that ancient. It was abandoned in the fifteenth century."

If her hallucination was correct, then she might, if she were very lucky, survive. There was still a village in the Tafilalt oasis. And water. She would also be somewhat close to her target—or, at least, on the proper continent. She estimated a three to four hour walk to reach the building.

She examined Hakimah again. "This is the Sijilmasa that sat at the northern end of the trade route that brought gold across the Sahara from West Africa?"

"Yes," Hakimah repeated. "But the gold isn't all that relevant to our purpose."

"'Our purpose?'"

"Yes." And then, before Marion could ask the obvious question: "do you know why the city was called Sijilmasa by its founder?"

"No." She wondered whether the figment could produce another glass of water. She was feeling thirsty again.

"According to Leo Africanus, who visited the ruins of the city in the early sixteenth century," Hakimah began, like some merciless tour guide sadistically imparting information to her tortured and dying audience, "it was founded by a Roman soldier fleeing from the Civil War in the first century BC. Leo Africanus said that 'Sijilmasa' was a corruption of *Sijillummesse*, camp Latin for 'somewhere near the borders of the town of Messa or Massa.'" She paused and then added helpfully, "Massa was a town further west, on the Atlantic."

"Fascinating." Marion hoisted the sack more securely over her shoulder. It was slipping as her strength waned.

"He was incorrect," Hakimah continued.

"Shame."

"Well," Hakimah amended. "Not entirely incorrect. The city was indeed founded by a Roman citizen fleeing the Civil War. Exiled by Julius Caesar. But not a soldier. A magician. Nigidius."

"Ah."

"He could predict the future and raise souls from the dead." Hakimah was still utterly unaffected by the heat. "A Pythagorean."

"Impressive."

"Leo Africanus was also correct that the name of the city derived from a corruption of the Latin," the hallucination continued, undeterred by Marion's lack of enthusiasm. "But not about which Latin phrase gave rise to that corruption."

They walked for a minute longer in silence until Marion, absurdly not wanting to be rude, encouraged her. "What was the Latin phrase, then?"

"*Sugiturlimes.* Or, eventually, elided, *Sigilimese.*" Hakimah smiled at Marion as though she'd revealed a remarkable and occult truth.

Marion thought for a moment. "'The border is imbibed?'"

"Well, that makes very little sense, Marion." Disappointed in her.

"True," Marion observed, watching the sand, forcing herself to continue trudging toward the shapes that were flirting with invisibility on the horizon.

"And so, what else might *limes* mean, Marion?" Like a school teacher.

"*Limes, limitis,*" Marion responded, obliging, not quite believing that she was now hallucinating an elementary Latin lesson before dying in the middle of the Sahara. "Masculine. Border, limit, track, path, riverbed—"

"Stop," Hakimah said. "That's what we're looking for. Riverbed."

"Ah."

"And *sugitur?*"

"Third person, singular, present, passive. From *sugo, sugere.* To drink, suck, take in—"

"Correct," she said. "The riverbed is taken in here."

"I don't understand—" Marion started to say, and then she stopped both speaking and walking. Dumbfounded.

Hakimah had moved aside a mound of sand with her foot, bent over, pulled up a slab of brick, and revealed a steep staircase of wood—cedar, Marion thought—leading into a subterranean cavern from which the unmistakable sound of a river emanated.

"This way," she said, stepping gracefully into the hole.

Bewildered, Marion followed her into the torchlit cavern, waiting docile while Hakimah secured the brick door above them. As they descended, and the wooden stairs became slick from the damp, her astonishment grew. The river, when they eventually left the stairs and stood on its bank, was enormous, as wide as the Thames, but much swifter. And the cavern was lofty, as though it had been deliberately improved, widened, and decorated.

"Some also call the ruins at the edge of the desert Tamanrasset. Rather than Sijilmasa," Hakimah said, gesturing Marion toward an improbable teak runabout, polished, gleaming, and operated by a quiet boy, not old enough for facial hair, wearing a djellaba.

"Tamanrasset," Marion said, focusing on the geography rather than on her overwhelmed rational faculties, "is two thousand miles away. In Algeria."

"It's a long river," Hakimah replied, helping Marion into the boat.

They sat quietly for two or three minutes while the boy maneuvered them upstream. Then Hakimah turned to her side, opened a compartment under her seat, produced two bottles of cold water, and handed one to Marion. Grateful, Marion drank the entire contents of the bottle and placed it on the seat next to her.

"When we reach the city—" Hakimah started.

"Which city?"

She wrinkled her forehead, perplexed. "Kur." Stating the obvious. "You called us."

"Oh." Marion looked down at Lydia, sleeping now in the canvas sack she held in her lap. "I understand."

"When we reach the city," Hakimah resumed, "you'll bathe, eat, and rest. Unfortunately, you won't interact with residents aside from myself. Although we can certainly see to it that the baby is cared for while you—"

"Lydia will stay with me," Marion said tersely.

Hakimah paused, taken aback by Marion's tone. Then she nodded. "Of course." Considered for a few seconds. "I shall answer your questions. When Khidr is prepared, he will see you."

"Oh," Marion repeated, bemused by Hakimah's apparently detailed knowledge of her assignment. And her lack of concern over it. "Thank you."

"We would, however, like to repair our table immediately."

"I'm sorry?"

"Our table," Hakimah said, "is missing a leg. We'd like to repair it."

"Oh," Marion said a third time. "Yes. Of course. Here it is."

She extracted the column from her canvas sack, keeping Lydia encased in the blankets, and passed it to Hakimah. Hakimah inclined her head, took the leg, and set it in her lap. "We'll reach the city in less than five minutes. You see the lights ahead."

Marion peered upriver and did in fact see what looked like a commonplace harbor in a wider part of the river—boats tied up to docks, two or three buoys, a collection of what must be electric lights on the exterior of dockside wooden buildings. It reminded her of the Thames at night. Except that she was under one of the most forbidding deserts in the world, just at the edge of inhabitable Morocco, having recently survived a crash in a plane piloted by a decomposing body savaged by enormous ants. She hugged Lydia, sleeping in the canvas sack, closer to her as the boat approached a vacant slip.

MARION had wondered how Hakimah would prevent her from interacting with Kur's inhabitants. But when they stepped off the deck of the runabout onto the wooden dock, the harbor was deserted. Even the boy who had transported them disappeared. She and Hakimah were alone in the damp city and, it seemed, would remain so.

Beckoning Marion, awkwardly, with the end of King Solomon's table leg, Hakimah led her up a paved hill toward a white, turreted castle—looking distinctly Almoravid—that was squatting, satisfied, as it surveilled the city. After preceding her through the open gates, still without any sign of living guards or citizens, she brought Marion through a tiled courtyard complete with an elaborate fountain also lit by some hidden electric light source. Finally, she showed her to a private pavilion consisting of a sitting area with a small pool, a bedroom furnished in European style, and a bath. A change of clothing was waiting for her on the bed.

"Please take all the time you need to refresh yourself," Hakimah said withdrawing backward through the doors to the sitting area. "And then join me by the water so that we may speak."

Marion put her sack on the bed, extracted Lydia, fed her, and removed her soiled nappy. Then she peeled off her own filthy clothing and left it on a chair that looked designed by Jack Pritchard. It was identical to a chair of which she was particularly fond in the drawing room of Jeffrey's London house, but she was too overwhelmed by the past few days to note the incongruity. Finally, holding Lydia against her waist, she walked into the bath.

While Lydia laughed and splashed in the warm, shallow water, Marion eradicated every trace she could find on her body of her days on the flying boat, in the cave, and walking through the desert. It took her longer than she had thought it would, but when she finished, she felt almost capable of meeting what would undoubtedly be an equally disturbing collection of experiences in the near future. Stepping out of the bath onto the geometric green and white tile, she unfolded a green towel that had been left on a marble bench and wrapped it around herself. Then she picked up Lydia and walked with her into the bedroom.

After putting a clean nappy on the baby, she turned to the clothing that had been chosen for her. It was a simple, also European-style, dress, white silk with black accents, and—when she held it up—meant to fall at least to the middle of her shin. The label read Madeleine Vionnet, which meant as little to her as labels ever did. Intuitively, she recognized the style to be one of which Jeffrey would approve. There were also sandals and appropriate, modest, underwear.

While Lydia pulled herself across the bed, still pleased after the bath, Marion slipped the dress over her head, slid her feet into the sandals, and plaited her hair. Then, gathering up the baby in her arms again, she returned to the sitting area. Hakimah was waiting for her there, arranging food on plates that had been set on a marble table to the side of the pool. Marion left Lydia near the water, noticing in passing that it was stocked with abundant, energetic, multicolored carp.

"Pomegranate?" Hakimah held out a fragile blue and white porcelain plate containing dates, orange slices, white cheese, and an artistically sliced wedge of pomegranate.

Wary, Marion sat on a sofa across from Hakimah, accepted the plate, and placed it to her side on a small table. She had nothing but respect for Mr. Atkins's argument that different netherworlds had different geographies and, presumably, different rules. But nothing in the world would persuade her to eat a pomegranate seed in Hakimah's company. She hoped her suspicions weren't too obvious. Or too arbitrary. Well aware that she was in no position to refuse water.

"Thank you." She accepted a glass of water with a mint leaf floating in it and took a sip.

Hakimah relaxed against her sofa and ate a dainty bite of a date. "What are your questions, Marion?"

Looking about at the dark yet glittering pavilion, the sound of the underground river noticeable in the background, and the disturbingly intelligent fish interacting with her daughter, she could have laughed. Instead, however, she elected to remember her assignment. To be direct. "Do you know why I've come?"

"Yes." Disinclined to elaborate.

"And—that isn't a problem?"

"Why would it be?" Hakimah finished her date and contemplated the orange slices, quiet and serious, before choosing one and popping it into her mouth.

Marion thought. "I—I don't know?"

"There you are then." Hakimah watched her for a few seconds, waiting. Then she spoke again. "What are your other questions?"

Marion blinked, trying to determine what she must say to bring her closer to completing her task. Taking another sip of water, she tried a different tack. "Was Basil Kingsbury here?"

"Yes."

"And—he left?"

"These," Hakimah said with what might have been a pout if her self-possessed face were capable of moving in that direction, "are uninteresting questions."

Marion gaped at her, not having realized that her conversation was being judged. Before collecting herself and drinking more water. Then a thought occurred to her and she nearly smiled. Flattery. Whatever these people were, they were operating according to an earlier code. She must flatter their power and their connections. "Did Musa ibn Nusayr, the governor of Ifriqiya and al-Andalus, servant of the Umayyad Caliph al-Walid ibn Abd al-Malik also visit you here?" She wished they were speaking Arabic. It would have sounded better.

Hakimah smiled, pleased that Marion was now understanding her role. "Indeed, he did. But before my time. Nigidius acted as his guide."

"The Nigidius exiled by Julius Caesar?" Marion frowned. "Surely Musa visited no earlier than the eighth century."

"Nigidius," Hakimah said, enjoying Marion's confusion, "lived a full life." When Marion didn't ask an additional question, Hakimah deigned to elaborate. "Musa," she said, "did not. He failed."

"In what way did he fail?" Marion asked, beginning to fear that she was missing something important. The conversation appeared to have a purpose of which Hakimah was aware, but which she was unwilling to explain to Marion. And Marion couldn't determine whether Hakimah assumed that Marion herself also knew what they were discussing, or whether she was deliberately mystifying her.

"It may have been the shaykh's fault," Hakimah said. "His translator. Nigidius refused to speak any language but Latin. Musa knew only Arabic. And so, when Musa was here, he was unable to understand the importance of his task. And then when he returned to the outside world, his story was— garbled. He failed to serve his purpose."

"His purpose?"

"Indeed." Hakimah ate another slice of orange, disinclined once again to clarify.

Marion finished her water, trying to decide what her next move ought to be in this surreal fog of a conversation. Then, unable to think of anything more sophisticated, she returned to flattery. "You said that you received a message sent to you from the cave in Anatolia. However did that message reach you from so very far away?" She tried to look amazed and astonished. "It seems impossible. Magical."

"Now that," Hakimah said, brightening, "is a very interesting question."

"Yes?" Marion couldn't decide whether she was supposed to thank Hakimah for her praise. And she was relieved when, a few seconds later, Hakimah continued on her own initiative.

"Magneto-inductive communication."

"What?"

"Magento-inductive communication," she repeated. When Marion remained baffled, she sighed, a disappointed school teacher. "When it reaches the surface, that's what it will be called. Not yet, I suppose. You see, Marion. We exist in the midst of rock," airy wave of her hand, "and water." Tilt of the head back toward the river. "We can't rely on signals moving through the atmosphere. And so, we use—and have always used, from the very, *very* beginning—magnetic fields that we generate in solid matter to transmit messages. When we must. The green stone at the base of each of the table's legs— call it *shamir* if you'd like—it produces magnetic fields that stretch through and across entire mountain ranges—" She stopped, irritated.

"But don't even begin to imagine 'magnetic mountains' sucking the metal out of ships and wrecking them." She pouted in earnest this time. "An entirely different sort of magnetism. The idiot." Then, recovering herself: "so, once the magnetic field has been generated by the rotating iron and

copper within the column, we can receive a signal from anywhere in the world. *Anywhere* in the world."
She paused again. "We can also move through space, but that's a conversation for another time."

Marion had followed only the tiniest fraction of Hakimah's explanation, but she felt it would
be unwise to admit to her increasing confusion. Instead, she said: "and so you—or Nigidius—explained
all of this to Musa, or to the shaykh, who translated for Musa?"

"Correct," she said. "In more detail than I've just described it to you. With diagrams. And
not only did Musa decline to fulfil his side of the agreement, but when he returned to the surface, he
deterred anyone who might want to take his place by publicizing his bizarre, self-aggrandizing account."

"Take his place?" Marion asked.

"Rotating horsemen and mermaids and robotic women beckoning his men to their
perdition." Hakimah was delicately ranting, ignoring Marion's question.

"But—how could he have made such egregious errors?" Marion asked. "Unless it was
deliberate?"

"It wasn't deliberate," Hakimah said. "It was stupidity."

"What sort of stupidity?"

"Nigidius," Hakimah said, "explained to him, in Latin, how our communications system
worked. Rotating iron, within copper, activated by the green stone. Simple. But when Nigidius said
ferrous, of iron, Musa heard *faris*, a horseman. A rotating bronze or copper horseman. Things
disintegrated from there. Their interpretation of our transport capabilities didn't even make it into the
stories, it was so fantastic."

Marion was beyond bewildered now. And so, she simply nodded, focusing on Lydia trying to
reach the fish in the pool.

"He could have had everything," Hakimah said, her voice cold. "Anything in the world. And
he failed."

Marion continued to watch Lydia for a moment. Then she looked back over at Hakimah,
troubled. "What was Musa expected to accomplish, then?"

Rather than answering, Hakimah stood and brushed down the green silk that enveloped her.
"Khidr will see you now."

Startled by her change in demeanor, Marion rose as well, leaving her empty glass on the
table. "Now?" She looked about the room. "Are you certain?"

"Yes," Hakimah said. "Follow me."

Scooping up Lydia, who was unwilling to leave the fish, but fortunately not so unwilling that
she began crying, she trotted after Hakimah. As they walked, she tried to make sense of the conversation
she'd just endured—and of why Hakimah had, in her torturous way, made her a gift of this apparently
occult information. Especially when she knew that Marion had arrived in the role of assassin.

Why bother pressing the history and—for lack of a better term—the technology on her if
she was not on their side? But the more she prodded the contours of the situation, the less confident
she was that she understood it. And so, after two or three minutes of walking, she pushed aside
Hakimah's remarks as irrelevant—focused on her assignment.

Following Hakimah through lofty marble corridors—most of them dark, frequently black,
but always lit by the same unnatural sources—Marion realized that she did have one other question. It
was a question prompted by curiosity, and it would do nothing to help her complete her task. But even
so, she felt little compunction about going beyond the bounds of her brief.

Catching up to Hakimah such that they were almost walking abreast, she looked over at her
imperious face. "Hakimah," she started. "Is this 'Kur,' here, the same 'Kur' that—that—" She stopped,
not knowing how to phrase the question.

"The same Kur as what?" Hakimah hadn't slackened her pace.

Marion thought for a moment and tried again. "Were you also visited by the Sumerians? Or
the Assyrians? Long before Nigidius and Musa?"

"Yes." Dismissive. "They watched the river sink. It saddened them."

"The river sank?"

"Yes." She remained silent for long enough that Marion thought she might not elaborate.
But then, stopping in front of two golden doors, twelve feet high, she faced Marion and spoke again. "It
went underground. Some claim that it went dry, but that theory is incorrect. There are now seven
entrances. Nigidius founded Sijilmasa at one of them." She pulled open a door with remarkably little
effort, given its size and bulk. "You'll enter here, make your obeisance, and submit to his commands."

Marion nodded, wondering whether Hakimah didn't in fact know why she had come. But
she couldn't enlighten her now. And so, deciding that on the whole she was pleased to be free of her

guide's maddening company, she entered the room. At least she could now develop an idea of the terrain, before finally completing this bewildering assignment.

THE room was large enough and dimly lit enough, by torches, that she couldn't make out its back wall. What she could see, however, was a great deal of gold—solid, molded, flaked, twined—more than she had ever encountered in one place. On the walls, over the furniture, melted-seeming over stairs and daises. Marble pillars also supported the ludicrously high ceiling. Which was gold. And, seated on a golden chair at the top of a marble stairway, was the distant figure of a tall, silent, straight-backed man.

As Marion stepped further into the room, she stumbled and came to a halt, noticing that the floor had been flooded by three or four feet of water. Perhaps from the river. She looked about for some sort of pier or bridge—or raft even—and when she saw nothing, she waited, perplexed.

The man in the chair, however, made no move to help or to approach her. He simply sat, watching. And so, after more than a minute, annoyed, she lifted the silk dress up over her knees with one hand, holding Lydia with the other, and waded out into the water. Which wasn't wet. Confused, she peered down at the floor until she heard laughter from the man sitting in the chair above her.

"I never tire of it," he said in English, standing and then bounding down the stairs. "It's marble." He jumped once or twice on the hard floor. "You see? Marble." He cocked his head. "You've got nice legs."

Blushing, she dropped her skirt. "Al-Khidr?"

"Call me George if you'd rather." He had a disconcerting Canadian accent.

"Is that what you'd prefer? Or that we speak Arabic? Or—or Latin?"

"I speak everything," he said, taking her arm and leading her, companionable, toward a less lofty part of the room. "I've had a long time to study. So, let's say English. And George."

As he walked with her into the alcove in which he apparently wanted to speak further with her, she took the opportunity to study his features. He was tall, no more than thirty years old, piercing green eyes with a slight tilt to them, a nicely trimmed white beard and moustache, and he was wearing—she imagined as a misguided nod to her own background—a Royal Navy dress uniform. He was entirely uninterested in Lydia. And, disquieting, he had no smell—which was an anomaly to Marion, who ordinarily picked up something of that sort off of everyone she met. Usually too much.

After a very long journey across the golden room, they reached the table whose leg had become familiar to her over the past week. He pulled out an uncomfortable looking golden chair and gestured her into it. Then he sat across the table from her in a similar chair. She held Lydia in her lap, trying not to fidget in what was the most disagreeable piece of furniture she'd ever occupied.

He leaned back, crossed his ankle over his knee, and rapped the leg of the table with his fist. "Thank you for bringing it back. The table wobbled."

"You're welcome." And then, after a few seconds, when he seemed to expect her to make conversation, she ventured: "I thought the table was in the Umayyad treasury."

"It was," he said. "But it always returns."

"Oh." She bounced Lydia two or three times in her lap to keep the baby from pulling herself, proprietary, up and over the tabletop. Looking beyond him, she saw a sizeable wall holding shelves and shelves of sealed copper bottles. She squinted, trying to see them more clearly in the dim firelight.

Noting her interest, he made a move as though to take one. "I can open a few, if you'd like—"

"No!" she said. "No. Thank you. I needn't see."

He shrugged and settled back into his chair. "They're a nuisance. Floating around, clogging up the river traffic. You wouldn't think there'd be so many of them, would you?"

She shook her head, resigned now to the realization that her interactions with him would be as frustrating as those she'd had with Hakimah. And so, coming to the point: "do you know why I'm here?"

He nodded. "You prefer poison, right?"

"I'm sorry?"

He didn't reply. And, after a moment of confused irritation, she tightened her lips. If he wanted to discuss her professional methods, there was no reason to disappoint him. Given the daft direction in which this project had already taken her. Inhabiting the chair as comfortably as she could, she responded with calm equanimity: "I use whatever's at hand. But I haven't taken on this sort of assignment for quite a while. I had planned to take a bit of time to assess my options."

"Unfortunately, that won't work. The *ad hoc* tactics. You have to use this." He reached into a long, golden box stored under the table and produced a fluid, brilliantly sharp, curved blade with a jeweled hilt. Damascus steel, without question. Mr. Aksu's old men would have been impressed. He set the sword, hilt toward her, on the table. "That ought to do it."

She looked at the sword, nonplussed. Then she raised her eyes to his face. "You want me to do this for you?"

"Yes."

"Why?"

"Marion," he said, "I am very, very old." He smiled at her, not a wrinkle marring his healthy, glowing face. "It's time."

She didn't touch the sword. "Why can't one of your followers do it?"

"They think it will bring about the apocalypse." His smile grew sheepish.

"Will it?"

"I don't *care*." His tone was as close to whining as Hakimah's face had been to pouting earlier. If only his magisterial voice were capable of operating in that register. "I've told you. I'm *old*. And bored."

She remained silent, thinking. Then, to cover her confusion, she placed Lydia on the marble floor to practice her crawling. Clapping her hands, gleeful, Lydia admired the liquid expanse before pulling herself in the direction of the shelves of copper jars. Moving quickly.

"Your superiors," he said, startling her out of her contemplation of her daughter, "have made an agreement with me, Marion. An agreement that they have neglected—for eight hundred years now—to satisfy. The others failed. You've come. You have a duty."

She blinked at him, unconvinced.

"You'd disobey your orders?" His green eyes bored into hers, but she had an impression of theatricality. His intensity didn't feel quite genuine.

"I'm not very good at loyalty," she eventually said, dropping her eyes. "Though I try."

He waited for a few seconds. And then, unexpectedly, he grinned, setting aside the intimidating glower. "I like that. You try." He reached over the sword and tapped the back of her hand with his fingertip, playful, jollying her into meeting his glance again. "I have a feeling that when you do try, you usually succeed. Certainly more than the last one I had here."

She moved her hand into her lap, and he leaned back, still smiling. Nothing was very serious to him. Even his potential assassination.

"The last one was Basil Kingsbury?" she asked.

"Poor Basil." He was laughing now.

"He wasn't sent by my organization," she said. "He isn't one of us."

"He's not?" He straightened one of the medals on his uniform and then looked up at her. "Forgive me, but it's hard to differentiate among you all sometimes. And whatever the case, I had to do something with him. He was fouling my cave. It was an interesting experiment, at any rate."

"I don't understand."

"My cave. In the Taurus Mountains. Basil took up residence." He almost snorted. "I waited for him to die. Of fear. Or starvation. Or even—though I flatter myself—of awe. Nothing doing. Too well trained. So, there he sat—persisting. Making the entire place stink." He arched a faintly greenish eyebrow. "Though it could have been worse. He could have left me nappies as an offering."

"They were clean," she retorted. "I felt guilty using up all of the torches."

"Guilt motivates you, then?" He watched her face. "When duty and loyalty don't?"

"No," she said, suspicious of his renewed interest. "My motivations aren't uniform." She paused. "I don't know what motivates me."

"Would you like to know why I sent Basil after Walther Wever, Antonio Locatelli, and Jose Sanjurjo?" he asked. A non-sequitur. "As the price of his freedom?"

"Why did you take all of his languages?" she asked instead, wanting, she didn't know why, to be obstructive.

"I didn't take his languages," he protested, hurt at the accusation. "Basil did that all on his own. Defense mechanism, I think your modern healers call it."

"Oh." She believed him. The Darija was so classically a symptom of something else. "Very well, then. So why did you remove Wever, Locatelli, and Sanjurjo?" She felt oddly as though she were speaking to an eight-year-old rather than to—whatever he was. She didn't want to puncture his childish pride.

He lowered his voice, prophetic. And yet still theatrical. "Wever," he intoned, "would have been captured by his enemies and given them false information, which would have led to the loss of many lives. Locatelli would have claimed loyalty to a noble cause, but he would have served a base one. And Sanjurjo would have taken Tariq's Mountain, and from there, he would have erected an unscalable wall across the entrance to the White Sea."

She stared at him. "Are you certain?"

He stared back at her, serious, for three long seconds. Then he burst out laughing. "Of course not." He continued laughing, wiping a tear from his eye. "But look at you! So somber. I like you."

She frowned at him.

"All three were bastards, Marion." He was still chuckling. "Why not? And it certainly caught the attention of your people. Terrified that they were facing competition. Sending you out here lickety-split. I feel much less neglected than I have in recent years."

She gazed down at the tabletop for a moment. Then, raising her eyes and noticing that Lydia was nearing the shelves of copper bottles, she pushed back her chair and stood. "Excuse me. I'm sorry. I must—" She ran across the floor and lifted Lydia into her arms. Then she twisted back to him, apologetic. "I was worried that she'd—cause damage—"

He had turned toward her, still sitting in his chair. Watching her now with an inscrutable expression. "You realize," he said, "that if I can't die, I'm entitled to choose my company. Those who will stay to share my—extensive—life." He rested an elbow on the table and set his cheek in his hand. "Basil bored me after a decade or two. And Hakimah, as you've undoubtedly noticed, is not what you'd call *compos mentis*. Which isn't her fault. It happens to the best of us after eleven hundred years." He rolled his eyes. "*Wisdom.* You, however, are interesting. And that," nodding at Lydia, squirming in her arms, "is fascinating. Eternal infant innocence. More intriguing an experiment even than Basil was."

When Marion stared at him, immobile and cold, he threw her an impudent smile. "Though I'll give you this one for free, Marion. That child is anything but harmless. And she will cause damage. Should she venture out again."

Marion held Lydia closer to her, her expression still icy. "You're trying to make me angry. To provoke me."

"Did it work?"

"No."

"Damn." He rose to his feet, facing her. "But that doesn't mean that my promise to you isn't genuine. Or consider it a threat rather than a promise if it suits your temperament better."

Without speaking, she circled around him until she was standing behind the table again, the hilt of the sword inches from her hand. Then, quickly, she lifted the sword in the hand that wasn't holding Lydia and backed toward the door.

"If you complete your assignment," he said, ignoring her self-protective movement, "Hakimah will let you take the green stone out with you. Along with its various, arcane instructions. Communication. Transportation. Destruction. All those capabilities your militaries are forever trying to perfect. Your superiors would be more than pleased."

"I'd like to think about it first," she replied, still backing toward the door.

He made a sudden move, as though to attack her, and she raised the sword, defensive. Then he relaxed, laughing again. "Are you threatening to kill me if I come any closer, Marion?"

She'd reached the doors, and she pushed one open, still watching him. "I don't know who or what you are, *George*. But I'm willing to bet that if I cut off your right arm at the shoulder, it would be an unpleasant experience for you."

"And who knows?" he added, tired now, turning to walk toward his throne. "I may even bleed to death if I'm lucky."

She slipped through the door and paused, testing the atmosphere for any hint of an ambush or attack. But there was nothing. Even Hakimah had disappeared. The corridor was vacant. A void.

Holding Lydia more securely against her waist, she retraced the route she'd taken from the pavilion, attuned now to the dead quality of the air. And once she'd reached the castle's central courtyard, her skin was crawling with fear, even though she'd faced not a single obstacle or challenge. She was desperate to escape the city. To reach the surface.

Deciding not to risk returning to the bedroom to retrieve her sack, she turned away from the pavilion and made her way to the main gates of the castle. Which were open. Unguarded, unwatched, and dead. Forcing herself to focus, not to give in to her mounting panic, she ran through the gates and down the hill until she reached the river and the dock. Her breath coming in shallow gasps in what now felt like insufficient air.

The runabout was still moored in its slip. She didn't know whether the boy in the djellaba was responsible for guarding it, but if he was, she certainly didn't see or sense him anywhere. Nor did she care. Untying the mooring lines at its bow and stern, she stepped into the cockpit—holding Lydia against her waist—and started the motor. Then she pushed off, settled the awkwardly large sword on the teak planks covering the bilge, and directed the boat downstream. She didn't know where the river ended, or surfaced, but wherever it was, it was preferable to the city. Frantic now, she moved the throttle as far forward as it would go, determined to get them out.

Once the boat had passed the riverbank and stairs down which Hakimah had led her from the desert, the lights illuminating the water's course thinned and then disappeared. And a half hour after that, her surroundings became pitch black. All she could sense was the smell of damp earth and the sound of the rushing current. But she didn't mind. The further the river took her from Kur, the calmer she would be. The earth smelled healthy. And the air was thickening again—returning to normal.

Finally beginning to relax, she held Lydia against her chest to eat. Less than twenty minutes later, they were both asleep in the cockpit of the boat, while the boat itself, unguided, continued its course downstream. Under the Sahara.

*W*HEN Marion woke, the runabout was grating along dirt and gravel in low—and decreasing—water. The river had exhausted itself. They had still not surfaced, but as the boat ran completely aground and skidded to a halt, she could see, above and ahead, an opening in the cavern that surrounded them. Sunlight.

The motor had already gone through its fuel while she and Lydia were sleeping, so Marion didn't trouble to cut it. Instead, and more pressing, she shifted the cushions and lifted the teak covers off the seats, looking for a stray piece of cloth she could use as a makeshift nappy. Lydia's last was sodden, and the baby wouldn't tolerate it much longer.

Eventually discovering the hold with the water bottles—which, squeamish, she left untouched—she found an anomalous set of linen tea towels. Fancy. Embroidered with pink dianthus. Bemused, she held one up, decided it would do, and changed Lydia. Then, holding the baby against her waist and retrieving the sword, she climbed out of the boat and waded through the five or six inches of water that were all that was left of the Tamanrasset River. Peering up at the sunlight that was still, thankfully, above her.

Scaling the cavern was more complicated than she had expected it to be, packed as the space was with layered slabs of stone that hindered, rather than aiding, her ascent. She also had to work through a series of arbitrarily curved tunnels that repeatedly wound back on themselves even as they brought her up to the surface. But she never lost sight of the sliver of sunlight. And she knew throughout her climb that she was moving in the proper direction rather than descending once more into subterranean darkness.

After reaching the top of the cavern, she wandered through eleven room-like compartments—more than reminiscent of a human dwelling or habitation. But she paid them little attention. Instead, she concentrated on pushing herself—sweating, breathing heavily, and dragging Lydia and the sword along with her—through a gap in the stone and dirt at the top edge of the last room. Which left her standing on a small mountain rising out of a gravelly desert.

But this desert was nothing like the bleak expanse in which the plane had crashed. From her vantage point, she could see sparse vegetation and buildings quite close by, no more than two miles away. Along with a welcome absence of dunes. There was also a well-used road leading toward a town or village, easily accessed from the hill on which she was standing.

Not a hill, she decided as she walked tentatively across the flat, gritty, surface. A tomb. One of the monumental dirt mounds she'd seen scattered across various edges of the North African desert. Although this one had been the subject of some thorough archaeological interest. There were marks of recent excavation in every cranny of the hilltop—despite the fact that, oddly, there were no archaeologists in sight.

Intrigued, she turned back to the hole from which she'd emerged and peered into it. Then she caught herself. Curiosity was not useful at this point. She must find a way back to London. To Ian. And—though mortifying—to the contrite report she'd submit to her superiors on her role in this disaster of an assignment. Besides, Lydia was becoming impatient, and the sword was both blisteringly hot and heavy.

"Drop your weapon, Dr. Bailey."

More baffled than frightened, she considered the steel blade in her hand. Puzzled. She supposed it was a "weapon," in a sense. Then, squinting, she tried to find the source of the voice.

"Drop it immediately."

Nick Trelawney, she now saw—crawling over the lip of the hilltop, a service revolver held expertly in two hands, aimed at her head. Speaking Darija.

He was flanked by five similarly armed soldiers, all with deadly serious expressions on their faces that were only slightly marred by their clownish short trousers and pith helmets. She felt a mild, atavistic sense of national embarrassment at the chosen uniform of the British officer abroad even as she bent over—slowly, harmlessly—and placed the sword on the ground at her feet. Nick made eye contact with one of the soldiers, who scrambled forward, grabbed the sword by its hilt, and dragged it back to his position at the edge of the hill.

"On the ground, Dr. Bailey. Kneeling. Hands behind your head." Nick still had the revolver trained on her. And he was still speaking Darija.

Exasperated, she shifted Lydia into a more comfortable position. "Really, Nick," she said in English. "How the hell am I supposed to do that?"

"Oh, thank God." A second or two later, Jeffrey climbed over the top of the hill to join Nick, who, true to character, blushed under his helmet. Though he didn't lower his revolver. Jeffrey was wearing long trousers and a white, civilian shirt. No uniform. He gestured to Nick and the soldiers to lower their weapons.

"The thought of having to communicate with you in that degraded patois until the alienists had sorted you was keeping me up at night." He ran a hand through his hair. "Though Basil seems finally to be coming to himself. He was correct about the tomb, at any rate."

"The tomb?"

Ignoring her, he stepped closer to them and touched the baby's nose with his fingertip. "Hullo Lydia. I've missed you, you know. While you were on the run with Mummy. Where's your giraffe?"

Lydia gave him a wide smile and held out her arms. He smiled back and took her from Marion, who didn't think to object or resist. Then she put her hands on both of his cheeks and babbled at him, excited.

"Of course, sweetheart," he said, turning away from Marion and carrying Lydia toward Nick. "You can tell me all about it very soon. But before that happens, Mr. Nick will take you to see a lovely desert camp. Full of date palms. And goats. And horses. No penguins, I'm afraid."

He hugged Lydia and handed her to Nick, who was now standing, his revolver holstered, at the edge of the hilltop. "Take her and the sword back to camp, Trelawney. Leave me Phillips and Staithes. We'll join you in an hour."

"Yes, sir." Nick took Lydia with the confidence of a man who had grown up in a large family. Then he began singing to her as he trudged back down the hill, followed by three of his soldiers. "The Grand Old Duke of York." Lydia didn't even whimper as she bounced along in his arms.

Jeffrey pulled his own revolver out of its holster and turned back to her. "Now you can get down, Marion. On your knees."

"Don't be an idiot." She walked toward the edge of the hill after Nick.

"Down, Marion." He lifted the revolver. "Now."

She stopped and looked at him, contemptuous. "You'll shoot me if I don't?"

"Shall we find out?"

Something about his expression made her think he might go through with it if she provoked him further. He looked angry. Exhaling in irritation, she knelt on the hot gravel and put her hands behind her head. "Lydia will want to eat soon," she said, looking up at him, annoyed. "And she'll need a new nappy."

"We've brought bottles."

"She won't take a bottle."

"She will if she's hungry enough," he said. "And Trelawney is eminently qualified to change a nappy."

She held his eyes, disdainful, her hands still behind her head. "Is that all? May I get up now?"

He let his gaze wander over her dress. Still fashionable, if damp and grubby. "You've been at a drinks reception?"

She didn't reply.

"You've been sheltering in that tomb, in that frock, the entire time?" He looked past her at the hole from which she'd emerged. "After you jettisoned the Blackburn Perth in Lake Sevan?" He paused. "The RAF are peeved, incidentally. They can't get the smell of psychoactive contraband out of the cabin."

"The tomb?" she repeated, looking behind her, confused.

"Nice choice," he commented. "That is, if you have been holidaying there. The last resting place of Tin Hinan, ancient Tuareg queen of the Sahara and Hoggar Mountains. Appropriate." He considered the mound. "We paid off the archaeologists to let us keep an eye on it for a week or two, once Basil finally remembered where he'd returned to the land of the living."

She blinked, confused. "I don't understand. The Hoggar Mountains?"

He watched her face for a few seconds, and then he began to smile, intrigued. "You don't know where you are, do you?"

"Of course I do," she retorted. "I—it's—" She thought for a moment. "North Africa."

The corner of his mouth went down. "Where in North Africa, Marion?"

"Morocco," she said.

"Wrong." He cocked his head. "But interesting." He considered for a moment longer. "Do you know how far you are from Morocco?"

"We weren't on the boat for more than half a day," she said. "Fifty miles?"

His eyebrows went up. "The—boat?"

"Yes," she said. "And I know I couldn't have slept for longer than a few hours."

"I suppose that explains why you've still got your clothing," he mused. "Basil claims to have swum."

"My knees hurt, Jeffrey." She dropped her hands from behind her head, not caring all that much whether he shot her. The heat was becoming unbearable.

"Where's her giraffe?" Jeffrey asked, allowing her to drop her hands, but cautioning her with the revolver to stay down. Uninterested in testing her story just yet.

"What?"

"Lydia's giraffe. Where is it?"

"I left it. We couldn't go back." She wiped a drop of sweat out of her eyes. "We'll buy another one."

"You remembered to bring Sindbad the Sailor's monstrosity of a sword with you, but you forgot her giraffe?" Angry.

"Jeffrey," she said, equally irritated. "If you'd been there, you would have seen—"

"If I'd been there?" he interrupted her. "If I'd been there? It was your decision, Marion, to drag my infant daughter along with you on her first kill." He stuffed his revolver into its holster, grabbed her arm, and lifted her roughly to her feet. "You might at least have remembered her giraffe. And found something more to cover her than a bloody tea towel."

"You don't understand—"

"On the contrary. What's not to understand? It's quite simple, isn't it? You sailed two thousand miles on a magical boat, uphill, from Morocco to the tomb of Tin Hinan. Overnight." His voice was snide now. "Lydia must have had a grand time."

"Two thousand miles?" She stared at him, not quite willing to comprehend his words. But then, in the face of his contempt, she rallied and shook off his hand. "It wasn't a magical boat. It was a perfectly normal, functional runabout. Teak." She paused, uncertain once again, as she considered what she was saying. "I think it was a Chris-Craft," she added weakly.

He nodded at the opening to the tomb. "You're saying there's a teak runabout down there. In Tin Hinan's grave. Nestled among the Roman coins and other burial detritus?"

"Yes." She glared at him.

"Staithes." He beckoned to one of the soldiers. "Would you please examine the enclosed part of the tomb? Try not to disturb the excavation. Let us know whether there's a boat in there, would you? Or any water?"

"Yes, sir."

The soldier approached the tomb's entrance and made his way into the first chamber. After that, he disappeared for a little over five minutes. Then he re-emerged. "There's no boat, sir. No water. Just the tomb."

Jeffrey turned to Marion, expressive. "Would you like to examine it yourself? To be certain—?"

"No." Then, thinking about the implications of his question, she shook her head vehemently. "Absolutely not."

She was surprised by the violent distress she felt at the thought of returning to the interior of the tomb. But as she watched him evaluating her response to his question, careful and professional, she tried to hide her disquiet. She couldn't let him sense how troubled she was by the memory of what was under the mound. "I must have made a mistake," she said to him, conciliatory. "You're right. The story is absurd. I—I'll try to remember what happened. Perhaps after I've had something to eat? Shall we go?"

Jeffrey examined her face more thoughtfully, his interest in her agitated reaction overt now. Then he spoke again: "before we leave, why don't we both go in one more time, simply to convince ourselves that—"

"No!"

She turned away from him to walk down the hill, but he took her arm and spun her back to face him. Holding her eyes, he laughed in disbelief. "You're terrified. I've never seen you like this."

"No," she said. "I'm not terrified. I'm tired. And hot. Dehydrated. I want to change out of this—this horrible—"

"Don't fault the dress, Marion. I believe it's a Madeleine Vionnet." He considered. "Beelzebub has good taste. And I can think of no better outfit for a bit of amateur archaeology—"

"No!" she shouted at him a fourth time. "Jeffrey, listen to me. Nothing will induce me to go in there again. *Nothing.*"

He watched her for two or three seconds. "Remarkable." Then, holding her arm, he walked with her down the hill, in the direction of the road and a waiting Austin 7, configured for use in the desert. "You realize, dear, that if the mood takes me, I can have you sealed up in there with the goblins for any length of time that pleases me. Should you choose not to be forthcoming."

"I have no reason not to be forthcoming."

He blinked in surprise and looked sidelong at her. "Curiouser and curiouser." He shook his head. "I never thought I'd hear those words coming out of that mouth. Whatever did they do to you, I wonder?"

She swallowed and kept walking, silent.

"Well, whatever it is, you can be proud of yourself." They'd reached the car, and he opened the door for her. She slid into the back seat, and he sat next to her. Staithes drove and Phillips sat in the front passenger seat. "You're damaged, obviously. But you've handled it infinitely better than Basil did, despite the public schoolboy training. You're at least recognizable. He's nothing more than an aggravating shell of his former self, with a taste for Cadbury's chocolate."

He put his hand over hers as the Austin sped away from the hill. "Though I would have expected nothing less from the most carefully groomed of my talent."

She withdrew her hand and wrapped her arms around her waist. Her eyes closed. Savoring the air, hot as it was, whipping through the windows of the car. She was ignoring everything he was saying, grateful simply to be out in the sunlight again.

*I*s he dead?"

"No."

"You failed?"

"I—I don't know."

She was, to her annoyance, still wearing the dress. But they had given her a glass of water and a plate of orange slices when the car had reached the collection of picturesque tents the soldiers had appropriated fifteen or sixteen miles outside the town of Abalessa.

Jeffrey was conducting their first interview in the largest of the tents, a cool expanse under dark, woven cloth. Brightly colored cushions along the edge of one flap. Clean matting underneath. A carved wooden table under the highest of the poles holding the structure aloft. There were two date palms outside the tent's entrance. And a goat. She had also noticed, a few hundred yards to their side as they'd entered, a paddock holding a sizeable herd of Barb horses.

"How can you not know? If he's alive, then you failed." He poured two glasses of mint tea and handed one to her.

She placed the glass of tea beside her on a small, cushioned cube. Then she shook her head, unable to explain her feeling that—though by any rational standards, she'd failed spectacularly—she'd done what she was meant to do.

Jeffrey sipped his tea and tried another tack. "Is he open to negotiation should we send an emissary to him?"

"Oh God, Jeffrey. Don't do that." She shuddered. "Stay away from him."

"Why?" Conversational. He wasn't pressing her.

She shook her head again. Then, trying in a childish way to redirect the discussion, she let her gaze wander over the comfortable, almost parodic, furnishings of the tent. "Why are you here rather than in the town?"

"Astonishing," he said after a few seconds had passed. "You are well and truly unnerved. Perhaps I ought to visit him myself to ask for professional advice. The most I've ever elicited from you

482

is a more or less heightened variation on your customary bad-tempered rage. Never this empty, aimless fear."

When she simply looked at him, he yielded. "Very well, darling. Let's chat, then. So," making himself comfortable on the cushion, "we had planned to use the city of Tamanrasset as our base. Modern. Well connected. Fifty miles away. And we had impeccable credentials as advisors to the French police on a matter of international automobile smuggling—having ourselves dealt recently with a similarly distressing criminal pattern in our Egyptian Protectorate."

He leaned against the cushions and put his hands behind his head. Relaxing further. "Sadly, we were less than six hours in the city, setting up our operation, when it became clear, first, that the French officials were in fact running the smuggling ring, and second, that they were no more convinced by our constabulary act than we were by their civilizing mission act. They were also eying our Austins in a worrisome manner.

"And so," he went on, looking up at the tent's ceiling, "we decamped. Under cover of darkness. We'd heard rumors of an outpost of the Kel Ahaggar confederation nearby—Berbers who remain less than enthusiastic about all that the French have offered them in the way of progress and prosperity. They weren't difficult to find." He dropped his eyes from the ceiling. "And here we are."

He reached for his tea and drank a few more swallows. "The clan's leadership isn't stupid. They know that we're as bad as the French. But they also have memories of their families being ripped apart thirty years ago during their resistance to French rule. Meaning that they're open to renegades fleeing the oppressive, automobile-snatching local government of Tamanrasset. They've given us this encampment—and our privacy—for as long as we might need it."

After pausing for a moment in thought, he continued. "I believe they were also softened by Trelawney's flawless, near-native fluency in Tahaggart."

She raised her eyebrows. "Nick speaks Tuareg?"

"You're surprised? He was your student, Marion." Then, as she frowned at the reminder: "when I asked him, he said that he'd spent six months in the early, disreputable part of his career picking up Berber dialects on the fringes of the desert. He enjoys the participles, apparently. I've cobbled together a bit myself since we've arrived." Complacent. Knowing how his freakish capacity to collect spoken languages irked her. "It's an interesting study. And the boy is also—"

"Ian?" She stood. "You've brought him here?"

"I wasn't going to leave him in London with servants. On his holiday. He fancied an adventure. Said you'd never taken him west of Egypt—"

"I want to see him." She moved toward the tent's entrance.

Jeffrey stood as well, blocking her way. "Sit down. We haven't finished talking."

"He'll want to see me."

"He doesn't know we found you."

"But—Lydia—"

"I don't think she's told him either." Impassive. "Sit."

She briefly considered attacking him, but before the thought had become coherent, she heard the unmistakable sound of Lydia's angry wailing outside the tent. Growing louder. Jeffrey wrinkled his forehead and turned toward the entrance, just as Nick, carrying the baby, pushed his way through it.

Lydia was wearing a skillfully pinned, clean nappy and a perfectly pressed, navy blue sailor dress. A tiny matching bow in her red hair. But she was pink-faced with rage, screaming, and pounding Nick's chest with her hands. Nick cast an apologetic look in Jeffrey's direction. "I'm sorry, sir, for the interruption." He managed, barely, to keep Lydia from squirming out of his grasp. "But she won't take a bottle."

"You've tried singing to her?"

"Yes, sir."

"What about the peas?"

"Private Buckley was obliged to change his uniform, sir." Uncomfortable. "They weren't to her taste."

Jeffrey sighed and stood back to let Nick hand the baby to Marion. Then, glancing back at Marion as she sat on a cushion and held Lydia to her chest, he said, "will twenty minutes be sufficient?"

She nodded as Lydia, overwrought, pulled open her dress of her own accord and began feeding. Then, leaning back against the pillows, she only half-noticed as Jeffrey and Nick, embarrassed, left her alone in the tent with the baby.

Lydia rapidly dropped into sleep once she'd finished eating, and Marion placed her on a cushion to her side before pouring herself another glass of tea and waiting for Jeffrey's return. When he did re-emerge from the blindingly bright exterior, he was carrying the sword she'd brought from Kur. He set it on the floor next to him and took up his position across the low table from her. He looked flushed from the brief time he'd spent in the blazing sun outside.

"We haven't any experts on hand to analyze this," he said, nodding at the sword and pushing his damp hair off his forehead, "but a cursory inspection suggests that it isn't your everyday Wootz steel blade." It was clear that he was no longer willing to indulge her squeamishness surrounding her time in Kur. He wanted to talk. And his voice was hard.

"I didn't examine it." Her eyes were averted. She couldn't look at it. "I suspect you're correct."

"He gave you this in exchange for the column?"

"He said the table wobbled." She frowned down at the collar of her dress, which was disarranged. Straightened it. "It wasn't really an exchange."

"Look at me." Impatient, irritated by her vague answers. When she raised her eyes to his, he continued, slow and emphatic: "did your target make you a gift of this sword?"

"Yes."

"What did he ask you to do with it?"

"Kill him."

"He *wanted* you to kill him?" Then, interested, he ran his fingertip over the sword's hilt. "With this?"

"Yes," she said. "He claimed that my ordinary—*ad hoc*—methods would be ineffective. Only the sword could destroy him."

Jeffrey lifted the sword in his hand and turned it in the dim light of the tent. Admiring. "Ah. King Solomon's Thunderbolt, then. Nothing better for killing dragons." He placed the sword back on the matting covering the floor. "Or slicing babies in half, should fighting dragons not be to one's taste."

"Slicing babies—?" She caught the reference just as she began to ask the question. But also just as she began to re-think her recent experiences. Growing excited, if ill, at the possibility that her assignment wasn't yet over.

"The famous judgement?" he said, mocking, not noticing her changed expression. "This very nice, very old bit of steel was its centerpiece, no? Thank goodness Lydia didn't pose him any juridical problems while you were both there. Though I have a feeling she would have given him a fight had he attempted it on her."

He turned his attention away from the sword. "Either way, you got the better end of the bargain. Less awkward than a broken piece of furniture. And it will make a lovely display for the Museum. Maugham will be more than pleased by your work."

She nodded and licked her dry lips. Wondering now whether she'd misinterpreted her entire assignment, misunderstood from the beginning—everything she'd been asked to do as well as all that she'd accomplished. Or had failed to accomplish. And she was yearning to find out. But she couldn't let him see her mind working. She held his eyes. "Fine, Jeffrey. Is that all? I'd like to talk with Ian now."

"No." He crossed his arms and watched her, attentive. Sensing her changed, charged aspect. "There must have been more to it. He's not the type to accept a refusal without a counterblow. A reprisal. What did he do when you declined to complete your task?"

"He threatened me." She lowered her eyes again.

"With what?"

"Immortality."

"Some threat." Then he smiled at her. "And yet, contrary mortal that you are, you didn't want it, did you? You told him precisely where he could put his everlasting life." His smile became a laugh. "I'll wager that Basil didn't do that. Or, at least not immediately. Took him a few decades to understand that he'd been hoodwinked."

She shivered in the hot tent and hugged her waist. Shook her head. He hadn't asked another question, and she felt no need to answer. To speak. She was also desperate to leave his company to determine whether her reappraisal of her superiors' orders was correct.

"Then what?"

"Then I left."

He watched her for a few more seconds, her eyes downcast, her breathing shallow. "That can't be all there was. What aren't you telling me?" His voice became bland. "Night is about to fall, dear. We can always go back to the tomb and—"

"After the threat," she said to stop him talking, "he offered me an assortment of—of very silly military technologies. Of the type that appeal to you people."

"Because your own organization is entirely immune to the attraction of technological preeminence."

She looked up and held his eyes, contemptuous and silent.

"Such as?" Impatient again.

"None of it made sense."

"Give me an example."

"Magneto-inductive communication."

He blinked. "I'm sorry?"

"Magneto-inductive communication."

"And what does that mean?" He had rested his cheek on his fist, weary.

"I have no idea." She leaned back against the cushions and closed her eyes. "I wasn't paying all that much attention."

"Why on earth not?" As pained as she was now.

"My assignment wasn't to collect information," she said, sullen. "My assignment was to remove him."

"And you're nothing if not monomaniacal." He paused. "But you didn't remove him, did you? What will you tell your organization?"

"That I failed." She opened her eyes and stared up at the ceiling. "I made a mistake."

He remained silent, thinking, for a number of seconds. Then he straightened and rolled back his shoulders. "So, our only course is to send someone in after you to clean up the mess you've made. It will be simple. Basil's still keen. Though it seems obvious that Tin Hinan's tomb is an exit rather than an entrance." He was thoughtful for another few seconds. "Where did you go in, Marion? Basil can't remember."

She shook her head. "I can't remember either."

"You're lying." He relaxed. "And not even troubling to hide it."

She turned to watch Lydia sleeping for nearly a minute. Then an idea occurred to her. A way to discover whether her reinterpretation of the project was correct. "Is Basil here?"

He nodded. "Yes. To the extent that he's ever anywhere."

"The entrance is near Sijilmasa," she said. "In the southern part of Morocco."

He examined her face, suspicious. "That was too easy. Are you lying?"

"No."

"No." He nodded. "You're not. Why the concession?"

"You'll never find it. It's at the head of an underground river. Invisible from the desert. They reveal themselves only when they know that you're coming. And they must be willing to let you enter." She paused. "And in any case, it can't be what I thought it was. The water would have flowed in the other direction. Toward the Atlantic rather than—up—here."

"The direction of the river's flow is the least fantastic part of the story you've been peddling, Marion." He stood. "And as for finding it, my own suspicion is that people haven't been trying hard enough. Certainly not from the air." He turned toward the tent's entrance and looked back at her. "The HP Hampden can drop a four-thousand-pound bomb. If there's anything at all to be exposed down there, that ought to do it for us."

As he pushed aside the tent flap to reveal orangish light—the sun setting—he continued: "I'm going now to radio a message to the chaps responsible for our informal airborne reconnaissance. They'll likely not have anything in place until tomorrow morning. But if I know them at all, once they've got their aircraft where they need to be, they'll provide us with more than satisfactory results. Perhaps even by the afternoon. I'll be certain to share them with you."

He kept his hand on the flap, watching for a few seconds as, distracted, she let her eyes rest on Lydia's sleeping face. Then, exasperated, he spoke further. "No despairing outburst, then? No beating of the breast over the fate of the innocents as our unfeeling imperial juggernaut crushes their fragile lives and culture?" He paused. "Nothing?"

"What?" She looked up at him. "No. Fine, Jeffrey. I understand." She turned back to Lydia.

"Fine," he echoed, muttering, as he passed through the tent's entrance. "And I'll be certain to get you the very best electro-convulsive therapy when we return to London. I wouldn't mind having a stern word with this St. George."

SHE was uncertain, once Jeffrey had left her alone with Lydia, whether she ought to seek out Basil or stay in place to allay suspicions about her compliance. Her decision, however, was made for her when less than five minutes after Jeffrey had disappeared, the flap covering the tent's entrance was pushed aside to reveal a figure in a blue Tuareg robe and *tagelmust*. Someone else had taken the initiative.

The figure briefly pulled down his face veil, exposing Basil's unremarkable features. Then he put a finger to his lips and pressed a coin-shaped medallion into her palm. She opened her hand and saw that it was the symbol of her organization—for use in emergencies, when an auxiliary lost in the field was unfamiliar with the local, predetermined identification cues. She handed the medallion back to him and nodded, waiting for him to speak.

Instead, he produced a second blue robe and *tagelmust* for her to wear over her dress, hair, and face. She stood, pulled the material over her head, and twisted on the *tagelmust*. After that, he pointed to the sword, which she hid under her robe, and gestured her out of the tent. As she left, she cast a quick guilt-ridden look at her sleeping daughter. She'd be gone for no more than a few hours. The sun was setting. If she was lucky, Lydia wouldn't even wake up. And if she did, then Jeffrey could try the peas a second time.

The only two soldiers they met as Basil led them toward the edge of the camp nodded politely and kept a respectful distance as they passed, which surprised Marion sufficiently to cause her to stumble. When they were a safe distance away, Basil explained: "they're here on forbearance. They know not to disturb any Tuareg who return to the tents."

He was speaking English—precise and fastidious, the sort affected by the type of boy who would have been bullied in a Victorian novel. But that he was speaking English at all was remarkable enough that she looked at him a second time. Useless. All she could see was a swath of indigo material moving along in the failing light.

A minute or two later, they reached the paddock of Barb horses, and Basil—without hesitation, with the look of a Tuareg noble—entered it and led out two mares that were already saddled. He brought one, chestnut and tossing its mane, toward her. "Can you ride? The cars can't manage the area we'll be crossing."

She approached the horse with a trepidation that it felt at once. Unimpressed, it snorted and twitched its tail. "Not very well, I'm afraid."

"Can you stay on?" Frustrated and bored. As though he'd expected her incompetence.

"Yes," she said, thinking she understood now why Khidr had tired of him after only two decades. She moved to the left side of the horse, passed Basil the sword, and tried to project calm. "I think so."

He helped her into the saddle and then handed the sword up to her. "You'll carry it, Dr. Bailey."

She set the sword precariously behind the pommel. It was odd to her that she should carry it given Basil's obviously superior riding skills. But he would explain it to her in time. Or not. He appeared to enjoy his secrets.

Once Basil had mounted his own grey mare, he led her at a trot away from the camp. When they were out of view of the soldiers, he stopped and pointed toward the red line of the setting sun. "It's an hour due west. They're expecting us. But we must hurry."

Without waiting for a response from her, he kicked his horse into a canter. Marion was startled, though grateful, when her own mare sped up without guidance from her. At least he'd given her an animal that knew how to follow.

The sun set quickly, but the reddish glow remained on the sand for the entire hour that they rode across the desert. It was only when she saw a campfire in the shelter of a cliff-like boulder that she realized that night had fallen. The stars were out by the time she and Basil had dismounted, secured their horses, and approached the fire. Which was abandoned. No one was waiting for them.

Basil, unsurprised by their absent reception, squatted and gazed into the flames. She squatted next to him and looked a question at him. It seemed for a moment that he wouldn't acknowledge her curiosity, but then he heaved a sigh and spoke. Still in his prim schoolboy English. "They'll arrive in less than an hour."

"Who?" She turned her attention to the fire.

"The people who've been waiting for that sword for far too many centuries."

She considered. "And they are?"

"Tin Hinan's line."

She nodded, watching the flames for a minute or two. Then, breaking the silence, she spoke again. "Mr. Kingsbury, would you tell me how you've come to be involved in this affair?"

"I don't see any reason why I ought to." The contempt was back in his voice. "There's no need for you to know."

"Perhaps," she said, "I want to know." And then, when he remained sulking and silent: "I have a feeling, Mr. Kingsbury, that there's a role I'm expected to play in whatever is about to happen. But it could be that I'll choose not to play that role. It could be that I'll take that sword and ride that horse all the way back to Abalessa without meeting 'Tin Hinan's line' at all. That would be embarrassing, Mr. Kingsbury, wouldn't it? Forgive me for suggesting that you couldn't easily stop me."

"Simply to make a point? You'd do that?" His voice was querulous.

"If you'd like."

"And you're the one they're all salivating over. *Both* sides. So useful." He snorted. "I find you average and predictable."

She stood. "Very well, Mr. Kingsbury—"

"Oh, sit down." Peevish. "You win."

She squatted. And waited.

"Our people," he began, "have been looking for a courier to move that sword from St. George to Tin Hinan for centuries now. Don't ask me why. Unlike you, I don't ask unnecessary questions to muddle up a perfectly straightforward operation." He stopped, as though expecting her to protest. When she didn't, he sighed heavily again and continued. "But a courier with the necessary qualifications was next to impossible to find."

"What were the qualifications?"

"St. George," he said, "would relinquish the sword only to someone who genuinely sought to kill him, but who then genuinely repented once he had the weapon in hand. It couldn't be an act. It couldn't be faked. It had to be deeply felt." Basil paused. "He's good at spotting deception."

She furrowed her brow, still staring into the fire. "That's odd. Why would he want that?"

Basil lifted a handful of sand and let it trickle through his fingers. "Who knows? Ask a Sufi." He wiped his hand on the blue material of his robe. "So they sent warrior after warrior. With orders to kill him. To believe in it. To want him dead. In the early days, their soldiers were more enamored of death and obedience than we tend to be. The hope was that one of them might, spontaneously, figure out the second half of the performance on site."

He sniggered unattractively. "Over and over again—I got this from St. George himself, during our endless, agonizing conversations. They'd arrive, declare themselves, kill him, and, well, it never finished happily for them. Through centuries, you understand, Dr. Bailey. Hundreds and hundreds of warriors, wading across that floor—into oblivion."

She swallowed, horrified by the thought of so many people absorbed into that dead, airless city. Prepared by Hakimah. And then gone. "But you escaped."

"Yes," he said. "They opted for a different strategy with me because, as you've so kindly noted, I'm no warrior."

"What was it?"

"They'd flipped me early on, during the War. In Mesopotamia." He looked down at his dusty fingernails. "A few weeks in close quarters with General Townshend was more than enough to convince me that I was due for a professional change. And I liked them. They were calm."

She nodded. Though she wouldn't have put it in the same words, her motivation for slipping into her role hadn't been all that different from his. "And then?"

"They had a job for me," he said. "But rather than sending me off to the cave with nothing more than orders to kill, they experimented with a modern approach. You know—briefing me properly, supplying detail, giving me an operational history, and explaining the paradox. Their idea was that I could persuade him beforehand that I wanted to kill him, receive the sword, and then *not* behave like some crazed berserker out for death or glory. Half a lie rather than a futile, deadly truth. I'm very intelligent, you see," he added, sounding both wistful and persecuted.

"You're not dead," she said, wanting to encourage him. "That's something."

He laughed, angry. "Right. So I made it there. A journey, I must admit, that was a tad more strenuous than I was expecting my first time out in the field for them to be. And then I approached him and told him that I'd come to kill him."

"And?"

"He laughed at me. He said that I must do better than that. That he wanted convincing." Basil paused. "But he also didn't refuse me entirely. He hinted that he could, under the proper circumstances, *be* convinced."

He went silent for a few further seconds. "I spent ages trying to prove my conviction to him. Ages. But he never produced the sword. He kept telling me that he might the next day. Or the next. On and on. Eventually, I knew I'd go mad if I stayed a minute longer. So—I swam. It was something of a surprise to me to discover when I surfaced that I'd wasted two decades there. It felt—less protracted."

She looked into his—young—face again, her respect growing. "I wouldn't have dared it. It's—extraordinary. What you've accomplished."

"But you weren't obliged to 'dare it,' were you, Dr. Bailey?" Scathing. Disliking her more for attempting to sympathize. "Because after centuries of failure, you were the perfect emissary. Both utterly dedicated and utterly unreliable."

She sensed a strange combination of envy and derision in his voice. Trying to placate him, she said, "they didn't brief me properly, though, Mr. Kingsbury. They didn't trust me. They trusted you."

"Yes. But that was the point, wasn't it? They needn't have trusted you. Instead, they sent you out in classic form—a proper medieval assassin. Knowing full well that you'd have a sniveling, modern change of heart at the crucial moment. When the pressure built. It's sordid, what you represent."

She wanted to disagree with him. To argue. But his dissection of her character was closer to her own feelings about her conflicted motivations than she liked to admit. Her inconstancy *was* sordid. And it was only growing more so as the years passed.

Rather than dwelling on it, she looked out over the moonlit desert and saw a group of three blue-robed Tuareg approaching on horseback. She turned back to Basil, grateful now that they wouldn't be continuing their conversation. "What do I do?"

"You retrieved the sword," he said. "You offer it to them. Old rules. There's no need to speak. Just stand up and present it."

She rose from her squatting position, took the sword by its hilt, and held it in front of her, the blade flat on both of her palms. The three figures slowed their horses to a walk and approached the campfire. Then, nodding, the first figure bent over, took the sword by the hilt, and turned the horse. After that, they galloped off into the darkness.

Once they'd disappeared, Basil stood, dusted down his blue robe, and pulled the *tagelmust* off his face and hair. Marion did the same, and they both remounted their horses. Without speaking, they cantered toward the camp. They'd been out for less than two hours.

When they were halfway back across the bleak expanse separating the tents from the boulder, they saw a contingent of Barb horses approaching them from the opposite direction. As they drew closer, they could see five British military uniforms. Marion frowned, uncertain as to what their response ought to be.

But once again, Basil took the initiative. Reining his horse to a halt, he spoke across the sand to Marion, who had, with more difficulty, also slowed her own mare. "I think it's best that I leave you now, Dr. Bailey. You'll understand, I'm sure."

With that, he slapped her horse into a not entirely controlled canter toward the soldiers, while he turned and rode off to the south. All that remained of him two minutes later was a white handkerchief that had blown from his neck to the sand as he was swallowed into the darkness. It was as though he'd never existed to begin with.

She had just regained some authority over the mare's movements when the soldiers—on the remainder of the Barb horses that Basil hadn't appropriated—reached her. Jeffrey, riding a large bay with annoying ease and confidence, came up on her right. Holding the reins of his own horse with his right hand, he reached over and twitched hers out of her control with his left. Surprised, she held the pommel to keep from tipping out of the saddle.

"Ride ahead," he said to the four soldiers who had accompanied him. "We'll return to camp later."

When the four horses were no longer visible, he turned to her, controlling both of their walking horses with expert assurance. The moon had turned the desert white. "You gave away King Solomon's sword."

"Yes." She was still holding the pommel, mistrusting her jittery mare about as much as the mare mistrusted her.

"Maugham," he said, ignoring her discomfort, "will want to speak with you about that when we return. I don't envy you the conversation."

"Maugham is your problem. Not mine." She wondered whether she could somehow snatch her reins back out of his hand. Unlikely. If she tried, she would find herself flat on her back on the desert sand.

"Do you think so, Marion?" His voice was smooth. "Not this time. He'll make it his business to be your problem. *King Solomon's sword*, for God's sake. You're in for it."

"Maugham," she started, "can—"

"Do you know?" he interrupted. "Once I'd completed my radio transmission to our Morocco contingent, I told our son that we'd searched the desert high and low and finally found you. He was overjoyed. So I brought him straight away to the tent to see his mother and his sister. Family tableau and all that."

"Oh God." She felt her chest clenching.

"You can imagine his—well, his complete lack of surprise when he discovered that you'd already left. Again."

"Oh." She tried to read his profile in the darkness. "What did you say to him?"

"What was I supposed to say? I told him that apparently you were back at work." He paused. "He said that it was all right, he understood, because you were bringing him a toy aeroplane." He looked over at her. "Do you have a toy aeroplane for him, dear?"

She shook her head in the darkness.

"Ah." He stopped their horses completely, leaned over, and spoke to her, his face close to hers. "The only reason, Marion, that I'm not abandoning you here, without a horse, to find your own bloody way back on foot, is that the demon girl you've produced refuses to take a bottle."

He moved away from her and then, without warning, kicked their horses into a wild, deliberately terrifying gallop toward the camp. She bit down hard on her lower lip to keep from crying out. She hated him.

London, England
September, 1936

Marion was sitting on a bench near the pond in Regent's Park, watching Ian warily circumvent a hostile swan on his way toward the water. He was returning to school in less than a week, and he was gratified to be spending the day with her before they began the dispiriting task of packing his trunk. He was also pleased that something had been done about the goose droppings. And that Lydia, sleeping in the pram, was unlikely to wake and demand his mother's attention.

The September air was warmer than normal, and Marion decided to remove her gloves. As she loosened the buttons under her left wrist, a woman wearing a navy-blue dress covered with tiny white polka dots sat on the other side of the bench. She and Marion exchanged an impersonal smile and then both turned their attention back to the pond. A minute or two later, the woman stood and walked off, leaving behind her on the bench a bright green leather satchel that didn't match her dress.

Marion knew better than to return the satchel to the woman who had left it. But still, she regarded it with a feeling somewhere between disbelief and resentment. Surely her people couldn't be encumbering her with another assignment already. She eyed the green leather with a feeling close to physical revulsion. But then, inwardly shrugging, she moved it onto her lap. She would simply refuse. They couldn't force her back into the field if she balked at going.

Glancing at Ian and Lydia to be certain that they were still, respectively, occupied and sleeping, she lifted the flap of the satchel and peered inside. Then, bemused, she pulled out a sheet of paper. Or, not paper. Papyrus. Not from her organization.

Although the papyrus was antique and crumbling to pieces, the writing on it was recent, in English, and expressed in a sprawling, nearly illegible hand:

Dear Marion,

I miss you. But perhaps someday we'll see one
another again. You left some things behind when
you departed. (Pls. see Encl.) I've also included a
few souvenirs. One is for you, one is for your girl,
and one is for your boy. I trust you'll manage to
sort out which is which. Don't let the girl open hers
until she's old enough to cause some damage. If you
don't know when that is, she certainly will. I hope
your return trip went smoothly.

Yours Sincerely,

George

p.s. Basil sends his regards. He still wants me dead!
We're having a grand time.

Baffled—and chilled—she set the papyrus to her side on the bench and reached further into the satchel. First, she pulled out Lydia's giraffe and wooden dolphin. Then, with some difficulty, she extracted a complicated model aeroplane made from a very thin, yet strong and flexible, sort of Bakelite. It was white and apparently meant to represent a vehicle from science fiction. "British Aircraft Corporation TSR-2" had been stenciled in tiny letters along the side. She wasn't certain that it was in keeping with Ian's collection, but she hoped at least he'd find it interesting.

After she'd left the toy aeroplane alongside the giraffe and the wooden dolphin, she reached into the bottom of the satchel and pulled out, first, an ancient copper bottle—smaller than those she'd seen, but menacing enough. And sealed. Shivering, she kept it in her lap. Then, forcing the satchel's opening wider, she used both hands to lift out a sheaf of papers wrapped in a thin sheet of old linen.

Intrigued, she began to unwrap the linen to identify the papers. Then, considering for a few seconds, she shook her head, re-secured the pages, and arranged them back in the bottom of the satchel. She didn't want to know. Perhaps she would never want to know. She thought wistfully of having sufficient strength of character to dispose of the volume altogether—while recognizing that doing so was beyond her meagre self-control.

But, she thought as she hooked Lydia's giraffe onto the pram and buried her wooden dolphin in the blankets next to her, she could certainly hide the papers away. In which case she might forget about them. Almost as effective as losing them. Almost.

She sighed, acknowledging her decrepit rationalization for what it was, and stopped trying to convince herself that she was acting responsibly. Instead, she focused on returning Ian's plane and Lydia's bottle to the satchel. The plane she'd present to Ian later that afternoon. The bottle—well, Lydia would know when she was ready for it.

She stood, hoisted the satchel's strap over her shoulder, and maneuvered Lydia's pram onto the path. Then, making eye-contact with Ian, she began to walk back toward the house. Ian ran across the grass and fell into step beside her, speciously docile and accommodating.

When they'd returned to the house and put Lydia to bed, Marion made her way to Jeffrey's study. Pausing outside the closed door, she considered for a moment, and then knocked.

"Yes?" Irritated.

She pushed open the door and found him lying on the sofa again, nearing the end of *Eyeless in Gaza*. He sat up when he saw her and put the book on the coffee table. "Is it a parody, do you think?" He looked, aggrieved, at the book. "It must be a parody. Mustn't it?"

"I don't know. I haven't read it." She sat in the chair opposite him. "Jeffrey, did Maugham's people identify the residue in the copper bottle Basil brought back with him?"

He shook his head. "They've got no idea. Passed it along to Section D. Though God knows what the alchemists want with it."

"Oh." Marion stood. "Thank you."

Jeffrey reclined back on the sofa and reached for the book. As he did so, he collected himself and stopped her. "Oh, Marion?"

"Yes?"

"Do you by any chance know what's become of the Jack Pritchard chair I had in the drawing room? From Isokon?"

"No." She frowned. "It's not there?"

He opened the book and focused on the page in front of him. "Vanished completely. Mrs. Bowen says it's as though some whirlwind swept it away." He glanced up at her and then back down at the book. "Bothersome. I liked that chair."

France, 1936

London, England
Hereford, Wales (Almost)
November, 1936

I am by birth a Lotharingian," he said, bending over and gazing into the rheumy eyes of a pale, thin boy kneeling against the bars of a wheeled metal cot.

Then, making a note on a clipboard he carried with him, he straightened, adjusted his white lab coat over his skeletal frame, and walked further along the narrow balcony toward the next cot. "My father was a direct descendant of the court physician to King Lothar II. Heir to a thousand-year-old medical practice in Aachen." He flicked his eyes toward Marion. "Aix-la-Chapelle, you'd call it." Something between a French and a German accent. Very faint.

He raised his pointed chin and gazed out over the rooftops of Bloomsbury, wreathed in damp fog. "Every generation of my mother's family presented ladies to Remiremont Abbey in the Vosges Mountains. For *more* than a thousand years."

Approaching a flushed, blonde girl lying prone in her cot, her eyes closed, he felt her throat with fingertips that looked colder than the glacial air, nodded to himself, and then continued speaking. "It is important, Dr. Bailey, for you to remember these things."

Marion nodded, bewildered. She was following on the heels of the doctor—whose name she still hadn't learned—carrying Lydia, now ten months old, and trying not to betray her astonishment that they were wandering the exterior balconies of the upper floors of Great Ormond Street Hospital on a bitingly cold November afternoon. Rather than speaking together in his office. The young patients, she had heard the nurses muttering to themselves, benefited from the fresh air.

Looking down into Lydia's face as she pressed a hand against the slimy brick wall to steady herself against a dirty gust whipped up from the street, she considered their point. The cold had gone quite a long way toward eliminating the baby's croup—Marion's excuse for her visit to the hospital. Lydia's breathing was almost normal. No wheezing at all.

"False croup," the doctor said, disconcertingly telepathic.

"I'm sorry?" Marion was standing beside him now that he'd stopped moving, gazing out over a city view that was almost completely obscured by the white mist.

He nodded at Lydia. "If the barking cough returns, take her for a walk outside in the cold. Throat exposed. It will pass in a day or two."

Marion glanced down at Lydia, frowned, and then returned her attention to the doctor. "Thank you," she offered. "But—was there anything else?"

Marion wasn't certain how persistent she ought to be. Or forthcoming. After receiving orders the previous afternoon directing her to Great Ormond Street Hospital, she had expected a quick, coded exchange with, perhaps, a cleaner. Or even a simple drop and retrieval.

Instead, she had now spent over an hour trailing this icy, cadaverous physician on his rounds, observing sickly children, while he told her in dizzying and irrelevant detail about his family's Frankish lineage. She was beginning to fear she'd misunderstood her brief. Or that she'd inadvertently crossed the wrong courier upon entering the building.

"Yes," he said, his expressionless pale blue eyes holding her own. "There is something else."

Marion nodded again, waiting for him to continue. Forcing herself not to fidget. Eventually, maintaining what was now physically uncomfortable eye contact, he did: "as Lothar's court physician, my father's ancestor had ample opportunity to observe the King's—behaviors. He observed, for example, that the King's family"—snide curve of a thin lip—"*spread*, quickly, throughout Lotharingia. From Aachen to Marseille. And beyond."

"And?" Marion shifted Lydia to her other hip. She was becoming impatient. And the balcony was frigid. The children were shivering in their wheeled cots.

"You know about the explosion in Marseille this past Monday? The sixteenth?" he asked in turn. "Forty people killed at the gunpowder factory?"

"I read about it in the newspaper." Refusing to be daunted by his veering conversation.

"It woke the family," he said, abruptly turning away from the opaque view and returning to the interior of the ward. The nurses, taking their cue from him, began wheeling the children inside as well.

"I don't understand." Marion was striding to keep up with him as he passed through the ward and into the corridor. When he stopped and turned to face her again, she nearly ran into him.

"You can put them back to sleep." If his eyes were capable of expressing sentiment, they would have shown tired skepticism. A touch of contempt. "I'm to give you this." He reached into the pocket of his lab coat, found a sealed brown envelope, five inches square, and handed it to her.

She stuffed the envelope into the pocket of her damp trench coat and shifted Lydia again. "Is that all?"

"You must consult a text from the Baquba collection," he continued tonelessly. "Ibn Wahshiyya bound together with Ibn Janah. Hidden in a sixteenth-century Ottoman tax register for the province of Raqqa."

"Oh." She looked down at her feet. Unhappy. "They can't access it themselves?"

"No." Unmoved. "Request the tax register. The rest of the material is well-concealed. No risk."

She nodded. "I understand. Thank you."

As she turned toward the stairway, he stopped her. "You'd also do well to investigate Hereford."

"Hereford?" She blinked at him. "Why?"

He drew a rattling breath, his eyes clouding. "Extensive family. King Lothar II's."

She watched as he turned to leave her, staggering against the wall. "Wait." She held Lydia closer to her chest, feeling suddenly more concerned than annoyed by his demeanor. "Are you all right?"

He looked back at her, his lips twisted in another thin smile. "No."

Then, supporting himself against the greenish bricks, he dragged his feet toward the dim end of the corridor. Leaving behind a smell, oddly, of fennel.

*W*HEN Marion returned to Chester Terrace, she left Lydia sleeping in the nursery and locked herself in her bedroom to examine the contents of the envelope. It was late afternoon and the light was fading, but Jeffrey hadn't yet returned from the office. Ian was away at school. She had at least a half hour to ruminate over her conversation at the hospital. After that, she'd approach Jeffrey about the volume from the Baquba collection—a task she was dreading.

Closing the heavy curtains against the twilit park, she sat at her functional desk, switched on the lamp, and examined the envelope in the circle of yellow light. It looked ordinary—suspiciously so. No markings or writing. A bulge at the center. Sealed with several unnecessary layers of adhesive cellophane tape. She opened a drawer in the desk, located a letter opener, and went to work on the thick tape.

Thirty seconds later, she concluded that the letter opener was useless. She set it aside and, deliberate and patient, picked at the layers of tape with her fingernails until she was able to pry apart the envelope's seal. Once it was open, she left it on the desktop, stood, and walked to the toilet to wash her hands. Her fingers were covered with adhesive and tiny bits of cellophane, which bothered her more than she liked to admit to herself.

After scrubbing the sticky residue from her hands, she glanced briefly at her reflection in the mirror—pale and restless—before returning to the desk. She sat, took a breath, and reached into the open envelope. Then she removed its contents and inspected them, before closing her eyes, swallowing, and leaning back in her chair, perturbed.

In the envelope, wrapped in tissue paper, had been a transparent disk of quartz, four and a half inches in diameter, engraved with episodes from the story of Susanna in the Book of Daniel. The "Susanna Crystal." One of the better guarded treasures of the British Museum.

If her people had stolen it, she was going to have even more difficulty than usual persuading Jeffrey to grant her access to the volume she wanted. He'd know that the Raqqa tax register was not what it appeared to be. And this project, she mused as she opened her eyes, was already difficult in all the wrong ways.

Chiding herself for her disloyalty to her organization, she straightened, held the crystal closer to the light, and peered at it, uncertain. The Susanna Crystal had been carved in the mid-ninth century for King Lothar II—as attested by an inscription in Latin along its edge. The crystal in her hands, although decorated with identical images, was engraved in Arabic. No Latin. It wasn't from the Museum.

Marion ran her fingertip over the letters, which were ornate and un-vowelled. Something about Lothar, "al-Awtari," "having made me"—just as in the Latin inscription. And then underneath, in more prominent letters, the name, "Susanna"—which was unusual, in that as far as she knew there was no explicit textual mention of Susanna or her story on the British Museum's version of the crystal.

"As far as she knew." Peeved again, she set the crystal on its envelope, put her elbows on the desktop, and held her fingertips against her temples. The Arabic inscription had mollified her, but she was still feeling out of her depth. The Franks and Carolingians—Lothar's family—were about as far removed from her area of expertise as it was possible for a geographical or chronological field to be. It was bizarre that her superiors had passed this along to her. And if they believed that she could do anything with what the doctor—proud Lotharingian that he was—had given her, they were sorely mistaken.

She pushed back her chair, stood, and slipped the crystal into her pocket. They must want her for only one purpose: to obtain the tax register for them. An unpleasant assignment, but not overly complex. She could finish it this evening, now that Jeffrey was—if the stir downstairs was any indication—returning to the house. After she'd retrieved the volume, she'd deliver it and the crystal to a courier who would forward them to a proper specialist.

As the sound of the front door closing drifted up the stairs to the bedroom, she wandered over to the windows, twitched back a curtain, and looked out over the park. Night had fallen, and she saw little more than the light of the desk lamp reflected, an unsettling jagged blur, just above her head. After waiting two or three minutes for him to reach his study, she let the curtain fall into place and, her fingers curled around the crystal in her pocket, left the room.

She descended to the first floor, paused for a split second outside the closed door to his study, and then knocked. She heard him walking across the room, before, a moment later, the door opened. When he saw her, he smiled and kissed her cheek. His hair was brushed back, and he still smelled of the autumn air on the street.

"Darling." He stood to the side. "Would you like a drink? Long day."

She nodded and crossed to the sofa, her hand still in her pocket. When she sat, he busied himself pouring scotch into two tumblers, returned to hand one to her, put his own on the coffee table, and sat in the armchair across from her. Then he unbuttoned his jacket and leaned back, still smiling at her. "And you? You've kept busy?"

She sipped her drink. "I took Lydia to the doctor. To see about her cough."

"Yes?"

"It should pass in a day or two." She paused. "Not diphtheria. I was worried."

"A relief." He sipped his own scotch and then held it on the arm of his chair. Waiting.

"Jeffrey, I need a volume from the Baquba collection." She took another quick swallow.

He leaned forward, opened a box on the coffee table, and selected a cigarette. "And what do we receive in return?"

"You can watch it travel," she said. "It's routine. But my superiors want the information. They're willing to let you follow it."

"Which volume?" He lit his cigarette and exhaled smoke at the ceiling.

"It's a sixteenth-century Ottoman tax register from Raqqa province," she said. "There are a number of registers in the library. Only one from Raqqa. If you've catalogued them, it will be easy to find."

He lifted his glass of scotch with the same hand that was holding the cigarette and observed the liquid. Then he set the glass on the table again without drinking. "Something's about to happen in Northern Iraq? Or Southeastern Anatolia? Urfa?"

"No," she said, irritated. "I've told you. It's a routine check. They want the background information. Send someone to watch—you'll see."

He sighed. "Very well. I'll dispatch a few of my Turkey people. They've become complacent anyway. It will do them good to concentrate for a while on the complete absence of activity in Urfa."

She frowned, confused. Then, rallying, she pressed him: "so—you'll bring me the volume, then?"

"What's really happening?"

Frustrated, she dropped her eyes to the glass in her lap before taking a breath and looking up at him. "I don't know exactly. But Maugham will find it interesting. And you have nothing to lose. It's a tax register. One of close to fifty in the collection. He's always saying he wants to watch my people operate. Here's his chance. They're offering an exchange."

He laughed. "Maugham wants nothing to do with you or your people at the moment. He's still resentful about King Solomon's sword." He took a drag of his cigarette. "As far as he's concerned,

495

you are out of commission. For a good long while. In fact, if he had his way, you'd be stashed in Chelsea as we speak. Which, now that Lydia's weaned, might do you some good—"

"Oh, stop it," she interrupted. "I understand. You're uninterested. I'll tell them—"

"This isn't about Hereford by any chance, is it?" He watched her reaction through the cigarette smoke.

"Hereford? How—? She stopped herself.

"Ah. It is about Hereford, then."

"What's happened in Hereford?" Trying to read his expression. Baffled.

"It's something of a relief, to be honest." He inhaled more smoke. Exhaled. "Liberated me from being sent to observe this Bakr Sidqi nonsense in Iraq. *Deus ex machina.* Though it's a shame about the schoolchildren."

"The schoolchildren?" She blinked, still confused. And then repeated: "what's happened in Hereford?"

He set his cigarette in an ashtray on the coffee table and stood. "I'll show you." Walked to his desk, retrieved his briefcase, and opened it. "If I'm lucky, what you see might shock you sufficiently to stop you trying to persuade me that your organization is now concerning itself with how many sheep the peasants of the northern Euphrates were assessed by the Ottoman government in the year 1558."

He glanced up at her as he removed two blank file folders and then a square of textile wrapped in thin paper. "I admit it freely, Marion. I haven't the energy for that conversation after the day I've had."

She watched, suspicious, as he brought the two folders and the square of cloth over to the coffee table. Then, as he sat, arranged all three between them, and took up his cigarette again, she shook her head, collecting herself. She didn't want to know about Hereford. At least, not yet.

But before she could formulate her thought, he held up his hand, preempting her. "Wait. You'll find this interesting. I give you my word."

She frowned at him, still on the verge of speech. And then, conceding, she remained silent.

"Thank you, darling." He leaned back and tapped his finger a few times on the arm of his chair. After that, as though coming to a decision, he began: "apparently, the local children in the area surrounding Hereford Cathedral play a game this time of year. November. Ghosts. 'Had rather thou shouldst painfully repent, than by my threat'nings rest still innocent.' That sort of thing."

"I don't think that poem lends itself to a children's game, Jeffrey."

"Doesn't it? Depends on one's childhood, I suppose." He took a drag from his cigarette, thoughtful, and continued: "whatever the case, they hide, play dead, stalk one another, presumably trespass into the disused parts of the building—though they've all denied doing anything of the sort now that they're being questioned by authoritative men wearing not quite civilian attire. That is," he amended, "those who remain to be questioned are denying any trespass."

"Who—remain?"

"Hmm." He observed the burning tip of his cigarette. "It seems that the game has taken on a few unpleasantly authentic twists over the past week or so." He raised his eyes to hers. "The apparition, for example, has been—less retiring—than it ordinarily is. Or has been in previous years. Sightings all over the place—both in the Cathedral and, on occasion, in the town itself. In bedrooms. By adults as well as children. And the children who've crossed it and gone missing—one, two, and now three—have remained missing. No contrite returns. No stumbling out of the wood the next morning, disheveled but healthy, with talk of the little people and their suspiciously Roman rites and festivals."

"Oh." She lowered her eyes and sipped her drink. Didn't know what else to say.

"The constabulary did investigate the disappearances at the beginning." He inhaled and blew smoke at the ceiling. "Without a great deal of enthusiasm, it's true. This sort of thing happens in Wales, after all."

"What?" She looked up at his complacent, amused expression. "How can you possibly—"

"Ah." He almost smiled. "I'd forgotten. It also happens up in your direction."

"Pig." She finished off her scotch and placed the empty glass on the table. "And Hereford isn't even—"

"Close enough." He was smiling overtly now.

"Why are you telling me this?"

"Yes." He took a sip from his own, nearly untouched glass and set it next to hers. "I'd almost forgotten. Thank you. So, a fourth child, a boy, was following the most recent victim of the vanishings. His older sister, I believe it was."

"Oh." She rubbed her cheek with her hand. "Oh Jeffrey, this is horrible—"

"The boy was brave," he spoke over her. "Because when his sister encountered the ghost, he first tried, he says, to rescue her—to 'pull her out' were his exact words. But he won't elaborate on what that means. When he couldn't extricate his sister, he says he tried to 'rip to pieces' the ghost itself."

He paused, choosing his next words carefully. "The boy's story coincides well with the evidence they found in the Cathedral. He himself was unconscious, lying on the floor at the north end of the nave. And surrounding him were torn pieces of very old cloth and very old paper. The boy is still alive, but gravely ill, and no one can identify his affliction."

Leaning forward, he unwrapped the piece of textile and then opened both folders. "They did what they could to put the cloth and the paper together into a coherent picture. It wasn't much, but it was enough to convince them to contact the office. For advice, if nothing else."

He stopped again, uncertain. Then, taking another drag of his cigarette, he continued. "Ordinarily, of course, the disappearance of a few disobedient, if imaginative, children—even accompanied by these unusual scraps of historical detritus—would have been insufficient to draw our attention." He crushed out the cigarette in an ashtray. "But there's a further chapter to the story."

"Yes?"

"The boy's illness," he said, his voice now bland, "looks remarkably like a reaction to an excruciatingly restricted concoction that the Porton Down alchemists have been in the process of brewing in Salisbury. In preparation for the War, you know."

"Porton Down?" She'd heard the reference before, but she couldn't place it. Except that it left her feeling uneasy.

"Yes." He lit another cigarette. "Chemical Defense Experimental Station. Not my field, obviously. And Salisbury is a hundred miles away. But the combination of the boy's symptoms and these papers," nodding at the folders on the table, "left them with little choice but to involve Maugham. And Maugham, as you'd expect, is charmed by the situation. He was still chuckling about it when I left him this evening. Rare opportunity to make inroads into War Office territory."

She stared at him for three silent seconds as understanding dawned. Then, disgusted, she stood and stalked to the other end of the room, wrapped her arms around her waist, and held his eyes. "You're abhorrent. All of you. Beyond despicable. You're—"

"Marion," he said. "I haven't finished—"

"You needn't finish," she spat back at him. "You've told me enough. You're saying that those monsters you have developing the gas and poison they claim is necessary to—"

"Marion—"

"They've been experimenting on—"

"They haven't been experimenting on anyone." Annoyed now.

"They haven't?" she shot at him. "Well, that's even better. So they've accidentally let it loose then, have they? Brilliant. And now there's a child dying, and they're so wrapped up in their clandestine and restricted and *satisfying* research that they're claiming—how did you put it?—that no one can 'identify his affliction?' So he'll die? Casualty of war?" She rammed her fists into her pockets. "And Maugham is charmed. Rubbing his hands over the potential expansion of his bureaucratic domain. *And you think that I'd—*"

"Marion." He stood, set his cigarette carefully in the ashtray, and walked toward her. "If you don't stop talking at once, I will deliver you to Chelsea, and you will hear the rest of this story from Maugham and Thacker. Tonight. Understood?"

"Fuck you." She wrapped her fingers around the crystal in her pocket and glowered up at him.

"I said that the researchers at Porton Down were in the *process* of developing the toxin." He waited, watching her face, for her to comprehend his meaning. "They haven't completed it yet. And from what they've admitted to Maugham—and, believe me, he can spot a deception, though he doesn't trust them any more than you do—they're nowhere near a satisfactory recipe."

"I don't understand."

"I think you do. And I think you can also imagine their consternation when this boy turned up with all of the symptoms of an illness they hadn't even perfected yet."

"One of their researchers was a double," she said. "It's the only explanation. They were further along than they'd realized. Someone smuggled it out of the laboratory."

He shook his head. "That was their first thought as well. But their material—which is very, very carefully stored—is all accounted for. As are their colleagues. And," he gestured her back toward the table, "there's also the evidence from the Cathedral. The cloth. The papers. They don't add up to a leak from the laboratory."

She threw him a cold look and returned to the sofa. Sat. Gazed, uninterested, at the items on the coffee table.

"Let me begin with the papers," he said, sitting across from her and turning the open folders to face her. "Or vellum, to be more accurate. Do you recognize them?"

On each side of the folders, close to a hundred small scraps of vellum had been painstakingly reassembled into four pages of medieval Arabic script in faded red ink. She chewed her bottom lip, trying to get a feel for the scribe's handwriting. Then, slowly, she began reading.

Five minutes later, she looked up at Jeffrey, who was patiently smoking his cigarette, watching her. "It's an account of the Frankish Queen Bertha's embassy to the Caliph al-Muktafi," she said. "I've read something like it before. Early tenth-century, isn't it?"

"The year 906," he said. "Do you notice anything interesting about it?"

She reconsidered the pages and then shook her head. "Not really. I remember the story. She sent gifts and a letter to the Caliph, offering an alliance. The Caliph's physician, Ishaq ibn Hunayn translated the letter for him. The Caliph himself was amused by the gifts but valued her proposal at what it was worth—which was not very much. He wrote a polite, noncommittal response. But the gifts and the exchange were unusual enough to enter three or four historical accounts. The classical historians found her ambition—refreshing—I think. The descriptions are a trifle patronizing."

"They did emphasize the exotic qualities of the gifts, though," he replied. "Just as the scraps we have here do. Fabulous hunting dogs. Hunting birds. Unusual slaves. Silk tents. A variety of rare textiles—including a robe made of byssus, or sea silk. A few unexpected surgical instruments—'beads' for extracting spearheads without pain and the like. Along with the usual—gold, silver, gemstones, etc."

"Yes," she said. "But this account of the gifts is no different from the others, is it? Same list. It's odd that it turned up in Hereford Cathedral, but manuscript pages of this sort did travel. It isn't unheard of."

"Re-read the copy of the letter she's supposed to have enclosed," he said. "In most versions of the exchange, remember, she writes openly at first, describing her offer, her background, and her gifts. But then she also encloses a secret message to be delivered privately to the Caliph by her envoy, an Arabic speaking eunuch."

He crushed out his cigarette. "The contents of that second message haven't made it into the historical accounts. No one knows what the private correspondence contained. Only, to quote most of the extant versions, that 'the matter must remain secret among ourselves. I wish you, myself, and this eunuch alone to be aware of it.'" He leaned back in his chair. "But there's an anomaly in this version of the private exchange. Read it again."

Obedient, she stared back down at the scraps arranged in the file folder. Then she found the description of Bertha's letter and concentrated on the language. "Oh." She lifted her eyes to his after a few minutes. "Yes. Interesting. 'The matter must remain secret among ourselves. I wish you, myself, and—and your Nabatean magician—?'" She paused, thought for a second or two, and then nodded to herself. "Yes. 'And your Nabatean magician alone to be aware of it.'" She sat back as well. "I think your scribe is having a joke."

"Given the circumstances under which we found those pages," he said, "it's rather a bleak joke." And then, when she remained quiet: "the cloth they collected from under the boy's unconscious body was byssus. Sea silk. Beautifully worked. And well over a thousand years old."

She nodded again, uncertain what he was suggesting. Unwilling to offer further interpretation. Then, intrigued, she turned her attention to the thin, gold, woven cloth resting on the white tissue paper. Tentatively, she ran her fingertips over it before, startled, she tensed, clenched her fist, and stiffened. She'd felt something like an electric shock shoot up through her elbow. And now, rubbing her fingertips together, she became uncomfortably aware again of the adhesive from the envelop. Gelatinous. Almost painful. She'd clearly not removed all of it from her hands.

"Marion." Concerned. "Are you all right? They assured us it was inert—"

"Inert?" She widened her eyes.

"Yes," he said. "There's some sort of chemical woven into the fabric. Unidentifiable. They've been testing their own sample in the laboratory. But we've all handled it without adverse effect. And they insisted—" He stopped speaking. And then, troubled, he walked around the coffee table, sat next to her on the sofa, and took her hand, chafing her fingers. "You don't feel ill?"

She gazed down at her hand in his. Shook her head. "No. I'm fine." She looked up at him. "It was a spark. The fabric must be dry. Or the air. I would already be feeling faint if it were—" She stopped. "I'm fine."

He nodded slowly, still holding her hand. "I'd very much like to know who this Nabatean magician was. And how Bertha, Queen of the Franks, got to know about him. And, of course, what she wrote in that secret letter to the Caliph." He paused. "You know her story? Her family?"

Startled by the question, and uncertain she wanted the conversation to drift too near the doctor from Great Ormond Street and his Lotharingian national pride, she shook her head. Silent. He watched her face for a few seconds and then cocked his own head, intrigued. "You do know. But you're lying about it. I can feel your pulse pounding. How odd."

She tried to pull back her hand, but, playful, he held it fast. "Why," he said, his fingertips now deliberately seeking out the underside of her wrist, "would you lie about something so trivial? I wasn't expecting this, Marion."

"I'm not lying." She forced herself to maintain eye contact with him.

"Very well." He smiled, still not relinquishing her wrist. "I'll give you a quick summary of her life and exploits, then. Heavens," laughing quietly, "that provoked a response, didn't it?"

She let her gaze fall to the table. Meeting his eye was useless. Remained silent.

"Queen Bertha," he began, his fingertips maintaining their pressure against her pulse, "was the illegitimate daughter of King Lothar II and his concubine—or, some say, common law wife—Waldrada. In the middle of the ninth century, the year 855, Lothar had been pressured by his family into a politically useful marriage with his formal wife, Theutberga, the daughter of the Count of Turin. He remained faithful, however, to Waldrada both during and after this marriage."

He repositioned his fingers on her wrist. "So besotted was he by Waldrada that he attempted to escape his formal marriage by accusing Theutberga not only of infertility—she produced no children—but also of incest. The Church was unimpressed by his conduct. The Pope cleared Theutberga of all wrongdoing and the local clergy initiated its own campaign against Waldrada—accusing her of witchcraft, as evidenced by first, Theutberga's sterility, and second, Lothar's less than moderate attraction to her. But Waldrada remained undefeated. Not only did she reign as *de facto* queen and bear him four children, including Bertha, but she retired with honor to Remiremont Abbey upon her—"

He paused, interested. "Remiremont Abbey?" He waited for a few seconds and then nodded, satisfied. "Yes, that elicited something as well. Care to respond, Marion?"

"Let go of my hand," she muttered.

"I haven't finished yet. Though I will remember this technique in the future. Fascinating results." He resumed. "So Waldrada entered Remiremont Abbey, never the most pious of convents. Known for its frightening and—perhaps 'potent' is the best word—canonesses. Over the centuries."

He considered. "But Theutberga did have a smaller, pyrrhic triumph of her own. When Lothar was persuaded by the Church to return to his proper wife, he commissioned a remarkable gem, the Susanna Crystal—" He raised his eyebrows, laughing in earnest now. "Good God, Marion. What have you done? Stolen it?" He shook his head. "No. I would have heard about something that extreme—"

She wrenched her hand out of his and wrapped her arms around her waist. "You're an idiot."

He leaned back, smiling at her sitting still and upright beside him. "At any rate, the Susanna Crystal was, according to most accounts, an apology. Susanna, like Theutberga, falsely accused of inappropriate sexual conduct—though obviously not incest—and then proved innocent by a king concerned above all with justice. All nicely depicted in detailed and artistic engravings."

"I can't see what this has to do with Bertha's embassy to the Caliph," she said, still irritated.

"I'll explain, then." Smug. "I think the Church wasn't half wrong about Waldrada—"

She laughed. "You mean that she was a witch? You would believe that sort of thing a thousand years later, wouldn't you? It's in your blood."

"Only when presented with irrefutable evidence, darling." He was still smiling. "I think she was—well educated. In certain ways. Seductively so, presumably, given Lothar's behavior. Surely you of all people know what that sort of knowledge does to a man—"

"Don't be—"

"And who can guess what she taught her daughter, Bertha? Lotharingia was one of the most important early centers for the transmission of Arabic scholarship into Europe. And by the tenth century, it was a cauldron of sorts, seething with European, African, and Asian scientific theories. An infertility recipe would have been child's play for a student of those—scholarly works." He was thoughtful for a moment longer. "But presumably Bertha offered the Caliph something a bit more significant than contraceptive spells."

He stood and gathered up the folders and the textile. "I'm curious to know why Bertha sent the surgical instruments along with her eunuch. To extract spearheads without pain and the like. As well as the byssus robe." Walking toward his open briefcase on the desk, he glanced back at Marion, still sitting rigid on the sofa. "And, given your reaction to my reference to the Susanna Crystal, I may look more carefully into its story as well. I don't believe for a moment that it was a peace offering by a repentant husband to his innocent and exonerated wife. It's obvious even a thousand years later that Lothar despised Theutberga—"

"I'm going to dress for dinner." She stood and walked toward the door.

"What about the Raqqa tax register?" He was arranging the material in his briefcase, not looking at her.

She stopped and turned to him. "You'll bring it to me?"

He closed his briefcase and faced her. "You're still saying it has nothing to do with Hereford?"

"Look at it yourself," she said stubbornly. "It's a tax register."

"I'd rather feel your pulse while you look at it. Less work."

"Are you going to bring it to me?"

"I'll discuss it with Maugham," he said finally. "But even if he agrees, you'll be waiting for at least a week until our own people vet it. You're plainly lying about its value. Our tedious task will be to determine why."

She nodded once, shortly. "Fine. I understand."

Then, before he could say more, she turned, shoved her hands into her pockets, her fingers curled around the crystal, and left the room.

LATE in the evening, three days later, Jeffrey appeared at her bedroom door with the volume. Sooner than she was expecting.

"It's a tax register," he said, annoyed. "From Raqqa Province. The years 1564 to 1565."

Marion, who had just emerged from the bath and was wearing a dressing gown and a towel over her hair, carefully tightened and knotted her belt. Then she looked up at him. "If you'll leave it on my desk, I'll skim it before I make my drop."

She had no intention of letting the volume out of her possession now, but he needn't know that. In fact, after having heard Jeffrey's account of the incidents in Hereford Cathedral, she understood that her organization had tapped her to examine the register with good reason. Although King Lothar and his family were far from her area of expertise, Bertha's embassy to the Caliph brought them quite a bit closer. And the sixteenth-century Ottoman tax register—along with whatever it concealed—was very much the sort of document she'd become used to decoding. She was confident that she could at least make a start on resolving whatever crisis was brewing. Put the family back to sleep, as the doctor had termed it.

"They claim there's nothing unusual about it," Jeffrey persisted, still cross.

"There isn't," she said, walking toward the door to take the volume from him. "I've told you, it's routine."

He made no move to hand her the pages. "You're lying. And Maugham's experts have missed something."

She threw him an irritated look. "If you don't believe me—or them—read it yourself, Jeffrey. I'll wait."

"You know perfectly well I won't find whatever's hidden in there," he said. "It's a tax register. A *tahrir defter*. Ottoman Turkish in *siyakat* script. I don't read illiterate bureaucratic scrawl."

"Your ignorance," she said, "doesn't signify my dishonesty. And your inability to read anything more than superficial Ottoman Turkish isn't a plot on the part of my organization. You've brought it all the way here. So now what? You're going to prevent me from working on it?"

He gave her an acid smile. "Follow me, dear. We'll work on it together. In my study. You read. I'll take notes." Then he turned and left the room, taking the volume with him.

Annoyed, she walked to her dressing table, sat, removed the towel, and pinned back her damp hair. Then, rising, she crossed to the bed, pulled on pyjamas, pushed her feet into slippers, and re-tied the belt of the dressing gown. Jeffrey hadn't yet changed out of the dark suit he'd worn to the office that morning, but she felt no need to make herself uncomfortable as well.

As she left her bedroom, she paused and felt the air. She had noticed over the past two or three days the lingering scent of anise or liquorice in the doorway, and it was pronounced this evening. A new cleaning product, presumably—although she was too inhibited to ask Mrs. Bowen about it. Whatever the case, she hoped the maids would stop using it. The scent left her uncomfortable, and the damp, sandy stain on the white wainscoting outside the room made it obvious that the product couldn't be all that effective.

By the time she'd reached the floor below, the scent had vanished, and she'd forgotten about it—steeling herself instead for what she knew would be an unusually unpleasant exchange with Jeffrey. After taking a quick breath and telling herself to keep calm, she pushed open the door to his study and entered. Prepared to protect her project.

He was sitting at his desk, paging through the tax register, his forehead wrinkled. He'd removed his jacket and tie, and he'd rolled up the sleeves of his white shirt, but otherwise he was still dressed for the office. There was a stack of writing paper and a pen in front of him. And when he heard her enter, he pointed to a chair on the other side of the desk. Without speaking.

She crossed the room, sat, and looked at him politely. Still quiet, he turned the volume to face her and then, holding her gaze, took up the pen. "They insist," he said, referring to Maugham's experts, "that there are no hidden pages and that the pages that we can see haven't been treated. No invisible writing. They also say that there's no evidence of encoded messages or prose in what they've translated. It's a *tahrir defter*. That's it."

She nodded and looked down at the first page of the register. It was conventional. A large *tuğra* followed by provincial divisions, populations, aggregate income. Turning the pages, she could find no overt evidence of the compositions by Ibn Wahshiyya and Ibn Janah that the doctor had told her were embedded in the volume. But then, if the evidence had been obvious, Jeffrey would already be making use of it.

"According to the register," he continued as he watched her familiarizing herself with the writing, "the revenue of Raqqa province accrued from the area surrounding Raqqa itself, the villages of the Balikh River, a tributary of the Euphrates, an area called the 'reed swamp'—*kapulı bük*—the area surrounding Jabar, and the nomadic tribes. To the extent, obviously, that the tax collectors could catch up to the last."

"Yes," she said. "I see that."

She was becoming anxious. The volume was a perfectly ordinary *defter*. She paged ahead and read the accounts of the taxes levied on wheat and barley for the river villages. Nothing unusual in the tables or the accounting. And certainly nothing to link these numbers to Ibn Wahshiyya or Ibn Janah. She read and re-read each list of figures, increasingly defeated.

Then, keeping her eyes averted from Jeffrey's, she went over in her mind what she knew of each of the writers whose works were supposed to be hidden in the register. Both lived centuries before the emergence of the Ottoman Empire—Abu Bakr ibn Wahshiyya in the early tenth century in Iraq, and Marwan ibn Janah at the beginning of the eleventh century in Spain. Both wrote in Arabic, though Ibn Janah was Jewish and Ibn Wahshiyya, although nominally Muslim, was sufficiently fascinated by his pagan "Nabatean" ancestry that he was, at best, heterodox in his beliefs.

Both wrote extensively on pharmacology, toxicology, and medicine—although only a small fraction of the corpus of each was extant. In fact, Ibn Janah was remembered primarily as a philologist on the basis of his dictionaries and studies of Hebrew grammar. And Ibn Wahshiyya was remembered as a small-time fortune teller and magician. Marion herself, however, had seen sections of both of their supposedly lost works, including a complete manuscript of Ibn Janah's medical study—*Kitab al-Talhis*—during her time in the Hagia Sophia library in Istanbul. And so she knew that there was more to their reputations than what scholars currently believed.

She also hadn't missed the connection between Ibn Wahshiyya, as a proudly Nabatean writer, and Queen Bertha's reference to the Caliph's "Nabatean magician." But she was leery of jumping to conclusions about Ibn Wahshiyya's life. Although he did spend time in Baghdad and Samarra in the same years that Bertha's embassy had approached the Caliph, Ibn Wahshiyya was notoriously not the sort of scholar to grace a respectable court. The hint of charlatanism, of disreputable, manipulative sleight-of-hand, that had haunted his reputation while he was alive had only grown more pronounced over the past thousand years. He was not a figure to associate with the higher echelons of Abbasid society.

In fact, when three of his more famous works had surfaced in the middle of the last century, European scholars had been—to their later mortification—overjoyed. His *Book of Nabatean Agriculture*, or *Kitab al-filaha al-Nabatiyya*, his work on alphabets in which he claimed to decipher Egyptian hieroglyphics centuries before the Rosetta Stone, and his *Book of Poisons*, or *Kitab al-sumum*, were more than historically important. They were a spectacular, unprecedented find.

And the reason for their significance, these scholars had determined, was that Ibn Wahshiyya hadn't composed the books himself in the tenth century, but had instead translated a set of Babylonian texts—thousands of years old, written in ancient Syriac, and preserved by his community—into Arabic.

His purpose, he had alleged, was to demonstrate to the world the knowledge that had been acquired and safeguarded by the Nabateans of Mesopotamia.

But when internal inconsistencies—and then the deciphering of cuneiform in 1857—cast doubt on Ibn Wahshiyya's claims, this same scholarly community turned on him. With a vengeance. And now, in 1936, his reputation was as tarnished as it had been in the 920s and 930s. He was untrustworthy—demonstrably dishonest—as much now as he had been then. Marion didn't want to join the company of scholars who had been fooled by him. She also couldn't quite believe that any Caliph would employ him as his personal "magician." At least not publicly.

But it was also worth noting that Ibn Wahshiyya wasn't entirely to blame for his bad reputation. One of the most significant marks against him, both during and after his lifetime, had been a quality for which Marion herself had a sneaking admiration: his preference for the company of peasants over the company of urban sophisticates. Yes, his claims to magic and sorcery had been laughable. His incantations were farcical. But worse even than his spells and recipes had been his belief—echoing, though she'd never admit it, her own—that the farmers of the Euphrates possessed arcane knowledge that the scholars in the cities had missed. Farmers living in precisely the area assessed by the Raqqa tax register.

Sighing, she turned another page. The connection was too tenuous. She couldn't see how whatever Ibn Wahshiyya may or may not have discovered in the tenth century could have been preserved in a bureaucratic document produced six hundred years later. Pressing her fingertips to her temples she stared down at the page in front of her. Supplemental data on a series of farms. "Two trees farm," "white sheep farm," "blessings farm," "spider farm"—*çiftlik-i ankabut*. She paused. An odd name, but not beyond the realm of possibility. Then she closed her eyes, frustrated. A few seconds later, sensing Jeffrey's goading smile, she opened them and looked across at him.

"You haven't found anything either," he said, pleased.

"There isn't anything to find," she retorted. "How many times—"

"Giving up, then?"

"Jeffrey, would you please just let me take this volume to my room to read?" She rubbed her eyes with her fists. "I can't do anything with you hovering over me like this."

"I'll return it to the collection," he said, reaching out to close the volume.

"No—" she started. Instinctively.

Then, looking down at his fingers obscuring the area above the description of the "spider farm," she stopped speaking. "Ankabutha" was the fanciful name that Ibn Wahshiyya had given to the most powerful of the supposedly ancient sorcerers who had composed the alleged originals from which his translations had derived. The one who could, among other things, raise the dead. And whose most potent spells were always to be found in the lost, rather than extant, manuscripts. "Jeffrey," she said, "would you please move your hand?"

Suspicious, he acquiesced, withdrawing his hand from the page, and she looked down. It was in typical *tahrir defter* format. Columns of names, numbers, produce, and figures. But the supplemental data was concerned with the wild or feral animals hunted and husbanded by the family who worked "spider farm," rather than with the domestic animals. And the term, "wild animals," was written, unusually, in Ottoman-inflected Arabic as *al-hayawanat al-wahshiyya*. Missing the first definite article: *hayawanat al-wahshiyya*. Smiling to herself, she read further: bees, lynxes, salamanders—

Jeffrey dropped his hand back over the page. "Care to read aloud, dear?"

She stared at the back of his hand. Furious and refusing to look up at him. It was entirely possible, she raged to herself, that what she had in front of her was a heavily cloaked, late translation into Ottoman Turkish of one of Ibn Wahshiyya's most provocative lost texts. Or, at least, of one of the more powerful of the recipes spelled out in the lost texts. And he was preventing her from reading it. She fantasized about ramming the pen into his hand. Then, controlling herself, she looked up at him. "If you'd like. Yes. I'll read it aloud. I've found the village that's been concerning my organization." She paused. "It will bore you."

"Try me." He removed his hand and took up the pen. "I'll take notes."

She nodded and considered the page. Astonished. It was brilliant work. If she hadn't known that she was looking for a composition by Ibn Wahshiyya, it would have read as nothing more than an assessment of a series of farms—perhaps unusual farms, but nothing outside the possible. Now that she knew what she was seeking, though, she could see that it was instead detailed instructions on—she swallowed—the "generation or growth of beings" and the "marshalling or mobilizing of beings." Nothing, unfortunately, about putting beings back to sleep—but she'd be patient and hope that something presented itself as she read further.

"Marion," Jeffrey said, startling her out of her train of thought. "Aloud. Now. If you continue to stare at it silently, I'll close it up and take it back to the library tomorrow."

"Very well." She took another breath. "Ankabut Farm. Feral animal husbandry. Bee-keepers. Lynx-catchers. Salamander-hunters. Scorpion-keepers—"

"Scorpion-keepers?" He raised his eyebrows.

"Yes," she said. "I believe the venom had market value in Urfa. Still does."

"Very well. Continue."

And so she did. Providing him with numerical details on each productive, growing, or decaying group of animals on the list. The number of coins they were assessed in tax. Their proportion to the village's adult male population. To the farm's adult male population. To the local mines and swamps. To the uncultivated land surrounding the farm.

It was difficult to draw the conclusions she was meant to draw from Ibn Wahshiyya's concealed instructions while also providing Jeffrey with the superficial tax record, but after a half hour, she'd fallen into a comfortable routine. She trusted herself to remember the details even without taking notes. And she was enjoying Jeffrey's palpable exasperation. If she was lucky, he'd become so disgusted by the mounting clerical minutiae that he'd hand the *defter* to her to finish without her pressuring him further at all.

And indeed, a little over an hour into her translation, he reached a breaking point. "Stop." He set his pen on the desk. Ran his hand through his hair. "You're getting something out of this beyond the accounting. I can tell. You've got that look about you that normal people wear when they've fallen in love."

She blinked up at him. Folded her hands in her lap. "I've transliterated and translated every word on every page that we've read." She turned the volume to face him. "You can decipher *siyakat* well enough to check. Is there anything I've kept from you? Tell me."

He didn't lower his gaze. "I've no doubt that you've scrupulously read each and every mark on these pages. That's not what I'm questioning." He watched her face. "I'm saying that you're drawing additional information out of those marks that you're not sharing with me."

She remained silent.

He turned the volume back to face her. "Continue. We'll keep this up all night if necessary."

She dropped her eyes to prevent him from seeing the flicker of annoyance. Then she continued. He paused to light a cigarette, but otherwise he didn't stop her. Nor did he falter in his note-taking. As he wrote, he underscored phrases that he sensed interested her. But she wasn't worried about his sensitivity to her reactions to the document. Even if she couldn't keep from betraying her fascination with certain pieces of the recipe, he'd never put the information together into a coherent set of instructions. She was safe.

After another hour had passed, she paused, confused by an entry in the list of crafts and occupations undertaken by the population of the village of "Kusama"—another of Ibn Wahshiyya's magicians. After transliterating it, she paused, frowning.

"What is it?" Jeffrey took a drag from his second cigarette.

She shook her head. "Nothing. It's unusual. Something about the revenue collected from a church." She paused. "No. From burials performed at a church? The church of the declaration? *Al-beyan*. Which houses a rock?" She stared down at the writing. "A rock of white water? *Kaya-yı ab-ı sefid*?"

She continued thinking, perplexed. And then, startled, she put her hand over her mouth. It wasn't the name of a church. It was the name of a person. Followed by directions to his tomb. She was to seek out the tomb of the "rock of white water," "Peter of Aquablanca" in the church of "*al-beyan*"—"Albion." Albion's church must be Hereford Cathedral. Where Peter of Aquablanca, or Aigueblanche, had been buried in the late thirteenth century.

This also meant that the translation in front of her was more than a translation. Ibn Wahshiyya had died by the middle of the tenth century. But someone, or some group, had continued his work. Spreading his scholarship as far as England and Wales in the thirteenth century. And then, hundreds of years after that, they had produced this document as a commentary on its travels.

She was about to resume reading, enthralled, but before she could gather her thoughts, Jeffrey stood, slammed the volume shut, turned to the wall behind him, and locked it up in his safe. Then he turned back to her. "I think that's sufficient for this evening."

She stood as well, staring at the closed door of the safe. "Why? Why would you do that? *Why?*"

"What are you drawing from that document?"

"Nothing," she said wildly. "*Nothing*. It's a tax register. Jeffrey, please—"

"We'll discuss it further tomorrow morning," he said, calm.

"Damn it." She strode across the room and glowered at him. She hadn't even reached the section by Ibn Janah. They were less than halfway through the volume. She must get it back from him. "This is infantile. I've done everything you asked. *Everything*. You can't take it away from me simply because you—you—"

"Good night, Marion." He walked to the door and opened it for her. "Sleep well. As I said, we'll talk tomorrow morning."

She wanted to hurt him. To throw something. Instead, she took a shaky breath, clenched her fists, and left his study. She'd seen this mood before. And she knew that she wouldn't change his mind.

As she climbed the stairs, though, she relaxed marginally. After all, she'd completed the difficult part of her task—locating the hidden texts. And if she could control her anger when Jeffrey spoke with her tomorrow, he'd grant her access to the register. He needed her analysis as much as her own organization did. And then, she'd continue to put the pieces together, suffering him as a bored and fretful audience if necessary. She'd worked under worse conditions.

When she reached her bedroom, she also realized that she was wretchedly tired. They'd been working, tense and combative, for over three hours, and it was nearing midnight. Grateful now for the respite, she drew the curtains over the windows, removed her dressing gown, and slipped between the cool covers of her bed. Closing her eyes with keyed up gratitude.

But despite her exhaustion, sleep eluded her. Under her closed eyes, her mind was alert and unable to relax. She felt watched. And although she was aware that her buzzing vigilance was a reaction to Jeffrey's decision to deny her solitary time with the *defter*—her instincts misbehaving after a more than trying evening—she couldn't damp it down. She'd felt eyes when none were there before—always after similarly difficult exchanges—and her rational mind was rarely able to convince her intuition to let down its defenses. She must let the feeling run its course.

A resolution that wasn't helped when, shortly after the clock downstairs struck a muffled two in the morning, Jeffrey himself entered her room and tried to climb into her bed. It was like him, she thought fuming, to consider their nightmarish conversation that evening as a prelude to a visit later in the night. When she felt him moving across the mattress, she curled into a ball in the corner of the bed and shook her head viciously.

"Absolutely not. Get out."

He obeyed without a word. Although he left an annoyingly cold spot on her sheet that she had difficulty warming with her body once he'd gone. And still, after that, she couldn't sleep. When shortly after three she heard Lydia awake and crying in the nursery, she was almost grateful for the excuse to leave the room. Pulling on her dressing gown, she shivered, sensing a draft. And as she walked down the shadowed corridor toward the nursery, she noted that the smell of anise, or perhaps it was fennel, was stronger than ever. Overpowering by the time she'd reached Lydia's cot.

Alicia was already bouncing and comforting the baby when Marion arrived. Looking tired. Without a word, she handed her to Marion, who held her close and kissed her hair. Lydia began to quiet, but she was still wide awake. Looking, fascinated, about the dark room.

"I'm sorry about this, Alicia." Marion gave the nurse an apologetic smile. "I'll take her to my room. Go to sleep."

"Let me close this window first, Lady Willcox." Alicia, still sleepy, walked to the source of the draft and pushed the window down. "I can't understand how it keeps opening in the night."

"You haven't been opening it?"

"In November? Of course not, Lady Willcox." She rubbed her eyes. "It's only been unbolting itself these past three or four nights. Since that awful smell started."

"The liquorice?" Marion's skin crawled. "I thought it was a new cleaning fluid. I was going to ask Mrs. Bowen about it."

If she weren't so groggy, Alicia would have looked almost roguish. "Oh no, Lady Willcox. Mrs. Bowen is out of her mind trying to get rid of it."

"Oh." Marion dropped her eyes to Lydia, who was already nodding off again. Then she looked back at Alicia, who was obviously desperate to get back to bed. "Good night, Alicia. And thank you."

"Of course, Lady Willcox."

When Alicia had left the room, Marion stood still, on guard, observing the window. Her instincts back on alert. Then, deciding that whatever was going to happen had already occurred, she carried Lydia with her to her own room. Before crawling into bed with the baby, she deliberately closed, and locked, her door. But she refused to gratify the paranoid part of her mind by searching the dressing room for ghostly intruders. If anyone did decide to do more than watch her, she knew how to respond. She wasn't completely bereft of training for this sort of situation. Aging though she might be.

T HE next morning, once she'd returned Lydia to the nursery, she descended to the dining room for breakfast. Wearing her dressing gown and pyjamas. Spoiling for a fight. Jeffrey was already there, similarly combative, but hiding it behind his toast and his *Times*. Marion was surprised to see that the table was free of flowers. She'd never seen it bare before. But she didn't comment.

Instead, after preparing her own toast and a cup of tea, she sat in her customary chair and observed the back of his newspaper. "You slept well last night, then?"

He folded his paper and set it on the table beside him. "Yes, dear. Thank you. You can take pride in having utterly exhausted me. I was asleep and dead to the world before midnight."

She frowned, confused.

After a few awkward seconds of silence had passed, he sipped his tea. "And you?"

She shook her head, quiet, deciding that it was best not to pursue that conversation. She'd obviously been mistaken about his visit. The victim of a strange—and disagreeable—dream. Then, coming to herself, she went on the offensive: "I'd like to go to Hereford today. With the *defter*."

"And yet you claim that your interest in the tax register is routine," he countered. "Nothing to do with the excitement in the Cathedral."

"Yes." She held his eyes. "I do claim that."

"You think that watching you work in Hereford is more important to me than tripping you up while you read the document."

"Yes." She waited.

He sighed. "And you're correct, of course. If I never hear another word about the irrigation practices of the peasants of the Balikh river, it will be too soon. You win." He finished his tea and stood. "I'll telephone the office to let them know our plans." Glanced at his wristwatch. "Will you be ready in thirty minutes? Hereford is a three-hour drive. We ought to leave early."

She nodded and took a bite of her toast. Then, as he left the dining room, she let herself relax. She was still unhappy about having lost the opportunity to look for Ibn Janah's contribution to the volume. But at least she could test her theories concerning the first half of the material. She was confident she'd find something of interest in the area surrounding Peter of Aigueblanche's tomb. And then she'd work out a means of retrieving her *defter*. Better to read it with more information at her disposal anyway.

Once she'd finished her breakfast, she walked up to her room to change into travelling clothing. But when she reached the door, she faltered, perplexed. The knob was visibly damp. And when she touched it, it felt sticky. Viscid. Pushing aside her unease, she opened the door and walked into the room just in time to hear plodding, wet footsteps retreating into her dressing room. Angry now, she followed the sound, switched on the light to the dressing room, and peered into the dim space.

Her clothing was undisturbed. But the scent of anise was acute. Narrowing her eyes, she pushed aside the rows of hanging dresses—most of which she never wore—and then stood, calculating, in front of the looming wardrobe. She'd never liked it. Even under the best of circumstances, it hinted at unspeakable things lurking and waiting for a moment of inattention, to pounce. But she wasn't about to let it intimidate her. Nerving herself, she opened its doors and each of the drawers in turn, the hairs on the back of her neck standing on end.

The clothing in the drawers was as she'd left it. Nothing was amiss. And even the smell was dissipating rather quickly now. Perhaps her sleepless night had left her prone to suggestion. Impressionable. Weak.

Satisfied that nothing was watching her, at least for the moment, she found her favorite loose wool trousers, a brown cashmere sweater that was unravelling at one sleeve, work boots, and the ratty tweed overcoat that she kept in her room for fear that Jeffrey would throw it away if he found it downstairs. She also stuffed underwear, socks, pyjamas, and—holding it tightly for a split second in her hand—the Susanna Crystal into an overnight bag to bring along with her. The gem might prove useful in deciphering whatever she found in the Cathedral.

After taking her clothing and the bag back to the bedroom, she left the clothes on the bed, removed her dressing gown and pyjamas, and went to the toilet. She turned to the mirror, opened the taps, and just had time to draw a breath in alarmed confusion before a pale, hairless, hominid thing with a smeared suggestion of a face and blind eyes leapt out at her from the bathtub, grabbed her by the hair, twisted her head, and pushed its mouth against hers. Although its features were no more than a misshapen scrawl across translucent skin, its lips were pronounced enough for her to feel them clamping over her own. Fat and wet. Reeking of fennel.

Its contact with her lasted no more than a few seconds, but it was sufficient to leave her stunned. Before, gagging, she pushed it off of her and—more by instinct than because she thought it would listen—hissed at it to get away from her. It moved back at once, crouching in the corner of the room, a handful of the hair it had ripped from her scalp clenched in its fist. Draped in scraps of rotting gold cloth.

After that, it turned its cloudy eyes toward hers and, without averting its unseeing gaze from her horrified face, lurched out of the room, making a noise that sounded like "yes." In Arabic. There was a small puddle of something liquid on the floor where it had been.

Marion turned back to the sink, shuddering in revulsion, unable to internalize what had happened. She ran the water as hot as she could, scrubbing at her face with the soap. Then she brushed her teeth three times, still tasting bile when she thought of the thing that had been touching her. Finally, once she'd cleaned herself as effectively as she could, she stared at her frantic reflection in the mirror, her skin rubbed raw and red, her teeth bloody where she'd tried to remove all evidence of the thing's mouth.

And after that, with an act of will, she controlled herself. She couldn't tell Jeffrey about this. She couldn't tell anyone. It obviously had to do with Lothar's and Waldrada's family, with whatever had woken up in Marseille, with Ibn Wahshiyya's instructions, and with what she'd eventually discover of Ibn Janah. Her assignment was not to discuss it, it was to put a stop to it. And given what she'd just experienced, she was very much looking forward to doing that. That thing, she inwardly screamed at herself, could not remain awake.

Still trembling, she left the sink, returned to the bed, and mechanically dressed herself. The fact that it had touched her while she was naked kept intruding itself into the corners of her mind, but she crushed the thought before it formed. She'd experienced worse. This was almost comic by comparison. And if she kept repeating that to herself, she might even begin to believe it. Pulling on her tweed overcoat and taking up her overnight bag, she walked resolutely out of the room and down the stairs.

Jeffrey was already waiting for her in the entryway, immaculate in a grey, double breasted wool overcoat, hat, and gloves, holding a small Goyard suitcase. When he saw her, wan, disheveled, and sloppily dressed, he raised an eyebrow. "It's Wales, Marion, not the Newgate exercise yard." He adjusted his hat. "You might at least make an effort."

"We'll stay the night?" Her voice sounded strange to her, but perhaps he wouldn't notice.

"Yes." Walking toward the stairs leading down to the garage. "The office keeps a farmhouse in Rowlstone. Ten miles from Hereford. Quiet enough to work, but close enough to watch the Cathedral."

She nodded, following him. When she reached the garage and he switched on the light, she halted on the bottom step, annoyed. He'd replaced his car. Again. And this new one—a low, two-seated roadster—was flimsy as well as extravagant. Thin metal conspicuously rivetted together along the back, over the ostentatiously long bonnet, and above the wheels.

He saw her staring at it and grinned. "Bugatti 57 Aerolithe Elektron Coupe. One of a kind."

"Oh." It didn't mean anything to her. The car was upsetting.

"They showed it last year at the Paris Motor Show," he continued, securing their cases behind the seats. "As a concept. But there weren't any takers. And so, when they brought it here to London a few months ago, I negotiated with Monsieur and quietly took possession. A crime to let it languish."

She didn't move from the staircase. "Why didn't anyone want it?"

"Aerolithe. 'The Meteorite.'" He walked around the car and opened the passenger door for her. "The body's made of a magnesium alloy to keep it lightweight. But magnesium's also unstable. It melts, you know. And catches fire. That's why they bolted it together rather than welding it." His smile grew. "But it's fast, Marion. Wait till you see. We'll be in Rowlstone before noon."

"It catches fire." She closed her eyes. Steadied herself. Opened them again. "That's insane, Jeffrey."

"Are you afraid?" Teasing. "You're aren't *afraid*, are you?"

"Why not take the train?" She felt tired. Unable to endure this exchange after what had happened in her bedroom.

"Privacy, Marion. Security." He returned to the driver's side, sat, and closed his door. Then he looked up at her through the open passenger-side door. "Your tax register is here in the car. I'm going to Hereford now. If you'd rather not accompany me, then I'll simply bear the ordeal without you."

Without speaking further, she walked to the car, lowered herself into the passenger seat, and closed her door. She knew better than to argue. She'd never convince him to travel inconspicuously.

Complacent, Jeffrey started the engine, which at least wasn't as loud as she'd expected it to be. And once they'd left his garage, she admitted that it did take them less than the usual hour to reach the empty route heading west out of the city. The other vehicles presumably giving them wide berth to keep from being caught up in any potential conflagration.

*W*HEN they'd been travelling for close to two hours, Jeffrey relaxed in his seat, shifted up, and glanced over at her. "We're still pretending that the tax register is unrelated to your interest in the Cathedral?"

"Yes." She looked out her window. Mud and damp grass.

He nodded. "Very well. But I've been doing my own research on Queen Bertha, or at least her family in Lotharingia, and Hereford. Care to listen?"

"Fine."

"You fear that if you respond at any length, you'll inadvertently spill something?" He smiled. "I'm flattered."

She remained silent. He laughed quietly and concentrated on driving for a moment or two. Then he spoke: "Hereford was disreputable nine hundred years ago. All sorts of questionable foreign theories seeping out of the Cathedral. Into the surrounding countryside. And beyond."

He looked over at her averted face. "It all started with the Danish King Canute the Great importing a court full of Lotharingian monks and scholars into England in 1015 after he'd subdued the country. Monks and scholars who, if not actually practicing Muslims and Jews, were by no means averse to what Muslim and Jewish philosophy could do for them. Moving gradually westward. Into Hereford." He scanned the empty road in front of them. "And then, a hundred or so years after that, there was the scandalous behavior of any number of monks of Hereford as recounted by William of Malmesbury."

"William of Malmesbury?" she asked. "The one who claimed that Pope Sylvester II made a deal with the devil for a prophetic talking head that betrayed him to a pair of demons who ripped out his eyeballs while he was reading a mass in Rome?" She watched the passing mud for a few seconds more. "Reliable source."

"Indeed," he said. "But Pope Sylvester wasn't the only monk with a weakness for forbidden knowledge to draw William's ire. Gerard of Hereford, for example, was also—according to William—tainted by an unseemly interest in the Arabic works of Muslim and Jewish sorcerers. Fascinated by prophecy. And he also, like Pope Sylvester, died suddenly and suspiciously, in 1108, of an illness that sufficiently frightened the canons of York once he'd become bishop there that they not only wouldn't bury him in the church, but wouldn't even 'let any earth be thrown on his body' outside of its gates.

"And then," he continued in a musing tone, "there was Roger of Hereford, a few decades later. Writing in the 1170s. Translating, in the face of stern opposition, Arabic treatises on astronomy, astrology, mathematics, medicine, and alchemy. Also interested in prophecy. Predicting the future. No talking head that we know of, but he may have merely kept it quiet."

He scanned the landscape for a minute or two and then turned onto a side road that wound through orchards of skeletal apple trees, bereft now of their leaves. Wet and grey. "Not to mention Gilbert Foliot, who had become Bishop of Hereford some years earlier, in 1148. Gilbert, intriguingly, was appointed to the Hereford position in Reims, when his predecessor died unexpectedly. Pleasant bit of former Lotharingia—almost—Reims. Where Gerbert of Aurillac, soon to become the ill-fated Pope Sylvester II had established a center for the study of Arabic-language sciences. And presumably also where Gilbert himself learned, as the chronicler Walter Map puts it, to lay to rest the revenants who were in the habit of wandering the streets of Hereford in the 1150s, infecting and terrifying the local residents with inexplicable maladies."

He peered through the windscreen at the muddy track stretched out in front of them. "According to the reports, Gilbert dug up the most offensive corpse, hacked it into pieces, and sprinkled it with holy water. Which would, once supposes, have been effective. Or, if not effective, then at least thorough." He paused. "And, of course, there was Peter of Aigueblanche. Bishop of Hereford in—"

He stopped and glanced over at her interested profile. "Hmm. At any rate—Peter of Aigueblanche. No explicit links to Muslim or Jewish scholarship written in Arabic—or, for that matter, to questionable Lotharingian knowledge. But he did spend a suspicious amount of time in recently Muslim Sicily. And he is supposed to have left 'a bad smell,' they say. The result, one assumes, of his own restless corpse protesting its burial at Hereford in 1268 rather than in Savoy, the land of his ancestors." He considered again. "And here, come to think of it, we do arrive full circle, back to Lothar II's family. Savoy having been wrested away from him upon the death of his father, Lothar I."

He slowed the car and turned onto a narrower dirt drive, flanked on either side by ditches full of rotting brambles and bracken fern. "The common theme," he continued as they drove now at almost a walking pace through the mud and gravel, "seems less the Hereford monks' disreputable interest in Muslim and Jewish scholarship, and less even their fascination with prophecy and the occasional apocryphal talking head, than it is the ongoing nuisance of their restless, foul-smelling, animated corpses. Wandering the streets. Causing trouble." He leaned forward, squinting out the fogged windscreen. "Wouldn't you agree?"

When she didn't respond, he also remained silent, focusing now on maneuvering the car. And after they'd crawled along the drive for fifteen minutes longer, the track finally opened, revealing a grassy circular area surrounded by a stone farmhouse, a sagging shed, and an empty barn with a stone tiled roof. Once Jeffrey had cut the engine, she opened her door and unfolded herself from the ludicrous car. Still not speaking. She didn't want to hear any more.

Instead, she watched the clouds, which were low and mud colored. The air both damp and biting. But she could nonetheless appreciate that on a brighter day, the house would be charming. It overlooked miles of pasture, down a sloping hill. An orchard to the side. Evidence of a picnic in the form of a wooden table surrounded by three chairs, now slick with moss. The broken, slimy stems of what must have been a well-conceived border, populated at this point by three or four sodden, slug-ravaged dahlias. It would have been a lovely house to visit three months earlier. She pulled her tweed coat more closely around her shoulders as a gust of wet air whistled up from the gully.

Jeffrey, extracting their luggage from the Bugatti, was unaffected by the weather. He walked up the path toward the front door—a solid, rectangular panel of worn wood that he pulled open to reveal a second, more polished and welcoming door, painted red with a small window embedded in it. This he pushed open, without unlocking, before standing to the side to let Marion enter the house.

The front door opened immediately into a large living area. Whitewashed walls and ceilings intersected by thick beams of dark wood. Two wide, mullioned windows looking out onto pasture. Scuffed wood plank floors covered with thin, shabby carpets. A collection of cushioned armchairs, old and comfortable-looking. And a wood-burning stove, which was radiating heat. The room was extravagantly warm.

Jeffrey, who had followed Marion, closed the door and left their bags to the side. Then he placed his hat and gloves on an unidentifiable piece of furniture inside the entry, apparently meant for that purpose, and hung his overcoat on a hook next to the door. "Domestics had advanced warning of our arrival," he said, nodding in the direction of the wood stove. "They'll have prepared us food as well. But there's time before dinner. Shall we unpack?"

She cautiously removed her tweed coat and left it on an armchair. "Yes. Fine."

He retrieved their bags and walked toward a steep, ladder-like staircase leading up to something between a loft and a bedroom as large as the living area. Nearly as warm too, Marion noted, as she followed him, still reserving judgement on the farmhouse. It was suspiciously comfortable. Pleasant. But its isolation worried her. She was entirely reliant on Jeffrey for transportation. And even if she tried to leave on foot, nothing in the miles of green pasture suggested a direction to take. Jeffrey had claimed that Hereford was nearby. But she could see no landmark in the disarmingly pretty landscape that would point her toward anything even resembling a town or a city.

Setting aside her apprehension, she examined the bedroom. It, too, was whitewashed with exposed beams. A single, tiny window looked out over the drive. But the bed was old and solid, covered in a thick, cheerful red and white quilt. And the wardrobe in which Jeffrey was arranging their luggage evoked furniture dimly remembered from her grandmother's house. Appealing. She'd keep on her guard.

She waited for Jeffrey to precede her back down the steps and then followed, not wanting to leave him alone with her overnight bag. Once they'd reached the ground floor, she made her way to a bookcase she'd seen against a far wall when she entered the building. Examined the spines of the books.

"Good idea," he said as he found a magazine—a two-decade old edition of *The Magnet*—and flopped into an armchair near the wood stove. "We've got a few hours before we must start foraging."

She pulled a book from the top shelf. *Five Children and It*. Shrugged and brought it back to an armchair near Jeffrey's. As she curled up in the chair and opened the book, she resolved to enjoy the atmosphere of the building. She had a sneaking suspicion that the office kept it for interrogations—and she didn't even want to know the nefarious purpose of the infantile collection of literature. But her suspicions by no means detracted from the room's calming air. The warm stove and the antics of the sand-fairy were leaving her almost grateful to Jeffrey for bringing her here.

When the light in the room dimmed, Jeffrey stood, fed the wood stove, and switched on three glass-covered, Edison bulb table lamps. "I'll try to start the oven."

She nodded, immersed in her story, not looking up at him. "Fine."

He smiled slightly and walked into the kitchen. She saw a yellow light through the door and then heard him doing battle with a coal-burning stove. Twenty minutes later, the smell of food convinced her to leave her book and wander into the kitchen. He was just removing a meat pie from an antique oven that brought back more conflicted memories than the wardrobe had. He'd also set two places at a wooden trestle table that took up much of the room, resting solidly on uneven flagstones. Bread, cheese, and mugs of cider.

He pulled out a chair for her. "Sit. I know your feelings about cider, but—"

"Under the proper circumstances," she said, sitting and pulling in her chair, "I can tolerate it. This looks delicious."

He served them both portions of the meat pie and sat across from her, ripping off a piece of his bread. "I was worried for a moment that the oven was unwilling to part with it. But eventually I managed to appeal to its better nature."

She took a bite of the pie. "It's good. What is it?"

"I don't know." Apologetic. "Domestics left it in the larder for us already made up. But fear not. They take their position seriously, and I can assure you that there's nothing more exotic in that pie than what every other farmer in the area is eating at the moment."

She smiled down at her plate. "I'm amenable to exotic, Jeffrey. You needn't worry."

"Nonetheless." He smiled as well. "We have a long day ahead of us tomorrow. Best not tempt fate."

She nodded, frowning now. Then they ate the rest of their dinner in silence, before cleaning up their plates—thick blue ceramic with lighthearted sunflowers painted in the middle—and moving upstairs to the bedroom.

By the time they had slipped under the quilt and into bed, Marion was more than sleepy, her fatigue from the previous night having caught up to her. And when Jeffrey switched off the table lamp beside him, she drifted instantly into unconsciousness. It was only when she felt him put his arm around her waist a few hours later, pulling her closer to him, that she emerged from her first sleep. But even then, she simply let him hold her, neither encouraging him nor resisting.

A moment or two later, however, a part of her mind registered the fact that Jeffrey slept on the other side of the bed. Disoriented, she opened her eyes. And saw, an inch or two away from her face, the misshapen, vestigial features of the thing that had accosted her in London. Pulling her head toward its own. Opening its translucent, slippery lips to close over hers.

Unable to control herself, she made a terrified squeaking sound before backing away from the thing. But the thing continued inexorably across the bed toward her, its mouth open. Cringing against Jeffrey, she covered her face with her hands, begging it over and over again, weak, useless, and irrational, to go away. It paused in its movement toward her, closed its mouth, bent its head in acquiescence, and slithered off the bed.

As she watched it scrabbling backward across the room, a second figure, glowing in its whitish wet skin and golden rags, emerged from behind the wardrobe. It also gazed blindly at her, almost thoughtful, before following the first figure in the direction of the ladder. When she realized that there was more than one of them, she lost what little self-control remained to her and let out a paralyzed sob. At which point the sound of a gunshot shattered the quiet air of the farmhouse.

Jeffrey, on his feet now, still wearing only pyjamas, was holding his revolver in two hands, carefully following the movements of the two things. But the figures, upon hearing—or sensing—the gun, were now floundering wetly down the stairs. Without speaking, Jeffrey followed them. He half climbed, half jumped to the ground floor, and Marion heard a second shot from the drive.

Chastising herself for her feeble reaction to the attack, she gathered her wits, left the bed, and made her way to the wardrobe. In the light of the table lamp Jeffrey had turned on downstairs, she could see a long smear of something like mucous across the door behind which they kept their luggage. And even without the light, she could smell the fennel. Ignoring her revulsion, she pulled open the door, wiping her hand on her pyjama top, and rummaged through her overnight bag.

When she found the Susanna Crystal and confirmed that the things hadn't taken it, she leaned back on her heels, grateful. Squeezed the gem tightly in her hand. Then, feeling the adrenaline draining from her nervous system, she began to return the crystal to her bag.

"What's that?"

She turned, startled, as Jeffrey switched on the lamp beside the bed. But she didn't speak.

"You weren't surprised by our visitors, Marion." He looked pointedly at the object in her hand. "Distressed, yes. But not surprised."

She shook her head, unable to respond.

"There was a third one outside," he continued, almost conversational. Placing his revolver next to the lamp. "But it was already on its way into the fields when I reached the door." He paused. "Do you know? I think that all three were motivated more by your order to decamp than they were by my clumsier methods of persuasion. Which I found interesting."

"Three of them?" Choking on the words.

"More than you expected?" He sat on the bed, watching her hands. "How many have you seen so far?"

"Just one." She hadn't moved from her squatting position by the wardrobe. Paralyzed again. "Where?"

"London."

"Ah." He wrinkled his forehead. "Yes. The smell. Mrs. Bowen will be pleased that it isn't a reflection on her housekeeping."

She stood slowly, looking stupidly at the crystal in her hand.

"In your bedroom, then?" he pressed her.

She nodded. "Also in Lydia's room."

He blinked, speciously calm, in what she recognized from experience as suppressed rage. "That thing," he said after two or three seconds of silence, "was in the baby's nursery and you chose not to tell me about it?"

When she said nothing, he rose from the bed, crossed the room in a single stride, and wrenched the crystal out of her hand. Held it to the light from the table lamp. "Oh dear. You did steal it from the Museum." He rubbed his thumb over the engravings. "Is what they have in the collection now a fake? Curators will have a fit."

She shook her head again. "Look at the inscription."

He peered at the gem more closely and then nodded. "I see. They were a pair. This one's the Arabic twin." He glanced over at her still standing partly dazed in the middle of the room. "So you think your guests were coming after this? They want it back?"

"It's the only explanation."

"But you want to keep it," he continued. "For your project."

She swallowed, but she didn't speak or move further.

"Care to tell me more, Marion? I think I deserve it." He sat back down on the edge of the bed.

"No," she finally said, looking at her feet. "And I don't think I'll sleep any more tonight. I'll read a book downstairs."

"What if I venture outside and tell them to come back and take it?" he asked.

"You won't," she said dully. "You're curious."

He smiled, but it turned into a yawn. "Well, if they do return to harass you, dear, you can let them know that I've got it now. Safe and sound under my pillow." And with that, he switched off the lamp, curled up under the quilt and closed his eyes. Holding the crystal tightly in his hand. Under his pillow.

After staring at his prone body in weary hatred for a few seconds, she dragged herself to the stairs, descended to the ground floor, and collapsed in the armchair. Took up the book. Reconciled to a second night without sleep. Following the further adventures of the children and It.

THE sun was rising pale and watery over the mud and grass when Jeffrey descended from the bedroom, wearing brown tweed trousers and carrying a matching jacket. Without speaking, Marion pushed herself up from her armchair, waited for him move away from the steps, and climbed up to the room to change into her own day clothes. A few minutes later, when she'd pinned back her hair, she found him in the kitchen, scrambling eggs on top of a now docile and well-behaved stove. He'd also begun to re-heat the living room.

When he saw her, he divided the eggs between two plates, added a piece of fried bread to each, and set the plates on the table next to a pot of hot tea. She sat, exhausted, poured herself a cup of tea without milk or sugar, and picked at the eggs with a fork. He sat across from her and took a bite of his fried bread.

"The Susanna Crystal is in my jacket," he said once he'd swallowed. "I thought it best to keep it with us. Should visitors call while we're at the Cathedral."

She nodded and sipped some tea. "Fine."

"Will you also want the *defter?*"

She thought for a few seconds, downing the rest of her tea and pouring herself a second cup. Then she decided it would be better not to have him watching her make line-by-line use of Ibn Wahshiyya's instructions. She'd remember what she needed well enough to reconnoiter the tomb.

"No." She drank the second cup of tea in a few grateful swallows.

"Very well." He had finished his eggs and was eyeing her plate. "You aren't hungry?"

"No. But thank you for preparing it." She took a few polite bites of the eggs and then stood and brought them to the monstrous sink that matched the ponderous stove. "The tea was sufficient. I'm grateful."

"Shall we leave straight away then?"

"Yes. Fine."

She walked through to the living area, retrieved her tweed overcoat, and watched as he pulled on his jacket and gloves. Then she followed him out to the grassy circle that fronted the house, stifled a sigh, and lowered herself into the passenger seat of his Bugatti. Closed her eyes and hoped that she might sleep for at least a few minutes on the road.

It took them a half hour to reach Hereford, ten minutes of which involved maneuvering the car down the farmhouse's driveway, which now consisted not only of mud, but of a thin layer of frost on top of the mud. As they bumped over the crusted tracks, she kept her eyes closed, pleased, despite the jarring ride, that they were likely not going fast enough for the magnesium to ignite. And when Jeffrey parked the car in a street across from the Cathedral's west front, she felt almost rested. Or, at least, her excitement about what she might discover in Peter of Aigueblanche's tomb was flooding her with enough artificial energy to make her forget that she hadn't slept for two nights.

When they entered the Cathedral, they walked the length of the nave, taking note of three or four devout-looking tourists who were visiting the building on a chilly November Tuesday. Upon reaching the north transept, Marion stopped and turned to Jeffrey. "I want to examine Peter of Aigueblanche's tomb and effigy."

"I knew it was Peter of Aigueblanche. You and your tells. May I watch?"

"I'd rather you didn't," she said, walking toward the stone sculpture.

"I know," he replied, following her.

When they neared the tomb, they stood side by side, observing it. It looked no different from any of the other tombs along the north side of the Cathedral. Cold and whitish-grey—protected by bars and, annoyingly, a long wooden bench secured just in front of it. She knelt backward on the bench, embarrassed and conspicuous, and peered more closely at the tomb, the effigy, and the stones surrounding each. Nothing struck her as unusual.

Glancing behind her to be certain no one was noticing her odd behavior, she put her hand through the bars and ran a finger along the top of the stone sarcophagus. Then, intrigued, she examined a rough, chipped section of its lid. The scars in the stone could be haphazard injuries done to the sculpture at some early point in its life. Or, she thought, pushing her face as close to the stone as she could, they might also be hieroglyphics. Ibn Wahshiyya's hieroglyphics. Six hundred years before the discovery of the Rosetta Stone.

She didn't have access to Ibn Wahshiyya's supposed translation of "ancient alphabets" in its complete form, though she knew there was a facsimile copy of it at the British Library. But she did remember the symbols for "going in," "going out," and "medicine" because those symbols, to her quiet amusement, had been faithfully reproduced near the reference to Peter of Aigueblanche in the tax register. And here they were once again: a little triangle on a pedestal, a circle with a square embedded in it, and something that looked like a capital letter "A" with a smaller letter "I" underneath it.

She thought for a moment further before deciding that, under the present circumstances, she was "going in." Looking for "medicine." And she was about to manipulate that section of the sarcophagus when Jeffrey bent over to whisper something in her ear. She jumped and pulled back her hand, startled. "Your inspection of Peter's mortal remains are attracting the curiosity of the deacon." He straightened and indicated a man walking toward them from the far end of the Cathedral. "I'll draw him off."

"Thank you." She turned back to the tomb, noting from the tail of her eye that Jeffrey had made contact with the deacon and was leading him to another part of the Cathedral. Pleased to be left in peace to work, she concentrated on the "going in" symbol. It was positioned just under a scrolled corner of the lid of the sarcophagus. Looking solid.

Confident in her interpretation, however, she pressed her palm against the scroll while pushing her thumb against the symbol. Less than a second later, a compartment opened, smooth and silent, embedded between the effigy and the lid. Wide enough to accommodate an adult hand's thickness.

She eyed the compartment, unenthusiastic. Unwilling to insert her fingers blindly into a centuries-old sarcophagus that was, at best, of ill repute. But then, without any other option presenting itself, she fortified herself, hunched her shoulders, and slid her hand into the opening. When nothing immediately unpleasant happened, she reached further in, feeling about until she encountered what felt like a roll of paper or parchment. Grabbed it and withdrew her arm.

Which was covered in a dark, reddish sludge, half liquid and half a crumbling sort of fungus, reeking of death and corruption. Swallowing hard, she shoved the papers as well as her hand into the pocket of her overcoat. Used her other hand to manipulate the "going out" symbol. By the time she'd closed the compartment, she was shivering and light-headed—a reaction to the smell and to the fact that she had no idea at all of what was adhering to the skin of her hand.

Jeffrey returned, alone, just as she was backing away—recoiling—from the tomb. When he saw her expression, he stopped, concerned. "You found what you were after?" He took her clean arm as they left the Cathedral. "No nasty surprises?"

"I want to wash my hands," she said through clenched teeth.

"Now?" They were crossing the street toward the car. "Surely you can wait until—"

She removed her other hand from her pocket, still holding the roll of crumbling paper, and showed it to him. The substance from the tomb was drying into a stinking brownish crust over her fingers. "Yes. Now."

He gazed down at her hand in silence for a few seconds. Then he nodded. "I saw a pub across the way."

As they entered the humid, convivial room, Jeffrey smiled down at her. "Does this mean that you'll finally dispose of that repellent coat? If so, I'll buy a few masses for the soul of Peter of Aigueblanche. I owe him."

"You're an ass." She walked in the direction of the lavatory, her hand shoved in her pocket, grasping the papers. And then she spent twenty minutes frantically running the lukewarm water over her fingers. Shuddering.

B<small>Y</small> the time they returned to the farmhouse, the sun was setting, and Marion was close to collapsing from fatigue. She had removed the sludge from her hand in the pub, and the meal they'd eaten had restored her equanimity. But she couldn't get the smell out of her coat, no matter how she tried.

And so, when Jeffrey took it from her, silent and expressive, and buried it under a pile of garden detritus behind the barn, she didn't protest. Took solace instead from the papers she'd retrieved from the tomb, which were unaffected by the substance. Clean, free of any stench, and—best of all—legible.

Neither felt hungry after their impromptu lunch, so rather than preparing dinner, they picked at a loaf of dark bread while they examined the document spread out on the trestle table between them. Three wide sheets of parchment. Written in educated Arabic.

"Thank God," Jeffrey said, pulling the first of the sheets toward him. "If it had been in *siyakat* I would have given up and left it to the vengeful dead."

He shook his head, playful but implacable, when she reached across to take the second sheet. "I think not, Marion. We'll switch roles this time. A change will do us good." He gathered all three sheets in front of him. "I'll read. You listen and interpret."

"But—"

"Or I can dispatch it to the office directly." He held her look. "After today, we may very well be in a position to take the next few steps on our own. Without your grudging assistance."

"Fine." She rubbed her eyes, too tired to fight him. "But you'll regret it."

"Arrogant." He shook his head, smiling down at the pages in front of him. "You know that I adore you, yes?"

She stood and poured herself a glass of cider. Leaned against the sink and watched him reading. Damping down her desire to hurt him and make off with both the pages from the tomb and the *defter*. Reminding herself that she had no transportation, and, more to the point, no notion of where he'd put the Susanna Crystal—except that it would be somewhere inaccessible to her. She took a sip of the cider and moved back to the table. Sat.

"This," he said, finishing the third page, "is a very strange document."

"What is it?" Neutral.

"At first, I didn't recognize it." He looked across at her. "But then, it started to sound familiar. If I'm not mistaken, it begins with an excerpt from Ibn Wahshiyya's *Nabatean Agriculture*."

"Oh." She dropped her eyes to the table.

"And you're not surprised by that. I should have known." He observed her downcast face. "What, then, does Ibn Wahshiyya have to do with recent events in the Cathedral? He's even less reputable than Hereford's own collection of medieval sorcerers. The last person we want involving himself in this crisis."

"Which bit is it?" Not answering his question.

"Where and when did you first come across a reference to Ibn Wahshiyya?" he countered. "Was it in that *defter*?"

"Which bit is it?" she repeated, stubborn.

"Thank you," he said. "I'll pass the tip along to Maugham's experts when I return it to them." He skimmed the first part of the initial page. "Perhaps if they know what they're looking for, it will offer up something more than useful detail on sixteenth-century Mesopotamian barley harvests."

She made an irritated movement but didn't reply. Then, careful and patient, she asked again: "which bit of *Nabatean Agriculture* is it, Jeffrey?"

"As I said before, it *begins* with an excerpt from Ibn Wahshiyya's work." He turned his attention to the second sheet of parchment. "But then it breaks off and continues with—an alternative interpretation of the Susanna story? Book of Daniel?" He paused, thoughtful. "Same handwriting, though. The same scribe wrote both."

"Oh," she repeated. She was impatient to read the document herself, but she didn't want to give him another opportunity to deny it to her. Drank more of her cider.

"The story of Susanna," he continued, still perusing the page in front of him, "is insignificant in the Muslim tradition, you know. It rarely appears in Islamic scholarship." He lifted his eyes. "Could this be a scrap of a Jewish commentary on Ibn Wahshiyya, do you reckon? I remember that back in the days when his name was being dragged through the mud by our own academics, one of the many absurdities that damned him in the eyes of the rationalists was that he claimed Spain for the Nabateans. The speech of *al-andalus* as *al-jaramiqa*, and the like. Which puts him at least in striking distance of the Jewish scholars of the region." He pushed back his hair from his forehead. "And, of course, Maimonides enjoyed him. To the lasting discredit of Maimonides."

"Which bit of *Nabatean Agriculture* is it?" she repeated, ready now to attack him whether or not it lost her the Susanna Crystal.

He smiled across the table at her. "It's obvious, isn't it? It's the bit where he hints that he— or, forgive me, his ancient Babylonian magician—can 'generate' not only plants and animals, but also men, by making use of a pre-existing dead but not yet corrupt body *or* by adding a carefully measured set of ingredients to inert matter that is undergoing putrefaction."

"Putrefaction." Speaking more to herself than to him.

"Yes," he said. "Decay. The process of being eaten by worms."

She almost smiled. "Eaten by worms." Then, keeping her voice neutral, she addressed him. "Jeffrey, please, let me read the passage. I must see it for myself."

"Oh, very well." Relenting. He turned the first page toward her. "Here."

She skimmed the text. Nodding. Yes. Nature's "womb" as a place of both decay and generation. Putrefaction as, first, change, and second, new growth. References to the ancient Babylonian secret of generating animals as farmers generate plants. And then, nodding again, her smile growing, the Sorcerer Ankabutha creating a human, recognizable as such in outer form, but unable to think or speak. Intriguingly—perhaps via a scribal slip—a *female* human in this version of the text. The fact that Ankabutha's recipe for the generation of this (female) human—not to mention, for those interested, a (female) sheep—is available to those who seek it. But that making humans in this way ought to be avoided as it leads to disorder. And so—" The page ended.

She looked up at Jeffrey. "What does he say on the next page?"

"Same as in all of the other extant versions of the manuscript. He claims to have read the recipe. He claims to know its location. But he's not going to reproduce it now. Perhaps later. In another work." He shrugged. "Typical charlatan behavior."

He pushed the second sheet of parchment toward her, and she frowned down at it. "And so," the text continued, "let's continue now with the growth of plants, a wonderful subject…" at which point the commentary ended.

She began to read the next section, which did resemble the Susanna story from the book of Daniel. But before she'd translated more than a line, Jeffrey pulled the page back again. "And so," he said, scanning the parchment, "Susanna here, just as in the original story, is falsely accused of promiscuity by the depraved elders. But after two or three lines of pious commentary, here," he pointed, "and here, the plot—strays."

He glanced up at her. "Granted, my memory may not be accurate, but if I'm not mistaken, in the orthodox version of the narrative, Daniel catches the elders in their lie by suggesting that they be questioned separately concerning their accusation. They trip up, quaintly, as a consequence of their faulty botanical knowledge. Providing contradictory details on the type of tree under which Susanna was alleged to have been enjoying herself. One says an oak, the other says a mastic. And thus, Susanna is proved innocent."

She nodded. "Yes. I remember."

He nodded as well. Then, pushing down a smile, he returned his attention to the parchment. "In this version, however, Susanna appears to have been a bit more enthusiastic. Or, if not that, the elders more creative." His lips were twitching, on the verge of laughter now. "Because, you see, according to the elders *here*, Susanna engaged in illicit carnal relations—" he cleared his throat: "'one time under a dead hoopoe bird, one time near the cauliflower and mung bean plants, where she left both blood and urine behind, one time under a fig tree, once while bathing in the brain of a donkey, the meat of a mouse, and the blood of man, seven more times under the fig tree, twenty-nine times under an oleander, and then—after resting for forty days—once in a bath of saffron and vinegar, and once more next to a live mouse. Before finally giving birth—witnessed, it says, by *Jayzil*, daughter of *Jirarid*, whatever she might be, to a fatal demon in the shape of a swallow-like bird.'"

He relaxed in his chair. "Heavens. One does understand the need for the forty-day rest in the midst of all that. Athletic girl, Susanna." He cocked his head. "Though you'd think that the pregnancy and the emergence of the terrifying demon-swallow would have obviated any need for Daniel's intervention."

"Jeffrey," she said, ignoring his crooked smile, "I want to look at the crystal again."

She'd been staring down at the tabletop as he'd translated the document, and she was now convinced that her intuition about the connection between Ibn Wahshiyya and the Susanna Crystal was correct. But she wanted to verify it. She looked up at him, hopeful.

"No," he said, arranging the three sheets of parchment into a pile for storage in his suitcase. His smile was gone.

"I give you my word that I won't take it," she said. "I'll examine it. That's all. If my hypothesis is correct, it will help you too. Please."

"What do you expect to find?" He pushed back his chair and stood, keeping the pages in his hand.

"You know I can't tell you." She stood as well. Faint from lack of sleep.

"Then we're at an impasse." He leaned across the table and kissed her cheek. "But chin up, dear, we'll chart a way through. We always have."

She watched him leave the kitchen and then observed the table for a few seconds longer. After that, rubbing her eyes with her fists, she followed him, pausing only to switch off the lamp. As she made her way to the stairs, she paid no attention to him sprawled out in an armchair, reading another edition of *The Magnet*. She meant to sleep. And if he was awake watching the door, perhaps her visitors would stay away for at least the first part of the night.

And indeed, she slept soundly for a good hour before she heard him climbing the stairs to join her. Leery at this point of trusting her unverified assumptions, she opened her eyes and sat up in bed to watch as his head emerged through the opening in the floor. She also watched as he changed into his pyjamas and crawled into bed beside her. And it was only when he'd turned off the lamp and was holding her against him that she allowed herself to drift back into unconsciousness.

Even in the midst of a deep, exhaustion-induced sleep, however, she was troubled by uncomfortable dreams. The worst involved an endless game with an untrained wet dog that repeatedly returned a spittle-soaked ball to her. She kept trying to throw the ball such that the dog wouldn't retrieve it, but always it came back to her. Eventually, she became so anxious that her mind propelled her into a state of semi-consciousness. Aware that it was pitch-black outside and that she was in a strange bed in Rowlstone.

And also that her hand, out of the covers and draped over the side of the bed, felt damp. Confused, she peered at the floor. Where a whitish, reeking body wrapped in rotting gold cloth was stretched out at length next to the bed, licking her fingers. Its mouth moving up into contact with her wrist.

She jerked back her arm, curled into a ball, and squeezed her eyes shut. When she opened them, the figure was climbing over the side of the bed, its mouth slack and wet. Its eyes blind, yet seeking. Converging on her.

At that, she screamed at it to get away. Never to come back. To go back where it came from. When it paused in its approach, she heard Jeffrey swearing on the other side of the bed. Then, before she knew what he was doing, he pushed her head down with his left hand and fired his revolver point blank at the thing.

Although the figure did recoil and lurch toward the stairs, the bullet didn't do it much damage. Nonetheless, Jeffrey strode across the floor after it. Professional and intent. She heard him fire another shot from the front door, but he didn't leave the house, and soon the sound of his steps on the ladder floated back up into the bedroom.

She was paying little attention to his movements. Sitting up in the bed, her arms wrapped around her knees, her forehead on her arms, she was weeping in dread. It was only when he replaced his revolver on the bedside table and sat on the edge of the bed beside her, that she raised her eyes to his.

"Just give it to them," she said. "I'm—unqualified—for this." Shaking now. "If they want the crystal, they can have it. And who knows? Perhaps they have good reason for coming after it. Perhaps we're the ones in the wrong." She took another shuddering breath. "Go out and leave it for them. They'll take it, and this will be over."

"I can't." He ran a hand through his rumpled hair.

"Why not? Your orders? You'd really rather please Maugham than put a stop to the nightly visits of those—those—horrible—" She choked on the words.

"Your Susanna Crystal," he said, inspecting his fingernails, "is in transit. I passed it to a colleague this morning." He looked back up at her. "The deacon in the Cathedral? Surely you could see he was too young."

"It isn't here?"

"No." He rose from the bed and found a dressing gown in the wardrobe. Wrapped it around himself and tied the belt. "It's on the continent by now, I daresay."

"Then why are they still coming?" She pressed the heels of her hands into her eyes. "Why did they visit again tonight?"

"I'm wondering the same thing." He sat on the bed next to her. "Perhaps they simply fancy you, darling."

For a good ten seconds, she thought through what he had told her. But then, the full implications of his words hit her—not only that the things were following her without any apparent reason, but that the crystal itself was out of her reach. Dropping her hands from her eyes, she glowered at him, incensed. "It's 'in transit?' You *gave it away?*" Then, before he could reply, and without considering the consequences, she leapt at him. "You fucking—"

He quickly had her wrists pinned behind her back. More efficient than she was, at least for the moment. "For heaven's sake, Marion. This is hardly the time." After two or three seconds, annoyed rather than entertained by her reaction, he let her arms go. Then he continued speaking as though nothing had happened, choosing his words carefully: "shall I tell you the other question that's been plaguing me the past few days?"

"What?" Rubbing her wrists.

"Why you're not dead." He adjusted the belt on his dressing gown.

"What do you mean?"

"The office," he said, "has been collecting reports on those—things—for close to two weeks now. The disturbance started in Marseille. Something to do with that munitions explosion. But since then, there have been incidents in countless cities throughout Europe and the Near East. Anywhere that can boast of having been a center of a particular occult type of medieval Muslim and Jewish scholarship."

"Oh."

"But in every other incident, the witnesses have finished dead. The merest touch has left them, at best, critically ill." He blinked at her. "You, however, appear to be immune. You alone."

"I'm meant to stop them," she said, her hands clasped tightly in her lap. "That's my assignment. The crystal would have been a—a guide to that assignment."

She didn't know, and didn't care, why she was unaffected by their contact. The contact was bad enough on its own. She rubbed her eyes again. "What I was going to tell you in the kitchen—about the crystal? It's this: I don't think that the Arabic 'Susanna' engraved on it refers to the Susanna story. 'Susanna' is a cipher. The letters are un-vowelled. They don't spell her name, they spell *sawwasna*—a verb related to 'they, feminine, decayed.' 'They became rotten or worm-eaten.' From *sawwasa*. And I wouldn't be remotely surprised if the Latin on the Museum's crystal—'Lothar, King of the Franks, caused me to be made,' *Lotharius Rex Francorum me fieri iussit*—refers not to the fact that he commissioned the engraving, but to a more fundamental act of creation. Or generation. The generation of the—the figures."

She dropped her hands into her lap. "Lothar—or, more likely, Waldrada and Bertha making use of Lothar—created them. My responsibility is the other half of the equation—destroying them. The document that Peter of Aigueblanche was guarding provides a preliminary recipe for that. And the crystal would have specified the next steps. You've wrecked your own project now as well as mine."

He smoothed out a wrinkle on the quilt. "Why are you so certain that our projects coincide?"

"What do you mean?"

"The office doesn't want them destroyed, Marion." He looked sidelong at her. "Contained, perhaps. Studied. But not eliminated. They're too potentially useful." He put his hands behind him on the bed and leaned back. "And so, yet again, we are working at cross purposes." He observed the ceiling. "Your orders may very well be to eliminate the creatures. Mine are different. To determine an origin story for them, to find a recipe for brewing a few more, ideally to collect a specimen—without poisoning myself in the process—and then to report back to Maugham."

She stared at his amused, if weary, profile. Then her brows rushed together. "That's monstrous."

"Perhaps." He stood, removed his dressing gown, and returned it to the wardrobe. "Interesting assignment, though. Better than most that come my way these days."

He walked to his side of the bed and slipped under the quilt. "More pressing for me at the moment, however, is what to do about you. You see, if Maugham discovers that you're resistant to whatever those things are spreading, he'll have you walled up in Porton Down, at the mercy of the alchemists, before we've left Wales." He rested his head on the pillow. "And I don't know that I'd approve of such a move."

"Hereford isn't in—"

"Close enough."

"You said they weren't experimenting on anyone," she persisted as she crawled under the covers as well.

"You're an exception," he said, switching off the light. "Too tempting. Your curse."

She closed her eyes, forcing herself to relax her rigid legs and back. At the moment, she was more worried about the things returning than she was about Maugham, who felt very far away. But up till now they'd visited only once every night. Which meant she'd had her requisite interaction with them. And so, perhaps, she could sleep now. If only she could stop shaking.

THEY left Rowlstone early the next morning, the flammable Bugatti just managing to negotiate the icy mud trough that the driveway had become during the night. And less than three hours later, they were climbing the stairs to the ground floor of Jeffrey's townhouse. When they reached the entryway, he turned to her, apologetic. Failing to remove his coat, hat, or gloves. "I'll be at the office for the remainder of the day. I trust you don't require anything further from me?"

She shook her head, her arms wrapped around her waist. "No."

"I'll send over two or three minders," he continued. "One for the house. One for Lydia's room. And one for you." He spoke over her when she opened her mouth to protest. "I'm well aware that you can lose any tail we affix to you, Marion. I won't even bother to send an intelligent one. The point is that this time perhaps you won't want to? In the name of at least one uninterrupted night's sleep?"

She closed her mouth and nodded. Quiet.

"Good." He turned toward the front door. "Thank you."

As she watched him take up his suitcase and leave, she stifled a scowl. Both the tax register and the pages from the tomb were leaving with him. And now that the Susanna Crystal was on the move, she had nothing to help her plan her next steps. Except her memory. As good a place to start as any. And so she turned, resolute, toward the stairs to the second floor.

When she opened the door to her bedroom, she hovered for a few seconds on the threshold, unable to force herself to enter. There was still a hint of anise in the air. Triggering a memory she immediately blocked, before—reproaching herself now—she aggressively pushed the door shut behind her and stalked toward the bed. She couldn't quite stop herself from inspecting both the dressing room and the bathtub before settling into work. But once she'd confirmed that nothing was waiting for her return, she walked with relative confidence to her desk. Prepared to focus on her project in peace.

She pulled a sheet of writing paper toward her and used a pencil to begin organizing her thoughts. The doctor at Great Ormond Street Hospital had mentioned Lotharingia, Hereford, and

Remiremont Abbey. Thus far, Lotharingia had recurred several times as a point of relevance—as the source of the Susanna Crystal, as Queen Bertha's family seat, and as the European origin of the demonic knowledge, at least as William of Malmesbury would have put it, that had afflicted the curious monks. Hereford, as she had seen herself, was as relevant to her project as Lotharingia had been.

Which meant that Remiremont Abbey in the Vosges Mountains of France must house at least a few pieces of information for her as well. Unlike Jeffrey, she had recognized the *Jayzil*, daughter of *Jirarid*, who had been mentioned in the alternative Susanna story, as Gisele, the daughter of Gerard the Great—one of the more prominent abbesses of Remiremont Abbey. Not dissimilar from Waldrada in her reputation for education and intelligence. And her father, Gerard the Great of Lotharingia, had died suspiciously, of perhaps poison, in Remiremont itself in 1070.

Marion was also confident that the series of locations in which Susanna was supposed to have behaved promiscuously was a superficially encoded recipe belonging to Ibn Wahshiyya. Its tone echoed much of what she'd read of his work, and the emphasis on blood and death suggested that it might very well be the recipe she was seeking: instructions for putting her visitors back to sleep.

But the prominent reference to Gisele and Gerard at the end of the account also made her wonder whether it wasn't something more. It was possible that at least some of the plants or fauna on the list would be represented in or around Remiremont Abbey. The story could be a map instead of a recipe. Or it could very well be both.

She set her pencil on the desktop, pushed back her chair, and stood. Thinking about the recipes had reminded her that she must go to the Library to re-read the published versions of the more famous, or notorious, treatises that Ibn Wahshiyya had written. She'd been fortunate to have recognized most of the references she'd encountered in her material. But she'd want more detailed notes on his work before she escaped to France.

And "escape" was the proper word for it, she sighed to herself as she wandered toward the door. She knew very well that she'd be unsuccessful should she try formally to cross borders. The office wanted her to stay in place, and she'd received no word from her own organization that they'd provided her an exit strategy. But she'd entered France quietly many times before, which meant that although the journey would be a nuisance, it was certainly not an impossibility.

At the moment, however, she didn't want to think about it. Instead—turning the knob of the door—she wanted to see Lydia. The baby would be waking from her morning nap, and Marion hoped to be in the room when she opened her eyes. Pleased to be ridding herself of her anxiety and irritation, she entered the corridor.

Where she gasped and took a terrified step backward—before gathering herself, embarrassed, and attempting to appear calm. Standing in front of her, as startled as she had been, was a tall, comically broad-shouldered man—or boy—his hand raised to knock on the door. Carefully cut dark blond hair. Carefully tailored grey city suit. Looking little more than twenty years old. Oxford, she decided. One of Jeffrey's.

"Forgive me, Dr. Bailey. I was about to knock. My name is Percy Lamb."

Of course it was. "How do you do, Mr. Lamb?"

"Sir Jeffrey has asked me—"

"I am going," she interrupted, "to spend an hour now with my daughter."

A second man—or boy—was loitering outside the nursery. Wearing the same suit? And haircut? She didn't want to know. Instead, as she walked, she spoke further to Percy, who was trotting along at her heels. "I see that your colleague will be taking care of us as well."

"Yes," he said. "Anthony—"

"Fine." She reached the door and turned to both of them, standing side by side, looking like highly educated, well-bred versions of a Lewis Carroll invention. "After I visit my daughter, Mr. Lamb, I'll walk to Bloomsbury to work in the Library. You may follow me then, if you'd like. Don't come in."

She closed the door in their faces and turned to Lydia's cot, exchanging an understanding and exasperated look with Alicia. And then, after spending close to two hours with Lydia, most of which involved picking out repetitive nursery rhymes on a badly-tuned xylophone, she left the nursery, nodded at Percy and Anthony, and descended to the ground floor. Grabbed a winter coat at random—something dark green with a pattern and wide fur collar and cuffs, Jeffrey's choice—and left the house.

The coat didn't match the rumpled working clothes she hadn't changed since returning from Hereford, but she didn't mind. More embarrassing was Percy obediently dogging her footsteps. Along with her realization that she must, equally obedient, let him follow. She picked up speed as she passed Great Portland Street. But, dejected, she then slowed and remained visible. She wanted to sleep tonight, and if Percy could make that happen, she would tolerate him.

When she reached the Museum, she left Percy—restless but docile—at the entrance, assuring him that if anything did attack her inside, she'd have more than enough protection in the form of exhibit guards. Then, as she walked toward the reading room, she felt a pang of guilt. He was, as Jeffrey had hinted, not their brightest recruit. But he was also a boy of good faith. She wondered whether she ought to have left him food before she went in. Or whether one only did that with dogs.

Then, as she reached the swinging doors of the reading room, she dismissed Percy from her mind. She knew the volumes she was seeking, and she had a good idea of their call numbers. Even so, after grabbing three request forms, she skimmed the catalogue to confirm her guess before writing out the information in triplicate and submitting the forms to the bored librarian behind the desk. She'd return tomorrow to collect and read the volumes.

As she stuffed the pink copies of the triplicate forms into the pocket of her coat, she glanced up for a second or two at the dome. Her visit had taken less than a half hour. She hoped, despite the short time, that Percy hadn't picked up a chill loitering outside in the biting November damp. Perhaps tomorrow—when she'd spend at least three or four hours reading—she'd suggest he tour the Museum itself. He looked as though he could do with some cultural stimulation. He might even enjoy it. Consider pursuing an alternative career.

Night was already falling when they returned to the house, and Marion was dreading having to withstand Jeffrey's questioning during dinner. But when they entered, Mrs. Bowen stopped her in the entryway to say that Jeffrey would be working late at the office. Delighted by the reprieve, Marion asked her to send a sandwich up to her room and then, still ignoring Percy, climbed the stairs and closed the bedroom door in his solicitous face. More than pleased by the outcome of the day.

After that, she changed into her pyjamas, consumed the sandwich when it arrived, and collapsed into bed. She woke once, sweating, just after midnight, when she sensed the knob of her door turning. But after waiting ten minutes for anything else to manifest itself, she relaxed and drifted back into sleep. She could feel the emptiness in the room. And it soothed her.

The next morning, she used the toilet and changed into a muted green wool dress—a concession to the mild formality of the Library—without violence or mishap. Then, timidly opening the door, she saw that Percy hadn't died in the night. He didn't even look tired or rumpled. Or, for that matter, bored.

But his type didn't bore. Insufficient imagination. And so, cheerful and loyal instead, he followed her down the stairs to breakfast—nodding at Anthony equally alert outside the nursery—where she convinced him to eat a plate of eggs. Then, wrapping up in the same coat she'd worn yesterday—grudgingly admitting that the collar did wonders to keep out the sleet that was spitting down on her—she walked, trailing Percy, to the Museum.

When she entered, she told him that she'd meet him at 1:00 near the exhibit of the pectoral cross from St. Cuthbert's tomb—which she had privately determined he would enjoy more than the display of paleolithic antiquities from the caves of Cresswell Crags. Or the Erasmus exhibit. Nonetheless, when she left him glumly perusing his catalogue, he was unenthusiastic. She wondered as she made her way to the reading room how he had ever attached himself to Jeffrey's specialized section of the service. Some unique, hidden talent, she assumed, which she'd discover to her detriment when the time came.

Pushing away the thought of whatever Percy might be hiding, she approached the entrance to the Reading Room with a degree or two of excitement. And after her customary superstitious glance up at the dome, she let the doors swing closed behind her, moving toward the librarian who had taken her requests the previous afternoon. Ordinarily, the librarians remembered patrons' orders without prompting. But should he need reminding, she had the three pink sheets in her hand.

When he was free—the researcher preceding her staggering away under the weight of eight or nine blank volumes—he turned his politely inquiring gaze in her direction. She arranged the sheets on the counter and began to speak. But before she could remind him of her name and request, he shook his head, cold yet civil. "I'm very sorry, Dr. Bailey." Though he looked more pleased than sorry. "The volumes you've requested aren't available."

"Oh." Surprised as well as disappointed. "Do you know when they will become available?"

"I'm afraid not." Disinclined to elaborate.

After a few seconds, she nodded, too inhibited to press him. "I understand. Thank you."

As she turned to go, he stopped her. "The patron who is using them has indicated a willingness to share."

She looked back at him, suspicious. This was not the scrupulously correct behavior of the staff she'd previously encountered at the Library. She pushed her hands into the pockets of her coat, uncertain she wanted to know the answer to the question she was about to ask. Steeling herself, however, she forced herself to formulate it: "who is currently using the volumes?"

"Professor Richard Maugham." He waited, still bland and polite.

"I see." She blinked. "Would you tell him that I'm grateful to him for the offer, but—"

"It isn't an offer, Dr. Bailey." He stood to the side and opened a gate leading to the other side of the counter. "If you'd walk this way? He's expecting you in his office."

She considered the gap in the counter for two or three seconds. Then she examined the insipid face of the librarian, waiting patiently for her to pass. Finally, deciding that the worst Maugham could do to her in the Library itself was enrage her—which he'd do at some point over the course of this project anyway—she stepped behind the desk.

The librarian closed the wooden gate with a click and opened a blank door into the stacks. He switched on a light, and Marion followed him through the labyrinth of metal and wooden cases until they'd reached the closed door of Maugham's office. Where she vowed that she'd remain calm. She might even pick up useful information from him. If she could only control her reactions to his sadistic conversation.

Maugham, sensing their presence behind the door, opened it before they could knock. He was dressed this morning with relative normality in a muted brown suit. But he'd also grown a pair of unruly white mutton chops, which, with his bald head, portly frame, and malice, gave him even more than usual the look of a mad, Dickensian barrister. Marion dropped her eyes to the ground, dreading the next few minutes. She was already angry.

"Thank you, Mr. Clutterbuck," he said, nodding at the librarian. "Dr. Bailey will find her own way back."

"Sir." The librarian almost bowed before melting into the stacks.

"Dr. Bailey," he continued, stepping to the side to allow her to enter the stagnant room. "So good of you to make time for me. Please come in."

She nodded in turn, walked through the door, and sat in one of the wooden chairs on casters he kept near his desk. The stuffed bird that had teetered at the top of his bookcase had been replaced by a small family of equally dead and stuffed hedgehogs. They saddened her, and she looked away.

Maugham, meanwhile, closed the door and walked around his desk to sit across from her. His hands clasped over his belly. The three volumes she had requested side by side in front of him on the desktop. But she remained silent, her gaze now directed toward her lap.

After the silence had become awkward, Maugham spoke again. "You owe me a sword, Dr. Bailey."

Confused she looked up at him. "That's why you wanted to see me?"

"No," he said. "Accounting."

"Oh." She looked back down at her hands. Waiting.

"Intriguing material you've requested from us." He opened the volume in the center. Ibn Wahshiyya's *Book of Poisons*.

"Background research," she replied. "As I explained to Mr.—Mr. Clutterbuck—my request isn't urgent. I'll continue without them."

"Continue what, Dr. Bailey?"

"My project, Professor Maugham."

"Ah." He let the silence linger again. Then, adjusting his spectacles, he peered down at a page he had marked and cleared his throat. "This spell, for example, on generating a poisonous cow-like creature that kills one's enemies on sight."

He began translating. "'Knead pure wheat flour, a man's blood, and olive oil together; set it aside; then take a cow and have sexual intercourse with it; then withdraw; then insert the dough you've made into the cow's vagina; then insert your penis and ejaculate into the cow; then caress the cow's neck and face; then take some oxblood—'"

"I'm interested in his work on alphabets, Professor Maugham." Cold. She wasn't about to let him embarrass her.

"Thank goodness," he said, closing the volume. "Not that we couldn't have found volunteers to sacrifice a bit of their recreational time on behalf of the Empire. In fact, if we sent a few of our people to Westminster to convince a promising young MP or three that it was all in aid of membership in some omnipotent secret society, I'm confident we'd have more interest than we knew what to do with."

He smiled to himself. "And, of course, we'd make good on our end of the bargain. Help their careers along, in our own small way, when they needed it. It's always useful to have a hold of that sort on one or two future Prime Ministers—"

"Is that why you've asked me to come here?" she interrupted again. "To discuss—" She faltered.

"The civil service," he supplied.

She remained silent.

"But you are correct, Dr. Bailey." He resettled his spectacles. "That is not why I've asked you here."

He continued smiling for a moment or two longer. Then, dismissing the role the office played in Great Britain's governance, he tapped the closed book in front of him with a fingertip. "I found particularly interesting," he said, "Ibn Wahshiyya's reliance in this composition on fennel-based recipes to prevent the decay of dead bodies. To keep them fresh, if I've understood properly."

She dropped her eyes back down to her lap. She hadn't remembered that part of the text. But now that he'd reminded her, it sounded familiar. And remembering those stray references was precisely the reason that she'd requested the volumes to begin with. She must take new notes. She couldn't trust her memory. Trying to keep her frustrated irritation off her face, she balled her hands into fists on her knees.

"You weren't similarly intrigued by those passages?" he prodded her when she didn't respond.

"I hadn't remembered them."

"I see." He fluffed out his right mutton chop. "Willcox mentioned to me a day or two ago that you'd been experiencing some housekeeping difficulties in your London home. Leakage. Odd smells. That sort of thing."

"I believe it was mildew," she said, raising her eyes again. "But it seems to have disappeared on its own. Thank you for your concern, Professor Maugham."

"Not at all, Dr. Bailey." He removed his spectacles and set them on his desk. Held the bridge of his nose between two fingers and closed his eyes. "Willcox didn't return home to you last night," he commented, trying another avenue of attack.

"No," she confirmed.

"You don't wonder where he's gone?"

"No."

He smiled, his eyes still closed. "Would you like me to tell you where he's gone?"

"No."

"Willcox," he said, opening his eyes and leaning back in his chair, "has gone after the people he sent to France." He paused again. "And do you know, Dr. Bailey, I've developed the distinct impression that he's worried about them. Which is unusual. For Willcox, that is."

"Why?" she countered. "He's always going on about how good talent is difficult to find. He wants to keep them informed and alive. What's unusual about that?"

"It's unusual, Dr. Bailey, because Willcox worries about you. Just you. No one else." He pursed his lips. "And so, the question thus becomes why is he *not* worried about you? Why is he not protecting his fragile wife from the dangers that so perpetually assail her? And why is he not sending you any other minder but our keen, yet limited, Mr. Lamb?" He leaned forward, conspiratorial. "It's almost as though he's convinced himself that you—and you *alone*—are specifically *not* in danger."

Silently ordering herself to think, to remain calm, she considered her next words carefully. And then, sitting up straight in her chair, maintaining eye contact, she replied: "he isn't worried about me, Professor Maugham, because he's taken my material. As you know. Without the Susanna Crystal or the documents, I'm neither a threat nor—nor in any danger. I'm neutral. There's no need to protect me. Jeffrey is possessive. Not irrational."

"Neutral." He nodded thoughtfully, mulling over her choice of words. "An interesting way of putting it. 'Non-reactive' might be more accurate."

"I don't understand, Professor Maugham."

"Hmm." He gathered up the three volumes and placed them into a battered imitation leather messenger bag. After which he looked across the desk at her. "I've been thinking, Dr. Bailey, that these volumes may be of more than a little interest to the technicians who are working at Lopcombe Corner to protect our shores from the threat of chemical and biological attack. I don't suppose you'd confer with them? A week or two on loan? For the sake of King and Country?"

"What?" She frowned, confused. Having failed to follow what she was certain must be a threat.

"Ah." Abashed. "Forgive me. Not Lopcombe Corner. Lopcombe Corner is nothing more than a disued RAF aerodrome in Salisbury. Empty. Of no interest to our nation's chemical defense project whatsoever. What I *meant* to say—" he waved a breezy hand in the air, "is the technicians who are working at 'Porton Down.' Also in Salisbury. A few miles down the road from Lopcombe Corner. The latter of which is, as I said, empty. Go and observe it for yourself, Dr. Bailey. Nothing there at all."

"I needn't observe it," she said, repressive. She still couldn't understand his threat, but the mention of Porton Down left her uneasy.

"As you wish." Losing interest. "The decision is entirely your own." He folded his hands over his stomach. "Please, though—even should you decide not to lend your assistance to our specialists in Salisbury—consider the volumes in that bag your own. With my compliments. Mr. Clutterbuck needn't know. I have the utmost confidence in your integrity. You'll return them to our collection when you've made good use of them."

She gazed down at the bag, bewildered. Something had happened, but she had no idea what it was. And although she was more than dubious about the wisdom of taking Maugham's bag, she did need to read the volumes it contained. Perhaps she could remove the material once she'd left the building and dispose of the bag? She suspected that doing so would be ineffective in preventing whatever he had initiated, but it was better than following his orders. Or leaving without the books. Cautiously, she reached for the handle.

"Thank you, Dr. Bailey," Maugham said as she hesitated. Uncertain. "That will be all." He was opening a drawer and removing a file folder. Radiating utter boredom at her continued presence in the room.

She stood, swallowed, and then quickly, with a forced gesture, took up the leatherette bag. As she was leaving, he spoke to her again, not raising his eyes from the file he was reading. "If you decide, Dr. Bailey, to follow your errant husband across the Channel, please know that you do so with our blessing." He scratched his left mutton chop as he read. "You won't be molested on your journey."

She was close to gaping at him now. "With my own passport, do you mean?"

"If you so choose," he said. "Or any of your other passports. Perhaps you or one of your aliases will find my sword floating about on the continent. One can always hope."

"I don't under—"

"Thank you, Dr. Bailey." Short tempered now. "You may leave."

She blinked, nodded a final time, shut the door, and made her way out of the stacks. Clutching Maugham's bag. Frightened and uncertain. She hoped, at least, that Percy had enjoyed St. Cuthbert's cross.

*H*ER first move upon exiting the reading room was to locate a rubbish bin in which to dispose of Maugham's leatherette briefcase. When she found one halfway down the corridor, she stopped, set the bag on a windowsill—noting through the glass the now drenching sleet slicing into the courtyard—and removed the three volumes. Then, rolling the bag into a tight cylinder—surprised by her irrational revulsion to it—she stuffed it into a nearly empty bin. After that, she gathered the books in her arms and descended into the galleries.

She felt lighter having rid herself of the bag. And though the palm of her hand was sticky where she'd been gripping its handle, she told herself that the unpleasant sensation was her own fault, having overreacted—again—to Maugham's prodding. Her palms weren't the only part of her body that had broken into a panic-stricken sweat over the past hour. Her entire body was dank.

Which meant, to her bemused surprise, that the dry, hot air produced by the Museum's excitable radiators was refreshing. Any air was refreshing after the close, suffocating miasma that was Maugham's office. She shuddered as she wandered in the direction of Anglo-Saxon antiquities.

When she found Percy, dutifully reading the brief history of the Viking invasion of 793 that accompanied the temporary St. Cuthbert exhibit, she was almost as pleased to see him as he was to be rescued by her. She found his guileless face soothing. And it was comforting to listen to him gamely expressing his appreciation of Anglo-Saxon Art History. As they left the Museum, she mused to herself that perhaps she did understand why they kept him at the office. He was calming. An antidote to the snidely vicious atmosphere in which its more competent functionaries thrived.

Once they'd exited the building, she suggested they take a taxi back to Chester Terrace, before allowing Percy—happy to be of use—to pay for it. And after they'd entered the building, she asked Mrs. Bowen to have another sandwich sent up to her for dinner. Then she left Percy in the corridor while she spent the afternoon and evening amusing Lydia. And then finally, Lydia having fallen asleep, she returned to her room, changed into pyjamas, ate her sandwich, and went to work on the volumes from the Library.

The more she thought about the Susanna story from Hereford, the more convinced she became that it was both a map and a recipe. True, it did resemble, in form, a spell from Ibn Wahshiyya's work—and she meant to spend the evening discovering which spell it was. But if the secret to stopping the things that had been awakened by the munitions explosion was so arcane that her organization wanted her following what was already a dizzyingly convoluted trail, it was unlikely to be available in an edited, published volume. The details of the story must point toward some set of actions she was expected to take on site, rather than to a concoction whose ingredients she was supposed to find. And that site must be Remiremont.

Her task tonight, therefore, was to find anomalies between the recipe as it had been recreated in the Hereford Susanna story and the recipe in these extant versions of Ibn Wahshiyya's work. Whatever those differences might be, they would provide her with an indication of where she ought to start once she'd reached the Abbey. They would serve as her guide.

With that in mind, she began skimming, first, the *Book of Poisons*—largely because it had been the volume to which Maugham had initially been attracted. And, to her satisfaction, she found the recipe before she was even a third of the way through the text. It was part of a spell for generating a swallow-like creature called "*farastuf*" out of a pit of decay and corruption. Anyone, Ibn Wahshiyya claimed, who looked at the creature that had been grown in this way would die within two hours or live only in pain, despair, and grief.

Reading slowly, she tried to identify any telling differences between the version of the spell she had in front of her and what Jeffrey had read to her in Hereford. But after three repetitions, she found that the only significant change was that in this published version, the magician was told to mix cauliflower with the leaf of the broad bean after splitting open a hoopoe bird, whereas the Hereford story described a mixture of cauliflower and mung bean. Sitting back in her chair, she blinked, nonplussed. She'd been hoping for something more pronounced.

But even if this was all there was, it was sufficient. The test would come when she examined the area surrounding the Abbey. There would, she was certain, be some hint at least of a hoopoe. The bird had been too prominent in the Susanna story not to play a role as guide. And once she'd found the bird, perhaps she'd also find some reference to mung beans. Allowing herself to feel a twinge of optimism, she continued skimming the first of the three volumes.

The clock in the entryway was striking midnight when she decided she was too tired to continue her work. There had been no sound of visitors in the hall, and she was comforted by the thought of Percy, enthusiastic and uncomplicated, stationed beyond her door. In fact, she thought to herself as she cleaned her teeth and crawled into bed, she might bring him along with her when she began her journey to France tomorrow. Perhaps he'd prove trivially useful.

As she lay in bed, staring up at the pink moulding along the edge of the ceiling, she considered her options. She had planned to ignore Maugham's tainted offer of safe passage across the Channel and to leave the country quietly. Losing Percy along the way. But without assistance from her organization, an invisible crossing would be difficult. Unnecessarily so.

It was obvious that Jeffrey, and therefore Maugham, already knew where she was going. He'd have one of his people investigate the Abbey even if he himself didn't. And whoever went to Remiremont on behalf of the office would have both the Susanna Crystal and the parchment with them. They'd already taken everything from her. Which meant she'd gain nothing by going under except delay and trouble.

And so, why not turn the journey into a holiday? Percy would make a pleasant travelling companion. If she brought him with her, she could even tell herself that she was watching the office—while avoiding the guilt she'd inevitably experience about abandoning him. She didn't want him to feel incompetent. He was the sort to take his responsibilities seriously.

Pleased by her decision, she let herself slip into unconsciousness. Oddly content at the thought of her upcoming voyage into France.

Remiremont, France
December, 1936

MARION purchased Percy and herself a sleeping coach on the Night Ferry train that had begun running between Victoria Station and *Gare du Nord* two months earlier. The train left London at nine in the evening, and arrived in Paris at nine the next morning, without stops or changes—the train carriages themselves having boarded the ferry and crossed the Channel without their passengers disembarking. Her plan was to see about transport from Paris to Remiremont once they'd arrived at *Gare du Nord.*

Percy was endearingly eager to experience the new train, but he hid his excitement under a barrage of stolid logistical questions that Marion eventually cut short by telling him that she'd meet him at 8:45 on platform two. He demonstrated his punctuality—another quality, perhaps, that commended him to the office—by appearing neat, composed, and well-scrubbed, carrying a crocodile-skin valise, not what she'd have expected of him, at 8:44. His composure shattered, however, once they'd boarded the train.

There were two bunks in the car, and more than enough room to change. But it was obvious from the moment they entered it that Percy had been concentrating on the mechanics of the train itself rather than on what a single sleeping coach entailed. He opened and then closed his mouth, gripped the handle of his valise, and swallowed, before turning to Marion, who was sliding the door shut. "I shall remain in the corridor tonight, Dr. Bailey. To keep watch. Should—should the creatures return."

"You've been awake for three days, Mr. Lamb." She placed her carpet bag on the tiny armchair in the corner of the carriage. "Take the opportunity to sleep. I'll work throughout the crossing, which means that you can use either bed. And I'll wait outside while you change."

"I haven't brought a change of clothing," he said. Too quickly.

She forced herself not to smile and avoided glancing at his valise. Then, as they felt the train pulling out of the station, she removed her overcoat, lowered herself into the armchair, and opened her bag. "I understand, Mr. Lamb. Good night, then."

"Good night, Dr. Bailey."

He stood rigid in the middle of the carriage for a few seconds. Then he took off his own overcoat and jacket, hung them to the side of the bed, climbed to the top bunk, and made a pretense of lying on his back to sleep. He hadn't removed his shoes or tie.

Marion, letting herself smile more freely now that he couldn't see her, opened Ibn Wahshiyya's volume on alphabets and hieroglyphs. His supposed study and translation of the Egyptian alphabet wouldn't tell her anything specific until she'd examined the Abbey. But she wanted nonetheless to prepare herself for what she would find there.

Her first task was to locate symbols in the volume that might be related to the ingredients listed in the Susanna story. It was a tedious process, but after close to two hours—at the end of which she heard Percy snoring—she had successfully found the figures for bean, blood, fig, and cauliflower, which she dutifully marked. In light pencil. Though, of course, Maugham would have been perfectly content with her marking up the book in any way she liked—or, for that matter, ripping out the pages in their entirety—if it got him closer to what he wanted.

Sighing, she turned to the second step of her preliminary research. To find symbols that resembled a hoopoe bird. After a mind-numbingly detailed search through each and every page of the volume, she identified three likely figures. All of which she also marked—though without a great deal of certainty as to what she would do with them when and if she encountered them in Remiremont.

The first of the three Ibn Wahshiyya had translated into Arabic as *daqqa*, which could mean anything from fragile, frail, or thin, to the act of pulverizing, grinding, or crushing. The word also suggested accuracy or painstaking care in measurement. She could imagine any one of those definitions becoming relevant to her search in the Abbey. Impossible to choose among them without further information at her disposal.

The second hieroglyph he had translated as *zalama*, *zulm*, or *zulam*. And once more, the multitude of meanings of those terms made it futile to guess its signification out of context. *Zalama and zulm* might refer to injustice, oppression, tyranny, or evil. But *zulam* could also mean darkness, gloom, or murkiness. And so, yet again, she was unable to do more than note the existence of the figure and its supposed translation—before moving on.

The final symbol was either *munqi* or *naqa*, both of which had to do with clarity, purity, and purification—but also with careful selection or with the elimination of the unnecessary. Both terms could similarly evoke the process of distillation. Which was, once more, both intriguing and vague to the point of uselessness.

After satisfying herself that she hadn't missed any additionally relevant figures in the volume, Marion closed the book, leaned back in the chair, and shut her eyes, fatigued. Although her findings had been suggestive, they'd brought her no closer to a practical strategy for working in the Abbey than she'd been before consulting the text. She was convinced that she would find some object, or perhaps concoction, in Remiremont that would help her to put Lothar's and Waldrada's creations back to sleep. But she still didn't know what that object would be. Or how and where she would acquire it. The book of alphabets had been no more useful to her than the book of poisons had been.

In fact, she was beginning to wonder now whether her initial failure to access the Ibn Janah material from the tax register was more of a liability than she'd imagined. Until this evening, she'd believed she could improvise without Ibn Janah's contribution. But as the conclusions she drew from Ibn Wahshiyya became increasingly diffuse, she felt ever more keenly the absence of what she suspected would have been a stabilizing influence. Ibn Janah—well-respected physician, lexicographer, and philologist—would have been the perfect counterbalance to the fanciful, grandiose, extravagant—and untrustworthy—Ibn Wahshiyya.

But wishing that she could consult Ibn Janah wouldn't bring his writing to her now. And even if it did magically appear, she'd be in no shape to read it. She could feel the train rocking in the midst of a choppy Channel squall, having now boarded the ferry. Which meant that focus was out of the question. And that it was time to sleep. Long past midnight. She hoped—glancing guiltily at the immobile bulk in the top bunk—that Percy wouldn't be scandalized that she had, after all, slept beneath him part of the way to France.

As she made her way to the bed, nauseated by the un-trainlike movement of the car, she heard a soft knocking on the carriage door. Thinking that it might be a porter asking about breakfast, she turned and slid the door open four or five inches. Wondering at the late hours of the staff. But before she could ask or answer any question from her visitor, a gummy white hand forced the door open the rest of the way. And standing in front of her was the smeared face and cloudy eyes of one of the things—its mouth opening and nearing her own. Questing.

Instinctively, she pushed the thing away, across the corridor, and slid the door shut. Shaking. More than nauseated now. But as she tried to lock it, she felt it being pulled from the other side. A white finger slipping between the frame and the edge of the flimsy handle.

"Oh God," she whispered. "No, no, no."

"Dr. Bailey?" Percy had swung down from his bed and was advancing on the door. About to grab the slick, oozing hand that had forced it two inches further open.

"Don't touch it!" she said. "Just—" She shook her head, and then, remembering what had worked in the past, she shouted at the door. "Go away! Go away and don't come back. Get out!"

Breathing heavily, she waited for three long seconds before the fingers withdrew from the crack. Leaving a slimy smudge on the handle. She slid the door completely shut and, with shaking hands, twisted the useless lock into place.

Then she turned to Percy. "Thank you, Mr. Lamb."

"I did nothing." He was staring at the wet spot on the door.

"You reminded me that I wasn't alone. For which I'm grateful."

"That smell," he said. "They briefed us. But I confess, I couldn't believe it. It's—" He faltered.

She sat on the bottom bunk and put her chin in her hands. "I could use a drink. I suppose it's too late to wake a porter?"

"I've got something," he said, coming to himself. "One moment." He loosened the clasps on his valise, opened the lid, and extracted two bottles. Of Vimto. Smiling, he opened one and handed it to Marion. "Cherry."

She took it, not quite believing that he was serious. But after trying a sip, she was overwhelmed by a protective affection for him. It was horrible. She could scarcely keep the cloying fizz down. But she'd never let him know that. Smiling up at him leaning manfully against the dark window of the carriage while he finished off his own bottle, she thanked him again. "It's delicious, Mr. Lamb. I feel better already."

*W*HEN they disembarked in Paris a few minutes before ten the next morning, Marion was uncertain about their next move. Her original strategy had been to board a local train, which would have brought them to Remiremont Station five hours later. More than enough time for them to find lodgings and examine at least the exterior of the Abbey. But after the visit from the thing, she was hesitant to trap them on another enclosed public conveyance. She didn't want them in a position from which they couldn't fight back.

As she considered, she watched the grindingly slow automobile traffic on the street outside *Gare du Nord* with growing envy. If she could convince Percy to borrow a stranger's car—preferably something bland and reliable—they'd be free to make their way south and east at their leisure. Absent undead followers. Without a car, they were at the mercy of both the rail timetables and the inquisitive French police. Neither of which would aid them in eluding Lothar's and Waldrada's creatures. She'd steal a car herself if only she knew how to drive.

As though sensing her thoughts, Percy turned to her, doubtful. She'd nearly fought him physically to prevent him from carrying her carpet bag as well as his valise, and he was unnerved after the defeat. But he was also watching the parade of automobiles inching past them toward Rue La Fayette with more than mild interest. "Would it be helpful," he finally asked, "for me to procure us private transport?"

She blinked up at him, surprised that he had that sort of network in Paris. Or in any city, for that matter. "*Can* you—procure—that sort of thing, Mr. Lamb?"

"Yes," he said. And then, looking anxious: "although I must warn you, Dr. Bailey, that my actions in—in acquiring the vehicle may not be entirely above board."

She continued to gaze up at him, bewildered now. The Vimto had been a surprise. But this current squeamishness, given his apparent choice of profession, was verging on the baffling. Finally, trying once again not to smile, she formulated a response: "may I ask you a question, Mr. Lamb?"

"Of course, Dr. Bailey."

"Did Sir Jeffrey tell you *anything* at all about me when he briefed you?"

He dropped his eyes to his shoes. "Yes." He swallowed. "But I believe that he may have been exaggerating." He looked quickly up at her, distressed by the hint of disloyalty. "Solely out of concern for you, Dr. Bailey. I'm confident that he expressed certain—qualms—concerning your conduct only because he wanted *me* on my guard. You see, I have on occasion failed to meet expectations. Sir Jeffrey understood that I simply could not fail him—or you—while undertaking this current assignment."

"Mr. Lamb," she said, charmed but keeping her voice grave, "there is no one in the world I'd rather have protecting me on this journey than you. You have been a marvel."

He nodded curtly, trying to keep his expression blank. "I'll see to that vehicle now, Dr. Bailey."

"Thank you, Mr. Lamb." She held her carpet bag in front of her with two hands. "I'll wait for you here."

She spent the next ten minutes watching the traffic, conscious of the scent of imminent snow under the onslaught of automobile exhaust. Taking in the familiar liquid greyness of the Parisian streets. Craving, by association, a strong cup of coffee.

Until, not believing her eyes, she saw Percy at the wheel of a five- or six-year-old Delaunay-Belleville TL6. Shining, black, and emphatically not bland. Though it was almost certainly reliable. She recognized the brand only because of its connection in her mind to the anarchist criminal gangs who had populated the newssheets twenty years ago, during her time at University. Presumably the vehicles they'd appropriated had been dependable. They'd have to have been.

She opened the passenger side door as he neared the pavement, before he'd come to a stop. Then she slipped into the seat and slammed the door shut, clutching her carpet bag in her lap. Without speaking, he picked up speed and skillfully maneuvered them away from the crowded streets surrounding the station and in the direction of the southeastern suburbs. When they'd safely passed the *Bois de Vincennes* twenty minutes later, she turned to him, surprised and impressed. "That was well done, Mr. Lamb."

"Thank you." His driving was fastidious but more than assertive.

"This is a remarkable vehicle," she continued, hoping not to offend him. "But—don't you think it might be missed?"

"Perhaps." He concentrated for a few moments on getting them over the Marne River. "Or perhaps they expect it to be stolen?"

She raised her eyebrows at what she thought might be a joke. "Like the Bonnot Gang's, you mean?"

He smiled, embarrassed at being caught out. "You're familiar with them?"

"They were celebrities of a sort when I was at University." She made a quick mental calculation. "But surely they were before your time."

"I used to read a series of adventure stories that was loosely based on their exploits. At school." He thought for a moment. "Absent the politics, of course. They inspired me to join the service, actually."

She was close to laughing now. "You can't have told Maugham that during your recruitment." Not, she continued silently to herself, that anything of Maugham's talent-spotting calculus would have surprised her. But an innocent and boyish middle-class admiration for one of the century's most notorious anarchist groups was whimsical even for him.

"Oh no," he said, shocked. "I came up with something banal about wanting to serve my country. Nothing about—" And then, horrified by what he had just said: "that is, I *do* wish to serve the nation. And—and the empire. But I also—" He stopped, flustered.

"You also appreciate a good getaway car," she supplied. "For which I, at least, am grateful. If your sole talent were loyalty to King and Country, we'd still be loitering outside *Gare du Nord*."

"Thank you for your understanding, Dr. Bailey." He glanced over at her and then dutifully back at the road.

"Nothing to understand," she replied, unfolding and peering down at a map she had found in a pocket in the side of the door. "Shall we stop in Troyes for lunch and petrol?"

He nodded. "And then, if all goes well, we ought to be in Remiremont by three this afternoon."

She continued examining the map. "I've been thinking. Since we aren't bound to the rail network, perhaps we ought to stay a few miles outside of the city? As a precaution?" Her eyes were still on the map. "We might find an inn in Le Tholy, for example. Ten or fifteen miles up the mountain."

He nodded again. "Simply direct me, Dr. Bailey. And I'll follow."

She smiled to herself as she closed the map. Then, without speaking further, she gazed out the window. They'd just passed the Yerres River. And she was very much looking forward to a spell of quiet research in the wilderness of the Vosges. With a simple and untroubling companion. For once.

Their journey to Le Tholy took longer than they'd estimated because once they passed Troyes, the stray flurries of snow they'd been encountering coalesced into a substantial storm. The road itself remained clear, if wet, until they climbed higher into the forested mountains. But by the time they reached Le Tholy itself, such light as there was had faded, and the ground was coated with three inches of accumulated snow.

Percy remained competent and unflustered as he navigated the car through the small town. When they parked in front of a promising inn on the town's outskirts, however, he also seemed relieved to be free of the wheel. And so, when he asked anxiously whether it might not be best to engage two rooms—about which he would enquire and for which he would pay—she agreed without protest. Then, demure and entertained, she waited for him in the car while he entered the building to discuss terms with the innkeeper.

He was pleased with himself when he returned to the car a few minutes later. Catching sight of the equally pleased faces of the innkeeper and his wife at the door—thin and inhospitable—she surmised that they were satisfied as well. He'd undoubtedly paid ten times the going rate for accommodation in the area.

And as she crunched through the snow, passing over the threshold of the building and nodding a greeting at them, she sensed that his nervousness had telegraphed to them precisely the impression he had hoped to avoid. Despite the fact that he could easily be her son, it was clear that both the innkeeper and his wife believed he'd be using only one of the two rooms he'd scrupulously hired. They were practically chortling.

Glancing at his solid back, she was glad that Percy himself was too buoyed up by his success in communicating their needs to the establishment's proprietors to notice the atmosphere he'd produced. And so, she kept her eyes averted, still demure, as she followed him up the stairs to the bedrooms on the first floor. No need to encourage or discourage the innkeepers in their assumptions. They were the sort best left unenlightened.

The inn conformed to a conventional plan—kitchen, dining room, and cavernous living area at ground level, with six small bedrooms along a corridor above. Wood floors. Painted flowers on the beams. Their own bedrooms were across from one another, at the end of the hall. And when she opened her door and took her bag from him—having let him carry it for her from the car—she saw in the light of a gibbous moon that had broken through the clouds of the dissipating storm that her windows overlooked a meadow and an attractive pond. Beyond which was forest.

But the effect of the moonlight on the untouched snow was eerie rather than enticing. The landscape malign in its frigid beauty. Dishonest. Though at least she'd spot any bodies lurching across the meadow toward her room. Nothing could cross or touch that expanse without violating it.

Sensing her thoughts, Percy hesitated outside her door. Then, clearing his throat, he spoke: "should you be disturbed or—or molested in the night, I do hope you'll summon me." He gestured toward his own door. "I'm here."

"Thank you, Mr. Lamb." She crossed the room and smiled at him. "I'll be certain to call. But I have a feeling that there will be no visitors tonight. They seem not to move quickly."

"Very well, Dr. Bailey. Good night, then."

"Good night." She closed the door and lowered the latch. Then, turning, she examined the furnishings. Carved wooden bed. Painted cuckoo clock on the wall. Feather pillows and white eiderdown. Like the town, the room was charming. Cozy. But disagreeably so. As though it were trying—feebly and dishonestly—to ward off the savagery of the mountains and the forest encroaching on it always less than a mile away. She shivered.

After that, collecting herself, she set about changing into her pyjamas and turning down the bed. She'd experienced similar reactions to this stretch of European forest before. The brightly painted shutters and clean interiors were cheery and delightful. The hospitality was impeccable and painstakingly respectable. But one nonetheless had the impression that it was best not to ask what was buried in the cellar. Not to ask anything at all, really.

As she turned off the lamp beside the bed and drifted into sleep, she found herself wishing, not for the first time, that Bertha's bewildering embassy to the Caliph al-Muktafi had sent her, a thousand years later, to Baghdad or Damascus rather than to the Vosges Mountains. Civilized cities. Less attractive to the not quite human.

A brilliant ray of sunlight reflecting off the blinding white meadow and then through a crack in the curtains woke Marion at seven the next morning. After a second or two of surprised relief that nothing had interrupted her sleep during the night, she sat up and pushed away the clinging eiderdown. Then she found the chair on which she'd left her clothing and changed into her wool trousers and work boots. Quickly cleaned her teeth, pinned back her hair, grabbed her overcoat and carpet bag before descending to the dining room. Percy, she suspected, had been awake and waiting for her since dawn.

He was sitting at the long communal dining table, wearing alpine hiking gear—a change of clothing on which she didn't comment. His corduroy trousers were tucked into thick woolen socks that she could imagine—but didn't—his mother having knit for him. He'd also placed a colorful wool hat topped by a fuzzy green ball on the table.

"Good morning, Dr. Bailey!" He sounded more energized than she would have expected him to be, until she saw the nearly empty pot of coffee to his side. Stronger than Vimto. But apparently he didn't know that.

"Good morning, Mr. Lamb." She sat across from him, set her carpet bag to her side, and lifted the coffee pot. "Is there any left?"

"Oh dear." His face fell. "I'll order more."

"No," she said. "I mustn't drink more than a cup, and it looks as though there's just that much in the pot."

She poured the coffee into a blue mug with a mischievous-looking sprite painted on it. Decided to drink it black and took a sip. "Shall we breakfast in Remiremont?"

"Yes." He jumped up from the table, pleased to be moving. "I'll go start the car." And with that, he pulled the wool hat down over his neatly arranged hair and tramped out of the building.

Marion finished her coffee, stood as well, and buttoned her overcoat. Then, taking up her carpet bag again, she followed him. The innkeepers hadn't made an appearance, but she assumed they were pleased to be spared the expense of preparing food for them. She shouted in the direction of the kitchen that she and Percy would return later in the afternoon, thought she heard an acknowledgment, and braced herself for the cold air and blinding snow.

Once she was through the door, she decided that Le Tholy was as disconcerting in daylight as it had been under the moon. Percy, sitting in the idling car, was a sharply delineated black shape against the backdrop of neatly split white meadow and shadowed forest. Shading her eyes with her hand, she trudged toward him, clutching her bag. And when she pulled herself into the passenger seat and shut the door, the gloom of the interior was an odd respite. She would, perhaps, not gaze out at the scenery as they made their way the ten miles into Remiremont. She might even close her eyes.

The Delaunay skidded periodically on the road away from Le Tholy, but by the time they were crossing the bridge over the Moselle, the snow had thinned to a light dust. The bare branches of what looked like maples and aspen were also appealing, spare over the calm, muted water of the river. Marion began to think—hope—that she would find Remiremont less jarring than the mountains that surrounded it. At the very least, she'd be able to lose herself in work.

And as they entered the town, they did catch sight of a few pedestrians scurrying from storefront to storefront. Otherwise, though, the streets were grimly empty. The small, urban squares creepily abandoned—and the car conspicuous as it navigated the quiet buildings. Ignoring the absence of public life, they left the car and made their way to a café across the street from the Abbey—open and occupied by two older men, who were smoking and hunched over newspapers.

Once there, they resolved to observe the church to get a better feel for its atmosphere. And so, occupying a table near a window with a view toward its façade—eighteenth-century, Marion noted, disappointed, as she put her bag next to her feet on the floor—they waited and watched. Looking for hints as to what sort of people might visit the building, and why.

When a stern woman approached them to inquire about food, Marion gave her a brief, distracted smile before ordering a second cup of coffee and a brioche. Percy, to the astonishment of both the proprietor and the two men reading newspapers, asked for the entire plate of marzipan biscuits he had seen under glass behind the counter. Along with a bottle of water. And then, once their plates arrived, unaware of the impression he was producing, he seriously and systematically annihilated the marzipan, while peering with self-conscious professionalism across at the church. But of course, he was a large boy. He could very well still be growing.

After an hour of observation, they decided that they might project sufficiently credible touristic interest in the building to enter it without drawing attention to themselves. Although Marion could already see that the only part of it that would help her would be the crypt, which was original, and tenth- or eleventh-century. Whatever bits of the fourteenth-century church that had survived the façade were too recent to yield information. And even had there been other parts of the compound that dated to earlier periods, she had a gloomy suspicion that the dead bodies were her target.

As they left the café, a thought occurred to Percy, and he slowed to a stop in the middle of the empty street. Fascinated and repelled. "Will there be nuns inside?"

"Only as visitors." She continued walking, and he trotted behind her. "The community was disbanded after the Revolution. But long before that, the ladies of Remiremont had become secular canonesses. I understand that they could even marry, if they chose to do so. The sole requirement for membership was written evidence of at least two hundred years of noble descent."

"Oh."

She couldn't tell whether he was disappointed or reassured. But either way, she was no longer paying him attention. They had entered the church, with its clean gothic vaulting, and she was concentrating now on how to get them into the crypt with as little delay as possible. They'd raise suspicion if they immediately descended below ground. But as close as they were to a concrete test of her hypothesis, she was itching to begin. She gripped the handle of her bag more tightly than was strictly necessary and gazed, frustrated, about the chapel.

After that, resentful but attempting to hide it, she led Percy around the cruciform aboveground building. Stared blankly up at the stained glass. Appreciated the sculpture. Before, feeling that they'd done their duty, she approached the door leading into the crypt.

She nodded a greeting at a young woman who was sketching the stairway and descended into the central room of the crypt. Then, pulling her overcoat around her shoulders as the subterranean air crept over them, she took in the stone floor and the whitewashed ceiling of the cavern. Antiseptic. Behind her, she could see Percy's breath rising in the air and the bobbing shadow that the fuzzy ball attached to his hat projected against the wall.

Uncertain, she walked the perimeter of the room, observing the squat, white sarcophagi and the bits and pieces of eleventh-century mural that remained on the walls. Then, ducking through a low, arched door, Percy obediently following on her heels, she continued to analyze the space. Despite the increasingly forbidding atmosphere.

Finally, intrigued, she approached a mural of a figure on horseback, half rubbed away, situated above a sarcophagus that was empty and open. Missing its stone cover. She considered the mural, frowning. Then, leaving her bag on the ground beside her, she crouched down to look more closely at the blank, erased bottom half. In the corner, she could just make out "Jirarid witnessed Susanna," etched shallowly in Arabic script. And underneath that, she found an equally shallow hoopoe bird symbol—the third of the set she had marked on the Night Train. Representing distillation rather than oppression, darkness, or fragility.

She sat back on her heels, perplexed. But then, noticing that the long "a" in the Arabic word "witnessed" had been blurred, and that two small dots had been added underneath, she understood. Gerard hadn't "seen" Susanna. He'd been a martyr—a *shahid*—to her. Not to the Susanna of the story, but to those, millennia later, who'd decayed. And his martyrdom—if the hoopoe bird hieroglyph was any indication—had taken the form of a "distillation."

Letting her eyes travel to the narrow, open sarcophagus beneath the mural, she felt ill. Knowing, without question, what had happened here. Gisele, the daughter of Gerard the Great, had kept his body, presumably fresh, in order to distill the necessary materials for generating those that decayed. He *had* been a martyr. Poisoned. And then distilled into ingredients for their recipe. Perhaps even as Lothar II, who had originally "caused them to be made" had been. Now that she understood the message, she could almost smell a centuries-old hint of anise or fennel in the air.

But, she reminded herself as her gorge rose, this realization by no means altered the direction of her project. Her assignment was to put the decaying things back to sleep. And she was confident now that the key to doing so was secreted somewhere near this empty tomb. Glancing over at Percy, clean and innocent in his hiking outfit, she felt corrupt herself. Implicated. Pushing down the feeling, she addressed him. "Mr. Lamb?"

"Yes?"

"I must examine this sarcophagus." She swept a strand of hair off her forehead. "Would you watch the door? Tell me whether I'm likely to be disturbed?"

"Of course, Dr. Bailey." He wandered toward the arch and positioned himself in line-of-sight to the stairway. Nodded back at her.

"Thank you." She knelt at the end of the shallow sarcophagus and peered at the rough, white stone. Then, finding the same set of hieroglyphs that had guided her in Hereford, she began to manipulate what looked upon superficial examination to be a cracked, loose surface near the base of the tomb. And when a compartment, identical to that in Peter of Aigueblanche's, opened not in the bottom half of the sarcophagus but in the floor beneath it, she was less pleased than she was perturbed.

They'd stored the body beneath the tomb. Not in it. To ward off inquisitive observers. As she gazed down at the opaque black crevice, the thought occurred to her that he may not even have been dead when they put him there. But then, viciously shoving away the morbid and unnecessary supposition, she ground her teeth and inserted her fingers into the opening in the stone floor.

When her fingertips brushed parchment, she was sickened. But she grabbed the pages and pulled them out of the hole. Unwilling to give up and admit failure this far into her assignment.

"Oh God." She stared down at her hand. It was coated with an orange-brown fluid, with the smell and consistency of well-aged vomit. Although the parchment, once again, was unaffected.

"What is it, Dr. Bailey?" Percy squinted back into the room at her crouching form.

"Nothing," she muttered, closing up the crevice and stuffing the parchment into her bag. "I'll want to wash my hand."

He took a few steps toward her as she straightened, and then he stopped, his eyes wide, gaping at her hand. "Oh dear." He whipped off his hat. "Use this. It will absorb the worst of it."

"I'm not going to ruin your hat, Mr. Lamb." She passed him and began climbing the stairs. "There's a toilet in the café. And if that doesn't work, I'll wash it in the river."

"But it could be harmful." He was striding to keep up with her.

"All the more reason not to wipe it on your hat." She led him out of the church and then crossed the street and entered the café. "Would you order us some eggs? You can't survive solely on Vimto and marzipan, you know."

"I don't see why not." He smiled at her. Shy. But pleased to have come up with a retort. She smiled back at him. "I won't be five minutes."

When she returned from the toilet, her hand free of contamination, the proprietor of the café was placing two cheese and sausage omelettes on their table. But rather than lingering, they ate quickly and silently, focusing on the food. And less than ten minutes later, grateful to be putting distance between themselves and the Abbey, they were making their way back to the car and then into the mountains toward Le Tholy. By the time they'd reached the inn, the road was almost bare of the previous night's snow.

Marion was pleased that Percy had been well enough trained not to ask her questions in the café. But she was surprised as well as pleased when he also had the tact not to become inquisitive in the car. And when they tramped up to their rooms, leaving wet, slushy footprints on the stairs, she was actually impressed that he left her to her own devices, claiming to need rest after rising so early. Increasingly, she was coming to understand what Maugham had seen in him.

She, however, contrary to her training, scarcely had the self-control to shrug off her overcoat before extracting the sheets of parchment from her bag to get a feel for their importance. They were two small, ripped pages, nothing like the elaborate illuminated sheets she'd found in Hereford. But even so, they felt valuable. She was confident that if she read them with care, she'd draw useful information out of them.

Casting about the room for a suitable place to work, she eventually sat cross-legged on the bed with the parchment spread out in front of her on the eiderdown. Then, intrigued, she examined the writing. Educated Arabic once again. A hand similar to what she'd seen in Hereford. These pages, however, were not only small, but nearly blank. The first contained four lines. Slowly, alert to anomalies or hidden signs, she translated:

> The mung bean is very small, with an eye like a black-eyed pea; I saw it once growing in the garden of our vizier, Ibn Shahid, but no one else in Cordoba had it; the vizier told me that Ibn Hasday, the Jew, brought it for him from the Orient.

And that was all. It was true that the reference to the mung bean caught her attention. But the rest was of little relevance. And if it was encoded, she couldn't begin to locate a meaningful message in it without context.

Although she did recognize the source—a section of Ibn Janah's work on pharmacology and medicine, *Kitab al-Talhis*, which she'd seen years ago, in pieces, in Istanbul. But the fact that she could venture an attribution only made her more uneasy, convincing her that whatever she had missed of the second part of the tax register had been a vital piece of the puzzle. The passage strongly suggested to her a code whose key had been buried in the *defter*.

She leaned back against the headboard of the bed and exhaled, frustrated. Wondering whether it would not only be difficult, but in fact counterproductive, to continue without that piece—without knowing what else Ibn Janah had written about putting the things back to sleep. She could very well be making the situation worse. Flailing about with only half of her instructions.

Feeling slightly desperate, she straightened, set the page to the side and focused on the second sheet of parchment. But after three or four minutes of translation, she was even more perplexed than she'd been before. In front of her was a short section of a description of John of Gorze's embassy to the Caliph of Cordoba in 953. Translated into Arabic. Gorze Abbey was a little over a hundred miles to the north of Remiremont—also a part of former Lotharingia. And John of Gorze, a polymath, had spent two or three years in Islamic Spain as an ambassador. But that was all she knew of him.

Even with that little information, however, she was confident that he couldn't have interacted with Ibn Janah. The timing was off. Ibn Janah had been born sometime close to the 970s in Cordoba, but he had spent most of his working life, after 1012, in the city of Saragossa. There was little to connect him to John's residence in Spain a good two decades before his birth. The passages must be unrelated.

Shrugging to herself, she skimmed the five or six lines describing John's impressions of cosmopolitan Muslim Cordoba. And then, smiling, she re-read the passage. Its centerpiece concerned John's favorable impression of "Rabbi Hasdai ibn Shaprut," the Jewish advisor to his embassy, who had provided him guidance on interacting with the Caliph's court. John had been astonished by Hasdai's extensive learning in all fields, including medicine, mathematics, and botany.

The Hasdai praised by John of Gorze was the same Hasdai who had brought the mung bean—a plant that Marion was convinced was a "mung bean" only in name—back to Cordoba in the mid-tenth century. A few decades after Bertha's embassy to the Caliph al-Muktafi. And a few years after Ibn Wahshiyya's supposed translations of the Nabatean books of sorcery. Meaning that there was a small—fragile—link between the two.

She knew that she was still missing a significant part of the story—something she would have found in the *defter* if Jeffrey hadn't taken it from her. But it was possible that if she and Percy travelled to Gorze and found the remnants of an Abbey garden, or even a pharmacological text, she'd be able to concoct the recipe. It was an unlikely course to take. But it was all she had.

And, she thought to herself, rolling up the parchment pages and stuffing them back into her carpet bag, it was best to leave tonight. Before the things—whose close presence she could feel now on her skin—caught up to them. All she must do was pack up her scant belongings before waking Percy from his nap. She hoped he was well enough rested for another evening drive through the mountains.

*W*HEN she crossed the corridor and knocked on his door, Percy wasn't sleeping. Instead, still wearing his wool socks, but having removed his hiking boots, he was eating a marzipan biscuit he'd saved from the café and reading a paperback edition of *The A.B.C. Murders*. He held the book in his hand, his place marked, when he opened the door.

"Forgive me, Mr. Lamb," she said. "But I'd like to leave Le Tholy this evening. For Gorze— a few hours to the north. Are you feeling rested?"

"Yes, of course, Dr. Bailey." He glanced back into his room, which bore no sign of having been occupied. The bed was conscientiously made. The furniture free of personal detritus. "It will take me a few minutes to pack."

"I'll meet you downstairs." Clutching her carpet bag, she descended to the dining room and sat at the end of the long table. Upright on the edge of a wooden chair. Nervous. Hunted. An irrational response to a charge in the atmosphere that she knew better than to dismiss. Something was closing in on them, and it was imperative that they move.

She gazed out one of the snugly curtained windows at the sun sinking behind the forest and meadow. Then, hearing Percy's boots clumping down the stairs, she rose from the chair to meet him. Jittery and relieved.

The innkeepers, who had also heard Percy on the staircase, emerged from the kitchen, inquisitive. And when he explained to them in his correct, schoolboy French that he and Marion would be leaving at once, they exchanged a slyly entertained look. Marion read "lovers' quarrel" in their expression and almost smiled herself.

But then, as her nerves reasserted themselves, she instead hugged her waist, her face blank, wishing that Percy would stop slowly and painfully explaining that their departure had nothing to do with the inn's hospitality. Anyone could see that the innkeepers were delighted to see the end of their guests. Especially having been overpaid a week's room and board for a single night and no food. Finally, however, he nodded politely and turned away from them, before following Marion—who had already ventured out onto the doorstep—in the direction of the car.

The sun was nearly gone by the time he'd started the engine and brought them onto the mountain road. And the patches of snow that had melted during the day were crusting over, the wet turf showing through, thick, heavy, and brownish. But they were well into the woods before the light disappeared completely, giving way to the partial illumination of a half-moon that kept pace with them as they traveled. Marion leaned back in her seat, pleased to be away from Le Tholy, and closed her eyes.

Thirty minutes later, as they passed through the town of Xamontarupt, she opened her eyes, peering out the window at the dark mountainside that was rising up, if gently, a few feet away from the ditch along the edge of the road. Five minutes after that, Percy slowed the car, leaned forward, and scanned the path in front of them. Then, shaking his head, he accelerated. Uncertain.

"What is it?" Marion asked.

"I don't know," he said. "I thought I saw something. An animal. Nothing of concern."

She nodded and looked out the windscreen as well. They were moving through a flat bit of landscape, still high, surrounded by conifers. No sign of habitation. It was, in fact, a peaceful stretch— until, without warning, Percy slammed on the brakes and the car skidded to a stop. Marion was shocked for a moment before understanding that his reflexes were quicker than hers. It was only once the car was idling at a diagonal across the road that she saw the animal.

A wolf. Though she had thought they were extinct in this part of France. And this wolf, from what she could see of it in the moonlight, was larger than wolves were supposed to be in Europe. Reddish. Immobile, dominating the middle of the road, legs straight, snarling at the car. A moment later, it was joined by four others, equally large, equally aggressive, pacing and circling.

She turned to Percy. "What do you think?"

"I'll drive through them."

He reversed and straightened the car. Then, slowly, he moved toward the first wolf, expecting it to give way as they approached. It didn't. Instead, once they'd neared it, it jumped up onto the long bonnet of the Delaunay, snarling at them through the windscreen. The other four wolves also closed in.

"Hmm," Percy remarked, demonstrating a sang-froid far removed from the terror of the boy who had recoiled at the thought of a single sleeping carriage. "Shall we see if it can hang on all the way to Gorze?"

She smiled at him. "It's your call, Mr. Lamb. I don't drive."

He frowned and shifted into first gear. But before he could accelerate, something that wasn't an animal began to pull open the passenger side door. Marion grabbed at the handle, unable to slam the

531

door shut again because a stinking white body had launched itself into her lap and, without hesitation, clamped its lips over her own.

Suffocating, she tried to push it off of her, while noting out of a frantic corner of her eye that there were at least three others following it, moving in her direction. Before she could free her mouth to order them away, she felt it lifted bodily away from her and pitched onto the road. And then, the car shuddered and stalled. Percy's foot had slipped off the pedal.

When, slow and unwilling, she turned to face him, he was slumped over the wheel, sweating, losing consciousness, and gasping for breath. His hands were covered with white, reeking sludge where he had grabbed the thing. His skin pallid. Cold, when she tentatively touched him.

"Oh no." She squeezed her eyes shut. "Oh no, Percy. You weren't supposed to touch it."

When she felt one of the things insinuating itself back into the car, she turned on it, close to hysteria, and shrieked at it to get away. Never to come back. And, as they always had in the past, the thing stopped, cowered, made the "yes" sound, and slunk into the forest.

But this time, she had no chance to recover from their presence. The moment it had retreated, it was replaced by a wolf, less inclined to listen to her orders. For a split second she locked eyes with it. Then, as it leapt, she threw up a useless hand to protect her face. The last thing she felt before she lost consciousness was the wolf's teeth ripping open the skin of her forearm.

UPON waking, she found herself reclining on a sofa, her arm bandaged, and a fire burning behind a stone hearth three or four feet in front of her. From the feel of the wound, the wolf had done little more than pierce her skin. Certainly no bones were broken. And as she gingerly sat upright, she felt no other damage to her body. Looking about the room, she hoped to see Percy, resting elsewhere, equally unharmed. But she was disappointed. The room was empty aside from herself.

Bracing her muscles, she rose to her feet, felt momentarily faint, mastered the dizziness, and inspected her surroundings. The room was brightly lit not only by the fire, but also by two chandeliers wired for electric bulbs. The floor was flagstone, covered with animal furs. And the furnishings, though rich, were minimal. In addition to the sofa, there was a low wooden table, three armchairs surrounding the table and facing the fire, and four storage trunks lined up against one wall. There weren't, as far as she could see, any windows in the walls. Although there was a door. Wooden and reinforced with iron bands. Opposite the hearth.

Deciding not to waste time deciphering her new situation—and worried about Percy—she walked toward the door, supporting her bandaged elbow with her left hand. When she reached for the handle and began to turn it, however, someone pushed it from the outside, and she stumbled back, on her guard.

"You're awake already, Dr. Bailey? How encouraging."

Spoken in French, but with a fifteenth- or sixteenth-century feel to it. By a round, cheerful woman—looking tired and harried, though suggesting that such was not her ordinary mien—of perhaps sixty years. She was wearing a white scarf over her greying curls, and a long white apron over a blue patterned dress. And carrying what Marion couldn't quite accept was a very large green glass of blood.

The woman closed the door behind her, crossed the room, and set the glass on the table. Then she turned back to Marion. "I'm Bertha." She smiled at an inward joke. "No relation, of course."

Marion nodded, uncertain as to whether she ought to continue her exploration of the building despite Bertha's return to the room. The small, round woman didn't look the type who could stop her physically. But then, if she'd had something to do with rescuing her from the wolf and the things, she must be well-disposed. She, herself, wasn't dead. Which she very well could have been. Warily, Marion retreated in the direction of the hearth.

"You look as though you could do with a meal," Bertha continued, lowering herself with a short, satisfied sigh into one of the armchairs. "Unfortunately, it's best that you don't eat for the next twelve hours."

Marion sat in the armchair across from her. "I had a companion with me. Is he—here as well?"

"Of course. Mr. Lamb." She leaned back in the chair and crossed her ankles. "He's in the infirmary. Our last bed. Which is why you've found yourself on the sofa. We're not quite set up for the undertaking that's been thrust upon us."

"And—who are you, then?" Marion found herself wishing that the glass of blood on the table might be replaced by a glass of water. Feeling dehydrated. And the blood, which was steaming less than a foot away from her, was disconcerting at best.

"You're less well-informed than I was led to believe you'd be, Dr. Bailey." Intrigued rather than accusatory.

"I'm less well-informed than I thought I'd be as well," Marion replied. "I may have missed—something important—along the way. But perhaps I'm nonetheless where I was originally meant to—arrive?" she added hopefully.

"Indeed, you are."

"Good." She paused. "And that is?" Unwilling to let the conversation continue until she knew Bertha's relation to her organization. Though the fact that Percy was apparently not dead left her less tense than she'd been a few minutes earlier.

"You are among," Bertha said, both pious and impish, "the Ladies of Remiremont. Or, the 'Lady' of Remiremont. The others are out and about. As they tend to be. I'm the Abbess. Holding the fort, no?" She frowned over at the row of closed trunks. "I've got the papers proving my ancestry somewhere or other, if you'd like to see them."

"The chapter was disbanded in the eighteenth century," Marion countered, her voice neutral.

"Don't be silly." Bertha's French still felt courtly and very old. "Of course we didn't disband. We went underground." She laughed again at some unexpressed joke.

When Marion simply looked at her, confused, Bertha continued, gesturing at the room. "This is one of my family's ancestral castles. Below ground, at least. Above ground is a ruin. Scads of them in the region. But we're rarely bothered. The peasants know that there's nothing of value to take here." Her smile deepened. "And then, of course, there is the Beast." She raised her eyebrows, conspiratorial. "The Beast of the Vosges."

"The—beast?"

"Yes. You met him." Her eyes grew sentimental. "He's an old softy when you get to know him." She brightened. "*Would* you like to get to know him?"

"No." Marion held her gaze. "Thank you. I was sufficiently impressed the first time."

Bertha nodded. "Yes. Most people are. Although he did find us an excellent vein." She turned her eyes to the glass of blood on the table. "I couldn't have selected a better one myself. And it spared you the trouble of parting with it while you were conscious."

"That's my blood?" She was on the defensive again, feeling that Bertha's aristocratic lack of empathy had just, if incrementally, crept over an invisible line into something more sinister.

"Yes. But it will want to heat, cool, and ferment for another seven hours before we use it." Bertha looked concerned herself, when Marion still did no more than gape back at her. "You don't know why you're here, do you, Dr. Bailey?"

"All I know is that I've failed," Marion said. "Even if I am here. This—situation—isn't right. Something's missing."

"No, nothing's missing. You haven't failed."

"Yes," Marion said, patient now. "I have. I was ordered to locate a—a recipe. And not only haven't I found it, but I have no idea where to pick up the trail again. I began with piecemeal information. Which led me astray." She hated herself for making excuses. Forced herself to stop.

"There is no recipe," Bertha replied.

"Of course there is."

Bertha shook her head. "No, there isn't."

"Yes, there—"

"That is to say," Bertha interrupted, "yes, once, long ago there was a recipe. Both for generating Waldrada's—descendants—and for putting them to sleep. But it was lost shortly after Gisele's time. All we have now is Ibn Janah's—"

"Ibn Janah?"

"Yes?" Bertha's black eyes twinkled, bird-like. "Ah. But I understand now. That would be the piece of the *defter* that you missed. We have it here, if it would comfort you to read it. In our library. Your husband had it with him—"

"*Jeffrey's* here?"

"My dear," Bertha sighed, looking elegantly haggard again, "everyone is here. We've been doing our best to collect them all in one place. Awaiting your arrival. The curious children. Various—agents. The merely unlucky. They're in stable condition. But I must say, we *are* pleased that you've—"

"Wait." Marion held up a hand. "Before you continue, tell me more about Ibn Janah."

Bertha glanced over at the glass of blood. "Very well. We do have seven hours." She settled herself more comfortably in the chair. "I'll start from the beginning." Then, gathering her thoughts, she did: "Waldrada, Lothar's wife, was a well-educated woman. A scientist. As many of those attached to Remiremont Abbey have been. As, indeed, am I. She, however, made a study of fertility and infertility. Generating and animating life. Ending it. Preventing its inception. She was unmatched in her knowledge of these fields."

Bertha paused. "But her true epiphany occurred when she received a gift of byssus—sea silk—from an admirer. Byssus, as you know, is cloth woven from the strands with which giant mussels attach themselves to the sea floor."

"Yes," Marion said in answer to a short break in Bertha's recitation. Recalling with misgiving the scraps of cloth and parchment ripped to pieces by the brave boy in Hereford.

"Somehow," Bertha continued, "the byssus that Waldrada received wasn't—yet—dead. Or perhaps she worked to keep it alive herself. It's difficult to know how she initiated her investigation. What we do know is that when she covered the recently dead body of one of her experiments with it, she noted certain promising chemical reactions occurring."

Bertha watched Marion for a few seconds to be certain that she was following the story, nodded to herself again when Marion appeared focused, and then resumed. "And so, over the years, Waldrada perfected her technique. On—dead matter. Using, among other materials, liquids she'd collected from her husband to craft her figures. But, to her dismay and frustration, she could never keep the bodies that she'd shaped cohesive. Minutes or, at best, hours later, the things she'd animated would disintegrate and die. Until she herself also died—as do we all—before she could do more than theorize the possibility of growing people in the same way that one might grow, for example, plants."

The Abbess now leaned forward in her chair. "It was Waldrada's daughter, Bertha, who discovered the missing piece of the puzzle that Waldrada had spent her life seeking. But Bertha—better placed and, in a way, better born—used diplomacy, rather than experimentation, to take that step forward."

The Abbess held her hands out to the fire and rubbed them together. They looked raw with work. "Knowing that her mother had made profitable use of the scientific discoveries that had been drifting out of the lands of the Caliphate, Bertha resolved to make discrete inquiries about the scholars there. And, eventually, her inquiries bore fruit. Her informers told her of a magician—of ill-repute but working in good faith—who was concerning himself with a set of problems similar to her own. Ibn Wahshiyya. And so, Bertha entered into a correspondence with him. She sent him her findings on the properties of byssus. And he, in turn, sent her a recipe for indefinitely preserving a dead body. Keeping it fresh. Open to regeneration. The foundation of that recipe, Dr. Bailey, was a rare type of fennel."

The abbess looked into the fire for a few seconds, clearly trying to decide how much more of the story Marion would, or could, understand. Then, frowning, she continued. "I've had the opportunity to read the papers that Waldrada left to our community. And I've also read much of what Bertha wrote. In addition, I've devoted many decades of my own life to the study of biology, chemistry, botany, and medicine." She smiled, wry. "But despite all of that, neither I nor anyone else familiar with Bertha's discovery has reproduced her results. There's always been an element missing."

She paused again. "If you're sympathetic, Dr. Bailey, I will tell you, in theory, in modern terms, how I believe the creatures were generated. Even if I've never replicated the feat myself."

Marion nodded. Quiet.

Bertha nodded in turn and went on. "Byssus," she said, "contains a unique combination of keratin and polyphenolic protein. When the mussel is living, both remain in liquid form. Somehow, Bertha preserved this liquid in the cloth, as it was being woven. Such that it could seep into whatever it touched. Or covered."

She folded her hands together on her lap. Modest. "Now, polyphenolic protein, in turn, contains elements called tyrosine and cysteine. Tyrosine is the building block of our—and any—nervous system. It generates neurotransmitters—Otto Loewi's recent discovery. Cysteine is an amino acid that crystallizes bodies. I made a study of it and other amino acids in Switzerland under one of Franz Hofmeister's students a decade ago. And I discovered that, again *theoretically*, the two together, when mixed with Ibn Wahshiyya's uncorrupt dead matter, can indeed animate a form that looks and acts—alive."

Bertha shrugged. Her hands still folded. "As I said, however, since Gisele, we haven't reproduced the experiment in practice." She flashed a smile at Marion. "Perhaps there's also something unique about Lotharingian seed. Lothar's? Gerard's? Who knows? I fear—not having taken advantage of our chapter's permission to marry—that I am not an expert in such matters."

"I see," said Marion, who had followed almost nothing of Bertha's scientific explanation. "But none of what you've described sounds dangerous. That is—harmful to others. If all Bertha was doing was creating—synthetic people—why do you now have an infirmary full of dying children and—and agents?"

"Yes. Well, that was Bertha's other great discovery," the Abbess replied. "The weapon. The secret that she sent to the Caliph al-Muktafi, courtesy of Ibn Wahshiyya. A secret, which, I fear, had less to do with the science of fertility and infertility than it had with the military implications of that science."

"And those implications were?" Marion rubbed the bandage over her wound. Uncertain that she wanted to know.

"When Bertha made her discovery," the Abbess explained, looking back at the fire, "she became a touch—obsessed. As any scientist would. And so, she began to purchase, and then hoard, the raw materials that went into her creations. Most especially, she outbid every competitor in the market for byssus. She bought it all. All of it. And she kept it in warehouses throughout her dominions. It was inevitable that at some point she would have found herself with a tainted batch. Mussels saturated with toxins. Saxitoxin, we call it now. Red tide."

"Oh." Marion thought she was beginning to understand.

"Given her ignorance of the danger she was in," the Abbess remarked, "it's astonishing that she survived. Because, you see, whatever kept the proteins and amino acids in the byssus active also preserved the saxitoxin. And when the tainted cloth animated that batch of figures, they too were flooded with the poison."

She cocked her head. "Interestingly, it didn't harm them. Perhaps since the creatures don't breathe, *per se*, they aren't adversely affected by the respiratory collapse that follows saxitoxin exposure. Again, who knows? What was important was that they were, themselves, deadly. Secreting sufficient neurotoxin from their pores to wipe out an army. Which," the Abbess concluded, "Bertha thought might interest the Caliph."

"But it didn't," Marion said. "Interest him, that is. He dismissed her embassy as—a bit of a joke."

"True," Bertha conceded. "It's difficult to know why. Although, once again, one can speculate. Ibn Wahshiyya, for example, wouldn't have been a respectable conduit for her communications to the court. Or perhaps the Caliph found the idea of poisonous hordes of undead soldiers dishonorable? Likely to run amok? There is a hint in Ibn Wahshiyya's own writing of what occurred at the meeting."

The Abbess crossed her ankles again. "Do you remember in his *Nabatean Agriculture*, he writes that the sorcerer 'Sabyatha' received the recipe for creating artificial humans from the messenger of the sun—'Bertha,' you know, meaning 'bright one?' This sorcerer then offered to generate a batch for his king. But the king, you'll recall, forbids him to do so. Tells him that the magic is unhelpful and will sow disorder—*fitna*—among people and nations. In short, in Ibn Wahshiyya's tale, the king simply didn't want it. He told his sorcerer to go back to brewing beneficial things like talismans and medicine."

Marion nodded again. She remembered the passage.

"My own impression," the Abbess commented, "is that Bertha was a better scientist than she was a strategist or ethicist. She was—enthusiastic—you understand?"

Marion considered. Then she frowned. "But she kept making them anyway."

"Unfortunately." Bertha looked embarrassed. "Thirty-six of them, to be exact. But now that her secret was out—if only among a select few—other interested parties began to respond to it. And so, whereas the Caliph dismissed it, a certain rabbi from Spain, travelling the region at the time, found it both compelling and—more so—disturbing. That rabbi's name was Hasdai ibn Shaprut."

"Oh." Marion waited. And then: "yes?"

"We believe that Hasdai met with Ibn Wahshiyya—or possibly with Ibn Wahshiyya's pupil, Ibn al-Zayyat, to whom he had dictated his supposed 'translations.' And from one or the other, Hasdai not only acquired the recipe, but also the beginning of an antidote to the toxin. Not to mention a means of putting the creations back to sleep. Ibn Wahshiyya was always conscientious—unlike Bertha—about concocting remedies for his potentially harmful spells."

"I see." Marion was increasingly regretting having missed the second section of the *defter*. At this point, she was on the verge of accepting the Abbess's polite, but likely not serious, offer to bring it to her to skim. For the moment, however, she held her curiosity in check.

"The mung bean," Bertha said, interrupting her thoughts.

"Yes," Marion confirmed. Then, perplexed: "how did you know?"

"I've taken the liberty of reading the pages you brought with you from Remiremont, as well as the pages Sir Jeffrey had with him when he was taken ill." She coughed quietly. "'Gerard was a martyr to Susanna'—that is, to the decaying things—'under the mung bean,' and the rest. 'Hasdai brought the mung bean to Cordoba from the East.' Where—and here I'm speculating rather than paraphrasing—he initiated Ibn Janah into its secret. Or perhaps he initiated Ibn Janah's teacher. The crucial point, Dr. Bailey, is that the 'mung bean' is the recipe for, and antidote to, Bertha's toxic artificial humans."

"No," Marion said, dejected. "I don't think it is. I had the same thought—or similar thoughts—when I read those passages. But there isn't anything concrete holding them together. It's all coincidental."

"That," said Bertha, "is only because you failed to read the second half of the tax register. Ibn Janah does explain the connections—although that explanation becomes meaningful only in retrospect. Do you remember the word for 'mung bean?'"

"Yes." She half-shrugged. "*Al-mash.*"

"Do you read Hebrew?"

"No."

"If you *had* studied Hebrew," Bertha said, "you'd have suspected, as I did, that the *al-mash* in that passage is a Hebrew term. Not Arabic. Consider the author—the Hebrew philologist, Ibn Janah. And the context."

"There is no context." Marion was feeling faint again. A psychological reaction to staring across the table at the large glass of her cooling blood.

"The context," Bertha pressed on, "comes from a different, yet related, tradition with which Ibn Janah—again, a respected student of Hebrew grammar—would have been more than familiar." She paused for a moment, organizing her thoughts. And then she resumed: "let me give you an example of this tradition. One example, of many. In the early thirteenth century, the prominent German rabbi, Eleazer of Worms—" she broke off. "You're familiar with his work?"

"I'm aware of his existence," Marion said. "Continue."

"Eleazer of Worms," Bertha resumed, "wrote the following about creating Golems." She paused again. "You know the lore of the Golem—"

"Yes, of course." Impatient.

"Of course," Bertha repeated. "Yes. So, to create a male Golem, Eleazer wrote, the initiate makes use of the sequence of Hebrew letters, AMSh. To create a female Golem, the sequence is AShM. To destroy the Golem, the sequence is ShMA. Does this sound at all familiar to you?"

"*Mash.*" Marion smiled slightly. "The mung bean."

"And consider the first line of the passage you rescued from Gerard in Remiremont," Bertha continued. "'The mung bean,' it reads, 'is a small seed.' But the word for 'seed' in that formulation is *habb*. Or, if you'd like, *habba*. Love, affection, procreation, generation—and so on. And so, another way of translating that line is 'the *MASh* is a tiny act of generation.' No?"

"Yes." She nodded again. "I see."

"I believe," Bertha continued, warming to her theme, "that it is also not a coincidence that the Vizier in the passage from Ibn Janah's work is called 'Ibn Shahid.'"

"Son of the martyr," Marion echoed. "Like Lothar. And Gerard."

"Did you also know," Bertha said, "that the 'mung bean' was famously introduced to the island of Pemba, the 'green island,' off Zanzibar, at approximately the same time that Hasdai brought it to Cordoba? And that Pemba is a notorious center for a certain type of medical practice that aims at the synthetic reanimation of dead human and animal matter? Its practitioners come to Pemba from all over the world, but particularly from the Caribbean, to study there."

She began to smile again. "My belief is that the 'mung bean' that made its way there was no more a—a legume than the fennel that Ibn Wahshiyya collected for his own work was your everyday carrot." Her eyes twinkled. "What do you think, Dr. Bailey?"

"Very well," Marion conceded. "You've convinced me. Bertha and Ibn Wahshiyya collaborated. The collaboration went in a problematic direction. The Caliph al-Muktafi wanted nothing to do with it. But Hasdai ibn Shaprut took the opportunity to acquire the recipe—and to concoct an antidote. Knowledge that he passed along, perhaps via an intermediary, to Ibn Janah." She rubbed her eyes. "But we still haven't found the recipe itself. I can't see how this all will end without—something more."

"As I said," Bertha replied, "we don't need the recipe. Ibn Janah discovered the antidote. The process for putting the creatures to sleep. But he feared that someone unscrupulous might destroy that knowledge if he simply wrote it down and preserved it. So instead, he hid it in a set of physical locations. We—that is, your superiors—already had an outline of the process as well as the first and last ingredients. Your assignment was to collect the rest."

"But I didn't collect it," Marion repeated, beginning once again to despair. "I collected nothing. Except the pages you've read."

"You did."

"Oh, for God's sake—"

"Dr. Bailey," Bertha spoke calmly, but disallowing further interruption, "the antidote that Ibn Janah developed must be incubated inside a living female body. It enters through the skin."

"What do you mean?" Her own skin beginning crawl.

"The first ingredient," Bertha said, "which, to repeat, we'd already distilled, was under the flap of the envelope that contained the Susanna Crystal. The envelope that Dr. Stumpp passed to you in London. You collected it, I believe, through your fingernails."

"Oh God."

"Your expertise led you to the second and third ingredients. We'd never have found them if you hadn't deciphered the *defter* and the pages from Hereford in the way that you did." Bertha nodded in brief, polite acknowledgment of Marion's skills. "Whatever adhered to your hands in the Cathedral and in the Abbey mixed with the ingredient from the envelop the moment they were absorbed by your skin."

She indicated the glass of blood on the table. "Those three ingredients form the basis of the medicine that will bring those who've been contaminated out of danger."

"But—" Marion swallowed. "But there must be hundreds of people who were exposed. Is there—enough blood?"

"There are sixty-six," Bertha said. "A drop each will be sufficient. With some left over should we learn of other victims. We'll mix it up in their food." A mischievous look quickly over her features. "Though I ought to warn you that there is one potential side effect. Given the traditional nature of this cure."

"Which is?" She didn't want to seem churlish, but she was feeling a proprietary displeasure at the thought of spreading her blood in so many directions. And the idea of some cultish side effect left her queasy.

"You've noticed that the creatures you've encountered have been—interested in you? Captivated?" Sounding entertained.

"Yes." Though she wouldn't have phrased it in those words.

"There may be a similar effect on our patients once they have taken their—eh—medicine," Bertha said.

"Do you mean to say that all sixty-six of those people—"

"The desire won't be nearly as strong in them as it has been in the creatures, who are, after all, human only in external form." Bertha's tone was reassuring, if still amused. "True humans are different. They have a will. And though this recipe has been reconfigured in sophisticated ways, it is at heart nothing more than a classic cure. Which means that, like all such spells, it will influence only those who are predisposed to the influence to begin with." She smiled at Marion. "In short, we can trust that most of our patients will recover and live because they have a will to live. Most of them are not, however, inclined to favor you. And so, they will not."

"You said," Marion replied, choosing not to pursue the topic further, "that you had the first and the final ingredients of the antidote. But thus far I've come into contact with only three substances. Where's the other?"

"It's here," Bertha said, drawing a stoppered jar out of the pocket of her apron. "The medicine that dissolves the toxin relies on three interactions. It will be ready in—six hours." She handed the bottle to Marion who, unthinking, took it and held it in her fist. "But the creatures themselves will go to sleep only upon contact with four ingredients." She nodded at the bottle. "When you're ready, rub that gel into your skin. After that, we'll wait—" she considered, "—eleven hours now, I believe. Once those eleven hours have passed, you'll touch each of the creatures—"

"All thirty-six of them?" She couldn't quite believe she was meekly accepting Bertha's plan.

"Yes. All thirty-six." Bertha cocked her head as though she could hear something. "They've gathered outside. Eager to enter. We're keeping the doors barred."

"That hasn't worked all that well in the past."

"We've taken special precautions."

"And how do you know this will be effective?" Marion retorted, unwilling to share in the joke. "You've already said that you failed to reproduce Bertha's and Ibn Wahshiyya's other experiments. Why will this succeed any better?"

"Two reasons," Bertha replied.

"Which are?"

"First," Bertha said, "you're alive. If the recipe had been ineffective, you'd have died after the first attack. But the ingredient under the envelope protected you. And you've grown stronger as you've absorbed the others."

"And the other reason?" Marion asked stubbornly.

"Because it's worked before." Bertha folded her hands in her lap again. "The tax register, remember, is a sixteenth-century document. Comparatively recent. Produced following an outbreak in the Ottoman Empire long after the written recipes from the tenth and eleventh centuries had been lost.

Whoever composed it did so on the basis of earlier instructions—now lost—in order to preserve the information for his Ottoman Turkish speaking colleagues. It worked. And the tax register then found its way into the Baquba collection—as reference material. And then, of course, the Baquba collection found its way to the British Library—"

Bertha smiled, conspiratorial, at Marion, who dropped her eyes. "And so, here we are. The point is, there have been other crises. Moments when the creatures have awoken. And these crises have all been resolved with reference to other instructions, secreted in other documents, stored in other collections. But, whenever and wherever they've been found, those instructions have always proved valid. Ibn Janah must have hidden the second and third ingredients in any number of protected places. Waiting to be discovered. Incubated. By volunteers such as yourself."

"I wasn't," Marion said, "a volunteer."

"You mean to say," Bertha countered, "that if you'd had the opportunity to read the *defter* in its entirety, to understand the implications of your assignment, you'd have refused?"

Marion remained silent.

"I thought not," Bertha said. "And it's time now to finish."

She waited.

Unhappy, Marion pulled the stopper out of the bottle with her left hand. Her right arm had started bleeding again. Then, gagging, she held her breath. The stench was unbearable.

Nonetheless, steeling herself, she poured the contents of the bottle—black, viscid, with an unhealthy sheen—into the palm of her right hand. After that, she set the empty bottle on the table, leaned back in the chair, and rubbed her hands together until both were covered with the vile gel. Then, sullen, she looked up at Bertha.

"Yes," Bertha said, standing. "That ought to do it. I'll bring you soap and water to clean your hands."

"Thank you." Marion rested her elbows on the arms of the chair in which she was sitting and tried to keep her hands from dripping on her clothing or further down her wrists. "Hurry, would you?"

Bertha was gone for less than five minutes. And when she returned, she was carrying two green glass bowls on pedestals—matching the glass in which she'd stored the blood—along with a towel and a bar of soap. There was warm water in each bowl, and Marion immersed her hands in the first, watching as the remnants of the ooze floated up to the surface.

The bowls, Marion thought irrelevantly as she scrubbed her hands with the astringent soap, were Maigelein. She'd seen an exhibit at the Museum. And she feared momentarily that she'd shatter one in her enthusiasm to remove the contaminant. Then, remembering her situation, she renewed her efforts with more vigor. Perhaps she'd break one deliberately.

When she finished, she used the towel to dry her abraded hands and sat on the edge of the sofa, both exhausted and faint. The scent was gone, but the fact that the concoction was inside of her— was *meant* to be inside of her—left her nauseated. She refused even to consider how she was going to touch, deliberately, the thirty-six undead things that were massed at the gate of the castle, waiting for her to attend to them. She wanted to cry.

Bertha, recognizing her state, tactfully removed the bowls and returned with a clean pillow— goose down—and a heavy blanket—some sort of large animal fur. She helped Marion to lie back on the sofa and then turned and fed the fire. Before she left the room, she smiled down at her. "You've done remarkable work, Dr. Bailey. We're grateful." She retrieved the glass of blood. "I'll wake you in five hours so that you can witness the effects of the medicine on our patients."

"Thank you." Marion moved her right arm into a more comfortable position. The wound was bothering her. "Good night."

"Good night." Bertha left the room and closed the door.

MARION was already awake, though still prone, with her eyes closed, when Bertha returned to the room. Given that they were underground, the light hadn't changed, but the hour felt to Marion like dawn. Which meant, she thought to herself, rising into a sitting position and wrapping the fur blanket around her shoulders, that she'd be welcoming the things at noon. For the best, perhaps. They were less active during the daylight.

Bertha hadn't changed her clothing. She was still wearing the blue dress and white apron. But she was also no longer carrying the glass of blood. It had presumably been distributed to those who needed it more. Sighing, she stood and dropped the blanket on the sofa. Giving herself a moment to keep from blacking out.

Then, following Bertha out the door, she walked in the direction of the infirmary. The passages of the castle were all brightly lit with electric bulbs—and in many cases disconcertingly modern hanging fixtures. But it was clear that the belowground parts of the building hadn't been designed with comfort in mind. The rooms, despite the bright lights and solid furnishings, evoked nothing more than a medieval dungeon.

And when Bertha led her down a steep, recently constructed staircase that dropped precipitously from a circular opening in the floor, it became apparent that the chamber—or set of chambers—that constituted the infirmary was a hastily reconfigured oubliette. At the bottom of the stairs were fifteen low cells, separated by a deliberately obfuscating collection of corridors, enclosed by thick stone walls. Each housed a quiet nurse and between three and five patients—grouped, it seemed, according to linguistic compatibility. When Marion, curious, peeked into an open doorway as she passed, she thought she saw the doctor—"Stumpp"—who had met her at Great Ormond Street Hospital, pale and unconscious, in a bed placed across the room from a group of children who were awake and chattering to one another in German.

Then, rattled, she strode to catch up to Bertha, who was leading her further into the warren of chambers. The nurses looked gentle, and the patients who weren't sleeping were certainly in good humor. But even the vases of hothouse flowers and cheerfully colored blankets on the clean, sturdy beds couldn't obscure from her the fact that the space was meant to torment its inhabitants rather than to heal them. She shuddered as Bertha led her lower yet, toward the sloping far end of the infirmary.

"We've administered the antidote now to each of our patients," Bertha said, turning to speak to Marion as they walked. "And it has already begun to take effect. All sixty-six are on the mend."

"I'm glad," Marion replied, noncommittal. She was still uncomfortable with her role in the process.

"I'm taking you now to see Mr. Lamb," she continued. "You were concerned about him."

"Thank you."

"He's in a room with his compatriots. The English travelers." Bertha glanced back again. "Your husband, Sir Jeffrey, is also there. You were less concerned about him, I believe."

"Hmm."

"They were the last to receive the medicine," Bertha informed her. "And so they haven't yet regained consciousness. But they will within the next half hour. You'll wait for them?"

"Yes," Marion said. "If that's acceptable?"

"Of course." Bertha stood to the side of a stone door—propped open with a rusting iron ball—and gestured Marion into the room. When she entered, a nurse smiled at her and rose from the chair in which she'd been sitting, watching her sleeping charges. Then, indicating to Marion that she ought to take the chair, the nurse left Marion alone with the three beds.

Jeffrey, wearing his dark blue pyjamas, was sleeping on his back on the first bed—his Goyard suitcase to the side. Percy, wearing only underwear and his woolen socks—which perhaps explained his behavior on the train—was sprawled out in the second bed, his crocodile-skin valise also to his side. The young man in the third bed Marion recognized as the deacon from Hereford Cathedral. Also in underwear. But without any obvious luggage.

Marion wrinkled her forehead for a few seconds, uncertain that any of the three would be pleased to see her upon waking. But then, deciding that Percy might be concerned about her if he woke alone, she took the chair and moved it to the side of his bed. The nurses had placed his hat with the fuzzy ball on top of the valise. She smiled when she recognized it and then sat next to him and brushed his rumpled hair off his forehead. He'd be horrified by his disheveled state when he regained his wits.

"You're very welcome."

Startled, she twisted in her chair. Jeffrey was sitting up in the bed, his arms crossed, smiling at her. "I had a feeling you'd enjoy him." He nodded in the direction of Percy's feet, his smile growing. "They're comfortable-looking socks. Homemade, I daresay."

"Jealous?" She was disgusted by his smug demeanor in the face of the boy's illness.

"What man wouldn't be jealous, Marion?" He covered a yawn with his hand. "Struggling up from near fatal unconsciousness only to find his beloved wife stroking and comforting a significantly younger rival." He looked at her more closely. "You are remarkably attractive at the moment, you know."

Sighing, she turned the chair so that it faced him. "He's a child, Jeffrey."

"Old enough to develop an infatuation. Though obviously you would have done all you could to discourage that sort of unprofessional attachment." His smile turned into a grin. "Wouldn't you, dear?"

"I'm glad," she said acidly, "that your illness hasn't left you weak. Or debilitated. That would have been a shame."

He laughed quietly. "Fear not. Percy's sacrifices to King and Country will be duly noted. He'll receive his gold star."

"You're making even less sense than you ordinarily do." She moved to turn the chair back.

"Darling," he said, still laughing, "after a decade and a half of failed surveillance, Percy Lamb is the first tail, ever, that's stuck to you throughout his assignment. *Ever.* I wouldn't be surprised if Maugham got him knighted when he returns. Though poor Percy himself will never understand why his career is as brilliant as it's bound to become."

"You're an idiot," she muttered, now resolutely turning the chair back toward Percy. Who had begun to snore.

"I wonder," Jeffrey said to her annoyed back, "what would happen if we attached him to you again. Would you remain sentimentally unwilling to lose him? Let the puppy follow even when it might compromise your project? If so, we may have finally solved one of the most provoking—"

"I think," she interrupted, standing, "that the nurse will want to examine you, now that you're feeling well. I'll—"

She was about to walk through the door when Bertha reappeared, flustered and embarrassed. After glancing over at Jeffrey and inclining her head in a distracted yet correct greeting, she addressed Marion. "My apologies, Dr. Bailey. But a situation has developed. The precautions we've taken to prevent our visitors from entering the castle have proved insufficient. They're at the door. You must attend to them now."

Marion nodded, tense, and began to follow her. But before they could leave the room, Jeffrey rose from his bed and stopped them, addressing Bertha in a surprisingly accomplished archaic French. "Please forgive me, Madame, for intruding myself upon your conversation. But I believe I may be of some assistance upstairs." He inclined his head as well. "With your permission, I'll follow and observe?"

"Don't let him come," Marion said to her. "At best he'll be a nuisance." She turned to Jeffrey. "Stay here."

Bertha hesitated, looking between Marion and Jeffrey, perplexed by their animosity. But then, visibly swayed by the fact that Jeffrey's French sounded like Pierre de Ronsard's, whereas Marion's sounded like a popular newsreel—or Jany Holt's—she cast Marion an apologetic look. "We haven't the time or the manpower to prevent him from attending, Dr. Bailey." She turned a stern face on Jeffrey. "Though he does so at his own risk."

"Of course, Madame." He smirked at Marion as they fell into step behind Bertha. She looked away from him. Hoped the stone floor was uncomfortable under his bare feet.

B‍ERTHA led them up four flights of heavy, stone stairs until they reached a set of unfurnished rooms that were half embedded in the ground and half protected by crumbling rock walls that extended into the air. At the end of the last of these rooms, Marion could see bleak white sky through an opening that had been blasted into the stone. Or, upon closer inspection, not blasted. Excavated. From the outside.

In fact, once her eyes had adjusted to the light, she could just make out three pairs of damp, white hands clawing rhythmically at the edges of the rock, widening the gap in the wall. Very soon, the opening would be large enough to admit a body—a realization that shocked her sufficiently to leave her standing and staring, aghast, at the busy, mindless fingers scratching through the stone.

Then, coming to herself, she turned to Bertha, who had backed against the far wall, dragging Jeffrey with her. "What do I do?"

"They'll come to you," Bertha said. "They're here for you. You needn't do anything."

Marion turned back to the crumbling gap and waited. Not moving from the center of the room. And when the first blind face pressed itself through the opening, before pulling itself to the floor, she stepped forward, tentatively reaching out to it.

But if she'd expected a methodical process, she was sorely disappointed. Once the first creature had slithered to the ground and begun lurching toward her, the others pressed through the hole in the wall as an accumulating swarm. And rather than approaching her singly, they thronged her, questing, their mouths open, dripping and fetid.

After less than five seconds, unable to perform her role with the dignity she thought she ought to bring to it, she staggered backward and then, when she felt the first of them touching her, sank to her knees, covering her face with her hands. And after that, she did all she could not to think or feel at all, as they came at her in a suffocating rush. Instead, she squeezed her eyes shut. Unwilling to watch. Clamped her teeth together, forcing herself not to make a sound.

And, finally, after what felt like an eternity, she perceived through her skin—the rest of her senses having shut down—that the press of bodies around her was thinning. Until eventually, she became aware that she was alone, kneeling on the stone floor in the middle of the room, her head buried in her arms. Warily, she removed her hands from her face and opened her eyes. Looked about her.

She was crouched at the center of a circle of fine, white powder. Scraps of golden cloth scattered throughout it. And, oddly, she felt clean. No scent of anise. The mucus-like liquid in which she'd been certain she was half-drowning moments before evaporated. If anything, her body felt refreshed. Younger.

Standing, she turned to the back of the room to look at Bertha and Jeffrey. Both were staring at her in astonishment. She swallowed and stepped fastidiously through the circle of dust. And then, hesitantly, she approached Bertha. Stopped. "Is it over?"

Bertha shook her head. "There were only thirty-five. I counted. It isn't over."

Marion frowned. "Are you certain you counted correctly? They weren't—orderly."

Jeffrey crossed the room, squatted, and peered down at the dust, curious. "No," he said after three or four seconds. "There is one missing. Madame is correct."

Marion turned to him, not wanting to ask the question. But then, forcing out the words, she said to him, slowly and carefully: "how do you know?"

"The last one," he said, switching to English, "is in Salisbury. Porton Down."

"What do you mean?"

"You took Maugham's briefcase, didn't you?" He straightened. "In your hand?"

"But I didn't keep it. I dropped it."

"Yes," he replied. "As you were meant to do. And good thing, too. We'd have been in a pretty mess if you'd chosen to bring it along with you."

"I don't understand."

"Then I'll explain. No reason not to now." He pushed his hands into pockets she hadn't realized were tailored into his pyjamas. "The alchemists at Porton Down concluded early on, soon after our holiday in Hereford, that your admirers were attracted to something physiological rather than to something external, like the crystal. Something that you must have been—secreting. And once they'd drawn that conclusion, they became equally convinced that they could analyze it, replicate it, and concoct a batch of their own to draw off one or two of your creatures for study. But they needed a workable sample of whatever it was you were discharging first." He paused. "It seems that the hair and clothing I provided them upon our return from Wales were insufficiently 'active.'"

He smiled at her, crooked and apologetic. "So they prepared the handle of the briefcase. Maugham then worked on you with his customary zeal. If you can believe it, he actually practiced for two or three days beforehand—assuming his role, and all that. As though the mere sight of him isn't enough to break you out into a panicked sweat." He shrugged. "And then they bagged the handle once you'd dropped it."

He considered. "I'd already crossed the Channel by the time they conducted their experiment, so I didn't know how it had fared. But given that one of your guests played truant just now, I'm confident that they succeeded."

When he saw her stunned face, he looked contrite. "Don't be angry, Marion. You've still disappointed Maugham, if it makes you feel better. He was certain once he'd decided to take you on, that he could push you not only into touching the briefcase but also into going to Salisbury on your own—dragging your followers along with you—to visit the lab. We had a wager. Which, of course, I've won."

He began to smile at her again. "He should have known that you're a precision instrument—responsive to one, and only one, handler. And let me repeat," he went on over her unvoiced protest, "I'm personally more than relieved that you did drop the briefcase. If you hadn't, Maugham would have collected you before you'd set foot in France, and Percy would never have had his adventure." He pushed at the white powder with a bare toe. "Not to mention that we'd all be dead."

She shook her head, unwilling to comprehend what he was telling her. Then, hating herself, she pounced on the least significant part of his revelation. "You gave those—those *ghouls*—my hair and clothing? As a *sample*?"

"Oh, calm down." He withdrew his toe. "It isn't as though they've made it into a poppet. They're scientists." He furrowed his brow. "At least I don't think they have. One never knows what they get up to in Lopcombe Corner." He paused. "I mean, Porton Down."

She took an angry step toward him. "You are the most—"

"Why are you attacking me?" He was laughing now. "Yes, I did give them a few strands of your hair. Along with some clothing that you really could do without. Your own people, meanwhile, have turned you into a walking petri dish. Why aren't you railing against them instead—"

"Sir Jeffrey," Bertha interrupted, shaking herself out of what had been a long few minutes of troubled contemplation. "You are aware, no, that there are—consequences—if the thirty-six are separated?"

"I would have been surprised, Madame, if there were not." He had switched back to his polished French. "But surely you understand that I have a duty to perform as well? My government will address those consequences when and if they arise."

Bertha held his look, uncharacteristically shaken. Then she spoke again. "The last time the creatures were separated," she said to him, "was in 1208. Months before the Albigensian Crusade. There are those who have suggested that the separation of the creatures precipitated the events, the deaths, of 1209. And of the decades that followed."

"There are always those," Jeffrey replied, "who seek to assign causes to what is in the end inexplicable. Outbreaks of catastrophic violence. Beyond reason. But Madame, the wise know that such outbreaks simply happen. No reason. No occult catalyst. Nothing."

Bertha blinked at him. Then, composed once more, she smoothed down the folds of her apron. "And, for our part, we have always endured those outbreaks. God grant your government a similar spirit of perseverance." She smiled, vague now, at Marion and left the room.

London, England
January 1, 1937

JEFFREY had dragged—or tricked, she wasn't quite certain how she'd found herself there—Marion to the Chelsea Arts Ball at Royal Albert Hall for New Year's Eve. He hadn't, however, managed to force her into the Arabian Princess outfit he'd hired for the evening. Nor had he himself been overly disappointed about abandoning his own turban and robe.

Once there, in ordinary evening dress, she had quietly enjoyed the spectacle and the champagne. Feeling even a mild sense of comradery with Jeffrey as they observed the drunken crush of celebrants. When they'd dutifully kissed under the falling balloons at midnight, she'd been almost free of anxiety—knowing that soon she'd be returning to Ian, home from school, and Lydia, a few weeks away from her first birthday.

Taking advantage of their relaxed near-friendliness, she risked speaking to him about France.

"Jeffrey?"

"Hmm?"

They were dancing. Something by Tommy Dorsey.

"I'm frightened." She looked up into his face. "I don't like that one of those things is awake."

"You worry that it will escape from the lab in Salisbury?" He kissed her temple. "It won't."

"No," she said. Then she waited while two mostly naked art students of uncertain gender fox-trotted past them. "No, it's not that. It's what Bertha said. I've been reading about the Albigensian Crusade. I'd never studied it before. It was horrific."

"It was also seven hundred years ago." He smiled down at her. "Darling, your life is already complicated. Don't take personal responsibility for history's humanitarian accidents. It's arrogant, if nothing else."

He deftly moved them around a puddle of champagne. "The Albigensian Crusade had nothing to do with the botched revival of a tenth-century science experiment gone wrong. As you know perfectly well, even if you've decided to torture yourself over it. And it will not be repeated."

"But—"

"It was a different time. The gloomy thirteenth century." He smiled politely at a girl dressed in a can-can outfit who was eyeing him over Marion's shoulder. "Utterly different psychology. Ripe for the Inquisition."

He maneuvered her through a pile of balloons. "The only Inquisition we've got now is Torquemada over there next to the punch bowl getting sick on Oliver Cromwell." He raised his eyebrows, impressed. "Remind me not to drink the punch."

"But—"

"No, Marion." He held her closer to him. "I will not let you terrify yourself for no good reason. Look at this room. It's a new year. 1937. Amazing advances are afoot. And our government has acquired a pet Golem." He laughed down at her. "Really, what's the worst that could happen?"

She looked up into his eyes. And behind the teasing glint she caught a flicker of fear, mirroring her own, quickly extinguished. Then she kissed his cheek and kept dancing.

Ethiopia, 1937

Istanbul, Turkey
March, 1937

IT was an unimpressive object. Half a foot tall, tarnished bronze, a circular base of perhaps five inches surmounted by a socket and neck of two or three inches. The exterior was engraved in a complicated floral motif, and at the edge of the base was a series of animals chasing one another, dominated by three rabbits with interlocking ears. A candlestick. Fourteenth- or fifteenth-century. Ilkhanid. Possibly Ottoman.

Marion ran a fingertip over the three ears shared by the three rabbits. Then she leaned back against the sofa and considered the floral scrollwork in the dim light of the glass lamp that stood in a corner of the room. It was close to midnight, and she and Jeffrey were sitting in the small library of his Istanbul house. The lamp illuminated the low, square table between them, throwing the candlestick into sharp relief. But the bookcases and recesses of the room were in shadow. A curtain drawn across the narrow window overlooking the building's courtyard.

"You say the boy had it with him at school?" She looked across the table at Jeffrey, who was watching her, impassive, as she inspected the candlestick.

"Yes. Harrow."

"And when he was discovered, the headmaster informed you?" She frowned. "Why?"

"The headmaster fancies himself an antiquarian." Jeffrey hadn't changed his attentive, yet otherwise blank, expression. "Once he'd sent the boy, Murdoch, back to his family, he took the opportunity to examine the candlestick himself. He concluded that the office might find it intriguing. He was correct."

"Why?" She returned her attention to the object.

It was an adequate, if not remarkable, example of its type. Valuable to certain collectors. And undoubtedly an odd artifact to find in the possession of a fourteen-year-old schoolboy. But hardly the sort of rare or influential find that interested Jeffrey's colleagues.

"Murdoch," Jeffrey said, "was corrupting the other boys with it. Frightening them. An unwholesome influence, according to the headmaster."

She made an irritated movement. "He's fourteen, Jeffrey. Dirty, perhaps. Not unwholesome. You're not telling me everything."

"I rarely do."

"His—the boy's—father is attached to the Consulate here?" Deciding to try another tack.

"His father's dead."

She blinked, annoyed now, and rose from the sofa. Then she crossed the room to a small cupboard below the lamp, opened it, withdrew a bottle of scotch and a glass, and poured herself a drink. "Would you like some?" she asked, not turning.

"Yes. Thank you."

She poured him a second glass, left the bottle in the cupboard, walked back across the room, and set the drink firmly in front of him. Returned to the sofa. "You are trying my patience, Jeffrey. You wanted me in Istanbul. I agreed to come. But if you don't start making some sense, I'm not going to stay much longer."

"You agreed to come because your own people want you in Istanbul as much as we do." He didn't touch his drink. "My nonsense has nothing to do with your movements."

She remained silent.

"Oh, very well." He raised his glass and took a small, polite sip. "Murdoch and his sister—she's eleven—were raised in India. Their parents died two years ago. Their father's younger brother—Sheridan Murdoch—became their guardian. Mr. Murdoch has been attached to the Istanbul Consulate for well on a decade now. He sent the boy to school this past year. The girl has remained in the city to be educated by a governess."

Marion nodded slowly, thinking. Then she drank from her glass. "And the candlestick?"

"We believe that Sheridan Murdoch collected it in Konya." Jeffrey had resumed his bland tone. "From a Sufi tomb."

"That's his role with the Consulate, then?" She took a bigger drink. "Looter?"

"Mr. Murdoch," Jeffrey said primly, "performs a number of consular functions for us."

"He'd been ordered to ransack the tomb?"

A few seconds passed, and then Jeffrey spoke again, choosing his words with care. "This is where the situation becomes complicated." He paused. "No. Any orders he received to inspect the tomb did not come from us."

"And so—"

"And so, when Murdoch minor filched his uncle's artifact to impress his disreputable schoolfriends, he exposed more than perhaps he meant to."

"Do you know who's running him?" She still found the candlestick an unprepossessing object to have caused the degree of trouble it apparently had.

"The boy?"

"His uncle."

"We think the Italians."

"Oh." She finished off her scotch. Uncertain she wanted to hear more. Then, deciding that it was better she bring a complete report back to her superiors, she suppressed a sigh and continued: "why?"

"You've been following recent events in Ethiopia?" A hint of a goading smile in his voice. "The excitement this past month?"

"It's difficult, Jeffrey, to remain unaware that the Italian military under Graziani slaughtered twenty thousand civilians, a quarter of the population of Addis Ababa, the weekend before last." She held his eyes. "Yes. I've been following recent events."

"You'd be surprised by what people fail to notice these days."

"But you've responded. Obviously."

"I?"

She didn't speak.

"We have an agreement with Italy." He dropped his eyes, demure. "Non-interference. We saw nothing."

"I don't remember any treaty. At least nothing public."

"Not a treaty. At least not since the unfortunate fall of Sir Samuel Hoare." He considered. "Which was for the best, really. He has time now to devote to his lawn tennis." He looked up at her, impish. "An informal agreement. A gentleman's agreement."

He waited, entertained, for a retort from her. When nothing came, he resumed, his voice once again blank, with perhaps a tinge of disappointment. "Best not provoke them at the moment, or so goes the general consensus. And to be honest, those who follow such things are more than a little impressed by Marshal Graziani's charmed existence. The man is indestructible. 'Viceroy of Italian Africa,' I believe he's called now. Can nothing touch him, do you think, nothing at all—?"

She stood. "I'm going to sleep."

"Mr. Murdoch," he continued as though she hadn't moved, "is not, however, indestructible. Agreement or not, we're less than well pleased by his promiscuity. Fraternizing with the competition, and all that. From what we've gathered, his activities—not least of which those surrounding this candlestick—are mixed up with the unfortunate events in Ethiopia."

"You're saying that this—" she nodded at the candlestick, "had something to do with the massacre? *This?*"

"I thought you were going to sleep." He lifted his glass and took another small sip.

Hostile, she sat. Watched his face.

"The excuse for the massacre," he said, putting his drink back down on the table, "was the attempted assassination of Marshal Graziani. But Mussolini had given orders for an undertaking of that sort long before any disaffected loyalists began lobbing grenades in the Marshal's direction. Waiting for an opportune moment. And though the rank and file soldiers killed indiscriminately, two or three trained sections were setting their sights on narrower targets."

He rested his elbow on the arm of his chair and his cheek against his fist. "Monks, from what we understand. Abducted rather than murdered. Interrogated. Questioned. According to our sources, they were pressed about—of all things—candlesticks." He blinked. "They—the monks, that is—appear not to have broken. We don't believe the Italians are any further along than they were two months ago when they sent Mr. Murdoch to Konya for the sample we've got in front of us. In fact, they've likely lost ground since the boy absconded with it."

She considered the dull bronze object in front of her on the table. Then she looked up at Jeffrey again. "You'll cut him loose?"

"Mr. Murdoch?" He shook his head. "No. We'll watch him. And you and I will visit him. Tomorrow, if you're willing."

"I don't want to visit him."

"I can't force you. But it will be worth your while, don't you think? Your people will want at least a bit of background information before they order you to incapacitate me and make off with the object, no?"

She frowned, thinking.

"A social call," he continued. "He and I meet on occasion when I'm in the city, so there won't be any suspicion. He'll enjoy you. You can commiserate with him over the trials of raising an incorrigible and delinquent boy."

She didn't rise to the bait. Though her chest tightened, as it always did, at the thought of Ian, miserable and abused in his fourth year at Temple Grove. Thus far this term, he hadn't attempted escape. But it was still early days. Lydia, now fourteen months old, was asleep in the next room.

She swallowed and nodded at him. "Yes. Fine. Tomorrow."

Before she could stand again, he stopped her. "Don't you want to see how it works?"

"Works?"

"The corrupting influence." He leaned forward and rested his own fingertips at the top of the socket. "Its unwholesomeness. The unhealthy atmosphere it generates." He grinned across at her mystified expression. "Surely you didn't think we'd go to all this trouble over a second-rate Seljuk—"

"Is it Seljuk?"

"We haven't determined its provenance yet." He rose from his chair and walked toward the lamp and cupboard. Continued speaking, with his back to her. "But its provenance is of less importance—for the moment—than its operation. Otherwise, it would hardly be worth the time we've taken to rescue it from the eternity it would otherwise have spent in some regional, backwater museum's storage facility."

He returned carrying an unused white wax candle, a cigarette lighter, and the bottle of scotch. Then he sat, set the bottle on the table, and inserted the candle into the socket of the candlestick. Opened the lighter.

"Wait," she said. "You haven't told me what it does."

"Difficult to describe." He flicked the lighter and lit the candle. "Best simply to experience it." He relaxed into his cushion and held his nearly untouched drink on the arm of his chair, watching her face.

She stared at the flame for a few seconds and then returned his look. "What do I do?"

"Anything you'd like. It takes effect regardless of your endeavors one way or the other." His lips twitched as she nodded, suspicious, and returned her attention to the candle.

As a minute or two passed and nothing happened, she let herself relax, enjoying the quiet room and serene evening. Whatever influence Jeffrey and the office had determined the candlestick produced, it was clearly too subtle to disorder her own sensibilities. She welcomed the opportunity to absorb the tranquil atmosphere of her favorite space in Jeffrey's two-century-old building.

She spent too little time here. And when she opened herself to it, she could almost feel, shivering a millimeter beyond the surface of her exposed skin, the calm, studious presence of the library's previous inhabitants, reading, thinking, breathing the slow air. Its centuries of habitation.

She let her gaze wander over the leather and gilt spines of those books she could make out in the shadows at the edge of the light. The dark, reassuring, paneled door. The breeze from the courtyard stirring the curtain covering the tall window. The pedestal displaying the marble sculpture of the small, perfect Satyr.

Then, uncertainty tugging at the corners of her mind, she narrowed her eyes, returning her attention to the agitated curtain. As she remembered, gradually, that the window in this room didn't open. That no breeze could force a curtain slowly and deliberately out, away from the wall, in that groping manner. Making a noise that sounded like bats or birds scrabbling just beyond her field of vision.

Still feeling herself more a passive, mildly interested observer than a participant in whatever was happening, she stared as something dark, more felt than seen, moved out from under the curtain and flowed with quiet deliberation toward the table. Liquid. But also purposeful. Seeking something specific.

And then, in a single moment, she abruptly recognized the situation for what it was, and her serene mood shattered. The shadow was gathering in every corner of the room, unaware of their presence, but nonetheless fumbling toward them. Hunched and curious, it explored the dwindling space between the unlit edges of the library and the pool of light in which she and Jeffrey sat. When it reached the lamp, the bulb flickered into darkness. The candle was also beginning to dim. Soon there would be nothing but black.

She tried to make a sound, to communicate with Jeffrey, to draw comfort from the existence of another human being in the room with her. But her throat constricted, and her pulse pounded painfully against her windpipe. No words came. When she dragged her eyes away from the anthropoid darkness that was attuned to her fear—growing and moving with intent in her direction, she saw that Jeffrey wouldn't help her. His eyes, blank and dead, stared over her shoulder at something she didn't want to imagine, something likewise moving toward her. His face was a mask, less human than the dark.

Summoning all that remained of her fortitude, she squeezed her eyes shut. Whatever was about to happen, she didn't want to see it. Couldn't see it. And then, her breathing shallow and rasping, she waited.

"You can open your eyes now." Jeffrey's voice was taunting, but there was a ragged quality to it.

She silently counted to five and then, cautiously, opened her eyes. The room was as it had been. The lamplight warm and mellow. The curtain still. The candle extinguished, a wisp of smoke rising from the blackened wick.

Jeffrey was filling her glass with scotch. His own was now empty. And despite his apparent calm, his forehead was damp with sweat. He replaced the bottle on the table. Without speaking, she took the glass and drank three large swallows, waiting impatiently for the burning heat to reach her stomach.

"You lasted longer than I thought you would," he commented, watching as she stared down at the glass in her hands. When she said nothing, he continued. "I feared there for a moment that you'd defeat me. It's interesting. A fragile mind like yours should have cracked easily. Just goes to show—"

"What were those things?"

"What things?" He had retrieved the lighter and was toying with the lid. Then, catching himself in the nervous movement, he set it next to the candlestick.

"Don't you dare pretend you didn't see them." She raised her glass, her hand shaking, and took another drink. "The shadows. The—the *things*."

"That's what you saw?"

"You saw them too." She wanted to shout, but managed to keep her voice in check.

"No," he said. "I didn't. Everyone sees something different."

"Everyone—? I don't understand. What did you see, then?"

He laughed. "We must have some secrets from one another, dear."

She turned her attention to the candlestick. The candle had burned down perhaps two inches. More than she would have expected in the short time she'd experienced its effects. Then she flicked her eyes back to Jeffrey's exhausted face. "It's a drug?"

He shook his head. "Not that we've been able to isolate."

"But the candle—"

"I borrowed it from the Consulate. I believe they order crates of them from Price's. And, as far as I know, Battersea is no less terrifying at the moment than it ever was." He paused. "The boy made use of candles filched from the chapel."

"Oh." She swallowed. Painfully. Something was still wrong with her throat.

"It's something to do with the candlestick," he said. "Not the candles."

"What is it?"

He sighed and stood. "We're hoping that Murdoch might provide us guidance in the matter. Our own experts are mystified."

She stood as well, unsteady. "You think he learned something at the tomb?"

"If Murdoch learned anything at the tomb," he replied, walking toward the door and opening it for her, "he's already sold it. But he may have picked up something without realizing he'd done so. We'll find out tomorrow."

She nodded, moving around the table, in the direction of the door. Keeping the curtained window as far away as possible. "Oh."

"We do know that there's at least one more," he said as she passed him onto the landing. "Candlestick, that is. Perhaps two. The behavior of the Italians in Ethiopia this past month indicates at the very least a small set. Collector's instinct gone mad and all that."

She stopped, took a calming breath as he closed the door, and then continued in the direction of their bedroom. She wouldn't let him provoke her. And she'd calm herself by looking in on Lydia before trying to force herself to sleep as well.

MR. Murdoch purchased property in the Islands when his niece and nephew joined his household," Jeffrey said, peering out a foggy window at the flat and opaque, yet still quietly menacing, water of the late winter Marmara Sea.

They were sitting on damp cushions in the overheated cabin of Murdoch's runabout. He had sent it to ferry them from the Karaköy pier to the public dock on Büyükada, the largest of Istanbul's Princes' Islands. Lydia, dressed in a green wool coat with her red hair in pigtails was climbing up and over Jeffrey's shoulder to grab the button holding the curtain back from the wet glass. She adored her father. Marion might not have been there.

"He thought," Jeffrey continued, grabbing Lydia and placing her back on his knee, "that the suburban atmosphere would suit them. A clean break from his disreputable life in Beyoğlu."

"What's he like?" Marion wiped the condensation away from the window on her side of the cabin and glanced outside. Grey water. Grey clouds. Salt spray. She wished they could be in the cockpit, but Murdoch's pilot had made it clear when they boarded that they were to stay below until they had docked at Büyükada.

"Untrustworthy," Jeffrey said, startling her out of her melancholy.

"What?"

"Mr. Murdoch," Jeffrey continued. "He's untrustworthy. Capricious. Irresponsible. I've always liked him." He kissed the top of Lydia's head, and she responded with a wide smile that soon turned into a new attempt to climb up his chest. "It's a pity about this Italian business. I blame the children."

"Why?" Marion wrinkled her forehead at Lydia's now precarious perch on Jeffrey's shoulder.

"I imagine he felt hemmed in. Trapped." He turned and unbuttoned the curtain for Lydia. Held her in place as she ripped it out of the groove above the window. "And since he couldn't outrun his unlooked-for parental responsibilities, he chose to prove his independence to himself and the world by disobeying us. Flouting the great authority figure. Surely you understand the motivation?"

"No," she said, coldly. "I don't."

"The children couldn't have made it easier for him," he mused, ignoring her reply. "From what I understand, they're monstrous. Like something out of the Brontës. But Mr. Murdoch has compensated in classic fashion by developing an infatuation for the girl's governess." He considered. "Perhaps her purity will redeem him."

His face clouded. "Damn it, I really do enjoy him. Such a shame, this situation." Then, relaxing as he lifted Lydia, triumphantly holding the ripped curtain in her fists, back down to his lap: "but if all goes well, nothing need change. We'll merely run him as a double, indefinitely, until he's a fat, old pensioner, and he need never know that his reputation's in tatters. Poor Mr. Murdoch."

Marion, never confident when reading Jeffrey's moods, tried to determine whether he was serious. Then, deciding that it didn't matter, she changed the subject: "why are you telling me this?"

"Last night you complained that I wasn't telling you enough." He smiled, and she held his look, silent. "It's your field," he eventually relented. "Ilkhanids, Turks, Italians. Failed assassination attempts. Difficult to find anything more tailor-made for your skill set."

"I don't work for you."

"Yes, dear. As you say."

"No," she continued, irritated, "I mean—"

"Yes, yes," he interrupted. "I know. You'll bolt at some awkward and provoking moment. Your aims are not our aims. Your organization is the enemy. As always." He bounced Lydia on his knee. "But the office has been keeping careful track of your progress with us, Marion. And your methods have, on average, been yielding us a good sixty to sixty-five percent success rate. Which is higher than we expect of even the most rabidly loyal of the remainder of our talent.

"Meaning," he concluded, tugging on one of Lydia's pigtails, "that we're satisfied with the situation as it stands. And so, presumably, are your own people. If not, they wouldn't keep throwing you across our path, would they?"

She closed her eyes, but otherwise she didn't reply.

"And personally," he resumed. "I find the candor of our working relationship—"

"We have no working relationship," she muttered.

"—refreshing. Infinitely less exhausting than the theatrics we'll be forced to perform for Mr. Murdoch, to take an example. Speaking of which," he said, glancing out the window at the approaching shore as the runabout's motor dropped to a lower, deeper register, "I believe we've arrived. I see his fiacre waiting for us beyond the dock. He's re-painted it. Purple."

He stood, smiling, and lifted Lydia to his waist. "Are you ready for your carriage, Lydia? Purple with white horses just for you?"

She made a sound that might have been "yes, Papa," as he climbed into the fresh, chilly air of the cockpit. Thus far, she hadn't settled on a name for her mother.

*T*HE ride in the fiacre took less than ten minutes, the vehicle clattering to a halt inside a pair of scrolled iron gates that protected a tall, wooden mansion painted a vivid turquoise. A hulking wisteria vine, just budding out, twined up to the roof of the building, splitting apart the elaborate white trim along each balcony. The flowers, Marion thought to herself as she stepped down from the fiacre, must clash jarringly with the turquoise wood. But, she mused, considering the bright, magenta purple vehicle in which they'd arrived, subtle arrangements of color were apparently not Sheridan Murdoch's strength.

She had little time to pursue the thought, as Mr. Murdoch himself—slim, energetic, and flirtatious—emerged from the house to welcome his guests. He wore a loose, white, cotton shirt, unbuttoned at the top, a hint of misplaced pre-Raphaelite about it. And as he held out his hand to shake Jeffrey's, he peered up at her from under long black eyelashes. When a gust of wind rose toward them from the water, he deliberately turned into it to let it whip across his curly—or curled?—hair.

"Willcox." He opened his eyes, wide and innocent, as he ran a caressing hand over Lydia's head. "A beautiful little girl. The very image of Ginnie." He glanced at Marion, a touch of spite behind the smile. "And, of course, her mother." He nodded at her. "Lady Willcox. I've heard so very much about you."

"How do you do, Mr. Murdoch?"

Through some occult sensitivity, Murdoch had already identified her as an unlikely target of seduction—and his only alternative mode was malice. Accustomed as she'd become to a steady stream of baroquely confusing antagonism from Jeffrey's acquaintances, however, Marion found Murdoch's innocent aggression almost refreshing. Though she tried to appear hurt by his nastiness. He clearly expected it, and she didn't want to disappoint.

Satisfied by her annoyance, he returned his attention to Jeffrey. "Please. Come in. The voyage is chilly this time of year."

Jeffrey clapped Murdoch on the shoulder with his free hand and rearranged Lydia on his hip. "Thank you, Murdoch. It's been too long. You'd only just settled when I was here last."

They walked through the front door into a tiled entry hall, also dominated by turquoise, and Jeffrey positioned Lydia on top of a wooden chest, carved and painted into clusters of grapes. Then he took Marion's coat and hat, hung them on a hook above the chest, placed his own coat and hat next to hers, and bent over to begin unlacing his shoes.

"Don't." Murdoch stopped him. "We don't. Must keep the children properly British." He turned away, muttering to himself as he walked further into the house. "Which means, one assumes, tramping mud and dirt all over the floors—"

"How are the children?" Jeffrey had gathered up Lydia again, and was striding to catch up to Murdoch. Marion, bemused, followed them more slowly, running a fingertip along the pink and gold wallpaper. Steadying herself.

"Outside," Murdoch said, not answering the question, as he pulled open two narrow white doors leading to a salon on the far side of the house. "With Lenore."

"Ah." Jeffrey had passed through the doors and his voice was muffled. But she could hear the laughter in it. "Lenore. Will I finally meet her, Murdoch? I'm beginning to doubt that she exists beyond your dreams and fancies."

Marion, only half listening, continued trailing them until she had also passed through the doors into a vast, light green room with a wall of windows overlooking a sloping garden. The Marmara was visible beyond the garden, down a cliff face, across thickly planted treetops. The city was a blur on the horizon. And, startlingly, a shaft of sunlight had just broken through the low clouds, producing a brilliant circle of gold at the center of the leaden water.

As the view presented itself to her, Marion stopped, surprised, and blinked. The contrast between the frothy interior—so sickly she could almost taste it at the back of her mouth—and the stark beauty of the view out the window left her unsettled. She tried to force herself back into an appropriately social attitude, but before she could muster her nerves, Murdoch had turned his lovely, mocking eyes in her direction.

"Tea, Lady Willcox?" He was holding up a fragile ceramic cup and saucer that, to her horror, matched the sea-green wallpaper. She swallowed, nodded, and took it from him.

"Thank you, Mr. Murdoch." Then, composing herself, she sat in a gilt armchair across from Jeffrey, who was already sipping from his own nightmarish cup. Taking a quick drink of the scalding sweet mint tea, she saw that Lydia had run across the room to peer out the window, down at the garden. "It's—an arresting view."

"You're very kind." He threw her a cocotte's smile that wouldn't have been out of place in a scene from a naughty music hall, before turning his bright face back to Jeffrey. "And no, Willcox. You will not meet her. I keep her to myself. I have few enough consolations."

"A shame," Jeffrey said. "But then, I suppose we all must have our consolations."

"Must we?" Murdoch glanced sidelong at Marion, now with an open sneer. "Hmm. Yes, I believe under certain, unfortunate circumstances we must."

Deciding that Murdoch had furnished her with all the excuse she needed to flee the crushing room, Marion set her cup and saucer on a side table—gently—and rose. She brushed down her skirt and smiled sweetly at Murdoch. "Do you think, Mr. Murdoch, that I might take Lydia outdoors while you and Jeffrey converse? As you can see, she's already fallen in love with your beautiful hyacinths."

He rose from his own chair, wearing a triumphant smile that mistook, or pretended to mistake, her boredom with his antics for jealousy. "By all means, Lady Willcox. You noticed the path at the side of the house? It will lead you into the garden. Pick a few for Lydia, if it makes her happy."

"Thank you." She crossed the room and scooped up Lydia, praying that the girl wouldn't balk at being separated from Jeffrey. Lydia, however, was more than willing to exchange her father's company for a visit to what she saw out the window, and she clung eagerly to Marion's neck. As they left the room, she threw a smile almost as accomplished as Murdoch's in the direction of the two men. Learning quickly.

After pausing in the entry hall to retrieve her coat and hat, Marion hurried out the door and found the flagstone walkway that led down the hill. When she reached the bottom of a flight of shallow, stone stairs, she placed Lydia on her feet on the wet grass and held her hand as they picked their way toward a carved, granite bench just beyond a magnolia tree covered in swelling, fuzzy buds, turning pink. Out of view of the windows.

Sitting on the bench was a woman, slender and tiny, smoking what, from her demeanor, must have been a superbly engrossing cigarette. She bore more than a passing resemblance to the author of a book that was making the rounds of Marion's more intellectually frantic friends. *House of Incest*, she reminded herself irrelevantly. Large black eyes, quizzical expression, rosebud mouth, dark, shingled hair—the woman was unseemly, somehow, in her sensible beret, cardigan, long wool skirt, and string shoes. Wicked in a manner that she'd never have been if she'd been wearing something more overtly feminine or revealing.

All the better for doing her job effectively, Marion supposed, as she encouraged Lydia to explore the flowers a few yards away from the bench. But the ensemble left her uncomfortable. She'd never liked Lenore.

Once she was satisfied that Lydia was well-occupied in examining the hyacinths, she picked her way through the overgrown grass to the bench and sat next to the woman.

"Hullo, Marion." Lenore inhaled smoke, luxuriantly, not bothering to look away from the view.

"Hullo."

They were speaking Turkish, as they always had, since they'd been thrown together professionally just after the War—although Lenore was equally comfortable in Armenian, Arabic, French, and English. Of Armenian background, she'd been politicized when still an adolescent after the extermination of her family. She and an older brother, who had taken refuge in France, were the sole survivors. The brother, still in Paris, was a significant figure in their organization.

Not that Lenore had fared professionally all that badly, Marion reminded herself, leaning awkwardly against the clammy stone back of the bench. As socially astute and sophisticated as she was political, Lenore, unlike Marion, was entertained, rather than tortured, by the ethical inconsistencies of their assignments. And Marion had the impression—had always had the impression—that Lenore found her own tormented loyalty to their cause clumsy. Laughable.

Forcing down her fear of provoking any bewildering ridicule, she turned to Lenore. "I met Murdoch."

"Oh?"

"He doesn't appear promising."

Lenore laughed. "He isn't."

"Oh." Marion tried to keep the repugnance out of her voice. "But you've nonetheless involved yourself in a—a relationship with him?"

"You've 'involved yourself in a relationship' with the other one, haven't you?"

"No." Marion tried to gather her thoughts. "That is, yes. I have. Obviously." She glanced over at Lydia, who was pulling the petals off a collection of ungainly purple double hyacinths. "But—I didn't mean—" She made another attempt. "Is Murdoch working for us, then?"

"Murdoch works for everyone." Lenore tossed her cigarette onto the wet grass. "He's accommodating."

"Then—then what's the point of—?"

Lenore shrugged. "Is *yours* working for us?"

"No, of course not." She shook her head, frustrated. "But I don't understand then why—"

"I've had worse." She looked down at her manicured fingernails. "He's grateful, at least. Poor Sheridan. I blame the children."

Marion gave up and gazed out at the view of the sea, still half watching Lydia as her daughter began to dig up the bed of hyacinths in its entirety. Lydia's arms were mud to the elbows. "Where are they? The children, that is."

"Around." Vague wave of a graceful white hand.

"Are they really so awful?" Marion peered further down the hill, trying to catch a glimpse of them.

"No," Lenore said. "They're perfectly ordinary. Boring. Which, to their distress, they know. And so, they compensate by taking their cues from Henry James. Tedious."

"Oh." Marion waited a few seconds for Lenore to elaborate, and then, when she didn't, she tried a direct question. "Lenore. My instructions are to evaluate this object, analyze its capabilities, and then determine which organizations or governments have an interest in collecting it. I'm assuming your instructions are the same. So why am I here? You seem to have everything well in hand."

"I do have everything well in hand." Lenore twisted to retrieve a hessian sack from behind the bench. "Or, I did. Until the project took on its current—cerebral—tone. At which point they determined that they wanted a contribution from you as well. Bookish drudgery is your terrain. Not mine." She dropped the sack into Marion's lap and then relaxed, folding her hands over her waist, and observed the sea.

Marion lifted the sack—though not before it had left a damp spot on her skirt—and peeked inside. Mismatched scraps and pages of vellum and paper. Very old. She re-secured the flap and placed the bundle to her side on the bench. "What is it?"

Lenore shrugged. "Music, as far as I can tell."

"Music?" She stared at the sack. "I know nothing about music. Why have they tapped me?"

"True," Lenore agreed. "You've never struck me as the musical type."

"Then why—?"

"Really, Marion." Lenore glanced over at her and then back out at the water. "Obviously, it's not music. Or not just music. The pages were cached with Sheridan's candlestick when he dug it up in Konya. Sheridan thought nothing of them—predisposed as he is to privilege the shiny object over the dusty paper. I passed along photos to my brother. He had them analyzed. His people in Paris have drawn provisional conclusions. But what they saw has convinced them that they want you on-site to sniff them or lick them or sleep on top of them or whatever it is that you do—"

Lenore abruptly rose from the bench and adjusted her hat. "And so here you are."

Marion rose as well, less steadily. "I see." She thought for a moment. "Shall I retrieve the candlestick as well? It won't be difficult. Jeffrey has it in—"

"No. We'll remove it at the proper time. It's safe enough where it is." She adjusted her tight governess's skirt. "More important is getting you to Venice without attracting excessive attention."

"*Venice?*" Marion was trying to keep up with Lenore's erratic conversation, but as usual she was feeling stupidly slow. Inept. "When?"

"Now," Lenore said. "Eugene is waiting outside the gates."

"But—" Marion stole another look at Lydia, who was coated in multiple layers of mud, flower petals, and grass. Half-running, half-crawling toward the steep edge of the cliff.

"I'll mind her," Lenore sighed, following Marion's gaze. "My job, after all."

"But—"

"It isn't difficult," Lenore said, patient and condescending, as she lifted the sack and shoved it into Marion's hands. "Walk up the stairs, open the gate, greet Eugene, follow his instructions. That's all. Can you manage it?" She picked her way across the devasted hyacinth beds and lifted Lydia to her hip. "Goodbye, Marion."

"But—Eugene?"

"An American post-doctoral student with an adventuresome streak. Music theory." She began walking with Lydia toward the other side of the house. "Tall, young. You'll figure it out."

And then she was gone.

$\mathcal{A}$FTER a few seconds of silent confusion, Marion shouldered the hessian sack, walked up the stairs, opened the gate, and found Eugene. He was difficult to miss. Rather than waiting in the back of one of the island's ubiquitous public fiacres, Eugene was leaning against a bright red Cushman scooter, smoking a cigarette. When he saw Marion, he gave her a little wave, dropped the cigarette and crushed it with the toe of a white and brown sport shoe.

"Do you think you can perch?" He pulled the scooter upright and indicated a flat seat that he'd lengthened with a piece of cloth-covered wooden plank.

She briefly considered her skirt, looser than Lenore's, but not meant for riding. Then, smiling at him, she nodded. "If you can balance."

"Nothing to it." He straddled the scooter and waited for her to balance herself behind him. "I'm on the other side of the island. Shouldn't take more than ten minutes."

"And then?" she asked, as she hitched up her skirt and he put the bike into gear.

"To Venice? Not on this." He laughed as they accelerated up the hill toward the island's rounded peak. "We'll be lucky if it gets us to the end of the road."

The journey was closer to five minutes than it was to ten, given that Eugene let momentum take them down the back side of the island once they'd cleared the ridge. He brought them to a clattering stop outside a wooden house that had once been as ostentatious as Sheridan's. Now, though, with peeling paint, missing roof tiles, rampant weeds, and slashed up into rental flats, it looked as though it might topple into the sea with the gentlest of earthquakes.

"Yes," he said as Marion slid from the makeshift seat of the scooter, holding the hessian bag up with one hand and the hem of her skirt down with the other, "it really is as bad as that. Worse inside. But it's got a dock, which will be useful later this evening."

She followed his look down a flight of decaying wooden stairs to what was, indeed, an equally rotten dock. Empty for the moment. "Yes. I see."

"And I don't spend much time here, anyway," he continued, as he secured the scooter and led her down a dirt alleyway toward a side-door that opened directly into his ground-floor flat. "My work is mostly on Heybeli Island. At the Halki monastery. I stay the night there whenever they let me."

"Music? That's your specialty?" She took in the dismal single room, cold tile floor, metal table, stained, brownish sink, and dusty sofa on which, she suspected, he slept as well as worked. No windows. An overpowering smell of sewage and mildew. The space must have been used for food storage before the house had been divided into flats. No one had ever been meant to live in it. She wondered how much he was paying for the privilege of making it inhabitable.

"Yes." He lit a paraffin lantern and hung it from a hook above the table. Then he moved two wooden stools into place on either side and gestured Marion onto the first. "Medieval instrumental music. Byzantine. Timurid."

"Timurid?" She was intrigued. "I didn't know there was any. That is, any—written notation." She blushed. "This isn't my field. I shouldn't be trying to have this conversation."

"No," he said, quickly. "No, you're right. There's no formal notation. But there's theory. Increasingly sophisticated and developed throughout the fourteenth and fifteenth centuries. That's the crux of my research." He glanced at the sack that Marion had set on the table. "How it developed. And that's also why I'm dying to see what you've got in that bag."

"Oh." A small dismay hit her as she realized that the boy—he couldn't be more than twenty-five years old—had been manipulated by her people into lending his expertise to her. He wasn't one of them. He didn't know what her organization did. She looked down at the table. Nor was it her place to enlighten him. Keeping her eyes averted, she nodded and began to empty the sack of its contents.

"I'm not as naïve as I appear to be," he said after a moment or two of awkward silence had passed.

She looked up at him. "What?"

"People think that about Americans," he said. "That we're gullible. I mean, we are. Usually. But let me assure you that I'm not an innocent. You seem embarrassed. Or ashamed. You needn't be."

She smiled wanly, thinking that the situation was worse than she'd feared. "Thank you, Eugene."

"You don't believe me. It's true. I'll be fine. My contact at the monastery explained to me your general—uh—aims. Before he showed me the photographs of the pages and made me the offer. I understand the arrangement, and I can protect myself."

"Offer?" She was organizing the papers on the scratched metal tabletop.

"Yes." He was peering down at those that were closest to him. "Once you've made use of the documents, I get first dibs on publishing them. Meantime, I close my eyes and have no recollection of what you've been doing here."

She pressed her lips together and nodded. Then, taking a breath, she looked at him again. "Eugene—"

"What?"

She dropped the empty sack on the floor next to her stool. "Don't let them distract you from your research."

"Impossible." He grinned at her. Then he turned an attentive face to the papers in front of them. "And so, what then do we have here? I've spent days studying copies of the photos. And your colleagues gave me a summary of their own findings. From Paris. The likely source of the pages." He scratched his cheek absentmindedly. "But nothing could do justice to the originals."

Marion considered the pages for a few seconds as well. Then she pushed aside her misgivings about using Eugene and spoke: "I'm seeing two separate scribes. Fifteen related sheets. Is that right?" She paused. "And then this larger, disconnected page of drawings. Shall we arrange them by handwriting? Date?" She paused again. "Are there dates?"

"Let me tell you what I've already concluded about them from the photos and the summaries," he said. "And then after that we can decide how to read them. Okay?"

"Yes," she nodded. "All right."

"So these," he indicated eight of the scraps, "all come from an early fifteenth-century manual on the proper use and arrangement of musical instruments. The writing is in Arabic, as you can see, but the only other extant copy of it is the Topkapı Palace Library, here in Istanbul. It was probably produced in an Ottoman milieu. Also, these aren't consecutive pages, and they aren't identical to those in the original. I took the photos with me to check against the manuscript in the library, and I discovered that these scraps are more detailed. Especially the diagrams. It's the same work, but those in the Topkapı manuscript are spare. These are—not."

"Hmm." She nodded. "Is there a title? An author? I don't see any indication here."

"It's an anonymous work. But there's a Sufi feel to it." He pointed to a thin line along the margin of the largest page. "And there is a title. Here, you see: *The revelation of anxieties and miseries in the exposition of musical instruments: Kashf al-ghumum wa'l kurab fi sharh 'alat al-tarab.*"

"Strange title. But yes, I see the Sufi influence. 'Revelation' or 'unveiling'—*kashf*. And the wordplay. 'Anxieties,' *ghumum*, comes from *'gam*,' the root for veiling or concealment. So, it could read, comically or paradoxically, as the revelation of concealment. Or the unveiling of veiling."

She paused. Then, speaking slowly, she hazarded an interpretation: "I wonder when *gam*— from the French *gamme*—also entered the Ottoman-Arabic lexicon as 'musical scale?' I mean, as a supplement to the original Arabic term for 'scale,' *maqam*? The orthography of *gam*/'anxiety' and *gam*/'musical scale' is different, but only just."

She mused in silence for a few more seconds. "Do you think the choice of terminology in the title was deliberate? The French, *gamme*, comes from *gamma ut*, doesn't it? Originally the lowest tone on the medieval musical scale?"

"Goodness." He was laughing. "They warned me about you. But that was—very fast." He shook his head, surprised. "Yes. You're absolutely right. And I hadn't thought of it. *Gam*, as a borrowed term for 'musical scale,' especially connoting very low tones, was familiar to musicians and theorists writing in Arabic, Persian, and Turkish a good two hundred years before this document appeared. There's no way that part of the title is an accident."

He rubbed the palm of his hand over his forehead, thinking. "So, let me understand where we are, then. The first part of the title is about how this low, bass tone, when simultaneously revealed and concealed, can produce anxiety? Sorrows—*kurab*?" She nodded, and he continued. "Which means that the second part, on the 'exposition of instruments of music,' could also read as, say, the 'dissection' of, perhaps 'tools of delight?'"

She made a face. "It doesn't make much sense, does it?"

"On the contrary," he said, "when you read the remainder of the pages, you'll wonder how I missed it before."

"Oh." She brightened. "Shall we do that now, then?"

He checked his wristwatch. Shook his head. "Later. If there's time, that is. I have to get you to your boat in one hour. Better that you have an overview of all the material before we go into detail. Besides, you seem to be more than capable of drawing useful conclusions without me."

"I know nothing about music."

"*Gamma ut?*" Skeptical.

"Yes, fine," she admitted. "But ask me to carry a tune and you'll be running for the hills."

"Understood," he said. Then he thought for a second longer. "This second set of pages," indicating the seven sheets of badly ripped and frayed vellum on the other side of the table, "is early fourteenth-century. A section from the tenth volume of Shihab al-Din al-'Umari's multi-volume world history. His discussion of singers and musicians. This passage—and these pages, unlike the others, *are* consecutive—tells the story of the last Abbasid Caliph's favorite court musician singing the Mongol Khan, Hulagu, to sleep after the latter's conquest of Baghdad in 1258. As far as I can tell, it's no different from any other version of the episode. You can read it for yourself."

She skimmed the pages. "Yes. The city falls. He's hiding in the streets. Hulagu's soldiers find him, and he identifies himself. He's brought to Hulagu's camp and told to perform." She read a few more lines. "He's terrified, but he boasts that he can sing so beautifully that anyone listening will fall asleep. Hulagu commands him to do so." She smiled slightly. "He persuades the Khan to drink a few cups of wine before he begins. Then he eventually produces his lute and a singing girl called Saba—Soft East Wind—?"

He nodded. "Yes. But 'Saba' is also a term for one of the more complex classical musical modes or scales—another *maqam*. I'm not certain it would have been developed by 1258. But it was certainly in evidence by the fourteenth century, when Shihab al-Din was writing under the Mamluks."

"Interesting." She blinked. "So, he says that he's accompanied during his performance, then, both by this—anthropomorphized, female musical mode—and also, a few lines later, by his lute, which he's tuned to a mode appropriate to 'sorrow and lethargy,' or—or 'discouragement'—'*huzn wa-futur.*' Why both modes, I wonder? And why the melancholy?"

"Taken together," he ventured, "or compounded, the two would create radically low tones. I'm sensing a theme."

"*Gamma ut?*"

"Potentially lower." He paused again. "Although at that point, the music would be theoretical. No one would be able to hear it."

"Oh." She gazed back down at the pages. Read a few more lines. "And the Khan fell asleep. The singer lived. And—" her finger ran off the edge of the last scrap, "that's it."

"As I said, it isn't any different from the other extant versions of the story." Apologetic.

"These pages," she said, ignoring the apology and running her fingertip along the edge of the last sheet, "are oddly frayed."

"Well," he said, "from what I understand, they've spent the past five or six centuries as packing paper."

She shook her head. "No. These have been ripped deliberately. Look." She brought two of the scraps together. "The edges match. And these—these lines drawn along the edges also join up." She wrinkled her forehead and began rearranging the papers on the table in front of her. Fitting the sections together.

Forgetting Eugene's presence for several minutes, she played with the pages. Then, smiling to herself, she leaned back, almost falling off the stool. After which, she straightened and gestured toward the result. "They make a picture. A strangely European-looking picture, given the text. But a picture." She cocked her head. "This doesn't look Mamluk to me."

Eugene stared down at the image for a full minute before he started laughing. "This is Germany. Also fourteenth-century."

"Germany? How is that possible?"

"I have no idea how it's possible," he said. "But I'd recognize these figures anywhere. St. John's Dance. They're afflicted by the Dancing Plague."

"I don't know what that is."

He rose from the stool and paced the tiny room. "It's a bizarre story, actually. There are outbreaks of it from the very early medieval period up until—well, in Italy, until now. But the most notorious eruptions were in the fourteenth century, primarily in Germany. But also, if less so, elsewhere—France, Switzerland, parts of England."

"What happened? Why did it happen?"

"No one knows *why* it happened," he said. "But the effect—*what* happened—was uniform throughout Europe. Groups of people—men, women, children, all social strata—would spontaneously begin dancing. Often the groups were small. But in some of the more fantastic cases, there were tens of thousands of people dancing."

He stopped pacing, turned to face her, and leaned against the sink. He was, she realized, an intense boy. Despite the sport shoes. "They couldn't stop," he told her. "They'd go on dancing for days, weeks. Until they dropped. Collapsed. Many of them died. But those who survived would, I guess, just snap out of it after a while. Go back to work. Forget that it had happened. Until, a few years or decades later, there would be another outbreak. They prayed to St. John the Baptist to lift the curse. To help them stop."

He paused. "Not that their prayers were much use. Those infected by the dancing plague ordinarily had to wait it out. Hope they survived. Eventually, the more extreme, widespread cases dwindled. By the Renaissance, they were few and far between. Although, again, you do hear every now and then of local outbreaks even now, in Italy. The tarantella."

"Oh." She rubbed her eyes with her fists. Feeling oppressed by the information she'd collected. It was all very interesting, but none of it coalesced into a meaningful picture. And nothing, from what she could see, had anything to do with Jeffrey's candlestick. She blinked at Eugene, still leaning against the sink. "Can you think of why this image would be hidden in Shihab al-Din's description of the visit of the Abbasid Caliph's musician to Hulagu's camp in 1258?"

"No." He pushed himself off the sink and lowered himself onto the stool. "I'm sorry. I wouldn't even have known it was there if you hadn't—"

"Right." She tapped her fingertips on the tabletop. "Well, let's set it aside for now." She moved the last large page of vellum to the center of the table, between them. "What about this, then?"

"That," he said, "is why you're going to Venice—" He checked his wristwatch again. "In twenty minutes."

"Oh?"

He smiled. "Yes. But in this case, I'm simply passing on information. This has nothing to do with my research. I'm no more than a conduit."

"Very well. Instructions, then?" She smiled as well, trying to ignore her misgivings about his open, almost childish enthusiasm. "But after that, if there's time, I would like to hear your thoughts on the first pages. We've covered little more than the title."

"Agreed." He leaned forward and pointed to a small image at the bottom corner of the vellum. "They told me to draw your attention to this."

Three hares elaborately composed in brown ink. Interlocking ears. When she saw them, she let out her breath, reassured that she'd finally seen something, anything, relevant to the candlestick. The rest of the sheet was covered in similarly elaborate animal representation. "Did my—my colleagues have a sense of where this page originated?" She ran her hand over the ancient-feeling ink strokes. "Or what I'm expected to do with it?"

"Apparently," he said, "this is a page from a fourteenth- or fifteenth-century Venetian pattern book. Used in the design and production of textiles. Silk, likely."

"Hmm."

"Ordinarily, it would be impossible to trace the textile on the basis of a single sheet," he said. "But your people ran into some luck. An old Venetian family—withered at this point to two elderly cousins—has been quietly selling pieces of lampas silk that match pages known to have been extracted from the same book. Your organization contacted the male cousin with a view to purchasing the textile. He refused. They want you to present him with this page. See if you can convince him to part with it on different terms."

"Steal it?"

"Gather information about it, if I've understood properly." He looked uncomfortable. "The message I'm meant to pass along to you is a little ambiguous."

"It always is." She thought. "Very well. I understand. Did they tell you anything about the motif? The three rabbits?"

"Just that it's widespread." He folded his hands on the table. "The earliest examples of it appear in caves in China. Then it shows up on a few pieces of Mongol coinage. Then in the marginal sculpture of European churches."

"In Germany?"

"Yes," he said. "As a matter of fact. And England. Devon primarily, they said."

"Hmm." It wasn't much, but at least a tenuous connection was forming. "I'll approach this family in Venice. Their name?"

"Rombulo."

She nodded. Then, trying to glance out the absent window for a sense of the time, she continued speaking. "What can you tell me about the pages from the instructional manual?"

He peered again at his wristwatch. "We've got five minutes. Then we'll have to make our way down to the dock. So I'll describe to you just the two most striking discrepancies I found between the pages here and those in the Topkapı Library manuscript."

"Good. Thank you."

He rotated one of the more complete pages around on the table so that it faced her. Pointed to a series of seven annotated drawings. "You can see here that these are diagrams of the proper method of playing classical instruments—pan pipes, tambourines, the *ud*, etc."

"Yes."

"The final instrument of this sequence in the Topkapı manuscript is a *santir*, a sort of dulcimer, right?" When she nodded, he indicated the final image on the page in front of her. "Here, it's a pneumatic organ."

"Interesting. Why the change?"

"I don't know," he said. "But it's striking. Musicians in the medieval Islamic world were aware of the organ. But it wasn't part of the classical canon. In fact, more often than not, the pneumatic organ was described as a weapon of war—the sort of thing tricky Greek armies would bring along with them into battle to disorient the enemy."

"I see."

"More than that, though," he continued, "look at the musician's face. All the other players are calm and stylized. This seventh figure is tortured. His expression is pained. Miserable."

She nodded again. Then she looked up at him. "And there's nothing in the text to indicate why the seventh figure has been replaced in this way?"

"Nothing," he said. "The text is dry. Didactic. Reminding readers that mastering perfect form is a prerequisite to mastering perfect tone. That sort of thing."

"What about the second discrepancy?"

"Right." He brightened and moved another sheet into position. "Now, in the complete version of the manuscript, this page is separated from the seven musicians by a great deal of exposition. Here, though, it follows directly from it."

"Yes," she said. "I see that." She stared down at ten overlapping circles of tightly spaced text. "What is it?"

"It's a common enough image. A diagram of the modes or scales and their astrological, natural, and medical correspondences. Which tone goes with which planet, humor, illness, emotion—you get the idea. Songs for healing. Songs for joy. Right?"

"Yes. I've seen similar arrangements in other texts."

He smiled. "But this is unusual. And utterly different from its counterpart in Topkapı."

"How?"

"Read these planetary correspondences." He indicated the first set of circles.

She concentrated on the page. "Saturn. Mars. Saturn. Mars. Saturn. Mars—ah yes. I see. Melancholy and fear. *Only* melancholy and fear."

"Precisely." He rested his fingertip against another circle. "Grief. Anxiety. Fear. No pleasure. No restfulness. No languor, even. No healing."

"Very interesting." She glanced up at him, brisk, and began rising from the stool. "Wonderful. Thank you, Eugene—"

"No, wait." He stopped her. "That isn't all."

She lowered herself back onto the stool. "No?"

"No." He thought for a few seconds. "Are you familiar at all with classical Islamic musical notation?"

She laughed. "No. Not remotely."

"All right." He considered. "What you have to understand, then, is that the purpose of diagrams such as these isn't to represent a static, unchangeable composition. There's little relation here to the staff notation that becomes popular in Europe between the fifteenth and seventeenth centuries. Musicians in the Islamic tradition were taught instead to read modes or pitches, or *distances* between modes and pitches, and these in turn would become a framework within which they'd be expected, when performing, to improvise. Their skill was evaluated on their ability to produce melodies spontaneously while nonetheless adhering to a pre-established set of modes. Composers were simultaneously performers."

He paused again, and then he spoke carefully. "Some of these modes leant themselves more easily to melodic interpretation. And some were more—'atmospheric' might be the best word for it. Less melody. Do you understand?"

"Yes," she said. "I think so. If in the simplest way."

"Good." He pointed to the circular diagram in front of her. "This diagram represents modes and pitches that are anti-melodic. Pure mood." He paused. "But they're also impossible to perform. If properly interpreted, they'd be too low on the scale for anyone to hear. Or any instrument to play, for that matter. They're for something entirely other than listening."

"Like the lullaby that Hulagu Khan commanded in 1258," she mused.

"And like the grief and fear, Saturn and Mars," he added, "that operate at the level below *gamma ut.*"

After a few seconds of silence, she nodded to herself and gathered the pages to return to the hessian sack. As she did so, she spoke. "I can't thank you enough for this, Eugene. You've done extraordinary work." When she'd secured the flap of her sack, she stood and smiled at him. "If it's the last thing I do, I'll see to it that these documents are delivered to you so that you can continue your analysis."

He stood as well, looking both embarrassed and pleased with himself. "I've enjoyed myself, Marion. You take more intellectual risks than the monks on Heybeli Island do."

"I certainly hope so." She pushed open the door, pleased to be out of the squalid flat. Then she scanned, perfunctory and professional, the side alley and their path to the dock. The night, which was dark under low clouds and the last sliver of a waning moon, felt empty. Quiet. Satisfied, she stood to the side to let Eugene lead her down the hill, a part of her mind still processing his interpretation of the material.

When they reached the dock, a sleek, thirty-foot pleasure boat—some sort of Elco—had half-moored to it with a temporary stern line. Its motor was running. Sounding impatient. Stepping over a splintered hole in the soft wood of the float she turned back and offered her hand to Eugene. "Thank you again. It's been a pleasure."

"I've enjoyed it as well," he said.

She climbed up over the transom, released the stern line, and opened the door to the boat's cabin. Then unable to stop herself, she turned back one last time. "Be careful, Eugene."

"I will." He smiled as the boat picked up speed away from the island, into the dark, choppy water.

Venice, Italy
March, 1937

THE voyage from Istanbul to Venice, fifteen hundred miles with stops for fuel at a series of joyless, politicized tourist destinations, took two weeks. Throughout, the boat's small crew was polite but uninterested in conversation. After supplying her with clothing, cash, and identification should she need it, they limited their interactions to comments on food and weather. Marion, in turn, spent her time familiarizing herself with what she now thought of as Eugene's documents.

She also, despite her intentions to the contrary, dwelled with increasing guilt on his role in her project. There had been no reason for her superiors to have informed him as extensively as they had—briefing him, unnecessarily and dangerously, not only on the material, but also on her movements. And the only conclusion she could draw from it was that they expected him to be interrogated and her to be followed. Which meant that representatives from Jeffrey's office had been waiting for Eugene after he'd seen her off at the dock.

She shifted uncomfortably in her berth at the thought of the naïve, enthusiastic child abruptly forced into an understanding of the danger into which he'd placed himself. Her own people would consider his difficulties as little more than a recruitment exercise—watching his reactions to determine how they might use him in the future. He himself would never be the same.

And although Marion had long since come to terms with the damage her early political choices had done to her personal and professional lives, even after years of work for her organization, she couldn't help cringing when she witnessed the demolition of an as-yet unsullied scholarly mind. It would be decades before Eugene recognized the extent of the injury that this seemingly harmless adventure had done to his work. But the injury had been done. His intellectual existence would never be free of management.

As the Elco moored alongside the partially constructed railway station at the north end of Venice's old city, she pushed away her thoughts of Eugene's predicament. She had a job to do. And if her superiors expected her to be followed, then they also expected her to play along—to do what she could to lose any tail attached to her. To keep the office close and visible, but always a step or two behind.

Venice not being a city she knew well, she resolved to rely on her reputation with Jeffrey's people rather than professional evasive tactics. Nodding her thanks to the crew of the boat, she took the bag they'd provided her, stepped up to the platform, and hailed a water-taxi. After accepting the pilot's inflated price, she directed him to one of the more hysterically sentimental of the hotels overlooking the Rialto Bridge.

Her tail, if there was one, would wait for whatever trick she was playing to reveal itself. No eye could accept at face value a decision to inhabit such an obvious and porous building. But in fact there was no trick. The hotel, maintained by her people, kept tucked in among its guest rooms of gilt mirrors, green and pink marble floors, and scrolled red and gold wallpaper, three bare cells. No view of the bridge. But safe and, for a number of centuries, hidden.

Only minimally aware of the sodden drizzle falling into the canal, Marion endured the voyage in the water-taxi, paid the pilot's fee without comment, and stepped with brisk focus into the hotel's reception area. Empty. Dull. Early March, with war looming, was not their busiest time. The short, angry man at the desk noted her appearance with a vague sneer, but he also waited for her to approach before openly acknowledging her presence.

"Reservation?" His book was closed. He wasn't expecting visitors, and he was manifestly in a mood to refuse accommodation to chance passers-by.

"Yes," she said in English. "Room Eight."

"With the Titian?"

"I believe it's a Tintoretto."

He grunted and unlocked a drawer in the reception desk. "Alessandro will show you." Shoving a key in her direction. Still angry.

She took the key and thanked him, but he'd returned his attention to the rain spattering the glass that fronted the canal. Bemused, she turned to a quiet boy who had appeared and shyly lifted her bag. He beckoned her not to the overwrought stairway leading up to the first floor of guest rooms, but instead through a narrow door to the side of what her brief glance told her was the dining room.

From there, they ascended a damp, wooden staircase to an additional door that hovered halfway between the second and third floors, embedded in a brownish wall obscured by flaking plaster. The boy set the bag on the tiny landing outside the door and gestured toward its handle. Nodding her thanks, she inserted the key into the modern-looking lock and then pushed open the door.

When the boy simply stood and watched as she crossed the threshold, she paused, disconcerted. Was she meant to tip him? Unexpected, but certainly not beyond the realm of possibility. Blushing, she faced him, searching her coat pockets for the non-existent change that the water-taxi's pilot had failed to give her. Before she could begin opening her bag, the boy, laughing, held up a hand. "No, no," he said in Italian. "You misunderstand."

"In what way?" Summoning up her own plodding, heavily accented Italian.

"The Rombulo cousins," he said, twisting away from her and trotting down the stairs, "sell carnival masks to foreigners in St. Mark's Square. They own a shop."

She pulled the door to Room Eight shut behind her. "What?" In English. "No, I'm sorry," in bad Italian. "What did you say?"

But the boy was gone.

Irritated, she turned back to the brown, mildewed wall and the door to her room. Then, deciding there was little point in tracking the boy, she pushed it open. In the blurry afternoon light seeping from somewhere overhead, she found, sitting on an unadorned wooden side table, a ceramic lamp with an orange cloth shade. She switched on the lamp, which threw a sickly beige glimmer over the room. A spare rectangle, little more than five feet wide and eight feet long, with an invisible ceiling soaring twenty feet above her. The source of the initial illumination was a roof-light, obscured by dirt and pigeon droppings.

The room, she noted as she placed her bag on the splintered wooden floor and closed the door behind her, contained a camp bed, a wicker chair, and the side table. Next to the lamp on the side table were a pitcher of water crafted from the same ceramic, and an incongruous shot glass from a local bar celebrated for its appeal to artists and fictional characters. She decided she'd drink directly from the pitcher.

Already bothered by the bilious color of the room, she removed the shade from the lamp. But unshaded, the bulb merely brought the rotting plaster and colonies of mold covering the walls into starker relief. Whereas the light from the ceiling, she determined upon switching off the lamp altogether, was insufficient for her work. And so, rubbing her eyes, defeated, she returned the shade to the lamp, turned on the bulb, and sat heavily on the camp bed. Removed her coat and boots, ignoring the wet chill in the air.

From her new vantage point, she noticed a second door opposite her on the far wall. Intrigued, she stood, walked the two paces toward it, used her small key to unlock it, and pulled it open. Then, pleased for the first time since entering the hotel, she smiled. A private stairway led, she could feel from the air circulating up from the dank floors below, to the outside. She'd be able to leave and return to her room without enduring the curiosity of the Grand Canal.

She was tempted to experiment with her escape route at once. But recognizing that both her professional unfamiliarity with the city and her need for proper sleep might compromise her sole advantage over any tail, she closed the door instead. She'd venture out the next morning. At least she'd have a destination. St. Mark's Square. A short walk. And there couldn't, she continued to herself, still feeling disgruntled as she switched off the lamp and reclined fully clothed into the camp bed, be more than twenty or thirty shops in the vicinity selling carnival masks. She'd be certain to give herself a fair amount of time to examine them all.

SHE next woke to light from the ceiling that told her nothing except that it was either day or a bright moonlit night. Her renewed energy led her to conclude the former. Sitting up, she switched on the orange lamp and ran her hands through her hair, pinning it into a knot at the base of her neck. Then she looked down at her wrinkled trousers and considered.

There was one change of clothing in her bag, a moderately presentable dress and shoes. Deciding to save those for an emergency—or, optimistically, an organized meeting with her targets— she pulled on her boots and buttoned the coat over the disheveled outfit in which she'd slept. Standing, she drank a few swallows of water from the pitcher, slipped her cash into an inside pocket of her coat, lifted the bag, and made for the door.

Once through, the door carefully locked behind her, she realized that the stairway had no external source of light. The slick, rotting stairs descended in complete darkness. Choosing not to dwell on how she'd ever manage to unlock the door upon her return—or, as she stumbled downward, what fungal or plant life was accumulating on the fingers she dragged along the wall to guide her—she eventually reached ground level. A puddle of fetid water that leaked over the top of her boots.

After feeling the wall for a panicked ten seconds, she found another door handle and pulled. Unlocked. Beyond it was a narrow, empty alley, stone buildings rising up three or four storeys on either side. She stepped through the door, shut it behind her, and began to wade through a steady five inches of dirty water in what she hoped, from the sound of swarming pigeons, was the direction of St. Mark's Square.

Although the alley was deserted, she could have touched the walls on either side of her with outstretched hands. She didn't, because the walls were coated with a layer of something wet, green, and toxic-looking. But the thought occurred to her when she wasn't concentrating instead on the overpowering stench of sewage—historic and centuries-old, no doubt, this being Venice—that came at her in waves from the standing water that only deepened as she neared what was now the combined sound of pigeons and shell-shocked tourists.

She emerged from the alley onto a street just to the south of the square. At the first café she met, she stopped, ordered an espresso and a croissant, and devoured both standing at the bar. Then, fortified, she walked, dripping, toward the square, in search of carnival masks. The overcast sky above her was a harsh, metallic yellow. Hostile. Unpleasant. But then, dismissing it, she focused on her task.

Her plan had been to spend the day painstakingly analyzing each and every gift shop before determining which she ought to approach first. Optimistically, she'd given herself two weeks, based on the boy's cryptic information, to encounter the Rombulo cousins. Less than three minutes after beginning her initial tour of the covered shops surrounding the square, however, she paused, examined a window, and rubbed her forehead in amused embarrassment. No wonder the boy had laughed at her.

Picked out in the red and gold script Marion associated with circus advertisements, was the single word, "Rombulo." The name obscured the entire top half of the glass window. Beneath it was a display of ornate masks, certain to appeal to passing customers. Clutching her bag to her shoulder, trying disguise her eagerness, she pushed through the door into the shop.

The smell of dry sandalwood, a welcome respite from the sewage, the pigeons, and the tactile dampness of the air outside, greeted her as the door swung shut behind her. And the shop, tiny but teeming with masks of every size, shape, and purpose, was overseen by an intelligent-looking girl, no more than twenty years old, writing in a journal. Not one of the Rombulo cousins. She looked up from her desk and smiled when Marion entered.

Rather than browsing the masks, Marion tried for immediate contact. Less flustered than she'd been at the hotel, she marshaled her correct, yet far from fluent Italian: "good morning. Would it be possible, I wonder, to speak with Mr. or Miss Rombulo?"

"I'm sorry," the girl replied, polite. "They aren't here at the moment. But I can pass them a message." Taking in Marion's disappointment, she continued, with sympathy: "they're very old, you see."

Marion nodded. "Yes. I understand." She paused. "I was hoping to ask them about the purchase of lampas silk."

"We sell masks here." The girl gestured toward her merchandise.

"Yes. But—"

"Would you be interested in our masks?"

Marion began to decline the offer, but something thinly insistent in the girl's tone stopped her. Swallowing, she nodded again. "Yes. Very well." She examined the girl's pleasant expression. "Is there any you'd recommend?"

"No." She stood and moved around the desk. "Whichever appeals to you."

"All right." Slowly, trying to determine whether she was missing some cue, she examined the masks closest to her. Then, lifting a white and grotesque, yet attractively gilded, Bauta, she turned to the girl. "This one?"

"Excellent choice." The girl took the mask from her and returned to the desk. Wrapping it gently in tissue paper, she settled it into a blue box that was as opulent as the mask itself. "The price is twenty-five lire."

Marion withdrew the cash from her pocket, still uncertain as to what the transaction meant, handed it to the girl, and took the box. "Thank you."

"Good day," the girl replied, returning her attention to her journal.

After a few seconds of awkward silence, Marion turned and left the shop, carrying the box in front of her, no more enlightened as to the Rombulos than she'd been when she first entered.

Still not registering the drizzle, she returned to the café she'd originally patronized, put the box on the bar, and ordered two more espressos and two more croissants. After paying and consuming both, she took the box and waded into the alley that led to her hotel. Giving a cursory glance to her surroundings, even though she still hadn't felt any eyes watching her. In fact, if she were relying solely on her sensitivity to the air, she'd be convinced that she had no followers at all. No one was remotely interested in her movements.

Once she'd returned to her room, she put the box, unopened, on the table next to the shot glass, spread out her coat and boots on the wicker chair in the unlikely hope that they'd dry, and lowered herself onto the camp bed. She'd continue familiarizing herself with Eugene's documents, and then she'd try again tomorrow. If the Rombulo cousins weren't in the shop, she'd press the girl further. Drop a hint about the drawing from the pattern book. Babble about rabbits and candlesticks. Anything to provoke their attention or interest.

Satisfied with what was at least a bit more of a plan than she'd had when she arrived in the city, she turned her attention to the story of Hulagu Khan's lullaby, her favorite text from Eugene's hoard.

THE next morning, confident in her strategy, she felt her way down the glutinous stairway, waded through the stench of the alley, consumed her espresso and croissant, and appeared at the Rombulos' shop just as the girl was opening it. The girl was, once again, alone. Marion gave her five minutes to settle herself, pretending with little enthusiasm to examine the leather goods in the window to the left of the carnival masks. Then, deciding she'd been patient enough, she stepped through the door into the shop.

"Good morning."

"Good morning," the girl replied. "You've been enjoying your mask?"

It was an odd question. "Yes?"

"You'd like to buy another, perhaps?" The girl rose from behind the desk.

"No," Marion said, on firmer ground. "I'd like, if possible, to speak to Mr. or Miss Rombulo."

"Unfortunately," the girl said, still polite, "they're away. I'm very sorry to disappoint. They rarely come to the shop."

"The piece of lampas silk that interests me," Marion pressed on, "is of an unusual design. I believe that Mr. or Miss Rombulo may be able to advise me on its provenance. Or—or its current whereabouts." She faltered, uncertain as to how much she ought to reveal to the girl. Then, determined not to lose her attention, she continued: "I have a drawing from a pattern book. Fourteenth-century. Perhaps fifteenth-century. I'd like to compare."

"Ah." The girl sat. "If you were to describe the characteristics of this drawing, I might pass the information to Mr. or Miss Rombulo."

"Yes." Marion gathered her thoughts. "All right. A motif of three rabbits or hares. Interlocking ears. Foliage. Similar to the engravings on a contemporary Ilkhanid or Ottoman candlestick that was found alongside it—" She went quiet, realizing how outlandish her description sounded. Then she waited. Fidgeting.

"Ah," the girl repeated after a few awkward seconds. "I see. I'll give them the message. It's possible that you will see them in the shop tomorrow morning." She stood. "You'd like to purchase a second carnival mask?"

"What?"

"A mask. Would you like to buy another?"

Marion stared at her for three or four seconds. Then, curt, she nodded. "Yes. Fine. This one." She held up a colorful Zanni mask with a six-inch nose. It would require a larger box.

"Excellent choice." The girl took the mask, wrapped it in tissue paper and fit it into a long, pink box covered in silver scrolls and musical staffs and notes.

When she'd finished, she handed Marion the box. "Good morning."

"Good morning." Marion left the shop without waiting for further conversation. Tried to convince herself that she was making progress. At the very least, Ian and Lydia would enjoy her growing collection of masks. Stopping briefly at the café for her espresso and croissants, she returned to her sodden room. The box felt unusually heavy.

THE next morning, she changed into the clean dress. Optimistic. She also, however, pushed her feet into the damp, unpleasant boots she'd been wearing since her arrival. Unwilling to wade through the alley and the pigeon detritus in the strapped heels that were meant to go with the more formal outfit. After shoving the shoes into her bag—careful not to damage the page from the pattern book she'd arranged at the top—she left the room quickly, refusing to acknowledge the likelihood that she'd arrive at the shop before the girl appeared to open it.

Once she'd reached the vicinity of St. Mark's Square, she paused, uncertain. She'd intended to change from the boots into the shoes as she neared the shop, but the drizzle had turned into a heavy rain—falling, somehow, both down and up—and the Square was no less flooded than her alley had been. She looked down at the tops of her boots and thought further, as a half-eaten bit of pastry attached to a clump of feathers drifted past her ankle. Then, shrugging the bag further up onto her shoulder, she strode in the direction of the shop, still wearing the boots. She'd make herself presentable later.

To her pleased surprise, the girl had already opened, and Marion could see her through the window, writing in her journal. Emboldened, Marion pushed through the door to discover that once again the girl was alone. She looked up from her writing.

"You would like to purchase a third mask?" Her tone was still nothing but polite.

"No." Marion crossed to the desk, set her bag down in front of the girl, and opened it. "No, I wouldn't."

She removed the shoes and placed them next to the bag. Although the girl glanced at them, she didn't comment. Focused instead on Marion's quiet anger. Then, carefully, she withdrew the page of the pattern book, moved the bag to the floor, and spread it on the desk in front of the girl.

"If possible," she said, "I would very much like to speak with Mr. or Miss Rombulo."

The girl let her eyes wander, uninterested, over the page. Then she returned her attention to Marion. "I'm very sorry, but Mr. and Miss Rombulo aren't here. They're very old, you see."

Marion nodded, silent, and returned the page to the bag. Closing it and holding the shoes in her hand, she turned to leave the shop. Livid.

"You would like to purchase a third mask?" The girl stood behind the desk.

Marion twisted, provoked, meaning to say something withering in her inept Italian. But something in the girl's otherwise placid face stopped her. And so, pushing down her anger, she nodded instead. Her eyes leveled on the girl, she chose a mask at random—a Columbina, silver—and held it out to her. "This one."

"Excellent choice."

The girl, concentrating on her work, wrapped the mask in tissue paper, and enclosed it in a yellow and white box. Then, smiling, she handed the box to Marion. "Good day."

"Right," she muttered in English as she took the box in the hand that wasn't holding her shoes. "Thank you ever so much."

Dejected, and uncertain as to what her next move ought to be, she waded in the direction of the café she'd been frequenting. Stood at the bar, drew a few annoyed looks as she set both the box and her shoes at her elbow, ordered an espresso, and, indulging herself, also asked for a large piece of chocolate cake.

With nowhere of interest to go, she lingered over the cake, letting herself enjoy it. Almost failing to notice when a tiny elderly woman and man pushed themselves through the crowded storefront into position beside her. It was only when the man, speaking English, commented on her cake that she turned to him, startled. "I'm sorry?"

"I said," he smiled up at her, "that you've made a wise decision. Switching from the croissants to the cake."

"Yes," she replied turning back to her plate. "I agree. Good cake."

"I believe you've been asking after us?" His voice was gentle. The barest trace of an Italian accent.

She considered the man standing next to her—thin, precise, balding, and dressed in a sober, dark wool suit that had clearly been hand crafted by a detail-obsessed tailor fifty or sixty years before. The woman to his side was no larger than a child of ten or eleven years. She beamed at Marion with iridescent artificial teeth that made it difficult for Marion to focus on any other part of her.

Blinking, trying to interpret the situation, Marion nodded. "Yes. Yes, I have been. Mr. and Miss Rombulo?"

"Veronica," the man said. "Please."

"And Giles," added the woman.

"Giles?"

"My father was an anglophile." His tone was apologetic.

"Oh. Marion. Marion Bailey."

563

"Shall we return to the shop to discuss your textile problem?" He flicked a drop of water off the immaculate cloth of his lapel.

"Yes. Of course." She smiled back at Veronica as she shouldered her bag and turned away from the bar. "Thank you for speaking with me."

"Don't forget your box, dear." Veronica nodded in the direction of the bar.

"Or your shoes," Giles added, as he walked through the press of bodies that had packed themselves into the café, attempting to escape the rain.

Too exhilarated to feel embarrassed, Marion collected the box and her shoes and followed them out, in the direction of the Square.

ALTHOUGH the rain had dwindled to a thick, yellowish mist by the time they were walking in the open, Marion was drenched below the knee when they reached the Rombulos' store. A surreptitious glance in the direction of Giles and Veronica told her that they had remained dry and unruffled. Some occult Venetian skill, she concluded, as Veronica reached into her slim handbag for a key to the locked door. The girl had vanished.

When they entered, the Rombulos led her to the back, where they unlocked a second door that opened onto a large, opulently furnished sitting room. The sort of place that French Romantic poets enjoyed eulogizing a hundred years before. But despite the riot of rich color that hit her as Giles, to her amusement, lit candelabra in each corner of the room, Marion concluded that they didn't spend a great deal of time here. The thick carpets and cushioned armchairs were coated by a layer of dust. And there was a stifled tomb-like quality to the air. This wasn't home.

Veronica closed the door behind them, and, still smiling, gestured Marion toward a tapestried armchair. Thanking her again, Marion sat, placed her shoes and the box on the floor to her side, and positioned her bag in her lap. Giles wandered over to a marble tabletop resting on scrolled iron legs at the far end of the room. Then, turning back to her, he held up a bottle. "Bourbon?"

"What?" She was nonplussed. It was 9:00 in the morning. She also thought she saw a half open, embossed leather box full of what couldn't possibly be human teeth on the table near where the bottle had stood.

"Bourbon, dear," Veronica supplied as she relaxed into a chair opposite Marion. "From America. We enjoy America. Minnie!"

"Dick Johnson!" Giles echoed, pouring three large drinks.

Veronica giggled as Giles, humming something from Puccini, brought them both glasses. Marion thanked him, took a sip, and left the glass on a table to her side. Next to a closed leather box that nothing in the world would induce her to open.

Once Giles had retrieved his own glass and sat down beside Veronica, he leaned back, crossed his knees, and threw an encouraging smile at Marion. "Lampas silk, then."

"Yes. I was—"

"Are you musical?" This from Veronica.

"I'm sorry?"

"Musical," Giles explained. "Can you sing? Are you aware of pitch? If I asked you for a clear A, could you produce it?"

She deflated. Certain now that her target was no closer than it had been before. It was becoming increasingly apparent that the Rombulos were addled. Pushing down her disappointment, she shook her head. "I'm afraid not. Aside from a few unsuccessful piano lessons as a child," she amended, trying for levity.

Giles and Veronica exchanged a glance. Then, after taking a healthy swallow of her bourbon, Veronica flashed her teeth in Marion's direction. "So much the better that you have your masks, then."

"I don't under—"

"You're impatient," Giles interrupted her, standing. "You want this." He walked to a crumpled velvet curtain obscuring a dark corner of the room and pushed it aside. Behind it, disguised as the reverse side of the cheaper, newer fabric, and protected in translucent wrapping, hung a centuries-old fall of silk, shimmering with animals, foliage, and what looked to be cartographic markings. When he moved the curtain, the dim corner of the chamber brightened, as though the brilliant threads running through the silk were their own light source.

She rose to her feet as well. "Oh—"

"You can't have it," Veronica said from her seat, still drinking the bourbon.

"No, of course not," she replied. "I wouldn't dream of—"

"But you can examine it," Giles spoke over her. "If you believe it would help."

"Thank you—"

"It won't help," Veronica continued. "You haven't the talent."

Marion reached for her bag. "I do have a document that may aid in—in interpreting it. I'd be happy to share it with—"

"What," Giles interrupted again, crossing the room and lowering himself into his chair, "do you know of the Rombulo family?"

Marion forced herself to remain calm. Sat back in her own chair. Quiet. Determined to appear polite. "Very little."

"You have a choice, then," he said. "You can begin at once and spend as long as you choose examining this jumble of silk. It will tell you nothing. Or you can sacrifice twenty minutes of your time listening to the story of our family's progenitor. After which, it is just possible that you'll be the first to draw a useful message out of what is otherwise a troublesome, if pretty, piece of decrepit cloth."

She subsided further into her chair and nodded. At the very least, she wanted to keep them in a forthcoming mood. "Thank you. I'm grateful to you for your guidance."

"Hmph," murmured Veronica, drunk now, her teeth slipping. "More than one can say about the others who've passed through here. Ruffians."

"Brigands," agreed Giles, sipping from his own glass. Then, focusing on a spot on the carpet in front of him, he began: "we are the last descendants of Pietro Rombulo—merchant, ambassador, and explorer. Since you know nothing of his life, I'll begin at the beginning. Pietro was born in the 1380s, in the south. Messina. Do you know it?"

"Yes," she said tersely. "A bit."

"Good. Northerners don't often appreciate it."

"A beautiful city," she replied mechanically. "Lovely Cathedral."

"Hmm." He hadn't raised his eyes from the spot on the carpet. "Pietro started life as a small merchant. But his heart was in adventure. He traveled all over the Mediterranean, to North Africa, the Levant, and back again, in the early 1400s. Building up his knowledge of the world and his trade. In 1407, however, he went further afield than he had before, to Ethiopia, where he worked to mutual benefit for that nation's Christian king. Whilst there, he married a daughter of the Ethiopian aristocracy, our ancestress."

He peered up at Marion, daring her to comment on his African blood. But she was too busy correlating the dates Giles was throwing at her with the dates she remembered from Eugene's summary of her material. She shook her head, irritated, thinking.

If Pietro had been travelling between Ethiopia and Italy in the early to mid-1400s, he could easily have played a part in the piecemeal narrative that had been buried alongside the candlestick. It's true that the story of Hulagu Khan's lullaby and the hidden images of the dancing plague contained within it were produced in the mid-1300s, fifty years before Pietro had lived. But the Topkapı manual, with its strange commentary on musical modes too low for humans to hear, was a near exact contemporary. And the vellum sheet from the pattern book would have been drawn near the end of Pietro's life, provided he hadn't met with any accidents during his travels. It was obviously the model for the silk she saw in front of her.

Intrigued, she nodded again, satisfied, and held Giles's look, waiting for his next comment. What he said confirmed her hypothesis. Dropping his gaze to the carpet, he continued: "for thirty years, Pietro acted as an intermediary between the Ethiopian court and Italian governing and trade bodies. In 1444, however, a disturbance of some sort—always described in vague terms—led the emperor Zara Yaqub to send Pietro on a longer voyage. To the east, rather than to the north. Through India, Ceylon, and then into China. Pietro returned in 1448. Whatever he learned there, in China, satisfied the Ethiopian court. The disturbance was quelled.

"At one point, the story of his travels between Ethiopia and China was recorded by a Dominican friar. That record is lost—" He broke off and glared over at Veronica, who had begun giggling into her glass again. She'd quietly refilled it and was drinking the bourbon like water. She'd also removed her teeth and set them on the table beside her.

Marion, her forehead wrinkled, thinking through the implications of what Giles was telling her, failed to notice. But when Giles remained silent, she prodded him. "And so, this piece of silk—"

"Pietro," he said, "commissioned this textile near the end of his life. He himself labored over the pattern book. And when the weaving was complete, he destroyed the models. Or, at least, that is what he told his family as he died."

"Oh." She gazed over his shoulder at the lampas silk hanging behind what was likely an eighteenth-century curtain of velvet. Attractive in its own right. But coarse and cheap compared to what it hid.

"I believe you have a page from a pattern book you'd like to show us," Giles prodded her in turn. "You mentioned to our shop girl that you'd benefit from our advice?"

"Yes," she replied hurriedly, snapping out of her silent contemplation. "Yes, of course." She opened the bag, which still rested on her lap, and drew out the sheet of decorated vellum.

"Ah," Giles affirmed, glancing at it. "It would seem, then, that Pietro lied. This is undeniably his work." He looked a question at Marion as he held out his hand for the page. More than willing, she gave it to him. After twenty seconds of running his eyes over the images, his lips thin, he stood. "I wonder…"

Walking unsteadily, he returned to the silk fabric hanging in the corner of the room. Marion, trying to keep her rising excitement in check, stood as well and followed.

"You see, there is a patch of the textile, here," indicating with his hand a rectangular area near the top right, roughly the size of the vellum page, "that is dull, faded. We've always told ourselves that this patch was simply worn. Because we had no other explanation. But we knew that we were rationalizing, given the second part of Pietro's legacy."

"What is the second part of his legacy?" Forcing the eagerness out of her voice.

"Pietro silenced the disturbance that concerned his emperor in the 1440s," Giles explained, "but that disturbance was, even at the time, one of many, scattered across the world. And so, Pietro charged his descendants with seeking out any others that might erupt and extinguishing them before they took hold. Which, he hinted, they were certain to do over the ensuing centuries."

"And you've had success in—in extinguishing these eruptions?" she ventured.

He shrugged, tired. "Not only don't we know where these disturbances are supposed to have taken place, we don't even know what they are. Or were." He considered the threads of the textile with eyes that had memorized their every detail and imperfection. "Pietro's message decayed. It's uncertain that even his own children were fully aware of what he had accomplished—or of what he was asking them to do."

He blinked, forcing his eyes away from the fabric. "What we do know is that this piece of silk," lifting his chin, "was meant to provide guidance. Perhaps this page will help us to decipher it."

Fluttering the delicate, nearly disintegrating fabric with his fingertips, he superimposed the vellum page onto the faded rectangle. Careful to match the ears of the hares on the latter to the identical interconnected ears that had been drawn onto the former. Then, with a shaky, astonished breath, he began, in an unhealthy wheeze, to laugh.

Veronica, bleary-eyed now, pushed herself up out of her chair. She was no taller standing that she'd been sitting. "What is it?" She tottered across the room. "What is it?"

Giles turned back to her, still holding the corners of the silk. "Veronica. This is it. Look."

Veronica pushed her face toward the cloth until her nose was nearly touching the three hares. And then, she too laughed. Something deeper and hoarser than the giggle she'd been directing into her bourbon. "Yes, Giles. Yes, I see it." She laughed again. "Obernai. Four leagues south of Strasbourg."

"Aix-la-Chapelle," he countered. "Bang in the center."

"Mongolia!" She wrinkled her forehead. "Or is it Gansu? China? Too far at any rate."

"Widecombe." His smile grew at the name. "Three leagues northeast of Plymouth."

"Basel," she continued, calming now. "In the Minster."

"And," he ended with a flourish, removing the vellum page while motioning Marion into her chair, "ten leagues south of Adigrat. Ethiopia." He was thoughtful as he himself also returned to his chair. "Somewhere in the vicinity of Mekelle. Which will simplify our work. We'll begin there."

"We?" Veronica, chuckling again, staggered back to her own chair and slumped into it. "*We*, Giles? We're too old. Long, long since too old."

"She's not, though." He nodded shortly in Marion's direction. "And she did say she wanted our guidance."

"Forgive me. But I don't—"

"No time," Veronica interjected. "No time for you to understand, dear."

"Listen," Giles said. "We must move quickly. We can't explain our deductions. They come of a lifetime of interpreting that damnable piece of cloth. But please believe us, your pattern has shown us where we must go to complete Pietro's work. Where the disturbances begin. As you can see, though," gesturing to Veronica and himself, "we're too old. We can't do it in person. You can."

"Do you even know what the disturbances are?" she asked, moved by his tone, but unconvinced that following his instructions would help her own project. She, too, was running out of time.

He laughed, audibly this time, but still shaking. "No, we do not."

"But we have an idea," Veronica countered. "And we have tools. Or," she said, her eyes twinkling over her empty mouth, "you have them."

"We made a gamble," Giles said when Marion looked perplexed.

"I haven't any tools beyond the pages I showed you." Marion paused in thought for a moment and then, when an idea hit her, began opening her bag again. "And a few additional texts I brought with me from—"

"Your masks," Veronica said. "Have you opened the boxes?"

"No."

"We thought not. Please do when you return to your room this evening." Veronica's drunkenness had evaporated. She sounded both sober and commanding. Though muffled without her teeth. "They're safe. The boy is watching them. One holds a bell. It's defensive. You'll know when to use it. The other is an inkwell. If you are who you claim to be, you'll recognize it. We disguised them should you be followed during your time in the city."

Marion blinked down at the third box on the floor next to her shoes. "And that—?"

"Identification," Giles said. "You're the British widow of an Italian war hero. It will gain you access to any social or professional milieu in the country. But now, of course, we know precisely where to insert you. There's a delegation of geologists leaving for Adigrat tomorrow morning—"

"You'll want to buy a new frock," Veronica said, thoughtful. "Perhaps two. And a suit—"

"Wait," Marion insisted. "Stop this." She fixed her eyes on Giles. "I don't understand what you're asking me to do."

They waited, irritated by her attempt to halt their momentum. Didn't reply. And so, irritated in turn, Marion spoke more slowly, enunciating each word: "and therefore, what happens now is this. First, you explain to me what you'd like me to accomplish. Second, you tell me where I must go to complete that task. And third, you convince me that it's in my interest to make this effort for you. After that, and *only* after that, will I decide whether I continue speaking to you about your ancestor and his legacy—and depart with this delegation tomorrow morning—or whether I return the masks to your girl this afternoon. Do you understand? Yes?"

Giles and Veronica, surprised by her sudden intractability, held one another's eyes for a long moment. And then, Giles spoke again. His voice quiet and his expression veiled. "You're correct. We've run ahead of ourselves." He gathered his wits about him. "First, we're asking you to take up Pietro's legacy. He and his Emperor built something dangerous in the fifteenth century, something that they couldn't fully control. The Emperor sent Pietro to China for instructions on how to suppress this— thing. Perhaps it originated in China. Or perhaps Chinese science had advanced enough at the time to counteract it. We don't know.

"What we do know," he continued, "is that Pietro succeeded upon his return from the Orient. At least for the time being. But he couldn't destroy it completely because it had spread in the decades before and after his voyage. The thing wasn't only in Ethiopia—in Africa—but also in Europe and Asia."

He gazed at Marion, gauging her understanding, and then concluded. "For centuries, we've known only in the most general terms where the outbreaks occurred. But now that you've brought us this pattern, we know *precisely where* in Africa, Europe and Asia it has been or will be. Please understand, we aren't asking you to travel to every one of these cities to find it. Only to Adigrat. Or, it seems, Mekelle, in Ethiopia. If you begin your work there, the others will be affected as well. That appears to have been the case in Pietro's time."

Marion nodded slowly. "Do you really have no idea what this—thing—is?"

"We've speculated," Giles said. "We're confident that it has something to do with music, for example. And, given the documents you're carrying in that bag—" he held up his hands, apologetic, "— the boy reported to us—we're even more convinced that music is the heart of the problem."

"But what music is as dangerous as Pietro suggests this thing was? And is?" Baffled.

"That we don't know," Giles admitted. "But the bell we've entrusted to you has been kept in our family for generations, for centuries, as a defensive weapon. Our fathers bequeathed it to us as the shield we'd wear when we battled this danger. And if the danger weren't musical, how could a tiny instrument like that protect us from it?"

"And the inkwell?"

"We're less certain about its use. But when you examine it, you'll form your own opinion." He held up his hand again, this time forestalling Marion's protest. "Forgive me, but it's best that you encounter it without prejudice."

"Fine," she said, not mollified, but willing to listen further. "So this danger, you're saying, can be suppressed, but not destroyed. It is, in some arcane way, musical. It has appeared, and perhaps continues to appear, in locations across three continents. It may have originated in China and moved west over the fourteenth and fifteenth centuries. Or, at least, the Chinese of the fifteenth century had knowledge of how to respond to it that Africans and Europeans of the time did not. One of its locations is about seventy miles south of Adigrat, in Ethiopia—"

"Closer to the city of Mekelle," Giles repeated. "And we even have an idea as to its whereabouts near Mekelle because we know that Pietro helped to found, until now inexplicably, a monastery in the mountains surrounding that city. This monastery is less well known than the others in the region, but if you are willing to travel on our behalf, we'll send a guide to accompany you who can direct you to the foot of the building complex."

"Women can't enter," Veronica added. "But it's improbable that the—the thing—is in the monastery itself. Perhaps in a chamber nearby. Underneath."

"I see," Marion said. "So, should I undertake this journey, I'd bring the bell and the inkwell with me into the mountains, to Pietro's monastery, and then I'd—"

"—determine how the information fits together," Giles continued, vague now. "Find a way to suppress whatever is beginning to erupt once again. I know it's not much of a starting point for your work, but it's more than anyone in the family has had for nearly five hundred years—"

"Wait," she repeated, suspicious again. "You said that this thing is 'beginning to erupt once again.' What does that mean? Has there been some—some change in the area? Are you aware of an alteration in its status? I must know that before I begin."

Giles paused, flustered for the first time that morning. Then, sighing, he resumed. "Political and military change, of course. Our government's policy in East Africa has been less than diplomatic. People aren't happy."

"So I understand." Carefully neutral.

"But the true source of our concern," he resumed, choosing his words more carefully, "is the mining. Recent changes that have been made to mining practices in the area."

"Mining practices."

"Yes," he said. "Ethiopia is, and always has been, rich in minerals. Gold, gemstones, salt, metals of all kinds. We believe there may be petroleum as well."

"Petroleum." Beginning to feel less sympathetic to the Rombulos.

"Please," he said. "Don't refuse us this task because your ethical commitments prevent cooperation with—with all Italians. Our family has maintained mines in Ethiopia since the fifteenth century. Through our ancestress. An Ethiopian, remember. Gold, primarily. But yes, before the last war, we contemplated expanding into other minerals. We've since reconsidered. We've had to. Marshal Graziani has taken personal control of our interests in the region. We have nothing."

"And that's why you want me to travel there? Because you want to reclaim your—your inheritance? That's the 'legacy?'"

"No," he said. Weary. "No, Veronica and I are quite content with our material resources as they stand. We have no desire to fight the Marshal over possession of our mines." He paused again. "Our concern instead is that when Graziani appropriated the mineral reserves this past month, he did so with the same—energy—with which our military occupied the rest of the country. And he has now, as a result, turned up a collection of local legends concerning a weapon secreted in the mountains. Said to do untold damage. Unstoppable. World-conquering. He became curious. He questioned the local monks—"

"Oh." Quiet now. "Yes, I understand."

"He hasn't discovered anything," Veronica said. "But he's sent emissaries in our direction. Looking for information. Smashing up the masks in the shop, yes?"

"We became—nervous," Giles added. "Which is why we avoided you upon your arrival. But this is also why we've taken you into our confidence. Your arrival in the city is providential. We look upon you as a—an answer to a plea we'd dared not even articulate. It was too fantastic. To discover the solution to the puzzle just as everything else unraveled. You can imagine, can't you, our eagerness to proceed? Can't you?"

"Yes," she said, embarrassed. "Yes, I understand." She leaned over the side of the chair, collected her shoes and box, shouldered her bag, and stood. "Very well. You're saying that my papers— British widow of an Italian war hero—are in this box? And I leave for Adigrat tomorrow?"

"Mekelle. A member of the delegation will meet you at 8:00 at your hotel." He rose and smiled as well. "At the front door." He held out the sheet of vellum. "Don't forget this."

She shook her head. "No, it belongs to you. You've made that very clear."

Veronica, still sitting, beamed up at her, toothless. "Do open the other boxes when you return to your room, dear. And buy yourself a new dress. Or two." She looked anxious for a moment, considering Marion's boots. "You'll have the money for that, won't you—?"

"Yes," Marion said, tired now. "Yes, I'll be fine. And I'll be certain to wear something suitable."

"Good, good," Veronica replied, losing energy. "Do you know, China is one of the few countries that refused to recognize our annexation of Ethiopia. Interesting, really—"

"Thank you once again for speaking with me," Marion spoke over her to Giles.

"Good day," he replied. "And good luck."

With that, she turned, left the room, and made her way out of the empty shop packed with masks. Once on the pavement, she tried to decide which of the off-putting windows was displaying clothing she could bear to purchase. But inevitably, she entered a shop at random. She was far more interested in what was waiting for her in her hotel room than in what Italian couturiers believed she ought to be wearing as she examined it.

*W*ADING back through the alley to her room while carrying her bag, her shoes, the box, and an unwieldy package containing newly purchased trousers, blouses, socks, gloves, and a hat took concentration. But she reached her cell and switched on the dull orange lamp without mishap. Once there, she spread out on the wicker chair a new pair of trousers, a blouse, the gloves, and the hat, in preparation for leaving quickly the next morning. All in shades of drab brown. She wasn't certain when her war hero husband was supposed to have died, but if her contacts wondered at her nondescript appearance, they could conclude that she was still in mourning. Marion herself sought simply to fade into uninteresting obscurity.

After less than a second of thought, she also left out her still damp—and now moldering—boots. They were far from fashionable. But she refused to contemplate wading across Venice in the heels tomorrow, and she couldn't imagine they'd be useful during her journey to the monastery in the mountains of Ethiopia. She shoved them down to the bottom of the bag she'd emptied of its contents and placed, gaping, on the camp bed. Before re-packing any more of the bag, she'd examine the Rombulos' boxes.

Blue, pink, and yellow, they sat side by side on the small table, nudging the now half-full pitcher of water. Pushing away an odd feeling of trepidation, she settled herself at the other end of the camp bed, reached for the first of them, the blue, and ripped open the girl's careful, decorative fastenings. She then removed the tissue in its entirety, held it in her lap, and probed inside for the mask.

There was no mask. Veronica had been telling the truth. Instead, she gradually revealed a four-inch tall silver instrument, a small, plain, perfect bell, of what was obviously great age. An unusually shaped clapper. She turned it over in her hands three or four times and then, shrugging inwardly, she held it up and shook it.

Nothing happened. No sound. No vibration. Nothing. Frowning, she shook it harder. Still nothing. Although, starting at the commotion, she did see that the pigeons that had been huddling over the roof-light, obscuring what little external illumination entered the cell, scattered upward in a noisy clump. Leaving behind them a new layer of excrement.

She glanced up at the distant glass, bewildered, and then returned her attention to the bell. Disappointed. Perhaps, she thought as she slipped it into the inside pocket of her coat, its use would become apparent when she'd reached the monastery. The Rombulos had said she'd know only at the moment when she ought to use it. A defensive weapon. She forced down her reviving irritation at their imprecise instructions and turned back to the table.

The second elongated pink box opened more easily, and the object hidden by the tissue paper was more substantial. Easier to expose. When she saw what she held in her lap, however, she widened her eyes, astonished. Unlike the bell, it was more than familiar to her. Famous. Or infamous. At least to those who travelled in Ilkhanid art, politics, and science.

Little more than five inches tall, it was a silver-inlayed inkwell. She could, within a minute of examining the inscription that ran along the lower rim—many of its letters stretching into figures, foliage, and animals—determine the date. Late thirteenth-century. The notorious property of the more influential of the Ilkhanid viziers.

And the inscription, she already knew—though she examined it to be certain—read: "let music be played and songs be sung when giving judgement, for only then will judgement be obeyed." A twisted sentiment for a state inkwell. The story was that when the vizier wielded it, neither force nor argument could thwart him. Opposition became mute.

She ran her fingertip along the elaborate panels depicting, first, aristocratic figures kneeling before a tall nobleman sounding a trumpet, second, onagers and dragons aligned in human-like configurations listening to a female figure playing a tambourine, and third, a hunting-scene that depicted intertwined Mars and Saturn figures halting rearing horses. She turned the inkwell over in her hands, and then she smiled.

On the bottom was a representation of the three hares, their ears interlocked. It surprised her that as often as she'd read thirteenth-, fourteenth-, and even fifteenth-century descriptions of this object, they'd never mentioned the hares. Only the inscription, the panels, and the inkwell's terrifying power to silence enemies of the state. And then, sometime in the late fifteenth century, the inkwell itself had been lost. For the best, many contemporary commentators had said, given the monstrous ill-luck that it brought to those influenced by it and, more so, to those who wielded it.

She wouldn't have expected it to turn up in Venice, attached to a story of a Sicilian merchant expanding his trade networks into North and East Africa. Or, to be honest with herself, she wouldn't have expected it to turn up at all. It bothered her that it was related to Sheridan's candlestick, and in turn to the treatises on music written over the next hundred years. The connection felt unhealthy.

And indeed, there was something wrong with it. Aside from small vent-like incisions in the metal around the top, there was no opening. No lid. No one could have used this as an aid in writing because there was no way to access the ink. She held the object in two hands in her lap and stared at it, baffled. It was, now that she examined it more closely, only superficially shaped like a traditional state or royal inkwell. Which meant that its function must have been something quite different. Indecipherable.

Squeezing her eyes shut for three or four seconds to stave off an incipient headache, she considered her situation as it now stood. She had collected a bell that made no sound and an inkwell that held no ink. Not to mention Sheridan's candlestick that darkened rather than illuminating its surroundings. And, with these objects in hand, she was expected tomorrow to infiltrate an Italian mining operation overseen by Mussolini's government, and from there convince a group of apocryphal, terrorized Ethiopian monks to help her disable an as-yet unnamed weapon or war device.

She opened her eyes, resigned. She might as well learn who she was going to be tomorrow. Turning her attention to the third, yellow, box, she opened it almost without interest. Withdrew the papers and, smiling slightly, the large sheaf of lire—Veronica's contribution—stuffed inside. Still smiling, she opened her passport. And then, she did let herself laugh. Belinda Storchio. Widow of Giovanni Storchio, recipient of the Gold Medal of Military Valour.

After staring down at the papers for a few seconds, she rubbed her forehead with her hand. Still laughing, she resolved to accept the situation as it presented itself. If the Rombulos' Puccini fixation left her exposed and their plans in ruins, they could blame themselves. She would merely hope that her colleagues on the journey to Mekelle tomorrow weren't overly musical.

And so, rather than dwelling on the myriad ways in which the project could go wrong, she began packing. The three empty boxes, pretty though they were, she would leave behind. Perhaps the boy would enjoy them. The bell she'd secure in her coat and keep on her. It was the most essential of the tools that the Rombulos had given her, and she didn't want to risk separation from it. She would have liked to keep the inkwell in a pocket as well, but it was too heavy. The bulge in her clothing would look awkward.

Unhappy, but uncertain what else she could do with it, she placed it at the bottom of the bag next to her shoes. But then, she rationalized, if her situation unraveled to a point at which her bag was being searched, she herself would already have been compromised. Protecting the inkwell would be the least of her concerns. Next, she re-packed Eugene's documents. She didn't expect she'd use them, but she also didn't want them lost for another four centuries. Somehow, she'd return them to Eugene. If he was still alive and undamaged.

After that, she packed the second pair of trousers she'd bought, the second blouse, the new socks and underwear, and half of Veronica's cash. The two changes of clothing she'd brought from the boat she'd leave here. They were damp and beginning to smell, and she'd be pleased when she saw the last of them.

And then, finally, looking up at the dark roof-light obscured by the returned, pacified pigeons, she decided to sleep. Drinking all but a few swallows of the water left in the pitcher, she switched off the lamp—hoping never to have to endure the beige light again—removed her dress, and relaxed into the camp bed for her welcome last night in the city. Ignoring her damp feet.

Mekelle, Ethiopia
March, 1937

WHEN the girl who had sold her the masks appeared in the hotel's reception area at 8:00 the next morning, Marion almost didn't recognize her. Gone was the distracted, bookish waif with the journal and the air of recondite intelligence. In her place was a practical professional who cast Marion a quick, dismissive glance before offering to carry her bag to the water-taxi idling outside. Although Marion had been waiting for over a half hour in the hotel's public rooms, the girl gave the impression that, first, they were late, and second, this was Marion's fault.

Bemused, Marion declined the offer of help with her bag and followed her out in the direction of the Grand Canal. She wasn't certain whether she was meant to recognize the girl or pretend that they hadn't met. But she followed the girl's lead. The Rombulos had moved people in and out of the city for many years. Their boy had been nothing but professional. And if they wanted her to act as though she'd never seen the girl, she could easily do so. She'd certainly worked with odder contacts than Giles and Veronica in the past.

Once they were sitting in the water-taxi and trundling up the Canal, the girl cast Marion a hard, empty hostess's smile. "We're pleased that you've agreed to join us, Mrs. Storchio." Precise, cool English. "Your familiarity with the customs and traditions of the Tigray region of Ethiopia will prove invaluable to our ongoing prospecting and exploration in the area."

So that was Marion's role. She was ill-equipped to perform it, but she believed she could satisfy the delegation in the small amount of time she'd spend with them. Before absconding in the direction of the monastery. Attempting to mimic the girl's businesslike demeanor, she smiled in turn. "Thank you, Miss—" She paused. "Forgive me, I'm afraid I don't know your name."

"Miss Sardou," she said. "Victoria Sardou."

Unable to keep a split-second of astonishment off her face, Marion rapidly schooled her expression. But she also cursed the Rombulos. They were either batty or deliberately courting danger. Either way, she didn't appreciate the unnecessary risks they were running with her person and her project. She spoke sweetly: "how do you do?"

"We'll arrive at Nicelli Aerodrome, at the north end of the Lido, in fifteen minutes," she said, dismissing Marion's tone. "From there we'll board our flight. Ala Littoria's ongoing cooperation with British Imperial Airways will significantly shorten our journey. We remain indebted to Great Britain for its support as we consolidate our own, Italian, African holdings. And, of course, our delegation is delighted to share our findings with our counterparts in the British Empire's mining sector."

Her discomfort growing, Marion dropped her eyes to her gloved hands, folded in her lap. "Indeed," she murmured.

Then she tried to determine whether she ought to engage "Victoria" in further conversation. On the one hand, she didn't trust herself to play with any degree of aptitude the role that the Rombulos had forced on her. Her skill set, such as it was, ran toward invisibility, evasion, and—her preference— working in a library. But the Rombulos wouldn't have known that. And they certainly wouldn't have known that when her own organization wanted someone who could dissemble, manipulate, or socialize, they tapped psychologically astute people like Lenore. Marion could scarcely manage the role that was her own personality. Adopting someone else's was a nightmare.

On the other hand, she felt confident that Victoria's chatter was more for the benefit of the water-taxi's pilot than it was for her—beyond informing her as to her persona. If Victoria worked for the Rombulos, then the clean, fascist, empty-headed optimism she was radiating couldn't be genuine. Inadequate though Marion was at reading behavior, she knew that the ambiguous girl with the journal in the empty shop was closer to Victoria's true character than the one currently domineering her in the boat. Steeling herself, she raised her eyes from her gloves.

Where she saw something like sympathy and resigned amusement flash across Victoria's face. "As a result of the cooperation between our two great nations," Victoria nonetheless resumed her monologue, "our flight between Venice and Mekelle will take less than three days. The Marshal has granted us use of his personal Savoia-Marchetti S.73, and we will stop five times for fuel at British and Italian airfields. Although we realize that our pace may cause discomfort, we will stop *only* for fuel. The aeroplane is well-equipped for long-distance flight, and we trust that you will sleep as necessary on-board."

"I understand." The thought of flying as the guest of Marshal Graziani left her not only uncomfortable, but queasy.

"Travelling today," Victoria continued, light and inexorable, "will be Mr. Colonna, a representative from the Ministry of Italian Africa, Mr. Pareschi, a representative from the Ministry of Industry and Commerce, Dr. Bonomi, a geologist from the University of Bologna, Dr. Rossi, a geomorphologist from the same, and yourself. I will serve as secretary to the delegation."

"Ah."

"But I believe we've arrived at our destination." She stood and held the edge of the cockpit as the water-taxi slowed into a mooring just below the empty airstrip. "You're certain you wouldn't like me to carry your case?"

"Yes," Marion said, standing as well and taking up her bag. "I'm certain. I'll carry it."

"Very well." Victoria stood to the side to let Marion precede her up to the dock. Then, stepping briskly behind her without paying the pilot of the water-taxi, she gestured toward a substantial propeller plane painted in a garish red and green that was idling at the end of the runway. The two of them half walked, half trotted to the stairs awaiting their approach. Then, breathing a bit heavily, they entered the cabin and found their seats just as a disdainful steward pulled the plane's door shut.

To her gratification, although she tried to hide it, the remainder of the plane's passengers were palpably enraged by her presence. She and Victoria were obviously late, and the others—largish men with varied moustaches and identical suits, already seated—glowered at them with something close to malevolence. But as the plane gathered speed for takeoff, Marion realized that their disgust with her presence derived from something more than tardiness. The men in the cabin were having difficulty restraining themselves from physical violence.

And indeed, once the plane had banked and leveled off, the most rotund of them leaned toward her and tapped her on the knee with his index finger. "Mrs. Storchio," he said in heavily accented English.

"Yes," Marion replied, itching to break his finger.

"I speak for all of us here. You are not welcome."

"Oh?" she said, hoping that her tone came out as querulous rather than grateful that she wouldn't be required to throw up the barrier herself.

"We have no interest, none whatsoever, in the customs and traditions of the Ethiopian people." He made the last eight words sound like the most depraved sort of pornography.

"I see."

"And we certainly do not appreciate the presence of a meddlesome, amateur English Lady Novelist among our specialists. We will thank you to keep quiet and stay out of our way. You understand, yes?"

"Yes, sir. I believe that I do." She hadn't realized that she was also a novelist. Wondered what she'd written, and whether her preferred language was English or Italian.

"Good," he grunted, and then leaned back in his seat.

Now that she was officially isolated from the rest of the delegation, she allowed herself a small hope that she'd manage to evade the attentions of the Italian government in the city. If she kept them convinced that she was as muddleheaded as they clearly thought her to be, they might even forget to report her absence should it come to their attention. Pleased and almost relaxed, she reclined in her own seat and allowed herself the luxury of examining the cabin in which she'd be passing the next three days.

It was well-appointed. But it was also tiring. Too much wood, too much gilt, and far too many cushions. Nonetheless, if there was ever an aeroplane cabin suited to sleep, this was it. She could, if she chose, remain cozily unconscious throughout the journey in its entirety. But, of course, she wouldn't. The thought of lowering her guard in the midst of this group of large, affronted men—most of them already snoring—distressed her. She'd sleep when she left Ethiopia. She could survive for a week or so without proper rest. Having done so many, many times in the past.

Glancing across the aisle at Victoria, prim, correct, and staring out the window, she imagined the girl felt similarly. And unexpectedly, this fragile comradery comforted her further—encouraged her to enjoy the excessively cushioned seat and mentally prepare for her encounter with the monastery.

THE flight, despite Victoria's soothing presence, was a misery. And when the plane landed at the partially constructed military airfield in Mekelle, Marion wanted nothing more than to sleep, to eat anything except sandwiches, and to drink anything but coffee. Instead, once the delegation had staggered out of the cabin and into the pleasant heat of the Enda Eyesus base, Victoria once again took charge. Leading them over the apron, she shook hands with a soldier awaiting them, and spoke to him in a low voice for a minute or two. Then, wearing her hostess smile again, she addressed Marion.

"The gentlemen will follow Captain Alberti to their quarters on the base," she said. "We have arranged for you to stay at a civilian hotel in the Italian quarter of the city. You will be quite comfortable, I assure you, Mrs. Storchio."

Thanking her, Marion shouldered her bag and followed Victoria toward a Fiat 508 painted a military green and waiting for them on the road leading out of the base. As she walked, she heard one of the delegates saying in loud Italian to the others, "if we're lucky, she'll be so comfortable she'll never leave." Followed by a collective laugh.

She ignored them, but as she and Victoria neared the car, she thought to herself that she'd rarely been so pleased to throw off a camouflage. Familiar though she was with widowhood, the role of self-appointed spokeswoman of the oppressed natives would have been difficult to maintain. Five minutes longer with the delegation and she was certain to have compromised herself. Victoria had rescued her.

Settling alongside the girl in the back seat of the Fiat, she allowed herself to luxuriate in the almost physical pleasure of ridding herself of social expectations. And once the driver had brought them out of the base and across Mekelle's rapidly expanding Italian neighborhood, she relaxed completely, her eyes closed, uninterested in the proliferating construction along the edges of the road. Encouraging her brain to suppress the unpleasant and unnecessary memories of both the flight and their arrival.

Eventually, however, the building projects tapered off, and the road turned to dirt. And a few minutes after that, the driver slowed, pulled over, and exited the car. Victoria smiled at Marion, who had grudgingly opened her eyes, and motioned her into the front passenger seat. Then, taking the driver's seat, Victoria gave a happy wave to the soldier, who grinned, waved in turn, and began walking back in the direction of the base. Still smiling to herself, Victoria accelerated toward an empty expanse of brown fields, interrupted periodically by striking green strips of vegetation. The higher mountains in the distance.

"Giles and Veronica saved him from the streets," she said when Marion turned back, curious, to catch a last glimpse of the soldier tramping home. "He tries to repay the favor whenever he can."

"I see."

They drove in silence for ten more minutes. Then Victoria spoke again. "Mekelle itself is approximately seven thousand feet above sea level. We'll take this road another six or seven hundred feet up, into the peaks. After that, we'll walk. Can you do that? I know you didn't sleep on the flight."

"Neither did you," Marion said.

"I'm used to it."

"I'll manage." Then she smiled. "Thank you for asking. And for not mentioning my age."

Victoria smiled as well. "There are canteens of water in the back."

They drove for two hours longer, the high plateau-like landscape giving way to a track, obviously meant for animals, to which the Fiat clung as it ascended a yellowish peak strewn with rocks and dust. Soon, the track vanished, and they were faced with a sheer rock face. Victoria cut the engine, opened the door, and stretched as she left the car. Then, reaching into the back, she rummaged about on the floor until she found trousers and a pair of hiking boots.

"Do you mind if I change here?" She blushed, looking like the girl from the shop again. "I can't climb in this." Gesturing toward her fashionable, secretarial skirt and heels.

"It will give me a chance to find my bearings," Marion replied. "Please do."

Grabbing one of the canteens of water, Marion turned away, drank several swallows, stuffed it, along with a spare into her bag, and gazed at the daunting landscape. She still wore her coat, which left her uncomfortably warm. If Victoria expected her to scale the cliff against which they'd stopped, it was just possible that her clothing, her lack of sleep, and the need for proper food would stand in the way. But she trusted that the girl's own condition would preclude excessive acrobatics. There must be another route up. Hidden.

Once Victoria had folded her skirt, left it on the driver's seat of the car along with her shoes, and taken a canteen of water for herself, she beckoned to Marion. "This way."

They approached a fissure in the rock that appeared superficially to be a shallow indentation but, upon investigation, revealed a narrow passage to the other side of the cliff. After squeezing their way through, they reached a track that wound further up the mountain and then disappeared into the horizon. Beckoning once more to Marion, Victoria spoke again.

"The monks are secretive. They prefer to remain hidden." She dabbed sweat off her face with a handkerchief as she walked. "Not that this stopped the Marshal, of course. When he became curious."

Marion nodded. The air was pleasantly rather than oppressively hot, but the coat was excessive, the bag was heavy, and she wanted to conserve her energy. She didn't know how long they'd be walking or what she'd encounter once they'd arrived at their destination.

"The monastery is a little over three miles up the hill," Victoria said. "Will you want to rest on the way?"

"No." She shrugged her bag up onto her shoulder. "I'll be fine."

As they walked, Marion allowed her mind to stray, continuing to ponder what they'd see once they'd reached the monastery. She occasionally ran her fingers over the bell secreted in the inside pocket of her coat. The presence of the Rombulos' "defensive weapon," useless though it had seemed in the hotel, comforted her here. The unusually stark, yet warm, air of the Tigray mountains raised her hackles. She'd rarely experienced a thin mountain atmosphere that was so suggestive of something just outside one's field of vision, watching and waiting.

Absorbed as she was in her thoughts, she at first failed to notice when Victoria slowed to a stop before surveying, astonished, a pile of rubble at the base of a recently scorched hillside. But when the girl turned back to her, hollow-eyed, she knew that something was wrong. And when, a few seconds later, Victoria strode over to a rope hanging from an outcropping above them and pulled it hard, only to duck out of the way as the rope's end fell heavily to the ground, she became alarmed. The rope had been roughly severed at the top. Graziani, or his representatives, had returned.

"The monks are gone." Victoria spoke with her back to Marion, staring up at the top of the hill, her hand shading her eyes. "The buildings are wrecked. They've been destroyed."

"Oh." Marion sat on a large rock that had embedded itself in the dirt. "I'm sorry."

"I don't know what to do." Victoria spun back. "I must return to the base. If I'm away overnight, they'll suspect me."

"I understand." Marion rubbed her eyes with her fists. "Go, then."

"But I can't leave you here. It's empty." She stared down at the heap of rope. "You haven't brought food." She considered, still agitated. "I know what we'll do. I'll drive you back. You'll remain Belinda Storchio. We'll put you on an aeroplane back to Venice—"

"No." Marion hadn't moved from her position seated on the rock. "No, I'd like to learn what happened here. Report to my own people. I'll find a way back on my own."

"I can't leave you here," Victoria repeated, beginning to sound frantic. "You could easily die."

"Victoria," Marion said, "I watched as we drove. This isn't a desert. There are countless villages. If I do find myself stranded, I won't die. A bit of discomfort. Some awkward interaction in a language I don't know. I've done it before. And shouldn't I be worrying about you instead? Potentially compromising yourself to an entire military base in the middle of a war zone? Go back. Do your job. I'm older than you are, and I know better."

Victoria stood motionless for a full minute longer. Then, with a wry smile, she adjusted her blouse. Embarrassed by her loss of control. "You're correct. Forgive me." She held out her hand to Marion. A strange combination of the waif from the shop and the secretarial fascist. Marion took it. "Good luck."

"And to you."

Then, without looking back, Victoria disappeared down the mountain trail.

ONCE the sound of Victoria's footsteps had receded into silence, Marion considered the expanse of dirt beneath the hill. It wasn't promising. At one end was the track that Victoria had taken. At the other end was the hillside, too steep to scale without the rope. And all about her were solid rock cliff faces. She reached into her bag, pulled out one of the canteens, and finished the water.

Then, placing the empty canteen and the bag on the ground next to the rock, she rose to her feet. If the start of the trail had been hidden by a fissure in a rock face, some part of the monastery complex, below the main building, might be hidden in a comparable manner. It was worth investigating.

Starting at the left edge of the trail, taking her time, she examined the cliff, searching for evidence of a path that led either further into the hill or through a wall toward another track. And gratifyingly, her survey took less than ten minutes. Just at the corner of the hillside that had been blackened by what must have been a flamethrower or some incendiary device, she found a fissure identical to what they'd encountered at the beginning of their hike. Less satisfied than she would have been had the monastery still been populated, she remembered the spot and returned to her bag.

When she reached it, she opened it, dug through to the bottom, and retrieved the inkwell. She didn't know what she'd meet on the other side of the fissure, and she wanted the objects on her person should she be forced to drop her bag. The bell she removed and held out in her hand like a pistol. She felt ridiculous, but the small ammunition comforted her.

Resigned now to her situation, she shouldered the bag and approached the fissure. Squeezed herself through the opening, hating the absence of any space to move. But the path between the rocks was short, less than ten yards. And once through, she found herself in a natural amphitheater with an unmistakable, deliberately chiseled stairway leading up to a platform, the top of which she couldn't see.

Walking slowly, testing the air, and unable to shake the feeling that something was watching her, she climbed the stairs. They brought her to a smooth, dirt floor of precise dimensions, an even fifteen-foot square. Its uniformity was broken only by an equally square hole at the far corner, and a rope attached to a wooden pole coiled up next to it.

Ignoring the dry wind that had begun buffeting her as she climbed, and disgruntled by the likelihood that she'd soon be lowering herself, blind, into some sort of pit, she walked to the edge of the hole. Sullen. Released her bag, lay on her stomach, and peered down. At least it wasn't completely dark. She could make out a clean, round chamber, lower than the level of the original path, but not dizzyingly far away, lit by well-spaced panels open to the sky.

Still half-unwilling, she dropped the rope into the chamber, put the bell in her pocket, secured her bag across her shoulders, and slid to the floor. Then, retrieving the bell, she looked about her, open to any stray intuition that she was attracting attention. She had the same sense of invisible observers she'd felt before, but it wasn't stronger here than it had been on the surface. The chamber wasn't any more dangerous than it appeared to be.

It was, however, much larger than she'd expected from the platform. A perfect circle surmounted by an equally perfect dome. And although the air was clean and dry, there was an underlying smell of rotting animal coming from a curve that she couldn't quite see. She'd investigate the smell first. Likely some unlucky bird or goat had flown or fallen through the hole and been unable to find its way out.

Still testing the air, she walked slowly in the direction of the smell until a disturbed shape on the floor against the far wall resolved itself in the dim light. Two steps closer and she could see what it was. Sheridan Murdoch. Pieces of Sheridan Murdoch. Wearing, improbably, an Italian military uniform that had, itself, been shredded to tatters.

Were it not for his hair, clumps of which had been ripped from his head, she wouldn't have recognized him. Both of his eyes had been gouged out and placed side by side three or four feet away from his body. One hand was charred beyond recognition into a pulpy mass of liquefied red and black. Perhaps the source of the scorch marks at the base of the first hill.

The other hand was missing all of its fingers. These had been stacked, like children's blocks, with precision next to his eyes. His tongue was gone altogether, a fact she could determine only because most of his upper teeth had been shattered and removed as well. He was also missing a foot, still wearing its shoe, and tossed as a kind of afterthought two yards away from the remainder of the scene.

It took her thirty seconds, stunned into immobility, to work through what she was seeing. But after that, with a strangled breath, she stumbled backward, clutching at her bell. Then, her hand shaking violently, she held it up and shook it as hard she could. Nothing. Pushing down her panic, she shook it again. She didn't know what she thought would happen, but she was confident that this was the moment the Rombulos had meant when they'd told her she'd know when to use it. She needed a shield.

When still nothing happened, she forced herself to stop shuddering, closed her eyes, and tried one more time. Then, lowering the bell, she felt the air. Something had changed. She opened her eyes and spun back, unable to see anything in the room aside from Sheridan's broken remains. But she knew that someone else was nearby. She could feel it. Angry now, she returned to the center of the circle.

"A lovely, pure G." Spoken in quiet Italian from the far side of the dome.

She strode, aggressively she hoped, in the direction of the voice. "Who are you?" In her bad Italian.

"A lovely, pure G." In English, this time. "Apologies, I mistook you for one of them. But, of course, you've brought the bell with you. And sounded it. Which means you couldn't possibly be a party to their destructiveness."

A small, smiling monk emerged from the shadows at the edge of the room. White robe and head covering. Thin sandals. She knew he hadn't been there before, which meant there must be some additional entrance to or exit from the chamber. A viewing room. But the dome's porousness, along with Sheridan's condition, left her wary rather than pleased.

When the monk moved further into the light, however, her wariness evaporated. Despite his calm demeanor, he was struggling to control what must have been enormous pain from a collection of shallow incisions across his face and body. Not to mention that one eye had been removed by the same tool that had worked on Sheridan. The monk had covered the wound with a clean square of cotton, but she could see its raw edges, seeping blood. Her aggression gave way to sympathy.

"Yes," the monk said, noting her changed stance. "But I was lucky. I could tell them what they wanted to know. And so, they left me my other one." He indicated Sheridan with a lift of his chin. "That one was less lucky. He tried to fool them with a fake. An obvious fake, as though he hardly expected them to believe him. And then, when they crushed that, he talked endlessly, on and on and on. But he couldn't satisfy them. Perhaps that's why they finished with his tongue."

He closed his eye for a moment. Then opened it again. "They left him here. Pulled up the rope. It took him two days to die, unfortunate man."

The monk, despite his words, was remarkably unperturbed by Sheridan's fate. His tone peaceful. Cold, even. Perhaps, Marion thought, he'd experienced so much violence recently that one more tortured body couldn't move him. Or, she mused in an icier vein, perhaps he believed, as she was trying to force herself not to, that Sheridan had brought his fate upon himself.

She was interrupted in her cogitation by the monk politely clearing his throat. "May I touch it?" He indicated the bell.

She handed it to him. "It doesn't work."

"On the contrary." He held it up and shook it, sustaining the movement. Nothing happened. "As I said, a perfect, pure G."

She remained silent.

"You aren't musical," he continued, with what might have been irony.

"No, I'm afraid not."

"Even if you were," he said, "you wouldn't hear it. We train for decades before we begin to appreciate music in that register. Our novices are chosen for their perfect pitch. The first ten years of their novitiate trains them in classical forms. From there, half devote themselves to the higher tones and half to the lower. I've immersed myself in the higher."

"I see."

He held out the bell to her and, pausing for a split second, she took it. She felt that she ought to leave it with him. That it belonged more to him than it did to her. She couldn't even tell when it was operational.

He smiled. "The work of the monastery is finished," he said, reading her thoughts. "Or, is finishing now. There's no need for you to leave the bell with me." He considered. "And, who knows? You may find that you need it. The high G, so the story goes, resolves the dangerous, lower chords that travelers such as yourself are wont to encounter. Negates them. Rendering them harmless."

She nodded, taking back the bell and replacing it in the pocket of her filthy coat. She'd only half understood what he'd said to her. "What was the work of your monastery, then? Aside from the music?"

"Only the music," he replied ambiguously. "But I believe you've come to finish that as well, haven't you?" He closed his eye and muttered something in Ge'ez.

"I've been charged with disabling a—a device." She wasn't certain how to translate the Rombulos' chaotic conversation to him. Or how to explain the nature of the documents she carried in her bag. "One of a number scattered across the globe. Do you know where that—the device—is? Nearby, perhaps?" she added hopefully.

"It is here," he said. "This room. Along with several others located in responsive settings in Europe, Africa, and the Orient. But all of them are one. Connected by deep machinery. If you destroy one, the others will be nullified. You've brought the tools with you?"

"Yes," she said, reaching into her pocket for the inkwell. "But—" pausing before taking a quick breath. Motivated by both curiosity and the thought of the report she'd submit to her people: "may I ask what this machinery is? What am I destroying? What music?"

"Deep music," he said simply. "Truly, nothing aside from music. But it strikes the heart rather than the ear." When she remained mystified, he explained further: "it's too low for our hearing, but it works wonders and horrors on our souls. And one can trace its journey across the civilized world by following the hares—their overlapping ears." He paused. "In the same way, one can witness its decadence.

"It began," he continued, falling into a narrative tone that must have told the story countless times before, "in the caves of China, as the music that accompanied enlightenment. Ecstatic music that moved those who experienced it to higher levels of existence. But as it travelled, it decayed into a tool for statesmen. A method of persuasion to be wielded when words failed to influence. A torture device. And then, inevitably, it became a weapon of war, shattering the souls of soldiers on the field of battle before they'd unsheathed their swords. Terrifying them into submission before the fight had even begun. While the chambers of resonance, such as this one, became ever more powerful and dominant."

He raised a hand toward the cloth covering his ruined eye, thought better of it, and let it fall to his side again. "In the fifteenth century, an Italian in the service of an Emperor thought he could restore the device to its spiritual glory. But he overestimated both his abilities and the purity of his followers. Our monastery has, since then, devoted itself to hiding this—thing. Halting its resurgence.

"Until now. My brothers are dead, and I've betrayed my vows." He gazed, still unmoved, at Sheridan's body parts. "That thing there is the inheritor of our legacy."

He stopped speaking for a few seconds, tired. Then, gathering his reserves, he pushed on. "But you've brought the tools. And we may yet succeed. The inkwell and the candlestick, yes? You have them with you?" He indicated two elaborate cavities on either side of the chamber. "As you can see, they fit into these stands. But we must take great care. Facing backward, they destroy the machinery. Facing forward, they activate it. Once we've lit the candle—"

"Only the inkwell." Her stomach dropped as she interrupted him, and she wrapped her arms around her waist. Then, swallowing, she looked him in the eye and said it louder: "I haven't got the candlestick. All I have with me is the inkwell."

"The inkwell," he repeated after a few seconds. "Not the candlestick. You've brought only one." Laughing, tears seeping out of his good eye, he began speaking rapidly to himself in Ge'ez. Shaking his head. Disintegrating.

Only the inkwell. At first, all she could feel was dull wretchedness. But then, gradually, she tasted bile in the back of her throat. Lenore had told her explicitly not to retrieve the candlestick from Jeffrey. She could easily have done so before setting off, but Lenore had insisted that their superiors wanted it to stay with him. And so, obedient, she had left it. Traipsed off to Venice without a backward glance.

For a few seconds, she believed that Lenore had acted out of spite. To weaken her standing in their organization. But then, swallowing the bile, she collected herself. As much as she disliked Lenore, she knew that her colleague wouldn't undermine her own project. Either their superiors had misunderstood the candlestick's importance, or they had their own reason for keeping the tools in separate hands until Marion had completed her analysis. Likely the latter. But now, they'd want her to bring the material together. And they'd want her to work quickly.

Which meant that her next step was clear. If sickening. The only way to access the candlestick was to resurface and return to Jeffrey. Rubbing her forehead with the heel of her hand, she faced the monk, who was still rocking back and forth on the balls of his feet and murmuring to himself in Ge'ez. "Is there any way," she asked him, "that you could get me to Khartoum, in Sudan? Or perhaps to Hargeisa, in Somaliland?" They were the two closest British imperial outposts that came to mind.

"Why?" His voice was edged with despair.

"I can collect the candlestick," she said. "I know where it is. But to do so, I must return to Great Britain."

"And when you find it? What do you do then?"

"I suppose—I suppose that I'll make my way back here—"

"No," he said. "Don't come back. This place is finished. Haunted. Wrong. There are other chambers. Can you find one elsewhere?"

She thought for a few seconds, remembering the Rombulos' excitement over the page from the pattern book. Widecombe, north of Plymouth. Among others. She nodded. "I'm aware of an additional one. You say that the tools must face backward, correct? Otherwise the device will be activated rather than destroyed?"

"Yes. As the candle burns down, the weight of the wax changes the pitch of the small pipes hidden at the base of the candlestick. Those pipes, along with the pipes at the base of the inkwell, can either block or open the larger pipes that have been driven into the earth below the chambers. It works on the same principle as a pneumatic organ. Except, across continents. Forward, the pipes open. Backward, they collapse. Permanently." Then, tottering, he began walking toward the far wall of the room. "This way. I'm in no condition to climb the rope."

Regaining something of his composure as she followed, he spoke further. "And yes, I'll send you to Hargeisa in Somaliland. A bit under eight hundred miles. We have a truck and petrol set aside against an emergency." He laughed again, the sound of anguish. "*An emergency*. What emergency? There are no more emergencies."

But a few seconds later, he collected himself once more and faced her even as he kept walking. "It will take you a week."

"Thank you," she said, trotting to catch up to his diminishing voice as it passed through an arched door that she hadn't noticed during her first examination of the room. A second chamber, evidently built as a viewing area. Protected acoustically against the dome. She wondered, with a pang of guilt, whether anyone would ever collect Sheridan's body.

THE journey between Tigray and British Somaliland took six days. A pleasant respite in the back of an Italian troop transport truck that the monks had appropriated and hidden in the mountains before Graziani's soldiers had eradicated the monastery. Marion had no language in common with the child—a shy boy of perhaps fourteen years of age—who drove her. And so, she spent her time gazing at the extraordinary landscape, sleeping among the canisters of petrol, and eating Italian military rations.

When, with a substantial bribe—all of Veronica's lire in exchange for a promise of safe passage back into Ethiopia for the boy—they crossed invisibly into Somaliland, she felt mild disappointment to be leaving the truck. It had calmed her. But at least she was rested and well-fed. Energetic for the first time since leaving Istanbul.

After exchanging a mutually inhibited goodbye with the boy, she even felt buoyed by a hint of optimism as she shouldered her bag and made for the headquarters of the local British Commissioner's office. When she saw the two-storey building, however, she paused—hiding across the street under the shade of a twisted acacia tree that must have been growing in that spot for a good fifty years before the neighborhood itself had been constructed. Trying to get a feel for the administration's likely reaction to her appearance.

The headquarters was the most prominent establishment in the area, but it was a modest example of its type. The ground floor was whitewashed stone and the first floor reddish brick surmounted by a row of arched windows. The door, watched in a haphazard way by a young uniformed soldier who clearly hadn't imagined he'd be spending his African adventure in this way, was of wood and painted green. It was, in short, disarming.

But even so, she wasn't certain how best to draw attention to herself. Creating a disturbance would be counterproductive. Walking inside and attempting to explain to them her baroque relationship to a Government office they'd never heard of would be even worse. Her only recourse, she finally decided, was to rely on her respectability. As much as she hated her respectability.

Lifting her bag, she crossed the street and approached the soldier, who appeared both astonished to see a figure of her sort wandering the interior of Somaliland and delighted that he would have something beyond the routine to occupy his attention. He straightened and stood somewhat at attention.

"Forgive me," she said when she reached him. "I'm afraid I'm in a spot of difficulty. I wonder whether one of your officers might help me?"

The soldier, baffled as he was by her presence, grinned. "Of course, Mrs.—"

"Lady Willcox," she supplied.

He blinked. "Lady Willcox, then. I'll show you upstairs."

She followed him into a low-ceilinged yet echoing hall and then up a flight of wooden stairs to a corridor lined with thin, fragile doors, all closed. He stopped at the furthest door away from the stairs and turned to her. "If you'd wait here?"

He pushed open the door, slipped through, and closed it behind him. Through the flimsy wall, she could hear every word of the conversation that ensued. A few moments later, the soldier opened the door and stood to the side to let her pass. "Captain Summers will have it fixed up for you in no time, Lady Willcox."

"Thank you." She nodded to him and walked into a room that she'd seen reproduced in countless colonial buildings in what felt like an infinite array of mandates, colonies, and protectorates. A scuffed wooden desk obscured by a mess of beige file folders. Photographs of family. Photographs of dogs. Metal bookshelves crammed with untouched monographs on the customs and habits of various native peoples. An empty glass pitcher. A portable fan, motionless. And a middle-aged functionary, less embittered than bewildered, wondering what had become of his childhood ambition to travel, an intrepid explorer, across uncharted wilds and wastelands.

Captain Summers had stood when she entered the room. Sleeves of the khaki uniform rolled up, the collar unbuttoned. Thinning brown hair. "Please sit down, Lady Willcox."

"Thank you." She set her bag next to the wooden chair that might have been taken from some Victorian school room, and sat.

Captain Summers sat as well, behind the desk, taking quick stock of her soiled, heavy coat, her disintegrating boots, and the ratted state of the plait into which she'd forced her filthy hair. "I confess," he said after a few seconds of silence. "I'm at a loss. How on earth have you turned up here?"

"I've misplaced my papers," she said, feeling her way forward.

"I see."

"My husband," she pushed on, "is Sir Jeffrey Willcox. He conducts research for the British Museum. We were separated during our travels."

"I see," he repeated, more weary now than interested or concerned. No doubt calculating the cost of sending out a search party to find and ransom the dimwit amateur. "And where did you lose Sir Jeffrey, Lady Willcox?"

"In Istanbul."

"I—" He stopped, defeated.

"Captain Summers," she said, once the pause had become awkward, "I would consider it a personal favor if you would place a call to Professor Richard Maugham at the British Museum to inform him that you've found me. My husband will have been troubled by my disappearance." When he didn't reply immediately, she spoke again: "I'll wait here."

He swallowed and stood. "Private Hanley will bring you tea, Lady Willcox. This may take some time."

"Thank you, Captain Summers."

True to his word, the soldier appeared fifteen minutes later with a more than presentable tray of tea, milk, sugar, and a plate of sandwiches. Maintaining her air of propriety while gorging herself on sandwiches and sweet, milky tea was difficult, but she liked to think she succeeded. No one was watching her anyway. Private Hanley had returned to his post downstairs once he'd deposited the tray.

After an hour of peaceful quiet, however, the corridor became animated. They had, she concluded, completed the call. An event that precipitated, first, a muffled argument in another room, second, the angry slam of a rickety door, and then finally, two agitated people stalking in her direction, stopping, and pacing away again. Captain Summers and an older, more imperious man. She could still hear every word that they said—although she wished that she couldn't. Closing her eyes, she hunched her shoulders and drank the dregs of her tea.

"...they don't *want* her detained, Summers," the other man was insisting. "They want her on an aeroplane to Croydon. Now."

"On whose authority?" Captain Summers was ranting. "Whose order? This is my administration. My town. Who knows what she's been doing in those mountains? What's in that bag? We don't know! We haven't inspected it. It would be the pinnacle of irresponsibility to send her on her way—"

"It would be the pinnacle of irresponsibility," the second man countered, "to do anything but that. Don't touch her. Don't touch her belongings. Get rid of her and forget you've seen her."

"I have a duty," Captain Summers raged, "to maintain a government here of British law and order. That does not involve looking the other way when some dubious Scottish bitch illegally skips across the *Italian* border with a sack full of God knows what and then sweetly orders me to phone up her unprincipled masters to send them her greetings."

"How old are you?" The other man's voice was quiet now.

"What?"

"I know how old you are," the man said. "You're fifty-one. And you're in bloody Hargeisa, 'maintaining British law and order.' Do you know why you're here, Summers?"

There was silence for a long minute. Marion could hear the call of an entirely un-English bird out the window. And then, inexorably, the other man continued: "you're here because you won't stop doing your damned duty. A mania, is it? Because I certainly fail to understand it. Why waste your life in this way? Why waste your wife's?"

Captain Summers didn't respond for a few, tense moments. Then, cursing with a resonance and creativity that led Marion to raise her eyebrows, he spoke loudly, nearly shouting, as his footsteps receded down the corridor. "Then you do it, Stafford. I won't have any part of it! I bloody *won't*."

Two or three seconds later, the office door opened, polite and quiet. A small, elderly man with floating white hair and a rough, permanently ruddy face entered the room. His eyes were kindly, with a hint of malicious intelligence. She recognized his type at once.

"Thank you for waiting, Lady Willcox," he said. "I trust you haven't been uncomfortable."

"Not at all," she replied, standing and shouldering her bag. "I'm grateful to you for helping me in my—my predicament. Mr.—?"

"Dr. Stafford," he said, standing to the side of the door to indicate that they should walk. "You're in luck. The RAF maintain an airstrip just outside town. Ordinarily it's deserted, but the border commission have been running reconnaissance these past days. We'll have you in Aden by nightfall. From there, I believe your husband has made arrangements for your return to London."

She hadn't realized they would work so quickly. And their eagerness left her apprehensive. "Thank you." She tried to keep her voice calm.

They left the building and he smiled as he held open the passenger door to an unexpected green Austin 7 that Private Hanley had driven to the front entrance. When she sat, Dr. Stafford closed the door and walked around to the driver's side. As he drove serenely in what she assumed was the direction of the RAF's airstrip, he spoke again. "You weren't expecting to find yourself in Hargeisa, were you, Lady Willcox?"

"And you were?" she retorted, remembering the argument in the corridor. She didn't want to make conversation with the administration here.

The corner of his mouth went down. "Ah well. We all end in Hargeisa eventually. Mark my words, Lady Willcox. When they've finished with you, you'll wash up in Somaliland as well." He paused, lost in thought. "Do you know, I haven't seen Richard Maugham for decades."

She refused to be drawn. But when he saw her frown, he smiled again. "He does leave a mark. I can sense it as well as you can. But fear not, I won't pry." He slowed the car alongside a stretch of dirt runway, empty aside from a futuristic-looking aeroplane. "And it looks as though we've arrived."

Marion climbed out of the Austin before he had the chance to help her or to open her door. He had no difficulty, however, in matching her stride as she approached the waiting plane. "You're in for a treat," he said. "Spanking new Westland Lysander. Still experimental, but I have a feeling they'll be playing an important role in the coming hostilities. They've got an atmosphere about them."

When the pilot took her bag to stuff into the small space beside the single passenger-observer's seat, she shook Dr. Stafford's hand. "Thank you once again."

"Not at all." He bowed a touch over her hand. "And don't worry about Captain Summers, Lady Willcox. He complains and complains, but he wouldn't have it any other way. Lone beacon of good, British sense in an otherwise barren wasteland of barbaric corruption. Your appearance on his doorstep will keep him blissfully irate for weeks. My compliments."

She let herself smile at him as she arranged the scarf and goggles over her head. And then, giving in, she nodded and waved as he shouted behind her: "give my regards to Maugham!"

Devon, England
March, 1937

DESPITE Jeffrey's remarkable organizational capacity, the journey from Aden to Croydon was even more torturous than the flight to Mekelle had been. But then, Marion's comfort would have been the last of his considerations. Over two sleepless days and nights, she was shuttled from leg to leg, more often than not in stripped out military aircraft. When she reached Croydon, sometime in the middle of March—she wasn't certain as to the day, much less the time—she was on the verge of exhausted tears. She mourned, deeply, the days of her childhood when mechanized air travel was the stuff of fantasy and novels of the distant future.

He was waiting alone at the edge of the apron when at last she dragged herself off the plane and down the ladder. Dark hat, dark wool double-breasted coat, dark gloves, comfortable in the cloudy, twilit damp. He kissed her on the temple as he took her bag and opened the passenger-side door of his least offensive car. A cream and black Wolseley Wasp, a few years old. Which meant, perhaps, that he and the office meant to be accommodating? She felt a small stab of hope.

But the first words out of his mouth once he'd stored her luggage and brought them onto the road north into the city quashed that optimism. "'Belinda?'"

"How is Lydia?"

"*Belinda*? Lost and helpless in Somaliland?" He glanced over at her. "Please tell me you've got a leopard-skin wrap under that coat."

"I'm tired, Jeffrey. Not now."

"Tired, are you?" He flipped on the Wolseley's headlights in the embryonic darkness. "You're lucky I'm not taking you to Chelsea. Maugham only relented because he's got happy memories of Hargeisa. Some rival whose exile there he organized at the end of last century." He peered through the windscreen and then leaned back. "I took advantage of his mood to negotiate a day or two of recovery for you before the onslaught."

"I met him," she said. "The exile."

"Oh?" Uninterested. "What's he like?"

"Intelligent. Engaging." She rubbed her eyes. "I imagine he reads a lot of Marcus Aurelius to keep himself sane. Ovid, maybe."

"Sounds about right."

"You know, the more I learn about Maugham, the more horrific—"

"Don't think about it."

She closed her eyes and relaxed against her seat. Didn't answer.

He drove in silence for five or six minutes and then, abruptly, spoke again. "She's learned the number five."

"What?"

"Lydia," he said. "You asked after her. She's learned the number five."

"Oh." She considered. "Only the number five?"

"Yes. Alicia and Mrs. Bowen are unhappy about it."

"Why? It's a bit early for numbers, but that shouldn't worry them. It isn't abnormal." Her eyes were still closed.

"No," he agreed. "But she's developed some sort of—attachment—to it. Throws an angry tantrum when she's presented with anything but five objects. Five dolls. Five apples." He paused. "Five shoes. It's trying."

"Oh." She thought for a few seconds more. Then a long-buried early memory came to her. "I was like that about the number seven."

"I should have known."

"Because it's yellow."

"What?"

"Seven is yellow," she repeated, without opening her eyes. "Six is blue. Five is brown. Nine is red—"

"Your brain," he commented before she could go further, "should be on display at the Natural History Museum."

"I liked yellow," she continued, ignoring him. "And it irritated me when the numbers, objects, and colors didn't match. Still does."

"Dear God," he muttered. "Poor Lydia."

"Ian hasn't got it," she said, opening her eyes and watching his profile. "He's too much like—" She stopped herself. Then: "is he still at school?"

"Yes," he said. "They've managed thus far to forestall any bids for freedom." He sighed. "Serves me right for tainting my impeccable lineage with your goblin blood. Can't be helped now, I suppose. We'll collect him in two weeks for his holiday."

Which gave her an idea as to the date. Later in March than she'd thought. She wondered where the missing weeks had gone. But then, unable to remain awake in the soothing motion of the car, she closed her eyes for the remainder of the journey.

*A*T first, all she could remember of her return to Jeffrey's London house was smelling Lydia's hair as her daughter slept in her pristine cot. When she woke after a fifteen-hour sleep to sunlight creeping through her bedroom's curtains, however, bits and pieces of the conversation she'd had the evening before began insinuating themselves into her mind. The onslaught. Maugham.

She rolled over onto her back and pushed her hands against her eyes. She'd deliberately placed herself into the orbit of the office because she had no other choice. She needed the candlestick. But now that she was here, she was far from confident that she could protect her interests. Vexed, she let her hands fall to her sides.

Then, reconciled to her situation, she sat up in the bed and pushed back her hair. Glanced at the clock on the bedside table. 10:00. She didn't know what day of the week it was, but she had a feeling that whatever it was, Jeffrey had stayed home. He'd want to report to Maugham on her condition and on her willingness to speak to them before taking her to Chelsea or the Museum for a proper interview. He would also have already examined the material she'd brought back with her—though she was confident he'd have little idea of what it meant or what he ought to do with it.

Steeling herself for the beginning of what were certain to be a distasteful few days, she stood barefoot on the thick carpet, walked to the toilet, cleaned her teeth, and washed her face. Then she found a clean pair of grey trousers and a grey blouse in the wardrobe, dressed quickly, pushed her feet into flat oxfords, and pinned back her hair. As she left the room, she met Mrs. Bowen, who told her that Jeffrey was waiting for her in his study. Once she'd eaten breakfast, of course.

Rather than putting off the inevitable, she ate a piece of toast, standing, in the dining room and then trudged back up the stairs to knock on the door to his study. When she entered, he was sitting in an armchair, skimming the treatise on misery, anxiety and the proper use of musical instruments. The other documents, the inkwell, and the bell were arranged together on the coffee table. To her quickly suppressed joy, the candlestick was there too, looking as though it belonged with the inkwell. She'd had difficulty imagining them as a pair until she'd seen them side by side.

He gestured her to the sofa opposite him. "I've left the bag in the cellar because of the smell. Is there anything I've missed? Anything hidden in it? Or can I bin it?"

"Get rid of it," she said, sitting. "There's nothing else."

"Good." He lifted a silver coffee pot from a tray on wheels that had been left near a wooden table to his side. "Coffee?"

"Thank you."

He poured them both cups, added milk and sugar to one, and handed it to her across the table. She held the cup in both hands, inhaled the steam, and took a sip. She'd be needing more than caffeine to see her through the next hours, but the coffee was at least a start. She took another, bigger, swallow, and waited.

He set his own cup on the table to his side and spoke: "when you abandoned Lydia in the mud at Murdoch's house, we reserved the tail for him rather than for you. He seemed the more valuable target. In hindsight, that was an error."

She knew better than to reply. He was trying to provoke her into defending herself. Or, if not that, at least showing curiosity. But she wouldn't speak unless he asked her a direct question. And even then, she'd withhold as much as she could.

He shot her an amused look. Knew what she was thinking. "At the time, it made sense. The Italians had discovered something. Murdoch had the relationship with the Italians. You hadn't. And if we'd followed you, chances are you'd have sensed it and shaken us off. Besides which, we'd picked up your boy at the dock."

She dropped her eyes and examined the coffee cup in her lap. She loathed the thought of Eugene fending off the attentions of Maugham's interviewers.

"He's not as delicate as you think he is, Marion." Jeffrey sipped his own coffee. "Given the American passport, we couldn't leave him with permanent damage. But we do have alternative strategies in place for that sort of situation, and under ordinary circumstances, he would have been talking to us within a few hours. We counted on him to spill—everything he knew about where you were going, what you were doing, and what you hoped to accomplish. A tail would have been redundant. A waste of resources."

He reached for a box on the coffee table, opened it, and extracted a cigarette. "As it was, he held out for two days." He thought for a moment, keeping the unlit cigarette between his fingers, and then corrected himself. "That is, he did drop bits and pieces here and there, but—remarkably for an untrained subject—he remained mostly intact."

She swallowed, keeping her gaze averted. She hated him for telling her this.

"Granted, we weren't working at top speed, and we were keeping him in a condition that allowed for future deniability." He shrugged. "But we also thought we had time. We were willing to wait."

He examined the tip of the unlit cigarette. "So we waited. We worked. We watched him. And at the end of two days, he was on the verge of crumbling. But then, just as he was about to talk to us, do you know what happened?" He lit the cigarette, inhaled, and blew smoke up at the ceiling. When she shook her head, still not speaking, he laughed. "Maugham received the order from on high. Higher even than *Maugham*, you understand."

He held her eyes. "Turn him loose. Eugene, the little American music student, is inviolate."

He moved an ashtray to the table next to his armchair and set the burning cigarette in it. "Well, that raised some eyebrows as you can imagine. Maugham was livid. But it didn't take him long to connect the dots. 'Eugene,' it seems, is Eugene Newland, son of Clement Newland, onetime heir to the most productive lode in California and current owner of Newland American Mining. And Newland American Mining," he continued, pedantic, "is quietly buying up every claim not only in Italian and French East Africa, but also in our very own British protectorates. Yankee commercialism making a right mockery of our Old-World thirst for conquest."

She was staring at him in astonishment. This was not the direction in which she'd expected the conversation to go. When he'd watched her reaction for a few seconds, he nodded and took up his cigarette again. "Good," he said, inhaling. "You didn't know. That will make our conversation with Maugham this afternoon less painful. And we'll stage it at the Museum rather than in Chelsea. I shudder to think what he would have done to you had you been aware of the boy's identity."

"I—"

"Yes?" He raised an eyebrow.

"Nothing." She took a quiet sip of coffee.

"Your people, however, knew all along. There can't be any doubt. They used him deliberately, throwing him in our way as a distraction while you slipped off in the other direction. In fact, I wouldn't be remotely surprised if it was their representatives who alerted the father when we collected the boy."

He took a speculative drag of the cigarette. "And if they're watching now—which they almost certainly are—they must be entertained to no end by the spectacle of Maugham trying to keep this project under wraps and under his control rather than giving it up to the Secretary for Mines. Young Harry Crookshank. Brought into the loop by Mr. Newland himself, if our sources at the Board of Trade are to be trusted. Maugham and Crookshank," he said dryly, "do not get on."

"Oh."

"I'm merely informing you as to the situation," he said. "so that Maugham's mood when you see him today doesn't alarm you."

Maugham's mood always alarmed her. She nodded and drank more coffee.

"We did, of course, despite our setbacks, learn a few things from Eugene." He placed the cigarette in the ashtray again and rested his cheek on his fist, his elbow on the arm of the chair. "I have a general idea of the tone of these documents, for example—which," he added when he saw her quick look, "we'll discuss later."

He paused. "And when he finally admitted that you'd gone to Venice—though not what you'd be doing in Venice—we watched the departure points. Belinda Storchio, the sole British passenger on Marshal Graziani's private flight to Mekelle, Ethiopia, wasn't difficult to identify. Especially given that we'd followed Murdoch and his Italian companions in the same direction—

"Ah," he interrupted himself when he saw her reaction to Sheridan's name, her inability to remember the wrecked body with any degree of composure. "Good. So you saw him too. That's helpful. Was it really so bad? Our tail relied on a third-party report—he couldn't cross the border."

He considered. "Of course, as far as we're concerned, it couldn't have ended more tidily. Murdoch cleaned himself up for us. The horrible children have been packed off to a second cousin in British Columbia. Perhaps if we're lucky they'll be eaten by a bear—"

"Stop it." She couldn't push the image of Sheridan's severed foot and fingers out of her head.

"I was joking about the bear."

"Stop it," she repeated.

"Hmm." He sipped his coffee. "You and Murdoch, then, both turned up in the same— monastery—?"

She kept her eyes averted.

He nodded, confident. "In the same monastery, in Tigray, Ethiopia. Murdoch, for obvious reasons, didn't make it out. You did. But rather than reporting to your own people, you chose to compromise yourself to the excitable Captain Summers of Hargeisa, Somaliland." He looked up at the ceiling. "Care to explain?"

"I need the candlestick."

"Why didn't you take it before you left for Venice?" He dropped his eyes from the ceiling, finished his coffee, and put the empty cup on the table.

"They told me not to."

"Odd. Why?"

"I don't know." She finished her own coffee. Then waited.

"But," he said, "I'm certain you have some guesses. You'll share those with Maugham this afternoon. Shall we leave after lunch?"

She nodded and stood. Prepared as she ever was to endure Maugham's claustrophobic office at the British Museum.

THE air was cool and clear under a sun that felt too high for March, and so they walked from Jeffrey's house to the Museum. The tulips had emerged, some already beginning to weaken and drop their petals. It was later in the month than she'd imagined. Distressingly so.

As they walked, she found herself regretting the days she'd lost in transit—the time on the boat, the aeroplanes, and even in the back of the transport truck all ran together into an anarchic absence of memory that resembled a period of unconsciousness. Unpleasant. She focused on a lone, late narcissus, wedged into a square of dirt between the pavement and a wall of white stone. It steadied her.

Far too soon, however, they reached the Museum and made their way through the Library, into the stacks, to Maugham's remote office. Upon Jeffrey's first knock, the door creaked open, wary, but then a split second later swung wide, revealing Maugham, genial and pernicious, waving them inside. When she stepped over the threshold, she braced herself against the familiar rush of hot, dry air and the overpowering smell of acrimony—Maugham's own or that of his visitors, she could never quite determine.

She tried with less success to block out the various tatty objects he'd arranged throughout the room to discomfit his interlocutors. Staring, despite herself, at the badger that had been added to the family of stuffed hedgehogs that lived atop the bookcase. Was it meant to be an allegory? A metaphor? If so, she failed to understand the message. But, she mused, as she sat in the unstable wooden chair on casters across from his desk, at least he'd shaved off his mutton chops since last they'd met.

Jeffrey, placing his briefcase to his side, sat next to her in the chair's twin. And Maugham, more like a pleased child than the thwarted bureaucrat for whom Jeffrey had prepared her, settled himself in the desk chair and folded his hands over a thin folder in front of him. Fixed Marion with a sympathetic gaze. "Poor Mr. Murdoch."

She felt her stomach harden. Didn't reply.

He opened the folder and examined a typed sheet contained within it. "You were there, Dr. Bailey. A witness. Did they really 'display his fingers and eyeballs as a warning to others who might betray them?'" He looked up at her. "That's from our third-party report."

She blinked. Still silent. Unwilling to let him goad her with morbid trivia.

"Hmm." He closed the folder. "I entirely understand your reticence. Who would have thought that a collection of monks could be so vicious? I was merely seeking confirmation that—"

"Monks?" Astonished.

"Yes," he said. "Quite. Monks. Who else would have separated Mr. Murdoch from his eyes, his fingers, his teeth, his left hand, his foot—" he glanced down at the closed file folder, "and his tongue? If I'm not mistaken? Monks, Dr. Bailey. Violent, savage monks."

"Graziani." she said, her voice strangled. "Marshal Graziani did it. The same lunatic who murdered twenty thousand people in Addis Ababa last month."

He pursed his lips, thoughtful. "No," he said eventually. "I think not. Marshal Graziani was nowhere near the mountains of Tigray on the day in question." He steepled his hands over the folder, prim. "And additionally, he's declared to us on his honor that the monks were to blame. Poor Mr. Murdoch," he repeated, his hand now over his heart. "But we'll take comfort in the fact that Graziani has dealt with them. They won't be assaulting any further innocent travelers, I can assure you. We're indebted to him for his kind regard—"

"I refuse to believe that you've absolved Italy of responsibility for this atrocity." She was trying and failing to keep her voice level. "Sheridan Murdoch was your own man. You trained him. You employed him. It's your *duty* to question the bald lies of that maniac butcher."

"It would have been ungentlemanly to cast doubt on his findings," Jeffrey interposed, bland. "He gave us his word."

She turned to stare at him, but he was busying himself brushing a speck of non-existent dust from the cuff of his trousers.

"And as for Mr. Murdoch," Maugham continued before she had the chance to speak again, "we believe that he was simply in the wrong place at the wrong time. These things happen in Africa. Loath as we are to admit it to ourselves."

She opened her mouth to retort, but he held up his hand. "And, let me be entirely open with you, Dr. Bailey. Distasteful as the situation is, it has left this department, at least, with a welcome moment to catch our breath. I believe Willcox has appraised you of the unfortunate situation with Crookshank, the Secretary for Mines?"

She couldn't think of any coherent reply.

"He has? Excellent." He resettled his spectacles on his nose. "Crookshank's original, entirely fantastic, demand was that we surrender Murdoch's artifact to Graziani, along with whatever information we may have accumulated concerning it, in exchange for a cooperative, rather than restrictive, interpretation of East African resource extraction.

"And not only Crookshank." He made a moue of distaste. "Our allies have been applying pressure as well. Because, you see, Dr. Bailey, it seems that Italy has finally struck a bit of long-delayed good luck." He pursed his lips further, looking even more like a petulant toddler. "Unlike our protectorate in Somaliland, which can produce cows—always helpful in keeping our boys in Aden fed— Italian Ethiopia, according to recent prospecting reports—" he opened the folder, turned over the page, and held up his spectacles to read, "—can potentially produce gemstones, gold, lead, nickel, silver, petroleum, and zinc."

"Don't forget the Norwegians," Jeffrey murmured.

"Ah yes." Maugham nodded his thanks to Jeffrey and closed the folder. "And potash. The Norwegians want it for fertilizer." He removed his spectacles. "In my day we used wood ash. But I suppose one can't halt the march of progress."

She could still think of nothing to say. And she had no idea what this monologue had to do with Sheridan. Or, for that matter, what it had to do with what she had thought was the purpose of the meeting—negotiating access to the candlestick. Despite her best intentions, Maugham and Jeffrey had left her stupefied. Again.

"A great deal of gold, Dr. Bailey," Maugham reiterated. "And a very great deal of petroleum."

She looked across the desk at him, silent.

"You wonder how all of this relates to Mr. Murdoch?" He held up his hand again, although she'd made no move to speak. "Only this. Less than a week ago, I was at my wits' end. I couldn't for the life of me muster a sufficiently convincing argument for keeping this investigation out of the hands of the Crookshanks of the world and in-house where it belongs.

"Wide-eyed and guileless, he enjoyed her bewildered stare. "But then, extraordinary as it is to state, salvation came in the form of Mr. Murdoch's severed foot and missing tongue." He tapped the folder with his index finger. "This very report, in fact. It rescued us from certain and ignoble defeat." He leaned forward over the desk, still nothing but charmed by the story he was telling. "The moment it arrived, I brought it to the attention of the mining people and, to say the least, it gave them pause. For, you understand, Dr. Bailey, it is one thing to send our boys as guests and observers to a well-ordered Italian colony, in search of gold and petroleum."

"And potash," Jeffrey supplied.

"And potash," Maugham agreed. "But it's another thing entirely to send them into the Italian interior when no one can guarantee their protection against murderous monks out to use European body parts as building materials. Even Crookshank recognized the validity of that argument.

"And so," he leaned back in his chair, pleased with himself, his hands folded over both his spectacles and his round stomach, "we now have time. Time to complete our investigation. Time to mourn the departed Mr. Murdoch. And time, most importantly, to learn why you've made the flattering choice, having narrowly escaped those same monks yourself, to send us your regards from Hargeisa rather than forcing us to chase you all over the continent as is your usual wont."

It took her a moment to realize that he'd stopped speaking and expected an answer. But, intellectually battered, she couldn't begin to formulate one. As much as she was aware that they'd deliberately fed her this bizarre concoction of shameless lies and what was, for all she knew, an accurate narrative of ministerial backbiting, she couldn't fathom what their purpose in doing so had been. Their motive was opaque—and the uncertainty left her shaky. Unable to decide what to tell them and what to hold back.

After staring at a spot on Maugham's desk for several seconds, she concluded that in the end it didn't matter. They could lead her in any direction that suited them, undermine her confidence all they liked, as long as she brought the inkwell and the candlestick together, traveled to Devon, and found the chamber, she would fulfill her promise to the Rombulos and the monk. She had no other goal.

She raised her eyes and looked across at Maugham. "I surfaced in Hargeisa because I'm trying to bring the candlestick—Sheridan Murdoch's candlestick—together with an inkwell that I collected in Venice. Jeffrey has the candlestick. I couldn't think of any other way to access it."

"Willcox had the candlestick in Istanbul as well," Maugham replied. "Why didn't you take it with you then? You've shown little hesitation for pilfering of that sort in the past."

"My instructions were to leave it."

"Why?"

"I don't know."

Maugham and Jeffrey exchanged a glance. Then, dropping that line of attack, Maugham asked her the question she'd been dreading since she'd landed in Croydon. "Why do you want them together?" He began cleaning the lens of his spectacles with a handkerchief he'd pulled with difficulty from the capacious pocket of his tweed jacket. "What do they do?"

"My understanding," she said, choosing not to waste time keeping the information back, "is that together they operate as a sort of—acoustic—weapon."

"An acoustic weapon." Maugham's voice gave nothing away.

"Yes," she said. "My—my informant confirmed a hypothesis that I'd drawn from the pages that Sheridan unearthed along with the candlestick. The inkwell, when brought together with the candlestick, produces sound below the range of human hearing that nonetheless profoundly influences its listeners. For the most part negatively. They hear nothing, but they feel fear, terror, despair. It—it shatters their souls, according to my source."

"Interesting." He replaced his spectacles. "How?"

"I don't understand the technology," she admitted. "He said that it works on the same logic as a pipe organ. Which was also corroborated by a leaf from among the documents. An image of a man in anguish working an organ. When the candle burns down, it compresses the pipes, and air begins to vibrate at a series of specific registers."

"So soldiers would do what?" Jeffrey asked. "Carry the candlestick into battle with them? The inkwell in the other hand? I can't imagine they'd last long on the field. And how do they protect themselves from the sound? Ear coverings?" He shook his head. "Outlandish."

"No," she said. "There were chambers—resonance chambers—hidden in areas where military leaders wanted to use the weapon. The inkwell and candlestick were inserted into special cavities in those chambers. And then, once the candle was lit, the pipes under the chambers compressed the air and sent the sound either out, abroad, or under certain circumstances back into the cavern."

She rubbed her eyes, hating the conversation, the room, everything about the moment. "I formed the impression in Ethiopia that the chamber's default position was resonance. There was a smaller, hidden viewing area that I discovered only by—by accident. I believe it was built to watch the effects of the sound on those inside. But the documents make clear that it can also be directed outward."

After a moment of thought, she explained further. "The references in them to the medieval 'dancing plagues' or 'dancing manias,' for example, must have been references to people under the influence of nearby chambers. I wouldn't be surprised if, at the height of their use, the chambers were a means of population control as much as military defense or offense."

She swallowed and stopped speaking, hoping they were satisfied. She'd deliberately avoided answering the second part of Jeffrey's question, unwilling to part with her knowledge of the bell. The Rombulos' gift was her only defense against whatever the office was intending to do with her material, and she wanted to keep it back from them. Nervous, and unable to look in his direction, she kept her eyes on Maugham, who was still fiddling with his spectacles.

"And so," Maugham eventually concluded, folding the spectacles and placing them to his side, "you'd like to take these artifacts back to Ethiopia with you. Brave the deranged monks a second time—"

"No," she interrupted. "No, there are chambers all over the world. The three rabbits with interlocking ears are a sign that one is close. Underground."

"The Tinners' Rabbits, you mean?" Maugham was chuckling to himself.

She frowned. "Yes. And there's a chamber nearby. In Devon. Widecombe-in-the-Moor, I believe."

"Devon?" Jeffrey considered. "That won't be difficult to investigate. A five-hour journey by car, we'd arrive late in the afternoon if we leave tomorrow morning." He flicked his eyes toward Maugham for a short second and then addressed Marion again. "And your people? What do they get out of you leading us to this site in Devon?"

"A report. They want to know what it does. Involving you was the only way."

He half smiled and then looked back at Maugham. "I suppose that must do for now." He dusted off his trousers and stood. "Satisfied, Maugham?"

"More than satisfied." Maugham stood as well. "Thank you, Dr. Bailey, for a charming conversation. I miss our chats when you're away. Until tomorrow, then."

Surprised by the abrupt—and painless—end to the interview, Marion rose more slowly. Tried to ignore the badger. And allowed Jeffrey to steer her out of the room.

THEY left London at 6:00 the next morning, before sunrise, in the Wolseley. Showing unexpected forbearance, Jeffrey didn't force Marion into the relentless, trivial conversation he ordinarily deployed to extract information from her. Instead, driving soberly, he let her sleep until the sun rose to their left, filling the car with watery, reddish light. When, two hours later, she couldn't keep her eyes closed any longer, she reached down to her feet and pulled an old Victorian guide to Dartmoor into her lap. All that Mrs. Bowen could find for her in the house on short notice.

As Jeffrey drove them along the empty trunk road, she skimmed the chapters, ignoring the ecstatic descriptions of health-giving walking tours, and focusing on the darker aspects of the region. She dwelled with particular attention on Widecombe-in-the-Moor. And after another two hours of careful reading, she closed the book and gazed, perplexed, out the window.

Then she turned to Jeffrey. "There's something wrong with Dartmoor."

The corner of his mouth went down. "Where to begin?"

"No, I mean its atmosphere. It's not right."

"Insufficiently grim for your tastes, dear?"

"No," she said, disregarding his tone. "The opposite, really." She opened the book and looked down at a page she had marked. "So much fear. Every conceivable horror story concentrated into one place. Ghosts, little people, demonic animals—"

"I believe the last of those was no more than the dastardly Mr. Stapleton out to cheat Sir Henry of his fortune." Jeffrey furrowed his brow. "And in the end, Holmes put it right."

"Look," she said, pointing at the page in her lap. "The devil even makes a not infrequent appearance."

"The place is haunted, Marion." He nodded out the windscreen at the landscape that surrounded them as they turned onto the winding local road that led them toward Widecombe-in-the-Moor. "Something of a disappointment, don't you think, if it were not?"

She closed the book and set it on the floor at her feet again. They'd be arriving at the Church of Saint Pancras, where they'd agreed to meet Maugham, in less than fifteen minutes. "I think it's more than that. These stories all originate in the fifteenth and sixteenth centuries. Something began to influence the area at the time. Some sort of reverberation."

"Perhaps." Unconvinced.

"Have you read the story of the Great Thunderstorm that hit this church in 1638?" she asked.

"I think I may have heard of it. The church was struck by lightning." He slowed as they passed between two rock walls backed by hedges, and then approached a low church with the tower appended in a haphazard way to its furthest end. "A few injuries. Burns. A noteworthy event in a town of this size."

"It was only afterward that they described it as a lightning strike," she corrected him. "At the time, they said something quite different. According to witnesses, the devil had targeted the church. Afflicting some with fire, some with a terrible thundering sound, some with overwhelming darkness. And then, there's a great deal of emphasis on the fact that they replaced the church's organ afterward." She looked at him. "Does it not sound familiar to you?"

He wedged the car against a continuation of the rock wall and cut the engine. "You think the weapon is under the church? Could be, I suppose. According to Maugham, it's crawling with your three-eared rabbits."

"No," she said. "Under the church would have been too prominent. Someone would have noticed. But the tale of the thunderstorm may be instructive." She reached down to collect the book and turned to push open her door. "Apparently the devil made two stops before and after his visit to the church. Once, they say, at an inn, in Poundsgate, to the south, and once at an inn, in Postbridge, to the north." She stood. "The detailed itinerary of the account makes me wonder."

"Do you think they're both involved?" he asked, opening his own door and standing as well, speaking to her over the top of the car.

"No." She shut her door and pulled her coat more tightly across her shoulders to stave off the damp wind. Hugged the book against her chest and leaned against the wall, behind which the tower rose, not quite straight. No tulips here. "But I do think it's one or the other. It shouldn't take long to determine which."

He retrieved his briefcase from the back seat, shut his own door, adjusted his hat, and walked around the car to stand beside her. "That will please Maugham. He dislikes uncertain casting about. Fieldwork. Says he's too old to enjoy the chase."

And then, just as he was speaking, Maugham himself arrived. Oddly, from the west. And even more oddly, driven in a London taxi. Marion had learned not to question Maugham's idiosyncratic methods of travel across Britain, but the taxi confounded her. She couldn't help staring as he climbed, flustered and patting down the pockets of his worn Ulster coat, out of the back of the black cab. The coat, for the first time in her experience, didn't look out of place.

He said something to the driver about waiting, he'd return in no time at all, and then looked up, smiling and jovial, at Marion and Jeffrey. "Rabbits, then." He squinted, unimpressed, at the church tower. Across the turf as though disappointed that the rabbits hadn't gathered to mark his arrival. Shook his head.

"Marion's been conducting research," Jeffrey said in response to Maugham's curiosity.

"Indeed?" Maugham beamed at her. "I wouldn't have it any other way. And?"

"She's narrowed our target to two sites. Both pubs. Not the church."

"Excellent. Churches dislike me. And I could use something warm to keep me going. Nearly noon, you see." He gestured toward the taxi. "Allow me to drive you?"

Marion and Jeffrey looked at one another, nonplussed, but before either could speak, Maugham's voice hardened. "I insist."

Half shrugging, they piled into the back of Maugham's taxi, Jeffrey in the middle, holding his briefcase on his knees, and Marion holding the book in her lap. Maugham looked a question at her, and she said, "the White Inn, Postbridge." She had a better feeling about the devil's departure point than about his point of arrival. And if she'd guessed incorrectly, the drive south wouldn't take more than a half hour.

"You heard the lady, my good man," Maugham shouted to the driver. "The White Inn, Postbridge."

The driver nodded and continued along the narrow street to the west and north. She felt a chill, which intensified as they gained speed, and she wrapped her arms around her waist. Compelled herself not to dwell on who or what the taxi driver actually was.

Less than twenty minutes later, they slowed to a stop in front of a long, whitewashed building, isolated and huddled against a barren grassy slope. A view of equally uninterrupted, pale moor sweeping out in a vista below. Exposed to the weather. Stark.

Marion wanted to examine it and the area surrounding it before entering the building. But before she could walk across the road and into the grass below, Jeffrey reached out and grabbed her arm. Tilted his head in Maugham's direction.

Maugham, having already made his muddled way though the wooden door, was surrounded by smiling staff, one trying to take his coat, another pointing the way into the dining room. Marion frowned at him, meaning to set out on her own anyway. But Jeffrey's grip and a glance at the immobile taxi driver, staring at her through the windscreen of the cab, convinced her otherwise.

Hostile, she allowed Jeffrey to lead her into the building, where they joined Maugham at a thick, unvarnished wooden table. Unnecessarily vigorous fire in a stone fireplace. The faintest smell of wet dog. Maugham was already ordering a rabbit pasty.

Jeffrey hung his coat on a hook to the side of the fire and held out his hand to take Marion's. She glared at him and sat across from Maugham, hugging the coat more tightly about her shoulders. Dropped the book in front of her on the table. Stared into the fire. Jeffrey sat next to her, caught the attention of the innkeeper, and ordered them both beer and ham.

Ignoring her sullen expression, Maugham appropriated the guide book, flipped through the pages until he found the ghost stories she'd been marking, and read them aloud to the empty dining room. Chuckling at the more lurid descriptions of the fates of those caught unaware on the moor. Until eventually, he reached a description of an unfortunate city-bred traveler who had been hauled screaming through the night by an angry east wind.

When he'd begun declaiming, Marion had blocked out his voice, choosing instead to nurse her spite at their enforced delay. But now, against her better inclinations, she listened more carefully. Concentrating. The story had snagged at the edges of her mind when she'd first read it that morning. At the time, she hadn't known why. Now, though, hearing it from Maugham, she stiffened.

"Wait," she said. "Read that bit again. About the east wind."

Maugham raised his eyebrows, turned the book, and handed it to her. "My compliments, Dr. Bailey."

She wrinkled her forehead and re-read the passage. And then, she sat back in her chair, thinking. "The east wind is female here. 'She' lifts him off the moor and drags him to his fate."

"Unusual," Jeffrey admitted after a few disappointed seconds. He and Maugham had apparently been hoping for something more. "I've never heard of a feminine east wind."

They stopped talking as the innkeeper's wife arrived with their food, but she'd heard them through the door. Smiling as she arranged their plates in front of them, she spoke to Jeffrey. "It's true, sir. But here, and in the villages nearby, the east wind has always been a lady. We've got the mask over there to prove it."

She lifted her chin in the direction of a round post supporting the room's ceiling, into which an elaborate female face had been carved, her cheeks distended to blow out the wind. Pushing back her chair with a disquieting screech, Marion crossed to the post to examine the mask. It was intricately carved, and very, very worn. She turned back to the innkeeper's wife. "Do you know how old this is?"

"Older than the building, dear. That much we know. The house was constructed around that post. Best not move it, they always say." She set the last glass of beer on the table. "We had a historian in here a few years ago who estimated that it was as early as the sixteenth century. Certainly the seventeenth. There's another out on the moor, same style, same age, though it's made of stone and terribly deteriorated compared to ours—"

"There's a second mask?" Marion had stuffed her fists into the pockets of her coat to steady herself. "Outdoors?"

"Yes, three miles down the hill. On a standing stone. You can't miss it." She rolled back her shoulders. "Visitors in the summer photograph themselves alongside it. It will be a brisker walk this time of year, but the weather ought to hold this afternoon. Don't leave it too late, though. There'll be something coming up in the evening, I can feel it."

"Thank you," Marion said. "That's—that's quite interesting."

"Not at all, dear." She turned to Jeffrey and Maugham. "Anything else, then? No? Enjoy your luncheon."

Nodding affably, she left.

Marion walked back across the room and sat in her chair. The plate of ham on the table in front of her turned her stomach, the smell overwhelming her overwrought sensitivities. "Jeffrey," she said. "That mask isn't English."

He'd cut a piece of ham and was holding it on his fork. "I can see that from here," he said. "Now that she's drawn our attention to it. Fascinating." He put the ham into his mouth and chewed. Swallowed. "What do you reckon? Ilkhanid? From this distance, I might even believe Chinese." He cut another piece of ham. "But yes, I concur. Those are not the traditional facial features of the Dartmoor peasant."

She stood again and paced the room. "How can you eat?"

She refused even to look at Maugham devouring his rabbit.

But neither responded.

"What is wrong with you?" she asked, her voice now shrill. "We can go now. Before dark. She said it's three miles away. You've read the documents, Jeffrey. Hulagu Khan was sung to sleep by a court musician accompanied by *Saba*, the female embodiment of the *east wind*. The lowest musical mode. Lower than human hearing. We've found her." When they simply continued eating, she stalked to the table and stared down at them. "Let's go."

"It's the country air, Dr. Bailey." Maugham had finished his pasty, leaned back in his chair, and folded his hands over his belly. "Leaves one peckish. In fact, I myself am thinking of dessert. I saw a sticky toffee pudding on the board that I can't very well leave behind. You, Willcox?"

"Coffee, Maugham. Thank you."

Marion blinked at them and made for the door. "I'll wait outside."

"Wherever gives you the greatest pleasure," Maugham said to her retreating back. "But do ask our driver if he'd like anything himself. I feel conscious-stricken thinking of him out there, deprived of sustenance in this growing chill."

Shaking her head, enraged, she walked out to the road and stared down the moor in the direction of the standing stone. Then, throwing a venomous look at the taxi driver, who hadn't changed his position, she strode back and forth in front of the inn. Attempting in vain to ward off the creeping cold. She thought she felt an east wind picking up. Classic harbinger of illness, terror, and mayhem. She was frantically curious to learn what that wind was hiding in the midst of all the emptiness stretched out below.

*W*HEN Jeffrey finally exited the inn, exchanging waves and smiles with the innkeeper, Marion was sitting, silent, in the back of the taxi. She'd given up walking to seek protection from the agitated eddies of sharp cold. The sun was also sinking, and she found herself taking a wan comfort in the presence of the driver, close by if taciturn, in the unnerving twilight. She was startled, in fact, when Jeffrey opened the door and peered into the back seat.

"I'm afraid we must walk, dear. No road in the direction we're heading. And, although I know it will disappoint you, Maugham has taken a room upstairs for the night. His days of trekking three miles across a moor in the darkness are behind him." He reached across her and retrieved his briefcase. She hadn't dared touch it in the presence of the driver. "I've got a few torches in here that will help us when the sun sets altogether. It promises to be an exciting outing."

She was equally surprised when the driver—a large man, well over six feet tall—exited the taxi along with her. Apparently, he'd be accompanying them. Additional protection from any headless horsemen, disembodied homicidal hands, or spectral dogs that assaulted them on the walk to the standing stone. Why Maugham and Jeffrey had staged the hike for nighttime she couldn't fathom.

But that question was far from prominent in her mind as they crossed into the wet, needle-thin grass and trudged down the hill. She couldn't contain her excitement. And a little over an hour later, when they'd reached the stone, as conspicuous as the innkeepers had promised it would be, her heart was pounding in her chest. It stood atop a circular mound that could have been natural, but also, quite easily, could have been not. She was pleased enough by the prospect that she could almost ignore the sound of the wind, like a swarm of noxious insects, coming at them from everywhere at once.

Tacitly allowing Marion to take the lead in examining the stone and its surroundings, Jeffrey and the driver stood back, illuminating the smoothly decayed face of the embodiment of the east wind with their torches. It floated just above eye level, cheeks enlarged to produce the breeze. She touched one cheek with her fingertip, shivered, and then cast the light of her own torch on the shorter grass beneath it. Her task would have been easier in the daylight.

Pushing away an unhelpful surge of the annoyance that had trailed her from the inn, she concentrated, walking around the stone and stopping to look more closely at its reverse side. Then she knelt in front of it and pushed her hands through the grass to feel the ground. As she worked, she set aside the torch. The texture of the earth was a more useful guide to her than the watery, white light from the bulb that merely emphasized the darkness of the rest of the moor.

When she'd crawled six or seven feet away from the stone, her hands lacerated in places from the sharp edges of the grass, she paused, intrigued. A square slab of granite, too evenly shaped to be natural, was embedded in the ground. It was obscured by grass and dirt—she wouldn't have seen it, even in daylight. But her fingers could sense its contours, and what she felt excited her.

She didn't want to risk losing contact with the granite by going back for the torch she'd left near the standing stone, and so, keeping her hands on the ground she turned to face Jeffrey and the driver. "Would you come and look at this?" Her voice was nearly inaudible in the wind. "I need assistance."

"Have you found something?" Jeffrey sounded miles away, but it took him less than twenty seconds to pick up her dropped torch and reach her, followed by the obediently plodding driver.

"Yes." She nodded at the stone under her fingertips. "I want to move this rock. Light will help."

He and the driver pointed their torches at the stone, and she ran her abraded fingertips along the edges until she found what felt like two intentionally carved hand holds. Then, taking a breath, she lifted and pulled at the slab, leaning back on her heels as she did so.

The slab moved more easily than she'd expected it to, and she nearly fell over backward. Pausing for a moment, she regained her balance. And then, slowly and carefully, she shifted the granite to the side sufficiently for them to shine a light into the opening. After a cursory inspection with the torches, it became clear that the entire mound on which the east wind's face stood was hollow. It was constructed of two domes—one, a small antechamber, over which they now stood, and one, a larger structure, similar to what she'd seen in Ethiopia. The antechamber mirrored the room from which the monk had emerged before making himself known in Tigray. The viewing area.

A thin, granite stairway wound into the antechamber, from which a fretful, cold gust, a peevish echo of the buzzing wail that assaulted the surface of the moor, seeped. Marion looked a question at Jeffrey, who nodded before handing her a torch. Then, testing her weight on each step, she descended to the floor. Jeffrey and the driver followed behind, lighting the walls and ceiling. The air in the room smelt suffocating, of wet dirt.

After they'd stood in the antechamber for close to a minute, examining the walls as well as they could with their insufficient light, Marion spoke. "This is it. It's identical to what I saw in Ethiopia."

"Good." Jeffrey aimed his torch through the arched door leading to the larger room. "And that's the resonance chamber?"

"Yes." She didn't move. She couldn't go to work until she'd retrieved the inkwell and candlestick. From Jeffrey's briefcase.

He peered through the door. "You're certain that the device is—is aimed inward? It won't affect anyone on the outside?"

"I can't be entirely certain," she said. "But yes, I'm confident that it's directed inward now. Pure resonance. If it were directed outward, we'd have seen evidence of disturbances near the standing stone."

Oddly, Jeffrey turned to the driver, seeking an acknowledgment of the exchange. The driver nodded once, and Jeffrey squatted, set the briefcase on the ground, and opened the lid. He stood and pointed his torch at the contents. "You know best how to proceed, Marion. Take what you need."

Surprised by his forthcoming attitude, she threw him a suspicious glance before kneeling beside the briefcase. She took the bell first and slipped it into the pocket of her coat, hoping that it looked like a move of negligible importance. She didn't think she'd need it, given her intentions, but she felt comforted by the closeness of the Rombulos' defensive weapon. Then, with more confidence, she took the inkwell and candlestick, one in each hand, and stood. "I'm ready."

"Would you like us to accompany you?" Nothing but courteous.

She couldn't believe that he was giving her a choice. Increasingly dubious, she shot him another, longer, appraising look. The only obstacle she'd been unable to work through on the walk over the moor had been how to keep Jeffrey and the driver occupied while she initiated the work of demolition. And yet, here they were, supplying her with ideal circumstances under which to complete her task. She didn't trust it. But when she examined Jeffrey's face in the meagre light, all she saw was concern for her condition and a touch of boredom.

"I'll go in alone." She swallowed. "Less chance of complications if only one of us has access to the mechanism. And you'll be protected in this room. It was built for that purpose. I think the acoustics are—are defensive in here. An audience can sense what's happening but remains unhurt."

Unexpectedly, he put out his hand and brushed a strand of damp hair off her forehead. "You'll be safe? You'll get out in time?"

The contact confused her. She thought abruptly of the bell, forced the thought down before she betrayed its importance, and then nodded. She wouldn't need it. Annoyed by the distraction, she pushed his hand away.

He smiled and reached into his own pocket. "Don't forget these, then."

A white candle and his lighter. She blinked, took them, and turned away from him. Something wasn't right, but she wasn't about to abandon her project now that she was on the verge of finishing it. He was merely trying to keep her unsteady. His default working strategy.

She dropped the lighter and candle into her other pocket, held the candlestick under her arm, and shone the light of the torch into the arched doorway. She walked through it cautiously, although she knew that nothing would be waiting for her on the other side but echoes and emptiness. Deserted acoustic perfection.

When she'd reached the far edge of the chamber, she had a brief, violent recollection of Sheridan's body smeared across the same wall under the dome in Ethiopia. The sludgy remnants of his hand. But she expunged the thought from her consciousness, focusing single-mindedly on making her way to the first wall cavity. She found it easily and investigated it with the torch. Backward, she repeated to herself. She must be certain to insert the first tool backward.

Resolute, wanting now to get the procedure finished, thinking of Lydia asleep in London and Ian preparing for his holiday from his hateful school, she shoved the inkwell into place in the cavity. Backward. It fit perfectly. She thought she could hear, or feel, the pipes under the wall coming into a sort of sucking contact with those in the inkwell. It unnerved her, but not enough to prevent her from walking to the other side of the dome, trailing her fingertips against the wall, until she found the second cavity. *Backward*, she said again. And again. Humming it to herself in her head.

She slid the candlestick into place, backward, with the same sense of something enormous, almost living, stirring beneath her feet. And then, without waiting further, she drew the candle and Jeffrey's lighter from her pocket and pushed the candle into the candlestick. Flicked the lighter. It didn't light. Frustrated, she flicked it two more times until she had a weak flame. Ignored the fact that her hand was shaking as she lit the candle. And then waited.

Three seconds later, she knew that something was wrong. After a blunt heave, she began to suffocate, as though damp sand were being poured into one of her lungs. And a trickle of something liquid drained deep inside her ear. A worrisomely necessary part of her brain turning to water and dripping away. She stumbled back, puzzled. And then, horribly cold. She could no longer see the candle. She must get out of the chamber.

Sensing that this would be her last rational thought until the invisible flame burned down, she twisted in the direction of the arched doorway, pointed her torch, and took half a step. With a popping sound, the torch went out. Startled and unthinking, she dropped it. Fell to her knees to retrieve it. Scrabbling on the ground, crawling in larger and larger circles, feeling for it. But it was nowhere nearby. She'd lost it.

Pushing herself into a half-upright crouch, she took another step in the direction of the doorway before falling to her knees again and screaming for Jeffrey. Nothing came in reply. She couldn't even be certain that she was facing the proper direction. There was only cold and darkness. A blackness like nothing she'd met in her sleeping or waking life.

Panic surged, but before it could overwhelm her, she pushed her hands against her ears and forced what remained of her useful mind to think. If she could find her way to a wall, she could at least demonstrate to herself, with tactile evidence, that she was experiencing a documented scientific effect within the confines of a finite room. The darkness might *seem* boundless, but it was nothing more than a clever mechanism. If she walked, she might even accidentally encounter the door. First, though, she would get herself off her knees.

With brutal determination, she forced herself upright and strode forward. Her hands still uselessly over her ears. Even if she hit herself in the face on the wall, it would be better than existing in this directionless vacuum. And so, ignoring the pressure on her chest and the dripping inside her head, she took five confident steps. Then, confused, her hands groping in front of her, five more. Then, silently counting in her head, she shuffled forward ten half-steps. And then, counting out loud in a thin, sobbing wail, fifty. One hundred. Another fifty. Until she couldn't bear it any longer and stopped. There was no wall. The chamber had given way to nothingness.

She dropped back to the floor, curled herself into a ball, and moaned. It had beaten her. She could do nothing but wait and hope she survived. Before she lost herself entirely, however, a small interior voice reminded her that she had the bell. The defensive weapon that the monk had assured her would add the inaudible high G to the chord. Neutralizing it. Still buckled up on the floor, she reached a tentative hand into the pocket of her coat. Nothing. With tears running down her cheeks, she tried the other pocket. Nothing. Rammed her fingers through the coat's seam. Nothing. Nothing but Jeffrey's fucking lighter.

In despair, she pulled out the lighter and tried to produce a flame, but something, some wind, some unthinkable intelligence, whipped it out of her fingers. She heard it clattering across the floor, a limitless expanse away from her, before it was enveloped in silence. And so then, finally, with no other options, she screamed up at the ceiling. Screamed and screamed. Over and over again. Willing herself to lose consciousness so that whatever was crushing her could finish the job without her awareness or participation.

"That's more than enough of that, I think."

She heard the voice out of a fog that extended from the edge of the moor through her eyes and into her brain. And she whimpered.

"Up you go, Marion. We can't carry you all the way back."

Hands hauling her to her feet, pushing her through the arched doorway. When she gripped the stone lintel above her head, unwilling to release the first material structure she'd felt since the darkness, they peeled her fingertips away and dragged her toward the stairway. Half carried her up onto the moor, where the open space and the shrieking wind brought her to her knees again, crying and clapping her hands over her ears.

"Stop it." He was standing above her. "Or I'll leave you here and collect you in the morning. We haven't further use for you this evening."

His voice touched a remaining intact part of her mind, and she staggered to her feet. She wouldn't survive a night alone in the company of the standing stone.

"Good." He held her arm, and, with the occasional assistance of the driver, they maneuvered her through the grass and back to the inn. Forcing her forward every time she froze in the face of a vicious gust of the east wind.

SOMEHOW, she found herself in an armchair next to a fire in a comfortable room upstairs at the inn. No one had removed her coat, and it still felt damp from the moor. She could remember little of her return from the resonance chamber aside from the wind, the concerned curiosity of the innkeepers—she'd taken a sudden chill, she'd recover—and the malicious curiosity of Maugham upon being deposited in the room.

Now, though, awake and, she thought, sane, she was certain that she'd sustained damage to her mind. Because she was hallucinating. If not, how could she be seeing Jeffrey handing the inkwell, the candlestick, and Eugene's material to Maugham's driver? Speaking to him in Italian? And how could the driver be shaking Jeffrey's hand, thanking him in native Italian? Depositing the objects in a large carrying case and exiting the room?

Jeffrey turned, laughing, to Maugham. "He's made off with your taxi."

"All for the best, my boy." Maugham was sitting in a second, shabby armchair across the fire from Marion. He lifted a poker and stirred the flames. "I'll stay on for a few more days. I've been enjoying the rabbit." Then, eyebrows raised, he leaned forward and looked closely at Marion. "Dr. Bailey has stopped screaming. Dare we hope for lucidity?"

She narrowed bloodshot eyes at Jeffrey. "You gave away my inkwell."

"Returned it to its rightful owner," Jeffrey corrected her, sitting on the edge of an elaborate four-poster bed.

"Who *was* that?" She struggled out of her coat and let it fall in a heap to the ground. It stank of fear.

"Ah yes," Maugham murmured. "Lucid and fractious. All is right with the world." He smiled at Marion. "The innkeepers will be relieved. They run a respectable establishment, and I'm afraid you've pushed them quite beyond their limits. Much as we've tried to explain to them that horror-stricken keening at a gibbous moon is entirely acceptable behavior up in your part of the country."

"*Who was that?*"

"Captain Alvaro. Attached to the Italian Embassy." Jeffrey put his hands behind him on the blanket and leaned back. "Military observer."

"Fuck." She would have felt rage if every chemical in her brain hadn't been tapped out on the moor.

"The Italians were suspicious of our motives," he said. "They wanted a demonstration of the device before they'd agree to negotiate. You supplied a more than adequate one. If you hadn't been making so much noise, you'd have seen Captain Alvaro's ample satisfaction for yourself."

"Oh, fuck." She wanted to cry. But she couldn't summon up tears either. "Jeffrey, they'll use it. They'll *use* it."

"We certainly hope they use it," Maugham said, poking at the fire again. "Otherwise this entire circus will have been for naught."

"What?"

"They'll use it, Marion, with the typical enthusiasm of Graziani's soldiers." Jeffrey hadn't moved. "We've all been watching him, yes? He's not what one would describe as a restrained and cautious man. So, they'll use it," he reached into his pocket and held up her bell, "but they'll use it without an antidote. Which means that three or four or five years from now, when we are inevitably at war with them—perhaps here, perhaps in East Africa, who knows—each and every one of our own people will be carrying one of these, whereas the Italians will be naked. Unprotected. And when we capture the chamber—or chambers, wherever we might encounter them—we'll gain total advantage in the amount of time it takes to light a candle."

She'd stopped listening when she saw the bell. But now that he'd finished, she stared at him, her eyes empty. "You took it from me."

"I traded you for the lighter," he said. "You should have felt it. Though I must admit, I find it adorable that whereas evading an army of surveillance experts across three continents is child's play for you, the pickpocketing techniques of the common street urchin overwhelm your strategic capacities. Someday, we'll be tourists together. I give you my word always to stand careful guard over your handbag."

"It wasn't worth it," she said, ignoring him. "Giving up access to that weapon for some potential—uncertain—military advantage."

"We've achieved more than a military advantage," Maugham replied, closing his eyes, content, in the warmth of the fire. "Of far greater significance, I've got that monkey, Crookshank, detached from my neck. The imbecile thinks he's won. Maneuvered me into negotiating with the Italian government against my inclinations. Thank heaven that's over with." He opened one eye. "Here's hoping he doesn't fall into a mineshaft in the not very distant future."

"But he did win," Marion said, her voice dull. "You *have* negotiated with the Italian Government."

"What happened tonight, Dr. Bailey, was not a negotiation, whatever Captain Alvaro may think. Do you really believe that we want those objects anywhere near what you unearthed out there on the moor?" Appalled. "And then what? When the war begins, we supply every citizen of Devon and possibly Cornwall with a bell that makes no noise, instructing them to tinkle it as loudly as they can when they feel jumpy? They're unhappy enough with gas masks. No, no—far better that Captain Alvaro takes those things with him to the ends of the earth. We want them nowhere near our shores."

"Then why—"

"Look, Marion." Jeffrey seemed tired now. "We needed information. Detail. Before, all we had from Murdoch was a vague sense that there was a device, somewhere in Africa, that could cause harm. We didn't know how it worked, what it did, or even where it was. We supposed that there must be a countermeasure to it, but we couldn't find evidence of that either. Still, though, that supposition left us with an advantage. Murdoch and the Italians were so focused on the weapon itself that it never occurred to them to locate a means of neutralizing it. *All* that interested us was the off-switch."

He pushed his hair off his forehead with one hand. "So yes, we did want a demonstration. But more than that, we wanted to counteract the effects of that hill. I watched you in the chamber. When you began digging about in your pocket, I knew that what I'd suspected before was correct. You'd avoided all reference to the bell during our conversations. The bell was the antidote."

"And so, I took a chance, using it when I entered the room to snuff out the candle. And it worked like a charm. Captain Alvaro was so enthralled by your broken state that he didn't even watch what I was doing." He smiled at her. "For which I thank you. We work well as a team, dear, don't you think?"

She tilted her head back on the chair and closed her eyes. She wanted to sleep for a month. Longer. But a few seconds later, Jeffrey was pulling her up, quiet laughter in his voice. "Come along, darling. Up you go again. It's late, and we must be getting home. Maugham will want to order his evening brandy."

She opened her eyes and looked at him, exhausted. "It's a six-hour journey, Jeffrey."

"All the more reason to be on our way." He lifted her stinking coat from the floor and helped her into it. "But we'll keep well away from the spooks and ghouls. I give you my word."

London, England
April, 1937

Upon her return to London, Marion had slept for twenty hours. She'd had little interest in remaining awake to experience the adrenaline drain that began soon after she'd folded herself into Jeffrey's car, and she'd been grateful that her body had agreed. As her mind had tucked away the more unthinkable memories of what she'd experienced on the moor, she'd remained blissfully unconscious in her bedroom. A willing partner to the most massive act of repression and forgetfulness she'd ever undertaken in a lifetime of repression and forgetfulness. When she'd risen from her bed on the last day of March, she'd felt clean and empty. Free of fever. Prepared to devote herself to Lydia's idiosyncratic grasp of numbers and colors.

Three days later, however, she realized that she'd never be liberated from the project until she'd submitted her report to her superiors. She'd been putting it off, telling herself that having failed so spectacularly, there was little point in rushing the post-mortem. They'd know what had happened. The details were unimportant. And embarrassing.

Eventually, though, sitting at the oak desk in her bedroom, staring at a drenching rain through the window over the side street, she'd begun to write. She'd recorded as much as she could remember—her tone a tad more highly strung than was perhaps appropriate in a document of the sort. And then, at the end, she had told them that the candlestick was her last project. She was finished. She'd then encoded the pages, destroyed the originals, and left the report in one of her drops. Satisfied.

Two days after, the weekend before she and Jeffrey would be collecting Ian for his holiday, she'd been sent instructions for a meeting. Which was only polite. They'd want to end the relationship amicably—as happy as she herself would have been with silence. Freedom and silence.

So now, in the second week of April, she had brought Lydia with her to the park. A bright, cold day. The tulips out in full force, glorying in the opulent mutations that would leave most of them dead by the end of the season. Marion kept Lydia well away from their beds—the Regent's Park horticulturists less understanding than Sheridan had been about toddlers ripping apart their efforts. Instead, she encouraged her daughter to explore the water, disregarding the likely result of such exploration, and perching herself on a nearby bench to wait.

A half hour later, she looked up at a man who had joined her on the bench. Samir. Which surprised her, given that the formulaic acknowledgment of her intentions should have involved a less prominent member of her organization. Certainly not Samir. He was wearing a dark blue, nearly black, spring wool coat, gloves, and no hat. Taking a risk. He shouldn't have been in London at all.

"You needn't have come." She was mumbling, embarrassed, tugging a seam that had begun to unravel along her green wool mittens.

"You can't quit, Marion. You know that." Looking across the expanse of damp grass at Lydia, who was on the edge of braving a lurch into the shallow, nearly freezing water of the lake.

"You can't possibly want to keep me on," she countered. "I've become useless."

"We'll tell you when you're useless." His American accent sounded out of place in the park.

"Samir." She turned to face him. "I'm benefitting the wrong side. With every project, I'm giving more and more to them. It isn't even a nasty joke any longer—this pretense that I'm working for them. I may as well be salaried."

"Hmm. Well, that's obviously up to you. But if you feel that you're being unfairly compensated—"

"Samir," she said, raising her voice. "Stop it. I can't do it anymore. I dislike failure. I don't handle it well. I'm old. I quit."

"You misunderstand our objectives," he replied after a few seconds of silence. "There *is* no wrong side. No opponents. We don't draw battle lines." He gazed sidelong at her. "Do you understand? There's *no enemy*. Instead, there are projects. On occasion, some governments are more accommodating to those projects than others. We pay little attention to their vacillating attitudes."

He stretched his legs in front of him and crossed his ankles. "And so, Marion, we tap you for the projects to which we believe you have the skill and capacity to contribute. Your current project was to locate and prime a reported, but unverified, sonic weapon on the shores of Great Britain. In preparation for what is looking to be a war of extreme proportions."

"I don't—"

"Let me finish."

She swallowed and nodded.

"Not only did you complete that task with remarkable competence and energy, but you also identified—if your report is accurate—similar weapons in Ethiopia, Germany, France, Switzerland, and perhaps also northern China. We're thrilled by your work. It's difficult to imagine an outcome any more successful."

"My job," she said, her voice raw, "wasn't to prime the weapon. It was to destroy it. I failed."

"The Rombulos, perhaps, expected you to destroy the weapon. We didn't. And we certainly never instructed you to do so."

"But—"

"And we never would have instructed you to destroy it because destroying it is self-evidently impossible." He smiled at Lydia, who had wisely taken a few steps back from the water. "Think about it, Marion. There was nothing in the documentation to suggest that the device could be destroyed. You said in your report that the Rombulos had it from their ancestor that doing so was a family legacy. But Pietro Rombulo, if anyone, would have known that it couldn't be done. He sailed all the way to China, and all they could tell him was how to put it to sleep for a few years."

He eyed her again. "If the inkwell and candlestick *had* been the means of sabotaging it, he would have used them himself. Not separated them, burying one in Konya, leaving the other to his descendants in Venice along with a cryptic tapestry, and then founding a monastery in Mekelle on the myth that the monks there were all waiting for the sublime moment when they'd grind the thing into the ground."

He shook his head. "No, that was obfuscation. He wanted to throw sufficient dust into the air to prevent anyone from resurrecting the trail to the device itself. And it worked. For five hundred years. Until we put you on the scent."

"You lied to me." Her voice was tired. "And you've lost the inkwell and candlestick. They're in Italy now. Ethiopia. Who knows? You've failed too."

"We always lie to you," he said. "And we haven't failed. Because, as you know perfectly well, we also lie to others. Others, in this case, who have excavated similar inkwells and similar candlesticks from all sorts of interesting places in their respective fields of expertise. Five resonance chambers you found. At least. Perhaps more. Did you really think there was only one set of tools to activate them?"

He stood and dusted down his coat. "So yes, go ahead and feel indignant that we kept your *particular* inkwell and your *particular* candlestick separate without telling you why. That's your right. But then," he looked down at her still sitting on the bench, "imagine if we hadn't separated them, and you'd been tempted by the monk's story to 'demolish' the machinery in Ethiopia. You'd be a lot more than resentful right now, wouldn't you?"

She stood as well. "I would have followed my instructions. If you'd trusted me."

"Perhaps. Perhaps not. You're a complicated read." He straightened his gloves. "But your instructions now are simple. Recuperate. Await further orders. Contact will come as usual."

She looked away from him toward Lydia, who was gathering her courage for another assault on the water. Then, her irritation growing again, she turned back to him. "Samir, I can't—"

But he was gone. No evidence of him across the expanse of the park. He'd disappeared. Swallowing her remark, she picked her way down the slope toward Lydia. Took her daughter's wet, mittened hand to lead her back in the direction of Jeffrey's house. Wondered whether it was too early to begin drinking. And decided that, emphatically, it was not.

Russia, 1937

London, England
October, 1937

SHE couldn't blame Jeffrey. After all, she didn't need a rucksack or wellingtons for a half-hour walk through the dry, dead leaves of Regent's Park. And her leave-taking of Lydia had been, despite her best professional intentions, effusive. Excessive. She was almost grateful to him for stopping her.

Not that her timing wasn't unfortunate. She'd have been out of Chester Terrace and on her invisible way without mishap if he hadn't returned unusually early from the office. Running into her like something out of Fred Karno just as she'd crossed the threshold of the house. He'd taken one look at her face, as startled as she'd been by the encounter, before appropriating the rucksack and helping her back through the door.

He'd then removed his hat, overcoat, and gloves, still holding the straps of her bag in one hand, and gestured her toward the stairs. Allowed her to walk in front of him to the floor above. Now, she was sitting on the worn leather sofa of his study, watching as he removed and examined each item of her hastily assembled luggage. Still wearing her boots and her waxed cloth Belstaff jacket. She'd received her instructions only three hours earlier; her packing had been haphazard.

Stifling a sigh, she let her gaze wander from Jeffrey, still wearing his repressive banker's suit as he arranged her possessions on his desk, to his closed briefcase on the floor by his feet, to the tall windows at the far end of the room. The curtains were open, and she watched, vacant, as a small, cold sun sank over the park. A shaft of light hit the surface of the desk just as he was finishing his inspection.

He squinted, irritated, left the empty rucksack hanging from the back of his equally imposing chair, and strode across the room to close the curtains. Then, still without speaking, he returned to a cabinet behind the desk, opened it, found a bottle of scotch, and poured them both drinks. He set hers on the coffee table in front of her, went back to his desk, took up a book he'd liberated from her rucksack, lifted his own glass, and sat in an armchair across from her. Tossed the book onto the table between them. Sipped his drink.

"Aristophanes. *Birds.*"

She nodded and tried to decide whether she could endure the conversation without alcohol. It was early in the evening yet, and she wanted her wits about her should another opportunity to depart present itself. Or, at the very least, should she find herself spending the next few hours with Lydia.

"Not your preferred light reading, I would have thought." He watched for a reaction. "Smutty."

Rather than replying, she blinked, half-noticing that his brushed-back blond hair was showing more grey than it had when last she'd thought about it. Reached for her own glass. Took a small swallow. Placed it on the table.

"Refreshing your Attic Greek, are you?"

"Yes. Why not?"

He put his glass next to the book and located a cigarette case in the inside pocket of his suit jacket, which he hadn't yet unbuttoned. Opened the case and selected a cigarette. Snapped the lid shut and returned it to his pocket. Then he lit the cigarette with a match and dropped the match into an ashtray he'd pulled over from her side of the table. Exhaled smoke. "I notice you've got a few pages of Evliya Çelebi's seventeenth-century travelogue stashed in there as well. His journey through the northwest Caucasus Mountains."

"Yes," she repeated. "*Why not?* Perhaps my Ottoman Turkish needs work too."

"You're going after Mr. Fyffes." He unbuttoned his jacket and relaxed into the chair.

She collected herself for a short moment. And then she gave up and grabbed her glass. Drained it. Left it empty on the coffee table and waited for the warmth to reach her stomach. It was useless to try to mislead him. Clear from his line of questioning that he already knew as much as she did about her assignment. Perhaps more. In fact, if she kept him talking, she might learn something. "Yes."

"You plan to run him down in Devon?"

"Yes."

"When did you receive your instructions?" He set his burning cigarette in the ashtray, stood, retrieved the bottle of scotch, and refilled her glass. Put the half-full bottle between them on the table.

"I took Lydia out to lunch a few hours ago." She wrapped her arms around her waist. "I also wanted to purchase something comforting for Ian now that you've incarcerated him in that hellhole for the foreseeable future."

"Eton," he said. "The hellhole is called Eton, dear."

"Yes. Eton. The hellhole." She lifted her glass and took another large swallow. Waiting now for it to dull her mind as well as her anger. "The courier crossed me then. It was—abrupt."

"Hmm." He nodded. "Your people must be on the same schedule as ours. Lucky I caught you."

She stared across at him, stony.

"Fancy a few days in Chelsea?" Bland. "We can't have you killing him, Marion. And I haven't the resources to keep you in place here—"

"I have no intention of killing him—" She stopped when she saw his face. Better to have let him believe that her assignment was a straightforward elimination. He'd tricked her. Again.

"You were saying?" He lifted his glass and took a small sip.

"Nothing."

"Shall I tell you about our own relationship with Mr. Fyffes?" he asked. "It might save you a journey to Devon. Wretched time of the year to go casting about on the downs in search of an eccentric Englishman who enjoys digging himself into rabbit burrows for months at a time under the bizarre impression that no one can see him. Especially if you *don't* intend to kill him afterward."

She thought for a few seconds, wondering how much she'd need to drink before his tone no longer provoked her. More than remained in the bottle, she suspected. Stifled another sigh. "Why would you tell me anything at all?"

"As I said, Marion, your people and mine appear to be working on the same schedule. At cross purposes, no doubt. But on the same schedule. It will save time if we pool our information. You'll have ample opportunity to thwart us later." He retrieved his cigarette and inhaled. "And Maugham wants you involved."

She didn't want to think about Maugham. Kept silent.

"Why else do you suppose I returned early today?" he persisted. "If not to make you an offer?"

He crushed out his cigarette in the ashtray. Looked across at her, mild and inquiring.

"Fine." She drained the glass a second time, reached for the bottle, and poured herself another few fingers. A trifle unsteady. Better to hear what he had to tell her, even if it was lies. "What's Fyffes to you, then?"

"An unwitting homing pigeon," he replied. "Same as he is to you. In fact," he reached into the pocket of his suit jacket and extracted two folded sheets of paper, "our courier retrieved this for you along with his own messages. In the interest of collegiality, and all that."

He set the papers on the table in front of her.

"Oh." She gazed down at them. Strings of Greek letters. Written across what looked to be the pages of a twenty- or thirty-year-old Ottoman-Turkish novel. They were almost certainly what she'd been tapped to collect. But she didn't want to appear too eager. Didn't touch them. Glanced up at him instead. "How did your courier get them?"

"Mr. Fyffes was distracted by his cat at the time. Simple extraction." He leaned back, holding his glass on the arm of his chair without drinking.

"His cat."

"Hmm." He ran a fingertip along the rim of his glass. "Mr. Fyffes keeps a feral cat with him in the ditch he's dug for himself on the downs. He believes that he and the cat share a special communion. Which means, among other things, that Mr. Fyffes spends quite a lot of time staring into the middle distance. Or, obviously, at the cat. Fails to notice when professionals are pilfering his papers."

"Oh." She was beginning to wish that she'd had a bit less to drink.

"Let me begin at the beginning, darling. You're looking demoralized." He considered for a few seconds. "And the beginning, as perhaps you're already aware, is Joseph Stalin."

He waited for a moment, watching her closed expression, and then nodded. "Yes. I can see that you *are* aware. But shall we fill in the background of Mr. Fyffes's recent adventures nonetheless? To be certain that we're on the same page?"

"Fine."

He sipped again from his still nearly untouched drink. "Stalin has been suffering recently from the pressures of his position. Great man, great responsibilities, a very great deal of paranoia, he's taken to recuperating with ever longer holidays on the Great Soviet Seaside. Sochi, on the eastern shore of the Black Sea, at the foot of the northwest Caucasus Mountains, has become his spa town of choice. So much so, in fact, that last year he commissioned a dacha for himself there. Surrounded by wilderness. And also by eight or nine cordons of the tightest security in Europe and Asia at the moment. You're familiar with both the dacha and the measures that have been taken to protect it?"

"Yes." She wanted to examine the papers on the coffee table more closely, but she forced herself to avoid looking at them. Held his eyes, sullen. What Jeffrey was telling her wasn't new.

"Good." He tapped the top of his glass. "Then you'll also know that when they broke ground on the dacha this past year, they encountered difficulties. Almost at once. Unusual difficulties. Abnormally large swarms of insects interfering with their work. Packs of wildlife digging at the building's foundations. Not to mention what our people inside Stalin's security forces have reported to us as elusive human spectators that, despite their menacing presence, no one could see, much less collect."

"Yes."

"All of these difficulties came to an abrupt halt when the builders stumbled across a cache of fifth- or fourth-century BC Greek pottery fragments—along with one perfect, unbroken vase—at the edge of their site." He took another sip of his drink. "When the vase was raised and cleaned, the interference evaporated. Spectators returned to their place of origin, wherever that might be. And construction came to a peaceful conclusion."

She nodded without speaking.

He smiled at her lack of response, set his glass on the coffee table, and rose from the chair. Then he retrieved his briefcase, opened it, and extracted an object wrapped in a linen sack. Removed the sack and put the object on the table beside his glass. "This vase."

"Oh."

She couldn't keep from staring. It was a small example of its type, perhaps ten inches tall. Black. Stylized orange and white figures enacting a dramatic scene around its circumference. Bird-like men interacting with the classic Athenian representation of Scythian archer-slaves imported from the Caucasus Mountains and eastern Black Sea.

The bird-men were speaking lines that she recognized from Aristophanes. And the Scythians were speaking conventional barbarian gibberish. Although, she realized as she stole a quick glance at the papers Jeffrey had shown her earlier, the gibberish letters were identical to those her people had copied and attached to Mr. Fyffes. Why not drop her vase instead, she wondered. And what was it about the modern Ottoman-Turkish pages themselves that bothered her?

"Please extend our apologies to your superiors, Marion."

"What?" She looked up at him.

"They did want to dispatch you the vase itself. Rather than those tatty paper copies of it." He looked smug. "But our own man pinched it from your envoy before she'd managed to smuggle it out of the dacha."

She was more annoyed that he'd so easily followed her line of thought than by the commentary on her colleague's skill. Tried to school her expression. And also, lowering her eyes again, tried to determine why the pages, almost more than the vase or the letter strings, irritated her subconscious—

"And into all of this excitement," he interrupted her meditation, "stumbled Mr. Fyffes."

"Right." She shook her head, clearing it of the confusion. If there was a connection to be made, it would come to her.

"By the time he arrived, Stalin's security people were well and truly spooked by the atmosphere surrounding the dacha. The animal swarms and the ghostly witnesses to the building's construction had mostly gone, it's true. But then, so had the vase. Which pointed to at least one or two remaining holes in their cordon. And more than that, there was a sense, still, of someone watching. Waiting. Not Mr. Fyffes, of course." A flicker of embarrassment passed over his face. "In fact, when Mr. Fyffes began blundering about in the woods on his 'big game hunt,' they were more relieved than otherwise. Something, finally, that they could intercept and interrogate."

"Big game hunt?"

"Yes." He drank the remainder of his scotch and placed the glass on the coffee table. "It's unclear to us—or to anyone else, for that matter—whether Mr. Fyffes genuinely can't distinguish between, say, an elephant and an authoritarian dictator, or whether he's thinking metaphorically. But in the end, the question is academic. Every year or so, he gets it into his head to go after one or the other with a rifle. Calls it 'big game hunting.' Everyone knows his proclivities so it's mostly harmless."

He paused for a moment. "Although the Foreign Secretary does send a polite warning to those with an interest in such things when he's been informed that Mr. Fyffes is on the prowl. But even that's primarily for form's sake. I don't believe Mr. Fyffes has once got off a shot. And my understanding is that the totalitarian security forces think of him as a kind of roving training drill. They look forward to his appearances when hunting season comes round."

"Why do you let him travel?" She knew that the question was irrelevant, but she couldn't help asking. "Why not take his rifle?"

"Mr. Fyffes is heir to one of the oldest estates in England." He reached into his pocket for his cigarette case. "Depriving him of his rifle would offend his ancestral gods."

"He's mentally incompetent. He buries himself in rodent warrens."

He removed and lit another cigarette. Returned the case to his pocket. "Your point?"

"Fine." The eccentricities of Mr. Fyffes were no longer of interest to her now that she wouldn't be tracking him in Devon. "So Fyffes chose a sensitive time to go waving his rifle about at Stalin. Then what?"

"They picked him up a few miles away from the dacha." He took a drag of the cigarette. "Brought him inside. Roughed him up a bit. He enjoys that too. Reminds him of his school days, he tells people."

She shoved away an image of Ian enduring Eton. "And?"

"And," he said, "according to our informant, Stalin's security people were shocked to discover that Mr. Fyffes had useful, viable information on him. He himself didn't know that, of course. If he had, he would have held out until they killed him—a dream come true. But instead, he let slip that some 'damned fool girl' had gotten in the way of his shot. If not, he insisted, he'd have taken down Koba easily. End of Soviet problem."

"A girl?" Her own courier hadn't mentioned a girl. But she didn't want to tip her hand to Jeffrey. "What sort of girl?"

"Unclear." He examined the tip of his cigarette. "But they weren't taking any chances. They scoured the forest surrounding the dacha until they found her. Or, at least, evidence of her. An enormous swarm of bees."

"What?"

"Indeed. The soldiers were sufficiently intimidated by its size to hesitate." He inhaled smoke. Exhaled up at the ceiling. "Just long enough for the girl, who'd been hiding in their midst, to shout something incomprehensible and disappear. At which point the bees also dispersed. No more girl. No more insects."

"They don't know what she said?" Marion rubbed her eyes. "That's farfetched. Are you certain your contact wasn't holding back on you?"

"Our contacts know better than to hold back." He smiled, impish. "You're merely peeved that he succeeded with his drop when yours failed."

She held his look. Silent.

"Most of Stalin's security forces are Russian," he relented. "They identified the girl's speech as Abkhaz. Western Caucasian, yes?"

"Oh."

"But an Abkhaz servant who allowed our man inside to interrogate him disagreed." He took another drag of the cigarette. "He was close enough to hear the girl, and he said that what she shouted was likely related to other languages of the northern Caucasus, but it wasn't a dialect he'd heard. And it certainly wasn't Abkhaz. He didn't share his thoughts with Stalin's security."

"And Fyffes?" She was staring again at the vase. Trying to piece together a narrative from what Jeffrey was telling her and what her own people had passed to her that afternoon.

"They dropped him in the woods." He crushed out his cigarette. "Let him think he'd eluded their attention as he limped back to the bay and stole a dinghy they'd left for him at the dock. Red sails, but Mr. Fyffes failed to appreciate the irony. Then, from the dinghy, he talked himself onto a merchant vessel that the Foreign Office had anchored offshore for that purpose, and—"

"Surely," she interrupted, "he wouldn't have believed that this string of good luck was pure coincidence. Were his suspicions not raised when there was an empty stateroom waiting and available for his supposedly clandestine use on his return journey?"

"Well." Embarrassed again. "They did offer him a stateroom. But he preferred less comfortable accommodation. Mr. Fyffes returned to London in an empty freshwater tank on deck. With the cover screwed down."

"What?"

"The second mate unscrewed it every few days to drop him food."

"*What?*"

"Marion," he said, "you're losing track of the relevant points of the story. Mr. Fyffes, regardless of his colorful travel arrangements, fulfilled his role as pack animal. The messages of both your contacts and ours—I'll leave ours to the side for now—have returned intact. And those messages are provocative, yes? Focus, dear, on what I'm telling you."

He gestured to the coffee table. "We have in front of us," pointing, "this classical Greek vase, those pages your people saw fit to copy from that vase, and an invisible girl who is almost certainly not Abkhaz possessed of a way with bees. Not to mention some jumpy Soviet security forces in Sochi." He paused. "What do you make of it?"

"There's more," she said. "What aren't you telling me?"

"You first."

"No."

"Always so bloody difficult. Very well. Our hypothesis is that the girl and her people are protecting some sort of object—or information—of interest to the Museum. The vase is part of it. But we believe there's more. A cache of artifacts, most likely. We think it might have something to do with the Nart Sagas. Caucasian equivalent of the Arthurian Legends, you know?"

"Why?"

He sighed. "You're relentless. Two additional points of interest, then. The first you've likely already considered. The Scythians on that vase are the ancestors not only of certain pockets of Iranians, but also of the populations of the northwestern Caucasus. At least, what's left of those populations since the Russians exterminated them in the 1860s. Their speech has remained unchanged through millennia of alien incursions. Which means, in turn, that the barbarian gibberish that this slave-archer is speaking is, at the very least, related to the languages that may or may not persist in the mountains beyond Sochi. Abkhaz, yes. But also dialects that wouldn't be familiar to a quasi-civilized Abkhaz-Soviet house servant."

She nodded and lifted the pages her people had sent her. Examined the strings of Greek letters. Peered at the essentially identical strings on the vase. A few stray gammas and thetas that the courier had failed to copy. But, even on the vase, the letters didn't look to her like a recognizable speech pattern, barbarian or otherwise.

Thoughtful, she put the pages back on the coffee table. "You believe that the barbarian speech represented on this vase is a transliteration into Greek letters of an actual Scythian language? Old speech of the northern Caucasus? And that the girl may have been speaking something like it? Hence the connection to—to ancient myths and treasures and—and the sort of objects that interest the Museum?"

"No," he said. Then he corrected himself. "That is, yes, there are theories floating about that the Scythian gibberish written in Greek letters in classical sources may have been a phonetic reproduction of what slaves from the eastern Black Sea were saying. But if that is true, this vase is not an example of it. Maugham has let his Classicists loose on it. They're certain. The letters attributed to the Scythians on this vase—and, incidentally, on your pages—aren't meaningful speech. They may be something else. The fact that your courier took the trouble to copy them, attach them to Mr. Fyffes, and dispatch them to you has certainly convinced Maugham that they are."

She lifted the pages again, puzzled. Didn't respond to his accusation. She thought she might now recognize their provenance—not the provenance of the letters, but of the pages—and she was becoming excited. But she kept her eyes downcast to keep from betraying her state of mind. If she was correct, the pages were as important as the information written on them.

"Anything you'd care to contribute, Marion?" His voice was once again bland.

She looked up at him. "No."

"I have a feeling you'll change your mind on that soon."

"Try me."

He smiled. "Second point of interest, then. A spot of luck at the office. When Maugham was tapping volunteers to decode that Greek letter string, he chanced upon one of our more intelligent and ambitious cataloguers."

"One of your 'cataloguers.'"

"Yes. One of our 'cataloguers.'" He threw her a mocking frown, leaned forward, and retrieved the vase. Turned it gently in his hand, examining it. "Fresh out of Trinity. Eager to prove his mettle. He'd been released into one of the more bewildering sections of the Baquba collection as an initiation rite. To determine what he was made of."

She tightened her lips, but otherwise she didn't respond.

Jeffrey himself kept his expression blank. "It was pure coincidence. The boy had been working his way through a series of medieval Arabic translations of classical Greek literature. Most of it was in scraps, but he'd been astonished only the day before by what looked to be a complete Arabic translation of *Birds* by Aristophanes."

"Oh." She hated that the discovery of a manuscript of that sort had happened under the auspices of the office. But she was intrigued, despite herself, that such a text might exist at all. She dropped her eyes again. Remained quiet.

"There's more," he said.

"Oh?" Her gaze still averted.

"This Scythian slave," turning the image on the vase toward her downcast eyes, "is reproduced precisely, in detail, on the margin of the first folio of the manuscript." He paused. "As is this string of gibberish Greek letters."

She stared at him. "But that vase is—is—"

"Fifth- or fourth-century BC. Yes."

"And the Arabic Aristophanes?"

He put the vase on the coffee table. "We think eleventh-century. Certainly no earlier than the ninth. There's a tag in the same handwriting by Hunayn ibn Ishaq, who died—"

"In the 870s. Yes." She was stunned by the implications. "So that Scythian archer and those Greek letters were recorded and copied over a—a thousand years?"

"There's more."

"*More?*" She chastised herself for failing to keep herself closed off, but she couldn't help it. His information was extraordinary.

"The Arabic translation of *Birds* is bound together with two additional manuscript fragments." He paused. Teasing.

"Yes?" Impatient. "And those are?"

"One is a very short section of Evliya Çelebi's travelogue. His *Seyahatname*." He glanced behind him at the detritus from his rucksack piled up on his desk. "Not that nineteenth-century bastardization you've got there, but a pristine set of passages from some as-yet unknown seventeenth-century copy. Only a few lines, though. His description of the languages of the northwestern Caucasus."

"Oh." She turned her attention to his briefcase, waiting for him to retrieve the folios. Clenching her fists in her lap.

"And then there's the third fragment," he continued.

"Yes?" Straightening her fingers out over her knees. Slowly. Painfully.

"A poem by Shams al-Din Muhammad Ibn Daniyal." He watched her face.

She frowned. The name was familiar to her, but she knew next to nothing about him. "He wrote shadow plays, didn't he? In Mamluk Cairo in the late thirteenth century. What does he have to do with the Caucasus?"

"We aren't certain." Jeffrey was still smiling at her in an unreadable manner. "But I know that you'll adore his poetry, Marion. Evocative language. Moving. *And,* the fact that all these passages— eleventh-, thirteenth-, and sixteenth-century—are concerning themselves with what Stalin's hapless security people dug up in Sochi leads us to speculate that, yes, there's something bigger there. Something worth investigating. Something, as I mentioned before, that our specialists believe may have to do with the distant and mythic, if perhaps bawdy, past."

She ignored his tone. Whatever was entertaining him, it wasn't relevant to her assignment. "Fine, Jeffrey. You win. I'll stay here and look over Maugham's material." She glanced back over at his briefcase. "I'll start tonight. I'll take it up to my room."

"I haven't got it here."

"What do you mean you haven't got it here?" The warmth from the scotch had dissipated, and now all she felt was the beginning of a dull headache. She wanted a cigarette, but she couldn't bring herself to ask him for one. She wished, just once, that they could have a conversation that didn't leave her feeling demolished.

"It's with Maugham." He retrieved the vase, her pages, and his briefcase and stood. Walked with them to his desk and, still standing, began wrapping the vase to replace in his briefcase. "In Chelsea."

She jumped to her feet. "Absolutely not."

He half shrugged. "Your decision, dear. If you'd rather make your way to Mr. Fyffes on the downs this evening, I'll not stop you a second time. Do try to avoid a chill."

She stared at him for five long seconds. And then, aiming for a reasonable tone, she spoke again. "Why not in the Library, Jeffrey? I'll read the material in Maugham's office. You'll watch. It will be safe."

"No." He snapped the briefcase shut and looked up at her. "Chelsea."

"*Why?*"

"Maugham wants you involved," he said. "But he doesn't want you anywhere near Stalin, the Black Sea, or the Caucasus. Your previous jaunts through the region have left him skittish. And when Maugham feels skittish, people like you find themselves on a short lead." He re-buttoned his suit jacket. "Not that I blame him given what happened the last time you ventured in that direction."

She pressed her fists into her eyes, thinking. Unable to summon up a useful response.

"Well?" Jeffrey remained standing behind his desk, his briefcase in hand. Ready to leave. "I must admit, Marion, were I in your position, I'd have been out the door and on my way to hole up with Mr. Fyffes in Devon ten minutes ago. Succumbing to this sort of temptation never ends well for you. You can't have forgotten."

She dropped her arms to her side. Held his eyes. "Fine. I'll come with you."

"To Chelsea?" He walked to the door, opened it, and stood to the side.

"Yes."

He smiled. "I thought so."

THE depot looked as sinister in the moonlight as it had when last she'd been stored there just after giving birth to Lydia. And the time before that, on her first return from Iraq. A stolid, squalid eighteenth-century terrace house, its desperate respectability only made what happened within its walls more horrific. But at least this time she was walking through the front door rather than being dragged, or wheeled, semi-conscious into the basement.

The five-storey building crouched at the edge of a row of dull, brick townhouses, a small, dead garden at the front and a failed attempt at sickly pink michaelmas daisies at the back. A laurel hedge blocking the ground-floor windows faced the street. The neighbors would have been the sort to wonder at the noise—and smell—that escaped the property, if the office hadn't taken the precaution of buying up all the adjacent houses in the row as well. Along with those on the streets parallel to it.

All of which meant that the optimistic recent construction in the area hadn't affected the depot. It remained the same dreary, blank edifice it had been in the 1770s when Maugham's predecessors had purchased it from a bankrupt, development-inclined brewer as a convenient holding pen for talent that couldn't be killed, but that also couldn't be allowed to circulate. Marion tasted something nasty in the back of her throat as Jeffrey waited for the pallid guard, a fixture of the building, to respond to their appearance outside the main entry.

When the guard had welcomed Jeffrey and cast a blank look at Marion, he indicated the narrow, thinly carpeted stairway to the right of the hall. "Fourth floor. Rear rooms. He's expecting you, Sir Jeffrey."

"Thank you, Mr. Leonard." Jeffrey stood to the side to allow Marion to precede him up the stairs.

As she climbed, she fought down a compulsion to turn, push Jeffrey to the side, and flee into the street. The back rooms at the top of the house were where they'd kept her on previous visits when they weren't working on her in the basement. If they'd simply wanted her to look over the manuscripts, they could have presented them to her in one of the public areas. Or at least in a room that didn't throw her into a panic. She didn't trust the scene they were setting. But, climbing past the third floor, Jeffrey uncomfortably close behind her, she forced herself to ignore the growing scent of damp cloth, old sweat, and the metallic hint of blood. She had no choice.

The door to the back rooms was cracked open when they reached it. It had been repurposed to swing outward, rather than inward, and it was fitted with an assortment of heavy locks. No handle or knob on the inside. Jeffrey pulled it further open and stood to the side again. Stumbling, she passed him into the low-ceilinged sitting area. A small window with discreet bars that couldn't be seen from the outside. Awkward, oddly angled walls that defied perspective. Dirty pink wallpaper that also covered the ceiling. And three mismatched, cheap lamps on low tables, all of which were on. Through the narrow doorway on the right, missing the door itself, Marion knew there was a tiny, windowless bedroom and an even tinier water closet.

Sitting in one of the four flimsy chairs placed around the decrepit table that occupied the greater part of the room, was Maugham. Wearing his spectacles and his customary look of corpulent, childlike malice. Fiddling with a cigarette lighter uncomfortably close to the brittle pages of what had to be the Baquba manuscript. A sheaf of writing paper and a pencil to the side.

He dropped the lighter and rose, genial and smiling, when they entered. Pursed his lips and took in the boots and Belstaff jacket that Marion was still wearing. "Apologies, Dr. Bailey, for dragging you away from the International Six Days Trial. Marjorie Cottle and her Triumph Tiger will feel your absence."

She ignored him, noted that there was, at least, a text on the table, and then glanced about the room. A neatly dressed, composed woman with smooth dark hair, middle-forties, was rising from a fifth chair in a dim corner. Margot Shields. Gracious, courteous, and one of the more frighteningly effective of the depot's interrogators, she gave Marion a sympathetic half-smile. From what Jeffrey had let drop, Margot had the most impressive record of Maugham's staff. And she never, ever used violence.

"Good evening, Margot." Jeffrey left his hat and gloves on one of the narrow tables just inside the door. Retained his coat against the room's chill.

"Good evening, Sir Jeffrey. Dr. Bailey." Margot, who was holding a writing pad and a pencil of her own, moved her chair further toward the table into the light, and sat again.

Jeffrey held out a chair for Marion, who sat as well, and then he settled himself beside Maugham. He put his briefcase on the table, opened it, and arranged the vase, the two pages from Fyffes, and Marion's copy of *Birds* next to the manuscript. Then he closed the briefcase, placed it on the ground by his feet, and looked, polite, at Maugham.

"The 18th of March, 1920." Maugham adjusted his spectacles. "Any thoughts, Dr. Bailey?"

She stared at him for a few seconds, mystified. "What?"

"March of 1920," he repeated. "Where were you?"

"I was at Cambridge." She wrinkled her forehead. "I'd received my D.Phil. in 1918, two years before. In 1920 I was working as Professor Dickinson's research assistant." She swallowed. Refused to look at Jeffrey. "I left in 1921."

Maugham and Jeffrey exchanged a glance. Then Maugham removed the spectacles and cleared his throat. "Let's try a different approach, shall we? Slower. Meandering. Perhaps it will jog your memory."

He gazed up at the ceiling. "In the spring of 1918, Enver Pasha, the Ottoman Empire's Minister of War and *de facto* leader, was celebrating an event nearly as momentous as the completion of your well-earned D.Phil. The founding, under his patronage, of the 'Northern Caucasus Political Society,' which he believed would act as a flashpoint for a new and glorious independence movement on the eastern shores of the Black Sea—a movement resistant to Russia and protected by the Ottomans."

She continued to gape at him, blank and confused.

"This dream," he continued, ignoring her empty reaction, "was not realized, obviously, given that the Russians had eradicated the native inhabitants of the region sixty years before, and that those who survived had emigrated almost in their entirety to Turkey. Not to mention that by the spring of 1918, the Ottoman Empire was—and largely thanks to Enver Pasha's earlier expansionist fantasies—dead. But Enver was never one to let logic, common sense, or indeed sanity stand in the way of his ambitions."

He paused, examined her face, and then pressed on, genial and pleasant, when she remained baffled. Shoving the spectacles into his pocket. "It also helped his cause that the Ottoman intelligence service at the time was both led, and disproportionately staffed, by the sons of the previous century's north Caucasian refugees. Indeed, it's possible that they prodded him, now and then, in the proper direction."

She blinked. "Yes. All right."

He twirled the lighter on the table. "Five or six months after initiating his pet project, Enver Pasha was obliged to drop it. Flee Entente-occupied, post-War Turkey. A romantic exile, he travelled first to Germany. And then, amusingly, to Russia, where he sold his services to the Soviets. Exit Enver."

He glanced over at her again. "But the Northern Caucasus Political Society, not to mention the Caucasian-flavored Ottoman, and now Turkish, intelligence community, flourished even in his absence. And a little over a year later, in January of 1920, a leader of the self-described 'Mountainous Republic of the Northern Caucasus'—one of the few left once the Russians had finished with them—approached Turkey's new *de facto* leader, Mustafa Kemal, later Atatürk, with a proposal. Atatürk, though three years away from proclaiming the Republic of Turkey, had, it seems, an aura of future influence about him. Unlike Enver, whose exploits by that time had acquired a whimsical Baron Munchausen quality."

She frowned. Unhappy with the direction the conversation was taking. But convinced now that she'd been correct in her appraisal of Fyffes's pages. She raised her eyes to Maugham's. "Yes. I've read something about that."

"Have you, Dr. Bailey?" He beamed at her. "Delighted to hear it." He furrowed his brow again, thoughtful. "No one is certain what this diplomat and Atatürk discussed. But the result of the conversation was a delegation of Turkish statesmen, composed primarily of members of the north Caucasian diaspora, that left for The East in February of 1920."

"Yes." She dropped her eyes to the tabletop. "I remember."

"A sort of cultural reconnaissance mission to determine the likely success of a nativist revolution in the mountains. From what we understand." Maugham flipped open the lighter and snapped it shut again. "They moved from Tbilisi in Georgia, to Baku in Azerbaijan, to Dagestan, and then by March of 1920, they were in Chechnya."

He turned wide, innocent eyes to Marion. "But Dr. Bailey, my original question remains: where were *you* in March of 1920?"

"Not in Chechnya."

"You also weren't in Cambridgeshire." He relaxed into his seat and folded his hands over his stomach. "Willcox remembers your absence."

"I may have been conducting research—"

"In Maykop?" Jeffrey was leaning forward now, his elbows on the table, his chin in his hands. "Up north in the Caucasian Republic of Adygea? Because that's where our source puts you on the 18th of March, 1920."

She twisted toward him. "Maykop is three hundred miles away from Chechnya. Which is it? Or are you suggesting I was in both at the same time?"

"No one is suggesting that you were in Chechnya, Dr. Bailey." Maugham hadn't moved, his hands still relaxed over his belly. "I said that the Turkish delegation was in Chechnya. You—well, we've yet to establish your whereabouts. I was merely providing you with context."

"Context for *what*?" She rubbed her temples with her fingertips. "This is a bizarre exchange, even for the two or you."

"The mission of the Northern Caucasus Political Society was, shall we say—elastic," Maugham continued, tapping an index finger against his stomach. "Bits and pieces of it broke off here and there. To pursue alternative, and less well-advertised, goals. For example, three delegates of Abkhaz descent travelled northwest, rather than northeast, once they'd reached Tbilisi. They disappeared. Certainly never reached Chechnya. Their colleagues presumed them dead."

Marion gazed down at the pages on the table in front of her. Wrinkled, dirty, and creased, they were nonetheless recognizable to her now. More than recognizable. Wrenching. Lines from a collection of Reşat Nuri Güntekin's short stories that had been published in Ottoman Turkish in 1919. She'd brought the book with her from Istanbul to read on the journey. And then, on a whim, she'd given it to her colleague, Ismail, before he and his two compatriots had left to explore the mountains to the north. Where they'd died.

She hadn't thought about him for decades. Although she'd tried, half-heartedly, to find him along the edges of the region in the weeks after he'd gone missing. Washing up, eventually, in Maykop. Whence she'd returned to Cambridge only to find Jeffrey attached to her mentor, Ronald Dickinson. Marking the end of her academic career.

Jeffrey startled her by covering the pages on the tabletop with his hand and moving them away from her. Lifting them and examining them himself. "You seem lost in thought, Marion."

She swallowed. "What does any of this have to do with—with that vase?" She pointed. "With the Aristophanes translation? With Evliya Çelebi?"

"Don't forget Ibn Daniyal." Jeffrey was still mulling over the two pages.

She scowled at him. "Why are you doing this?"

"Did your organization send you to the northern Caucasus in March of 1920, Dr. Bailey?" Maugham was looking at the ceiling again.

"I was twenty-seven years old. What organization? There was no organization. I had no affiliations." She rubbed her eyes. "Yes, fine, I did follow them. There's no need to deny it. But my motivation was curiosity. It was an opportunity." She turned again to Jeffrey, who was immersed in the pages. "This is an unproductive line of questioning. You know that as well as I do. What can you possibly gain from it?"

"Your work in the Caucasus over the past fifteen years, Marion, has been—suspiciously—competent." He placed the pages face down on the table. "Too competent. So much so, in fact, that it leads one to wonder how deep your channels there run. And, given this emergent problem in the area, it's worth our while to dredge up whatever buried information you may have neglected to mention to us in previous conversations concerning your contacts in the region."

"My work in the Caucasus," she shot back at him, "has been no more and no less competent than my work everywhere else. You've simply been singularly arse-backwards there. It's not a plot, Jeffrey. You're inept."

"Really, Dr. Bailey." Maugham was fishing his spectacles out of his pocket again. "There's no need for that sort of language."

"On the contrary," she retorted, "there's every need—"

"Why," Jeffrey interrupted, pushing the papers back toward her, "did your organization dispatch this message to you on pages ripped from a twenty-year-old collection of Turkish short stories?"

She shivered as her fingertips brushed them. There wasn't any doubt. These pages were from the book she'd given to Ismail. Which meant that there was a plausible chance that he was alive. Contacting her through her colleagues. Inviting her to find him after nearly two decades, now that whatever had been ignited in the Caucasus was erupting.

She'd known at the time, when he and his colleagues had splintered off toward the north, that they'd been searching for something specific; she'd simply not asked. Aware that she was with them on sufferance, and that her presence demanded discretion. But now—nothing would induce her to betray to Maugham their possible connection to the recent commotion surrounding Stalin's dacha. Or their quiet departure from the delegation in 1920.

She raised her eyes to Jeffrey's. "Perhaps," she said, "they'd run out of clean paper."

Jeffrey looked across her toward Maugham, who shook his head. Then, leaving the pages, he reached for the manuscript, dragged it into place, and positioned it in front of her. Leaned back in his own chair. "Fair enough." Neutral. "Would you like to examine the volume from the Baquba collection now?"

She blinked at him, more disturbed than reassured by his abandonment of the question. If he and Maugham were satisfied by her answers, she was in a weaker position than she'd believed. But she also knew that she couldn't begin to determine their motivation without collecting further information. And even then, she'd be at a loss. And so, sullen once more, she nodded. Quiet. She'd wait for the trick to reveal itself.

But there was no trick, apparently. Instead, smiling and open, Jeffrey moved his chair to give her space. Stood and walked to the grimy window and leaned against it, watching her. "You'll let us know whether you require additional material?"

She cleared her throat and nodded again. "Yes. Thank you."

FEELING anxious and on display, she ran her fingertips over the cover of the document. Opened it. Took up a pencil and moved a leaf of the writing paper to her side. As Jeffrey had said, the Scythian archer from the vase was reproduced in astonishingly precise detail in the margin of the first folio. And, should there be any doubt that the reproduction was deliberate, the Scythian's barbarian speech was also copied, with careful accuracy, in Greek letters. The reproduction, over centuries, of both the image and the letter string gave her chills. The obvious place to begin.

First, though, she must verify that while the Scythian on the front of the vase had not been taken from Aristophanes, the scene on the reverse side, depicting the bird-men, had. A simple task of comparing the text on the vase to her Greek *Birds*. She flipped rapidly through her modern edition of the play.

And yes, she confirmed after less than an hour, the left bird-man on the vase was quoting an early speech of Tereus, the bird king, summoning the fellowship of birds. Lines that began Ἴτω τις ὧδε τῶν ἐμῶν ὁμοπτέρων, ὅσοι τ' εὐσπόρους ἀγροικῶν γυας... The central bird-figure was quoting a speech by the chorus invoking the muse, which began Μοῦσα λοχμαίαι... And the third image was from a later speech, also by the chorus, praising the city of the birds, which began τοιαδε κυκνοι...

It was an arbitrary collection of moments to commemorate on the vase. But together they at least gestured toward a coherent message. The letters attributed to the Scythian, however, were nonsense. Not even reminiscent of the Classical Athenian mockery of harsh barbarian speech.

She peered at the lines, perplexed. Unconsciously memorizing them in adherence to her training. And then, meditative, she compared, character by character, the letter string on the vase to the letters on the first page of the manuscript. They were, as they appeared to be, identical: γτοσο μβτ βββ νγσγπ μυηορζ κ γαωβθβα αγγ ιαιζζαρκξε ζονξ

Meaningless. She thought further. Concluded that the spaces, carefully demarcated, must be important. Noticed also that whereas her own courier had left out the gammas and thetas, the γ's and θ's, when copying the message, those letters were larger in the writing on the vase—and they were written in red, as opposed to brown, ink in the manuscript. Which must be significant as well.

She sighed. Skimmed the tag from Hunayn ibn Ishaq. A short statement on the difficulty and uselessness of translating Aristophanes into Arabic. Meant to be ironic, she assumed, given that what followed was a complete Arabic version of the latter's *Birds*. She didn't think the translation was Hunayn ibn Ishaq's work.

Then she stopped herself again. She couldn't waste her time wondering about the provenance of the translation, painstakingly reading every line of it—as curious as she was to see how its anonymous author had rendered it in Arabic. Better to turn immediately to the passages in the manuscript that had appeared on the vase. Ascertain whether there were discrepancies between the Arabic translations and the original Greek. There must have been a reason for preserving those moments on the vase, and she ought to be able to discover that reason through slips or errors in the translated manuscript. From there, she'd examine the Scythian archer's speeches, which would also yield interesting results. Satisfied, she began her work.

It took her less than fifteen frustrated minutes to conclude that the three sections that had appeared on the vase were translated from the Greek into Arabic without inconsistencies. Carefully. Rationally. Dutifully. And therefore entirely without significance to her.

Rubbing her left eye with her hand, she turned to the scenes in the manuscript depicting the Scythian slave-archer instead. Hoping for something more promising. And, after reading only half a line, her frustrated discouragement turned to interest. Not only was the Scythian slave in the Arabic translation of the play speaking gibberish, but he was speaking an entirely different gibberish to what had appeared on the vase or on the cover of the manuscript. Not to mention in the original *Birds*. This was no transliteration of meaningless Greek letters. Nor was it a translation of the play. It was something new. Composed deliberately. And shorter.

Frowning, she tried to make sense of the one line attributed to the Scythian:

احط دحد بشطظ ثذ تعبسنثح ذ جبخغج بز وث ح بعس طابج.

It certainly wasn't in any language familiar to her. In fact, as she gazed down at it, it reminded her more than anything of a basic, bureaucratic key code: a string in which each letter corresponded to a discrete number, and each space denoted either zero or a return to a new line.

Shaking her head to clear it of her wandering thoughts, she told herself that the string couldn't be a key. First, the cipher was childishly simple, not even the proper, alphanumeric *abjad* code used by classical scholars. Whereas whoever had put together this manuscript had been working across centuries of highly-educated obfuscation. And second, there was no encoded text beyond the Scythian speech itself to which she could apply the number string once she'd unraveled it.

Nonetheless, only half-consciously, she made a mental note of the numbers the string represented, leaving aside the tens, fifties, hundreds, and thousands that would have appeared in the more complex *abjad*. She kept the correspondences as simple as possible, taking the letters y, n, r, q, and the rest at face value, rather than as ten, fifty, two-hundred, one-hundred, and the like: (1, 6) (16, 5, 8) (2, 13, 17, 5) (9, 4) (6, 3, 12, 2, 18, 3) (11) (5, 2, 0, 7, 7, 2, 11) (28, 4) (6) (2, 18, 12) (5, 2, 1, 16, 0). Memorized it. Reminded herself that the letters could read either right to left or left to right depending on whether the intended audience preferred Greek or Arabic script.

Recalling the Greek led her to consider another—unlikely yet possible—reason for the letter strings. If the nonsense Arabic in the manuscript was a numeric key-code, the nonsense Greek on the vase might be something similar. Worth trying. Also, if there was a numeric underpinning to the Greek letter string, that would explain the seemingly random choice of bird-man scenes to represent graphically. Those scenes would be the encoded texts.

After a quick calculation, she determined, leaving aside the gammas and thetas, and assuming that the spaces equaled zero, that the string read something like: γ, 19, 15, 1, 47, 0, 0, 12, 2, 19, 0, 2, 4, 2, 0, γ, 13, 3, 18, 4, 16, 0, 12, 0, 20, 7, 15, 17, 6, 6, 42, 3, 1, 24, 2, 9, 2, 1, 0, 0, 1, 3, 3, 0, 9, 1, 9, 6, 6, 1, 17, 10, 6, 5, 0, 6, 27, 13, 6.

Feeling foolish, but curious nonetheless, she opened her copy of *Birds* and turned to the first scene represented on the vase: Tereus, the bird-king's, speech. The conventional method of decoding using a string of this sort was to start from some pre-arranged point, and then strike out a certain number of letters to reveal the message. Inwardly shrugging, she left aside the first two lines of repetitive bird call and began counting at Tereus's first invocation of the "feathered fellowship." Nothing. But what was she expecting?

Deciding to try a further experiment, she began decoding at the first gamma instead, which appeared, in that speech, in the word, ἀγροικων. Circled the γ and counted forward 19: λ. Circled it and counted forward 15: ω. Circled it and counted forward 1: σ. Counted forward 47: σ. And a space, which meant 0: α. She blinked: γλωσσα. Tongue. Or language.

Bemused, she stared down at the page. And then, frightened lest she show her hand to Jeffrey or Maugham, she crossed out the letters she'd highlighted and continued to decode without taking notes. Forcing herself to keep her amazement in check, she read through all three passages depicted on the vase, always beginning her count with the gammas and thetas.

And when she'd finished, she had, to her entertained astonishment, a message. A message, however, that left her as baffled as the original gibberish had. But it was unquestionably internally meaningful: γλωσσα των πτηνων, γλωσσα των σμηνων, και των θἐων, σμηνο καλεετε, φεβεσθε.

There were spelling and grammatical errors—the fault of her decoding, a product of the vase's burial in the dirt for two thousand years, or the result of the manuscript's reproduction of an eroded key. But the message, such as it was, was clear: "language of the birds, language of the swarms, and of the gods, call the swarm, fear it."

She had no notion of what to make of it. But it did echo, if in an attenuated way, the events that Jeffrey and her contact had described to her earlier. Swarms and unknown languages. Fear. Gods and animals behaving inexplicably. She also thought that she understood now why the office had concerned itself with whatever objects or artifacts this material was on the verge of exposing. Not to mention why Ismail and his two colleagues would have taken the risk of travelling alone into the northern Caucasus mountains twenty years ago.

For though the warning in the text was obvious, so too was the power. And the "language of the birds," she well knew, was as much a classic accompaniment of the heroic treasure-quest in the Caucasian Nart Sagas as it was in every other Asian and European mythological system. It made sense that those who stumbled across clues to its whereabouts, be it an eleventh-century translator of Aristophanes, a thirteenth-century Mamluk poet, a seventeenth-century Ottoman traveler, or for that matter, Jeffrey's office would want to act on them. They were, proverbially, an invitation to action.

Her own response to the messages was less exalted—not one to trust epic calls to arms. If a variation on the simple number-letter code worked for the Greek Aristophanes, then there was every possibility that it would work for at least part of the manuscript from the Baquba collection too. She merely had to determine which bits of the three texts had been encoded, and then apply the key. Cautious, but edgy, she turned her attention to the scrap of Evliya Çelebi's travelogue that followed the translation of *Birds*.

She'd worked with versions of this seventeenth-century Ottoman-Turkish travel narrative before, with varying degrees of both trauma and success. And she was pleased to see that what had been bound into the manuscript was a short, rather than extensive, excerpt. Nothing more than his commentary on the languages of the Caucasus. Four folios rather than ten volumes. She'd have little difficulty spotting discrepancies between this text and those she knew.

But as she skimmed them, it became clear that the pages began in the same way that every other copy of this section of the *Seyahatname* did. With interesting, but hardly complex, phonetic translations between Turkish and Caucasian speech. Evliya himself was Abkhaz on his mother's side, and he initiated his description with the language he knew: "the strange and odd Abaza tongue." From there, he moved on to the related Ubykh language, which he called "the Sadşa-Abaza tongue." From Ubykh, he described Georgian, or "the Şavşad-Georgian tongue," and then, finally, Circassian, or "the Circassian-Mamluk tongue."

As she delved deeper into the passages, her irritation mounted. The text was identical to at least two other existing manuscript copies of which she was aware. There was nothing in it that hinted even quietly at an embedded additional message.

Pushing away a creeping exhaustion—though there were no clocks in the room, she knew that it must be close to midnight—she stared, unseeing, at the lines in front of her. Willing them to make some sense. She didn't want to move on to the Ibn Daniyal until she had an idea as to why the Evliya Çelebi had been included in the volume.

Then, her eye resting on the heading above the Ubykh, *Lisan-i Sadşa-Abaza*, "The Sadşa-Abaza tongue," she noticed that the word "*Abaza*" had been struck through. Not strongly, but distinctly. She'd seen it on her first reading, but at the time she'd merely smiled at the coincidence of the scribe echoing modern scholarly confusion over Evliya's implication that Ubykh was a variant of Abkhaz. As a native-speaker of Abkhaz, he would have known that Ubykh and Abkhaz, though somewhat mutually intelligible, were not identical dialects.

Now, though, she wondered. The word "*Sadşa*" was also elongated, the ـصـ and the ـشـ excessively far apart from one another. With a faint line between the two. Indeed, the title, in this way, read almost less as *Lisan-i Sadşa* and more as *Lisan-i sada-yı şeh*. "The language of the echo of power."

Poetic. And more than reminiscent of the invocations and warnings she'd drawn from the Greek passages.

It was also intriguing that the section that leant itself to further investigation was the passage on Ubykh. Of all the languages of the Caucasus, Ubykh was the most fragile. The least visible. Whereas the others continued to flourish, if on a small scale, both in the region and in the diaspora community, Ubykh was nearly gone. Almost no one spoke it—at least, not properly. And, more perplexing, no one appeared capable of learning it. It was a tongue on the verge of extinction.

None of that, however, altered the fact that the pages in front of her were still no different from every other copy of Evliya's work in circulation. Yes, the Ubykh passages were intriguing. Yes, the heading was rendered oddly. But they weren't close to revealing an extended, alternative message to her.

Unless, she mused, Evliya himself, when he composed these sections, already knew about the key-code. If so, he could have written the message into his original text. Which *would* mean that the other versions would look the same: rather than developing a key to draw meaning out of a pre-existing original, as with the Aristophanes, it was possible that he wrote the original with the key in mind.

Rubbing her eyes again and deciding that she ought, at least, to eliminate that possibility, she re-read the lines. Focusing, fatigued, on the passage before her: phonetic translations from Ottoman-Turkish into Ubykh of various words and phrases. Numbers from one through twelve. Food items: "bread," "meat," "water," "cheese," and others. Verbs: "come," "sit," don't go," and others. And then, a stilted conversation: "where are you going?" "I've got something to do, I'm going." "Where are you going?" "We're going to steal." "Where did you go?" "We went to the country of the Arids." Without enthusiasm, she applied the string of letters in two or three conventional ways to the first few lines. Nothing.

Then, her mind straying as her exhaustion mounted, she noted in passing that Evliya had reversed the numbers that compose "eleven" and "twelve" in Ubykh—writing them as "one-ten" and "two-ten" rather than "ten-one" and "ten-two." As he had, she reminded herself with some asperity, in every other version of the text. Commentators had flagged that error before. But, when her attention returned to the odd dialogue he'd reproduced immediately afterward, she reconsidered the import of this reversal.

Of all the generic conversations that he could have translated as an example for the benefit of his readers, Evliya had chosen a bizarre exchange about thieving from the "land of the Arids"— *Aridler vilayeti*. This "land of the Arids" had always mystified his readers, with most concluding, unsatisfactorily, that the Arids were an unidentified neighboring population of the seventeenth century. Who no longer existed today.

But if one wanted to translate the phrase in a naïvely literal way, it could also be read as the land of the backwards or "backward land." Which was silly, of course. Except, she thought—*except* that the reversed numerals, along with an intention to steal something from this backward land might lead a reader to wonder.

Smiling to herself more in embarrassment than in any sort of confidence, she began to apply the key backward, from the bottom, moving up one line at each space. Slowly, she started with 1, circled the letter, and then 6, circled the letter, moved up a line, tried 16, circled the letter, 5, and then 8. Read the result: *dil-i kuş*, "the language of the bird." More or less. But it was enough.

Keeping her eyes down, averted from her audience, she scribbled out the phrase she'd deciphered, and then she continued, once again without taking notes, memorizing. Twenty minutes later, she'd extracted, or "stolen": *dil-i kuş, dil-i küme, dil-i tanrı, davet edin, dehşete düşün*. The language of the bird, the language of the swarm, the language of god, call it, fear it. She still didn't know what it meant. But something was obviously there. And there was a good chance that she'd discover what that something was when she examined the Ibn Daniyal. Shaky, but flooded now with a restless, keyed up energy, she turned to the beginning of the third text—the poem.

"She has something."

Taken aback, Marion raised her eyes. It was Margot. She was standing, holding her writing pad, and looking, once again apologetic, in her direction.

Jeffrey pushed himself up off the meager windowsill. "I believe you're correct, Margot. Extraordinary. Even I wasn't certain yet." He strode across the room to the table, retrieved the manuscript, and arranged it and the vase in his open briefcase.

Marion blinked, baffled, her vision blurry from concentrating on the letters. Her hands hovering in the air above where the manuscript had been. "I haven't—"

"Yes?" This from Maugham, who was still sitting across from her at the table.

She blinked again. "I haven't found anything yet. I need more time."

Maugham looked over at Margot, who shook her head, almost ashamed-seeming by her role. "No. She's got it. There may be pieces missing. But she's ready to bolt, even without the information she's not gathered."

Marion pushed back her chair and stood. "But I haven't—"

Then, stopping herself, she realized that Margot was correct. She did have enough at this point to begin work in the field. The Ibn Daniyal would have helped. But far better to seek out Ismail with her findings. She could retrieve the last part later. Either way, the office wouldn't be a part of it.

Satisfied with her position, she addressed Jeffrey, composed now. "Fine. If you'd rather keep it from me, I understand. I don't need it. Let's go home."

He cast her a thin smile. Then he turned to Margot. "Would you assist Mr. Leonard downstairs, Margot? The situation in the cellar sounds as though it's deteriorated."

"Yes, of course, Sir Jeffrey. Dr. Bailey." She nodded at them both and left the room.

For the first time since she'd begun working, Marion registered through the partially open door the sound of high-pitched screams, identifiable somehow as adult and male, floating up from the lower storeys. They had started more than an hour before, but she'd unconsciously blocked them out as she'd concentrated on the document. Now, she no longer could.

Nervous, she addressed Jeffrey again. "Let's go."

Maugham, who had remained sitting, peered up at her. "You were enthralled by what you were reading, Dr. Bailey. Charming to watch. And yet, you say, you found nothing?"

Without responding, she took a step toward the door. And stopped. Pulling it open from the outside, wearing his obsessively belted and buttoned mackintosh and monstrously bad skin, was Eric Thacker. Incapable and violent. There was only one explanation for his appearance, and she knew better than to wait for him to attack her.

Ignoring her exhaustion, and clownishly hobbled by her wellingtons, she launched herself at him, kneed him in the groin, inadvertently ripped a button off his coat, and pushed past him into the corridor. Where she encountered Mr. Leonard. He swung a truncheon at her face, but she ducked and shoved him down the stairs. Briefly grateful for the customary absence of firearms in the depot. They tried to keep a low profile here.

He stumbled and fell, and she began to jump over him, but Jeffrey, who'd stepped past Thacker, grabbed her arm and pulled her back toward the doorway. She turned to kick him, or bite his hand, but Thacker, joining him in the corridor, snarled his fingers into her hair and, holding her in place, slammed his fist into her stomach. Dragged her into the room and threw her bodily against the window.

She was doubled over, retching, but still reaching for a chair to throw at him, when he strode toward her and kicked her hard at the base of her spine. She flattened onto the floor, tears streaming out of her eyes, just in time to see him readying another kick. Instinctively, she covered her head with her arms.

"That's sufficient, Thacker." Maugham had stood, and he was dropping the unused lighter into his jacket pocket. Adjusting his spectacles. "We'll want her lucid tomorrow."

"She ruined my overcoat."

"Willcox will make it good." They were moving away from her, through the door.

"I most certainly will not." A hint of exasperation in his voice. And then: "there was no need to disarrange her hair, Thacker. I like her hair."

"Chin up, Mr. Leonard," Maugham was already out in the corridor, addressing the guard. "No harm done. Up you go—"

And then the door was shut and locked, and she couldn't hear any more. At least, nothing more than the distant sound of the screaming from the basement. An echo of street traffic. The damp, cold fear of the room.

She dropped her arms from over her head, pushed herself up onto her knees, and moved her hair out of her face. Looked about the empty room. Rose to her feet, a bit unsteady. And then, giving in to the staggering rage that surged up inside of her, she grabbed the lamp closest to her and hurled it with all her strength against the wall.

It was too cheap to break. With a thud, it fell to the ground, still glowing, casting an ominous shadow across the already nightmarish pink walls. Rolling gently, back and forth, on the thin carpet.

Without troubling to switch it off, she made her way to the dank bedroom, lowered herself onto the bare mattress of the thin, single bed, and cried herself into inertia. She should have seen this coming. She should have known. She'd never, ever learn.

THEY left her to brood, and to pace the dismal set of rooms, until nearly noon the next day. She had woken before dawn, her abdomen aching, and something off, wrong, with her lower vertebrae. Ignoring the pain, she'd eased herself into a sitting position on the metal bed and considered her situation. Still wearing the boots, which now stank. And her Belstaff jacket, the buckles of which had dug into her side during the night.

After entertaining a brief, foolish hope that one of the pockets of the jacket might contain a weapon or a tool to force the door, she methodically searched her clothing. Nothing. A few stray threads and a note to herself on promising starting points for her aborted search of Devon. She'd packed her tools in the rucksack. Jeffrey would never have left her the jacket otherwise.

Irritated, she unbuttoned it and shrugged it off onto the mattress. The house was cold, but the clammy feel of the waxed cloth was making her skin crawl. Better to shiver beneath a thin cotton shirt in the frigid air of the tiny bedroom.

Pushing herself onto her feet, careful not to cause further damage to her stomach or back, she walked to the degrading, open toilet. Also familiar from previous incarcerations. At least there were no windows in this part of the room. She used it quickly, squeamishly, trying not to touch any part of it, and then she dragged herself to the larger sitting room.

The lamps were still on, the one on its side resting on the floor. But the window was also turning from blue-black to whitish-grey. Pacing the room without turning off the bulbs, she noted that Jeffrey had left the two pages her organization had attached to Fyffes on the table. The rest of the material was gone.

When the ache in her back became intolerable, she used her hands to ease herself into one of the chairs still scattered haphazardly around the table, and waited. Fretting. Angry. Until the yellow-grey exterior light and the remote sounds of the street told her that it was no longer just past dawn, but late morning. Perhaps the middle of the day. Then she pressed her fists into her eyes, willing herself to disengage. To remain professional.

Eventually, the door opened, and Mr. Leonard appeared on the threshold. He held the truncheon in one hand and a ceramic cup of foul-smelling coffee in the other. Impassive and undamaged by their interaction the night before. He was closely followed by Jeffrey, carrying a slice of stale-looking sponge cake on a small plate. His briefcase in the other hand.

Jeffrey, to her annoyance, looked well-rested and clean, wearing a different, if equally subdued black suit and blue tie under his wool overcoat. His hair brushed back. His face smooth. Smelling of Chester Terrace. After setting the plate on the table in front of her, he walked through the room, switching off the lamps. Returned the one she'd thrown against the wall to its table.

Then he turned to Mr. Leonard. "Thank you. I'll knock when we've finished."

Mr. Leonard nodded, placed the cup of coffee on the table beside the plate, backed through the door and closed it. She heard the locks clicking into place. Didn't touch the food.

Without removing his overcoat, Jeffrey sat in the chair across from Marion, retrieved his briefcase, opened it and found the manuscript. Pushed it across the table toward her. Glanced, with fastidious distaste, at the room. "This is Thacker's territory. I dislike it here."

"So do I, Jeffrey." Failing to keep the aggrieved belligerence out of her voice.

"Necessity." He nodded at the plate. "You'll want to eat something."

She examined the cup. Pink flowers. And a faint but unmistakable smudge of some other woman's lipstick on the rim. Also familiar. Her stomach lurched. But she picked at the dry, crumbling cake nonetheless. Trying to appear compliant. There was a tap next to the toilet. Perhaps she could drink from that.

He watched her for a few seconds, sighed slightly, and then spoke again. "We have two courses open to us. We can discuss your movements and contacts in the north Caucasus in 1920. Or we can discuss what you learned last night from this volume. Which would you prefer?"

She kept her eyes averted, concentrating on demolishing the cake. It was now more than half collapsed into desiccated, yellow crumbs. And she'd thus far avoided eating any. She knew she'd regret not taking in what energy she could, but the thought of ingesting what came from the depot's kitchen left her queasy. Distraught.

"Or," he continued, "you might look over the third text. The Ibn Daniyal. What do you say?"

She raised her eyes to his, suspicious. There was a hint of gloating amusement behind his bland expression that she couldn't analyze. Best not try. If he wanted to risk her completing her investigation without any gain for the office, she wouldn't dissuade him. Still distrustful, she pulled the manuscript closer to her and opened it, locating the beginning of the poem. Began reading. Stopped almost immediately. Annoyed again. "Oh."

He was watching her closely, fighting down laughter. "Aren't you going to continue?"

She ignored him and turned her attention back to the folio. She'd been aware of Ibn Daniyal and his work, but she was by no means familiar with it. He'd been a notoriously—dangerously—incompetent eye-doctor in thirteenth-century Cairo, practicing under Mamluk rule. But he'd also had a reputation as a writer of popular, sometimes vulgar, and always virtuoso, shadow plays and burlesque verse. She'd read bits and pieces of two of his poems satirizing the Mamluk government's periodic campaigns against vice. And she could understand their appeal. But she hadn't enjoyed them. They were, as Jeffrey would have put it, smutty. Similar, now that she thought about it, to the work of Aristophanes.

This ode, though, topped any that she'd previously read in terms of sheer pornographic glee. Framed loosely as an elegy, in which the narrator, as lover, mourns the loss of the departed beloved, it subverted the genre by substituting the devil, Iblis, as the lover and the indecent, licentious citizens of Cairo as the beloved. Which gave Ibn Daniyal the opportunity to explore in obscene, lascivious detail the myriad activities that both the lover and beloved had enjoyed together.

When the Mamluk Sultan curbed and suppressed vice in the city, Iblis laments, Cairo's pimps, prostitutes, strippers, drug dealers, addicts, and gamblers were taken from him. And along with those pimps, prostitutes, strippers, drug dealers, addicts, and gamblers, also disappeared, for fifty explicit verses, their pastimes. Not to mention the various, often acrobatic, ways in which Iblis himself joined in these pastimes.

"I'm partial myself to verses thirty through thirty-three," Jeffrey commented, interrupting her impatient, silent examination of the document. "Brilliant character sketch of Iblis."

Inwardly protesting, but willing to take any hint Jeffrey might provide her, she moved ahead to the thirtieth verse. Skimmed it and those that followed. Exhaled, cross: "'Oh Iblis,' I asked, 'why are you so sad?'/And Iblis replied, 'You moron, you've got your head up your sister's cunt/why do you think I'm upset? My troops have all evaporated, my position is undermined, and I've lost all my power…'" And so on.

"One wonders," Jeffrey mused, "what Milton would have made of it. Infinitely more effective, I think, than all that vacuous carrying on about the honor of reigning in hell rather than serving in heaven. Cuts direct to the point. Don't you agree, dear?"

"If you won't let me concentrate," she muttered, "I'll get nothing out of this. Would you shut up, Jeffrey?"

"As you wish." He set his chin in his hands, his elbows on the table. "I'll content myself with watching."

She spent another fifteen minutes reading and re-reading the fifty verses. The document was not any longer than the passages from the travelogue had been. And despite the scatological content, its Arabic was clean and elegant. But she couldn't force her mind to make any more of it than the shrieking, dirty farce that operated at the surface. The combination of gritty sleeplessness, the pain in her back and abdomen, and wretchedness at her current circumstances left her mind dull. Useless.

She wiped a strand of lank hair off her face, closed the volume, and pushed it away from her. "I can't do anything with it."

Jeffrey relaxed in his chair. Thoughtful. "If you'd give me a hint as to what you found last night, I may be able to help you. I, personally, feel something of an affinity for poor, beleaguered Iblis."

She shot him an annoyed look. Didn't respond.

"Very well." He stood and gathered up the manuscript. "Then I suppose we must move the conversation downstairs."

"Oh God." She stared up at him. "Jeffrey, I swear to you, whatever you do to me down there, I will *not*—"

"Of course you will." He considered. "Or, would." Then he moved toward the door. "But you misunderstand me. As I said, that scenario is Thacker's specialty." He knocked and she heard the locks on the outside of the door turning. "No. There's someone I'd like you to meet. Downstairs. Waiting."

Unsteady, her head buzzing, she rose to her feet. Rubbed her hand against the base of her spine. "I don't want to do this."

"You're not supposed to want to do it, Marion." He stood to the side and gestured her toward the open door.

Hating the damp feel of her feet in the soggy boots, and wishing now that she'd worn her jacket to cover her thin shirt, she approached the corridor. Paused briefly at the sight of Mr. Leonard. Then swallowed and allowed him to lead her, Jeffrey following, down the dim stairs.

*W*HEN they reached the concrete basement, Mr. Leonard paused beside a blank metal door and produced a keyring like something out of an amateur theatrical production of the Arthurian

Legend. He chose a benign, modern-looking key from the otherwise ponderous twist of dangling metal, and unlocked the cell. Pulled open the door and moved to the side.

Jeffrey stood to the other side and indicated with his hand that she ought to enter. After casting him a split-second look of uneasiness, she obeyed.

"I'll leave the two of you to reminisce," Jeffrey said and closed the door from the outside. She heard Mr. Leonard locking it.

What she saw in the room didn't surprise her after what she'd experienced the previous evening. Though perhaps it should have. Ismail had been in his late thirties when he'd allowed her to attach herself to the edges of the delegation travelling from Turkey. He'd been tall, friendly, and fit, unimpaired by the recent War, with a semi-ironic interest in shooting and, even more self-mocking, boxing.

Now, in his early fifties, he was diminished. Skeletal. His formerly black hair was white, and there was yellowish stubble across his chin. He was sitting, hunched, on the bare, ripped mattress that failed to fill the narrow bedframe. Wearing a tan undershirt, beltless brown pyjama bottoms, and no shoes. There was a scabbed cut running for more than a foot along the inside of his left arm. Though, Marion noted, a trifle cool, it was old. It couldn't have been inflicted over the past few days.

He pushed back his shoulders and half-smiled at her when she entered the room. As though also expecting her. "They're listening outside the door." He spoke in Turkish.

"Yes," she said, also in Turkish. "I know."

"It's started."

"Yes," she repeated.

"You mustn't trust me, Marion."

"I know." She walked the three paces across the room and sat next to him on the mattress. Looked straight ahead. "How did this happen to you?"

He leaned back and examined her, sideways. Shook his head, his smile rueful. "You were so pure then. So certain."

"And now look at me. Tainted and baffled."

"You're better this way. Human."

She remembered, irrelevantly, the joking presumption among the other hangers-on that had followed the delegation that she'd been infatuated with Ismail. An infatuation that he himself had not returned. She'd been confused and mildly insulted at the time, uncertain as to how to prove that her interest in him was friendly and intellectual rather than—otherwise.

But now, nearly twenty years later, comprehension clicked. The story had been an affectionate joke that she'd failed, as usual, to understand. Gossip to pass the time. And perhaps, without fully realizing it, she had felt more than friendly toward Ismail. She blushed, ashamed of her pure, certain, twenty-seven-year-old self.

"How did this happen to you?" she asked again, pushing away the two-decade-old humiliation. She'd examine her social confusion later.

"Where shall I begin?" He rubbed a thumb along the scab inside his arm.

"Why not with how you got here? To this room." She ran appalled eyes over the grimy basement cell. Reminded herself that everything they said in here was noted and analyzed.

"Ah," he said. "That one is easy. "The British traded for me. Gave Stalin an informant he wanted more."

"Stalin?" Her voice was small.

"Yes. From what I overheard in transit, they delivered him some unfortunate Trotskyite they'd had in storage for years. Couldn't find a use for him." Unlike Marion, he gazed about the room with something like satisfaction. "I think I got the better end of the bargain. The people here are certainly—baroque. But aside from that scrofulous, angry one—"

"Eric Thacker," she said.

"—whatever. Aside from him, they've been nothing but polite." He glanced sidelong at her again, embarrassed. "At the same time, Marion, you mustn't trust this situation. I was never one for the intelligence services—Ottoman, Turkish, Circassian, Russian, British or otherwise. I preferred the adventure and the chase. But I can spot a compromised actor when I see one, and there are few more contaminated than I am at the moment."

"I know," she repeated. It wasn't important. "It doesn't matter. How long have you been here?"

"A week?" He let his eyes wander the blank, windowless walls of the cell, squinting, as though that would help him to answer. He had a scar running from the corner of his right eyebrow to his ear.

She thought for a moment. If Ismail had been here a week, it meant that Jeffrey had lied about the immediacy of his information. That didn't surprise her, but it did alter her interpretation of her own organization's orders. She stored the discrepancy in the back of her mind to consider later. Then she spoke again. "And Stalin? How long did his people have you?"

"Two months, perhaps." He licked his dry, cracked lips. "Since they finished work on the dacha. I came down from the mountains when construction began, in order to—"

He stopped speaking when he saw her look, quickly apprehensive, toward the locked door. Then his smile deepened, exposing stark wrinkles in his cheeks. "Still highly-strung." He patted the top of her hand. "They know everything, Marion. There's nothing I can say to you here that will compromise me further."

She didn't believe him. But she knew better than to tell him that while they had an audience. "So the dacha was a—a threat? To what you were doing in the mountains?"

"Stalin picked an unfortunate building site." He stared across the room at the wall. "But the mountains were about to explode anyway."

She chose her next words with care, unable to ignore her creeping sensitivity to the listeners beyond the door of the cell. "And what you were doing in the mountains had—had—"

"Had to do with the Nart Sagas, yes."

"But that was a joke." She turned to the side to take in his still ironic profile.

"In a way," he said, "yes. But also not. The War had ended. Our country was ruined. Our land occupied. Everything was a little—satirical—at the time. If not, we'd have lost our minds. Or become Atatürk." An unexpected twist of contempt in his tone.

"And Atatürk—"

"Yes," he said. "This is where the story begins. Both Enver Pasha and Atatürk knew that a national independence movement in the northern Caucasus, of all places, was an absurdity. As did everyone who joined the delegation in 1920—"

"Ismail," she interrupted him. "Are you certain that you want to—"

He smiled, exasperated now, at the door. "They *know*, Marion. And even if I hadn't confirmed it for them, it's obvious when you look back at the moment. Objectively. Historically. Think about it. Did you really believe when you crossed the border from Turkey into the power vacuum that was the Caucasus that the eradicated, non-existent population of—" he waved his hand, looking for an example, "—of the Republic of Adygea was going to defeat the Soviet Army? With what? The eagle that used to annoy Prometheus?"

"At the time I did," she said quietly. "But you're right. In hindsight, it's clear that a revolution of that sort was doomed to failure."

"What the Russians didn't know," he said, "was that although an independence movement was impossible, and the delegation an earnest, pompous spectacle, the mountains did hide a different sort of threat. Or promise, I suppose, depending on how you look at it."

He closed his eyes, weary. "Enver Pasha and Atatürk, unlike the Russians, did know about it. From the refugees that staffed their intelligence services and also from the occasional stray visitor—like that damned renegade from the 'Mountainous Republic of the Northern Caucasus'—who piqued Mustafa Kemal's interest. And Enver and Atatürk wanted it. They thought they could tuck it neatly and comfortably into the Turkish sphere of influence. No need to shore up the borders of a sickly independent republic if their people underground could control the region from the inside."

"And you were—"

"One of the people underground." He opened his eyes, put his hands behind him on the mattress, and leaned back. Grimaced in pain. Something had been done to him within the last day or two. Something that left no marks. Something British. She silently cursed Jeffrey and Maugham, but she didn't let Ismail guess that she'd noticed.

"You found it?"

"No." He half-smiled in the direction of the closed door. "But we found evidence of it. Enough to convince us that no one—not the Russians, not the Turks, not the British—" he nodded, polite, at the door, "—*no one* should lay claim to it. It was best left inert."

"And so, you've spent the past two decades in the mountains searching for it solely to—to hide it more effectively?" Perplexed.

"Quixotic, isn't it?" He grinned again, looking like the young man who had appropriated her collection of short stories and disappeared into the forest in 1920.

"But then it—it activated on its own." She was beginning to understand, to piece together a narrative that almost satisfied her. Large sections were missing, but she thought she knew now at least generally what her organization wanted from her. And possibly also from Ismail.

"So it seems." He looked up at the low, mildewed ceiling of the cell. "And as a result of its unilateral decision to return to life, I am now the carefully tended guest of this delightful London lodging house." He frowned. "At least, I assume we're in London. I haven't had much opportunity to take in the sights."

"Yes," she said absentmindedly, mulling over what Ismail had told her. "Chelsea."

"Ah." It obviously meant nothing to him.

"But only until we have you back on your feet again, Ismail." Mr. Leonard had unlocked and opened the door, and Jeffrey was smiling down at them, his hands in the pockets of his overcoat. Also speaking Turkish.

"Ah yes," Ismail replied. "My feet. I feared I'd never be on them again, after the attention they received in Russia."

Marion, unthinking, glanced down at his bare feet. Then, drawing in her breath in sympathetic horror, she looked up at his face. His toenails were missing.

"Pure and certain," Ismail murmured. He patted her hand again.

"It's time, Marion," Jeffrey said in English. "Ismail needs rest. And you haven't eaten. The two of you will have further opportunities to converse later."

She rose from the mattress, obedient, and took a step toward the corridor. But then, feeling foolish once again, she turned, bent over, and kissed Ismail on the cheek. It had been nearly two decades, and he still left her flushed and confused.

T HE cold coffee and the withered, pulverized sponge cake remained on the table when she and Jeffrey returned to the rooms upstairs. Once Mr. Leonard had locked the door behind them, Jeffrey pulled out a chair for her, gestured toward it, and nodded at the plate. "Finish it."

She sat, and he sat beside her.

"It's inedible."

He held her eyes, cold and silent.

After a few mutinous seconds, she swallowed the bitter saliva at the back of her throat, took a tiny piece of the cake, put it in her mouth, and chewed. Lifted the floral cup, turned the lipstick smudge away from her, and washed down the cake with the rancid liquid. Looked at him for approval.

"Good. Keep eating. I'll talk." He leaned back in the chair. "Maugham wants to send Ismail with the unit he's planning to drop in the Caucasus later this month. As a caged canary." He noticed she'd stopped eating and nudged the plate toward her. "More."

Fighting down nausea, she ate another bite and drained the coffee. Didn't speak.

Satisfied, Jeffrey continued. "But he can't exert the proper pressure until you've spilled what you extracted from the manuscript last night." He watched her picking at the cake, his expression blank. "You've landed us in a bizarre situation, Marion. You and your friend."

Holding the bridge of his nose between his thumb and index finger, he explained, though she hadn't replied. "Because, you see, Ismail—our unwilling scout—though on site for twenty years, has no idea what he's seeking. The past week has convinced us of that. You—our unwilling analyst—are fully aware of our target. But Maugham won't let you within a thousand miles of the site. Which means that my unenviable task is to convince the two of you to work together without Ismail discovering what we're looking for or you leaving London. Classic Maugham setup."

"I don't know what it is." She pushed the empty plate away from her. Wanted to smash it on the floor instead. "Your 'target.'"

"You've got a few good guesses, though." He pressed his hands into the pockets of his coat. The room was almost cold enough to see his breath. "You were electrified last night."

She flicked her eyes up to his and then down toward the tabletop. Remained quiet.

"What did you learn from the Aristophanes and the Evliya Çelebi?" Bored. He didn't expect her to answer.

She wrapped her arms over her chest and rubbed her shoulders. Wishing she had more than the cotton shirt to cover herself. The hairs on the back of her neck were standing on end.

"Would you like to complete your analysis of the poem? Now that you've eaten and rested?" He pulled the manuscript toward her and opened it to the Ibn Daniyal.

She considered it, tempted. But then Ismail's warning returned to her. He'd never been prone to nervous exaggeration. And even in his current state, there'd been a vestige of his playful, grounded, and always sane wit. If he believed that the object in the north Caucasus was best left alone, she wouldn't question his interpretation. He'd had nearly twenty years to come to that conclusion. She raised her eyes to Jeffrey's. Shook her head.

He sighed, impatient. Retrieved the manuscript. Sat up straighter in the chair and folded his hands over it. "Shall I read it to you instead?"

"What? No."

"Very well." He cleared his throat and began translating the Arabic, his smile now growing. "I saw Iblis in a dream, bereft and heartbroken/ one eye blind, the other red with dripping tears/ Lamenting, 'woe, despair, unmatched pain!'/ He was surrounded by his fellows, few in number but great in heart/ First, there was the catamite, with a face like a full moon/ his eyes triumphant over his conquests yet sorrowful/ his flexible limb the bright sun, his soft pubic hair the shadow/ embracing him is like sucking sweet fruit/ fucking the fig along with the date—"

"Stop it, Jeffrey." She was huddled in the chair, her eyes downcast, her arms around her waist. "This is embarrassing."

But he didn't. Instead, he read through every one of the increasingly explicit fifty verses before blinking, setting aside the volume, and addressing her. Reflective. "Any thoughts?"

"*Why?*" she asked him. "What was the purpose of that? Spite? Because I've told you, I'm no longer reading any of it. Not the Aristophanes. Not the Evliya. Not *that*. Nothing."

He half shrugged and gazed out the window. Night was falling. The glass was turning from yellow-grey to dirty blue. "Why not? We'd be sitting here in awkward silence, otherwise. Waiting for Mr. Leonard to bring you your next meal."

She pressed her hands against her eyes. Dropped them a few seconds later. Noted the darkness filling the room. "I want to go home."

He laughed. "Direct. I'll give you that." He lifted his chin, still smiling. "What did you learn from the Aristophanes?"

She didn't respond.

"What did you learn from the Evliya Çelebi?"

She remained quiet.

He stood. "See you tomorrow, darling. I'll give Lydia your apologies."

"Pig."

He walked throughout the room, turning on the lights. Then he returned to the table, straightened the manuscript and the two sheets from Fyffes, leaned over, and kissed the top of her head. Approached the door. Knocked to be let out. Didn't speak as he stepped into the corridor.

When the room was closed and locked, she shoved back her own chair, strode over to the nearest lamp, and threw it hard against the door. It bounced harmlessly onto the ground, where it rolled languidly on its side. Still shining.

Then, paying no attention to it, she stalked into the bedroom and threw herself onto the bare mattress, pulling the clammy Belstaff jacket over her to try to keep warm. Refusing to think about her situation. Refusing to consider how she'd deflect Jeffrey's attention tomorrow. Shivering and nauseated from the coffee and the cake.

THE next morning, she pulled off her boots, too revolted by the feel of her damp, sweating feet in the constricted rubber to bear wearing them any longer. And she forced herself into the jacket—her muscles aching both from Thacker's attack and from shuddering against the cold all night. Then she ran the tap next to the toilet and forced herself to drink three swallows of the metallic water.

After that, she wandered into the larger room, inspecting the dingy glass of the window to determine the time. Gave up after a few seconds and settled herself at the table. Resisting the temptation to page through the manuscript Jeffrey had left for her the night before. She didn't want to learn anything more. She wanted nothing to do with it.

The door opened earlier than it had the previous morning, as she was still musing over the two pages from Fyffes to keep her mind at a distance from the manuscript. Mr. Leonard was once again carrying his truncheon and a cup of coffee—no smudge of lipstick this time. And Jeffrey had a slice of what looked like the same sponge cake along with his briefcase. He was wearing wool trousers, a white cotton shirt, and a pullover under his coat. Casual. Saturday, she realized. Already losing track of the calendar.

When Mr. Leonard had closed and locked the door, Jeffrey set the plate of cake on the table and walked over to the lamp on the floor. Bent over to retrieve it. Cast her an amused look halfway down. "Unless you prefer it this way?"

Toying with the two sheets from Fyffes, she didn't respond. He smiled and placed it upright on the table. Sat in the chair beside her and nodded at the cake and coffee. "Eat."

She decided to force down the coffee first. Lifted the cup a half inch off the table before realizing that the handle was sticky. Released it in disgust, wiping her fingertips on her trousers. The slice of cake had two dead fruit flies embedded in the moldy-looking icing sugar. She wondered whether Jeffrey had chosen it deliberately. Attention to detail.

"I said, eat." He smelled of the clean autumn air of the Park. He must have walked part of the way here.

She tore a piece from the underside of the cake and forced it down. Held his eyes.

"Good." He paused. "Any new thoughts about the manuscript?"

She pushed the two pages from the collection of short stories across the table at him. "You took these from Ismail. He'd preserved them for seventeen years. To use to identify himself should that become necessary. Even when Stalin had him in Russia, he'd kept hold of them. But when you collected him, you lifted them. Marked them up with Greek from the vase. Left out the gammas and thetas because those were highlighted in the first folio. Told me your courier had retrieved them from Fyffes. You wanted to get me talking about my work in the Caucasus."

"Did we?"

"My instructions," she said, "were to fetch two pages from Fyffes. I failed to do so. My next move, Jeffrey, is to go to Devon to complete my assignment. I don't give a damn about your manuscript."

"Mr. Fyffes is no longer in Devon." He rubbed his cheek with his hand. "Last anyone heard of him, he was making his way toward the Pyrenees. He's apparently got it into his head that some Basque octogenarian there is a warlock in disguise. Bewitched Mr. Fyffes's deceased friend's pet polecat. Mr. Fyffes means to put a stop to all that before it blossoms into a threat to the security of our sceptered isle." He considered. "Or, at least, to the security of the polecats of our sceptered isle."

She blinked. Said nothing.

"We've already got your pages," he explained patiently. "The proper pages. Off Fyffes when he was still in the ditch in Devon."

"Where are they?"

He smiled at her.

"What were they?"

"You're not eating."

She took a large piece off the bottom of the cake, forced it into her mouth, chewed and swallowed.

"The coffee too."

Avoiding the handle and taking the cup between two fingertips, she drained the coffee. Set the empty cup back on the table. Shuddered. *"What were they?"*

"What do you think they were?" He watched her. "Any guesses?"

"No."

"Would you consider a trade?" Mild. "We'll grant you supervised access to your pages. You tell us what you drew from the volume. Along with any stray memories you might have of your time in the northern Caucasus in 1920."

"No."

"Very well." He stood and buttoned his overcoat. "See you tomorrow."

"That's it?" She stood as well.

"Yes," he said. "I must get back. I'm taking Lydia to the zoo. She misses you, darling. Can't understand why Mummy's avoiding her."

"Pig."

He smiled, kissed her cheek, and left. She threw the lamp at the door.

*W*HAT felt like six or seven days later, she was having difficulty moving herself about the room or effectively marking the passage of time. The water in the tap did little to hydrate her, the monotonous, incessant conversations with Jeffrey were driving her into intermittent, hysterical rages, and her dank clothing gave her a creeping horror wherever it touched her skin. She also suspected that they were dosing the coffee with a sedative or narcotic. Wanting her compliant rather than intelligent, now that they'd tricked her into working through most of the manuscript for them. She recognized the symptoms.

But she easily fought them down. Having experienced the depot before, she knew better than to believe that her emotions or sensory responses to its environment were natural. Which meant that she could analyze the fluctuations of her brain chemistry from a somewhat objective distance, retain vestiges of her dignity, and allow Jeffrey to talk at her. While waiting. In the meantime, she thought about Ismail downstairs, who was undoubtedly undergoing far worse.

When Jeffrey put the plate in front of her a week later—the slices of sponge cake had given way to equally vile hunks of caraway seed loaf—his affect had changed. He watched, silent, as she consumed the cake and drank the coffee. No longer needing to prod her. Then he tapped his fingers on the table a few times, thinking.

"Ismail has finally agreed to act as tour guide," he said as she ate. "He'll lead Maugham's team to the source of the disturbances up beyond Sochi."

"Oh." She tried to sound neutral. It was bound to happen eventually. No one stood up to them forever.

"But he'll do so only provided you accompany us." The corner of his mouth went down. "Is there anything you'd like to confess to me, dear? As your husband? His refusal to travel without you, even after a great deal of compelling persuasion, has left me suspicious. Jealous. Confused."

"Don't be revolting." But she was surprised. Ismail presumably had a plan in mind, but she couldn't fathom how her presence in the region would help him to achieve it. It didn't matter. She kept her eyes on the empty, floral plate, refusing to engage.

"Maugham," Jeffrey pressed on, "is unhappy about this outcome. In fact, his initial reaction was to order us to increase the pressure on Ismail. Couldn't believe that a few more days of carefully reasoned argument wouldn't convince him to undertake the journey alone."

"Oh."

"I must admit, at this point I'm nearly as jealous of your influence on Maugham as I am of your effects on Ismail. Never in my life would I have imagined Richard Maugham—omniscient, unscrupulous scourge of five different ministries—thrown into confusion by some expendable, if always charming, bit of talent. Yet, the circumstances are undeniable. You've got him by the—" he cleared his throat. "That is to say, the thought of you at large in the Caucasus, even under the closest of supervision, has terrorized him. He's abject."

She swallowed. Didn't raise her eyes.

"Nonetheless," he said, "he's changed his mind and agreed to accept Ismail's conditions. We need a scout capable of walking, and any more carefully reasoned argument from us would find Ismail leading us up the mountain in a sedan chair."

She dropped her face into her hands, but she didn't speak. She hated this.

"I also suggested to him that you yourself might be inclined to spill once you were on-site." He glanced about the room with his customary distaste. "God knows the depot hasn't worked its magic."

"I won't."

"We'll see."

She looked up at him. "'We?' You don't hike."

"I'm capable of climbing a mountain, Marion." Exasperated. "I merely prefer to do more interesting things unless there's some reason for it."

"I'm not going."

"The team thus far," he said, ignoring her, "consists of you, me, Ismail, Trelawney, Gardiner, and three of Gardiner's subordinates. I've got Russian, Turkish, and Persian. Trelawney's got some Circassian in addition to the rest. You've got twenty-three different dialects of old Turkic and Persian. We ought to manage. Maugham will pull some strings to get us in unnoticed. We don't want Ismail attracting Stalin's attention again."

"I said, I'm not going."

He stood. "You'd rather stay here?"

She felt, for the first time since her incarceration, on the verge of public tears. Blinked them away. "No."

"I thought not." He walked to the door and knocked. And then, as Mr. Leonard turned the locks on the outside, he took in the room a final time. "Any furniture you'd like to abuse before taking your leave of the place?"

She shook her head, stood, and followed him. Wondered how long it would take to wash the stench of Chelsea off her skin when she'd returned to Chester Terrace. And how many days the drug they'd been giving her would linger in her system. At this point, she had to hold Jeffrey's arm to keep her balance as they descended the narrow, fetid staircase.

The Northern Caucasus
November, 1937

"YOU aren't frightened?" Jeffrey was seated and leaning against the freezing, stripped-out fuselage of the Whitley bomber that had flown them, with three stops for fuel, from the RAF station in North Yorkshire. Twenty-five hundred miles. His knees up. Gloved hands relaxed over his pack. He was already strapped into his parachute.

"No," she said shortly. Uninterested in talk. "I've done it before."

"I don't believe it." His smile was hardly visible through his winter headgear. "When could you possibly have done this before?"

"Training," she muttered. "I like it."

He laughed and peered down the length of the cabin. Arthur Gardiner and his three colleagues were waiting, calm and silent, nearer the tail of the plane. Sitting in a position similar to Jeffrey's, conserving their energy for the jump. Nick Trelawney was more visibly excited, though in his customary repressed and correct manner. He'd been elated when informed that Maugham had arranged for them to travel invisibly into Russia on one of the experimental paratroop transports. A newly designed bomber with the rear gun turret removed.

Ismail, however, even covered in layers of clothing, was deathly pale and cadaverous. His eyes closed. Deep lines etched on what showed of his face.

Jeffrey scrutinized Ismail's bent figure, sitting with legs straight out, more like a doll than a human being. "Ismail disagrees with you. He's terrified."

"He's not terrified," she snapped back at him. "He's recovering. After what you've done to him, it's a miracle he could climb into the plane, much less jump out of it."

"He seemed more resilient when we began work on him." Contrite. Though sorrier about his miscalculation than about Ismail's broken condition. "But he's the sort to keep hidden reserves. He'll hold up."

"Prick." She looked away from him.

The plane banked and turned sharply. A signal for Gardiner to check his wristwatch and begin unsnapping the cloth where the rear gun had been. When the plane was flying level and its tail open, he looked back for confirmation. At a nod from Jeffrey, he turned, grabbed the bars on either side of the gap, and pushed himself out, keeping straight and rigid. Gardiner was followed by the first of his subordinates. Then Marion and Ismail. And finally, Jeffrey, Nick, and the last two soldiers.

Ismail had directed them to the Lago-Naki plateau, equidistant between Sochi and Maykop, a sparsely inhabited area of meadow and forest six thousand feet above sea level. They'd dropped from the plane eight hundred feet above that. Their jump formation textbook. And less than an hour later, the sky quiet and empty, they were regrouping at the edge of a shallow river skirting an outcropping of bare rock that sliced through an expanse of green.

Marion had seen cows as she descended, which suggested farmers or shepherds. But she had landed well away from the field. Ismail needed rest, and Gardiner wanted to find his bearings, before they pushed onward. Which meant that they couldn't draw attention to themselves. They expected to make camp for at least a day and a night in the meadow.

She found their plan increasingly appealing as she opened herself to the atmosphere of the place. Although the air was thin and cold, there was no indication of snow—and the river, though austere, was welcoming rather than hostile. She followed Jeffrey's and Gardiner's lead with equanimity.

Once they'd collected and hidden the parachutes, they walked further along the stream until they reached the edge of a stand of conifers. Assuming that whoever cared for the livestock would be unlikely to explore the forest as dusk was falling on a November evening, they took shelter beyond the first line of trees. Gardiner found a clearing, posted two of his subordinates to watch, and worked with Nick to make a fire.

He and Jeffrey then distributed tinned bacon and packets of biscuits before they worked their way into their French Elephant's Foot sleeping bags to endure the night. The air was by no means unbearable. But it was well below freezing once the light had gone, and no one felt like talking. Marion calmed herself by thinking that, at least, she was no longer in Chelsea.

The next morning, Jeffrey lowered himself to the ground beside Ismail, who had sat up, sallow and sweating, in his sleeping bag. Otherwise, he'd not moved. His eyes glassy with pain.

"How are you feeling?" Jeffrey asked him in Turkish.

"I'd like to move north today." Ismail pushed himself out of the bag and pulled on his boots. "Best remain a moving target."

"Good." Jeffrey rose, dusted off his trousers, and addressed Gardiner. "We'll leave shortly."

When Gardiner nodded and began supervising the erasure of evidence of their camp, Jeffrey turned back to Ismail. "We agreed that you'd provide information about our destination when we'd reached the mountain. We are now on the mountain. Where are we going?"

"A little less than thirty miles west of Maykop." Ismail suppressed a wince of pain as he adjusted the straps of his rucksack. "There's a village nearby, but we'll avoid it"

"We've landed seventy miles south of Maykop." Jeffrey was arranging his own pack with more precision. "Why are we here? Why not touch down closer to our target? To the west?"

"It can be approached only from the south." Talking appeared to cause Ismail further pain. "And we must move with circumspection. You don't want to draw its attention before you're ready."

Jeffrey held his eyes for a silent five seconds. "What is it, Ismail?"

"I don't know." He smiled. Beaten. "You of all people know that I don't know."

"Marion," Jeffrey said levelly, turning away from Ismail. "What is it?"

She'd been hovering at the edges of their conversation, eavesdropping. But she merely gazed back at him, cold. Her pack tightened over her shoulders. Prepared to move.

Then, distracted, she brushed a brown spider off her lower arm. Watched it lower itself to the needle-covered floor of the clearing. She'd been surprised by their numbers so late in the season. Thinking that the early morning frosts ought to have put them to sleep for the year. An alien climate.

"Oh, very well." Irritated, Jeffrey didn't push her.

Instead, examining the stand of trees, he made certain that they'd left nothing behind to betray their presence. Then, satisfied, he and Gardiner led them out of the forest, in the direction of the river. The water flowed from the north to the south, and here it was less than six inches deep. If they kept to it, they'd be invisible to any dogs attached to the farms they'd seen on the way down. As a group, they were more than capable of communicating with the populations of the region. But no one would take them for native inhabitants. Better, as Ismail had said, to remain moving targets.

When the river veered to the east on the second day of their hike, they walked across a meadow at a higher elevation, its knee-high grass turning bronze-red in the cold. And then, at the edge of the meadow, they startled a griffon vulture feeding on the carcass of some days-dead ungulate. Intriguing, until the sky became dark with tens, hundreds, of the birds converging on the same spot. Circling. Their numbers felt unnatural, especially when only one, long-dead deer was drawing them. Ignoring her disquiet, Marion looked in the other direction. At the sharp, snow-covered peaks surrounding them.

Only once were they forced to exert themselves in a true alpine climb. Half a day, when they reached proper freezing level, crunched and slipped through three or four inches of new snow coating bare, grey rock, and then slid down into another dying meadow. Ismail, drawing on the reserves Jeffrey claimed he had retained, kept up without difficulty. In fact, he was gaining strength as they neared their target.

When they were within ten miles of Maykop, after a week of hiking eight or nine miles per day, he drew up beside Jeffrey and stopped him. Healthy and almost smiling. "We'll want to camp here for the night. I'll provide you more detailed instructions on our next steps tomorrow morning."

"Tonight," Jeffrey said, bland. "You'll provide the information tonight."

At which point a massive herd of goats—bezoar ibexes—thundered through a ravine a few hundred yards away from them. Marion stared. She hadn't thought that ibexes were stampeding animals. Or that they moved in such large groups. Brushing down the sleeves of her coat again, she noted that the spiders were becoming more abundant the further north they moved. Annoyed by her nervousness, she crushed the thought. Concentrated on preparing her sleeping bag for the evening. Curious, and cautiously pleased, about Ismail's changed, charged energy.

THEY never saw the next morning. Long before the sun rose over the bare oak forest in which they'd camped, the sound of a strangled shout from one of Gardiner's patrols woke them. The fire had been extinguished and their surroundings were black. No moon. No stars. Only the ragged sound of the patrol breathing a hundred yards away.

Gardiner and the third of his subordinates were running in the direction of the sound, their weapons drawn, before Marion had the chance to struggle out of her sleeping bag. Bleary-eyed, she watched Jeffrey and Nick following closely on their heels. Ismail was less agitated. Taking his time to tie and secure his boots before moving into the darkness.

By the time Marion had caught up to Jeffrey, Gardiner was shining a torch over the frail, crumbling dry leaves that coated the floor of the wood. Searching for a trail. One of his patrols, unconscious but alive, was lying injured at the center of nine slender trunks of an oak tree that had grown, in a lop-sided and sinister ring, from a single root. The second, conscious but silent, his nostrils flaring in pain, was staring wide-eyed at the blind wood. Both legs lacerated and bleeding.

Gardiner, squatting next to the conscious soldier, supported his shoulders with his arm. Moved him upright. "What happened?"

"An animal, sir. Vicious. Fast. I've never seen anything like it." The patrol was working hard to control his shaking.

Gardiner squinted across the clearing. "It took your weapons?"

"Must have done."

"Then it wasn't an animal, was it?"

Pale grin. "That's why you're in command, sir. Superior intelligence. But I know what I saw."

"Right." Gardiner's smile tilted. Then he helped the man to lean against the trunk of a tree. "And I mean to use that superior intelligence of mine to rip our shy werewolf another arseho—"

But before he could finish his sentence, the branches of the bare trees surrounding the clearing were disturbed by a humming wind, and the third of Gardiner's men was pulled bodily into the darkness. A quick intake of breath, and Nick was gone as well. Only Jeffrey, Gardiner, and Marion remained. Ismail had still not emerged from the camp.

Marion, feeling more spectator than potential target of the assault, exchanged a confused glance with Jeffrey, before she heard Gardiner crashing to the ground behind her. She twisted back, searching for him, and saw nothing but the torch lying on the otherwise empty dirt. Slowly, she turned back toward Jeffrey. But he was gone. Nothing. And so, she waited. Wondering why she'd been spared.

A few seconds later, she spotted a paraffin lamp glowing beyond the first line of trees. And then another. And then ten more. Twenty. Bobbing slowly toward her clearing. When they reached her, she smiled. Walking in their midst, looking as though he was back where he belonged, was Ismail. Speaking to their leader in what she assumed was another north Caucasian dialect.

They were dressed as ordinary villagers. Healthy certainly, but also soft and civilian. No super-human shock forces here. Rather, men, women, and children, smiling at her a trifle embarrassed, a trifle pleased by their intervention in her expedition.

Behind them, secured in a second clearing, she could just make out by the light of their lamps Gardiner, Nick, Jeffrey, and the three patrols. Jeffrey was the only one who was still conscious, on his knees, his arms and legs secured with rope, a rag stuffed into his mouth. His expression, from what she could see of it, was more bored than angry or distraught.

Ismail detached himself from the group, walked behind her, and retrieved Gardiner's torch. Handed it to the leader of the villagers with what Marion understood to be thanks. Took his rucksack and hers from one of the boys, who had been carrying them. Then he addressed Marion in Turkish.

"He says he can't kill them. Although that would be the simplest solution. Even if the British government denies that they've been here, which it would, there'd be an unofficial inquiry. And that inquiry would become an excuse for Stalin to send soldiers to restore order." He flicked his eyes toward the leader. "The village can't survive another round of that."

"I understand." She peered at the prone bodies in the clearing again. She'd have felt guilty leaving them all for dead.

"He also," Ismail continued, "can't detain them without a trial. The inspector tours the village on a monthly, and sometimes weekly, schedule. Confining a collection of angry foreigners in the collective stockroom for no official reason would require a larger bribe than he can afford at the moment. He also wouldn't be able to hide them because the village is too small."

"Oh." She couldn't grasp where Ismail was going with this information.

"So," Ismail explained, "there must be a trial. Which shouldn't pose a problem. They were trespassing on village land. The evidence is clear."

"I see."

"But the trial can take place only after sufficient time has passed for all parties to prepare their cases." Ismail looked down at the ground, a small smile on his face. "They take their criminal procedure seriously here."

"Oh." Beginning to follow Ismail's meaning.

"That pre-trial period," he said, "can take a week. A month. Six months." His smile was growing. "A year. Five years—"

"Marion." Jeffrey had managed to spit the rag onto the ground in front of him. He was speaking Turkish. "You can't possibly believe that this collection of antediluvian peasants is capable of detaining a unit of trained British soldiers for more than a few hours. If you don't put a stop to this idiocy at once, you will sorely regret it."

She blinked at him. And then she turned to Ismail. "A year." Long enough to extract Ian from Eton. To introduce Lydia to Edinburgh. To begin work on a new—"

"*Marion*—" But one of the village women had retrieved the rag and stuffed it back into his mouth.

Ismail, glancing over at Jeffrey, addressed the leader again. Exchanged a few comments. Laughed. And then he pointed Marion toward the darker part of the forest as he handed her one of the rucksacks. "We'll separate from them here. Reduce the chances that the villagers will be associated with our movements should we be caught."

She nodded, adjusted the straps over her shoulders, and walked beside him. "Won't you need the torch?"

"No." He held her elbow and guided her over a fallen tree trunk. "I hope that's acceptable to you. I know the way in the dark. We'll travel by night, camp during the day. It will take us two days to reach it."

"I understand." She began to walk. "I'll try to keep up."

He nodded without reply.

At first, she could see nothing of the forest. And, squinting behind her, there was no evidence that the villagers had been in the clearing at all. But moving by instinct, following the sound of Ismail's steps, she gradually fell into a comfortable rhythm.

And then, to be certain she wasn't losing him, she spoke. "Do you know what it is? I mean, this—this artifact? You held back at the depot, but I wasn't certain whether you were obfuscating there. Remaining intact."

"No. Truly, I don't. Those last few days—" He paused, exuding discomfort even in the pitch dark. "Those last few days in London, I'd have told them if I could have. At the time, I wished I could." He stopped and indicated to her a boulder she'd need to circumvent. "I do, though, have some guesses about it, which I didn't share with them. I also won't share them with you just yet. Better to wait till we arrive, so you can draw your own conclusions."

"Ismail," she began. "I've already drawn at least provisional conclusions. Remarkable ones. Those manuscripts they had in Chelsea—"

"Stop! Don't tell me." There was laughter in his voice.

"Why not?"

"What I said before still applies." He'd slowed to make his way through a stand of narrowly spaced conifers. The needles brushing their arms and cheeks. "I'm compromised. The less I know, the better."

She pushed the last wing-like branch out of her face and followed him into another small, black clearing. Confused. Everyone was compromised. Only someone very young or very stupidly indoctrinated would think otherwise. Why would he insist that he was less to be trusted than anyone else?

And then, finally, it hit her. He had a family. He hadn't disappeared here, he'd settled. And, of course, both the Russians and the British would use that. Had used that. When he'd finished this task, he'd be forced to report back to one. Or the other. Or both. Just, she sighed to herself, as she would.

As though reading her thoughts, Ismail spoke again. Veering away from talk of their target. "This organization of yours," he began, "they mentioned it in London. Persistently. Thought I was attached to it as well." She felt him glance back at her, curious. "Was it running you then? When you joined our delegation?"

"I hardly joined your delegation, Ismail." She hurried to keep up with his fading voice. If she lost him in the dark, in these woods, she'd never find her way out. "I affixed myself to its margins. Out of curiosity."

"Not infatuation?"

"Stop it."

The smile was evident in his tone. "But you couldn't have been tapped by them then, could you? You were so raw. Innocent. Would they have found you useful?"

She mused, walking over decades' worth of fallen pine needles. Then, eventually, she spoke again. "I thought at the time that I was attached—tenuously attached, mind you—to Ottoman

Intelligence. As I had been, from the beginning of the War. When it broke out in 1914, I was studying for my degree, but I'd already become indignant over British policy in the area. In an undergraduate sort of way, true. But that didn't make my feelings any less strong. The War was a catalyst."

She stopped speaking, uncertain of what to say next. He prodded her. "Yes?"

"And so," she resumed, "when the opportunity presented itself, I offered them my services. Mostly as a courier. Far from indispensable. But I was in Istanbul for research quite frequently, even when it became off-limits to British citizens. Inviolate international scholarly community, you know. They used that."

She felt damp seep into her boots as they crossed a shallow streamlet. "But then the War finished. Badly, as you'll recall. And I was at loose ends. I thought that my adventures, such as they were, were over. When suddenly, after fifteen months of silence, my handler reappeared with new instructions. Follow the delegation. Gather impressions of the region. Nothing specific, or—or violent. I'd likely have gone anyway, given the opportunity."

"I see." He'd stopped in a sticky, dark glade and was finding his bearings.

She waited beside him until she felt, rather than saw, him nod and move again. Then, following, she continued. "Since then, I've had more than a decade to watch my people recruit new talent. Some willing. Others less so. And in hindsight, from what I've seen, I think it's possible that my instructions in 1920 came from them rather than from the Ottoman government."

She shrugged in the darkness. "It could be that they were running me even before that. During the War. To watch how I'd react. Again, I've seen similar recruitment exercises many, many times since then."

"Hmm." Ismail walked in silence for close to five minutes. She had to work to follow him, listening for the sound of his boots crushing the brittle leaves. Then, pausing again, he led them down into a ravine. Squatted against a boulder to the side of another pebbled stream. "The sun will be rising in less than an hour. We'll stop here."

She sat next to him, leaning against the rock. Wind had blown it clean, and its white and grey surface felt close to sterile. But the air was beginning to take on a fertile, pre-dawn smell. And the water was a whispering sound and intermittently cold mist against her face. She looked forward to watching it when she could see again.

"He's your husband?"

Startled, she turned to him. Could just make out his profile now against a dark blue background. "Yes."

"Odd." And then, when he sensed her discomfort. "I mean, not odd as a choice." He considered. "No, I take it back. That's strange as well. But to me, it's more surprising that you married at all."

She laughed, stung. "What does that mean?"

"You were always so vestal, Marion. That's why they teased you, you know." He glanced over at her. The sun had begun to climb over the edge of the ravine, and her face was white in the reflected light. "You made even the Turkish girls look promiscuous, which, believe me, took some doing." He shook his head. "And now I come back after twenty years to find you wed to that—that insufferable, urbane wanker."

She felt herself blushing. Couldn't think of any way to explain her relationship to Jeffrey. And so instead, she took refuge in remembering her earlier years. "I was married before," she told him. "To someone else. In Egypt."

"A good place to be married." Amused by the non-sequitur.

"He was—" She paused, uncertain what to say about Tariq. She herself hardly knew what she thought of him anymore. More than a decade now without him. "He died. That is, Jeffrey killed him." She stopped herself again. "I mean, Jeffrey orchestrated the circumstances under which he was murdered."

"And so," Ismail was laughing now, "you thought to yourself, why not marry 'Jeffrey' instead?"

Confused, she squeezed her eyes shut. She couldn't begin to put her decisions over the past fifteen years into any kind of coherent narrative. Opened her eyes and gazed out at the river. Smooth round pebbles. A lynx, suspicious and supercilious, staring at them from the opposite shore.

Ismail covered her hand with his. "You haven't changed all that much, you know. Despite your tainted, competent uncertainty. Always so confounded by human interaction. I'll bet you'd prefer the company of that cat right now."

She half smiled, still looking across the water at the lynx. Disdainful, it drank from the shallow stream and disappeared into the trees that edged the ravine.

"I'm married as well," he offered quietly, as though admitting to membership in some unscrupulous political organization.

"I guessed it," she said. "At least some of those lines on your face are the product of child-rearing rather than politics. I can tell. I've got them too."

"Two girls and a boy," he said. "Eight, twelve, and fourteen. You?"

"A boy and a girl. Both Jeffrey's. Eleven and two." She squinted over at him. The sun had climbed higher and was reflecting blindingly off the water. His girls must adore him. He looked the perfect father. "Are they here?"

"In the area."

"I understand." And she did understand. More thoroughly than he seemed to imagine.

Relaxing further against the rock, she closed her eyes, enjoying the feel of the sun against her skin. Although the night had been hectic, and the walk arduous, she felt little inclination to eat. The sharp, flawless air precluded anything so corporeal. In fact, she could imagine remaining in this spot, in this position, for centuries. Eons. Waiting out whatever cataclysm Jeffrey, Maugham, and their like were preparing for the world. Watching for the return of the lynx.

But then, as the sun rose higher and the light became mundane, she remembered her assignment. There were questions she wanted to ask Ismail, now that he was no longer—directly, at least—under the thumb of the office. She straightened her back against the rock and glanced sidelong at him. His eyes were closed as well, but he was awake.

"Ismail, I know that you don't want me telling you anything about my findings in Chelsea." She rubbed her palm against her knee. Enjoying the feel of the coarse cloth of the military fabric. "But it would help me to talk about them. To order my thoughts."

"I'm no historian," he said. His eyes remained closed. "I'm not sure what I can contribute."

"Nonetheless—" She stopped to consider. She felt ashamed now of her refusal to examine the Ibn Daniyal in Chelsea. Stared at the water, uneasy. And then, she resumed: "there were three manuscript fragments bound together into a single volume from a collection that had been hidden in Iraq."

"Don't tell me what they were."

"I won't." She rubbed her palms together, bringing the blood to the surface of her skin. "But I'll tell you about them."

"Carefully."

"Yes," she agreed. "Carefully."

She watched a swarm of dragonflies, too late for the season, hover over the running water for a few seconds before exploding upward and outward. Gone. "Two of the documents made sense. Or, at least, a kind of sense. There were connections between them and the people and history of the Caucasus."

"And the third?" Drowsy now.

She spoke briskly to keep him awake and interested. "The third was strange. Irrelevant and—and offensive." She blushed. "At least, I found it offensive. Others might think it clever. But the point is that there was nothing in it of the slightest applicability to this region. It was—comically inappropriate."

"Perhaps its inclusion was an error," he offered. "These were old documents, correct? Who knows where they were kept, or who had a hand in compiling them, over the centuries?"

"No," she said slowly. "No, I don't think so. This was a deliberate inclusion. I could feel it. Though I didn't understand it."

"What part of it didn't you understand?" He sounded entirely uninterested. Resting properly for the first time since London. Or, she corrected herself, since the Russians had collected him months earlier.

But she continued speaking anyway. Unable to relax herself. Willing Ismail to follow. "It was a poem composed in the thirteenth century by an Arab doctor living in Cairo under the Mamluk Sultan, Baybars." She closed her eyes as well. "And, I suppose, that's all you need know. It's inexplicable. What possible link could there be between a Mamluk poet writing in the thirteenth century and this ancient Caucasian artifact you've been describing?"

"Aside from the obvious, you mean." Ismail was still reclined, on the verge of sleep.

She was silent for five long seconds. And then: "what do you mean the obvious?"

"Well." He opened his eyes and looked at her, surprised by her lack of understanding. "You know. I'm no historian, but even I'm aware that the Mamluk sultans were, you might say, native sons. Baybars came from here."

She did know that, of course. Though it hadn't occurred to her. But—her momentary excitement ebbing—she shook her head. The Mamluks were Turks. From the steppes. Too far north. Baybars himself was Kipchak. Reluctantly, she let the thought go. "No. It's too tenuous."

Ismail, though, was excited and awake himself now, albeit in his self-mocking, half-joking way. "Why?" Injured. "The steppes are a lot closer than Cairo, at any rate."

"The Mamluks were Turks." Exasperated.

"You forget, Marion. You're in the Caucasus. Those designations don't mean anything here." He was sitting further upright now. "How many times have hordes like the damned Russians swept through here? The Mongols? They always leave a bit of themselves behind. Turks too. How can you claim to tell the difference?"

She wasn't going to be browbeaten by his specious cosmopolitanism. "Russians," she said, "speak Russian. Circassians speak Circassian. Mongols speak—" She stopped, annoyed to have fallen into her own conversational trap. More exhausted than she realized.

"Baybars spoke Arabic." He was still smiling. "And you and I are speaking Turkish. What does that tell you?"

"You don't understand—"

"I'm teasing." The lines around his eyes had deepened. Warm. "And yes," he conceded, "Baybars was Kipchak. According to all of the most reliable sources." He re-settled his shoulders against the rock and closed his eyes again. "It's an interesting coincidence, though. My immigrant father, you know—also not an historian, to be clear—used to claim Sultan Baybars as one of our own. An early success in our centuries-long emigration."

"As Abkhaz?" She watched his profile, also smiling. "That's silly."

"Not Abkhaz. Ubykh."

Her smile faded. "You're Abkhaz."

"I," he said, "am Turkish. But my forefathers were Ubykh. Not Abkhaz. Never Abkhaz."

"But you ran that journal in Istanbul." She was frowning at him now, a worrisome thought forming at the back of her mind. "For the promotion of Abkhaz language and culture. And you helped to found that society. On Abkhaz literary—"

"Ubykh," he interrupted her, laughter still in his voice, "is a language with eighty-four consonants and two vowels. *No one* can speak it. Even in the diaspora. It's embedded in the land. Here. Nowhere else. Doesn't travel. Can you imagine trying to 'promote' that in a city full of French-speaking Turks? Nothing *but* vowels in those languages. Abkhaz is friendlier. Easier to collect subscriptions to support a language that doesn't terrorize everyone who hears it."

"It is a coincidence," she echoed him after a few seconds, only half responding to what he was saying.

The scrap from Evliya Çelebi had focused narrowly on Ubykh. Not Abkhaz. Not Circassian. Not Georgian. The code had been embedded in the Ubykh sections. And now, following the evidence that Ismail had uncovered over the past two decades, they were entering the historic Ubykh homeland. Had the Ubykhs themselves hidden something before the Russians had destroyed them? Something having to do with their language—

"Not to mention," he was continuing, "that Ubykh culture is one long story of eradication by superior enemy forces. We were always the region's death-or-glory types. Short lives. Great fame. Very, *very* small numbers. That sort of thing. Also difficult to sell to a charitable urban audience. And so," he yawned, "I threw my support behind the Abkhazians. Cut my losses. My father didn't mind. He was always suspicious of outside interest in our culture anyway. Better to deflect attention away. The Ubykhs in Turkey, incidentally, who claim to be speaking the language—well, they aren't. None of us do. We prefer not to advertise."

"He claimed that Baybars was Ubykh," she repeated. "Your father, I mean."

"Oh no." Ismail was laughing openly, his eyes still shut. "Your tone has gone distressingly earnest. Please don't let what I've said influence your interpretation of whatever it was you read in London. You said you wanted to talk. I'm acting as a receptive listener. No more. God forbid I lead you further astray."

"But—"

"My father," he said, "claimed not only Baybars as Ubykh, but most of the heroes of the Nart Sagas, not to mention Prometheus, Circe, Medea, the Amazons, and the mothers of all of the Ottoman sultans after Selim the Grim. Oh yes, and Polyphemus the cyclops. He wasn't an understated man. Not the sort of informant to serve as the basis for a scholarly theory."

"I see." She tried to keep her tone neutral, but even his last statement left her more intrigued than discouraged. Circe and Medea were interesting additions to the list. From the eastern Black Sea, of course. But they were also notorious sorceresses who had a way with animals. Aristophanes undoubtedly would have had something to say to Ismail's father—

"Stop!" he repeated, still entertained. "Look at you. It's worse than I thought."

"It's not," she retorted. "I'm curious. I hadn't thought in this direction before, and it's given me a new perspective on the documents. I haven't been carried away."

"Not you," he agreed. "But really, Marion. We're both fatigued. Enervated. We need sleep. So do try to put it out of your head and rest for a few hours. When the sun goes down, we'll move again. We ought to reach our target before the light returns. And then," he yawned a second time, "you'll have something more concrete than my displaced father's lost heritage to work with. Trust me, it's extraordinary."

"Your father sounds extraordinary." She rested her head against his shoulder and closed her eyes.

"He would have liked you," Ismail replied. "Pure and certain."

THEIR second night of trekking through the blind, black forest was less peaceful than the first. Although the trees and undergrowth remained uniform—stands of bare oaks followed by larger sections of conifer—the air was disturbed. Eddies of wind from multiple directions at once that suggested imminent rain, but that remained dry and frigidly desiccating. The constant movement of animals through the groundcover, animals, however, that couldn't be nocturnal. Wrong in the darkness. Too large. Too numerous. Insufficiently furtive.

But they pressed on despite the inhospitable atmosphere. Marion had the sense that Ismail was hurrying now. Careful to remain within shouting distance, but impatient to reach their goal. On occasion, she had to stop, filter out the scrabbling animal noises, and locate the distant crunching of his steps, before half-jogging to catch up to him. Infected by his mood, she couldn't bring herself to resume conversation with him.

Despite their nervousness, they reached their destination without mishap a good two hours before sunrise, Ismail panting from the exertion, his hand against a tree. She couldn't see what their target was—and only recognized Ismail because she ran into him—but he seemed relieved. Gave her a little hug when she stumbled across him. "This is it."

"I can't see anything."

A short laugh. "I'd be concerned if you could. We'll wait now. Watch the sun rise over it."

"I'd like to sit," she said. "Regain my breath. Will that be all right?"

"Yes." He held her by the arm and helped her sink to the ground next to him. "Beside me. Facing this direction. When the sky begins to change color, don't move."

Nonplussed, she nodded, though she knew he couldn't see her, and waited. Forty-five minutes later, the black outlines of bare oak trees became visible against a slightly less black sky. And, five minutes after that, she became aware that they were sitting at the edge of a glade. Fallen leaves and pebbles surrounding, and partially covering, a squat structure, still in shadow. Then, less than a minute later, a line of orange appeared above the horizon beyond the oak trees. Distended into reddish pink. They were facing east.

And as the sun broke over the horizon, it illuminated in stark relief against a blurry dawn a ring of standing stones. At their center was a hut or altar made of the same material, half fallen-in. She nearly laughed as the monument revealed itself. If she hadn't known better, she'd have thought herself in Wales or the Orkneys. Even the hostile, inhospitable air felt similar.

Smiling, she turned to Ismail, about to speak. But he shook his head firmly and pointed toward the stones. Bemused, she returned her attention to the dolmens, watching the warm sunrise dissolve into ordinary daylight. And, just as she was beginning to fidget, wondering why Ismail refused to move, her eyes widened.

From a small, round opening at the front of the altar, a foot or so above the ground, three or four spiders emerged. And then ten more. And then a hundred. Until the opening was clogged with spiders crawling out and falling or lowering themselves to the ground. Thousands upon thousands of them. For well over five minutes.

After which—and dispelling any hope that this arachnid behavior was, in some obscure zoological way, natural—came sparrows. Floods of them. Straining and pushing themselves through the gap in the rock before taking flight above the bare, slumbering oak trees. Flocking in the pale blue sky before dispersing and then plummeting toward the ground. Aggressive and deliberate. Frightening.

And then finally, once the rock had disgorged the last sparrow, came catfish. Falling wetly to the ground, crushing the less agile spiders. Crawling and flopping toward some nonexistent water source. Swarming, if turgidly, in the same martial, dangerous manner that the sparrows had.

Cringing back, Marion glanced again at Ismail. But, once more, he merely shook his head, firm, and pointed. Less acquiescent now, but unwilling to risk attracting the attention of the animals, she remained still, observing. A little over ten minutes later, when the sun was well above the glade, the spiders began to bury themselves under the fallen oak leaves. Digging themselves into the ground where the wind had blown it bare.

Looking up, she saw that the sparrows had also vanished. And the sky was empty. Clean. Too quiet. While the catfish, making a bit more noise, scuttled out beyond the stone circle, away from Ismail and Marion, toward what she assumed was some pond or stream known only to them. And then, ominously, pregnantly, the clearing was quiet.

Marion waited a full minute before addressing Ismail, who was rising to his feet, helping her up at the same time. And even then, she wasn't certain what to say. Rubbing her eyes with her fists, she finally spoke. "What was that?"

"Unimportant," he said briskly.

"*Unimportant?*"

"Or," he amended, "irrelevant. I'll show you the ruin now. Evidence that the object is nearby."

"How," she asked, rooted in place, "could what we just saw be irrelevant? What *was* that?"

"I don't know." Politely tolerant of her reaction. "Do you?"

She had a few ideas. Didn't like them. "No."

"Then we'll ignore it."

"How do you know it won't come back? What happens if we get in its way?" She hadn't moved. Couldn't force herself to walk in the direction of the stones.

"We won't get in its way." He'd adjusted the straps of his rucksack, and he was beckoning her to follow him in the direction of the stone circle. Impatient. "It happens at dawn and at sunset. Only at dawn and at sunset. Different animals every time. I've watched. We'll be safe. More important now is for you to look at the stones."

Pushing down further protest, she followed him into the clearing. Recognizing, despite her queasy stomach, the site for the remarkable find that it was. Wondering how many inert spiders she was treading underfoot as she crunched through the fallen leaves. "It *is* extraordinary, Ismail." Wanting, ambiguously, to reassure him. When she passed the closest standing stone, she brushed its rough surface with her fingertip. Shivered. "I had no idea that these formations appeared in the Caucasus. Reminds me of home."

He gazed, unimpressed, about the clearing. Took in the stones. "No," he said after a few seconds. "Not this. These are everywhere. Most are fallen or buried in the ground. But a few, like these, have remained upright. This isn't what I'm showing you."

"It isn't?" If not this, then what? "But—"

"The villagers have always known about the dolmens. And they know to stay away at dawn and sunset. As will we." He shrugged as he left the last of the standing stones behind and continued into the forest. "I've no doubt some Russian archaeologist will show up in a few years' time to develop a self-serving theory about them. Proof of ancient Slavic roots in the region. Something like that.

"They're mostly bronze-age," he added, still indifferent. "From what I understand. But what I want to show you is the use that more recent visitors have found for them. Visitors from the same period as your Mamluk poet, now that I think of it. Give or take a century. Which is interesting in its own right."

Silent, she followed him. Astonished that there could be more to show her than these haunting, alien structures. They shivered the air around her. Unsympathetic. Just as they did at home. She tried to avoid them there as well.

But she was nonetheless disappointed when he stopped triumphantly at nothing more than a small hill of pebbles scattered to the side of a rotting tree trunk. No megaliths. In fact, there was little to indicate that the pebbles hadn't collected there randomly. The product of wind, erosion, or the activity of normal animals.

Ismail himself, though, energetic now, didn't notice her unenthusiastic response. He slipped off his rucksack, set it at the foot of a tree, and began pushing piles of leaves aside. Revealing a cluster of narrow apertures in the ground.

Marion dropped her rucksack as well. "Can I help?"

"No." He stood, panting. "That's it. These will allow light to enter. Natural light. I'm not brave enough to risk artificial light in there."

"In where?" She let her eyes wander over the pile of pebbles. Unimpressed.

"As I said before, there are dolmens distributed all over this region. Mostly fallen or sunk underground." He shoved aside the pebbles until he'd exposed a round hole, similar to the one from which the spiders, sparrows, and catfish had emerged a few hours earlier. "This leads to a stone gallery. Quite small. And partially ruined. But remarkable."

The back of her neck prickled. "A tomb?"

"I haven't found any bodies." He lowered himself feet-first through the hole. "I don't think these are tombs."

"Good." She'd have followed him anyway. But she was pleased she wouldn't be meeting any territorial ghosts. This part of the forest was unnerving enough as it stood.

Once his head had disappeared into the structure, she sighed and pushed her own feet through the hole. Felt empty space beneath her, lowered herself further, keeping hold of the edges of the opening. Allowing herself, eventually, to swing at full length from the lip. Still not touching the ground.

A quick peek down told her that she must drop three or four feet further. The light from Ismail's apertures was more than sufficient to illuminate the small chamber. And Ismail himself was standing to the side of the room, waiting for her. Releasing her grip, she fell to the stone floor, straightened, and looked about her.

It was a surprising structure to find hidden beneath the forest in this sparsely populated section of the northwest Caucasus. But though she tried not to show it, it wasn't overwhelming. A cube, approximately twelve feet in every direction, constructed of roughly worked stone pillars supporting the stone ceiling. Otherwise bare. No bodies. Although the room felt as though it wouldn't decline collecting some. She pushed the feeling away and looked at Ismail.

"This way," he said. "There's a smaller chamber here. Beyond this fallen pillar. I'll crawl under it first, you follow. When you're through, the light will return. From above."

She nodded and prepared to push behind him through the narrow tunnel. Having encountered more daunting underground passages in the past, she didn't panic in the close darkness. But she was reassured when the tunnel opened into another cubical chamber. Light falling into the room from a shaft that dimly reached the surface. Five feet in all directions this time. They had to crouch.

"What do you think?" Ismail was smiling in the greyish-yellow air.

She examined the room, uncertain of what to expect. Her neck bent uncomfortably under the low ceiling. And then, stiffening in disbelief, she peered more closely at the walls. The ceiling. The floor. Every inch of the cube was covered in tiny, carved letters. Greek on the ceiling and the west wall. Arabic on the three other walls and the floor. The Greek fading but legible. The Arabic brighter and better preserved, but still very old. Marion silently accepted Ismail's conjecture that it was thirteenth-century. Stunned, she pressed her palm against the cold ceiling. And then against the east wall.

"There's more," he said.

"More?"

"Yes." He knelt in the darkest corner of the room and felt about until he retrieved a cloth-covered object, beckoned Marion toward him, and then removed the cloth when she was squatting beside him. "This was waiting in the center of the floor when I found the chamber. I moved it when I stumbled across the shaft to the surface. I didn't want to take it with me because—" He paused. "If I had, it would be in Moscow now. You may have a better idea as to why it was here than I have."

He handed it to her, and she moved into the light, sitting cross-legged on the floor to examine it. An astrolabe. Bronze inlaid with gold and silver. Three additional plates attached to it. Mamluk, she guessed by the markings. Although, turning them in her hand, her brow furrowed, she saw that the plates were wrong. The latitude numbers made no sense. And the choice of stars and constellations on the "spider" or rete were unusually obscure. Canis Minor, she thought. A few others. Useless.

The astrolabe itself was also attributed to an odd artist: *al-Qawwas*, "the archer." An unknown. Ordinarily, these instruments were proudly claimed by astronomers listed prominently in the biographical dictionaries. This one, against the norm, was effectively anonymous.

Nonplussed, she turned it over in her hands. And nearly dropped it. Sketched into the Sagittarius position of the sequence of astrological signs was not the conventional abstract arrow or centaur, but her Scythian slave-archer. Uncontestably the same figure. Identical to those in the manuscript and on the classical vase. She shoved the instrument back into Ismail's hands. "I can't take this. It belongs here."

"There will be Russian archaeologists here before the year is out," he said shortly. "Someone must take it. I also intend to destroy this room. I don't know what it does or what it leads to, but whatever it is, they can't know about it." He peered at her face in the dim light. "I'd hoped you'd draw something valuable from it, maybe inform this organization of yours of its existence. They could, perhaps, help to—to deflect attention away from it? Or at the very least use it properly? The impression I formed in London was that your people do that sort of thing."

When she said nothing, his voice became ironic again. "Who would have thought, in 1920, that seventeen years later I'd be begging innocent, credulous Marion Bailey for her protection and influence?"

She rose into a semi-standing position. Disliking his tone, which reminded her of Jeffrey's. "What about the engravings? Have you read them?"

"I can't read Greek." He stood, crouching, as well. "But I've spent time with the Arabic script. It isn't in any language I've seen. Though it's evocative."

"What do you mean?"

"Try for yourself." He gestured toward the east wall. "My advice is to read it aloud, phonetically. As much as that's possible in Arabic letters."

Nodding, she squinted at a line of letters that ran across the room at eye-level. Tried to draw meaning out of it. Couldn't do so. And then, taking Ismail at his word, she began, painstakingly, to recite the sounds. Nothing. Except, following a few seconds of recitation, a scurrying sound behind the walls. After which, three mice skittered across the floor, disappearing into a hole on the other side. She stopped reading, disappointed.

"I'm getting nothing from this." She glanced over at him for corroboration.

"Try the Greek." He twisted his neck to observe the ceiling. "I've been curious. Couldn't ask anyone for help, obviously."

She looked up at the ceiling as well. Nonsense. Lines and lines and lines of nonsense. But then, with a small sigh, she began reciting. Almost at once, the three mice reappeared, trailed by eight others. And a throng of the brown spiders toppled into the room from the surface, through the shaft, landing on her head. Startled and annoyed, she stopped speaking and stepped back. The scrabbling noises ceased.

"Nothing," she said. "It's gibberish."

"It's Ubykh. The Greek script is even closer than the Arabic."

"You understand it?" She stared at him. "Why didn't you tell me? This is astonishing. Extraordinary. It—"

"I don't understand it."

"Then how do you know it's Ubykh? I thought you could speak it."

"I can tell from the sound." He examined the ceiling, as though to avoid her gaze. "And there's an echo of a meaning in it. Like—like perhaps when you read poetry in the oldest dialects of English? Anglo-Saxon? You sense something. It's there. You may not understand it, but you feel the deep history."

"I certainly don't," she muttered in English.

He dropped his eyes and smiled, breaking the mood. Responded in Turkish. "I've been told, by people who know about such things, that the only city in the world whose inhabitants speak a more frightening dialect than Ubykh is Glasgow."

"They'd also be more than willing to match you horn for horn in the consumption of fermented milk and grain products," she replied. Then, discouraged and glancing about the small chamber, she continued. "I'd like to take rubbings of these engravings. All of them. And perhaps also copy them into my notebook. It will take several days, but that's the only way I'll have a chance of deciphering them." She squinted up at the bright sky through the shaft. "Have we time for that?"

"I think so." He was wrapping the astrolabe in its cloth. "This part of the forest rarely sees visitors. The air puts off intelligent people. Less intelligent people don't make it past the animals. So yes, we'll be safe. We'll camp in the next clearing."

"What about dawn and sunset?"

"We're at the far edge of the disturbances." He slipped the wrapped instrument into his jacket. "The clearing is beyond it."

"Good. Then I suppose I'll begin work tomorrow." She grinned at him, feeling inexplicably lighthearted. "Thank you for this, Ismail. You were right. I wouldn't have believed it without experiencing it in person."

IT took five days, crawling back and forth through the tunnel to the small chamber, for Marion to copy the lines of text to her satisfaction. Since the strings of letters were meaningless, she had to double check each entry in her notebook. And once she had the rubbings in front of her—a thick sheaf of filmy pages—she was irritated to discover her many errors. She'd always thought herself a careful copyist.

On the sixth day, finally content with both her rubbings and her copies, she rolled the pages into a tube, protected them with cardboard casing, and secured them in her rucksack. It was just past noon, the air was hovering a few degrees above freezing, and her eyes ached from a week of staring into the dim light of the five-foot cube. Stretching her neck, she searched the clearing for Ismail.

When she saw him, reclined against a tree, reading what she hoped wasn't a collection of late-Ottoman short stories, she waded through the carpet of fallen leaves in his direction. Holding her rucksack in her hand. Her breath heavy in the air. "I've got everything I can from it."

He pushed himself up, flicking a snail off the sleeve of his jacket. "Good. I'll take you to the coast road, then. We won't have difficulty finding a reputable lorry-driver to transport you down. They travel between Maykop and Tuapse two or three times per week." He paused, briefly shy. "Unless you'd rather meet my family? We'd be honored to have you."

She was tempted. And curious. But she declined. "It's better that I move quickly. When I cross my contact, I'll pass along your proposal. About—about this site, I mean. And the Russians."

"Thank you." He frowned at the nearly invisible disturbances in the leaves matching the contours of the gallery beneath the surface. "I'll finish things off, then."

She watched as he trudged toward the opening, carrying three pipe bombs she'd seen him constructing as she'd moved in and out of the chamber. "Is there anything I can do?"

He shook his head and squatted at the stone gap. Thought for a moment. And then, setting the explosives on the ground, he leaned back on his heels. Looked back at her, sheepish. "I can't do it."

"Are you certain?"

"Yes." He stood, brushing down his trousers. "I thought I could. I left these components with the villagers intending to. But—" His expression flickered between frustrated and ironic.

"It's better this way," she said. "I wouldn't have tried to stop you. It's your find. But destroying it felt excessive to me." She walked toward him and stood beside him, looking down at the opening. "Even if the Russians do stumble across the site, they'll make nothing of the writing. They haven't got the explanatory material. Not to mention," she added, reaching into her jacket and retrieving the astrolabe, "you've got this."

"No." He refused to take it. "You've got it."

Displeased, she shoved it into an inside pocket of the shirt she wore beneath her pullover and jacket. She'd force him to accept it as they moved toward the coast road. Or, if that failed, she'd trick him and hide it on him before they separated. Something told her that the astrolabe wasn't meant to leave the Caucasus. She didn't want it.

Reading her thoughts, he cast her a wary smile, stepped away, and squatted again. Began obscuring the entrance to the gallery. Piling leaves and dirt across a makeshift wooden cover. Moving a fallen tree trunk into place above that.

Following his lead, Marion wandered through the clearing, hiding the shafts that lit the chamber and attempting as much as possible to disguise her own footprints in the process. She was just dragging a large, crumbling rock into place when she stopped, straightened, and listened. Knit her brows. And then, moving quickly, she left the rock, retrieved the rucksacks, and tossed one to Ismail.

He caught it in one hand, perplexed. "What is it?"

"Steps. Someone's coming." She tightened the straps over her shoulders. Nervous.

"Animals," he said, nonetheless obediently lifting his own rucksack into place. "No one comes here."

She shook her head. "Listen."

The footsteps were louder now. Running. More than one.

"Shit." He took her arm. "Come. I know a back way out."

"Wait," she said, kneeling to take up two of his pipe bombs. "Before we move, I have a better use for these. Whoever this is, they know we're here. No purpose in being furtive. Let's slow them down."

Nodding, he took a lighter from an external pocket of his rucksack, made eye-contact with her, and lit both fuses. They threw the pipes in the direction of the converging runners. And then, scooping up the last, unlit, pipe to use later, Marion followed him into the forest.

They pushed through a wide belt of conifers before sliding down a ravine and running along a section of stream. Perhaps, she thought hectically, the ultimate destination of the catfish. But, though a satisfying explosion followed their deployment of the pipes, and though they were moving fast, the steps were soon gaining on them again. At one point she saw a dark figure through the bare trunks of the oak trees.

When it became clear that they'd never outrun their pursuers, Marion reached out for Ismail's shoulder and pulled him into the cover of an overhanging boulder. "We can't stay together. It's too easy for them."

"How will you find your way out?" He was sweating hard. The days in storage catching up to him—distressingly plain in his taut, grey face.

"Which way to the road?"

"Northwest."

"Good." She nodded. "I'll keep to the northwest. I'll find it. But for the moment, I'm going to make some noise. When I've left, and when you've heard them following me, throw that last pipe. Wait till I've drawn them off, and then go."

"I'd argue, but—"

"You know better," she finished for him. Then, hating herself for blushing, she kissed his cheek again. "I'm glad you didn't die in 1920."

"You see?" He kissed her forehead. "Utterly infatuated. Poor girl."

"Idiot."

She crept out from under the rock and made her way five hundred yards to the south, where a trail marked by deer cut through some of the oldest pines she'd seen in the area. Then, jumping up, she pushed loudly through the trees, kicking up leaves as she went.

A few seconds later, she heard the renewed sound of the running steps. And a minute after that, the third pipe bomb exploding behind her. Using the confusion caused by the pipe, she left the deer path and sprinted with all her strength away from the rock. Still making enough noise to attract the runners.

When she was certain they were following her, she slowed, searching for cover. She couldn't run indefinitely, though she was beginning to fear that her pursuers could. Their momentum hadn't flagged. As she was considering possibilities, looking in the undergrowth for a gap or indentation in which to bury herself, she stumbled, horrified, to a halt.

In front of her wasn't a small ravine of the sort she'd seen repeatedly in this wood, but a canyon. Well over one hundred feet tall. Stretching out miles in both directions. Impassible. Mocking. And though the river at the bottom was wide and deep, it looked frigid. And so very far away.

She cast a quick, involuntary glance behind her. Needn't have. She could hear the footsteps closing in on her. Slowing as they also registered her situation. She thought that she could see a trace of more than one of the figures now. No choice.

And so, taking a deep breath, and cursing the fact that she'd failed to return the astrolabe to Ismail, she jumped. Rigid and straight. Forcing herself not to think for the five, long, sickening seconds that she plummeted toward the water.

When she hit, she didn't die. Which annoyed her. Alive, she was forced to suffer the shock of the needle-cold water and the unendurable pain of clawing her way to the surface. Alive, she was also compelled to drag herself onto a shelf of horizontal rock, crying and shivering, miserably conscious. And finally, alive, she heard, after a half hour of drifting in and out of darkness, an exasperated voice speaking English.

"Marion, damn it. You stupid—"

SHE struggled into consciousness in what she at first took to be the guest room of a respectable, but not luxurious, hotel. Clean white walls. Clean white wood floor. Clean white linen on her wide single bed. And, turning to her side, before groaning in dismay, clean white bars over the large window.

When she sat up, she saw that she herself was wearing a white cotton nightgown. Her hair loose. She examined the room for evidence of additional clothing, but there was no wardrobe. Nor was there any luggage. Instead, there was an armchair in striped yellow and white silk and a white fur rug beside the bed. A yellow dressing gown arranged over the chair. A pair of fur slippers on the rug.

There was also a low, whitewashed table placed under the window, through which bright sunlight poured, illuminating the room. Though she couldn't see it from her position in the bed, she sensed water nearby. The light felt maritime. Tropical perhaps. A hint of the South of France.

She pushed the bedclothes off her legs, noted in passing that she hadn't been damaged by her jump into the river, and swung her feet onto the rug. Slid them into the slippers, which fit perfectly and felt new. Stood cautiously, and—when no stray spasms of pain stopped her—walked with more confidence toward one of the two pale-yellow doors in the room. One, she imagined, a toilet and the other leading to a corridor.

The first door was locked. The corridor, most likely. Discouraged, but not surprised after the barred window, she moved toward the second door. The toilet. Turned the knob. It was also locked. Perturbed, she gazed about the room. She wasn't in need of it immediately, but she did wonder what she was expected to do when the time came. No evidence that she could see of a chamber pot.

Bemused, she wandered to the window and looked out. An immaculate green lawn. Empty. And a high white wall. She couldn't see beyond the wall, but she remained convinced that it blocked some subtropical body of water. The light was too bleached and buoyant to be anything but the sunshine of a coastal town. Even in the room, she could feel its warmth.

She was interrupted in her contemplation of the view, or absence of it, by a door opening. To the corridor. Through it passed a young woman wearing a starched nurse's uniform, who stumbled to a halt, stared at her in horror, dropped the tray of food she was carrying, and abruptly shut the door again.

Marion blinked and contemplated the tray. The shattered tea pot. The pool of milk. The three-minute egg smashed sideways in its cup. And the four pieces of unscathed toast. She debated retrieving and eating the toast, but then concluded she wasn't all that hungry. Instead, she walked to the armchair, examined the dressing gown, and wrapped it around her, tying the belt. Quilted like a grandmother's, but also new. Then, sitting in the chair, she waited.

Less than five minutes later, the door opened and the same nurse, blushing, knelt in the open frame and cleaned the mess. When she'd backed out of the room, a second, older, sturdier nurse accompanied by two male orderlies took her place. The second nurse smiled at her, unpleasant. When Marion said nothing, the nurse addressed her in English with a heavy French accent. "Please forgive Nurse Voisin. She was startled to find you awake and out of bed. Would you be so kind as to come with me?"

After a split-second of hesitation, Marion complied. Nodding silently, she rose from the chair. The nurse led her into a corridor that matched the room. Clean, hygienic, lacking in character. Respectable. The orderlies followed. They walked past eight identical doors until they reached an open office, paneled in dark wood. Sitting behind a desk that mimicked the walls was a young man, tall, thin, blond, who stood and smiled professionally when they entered. Once Marion was seated in the chair, the nurse withdrew, closing the door, taking the orderlies with her.

"Good morning. You look well." The man sat behind the desk and observed Marion with open good humor and equally open interest. The same French-accented English.

"Good morning. Thank you."

"Dr. Pinel is occupied today, but he is very much looking forward to speaking with you tomorrow morning."

She nodded. It meant nothing to her.

"I am Dr. Dagonet. Shall we begin?" He opened a leather notebook on the desk in front of him and took up a thick, Montblanc pen.

But before he could continue, she preempted him. "Where am I?"

"Where do you think you are?"

This annoyed her. But she wasn't yet ready to go on the offensive. Biting back a nasty retort, she said, "I last remember joining a communal hike through the mountain wilderness. I'm not certain what happened to me after that."

"Yes," he said, making a note. "That coincides with our information. You were discovered injured and raving in the local mountains in December of 1937. Your rescuers did what they could for you before bringing you here to recover. You're lucky to be alive."

"December of 1937?" A pit opened at the bottom of her stomach. "And what is the date today?"

"Today is the twenty-third of September, 1938."

"That's impossible."

"On the contrary." He turned a small desk calendar toward her.

She didn't look at it. "I can't stay here."

"Where will you go?" He was still taking notes.

"Home. Britain."

"Ah." He made another note. Looked up at her. "You had no identification when you were found. We presumed Britain, but we couldn't be positive. We also don't know your name."

"If I had no identification, then how could you presume Britain?"

"You were raving." He set the pen carefully to the side of the notebook. "In English. What is your name?"

"Marion." Aggressive.

"Yes?" He took up the pen again.

"Bailey."

"Very good." He wrote it down.

"I want to contact my family."

"Excellent." He held the pen above the page expectantly. "And their names?"

But she hesitated. Uncertain that she wanted Jeffrey to find her. Or Maugham. They knew nothing about the documents or the dolmens. And it was possible, even after the time that had apparently passed, that she could salvage her project.

"Not yet." She lowered her eyes.

"I'm sorry?"

"I'll contact them upon my return." She let her gaze wander the room. "If you'd make a package of my belongings, I'll leave and purchase passage home. I—I will also settle any accounts you may have opened in my name here."

"We can't allow you to leave without the consent of a guardian." Sympathetic. "I'm sorry Mrs. Bailey."

"Dr. Bailey."

"Ah." He made another note.

"What possible reason could you have for keeping me here?" Trying to maintain a neutral tone. "I've been ill. Not mad."

"You've been raving," he repeated. "Delirious. We're pleased that you've come out of it, but we can't release you without the consent of a guardian or, at the very least, further observation." He achieved the neutral tone at which she'd failed.

"Further observation."

"Yes. But Dr. Pinel is better able than I to explain to you the process. Tomorrow. In the meantime, you may find it soothing to take the air. Nurse Voisin will accompany you."

He pressed a button on the desk, and she heard a muffled buzzing from the corridor. A few seconds later, the door opened and the younger, frailer nurse, looking recovered, appeared. Dr. Dagonet stood, indicating that their meeting had ended. "Mrs. Bailey," he said to the nurse, "will take part in the croquet this morning. Please escort her to the lawn, Nurse Voisin."

Marion stood as well. "I'll return to my room."

"Of course, Mrs. Bailey." Dr. Dagonet arranged himself behind the desk. Paid them no further attention. And Nurse Voisin, after taking Marion's elbow and helping her out of the office, brought her to the lawn. Not her room. But also, no longer empty.

Six patients, dressed in sleepwear, were assailing the balls with varying degrees of enthusiasm and competence. The youngest was at least twenty-five years older than Marion. Tottering over the turf and reprimanding each hoop in turn for having failed to attract the ball. With some violence.

Marion addressed the nurse. "I don't play."

"But you're English."

"Scottish."

"What?"

"Nothing." She considered making use of one of the mallets to put an end to the farce, but the close attention of the six orderlies loitering at the edges of the game convinced her to bide her time. Something had clearly gone awry between her leap into the canyon and whatever was happening here. It would be worth learning more before she scaled what she had to admit, upon closer inspection, was a substantial and serious wall.

Eying one of the chairs that had been scattered in viewing distance of the croquet, she lowered herself into the reclined position that was the only posture it allowed. Tried to avoid the feeling that she was travelling on some doomed cruise ship. Gazed up at the nurse, who was standing, relieved now, to her side.

"I'll watch."

"Excellent idea, Mrs. Bailey."

And so, they did. For six hours. Until the last of the croquet players—tenacious despite their advanced age—had been led chattering away, and the sun was setting beyond the wall. Into what Marion remained certain was water. The town faced west.

As she allowed the nurse to help her back to her room, she also concluded that the air felt less like the South of France and more like the eastern Black Sea. Leaving the French-speaking staff a mystery, it's true. But according perfectly with a recent, rather than year-old, sojourn in the western Caucasus mountains. She'd take care to examine Dr. Pinel with close attention tomorrow.

And so, the next morning, after Nurse Voisin had brought her breakfast and unlocked the door to the toilet, Marion spent time considering her most effective approach to the imminent meeting. Remained meditative as she changed into a freshly laundered nightdress. But also uncertain.

As she belted the quilted dressing gown, she looked up at Nurse Voisin from under her brows. "May I have day clothes?"

"Why?" Mystified. "Aren't you comfortable?"

"I'd prefer less informal clothing."

"You must ask Dr. Pinel."

"I will."

She followed the nurse into the corridor, where the same two orderlies were waiting. But they walked this time in the opposite direction along the corridor, until they reached an imposing door at the end of the wing. One of the orderlies pushed a button set to its side, and then opened the door when it buzzed in return. Helped her into a cavernous, strangely ceremonial room. Like the reception hall of some provincial palace.

Arched windows covered two of its walls, though still showing no more than lawn, barrier, and bright, white sunlight. The other two walls were decorated by baroque bookcases. Pristine and untouched. Matching, perhaps deliberately, the red and blue Bukhara carpet that Marion could tell from where she was standing was fake. Given its prominent position on the floor, she suspected that its owner could not.

And finally, situated disconcertingly at the precise center of the room were a broad wooden desk, a leather chair on rollers behind it, and two smaller leather chairs on scrolled feet in front of it. A standing lamp hovered to the back and side of the larger chair, flickering off and on with a maddening lack of regularity. Every time the bulb twitched into life, it emitted a nearly inaudible hissing sound.

The man who rose to greet his visitors was tiny, meticulous, portly, and dark. Bright eyes. Pointed beard and moustache. When he stood, he was shorter than the chair. And his dour, black three-piece suit might have fit a child. If the ghostly sort of child inclined to haunt suggestible governesses. As Nurse Voisin helped her to sit, Marion found herself on the edge of inconvenient laughter.

When the door had closed on the nurse and the orderlies, Dr. Pinel sat across from her and pulled a leather notebook similar to Dr. Dagonet's—or perhaps the same one?—into place in front of him. Took up an ink pencil. Gazed, calm and confident, into Marion's eyes.

And then he spoke.

Incomprehensibly.

His French accent was so heavy that she was forced to ask him to repeat himself. Which, obliging, he did—again and again—until finally, after multiple iterations, she heard him say with impeccable, if impenetrable, grammar: "I am gratified to find you composed and well. We feared that you might do yourself harm. Is there anything you would like to share with me?"

"No. Nothing."

He made a note, wet his lips, and said something in his heavy accent. She asked him to repeat it. He did. She still couldn't understand. And so, her irritation getting the better of her, she said, in French: "would you rather we speak French? Our conversation may move more quickly."

He furrowed his brow. "I'm sorry, I do not understand."

She repeated herself. He shook his head.

Then, in English, she said, slowly: "I said, we can speak French if you'd like."

He stared at her. "You believed you were speaking French?"

"I was speaking French."

He raised his eyebrows. Made a longer note. "Fascinating."

"What does that mean?" Then, deciding it didn't matter. "Where am I?"

"Where do you think you are?"

She tightened her shoulders in irritation. "All right. I think I'm in Sochi. Where do you think I am?"

"Interesting." He wrote a few further silent lines.

"Where am I?"

"What other languages do you believe you speak?" He folded his hands over the open notebook.

"Oh, for God's sake." She stood. "I'm leaving. Thank you for your help."

He pressed a button on his desk, and she heard the buzzer from outside the door. It opened at once, and five orderlies entered. "Mrs. Bailey is agitated. Room Eighteen. Water Therapy. Five minutes." He dropped his eyes to the notebook and began writing.

They nodded in the direction of his uninterested, balding head, and two grabbed her by the arms, propelling her out of the room. Dragged her through the doorway. Hitting her wrist, hard, against the frame.

More astonished than frightened, she allowed them to guide her, eventually walking her through a narrow corridor situated at a right angle to the office, down a flight of stairs into a below-ground set of rooms, and into a small, tiled chamber. Eight feet square with a very high ceiling. A wooden chair with arm and leg restraints, bolted to the floor. A large drain underneath. An even larger spigot above. Like a prurient lithograph of eighteenth-century Bedlam.

When she saw it, she re-thought her compliance. Bucked backward against the door, and then the wall. But the orderlies easily overpowered her and steered her into the chair, strapping her wrists, ankles, and forehead to the wood. When she was immobile, all but one of the men left the room. The one who remained, without pause, speech, or warning, twisted a metal handle attached to an exposed pipe that ran up the side of the wall. A few seconds later, torrents of frigid water cascaded onto her head.

For the first few moments, all she felt was pain. The water, falling from twelve or fifteen feet above her, hit the top of her head like bags of solid, wet sand. Bruising her scalp. Breaking her neck, no doubt, if her forehead weren't strapped upright. Thirty seconds after that, she became aware of the cold, her body shivering, and then convulsing, in the near-freezing deluge.

But once a minute had passed, only one thought occupied her mind. She couldn't breathe. They meant to kill her. She'd suffocate. She opened her mouth to speak to the monstrous, soft, orderly, but she closed it again when water coursed down her windpipe. She couldn't cough it out. She couldn't move into any other position. And only when she was certain she would die in the next instant, did the water stop.

No more than half-conscious of the orderly as he approached the chair, she twisted feebly in shame. She might as well have been naked with the protection that the drenched cotton nightgown provided her. But he wasn't interested in her physical state or her humiliation. Instead, after tapping the tip of a syringe, he shoved a needle into her neck. She was unconscious before he unstrapped the restraints on the chair.

SHE woke the next morning in the bedroom. Wearing a new nightgown. Her hair dry and brushed onto the pillow. And when she sat up, although her head was pounding and her neck was stiff with pain, she was otherwise undamaged. She could tell from the light in the room, however, that she'd slept later than she ordinarily did. And before she'd had time to climb out of the bed and belt her dressing gown, Nurse Voisin had arrived with the key to the toilet and her breakfast.

Once she'd eaten, they took her to Dr. Pinel. He greeted her in the same manner he had the day before, as though nothing untoward had occurred, opened the leather notebook, and took up his pen. "What other languages do you believe you speak, Mrs. Bailey?" His tone, beneath the French accent, was bored.

She swallowed. "I've studied a number of languages. I don't speak all of them well."

"Yes?"

"Classical Greek and Latin." She stared down at her lap. "Arabic, Persian, and Turkish. A few Romance languages. Some German."

"Ah." He made a note. And then he opened a drawer in his desk. "So if I were to provide you with a page of, say, Greek or Arabic, you could translate it for me?"

"Yes." Then, capitulating to the torment of the room: "would you turn off the lamp, please?"

He frowned and looked behind him. "It bothers you?"

"It's intolerable."

"Interesting." He wrote a few further lines in the notebook. Then, still focused on his writing, he pulled two pages from the open drawer and arranged them in front of her on the desk. Negligent. Without touching the flickering lamp. "These, for example."

Mildly interested, she glanced down at them. And then, outraged, she raised her eyes to his. "You can tell them for me, 'Dr. Pinel,' that they're even greater nitwits than I believed if they expect this facile idiocy to work." The pages were her rubbings from the gallery walls. Wrinkled from the water, but carefully preserved and unmistakable. "You moron."

"Forgive me." Bewildered. "Are you saying that you can't read them?"

"Fuck you."

636

"You told me, Mrs. Bailey, that you'd studied," consulting the notebook, "'a number of languages.' Greek and Arabic among them." He indicated the pages with his fingertip. "That is Greek, and this is Arabic. Please demonstrate your competency."

"Fuck you."

Nodding, he made another note. "A classic defense mechanism. Aggression directed outward when the patient's delusion is shown to be false. Fascinating."

"Fuck. You."

He settled his finger on the button, but he didn't depress it. "Are you certain there isn't anything more you'd like to say to me, Mrs. Bailey?"

"*Fuck you.*"

He pushed the button. When the orderlies appeared, he closed his leather notebook. "Room Eighteen. Water Therapy. Ten minutes."

This time, she lost consciousness before the orderly had turned off the spigot. And she had no idea whether he'd stopped it once she was gone or waited the entire ten-minute period. Although, when she woke the next morning, dry and clean, her neck wasn't stiff—meaning that he'd refrained from using the needle. Economical. Perhaps he injected the drugs only when she hadn't already fainted? She stored the information away for later use.

But mostly, she forced herself to conserve energy and shut herself down. Because over the next six days, Nurse Voisin brought her every morning to the doctor, who sent her every noon to Room Eighteen for varying, arbitrary, periods. Never more than fifteen minutes. But also never less than five. And, observing to the extent that she was able, she was confident by the end of the week that the orderlies were running a side business in the medicine. Any excuse not to use the syringe.

On the seventh day, therefore, she conducted an experiment. Forcing herself to slump, fainting, under the deluge, she mimicked unconsciousness before the shower had incapacitated her. The position was next to impossible to maintain because the orderly did keep the spigot on for precisely the length of time stipulated by Dr. Pinel. But when the water had ceased, he also slipped the unused syringe into the pocket of his white smock. Loosened the restraints with surprising gentleness. And then lifted her bodily onto a gurney that the four others had wheeled into the room.

By the time they had brought her back to bed via a rear corridor and a service lift, she herself had transferred the syringe from his pocket to a damp fold of her saturated nightgown. And when Nurse Voisin arrived in the evening to dry her hair and change her clothing, it was the work of a few seconds to immobilize her with the drug and leave her unconscious in the newly made bed.

Marion then appropriated the nurse's outfit for herself. It wouldn't fool careful observers. And Nurse Voisin being tiny, it was unflatteringly short and tight. But to explore the darker parts of the building at night, it would serve. She meant to search Dr. Pinel's office. And then, once she'd retrieved her pages, to take on the wall.

When the building was silent, and the absent view out the window told her that it was close to midnight, she slipped from her room into the empty corridor. Walked in the direction of Dr. Pinel's office. Trusting in her uniform to keep any distant staff at bay.

But when she reached the office, she stopped short. Irritated. A light—strong, without flickering—shone from under the door, and she could hear muffled voices. With a furtive glance behind her, she drew closer to the wall. If she heard them rising to leave, she'd hide herself. But in the meantime, any information she might obtain before retrieving her papers would help. Gradually, as she concentrated, the voices resolved themselves into something comprehensible.

The first was Dr. Pinel. But his speech had changed. In place of the plodding French accent, he was speaking a quick, native English, with the subtlest hint of South London. She pressed her fingertips to her temples, even as she strained to follow him. The situation had crossed a line from horrific to surreal.

"…weeks. Perhaps months. She's neurotic. Phobic. But not suggestible. Which I think you already knew."

"We haven't got months." It was Jeffrey, and she felt close to gagging on the information.

"My advice is to move her to a proper prison. Work on her there." Dr. Pinel again. "We haven't the tools in this facility to shift her into the state you require."

"We'll provide you additional staff. Medicines. Machines, if you feel it would help."

"No. You fail to understand." Frustrated. "The others you've brought me, they've begun the process sound."

"She's sound."

"She's the least mentally sound individual I've encountered in twenty years of practice. Wait—" when Jeffrey must have moved to interrupt. "Let me explain myself. The patients you've installed here thus far have all been normal and sane, yes? They've had a sense of what to expect of the world and of how to react to what we, collectively, consider appropriate stimuli. That means that when we've turned the world upside down, when we've assaulted them with abnormal or inappropriate stimuli, they've broken. Some sooner. Some later. But they've all cracked. There's been no other option open to them."

"Fine."

"This one." Dr. Pinel cleared his throat. "She expects nothing of the world. She has no notion of how to react to even the most mundane of experiences. Each and every incident in her life strikes her as unique, and she reacts to it as a shock. As a distasteful surprise. It's a fascinating illness—and I'd welcome the opportunity to study it further. I don't know, for example, whether her condition is biological or the result of some emotional trauma—I'd hypothesize the former given the unusual cognitive skills that appear to accompany it. But the result is the same."

"And what is the result?" Annoyed.

"The mechanisms she's developed to cope with her daily life—that is, interactions with strangers, marital relations, professional encounters, all of it—are so elaborate, so baroque, that they protect her from any assault we might mount on her here. Physical or mental. What she suffers from, say, isolation, mescaline, or water therapy is no different to her emotionally and psychologically than what she suffers from walking down a crowded street, attending a dinner party, or the random flickering of a light bulb. Her defenses against both sets of experiences are identical."

"It was a nice touch." The annoyance replaced by a quiet amusement. "The lamp."

"It was an experiment."

"Which told you?"

"A great deal. The others have all at one point or other begged us to stop the water. Attempted to negotiate. To restore rationality to their treatment." Dr. Pinel paused. "This one endured the water without complaint." He paused again. "And then she asked me to turn off the lamp."

"So?"

"She's already broken, Sir Jeffrey. I'm sorry. We can't break her any further."

As she'd listened to their conversation, she'd rested her forehead against the door, increasingly dismayed. And she failed to notice, therefore, when three orderlies approached her from behind until they were pinioning her arms. Activating the buzzer on the door. Clapping a hand over her mouth.

The voices inside stopped abruptly. And then, after a second of tense silence, there was a short buzz in return and Dr. Pinel, his French accent back in place: "yes? Enter."

The orderlies pushed open the door and dragged her into the room. Dr. Pinel ran his eyes over her clothing, weary and unsurprised. Jeffrey did the same, but his expression was more complicated. He was dressed like a banker again. "I like your uniform—"

"Room Eighteen," Dr. Pinel interrupted him. "Water therapy. Thirty minutes."

When they forced her from the office and back in the direction of the staircase, Jeffrey followed. And once they'd strapped her into the wooden chair, he gestured them out of the room, murmuring that he'd take responsibility for agitation on the part of the patient. Then finally, when he and Marion were alone, he leaned against the wall, watching her, his hand toying with the spigot. "You were content," he said, "to abandon me to those troglodytes for a year. *A year.* Have you any idea what the food was like?"

"What day is it?"

"*A year*, you bitch." He twisted the spigot.

She squeezed her eyes shut. But only two or three drops fell before he turned it off again. Wary, she opened her eyes. Then she turned her head as far as it would go in the restraints and glared at him. "Go ahead. I'm used to it."

"Enjoy it, do you?"

"Fuck you."

"If it hadn't been for Trelawney's impeccable linguistic training," he resumed, releasing the spigot and crossing his arms, "we'd be mired in that pit even now. Thank God he'd advanced sufficiently in his Circassian dialects to make himself understandable to the impressionable girl who brought his food. Convinced her to pass the time teaching him her own debased tongue." He ran a hand through his hair. "And so, four days later, the girl was unlocking our shackles and putting us on your trail. From there, it was easy."

"So that's how a 'unit of trained British soldiers' escapes captivity, then?" She laughed. "Prostitution?"

"Now, now, dear. You've already had your time with Trelawney. No need for jealousy." He pushed himself off the wall and walked toward her. Stood in front of the chair, looking down at her. "I don't think I've seen you quite this abject since Iraq. Though the nurse's uniform does lend a certain confused, fancy dress feel to the situation."

"Perfect," she muttered. "Acting the passive whore and petty retaliation. All the marks of the true English officer."

"No, there's more to this than retaliation." He remained where he stood. "Though I did warn you about that."

"What more could there be?" She squeezed her hands into fists under the straps. "You've wrecked the scene that you concocted here, Jeffrey. I heard your entire conversation with that contemptible pantomime doctor. After tonight, I'll never believe that this—this stage set is a hospital."

"How do you know you're not hallucinating as we speak?"

"Don't be a prat."

He returned to the wall. Rested his hand loosely over the spigot. "You're correct. You're not hallucinating. But, even so, Maugham isn't certain that he wants you released. He feels that you've become complacent. Spoiled. That you've forgotten what we're capable of doing to you should you cross certain, tacitly agreed upon boundaries of behavior. And after that incident in the mountains, I must admit that I don't entirely disagree with him."

"What you're capable of doing to me? *What you're capable of doing to me?*" She drew in her breath, ragged, a split second image of her agonizing existence since Jeffrey had reappeared in her life streaking across her consciousness. "Are you fucking insane?"

"No, you are." He twisted the spigot and a small stream of water descended onto her head before he stopped it. "Whoops. Slip of the hand. Apologies."

"Oh, go drown some kittens, Jeffrey." She slumped into the chair to the extent that she could. Contemptuous. "This bores me."

He laughed and crossed his arms again. Leaving the spigot. "If I instruct Dr. Pinel to suspend the water therapy for a few weeks would you be willing to complete your work for us here? It's a lovely climate. Warm. Clean air."

"No."

"You've still not seen the pages we lifted from Mr. Fyffes. Aren't you curious?"

"No."

"In Chelsea?"

"Absolutely not."

"What if I tell him to increase the water therapy? Twice daily? Four times?"

"Go ahead."

He sighed. "Is there anywhere you'll consider resuming your work? Along with access to those pages? And don't say alone and unsupervised, because that won't happen."

She remained silent in the chair for over a minute, her eyes closed. Thinking. She couldn't let the project go. And she must, at the very least, pass Ismail's message to her superiors. Which she most certainly couldn't do from here. Wherever it was. And so, slowly capitulating, she opened her eyes and stared at the wall across from her. "Suffolk. Virginia's."

"Suffolk." He raised his eyebrows. "You've got quite a bit of faith in my sister."

"Yes."

"Hmm. Ginnie'll be delighted to hear it."

He opened the door to the chamber and stepped into the corridor. A few seconds later, he returned with the orderly's syringe. Squinting at the tip of the needle.

"Suffolk it is, then."

He shoved the needle into her neck.

Suffolk, England
November, 1937

$\mathcal{S}$HE remained unconscious throughout their return journey to Britain. And she never discovered whether the hospital had indeed been in Sochi or in the south of France. Or, for all she knew, in Hastings. As Jeffrey drove her down the avenue of yew trees that fronted his sister's house, she found that she didn't care. At least the bleak evening wind that hit her as she exited the car in Suffolk left no doubt that it could only be November. And Jeffrey no longer pretended the year was anything but 1937. She'd lost, at most, three weeks.

When she walked through the Elizabethan door into Virginia's raftered, chaotic, and always disorienting entry hall, she realized that she was also, if grimly, looking forward to resuming her work. She'd outmaneuver the office when the moment came. She'd done so before. And this time, she'd also be fulfilling her obligation to Ismail. Completing the job she'd only half understood when they'd set out from Istanbul toward Georgia in March of 1920.

As Virginia greeted them with affection and open curiosity, Marion was struck, as she always was, by her similarity to Jeffrey. Intelligently malicious and aggressively beautiful even at fifty, Virginia was more like his twin than his older sister—which, as usual, left Marion questioning the trust she placed in her. But Teddy, overweight and dressed in his threadbare smoking jacket, allayed any mounting concern.

He was delighted to see Marion—a defensive ally in the silent, scorched-earth warfare that persisted between brother and sister. Smiling, he kissed her cheek as he took her coat. Marion had never met their eldest brother, George. Nor, given Teddy's occasional, cryptic references to him, did she want to.

"We're nearly full up, Jeffie." Virginia pressed her cheek to her brother's. "You might have warned me that you'd invited the entire shop here. We'd have advised the blacksmiths to make up a few additional effigies of Old Clem."

"Trelawney's come too?" Distracted. Less willing than he ordinarily was to return Virginia's sniping.

She looked thoughtful. Mocking. "Yes, Nick arrived this morning. I've put him in the Blue Room. And then Arthur Gardiner and his three morose and serious friends turned up quick on his heels. They appeared unhappy to be housed in separate rooms, but they can remedy that in the night if they must. Arthur's bed is large enough. They're together off the second-floor gallery."

She considered further. "Oh yes, and a flighty girl called Lucy came just after tea. Wearing a lot of red. More than a little interested in Nick, I sensed, so I put her three rooms away from him. Close enough not to hinder young love, but far enough away to throw up some obstacles to make it interesting. And, of course, Mrs. Bowen and Alicia brought Lydia yesterday afternoon. She's sleeping in the nursery. Did I do right, Jeffie?"

"Poor Trelawney," he murmured. "But yes. Perfect. Lucy Peters may calm him."

"If Nick were any calmer, he'd be dead."

"And Maugham?" He ignored her.

"Maugham," she said, "came with Eric Thacker."

"Oh?"

"Yes." She twitched the embroidered silk shawl she'd arranged over her shoulders. "I told him that there are limits."

"Where are they?"

"Maugham is in the East Wing with the ghost. Mr. Thacker is elsewhere."

"Where 'elsewhere?'" Irritated.

"A driftwood hut on the beach? In town? I've no idea." She gazed at him, imperious. Humorous. "He doesn't set foot in this house, Jeffie"

"He's a necessary evil, Ginnie."

"He is," she said, "neither necessary nor evil. Merely dull and grotesque."

Before he could argue, she addressed Marion. "You and Jeffie are in your usual room on the first floor." She pressed a key into Marion's hand. "And this is the unique key to the second-floor room above it. Should Jeffie go on the rampage he's clearly planning, use it. There's a large window. And a well-secured drainpipe."

"And now I know she's got it," Jeffrey said.

"Yes," Virginia replied patiently. "It's a subtle psychological game on my part. You know about those, don't you, Jeffie? Here's how it works: if you know that she's got access to the Room with the Lock on the Door and the Drainpipe and the Escape Route and whatever else those Bloomsbury types demand, perhaps you won't do anything too painfully obvious."

"I'm not feeling all that subtle these days." Looking at Marion, however, rather than at Virginia. And then, tired: "let's go upstairs, dear."

As Marion climbed the stairs beside him, she added one additional guest to Virginia's list of visitors. Her courier. She'd managed, between regaining consciousness in London and being shuffled into Jeffrey's car to Suffolk, to signal, if obliquely, her people. Not enough to explain her discoveries or her situation. But sufficient to alert them that she'd be working at Virginia's and Teddy's. And that, when she'd unraveled the knot of material, she'd pass her findings to them.

The courier would be waiting, watching her, prepared to disappear when the time came. And that invisible presence, just beyond the boundaries of the house, calmed her. Left her almost optimistic. Ready to begin thinking again. Open herself to stimuli from the outside world.

When they reached the familiar, ironic, and richly furnished room—overwhelming fire under the solid mantle, wood paneling, thick carpets, and carved bed—Jeffrey threw himself into an armchair and watched her walk to the mullion windows to look out over the moonlit yews. After a few seconds of silence, he spoke. Irritated again. "That key won't help, you know. The drainpipe is exposed, and it descends to an open bit of turf at the front of the house. Gardiner will have someone on it before you've even unlatched the window."

"I know." She didn't leave the window. "Its purpose isn't strategic. It's emotional. A comfort. Virginia understands."

"What Ginnie understands," he said, "is that if your side and mine are sufficiently mutually destructive, she can pick up the pieces and bring what's left to her own department. She's not some housewife, Marion. She's done it before. You *know* she's done it before. Do you really want George involved again?"

"I can't honestly see the difference between you and George." She turned. "Except that George's office doesn't use water."

"No. George's office uses rocket-propelled missiles." He tilted his head. "Is that better? You're the expert on ethics, darling."

"I'm tired." She removed her shoes and sat on the edge of the bed. "I don't want to do this."

"I'd have thought that after all those days and weeks of rest, you'd be more than ready to—"

"Stop it." She unbuttoned her shirt.

"Very well." He rose and walked to the bed as well. Paused to look down at her, smiling and speculative. "I don't suppose—?"

"Don't be daft."

"I did very much like the nurse's uniform."

"I said, stop it."

"Oh, very well," he repeated. "Let me prepare you for tomorrow, then, and we'll go to sleep."

"Fine." She rolled down her stockings.

He sat and spoke as he removed his own shoes. "Virginia's reserved the library for your work. The material, all of it, including the pages from Mr. Fyffes, is there. But you won't enter or leave the library without an escort. Trelawney and Lucy Peters will also be on hand to observe you."

"I won't—"

"No," he said. "We understand that. No one will be persuading you to explain yourself. But if you want access to the papers, you must accept their presence in the room. Miss Peters has no languages, but she's the best codebreaker we've got. And Trelawney—well, you know his skill set."

"I don't like it," she said.

"We don't like it either. But that's in the nature of a compromise, isn't it, Marion? We recognize the risk we're running in letting you at this material in a porous location. And we have no doubt that you'll bolt the moment you've got what you're seeking. But at this point, Maugham can't see any other way forward. He *wants* to increase the pressure. Out of spite. But he also knows that he can't expect a performance if he breaks the acrobat's legs."

"Lovely."

"Not that he didn't consider it." Jeffrey straightened, stretched, and began unbuttoning his own shirt. "Breaking your legs, that is. Thacker's contribution. Doing so wouldn't affect your mind, and it would certainly slow your descent down the proverbial drainpipe." He yawned. "But we mustn't risk provoking another tantrum on your part. Better to watch and wait. Hopefully, we won't regret it."

"I'm going to sleep now, Jeffrey." She reached up and switched off the bedside lamp. "I'm uninterested in your conversations with Maugham."

"Nonetheless, in the interest of collegiality—"

"Good night."

"Good night, dear."

$\mathcal{A}$ long table in the middle of the library had been cleared for Marion's use. Ordinarily invisible under the detritus of whatever caught the interest of Virginia's and Teddy's family, including bits and pieces of plants and animals they'd brought indoors weeks or months earlier, it was now spotless. Marion hadn't understood before what a substantial piece of furniture it was. Heavy and satisfied, like the rest of the weighty, Elizabethan structure.

But she had little time to pursue the thought. Nick and Lucy were already waiting when she and Jeffrey entered the room. Nick nervously immersed in *The Natural History of Vegetables*, the second volume of *The New and Accurate System of Natural History*, signed and annotated by its eighteenth-century author. Ignoring Lucy. And Lucy, in a pink dress, red lipstick, and very high heels, standing precariously on her toes, reaching for a volume of Buffon shelved just above his head.

Marion hadn't seen Lucy since Maugham had staged her execution four years previously. Lucy would be in her mid-twenties now. Hardened, Marion noted. Though she'd been hard, if sweet, before. It was a relief to Marion that Lucy, whose sole skill was cryptanalysis, had no interest in psychology. If she noticed Marion at all, it was with the contemptuous confidence that Marion was too old to be a rival.

Lucy's inner arm brushed Nick's cheek as the door opened, and, blushing, he dropped the volume he was reading. Before he could bend to retrieve it, Jeffrey had crossed the room, picked it up, and re-shelved it. "Coward."

"Sir?"

"For future reference, Trelawney," Jeffrey indicated the shelves in front of him, "eighteenth-century botany." Then, turning, he pointed across the room. "The modern Arabic novel. Unless you've acquired a new hobby since last we spoke?"

"No, sir."

"I thought not."

"Good morning, Miss Peters." Jeffrey nodded at her.

"Good morning, Sir Jeffrey." Lucy had retreated into herself. Frightened by his curt, cold boredom.

"As you all know," Jeffrey walked to the table, "this situation is ideal for none of us." He didn't sit. Instead, he stood looking down at the material placed at intervals along the table's perimeter. "Trelawney, you've read through these pages and examined the astrolabe. You're as familiar with it as Marion is. I want you to watch what she does with it. Deduce from her process something of the message contained in it. We're looking for references to an artifact. Likely ancient Caucasian. Potentially related to the Nart Sagas. Its use. Its location. Why Stalin's holiday cottage might have prompted its re-emergence. You understand?"

"Yes, sir."

"Miss Peters." He continued to gaze down at the papers. "Try to fight the tedium. You're here because Maugham believes you're a sufficiently skilled codebreaker that the language barrier won't prove an obstacle to your analysis. You've got a remarkable mind. Use it. If you've got questions about the content of the material, ask Trelawney. He's here to help you."

"I will, Sir Jeffrey."

"I've no doubt." He beckoned Marion to the table. When she'd obediently approached, he indicated the books and pages spread out on it. "A modern edition of Aristophanes's *Birds*, in Attic Greek. The manuscript from the Baquba collection, which includes, first, the medieval Arabic translation of *Birds*, second, Evliya Çelebi in Ottoman Turkish on the languages of the Caucasus, and third, Ibn Daniyal's poem mourning the Mamluk Sultan Baybar's campaign against vice. The meaningless Greek and Arabic pages you had on you when we fished you from the river near Maykop. The two pages Mr. Fyffes obligingly brought back from his own, equally eventful holiday in the eastern Black Sea. The vase, ancient Athenian, we pinched from Stalin's dacha. And the astrolabe you really ought to have dropped before jumping, if you had any respect at all for near-millennium-old antiquities."

He looked up at her. "Have I missed anything?"

"No." She was already focusing, hungry, on the two pages she'd been tapped to liberate from Fyffes. She thought she could see a miniature copy of the Scythian archer at the corner of the first. "It's all here."

"Good." He put his hand flat on the table and tapped his fingers. "I'll be in and out. As will food, tea, coffee, and anything else you'll want to keep you going. But know this now, Marion: Trelawney and Miss Peters will refrain from asking you questions, and they'll give you the space you need to work. Any notes you write, however, are theirs. And, though we'll take it as read that you'll attempt to mislead them, you won't go too far. If you cross any lines, things will become unpleasant. Thacker, I've been informed, has found himself a room above the pub in town. He's close. And angry."

"Yes," she said, already preoccupied. "Fine. I understand."

"Enjoy yourselves." He cast another dissatisfied glance about the room. "I'll be introducing Lydia to one of Anne's castoff Shetlands, if you want me." Then he turned and left them alone.

Once he was gone, Marion lost no time. Without addressing Nick or Lucy, she pulled out a chair, sat, and moved the pages from Fyffes closer to her. She knew what she was seeking. Some connection, no matter how tenuous, among the swarms of animals that had hindered Stalin's building project, the swarms that Ismail had shown her emerging from the dolmens, the swarms referenced in the Greek Aristophanes, and those referenced in Evliya Çelebi's reproduction of the languages of the northwest Caucasus.

She was convinced that the connection would show itself when she analyzed the pages her people had instructed her to retrieve. If they'd taken the trouble to move them from the Caucasus to Devon, they'd have had a sense of the text's power already. Her role was to determine what form that power took. Or, in Jeffrey's language, to identify the object—and then locate it.

As she skimmed the first of the pages, she discovered that location wouldn't be a problem. Or, not the ordinary sort of problem. The document had been ripped from a medieval Arabic geographical table of cities and their coordinates—a list of place names, star signs associated with the names, latitudes, and longitudes, with the shore of the Atlantic Ocean taken as the base meridian. Nothing unique or distinctive about them.

Like the astrolabe, the pages felt Mamluk and thirteenth-century to her. In fact, she nodded to herself as she turned to the second scrap, they too were signed by *Al-Qawwas*, the archer. The Scythian. The same hand that had calibrated the tool had produced the table. That helped.

But she still didn't know what to do with them. The cities enumerated were random—global. And by no means unusual. Damascus. Cairo. Mecca. A few, she could see from the coordinates, were in the Caucasus. But the points on the eastern Black Sea weren't emphasized. No unusual ink or stray markings. And they certainly didn't constitute the majority of the entries. As she would have expected for a Mamluk work, its focus was Egypt and Syria.

Disappointed, she pushed the pages away. Chewed her lip. The material from Fyffes, she was gradually, grudgingly admitting to herself, was pointing her straight back to Ibn Daniyal. Just as the astrolabe had done before. There must be something in the Mamluk poem that would help her to use the Mamluk geographical coordinates and the Mamluk astrolabe. But she wasn't ready for Ibn Daniyal. Feeling too fragile.

And so, she turned her attention to the rubbings from the underground gallery near Maykop. Squashed the concern for Ismail that they incited. Sounded out the Arabic, half whispering, trying to make sense of the language. After thirty seconds of fruitless murmuring, she paused and brushed four or five ants off her arm. Observed them, perplexed, as they sped across the tabletop and hid themselves in a deep crack at its edge. In November? Presumably the heat and old paper in the library had kept them active.

Then she paged forward to the Greek. Read a few lines of that as well, also half-aloud. Smiled when she heard a squeak from Lucy as a mouse rattled along the wainscoting. And then another. Lost the smile and looked up, frowning, at the sound of a swallow beating itself against the room's clerestory windows.

They'd done a remarkable job of cleaning the table, she muttered to herself, but the rest of the room remained under siege by the wildlife Virginia's children had transported over years and decades to this part of the house. As she continued to read under her breath, she found herself as jittery as Lucy sounded. Kicking the tip of her shoe against encroaching animals. And was that a pine marten slinking behind the shelves devoted to country house hedge mazes and labyrinths?

Finally, too distracted to read properly, she stopped. Shook her head. She could make nothing of it. Dull and frustrated, she stood and walked to the coffee service in the far corner of the room. Poured herself a cup, added milk and sugar, and examined the volumes in the shelf above it. Danish Architecture of the nineteenth century. Continued to ignore Nick trying to ignore Lucy. And very much appreciated the caffeine when it hit her bloodstream.

Energized but resigned, she returned to the table, where she retrieved the Baquba manuscript and found Ibn Daniyal's elegy. Took another sip of the coffee and began reading. As she read, her attention wandered, half-hearing Lucy appropriating the pages from Fyffes and bringing them to Nick. After which, she sat primly in an armchair, arranged the papers in her lap, and asked him in a loud whisper what they were.

Nick, who was forced to lean over her to examine the pages, spoke softly. Reminding Marion unpleasantly of his demeanor when he'd worked as her research assistant. She wrinkled her forehead, peered at the poem, and tried to disregard his voice. But the whispering, bouncing across the acoustical pandemonium that was the ceiling of the library, forced itself into her consciousness. She couldn't block it out.

"It's a section of geographical work," he was saying. "Probably from the thirteenth century. So, you see, here," artlessly pointing at the line that obscured her thighs, "is the city of Beirut. Longitude 59.3, latitude 34.0. And then, say, here, is Genoa. Longitude 43.0, latitude, 39.3. Or, further down, here, Mecca. Longitude, 67.0, latitude, 21.2." He straightened, aware, suddenly, of his proximity to her legs. "And so on."

"But it's inaccurate." Pouting. Marion had the impression from the sound of her voice that she was chewing gum. "The latitudes are about right. But the longitudes are nowhere near those cities."

Nick paused. A surprised silence. "I hadn't realized you were familiar with the science of navigation, Miss Peters."

"I memorized them all when I was ten, didn't I?" She snapped her gum. "Bored at school. Something to do."

"I see." Scared.

"But, as I mentioned, these longitudes," gesturing toward the pages in her lap, "if you've read them properly, are wrong."

"No," he said recovering himself. "That is, yes, by our own reckoning, they're wrong. But we take Greenwich as our zero meridian. As does the rest of the civilized world, Miss Peters. You understand?"

"Hmm." Torn between pressing him to explain himself further and demonstrating her sophisticated comprehension of the mathematics.

"Right." He took a breath. "So, erm, the geographer who compiled this list was working in the thirteenth-century, most likely in Cairo. He wouldn't have been aware of Greenwich as the zero meridian."

"Pity."

"Yes. Geographers and astronomers in his milieu would have taken different base meridians. Some chose their place of writing. Others, following Ptolemy, took the Canary Islands. And others, like this *al-Qawwas*, took the Atlantic shore." He cleared his throat. "In practice, this means that we must subtract approximately thirty-three from the longitude listed here to determine a longitude based on Greenwich as the zero meridian. So—"

"Yes." A split second silence. "Yes, now they're correct. But where are the numbers? I may not be able to read the alphabet, but I can distinguish letters from numbers. There aren't any on these pages."

"Medieval geographers expressed coordinates in *abjad* code," he said. Uncertain.

Marion smiled to herself as she re-read the poem. The students he'd helped her teach at Durham were never so petulant. Nor so quick. She wished she could appreciate Lucy's horrible personality as much as she did her mind. Hobbled by envy, most likely. She'd have given anything to approach the world with Lucy's bullet-proof confidence. Though she was enjoying the effect it was having on Nick.

"What's that?" The sound of Lucy's stockings rubbing together as she re-crossed her legs. "*Abjad?*"

"A very basic code. Each letter represents its corresponding number in the alphabet."

"That's it?" Contemptuous and amused.

"Essentially. Along with a few tricks. The letter 'y,' for example, is ten, the letter 'n' is fifty, 'q' is one hundred, that sort of thing. So, for example, 'bq' is one hundred two."

Lucy stood abruptly, walked to the table, retrieved a sheet of writing paper and a pencil, and handed them to Nick. "Write it down for me to memorize."

"Oh." Nick took the pencil, flustered. "Yes, of course. Excellent idea, Miss Peters. It won't take five minutes."

"Thank you, love." She wandered the room, brushing her fingertips against the spines of the books, as he worked. Smirking.

And Marion, surprised that their exchange had helped her, reconsidered her strategy. She had been approaching the poem entirely wrong. Searching for an embedded message or literary meaning. A description of whatever this missing object might be. What it might do.

But Nick's explanation of the coordinates forced her to consider the simpler possibility that the poem was precisely what it purported to be: a lament for the lost beloved. The satirical theme and the scatological content certainly distracted the audience. Perhaps, though, they were meant to. To mask the underlying theme. Redirect the attention of the chance reader, but draw the attention of a reader looking deeper. Because, fundamentally, the message was there for anyone to find: Baybars had destroyed something important; but that something might be restored or found.

Silently thanking Lucy, she turned her attention to the two climactic lines of the elegy— those where the narrator pleads with Iblis to return him to a land where the "vice" that had been eliminated might be reclaimed. The land of the lost beloved. She read the section once again. Slowly. Carefully: "I cried, 'Oh Iblis, take us far away from here, on a long journey/But whatever happens, never live in Egypt, though it's familiar, go nowhere near…'" If any part of the composition suggested a place, a lost location, this was it. All the better that it was "far from Egypt."

And then, as she was considering her next step, she noticed to her surprise a faint, yet deliberate, ع added to the end of the second line. The alteration to the text that she'd been seeking, and failing to find. Every other line of the poem ended with ون. And, more to the point, the letter ع represented one thousand in *abjad* code.

Out of curiosity, she calculated the *abjad* number of the two lines together: 6347. Added the spare ع, and calculated 7347. Moved the decimal point over: 73.47. A longitude that would place her squarely in the Caucasus. But, more than that, there was the aesthetic quality of 7347 as the total. Twenty-one, or three sevens, taken together. Not to mention that the ون at the end of each line, produced 205. Another seven.

Enjoying herself, and keeping to threes and sevens, she played with the first three words of the first line, calculated their value, and found 724. Moved the decimal: 72.4. A longitude also in the Caucasus. Then she tried the next three words—and raised her eyebrows: 445. The latitude 44.5 was within a few miles of Maykop if the longitude remained 73. Still keeping to threes and sevens, she added the first three words of the first line to the second line in its entirety: 4462, or 44.62. Another perfect latitude.

Fifteen minutes later, using the same process, she'd produced fifteen sets of coordinates, all within a forty-mile radius of Maykop, with 44.5 and 44.62 as the greatest latitude spread, and, taking Greenwich as the zero meridian, 39.4 and 40.3 as the greatest longitude spread. She'd found her location. Or, to be accurate, her locations. The poem told the reader to flee Egypt because the beloved had been lost there. But the beloved existed elsewhere. Far away. In a set of places specified with scientific, rather than poetic, precision, by the coordinates hidden in the text.

Draining her cold coffee, she pushed away the manuscript and stood again. She'd committed nothing to paper. But she could easily recalculate the location, even if, unlike Lucy, she didn't trust her ability to retain the coordinates in her memory. She'd deciphered the code. The numbers would always be there, waiting for her to find.

Pleased, she walked over to where Nick was writing, and lifted the list of coordinates. "I want these."

"Hmm?" He looked up at her. "Yes, of course, Dr. Bailey. I was just finishing."

"Thank you."

She knew that her interest in them now was obvious, but she couldn't think of any way to retrieve them furtively. And, she told herself as she sat back in her chair, she was far enough ahead of them that it didn't matter. She'd have sufficient information for her courier by nightfall. If not earlier. All she had left to do was determine how this object beloved by Iblis worked.

Running her finger along the list, she skimmed the entries. Uncertain of what she wanted to find. But, true to form, it found her instead. Midway through the second page, fifteen sets of coordinates, identical to those she'd derived from the poem, appeared one after the other. All associated with the North Caucasian city of Balanjar. The lost city of Balanjar. The fabled town had been destroyed in the twelfth century. Though it was ordinarily thought to have existed further to the east, in Dagestan. Or, that's where archaeologists kept looking for it.

She stared down at the coordinates, star signs, and city-name, confused. There could be no doubt. Balanjar. Vanished in the mountain forests, according to this document, near Maykop. It had an odd history. Repeatedly overrun by Arab, Mongol, and Turkic militaries, it had nonetheless thrived until the end of the Khazar Khanate, after which it had disappeared without a trace. Too quickly not to be suspicious.

Baybars would have known about it, she mused, even if only by reputation. He would also have known of the disconcerting tendency on the part of its inhabitants to call on groups and rings of objects and animals to protect its ramparts. Confusing the enemy with the unusual strategy. Not that the strategy was all that successful in the end, it's true.

Still half-distracted, she considered the astrological symbols and stars associated with the town. Libra. Venus. *Al-ghumaisa*, the "bleary-eyed one." Identified with Procyon, the "unfortunate star," in the constellation Canis Minor. Intrigued, she pulled the Ibn Daniyal back into position. Iblis was described repeatedly as "unfortunate" and "bleary-eyed" in the poem. As were his partners in vice. And, she read rapidly, yes, the star sign of the whores, pimps, gamblers, and drug addicts lost to him was, unsurprisingly, Libra. Protected by Venus.

Once she'd forged that connection, introducing Canis Minor to the portrait was simple. Her heart thudding, she reached for the astrolabe, found the plate with what had seemed before the obscure constellation of Canis Minor, situated it, and twisted it until Procyon was in Libra. Read the nonsense markings and incorrect latitudes inscribed beside it. "Balanjar." "4462, 7347."

Her intuition against taking the astrolabe from Ismail had been correct. The tool did belong in the Caucasus. Nowhere else. She had no doubt now that if her people returned it to the region, aligned the first plate with Procyon in Libra, and triangulated using the coordinates she'd derived from the poem, they'd find their object. The only question that remained was what this lost, beloved thing could be.

She was just reconsidering the passages from Evliya Çelebi when she raised her head, sensing a change in the room. Perplexed, she looked about her. Nick and Lucy had left. And, scanning the table, they'd taken her rubbings of the gallery walls with them.

Uneasy, but refusing to be sidetracked now that she'd nearly completed her analysis, she returned her attention to the travelogue. Before she could read more than two or three lines, she was distracted by the sound of people entering the room. Irritated, she looked up again. Blinked. Nick and Lucy. Followed by Maugham, Jeffrey, Thacker, and Gardiner. Her anxiety growing, she swallowed. But she didn't speak.

"Trelawney," Maugham announced, occupying a chair at the far end of the table, "believes he's found something. He'd like you to check his work, Dr. Bailey. If you'd be so kind?"

JEFFREY sat across from Marion at the other end of the table, nearer the door. Exhausted in muddy riding clothes. Lydia, it appeared, had not taken to Anne's Shetland. Nick used the chair to the right of Jeffrey, and Lucy pulled another chair close enough to Nick's to touch him. Thacker and Gardiner remained standing, hovering near the door. Her disquiet spiked as she recognized their carefully choreographed arrangement. Exiting the room without their permission would be next to impossible.

She chose not to think about it. Instead, slicing through her nervousness, she noted that Maugham was wearing a leather apron and a tall, cloth hat over his tweeds. Which took her a moment of silent confusion to comprehend. And then, yes: St. Clement's Day. He was attending their meeting dressed as a Victorian blacksmith. A befuddled Victorian blacksmith. Not a good sign. She stifled a sigh and looked across the table at Nick. Unwilling to hear what he had to say, but unable to think of a way of getting out of it.

"Dr. Bailey," Maugham continued, extracting a miniature blacksmith's hammer from a pocket of the apron and tapping it experimentally against the side of the table, "is itching to hear your piece, Trelawney. Observe her excitement. Proceed, please."

"Yes." Nick cleared his throat. Spread four of the pages from her rubbings on the tabletop between them. "I'll be brief. I believe that these are Greek and Arabic transliterations of a north Caucasian dialect. They aren't encoded. There's no message embedded in them."

"Dr. Bailey, your response?"

"I disagree."

Jeffrey smiled at his dirty hands. Lydia must have insisted that he remove his gloves during their lesson. "Well done, Trelawney."

She frowned at them both. Set aside the thought of Lydia. "Can you translate it, then, Nick? Because I certainly can't. If it's a north Caucasian dialect, what does it say?"

"I can't translate it. I haven't derived any meaning from it." Calm and reasonable. Refusing to be drawn.

"Then how do you know what it is?"

"The sound," he said simply. "And the feel."

"The feel?" She raised her eyebrows. "And I thought you were meant to be the rational one."

He cleared his throat again, still unruffled, and read a line of the Arabic page. Then a line of the Greek. He was about to explain himself when six bats fluttered down from behind a rafter, disturbed the pages on the table with their flapping wings, and disappeared into one of the darker recesses of the room. Lucy shrieked and grabbed Nick's arm. And Thacker, jumping, let out a guttural oath from the door. Night was falling beyond the glass.

"I must say, Willcox." Maugham watched, delighted and wide-eyed, as the bats flurried throughout the library. "I don't think much of your sister's housekeeping. Has she considered a cat, I wonder? It might take care of the pine marten in the corridor too."

Jeffrey, who'd quashed his own surprise, shook his head and addressed Nick again. "What do you mean, 'the feel?'"

"Caucasian languages," Nick began slowly, "are ancient. Distinct. They developed over millennia in the mountains, largely untainted by external linguistic contact. They're easily identifiable."

"In what way?"

"In part by the sound, of course. But there's something deeper than that. Unlike most other modern languages, the Caucasian languages are what scholars of linguistics have begun to call 'ergative.' A term of art. No one has published yet, but the categorization is becoming accepted in the field. I've attended a few symposia."

He paused to gather his thoughts, and then, plodding and methodical, he resumed. "The languages of the Caucasus aren't the only tongues of that kind. Another example is Basque. The Eskimo languages. Mayan was. Etruscan too, some speculate. And there are other languages with mild ergative tendencies. Kurdish is one. But those of the Caucasus, and especially of the northwest Caucasus, are particularly so.

"In practice," he explained when no one responded, "this means that they diverge from most other languages in the world, which are what one would call nominative, by not privileging the subject who acts. Ergative languages, instead, privilege the action itself. Or, put differently," warming to his theme, "one might argue that whereas nominative languages are echo-chambers, referencing the speaking, acting human, the languages of the north Caucasus, Basque, Mayan, and the rest, reference the work that speech does on the world." He hesitated. "One can feel that in the rhythm of the language. I can feel it. It's there."

He placed his hand over the page closest to him. "These lines, I'm confident, are taken from a previously unknown north Caucasian text. They aren't subordinate to a speaking human. They do their own work."

When he stopped speaking, Maugham and Jeffrey exchanged a glance. Then, once more, Maugham addressed Marion. "Response, Dr. Bailey?"

But she'd stopped listening. As Nick had spoken, describing in a stripped back, inhibited way what Ismail had also tried to explain to her, she'd reconsidered, once again, her interpretation of the material. And now, finally, she knew what her organization was meant to find. It wasn't an object, an artifact, a tool, or a weapon. Nor was it anything as grandiose as a lost city. It was a language. Speech: the language of the birds, the language of the swarms, and, in fact, the language of the gods. The coordinates she'd extracted would, if her colleagues set the astrolabe properly, triangulate to the location of a powerful and legendary tongue.

And this speech *was* mythical. Since antiquity, secreted among the "mountain of tongues," as the medieval Arabs had called the Caucasus region, was a single tongue, the most dynamic of dynamic languages, that would work on the world rather than referencing the meagre human speaker. As Ismail's father had hinted, Circe and Medea had known it. But so, according to the legends, had King Solomon. The figurehead of the Argo, sailing back from the eastern Black Sea. The sorceresses, heroes, and gods of the Nart Sagas. While Sufis and European alchemists had sought it as the Green Language understood by the birds.

Aristophanes, too, had known about it. And although he hadn't himself hidden the message in his comedy, others had used the play and the vase as vehicles in which to transport intelligence of its existence to those who would make use of it later. A method that worked equally well more than a fifteen hundred years after that, when Sultan Baybars, as a "native son" of the region, ordered it destroyed.

And also when Ibn Daniyal, writing in a style that more than self-consciously echoed that of Aristophanes, produced a message that would send the initiated seeker, or at least the seeker with the open mind, back to the linguistic source. Reviving the lost beloved, who always disappeared, but never died. And Evliya Çelebi, himself Abkhaz, had preserved and copied the message in the seventeenth century. Another link in the chain.

But then, in the 1860s, an unexpected chapter in the story had unfolded. The Russians had massacred and displaced the entire population of the region. Those who'd survived emigrated to Anatolia. And in Anatolia, the ordinary tongues of the mountains thrived well enough. As artifacts, perhaps, but with a significant enough diaspora community to keep them alive.

Ubykh, however, did not. A few refugees here and there in Turkey claimed to speak it, but as Ismail's father had said, they'd never spoken it properly. Because Ubykh could only be produced on the eastern shores of the Black Sea. Never elsewhere. Which meant in turn that some of its speakers must have stayed behind when the Russians had undertaken their slaughter. Gone into hiding. Preserved the tongue and its embeddedness in the land. Without Russian awareness.

One of them had approached Enver Pasha and Mustafa Kemal Atatürk at the end of the First World War with word of its preservation. Precipitating Marion's unwitting integration into the tale. And one of them had been disturbed by the construction of Stalin's dacha. The girl. Calling up the swarms to hinder construction and, when that failed, to mask her escape—

"Dr. Bailey?" Maugham's voice was light and menacing.

She must appropriate the astrolabe and the list of coordinates. Get herself out of the room. Once outdoors, the courier would know what to do. It was dark. She'd have every advantage. But how to leave the room when Thacker and Gardiner were loitering at the door?

"Catatonia doesn't become you, Dr. Bailey." Maugham raised a fiendish eyebrow and brandished the toy blacksmith's hammer. "Don't make me use this."

She continued to think.

"I'm feeling an unexpected pang of sympathy for Dr. Pinel, Willcox. What was it he said about—"

She pushed back her chair, stood, and snatched the astrolabe and coordinates, while pulling a sheet of the tracing paper—the Greek, with vowels, easier to sight-read aloud—from under Nick's hand. Stepped back, held the paper up to her face, and took a breath.

"Damn it." Jeffrey stood as well. Fatigued. Lydia must have wrecked him this afternoon.

The language wouldn't attain full force outside of the region. And she was anything but a native speaker. But she'd seen already what it could do. And perhaps spoken loudly, with intent, it would conjure up something more than dormice and house spiders. Facing the door, she shouted the first three lines.

Starlings. Hundreds of them. Pitching down from the ceiling of the room in the direction of Gardiner and Thacker. Utterly unswayed by the solid wood walls into which they were flying.

"Jesus Christ!" Thacker fell to the ground and covered his head with his hands.

Gardiner, after a brief attempt to knock the first wave out of the way, stumbled backward as well.

And she took her opportunity. Running in the wake of the birds, she jumped over Thacker, pulled open the door, and sprinted into the corridor toward the entry hall. Passing Teddy, who was walking absentmindedly in the direction of the music room. Sheet music in one hand. Lydia, giggling, in the other.

She didn't stop. "I'm going out."

He squinted toward the library. "Ah. They'll be following hard on, then?"

"Yes. Any second." Reaching the front door.

"Oh dear." He dropped his music, which fanned out into treacherous disarray on the floor. Delighting Lydia, who pulled her uncle's ear. "Clumsy of me. Ought to slow them down a bit, though."

"Thank you, Teddy."

"Hmm?" He bent over, grunting, to retrieve the pages. Set Lydia down to caper about, stomping on them. "Oh, Marion?"

"Yes?" She was already out the door, but she paused.

"Our gardener bumped into that lovely Irish girl who's always skulking about here when you're in residence." He looked up and saw Thacker sprinting down the corridor. Pulled Lydia back into his arms. Let another piece of sheet music slide across the floor. "Said she had some excellent advice about overwintering dahlias."

He nodded to himself, pleased by the thought of the healthy tubers. "Anyhow, she's been spending her time recently out beyond the stables. Thought you might want to know."

"*Thank you,* Teddy. Bye, bye, Lydia."

"Bye, bye, Mummy. Don't whap the ponies. Father says it's wrong."

"I'll try not to, Lydia." She smiled quickly and was running through the damp meadow, in the direction of the horses, less than thirty seconds later. Though she could already hear pounding, angry, footsteps gaining behind her. Thacker and Gardiner had overcome Teddy's obstacle.

When she'd reached the stables and turned a corner, out of view of the house, she nearly ran into the courier, dressed in black, jumping neatly and silently to the ground from the low roof of the structure. Breathing hard, she shoved the astrolabe and the papers in the girl's direction. The courier, quiet and competent, secured them inside the complex jacket she wore for that purpose.

Then, entertained, she looked up under her brows at Marion. "You're more agile than you were when last I saw you."

"Yes." Having regained her breath. "It comes of not being in labor."

"That would do it." She tilted her head. "How's Arthur Gardiner?"

"Approximately fifteen seconds away."

"All the time in the world." She smiled. "Any message?"

"Tell them to use the astrolabe to triangulate the Balanjar coordinates." She glanced behind her, worried now. "Procyon in Libra."

"Understood. Anything more?"

"I'll drop a report when the situation is less scalding. For now, tell them that they're seeking the language of the birds." The footsteps were rounding the corner of the stable. "The lost tongue. Not an artifact."

"Understood."

And she was gone. Just as Marion felt Thacker coming at her from the edge of the building. Instinctively, she ducked. And then, once she'd turned, she stumbled backward, wide-eyed. He had a cricket bat.

He was readying for another swing, when Jeffrey, stepping up behind him, pulled the bat out of his hand. "Too late, Thacker." He tossed it to the side and addressed Gardiner. "I believe that was your little Irish friend."

"I'll catch her."

"Leave it." He reached down, grabbed Marion's arm, and pulled her to her feet. "Marion will tell us all we want to know. She's memorized it. Even if she didn't intend to. Her brain's revenge for her lifelong mistreatment of it."

"Without the astrolabe and list of coordinates," she said as he spun her back and began walking her toward the house, "there's nothing you can do. Even if I were to talk to you. Which I won't."

"You will," he said.

She looked behind her, nervously, as Thacker retrieved his cricket bat.

As the four of them tramped through the door, bleak of purpose, Teddy was backing out of the music room, juggling Lydia, a child's violin, and a stand in his hands. He smiled sheepishly at Marion when he saw her in their midst. Jeffrey holding her arm.

"I trust you found your friend?" He placed the stand in the middle of the corridor. Bounced Lydia a few times on his hip.

"Yes. We had a profitable conversation."

"Good show. Pleased to hear it."

"Did you whap the pony, Mummy?" Lydia was reaching for the violin's bow, which Teddy was holding higher and higher in his other hand.

"Yes," she said. "I did. Hard."

"Mummy," Jeffrey said, "did *not* whap the pony. No one whaps the ponies."

"I do," Marion retorted. "I whap them constantly. Ponies make me angry."

"They make me angry too, Mummy—"

"Teddy," Jeffrey interrupted, "we mustn't keep Aunt Ginnie waiting for Lydia's recital. That would be a shame, wouldn't it?"

Teddy smothered a laugh, lifted the stand, and walked with it in the direction of the staircase. Smiling, half-embarrassed and half-conspiratorial, as he passed Marion. "I'll leave you all to it then."

Jeffrey maneuvered her down the hall and back into the library, where a fire was now burning in the stone hearth. He twisted one of the armchairs that ordinarily flanked it such that it faced the room, and shoved her down into it. When she'd collected herself, she noticed that Maugham, Nick, and Lucy were still sitting at the table. Nick embarrassed, Lucy bright and eager, and Maugham occupied by his miniature hammer.

She remembered Lucy's excitement four years earlier. During her execution. Strange girl. Though she agreed with Virginia that Lucy might be the only solution to Nick's catastrophic decency. A thin wedge driven into the otherwise unassailable probity with which he shielded himself from the world. Not to mention his job.

"Use these." Thacker had thrown the cricket bat onto the table and taken up a pair of tongs that had been left in the fire. Their tips red hot. He shoved the tongs at Jeffrey.

"Don't be an ass." Jeffrey replaced them in their stand by the fireplace.

"She won't talk otherwise."

"She won't talk anyway."

"Then why are we doing this, Willcox?" Thacker was spitting as he shouted. His pocked face blotchy and flushed.

"I've told you," he said, looking down at Marion. "It's there in her head. Just a matter of coaxing it out. Gently. Ideally, while she's looking the other way."

"Thacker," Maugham said, still absorbed in the toy hammer, "use the fire. Gardiner, hold her still." He sighed, dropped the hammer into the pocket of his leather apron, and stood. "I've lost patience."

"Thank God." Thacker reached behind Jeffrey and retrieved the tongs. Thrust them back into the fire.

Marion, panicking, pushed herself out of the chair, but before she could rise, Gardiner was behind her, pinioning her arms behind her back. Keeping her in place.

Jeffrey, who had been left momentarily off-guard by the departure from his strategy, regained his composure. Then, looking down at the floor, he pushed his fists into the pockets of his riding breeches. Looking like some outmaneuvered eighteenth-century rake. "Just keep it away from her face."

"Start with the shoulder." Maugham straightened the cloth hat over his bald head and the wisps of white hair that floated across it. He nodded at Jeffrey.

Exhaling, annoyed now, Jeffrey knelt in front of her and unbuttoned her shirt. Methodical and correct. Distant. "Given that performance with the starlings, Marion, we've got a fair idea of *what* your material was hiding. Care to tell us where the rest of it is? How it works? Before Thacker gets to work?"

She stared back at him, cold.

"Thought not." He pushed her open shirt down to expose her right shoulder. "Enjoy, then. Try not to make too much noise." He straightened her collar. "Or smell."

"Ready." Thacker had pulled the tongs from the fire. They were glowing again.

Jeffrey kissed her forehead, stood, and backed away. Thacker, concentrating now, performing the only part of his job at which he excelled, moved the tips with precision toward her bare skin. Then, after a moment of hesitation, which lasted an eternity in Marion's mind, he pressed them downward over her shoulder, and squeezed. Ten seconds. The smell and sound of burning meat permeated the room.

And Marion, who had vowed not to make a sound, not to perform for them, stiffened against Gardiner's arms. And screamed. When, after ten seconds, Thacker withdrew the tongs to return to the fire, she broke into sobs. Aware of nothing in the room apart from her ruined shoulder. Unable to remember where she was, or why she was in this position.

A few seconds later, Maugham took Thacker's place, put his hands on his knees, and peered into her tear-streaked face. "You do work yourself into a state, Dr. Bailey."

He retrieved the toy hammer from his pocket and tapped it playfully against her blistered and bleeding skin, eliciting another whimper. "Before Thacker resumes, is there any information you'd care to pass along to Trelawney or Miss Peters to aid them in their research? A hint to Miss Peters, for example, of what that list of coordinates told you?" He waited. "Anything at all?"

When she said nothing, he straightened and nodded at Jeffrey. "Other shoulder."

Still irritated, but only mildly so, as though he'd expected this denouement all along, Jeffrey stepped toward the chair to expose her left shoulder. But before he could pull the cloth of her shirt down further, Virginia threw open the door at the far end of the room and stalked toward them. Angry. Holding the tiny violin. Her turquoise silk dressing gown billowing out behind her. They all turned to face her.

When she reached Jeffrey, she slapped him. Hard. "You have made an utter fiasco of Lydia's Schumann. She's distraught. What is *wrong* with you? You can't keep quiet for ten minutes?"

"Her Schumann?" Maugham sounded intrigued.

"The Happy Farmer." Incensed. "Teddy was accompanying her. Or trying to accompany her—" She twisted toward the fireplace. "What *is* that smell?" Astonished, she noticed Marion for the first time. "Oh, for heaven's sake!"

Then, moving from incensed to livid, she turned on Jeffrey again. "That," pointing at Marion, "is for upstairs. In private. The bedroom. Not the library. Can you imagine how Mrs. Galbraith would've reacted if she'd walked in to tidy the shelves?"

"You've used the library," he said, petulant. Rubbing his cheek. Sounding nine years old. "I've seen it. Heard it too."

"I've used the library," she snapped back at him, "when there was some hope left to my project. You and this—this *Boy's Own Snatch Squad*—are acting purely out of pique."

"There's still time—"

"There's no time," she spoke over him. "Her courier's gone. She's outsmarted you, Jeffie." She took a step closer to him. "Don't be a sore loser on top of everything else." Glanced at Marion. "Congratulations, Marion."

"Thank you." Her voice barely audible.

"We don't need the courier," he insisted. "If we can get the location out of her—"

"No. You do need the courier. You've lost." She grabbed the tongs from Thacker, who'd been watching, bewildered, as the metal cooled in his hand. Shoved them back into the stand. "Mr. Thacker, you will leave this house. If I see you near it again, I will set the dogs on you." Still holding the toy violin.

Reddening, Thacker looked over at Maugham, who nodded and shooed him away. With a last, lingering gaze at Marion's untouched left shoulder, he slunk from the room. Failing to slam the door behind him.

"Marion," she said once he'd left, "Dr. Gaunt will attend to your wound. I'll telephone him now. Mr. Gardiner, if you'd be so kind as to—"

"Virginia," Maugham finally intervened, "we have unfinished business with Dr. Bailey. You've had your say. Please leave now."

"I think not."

"Don't make me do something we'd both regret."

She turned on him, her eyebrows raised, smiling sweetly. "Your office, Professor Maugham, concerns itself with the identification and collection of papers, artifacts, and antiquities of national import. For the Museum and Library. You've got your papers. There." Pointing to the remaining rubbings on the table. "I've got evidence of their import to the nation in the form of bat and polecat carcasses all over my house. There *is* nothing else. Nothing in the way of an artifact. The scene you've arranged here is in aid of nothing at all except petty, personal revenge."

"On the contrary—"

"When I leave this room," she interrupted, "I will telephone either Dr. Gaunt or George. If George, I will explain to him that you are recklessly wasting government resources on a private vendetta against a useful, if sometimes wayward, acquisition. His ministry is not unaware of your less than dispassionate attitude toward her." She stared at him, icy. "Perhaps you've simply grown too old for this position."

He pushed his hands into the pockets of his leather apron. His fist gripping the toy hammer was visible through the material. But his voice was steady. "Your father would have been saddened by your misplaced loyalty, Virginia. I myself am saddened by it. A disappointment to your family. Your position."

"My father," she replied, "would have been saddened by that hat. He'd have found my misplaced loyalty diverting." And then, still holding the violin, she left the room.

Maugham, looking indeed older than he had moments before, adjusted the hat. Turned to Jeffrey. "That," pointing at Marion, "never sets foot in the Caucasus again, Willcox. Do you understand me? *Never.* Or far from metaphorical heads will roll." Then, beckoning to Gardiner, he walked toward the door. "Would you accompany me, Mr. Gardiner? A few details remain to be discussed."

"Of course, sir." Gardiner straightened and trailed Maugham. Cast a quick, amazed look at Jeffrey as he passed. Smirked toward Nick, sitting silent at the table next to Lucy. And then he was gone as well.

Jeffrey, after a few seconds of silence, crouched in front of Marion again. Pulled her shirt up over her left arm. Kept the right, oozing blood, exposed. "Can you walk?"

"It was my shoulder, idiot." She held her shirt together with her left hand and allowed him to help her rise from the chair. "You're a toad."

"You smell of an accident in the kitchen."

"Fuck you."

They left.

And Nick and Lucy were alone in the room.

London, England
December, 1937

IAN had survived his first term at Eton with wounds only slightly less agonizing than Marion's. But he was home now for six weeks, and she was reveling in the time she spent with him. More tolerant than he'd been before of her tendency toward protectiveness, he'd allowed her to take him and Lydia to the zoo and then, afterward, a brightly colored, childish tea room. Had patiently appreciated the miserable African animals enduring the ice and dusting of snow. And had allowed Lydia to climb over his back and shoulders upon their return, re-enacting some scene she'd witnessed and stored for later use.

Now, nearing midnight, they were both sleeping. And Marion had crept down to the dark dining room with a bottle of scotch and a glass. Wanting to work through her memories of the preceding months. Understand them. And lock them away.

A few days after her return from Suffolk, she'd dropped a report for her superiors, emphasizing Ismail's request that their find in the Caucasus be protected and hidden rather than exposed or weaponized. She'd received an acknowledgment—positive-sounding—a few days after that. Which was all she could expect from them. More than she ought to expect.

And, better, Maugham had kept his distance. From what Jeffrey had let slip, the pages she'd copied from the walls of the underground gallery had been duly catalogued in the British Library as "Nart Sagas—Fragments and Apocrypha." Which meant that no one would ever see or read them again. The office had dropped the project.

So why was she anxious? Frowning, she opened the bottle and poured a large helping into her glass. Swallowed it and waited for it to go to work. But before it had passed into her blood, she heard footsteps at the door and looked up. Jeffrey. Wearing pyjamas and a dressing gown, carrying a thick, brown envelope in one hand, a tumbler in the other.

He held up the tumbler. "Mind if I join you?"

She pushed the bottle toward him.

He sat, placed the envelope on the table, and poured himself two or three fingers. Sipped and nodded at the envelope. "Dr. Pinel's report. Good news. You've narrowly escaped sectioning."

She reached for the bottle and poured herself more. "It's midnight. Don't you ever stop?"

"Midnight makes it worse." He smiled at her over the lip of his glass.

"Why?" She drained the glass. "Why, *why* do you do this?"

"Marion, I can't help it." He finished off his own drink, set the glass on the table, and watched her. "Your mind is endlessly fascinating to me. Unique in all my experience. I keep thinking that I've won, that I've tortured it into submission, that it's broken. But then, somehow, it always wriggles free. And so, I start over. How could I not, my love?"

"I wouldn't have lasted," she said, ignoring his comment. Admitting to him and to herself what had bothered her over the past weeks. "If Thacker had continued. I'd have talked to you." She rubbed her eyes with her fists. "I'm old. Weak. Another—another—"

"No one withstands it," he said. "No matter how young or strong. Not even Mr. Fyffes. It's Thacker's skill." He shrugged. "But his results are slipshod. Yes, you'd have talked. Tried to talk. Kept talking. Perhaps even given us a bit more than we already had. But it wouldn't have been useful. And he'd have ruined your mind for the rest. Counterproductive when the accounts are in."

"Oh."

"That's why Maugham uses him only as a last resort." He ran his fingertip along the edge of the empty glass. "You might think of it as a compliment."

"Right."

"No," he said. "Truly. In all the time I've known Maugham, I've never seen him set Thacker on one of our own during a debriefing. It's a testament to your influence. He's frightened."

"I'm not one of your own."

"Always and forever, darling." He rose, taking up his empty glass. "But that's a conversation for the morning." He turned back as he passed through the door. "Read the report, Marion. You'll find it distracting. Lift you out of this mood, yes?"

She spent the remainder of the night alone in the dining room, finishing the bottle of scotch. Staring, resentful, at the closed, brown envelope.

Iraq, 1938

London, England
March, 1938

Both had been educated in medicine, though neither had practiced. Our man on the scene wondered whether this common background in abandoned surgical discipline might have had something to do with their unfortunate allure to the gibbon. It certainly aided in their innovative suicides."

Maugham fed the monkey a piece of cheese. It spit it out. Puzzled, he considered the wet, whitish chunk on the floor of the drawing room. Illuminated by the glow of the glass lamps, turned up against the twilit drizzle beyond the uncurtained windows.

He had arrived unannounced at the door to Jeffrey's Chester Terrace house a few minutes before, bearing both the monkey and news of the demise of two elderly functionaries at the British Embassy in Baghdad. Each, according to Maugham, had prepped himself and then surgically removed his own liver and kidneys. Upon the urging, so said their colleagues, of an insistent and hectoring gibbon. Resulting in their deaths.

"*That* gibbon?" Jeffrey, sitting beside Marion on their sofa, lifted his gaze from the spot of cheese on the floor to the monkey itself. Not troubling to mask his revulsion.

Maugham fed it another piece of cheese. It spit it out. "No, no. Not this one. The gibbon that put paid to Mr. Jennings and Mr. Barton was invisible. At least according to witnesses. Similar to this, though. Same form. Same behavior." He furrowed his brow. "Does it not like cheese? I was assured that—"

"If it was invisible," Jeffrey began, "how could there be—"

"It's not a gibbon." Marion spoke quietly. Unwilling to remain passive in the room while they dissected the adventures of what Maugham continued to insist was an invisible monkey terrorizing Baghdad. The second piece of cheese had landed uncomfortably close to her shoe, and she wanted the meeting over before she brushed it with her toe. "Gibbons haven't got tails."

Jeffrey raised surprised eyebrows at her.

"I've been spending time with Lydia at the zoo," she muttered. "That's a mangabey. Not a gibbon."

Maugham tried to pat the monkey—silky black fur, red eyes, sinuous tail—perched now on the edge of his armchair. It reared back and showed its teeth. Threatening. But it didn't move or attack. "Delightful creature." He ate a piece of the cheese himself. "And of course, as always, Dr. Bailey is correct. This isn't a gibbon. Nor was its counterpart in Baghdad. I merely like the word." He chewed and swallowed. "Gibbon. Gibbon. Gibbon—"

"Maugham," Jeffrey interjected. The monkey was eyeing him. Cool and dangerous. "Could these deceased diplomats have contracted a parasite? Brain fever? What reason is there to discount hallucination?" He narrowed his own eyes at the monkey. "Enchanted though I am by the thought of a ghostly, murderous ape on the loose in Mesopotamia."

"Not an ape," Maugham corrected him. "It has a tail."

"An invisible tail."

Maugham grunted. Reached into his trouser pocket and pulled out two frayed pieces of a small beige card. Held one up, nearsighted, to examine it. The monkey grabbed it. Ate it. Uncharacteristically flustered, Maugham pushed another piece of cheese into the monkey's face. It spit the cheese onto the floor.

"Here," he said, shoving the second half of the card at Jeffrey. "Before it consumes my evidence."

Jeffrey accepted the card with ill grace, avoiding eye contact with the monkey, which had begun pulling itself in his direction the moment the card was out of Maugham's hand. Examined it quickly and crammed it into the inside pocket of his own jacket. "Catalogue card. From the Baquba collection."

"Correct. That half was found in Mr. Barton's mouth." Maugham, irritated, brushed the monkey's paw off his bald head. The monkey put it back. Began patting Maugham's scalp. "The other half was retrieved from the mouth of Mr. Jennings."

"Oh." Marion continued to contemplate the cheese on the ground. She disliked the tone of the conversation. Wanted to leave, but knew they'd only brief her more aggressively later if she refused to listen now.

"Indeed." Maugham ate another piece of cheese. "There's no doubt that their deaths were suicide. They were alone in their offices, and they died by their own hand. Which means either that each placed half of the card in his mouth prior to removing his own organs—and retained it there throughout the process—or that something wedged it between their lips afterward. We're inclined toward the latter explanation."

"I see." Jeffrey's voice was neutral.

"Also," Maugham continued, "Mr. Jennings and Mr. Barton were unacquainted. They worked in different departments, at opposite ends of the city, and no one had seen them interact. The only connection between the two is that in the weeks leading up to their deaths, they'd each confided to friends that they'd been troubled, as you say, Willcox, by hallucinations. A chattering black monkey that wouldn't let them be. Neither was vocal about the persecution because neither wanted to end his career under care. But once they'd done away with themselves, their statements were compared. Identical."

"And the catalogue card?"

"Refers us to a fourteenth-century bestiary by Muhammad ibn Musa al-Damiri. *Hayat al-Hayawan*. Catalogued and stored nearly a decade ago with the rest of the Baquba material."

"Oh." Marion rubbed her eyes. She'd encountered the bestiary before. When it was still under Baquba. And at the time, she'd left it severely alone—a volume with an air of evil about it. She shuddered, remembering the split-second flash of eyes, fur, and something worse that had sliced through her mind when she'd brushed a stray fingertip across its cover. Thinking back, she was surprised that it had taken so long for the book to come into its own in London.

"Thoughts, Dr. Bailey?" Maugham's expression mirrored that of the mangabey now draped, immobile, over his shoulder.

"Mr. Jennings and Mr. Barton were a provocation," she said. "Ignore it. Ignore them. Don't touch it."

"Can't."

"Why not?"

"Because, Dr. Bailey," he held up a finger, which the monkey failed to grab, Maugham adapting to his situation quickly, "the gibbon is on the move."

"How do you know? It's invisible." Jeffrey gazed, affronted, across at the mangabey. "Is there a smell? That one's got a distinct atmosphere about it."

"Jealous, Willcox?" Maugham patted the monkey's head, which it allowed this time, holding Jeffrey's look. "And no. No smell. Nothing more than a trail of human organs. From what we gather, it's following the route of the Simplon Orient Express. Baghdad, Istanbul, Sofia, Belgrade, Venice, etc. etc. An invisible monkey sighting at every stop. An undistinguished official with lost surgical training attempting to remove his own entrails a day or two later. Mr. Jennings and Mr. Barton are the only ones to have succeeded thus far. Likely because the monkey stayed with them a bit longer than he has with the others. To be honest, we've become bored by the whole affair. Very much like it resolved."

"Has it bought a ticket, I wonder?" Jeffrey brushed a speck of dust off his knee.

"It's crossed the water," Maugham said, ignoring him. "Spotted in London."

"*If it's invisible*," Jeffrey reiterated, "*then how can it*—"

"Clairvoyants." Unperturbed. "Not our branch. Liaising for the duration of this project."

Jeffrey stood. "Thank you, Maugham. This has all been quite fascinating. Marion and I are delighted to have met your atrocious gibbon. Pleased to see you and it getting on so well. Unfortunately, however, you appear to have mistaken us for recruits into your faithful army of Snergs. I suggest you take all this up with them."

"It's found itself a nest in the city," Maugham persisted. "A home. Protected and untouchable. In the residence of one Dr. Clarissa Harbottle, formerly of Cambridge University."

"Oh." Marion had remained seated on the sofa. Frowning at the cheese on the floor.

Jeffrey peered down at her for a moment or two. Then, weary, he lowered himself to her side. Looked across at Maugham. "Let me guess, Marion. Dr. Clarissa Harbottle. Having been driven out of the academy by the unrelenting derision of the establishment, she now devotes her considerable intellectual powers to destabilizing the scholarly edifice she once sought to climb? Chipping away at it. Bitter and potent."

"The solution," she mumbled to the floor, "is not to drive us out with such unfettered glee."

"The solution," he snapped back at her, "is not to let you in to begin with."

"Nonsense, Willcox." Maugham had finished his cheese and was crumpling the empty bag into his pocket. "What fun would that be? Dr. Bailey will visit Dr. Harbottle and her invisible monkey tomorrow. Separate the one from the other. Bring the monkey to us. A resolution. No more jumpy clerks terrified of the Orient Express. Quite the relief."

"Clarissa and I haven't spoken for over a decade," she said. "And even if we had, I—"

"Then reacquaint yourself." Maugham stood himself, allowing the monkey to scramble up his arm and cling to his shoulder.

She scowled up at him. "The monkey, Professor Maugham, is invisible. How am I supposed—"

"We can always send Thacker in your place, Dr. Bailey." Buttoning his jacket. "He's recently discovered arson."

"But—"

"She'll go tomorrow morning." Jeffrey rose and shook Maugham's hand. "Thank you, Maugham. Good evening."

"Willcox." He nodded down at Marion. "Dr. Bailey."

As he left, the monkey lifted a small, painted china dog from the mantelpiece and dropped it into the pocket of Maugham's jacket. They made no attempt to retrieve it.

CLARISSA Harbottle lived in a decrepit red brick house of three-storeys in Westminster. Inherited from an equally decrepit great-uncle. She was fifteen years older than Marion, but even when they'd known one another at Cambridge twenty years before, Clarissa had been haggish. Unapproachable.

Marion paused at the base of the iron bannister that twisted up to the front door, collecting herself. She and Clarissa had each been, in her own way, demolished by the academy. Both had responded by attacking it and the political architecture that supported it. But whereas Marion's reaction had led her further and further afield, into wider and ever more bleak and barren terrain, Clarissa's had left her compressed into the cramped and tortured crevices of this house. Only this house. Abandoning the rest of the building—not to mention the outside—to her botanical and zoological collection. The result of having failed at biology rather than at The Orient. Marion didn't want to see Clarissa again.

As she was standing, morose, on the lowest of the five steps leading to the entry, the door cracked open. A stream of vile brown smoke from a cigarillo, the smell hitting Marion's amygdala like a battering ram, escaped the house. She remembered the cigarillo's scent too well. Its thick fug hanging low over angry, ranting conversations she'd thought she'd forgotten. She very, very much did not want to renew her acquaintance with Clarissa.

"Go on, then." A voice unused to communicating with humans trickled past the smoke. "You've been planted there for ten minutes. Leave or walk up."

"Good morning, Clarissa." She climbed the stairs and squeezed sideways through the door.

"You look old." Clarissa had shoved a candle dripping over an ancient bronze candlestick into her face. The cigarillo extinguished in the soft wax. Gawking, rude, at her middle-aged skin.

The rest of the entry hall was lit by two additional candles. Dim. Filthy. Emphasizing rather than dulling the feel of countless things climbing, scurrying, and oozing along the floor and walls.

Marion blinked in astonishment. Clarissa herself looked more than old. A nightmarish Elizabethan caricature of a Greek Sibyl. Wild, curling grey hair to her waist. Overgrown eyebrows meeting above her nose. Bits of half-chewed meat crammed between loose teeth. Not to mention a purplish fungal growth that spread across her wrist and lower arm.

She was wearing a man's dressing gown with a sticky, stiff brown stain down the front. And nothing else. Bare feet. Horrible feet.

"You've come for *it*, haven't you?" Clarissa turned and walked into the blackness of the ground floor's central corridor.

"It?" Marion followed. Hurrying to keep within the sparse light of the candle rather than leaving herself open to the things that filled the shadow it left behind.

"Or, perhaps, it's come for you." Clarissa pushed open a door and gestured Marion into a vaulted conservatory.

The room was as dim as the corridor had been, crawling with contorted vines, the width of a man's thigh or broader, that obscured the glass and dripped liquid—unidentifiable—over the puny bits and pieces of furniture still visible under the growth. In the damp, the strands of Clarissa's grey hair and the flecks of her dead skin hadn't yet turned to dust. Fallen hair coated every surface. Mingling with tendrils from the vines. It was also the primary ingredient in the nests that the room's teaming animals had built along the edges of the walls and under the larger trees.

Marion swallowed. "For me?"

"The monkey." Clarissa threw herself onto a rusting iron stool, taking longer than strictly necessary to re-secure the dressing gown that gaped open at her movement.

Marion colored and looked away. Then, once she was certain that Clarissa had safely tied her belt, she sat on a three-legged stool opposite. Relieved. At least she needn't explain herself. "I won't take it if you'd rather I didn't. I don't like this situation. But if I hadn't agreed to visit you, they'd have hurt you. My contacts. I wanted to prevent that."

"Hurt me?" Entertained. "Wouldn't mind seeing them try." And then, when Marion said nothing: "it's better that you came. The monkey wants you. Not them."

"You said that before." She held out a hand to steady herself on the stool, one leg of which was sinking into a tangle of colocasia tubers. "I don't understand."

"Nothing to understand." Clarissa scratched a running sore on the inside of her leg. "It wants you."

"Yes, but—" And then she stopped short. Squinted up into the shade of a twenty-foot cycad from the top of which dim red eyes gazed down at her. Eyes surrounded by a greyish shadow that, as it descended the trunk, resolved itself into a sleek black monkey. Very long tail.

But the monkey wasn't right. Its expression was too intense. Jeering. And not in the accidental manner of Maugham's mangabey, but with a premeditated intentionality that was sorely amiss in the face of something not human.

As it neared, she could hear it chattering to itself. And though no specific sound it made coalesced into a meaningful word, the effect of its muttering was that if she listened, she'd understand. To her detriment. The animal was flinging verbal fecal matter at her. Nonsense, but with a smell and a feel. It stank of shame.

"Thought so." Clarissa watched her reaction, smug.

"That's it, then? Over there?"

"Wouldn't know."

"What do you mean you wouldn't know?"

"I can't see it."

"But it's just there." Like a toddler, Marion pointed, eager, over Clarissa's shoulder. Where the monkey had perched for a half second before scuttering under the stool. Still watching her, composed, with its cold, red expression.

"I can't see a thing."

"If you can't see it," Marion said, echoing Jeffrey as she followed the monkey's movement across the floor with wide, sick eyes, "then how do you know what it is?"

"The animals can see it. Or sense it. And I've come across the stray print in the dust since it arrived. Simple to identify if you know what you're seeing."

Now that Clarissa had mentioned the other animals, Marion noticed the silence. The scurrying, scrabbling, and oozing had come to an abrupt halt since the monkey had climbed from the cycad. Even the dripping of the trees was muffled. All she could hear in the enormous, vaulted room were its obscene mutterings and Clarissa's grating breath.

"Why can I see it?" The monkey was circling her stool, grinning and contemptuous.

"The conventional answer to that question," Clarissa said, scratching at her matted grey hair and dislodging a clump of scalp, "is guilt."

"Guilt?"

"Jahiz. Al-Damiri. Ibn Qutayba. Take your pick." She examined her ragged, brown fingernails. "But you know more about that side of the story than I do, Marion." Referring to her by name for the first time. "There's also metamorphosis. Monkeys represent transmutation. Usually in an undesirable direction. And corruption. Corrupted morals. Any of this ring true? Any transformation, taint, or guilt you've not yet come to terms with? Needn't be adultery. That was always a bit of a red herring. Though, perhaps, the simplest to remedy."

The monkey had faded into the maroon shade of a pornographic aristolochia vine, though its eyes still fixed her in place on the unstable stool. She closed her own. Which did nothing to dampen the chattering that felt now as though it were coming from inside her head. Returned her attention to Clarissa. Opened her eyes. "Guilt."

"Hmm."

"It was attached to al-Damiri's bestiary. I remember it. Impressions of it. Behind my eyes." She stared at the red glow that failed to illuminate the shadow at the edge of the conservatory. "It wants to go home. It isn't my own guilt."

"I wouldn't know."

"I may be able to convince them." She considered. "If the alternative is a rising tide of deranged, dead bureaucrats, they'll listen—"

"I also don't care." Clarissa rose from the stool, not troubling to re-tie her dressing gown, which hung open to reveal a body not demonstrably different from that of the invisible monkey. Larger. Flaccid. Less sleek. But otherwise remarkably similar. "You bore me, Marion. You aren't what you were."

When Marion stood as well, the monkey moved sideways, stalking her, out from under the vine. Then it streaked across the floor, tumbling under her feet, forcing her to trip into a thin palm that dumped a leaf-full of yellow liquid into her hair. Righting herself, she squinted about her. She hadn't felt the monkey. It was as intangible to her as it was invisible to others. But its effect on her mind was that of a real animal. She didn't want to make contact with it. To step on it.

Clarissa laughed, unpleasant, and made her way to the conservatory door. Opened it for her. "Go away. You'll find your own way out. My regards to your terrifying contacts."

Baquba, Iraq
April, 1938

JEFFREY and Marion took the train to Baghdad. The slow train. Unable to ignore the persistent menace of the monkey, Marion had refused outright to board an aeroplane—the thought of its materialization in the cockpit or outside her window leaving her jittery. Ill. More so, even, than its constant, if random, presence at the tail of her eye once she'd left Clarissa's Dickensian nightmare of a home.

But she was grateful, despite the monkey's companionship, to be moving at all. Surprised by Maugham's willingness to relinquish al-Damiri's bestiary to Baquba. Though perhaps she shouldn't have been. Bowing as he was to the combined imperative of her own agitation, two or three stomach-turning accidents in the stacks, and the likelihood that additional functionaries would soon be doing away with themselves using even more acrobatic methods. He wanted the monkey out of Britain. And Baquba was as good a place as any to contain it.

Not that the weeks on the train had been enjoyable. The monkey's carping mutter was just haphazard and just intelligible enough to snag at her shredded attention. Catching her mid-sentence when she made an effort to speak. Mid-thought when she didn't. Wrecking any coherent set of ideas as it dropped into a spare moment of silence or emerged imperceptibly from the shuddering of the locomotive's wheels over the tracks. And then disappeared again—while she herself tripped over her feet or tumbled down stairways or collided with walls, trying to avoid the absent touch of the animal that remained, tauntingly, on the move. Behind her. Crouching and ready to spring.

Even worse than her own fractured mind and wrecked body was the monkey's effect on those near her. At first, she'd thought that strangers were, reasonably, shying away from her own peculiar behavior. Lowering their eyes and passing rapidly in the street because, despite her dogged intention to the contrary, she couldn't help staring at the aggressive animal draped about their shoulders or hanging off their necks, shrieking abuse in her direction.

But gradually, she came to understand that there was more to their antipathy than her eccentric conduct. Although they could see nothing, they could sense that the air about her was off. Pick up something that wasn't quite a smell, but might very well have been. Enough to drive away all but those required to interact with her.

And even those forced into contact with her were hostile. Jeffrey, for example, had suggested that they rest for two or three nights in Paris before boarding the train south. But when they'd found their hotel—walking because no taxi would stop for them—the clerk explained that there'd been an error. No room was available. Nor was there a room in any of the six additional hotels they'd tried. Eventually, without speaking to one another about it, they'd changed their tickets and boarded a night train out of Paris.

But the confined space of the train only made her spectral stench more offensive. When they entered the dining car, it emptied. When she chanced upon a boy and his mother in the corridor, the boy let out a sob and ran in the opposite direction. His mother looking her up and down in fear and disgust. The porters, contemptuous and facing away from her, held the door for her a touch longer than was necessary to allow it through. And even Jeffrey, who pretended that nothing was wrong, left an instinctive space between them when he walked behind her. As though he could sense the thing between them. His playfulness long since gone.

Once they left the train in Baghdad, they didn't even try to recuperate from the journey. Instead, Jeffrey appropriated a vehicle from the Embassy, hefted their unnecessary luggage into the back, and sped out of the city in the direction of Baquba. He was as anxious as she was to put the manuscript to rest.

As they neared the grove of date palms at the outskirts of town, though, she felt more ambivalent than she'd expected to be. She hadn't visited the site since Jeffrey had looted it. Had never seen the chambers empty. The scrolls and volumes gone. And she wasn't certain that she could face the vacant rooms with any degree of composure. But when the reddish eyes of the monkey emerged out of an orange sunset beyond the trees, she set aside her personal aversion to the place. The manuscript expected to return. She had no choice.

Opening her door before Jeffrey had brought the car to a stop, she took up the wrapped pages and stood. Shaded her eyes against the last of the sun and the flat, black relief of the monkey on the horizon. Took a step. Jeffrey, who had followed her, took a few steps in the same direction before reconsidering and stopping. "We've kept a watch on it," he said. "Maintained the structure. There's no danger. Would you like me to accompany you or would you rather do this alone?"

She thought for a moment. Debating whether her fear of being alone underground with the monkey exceeded her rage at what Jeffrey had done to the site. Decided she preferred rage. "Come with me. You go first."

"Very well." He walked into the stand of trees, casting a torch over the ground until he found the trapdoor. Squatted, pulled it up by its loop, secured it, and handed the torch to Marion. Lowered himself onto the ladder. As he descended, she illuminated the rungs for him. Ineffectively. Trying to keep the monkey's shadow from playing over the walls.

Once he was down, she tossed him the torch, closed her eyes and lowered herself as well. Working by feel and suffering the screaming insults of the monkey rather than risking a fall because of something she thought she'd seen on the ladder or the floor. When she reached the bottom, she swallowed, squeezed her eyes tightly together for a further five seconds, and then opened them. Looked about her.

Before she could react to the dry, sterile room and the growing lump in her throat, Jeffrey blocked her thought. "Do what we've come here to do, Marion. Don't think about the rest."

She swallowed again, nodded, and approached the lectern at the center of the chamber. Empty. Placed the wrapped book on top of it. And stepped back. Uncertain.

Then, confused and unwilling to hope, she raised her head. The air was different. Noticeably so. There was no chattering. No muttering on the edge of audibility. No invisible black form about to blossom into horrible coherence. Suspicious, she let her eyes wander across the darker fringes of the room. No dull eyes. She felt, oddly, like crying.

"It's gone?" His voice was edgy. Impatient.

"Yes."

"Thank God." He moved toward the ladder. "Let's go. I loathe this place."

She took the torch he handed to her and lit the rungs of the ladder. Surprised. "It's your legacy, Jeffrey. All of your work."

"There are other things than work."

When he reached the top, she tossed him the torch and began climbing the ladder herself. Didn't reply.

TWO weeks later, they were on an Imperial Airways flight over Bulgaria. Heading home. The cabin was empty aside from the two of them, and the only crew were in the cockpit. The atmosphere, despite the engines, was tranquil.

Marion had slept for a full day and night once they'd returned to Baghdad. In a hotel. The staff delighted to take them when they'd turned up, without a reservation, in the lobby. No revolted glances over her shoulder or at her feet. No sudden absence of accommodation.

After that, she'd walked deliberately, provocatively, through the most crowded and public parts of the city she could find, and drunk cup after cup of coffee in the most teeming cafés she knew. No disgust. No invisible quarantine. The atmosphere surrounding her was no more abhorrent than it had ever been. But it had still taken her another three days to begin scanning her environment without the preemptive rush of adrenaline that announced the potential appearance—or not—of red eyes reflected from a window or consolidating at knee-level in some dark alley.

Now, recuperated, she was sitting across from Jeffrey, reading a magazine. Something about cinema stars. He was smoking a cigarette, looking out the window. As quietly relieved as she was by the empty cabin and the rhythmic hum of the engines.

Bored, she closed the magazine in her lap and looked up. Into the grinning face of the monkey. Pulling itself up and over the seat in front of her. Murmuring to itself. And then, to her.

"Oh, damn." Jeffrey, having turned from the window, caught her white, terrified eyes.

She shook her head. Speechless. The monkey didn't move. But it did mutter more pointedly.

"What will you do, Marion?"

She shook her head again. Distraught. But then, gradually, anger supplanted her fear. Her thoughts, she noted in a pristine, unaffected part of her mind, were coming as logically and precisely as ever—cleaving through what was now the impotent chatter of the animal. It wasn't gone. But it didn't matter to her anymore.

"Marion?"

"I think," she said, "that I'm going to give it a name."

"I'm sorry?"

"A name. It hasn't got a name." She glared across at the monkey. "What do you think of Fluffy?"

"I've always been partial to 'Fluffy.'"

"Good."

He smiled, weak and uncertain. "Are you confident that you can handle this, Marion? It seems—extreme."

"*This?*" She smiled back at him. "*This?* This is nothing. I've survived worse." She cast a cold, calculating, and contemptuous look at the monkey. Which, slowly and meekly, lowered itself into its seat. And she didn't see it or hear from it for the remainder of the flight.

Jeffrey smoked his cigarette for a few minutes longer, observing the window. Then, without facing her, he spoke again. "I'm very fond of you, you know."

"Yes," she said to her own window. "I know."

He smoked a bit more. "Shall we go back and retrieve the manuscript, do you think? A shame to let it languish there in that dismal cavern."

She watched the clouds passing beneath them. Didn't reply.

Epilogue: London, 1967

London, England
May, 1967

MOTHER never rid herself of the monkey. Lydia and I used to see it occasionally. Its shadow. On darker nights. And it drove Mrs. Bowen batty. Dusty paw prints everywhere, no culprit in sight."

But his friend wasn't to be deterred. "Come on, John." Nodding at the package. "Open it. The monkey's a diversion."

"Fluffy? A diversion?"

"Open it."

"Really, after all that I've said, you aren't nervous? Think of how dangerous this composition must be to have put off my mother. She was game for anything."

"After all that you've said," John's friend replied, "I'm even more eager to see that thing unwrapped. Whilst also coming to terms with the fact that your name, apparently, is 'Ian.'"

"My name," he said, "is John."

"May I call you 'Ian?'"

"No."

The sun had set, and John's friend was sitting upright in the chair, buttoning his jacket. May in London was still May. "It's a pity we didn't unearth it when she was alive. I apologize for that."

"No. It would have been worse then. Catastrophic."

"Then?"

"Yes." He frowned. "I thought you knew. Mother and father both died in the Blitz. He had some idea about protecting her from one of Maugham's sprees. Spirited her away to Exeter in May of 1942. Bad decision. Whatever that package is, it wouldn't have helped the war effort."

"I'm sorry," his friend repeated. "I didn't know."

"Lydia and I were raised in Suffolk by my Aunt Ginnie and Uncle Teddy." He forced a smile. "But at least I got to leave that awful school."

"Eton?"

"Hmm." Not catching the irony. "Lydia scarcely remembers them. Though her antics now may trace their antecedents to 1942." He considered. "I do miss her quite a lot sometimes. Mother."

"Not your father?"

"Father," John said, "wouldn't have approved of my missing him. Sentiment."

John's friend rose from the chair into what was now twilight. He didn't take the package. "I'll leave it here with you. Open it or not, as you see fit." Passed through the door into the flat, and then, thinking, turned. "Don't bring it back. It's not meant for the Museum."

"I won't. And thank you."

John continued to scrutinize the package as he heard the door click shut. And then he unraveled the twine.

The End

English-Language Bibliography

Aga-Oglu, Mehmet. "A Brief Note on Islamic Terminology for Bronze and Brass," *Journal of the American Oriental Society* (64) (4) (Oct.-Dec., 1944): 218-223.

Al-Faruqi, Lois Ibsen. "The Suite in Islamic History and Culture," *The World of Music* (27) (3) (1985): 46-66.

Al-Hamdani, Husain, F. "The History of the Ismaili Dawat and Its Literature During the Last Phase of the Fatimid Empire," *The Journal of the Royal Asiatic Society* (1) (Jan., 1932): 126-136.

Ambros, Edith. "The Leta'if of Faqiri, Ottoman Poet of the 16th Century," *Wiener Zeitschrift für die Kunde des Morgenlandes* (80) (1990): 59-78.

Atil, Esin. "Two Il-Hanid Candlesticks at the University of Michigan," *Kunst des Orients* (8) (1972): 1-33.

Baer, Eva. "The Nisan Tasi: A Study in Persian-Mongol Metal Ware," *Kunst des Orients* (9) (1973): 1-46.

Baldry, John. "Anglo-Italian Rivalry in Yemen and 'Asir, 1900-1934," *Die Welt des Islams* (17) (1976-1977): 155-193.

Başgöz, İlhan. "Functions of Turkish Riddles," *Journal of the Folklore Institute* (2) (2) (June, 1965): 132-147.

Bates, Michael L. "Notes on Some Ismaili Coins from Yemen," *Museum Notes* (18) (1972): 149-162.

Blackburn, J. Richard. "The Collapse of Ottoman Authority in Yemen, 968/1560-976/1568," *Die Welt des Islams* (19) (1979): 119-176.

Çağman, Filiz and Tanindi, Zeren. "Remarks on Some Manuscripts from the Topkapi Palace Treasury in the Context of Ottoman-Safavid Relations," *Muqarnas* (13) (1996): 132-148.

Carey, Moya, "The Gold and Silver Lining: Shams al-Dīn Muhammad B. Mu'ayyad al-'Urdī's Inlaid Celestial Globe (C. Ad 1288) from the Ilkhanid Observatory at Marāgha," *Iran*, (47) (2009): 97-108.

Carlson, Marvin. "The Arabi Aristophanes," *Comparative Drama* (47) (2) (Summer, 2013): 151-166.

Casale, Giancarlo. "Global Politics in the 1580s: One Canal, Twenty Thousand Cannibals, and an Ottoman Plot to Rule the World," *Journal of World History* (18) (3) (Sept. 2007): 267-296.

Catford, J.C. "Mountain of Tongues: The Languages of the Caucasus," *Annual Review of Anthropology* (6) (1997): 283-313.

Christys, Ann. "The Queen of the Franks offers gifts to the caliph al-Muktafi," in Davies, Wendy, ed. *The Language of Gift in the Early Middle Ages* (Cambridge: Cambridge University Press, 2010): 149-170.

Colarusso, John. *Nart Sagas from the Caucasus*. (Princeton: Princeton University Press, 2002).

Comrie, Bernard. "Linguistic Diversity in the Caucasus," *Annual Review of Anthropology* (37) (2008): 131-143.

Cook, Michael. "Ibn Qutayba and the Monkeys," *Studia Islamica* (89) (1999): 43-74.

Coutts, Howard, Evans, Mark, and Monnas, Lisa. "An Early Italian Textile Drawing in the Victoria and Albert Museum," *The Burlington Magazine* (150) (Jun., 2008): 389-392.

Ergene, Boğaç A. "On Ottoman Justice: Interpretations in Conflict (1600-1800)," *Islamic Law and Society* (8) (1) (2001): 52-87.

Farah, Caesar E. "Yemeni Fortification and the Second Ottoman Conquest," *Proceedings of the Seminar for Arabian Studies* (20) (1990): 31-42.

Friberg, Jören. "Seven-Sided Star Figures and Tuning Algorithms in Greek, Mesopotamian, and Islamic Texts," *Archiv für Orientforschung* (52) (2011): 121-155.

Fudge, Bruce. "Signs of Scripture in 'The City of Brass,'" *Journal of Qur'anic Studies* (8) (1) (2006): 88-118.

Gingeras, Ryan. "The Sons of Two Fatherlands: Turkey and the North Caucasian Diaspora, 1914-1923," *European Journal of Turkish Studies* (2011): 2-17.

Goodrich, Thomas D. "Tarih-i Hind-i Garbi: An Ottoman Book on the New World," *Journal of the American Oriental Society* (107) (2) (1987): 317-319.

Guo, Li. "Paradise Lost: Ibn Daniyal's Response to Baybars' Campaign Against Vice in Cairo," *Journal of the American Oriental Society* (121) (2) (April-June, 2001): 219-235.

Guo, Li. "The Devil's Advocate: Ibn Daniyal's Art of Parody in His Qasidah No. 71," *Mamluk Studies Review* (2003): 177-208.

Haines, John. "The Arabic Style of Performing Medieval Music," *Early Music* (29) (3) (Aug., 2001): 369-378.

Halasi-Kun, Tibor. "Evliya Çelebi as Linguist," *Harvard Ukrainian Studies* (3) (1) (1979-1980): 376-382.

Hämeen-Anttila, Jaakko. "Artificial Man and Spontaneous Generation in Ibn Wahshiyya's al-Filāha an-Nabatiyya," *Zeitschrift der Deutschen Morgenländischen Gesellschaft* (153) (1) (2003): 37-49.

Hämeen-Anttila, Jaakko. *The Last Pagans of Iraq: Ibn Wahshiyya and His Nabatean Agriculture* (Leiden, Brill: 2006).

Hamori, Andras. "An Allegory from the Arabian Nights: The City of Brass," *Bulletin of the School of Oriental and African Studies* (34) (1) (1971): 9-19.

Hathaway, Jane. "The Mawza Exile at the Juncture of Zaydi and Ottoman Messianism," *AJS Review* (29) (1) (April, 2005): 111-128.

Hathaway, Jane. "The Ottomans and the Yemeni Coffee Trade," *Oriente Moderno* (25) (1) (2006): 161-171.

Hepper, Nigel F. "Current Research on the Plant Specimens from the Niebuhr and Forsskal Yemen Expedition, 1761-63," *Proceedings of the Seminar for Arabian Studies* (17) (1987): 81-90.

Hillenbrand, Robert. "Mamluk and Ilkhanid Bestiaries: Convention and Experiment," *Ars Orientalis* (20) (1990): 149-187.

Johns, Jeremy and Savage-Smith, Emilie. "The Book of Curiosities: A Newly Discovered Series of Islamic Maps," *Imago Mundi* (55) (2003): 7-24.

Kennedy, E.S. "An Islamic Computer for Planetary Latitudes," *Journal of the American Oriental Society* (71) (1) (Jan., 1951): 13-21.

Kennedy, E.S. "The Planetary Theory of Ibn al-Shatir," *Isis* (50) (3) (Sept. 1959): 227-235.

King, David A. "The Astronomy of the Mamluks," *Isis* (74) (4) (Dec., 1983): 531-555.

Kornbluth, Genevra. "Susanna and Saint Eligius: Romanesque Reception of a Carolingian Jewel," *Studies in Iconography* (16) (1994): 37-51.

Kornbluth, Genevra. "The Susanna Crystal of Lothar II: Chastity, the Church, and Royal Justice," *Gesta* (31) (1) (1992): 25-39.

Kortepeter, Carl M. "Ottoman Imperial Policy and the Economy of the Black Sea Region in the Sixteenth Century," *Journal of the American Oriental Society* (86) (2) (Apr.-June, 1966): 86-113.

Kuromiya, Hiroaki and Mamoulia, Georges. "Anti-Russian and Anti-Soviet Subversion: The Caucasian-Japanese Nexus, 1904-1945," *Europe-Asia Studies* (61) (8) (Oct., 2009): 1415-1440.

Leiser, Gary and Dols, Michael. "Evliya Chelebi's Description of Medicine in Seventeenth-Century Egypt, Part I: Introduction," *Sudhoffs Archiv* (71) (2) (1987): 197-216.

Leoni, Stefano. "Kanz al-Tuhaf (Al-Musiqi). The Casket of (Music) Rarities: Ars Musica and Musica Practica between Islam and Christianity," *International Review of the Aesthetics and Sociology of Music* (27) (2) (Dec., 1996): 167-183.

Levey, Martin. "Medieval Arabic Toxicology: The Book of Poisons of Ibn Wahshiya and Its Relation to Early Indian and Greek Texts," *Transactions of the American Philosophical Society* (56) (7) (1966): 1-130.

Lowe, Kate. "'Representing' Africa: Ambassadors and Princes from Christian Africa to Renaissance Italy and Portugal, 1402-1608," *Transactions of the Royal Historical Society* (17) (2007): 101-128.

Makdisi, John. "The Islamic Origins of the Common Law," *North Carolina Law Review* (77) (1998-1999): 1635-1740.

Mallet, Alex. "A Trip down the Red Sea with Reynald of Chatillon," *Journal of the Royal Asiatic Society* (18) (2) (April, 2008): 141-153.

Mayor, Adrienne, Colarusso, John and Saunders, David. "Making Sense of Nonsense Inscriptions Associated with Amazons and Scythians on Athenian Vases," *Hesperia: The Journal of the American School of Classical Studies at Athens* (83) (3) (July-September 2014): 447-493.

Melikian-Chirvani, A.S. "State Inkwells in Islamic Iran," *The Journal of the Walters Art Gallery* (44) (1986): 70-94.

Mozaffari, S. Mohammad and Zotti, Georg. "Ghāzān Khān's Astronomical Innovations at Marāgha Observatory," *Journal of the American Oriental Society*, (132) (3) (July-September 2012): 395-425.

Netton, Ian Richard. "Towards a Modern Tafsir of Surat al-Kahf: Structure and Semiotics," *Journal of Qur'anic Studies* (2) (1) (2000): 67-87.

Özdemir, Lale. *Ottoman History Through the Eyes of Aşıkpaşazade* (Istanbul: The Isis Press, 2013).

Pacholczyk, Jozef. "Music and Astronomy in the Muslim World," *Leonardo* (29) (2) (1996): 145-150.

Pancaroğlu, Oya. "The Itinerant Dragon-Slayer: Forging Paths of Image and Identity in Medieval Anatolia," *Gesta* (43) (2) (2004): 151-164.

Pankhurst, Richard. "Early Contacts Between Italy and Ethiopia, and the Beginnings of Italian Scholarship on Ethiopia," *Africa: Rivista trimestrale di studi e documentazione dell'Istituto italiano per l'Africa e l'Oriente* (50) (3) (Sept. 1995): 399-403.

Paviot, Jacques. "England and the Mongols, 1260-1330," *Journal of the Royal Asiatic Society* (10) (3) (Nov., 2000): 305-318.

Rapoport, Yossef and Savage-Smith, Emilie. *Lost Maps of the Caliphs: Drawing the World in Eleventh-Century Cairo* (Chicago: University of Chicago Press, 2018).

Sabra, A. I. "The 'Commentary' that Saved the Text: The Hazardous Journey of Ibn al-Haytham's Arabic 'Optics,'" *Early Science and Medicine* (12) (2) (2007): 117-133.

Salvadore, Matteo. "The Ethiopian Age of Exploration: Prester John's Discovery of Europe, 1306-1458." *Journal of World History* (21) (4) (December, 2010): 593-627.

Sayılı, Aydın. *The Observatory in Islam and Its Place in the General History of the Observatory* (Ankara: Türk Tarih Kurumu Basımevi, 1988).

Shalem, Avinoam, "Jewels and Journeys: The Case of the Medieval Gemstone Called al-Yatima," *Muqarnas* (14) (1997): 42-56.

Shiloah, Amnon. "Musical Scenes in Arabic Iconography," *Music in Art* (33) (2008): 283-300.

Sinor, Denis. "Mongols in the West," *Journal of Asian History* (33) (1) (1999): 1-44.

Smith, Clive. *Lightning Over Yemen: A History of the Ottoman Campaign, 1569-71* (London: I.B. Tauris, 2002).

Tietze, Andreas. *The Koman Riddles and Turkic Folklore* (Berkeley: University of California Press, 1966).

Trablousi, Samer. "The Queen was Actually a Man: Arwa Bint Ahmad and the Politics of Religion," *Arabica* (50) (Jan., 2003): 96-108.

Tuczay, Christa A. "Motifs in 'The Arabian Nights' and in Ancient and Medieval Literature: A Comparison," *Folklore* (116) (3) (Dec., 2005): 272-291.

Van Gelder, Geert Jan. "Sing Me to Sleep: Safī Al-Dīn Al-Urmawī, Hülegü, and the Power of Music," *Quaderni di Studi Arabi* (7) (2012): 1-9.

Wardwell, Anne E. "Flight of the Phoenix: Crosscurrents in Late Thirteenth- to Fourteenth-Century Silk Patterns and Motifs," *The Bulletin of the Cleveland Museum of Art* (74) (Jan., 1987): 2-35.

Wheeler, Brannon M. "Moses or Alexander? Early Islamic Exegesis of Qur'an 18: 60-65," *Journal of Near Eastern Studies* (57) (3) (Jul., 1998): 191-215.

Willis, John M. "Colonial Policing in Aden, 1937-1967," *The Arab Studies Journal* (5) (1) (Spring 1997): 57-91.

Willis, John M. "Making Yemen Indian: Rewriting the Boundaries of Imperial Arabia," *International Journal of Middle East Studies* (41) (1) (2009): 23-38.

Winter, S. H. "The Province of Raqqa Under Ottoman Rule: 1535-1800," *Journal of Near Eastern Studies* (68) (4) (Oct., 2009): 253-268.

Wright, O. "'Abd al-Qādir al-Marāghī and 'Alī B. Muhammad Binā'ī: Two Fifteenth-Century Examples of Notation Part 1: Text," *Bulletin of the School of Oriental and African Studies* (57) (3) (1994): 475-515.

Wright, Owen. "On the Concept of a 'Timurid Music,'" *Oriente Moderno* (76) (1996): 665-681.